DON
QUIXOTE

The Ingenious Gentleman

DON QUIXOTE

DE LA MANCHA

Miguel de Cervantes

COMPLETE IN TWO PARTS

*Translation from the Spanish, with a Critical Text
Based upon the First Editions of 1605 and 1615, and with Variant
Readings, Variorum Notes, and an Introduction by*
SAMUEL PUTNAM

THE MODERN LIBRARY · NEW YORK

THE MODERN LIBRARY
is published by

RANDOM HOUSE, INC.

CONTENTS

"*. . . el que lee mucho y anda mucho, vee mucho y sabe mucho.*"

DON QUIXOTE (Part Two, Chapter xxv)

TRANSLATOR'S INTRODUCTION

Toda afectación es mala.
CERVANTES

I

THE four-hundredth anniversary of the birth of Miguel de Cervantes Saavedra, one of the world's best-beloved writers, whose masterpiece has been translated into more languages than any other work with the exception of the Bible, came near to passing wholly unobserved in this country in 1947. There were, it is true, a certain number of academic tributes, but our men of letters, who should have been especially concerned, and the more literate reading public were for the most part unaware of the occasion, or would have been if the timely appearance of Aubrey F. G. Bell's fine study, *Cervantes,* had not served to remind them of it.[1]

Mr. Bell is a scholar who has devoted a long and useful life to the task of making the English-speaking peoples better acquainted with the treasure house of Iberian culture, and as he looks out over the present scene he is inclined to be rather pessimistic with regard to the fate of the Ingenious Gentleman of La Mancha in this modern age. "The question arises," he says, "whether *Don Quixote* as a universal classic has not now joined Dante and Milton, Shakespeare and the Bible, in being universally praised but comparatively seldom read." He then goes on to speak of an inquiry he had made "among a dozen persons of keen intelligence and wide reading and culture" which "elicited some disconcerting results."[2] To begin with, "six of the twelve persons consulted had not read *Don Quixote,* and not one of the twelve (they were not Spanish scholars) spoke of it with unqualified admiration." Mr. Bell's parenthesis is significant, for the individuals whom he interviewed were naturally dependent upon English-language translations, "none of which do justice to the Spanish original," and hence it is not surprising if they found this great classic, which for more than three centuries has enjoyed so tremendous a popularity, to be dull and all but unreadable.

It is not, however, in our country alone that Cervantes' readers would seem to be falling away. Nearly forty years ago, in the charming introduction that he wrote for his popular edition of *Don Quixote*, the late Francisco Rodríguez Marín, to whom all students in this field owe so much, is to be heard complaining that the work is little read in the Spain of today, being absent from many cultured homes, while certain schoolmasters regard it as "antiquated"; and he adds the biting comment that more people pretend to have read it than have actually done so. With this Mr. Bell would agree. "Even in Spain today," he notes, "it cannot be said that *Don Quixote* is really popular. New editions appear at moderate prices, but they have only a faint appeal to the millions, who confine their reading to the cheaper newspapers." [3]

There are some—Mr. Bell is one of them—who would explain all this by what they see as the degeneration of our times. They tell us that, having abandoned a primitive, close-to-the-soil simplicity, we have lost our hold upon life's deepest meaning, the "eternal verities," and that as a consequence genius is threatened with banishment and the classics with a living death. In the case of the English-language reader at least, we have already witnessed the practical interment of more than one work that once was the mirror of an age: the *Orlando Furioso*, the *Faerie Queene*, and (if we are to be honest with ourselves) even the *Divine Comedy*, in spite of such excellent renderings of the Dante poem as those by Laurence Binyon and Professor Fletcher. How many others are there that might be mentioned?

With the term "classic" we commonly associate the idea of immortality; but can it be that, in place of being deathless, these masterpieces in the end must inevitably lose their vital appeal and be nicely bound, embalmed, and laid upon the shelf? "Nothing that is human is eternal but is ever declining from its beginning to its close"—these are the words of Don Quixote's creator.[4] Would he have applied them to his own work and similar manifestations of the human spirit? It is a kind of heresy to believe so. Homer's age or that of Dante or of Cervantes is far removed from ours, but a basic faith in that humanity of which the *Iliad* and the *Odyssey*, the *Divine Comedy* and *Don Quixote*, afford us a supreme artistic expression forbids us to doubt the enduring germ of life that is in them and compels us to look for other causes of the neglect into which they have undeservedly fallen.

The truth of the matter is that the modern reader and his civilization are not altogether to blame. It is characteristic of great works of art that they have something new to say to each succeeding age that discovers them, whether it be a period in the life of the individual or of the world; [5] and it well may be that a particular work will speak more clearly to one era than to another, but at no time can it fail to have a message for those whose ears are attuned to it and whose minds are properly receptive. Certainly, the profound faith of a Cervantes, his cheerful acceptance of life in its simplest and sublimest terms, with all its tragedy and all its enveloping mystery, is not an easy one for us to attain today, and there are many who will spurn it; yet on the other hand there are many also who would welcome it if—and this is the point—they could but come to grips with the author's mind, with what he thought and what he really wrote, shorn of irrelevancies and presented with the greatest possible fidelity, clarity, and simplicity.

The problem, then, is how to overcome those obstacles that have unavoidably been erected by time and distance and that tend to bar the way to a full and satisfying comprehension of the classics, and here is where the task of the scholar and translator begins. In a sense it may be said that such works, especially where the medium of translation is involved, need to be brought back to their original luster, as precious antiques from time to time need to be refurbished; but this must be done with the utmost care and reverence, with no attempt at "improvement" or a modernization that would represent a betrayal of the original. This is far more readily accomplished in the case of prose than of poetry, the adequate rendering (re-creation) of a poem being a miracle that rarely occurs, for which reason it is that some of the most satisfactory versions of poetical masterpieces have been done in prose and not in verse.[6] What an all but insuperable stumbling block *terza rima* has proved to be for the translator of Dante!

There can be no doubt that the life view which a classic embodies may limit its audience in another and remote era. The spirit of the age of chivalry as reflected in Ariosto is one that is foreign to all but a handful of present-day readers; and what of Dante, who stands like a magnificent Janus-headed statue on the threshold between the late Middle Ages and the early Renaissance? The *Divine Comedy* and the *Iliad* are perhaps the two works in all literature that may be said really to sum up and embody an age, but time has laid its hand upon both of them, rendering popular comprehension and appreciation increasingly difficult. As a result they are coming more and more to be relegated to the famous Five-Foot Shelf or some pedagogic list of the world's great books.[7]

With *Don Quixote* the case is different. It is a work essentially popu-

lar in inspiration,[8] which the peoples of the earth at once claimed as
their own, making of it for centuries a phenomenal and world-wide
best-seller. While no book could be more thoroughly, unmistakably
Spanish and of its age, it still, by reason of the fascinating story it tells,
its rich vein of humor, and the wealth of wisdom that it contains, has
an appeal for readers of every land that is in reality timeless. And this
is not to speak of its importance, the interest it should hold for writers,
critics, and students of literature, as the prototype of the modern novel.[9]
If, then, it shows signs of losing today the enormous popularity that it
once enjoyed, other explanations must be found.

Even in Spain, as Rodríguez Marín observes, the modern reader of
Don Quixote encounters certain difficulties. For the very reason that
it is so immersed in its period, so filled with topical allusions, a classic
not infrequently grows more and more obscure in the course of the
centuries. This is true of Dante, Rabelais, and, to a lesser degree, Cervantes. And so it is not strange that the ordinary cultured twentieth-century
Spaniard should stand in need of the services of an annotator, a specialist,
if the text of *Don Quixote* is to be perfectly clear to him. Nor is it
merely a question of the numerous references to contemporary personages and events; the author's language as well often calls for clari-
fication. Like Rabelais, Cervantes drew upon the rich and racy idiom
of the people and, in particular, the speech of the Andalusian countryside, making use often of expressions that have not been preserved in
the lexicons and must be run down to their sources.[10]

As for the foreign reader who is unfamiliar with Spanish, he has the
additional handicap of being forced to rely upon the linguistic knowledge, textual fidelity, literary ability, and faithfulness to the spirit of
the work that may or may not be possessed by the one who has undertaken to translate it. In this regard the English-speaking public has had
on the whole an unfortunate experience, especially here in America
where "the odious Motteux translation," as Bertram D. Wolfe has
termed it, has been the medium through which most of us, including
most American writers, have formed our impression of this "father of
all novels, and the novel most nearly coextensive with humanity." [11]
In discussing what he sees as "the underestimation of one of the world's
greatest works," Mr. Wolfe says:

   . . . most of all, it is due to the wretched but time-hallowed translation of Motteux, who was traducer more than translator, who was
too lazy and swift of pen to stop for rhythms and subtle meanings
where they eluded his first dip into the inkpot, and who, miscon-

ceiving Cervantes as another Rabelais, did not hesitate to change the tenor and mood of the whole work into a gross caricature of itself by keying his extravagant slapstick English to a different conception of the characters. Since he thereby substitutes two rather ridiculous fools of low comedy for Cervantes' two lovable ones of high humor and deep humanity, it is not surprising that so many readers have failed to reach the richer Part II or go much beyond the windmills and the blanket-tossing in Part I. Appalled by the surfeiting prospect of a thousand pages of belly laughs, how many have abandoned the work without suspecting that Sancho and Don Quixote grow steadily in character and significance, grow together in oneness until they are the two inseparable poles of a single human archetype, insinuate themselves into our hearts until we begin to resent the pranks that are played upon them and to consider the players of the pranks more foolish than the ever-more-admirable butts of their jokes? Still less can the too-soon-wearied reader sense the wealth of sanity, philosophy, wisdom and essential humanity that is embodied in their peculiar madness.

This is stern censure, but there are few competent critics who would not concur in it. *Traduttori traditori*, the old proverb has it. By thus betraying the entire character and animating spirit of a great work, a translator may condemn his author to something like oblivion for a huge body of readers to whom the original is inaccessible. It is enough to inspire fear and trembling in one who practices the trade, if indeed it does not lead him to abandon his calling once and for all, when he thinks of the harm he conceivably may do.

But Motteux was not the only offender by any means. It is worth our while to glance for a moment at the rather curious history of the English versions of *Don Quixote*.

II

The popularity of the tale was instantaneous. The ink was scarcely dry on the first printing in 1605 before pirated editions were under way,[12] and within seven years after the publication of Part II in 1615 the book had been translated into French, German, Italian, and English.[13] The first of the foreign-language renderings was Thomas Shelton's version of Part I, which was published at London in 1612 but was probably made about 1608, Part II appearing in 1620.[14] Shelton had the advantage of being a contemporary of the author and his "fine old crusted English," as the scholarly nineteenth-century translator John

Ormsby describes it,[15] is that of Shakespeare's day. For this reason his
Don Quixote, like Urquhart's Rabelais, remains a cherished item on
many a library shelf even though it is far from satisfactory as a carrying-
over of Cervantes' text. For one thing, it was done with extreme haste
—the First Part, he informs us, was completed in forty days! What is
more, it is often, to quote Ormsby once again, "barbarously literal,"
with no regard to the variety of fine shadings of certain Spanish words
as employed by the author.

But Shelton at least does not undertake to improve or expand upon
the original or to turn those two superb creations, Don Quixote and
Sancho Panza, into a pair of English clowns in the manner of Motteux.
His language is pleasingly colloquial and of his time; he avoids the
affectation of an archaic style that, save in passages where the romances
of chivalry are definitely being parodied, is wholly uncalled for in the
case of Cervantes.

It was well toward the end of the seventeenth century, in 1687, that
the second and by all odds the worst English version—it cannot be called
a translation—appeared from the pen of John Phillips, nephew of the
poet Milton. This is truly a disgraceful performance, coarse and clowning, based not upon the Spanish original but upon Shelton and the
French work by Filleau de Saint-Martin with its gross distortions of
Cervantes' text.[16] The less said of Phillips the better. In 1700 Captain
John Stevens published his revision of Shelton, and in that same year
what is commonly known as the Motteux version ("translated from
the original by several hands and published by Peter Motteux") took
its place upon the bookstalls.

Peter Anthony Motteux was a tea merchant who dabbled in literature, and it might have been better if he had confined himself to the
China trade. How much of the *Don Quixote* is by him and how much
by the other "hands," it is impossible to say.[17] In any event it seems
certain that, in place of having been done "from the original," it is
rather a pastiche of Shelton, Phillips, and Filleau de Saint-Martin. A
fifth edition in 1725 was revised by J. Ozell, and this is the one that is
best known in America today. In 1822 the five-volume edition of
Motteux by John Gibson Lockhart was published at Edinburgh, the
notes of the Spanish commentator Juan Antonio Pellicer being taken
over without credit to their author.[18]

As to the general character of the Motteux "translation," the opinion
we have heard expressed by Bertram D. Wolfe is identical with that of
leading specialists in the field of Hispanic studies. "Worse than worth-

less" is Ormsby's verdict; "the very worst," says Richard Ford.[19] The prevailing slapstick quality of the work, especially where Sancho is involved; the obtrusion of the obscene where it is not to be found in Cervantes; the slurring over of difficulties through omissions or by expanding upon the text; [20] the substitution of English for Spanish proverbs where there is often no close correspondence—these and other grave faults fully support the judgment that has been pronounced by Motteux's critics.

From all of this it may be seen that Cervantes was very badly handled by his early English-language translators, and the reason for it may be found in the fact that *Don Quixote* was looked upon as being in essence a farcical production designed solely to provoke side-splitting laughter of the more ribald sort. True, there is plenty of humor in its pages, which accounts for the favor with which it has been received by the simple and wise of heart all over the earth, but Cervantes' humor is of that higher kind that consists in a perception of the incongruous and, as Mr. Bell has pointed out, in the ability to see both sides of a question. This is a humor and a wisdom—the two are one—that is of the people and is incomprehensible to men like John Phillips, Peter Motteux and his collaborators, Ned Ward, and Edmund Gayton. Because *Don Quixote* was a popular work, they assumed that it must be low comedy; and, possessing little or no acquaintance with Spanish or with Spain and its inhabitants, they thought that the way to translate a Spanish peasant was to make of him at best a Shakespearean buffoon. Accordingly, Gayton from his Oxford study gives us his smut-filled *Festivous Notes*, and Ward a *Don Quixote* "translated into Hudibrastick verse." [21]

It is to a reaction against this betrayal of the text and spirit of Cervantes' masterpiece, particularly as represented by Motteux, that we owe our first truly faithful English version of it: that by Charles Jervas, who was a portrait painter by profession and who, owing to a printer's error, has come to be known to posterity as Charles Jarvis. Jarvis [22] was a contemporary of Pope; [23] his translation appeared in 1742, three years after his death. It has since run through nearly a hundred printings (ninety-nine to be exact, down to 1933), which shows that it has met with widespread approval on the part of the reading public; yet for one reason or another critics in the past have been especially harsh toward it, and some have even had the bad taste to prefer Motteux.[24] The worst that may be said about Jarvis is that he is inclined to be ponderous and dull, but there are many who will prefer this dullness to a pumped-up vitality and out-of-place clowning that are in reality a desecration.[25]

The version published by T. G. Smollett in 1755 merits little consideration as it is merely a working over of Jarvis. In 1769 George Kelly brought out what purports to be a translation but is actually a twofold theft: that of Motteux's text and Jarvis's notes.[26] Charles Henry Wilmot's abridgment (1774) was not made from the Spanish, and Mary Smirke's *History of Don Quixote* (1818) and the work of the same title by J. W. Clarke (1867) are no more than revisions.[27]

Such were the unfortunate adventures, down to the latter half of the nineteenth century, of the Knight of the Mournful Countenance as he fared forth in English garb. As should be evident by now, he had with one or two exceptions been made the victim of literary hacks and impostors, without a knowledge of Spanish and with no respect for their author, who were simply out to turn an easy penny. It was not until the 1880's that a new, scholarly, and conscientious type of Cervantes translator began to appear. The version by Alexander J. Duffield (1881) and those by John Ormsby (1885) and Henry Edward Watts (1888) may be said to mark the turning point. Here were men who knew and loved Spain, its language, its people, and its literature, and from now on, during the turn-of-the-century decades, many of these Hispanic students and Cervantes specialists, like Ormsby, James Fitzmaurice-Kelly, Robinson Smith, Aubrey F. G. Bell, and others, were to tramp, faithfully and enthusiastically, those same monotonous plains of La Mancha over which Don Quixote and Sancho had ridden in the pages of their chronicler. They would stop at the same roadside inns, little changed by the centuries, encountering there the same stone watering troughs and "starry" garrets and the same human types, as they listened to more than one proverb that had dropped from Sancho Panza's lips.

It is scholars such as these who are to be credited with having restored *Don Quixote* to its rightful place among the classics as a serious work that not only is important from the point of view of the history of the novel, but that holds a deeper meaning for those that would seek it, while at the same time losing nothing of its appeal as a masterpiece of humor. If none of those who tried their hand at turning the book into English wholly succeeded in the formidable task—and we have heard what Mr. Aubrey Bell has to say as to this—their failure is not to be ascribed to any lack of background, of good will and integrity, or even of literary ability, but rather is to be explained by other factors. Both Duffield and Watts, for example, believed that an archaic style was the only one suited for an English rendering, while Ormsby, in his striving for a minute verbal accuracy (not to be confused with literalness) and a strict adherence to the Spanish text, is seemingly willing to sacrifice all thought of style and sentence clarity.

But despite what has just been said, Ormsby remains a translator whom present-day Cervantists respect most highly.[28] On the linguistic side his contribution is outstanding. He was the first to insist that Cervantes wrote an essentially modern Spanish[29] and that there was no excuse for employing an antiquated idiom in rendering an author who had declared that "all affectation is bad."[30] He was the first also to make a close study of the nuances of certain key words as they occur in different parts of the work, in which respect he anticipated the labors of the semantics investigator.[31] One often becomes impatient with his long, tangled sentences and obscure pronoun antecedents, but one is none the less grateful to him for his painstaking honesty and the light he has thrown on Cervantes' vocabulary. He is, indeed, so likely to use the inevitable word or expression that a subsequent translator will be hard put to it to find a better one.

The latest English version is by Robinson Smith. First published in 1908, it has been reprinted four times, a fifth and new edition having been brought out on this side of the Atlantic by the Hispanic Society of America in 1932.[32] Smith is of that new race of *cervantistas* that began with Duffield, Ormsby, Watts, Fitzmaurice-Kelly, and others at the end of the last century. Like Duffield and Watts, he is concerned with patiently carving out a flavorous and somewhat mannered prose which he believes will do justice to the original, and, like Ormsby, he is extremely meticulous in his choice of words. Perhaps the chief criticism to be made of his translation, although this is largely a matter of one's personal taste and feeling for the author, is that it is a bit too mannered, a little stiff, with somewhat of the rigidity of a carving, and hence is lacking in the freedom and ease, the vitality, and the fluency combined with terseness that is so characteristic of Cervantes' own prose. The verse is omitted entirely (which, it must be confessed, is no great loss), and the copious notes follow the pattern set by the older commentators who concentrated their attention upon the literature of chivalry.

III

What, then, it may be asked, can be the excuse for yet another attempt to bring over into English the adventures of the inimitable Knight? Is the task really one that is impossible to accomplish? Mr. Bell asserts as an "undeniable fact" that "the best of Cervantes is untranslatable," and he and others would advise the reader to master Spanish and turn to the original. It would, of course, be an ideal state of affairs if the great body of readers were able to do so, but unfortunately, in connection with this and other classics, it remains an ideal. Are the classics for that reason to go unread? Or must the translator rather keep hammering away at what he knows can only be wrought by a kind of miracle? Cervantes himself has some harsh things to say about the craft: see his remarks on the translation of poetry in Part I, Chapter VI, and on translations in general in Part II, Chapter LXII:

> But for all of that, it appears to me that translating from one language into another, unless it be from one of those two queenly tongues, Greek and Latin, is like gazing at a Flemish tapestry with the wrong side out: even though the figures are visible, they are full of threads that obscure the view and are not bright and smooth as when seen from the other side.

"And yet," says Ormsby, "of all great writers there is not one that is under such obligations to translation as Cervantes. The influence of Homer and Virgil would be scarcely less if they had never been translated; Shakespeare and Milton wrote in a language destined to become the most widely read on the face of the globe, and no reader of any culture needs an interpreter for Molière or Le Sage. But how would Cervantes have fared in the world if, according to his own principles, he had been confined to his native Castilian?" [33]

The fact of the matter is that Cervantes was very much gratified that his book, during the few years of life that remained to him, had found so large an audience in foreign countries: "In short, I feel certain that there will soon not be a nation that does not know it or a language into which it has not been translated." [34]

For one thing, in connection with the English rendering of *Don Quixote*, there would appear to be reason for believing that the translator's two basic problems have not as yet been solved: that of attaining a style which, like the original, shall be free of affectation—colloquial and modern without being flagrantly "modernized"; and that of combining textual and linguistic fidelity with a readable prose. But an even more urgent consideration is the need of a version which shall take full advantage of the great strides in Cervantes scholarship that have been made since the beginning of the century, as regards the critical reconstruction of a text based upon the first Spanish editions of 1605 and 1615, and in the field of specialized lexicography and literary-historical research.

It is the year 1905, marking the three-hundredth anniversary of the first publication of *Don Quixote*, that seems to have provided the impetus for a whole series of important studies by inspiring the Cervantist with a fresh enthusiasm for his subject. In that year Don Clemente Cortejón y Lucas began the publication of his critical edition with variants and notes, a work that was completed in 1913,[35] and it was during this period that the Hispanic Society of America brought out its reprint of the first and fourth La Cuesta editions (1605, 1615). In 1905, also, Don Julio Cejador y Frauca made an extremely valuable contribution with his treatise on Cervantes' vocabulary and syntax,[36] and Rodríguez Marín about this time entered upon his lifelong and monumental task of editing and annotating *Don Quixote*, his first and more popular edition of 1911–13 being followed in 1927–28 by his new critical edition, which constitutes a veritable landmark. In 1914 the late Rudolph Schevill, an American scholar,[37] and Don Adolfo Bonilla y San Martín published the first two volumes in their *Obras Completas* series, culminating with a *Don Quixote* edited by Schevill, the four volumes of which appeared during the years 1928–41.[38]

It is obvious that this wealth of new scholarship came too late for Duffield, Ormsby, and Watts to be able to avail themselves of it, and Smith's original version was completed some time before Rodríguez Marín's edition and that by Schevill had seen the light of day.

One of the most important accomplishments of the modern specialist has been a reconstruction of the text of the first editions, such as that achieved by Professor Schevill. In the past the best of the English-language translators of *Don Quixote* have had a very unsatisfactory text from which to work and too often have relied upon later printings and the "emendations" to be found in them;[39] whereas the principle followed by textual critics of today, as in the case of this work, is the one laid down by Schevill, to the effect that the first editions are to be treated with the same reverence as if they were the original manuscript itself and must accordingly be employed as the scientific base for any edition—and this applies to any translation as well—that aims at being definitive.[40]

There is a valid reason for such an attitude. The latest authorities appear to be agreed that Cervantes never read over his manuscript before sending it to the printer; had he done so he would have avoided more than one minor inconsistency and the confusion over the theft of Sancho's ass in Part I.[41] And it is equally apparent that he did not make any corrections either in the proofs or when a new edition was put out by his own publisher.[42] This is understandable if we remember his uncertain health and failing eyesight—let us not forget that he was on the verge of sixty when he wrote Part I, and that Part II was composed in the seventh decade of his life. There would seem, then, to be nothing to do but rely upon the first editions in the absence of a manuscript; nor should their text be departed from by editor or translator save for very good reason. This is the opinion of such scholars as Schevill and Rodríguez Marín. As Fitzmaurice-Kelly has put it, no attempt should be made to correct or improve upon the author, but one should rather strive, in cases of doubt and where possible, to determine *what he wrote*.

It is Schevill's reconstructed text that has been used as a base for this translation; where another reading has been adopted the fact has been noted and the explanation given. Other important variants that have a bearing upon the English version will also be found.

As to the general character of my rendering, I would once more stress the point that I have striven to avoid on the one hand an antiquated style and vocabulary, and on the other hand any modernism that would be out of place and savor of flippancy. Cervantes, it may be repeated, wrote the language of his day or he would never have been so popular, and there is therefore no excuse for making him out to be archaic save where he is deliberately seeking such an effect with humorous intent. There is, of course, the argument that in dealing with any work that is removed by centuries from our own era there should be some stylistic indication of its period; but in the present instance this is hardly necessary, the subject matter in itself providing about all that is needed in the way of a chronological differentiation. In this regard the translator should confine himself at most to the delicate nuance and turn of phrase rather than endeavor to maintain a painfully wrought manner and idiom which after all do not reflect his author.

Cervantes, when all is said, is one of the most modern of Spanish writers, and hence stands in no need of modernizing. Aside from certain changes in the shadings of words and a few locutions that have since been dropped from general usage, and apart from the semantics of his highly personal vocabulary, his Spanish is in essence the Spanish of today; [43] in this respect he differs radically from a writer like Rabelais whose language is still middle, not modern, French. And so the thing to do would seem to be, simply, to leave him alone, let him speak for himself, while his translator strives for perfect naturalness and shuns all affectation.

One cannot, however, lay down any hard-and-fast rule in drawing the line between that which is affectedly quaint and that which is honestly modern. This question comes up in connection with the title of the work: *The Ingenious Gentleman, Don Quixote de la Mancha.* "Ingenious," needless to say, is not, or was not originally, a proper translation of *ingenioso.* In his first edition Robinson Smith substitutes "imaginative" for "ingenious," and in his fifth and revised edition of 1932 he employs "visionary." Now, either "visionary" or "imaginative" is unquestionably closer to the original if one does not take into account the semantic associations; but it seems to me that by this time the word "ingenious" in the sense that the literal-minded Shelton gave it has so embedded itself in our consciousness as we think of Don Quixote that it would be a mistake to change it on the title-page. And similarly with the spelling of the Knight's name: Smith later adopts the modern form, *Quijote,* which to most American readers would be as disturbing —and distracting—as it is to see Mexico spelled Méjico. Has not the adjective quixotic long been a part of our language? [44]

On the other hand I cannot, as Ormsby does, feel a pang at parting with such an expression as "Curious Impertinent," which is one of the worst linguistic barbarisms ever coined. Ormsby's substitute, "Tale of the Ill-Advised Curiosity," would have been all right if he had omitted the definite article (the phrase "ill-advised curiosity" occurs a time or two in the course of the narrative); but inasmuch as the original here cannot be translated concisely or with any degree of literalness, I have felt free to expand upon it and try to give what I take to be the meaning of the episode "Story of the One Who Was Too Curious for His Own Good."

In the present version names of persons other than monarchs have been retained in their original form; thus, Luscinda, Dorotea, Grisóstomo (in place of Chrysostom), Lotario, Ambrosio, Anselmo, etc. This has been done not only as a matter of principle, but for the sake of consistency as well. Why should a translator in one and the same chapter Anglicize Grisóstomo and let Ambrosio stand? [45] I have likewise preferred the Italian Orlando to the Spanish Roldán or the French Roland. But in the case of geographical names the form current in English has been used: Andalusia in place of Andalucía, Cordova in place of Córdoba, Saragossa in place of Zaragoza, etc.

Something should be said as to the rendering of certain other words. I have not followed Ormsby's example by leaving such terms as *alforjas* and *bota* in the original, a procedure that inevitably tends to slow up the average reader. In the case of *alforjas*, "saddlebags" would appear to be a near enough equivalent, one approved by the Spanish-English lexicographer, while in the latter case "wine flask," or even "flask," may serve, providing it is made clear—by a note rather than by an obtrusive circumlocution in the text—that *bota* is not our "bottle." And the same would apply to *cura*, which previous translators, including Ormsby, have rendered as "curate." As for *rucio*, the common term for Sancho's ass, it raises another point. I have rejected "Dapple" as being, by now at least and here in America, too quaint, as laying too much stress upon a mere adjective that as a noun has come to mean simply a donkey. *Rucio* originally means a light silver-gray color as applied to a horse, and I have accordingly translated it, as best suited the context, sometimes as "gray" (a noun) and sometimes as "ass" or "donkey." "Dapple," I must confess, is for me a little too unpleasantly reminiscent of the old light-and-merry school.

One of the most noticeable innovations that I have made, and to my mind one of the most important so far as modern readability is concerned, lies in the substitution of "you" for "thou" in Don Quixote's speeches addressed to Sancho and in other passages where an archaic effect is not sought; "thou" has been used in the more high-flown apostrophes of the Knight to his ladylove, some of the verse, and places of that sort. After all, the second person singular as a form of address in speaking to intimates and social inferiors still persists in Spanish and other languages, yet we would not employ "thou" in translating a contemporary novel. Why, then, should we make Cervantes out to be more archaic or mannered than he is? I have never been able to understand why Ormsby, who stresses the modern character of his author's prose, should have seen fit to retain this antiquated form.

On the other hand there is a very definite old-fashioned flavor to *vuessa merced* [46] that is not to be sacrificed, as it accords admirably with the gentle humor of the tale and with the portrait of the eldering country gentleman of La Mancha in the opening chapter of the book. As a translation I have preferred "your Grace" to "your Worship," [47] though there are objections that may be raised to the use of either one.

Properly speaking, I think I may say that I have in reality "modernized," that is, taken some liberties with, only the punctuation, paragraphing,[48] the dialogue transitions now and then, and to a certain degree the sentence structure. This is something the modern translator is compelled to do if he is not to betray the spirit by too faithful an adherence to the letter. The Spanish language in general, and the Spanish of Cervantes in particular, have a terseness which, one may as well admit it, cannot be carried over into English; but with Cervantes this is a terseness that is achieved *within* a long and sprawling sentence marked by an intricate interweaving of clauses loosely connected by a series of *que's* and relative pronouns. Any attempt to preserve this sentence structure—and Ormsby does attempt it—can lead only to obscurity in English, as it sometimes does in Spanish,[49] conveying an impression of dullness which is decidedly unfair to the author.

Something also has to be done with regard to pronoun antecedents or the result is confusion, as in this sentence fragment from the passage describing Camacho's wedding in Part II, Chapter xxi, in the Ormsby version (I have here indicated within brackets the person to whom the pronoun refers): "Camacho was listening to all this, perplexed and bewildered and not knowing what to say or do; but so urgent were the entreaties of Basilio's friends, imploring him [Camacho] to allow Quiteria to give him [Basilio] her hand so that his [Basilio's] soul, quitting this life in despair, should not be lost . . ." In order to avoid such an effect as this it is often necessary to introduce a word or two not found in the text, but they should always be words that are in consonance with it, such as the author himself employed.[50] And the same principle should be observed where extra words are (sparingly) introduced for the sake of cadence or rhythm.

Among the most modern and surprising aspects of Cervantes' art as a novelist is the freedom and fluency of his dialogue. Here I have merely endeavored to vary the transitions a little, as the author does at times, through the employment of some locution other than the constant "said" or "replied" that will not be out of context.

Cervantes' greatness as a writer, like that of Shakespeare in a way, lies in the sweep of the whole rather than in minute particulars or the details of polished craftsmanship. "Careless" and "slovenly" are adjectives that have been used by his most devoted admirers in speaking of his method of composition; and that there is a basis for the charge must be evident to any reader who observes the rather numerous contradictions and inconsistencies. If I, like other translators, editors, and commentators, have called attention to some of these in my notes, the reader may be assured that this has not been done out of any desire to pick flaws in a masterpiece, but simply in order to present as true a picture as possible of the writer and his work.

One evidence of the carelessness and undoubted haste with which the author of *Don Quixote* wrote is to be seen in his frequent word repetitions. He will sometimes use the same verb three times within a couple of lines; [51] he is fond of piling up synonyms or near-synonyms, whether verbs, adjectives, or nouns, for the pleasure of doing so; [52] and he is also inclined to overwork the superlative; in all of which it may be there is to be discerned a trace of the Góngora influence. This poses yet another problem for the translator, one which he must solve with only his literary conscience to guide him as he strives to convey the feeling of the original without undue offense to modern canons of taste.

Regarding Cervantes' verse there is not a great deal that need be said. His was the misfortune of being a poet by temperament, in his attitude toward and feeling for life, but unsuccessful in the practice of his art. He is at his best in certain passages of the *Journey to Parnassus*,[53] an occasional ballad, a stray sonnet or two. Perhaps the only pieces in the *Don Quixote* that merit serious consideration are Antonio's Ballad in Part I, Chapter XI, and Grisóstomo's Song in Part I, Chapter XIV, and they are chiefly remarkable for their intricate use of assonant and medial rhymes, as experiments in versification, rather than as poems in the true sense of the word. Between the verse in Part I and that in Part II there is a difference to be noted: in the former instance Cervantes is taking himself seriously as a poet and upon occasion introduces into the text a sonnet he had composed years before and which he obviously thinks is worthy of being preserved; whereas in the latter part of the work he is for the most part frankly writing doggerel. But in either case the verse is not of a high order, and the problem of how to treat it in another language becomes a somewhat embarrassing one for any translator.

Smith, as has been stated, employs the simple expedient of omitting the verse entirely. Duffield makes use of the version of James Y. Gibson.[54] Ormsby, who possesses a metrical gift, will sometimes abandon the original form for one in which he can move about more freely, and again he will seek to achieve the impossible by imitating the Spanish assonance, the result being a surprising and not unpleasing, even if not wholly satisfying, *tour de force*. As for the renderings in the Motteux version, especially after they have gone through the hands of subsequent editors and revisers, it may merely be said that they bear little if any resemblance to the original. For my part I have not felt that it was desirable, assuming it could be done, to make Cervantes' work as a versifier appear better than it is, and in the case of the metrically more interesting pieces, I have made no effort to reproduce the assonance and similar intricacies, but I have preserved the rhyme schemes.

I V

So much for translation and the problems involved; and now a final word as to the notes.

It seems to be the fate of writers of the stature of Cervantes, Rabelais, Dante, and Shakespeare to attract about them a swarm of that frequently terrible species known as commentator. Running off on innumerable tangents and becoming the victims of some interpretative *idée fixe* or other, many of them impress one as being far madder than the windmill-tilting Don Quixote ever was and almost as amusing at times,[55] and are capable of all but burying their author under a host of impertinences and irrelevancies that are annoying in the extreme. Fitzmaurice-Kelly, Duffield, Rodríguez Marín, and others have had their say as to this tribe, and in the Prologue to Part I Cervantes himself pokes fun at their pomposity and mock-erudition.

This, of course, is not to imply that all commentators are of this sort. From an early date two types are to be distinguished. The venerable dean of one school is that English clergyman, the Reverend John Bowle, who in 1781 published a six-volume Spanish edition, three volumes of which were filled with notes;[56] Bowle, to whom all his successors will freely acknowledge a considerable debt, was a man of wide reading in the literature of chivalry, which with him becomes an obsession,[57] and in this respect he has had all too many followers. The other school was founded by Don Juan Antonio Pellicer with his edition of 1797-98, where in his distinguished commentary he turns his attention to Spanish folklore rather than the old romances, and in this sets a precedent for the editor of today.

Then, in 1833-39, came Don Diego Clemencín's six quarto volumes with extensive notes devoted to clearing up linguistic difficulties and obscure allusions. His contribution is well summarized by Ormsby, who states that "Clemencín . . . has done more toward the elucidation of *Don Quixote* than all the rest of the commentators and annotators together."[58] In the past he has been unpopular in certain quarters by reason of his critical temper, his impatience with Cervantes' careless writing, an attitude which to those who insist upon a blind, unreasoning adulation is an unforgivable sin.

The modern Cervantist realizes that criticism is not incompatible with reverence, a reverence that is best shown on the part of editor and translator by adhering as strictly as possible to the most satisfactory text that can be established, and on the part of the annotator by confining oneself on the whole to making that text clear and intelligible to the present-day reader. This type of commentator will look upon the life of Cervantes' century, of sixteenth-century Spain, as being of greater importance than all the minutiae of chivalry already so well explored, and will deem a cooking or cosmetic recipe—for *manjar blanco* or "angel water"—to be of far more interest than an obscure and long-forgotten incident in the *Orlando Furioso* or the *Amadis of Gaul*. He will not neglect allusions of the latter sort, but his stress will be on the aspects of daily life, on Sancho's proverbs, on folk customs, popular traditions, and the like.[59]

The notes to this translation, it may be remarked, are not intended for scholars or special students but for the general reading public; like Rodríguez Marín in his popular edition, I have had in mind those who know little about Cervantes rather than those who know much.[60] For this reason they have been held down to a minimum, and I have endeavored to keep them as concise as possible. I not only have made no attempt to trace all the references and parallels to the literature of chivalry, but have avoided going into the subject of the influence of *Don Quixote* upon our own and other modern literatures, as that would open up too vast a field. My guide always has been intelligibility for the modern reader.

In connection with the textual variants I have naturally limited myself to those more important ones that affect the English version. Where I have quoted the Spanish text I have retained the orthography of the first editions. In cases where I have wished to compare my translation with the work of my predecessors, I have usually cited Motteux, Ormsby, Jarvis, or Shelton, occasionally Duffield, as being the ones best known and most accessible in America. Like Ormsby I have paid particular attention to the proverbs, since they represent that wealth of popular wisdom that is one of the outstanding traits of the Spanish people.[61]

For the material in the variorum notes I am under a special debt to Rodríguez Marín, Schevill, Ormsby, and such older commentators as Pellicer, Clemencín, Hartzenbusch, and Don Juan Calderón, and I must also express my obligation to Cortejón, Cejador, Covarrubias, and Cor-reas.[62] Professor Raymond L. Grismer's *Cervantes: A Bibliography* has been an invaluable aid.[63]

V

With this I bring to a close a task that was begun in Europe some sixteen years ago, the result of an impulse deriving from a sojourn in Spain in the late 1920's. In the course of those years I have read Cer-vantes' own works, his commentators, translators, critics, and imitators, only to realize how he in the end inevitably eludes them all. In the meanwhile, as time and the exigencies of a troubled world permitted, I have labored over this version, which I had vainly hoped to complete by 1947. I can only say that it has not been done carelessly or in haste, but with that love and reverence that are due so great and lovable a writer. I now present it simply for what it is: the result of one man's— a translator's—prolonged communings with one of the fine, rare spirits of our "usable past."

SAMUEL PUTNAM

Philadelphia, 1948

A NOTE ON THE AUTHOR OF

DON QUIXOTE

THE life of Miguel de Cervantes Saavedra like that of Shakespeare is largely shrouded in darkness, a darkness that modern scholarship has not succeeded in dispelling to any considerable extent.[1] We do not even know the exact date on which he was born, but we do know that his birth occurred in the little town of Alcalá de Henares near Madrid and that he was christened there, in the church of Santa Maria, on October 9, 1547. The son of a wandering ne'er-do-well apothecary-surgeon, he came of an old family of Northern Spain that had seen better days but was now harassed by debt and poverty. Cervantes was to be accustomed as long as he lived to the condition of penniless gentleman.

For the first twenty-one years his biography is a blank, there being no definite evidence as to the whereabouts of his family or the nature of his schooling. It is believed that he may have attended the Jesuit college in Seville, but there is nothing to show that he had any university education. The first dependable date that we have following his christening is 1568, at which time he was a student in the City School of Madrid. Meanwhile, it is possible that he had left his studies for a period of service with the army in Flanders. In December 1569 he is to be found in Rome, serving as chamberlain to Cardinal Acquaviva, and from there he writes home for a certificate of legitimacy, setting forth that he is of "old Christian" stock, in order that he may be able to enter his Majesty's armed forces. He then enlisted in the Spanish legion stationed in Italy and in 1571 took part in the campaign under John of Austria that culminated on October 7 in the naval battle of Lepanto and a decisive victory over the Turks.

Lepanto from that time forth was to be a magic word in Cervantes' vocabulary, marking what obviously was for him the high point of his career; for he remained to the end of his days the old soldier reliving the past and priding himself on his honorable scars.[2] And he had good reason to remember that famous battle, for a maimed left hand was ever there to remind him of the heroism he had displayed. Though ill with malarial fever, he had insisted that his comrades carry him on deck that he might join in the fight, and even after he had been wounded, he fought on. Two of the wounds were in the chest, and a third shattered his hand, rendering it useless for the rest of his life.

Cervantes also participated in the Tunis campaign in the fall of 1573, and in November of the following year his military service ended with letters of commendation to the King given him by John of Austria and by the Duke of Sessa, Spanish viceroy in Naples. He was a model soldier, and this fact—which must have resulted in his close confinement to camp and barracks—may go to explain the rather superficial impressions that he seems to have derived from contact with the culture of the Italian Renaissance.[3] In September 1575 he and his brother Rodrigo, who was also serving on the peninsula, embarked for Spain and on the way were captured by Algerian pirates, an experience that is reflected in the captive's tale in Part I of *Don Quixote*.[4] After five years' imprisonment by the Moors he was finally ransomed by his family and friends and by December 1580 was back in Madrid.

Miguel was now thirty-four years of age, and it was about this time, in the early 1580's, that he turned to writing and, in particular, to the theater, while eking out a livelihood by any means that was afforded him.[5] He may even have returned to the colors in the campaign of the Azores, but this is not likely. It was during this period that he became the father of a bastard daughter, Isabel, whose mother was perhaps an actress; for he was now in contact with the world of actors and managers and is said to have written between twenty and thirty plays in the course of three years, although none of them was produced and only two have come down to us.[6]

He did not confine his efforts to the theater, however, but also tried his hand at the pastoral romance, then at the height of its popularity. His first published work, *La Galatea* (1585), was in this genre and revealed the influence of such writers as Montemayor, Gil Polo, and Montalvo. Even as he was struggling for a foothold in the literary world, he was married, in 1584, to the daughter of a well-to-do peasant of Esquivias. She brought him little dowry, and, while they had no children, Cervantes was saddled for the rest of his life with a houseful of womenfolk to support, including his two sisters, his illegitimate daughter, his niece, and a maidservant, in addition to his wife. He must, accordingly, have rejoiced when in 1588 he was appointed deputy purveyor to the fleet, with the task of requisitioning supplies for the Invincible Armada. He did not know all the trouble that was in store for him in connection with this post.

The territory assigned to him was Andalusia, and it was while roaming the countryside as a government commissary that he became familiar with the colorful folk speech and folklore of that province, of which he has given us a vivid reflection in more than one passage of *Don Quixote*. This for him was doubtless the more agreeable side of his new employment, but it was not so pleasant when he found himself temporarily excommunicated for having confiscated supplies belonging to the dean of the cathedral of Seville; and the worst was yet to come. The peasants made it hard for him, and Cervantes was no bookkeeper; he soon came up with a shortage in his accounts. As a result, he was thrown into jail on two occasions (1592 and 1597) and possibly a third time, in 1602. This gave rise to the legend, for there is no evidence to support it, that Part I of *Don Quixote* was composed in a prison cell. One thing that the author did gain from the experience was a first-hand acquaintance with underworld types and their jargon, as is clearly to be seen from from his *Exemplary Novels*[7] and his plays.

All this took place while Cervantes was engaged in a losing battle with poverty and an ill luck that seemed constantly to pursue him. Dissatisfied with his lot, he had applied to the King, in May 1590, for an overseas appointment but had been told to "look for something nearer home." In literature he fared little better than in practical life. In 1595 he won a first prize, consisting of three silver spoons, in a poetry contest at Saragossa, and three years later (1598) his sonnet "At the Bier of King Philip II in Seville" attracted some attention, but that was about all he had to show. In the meantime, as his poems and stories went unpublished, he would appear to have moved his burdensome household from one city to another. In November 1598 he was in Seville, but from then until 1603, when he was summoned to Valladolid [8] in connection with the money that he owed the Crown, we have no knowledge as to his whereabouts.[9] Wherever he was in the early years of the seventeenth century, he must have been at work on his masterpiece.

It was, then, not in the glow of youth nor in the mature vigor of middle age, but in his later fifties, as an old and ailing man ground down by poverty and hardship and sadly in need of funds, that Miguel de Cervantes sat down to write a book that was to prove to be the first modern novel and one of the greatest—many would say the greatest—of all time.[10] He was in his fifty-eighth year when Part I was put on sale by the Madrid bookseller Francisco de Robles, in 1605, and sixty-eight when the superb Part II came off the press of Juan de la Cuesta.

How did *Don Quixote* come to be written? What was the inspiring purpose in the author's mind? There is every reason to believe that, spurred on by want, Cervantes began the work with the object of making a little money and that he laid aside his poems, plays, and pastoral novels, which he looked upon as more serious productions, in order to compose a tale that would have a widely popular appeal, one designed, as he put it, "for the universal entertainment of the peoples." [11] And so, what could be more natural than that he should have conceived the idea of a parody or satire, not on the institution of chivalry, as has wrongly been assumed in the past, but on those romances dealing with knights-errant and their fantastic adventures that, having enjoyed so tremendous a vogue in the sixteenth century, had some while since begun to fall into disrepute with discerning readers? The theme was there, ready at hand, and offered unlimited possibilities.[12]

This may be said to have been Cervantes' original intention; it was a task similar to the one that Richardson was to undertake in his *Pamela* during the following century. The pretense, the fiction (for it is scarcely more than that) of an attack on the books of chivalry is kept up throughout; but as the story develops and deepens beyond the author's expectations as well as those of the reader, *Don Quixote* becomes nothing less than a novelistic treatment of the essential nature of human life and man's greatest metaphysical problem: that of illusion and reality. It is a problem as old as Plato—and a good deal older—and as new as Jean-Paul Sartre.[13] It is one that, as Lionel Trilling has rightly observed, has always been the serious novelist's chief concern. In this light, there can no longer be any question as to Don Quixote's "madness" in the ordinary acceptation of that term. In Waldo Frank's finely expressive phrase, he is "a man possessed, not a madman." [14]

This aspect of the work, however, could not have been apparent to Francisco de Robles when Cervantes presented his manuscript for publication. Indeed, it does not become fully evident until Part II is reached; for the author was to grow with the book, and there is an appreciable gulf between the first and second parts. What Robles must have seen was a story that was sufficiently amusing, with enough good laughs in it, to justify his taking a chance on it. The aging author, on the other hand, amid all the luminaries of Spain's Golden Age, was practically unknown and might well have been described as a literary failure. Cervantes, it appears, had given readings from the manuscript before the book was published, and the great Lope de Vega had declared that "there is none so foolish as to praise *Don Quixote*." The result was that Robles did not take the trouble to protect his own and the author's rights outside of Castile.

Then the miracle occurred. The work was pirated almost at once, and there were five printings within a year, including a second authorized one, the publisher meanwhile having secured the rights not only for Castile but for Aragon and Portugal as well. All Spain was now laughing over Don Quixote's "adventures" and Sancho's drolleries, and foreign editions and translations were not long in coming. Cervantes had lived to see himself famous, almost overnight, but his material burdens were not lightened to any extent [15] and misfortune continued to dog his steps. In 1605, even as Part I was appearing upon the stalls, he became involved in an investigation concerning the death of a nobleman slain in a duel, which may have led him to go into hiding, since we do not know where he was from 1605 to 1608.

From 1608 until his death in 1616, Cervantes' chief residence was at Madrid, where he labored upon Part II of the *Don Quixote*, his

Exemplary Novels and his plays, his long poem, the *Journey to Parnassus*, and, assuming it was written at this time, his *Persiles and Sigismunda*.[16] And all this, it is to be remembered, between the ages of fifty-eight and sixty-nine! In 1610 he was deeply disappointed when left out of a group of literary men who were accompanying his patron, the Count of Lemos, to Rome. The *Exemplary Novels* were published in 1613 and the *Journey to Parnassus* the following year. It was in 1614, also, that the spurious and vicious "sequel" to *Don Quixote*, signed by one Alonso Fernández de Avellaneda, fell into his hands, and this induced him to hurry the completion of Part II, which appeared in 1615, together with his *Eight Comedies and Eight Interludes*. The *Persiles and Sigismunda* was not published until 1617, a year after his death.

In his last days Cervantes turned to the Church for comfort, joining the Tertiary Order of St. Francis, and it was the Franciscans who carried him to his grave. His death, due to dropsy, occurred on April 23 (New Style),[17] but the place of his burial remains unknown.

PART ONE

The Ingenious Gentleman

DON QUIXOTE

DE LA MANCHA

PART ONE: CONTENTS

Certificate of Price

I, Juan Gallo de Andrada, scrivener of the Chamber of our master the King, in behalf of those who reside in his Council, do hereby certify and affirm that, those lords having seen a book entitled *The Ingenious Gentleman of La Mancha*, composed by Miguel de Cervantes Saavedra, they have estimated the value of each sheet of the said book at three and a half maravedis, and inasmuch as it contains eighty-three sheets, the value of the paper in the said book amounts to two-hundred-ninety maravedis and a half, at which price they have licensed it to be sold; and they have commanded that this certificate of price be placed in the front of the book, which may not be sold without it. As witness these presents, in Valladolid, on the twentieth day of the month of December of the year one-thousand-six-hundred-and-four.

JUAN GALLO DE ANDRADA

Certificate of Errata

THIS book contains nothing worthy of note that does not correspond to the original. In witness of the corrections made, in the College of the Mother of God of the Theologians of the University of Alcalá, on the first of December of the year one-thousand-six-hundred-and-four.

THE LICENTIATE FRANCISCO MURCIA DE LA LLANA

Royal Privilege

THE KING

INASMUCH as we have been informed, Miguel de Cervantes, that you have composed a book entitled *The Ingenious Gentleman of La Mancha*, which book has cost you much labor and is a very useful and profitable work; and inasmuch as you have petitioned and entreated us to grant you the license and authority to have it printed, along with a

Privilege for such time as we in our good grace might see fit to specify; and inasmuch as the said book has been duly scrutinized by our Council in accordance with our recent decree regarding the printing of books, it has been decided that we should grant you this scroll for the said purpose, the which we right willingly do.

With this object in view, by way of showing you grace and favor, we do hereby grant you, or the person you shall employ and none other, license and authority to print the said book entitled *The Ingenious Gentleman of La Mancha*, of which mention has been made above, in all these our realms of Castile, throughout the time and space of ten years current from the day of the date of this our scroll. It is further provided that any person or persons who without your permission shall print or sell the said book or cause it to be printed or sold shall lose the printing which he has made of it along with the type and the forms and shall in addition incur the penalty of a fine of fifty thousand maravedis for each such offense, one third of the said fine to go to the plaintiff, one third to our Chamber, and the remaining third to the judge who shall sentence him.

Withal, each time that you shall have the said book printed in the course of the said ten years, you shall bring it before our Council that each page may be endorsed and the work signed at the end by Juan Gallo de Andrada, our scrivener of the Chamber, in behalf of those in residence; this by way of seeing that the said printing conforms to the original; or you shall take public oath that the said printing has been seen and corrected by the reader appointed by us and has been found to be in conformity with the original; and there shall be printed also a list of the errata pointed out by him for each of the books published; and, finally, the price of each volume shall be duly fixed as provided by law.

And we do hereby command the printer who shall print the said book that he shall not print the beginning nor the first sheet of it nor deliver more than a single book along with the original to the person who pays the cost of the printing or any other person whomsoever until, first and foremost, the said book shall have been corrected and its price fixed by our Council. Only when this shall have been done and under no other circumstances may the beginning and the first sheet be printed, and after it shall be printed this our scroll and approbation, together with the certificate of price and the errata; this under pain of incurring those penalties provided in the laws and regulations of these our realms.

And we do hereby command the members of our Council and all others whomsoever charged with enforcing their decrees, to keep and observe this our scroll and that which is contained therein.

Done in Valladolid, on the twenty-sixth day of the month of September of the year one-thousand-six-hundred-and-four.

I, THE KING

By command of our master, the King,

JUAN DE AMEZQUETA

To the Duke of Béjar

MARQUIS OF GIBRALEÓN, COUNT OF BENALCÁZAR AND BENARES, VISCOUNT OF LA PUEBLA, LORD OF THE BOROUGHS OF CAPILLA, CURIEL, AND BURGUILLOS.

TRUSTING in that good reception and those marks of honor that your Excellency is in the habit of according to books of every sort, being a prince so inclined by nature to favor the fine arts, especially those works that by their nobility do not lower themselves to the service and profit of the vulgar, I have resolved to bring to light THE INGENIOUS GENTLEMAN, DON QUIXOTE OF LA MANCHA under the shelter of your Excellency's most illustrious name; and with that respect that I owe to one so great I do hereby beseech you to receive it and graciously to take it under your protection. Thus, even though barren of those precious ornaments of elegance and erudition in which works composed in the houses of the learned are accustomed to go clad, in your august shadow it may safely dare to appear before the judgment of those who, not content to confine themselves within the bounds of their own ignorance, are wont to condemn with much severity and less justice all writings that are strange to them. If your Excellency in your wisdom will but deign to look upon my worthy desire, I feel sure that you will not disdain this offering by reason of the scant service that it renders you.

MIGUEL DE CERVANTES SAAVEDRA

Prologue

IDLING READER, you may believe me when I tell you that I should have liked this book, which is the child of my brain, to be the fairest, the sprightliest, and the cleverest that could be imagined; but I have not been able to contravene the law of nature which would have it that like begets like. And so, what was to be expected of a sterile and uncultivated wit such as that which I possess if not an offspring that was dried up, shriveled, and eccentric: a story filled with thoughts that never occurred to anyone else, of a sort that might be engendered in a prison where every annoyance has its home and every mournful sound its habitation? [1] Peace and tranquillity, the pleasures of the countryside, the serenity of the heavens, the murmur of fountains, and ease of mind can do much toward causing the most unproductive of muses to become fecund and bring forth progeny that will be the marvel and delight of mankind.

It sometimes happens that a father has an ugly son with no redeeming grace whatever, yet love will draw a veil over the parental eyes which then behold only cleverness and beauty in place of defects, and in speaking to his friends he will make those defects out to be the signs of comeliness and intellect. I, however, who am but Don Quixote's stepfather, have no desire to go with the current of custom, nor would I, dearest reader, beseech you with tears in my eyes as others do to pardon or overlook the faults you discover in this book; you are neither relative nor friend but may call your soul your own and exercise your free judgment. You are in your own house where you are master as the king is of his taxes, for you are familiar with the saying, "Under my cloak I kill the king." [2] All of which exempts and frees you from any kind of respect or obligation; you may say of this story whatever you choose without fear of being slandered for an ill opinion any more than you will be rewarded for a good one.

I should like to bring you the tale unadulterated and unadorned, stripped of the usual prologue and the endless string of sonnets, epigrams, and eulogies such as are commonly found at the beginning of books. For I may tell you that, although I expended no little labor upon the work itself, I have found no task more difficult than the composition of this preface which you are now reading. Many times I took up my pen and many times I laid it down again, not knowing what to write. On one occasion when I was thus in suspense, paper before me, pen over my ear, elbow on the table, and chin in hand, a very clever friend of mine came in. Seeing me lost in thought, he inquired as to the reason, and I made no effort to conceal from him the fact that my mind was on the preface which I had to write for the story of Don Quixote, and that it was giving me so much trouble that I had about decided not to write any at all and to abandon entirely the idea of publishing the exploits of so noble a knight.

"How," I said to him, "can you expect me not to be concerned over what that venerable legislator, the Public, will say when it sees me, at my age, after all these years of silent slumber, coming out with a tale that is as dried as a rush, a stranger to invention, paltry in style, impoverished in content, and wholly lacking in learning and wisdom, without marginal citations or notes at the end of the book when other works of this sort, even though they be fabulous and profane, are so packed with maxims from Aristotle and Plato and the whole crowd of philosophers as to fill the reader with admiration and lead him to regard the author as a well read, learned, and eloquent individual? Not to speak of the citations from Holy Writ! You would think they were at the very least so many St. Thomases and other doctors of the Church; for they are so adroit at maintaining a solemn face that, having portrayed in one line a distracted lover, in the next they will give you a nice little Christian sermon that is a joy and a privilege to hear and read.

"All this my book will lack, for I have no citations for the margins, no notes for the end. To tell the truth, I do not even know who the authors are to whom I am indebted, and so am unable to follow the example of all the others by listing them alphabetically at the beginning, starting with Aristotle and closing with Xenophon, or, perhaps, with Zoilus or Zeuxis, notwithstanding the fact that the former was a snarling critic, the latter a painter. This work will also be found lacking in prefatory sonnets by dukes, marquises, counts, bishops, ladies, and poets of great renown; although if I were to ask two or three colleagues of mine, they would supply the deficiency by furnishing me with productions that could not be equaled by the authors of most repute in all Spain.

"In short, my friend," I went on, "I am resolved that Señor Don Quixote shall remain buried in the archives of La Mancha until Heaven shall provide him with someone to deck him out with all the ornaments that he lacks; for I find myself incapable of remedying the situation, being possessed of little learning or aptitude, and I am, moreover, ex-

tremely lazy when it comes to hunting up authors who will say for me
what I am unable to say for myself. And if I am in a state of suspense
and my thoughts are woolgathering, you will find a sufficient explanation in what I have just told you."

Hearing this, my friend struck his forehead with the palm of his hand
and burst into a loud laugh.

"In the name of God, brother," he said, "you have just deprived me of
an illusion. I have known you for a long time, and I have always taken
you to be clever and prudent in all your actions; but I now perceive that
you are as far from all that as Heaven from the earth. How is it that
things of so little moment and so easily remedied can worry and perplex
a mind as mature as yours and ordinarily so well adapted to break down
and trample underfoot far greater obstacles? I give you my word, this
does not come from any lack of cleverness on your part, but rather from
excessive indolence and a lack of experience. Do you ask for proof of
what I say? Then pay attention closely and in the blink of an eye you
shall see how I am going to solve all your difficulties and supply all those
things the want of which, so you tell me, is keeping you in suspense, as
a result of which you hesitate to publish the history of that famous Don
Quixote of yours, the light and mirror of all knight-errantry."

"Tell me, then," I replied, "how you propose to go about curing my
diffidence and bringing clarity out of the chaos and confusion of my
mind?"

"Take that first matter," he continued, "of the sonnets, epigrams, or
eulogies, which should bear the names of grave and titled personages:
you can remedy that by taking a little trouble and composing the pieces
yourself, and afterward you can baptize them with any name you see
fit, fathering them on Prester John of the Indies or the Emperor of
Trebizond, for I have heard tell that they were famous poets; and supposing they were not and that a few pedants and bachelors of arts
should go around muttering behind your back that it is not so, you should
not give so much as a pair of maravedis for all their carping, since even
though they make you out to be a liar, they are not going to cut off the
hand that put these things on paper.

"As for marginal citations and authors in whom you may find maxims
and sayings that you may put in your story, you have but to make use
of those scraps of Latin that you know by heart or can look up without
too much bother. Thus, when you come to treat of liberty and slavery,
jot down:

Non bene pro toto libertas venditur auro.[3]

And then in the margin you will cite Horace or whoever it was that said it. If the subject is death, come up with:

> Pallida mors aequo pulsat pede pauperum tabernas
> Regumque turres.[4]

If it is friendship or the love that God commands us to show our enemies, then is the time to fall back on the Scriptures, which you can do by putting yourself out very little; you have but to quote the words of God himself:

> Ego autem dico vobis: diligite inimicos vestros.

If it is evil thoughts, lose no time in turning to the Gospels:

> De corde exeunt cogitationes malae.[5]

If it is the instability of friends, here is Cato for you with a distich:

> Donec eris felix multos numerabis amicos;
> Tempora si fuerint nubila, solus eris.[6]

With these odds and ends of Latin and others of the same sort, you can cause yourself to be taken for a grammarian, although I must say that is no great honor or advantage these days.

"So far as notes at the end of the book are concerned, you may safely go about it in this manner: let us suppose that you mention some giant, Goliath let us say; with this one allusion which costs you little or nothing, you have a fine note which you may set down as follows: *The giant Golias or Goliath. This was a Philistine whom the shepherd David slew with a mighty cast from his slingshot in the valley of Terebinth, according to what we read in the Book of Kings,* chapter so-and-so where you find it written.[7]

"In addition to this, by way of showing that you are a learned humanist and a cosmographer, contrive to bring into your story the name of the River Tagus, and there you are with another great little note: *The River Tagus was so called after a king of Spain; it rises in such and such a place and empties into the ocean, washing the walls of the famous city of Lisbon; it is supposed to have golden sands,* etc. If it is robbers, I will let you have the story of Cacus,[8] which I know by heart. If it is loose women, there is the Bishop of Mondoñedo,[9] who will lend you Lamia, Laïs, and Flora, an allusion that will do you great credit. If the subject is cruelty, Ovid will supply you with Medea; or if it is enchantresses and witches, Homer has Calypso and Vergil Circe. If it is valorous captains, Julius Caesar will lend you himself, in his *Commentaries,* and Plutarch will furnish a thousand Alexanders. If it is loves, with the ounce or two of Tuscan that you know you may make the acquaintance of Leon the Hebrew,[10] who will satisfy you to your heart's content. And in case you do not care to go abroad, here in your own house you have Fonseca's *Of the Love of God*,[11] where you will encounter in condensed form all that the most imaginative person could wish upon this subject. The short of the matter is, you have but to allude to these names or touch upon those stories that I have mentioned and leave to me the business of the notes and citations; I will guarantee you enough to fill the margins and four whole sheets at the back.

"And now we come to the list of authors cited, such as other works contain but in which your own is lacking. Here again the remedy is an easy one; you have but to look up some book that has them all, from A to Z as you were saying, and transfer the entire list as it stands. What if the imposition is plain for all to see? You have little need to refer to them, and so it does not matter; and some may be so simple-minded as to believe that you have drawn upon them all in your simple unpretentious little story. If it serves no other purpose, this imposing list of authors will at least give your book an unlooked-for air of authority. What is more, no one is going to put himself to the trouble of verifying your references to see whether or not you have followed all these authors, since it will not be worth his pains to do so.

"This is especially true in view of the fact that your book stands in no need of all these things whose absence you lament; for the entire work is an attack upon the books of chivalry of which Aristotle never dreamed, of which St. Basil has nothing to say, and of which Cicero had no knowledge; nor do the fine points of truth or the observations of astrology have anything to do with its fanciful absurdities; geometrical measurements, likewise, and rhetorical argumentations serve for nothing here; you have no sermon to preach to anyone by mingling the human with the divine, a kind of motley in which no Christian intellect should be willing to clothe itself.

"All that you have to do is to make proper use of imitation in what you write, and the more perfect the imitation the better will your writing be. Inasmuch as you have no other object in view than that of overthrowing the authority and prestige which books of chivalry enjoy in the world at large and among the vulgar, there is no reason why you should go begging maxims of the philosophers, counsels of Holy Writ, fables of the poets, orations of the rhetoricians, or miracles of the saints; see to it, rather, that your style flows along smoothly, pleasingly, and sonorously, and that your words are the proper ones, meaningful and well placed, expressive of your intention in setting them down and of what you wish to say, without any intricacy or obscurity.

"Let it be your aim that, by reading your story, the melancholy may be moved to laughter and the cheerful man made merrier still; let the simple not be bored, but may the clever admire your originality; let the grave ones not despise you, but let the prudent praise you. And keep in mind, above all, your purpose, which is that of undermining the ill-founded edifice that is constituted by those books of chivalry, so abhorred by many but admired by many more; if you succeed in attaining it, you will have accomplished no little."

Listening in profound silence to what my friend had to say, I was so impressed by his reasoning that, with no thought of questioning them, I decided to make use of his arguments in composing this prologue. Here, gentle reader, you will perceive my friend's cleverness, my own good fortune in coming upon such a counselor at a time when I needed him so badly, and the profit which you yourselves are to have in finding so sincere and straightforward an account of the famous Don Quixote de la Mancha, who is held by the inhabitants of the Campo de Montiel region [12] to have been the most chaste lover and the most valiant knight that had been seen in those parts for many a year. I have no desire to enlarge upon the service I am rendering you in bringing you the story of so notable and honored a gentleman; I merely would have you thank me for having made you acquainted with the famous Sancho Panza, his squire, in whom, to my mind, is to be found an epitome of all the squires and their drolleries scattered here and there throughout the pages of those vain and empty books of chivalry. And with this, may God give you health, and may He be not unmindful of me as well. VALE.

PREFATORY POEMS

Urganda the Unknown

FOR THE BOOK OF DON QUIXOTE DE LA MANCHA[1]

If to win the worthy be thine ambition,
O book, then let the foolish chatter
As much as they please, it will not matter,
For thy desire has had fruition.
To bake bread for fools is not thy mission:
Hand raised to mouth, they're hungry still,
But taste thee the dunces surely will,
And each his fingers will greedily lick
To prove he appreciates the trick
Of such fine fare and would eat his fill.

Experience shows that he who reaches
A tree that's goodly, fair, and thriving,
Is bound to find there, upon arriving,
A pleasing shade; let none impeach
This lesson life itself would teach.
Draw near; thy star benign is showing
A regal tree in Béjar [2] that's growing.
In way of fruit this tree doth bear
One who a princely crown doth wear;
'Tis an Alexander his shade bestowing.

Thou shalt relate the high emprises
Of a Manchegan [3] gentleman whose reading
Had turned his head with tales of bleeding
Knights-errant, damsels, love's surprises,
And all of chivalry's disguises.
By deeds of valor he sought to gain
His lady's love, and ease his pain;
His model Orlando Furioso,
And Dulcinea del Toboso
Was the one whose favor he would obtain.

No hieroglyphs upon thy shield,[4]
No pictures to display thy pride;

17

Better by far a humbler stride,
Then envy's weapon none can wield
By saying all that thou dost yield
Is an old story quite banal
Of Alvaro de Luna [5] or Hannibal
Or of King Francis his fate bemoaning
As at Madrid he lies a-groaning. [6]
So, close the door on their cabal.

Seeing it was not Heaven's pleasure
To make thee learned as black John, [7]
Do not the cloak of learning don
By quoting Latin in over-measure,
Displaying thy philosophic treasure
In long and windy argument,
Until some fellow irreverent,
Twisting his mouth at thine ear shall say:
"Why give me flowers, anyway?
On me such bounty is misspent."

Seek not to know or to portray
The lives of others; mind thine own
And leave thy neighbor's life alone.
Be wise in this and in the play
Thou givest thy wit—there may come a day
When the word spoken in lightsome jest
Will come winging home with thee to rest;
And ever seek an honest fame,
For he is doomed to perpetual blame
Who nonsense prints and calls it best.

Remember, 'tis a foolish thing,
Dwelling beneath a roof of glass,
To stone thy neighbors as they pass,
For they likewise may pebbles fling.
Seek rather to please in everything
The man of taste and judgment fine,
That he may ponder every line;
If damsels be thy audience,
Thou shalt be spurned by those with sense,
To fools thou dost thyself consign.

Amadis of Gaul

TO DON QUIXOTE DE LA MANCHA[8]

SONNET

Thou who didst imitate my own sad life,
So full of loneliness and love's disdain
As on the Poor Rock[9] I endured my pain—
My days once joyful now with sorrow rife,
To pay love's penance was my constant strife—
Thou knowest the taste of tears; for thee most vain
Were silver, tin, or copper plate; thou wert fain
To make of the earth thy table and chatelaine.
But rest assured, thou livest eternally,
Or as long as blond Apollo in that fourth sphere
Doth guide on their heavenly course his fiery steeds.
Thy fame and valor shall unsullied be,
Thy fatherland remain without a peer,
And peerless the chronicler of thy brave deeds.

Don Belianís of Greece[10]

TO DON QUIXOTE DE LA MANCHA

SONNET

In slashing, smashing, bruising, in word and deed,
I was the foremost knight of errantry,
In pride, in valor, in dexterity.
A myriad wrongs I righted, did ever heed
The call of those who were in direst need;
My famed exploits shall endure eternally.
Deep-versed was I in love and ecstasy,
And on the field of honor I did bleed.
A giant for me was but a dwarf. No boon
Luck did deny me; I was ever wise
And brought her by the forelock to my feet.
But though my fortune rides the horn o' the moon,
I envy still thy deeds of high emprise,
O great Quixote, who dost with me compete!

The Lady Oriana [11]

TO DULCINEA DEL TOBOSO

O lovely Dulcinea, could I with thee
But exchange my Miraflores [12] of such renown,
London for El Toboso, thy little town,
How great a comfort and relief 'twould be!
Could I but once my soul and body see
Dressed in thy love as in a daily gown,
And behold that famous knight (thy love his crown)
Performing some brave feat of chivalry!
Ah, then, I might remain fully as chaste
With Amadis [13] as thou with thy lover bold,
The gallant Don Quixote without blame!
Then I'd not envy, but envied be, nor waste
My life in sorrow for the time that's told;
Joy would be mine, no cost to my good name!

Gandalin, Squire to Amadis of Gaul,

TO SANCHO PANZA, DON QUIXOTE'S SQUIRE

Hail, celebrated one, Fortune was kind
When she did set thee to the squire's trade,
And wise as well—ah, she no blunder made;
No great calamity e'er came to find
Thee out, but men still fondly call to mind
That thou didst erstwhile leave sickle and spade
For the pursuit of arms, all unafraid;
Thy squire's simplicity puts far behind
The haughty pride that would defy the moon.
I envy thee thine ass, thy name, thy sense,
And those saddlebags that thou didst wisely stuff.
Sancho, hail once again! And very soon
May our Spanish Ovid [14] do thee reverence
By giving thee a famous kick-and-cuff. [15]

Donoso, Interlarded Poet,[16]

TO SANCHO PANZA AND ROCINANTE

TO SANCHO PANZA

I am Sancho Panza, squi—	(squire)
Of the Manchegan Don Quixo—	(Quixote)
Who did withdraw to a place remo—	(remote)
That I might from his service reti—.	(retire)
Villadiego [17] known as the Si—	(Silent)
Is said to have found that the real se—	(secret)
Of a good life was a pleasant re—;	(retreat)
His words you'll find if in that divine boo—,	(book)
The *Celestina*,[18] you choose to loo—,	(look)
Or 'twould be divine if more discree—.	(discreet)

TO ROCINANTE

I am Rocinante, the famous stee—,	(steed)
Great Babieca's [19] great grandso—.	(grandson)
'Twas the sin of leanness that for me wo—	(won)
My master (I met his every nee—),	(need)
Don Quixote of far-famed dee—.	(deed)
I ran my race in my own good ti—,	(time)
And can say no stable mate of mi—	(mine)
Ever stole my barley by dint of hoo—;	(hoof)
From Lazarillo [20] I learned, in soo—	(sooth)
With a straw to take the blind man's wi—.	(wine)

Orlando Furioso

TO DON QUIXOTE DE LA MANCHA

SONNET [21]

If thou art not a Peer,[22] no peer hast thou,
But amongst a thousand Peers, a peer thou art,
When thou art present, thou dost stand apart.
Victor invincible, unvanquished up to now.

Quixote, I am Orlando. Hast heard how
I sailed far seas for her who held my heart?
Love for Angelica [23] my course did chart;
My valor on Fame's altar laid its vow,
Held back oblivion. It is not meet
To rival thee in prowess or in fame,
E'en though our loss of sense be a common bond;
But thou mayest very well with me compete,
Though neither Moor nor Scythian didst tame:
In our ill-fated loves we correspond.

The Knight of the Sun [24]

TO DON QUIXOTE DE LA MANCHA

My sword, though valiant, did never equal thine,
Phoebus of Spain, O thou most courteous knight,
Nor was my arm as powerful in the fight,
Though it lightning-flashed all while the sun did shine.
Empires I wanted not. I did decline
The rosy Orient's crown for the countenance bright
Of Claridiana, filled with dawn's own light,
For she was my Aurora blest, divine.
Miraculous my love for her and rare;
And banished by her decree, my mighty arm
Caused hell in all its fury to fear my rage.
But thou, Gothic Quixote, shinest everywhere
Immortal, thanks to Dulcinea's charm,
While she is ever famous, honored, sage.

Solisdan [25]

TO DON QUIXOTE DE LA MANCHA

Señor Quixote, your fancies turned your head,
But none shall reprehend your lack of guile
Or take you for a man that's base and vile;
Your deeds speak for themselves when all is said.

You went about the world in knightly style,
Undoing wrongs and suffering the while
A myriad drubbings; but be comforted.
If the beauteous Dulcinea did prolong
Love's agony and pitied not your pain,
In such a case there's one thing you may do:
Reflect that Sancho Panza was not strong
As a go-between a lady's love to gain;
He was a dunce, she cruel, no lover you.

DIALOGUE BETWEEN BABIECA[26] AND ROCINANTE

SONNET

B. How comes it, Rocinante, you are so lean?
R. From working overmuch and eating never.
B. But straw and barley they must give you ever?
R. Not one mouthful, my master is so mean.
B. Come, come, sir, you are quite ill bred, I ween.
   You talk like an ass; our acquaintance we must sever.
R. A lifelong ass is he—at least not clever—
   And in love the biggest ass was ever seen.
B. To love is foolish, then? R. It is not wise.
B. You grow metaphysical. R. From lack of food.
B. Why not complain of the squire? R. Ah, what's the use?
   How in my sorrow can I sermonize
   When master and man are of the selfsame brood
   And both are hacks like me,[27] fit for abuse?

The Ingenious Gentleman

DON QUIXOTE

DE LA MANCHA

Part One

CHAPTER I. *Which treats of the station in life and the pursuits of the famous gentleman, Don Quixote de la Mancha.*

IN A village of La Mancha the name of which I have no desire to recall,[1] there lived not so long ago one of those gentlemen who always have a lance in the rack, an ancient buckler, a skinny nag, and a greyhound for the chase. A stew with more beef than mutton in it, chopped meat for his evening meal, scraps [2] for a Saturday, lentils on Friday, and a young pigeon as a special delicacy for Sunday, went to account for three-quarters of his income. The rest of it he laid out on a broadcloth greatcoat and velvet stockings for feast days, with slippers to match, while the other days of the week he cut a figure in a suit of the finest homespun. Living with him were a housekeeper in her forties, a niece who was not yet twenty, and a lad of the field and market place who saddled his horse for him and wielded the pruning knife.

This gentleman of ours was close on to fifty, of a robust constitution but with little flesh on his bones and a face that was lean and gaunt. He was noted for his early rising, being very fond of the hunt. They will try to tell you that his surname was Quijada or Quesada—there is some

difference of opinion among those who have written on the subject—
but according to the most likely conjectures we are to understand that
it was really Quejana. But all this means very little so far as our story
is concerned, providing that in the telling of it we do not depart one
iota from the truth.

You may know, then, that the aforesaid gentleman, on those occasions
when he was at leisure, which was most of the year around, was in the
habit of reading books of chivalry with such pleasure and devotion as to
lead him almost wholly to forget the life of a hunter and even the administration of his estate. So great was his curiosity and infatuation in
this regard that he even sold many acres of tillable land in order to be
able to buy and read the books that he loved, and he would carry home
with him as many of them as he could obtain.

Of all those that he thus devoured none pleased him so well as the ones
that had been composed by the famous Feliciano de Silva,[3] whose lucid
prose style and involved conceits were as precious to him as pearls; especially when he came to read those tales of love and amorous challenges
that are to be met with in many places, such a passage as the following,
for example: "The reason of the unreason that afflicts my reason, in such
a manner weakens my reason that I with reason lament me of your comeliness." And he was similarly affected when his eyes fell upon such lines
as these: ". . . the high Heaven of your divinity divinely fortifies you
with the stars and renders you deserving of that desert your greatness
doth deserve."

The poor fellow used to lie awake nights in an effort to disentangle
the meaning and make sense out of passages such as these, although
Aristotle himself would not have been able to understand them, even if
he had been resurrected for that sole purpose. He was not at ease in his
mind over those wounds that Don Belianís [4] gave and received; for no
matter how great the surgeons who treated him, the poor fellow must
have been left with his face and his entire body covered with marks
and scars. Nevertheless, he was grateful to the author for closing the
book with the promise of an interminable adventure to come; many a
time he was tempted to take up his pen and literally finish the tale as
had been promised, and he undoubtedly would have done so, and would
have succeeded at it very well, if his thoughts had not been constantly
occupied with other things of greater moment.

He often talked it over with the village curate, who was a learned man,
a graduate of Sigüenza,[5] and they would hold long discussions as to who
had been the better knight, Palmerin of England or Amadis of Gaul; but

Master Nicholas, the barber of the same village, was in the habit of saying that no one could come up to the Knight of Phoebus, and that if anyone *could* compare with him it was Don Galaor, brother of Amadis of Gaul, for Galaor was ready for anything—he was none of your finical knights, who went around whimpering as his brother did, and in point of valor he did not lag behind him.

In short, our gentleman became so immersed in his reading that he spent whole nights from sundown to sunup and his days from dawn to dusk in poring over his books, until, finally, from so little sleeping and so much reading, his brain dried up and he went completely out of his mind. He had filled his imagination with everything that he had read, with enchantments, knightly encounters, battles, challenges, wounds, with tales of love and its torments, and all sorts of impossible things, and as a result had come to believe that all these fictitious happenings were true; they were more real to him than anything else in the world. He would remark that the Cid Ruy Díaz had been a very good knight, but there was no comparison between him and the Knight of the Flaming Sword,[6] who with a single backward stroke had cut in half two fierce and monstrous giants. He preferred Bernardo del Carpio, who at Roncesvalles had slain Roland despite the charm the latter bore, availing himself of the stratagem which Hercules employed when he strangled Antaeus, the son of Earth, in his arms.

He had much good to say for Morgante who, though he belonged to the haughty, overbearing race of giants, was of an affable disposition and well brought up. But, above all, he cherished an admiration for Rinaldo of Montalbán,[7] especially as he beheld him sallying forth from his castle to rob all those that crossed his path, or when he thought of him overseas stealing the image of Mohammed which, so the story has it, was all of gold. And he would have liked very well to have had his fill of kicking that traitor Galalón,[8] a privilege for which he would have given his housekeeper with his niece thrown into the bargain.

At last, when his wits were gone beyond repair, he came to conceive the strangest idea that ever occurred to any madman in this world. It now appeared to him fitting and necessary, in order to win a greater amount of honor for himself and serve his country at the same time, to become a knight-errant and roam the world on horseback, in a suit of armor; he would go in quest of adventures, by way of putting into practice all that he had read in his books; he would right every manner of wrong, placing himself in situations of the greatest peril such as would redound to the eternal glory of his name. As a reward for his valor and the

might of his arm, the poor fellow could already see himself crowned
Emperor of Trebizond at the very least; and so, carried away by the
strange pleasure that he found in such thoughts as these, he at once set
about putting his plan into effect.

The first thing he did was to burnish up some old pieces of armor, left
him by his great-grandfather, which for ages had lain in a corner, moldering and forgotten. He polished and adjusted them as best he could, and
then he noticed that one very important thing was lacking: there was
no closed helmet, but only a morion, or visorless headpiece, with turned
up brim of the kind foot soldiers wore. His ingenuity, however, enabled
him to remedy this, and he proceeded to fashion out of cardboard a
kind of half-helmet, which, when attached to the morion, gave the appearance of a whole one. True, when he went to see if it was strong
enough to withstand a good slashing blow, he was somewhat disappointed; for when he drew his sword and gave it a couple of thrusts, he
succeeded only in undoing a whole week's labor. The ease with which
he had hewed it to bits disturbed him no little, and he decided to make
it over. This time he placed a few strips of iron on the inside, and then,
convinced that it was strong enough, refrained from putting it to any
further test; instead, he adopted it then and there as the finest helmet
ever made.

After this, he went out to have a look at his nag; and although the
animal had more *cuartos*, or cracks, in its hoof than there are quarters
in a real,[9] and more blemishes than Gonela's steed which *tantum pellis
et ossa fuit*,[10] it nonetheless looked to its master like a far better horse
than Alexander's Bucephalus or the Babieca of the Cid. He spent all of
four days in trying to think up a name for his mount; for—so he told
himself—seeing that it belonged to so famous and worthy a knight, there
was no reason why it should not have a name of equal renown. The kind
of name he wanted was one that would at once indicate what the nag
had been before it came to belong to a knight-errant and what its present
status was; for it stood to reason that, when the master's worldly condition changed, his horse also ought to have a famous, high-sounding appellation, one suited to the new order of things and the new profession
that it was to follow.

After he in his memory and imagination had made up, struck out, and
discarded many names, now adding to and now subtracting from the
list, he finally hit upon "Rocinante," a name that impressed him as being
sonorous and at the same time indicative of what the steed had been when

it was but a hack,[11] whereas now it was nothing other than the first and foremost of all the hacks in the world.

Having found a name for his horse that pleased his fancy, he then desired to do as much for himself, and this required another week, and by the end of that period he had made up his mind that he was henceforth to be known as Don Quixote,[12] which, as has been stated, has led the authors of this veracious history to assume that his real name must undoubtedly have been Quijada, and not Quesada as others would have it. But remembering that the valiant Amadis was not content to call himself that and nothing more, but added the name of his kingdom and fatherland that he might make it famous also, and thus came to take the name Amadis of Gaul, so our good knight chose to add his place of origin and become "Don Quixote de la Mancha"; for by this means, as he saw it, he was making very plain his lineage and was conferring honor upon his country by taking its name as his own.

And so, having polished up his armor and made the morion over into a closed helmet, and having given himself and his horse a name, he naturally found but one thing lacking still: he must seek out a lady of whom he could become enamored; for a knight-errant without a lady-love was like a tree without leaves or fruit, a body without a soul.

"If," he said to himself, "as a punishment for my sins or by a stroke of fortune I should come upon some giant hereabouts, a thing that very commonly happens to knights-errant, and if I should slay him in a hand-to-hand encounter or perhaps cut him in two, or, finally, if I should vanquish and subdue him, would it not be well to have someone to whom I may send him as a present, in order that he, if he is living, may come in, fall upon his knees in front of my sweet lady, and say in a humble and submissive tone of voice, 'I, lady, am the giant Caraculiambro, lord of the island Malindrania, who has been overcome in single combat by that knight who never can be praised enough, Don Quixote de la Mancha, the same who sent me to present myself before your Grace that your Highness may dispose of me as you see fit'?"

Oh, how our good knight reveled in this speech, and more than ever when he came to think of the name that he should give his lady! As the story goes, there was a very good-looking farm girl who lived near by, with whom he had once been smitten, although it is generally believed that she never knew or suspected it. Her name was Aldonza Lorenzo, and it seemed to him that she was the one upon whom he should bestow the title of mistress of his thoughts. For her he wished a name that should

not be incongruous with his own and that would convey the suggestion
of a princess or a great lady; and, accordingly, he resolved to call her
"Dulcinea del Toboso," she being a native of that place. A musical
name to his ears, out of the ordinary and significant, like the others he
had chosen for himself and his appurtenances.

CHAPTER II. *Which treats of the first sally that
the ingenious Don Quixote made from his native heath.*

HAVING, then, made all these preparations, he did not wish to lose
any time in putting his plan into effect, for he could not but blame himself for what the world was losing by his delay, so many were the wrongs
that were to be righted, the grievances to be redressed, the abuses to
be done away with, and the duties to be performed. Accordingly, without informing anyone of his intention and without letting anyone see
him, he set out one morning before daybreak on one of those very hot
days in July. Donning all his armor, mounting Rocinante, adjusting his
ill-contrived helmet, bracing his shield on his arm, and taking up his
lance, he sallied forth by the back gate of his stable yard into the open
countryside. It was with great contentment and joy that he saw how
easily he had made a beginning toward the fulfillment of his desire.

No sooner was he out on the plain, however, than a terrible thought
assailed him, one that all but caused him to abandon the enterprise he had
undertaken. This occurred when he suddenly remembered that he had
never formally been dubbed a knight, and so, in accordance with the
law of knighthood, was not permitted to bear arms against one who
had a right to that title. And even if he had been, as a novice knight he
would have had to wear white armor,[1] without any device on his shield,
until he should have earned one by his exploits. These thoughts led him
to waver in his purpose, but, madness prevailing over reason, he resolved
to have himself knighted by the first person he met, as many others had
done if what he had read in those books that he had at home was true.
And so far as white armor was concerned, he would scour his own the

first chance that offered until it shone whiter than any ermine. With this he became more tranquil and continued on his way, letting his horse take whatever path it chose, for he believed that therein lay the very essence of adventures.

And so we find our newly fledged adventurer jogging along and talking to himself. "Undoubtedly," he is saying, "in the days to come, when the true history of my famous deeds is published, the learned chronicler who records them, when he comes to describe my first sally so early in the morning, will put down something like this: 'No sooner had the rubicund Apollo spread over the face of the broad and spacious earth the gilded filaments of his beauteous locks, and no sooner had the little singing birds of painted plumage greeted with their sweet and mellifluous harmony the coming of the Dawn, who, leaving the soft couch of her jealous spouse, now showed herself to mortals at all the doors and balconies of the horizon that bounds La Mancha—no sooner had this happened than the famous knight, Don Quixote de la Mancha, forsaking his own downy bed and mounting his famous steed, Rocinante, fared forth and began riding over the ancient and famous Campo de Montiel.' " [2]

And this was the truth, for he was indeed riding over that stretch of plain.

"O happy age and happy century," he went on, "in which my famous exploits shall be published, exploits worthy of being engraved in bronze, sculptured in marble, and depicted in paintings for the benefit of posterity. O wise magician, whoever you be, to whom shall fall the task of chronicling this extraordinary history of mine! I beg of you not to forget my good Rocinante, eternal companion of my wayfarings and my wanderings."

Then, as though he really had been in love: "O Princess Dulcinea, lady of this captive heart! Much wrong have you done me in thus sending me forth with your reproaches and sternly commanding me not to appear in your beauteous presence. O lady, deign to be mindful of this your subject who endures so many woes for the love of you."

And so he went on, stringing together absurdities, all of a kind that his books had taught him, imitating insofar as he was able the language of their authors. He rode slowly, and the sun came up so swiftly and with so much heat that it would have been sufficient to melt his brains if he had had any. He had been on the road almost the entire day without anything happening that is worthy of being set down here; and he was on the verge of despair, for he wished to meet someone at once with whom he might try the valor of his good right arm. Certain authors say that his first adventure was that of Puerto Lápice, while others state that it was that of the windmills; [3] but in this particular instance I am in a position to affirm what I have read in the annals of La Mancha; and that is to the effect that he went all that day until nightfall, when he and his hack found themselves tired to death and famished. Gazing all around him to see if he could discover some castle or shepherd's hut where he might take shelter and attend to his pressing needs, he caught sight of an inn [4] not far off the road along which they were traveling, and this to him was like a star guiding him not merely to the gates, but rather, let us say, to the palace of redemption. Quickening his pace, he came up to it just as night was falling.

By chance there stood in the doorway two lasses of the sort known as "of the district"; they were on their way to Seville in the company of some mule drivers who were spending the night in the inn. Now, everything that this adventurer of ours thought, saw, or imagined seemed to him to be directly out of one of the storybooks he had read, and so, when he caught sight of the inn, it at once became a castle with its four turrets and its pinnacles of gleaming silver, not to speak of the drawbridge and moat and all the other things that are commonly supposed to go with a castle. As he rode up to it, he accordingly reined in Rocinante and sat there waiting for a dwarf to appear upon the battlements and blow his trumpet by way of announcing the arrival of a knight. The dwarf, however, was slow in coming, and as Rocinante was anxious to reach the stable, Don Quixote drew up to the door of the hostelry and surveyed the two merry maidens, who to him were a pair of beauteous damsels or gracious ladies taking their ease at the castle gate.

And then a swineherd came along, engaged in rounding up his drove of hogs—for, without any apology, that is what they were. He gave a blast on his horn to bring them together, and this at once became for Don Quixote just what he wished it to be: some dwarf who was heralding his coming; and so it was with a vast deal of satisfaction that he presented himself before the ladies in question, who, upon beholding a man in full armor like this, with lance and buckler, were filled with fright and made as if to flee indoors. Realizing that they were afraid, Don Quixote raised his pasteboard visor and revealed his withered, dust-covered face.

"Do not flee, your Ladyships," he said to them in a courteous manner and gentle voice. "You need not fear that any wrong will be done you, for it is not in accordance with the order of knighthood which I profess to wrong anyone, much less such highborn damsels as your appearance shows you to be."

The girls looked at him, endeavoring to scan his face, which was half hidden by his ill-made visor. Never having heard women of their profession called damsels before, they were unable to restrain their laughter, at which Don Quixote took offense.

"Modesty," he observed, "well becomes those with the dower of beauty, and, moreover, laughter that has not good cause is a very foolish thing. But I do not say this to be discourteous or to hurt your feelings; my only desire is to serve you."

The ladies did not understand what he was talking about, but felt more than ever like laughing at our knight's unprepossessing figure. This increased his annoyance, and there is no telling what would have happened if at that moment the innkeeper had not come out. He was very fat and very peaceably inclined; but upon sighting this grotesque personage clad in bits of armor that were quite as oddly matched as were his bridle, lance, buckler, and corselet, mine host was not at all indisposed to join the lasses in their merriment. He was suspicious, however, of all this paraphernalia and decided that it would be better to keep a civil tongue in his head.

"If, Sir Knight," he said, "your Grace desires a lodging, aside from a bed—for there is none to be had in this inn—you will find all else that you may want in great abundance."

When Don Quixote saw how humble the governor of the castle was—for he took the innkeeper and his inn to be no less than that—he replied, "For me, Sir Castellan, anything will do, since

> *Arms are my only ornament,*
> *My only rest the fight, etc."*

The landlord thought that the knight had called him a castellan because he took him for one of those worthies of Castile,[5] whereas the truth was, he was an Andalusian from the beach of Sanlúcar, no less a thief than Cacus himself, and as full of tricks as a student or a page boy.

"In that case," he said,

> *"Your bed will be the solid rock,*
> *Your sleep: to watch all night.*[6]

This being so, you may be assured of finding beneath this roof enough to keep you awake for a whole year, to say nothing of a single night."

With this, he went up to hold the stirrup for Don Quixote, who encountered much difficulty in dismounting, not having broken his fast all day long. The knight then directed his host to take good care of the steed, as it was the best piece of horseflesh in all the world. The innkeeper looked it over, and it did not impress him as being half as good as Don Quixote had said it was. Having stabled the animal, he came back to see what his guest would have and found the latter being relieved of his armor by the damsels, who by now had made their peace with the new arrival. They had already removed his breastplate and backpiece but had no idea how they were going to open his gorget or get his improvised helmet off. That piece of armor had been tied on with green ribbons which it would be necessary to cut, since the knots could not be undone, but he would not hear of this, and so spent all the rest of that night with his headpiece in place, which gave him the weirdest, most laughable appearance that could be imagined.

Don Quixote fancied that these wenches who were assisting him must surely be the chatelaine and other ladies of the castle, and so proceeded to address them very gracefully and with much wit:

> "Never was knight so served
> By any noble dame
> As was Don Quixote
> When from his village he came,
> With damsels to wait on his every need
> While princesses cared for his hack . . ."[7]

"By hack," he explained, "is meant my steed Rocinante, for that is his name, and mine is Don Quixote de la Mancha. I had no intention of revealing my identity until my exploits done in your service should have made me known to you; but the necessity of adapting to present circumstances that old ballad of Lancelot has led to your becoming acquainted with it prematurely. However, the time will come when your Ladyships shall command and I will obey and with the valor of my good right arm show you how eager I am to serve you."

The young women were not used to listening to speeches like this and had not a word to say, but merely asked him if he desired to eat anything.

"I could eat a bite of something, yes," replied Don Quixote. "Indeed, I feel that a little food would go very nicely just now."

He thereupon learned that, since it was Friday, there was nothing to be had in all the inn except a few portions of codfish, which in Castile is called *abadejo,* in Andalusia *bacalao,* in some places *curadillo,* and elsewhere *truchuella* or small trout. Would his Grace, then, have some small trout, seeing that was all there was that they could offer him?

"If there are enough of them," said Don Quixote, "they will take the place of a trout, for it is all one to me whether I am given in change eight reales or one piece of eight. What is more, those small trout may be like veal, which is better than beef, or like kid, which is better than goat. But however that may be, bring them on at once, for the weight and burden of arms is not to be borne without inner sustenance."

Placing the table at the door of the hostelry, in the open air, they brought the guest a portion of badly soaked and worse cooked codfish and a piece of bread as black and moldy as the suit of armor that he wore. It was a mirth-provoking sight to see him eat, for he still had his helmet on with his visor fastened,[8] which made it impossible for him to put anything into his mouth with his hands, and so it was necessary for one of the girls to feed him. As for giving him anything to drink, that would have been out of the question if the innkeeper had not hollowed out a reed, placing one end in Don Quixote's mouth while through the other end he poured the wine. All this the knight bore very patiently rather than have them cut the ribbons of his helmet.

At this point a gelder of pigs approached the inn, announcing his arrival with four or five blasts on his horn, all of which confirmed Don Quixote in the belief that this was indeed a famous castle, for what was this if not music that they were playing for him? The fish was trout, the bread was of the finest, the wenches were ladies, and the innkeeper was the castellan. He was convinced that he had been right in his resolve to sally forth and roam the world at large, but there was one thing that still distressed him greatly, and that was the fact that he had not as yet been dubbed a knight; as he saw it, he could not legitimately engage in any adventure until he had received the order of knighthood.

CHAPTER III. *Of the amusing manner in which Don Quixote had himself dubbed a knight.*

WEARIED of his thoughts, Don Quixote lost no time over the scanty repast which the inn afforded him. When he had finished, he summoned the landlord and, taking him out to the stable, closed the doors and fell on his knees in front of him.

"Never, valiant knight," he said, "shall I arise from here until you have courteously granted me the boon I seek, one which will redound to your praise and to the good of the human race."

Seeing his guest at his feet and hearing him utter such words as these, the innkeeper could only stare at him in bewilderment, not knowing what to say or do. It was in vain that he entreated him to rise, for Don Quixote refused to do so until his request had been granted.

"I expected nothing less of your great magnificence, my lord," the latter then continued, "and so I may tell you that the boon I asked and which you have so generously conceded me is that tomorrow morning you dub me a knight. Until that time, in the chapel of this your castle, I will watch over my armor, and when morning comes, as I have said, that which I so desire shall then be done, in order that I may lawfully go to the four corners of the earth in quest of adventures and to succor the needy, which is the chivalrous duty of all knights-errant such as I who long to engage in deeds of high emprise."

The innkeeper, as we have said, was a sharp fellow. He already had a suspicion that his guest was not quite right in the head, and he was now convinced of it as he listened to such remarks as these. However, just for the sport of it, he determined to humor him; and so he went on to assure Don Quixote that he was fully justified in his request and that such a desire and purpose was only natural on the part of so distinguished a knight as his gallant bearing plainly showed him to be.

He himself, the landlord added, when he was a young man, had followed the same honorable calling. He had gone through various parts of the world seeking adventures, among the places he had visited being the Percheles of Málaga, the Isles of Riarán, the District of Seville, the Little Market Place of Segovia, the Olivera of Valencia, the Rondilla of Gra-

nada, the beach of Sanlúcar, the Horse Fountain of Cordova, the Small
Taverns of Toledo, and numerous other localities [1] where his nimble
feet and light fingers had found much exercise. He had done many
wrongs, cheated many widows, ruined many maidens, and swindled not
a few minors until he had finally come to be known in almost all the
courts and tribunals that are to be found in the whole of Spain.

At last he had retired to his castle here, where he lived upon his own
income and the property of others; and here it was that he received all
knights-errant of whatever quality and condition, simply out of the
great affection that he bore them and that they might share with him their
possessions in payment of his good will. Unfortunately, in this castle
there was no chapel where Don Quixote might keep watch over his arms,
for the old chapel had been torn down to make way for a new one;
but in case of necessity, he felt quite sure that such a vigil could be maintained anywhere, and for the present occasion the courtyard of the
castle would do; and then in the morning, please God, the requisite ceremony could be performed and his guest be duly dubbed a knight, as
much a knight as anyone ever was.

He then inquired if Don Quixote had any money on his person, and
the latter replied that he had not a cent, for in all the storybooks he had
never read of knights-errant carrying any. But the innkeeper told him
he was mistaken on this point: supposing the authors of those stories
had not set down the fact in black and white, that was because they did
not deem it necessary to speak of things as indispensable as money and
a clean shirt, and one was not to assume for that reason that those knights-
errant of whom the books were so full did not have any. He looked upon
it as an absolute certainty that they all had well-stuffed purses, that they
might be prepared for any emergency; and they also carried shirts and
a little box of ointment for healing the wounds that they received.

For when they had been wounded in combat on the plains and in desert
places, there was not always someone at hand to treat them, unless they
had some skilled enchanter for a friend who then would succor them,
bringing to them through the air, upon a cloud, some damsel or dwarf
bearing a vial of water of such virtue that one had but to taste a drop
of it and at once his wounds were healed and he was as sound as if he had
never received any.

But even if this was not the case, knights in times past saw to it that
their squires were well provided with money and other necessities, such
as lint and ointment for healing purposes; and if they had no squires—
which happened very rarely—they themselves carried these objects in

a pair of saddlebags very cleverly attached to their horses' croups in such a manner as to be scarcely noticeable, as if they held something of greater importance than that,² for among the knights-errant saddlebags as a rule were not favored. Accordingly, he would advise the novice before him, and inasmuch as the latter was soon to be his godson, he might even command him, that henceforth he should not go without money and a supply of those things that have been mentioned, as he would find that they came in useful at a time when he least expected it.

Don Quixote promised to follow his host's advice punctiliously; and so it was arranged that he should watch his armor in a large barnyard at one side of the inn. He gathered up all the pieces, placed them in a horse trough that stood near the well, and, bracing his shield on his arm, took up his lance and with stately demeanor began pacing up and down in front of the trough even as night was closing in.

The innkeeper informed his other guests of what was going on, of Don Quixote's vigil and his expectation of being dubbed a knight; and, marveling greatly at so extraordinary a variety of madness, they all went out to see for themselves and stood there watching from a distance. For a while the knight-to-be, with tranquil mien, would merely walk up and down; then, leaning on his lance, he would pause to survey his armor, gazing fixedly at it for a considerable length of time. As has been said, it was night now, but the brightness of the moon, which well might rival that of Him who lent it, was such that everything the novice knight did was plainly visible to all.

At this point one of the mule drivers who were stopping at the inn came out to water his drove, and in order to do this it was necessary to remove the armor from the trough.

As he saw the man approaching, Don Quixote cried out to him, "O bold knight, whoever you may be, who thus would dare to lay hands upon the accouterments of the most valiant man of arms that ever girded on a sword, look well what you do and desist if you do not wish to pay with your life for your insolence!"

The muleteer gave no heed to these words—it would have been better for his own sake had he done so—but, taking it up by the straps, tossed the armor some distance from him. When he beheld this, Don Quixote rolled his eyes heavenward and with his thoughts apparently upon his Dulcinea exclaimed, "Succor, O lady mine, this vassal heart in this my first encounter; let not your favor and protection fail me in the peril in which for the first time I now find myself."

With these and other similar words, he loosed his buckler, grasped his lance in both his hands, and let the mule driver have such a blow on the head that the man fell to the ground stunned; and had it been followed by another one, he would have had no need of a surgeon to treat him. Having done this, Don Quixote gathered up his armor and resumed his pacing up and down with the same calm manner as before. Not long afterward, without knowing what had happened—for the first muleteer was still lying there unconscious—another came out with the same intention of watering his mules, and he too was about to remove the armor from the trough when the knight, without saying a word or asking favor of anyone, once more adjusted his buckler and raised his lance, and if he did not break the second mule driver's head to bits, he made more than three pieces of it by dividing it into quarters. At the sound of the fracas everybody in the inn came running out, among them the innkeeper; whereupon Don Quixote again lifted his buckler and laid his hand on his sword.

"O lady of beauty," he said, "strength and vigor of this fainting heart of mine! Now is the time to turn the eyes of your greatness upon this captive knight of yours who must face so formidable an adventure."

By this time he had worked himself up to such a pitch of anger that if all the mule drivers in the world had attacked him he would not have taken one step backward. The comrades of the wounded men, seeing the plight those two were in, now began showering stones on Don Quixote, who shielded himself as best he could with his buckler, although he did not dare stir from the trough for fear of leaving his armor unprotected. The landlord, meanwhile, kept calling to them to stop, for he had told them that this was a madman who would be sure to go free even though he killed them all. The knight was shouting louder than ever, calling them knaves and traitors. As for the lord of the castle, who allowed knights-errant to be treated in this fashion, he was a lowborn villain, and if he, Don Quixote, had but received the order of knighthood, he would make him pay for his treachery.

"As for you others, vile and filthy rabble, I take no account of you; you may stone me or come forward and attack me all you like; you shall see what the reward of your folly and insolence will be."

He spoke so vigorously and was so undaunted in bearing as to strike terror in those who would assail him; and for this reason, and owing also to the persuasions of the innkeeper, they ceased stoning him. He then permitted them to carry away the wounded, and went back to watching his armor with the same tranquil, unconcerned air that he had previously displayed.

The landlord was none too well pleased with these mad pranks on the part of his guest and determined to confer upon him that accursed order of knighthood before something else happened. Going up to him, he begged Don Quixote's pardon for the insolence which, without his knowledge, had been shown the knight by those of low degree. They, however, had been well punished for their impudence. As he had said, there was no chapel in this castle, but for that which remained to be done there was no need of any. According to what he had read of the ceremonial of the order, there was nothing to this business of being dubbed a knight except a slap on the neck and one across the shoulder, and that could be performed in the middle of a field as well as anywhere else. All that was required was for the knight-to-be to keep watch over his armor for a couple of hours, and Don Quixote had been at it more than four. The latter believed all this and announced that he was ready to obey and get the matter over with as speedily as possible. Once dubbed a knight, if he were attacked one more time, he did not think that he would leave a single person in the castle alive, save such as he might command be spared, at the bidding of his host and out of respect to him.

Thus warned, and fearful that it might occur, the castellan brought out the book in which he had jotted down the hay and barley for which the mule drivers owed him, and, accompanied by a lad bearing the butt of a candle and the two aforesaid damsels, he came up to where Don Quixote stood and commanded him to kneel. Reading from the account book—as if he had been saying a prayer—he raised his hand and, with the knight's own sword, gave him a good thwack upon the neck and another lusty one upon the shoulder, muttering all the while between his teeth. He then directed one of the ladies to gird on Don Quixote's sword, which she did with much gravity and composure; for it was all they could do to keep from laughing at every point of the ceremony, but the thought of the knight's prowess which they had already witnessed was sufficient to restrain their mirth.

"May God give your Grace much good fortune," said the worthy lady as she attached the blade, "and prosper you in battle."

Don Quixote thereupon inquired her name, for he desired to know to whom it was he was indebted for the favor he had just received, that he might share with her some of the honor which his strong right arm was sure to bring him. She replied very humbly that her name was Tolosa and that she was the daughter of a shoemaker, a native of Toledo who lived in the stalls of Sancho Bienaya.[3] To this the knight replied that she would do him a very great favor if from then on she would call her-

self Doña Tolosa, and she promised to do so. The other girl then helped
him on with his spurs, and practically the same conversation was repeated.
When asked her name, she stated that it was La Molinera and added that
she was the daughter of a respectable miller of Antequera. Don Quixote
likewise requested her to assume the "don" and become Doña Molinera
and offered to render her further services and favors.

These unheard-of ceremonies having been dispatched in great haste,
Don Quixote could scarcely wait to be astride his horse and sally forth
on his quest for adventures. Saddling and mounting Rocinante, he embraced his host, thanking him for the favor of having dubbed him a
knight and saying such strange things that it would be quite impossible
to record them here. The innkeeper, who was only too glad to be rid of
him, answered with a speech that was no less flowery, though somewhat
shorter, and he did not so much as ask him for the price of a lodging, so
glad was he to see him go.

CHAPTER IV. *Of what happened to our knight when he sallied forth from the inn.*

DAY was dawning when Don Quixote left the inn, so well satisfied
with himself, so gay, so exhilarated, that the very girths of his steed all but
burst with joy. But remembering the advice which his host had given him
concerning the stock of necessary provisions that he should carry with
him, especially money and shirts, he decided to turn back home and
supply himself with whatever he needed, and with a squire as well; he
had in mind a farmer who was a neighbor of his, a poor man and the
father of a family but very well suited to fulfill the duties of squire to
a man of arms. With this thought in mind he guided Rocinante toward
the village once more, and that animal, realizing that he was homeward
bound, began stepping out at so lively a gait that it seemed as if his feet
barely touched the ground.

The knight had not gone far when from a hedge on his right hand he
heard the sound of faint moans as of someone in distress.

"Thanks be to Heaven," he at once exclaimed, "for the favor it has shown me by providing me so soon with an opportunity to fulfill the obligations that I owe to my profession, a chance to pluck the fruit of my worthy desires. Those, undoubtedly, are the cries of someone in distress, who stands in need of my favor and assistance."

Turning Rocinante's head, he rode back to the place from which the cries appeared to be coming. Entering the wood, he had gone but a few paces when he saw a mare attached to an oak, while bound to another tree was a lad of fifteen or thereabouts, naked from the waist up. It was he who was uttering the cries, and not without reason, for there in front of him was a lusty farmer with a girdle who was giving him many lashes, each one accompanied by a reproof and a command, "Hold your tongue and keep your eyes open"; and the lad was saying, "I won't do it again, sir; by God's Passion, I won't do it again. I promise you that after this I'll take better care of the flock."

When he saw what was going on, Don Quixote was very angry. "Discourteous knight," he said, "it ill becomes you to strike one who is powerless to defend himself. Mount your steed and take your lance in hand"—for there was a lance leaning against the oak to which the mare was tied—"and I will show you what a coward you are."

The farmer, seeing before him this figure all clad in armor and brandishing a lance, decided that he was as good as done for. "Sir Knight," he said, speaking very mildly, "this lad that I am punishing here is my servant; he tends a flock of sheep which I have in these parts and he is so careless that every day one of them shows up missing. And when I punish him for his carelessness or his roguery, he says it is just because I am a miser and do not want to pay him the wages that I owe him, but I swear to God and upon my soul that he lies."

"It is you who lie, base lout," said Don Quixote, "and in my presence; and by the sun that gives us light, I am minded to run you through with this lance. Pay him and say no more about it, or else, by the God who rules us, I will make an end of you and annihilate you here and now. Release him at once."

The farmer hung his head and without a word untied his servant. Don Quixote then asked the boy how much his master owed him. For nine months' work, the lad told him, at seven reales the month. The knight did a little reckoning and found that this came to sixty-three reales; whereupon he ordered the farmer to pay over the money immediately, as he valued his life. The cowardly bumpkin replied that, facing death as he was and by the oath that he had sworn—he had not sworn any

oath as yet—it did not amount to as much as that; for there were three
pairs of shoes which he had given the lad that were to be deducted and
taken into account, and a real for two blood-lettings when his servant
was ill.

"That," said Don Quixote, "is all very well; but let the shoes and the
blood-lettings go for the undeserved lashes which you have given him;
if he has worn out the leather of the shoes that you paid for, you have
taken the hide off his body, and if the barber [1] let a little blood for him
when he was sick, you have done the same when he was well; and so
far as that goes, he owes you nothing."

"But the trouble is, Sir Knight, that I have no money with me. Come
along home with me, Andrés, and I will pay you real for real."

"I go home with him!" cried the lad. "Never in the world! No, sir, I
would not even think of it; for once he has me alone he'll flay me like a
St. Bartholomew."

"He will do nothing of the sort," said Don Quixote. "It is sufficient
for me to command, and he out of respect will obey. Since he has sworn
to me by the order of knighthood which he has received, I shall let him
go free and I will guarantee that you will be paid."

"But look, your Grace," the lad remonstrated, "my master is no knight;
he has never received any order of knighthood whatsoever. He is Juan
Haldudo, a rich man and a resident of Quintanar."

"That makes little difference," declared Don Quixote, "for there may
well be knights among the Haldudos,[2] all the more so in view of the fact
that every man is the son of his works." [3]

"That is true enough," said Andrés, "but this master of mine—of what
works is he the son, seeing that he refuses me the pay for my sweat and
labor?"

"I do not refuse you, brother Andrés," said the farmer. "Do me the
favor of coming with me, and I swear to you by all the orders of knighthood that there are in this world to pay you, as I have said, real for real,
and perfumed at that." [4]

"You can dispense with the perfume," said Don Quixote; "just give
him the reales and I shall be satisfied. And see to it that you keep your
oath, or by the one that I myself have sworn I shall return to seek you
out and chastise you, and I shall find you though you be as well hidden as
a lizard. In case you would like to know who it is that is giving you this
command in order that you may feel the more obliged to comply with
it, I may tell you that I am the valorous Don Quixote de la Mancha,
righter of wrongs and injustices; and so, God be with you, and do not

fail to do as you have promised, under that penalty that I have pronounced."

As he said this, he put spurs to Rocinante and was off. The farmer watched him go, and when he saw that Don Quixote was out of the wood and out of sight, he turned to his servant, Andrés.

"Come here, my son," he said. "I want to pay you what I owe you as that righter of wrongs has commanded me."

"Take my word for it," replied Andrés, "your Grace would do well to observe the command of that good knight—may he live a thousand years; for as he is valorous and a righteous judge, if you don't pay me then, by Roque,[5] he will come back and do just what he said!"

"And I will give you my word as well," said the farmer; "but seeing that I am so fond of you, I wish to increase the debt, that I may owe you all the more." And with this he seized the lad's arm and bound him to the tree again and flogged him within an inch of his life. "There, Master Andrés, you may call on that righter of wrongs if you like and you will see whether or not he rights this one. I do not think I have quite finished with you yet, for I have a good mind to flay you alive as you feared."

Finally, however, he unbound him and told him he might go look for that judge of his to carry out the sentence that had been pronounced. Andrés left, rather down in the mouth, swearing that he would indeed go look for the brave Don Quixote de la Mancha; he would relate to him everything that had happened, point by point, and the farmer would have to pay for it seven times over. But for all that, he went away weeping, and his master stood laughing at him.

Such was the manner in which the valorous knight righted this particular wrong. Don Quixote was quite content with the way everything had turned out; it seemed to him that he had made a very fortunate and noble beginning with his deeds of chivalry, and he was very well satisfied with himself as he jogged along in the direction of his native village, talking to himself in a low voice all the while.

"Well may'st thou call thyself fortunate today, above all other women on earth, O fairest of the fair, Dulcinea del Toboso! Seeing that it has fallen to thy lot to hold subject and submissive to thine every wish and pleasure so valiant and renowned a knight as Don Quixote de la Mancha is and shall be, who, as everyone knows, yesterday received the order of knighthood and this day has righted the greatest wrong and grievance that injustice ever conceived or cruelty ever perpetrated, by snatching the lash from the hand of the merciless foeman who was so unreasonably flogging that tender child."

At this point he came to a road that forked off in four directions, and at once he thought of those crossroads where knights-errant would pause to consider which path they should take. By way of imitating them, he halted there for a while; and when he had given the subject much thought, he slackened Rocinante's rein and let the hack follow its inclination. The animal's first impulse was to make straight for its own stable. After they had gone a couple of miles or so Don Quixote caught sight of what appeared to be a great throng of people, who, as was afterward learned, were certain merchants of Toledo on their way to purchase silk at Murcia. There were six of them altogether with their sunshades, accompanied by four attendants on horseback and three mule drivers on foot.

No sooner had he sighted them than Don Quixote imagined that he was on the brink of some fresh adventure. He was eager to imitate those passages at arms of which he had read in his books, and here, so it seemed to him, was one made to order. And so, with bold and knightly bearing, he settled himself firmly in the stirrups, couched his lance, covered himself with his shield, and took up a position in the middle of the road, where he paused to wait for those other knights-errant (for such he took them to be) to come up to him. When they were near enough to see and hear plainly, Don Quixote raised his voice and made a haughty gesture.

"Let everyone," he cried, "stand where he is, unless everyone will confess that there is not in all the world a more beauteous damsel than the Empress of La Mancha, the peerless Dulcinea del Toboso."

Upon hearing these words and beholding the weird figure who uttered them, the merchants stopped short. From the knight's appearance and his speech they knew at once that they had to deal with a madman; but they were curious to know what was meant by that confession that was demanded of them, and one of their number who was somewhat of a jester and a very clever fellow raised his voice.

"Sir Knight," he said, "we do not know who this beauteous lady is of whom you speak. Show her to us, and if she is as beautiful as you say, then we will right willingly and without any compulsion confess the truth as you have asked of us."

"If I were to show her to you," replied Don Quixote, "what merit would there be in your confessing a truth so self-evident? The important thing is for you, without seeing her, to believe, confess, affirm, swear, and defend that truth. Otherwise, monstrous and arrogant creatures that you are, you shall do battle with me. Come on, then, one by one, as the order of knighthood prescribes; or all of you together, if you will have it so, as is the sorry custom with those of your breed. Come on, and I will await you here, for I am confident that my cause is just."

"Sir Knight," responded the merchant, "I beg your Grace, in the name of all the princes here present, in order that we may not have upon our consciences the burden of confessing a thing which we have never seen nor heard, and one, moreover, so prejudicial to the empresses and queens of Alcarria and Estremadura,⁶ that your Grace will show us some portrait of this lady, even though it be no larger than a grain of wheat, for by the thread one comes to the ball of yarn; ⁷ and with this we shall remain satisfied and assured, and your Grace will likewise be content and satisfied. The truth is, I believe that we are already so much of your way of thinking that though it should show her to be blind of one eye and distilling vermilion and brimstone from the other, nevertheless, to please your Grace, we would say in her behalf all that you desire."

"She distills nothing of the sort, infamous rabble!" shouted Don Quixote, for his wrath was kindling now. "I tell you, she does not distill what you say at all, but amber and civet wrapped in cotton; ⁸ and she is neither one-eyed nor hunchbacked but straighter than a spindle that comes from Guadarrama.⁹ You shall pay for the great blasphemy which you have uttered against such a beauty as is my lady!"

Saying this, he came on with lowered lance against the one who had spoken, charging with such wrath and fury that if fortune had not caused Rocinante to stumble and fall in mid-career, things would have gone badly with the merchant and he would have paid for his insolent gibe. As it was, Don Quixote went rolling over the plain for some little distance, and when he tried to get to his feet, found that he was unable to do so, being too encumbered with his lance, shield, spurs, helmet, and the weight of that ancient suit of armor.

"Do not flee, cowardly ones," he cried even as he struggled to rise. "Stay, cravens, for it is not my fault but that of my steed that I am stretched out here."

One of the muleteers, who must have been an ill-natured lad, upon hearing the poor fallen knight speak so arrogantly, could not refrain from giving him an answer in the ribs. Going up to him, he took the knight's lance and broke it into bits, and then with a companion proceeded to belabor him so mercilessly that in spite of his armor they milled him like a hopper of wheat. The merchants called to them not to lay on so hard, saying that was enough and they should desist, but the mule driver by this time had warmed up to the sport and would not stop until he had vented his wrath, and, snatching up the broken pieces of the lance, he began hurling them at the wretched victim as he lay there on the ground. And through all this tempest of sticks that rained upon him Don Quixote never once closed his mouth nor ceased threatening Heaven and earth and these ruffians, for such he took them to be, who were thus mishandling him.

Finally the lad grew tired, and the merchants went their way with a good story to tell about the poor fellow who had had such a cudgeling. Finding himself alone, the knight endeavored to see if he could rise; but if this was a feat that he could not accomplish when he was sound and whole, how was he to achieve it when he had been thrashed and pounded to a pulp? Yet nonetheless he considered himself fortunate; for as he saw it, misfortunes such as this were common to knights-errant, and he put all the blame upon his horse; and if he was unable to rise, that was because his body was so bruised and battered all over.

CHAPTER V. *In which is continued the narrative of the misfortune that befell our knight.*

SEEING, then, that he was indeed unable to stir, he decided to fall back upon a favorite remedy of his, which was to think of some passage or other in his books; and as it happened, the one that he in his madness now recalled was the story of Baldwin and the Marquis of Mantua, when Carloto left the former wounded upon the mountainside,[1] a tale that is known to children, not unknown to young men, celebrated and believed in by the old, and, for all of that, not any truer than the miracles of Mohammed. Moreover, it impressed him as being especially suited to the straits in which he found himself; and, accordingly, with a great show of feeling, he began rolling and tossing on the ground as he feebly gasped out the lines which the wounded knight of the wood is supposed to have uttered:

"Where art thou, lady mine,
That thou dost not grieve for my woe?
Either thou art disloyal,
Or my grief thou dost not know."

He went on reciting the old ballad until he came to the following verses:

"O noble Marquis of Mantua,
My uncle and liege lord true!"

He had reached this point when down the road came a farmer of the same village, a neighbor of his, who had been to the mill with a load of wheat. Seeing a man lying there stretched out like that, he went up to him and inquired who he was and what was the trouble that caused him to utter such mournful complaints. Thinking that this must undoubtedly be his uncle, the Marquis of Mantua, Don Quixote did not answer but went on with his recitation of the ballad, giving an account of the Marquis' misfortunes and the amours of his wife and the emperor's son, exactly as the ballad has it.

The farmer was astounded at hearing all these absurdities, and after removing the knight's visor which had been battered to pieces by the blows it had received, the good man bathed the victim's face, only to discover, once the dust was off, that he knew him very well.

"Señor Quijana," he said (for such must have been Don Quixote's real name when he was in his right senses and before he had given up the life of a quiet country gentleman to become a knight-errant), "who is responsible for your Grace's being in such a plight as this?"

But the knight merely went on with his ballad in response to all the questions asked of him. Perceiving that it was impossible to obtain any information from him, the farmer as best he could relieved him of his breastplate and backpiece to see if he had any wounds, but there was no blood and no mark of any sort. He then tried to lift him from the ground, and with a great deal of effort finally managed to get him astride the ass, which appeared to be the easier mount for him. Gathering up the armor, including even the splinters from the lance, he made a bundle and tied it on Rocinante's back, and, taking the horse by the reins and the ass by the halter, he started out for the village. He was worried in his mind at hearing all the foolish things that Don Quixote said, and that individual himself was far from being at ease. Unable by reason of his bruises and his soreness to sit upright on the donkey, our knight-errant kept sighing to Heaven, which led the farmer to ask him once more what it was that ailed him.

It must have been the devil himself who caused him to remember those tales that seemed to fit his own case; for at this point he forgot all about Baldwin and recalled Abindarráez, and how the governor of Antequera, Rodrigo de Narváez, had taken him prisoner and carried him off captive to his castle.[2] Accordingly, when the countryman turned to inquire how he was and what was troubling him, Don Quixote replied with the very same words and phrases that the captive Abindarráez used in answering Rodrigo, just as he had read in the story *Diana* of Jorge de Montemayor,[3] where it is all written down, applying them very aptly to the present circumstances as the farmer went along cursing his luck for having to listen to such a lot of nonsense. Realizing that his neighbor was quite mad, he made haste to reach the village that he might not have to be annoyed any longer by Don Quixote's tiresome harangue.

"Señor Don Rodrigo de Narváez," the knight was saying, "I may inform your Grace that this beautiful Jarifa of whom I speak is not the lovely Dulcinea del Toboso, in whose behalf I have done, am doing, and shall do the most famous deeds of chivalry that ever have been or will be seen in all the world."

"But, sir," replied the farmer, "sinner that I am, cannot your Grace see that I am not Don Rodrigo de Narváez nor the Marquis of Mantua, but Pedro Alonso, your neighbor? And your Grace is neither Baldwin nor Abindarráez but a respectable gentleman by the name of Señor Quijana."

"I know who I am," said Don Quixote, "and who I may be, if I choose: not only those I have mentioned but all the Twelve Peers of France and the Nine Worthies as well; for the exploits of all of them together, or separately, cannot compare with mine."

With such talk as this they reached their destination just as night was falling; but the farmer decided to wait until it was a little darker in order that the badly battered gentleman might not be seen arriving in such a condition and mounted on an ass. When he thought the proper time had come, they entered the village and proceeded to Don Quixote's house, where they found everything in confusion. The curate and the barber were there, for they were great friends of the knight, and the housekeeper was speaking to them.

"Señor Licentiate Pero Pérez," she was saying, for that was the manner in which she addressed the curate, "what does your Grace think could have happened to my master? Three days now, and not a word of him, nor the hack, nor the buckler, nor the lance, nor the suit of armor. Ah, poor me! I am as certain as I am that I was born to die that it is those cursed books of chivalry he is always reading that have turned his head; for now that I recall, I have often heard him muttering to himself that he must become a knight-errant and go through the world in search of adventures. May such books as those be consigned to Satan and Barabbas, for they have sent to perdition the finest mind in all La Mancha."

The niece was of the same opinion. "I may tell you, Señor Master Nicholas," she said, for that was the barber's name, "that many times my uncle would sit reading those impious tales of misadventure for two whole days and nights at a stretch; and when he was through, he would toss the book aside, lay his hand on his sword, and begin slashing at the walls. When he was completely exhausted, he would tell us that he had just killed four giants as big as castle towers, while the sweat that poured off him was blood from the wounds that he had received in battle. He would then drink a big jug of cold water, after which he would be very calm and peaceful, saying that the water was the most precious liquid which the wise Esquife, a great magician and his friend, had brought to him. But I blame myself for everything. I should have advised your Worships of my uncle's nonsensical actions so that you could have done something about it by burning those damnable books of his before things came to such a pass; for he has many that ought to be burned as if they were heretics."

"I agree with you," said the curate, "and before tomorrow's sun has set there shall be a public *auto de fe*, and those works shall be condemned to the flames that they may not lead some other who reads them to follow the example of my good friend."

Don Quixote and the farmer overheard all this, and it was then that the latter came to understand the nature of his neighbor's affliction.

"Open the door, your Worships," the good man cried. "Open for Sir Baldwin and the Marquis of Mantua, who comes badly wounded, and for Señor Abindarráez the Moor whom the valiant Rodrigo de Narváez, governor of Antequera, brings captive."

At the sound of his voice they all ran out, recognizing at once friend, master, and uncle, who as yet was unable to get down off the donkey's back. They all ran up to embrace him.

"Wait, all of you," said Don Quixote, "for I am sorely wounded through fault of my steed. Bear me to my couch and summon, if it be possible, the wise Urganda to treat and care for my wounds."

"There!" exclaimed the housekeeper. "Plague take it! Did not my

heart tell me right as to which foot my master limped on? To bed with
your Grace at once, and we will take care of you without sending for
that Urganda of yours. A curse, I say, and a hundred other curses, on
those books of chivalry that have brought your Grace to this."

And so they carried him off to bed, but when they went to look for
his wounds, they found none at all. He told them it was all the result of
a great fall he had taken with Rocinante, his horse, while engaged in com-
bating ten giants, the hugest and most insolent that were ever heard of
in all the world.

"Tut, tut," said the curate. "So there are giants in the dance now, are
there? Then, by the sign of the cross, I'll have them burned before nightfall tomorrow."

They had a thousand questions to put to Don Quixote, but his only
answer was that they should give him something to eat and let him sleep,
for that was the most important thing of all; so they humored him in
this. The curate then interrogated the farmer at great length concerning
the conversation he had had with his neighbor. The peasant told him
everything, all the absurd things their friend had said when he found him
lying there and afterward on the way home, all of which made the
licentiate more anxious than ever to do what he did the following day,
when he summoned Master Nicholas and went with him to Don
Quixote's house.

CHAPTER VI. *Of the great and diverting scru-
tiny which the curate and the barber made in the library
of our ingenious gentleman.*

As Don Quixote was still sleeping, the curate asked the niece for the
keys to the room where those books responsible for all the trouble were,
and she gave them to him very willingly. They all went in, the housekeeper too, and found more than a hundred large-sized volumes very
well bound and a number of smaller ones. No sooner had the housekeeper

laid eyes on them than she left the room, returning shortly with a basin
of holy water and a sprinkling-pot.

"Here, Señor Licentiate," she said, "take this and sprinkle well, that
no enchanter of the many these books contain may remain here to cast
a spell on us for wishing to banish them from the world."

The curate could not but laugh at her simplicity as he directed the
barber to hand him the volumes one by one so that he might see what
their subject matter was, since it was possible that there were some there
that did not deserve a punishment by fire.

"No," said the niece, "you must not pardon any of them, for they are
all to blame. It would be better to toss them out the window into the
courtyard, make a heap of them, and then set fire to it; or else you can
take them out to the stable yard and make a bonfire there where the
smoke will not annoy anyone."

The housekeeper said the same thing, both of them being very anxious
to witness the death of these innocents, but the curate would not hear
of this until he had read the titles. The first that Master Nicholas handed
him was *The Four Books of Amadis of Gaul.*

"There seems to be some doubt about this one," he said, "for according
to what I have heard, it was the first romance of chivalry to be printed
in Spain and is the beginning and origin of all the others; but for that
very reason I think that we should condemn it to the flames without any
mercy whatsoever as the work that supplied the dogmas for so vile a
sect."

"No, my dear sir," said the barber, "for I have heard that it is better
than all the other books of this sort that have been composed, and inasmuch as it is unique of its kind, it ought to be pardoned."

"True enough," said the curate, "and for that reason we will spare its
life for the present. Let us see the one next to it."

"It is the *Exploits of Esplandián,*[1] legitimate son of Amadis of Gaul."

"Well, I must say," the curate replied, "that the father's merits are
not to be set down to the credit of his offspring. Take it, Mistress Housekeeper; open that window and throw it out into the stable yard; it will
make a beginning for that bonfire of ours."

The housekeeper complied with a great deal of satisfaction, and the
worthy Esplandián went flying out into the yard to wait as patiently
as anyone could wish for the threatened conflagration.

"Let's have some more," said the curate.

"This one coming next," said the barber, "is *Amadis of Greece;*[2] in fact, all those on this side, so far as I can see, are of the same lineage—descendants of Amadis."

"Then out with them all," was the curate's verdict; "for in order to be able to burn Queen Pintiquinestra and the shepherd Darinel and his elegies and the author's diabolic and involved conceits, I would set fire, along with them, to the father that bore me if he were going around in the guise of a knight-errant."

"I agree with you on that," said the barber.

"And I also," put in the niece.

"Well, since that is the way it is," said the housekeeper, "to the stable yard with them."

They handed her a whole stack of them, and, to avoid the stair, she dumped them out the window into the yard below.

"What is that tub there?" inquired the curate.

"That," replied the barber, "is *Don Olivante de Laura*." [3]

"The author of this book," observed the curate, "was the same one who composed the *Garden of Flowers*, and, in truth, there is no telling which of the two is the truer, or, to put it better, less filled with lies; I can only say that this one is going out into the yard as an arrogant braggart."

"The next," announced the barber, "is *Florismarte of Hircania*." [4]

"So, Señor Florismarte is with us, is he? Then, upon my word, he is due in the yard this minute, in spite of his strange birth and imaginary adventures, for the stiffness and dryness of his style deserve nothing better. Out with him, and with the other as well, Mistress Housekeeper."

"With great pleasure," she said, and she gleefully carried out the order that had been given her.

"This," said the barber, "is *Platir the Knight*." [5]

"A very old book," said the curate, "and I find nothing in it deserving of clemency. Let it accompany the others without appeal."

Once again sentence was carried out. They opened another volume and saw that its title was *The Knight of the Cross*.[6]

"Out of respect for a name so holy as the one this book bears, one might think that its ignorance should be pardoned; but you know the old saying, 'The devil takes refuge behind the cross,' so to the fire with it."

"And this," said the barber, taking up yet another, "is *The Mirror of Chivalry*." [7]

"Ah, your Grace, I know you," said the curate. "Here we have Sir

Rinaldo of Montalbán with his friends and companions, bigger thieves than Cacus, all of them, and the Twelve Peers along with the veracious historian Turpin.[8] To tell you the truth, I am inclined to sentence them to no more than perpetual banishment, seeing that they have about them something of the inventiveness of Matteo Boiardo,[9] and it was out of them, also, that the Christian poet Ludovico Ariosto wove his tapestry —and by the way, if I find him here speaking any language other than his own, I will show him no respect, but if I meet with him in his own tongue, I will place him upon my head." [10]

"Yes," said the barber, "I have him at home in Italian, but I can't understand him."

"It is just as well that you cannot," said the curate. "And for this reason we might pardon the Captain [11] if he had not brought him to Spain and made him over into a Castilian, depriving him thereby of much of his native strength, as happens with all those who would render books of verse into another language; for however much care they may take, and however much cleverness they may display, they can never equal the original. I say, in short, that this work and all those on French themes ought to be thrown into, or deposited in, some dry well until we make up our minds just what should be done with them, with the exception of one *Bernardo del Carpio*, which is going the rounds, and another called *Roncesvalles;* [12] for these books, if they fall into my hands, shall be transferred to those of the housekeeper at once, and from there they go into the fire without any reprieve whatever."

The barber thoroughly approved of everything, being convinced that the curate was so good a Christian and so honest a man that he would not for anything in the world utter an untruth. Opening another book, he saw that it was *Palmerin de Oliva*, and next to it was one entitled *Palmerin of England*.[13]

The curate took one look at them. "Let this olive," he said, "be sliced to bits and burned until not even the ashes are left; but let this palm of England be guarded and preserved as something unique, and let there be made for it another case such as Alexander found among the spoils of Darius and set aside for the safekeeping of the works of the poet Homer. This book, my good friend, is deserving of respect for two reasons: first, because it is very good; and second, because it is reputed to have been composed by a wise and witty king of Portugal. All the adventures at Miraguarda's castle are excellently contrived, and the dialogue is clear and polished, the character and condition of the one who is speaking being observed with much propriety and understanding. And so, saving your good pleasure, Master Nicholas, I say that this book and *Amadis of Gaul* should be spared the flames, but all the others without more ado about it should perish."

"No, my friend," replied the barber, "for this one that I hold here in my hand is the famous *Don Belianís*." [14]

"Well," said the curate, "the second, third, and fourth parts need a little rhubarb to purge them of an excess of bile, and we shall have to relieve them of that Castle of Fame and other worse follies; but let them have the benefit of the overseas clause,[15] and, providing they mend their ways, they shall be shown justice and mercy. Meanwhile, friend, take them home with you and see to it that no one reads them."

"I shall be glad to do so," the barber assented. And not wishing to tire himself any further by reading these romances of knighthood, he told the housekeeper to take all the big ones and throw them into the yard. This was not said to one who was deaf or dull-witted, but to one who took more pleasure in such a bonfire than in the largest and finest tapestry that she could have woven. Snatching them up seven or eight at a time, she started flinging them out the window; but taking too big an armful, she let one of them fall at the barber's feet. Curious to see what it was, he bent over and picked it up. It was *The History of the Famous Knight, Tirant lo Blanch*.[16]

"Well, bless my soul!" cried the curate, "if that isn't *Tirant lo Blanch!* Let me have it, my friend, for I cannot but remember that I have found in it a treasure of contentment and a mine of recreation. Here we have Don Quirieleison de Montalbán, that valiant knight, and his brother, Tomás de Montalbán, and the knight Fonseca, along with the combat which brave Tirant waged with the mastiff, as well as the witty sayings of the damsel Placerdemivida and the amours and deceits of the Empress, who was enamored of Hipólito, her squire. Tell the truth, friend, and admit that in the matter of style this is the best book in the world. Here knights eat and sleep and die in their beds and make their wills before they die and do other things that are never heard of in books of this kind. But for all that, I am telling you that the one who needlessly composed so nonsensical a work deserves to be sent to the galleys for the rest of his life. Take it along home with you and read it and see if what I say is not so."

"That I will," said the barber, "but what are we going to do with these little ones that are left?"

"Those, I take it," replied the curate, "are not romances but poetry." Opening one of them, he saw that it was Jorge de Montemayor's *Diana*, and being under the impression that all the rest were of the same sort, he added, "These do not deserve to be burned like the others, for they are not harmful like the books of chivalry; they are works of imagination such as may be read without detriment."

"Ah, but Señor!" exclaimed the niece, "your Grace should send them to be burned along with the rest; for I shouldn't wonder at all if my uncle, after he has been cured of this chivalry sickness, reading one of these books, should take it into his head to become a shepherd and go wandering through the woods and meadows singing and piping, or, what is worse, become a poet, which they say is an incurable disease and one that is very catching."

"The young lady is right," said the curate. "It would be just as well to remove this stumbling block and temptation out of our friend's way. And so, to begin with Montemayor's *Diana*, I am of the opinion that it should not be burned, but rather that we should take out of it everything that has to do with that enchantress Felicia and her charmed potion, together with nearly all the longer verse pieces, while we willingly leave it the prose and the honor of being first and best among books of its kind."

"This one coming up now," said the barber, "is *The Second Part of La Diana*, 'by the Salamancan'; and here is yet another bearing the same title, whose author is Gil Polo." [17]

"As for the Salamancan's work," said the curate, "let it go to swell the number of the condemned out in the stable yard, but keep the Gil Polo as if it were from Apollo's own hand. Come, my friend, let us hurry, for it is growing late."

"This," said the barber as he opened another volume, "is *The Ten Books of the Fortunes of Love*, composed by Antonio de Lofraso, the Sardinian poet." [18]

"By the holy orders that I have received," the curate declared, "since Apollo was Apollo, since the Muses were Muses and poets were poets, so droll and absurd a book as this has not been written; in its own way it is unique among all those of its kind that have seen the light of day, and he who has not read it does not know what he has missed. Give it to me, my friend, for I am more pleased at having found it than if they had presented me with a cassock of Florentine cloth."

Saying this, he laid the book aside with great glee as the barber went on, "Those that we have here are *The Shepherd of Iberia*, *The Nymphs of Henares*, and *The Disenchantments of Jealousy*." [19]

"Well," said the curate, "there is nothing to do with those but to turn them over to the housekeeper's secular arm; and do not ask me why, or we shall never be finished."

"And this is *Filida's Shepherd*." [20]

"He is no shepherd but a polished courtier. Guard him as you would a precious jewel."

"And this big one that I am handing you now is called *Treasury of Various Poems*." [21]

"If there were not so many of them," remarked the curate, "they would be held in greater esteem. This is a book that must be weeded out and cleansed of certain trivialities among the many fine things that it contains. Keep it, for the reason that its author is my friend and out of respect for other more heroic and lofty works that he has produced."

"This," said the barber, "is the *Song Book* of López de Maldonado." [22]

"Another great friend of mine; and when he himself recites or, better, sings his verses, all who hear them are filled with admiration for the charm and sweetness of his voice. His eclogues are a bit too long; for that which is good never did exist in great abundance.[23] Put it with the others that we have laid aside. But what is that one next to it?"

"*La Galatea* of Miguel de Cervantes," said the barber.

"Ah, that fellow Cervantes and I have been friends these many years, but, to my knowledge, he is better versed in misfortune than he is in verses. His book has a fairly good plot; it starts out well and ends up nowhere. We shall have to wait for the second part which he has promised us, and perhaps when it has been corrected somewhat it will find the favor that is now denied it.[24] Meanwhile, keep it locked up in your house."

"That I will gladly do," replied the barber. "And here we have three more—I will hand them to you all together: the *Araucana* of Don Alonso de Ercilla; the *Austriada* of Juan Rufo, magistrate of Cordova; and the *Monserrate* of Cristóbal de Virués, the poet of Valencia." [25]

"These three books," said the curate, "are the best that have been written in heroic verse in the Castilian tongue and may well compete with the most famous of Italy; keep them as the richest jewels of poetry that Spain has to show."

By this time his Reverence was too tired to look at any more books and accordingly decided that the rest should be burned without further inspection. The barber, however, had already opened one called *The Tears of Angélica*.[26]

"I should have wept myself," said the curate when he heard the title, "if I had sent that one to the flames; for its author was one of the most famous poets in the world, and not in Spain alone, and he was most happy in the translation that he made of certain of the fables of Ovid." [27]

CHAPTER VII. *Of the second sally of our good knight, Don Quixote de la Mancha.*

AT THAT instant Don Quixote began shouting, "Here! here! good knights, now is the time to show the strength of your mighty arms, for they of the court are gaining the better of the tourney!"

Called away by this noise and uproar, they went no further with the scrutinizing of those books that remained; and as a consequence it is believed that *La Carolea* and the *León of Spain* [1] went to the fire unseen and unheard, along with *The Deeds of the Emperor* as set down by Don Luis de Avila,[2] for these undoubtedly must have been among the works that were left, and possibly if the curate had seen them he would not have passed so severe a sentence upon them.

When they reached Don Quixote's side, he had already risen from his bed and was shouting and raving, laying about him on all sides with slashes and back-strokes, as wide awake as if he had never been asleep. Seizing him with their arms, they forced him into bed.

When he had quieted down a little he turned to the curate and said, "Most certainly, Señor Archbishop Turpin, it is a great disgrace for us who call ourselves the Twelve Peers so carelessly to allow the knights of the court to gain the victory in this tournament, seeing that previously we adventurers had carried off the prize for three days running."

"Be quiet, my friend," said the curate, "for, God willing, luck may change, and that which is lost today shall be won tomorrow. For the present, your Grace should look after your health, for you must be very tired, if not, perhaps, badly wounded."

"Wounded, no," said Don Quixote, "but bruised to a pulp, there is no doubt of that; for that bastard of a Don Orlando flayed me with the trunk of an oak, and all out of envy, because he knows that I am his only rival in feats of valor. But my name is not Rinaldo of Montalbán if on arising from this couch I do not make him pay for it in spite of all his enchantments. In the meantime, you may bring me something to eat, for I think that would do me more good than anything else. I will see to avenging myself in due course."

They did as he asked, brought him a bite of supper, and he once more fell asleep, while the others wondered at the strange madness that had laid hold of him. That night the housekeeper burned all the books there were in the stable yard and in all the house; and there must have been some that went up in smoke which should have been preserved in everlasting archives, if the one who did the scrutinizing had not been so indolent. Thus we see the truth of the old saying, to the effect that the innocent must sometimes pay for the sins of the guilty.

One of the things that the curate and the barber advised as a remedy for their friend's sickness was to wall up the room where the books had been, so that, when he arose, he would not find them missing —it might be that the cause being removed, the effect would cease— and they could tell him that a magician had made away with them, room and all. This they proceeded to do as quickly as possible. Two days later, when Don Quixote rose from his bed, the first thing he did was to go have a look at his library, and, not finding it where he had left it, he went from one part of the house to another searching for it. Going up to where the door had been, he ran his hands over the wall and rolled his eyes in every direction without saying a word; but after some little while he asked the housekeeper where his study was with all his books.

She had been well instructed in what to answer him. "Whatever study is your Grace talking about?" she said. "There is no study, and no books, in this house; the devil took them all away."

"No," said the niece, "it was not the devil but an enchanter who came upon a cloud one night, the day after your Grace left here; dismounting from a serpent that he rode, he entered your study, and I don't know what all he did there, but after a bit he went flying off through the roof, leaving the house full of smoke; and when we went to see what he had done, there was no study and not a book in sight. There is one thing, though, that the housekeeper and I remember very well: at the time that wicked old fellow left, he cried out in a loud voice that it was all on account of a secret enmity that he bore the owner of those books and that study, and that was why he had done the mischief in this house which we would discover. He also said that he was called Muñatón the Magician."

"Frestón, he should have said," remarked Don Quixote.

"I can't say as to that," replied the housekeeper, "whether he was called Frestón or Fritón; [3] all I know is that his name ended in a *tón*."

"So it does," said Don Quixote. "He is a wise enchanter, a great enemy of mine, who has a grudge against me because he knows by his arts and learning that in the course of time I am to fight in single combat with a knight whom he favors, and that I am to be the victor and he can do nothing to prevent it. For this reason he seeks to cause me all the trouble that he can, but I am warning him that it will be hard to gainsay or shun that which Heaven has ordained."

"Who could doubt that it is so?" said the niece. "But tell me, uncle, who is responsible for your being involved in these quarrels? Would it not be better to remain peacefully here at home and not go roaming through the world in search of better bread than is made from wheat, without taking into consideration that many who go for wool come back shorn?" [4]

"My dear niece," replied Don Quixote, "how little you understand of these matters! Before they shear me, I will have plucked and stripped the beards of any who dare to touch the tip of a single hair of mine."

The niece and the housekeeper did not care to answer him any further, for they saw that his wrath was rising.

After that he remained at home very tranquilly for a couple of weeks, without giving sign of any desire to repeat his former madness. During that time he had the most pleasant conversations with his two old friends, the curate and the barber, on the point he had raised to the effect that what the world needed most was knights-errant and a revival of chivalry. The curate would occasionally contradict him and again would give in, for it was only by means of this artifice that he could carry on a conversation with him at all.

In the meanwhile Don Quixote was bringing his powers of persuasion to bear upon a farmer who lived near by, a good man—if this title may be applied to one who is poor—but with very few wits in his head. The short of it is, by pleas and promises, he got the hapless rustic to agree to ride forth with him and serve him as his squire. Among other things, Don Quixote told him that he ought to be more than willing to go, because no telling what adventure might occur which would win them an island, and then he (the farmer) would be left to be the governor of it. As a result of these and other similar assurances, Sancho Panza forsook his wife and children and consented to take upon himself the duties of squire to his neighbor.

Next, Don Quixote set out to raise some money, and by selling this thing and pawning that and getting the worst of the bargain always, he finally scraped together a reasonable amount. He also asked a friend of his for the loan of a buckler and patched up his broken helmet as well as he could. He advised his squire, Sancho, of the day and hour when they were to take the road and told him to see to laying in a supply of those things that were most necessary, and, above all, not to forget the saddlebags. Sancho replied that he would see to all this and added that he was also thinking of taking along with him a very good ass that he had, as he was not much used to going on foot.

With regard to the ass, Don Quixote had to do a little thinking, trying to recall if any knight-errant had ever had a squire thus asininely mounted. He could not think of any, but nevertheless he decided to take Sancho with the intention of providing him with a nobler steed as soon as occasion offered; he had but to appropriate the horse of the first discourteous knight he met. Having furnished himself with shirts and all the other things that the innkeeper had recommended, he and Panza rode forth one night unseen by anyone and without taking leave of wife and children, housekeeper or niece. They went so far that by the time morning came they were safe from discovery had a hunt been started for them.

Mounted on his ass, Sancho Panza rode along like a patriarch, with saddlebags and flask, his mind set upon becoming governor of that island that his master had promised him. Don Quixote determined to take the same route and road over the Campo de Montiel that he had followed on his first journey; but he was not so uncomfortable this time, for it was early morning and the sun's rays fell upon them slantingly and accordingly did not tire them too much.

"Look, Sir Knight-errant," said Sancho, "your Grace should not forget that island you promised me; for no matter how big it is, I'll be able to govern it right enough."

"I would have you know, friend Sancho Panza," replied Don Quixote, "that among the knights-errant of old it was a very common custom to make their squires governors of the islands or the kingdoms that they won, and I am resolved that in my case so pleasing a usage shall not fall into desuetude. I even mean to go them one better; for they very often, perhaps most of the time, waited until their squires were old men who had had their fill of serving their masters during bad days and worse nights, whereupon they would give them the title of count, or marquis at most, of some valley or province more or less. But if you live and I live, it well may be that within a week I shall win some kingdom with others dependent upon it, and it will be the easiest thing in the world to crown you king of one of them. You need not marvel at this, for all sorts of unforeseen things happen to knights like me, and I may readily be able to give you even more than I have promised."

"In that case," said Sancho Panza, "if by one of those miracles of which your Grace was speaking I should become king, I would certainly send for Juana Gutiérrez, my old lady, to come and be my queen, and the young ones could be infantes."

"There is no doubt about it," Don Quixote assured him.

"Well, I doubt it," said Sancho, "for I think that even if God were to rain kingdoms upon the earth, no crown would sit well on the head of Mari Gutiérrez,[5] for I am telling you, sir, as a queen she is not worth two maravedis. She would do better as a countess, God help her."

"Leave everything to God, Sancho," said Don Quixote, "and he will give you whatever is most fitting; but I trust you will not be so pusillanimous as to be content with anything less than the title of viceroy."

"That I will not," said Sancho Panza, "especially seeing that I have in your Grace so illustrious a master who can give me all that is suitable to me and all that I can manage."

CHAPTER VIII. *Of the good fortune which the valorous Don Quixote had in the terrifying and never-before-imagined adventure of the windmills, along with other events that deserve to be suitably recorded.*

AT THIS point they caught sight of thirty or forty windmills which were standing on the plain there, and no sooner had Don Quixote laid eyes upon them than he turned to his squire and said, "Fortune is guiding our affairs better than we could have wished; for you see there before you, friend Sancho Panza, some thirty or more lawless giants with whom I mean to do battle. I shall deprive them of their lives, and with the spoils from this encounter we shall begin to enrich ourselves; for this is righteous warfare, and it is a great service to God to remove so accursed a breed from the face of the earth."

"What giants?" said Sancho Panza.

"Those that you see there," replied his master, "those with the long arms some of which are as much as two leagues in length."

"But look, your Grace, those are not giants but windmills, and what appear to be arms are their wings which, when whirled in the breeze, cause the millstone to go."

"It is plain to be seen," said Don Quixote, "that you have had little experience in this matter of adventures. If you are afraid, go off to one side and say your prayers while I am engaging them in fierce, unequal combat."

Saying this, he gave spurs to his steed Rocinante, without paying any heed to Sancho's warning that these were truly windmills and not giants that he was riding forth to attack. Nor even when he was close upon them did he perceive what they really were, but shouted at the top of his lungs, "Do not seek to flee, cowards and vile creatures that you are, for it is but a single knight with whom you have to deal!"

At that moment a little wind came up and the big wings began turning.

"Though you flourish as many arms as did the giant Briareus," said Don Quixote when he perceived this, "you still shall have to answer to me."

He thereupon commended himself with all his heart to his lady Dulcinea, beseeching her to succor him in this peril; and, being well covered with his shield and with his lance at rest, he bore down upon them at a full gallop and fell upon the first mill that stood in his way, giving a thrust at the wing, which was whirling at such a speed that his lance was broken into bits and both horse and horseman went rolling over the plain, very much battered indeed. Sancho upon his donkey came hurrying to his master's assistance as fast as he could, but when he reached the spot, the knight was unable to move, so great was the shock with which he and Rocinante had hit the ground.

"God help us!" exclaimed Sancho, "did I not tell your Grace to look well, that those were nothing but windmills, a fact which no one could fail to see unless he had other mills of the same sort in his head?"

"Be quiet, friend Sancho," said Don Quixote. "Such are the fortunes of war, which more than any other are subject to constant change. What is more, when I come to think of it, I am sure that this must be the work of that magician Frestón, the one who robbed me of my study and my books, and who has thus changed the giants into windmills in order to deprive me of the glory of overcoming them, so great is the enmity that he bears me; but in the end his evil arts shall not prevail against this trusty sword of mine."

"May God's will be done," was Sancho Panza's response. And with the aid of his squire the knight was once more mounted on Rocinante, who stood there with one shoulder half out of joint. And so, speaking of the adventure that had just befallen them, they continued along the Puerto Lápice highway; for there, Don Quixote said, they could not fail to find many and varied adventures, this being a much traveled thoroughfare. The only thing was, the knight was exceedingly downcast over the loss of his lance.

"I remember," he said to his squire, "having read of a Spanish knight by the name of Diego Pérez de Vargas, who, having broken his sword in battle, tore from an oak a heavy bough or branch and with it did such feats of valor that day, and pounded so many Moors, that he came to be known as Machuca,[1] and he and his descendants from that day forth have been called Vargas y Machuca. I tell you this because I too intend to provide myself with just such a bough as the one he wielded, and with it I propose to do such exploits that you shall deem yourself fortunate to have been found worthy to come with me and behold and witness things that are almost beyond belief."

"God's will be done," said Sancho. "I believe everything that your Grace says; but straighten yourself up in the saddle a little, for you seem to be slipping down on one side, owing, no doubt, to the shaking-up that you received in your fall."

"Ah, that is the truth," replied Don Quixote, "and if I do not speak of my sufferings, it is for the reason that it is not permitted knights-errant to complain of any wound whatsoever, even though their bowels may be dropping out."

"If that is the way it is," said Sancho, "I have nothing more to say; but, God knows, it would suit me better if your Grace did complain when something hurts him. I can assure you that I mean to do so, over the least little thing that ails me—that is, unless the same rule applies to squires as well."

Don Quixote laughed long and heartily over Sancho's simplicity, telling him that he might complain as much as he liked and where and when he liked, whether he had good cause or not; for he had read nothing to the contrary in the ordinances of chivalry. Sancho then called his master's attention to the fact that it was time to eat. The knight replied that he himself had no need of food at the moment, but his squire might eat whenever he chose. Having been granted this permission, Sancho seated himself as best he could upon his beast, and, taking out from his saddle-bags the provisions that he had stored there, he rode along leisurely behind his master, munching his victuals and taking a good, hearty swig now and then at the leather flask in a manner that might well have caused the biggest-bellied tavernkeeper of Málaga to envy him. Between draughts he gave not so much as a thought to any promise that his master might have made him, nor did he look upon it as any hardship, but rather as good sport, to go in quest of adventures however hazardous they might be.

The short of the matter is, they spent the night under some trees, from one of which Don Quixote tore off a withered bough to serve him as a lance, placing it in the lance head from which he had removed the broken one. He did not sleep all night long for thinking of his lady Dulcinea; for this was in accordance with what he had read in his books, of men of arms in the forest or desert places who kept a wakeful vigil, sustained by the memory of their ladies fair. Not so with Sancho, whose stomach was full, and not with chicory water. He fell into a dreamless slumber, and had not his master called him, he would not have been awakened either by the rays of the sun in his face or by the many birds who greeted the coming of the new day with their merry song.

Upon arising, he had another go at the flask, finding it somewhat more flaccid than it had been the night before, a circumstance which grieved his heart, for he could not see that they were on the way to remedying the deficiency within any very short space of time. Don Quixote did not wish any breakfast; for, as has been said, he was in the habit of nourishing himself on savorous memories. They then set out once more along the road to Puerto Lápice, and around three in the afternoon they came in sight of the pass that bears that name.

"There," said Don Quixote as his eyes fell upon it, "we may plunge our arms up to the elbow in what are known as adventures. But I must warn you that even though you see me in the greatest peril in the world, you are not to lay hand upon your sword to defend me, unless it be that those who attack me are rabble and men of low degree, in which case you may very well come to my aid; but if they be gentlemen, it is in no wise permitted by the laws of chivalry that you should assist me until you yourself shall have been dubbed a knight."

"Most certainly, sir," replied Sancho, "your Grace shall be very well obeyed in this; all the more so for the reason that I myself am of a peaceful disposition and not fond of meddling in the quarrels and feuds of others. However, when it comes to protecting my own person, I shall not take account of those laws of which you speak, seeing that all laws, human and divine, permit each one to defend himself whenever he is attacked."

"I am willing to grant you that," assented Don Quixote, "but in this matter of defending me against gentlemen you must restrain your natural impulses."

"I promise you I shall do so," said Sancho. "I will observe this precept as I would the Sabbath day."

As they were conversing in this manner, there appeared in the road in front of them two friars of the Order of St. Benedict, mounted upon dromedaries—for the she-mules they rode were certainly no smaller than that. The friars wore travelers' spectacles and carried sunshades, and behind them came a coach accompanied by four or five men on horseback and a couple of muleteers on foot. In the coach, as was afterwards learned, was a lady of Biscay, on her way to Seville to bid farewell to her husband, who had been appointed to some high post in the Indies. The religious were not of her company although they were going by the same road.

The instant Don Quixote laid eyes upon them he turned to his squire. "Either I am mistaken or this is going to be the most famous adventure that ever was seen; for those black-clad figures that you behold must be, and without any doubt are, certain enchanters who are bearing with them a captive princess in that coach, and I must do all I can to right this wrong."

"It will be worse than the windmills," declared Sancho. "Look you, sir, those are Benedictine friars and the coach must be that of some travelers. Mark well what I say and what you do, lest the devil lead you astray."

"I have already told you, Sancho," replied Don Quixote, "that you know little where the subject of adventures is concerned. What I am saying to you is the truth, as you shall now see."

With this, he rode forward and took up a position in the middle of the road along which the friars were coming, and as soon as they appeared to be within earshot he cried out to them in a loud voice, "O devilish and monstrous beings, set free at once the highborn princesses whom you bear captive in that coach, or else prepare at once to meet your death as the just punishment of your evil deeds."

The friars drew rein and sat there in astonishment, marveling as much at Don Quixote's appearance as at the words he spoke. "Sir Knight," they answered him, "we are neither devilish nor monstrous but religious of the Order of St. Benedict who are merely going our way. We know nothing of those who are in that coach, nor of any captive princesses either."

"Soft words," said Don Quixote, "have no effect on me. I know you for what you are, lying rabble!" And without waiting for any further parley he gave spur to Rocinante and, with lowered lance, bore down upon the first friar with such fury and intrepidity that, had not the fellow tumbled from his mule of his own accord, he would have been hurled to the ground and either killed or badly wounded. The second religious, seeing how his companion had been treated, dug his legs into his she-mule's flanks and scurried away over the countryside faster than the wind.

Seeing the friar upon the ground, Sancho Panza slipped lightly from his mount and, falling upon him, began stripping him of his habit. The two mule drivers accompanying the religious thereupon came running up and asked Sancho why he was doing this. The latter replied that the friar's garments belonged to him as legitimate spoils of the battle that his master Don Quixote had just won. The muleteers, however, were lads with no sense of humor, nor did they know what all this talk of spoils and battles was about; but, perceiving that Don Quixote had ridden off to one side to converse with those inside the coach, they pounced upon Sancho, threw him to the ground, and proceeded to pull out the hair of his beard and kick him to a pulp, after which they went off and left him stretched out there, bereft at once of breath and sense.

Without losing any time, they then assisted the friar to remount. The good brother was trembling all over from fright, and there was not a speck of color in his face, but when he found himself in the saddle once more, he quickly spurred his beast to where his companion, at some little distance, sat watching and waiting to see what the result of the encounter would be. Having no curiosity as to the final outcome of the fray, the two of them now resumed their journey, making more signs of the cross than the devil would be able to carry upon his back.

Meanwhile Don Quixote, as we have said, was speaking to the lady in the coach.

"Your beauty, my lady, may now dispose of your person as best may please you, for the arrogance of your abductors lies upon the ground, overthrown by this good arm of mine; and in order that you may not

pine to know the name of your liberator, I may inform you that I am
Don Quixote de la Mancha, knight-errant and adventurer and captive
of the peerless and beauteous Doña Dulcinea del Toboso. In payment
of the favor which you have received from me, I ask nothing other than
that you return to El Toboso and on my behalf pay your respects to
this lady, telling her that it was I who set you free."

One of the squires accompanying those in the coach, a Biscayan, was
listening to Don Quixote's words, and when he saw that the knight did
not propose to let the coach proceed upon its way but was bent upon
having it turn back to El Toboso, he promptly went up to him, seized
his lance, and said to him in bad Castilian and worse Biscayan,² "Go,
caballero, and bad luck go with you; for by the God that created me, if
you do not let this coach pass, me kill you or me no Biscayan."

Don Quixote heard him attentively enough and answered him very
mildly, "If you were a *caballero*, which you are not, I should already
have chastised you, wretched creature, for your foolhardiness and your
impudence."

"Me no *caballero?*" cried the Biscayan.³ "Me swear to God, you lie
like a Christian. If you will but lay aside your lance and unsheath your
sword, you will soon see that you are carrying water to the cat! ⁴ Biscayan on land, gentleman at sea, but a gentleman in spite of the devil,
and you lie if you say otherwise."

" ' "You shall see as to that presently," said Agrajes,' " Don Quixote
quoted.⁵ He cast his lance to the earth, drew his sword, and, taking his
buckler on his arm, attacked the Biscayan with intent to slay him. The
latter, when he saw his adversary approaching, would have liked to dismount from his mule, for she was one of the worthless sort that are let
for hire and he had no confidence in her; but there was no time for this,
and so he had no choice but to draw his own sword in turn and make
the best of it. However, he was near enough to the coach to be able to
snatch a cushion from it to serve him as a shield; and then they fell upon
each other as though they were mortal enemies. The rest of those present
sought to make peace between them but did not succeed, for the Biscayan
with his disjointed phrases kept muttering that if they did not let him
finish the battle then he himself would have to kill his mistress and anyone else who tried to stop him.

The lady inside the carriage, amazed by it all and trembling at what
she saw, directed her coachman to drive on a little way; and there from
a distance she watched the deadly combat, in the course of which the
Biscayan came down with a great blow on Don Quixote's shoulder,

over the top of the latter's shield, and had not the knight been clad in armor, it would have split him to the waist.

Feeling the weight of this blow, Don Quixote cried out, "O lady of my soul, Dulcinea, flower of beauty, succor this your champion who out of gratitude for your many favors finds himself in so perilous a plight!" To utter these words, lay hold of his sword, cover himself with his buckler, and attack the Biscayan was but the work of a moment; for he was now resolved to risk everything upon a single stroke.

As he saw Don Quixote approaching with so dauntless a bearing, the Biscayan was well aware of his adversary's courage and forthwith determined to imitate the example thus set him. He kept himself protected with his cushion, but he was unable to get his she-mule to budge to one side or the other, for the beast, out of sheer exhaustion and being, moreover, unused to such childish play, was incapable of taking a single step. And so, then, as has been stated, Don Quixote was approaching the wary Biscayan, his sword raised on high and with the firm resolve of cleaving his enemy in two; and the Biscayan was awaiting the knight in the same posture, cushion in front of him and with uplifted sword. All the bystanders were trembling with suspense at what would happen as a result of the terrible blows that were threatened, and the lady in the coach and her maids were making a thousand vows and offerings to all the images and shrines in Spain, praying that God would save them all and the lady's squire from this great peril that confronted them.

But the unfortunate part of the matter is that at this very point the author of the history breaks off and leaves the battle pending, excusing himself upon the ground that he has been unable to find anything else in writing concerning the exploits of Don Quixote beyond those already set forth.[6] It is true, on the other hand, that the second author of this work could not bring himself to believe that so unusual a chronicle would have been consigned to oblivion, nor that the learned ones of La Mancha were possessed of so little curiosity as not to be able to discover in their archives or registry offices certain papers that have to do with this famous knight. Being convinced of this, he did not despair of coming upon the end of this pleasing story, and Heaven favoring him, he did find it, as shall be related in the second part.[7]

CHAPTER IX. *In which is concluded and brought to an end the stupendous battle between the gallant Biscayan and the valiant Knight of La Mancha.*

IN THE first part of this history we left the valorous Biscayan and the famous Don Quixote with swords unsheathed and raised aloft, about to let fall furious slashing blows which, had they been delivered fairly and squarely, would at the very least have split them in two and laid them wide open from top to bottom like a pomegranate; and it was at this doubtful point that the pleasing chronicle came to a halt and broke off, without the author's informing us as to where the rest of it might be found.

I was deeply grieved by such a circumstance, and the pleasure I had had in reading so slight a portion was turned into annoyance as I thought of how difficult it would be to come upon the greater part which it seemed to me must still be missing. It appeared impossible and contrary to all good precedent that so worthy a knight should not have had some scribe to take upon himself the task of writing an account of these unheard-of exploits; for that was something that had happened to none of the knights-errant who, as the saying has it, had gone forth in quest of adventures, seeing that each of them had one or two chroniclers, as if ready at hand, who not only had set down their deeds, but had depicted their most trivial thoughts and amiable weaknesses, however well concealed they might be. The good knight of La Mancha surely could not have been so unfortunate as to have lacked what Platir and others like him had in abundance. And so I could not bring myself to believe that this gallant history could have remained thus lopped off and mutilated, and I could not but lay the blame upon the malignity of time, that devourer and consumer of all things, which must either have consumed it or kept it hidden.

On the other hand, I reflected that inasmuch as among the knight's books had been found such modern works as *The Disenchantments of Jealousy* and *The Nymphs and Shepherds of Henares*, his story likewise must be modern, and that even though it might not have been written down, it must remain in the memory of the good folk of his village and the surrounding ones. This thought left me somewhat confused and more than ever desirous of knowing the real and true story, the whole story, of the life and wondrous deeds of our famous Spaniard, Don Quixote, light and mirror of the chivalry of La Mancha, the first in our age and in these calamitous times to devote himself to the hardships and exercises of knight-errantry and to go about righting wrongs, succoring widows, and protecting damsels—damsels such as those who, mounted upon their palfreys and with riding-whip in hand, in full possession of their virginity, were in the habit of going from mountain to mountain and from valley to valley; for unless there were some villain, some rustic with an ax and hood, or some monstrous giant to force them, there were in times past maiden ladies who at the end of eighty years, during all which time they had not slept for a single day beneath a roof, would go to their graves as virginal as when their mothers had borne them.

If I speak of these things, it is for the reason that in this and in all other respects our gallant Quixote is deserving of constant memory and praise, and even I am not to be denied my share of it for my diligence and the labor to which I put myself in searching out the conclusion of this agreeable narrative; although if heaven, luck, and circumstance had not aided me, the world would have had to do without the pleasure and the pastime which anyone may enjoy who will read this work attentively for an hour or two. The manner in which it came about was as follows:

I was standing one day in the Alcaná, or market place, of Toledo when a lad came up to sell some old notebooks and other papers to a silk weaver who was there. As I am extremely fond of reading anything, even though it be but the scraps of paper in the streets, I followed my natural inclination and took one of the books, whereupon I at once perceived that it was written in characters which I recognized as Arabic. I recognized them, but reading them was another thing; and so I began looking around to see if there was any Spanish-speaking Moor near by who would be able to read them for me. It was not very hard to find such an interpreter, nor would it have been even if the tongue in question had been an older and a better one.[1] To make a long story short, chance brought a fellow my way; and when I told him what it was I wished and placed the book in his hands, he opened it in the middle and began reading and at once fell to laughing. When I asked him what the cause of his laughter was, he replied that it was a note which had been written in the margin.

I besought him to tell me the content of the note, and he, laughing still, went on, "As I told you, it is something in the margin here: 'This Dulcinea del Toboso, so often referred to, is said to have been the best hand at salting pigs of any woman in all La Mancha.' "

No sooner had I heard the name Dulcinea del Toboso than I was astonished and held in suspense, for at once the thought occurred to me that those notebooks must contain the history of Don Quixote. With this in mind I urged him to read me the title, and he proceeded to do so, turning the Arabic into Castilian upon the spot: *History of Don Quixote de la Mancha, Written by Cid Hamete Benengeli, Arabic Historian.* It was all I could do to conceal my satisfaction and, snatching them from the silk weaver, I bought from the lad all the papers and notebooks that he had for half a real; but if he had known or suspected how very much I wanted them, he might well have had more than six reales for them.

The Moor and I then betook ourselves to the cathedral cloister, where I requested him to translate for me into the Castilian tongue all the books that had to do with Don Quixote, adding nothing and subtracting nothing; and I offered him whatever payment he desired. He was content with two arrobas of raisins and two fanegas [2] of wheat and promised to translate them well and faithfully and with all dispatch. However, in order to facilitate matters, and also because I did not wish to let such a find as this out of my hands, I took the fellow home with me, where in a little more than a month and a half he translated the whole of the work just as you will find it set down here.

In the first of the books there was a very lifelike picture of the battle between Don Quixote and the Biscayan, the two being in precisely the same posture as described in the history, their swords upraised, the one covered by his buckler, the other with his cushion. As for the Biscayan's mule, you could see at the distance of a crossbow shot that it was one for hire. Beneath the Biscayan there was a rubric which read: "Don Sancho de Azpeitia," which must undoubtedly have been his name; while beneath the feet of Rocinante was another inscription: "Don Quixote." Rocinante was marvelously portrayed: so long and lank, so lean and flabby, so extremely consumptive-looking that one could well understand the justness and propriety with which the name of "hack" had been bestowed upon him.

Alongside Rocinante stood Sancho Panza, holding the halter of his ass, and below was the legend: "Sancho Zancas." The picture showed him with a big belly, a short body, and long shanks, and that must have been where he got the names of Panza y Zancas [3] by which he is a number of times called in the course of the history. There are other small details that might be mentioned, but they are of little importance and have nothing to do with the truth of the story—and no story is bad so long as it is true.

If there is any objection to be raised against the veracity of the present one, it can be only that the author was an Arab, and that nation is known for its lying propensities; but even though they be our enemies, it may readily be understood that they would more likely have detracted from, rather than added to, the chronicle. So it seems to me, at any rate; for whenever he might and should deploy the resources of his pen in praise of so worthy a knight, the author appears to take pains to pass over the matter in silence; all of which in my opinion is ill done and ill conceived, for it should be the duty of historians to be exact, truthful, and dispassionate, and neither interest nor fear nor rancor nor affection should swerve them from the path of truth, whose mother is history, rival of time, depository of deeds, witness of the past, exemplar and adviser to the present, and the future's counselor. In this work, I am sure, will be found all that could be desired in the way of pleasant reading; and if it is lacking in any way, I maintain that this is the fault of that hound of an author rather than of the subject.

But to come to the point, the second part, according to the translation, began as follows:

As the two valorous and enraged combatants stood there, swords upraised and poised on high, it seemed from their bold mien as if they must surely be threatening heaven, earth, and hell itself. The first to let fall a blow was the choleric Biscayan, and he came down with such force and fury that, had not his sword been deflected in mid-air, that single stroke would have sufficed to put an end to this fearful combat and to all our knight's adventures at the same time; but fortune, which was reserving him for greater things, turned aside his adversary's blade in such a manner that, even though it fell upon his left shoulder, it did him no other damage than to strip him completely of his armor on that side, carrying with it a good part of his helmet along with half an ear, the headpiece clattering to the ground with a dreadful din, leaving its wearer in a sorry state.

Heaven help me! Who could properly describe the rage that now entered the heart of our hero of La Mancha as he saw himself treated in this fashion? It may merely be said that he once more reared himself in the stirrups, laid hold of his sword with both hands, and dealt the Biscayan such a blow, over the cushion and upon the head, that, even so good a defense proving useless, it was as if a mountain had fallen upon his enemy. The latter now began bleeding through the mouth, nose, and ears; he seemed about to fall from his mule, and would have fallen, no doubt, if he had not grasped the beast about the neck, but at that moment his feet slipped from the stirrups and his arms let go, and the mule, frightened by the terrible blow, began running across the plain, hurling its rider to the earth with a few quick plunges.

Don Quixote stood watching all this very calmly. When he saw his enemy fall, he leaped from his horse, ran over very nimbly, and thrust the point of his sword into the Biscayan's eyes, calling upon him at the same time to surrender or otherwise he would cut off his head. The Biscayan was so bewildered that he was unable to utter a single word in reply, and things would have gone badly with him, so blind was Don Quixote in his rage, if the ladies of the coach, who up to then had watched the struggle in dismay, had not come up to him at this point and begged him with many blandishments to do them the very great favor of sparing their squire's life.

To which Don Quixote replied with much haughtiness and dignity, "Most certainly, lovely ladies, I shall be very happy to do that which you ask of me, but upon one condition and understanding, and that is that this knight promise me that he will go to El Toboso and present himself in my behalf before Doña Dulcinea, in order that she may do with him as she may see fit."

Trembling and disconsolate, the ladies did not pause to discuss Don Quixote's request, but without so much as inquiring who Dulcinea might be they promised him that the squire would fulfill that which was commanded of him.

"Very well, then, trusting in your word, I will do him no further harm, even though he has well deserved it."

CHAPTER X. *Of the pleasing conversation that took place between Don Quixote and Sancho Panza, his squire.*

BY THIS time Sancho Panza had got to his feet, somewhat the worse for wear as the result of the treatment he had received from the friars' lads. He had been watching the battle attentively and praying God in his heart to give the victory to his master, Don Quixote, in order that he, Sancho, might gain some island where he could go to be governor as had been promised him. Seeing now that the combat was over and the knight was returning to mount Rocinante once more, he went up to hold the stirrup for him; but first he fell on his knees in front of him and, taking his hand, kissed it and said, "May your Grace be pleased, Señor Don Quixote, to grant me the governorship of that island which you have won in this deadly affray; for however large it may be, I feel that I am indeed capable of governing it as well as any man in this world has ever done."

To which Don Quixote replied, "Be advised, brother Sancho, that this adventure and other similar ones have nothing to do with islands; they are affairs of the crossroads in which one gains nothing more than a broken head or an ear the less. Be patient, for there will be others which will not only make you a governor, but more than that."

Sancho thanked him very much and, kissing his hand again and the skirt of his cuirass, he assisted him up on Rocinante's back, after which the squire bestraddled his own mount and started jogging along behind his master, who was now going at a good clip. Without pausing for any further converse with those in the coach, the knight made for a near-by wood, with Sancho following as fast as his beast could trot; but Rocinante was making such speed that the ass and its rider were left behind, and it was necessary to call out to Don Quixote to pull up and wait for them. He did so, reining in Rocinante until the weary Sancho had drawn abreast of him.

"It strikes me, sir," said the squire as he reached his master's side, "that it would be better for us to take refuge in some church; for in view of the way you have treated that one with whom you were fighting, it would be small wonder if they did not lay the matter before the Holy Brotherhood [1] and have us arrested; and faith, if they do that, we shall have to sweat a-plenty before we come out of jail."

"Be quiet," said Don Quixote. "And where have you ever seen, or read of, a knight being brought to justice no matter how many homicides he might have committed?"

"I know nothing about omecils," [2] replied Sancho, "nor ever in my life did I bear one to anybody; all I know is that the Holy Brotherhood has something to say about those who go around fighting on the highway, and I want nothing of it."

"Do not let it worry you," said Don Quixote, "for I will rescue you from the hands of the Chaldeans, not to speak of the Brotherhood. But answer me upon your life: have you ever seen a more valorous knight than I on all the known face of the earth? Have you ever read in the histories of any other who had more mettle in the attack, more perseverance in sustaining it, more dexterity in wounding his enemy, or more skill in overthrowing him?"

"The truth is," said Sancho, "I have never read any history whatsoever, for I do not know how to read or write; but what I would wager is that in all the days of my life I have never served a more courageous master than your Grace; I only hope your courage is not paid for in the place that I have mentioned. What I would suggest is that your Grace allow me to do something for that ear, for there is much blood coming from it, and I have here in my saddlebags some lint and a little white ointment."

"We could well dispense with all that," said Don Quixote, "if only I had remembered to bring along a vial of Fierabrás's balm, a single drop of which saves time and medicines."

"What vial and what balm is that?" inquired Sancho Panza.

"It is a balm the receipt for which I know by heart; with it one need have no fear of death nor think of dying from any wound. I shall make some of it and give it to you; and thereafter, whenever in any battle you see my body cut in two—as very often happens—all that is necessary is for you to take the part that lies on the ground, before the blood has congealed, and fit it very neatly and with great nicety upon the other part that remains in the saddle, taking care to adjust it evenly and exactly. Then you will give me but a couple of swallows of the balm of which I have told you, and you will see me sounder than an apple in no time at all."

"If that is so," said Panza, "I herewith renounce the governorship of the island you promised me and ask nothing other in payment of my many and faithful services than that your Grace give me the receipt for this wonderful potion, for I am sure that it would be worth more than two reales the ounce anywhere, and that is all I need for a life of ease and honor. But may I be so bold as to ask how much it costs to make it?"

"For less than three reales you can make something like six quarts," Don Quixote told him.

"Sinner that I am!" exclaimed Sancho. "Then why does your Grace not make some at once and teach me also?"

"Hush, my friend," said the knight, "I mean to teach you greater secrets than that and do you greater favors; but, for the present, let us look after this ear of mine, for it is hurting me more than I like."

Sancho thereupon took the lint and the ointment from his saddlebags; but when Don Quixote caught a glimpse of his helmet, he almost went out of his mind and, laying his hand upon his sword and lifting his eyes heavenward, he cried, "I make a vow to the Creator of all things and to the four holy Gospels in all their fullness of meaning that I will lead from now on the life that the great Marquis of Mantua did after he had sworn to avenge the death of his nephew Baldwin: not to eat bread off a tablecloth, not to embrace his wife, and other things which, although I am unable to recall them, we will look upon as understood—all this until I shall have wreaked an utter vengeance upon the one who has perpetrated such an outrage upon me."

"But let me remind your Grace," said Sancho when he heard these words, "that if the knight fulfills that which was commanded of him, by going to present himself before my lady Dulcinea del Toboso, then he will have paid his debt to you and merits no further punishment at your hands, unless it be for some fresh offense."

"You have spoken very well and to the point," said Don Quixote, "and so I annul the vow I have just made insofar as it has to do with any further vengeance, but I make it and confirm it anew so far as leading the life of which I have spoken is concerned, until such time as I shall have obtained by force of arms from some other knight another headpiece as good as this. And do not think, Sancho, that I am making smoke out of straw; there is one whom I well may imitate in this matter, for the same thing happened in all literalness in the case of Mambrino's helmet which cost Sacripante so dear." [3]

"I wish," said Sancho, "that your Grace would send all such oaths to the devil, for they are very bad for the health and harmful for the conscience as well. Tell me, please: supposing that for many days to come we meet no man wearing a helmet, then what are we to do? Must you still keep your vow in spite of all the inconveniences and discomforts, such as sleeping with your clothes on, not sleeping in any town, and a thousand other penances contained in the oath of that old madman of a Marquis of Mantua, an oath which you would now revive? Mark you, sir, along all these roads you meet no men of arms but only muleteers and carters, who not only do not wear helmets but quite likely have never heard tell of them in all their livelong days."

"In that you are wrong," said Don Quixote, "for we shall not be at these crossroads for the space of two hours before we shall see more men of arms than came to Albraca to win the fair Angélica."

"Very well, then," said Sancho, "so be it, and pray God that all turns out for the best so that I may at last win that island that is costing me so dearly, and then let me die."

"I have already told you, Sancho, that you are to give no thought to that; should the island fail, there is the kingdom of Denmark or that of Sobradisa,[4] which would fit you like a ring on your finger, and you ought, moreover, to be happy to be on *terra firma*.[5] But let us leave all this for some other time, while you look and see if you have something in those saddlebags for us to eat, after which we will go in search of some castle where we may lodge for the night and prepare that balm of which I was telling you, for I swear to God that my ear is paining me greatly."

"I have here an onion, a little cheese, and a few crusts of bread," said Sancho, "but they are not victuals fit for a valiant knight like your Grace."

"How little you know about it!" replied Don Quixote. "I would inform you, Sancho, that it is a point of honor with knights-errant to go for a month at a time without eating, and when they do eat, it is whatever may be at hand. You would certainly know that if you had read the histories as I have. There are many of them, and in none have I found any mention of knights eating unless it was by chance or at some sumptuous banquet that was tendered them; on other days they fasted. And even though it is well understood that, being men like us, they could not go without food entirely, any more than they could fail to satisfy the other necessities of nature, nevertheless, since they spent the greater part of their lives in forests and desert places without any cook to prepare their meals, their diet ordinarily consisted of rustic viands such as those that you now offer me. And so, Sancho my friend, do not be grieved at that which pleases me, nor seek to make the world over, nor to unhinge the institution of knight-errantry."

"Pardon me, your Grace," said Sancho, "but seeing that, as I have told you, I do not know how to read or write, I am consequently not familiar with the rules of the knightly calling. Hereafter, I will stuff my saddlebags with all manner of dried fruit for your Grace, but inasmuch as I am not a knight, I shall lay in for myself a stock of fowls and other more substantial fare."

"I am not saying, Sancho, that it is incumbent upon knights-errant to eat only those fruits of which you speak; what I am saying is that their ordinary sustenance should consist of fruit and a few herbs such as are to be found in the fields and with which they are well acquainted, as am I myself."

"It is a good thing," said Sancho, "to know those herbs, for, so far as I can see, we are going to have need of that knowledge one of these days."

With this, he brought out the articles he had mentioned, and the two of them ate in peace, and most companionably. Being desirous, however, of seeking a lodging for the night, they did not tarry long over their humble and unsavory repast. They then mounted and made what haste they could that they might arrive at a shelter before nightfall; but the sun failed them, and with it went the hope of attaining their wish. As the day ended they found themselves beside some goatherds' huts, and they accordingly decided to spend the night there. Sancho was as much disappointed at their not having reached a town as his master was content with sleeping under the open sky; for it seemed to Don Quixote that every time this happened it merely provided him with yet another opportunity to establish his claim to the title of knight-errant.

CHAPTER XI. *Of what happened to Don Quixote in the company of certain goatherds.*

H E W A S received by the herders with good grace, and Sancho having looked after Rocinante and the ass to the best of his ability, the knight, drawn by the aroma, went up to where some pieces of goat's meat were simmering in a pot over the fire. He would have liked then and there to see if they were done well enough to be transferred from pot to stomach, but he refrained in view of the fact that his hosts were already taking them off the fire. Spreading a few sheepskins on the ground, they hastily laid their rustic board and invited the strangers to share what there was of it. There were six of them altogether who belonged to that fold, and after they had urged Don Quixote, with rude politeness, to seat himself upon a small trough which they had turned upside down for the purpose, they took their own places upon the sheep hides round about. While his master sat there, Sancho remained standing to serve him the cup, which was made of horn. When the knight perceived this, he addressed his squire as follows:

"In order, Sancho, that you may see the good that there is in knight-errantry and how speedily those who follow the profession, no matter what the nature of their service may be, come to be honored and esteemed in the eyes of the world, I would have you here in the company of these good folk seat yourself at my side, that you may be even as I who am your master and natural lord, and eat from my plate and drink from where I drink; for of knight-errantry one may say the same as of love: that it makes all things equal."

"Many thanks!" said Sancho, "but if it is all the same to your Grace, providing there is enough to go around, I can eat just as well, or better, standing up and alone as I can seated beside an emperor. And if the truth must be told, I enjoy much more that which I eat in my own corner without any bowings and scrapings, even though it be only bread and onions, than I do a meal of roast turkey where I have to chew slowly, drink little, be always wiping my mouth, and can neither sneeze nor cough if I feel like it, nor do any of those other things that you can when you are free and alone.

"And so, my master," he went on, "these honors that your Grace
would confer upon me as your servant and a follower of knight-errantry
—which I am, being your Grace's squire—I would have you convert,
if you will, into other things that will be of more profit and advantage
to me; for though I hereby acknowledge them as duly received, I renounce them from this time forth to the end of the world."

"But for all that," said Don Quixote, "you must sit down; for whosoever humbleth himself, him God will exalt." And, laying hold of his
squire's arm, he compelled him to take a seat beside him.

The goatherds did not understand all this jargon about squires and
knights-errant; they did nothing but eat, keep silent, and study their
guests, who very dexterously and with much appetite were stowing
away chunks of meat as big as your fist. When the meat course was
finished, they laid out upon the sheepskins a great quantity of dried
acorns and half a cheese, which was harder than if it had been made
of mortar. The drinking horn all this while was not idle but went the
rounds so often—now full, now empty, like the bucket of a water
wheel [1]—that they soon drained one of the two wine bags that were on
hand. After Don Quixote had well satisfied his stomach, he took up
a handful of acorns and, gazing at them attentively, fell into a soliloquy.

"Happy the age and happy those centuries to which the ancients gave
the name of golden, and not because gold, which is so esteemed in this
iron age of ours, was then to be had without toil, but because those who
lived in that time did not know the meaning of the words 'thine' and
'mine.' In that blessed era all things were held in common, and to gain
his daily sustenance no labor was required of any man save to reach
forth his hand and take it from the sturdy oaks that stood liberally inviting him with their sweet and seasoned fruit. The clear-running fountains and rivers in magnificent abundance offered him palatable and
transparent water for his thirst; while in the clefts of the rocks and the
hollows of the trees the wise and busy honey-makers set up their republic so that any hand whatever might avail itself, fully and freely, of
the fertile harvest which their fragrant toil had produced. The vigorous
cork trees of their own free will and grace, without the asking, shed
their broad, light bark with which men began to cover their dwellings,
erected upon rude stakes merely as a protection against the inclemency
of the heavens.

"All then was peace, all was concord and friendship; the crooked
plowshare had not as yet grievously laid open and pried into the merciful bowels of our first mother, who without any forcing on man's part

yielded her spacious fertile bosom on every hand for the satisfaction, sustenance, and delight of her first sons. Then it was that lovely and unspoiled young shepherdesses, with locks that were sometimes braided, sometimes flowing, went roaming from valley to valley and hillock to hillock with no more garments than were needed to cover decently that which modesty requires and always has required should remain covered. Nor were their adornments such as those in use today—of Tyrian purple and silk worked up in tortured patterns; a few green leaves of burdock or of ivy, and they were as splendidly and as becomingly clad as our ladies of the court with all the rare and exotic tricks of fashion that idle curiosity has taught them.

"Thoughts of love, also, in those days were set forth as simply as the simple hearts that conceived them, without any roundabout and artificial play of words by way of ornament. Fraud, deceit, and malice had not yet come to mingle with truth and plain-speaking. Justice kept its own domain, where favor and self-interest dared not trespass, dared not impair her rights, becloud, and persecute her as they now do. There was no such thing then as arbitrary judgments, for the reason that there was no one to judge or be judged. Maidens in all their modesty, as I have said, went where they would and unattended; whereas in this hateful age of ours none is safe, even though she go to hide and shut herself up in some new labyrinth like that of Crete; for in spite of all her seclusion, through chinks and crevices or borne upon the air, the amorous plague with all its cursed importunities will find her out and lead her to her ruin.

"It was for the safety of such as these, as time went on and depravity increased, that the order of knights-errant was instituted, for the protection of damsels, the aid of widows and orphans, and the succoring of the needy. It is to this order that I belong, my brothers, and I thank you for the welcome and the kindly treatment that you have accorded to me and my squire. By natural law, all living men are obliged to show favor to knights-errant, yet without being aware of this you have received and entertained me; and so it is with all possible good will that I acknowledge your own good will to me."

This long harangue on the part of our knight—it might very well have been dispensed with—was all due to the acorns they had given him, which had brought back to memory the age of gold; whereupon the whim had seized him to indulge in this futile harangue with the goatherds as his auditors. They listened in open-mouthed wonderment, saying not a word, and Sancho himself kept quiet and went on munching acorns, taking occasion very frequently to pay a visit to the second wine bag, which they had suspended from a cork tree to keep it cool.

It took Don Quixote much longer to finish his speech than it did to put away his supper; and when he was through, one of the goatherds addressed him.

"In order that your Grace may say with more truth that we have received you with readiness and good will, we desire to give you solace and contentment by having one of our comrades, who will be here soon, sing for you. He is a very bright young fellow and deeply in love, and what is more, you could not ask for anything better than to hear him play the three-stringed lute."

Scarcely had he done saying this when the sound of a rebec was heard, and shortly afterward the one who played it appeared. He was a good-looking youth, around twenty-two years of age. His companions asked him if he had had his supper, and when he replied that he had, the one who had spoken to Don Quixote said to him, "Well, then, Antonio, you can give us the pleasure of hearing you sing, in order that this gentleman whom we have as our guest may see that we of the woods and mountains also know something about music. We have been telling him how clever you are, and now we want you to show him that we were speaking the truth. And so I beg you by all means to sit down and sing us that love-song of yours that your uncle the prebendary composed for you and which the villagers liked so well."

"With great pleasure," the lad replied, and without any urging he seated himself on the stump of an oak that had been felled and, tuning up his rebec, soon began singing, very prettily, the following ballad:

THE BALLAD THAT ANTONIO SANG [2]

> *I know well that thou dost love me,*
> *My Olalla, even though*
> *Eyes of thine have never spoken—*
> *Love's mute tongues—to tell me so.*
> *Since I know thou knowest my passion,*
> *Of thy love I am more sure:*
> *No love ever was unhappy*
> *When it was both frank and pure.*
> *True it is, Olalla, sometimes*
> *Thou a heart of bronze hast shown,*
> *And it seemed to me that bosom,*
> *White and fair, was made of stone.*

Yet in spite of all repulses
And a chastity so cold,
It appeared that I Hope's garment
By the hem did clutch and hold.

For my faith I ever cherished;
It would rise to meet the bait;
Spurned, it never did diminish;
Favored, it preferred to wait.

Love, they say, hath gentle manners:
Thus it is it shows its face;
Then may I take hope, Olalla,
Trust to win a longed for grace.

If devotion hath the power
Hearts to move and make them kind,
Let the loyalty I've shown thee
Plead my cause, be kept in mind.

For if thou didst note my costume,
More than once thou must have seen,
Worn upon a simple Monday
Sunday's garb so bright and clean.

Love and brightness go together.
Dost thou ask the reason why
I thus deck myself on Monday?
It is but to catch thine eye.

I say nothing of the dances
I have danced for thy sweet sake;
Nor the serenades I've sung thee
Till the first cock did awake.

Nor will I repeat my praises
Of that beauty all can see;
True my words but oft unwelcome—
Certain lasses hated me.

One girl there is, I well remember—
She's Teresa on the hill—
Said, "You think you love an angel,
But she is a monkey still.

"Thanks to all her many trinkets
And her artificial hair
And her many aids to beauty,
Love's own self she would ensnare."

She was lying, I was angry,
And her cousin, very bold,
Challenged me upon my honor;
What ensued need not be told.

Highflown words do not become me;
I'm a plain and simple man.
Pure the love that I would offer,
Serving thee as best I can.

Silken are the bonds of marriage,
When two hearts do intertwine;
Mother Church the yoke will fasten;
Bow your neck and I'll bow mine.

Or if not, my word I'll give thee,
From these mountains I'll come down—
Saint most holy be my witness—
Wearing a Capuchin gown.

With this the goatherd brought his song to a close, and although Don Quixote begged him to sing some more, Sancho Panza would not hear to this as he was too sleepy for any more ballads.

"Your Grace," he said to his master, "would do well to find out at once where his bed is to be, for the labor that these good men have to perform all day long does not permit them to stay up all night singing."

"I understand, Sancho," replied Don Quixote. "I perceive that those visits to the wine bag call for sleep rather than music as a recompense."

"It tastes well enough to all of us, God be praised," said Sancho.

"I am not denying that," said his master; "but go ahead and settle yourself down wherever you like. As for men of my profession, they prefer to keep vigil. But all the same, Sancho, perhaps you had better look after this ear, for it is paining me more than I like."

Sancho started to do as he was commanded, but one of the goatherds, when he saw the wound, told him not to bother, that he would place a remedy upon it that would heal it in no time. Taking a few leaves of rosemary, of which there was a great deal growing thereabouts, he mashed them in his mouth and, mixing them with a little salt, laid them on the ear, with the assurance that no other medicine was needed; and this proved to be the truth.

CHAPTER XII. *Of the story that one of the goatherds told to Don Quixote and the others.*

J UST then, another lad came up, one of those who brought the goatherds their provisions from the village.

"Do you know what's happening down there, my friends?" he said.

"How should we know?" one of the men answered him.

"In that case," the lad went on, "I must tell you that the famous student and shepherd known as Grisóstomo died this morning, muttering that the cause of his death was the love he had for that bewitched lass of a Marcela, daughter of the wealthy Guillermo—you know, the one who's been going around in these parts dressed like a shepherdess."

"For love of Marcela, you say?" one of the herders spoke up.

"That is what I'm telling you," replied the other lad. "And the best part of it is that he left directions in his will that he was to be buried in the field, as if he were a Moor, and that his grave was to be at the foot of the cliff where the Cork Tree Spring is; for, according to report, and he is supposed to have said so himself, that is the place where he saw her for the first time. There were other provisions, which the clergy of the village say cannot be carried out, nor would it be proper to fulfill them, seeing that they savor of heathen practices. But Grisóstomo's good friend, the student Ambrosio, who also dresses like a shepherd, insists that everything must be done to the letter, and as a result there is great excitement in the village.

"Nevertheless, from all I can hear, they will end by doing as Ambrosio and Grisóstomo's other friends desire, and tomorrow they will bury him with great ceremony in the place that I have mentioned. I believe it is going to be something worth seeing; at any rate, I mean to see it, even though it is too far for me to be able to return to the village before nightfall."

"We will all do the same," said the other goatherds. "We will cast lots to see who stays to watch the goats."

"That is right, Pedro," said one of their number, "but it will not be necessary to go to the trouble of casting lots. I will take care of the flocks for all of us; and do not think that I am being generous or that I am not

as curious as the rest of you; it is simply that I cannot walk on account of
the splinter I picked up in this foot the other day."

"Well, we thank you just the same," said Pedro.

Don Quixote then asked Pedro to tell him more about the dead man
and the shepherd lass; to which the latter replied that all he knew was
that Grisóstomo was a rich gentleman who had lived in a near-by village.
He had been a student for many years at Salamanca and then had returned
to his birthplace with the reputation of being very learned and well read;
he was especially noted for his knowledge of the science of the stars and
what the sun and moon were doing up there in the heavens, "for he would
promptly tell us when their clips was to come."

"*Eclipse*, my friend, not *clips*," said Don Quixote, "is the name applied
to the darkening-over of those major luminaries."

But Pedro, not pausing for any trifles, went on with his story. "He
could also tell when the year was going to be plentiful or estil—"

"*Sterile*, you mean to say, friend—"

"*Sterile* or *estil*," said Pedro, "it all comes out the same in the end. But
I can tell you one thing, that his father and his friends, who believed in
him, did just as he advised them and they became rich; for he would say
to them, 'This year, sow barley and not wheat'; and again, 'Sow chickpeas
and not barley'; or, 'This season there will be a good crop of oil, but
the three following ones you will not get a drop.' "

"That science," Don Quixote explained, "is known as astrology."

"I don't know what it's called," said Pedro, "but he knew all this and
more yet. Finally, not many months after he returned from Salamanca,
he appeared one day dressed like a shepherd with crook and sheepskin
jacket; for he had resolved to lay aside the long gown that he wore as
a scholar, and in this he was joined by Ambrosio, a dear friend of his
and the companion of his studies. I forgot to tell you that Grisóstomo
was a great one for composing verses; he even wrote the carols for
Christmas Eve and the plays that were performed at Corpus Christi by
the lads of our village,[1] and everyone said that they were the best ever.

"When the villagers saw the two scholars coming out dressed like shepherds, they were amazed and could not imagine what was the reason
for such strange conduct on their part. It was about that time that
Grisóstomo's father died and left him the heir to a large fortune, consisting of land and chattels, no small quantity of cattle, and a considerable
sum of money, of all of which the young man was absolute master; and,
to tell the truth, he deserved it, for he was very sociable and charitably
inclined, a friend to all worthy folk, and he had a face that was like a

benediction. Afterward it was learned that if he had changed his garments like this, it was only that he might be able to wander over the wastelands on the trail of that shepherdess Marcela of whom our friend was speaking, for the poor fellow had fallen in love with her. And now I should like to tell you, for it is well that you should know, just who this lass is; for it may be—indeed, there is no maybe about it—you will never hear the like in all the days of your life, though you live to be older than Sarna." [2]

"You should say *Sarah*," Don Quixote corrected him; for he could not bear hearing the goatherd using the wrong words all the time.[3]

"The itch," said Pedro, "lives long enough; and if, sir, you go on interrupting me at every word, we'll never be through in a year."

"Pardon me, friend," said Don Quixote, "it was only because there is so great a difference between Sarna and Sarah that I pointed it out to you; but you have given me a very good answer, for the itch does live longer than Sarah; and so go on with your story, and I will not contradict you any more."

"I was about to say, then, my dear sir," the goatherd went on, "that in our village there was a farmer who was richer still than Grisóstomo's father. His name was Guillermo, and, over and above his great wealth, God gave him a daughter whose mother, the most highly respected woman in these parts, died in bearing her. It seems to me I can see the good lady now, with that face that rivaled the sun and moon; [4] and I remember, above all, what a friend she was to the poor, for which reason I believe that her soul at this very moment must be enjoying God's presence in the other world.

"Grieving for the loss of so excellent a wife, Guillermo himself died, leaving his daughter Marcela, now a rich young woman, in the custody of one of her uncles, a priest who holds a benefice in our village. The girl grew up with such beauty as to remind us of her mother, beautiful as that lady had been. By the time she was fourteen or fifteen no one looked at her without giving thanks to God who had created such comeliness, and almost all were hopelessly in love with her. Her uncle kept her very closely shut up, but, for all of that, word of her great beauty spread to such an extent that by reason of it, as much as on account of the girl's wealth, her uncle found himself besought and importuned not only by the young men of our village, but by those for leagues around who desired to have her for a wife.

"But he, an upright Christian, although he wished to marry her off as soon as she was of age, had no desire to do so without her consent,

not that he had any eye to the gain and profit which the custody of his
niece's property brought him while her marriage was deferred. Indeed,
this much was said in praise of the good priest in more than one circle
of the village; for I would have you know, Sir Knight, that in these little
places everything is discussed and becomes a subject of gossip; and you
may rest assured, as I am for my part, that a priest must be more than
ordinarily good if his parishioners feel bound to speak well of him, especially in the small towns."

"That is true," said Don Quixote, "but go on. I like your story very
much, and you, good Pedro, tell it with very good grace."

"May the Lord's grace never fail me, for that is what counts. But to
go on: Although the uncle set forth to his niece the qualities of each
one in particular of the many who sought her hand, begging her to
choose and marry whichever one she pleased, she never gave him any
answer other than this: that she did not wish to marry at all, since being
but a young girl she did not feel that she was equal to bearing the
burdens of matrimony. As her reasons appeared to be proper and just,
the uncle did not insist but thought he would wait until she was a little
older, when she would be capable of selecting someone to her taste. For,
he said, and quite right he was, parents ought not to impose a way of
life upon their children against the latters' will. And then, one fine day,
lo and behold, there was the finical Marcela turned shepherdess; and
without paying any attention to her uncle or all those of the village
who advised against it, she set out to wander through the fields with the
other lasses, guarding flocks as they did.

"Well, the moment she appeared in public and her beauty was uncovered for all to see, I really cannot tell you how many rich young
bachelors, gentlemen, and farmers proceeded to don a shepherd's garb
and go to make love to her in the meadows. One of her suitors, as I have
told you, was our deceased friend, and it is said that he did not love but
adored her. But you must not think that because Marcela chose so free
and easy a life, and one that offers little or no privacy, that she was
thereby giving the faintest semblance of encouragement to those who
would disparage her modesty and prudence; rather, so great was the
vigilance with which she looked after her honor that of all those who
waited upon her and solicited her favors, none could truly say that she
had given him the slightest hope of attaining his desire.

"For although she does not flee nor shun the company and conversation of the shepherds, treating them in courteous and friendly fashion,
the moment she discovers any intentions on their part, even though it

be the just and holy one of matrimony, she hurls them from her like a catapult. As a result, she is doing more damage in this land than if a plague had fallen upon it; for her beauty and graciousness win the hearts of all who would serve her, but her disdain and the disillusionment it brings lead them in the end to despair, and then they can only call her cruel and ungrateful, along with other similar epithets that reveal all too plainly the state of mind that prompts them. If you were to stay here some time, sir, you would hear these uplands and valleys echo with the laments of those who have followed her only to be deceived.

"Not far from here is a place where there are a couple of dozen tall beeches, and there is not a one of them on whose smooth bark Marcela's name has not been engraved; and above some of these inscriptions you will find a crown, as if by this her lover meant to indicate that she deserved to wear the garland of beauty above all the women on the earth. Here a shepherd sighs and there another voices his lament. Now are to be heard amorous ballads, and again despairing ditties. One will spend all the hours of the night seated at the foot of some oak or rock without once closing his tearful eyes, and the morning sun will find him there, stupefied and lost in thought. Another, without giving truce or respite to his sighs, will lie stretched upon the burning sands in the full heat of the most exhausting summer noontide, sending up his complaint to merciful Heaven.

"And, meanwhile, over this one and that one, over one and all, the beauteous Marcela triumphs and goes her own way, free and unconcerned. All those of us who know her are waiting to see how far her pride will carry her, and who will be the fortunate man who will succeed in taming this terrible creature and thus come into possession of a beauty so matchless as hers. Knowing all this that I have told you to be undoubtedly true, I can readily believe this lad's story about the cause of Grisóstomo's death. And so I advise you, sir, not to fail to be present tomorrow at his burial; it will be well worth seeing, for he has many friends, and the place is not half a league from here."

"I will make a point of it," said Don Quixote, "and I thank you for the pleasure you have given me by telling me so delightful a tale."

"Oh," said the goatherd, "I do not know the half of the things that have happened to Marcela's lovers; but it is possible that tomorrow we may meet along the way some shepherd who will tell us more. And now it would be well for you to go and sleep under cover, for the night air may not be good for your wound, though with the remedy that has been put on it there is not much to fear."

Sancho Panza, who had been sending the goatherd to the devil for talking so much, now put in a word with his master, urging him to come and sleep in Pedro's hut. Don Quixote did so; and all the rest of the night was spent by him in thinking of his lady Dulcinea, in imitation of Marcela's lovers. As for Sancho, he made himself comfortable between Rocinante and the ass and at once dropped off to sleep, not like a love-lorn swain but, rather, like a man who has had a sound kicking that day.

CHAPTER XIII. *In which is brought to a close the story of the shepherdess Marcela, along with other events.*

DAY had barely begun to appear upon the balconies of the east when five or six goatherds arose and went to awaken Don Quixote and tell him that if he was still of a mind to go see Grisóstomo's famous burial they would keep him company. The knight, desiring nothing better, ordered Sancho to saddle at once, which was done with much dispatch, and then they all set out forthwith.

They had not gone more than a quarter of a league when, upon crossing a footpath, they saw coming toward them six shepherds clad in black sheepskins and with garlands of cypress and bitter rosebay on their heads. Each of them carried a thick staff made of the wood of the holly, and with them came two gentlemen on horseback in handsome traveling attire, accompanied by three lads on foot. As the two parties met they greeted each other courteously, each inquiring as to the other's destination, whereupon they learned that they were all going to the burial, and so continued to ride along together.

Speaking to his companion, one of them said, "I think, Señor Vivaldo, that we are going to be well repaid for the delay it will cost us to see this famous funeral; for famous it must surely be, judging by the strange things that these shepherds have told us of the dead man and the homicidal shepherdess."

"I think so too," agreed Vivaldo. "I should be willing to delay our journey not one day, but four, for the sake of seeing it."

Don Quixote then asked them what it was they had heard of Marcela and Grisóstomo. The traveler replied that on that very morning they had fallen in with those shepherds and, seeing them so mournfully trigged out, had asked them what the occasion for it was. One of the fellows had then told them of the beauty and strange demeanor of a shepherdess by the name of Marcela, her many suitors, and the death of this Grisóstomo, to whose funeral they were bound. He related, in short, the entire story as Don Quixote had heard it from Pedro.

Changing the subject, the gentleman called Vivaldo inquired of Don Quixote what it was that led him to go armed in that manner in a land that was so peaceful.

"The calling that I profess," replied Don Quixote, "does not permit me to do otherwise. An easy pace, pleasure, and repose—those things were invented for delicate courtiers; but toil, anxiety, and arms—they are for those whom the world knows as knights-errant, of whom I, though unworthy, am the very least."

No sooner had they heard this than all of them immediately took him for a madman. By way of assuring himself further and seeing what kind of madness it was of which Don Quixote was possessed, Vivaldo now asked him what was meant by the term knights-errant.

"Have not your Worships read the annals and the histories of England that treat of the famous exploits of King Arthur, who in our Castilian balladry is always called King Artús? According to a very old tradition that is common throughout the entire realm of Great Britain, this king did not die, but by an act of enchantment was changed into a raven; and in due course of time he is to return and reign once more, recovering his kingdom and his scepter; for which reason, from that day to this, no Englishman is known to have killed one of those birds. It was, moreover, in the time of that good king that the famous order of the Knights of the Round Table was instituted; and as for the love of Sir Lancelot of the Lake and Queen Guinevere, everything took place exactly as the story has it, their confidante and go-between being the honored matron Quintañona; [1] whence comes that charming ballad that is such a favorite with us Spaniards:

> Never was there a knight
> So served by maid and dame
> As the one they call Sir Lancelot
> When from Britain he came— [2]

to carry on the gentle, pleasing course of his loves and noble deeds.

"From that time forth, the order of chivalry was passed on and propagated from one individual to another until it had spread through many and various parts of the world. Among those famed for their exploits was the valiant Amadis of Gaul, with all his sons and grandsons to the fifth generation; and there was also the brave Felixmarte of Hircania,[3] and the never sufficiently praised Tirant lo Blanch; and in view of the fact that he lived in our own day, almost, we came near to seeing, hearing, and conversing with that other courageous knight, Don Belianís of Greece.

"And that, gentlemen, is what it means to be a knight-errant, and what I have been telling you of is the order of chivalry which such a knight professes, an order to which, as I have already informed you, I, although a sinner, have the honor of belonging; for I have made the same profession as have those other knights. That is why it is you find me in these wild and lonely places, riding in quest of adventure, being resolved to offer my arm and my person in the most dangerous undertaking fate may have in store for me, that I may be of aid to the weak and needy."

Listening to this speech, the travelers had some while since come to the conclusion that Don Quixote was out of his mind, and were likewise able to perceive the peculiar nature of his madness, and they wondered at it quite as much as did all those who encountered it for the first time. Being endowed with a ready wit and a merry disposition and thinking to pass the time until they reached the end of the short journey which, so he was told, awaited them before they should arrive at the mountain where the burial was to take place, Vivaldo decided to give him a further opportunity of displaying his absurdities.

"It strikes me, Sir Knight-errant," he said, "that your Grace has espoused one of the most austere professions to be found anywhere on earth—even more austere, if I am not mistaken, than that of the Carthusian monks."

"Theirs may be as austere as ours," Don Quixote replied, "but that it is as necessary I am very much inclined to doubt. For if the truth be told, the soldier who carries out his captain's order does no less than the captain who gives the order. By that I mean to say that the religious, in all peace and tranquility, pray to Heaven for earth's good, but we soldiers and knights put their prayers into execution by defending with the might of our good right arms and at the edge of the sword those things for which they pray; and we do this not under cover of a roof but under the open sky, beneath the insufferable rays of the summer sun and the biting cold of winter. Thus we become the ministers of God on earth, and our arms the means by which He executes His decrees. And just as war and all the things that have to do with it are impossible without toil, sweat, and anxiety, it follows that those who have taken upon themselves such a profession must unquestionably labor harder than do those who in peace and tranquility and at their ease pray God to favor the ones who can do little in their own behalf.

"I do not mean to say—I should not think of saying—that the state of knight-errant is as holy as that of the cloistered monk; I merely would imply, from what I myself endure, that ours is beyond a doubt the more laborious and arduous calling, more beset by hunger and thirst, more wretched, ragged, and ridden with lice. It is an absolute certainty that the knights-errant of old experienced much misfortune in the course of their lives; and if some by their might and valor came to be emperors, you may take my word for it, it cost them dearly in blood and sweat, and if those who rose to such a rank had lacked enchanters and magicians to aid them, they surely would have been cheated of their desires, deceived in their hopes and expectations."

"I agree with you on that," said the traveler, "but there is one thing among others that gives me a very bad impression of the knights-errant, and that is the fact that when they are about to enter upon some great and perilous adventure in which they are in danger of losing their lives, they never at that moment think of commending themselves to God as every good Christian is obliged to do under similar circumstances, but, rather, commend themselves to their ladies with as much fervor and devotion as if their mistresses were God himself; all of which to me smacks somewhat of paganism."

"Sir," Don Quixote answered him, "it could not by any means be otherwise; the knight-errant who did not do so would fall into disgrace, for it is the usage and custom of chivalry that the knight, before engaging in some great feat of arms, shall behold his lady in front of him and shall turn his eyes toward her, gently and lovingly, as if beseeching her favor and protection in the hazardous encounter that awaits him, and even though no one hears him, he is obliged to utter certain words between his teeth, commending himself to her with all his heart; and of this we have numerous examples in the histories. Nor is it to be assumed that he does not commend himself to God also, but the time and place for that is in the course of the undertaking."

"All the same," said the traveler, "I am not wholly clear in this matter; for I have often read of two knights-errant exchanging words until, one word leading to another, their wrath is kindled; whereupon, turning their steeds and taking a good run up the field, they whirl about and bear down upon each other at full speed, commending themselves to their ladies in the midst of it all. What commonly happens then is that one of the two topples from his horse's flanks and is run through and through with the other's lance; and his adversary would also fall to the ground if he did not cling to his horse's mane. What I do not understand is how the dead man would have had time to commend himself to God in the course of this accelerated combat. It would be better if the words he wasted in calling upon his lady as he ran toward the other knight had been spent in paying the debt that he owed as a Christian. Moreover, it is my personal opinion that not all knights-errant have ladies to whom to commend themselves, for not all of them are in love."

"That," said Don Quixote, "is impossible. I assert there can be no knight-errant without a lady; for it is as natural and proper for them to be in love as it is for the heavens to have stars, and I am quite sure that no one ever read a story in which a loveless man of arms was to be met with, for the simple reason that such a one would not be looked upon as a legitimate knight but as a bastard one who had entered the fortress of chivalry not by the main gate, but over the walls, like a robber and a thief."

"Nevertheless," said the traveler, "if my memory serves me right, I have read that Don Galaor, brother of the valorous Amadis of Gaul, never had a special lady to whom he prayed, yet he was not held in any the less esteem for that but was a very brave and famous knight."

Once again, our Don Quixote had an answer. "Sir, one swallow does not make a summer. And in any event, I happen to know that this knight was secretly very much in love. As for his habit of paying court to all the ladies that caught his fancy, that was a natural propensity on his part and one that he was unable to resist. There was, however, one particular lady whom he had made the mistress of his will and to whom he did commend himself very frequently and privately; for he prided himself upon being a reticent knight."

"Well, then," said the traveler, "if it is essential that every knight-errant be in love, it is to be presumed that your Grace is also, since you are of the profession. And unless it be that you pride yourself upon your reticence as much as did Don Galaor, then I truly, on my own behalf and in the name of all this company, beseech your Grace to tell us your lady's name, the name of the country where she resides, what her rank is, and something of the beauty of her person, that she may esteem herself fortunate in having all the world know that she is loved and served by such a knight as your Grace appears to me to be."

At this, Don Quixote heaved a deep sigh. "I cannot say," he began, "as to whether or not my sweet enemy would be pleased that all the world should know I serve her. I can only tell you, in response to the question which you have so politely put to me, that her name is Dulcinea, her place of residence El Toboso, a village of La Mancha. As to her rank, she should be at the very least a princess, seeing that she is my lady and my queen. Her beauty is superhuman, for in it are realized all the impossible and chimerical attributes that poets are accustomed to give their fair ones. Her locks are golden, her brow the Elysian Fields, her eyebrows rainbows, her eyes suns, her cheeks roses, her lips coral, her teeth pearls, her neck alabaster, her bosom marble, her hands ivory, her complexion snow-white. As for those parts which modesty keeps covered from the human sight, it is my opinion that, discreetly considered, they are only to be extolled and not compared to any other."

"We should like," said Vivaldo, "to know something as well of her lineage, her race and ancestry."

"She is not," said Don Quixote, "of the ancient Roman Curtii, Caii, or Scipios, nor of the modern Colonnas and Orsini, nor of the Moncadas and Requesenses of Catalonia, nor is she of the Rebellas and Villanovas of Valencia, or the Palafoxes, Nuzas, Rocabertis, Corellas, Lunas, Alagones, Urreas, or Gurreas of Aragon, the Cerdas, Manriques, Mendozas, or Guzmanes of Castile, the Alencastros, Pallas, or Menezes of Portugal; but she is of the Tobosos of La Mancha, and although the line is a modern one, it well may give rise to the most illustrious families of the centuries to come. And let none dispute this with me, unless it be under the conditions which Zerbino has set forth in the inscription beneath Orlando's arms:

These let none move
Who dares not with Orlando his valor prove." [4]

"Although my own line," replied the traveler, "is that of the Gachupins [5] of Laredo, I should not venture to compare it with the Tobosos of La Mancha, in view of the fact that, to tell you the truth, I have never heard the name before."

"How does it come that you have never heard it!" exclaimed Don Quixote.

The others were listening most attentively to the conversation of these two, and even the goatherds and shepherds were by now aware that our knight of La Mancha was more than a little insane. Sancho Panza alone thought that all his master said was the truth, for he was well acquainted with him, having known him since birth. The only doubt in his mind had to do with the beauteous Dulcinea del Toboso, for he knew of no such princess and the name was strange to his ears, although he lived not far from that place.

They were continuing on their way, conversing in this manner, when they caught sight of some twenty shepherds coming through the gap between two high mountains, all of them clad in black woolen garments and with wreaths on their heads, some of the garlands, as was afterward learned, being of cypress, others of yew. Six of them were carrying a bier covered with a great variety of flowers and boughs.

"There they come with Grisóstomo's body," said one of the goatherds, "and the foot of the mountain yonder is where he wished to be buried."

They accordingly quickened their pace and arrived just as those carrying the bier had set it down on the ground. Four of the shepherds with sharpened picks were engaged in digging a grave alongside the barren rock. After a courteous exchange of greetings, Don Quixote and his companions turned to look at the bier. Upon it lay a corpse covered with flowers, the body of a man dressed like a shepherd and around thirty years of age. Even in death it could be seen that he had had a handsome face and had been of a jovial disposition. Round about him upon the bier were a number of books and many papers, open and folded.

Meanwhile, those who stood gazing at the dead man and those who were digging the grave—everyone present, in fact—preserved an awed silence, until one of the pallbearers said to another, "Look well, Ambrosio, and make sure that this is the place that Grisóstomo had in mind, since you are bent upon carrying out to the letter the provisions of his will."

"This is it," replied Ambrosio; "for many times my unfortunate friend told me the story of his misadventure. He told me that it was here that he first laid eyes upon that mortal enemy of the human race, and it was here, also, that he first revealed to her his passion, for he was as honorable as he was lovelorn; and it was here, finally, at their last meeting, that she shattered his illusions and showed him her disdain, thus bringing to an end the tragedy of his wretched life. And here, in memory of his great misfortune, he wished to be laid in the bowels of eternal oblivion."

Then, turning to Don Quixote and the travelers, he went on, "This body, gentlemen, on which you now look with pitying eyes was the depository of a soul which heaven had endowed with a vast share of its

riches. This is the body of Grisóstomo, who was unrivaled in wit, unequaled in courtesy, supreme in gentleness of bearing, a model of friendship, generous without stint, grave without conceit, merry without
being vulgar—in short, first in all that is good and second to none in
the matter of misfortunes. He loved well and was hated, he adored and
was disdained; he wooed a wild beast, importuned a piece of marble,
ran after the wind, cried out to loneliness, waited upon ingratitude, and
his reward was to be the spoils of death midway in his life's course—a
life that was brought to an end by a shepherdess whom he sought to
immortalize that she might live on in the memory of mankind, as those
papers that you see there would very plainly show if he had not commanded me to consign them to the flames even as his body is given to
the earth."

"You," said Vivaldo, "would treat them with greater harshness and
cruelty than their owner himself, for it is neither just nor fitting to carry
out the will of one who commands what is contrary to all reason. It
would not have been a good thing for Augustus Caesar to consent to
have them execute the behests of the divine Mantuan in his last testament. And so, Señor Ambrosio, while you may give the body of your
friend to the earth, you ought not to give his writings to oblivion. If out
of bitterness he left such an order, that does not mean that you are to
obey it without using your own discretion. Rather, by granting life to
these papers, you permit Marcela's cruelheartedness to live forever and
serve as an example to the others in the days that are to come in order
that they may flee and avoid such pitfalls as these.

"I and those that have come with me know the story of this lovesick
and despairing friend of yours; we know the affection that was between
you, and what the occasion of his death was, and the things that he
commanded be done as his life drew to a close. And from this lamentable
tale anyone may see how great was Marcela's cruelty; they may behold
Grisóstomo's love, the loyalty that lay in your friendship, and the end
that awaits those who run headlong, with unbridled passion, down the
path that doting love opens before their gaze. Last night we heard of
your friend's death and learned that he was to be buried here, and out
of pity and curiosity we turned aside from our journey and resolved to
come see with our own eyes that which had aroused so much compassion
when it was told to us. And in requital of that compassion, and the desire
that has been born in us to prevent if we can a recurrence of such tragic
circumstances, we beg you, O prudent Ambrosio!—or, at least, I for

my part implore you—to give up your intention of burning these papers and let me carry some of them away with me."

Without waiting for the shepherd to reply he put out his hand and took a few of those that were nearest him.

"Out of courtesy, sir," said Ambrosio when he saw this, "I will consent for you to keep those that you have taken; but it is vain to think that I will refrain from burning the others."

Vivaldo, who was anxious to find out what was in the papers, opened one of them and perceived that it bore the title "Song of Despair."

Hearing this, Ambrosio said, "That is the last thing the poor fellow wrote; and in order, sir, that you may see the end to which his misfortunes brought him, read it aloud if you will, for we shall have time for it while they are digging the grave."

"That I will very willingly do," said Vivaldo.

And since all the bystanders had the same desire, they gathered around as he in a loud clear voice read the following poem.

CHAPTER XIV. *In which are set down the despairing verses of the deceased shepherd, with other unlooked-for happenings.*

GRISÓSTOMO'S SONG [1]

Since thou desirest that thy cruelty
Be spread from tongue to tongue and land to land,
The unrelenting sternness of thy heart
Shall turn my bosom's hell to minstrelsy
That all men everywhere may understand
The nature of my grief and what thou art.
And as I seek my sorrows to impart,
Telling of all the things that thou hast done,
My very entrails shall speak out to brand

Thy heartlessness, thy soul to reprimand,
Where no compassion ever have I won.
Then listen well, lend an attentive ear;
This ballad that thou art about to hear
Is not contrived by art; 'tis a simple song
Such as shepherds sing each day throughout the year—
Surcease of pain for me, for thee a prong.

   Then let the roar of lion, fierce wolf's cry,
The horrid hissing of the scaly snake,
The terrifying sound of monsters strange,
Ill-omened call of crow against the sky,
The howling of the wind as it doth shake
The tossing sea where all is constant change,
Bellow of vanquished bull that cannot range
As it was wont to do, the piteous sob
Of the widowed dove as if its heart would break,
Hoot of the envied owl,[2] ever awake,
From hell's own choir the deep and mournful throb—
Let all these sounds come forth and mingle now.
For if I'm to tell my woes, why then, I vow,
I must new measures find, new modes invent,
With sound confusing sense, I may somehow
Portray the inferno where my days are spent.

   The mournful echoes of my murmurous plaint
Father Tagus[3] shall not hear as he rolls his sand,
Nor olive-bordered Betis;[4] my lament shall be
To the tall and barren rock as I acquaint
The caves with my sorrow; the far and lonely strand
No human foot has trod shall hear from me
The story of thine inhumanity
As told with lifeless tongue but living word.
I'll tell it to the valleys near at hand
Where never shines the sun upon the land;
By venomous serpents shall my tale be heard
On the low-lying, marshy river plain.
And yet, the telling will not be in vain;
For the reverberations of my plight,
Thy matchless austerity and this my pain,
Through the wide world shall go, thee to indict.

   Disdain may kill; suspicion false or true

May slay all patience; deadliest of all
Is jealousy; while absence renders life
Worse than a void; Hope lends no roseate hue
Against forgetfulness or the dread call
Of death inevitable, the end of strife.
Yet—unheard miracle!—with sorrows rife,
My own existence somehow still goes on;
The flame of life with me doth rise and fall.
Jealous I am, disdained; I know the gall
Of those suspicions that will not be gone,
Which leave me not the shadow of a hope,
And, desperate, I will not even grope
But rather will endure until the end,
And with despair eternally I'll cope,
Knowing that things for me will never mend.

Can one both hope and fear at the same season?
Would it be well to do so in any case,
Seeing that fear, by far, hath the better excuse?
Confronting jealousy, is there any reason
For me to close my eyes to its stern face,
Pretend to see it not? What is the use,
When its dread presence I can still deduce
From countless gaping wounds deep in my heart?
When suspicion—bitter change!—to truth gives place,
And truth itself, losing its virgin grace,
Becomes a lie, is it not wisdom's part
To open wide the door to frank mistrust?
When disdain's unveiled, to doubt is only just.
O ye fierce tyrants of Love's empery!
Shackle these hands with stout cord, if ye must.
My pain shall drown your triumph—woe is me!

I die, in short, and since nor life nor death
Yields any hope, to my fancy will I cling.
That man is freest who is Love's bond slave:
I'll say this with my living-dying breath,
And the ancient tyrant's praises I will sing.
Love is the greatest blessing Heaven e'er gave.
What greater beauty could a lover crave
Than that which my fair enemy doth show
In soul and body and in everything?

E'en her forgetfulness of me doth spring
From my own lack of grace, that I well know.
In spite of all the wrongs that he has wrought,
Love rules his empire justly as he ought.
Throw all to the winds and speed life's wretched span
By feeding on his self-deluding thought.
No blessing holds the future that I scan.

Thou whose unreasonableness reason doth give
For putting an end to this tired life of mine,
From the deep heart wounds which thou mayest plainly see,
Judge if the better course be to die or live.
Gladly did I surrender my will to thine,
Gladly I suffered all thou didst to me;
And now that I'm dying, should it seem to thee
My death is worth a tear from thy bright eyes,
Pray hold it back, fair one, do not repine,
For I would have from thee no faintest sign
Of penitence, e'en though my soul thy prize.
Rather, I'd have thee laugh, be very gay,
And let my funeral be a festive day—
But I am very simple! knowing full well
That thou art bound to go thy blithesome way,
And my untimely end thy fame shall swell.

Come, thirsting Tantalus from out Hell's pit;
Come, Sisyphus with the terrifying weight
Of that stone thou rollest; Tityus, bring
Thy vulture and thine anguish infinite;
Ixion with thy wheel, be thou not late;
Come, too, ye sisters ever laboring;
Come all, your griefs into my bosom fling,
And then, with lowered voices, intone a dirge,
If dirge be fitting for one so desperate,
A body without a shroud, unhappy fate!
And Hell's three-headed gateman, do thou emerge
With a myriad other phantoms, monstrous swarm,
Beings infernal of fantastic form,
Raising their voices for the uncomforted
In a counterpoint of grief, harmonious storm.
What better burial for a lover dead?

Despairing song of mine, do not complain,

Nor let our parting cause thee any pain,
For my misfortune is not wholly bad,
Seeing her fortune's bettered by my demise.
Then, even in the grave, be thou not sad.

Those who had listened to Grisóstomo's poem liked it well enough, but the one who read it remarked that it did not appear to him to conform to what had been told him of Marcela's modesty and virtue, seeing that in it the author complains of jealousy, suspicion, and absence, all to the prejudice of her good name. To this Ambrosio, as one who had known his friend's most deeply hidden thoughts, replied as follows:

"By way of satisfying, sir, the doubt that you entertain, it is well for you to know that when the unfortunate man wrote that poem, he was by his own volition absent from Marcela, to see if this would work a cure; but when the enamored one is away from his love, there is nothing that does not inspire in him fear and torment, and such was the case with Grisóstomo, for whom jealous imaginings, fears, and suspicions became a seeming reality. And so, in this respect, Marcela's reputation for virtue remains unimpaired; beyond being cruel and somewhat arrogant, and exceedingly disdainful, she could not be accused by the most envious of any other fault."

"Yes, that is so," said Vivaldo.

He was about to read another of the papers he had saved from the fire when he was stopped by a marvelous vision—for such it appeared—that suddenly met his sight; for there atop the rock beside which the grave was being hollowed out stood the shepherdess Marcela herself, more beautiful even than she was reputed to be. Those who up to then had never seen her looked on in silent admiration, while those who were accustomed to beholding her were held in as great a suspense as the ones who were gazing upon her for the first time.

No sooner had Ambrosio glimpsed her than, with a show of indignation, he called out to her, "So, fierce basilisk of these mountains, have you perchance come to see if in your presence blood will flow from the wounds of this poor wretch whom you by your cruelty have deprived of life? Have you come to gloat over your inhuman exploits, or would you from that height look down like another pitiless Nero upon your Rome in flames and ashes? Or perhaps you would arrogantly tread under foot this poor corpse, as an ungrateful daughter did that of her father Tarquinius? Tell us quickly why you have come and what it is that you want most; for I know that Grisóstomo's thoughts never failed to obey you in life, and though he is dead now, I will see that all those who call themselves his friends obey you likewise."

"I do not come, O Ambrosio, for any of the reasons that you have mentioned," replied Marcela. "I come to defend myself and to demonstrate how unreasonable all those persons are who blame me for their sufferings and for Grisóstomo's death. I therefore ask all present to hear me attentively. It will not take long and I shall not have to spend many words in persuading those of you who are sensible that I speak the truth.

"Heaven made me beautiful, you say, so beautiful that you are compelled to love me whether you will or no; and in return for the love that you show me, you would have it that I am obliged to love you in return. I know, with that natural understanding that God has given me, that everything beautiful is lovable; but I cannot see that it follows that the object that is loved for its beauty must love the one who loves it. Let us suppose that the lover of the beautiful were ugly and, being ugly, deserved to be shunned; it would then be highly absurd for him to say, 'I love you because you are beautiful; you must love me because I am ugly.'

"But assuming that two individuals are equally beautiful, it does not mean that their desires are the same; for not all beauty inspires love, but may sometimes merely delight the eye and leave the will intact. If it were otherwise, no one would know what he wanted, but all would wander vaguely and aimlessly with nothing upon which to settle their affections; for the number of beautiful objects being infinite, desires similarly would be boundless. I have heard it said that true love knows no division and must be voluntary and not forced. This being so, as I believe it is, then why would you compel me to surrender my will for no other reason than that you say you love me? But tell me: supposing that Heaven which made me beautiful had made me ugly instead, should I have any right to complain because you did not love me? You must remember, moreover, that I did not choose this beauty that is mine; such as it is, Heaven gave it to me of its grace, without any choice or asking on my part. As the viper is not to be blamed for the deadly poison that it bears, since that is a gift of nature, so I do not deserve to be reprehended for my comeliness of form.

"Beauty in a modest woman is like a distant fire or a sharp-edged sword: the one does not burn, the other does not cut, those who do not come near it. Honor and virtue are the adornments of the soul, without which the body is not beautiful though it may appear to be. If modesty is one of the virtues that most adorn and beautify body and soul, why should she who is loved for her beauty part with that virtue merely to satisfy the whim of one who solely for his own pleasure strives with all his force and energy to cause her to lose it? I was born a free being, and in order to live freely I chose the solitude of the fields; these mountain trees are my company, the clear-running waters in these brooks are my mirror, and to the trees and waters I communicate my thoughts and lend them of my beauty.

"In short, I am that distant fire, that sharp-edged sword, that does not burn or cut. Those who have been enamored by the sight of me I have disillusioned with my words; and if desire is sustained by hope, I gave none to Grisóstomo or any other, and of none of them can it be said that I killed them with my cruelty, for it was rather their own obstinacy that was to blame. And if you reproach me with the fact that his intentions were honorable and that I ought for that reason to have complied with them, I will tell you that when, on this very spot where his grave is now being dug, he revealed them to me, I replied that it was my own intention to live in perpetual solitude and that only the earth should enjoy the fruit of my retirement and the spoils of my beauty; and if he with all this plain-speaking was still stubbornly bent upon hoping against hope and sailing against the wind, is it to be wondered at if he drowned in the gulf of his own folly?

"Had I led him on, it would have been falsely; had I gratified his passion, it would have been against my own best judgment and intentions; but, though I had disillusioned him, he persisted, and though I did not hate him, he was driven to despair. Ask yourselves, then, if it is reasonable to blame me for his woes! Let him who has been truly deceived complain; let him despair who has been cheated of his promised hopes; if I have enticed any, let him speak up; if I have accepted the attentions of any, let him boast of it; but let not him to whom I have promised nothing, whom I have neither enticed nor accepted, apply to me such terms as cruel and homicidal. It has not as yet been Heaven's will to destine me to love any man, and there is no use expecting me to love of my own free choice.

"Let what I am saying now apply to each and every one of those who would have me for their own, and let it be understood from now on that if any die on account of me, he is not to be regarded as an unfortunate victim of jealousy, since she that cares for none can give to none the occasion for being jealous; nor is my plain-speaking to be taken as disdain. He who calls me a wild beast and a basilisk, let him leave me alone as something that is evil and harmful; let him who calls me ungrateful cease to wait upon me; let him who finds me strange shun my acquaintance; if I am cruel, do not run after me; in which case this wild beast, this basilisk, this strange, cruel, ungrateful creature will not run after them, seek them out, wait upon them, nor endeavor to know them in any way.

"The thing that killed Grisóstomo was his impatience and the impetuosity of his desire; so why blame my modest conduct and retiring life? If I choose to preserve my purity here in the company of the trees, how can he complain of my unwillingness to lose it who would have me keep it with other men? I, as you know, have a worldly fortune of my own and do not covet that of others. My life is a free one, and I do not wish to be subject to another in any way. I neither love nor hate anyone; I do not repel this one and allure that one; I do not play fast and loose with any. The modest conversation of these village lasses and the care of my goats is sufficient to occupy me. Those mountains there represent the bounds of my desire, and should my wishes go beyond them, it is but to contemplate the beauty of the heavens, that pathway by which the soul travels to its first dwelling place."

Saying this and without waiting for any reply, she turned her back and entered the thickest part of a near-by wood, leaving all present lost in admiration of her wit as well as her beauty. A few—those who had felt the powerful dart of her glances and bore the wounds inflicted by her lovely eyes—were of a mind to follow her, taking no heed of the plainly worded warning they had just had from her lips; whereupon Don Quixote, seeing this and thinking to himself that here was an opportunity to display his chivalry by succoring a damsel in distress, laid his hand upon the hilt of his sword and cried out, loudly and distinctly, "Let no person of whatever state or condition he may be dare to follow the beauteous Marcela under pain of incurring my furious wrath. She has shown with clear and sufficient reasons that little or no blame for Grisóstomo's death is to be attached to her; she has likewise shown how far she is from acceding to the desires of any of her suitors, and it is accordingly only just that in place of being hounded and persecuted she should be honored and esteemed by all good people in this world as the only woman in it who lives with such modesty and good intentions."

Whether it was due to Don Quixote's threats or because Ambrosio now told them that they should finish doing the things which his good friend had desired should be done, no one stirred from the spot until the burial was over and Grisóstomo's papers had been burned. As the body was laid in the grave, many tears were shed by the bystanders. Then they placed a heavy stone upon it until the slab which Ambrosio was thinking of having made should be ready, with an epitaph that was to read:

Here lies a shepherd by love betrayed,
His body cold in death,
Who with his last and faltering breath
Spoke of a faithless maid.
He died by the cruel, heartless hand
Of a coy and lovely lass,
Who by bringing men to so sorry a pass
Love's tyranny doth expand.

They then scattered many flowers and boughs over the top of the grave, and, expressing their condolences to the dead man's friend, Ambrosio, they all took their leave, including Vivaldo and his companions. Don Quixote now said good-by to the travelers as well, although they urged him to come with them to Seville, assuring him that he would find in every street and at every corner of that city more adventures than are to be met with anywhere else. He thanked them for the invitation and the courtesy they had shown him in offering it, but added that for the present he had no desire to visit Seville, not until he should have rid these mountains of the robbers and bandits of which they were said to be full.

Seeing that his mind was made up, the travelers did not urge him further but, bidding him another farewell, left him and continued on their way; and the reader may be sure that in the course of their journey they did not fail to discuss the story of Marcela and Grisóstomo as well as Don Quixote's madness. As for the good knight himself, he was resolved to go seek the shepherdess and offer her any service that lay in his power; but things did not turn out the way he expected, as is related in the course of this veracious history, the second part of which ends here.

CHAPTER XV. *In which is related the unfortunate adventure that befell Don Quixote when he encountered certain wicked Yanguesans.*

THE learned Cid Benengeli tells us that, upon taking leave of their hosts and all those who had attended the shepherd Grisóstomo's funeral, Don Quixote and his squire entered the same wood into which they had seen the shepherdess Marcela disappear, and that, having journeyed in the forest for more than two hours, looking for her everywhere without being able to discover her, they finally came to a meadow covered with fresh young grass, alongside the cool and placid waters of a mountain stream which irresistibly invited them to pause there during the noontide heat, for the sun was now beating down upon them. The two of them accordingly dismounted and, turning Rocinante and the ass out to feed upon the plentiful pasturage, proceeded to investigate the contents of the saddlebags, after which, without further ceremony, master and man sat down together very peaceably and sociably to eat what they had found there.

Now, Sancho had not taken the trouble to put fetters on Rocinante, knowing the hack to be so tame and so little inclined to lust that, he felt certain, all the mares in the Cordovan meadowlands would not be able to tempt him to an indiscretion. But fate and the devil—who is not always sleeping—had ordained that a herd of Galician ponies belonging to some carters of Yanguas [1] should be feeding in this same valley; for it was the custom of these men to stop for their siesta in some place where grass and water were to be had for their teams, and as it happened, the spot the Yanguesans had chosen on this occasion was not far from where Don Quixote was.

Then it was that Rocinante suddenly felt the desire to have a little sport with the ladies. The moment he scented them, he abandoned his customary gait and staid behavior and, without asking his master's leave, trotted briskly over to them to acquaint them with his needs. They, however, preferred to go on eating, or so it seemed, for they received him with their hoofs and teeth, to such good effect that they broke his girth and left him naked and without a saddle. But the worst of it was when the carters, seeing the violence that he was offering their mares, came running up with poles and so belabored him that they left him lying there badly battered on the ground.

At this point Don Quixote and Sancho, who had witnessed the drubbing that Rocinante received, also ran up, panting. It was the master who spoke first.

"So far as I can see, friend Sancho," he said, "those are not knights but low fellows of ignoble birth; and so you may very well aid me in wreaking a deserved vengeance upon them for the wrong they have done to Rocinante in front of our very eyes."

"What the devil kind of vengeance are we going to take," asked Sancho, "seeing there are more than twenty of them and not more than two of us, or maybe only one and a half?"

"I," replied Don Quixote, "am worth a hundred." Without saying anything more, he drew his sword and fell upon the Yanguesans, and, moved and incited by his master's example, Sancho Panza did the same. At the first slashing blow he dealt, the knight laid open the leather jacket that the man wore along with a good part of one shoulder. Seeing themselves assaulted like this by two lone individuals while they were so many in number, the Yanguesans again ran up with their poles and, surrounding their assailants, began flaying them with great ardor and vehemence. The truth is that the second blow sufficed to lay Sancho low, and the same thing happened with Don Quixote, all his dexterity and high courage availing him not at all. As luck would have it, he fell at Rocinante's feet, for the animal had not yet been able to rise; all of which goes to show what damage poles can do when furiously wielded by angry rustics. When the Yanguesans saw what mischief they had wrought, they lost no time in loading their teams and were soon off down the road, leaving the two adventurers in a sorry plight and a worse mood.

The first to recover his senses was Sancho Panza. Finding himself beside his master, he called out to him in a weak and piteous voice, "Señor Don Quixote! Ah, Señor Don Quixote!"

"What do you want, brother Sancho?" said the knight in the same feeble, suffering tone that the squire had used.

"I'd like, if possible," said Sancho, "for your Grace to give me a couple of draughts of that ugly Bras,[2] if you happen to have any of it at hand. Perhaps it would be as good for broken bones as it is for wounds."

"If I only did have some of it, wretch that I am," said Don Quixote, "what more could we ask for? But I swear to you, Sancho Panza, on the word of a knight-errant, that before two days have passed, unless fortune should rule otherwise, I shall have it in my possession, or else my hands will have failed me."

"But how many days do you think it will be, your Grace, before we are able to move our feet?" Sancho wanted to know.

"For my part," said his well-cudgeled master, "I must confess that I cannot answer that question. I hold myself to blame for everything. I had no business putting hand to sword against men who had not been dubbed knights and so were not my equals. Because I thus violated the laws of knighthood, the God of battles has permitted this punishment to be inflicted upon me. For which reason, Sancho, you should pay attention to what I am about to say to you, for it may have much to do with the safety of both of us. Hereafter, when you see a rabble of this sort committing some offense against us, do not wait for me to draw my sword, for I shall not do so under any circumstances, but, rather, draw your own and chastise them to your heart's content. If any knights come to their aid and defense, I will protect you by attacking them with all my might; and you already know by a thousand proofs and experiences the valor of this, my strong right arm."

For the poor gentleman was still feeling puffed up as a result of his victory over the valiant Biscayan. His advice, however, did not strike Sancho as being so good that he could let it pass without an answer.

"Sir," he said, "I am a peaceful man, calm and quiet, and I can put up with any insult because I have a wife and young ones to support and bring up; and so let me advise your Grace, since it is not for me to lay down the law, that under no consideration will I draw my sword, either against rustic or against knight, but from now on, as God is my witness, I hereby pardon all wrongs that have been done or may be done to me by any person high or low, rich or poor, gentleman or commoner, without excepting any rank or walk in life whatsoever."

"I wish," said his master, "that I had a little breath so that I could speak to you without so much effort; I wish the pain in this rib would subside somewhat so that I might be able, Sancho, to show you how wrong you are. Come now, you sinner, supposing that the wind of fortune, which up to now has been so contrary a one, should veer in our favor, filling the sails of our desire so that we should certainly and without anything to hinder us be able to put into port at one of those islands that I have promised you, what would happen to you if, winning the victory, I were to make you the ruler of it? You will have rendered that impossible by not being a knight nor caring to become one, and by having no intention of avenging the insults offered you or defending your seignorial rights.

"For you must know that in newly conquered kingdoms and provinces the minds of the inhabitants are never tranquil, nor do they like their new lord so well that there is not to be feared some fresh move on their part to alter the existing state of affairs and, as the saying goes, see what their luck will bring. And so it is necessary that the new ruler possess the ability to govern and the valor to attack or defend himself as the case may be."

"Well, in the present case," said Sancho, "I can only wish I had that ability and that valor of which your Grace speaks; but I swear to you on the word of a poor man that I need a poultice more than I do an argument. If your Grace will try to rise, we will help Rocinante up, although he does not deserve it, seeing that he is the principal cause of this thrashing we have received. I never would have thought it of him; I always took him to be as chaste and peaceful as I am. Oh, well, they say it takes a lot of time to get to know a person and nothing in this life is certain. Who would have thought that those mighty slashes your Grace gave that poor knight-errant would be followed posthaste by such a tempest of blows as they let fall upon our shoulders?"

"Your shoulders, at any rate," observed Don Quixote, "ought to be used to such squalls as that, but mine, accustomed to fine cambric and Dutch linen, naturally feel more acutely the pain of this misfortune that has befallen us. And if I did not imagine—why do I say imagine?— if I did not know for a certainty that all these discomforts are the inevitable accompaniment of the profession of arms, I should straightway lay me down and die of pure vexation."

"Sir," replied the squire, "seeing that these mishaps are what one reaps when one is a knight, I wish your Grace would tell me if they happen very often or only at certain times; for it seems to me that after two such harvests, there will not be much left of us for the third, unless God in His infinite mercy sees fit to succor us."

"Be assured, friend Sancho," said Don Quixote, "that the life of knights-errant is subject to a thousand perils and misadventures. At the same time, it is within the power of those same knights to become at almost any moment kings and emperors, as experience has shown in the case of many different ones whose histories I know well. If this pain of mine permitted me, I could tell you right now of some who merely by the might of their arm have risen to the highest stations such as I have mentioned; yet these very ones, both before and after, endured various troubles and calamities.

"There was the valorous Amadis of Gaul, who fell into the power of his mortal enemy, Arcalaus the enchanter, who, after he had taken him prisoner and had bound him to a pillar in the courtyard, is known for a fact to have given him more than two hundred lashes with his horse's reins. And there is a certain author of no little repute, though his name is not widely known, who tells us how the Knight of the Sun, in a certain castle, was caught in a trapdoor that opened beneath his feet; on falling through the trap, he found himself in a deep underground pit, bound hand and foot, and they gave him one of those so-called clysters of sand and snow-water that all but finished him. Indeed, if in this great peril a magician who was a great friend of his had not come to his aid, it would have gone very badly with the poor knight.

"And so I well may suffer in the company of such worthy ones; for the indignities that they endured are worse than those that we have had to suffer. I would inform you, Sancho, that those wounds that are inflicted by any instruments that chance to be in the assailant's hand do not consti- tute an affront, as is expressly laid down in the dueling code. Thus, if the shoemaker strike another with the last that he holds, although it is really of wood, it cannot for that reason be said that the one attacked with it has been cudgeled. I tell you this in order that you may not think that, because we have been beaten to a pulp in this combat, an affront has thereby been offered us; for the arms that those men bore and with which they pommeled us were nothing other than stakes, and none of them, so far as I can recall, carried a rapier, sword, or dagger."

"They did not give me time to see what they carried," said Sancho, "for I had no sooner laid hands on my blade than they made the sign of the cross over my shoulder with their clubs, taking away the sight of my eyes and the strength of my feet, after which they went off and left me lying here where I am now, and I am not taking the trouble to think whether or not those blows they gave me with their poles were an affront; all I can think of is the pain they have caused me, which is as deeply im- printed on my memory as it is on my shoulders."

"But with all that, brother Panza," said Don Quixote, "I must remind you that there is no memory to which time does not put an end and no pain that death does not abolish."

"Well," said Panza, "what greater misfortune could there be than that of having to wait on time and death? If this trouble of ours were one of those that are cured with a couple of poultices, it would not be so bad. But I am beginning to think that all the plasters in a hospital will not be enough to put us in shape again."

"Leave all that," said Don Quixote, "and draw strength from weakness as I propose to do. Come, let us see how Rocinante is; for, it appears to me, the poor beast has had the worst of this mishap."

"I am not surprised at that," said Sancho, "in view of the fact that he is a knight-errant also. What does astonish me is that my donkey should have gone free and without costs while we have come off without our ribs." [3]

"Fortune," said Don Quixote, "always leaves a door open in adversity as a means of remedying it. What I would say is, this little beast may take the place of Rocinante now by carrying me to some castle where I may be healed of my wounds. And I may add that I do not look upon it as a disgrace to go mounted like that, for I recall having read that good old Silenus, the tutor and instructor of the merry god of laughter, when he entered the city of the hundred gates,[4] was pleased to do so mounted upon a very handsome ass."

"That may very well be," said Sancho, "but there is a big difference between going mounted and being slung across the animal's flanks like a bag of refuse."

"Wounds received in battle," replied Don Quixote, "confer honor, they do not take it away; and so, friend Sancho, say no more, but, as I have already told you, lift me up the best you can and place me on the ass in any fashion that pleases you, and we will then be on our way before night descends upon us here in this wilderness."

"But I thought I heard your Grace say," remarked Panza, "that it is very fitting for knights-errant to sleep out in the cold wastes and desert places the better part of the year, and that they esteem it a great good fortune to be able to do so."

"That," said Don Quixote, "is when they have no choice in the matter or when they are in love; and, it is true, there have been knights who for two years' time have remained upon a rock, in sun and shade and through all the inclemencies of the heavens, without their ladies knowing anything about it. One of these was Amadis, who, under the name of Beltenebros, took up his lodging on the rock known as Peña Pobre, remaining there either eight years or eight months, I am not quite certain as to the exact length of time; what matters is that he was there doing penance for some slight offense that he had given to his lady Oriana. But let us quit this talk, Sancho, and make haste before something happens to the ass as it did to Rocinante."

"There will be the devil to pay in that case," said Sancho; and venting himself of thirty "Ohs" and "Ahs" and sixty sighs and a hundred-twenty imprecations of various sorts, with curses for the one who had got him into this, he arose, pausing halfway like a Turkish bow bent in the middle, without the power to straighten himself. It was with the greatest difficulty that he succeeded in saddling his ass, which, making use of the unwonted freedom it had enjoyed that day, had wandered off some little distance. He then managed to get Rocinante on his feet, and if that animal had possessed the power to complain, you may be sure that he would have been an equal for Sancho and his master.

The end of the matter was, Sancho seated Don Quixote upon the donkey, tying Rocinante on behind, and then started off leading the ass by the halter, proceeding more or less in the direction in which he thought the main highway ought to be; and as chance was now guiding their affairs from good to better, he had gone but a short league when there before them was the road—not only the road but an inn, which greatly to Sancho's disgust and his master's delight had, of course, to be a castle. The squire stubbornly insisted that it was not a castle but a hostelry, while his master maintained the contrary. The argument lasted so long that they had reached the inn before it was ended, and with the point still unsettled, Sancho entered the gateway, followed by his cavalcade.

CHAPTER XVI. *Of what happened to the ingenious gentleman in the inn which he imagined was a castle.*

UPON seeing Don Quixote thus slung across the ass, the innkeeper inquired of Sancho what was wrong. The squire replied that it was nothing; his master had fallen from a cliff and bruised a few ribs, that was all. Now, the innkeeper had a wife who was not the kind one would expect to find among women of her calling, for she was naturally of a charitable disposition and inclined to sympathize with those of her neighbors who were in trouble. She accordingly came running up to take care of her injured guest and called upon her daughter, who was young and very good-looking, to lend her a helping hand.

Serving in the inn, also, was a lass from Asturia, broad-faced, flat-headed, and with a snub nose; she was blind in one eye and could not see very well out of the other. To be sure, her bodily graces made up for her other defects: she measured not more than seven palms from head to foot, and, being slightly hunchbacked, she had to keep looking at the ground a good deal more than she liked. This gentle creature in turn aided the daughter of the house, and the two made up a very uncomfortable bed for Don Quixote in an attic which gave every evidence of having formerly been a hayloft and which held another lodger, a mule driver, whose bed stood a little beyond the one they had prepared for our friend.

The muleteer's couch was composed of the packsaddles and blankets from his beasts, but it was a better one for all of that. The other consisted merely of four smooth planks laid upon two trestles of uneven height, and had a mattress so thin that it looked more like a counterpane, with lumps which, had they not been seen through the rents to be of wool, might from the feel of them have been taken for pebbles. To cover him, the knight had a pair of sheets made of the kind of leather they use on bucklers and a quilt whose threads anyone who chose might have counted without missing a single one.

On this wretched pallet Don Quixote stretched himself out, and then the innkeeper's wife and daughter proceeded to cover him from top to toe with plasters while Maritornes (for that was the Asturian girl's name) held the light. As she applied the poultices, the mistress of the house remarked that he was so black-and-blue in spots that his bruises looked more like the marks of blows than like those caused by a fall.

"They were not blows," said Sancho, adding that the rock had many sharp points and jutting edges and each one had left its imprint. "If your Ladyship," he went on, "can manage to save a little of that tow, it will come in handy, for my loins also hurt me a little."

"So, then," replied the innkeeper's wife, "you must have fallen too."

"I did not fall," said Sancho Panza, "but the shock I had at seeing my master take such a tumble makes my body ache as if I had received a thousand whacks."

"That may very well be," said the daughter, "for I have often dreamed that I was falling from a tower and yet I never reached the ground, and when I awoke from my dream I would feel as bruised and broken as if I had really fallen."

"The point is, lady," Sancho explained, "that I was not dreaming at all, but was more wide awake than I am at this minute, and yet I find myself with scarcely less bruises than my master, Don Quixote."

"What did you say the gentleman's name was?" asked Maritornes, the Asturian.

"Don Quixote de la Mancha," replied Sancho, "and he is a knightly adventurer and one of the best and bravest that the world has seen for a long time."

"What is a knightly adventurer?" the girl wished to know.

"Are you so unused to the ways of the world that you don't know that?" he said. "Then let me inform you, my sister, that it is something that can be summed up in two or three words: well thrashed and an emperor; today, he is the most wretched and needy creature that there is, and tomorrow he will have the crowns of two or three kingdoms to give to his squire."

"If that is so," said the innkeeper's wife, "how does it come that you, being this worthy gentleman's squire, have not so much as an earldom, to judge by appearances?"

"It is early yet," was Sancho's answer. "We have been looking for adventures for only a month now, and so far have not fallen in with what could rightly be called one. Sometimes you look for one thing and you find another. The truth is, once my master Don Quixote is healed of this wound or fall, providing I am none the worse for it all, I would not exchange my expectations for the best title in all Spain."

The knight had been following this conversation very closely; and at this point, raising himself up in the bed as well as he was able, he took the landlady's hand and said to her, "Believe me, beautiful lady, you well may call yourself fortunate for having given a lodging in this your castle to my person. If I myself do not tell you of my merits, it is for the reason that, as the saying goes, self-praise is degrading; but my squire can inform you as to who I am. I will only say that I have written down in my memory for all eternity the service which you have rendered me, that I may give you thanks as long as life endures. And I would to high Heaven that love did not hold me so captive and subject to its laws, and to the eyes of that beauteous but ungrateful one whose name I mutter between my teeth; [1] for then the orbs of this lovely damsel here would surely be the mistress of my liberty."

The landlady, her daughter, and the worthy Maritornes were very much bewildered by these remarks of the knight-errant; they understood about as much of them as if he had been speaking Greek, although they were able to make out that he was offering them flattery and compliments. Being wholly unused to such language, they could but stare at him in amazement, for he seemed to them a different kind of man than any they had known. And so, thanking him in their own idiom, which was that of a wayside tavern, they left him, while Maritornes looked after Sancho, who had no less need of attention than did his master.

The mule driver had arranged with the Asturian to have a little sport with her that night, and she had given him her word that, as soon as the guests were quiet and her master and mistress asleep, she would come to him and let him have his way. It was commonly said of the good lass that she never made such a promise without keeping it, even though it was in a forest and without witnesses, for she prided herself greatly upon being a lady and did not look upon it as any disgrace to be a servant in an inn, for, as she was in the habit of saying, it was misfortunes and ill luck that had brought her to such a state.

Don Quixote's hard, narrow, cramped, makeshift bed stood in the middle of this starry stable [2] and was the first that one encountered upon entering the room. Next to it was that of his squire, Sancho, which consisted solely of a cattail mat and a blanket that looked as if it was of shorn canvas rather than of wool. And beyond these two was that of the mule driver, made up, as has been said, of packsaddles and all the trappings of his two best mules, although he had twelve of them altogether, sleek, fat, and in fine condition; for he was one of the richest carters of Arévalo, according to the author of this history who knew him well and makes special mention of him—some say they were related in one way or another. In any event, Cid Hamete Benengeli was a historian who was at great pains to ascertain the truth and very accurate in everything, as is evident from the fact that he did not see fit to pass over in silence those details that have been mentioned, however trifling and insignificant they may appear to be.

All of which might serve as an example to those grave chroniclers who give us such brief and succinct accounts that we barely get a taste, the gist of the matter being left in their inkwells out of carelessness, malice, or ignorance. Blessings on the author of the *Tablante de Ricamonte* [3] and the one who wrote that other work in which are related the deeds of Count Tomillas—with what exactitude they describe everything!

But to go on with our story, the mule driver, after he had looked in on his beasts and had given them their second feeding, came back and stretched out on his packsaddles to await that model of conscientiousness, Maritornes. Sancho, having been duly poulticed, had also lain down and was doing his best to sleep, but the pain in his ribs would not let him. As for Don Quixote, he was suffering so much that he kept his eyes open like a rabbit. The inn was silent now, and there was no light other than from a lantern which hung in the middle of the gateway.

This uncanny silence, and our knight's constant habit of thinking of incidents described at every turn in those books that had been the cause of all his troubles, now led him to conceive as weird a delusion as could well be imagined. He fancied that he had reached a famous castle—for, as has been said, every inn where he stopped was a castle to him—and that the daughter of the lord (innkeeper) who dwelt there, having been won over by his gentle bearing, had fallen in love with him and had promised him that she would come that night, without her parents' knowledge, to lie beside him for a while. And taking this chimerical fancy which he had woven out of his imagination to be an established fact, he then began to be grieved at the thought that his virtue was thus being endangered, and firmly resolved not be false to his lady Dulcinea del Toboso, even though Queen Guinevere with her waiting-woman Quintañona should present themselves in person before him.

As he lay there, his mind filled with such nonsense as this, the hour that had been fixed for the Asturian's visit came, and an unlucky one it proved to be for Don Quixote. Clad in her nightgown and barefoot, her hair done up in a fustian net, Maritornes with silent, cautious steps stole into the room where the three were lodged, in search of the muleteer. She had no sooner crossed the threshold, however, than the knight became aware of her presence; and, sitting up in bed despite his poultices and the pain from his ribs, he held out his arms as if to receive the beautiful maiden. The latter, all doubled up and saying nothing, was groping her way to her lover's cot when she encountered Don Quixote. Seizing her firmly by the wrists, he drew her to him, without her daring to utter a sound.

Forcing her to sit down upon the bed, he began fingering her nightgown, and although it was of sackcloth, it impressed him as being of the finest and flimsiest silken gauze. On her wrists she wore some glass beads, but to him they gave off the gleam of oriental pearls. Her hair, which resembled a horse's mane rather than anything else, he decided was like filaments of the brightest gold of Araby whose splendor darkened even that of the sun. Her breath without a doubt smelled of yesterday's stale salad, but for Don Quixote it was a sweet and aromatic odor that came from her mouth.

The short of it is, he pictured her in his imagination as having the same appearance and manners as those other princesses whom he had read about in his books, who, overcome by love and similarly bedecked, came to visit their badly wounded knights. So great was the poor gentleman's blindness that neither his sense of touch nor the girl's breath nor anything else about her could disillusion him, although they were enough to cause anyone to vomit who did not happen to be a mule driver. To him it seemed that it was the goddess of beauty herself whom he held in his arms.

Clasping her tightly, he went on to speak to her in a low and amorous tone of voice. "Would that I were in a position, O beauteous and high-born lady, to be able to repay the favor that you have accorded me by thus affording me the sight of your great loveliness; but Fortune, which never tires of persecuting those who are worthy, has willed to place me in this bed where I lie so bruised and broken that, even though my desire were to satisfy yours, such a thing would be impossible. And added to this impossibility is another, greater one: my word and promise given to the peerless Dulcinea del Toboso, the one and only lady of my most secret thoughts. If this did not stand in the way, I should not be so insensible a knight as to let slip the fortunate opportunity which you out of your great goodness of heart have placed in my way."

Maritornes was extremely vexed and all a-sweat at finding herself held fast in Don Quixote's embrace, and without paying any heed to what he was saying she struggled silently to break away. Meanwhile, the mule driver, whose evil desires had kept him awake, had been aware of his wench's presence ever since she entered the door and had been listening attentively to everything that Don Quixote said. Jealous because the Asturian lass, as he thought, had broken her word and deserted him for another, he came up to the knight's cot and, without being able to make head or tail of all this talk, stood there waiting to see what the outcome would be.

When he saw that the girl was doing her best to free herself and Don Quixote was trying to hold her, he decided that the joke had gone far enough; raising his fist high above his head, he came down with so fearful a blow on the gaunt jaws of the enamored knight as to fill the poor man's mouth with blood. Not satisfied with this, the mule driver jumped on his ribs and at a pace somewhat faster than a trot gave them a thorough going-over from one end to the other. The bed, which was rather weak and not very firm on its foundations, was unable to support the mule-teer's added weight and sank to the floor with a loud crash. This awoke the innkeeper, who imagined that Maritornes must be involved in some brawl, since he had called twice to her and had received no answer. Sus-picious of what was going on, he arose, lighted a lamp, and made his way to the place from which the sound of the scuffle appeared to be coming. Frightened out of her wits when she heard her master, for she knew what a terrible temper he had, the girl took refuge beside Sancho Panza, who was still sleeping, and huddled herself there like a ball of yarn.

"Where are you, whore?" cried the landlord as he came in; "for I am certain that this is all your doing."

At that moment Sancho awoke and, feeling a bulky object almost on top of him and thinking it must be a nightmare, began throwing his fists about on one side and the other, giving Maritornes no telling how many punches. Feeling the pain, the wench cast all modesty aside and let him have so many blows in return that he very soon emerged from his sleepy state. When he saw himself being treated like this by an unknown assail-ant, he rose the best way he could and grappled with her, and there then began between the two of them the prettiest and most stubbornly fought skirmish that ever you saw.

When the muleteer perceived by the light of the lamp what was hap-pening to his lady, he left Don Quixote and went to her assistance. The innkeeper also came over to her, but with different intentions, for he meant to punish the girl, thinking that, undoubtedly, she was the cause of all the disturbance that prevailed. And so, then, as the saying goes, it was "the cat to the rat, the rat to the rope, the rope to the stick." [4] There was the mule driver pounding Sancho, Sancho and the wench flaying each other, and the landlord drubbing the girl; and they all laid on most vigorously, without allowing themselves a moment's rest. The best part of it was, the lamp went out, leaving them in darkness, whereupon there ensued a general and merciless melee, until there was not a hand's breadth left on any of their bodies that was not sore and aching.

As chance would have it, there was lodged at the inn that night a patrolman of the old Holy Brotherhood of Toledo,[5] who, hearing all this uproar and the sounds of a struggle, at once snatched up his staff of office and the tin box containing his warrants and went groping his way through the darkness to the room above, as he cried, "Hold, in the name of the law! Hold, in the name of the Holy Brotherhood!" The first one whom he encountered was the well-pommeled Don Quixote, who lay flat on his back and senseless on his broken-down bed. Grasping the knight's beard, the officer cried, "I charge you to aid the law!" But when he perceived that the one whom he thus held did not budge nor stir, he concluded that the man must be dead and the others in the room his murderers. Acting upon this suspicion, he called out in a booming voice, "Close the gateway of the inn! See that no one leaves, for someone here has killed a man!"

This cry startled them all, and each one left off his pommeling at the point where he was. The innkeeper then retired to his room, the mule driver to his packsaddles, and the wench to her stall, the poor unfortunate Don Quixote and Sancho being the only ones that could not move. The officer now let go of our friend's beard and left the room to go look for a light, that he might arrest the offenders. He did not find any, however, for the innkeeper had taken care to put out the lantern when he retired to his room, and the representative of the Holy Brotherhood was accordingly compelled to have recourse to the hearth, where with a great deal of time and trouble he finally succeeded in lighting another lamp.

CHAPTER **XVII**. *Wherein is continued the account of the innumerable troubles that the brave Don Quixote and his good squire Sancho Panza endured in the inn, which, to his sorrow, the knight took to be a castle.*

HAVING by this time recovered from his swoon, Don Quixote called to his squire in the same tone of voice that he had used the day before as they lay stretched out in the "vale of stakes." [1] "Sancho, my friend, are you asleep? Are you asleep, friend Sancho?"

"How do you expect me to sleep, curses on it?" replied the squire, who was filled with bitterness and sorrow. "I think all the devils in Hell must have been after me tonight."

"You are undoubtedly right about that," said his master; "for either
I know little about it or this castle is an enchanted one. I may as well
tell you—but first you must swear that you will keep it a secret until after
I am dead."

"I swear," said Sancho.

"I ask that," Don Quixote went on, "because I hate taking away anyone's good name."

"I told you," Sancho repeated, "that I will say nothing about it until
your Grace has reached the end of his days; and please God I may be
able to reveal it tomorrow."

"Do I treat you so harshly, Sancho, that you wish to see me die so
soon?"

"It is not for that reason," said Sancho. "It is just that I am opposed to
keeping things too long—I don't like them to spoil on my hands."

"Be that as it may," said Don Quixote, "I am willing to trust your
friendship and your courtesy. And so I may tell you that one of the
weirdest adventures happened to me that I could possibly describe. To
make a long story short, you must know that, a short while ago, the
daughter of the lord of this castle came to me. She is the most genteel
and lovely damsel to be found in many a land. How can I describe to
you the grace of her person, her sprightly wit, or all those other hidden
charms which, in order to keep faith with my lady Dulcinea, I must
leave untouched and pass over in silence? I can only say that Heaven
was envious of this gift that fortune had placed in my hands—or it may
be (and this is more likely) that this castle, as I have remarked to you,
is enchanted; at any rate, just as I was engaged with her in most sweet
and amorous parley, without my seeing him or knowing whence he came,
a monstrous giant seized me by the arm and gave me such a blow on the
jaw that my mouth was bathed in blood; and after that he flayed me in
such a manner that I am even worse off today than yesterday, when those
carters on account of Rocinante's excesses did us that wrong with which
you are acquainted. I therefore can only conjecture that the treasure of
this damsel's beauty must be in the keeping of some enchanted Moor,
and that it is not for me."

"Nor for me either," said Sancho; "for more than four hundred Moors
have been mauling me and have made such a job of it that the thrashing
those fellows gave me with their poles was but cakes and gingerbread
by comparison. But tell me, sir, what name do you give to this fine and
rare adventure which has left us where we are now? Your Grace, it is
true, did not have quite so bad a time of it, with that incomparable beauty

in your arms that you have been telling me about; but what was there in it for me except the worst beating that I hope to receive in all my born days? Pity me and the mother that bore me, for I am not a knight-errant nor ever expect to be, yet I always get the worst of whatever's coming!"

"So, you were beaten too, were you?" said Don Quixote.

"Did not I tell you I was, curses on it?" said Sancho.

"Well, do not let it worry you, my friend," said the knight; "for I will now make some of that precious balm and we shall both of us be healed in the blink of an eye."

The officer of the Brotherhood had lighted his lamp by this time and now came in to have a look at the one he thought was dead. The moment Sancho caught sight of him, in his nightgown, with a lamp in his hand, a towel around his head, and an evil-looking face, the squire turned to his master and said, "Could this be the enchanted Moor coming back to give us some more punishment, if there is any left in the inkwell?"

"No," replied Don Quixote, "it cannot be; for those who are under a spell do not let themselves be seen by anyone."

"If they do not let themselves be seen," remarked Sancho, "they certainly make themselves felt; if you do not believe it, let my ribs speak for me."

"Mine," said Don Quixote, "could tell the same story; but that is not a sufficient reason for believing that he whom we see here is the enchanted Moor."

Upon seeing them talking together so calmly, the officer did not know what to make of it, although the knight, true enough, was still flat on his back and unable to move, on account of his plasters and because he was still so stiff and sore.

"Well," said the officer coming up to him, "and how goes it, my good man?"

"If I were you," said Don Quixote, "I would speak a little more politely. Is it the custom in this country to address knights-errant in such a fashion, you dunce?"

Unable to bear being treated so ill by one whose appearance was so unimpressive, the patrolman raised his lamp with all the oil that was in it and let him have it over the head, a good stiff blow at that; after which, in the darkness, he slipped out of the room.

"Undoubtedly, sir," said Sancho, "that must be the enchanted Moor. He must be keeping the treasure for others, seeing all that he gives us is punches with his fist and blows with the lamp."

"Yes," said Don Quixote, "that is it; but no notice is to be taken of such things where enchantments are concerned, nor should one be angry or annoyed by them. Since these are invisible and fanciful beings, we should find no one on whom to take revenge even if we were to go looking for him. Arise, Sancho, if you can, summon the governor of this fortress, and tell him to let me have a little oil, wine, salt, and rosemary that I may make that health-giving balm. I think that truly I have need of it now, for there is much blood coming from the wound which that phantom gave me."

His bones aching all over, Sancho got to his feet and went out into the darkness to look for the landlord. On the way he met the officer, who was listening to find out what happened to his enemy.

"Sir," said the squire, "whoever you may be, kindly do us the favor of giving us a little rosemary, oil, salt, and wine, for they are needed to heal one of the most gallant knights-errant that ever walked the earth; he lies now in that bed, badly wounded at the hands of the enchanted Moor who is lodged in this inn."

Hearing this, the officer thought the man must be out of his senses, but inasmuch as day was already dawning, he threw open the inn door and told the proprietor what it was that Sancho required. The innkeeper provided all the things mentioned, and Sancho then took them to Don Quixote, who was lying there with his hands to his head, complaining of the pain from the blow that had been dealt him with the lamp, although the fact of the matter was that it had done him no more harm than to raise a couple of rather large bumps, while what he fancied to be blood was in reality nothing other than sweat, due to the anxiety he felt over the tempest that had but recently subsided.

Taking the ingredients, he now made a compound of them, mixing them all together and boiling them for some little while until he thought they were properly steeped. He then asked for a small vial into which he might pour the liquid, but as there was none to be had, he resolved to make use of an oil flask made of tinplate which the innkeeper presented to him free of charge. Above this flask he muttered more than eighty Our Fathers and as many Hail Marys and other prayers, each word being accompanied by the sign of the cross in way of benediction. All of which was witnessed by Sancho, the landlord, and the officer of the Holy Brotherhood. As for the carter, he had quietly gone out to look after his mules.

Having done this, the knight wished to try out the virtues of this precious balm, as he fancied it to be, and so he drank what remained in the pot, amounting to nearly half a quart. No sooner had he swallowed it than he at once began to vomit and kept it up until there was absolutely nothing left in his stomach; and with all his anxiety and the agitation of vomiting, a most copious sweat broke out upon him, whereupon he asked them to throw some covering over him and leave him alone. They did so, and he slept for more than three hours, at the end of which time he awoke, feeling greatly relieved in body and especially in his much battered bones. This led him to believe that he had been cured and that he had indeed discovered Fierabrás's balm; from now on he would be able to face with no fear whatsoever any kind of destruction, battle, or combat, no matter how perilous the undertaking.

Marveling at the change for the better that had been wrought in his master, Sancho Panza asked that what remained in the pot, which was no small quantity, be given to him. Don Quixote consented; and, taking the kettle in both hands, with good faith and right good will, the squire gulped down only a trifle less than his master had taken. Now, Sancho's stomach was not so delicate as the knight's, for he did not vomit at first but suffered such cramps and nausea, perspired so freely, and felt so faint, that he thought surely his last hour had come; and, finding himself in such misery and affliction, he cursed the balm and the thief who had given it to him.

"It is my opinion, Sancho," said Don Quixote, "that all this comes of your not having been dubbed a knight, for which reason this liquor is not suited to you."

"If your Grace knew that all the time," replied his squire, "then, curse me and all my kin, why did you let me taste it?"

At this point the beverage took effect and poor Sancho began to discharge at both ends and with such force that neither the cattail mat on which he had dropped down nor the coarse linen coverlet that had been tossed over him was of much use afterward. The sweat poured off him in such abundance, accompanied by such spasms and convulsions, that not only he but all who saw him thought that he was dying. This untoward squall kept up for nearly two hours, and when it was over he was not left in better condition as his master had been, but was so tired and weak that he was not able to stand.

But Don Quixote, who, as has been said, felt greatly relieved and quite himself again, was all for setting out at once in search of adventures; for, as he saw it, every moment that he tarried he was cheating the world and the needy ones in it of his favor and assistance—especially in view of the sense of security and confidence which the possession of his balm now afforded him. Accordingly, impelled by this desire, he himself saddled Rocinante and the ass and then aided his squire to clothe himself and straddle his beast, after which the knight mounted his steed and prepared to ride away. As he passed a corner of the inn, he seized a pike that was standing there to serve him as a lance.

All the guests in the hostelry, more than twenty persons, stood around watching, among them the innkeeper's daughter, and the knight in turn could not keep his eyes off the lass; every so often he would heave a sigh which it seemed must come from the depths of his entrails, but the others thought it must be from the pain in his ribs—at least, those who had seen him covered with plasters as he had been the night before were of this opinion.

As the two rode up to the gateway of the inn, Don Quixote called to his host and said to him, gravely and calmly, "Many and great are the favors, Sir Governor, which I have received in this your castle, and I shall be under obligations to you all the days of my life. If I can repay you by avenging the wrong done you by some haughty foe, you know that my profession is none other than that of helping those who cannot help themselves, avenging those who have been wronged, and chastising traitors. Search well your memory, and if you find anything of this sort with which to entrust me, you have but to speak, and I promise you by the order of chivalry which I have received to see that you are given satisfaction and are paid in accordance with your wishes."

The innkeeper's manner was equally tranquil as he replied, "Sir Knight, I have no need of your favor nor that you should avenge me of any wrong; for I can take such vengeance as I see fit when the need arises. The only thing needed in this case is for your Grace to pay me what you owe me for last night, including straw and barley for the two animals, your supper, and beds."

"Then this is an inn, is it?" said Don Quixote.

"And a very respectable one," replied the innkeeper.

"In that case I have been laboring under a mistake all this time," said the knight; "for the truth is, I thought it was a castle, and not a bad one at that. However, seeing it is not a castle but an inn, the only thing for you to do is to overlook the payment, since I cannot contravene the rule of knights-errant, none of whom, I am sure—at least, up to now, I have read nothing to the contrary—ever paid for his lodging or anything else when he stopped at an inn; for any hospitality that is offered to knights is only their just due, in return for all the hardships they suffer as they go in quest of adventures day and night, in summer and in winter, on horseback and on foot, enduring hunger and thirst and heat and cold, being subject to all the inclemencies of Heaven and all the discomforts of earth."

"I have little to do with all that," said the landlord. "Pay me what you owe me and let us hear no more of these accounts of chivalry. The only accounts that interest me are those that are due me."

"You are but a stupid, evil-minded tavernkeeper," was Don Quixote's answer; and, putting spurs to Rocinante and bringing his lance into position, he sallied out of the inn with no one to stop him. Without looking back to see if his squire was following him, he rode along for some distance. The innkeeper, meanwhile, seeing him leave like this without settling his account, straightway made for Sancho Panza, who said that since his master would not pay, neither would he, for being squire to a knight-errant as he was, he came under the same rule with regard to inns and taverns.

The landlord grew very indignant at this and began to threaten him, telling him that if he did not pay he would regret it. But Sancho replied that, by the law of knighthood which his master had received, he would not part with a single coronado,[2] even though it cost him his life; for if the worthy and ancient custom of knights-errant was to be violated, it would not be by him, nor would the squires of those knights who were yet to come into the world have any cause to complain of him or to reproach him for breaking so just a code.

As poor Sancho's ill luck would have it, stopping at the inn that day were four wool carders of Segovia, three needlemakers from the vicinity of the Horse Fountain of Cordova, and a couple of lads from the Fair of Seville,[3] merry fellows all of them, well intentioned, mischievous, and playful. They now, as if moved and instigated by one and the same impulse, came up to Sancho and pulled him off his donkey, and then one of them entered the inn to get the blanket off the host's bed. Throwing Sancho into it, they glanced up and saw that the roof was a little too low for the work in hand; so they went out into the stable yard, which was bounded only by the sky above. Placing the squire in the middle of the blanket, they began tossing him up and down, having as much sport with him as one does with a dog at Shrovetide.

The cries of the poor wretch in the blanket were so loud that they reached his master's ears. Reining in his steed to listen attentively, Don Quixote at first thought that it must be some new adventure that awaited him, until he came to distinguish clearly the voice of his squire. Turning about then, he returned to the inn at a painful gallop and, finding it closed, started circling the hostelry to see if he could find an entrance of some sort. The moment he reached the walls of the stable yard, which were not very high, he saw the scurvy trick that was being played on Sancho. He saw the latter going up and down in the air with such grace and dexterity that, had the knight's mounting wrath permitted him to do so, it is my opinion that he would have laughed at the sight.

He then endeavored to climb down from his horse onto the wall, but he was so stiff and sore that he was unable to dismount; whereupon, from his seat in the saddle he began hurling so many insults and maledictions at those who were doing the tossing that it would be quite impossible to set them all down here. The men in the yard, however, did not for this reason leave off their laughing sport, nor did the flying Sancho cease his lamentations, mingled now with threats and now with entreaties, all of which were of no avail until his tormentors saw fit to stop from pure exhaustion. After that, they brought his ass and set him upon it, bundling him in his greatcoat. Seeing him so done in, Maritornes felt sorry for him and, in order to refresh him, brought him a jug of water which she got from the well that it might be cooler. Taking the jug and raising it to his mouth, Sancho paused at sound of his master's words.

"Sancho, my son, do not drink that water. Do not drink it, my son, for it will kill you. Do you not see? I have here the most blessed balm"— and he showed him the vial containing the beverage—"of which you have but to imbibe two drops and you shall be healed without a doubt."

At this, Sancho rolled his eyes and cried out in a voice that was even louder than his master's, "Can it be your Grace has forgotten that I am not a knight, or do you want me to vomit up what guts I have left from last night? Keep your liquor and to the devil with it; just leave me alone, that's all."

Even as he finished saying this he started to take a drink; but perceiving at the first swallow that it was only water, he stopped and asked Maritornes to bring him some wine instead. She complied right willingly, paying for it out of her own money; for it is said of her that, although she occupied so lowly a station in life, there was something about her that remotely resembled a Christian woman. When he had drunk his fill, Sancho dug his heels into his ass's flanks, and the gate of the inn having been thrown wide open for him, he rode away quite well satisfied with himself because he had not had to pay anything, even though it had been at the expense of those usual bondsmen, his shoulders.

The truth is, the innkeeper had kept his saddlebags, but Sancho was so excited when he left that he did not notice they were gone. Once the two unwelcome guests were safely outside, the landlord was all for barring the gate; but the blanket-tossers would not hear of this, for they were fellows to whom it would not have made a penny's worth of difference if Don Quixote had really been one of the Knights of the Round Table.

CHAPTER XVIII. *In which is set forth the conversation that Sancho Panza had with his master, Don Quixote, along with other adventures deserving of record.*

BY THE time Sancho reached his master, he was so exhausted and felt so faint that he was not even able any longer to urge on his beast.

"Well, Sancho," said Don Quixote when he saw him, "I am now convinced that yonder castle or inn is without a doubt enchanted; for what sort of creatures could they be who had such atrocious sport with you if not phantoms from another world? The thing that confirms me in this belief is the fact that, when I was alongside the stable-yard wall, witnessing the acts of that sad tragedy, it was not possible for me to climb it or even so much as get down off Rocinante, and that shows they must have cast a spell on me. But I swear to you, by the sword of a knight, that if I had been able to dismount and come over that wall, I should have wreaked such vengeance in your behalf that those villainous knaves would never have forgotten their little jest; and I should have done this even though it be against the laws of knighthood; for as I have told you many times, it is not permitted that a knight raise his hand against one who is not of his calling, save it be in defense of his own life and person in a case of great and urgent necessity."

"I would have avenged myself, if I had been able," said Sancho, "whether I had been dubbed a knight or not; although it is my opinion that those who had such sport with me were not phantoms or human beings under a spell as your Grace says, but flesh-and-blood men like us. They all had names, for I heard them calling one another by them as they were tossing me. There was one who was called Pedro Martínez, and another Tenorio Hernández, and the innkeeper's name was Juan Palomeque the Left-Handed. And so, Señor, your not being able to leap over the stable-yard wall or even get down off your horse was due to something other than enchantments. What I make out of it all is that these adventures that we go looking for will end by bringing us so many misadventures that we shan't know which is our right foot. The best and most sensible thing to do, in my judgment, would be for us to return home, now that it is harvest time, and stop running about from Ceca to Mecca and from pail to bucket, as the saying goes." [1]

"How little you know, Sancho, about the matter of chivalry!" Don Quixote replied. "Hush, and have patience; the day shall come when you will see with your own eyes how honorable a calling it is that we follow. For tell me, if you will: what greater pleasure or satisfaction is to be had in this world than that of winning a battle and triumphing over one's enemy? None, undoubtedly none."

"That may be," said Sancho; "I cannot say as to that; but one thing I know is that since we have been knights-errant, or since your Grace has been one, for I am not to be counted among that honored number, we have not won a single battle, unless it was with the Biscayan, and even there your Grace came out with half an ear and half a helmet the less. Since then, all that we have had has been poundings, punches, and more poundings; and over and above that, I got the blanketing at the hands of certain persons who were under a spell, and so I do not know what that pleasure of conquering an enemy, of which your Grace speaks, is like."

"That," said Don Quixote, "is the thing that vexes me, and I can understand that it should vex you as well, Sancho. But from this time forth I shall endeavor to have at hand some sword made by so masterful an art that anyone who carries it with him cannot suffer any manner of enchantment. It may even be that fortune will procure for me the blade of Amadis,[2] the one he bore when he was called the Knight of the Flaming Sword. It was one of the best that ever a knight had in this world, for in addition to the aforesaid virtue which it possessed, it cut like a razor, and there was no suit of armor, however strong or enchanted it might be, that could withstand it."

"It would be just my luck," said Sancho, "that if your Grace did find a sword like that, it would be of use only to those who had been dubbed knights; as for the squires, they are out of luck."

"Never fear, Sancho," said his master, "Heaven will do better by you than that."

As they went along conversing in this manner, Don Quixote caught sight down the road of a large cloud of dust that was drawing nearer.

"This, O Sancho," he said, turning to his squire, "is the day when you shall see the boon that fate has in store for me; this, I repeat, is the day when, as well as on any other, shall be displayed the valor of my good right arm. On this day I shall perform deeds that will be written down in the book of fame for all centuries to come. Do you see that dust cloud rising there, Sancho? That is the dust stirred up [3] by a vast army marching in this direction and composed of many nations."

"At that rate," said Sancho, "there must be two of them, for there is another one just like it on the other side."

Don Quixote turned to look and saw that this was so. He was overjoyed by the thought that these were indeed two armies about to meet and clash in the middle of the broad plain; for at every hour and every moment his imagination was filled with battles, enchantments, nonsensical adventures, tales of love, amorous challenges, and the like, such as he had read of in the books of chivalry, and every word he uttered, every thought that crossed his mind, every act he performed, had to do with such things as these. The dust clouds he had sighted were raised by two large droves of sheep coming along the road in opposite directions, which by reason of the dust were not visible until they were close at hand, but Don Quixote insisted so earnestly that they were armies that Sancho came to believe it.

"Sir," he said, "what are we to do?"

"What are we to do?" echoed his master. "Favor and aid the weak and needy. I would inform you, Sancho, that the one coming toward us is led and commanded by the great emperor Alifanfarón, lord of the great isle of Trapobana. This other one at my back is that of his enemy, the king of the Garamantas, Pentapolín of the Rolled-up Sleeve, for he always goes into battle with his right arm bare." [4]

"But why are they such enemies?" Sancho asked.

"Because," said Don Quixote, "this Alifanfarón is a terrible pagan and in love with Pentapolín's daughter, who is a very beautiful and gracious lady and a Christian, for which reason her father does not wish to give her to the pagan king unless the latter first abjures the law of the false prophet, Mohammed, and adopts the faith that is Pentapolín's own."

"Then, by my beard," said Sancho, "if Pentapolín isn't right, and I am going to aid him all I can."

"In that," said Don Quixote, "you will only be doing your duty; for to engage in battles of this sort you need not have been dubbed a knight."

"I can understand that," said Sancho, "but where are we going to put this ass so that we will be certain of finding him after the fray is over? As for going into battle on such a mount, I do not think that has been done up to now."

"That is true enough," said Don Quixote. "What you had best do with him is to turn him loose and run the risk of losing him; for after we emerge the victors we shall have so many horses that even Rocinante will be in danger of being exchanged for another. But listen closely to what I am about to tell you, for I wish to give you an account of the principal knights that are accompanying these two armies; and in order that you may be the better able to see and take note of them, let us retire to that hillock over there which will afford us a very good view."

They then stationed themselves upon a slight elevation from which they would have been able to see very well the two droves of sheep that Don Quixote took to be armies if it had not been for the blinding clouds of dust. In spite of this, however, the worthy gentleman contrived to behold in his imagination what he did not see and what did not exist in reality.

Raising his voice, he went on to explain, "That knight in the gilded armor that you see there, bearing upon his shield a crowned lion crouched at the feet of a damsel, is the valiant Laurcalco, lord of the Silver Bridge; the other with the golden flowers on his armor, and on his shield three crowns argent on an azure field, is the dread Micocolembo, grand duke of Quirocia. And that one on Micocolembo's right hand, with the limbs of a giant, is the ever undaunted Brandabarbarán de Boliche, lord of the three Arabias. He goes armored in a serpent's skin and has for shield a door which, so report has it, is one of those from the temple that Samson pulled down, that time when he avenged himself on his enemies with his own death.

"But turn your eyes in this direction, and you will behold at the head of the other army the ever victorious, never vanquished Timonel de Carcajona, prince of New Biscay, who comes with quartered arms—azure, vert, argent, and or—and who has upon his shield a cat or on a field tawny, with the inscription *Miau*, which is the beginning of his lady's name; for she, so it is said, is the peerless Miulina, daughter of Alfeñiquén, duke of Algarve. And that one over there, who weights down and presses the loins of that powerful charger, in a suit of snow-white armor with a white shield that bears no device whatever—he is a novice knight of the French nation, called Pierres Papin, lord of the baronies of Utrique. As for him you see digging his iron spurs into the flanks of that fleet-footed zebra courser and whose arms are vairs azure, he is the mighty duke of Nervia, Espartafilardo of the Wood, who has for device upon his shield an asparagus plant with a motto in Castilian that says 'Rastrea mi suerte.' " [5]

In this manner he went on naming any number of imaginary knights on either side, describing on the spur of the moment their arms, colors, devices, and mottoes; for he was completely carried away by his imagination and by this unheard-of madness that had laid hold of him.

Without pausing, he went on, "This squadron in front of us is composed of men of various nations. There are those who drink the sweet waters of the famous Xanthus; woodsmen who tread the Massilian plain; those that sift the fine gold nuggets of Arabia Felix; those that are so fortunate as to dwell on the banks of the clear-running Thermodon, famed for their coolness; those who in many and diverse ways drain the golden Pactolus; Numidians, whose word is never to be trusted; Persians, with their famous bows and arrows; Medes and Parthians, who fight as they flee; Scythians, as cruel as they are fair of skin; Ethiopians, with their pierced lips; and an infinite number of other nationalities whose visages I see and recognize although I cannot recall their names.

"In this other squadron come those that drink from the crystal currents of the olive-bearing Betis; [6] those that smooth and polish their faces with the liquid of the ever rich and gilded Tagus; those that enjoy the beneficial waters of the divine Genil; [7] those that roam the Tartessian plains with their abundant pasturage; [8] those that disport themselves in the Elysian meadows of Jerez; [9] the men of La Mancha, rich and crowned with golden ears of corn; others clad in iron garments, ancient relics of the Gothic race; those that bathe in the Pisuerga, noted for the mildness of its current; [10] those that feed their herds in the wide-spreading pasture lands along the banks of the winding Guadiana, celebrated for its underground course; [11] those that shiver from the cold of the wooded Pyrenees or dwell amid the white peaks of the lofty Apennines—in short, all those whom Europe holds within its girth."

So help me God! How many provinces, how many nations did he not mention by name, giving to each one with marvelous readiness its proper attributes; for he was wholly absorbed and filled to the brim with what he had read in those lying books of his! Sancho Panza hung on his words, saying nothing, merely turning his head from time to time to have a look at those knights and giants that his master was pointing out to him; but he was unable to discover any of them.

"Sir," he said, "may I go to the devil if I see a single man, giant, or knight of all those that your Grace is talking about. Who knows? Maybe it is another spell, like last night."

"How can you say that?" replied Don Quixote. "Can you not hear the neighing of the horses, the sound of trumpets, the roll of drums?"

"I hear nothing," said Sancho, "except the bleating of sheep."

And this, of course, was the truth; for the flocks were drawing near.

"The trouble is, Sancho," said Don Quixote, "you are so afraid that you cannot see or hear properly; for one of the effects of fear is to disturb the senses and cause things to appear other than what they are. If you are so craven as all that, go off to one side and leave me alone, and I without your help will assure the victory to that side to which I lend my aid."

Saying this, he put spurs to Rocinante and, with his lance at rest, darted down the hillside like a flash of lightning.

As he did so, Sancho called after him, "Come back, your Grace, Señor Don Quixote; I vow to God those are sheep that you are charging. Come back! O wretched father that bore me! What madness is this? Look you, there are no giants, nor knights, nor cats, nor shields either quartered or whole, nor vairs azure or bedeviled. What is this you are doing, O sinner that I am in God's sight?"

But all this did not cause Don Quixote to turn back. Instead, he rode on, crying out at the top of his voice, "Ho, knights, those of you who follow and fight under the banners of the valiant Pentapolín of the Rolled-up Sleeve; follow me, all of you, and you shall see how easily I give you revenge on your enemy, Alifanfarón of Trapobana."

With these words he charged into the middle of the flock of sheep and began spearing at them with as much courage and boldness as if they had been his mortal enemies. The shepherds and herdsmen who were with the animals called to him to stop; but seeing it was no use, they unloosed their slings and saluted his ears with stones as big as your fist.

Don Quixote paid no attention to the missiles and, dashing about here and there, kept crying, "Where are you, haughty Alifanfarón? Come out to me; for here is a solitary knight who desires in single combat to test your strength and deprive you of your life, as a punishment for that which you have done to the valorous Pentapolín Garamanta."

At that instant a pebble [12] from the brook struck him in the side and buried a couple of ribs in his body. Believing himself dead or badly wounded, and remembering his potion, he took out his vial, placed it to his mouth, and began to swallow the balm; but before he had had what he thought was enough, there came another almond,[18] which struck him in the hand, crushing the tin vial and carrying away with it a couple of grinders from his mouth, as well as badly mashing two of his fingers. As a result of these blows the poor knight tumbled from his horse. Believing that they had killed him, the shepherds hastily collected their flock and, picking up the dead beasts, of which there were more than seven, they went off down the road without more ado.

Sancho all this time was standing on the slope observing the insane things that his master was doing; and as he plucked savagely at his beard he cursed the hour and minute when luck had brought them together. But when he saw him lying there on the ground and perceived that the shepherds were gone, he went down the hill and came up to him, finding him in very bad shape though not unconscious.

"Didn't I tell you, Señor Don Quixote," he said, "that you should come back, that those were not armies you were charging but flocks of sheep?"

"This," said Don Quixote, "is the work of that thieving magician, my enemy, who thus counterfeits things and causes them to disappear. You must know, Sancho, that it is very easy for them to make us assume any appearance that they choose; and so it is that malign one who persecutes me, envious of the glory he saw me about to achieve in this battle, changed the squadrons of the foe into flocks of sheep. If you do not believe me, I beseech you on my life to do one thing for me, that you may be undeceived and discover for yourself that what I say is true. Mount your ass and follow them quietly, and when you have gone a short way from here, you will see them become their former selves once more; they will no longer be sheep but men exactly as I described them to you in the first place. But do not go now, for I need your kind assistance; come over here and have a look and tell me how many grinders are missing, for it feels as if I did not have a single one left."

Sancho went over and almost put his eyes into his master's mouth. Now, as it happened, this was just the moment when the balm in Don Quixote's stomach began to work, and he promptly discharged its entire contents with more force than a musket straight into the beard of his good-hearted squire.

"Holy Mary!" exclaimed Sancho, "and what is this that has happened now? This sinner must surely be mortally wounded, for he is vomiting blood from the mouth."

When he investigated a little more closely, however, he discovered from the color, taste, and smell that this was not blood but balm from the vial from which he had seen his master drinking; and so great was the disgust he felt that, his stomach turning over, he now vomited up his insides all over Don Quixote and both of them were in a fine state indeed. Sancho then made for his saddlebags to get something with which to wipe the vomit off them, and when he found the bags were missing, it was more than he could do to contain himself. Cursing himself anew, he made up his mind that he would leave the knight and return home, even though he did lose what was coming to him for his services, along with all hope of becoming governor of that promised island.

Don Quixote then rose and, with his left hand to his mouth to keep his teeth from popping out, grasped Rocinante's reins in the other hand—for the animal had not stirred from his side, so loyal and well trained was he—and went over to where the squire was bending above his donkey with his hand to his cheek like one lost in thought.

Seeing him so downcast, his master said to him, "Bear in mind, Sancho, that one man is worth no more than another unless he does more. All these squalls that we have met with are merely a sign that the weather is going to clear and everything will turn out for the best; for it is impossible that either good or evil should be lasting; and from this it follows that, the evil having lasted so long, the good must be near at hand. And so you should not grieve for the misfortunes that have befallen me, since you have had no part in them."

"How is that?" replied Sancho. "I suppose the one they tossed in a blanket yesterday was somebody else than my father's son? And my saddlebags, which are gone now, did they belong to some other person?"

"You mean to say your saddlebags are missing, Sancho?"

"Yes," replied the squire, "that they are."

"Well, in that case, we shan't have anything to eat today," said Don Quixote.

"Not unless these meadows have some of those herbs which your Grace was saying he knows so well, with which unfortunate knights-errant like your Grace are in the habit of supplying their needs."

"So far as that goes," said his master, "right now I would rather have a quarter of a loaf or a loaf of bread and a couple of pilchards' heads than all the herbs that Dioscorides describes, even with Dr. Laguna's commentary.[14] But, nevertheless, Sancho, mount your ass and follow me; for inasmuch as God is the provider of all things, He will not fail us, especially seeing that we are so active in His service; for gnats never lack the air, grubs the earth, nor polliwogs the water; and He is so merciful that He causes His sun to shine on the good and the bad and the rain to fall on the just and the unjust."

"It strikes me," said Sancho, "that your Grace is better fitted to be a preacher than a knight-errant."

"Knights-errant," was Don Quixote's rejoinder, "have always known, and have to know, everything; for they might be called upon to deliver a sermon or make a speech in the middle of the open country, just as if they were graduates of the University of Paris; from which it may be deduced that the lance never yet blunted the pen nor the pen the lance." [15]

"That may all very well be as your Grace says," replied Sancho, "but let us leave here at once and go look for a lodging for tonight; and God grant it may be someplace where there are no blankets or blanket-tossers, nor phantoms nor enchanted Moors, for if I come upon any of those, I'll have nothing whatever to do with them." [16]

"Pray God, then, my son," said Don Quixote, "and lead the way where you will; for this time I will leave the lodging to your choice. But, first, put your finger in my mouth and feel how many teeth and grinders are missing on this right side of my upper jaw, for that is where the pain is."

Sancho did as he was told. "How many grinders did your Grace have on this side?"

"Four besides the double tooth and all of them whole and healthy."

"Mind what you are saying, your Grace," Sancho warned.

"I am telling you: four, if not five," said Don Quixote; "for in all my life I have never had a tooth or grinder pulled, nor has any fallen out or been destroyed by decay or abscess."

"Well, in this lower jaw," Sancho went on, "your Grace has not more than two grinders and a half left; and in the upper jaw, there is not even a half, there is none at all—it is all as smooth as the palm of your hand."

"How unfortunate I am!" cried Don Quixote as he heard this sad news from his squire. "I would rather they had robbed me of an arm so long as it was not my sword arm. For I must tell you, Sancho, that a mouth without grinders is like a mill without a millstone, and a tooth is more to be prized than a diamond. But to all this we are subject, those of us who follow the arduous profession of knighthood. So mount, my friend, and lead on, and I will follow at whatever pace you will."

Sancho obeyed, heading in the direction in which he thought they might be able to find a lodging without leaving the highway, which at this point was a much-traveled stretch of road. They went along slowly, for Don Quixote's jaws were hurting him so much that he could think of nothing else and was in no mood to make haste. Perceiving this, Sancho sought to divert him and to take his mind off his troubles by small talk of one kind or another; and some of the things he said to him are set forth in the chapter that follows.

CHAPTER **XIX**. *Of the shrewd things that Sancho Panza said to his master and the adventure that happened to him in connection with a dead body, along with other famous events.*

"IT SEEMS to me, sir, that all these misadventures that have happened to us of late are without any doubt a punishment for the sin your Grace committed against the order of knighthood by failing to keep the vow that you made not to eat bread off a tablecloth, or embrace the queen, and all the rest of it; your Grace swore not to do any of these things until you had taken a helmet from that Moor Malandrino [1] or whatever his name is, I don't rightly remember."

"There is much in what you say, Sancho," replied Don Quixote, "but to tell you the truth, I had forgotten about it; and you may be sure that it was because you had failed to remind me in time that the business of the blanket occurred. But I will see to making amends for it all; for in knighthood there are ways of adjusting everything."

"Why," said Sancho, "did I take some kind of oath, then?"

"It makes no difference whether you did or not," said Don Quixote. "It appears to me that you are not wholly clear of complicity in this matter, and so it will not be a bad thing to provide ourselves with a remedy."

"In that case," said his squire, "will your Grace please be sure not to forget the remedy as you did the vow? For who knows. the phantoms may take it into their heads to have sport with me again, and with your Grace as well, if they see you so stubborn."

While they were engaged in this and similar talk, night descended upon them as they were going along the highway, before they had as yet found a lodging; and what made matters worse, they were very hungry, for with their saddlebags they had lost their entire pantry and store of provisions. And on top of all their misfortunes, they now had an experience which, if it was not a real adventure, certainly had all the earmarks of one. Although it was already quite dark, they continued on their way, for Sancho was sure that, since this was a main highway, they would have to go but a league or two before they came upon some kind of inn. And as they were riding along through the darkness like that, the squire hungry and the master with a great desire to eat, they suddenly saw coming toward them a great number of lights which looked exactly like moving stars. Sancho was stunned by the sight, while Don Quixote did not feel altogether easy about it, and the one pulled on the halter of his ass, the other on his horse's reins. They sat there watching closely, trying to make out what these lights could be, which were all the time coming nearer—and the nearer they came, the bigger they seemed. Sancho was shaking like someone who had had a dose of mercury, and his master's hair was standing on end. Then Don Quixote managed to pluck up a little courage.

"There can be no doubt, Sancho," he said, "that this is going to be a very great and perilous adventure in which it will be necessary for me to display all my strength and valor."

"Poor me!" said his squire. "If by any chance this is to be another adventure with phantoms, where am I going to find the ribs to bear it?"

"Phantoms or not," said the knight, "I will not permit them to touch the nap of your garments. If they had sport with you last time, it was only because I was unable to get over the stable-yard wall; but here we are in the open where I can wield my sword as I like."

"And what if they enchant and benumb you as they did before, what difference will it make whether or not you are in the open?"

"Nonetheless," replied Don Quixote, "I beg of you, Sancho, to keep up your courage; for experience will teach you what mine is."

"Very well, I will keep it up, God willing," was Sancho's answer.

Retiring then to one side of the road, the two of them continued watching attentively to see what those moving lights could be; and it was not long before they caught sight of a large number of white-shirted figures,[2] a vision so frightening that Sancho lost what courage he had.

His teeth began chattering like those of a person who has the quartan fever, and they chattered more than ever as the apparition came near enough to be distinguishable; for there were some twenty of those shirted figures, all mounted on horseback and with lighted torches in their hands, and behind them came a litter covered with mourning, followed by six other riders all in black down to the feet of their mules, for it was obvious from their leisurely gait that these animals were not horses. As the cavalcade approached, it could be seen that the shirted ones were muttering something to themselves in a low and mournful tone of voice.

This weird vision, at such an hour and in so out-of-the-way a place, was sufficient to strike terror to Sancho's heart, and his master would have felt the same way had he been anyone else than Don Quixote. As it was, the former had by now reached the end of his strength, but not so the latter, whose vivid imagination was already at work and who saw here another adventure out of his storybooks. The litter had to be a bier, bearing some knight either dead or badly wounded, and it was for him, Don Quixote, and him alone, to exact vengeance; and so, without another word, he rested his lance, settled himself well in the saddle, and, with highborn mettle and intrepid bearing, took up his stand in the middle of the road along which the shirted figures had to pass.

When they were close upon him, he raised his voice and cried, "Halt, knight, or whoever you may be, and give an account of yourself; tell me whence you come and whither you are bound, and who it is that you bring with you on that bier; for to all appearances either you have done some wrong or some wrong has been done to you, and it is fitting and necessary that I should know of it, either to punish you for your evil deeds or to avenge you for the misdoings of another."

At this point, one of the figures spoke up. "We are in a hurry," he said, "and the inn is far, and we cannot stop to give you the information that you seek." And, so saying, he spurred his mule forward.

Don Quixote was greatly put out at such a reply and, seizing the mule by the bridle, he repeated, "Halt, I say, and show a little better breeding by giving me an answer to my questions. Otherwise, you shall all do battle with me."

Now, the mule as it happened was a little shy, and when Don Quixote laid hold of the bridle, it reared on its hind legs and threw its master to the ground. A lad who was on foot, upon seeing the shirted one fall, began reviling the knight; but our friend's wrath was up, and without further delay he brought his lance into position and bore down upon one of those who were clad in mourning, wounding him badly and tumbling him from his mount. Then he turned upon the others, and it was something to see the dexterity with which he attacked and routed them. It seemed as if at that moment Rocinante had sprouted wings, so proud-stepping and light-footed did he show himself to be.

All these shirt-wearers were timid folk, without arms, and so, naturally enough, they speedily quit the fray and started running across the fields, still bearing their lighted torches in their hands, which gave them the appearance of masked figures darting here and there on some night when a fiesta or other celebration is being held. Those who wore the mourning, on the other hand, wrapped and swathed in their skirts and gowns, were unable to move; and, accordingly, with no risk to himself, Don Quixote smote them all and drove them off against their will; for they thought that this surely was no man but a devil straight out of Hell who had come to rob them of the body that they carried on the litter.

Sancho watched it all, greatly admiring his master's ardor. "No doubt about it," he told himself, "he is as brave and powerful as he says he is."

There was a flaming torch that had been stuck in the ground near the first one who had fallen from his mule; and by its light Don Quixote could be seen coming up to the fellow, sticking the point of his lance in his face, and calling upon him to surrender as he valued his life.

"I am prisoner enough as it is," the man said; "for my leg is broken and I cannot stir. I beg your Grace, if you are a Christian knight, not to slay me; if you were to do so, you would be committing a great sacrilege, for I am a licentiate and have already taken my first orders."

"Well," said Don Quixote, "what in the devil brings you here if you are a churchman?"

"What, sir?" said the man on the ground. "My bad luck, that's all."

"Still worse luck awaits you," said Don Quixote, "if you do not answer to my satisfaction all those questions that I put to you in the first place."

"Your Grace shall be easily satisfied as to all that," replied the licentiate. "To begin with, I may tell your Grace that, although I said I was a licentiate, I am really but a bachelor, and my name is Alonso López, a native of Alcobendas. I come from the city of Baeza with eleven other priests, the ones that are carrying the torches. We are on our way to the city of Segovia, accompanying the corpse that is in that litter, the body of a gentleman who died in Baeza, where he was first interred; and now we are taking his bones to their last resting place in Segovia, where he was born."

"And who killed him?" demanded Don Quixote.

"God," said the bachelor, "by means of a pestilential fever that took him off."

"In that way," said the knight, "Our Lord has absolved me of the trouble of avenging him, as I should have had to do had he met his death at the hands of another; but He who slew him having slain him, there is nothing to do but be silent and shrug one's shoulders, and I should do the same if it were I whom He was slaying. I would have your reverence know that I am a knight of La Mancha, Don Quixote by name, and it is my calling and profession to go through the world righting wrongs and redressing injuries."

"I do not know what you mean by righting wrongs, seeing that you found me quite all right and left me very wrong indeed, with a broken leg which will not be right again as long as I live; [3] and if you have redressed any injury in my case, it has been done in such a way as to leave me injured forever. It was a great misadventure for me to fall in with you who go hunting adventures."

"Everything," replied Don Quixote, "does not occur in the same manner. The big mistake you made, Sir Bachelor Alonso López, was in coming as you did, by night, dressed in those surplices, bearing lighted torches and praying, all of which gave the appearance of something evil and of the other world. I accordingly could not fail to fulfill my obligation by attacking you, and I would have done so even though I knew for a certainty that you were devils out of Hell; for such I took you to be all the time."

"Since that is the way fate has willed it," said the bachelor, "I beseech your Grace, Sir Knight-errant—whose errantry has done me so bad a turn—I beseech you to help me up from under this mule, for one of my legs is caught between the stirrup and the saddle."

"Why," exclaimed Don Quixote, "I might have talked on until tomorrow! How long were you going to wait to tell me of your distress?"

He then called to Sancho to come, but the squire did not see fit to do so, being engaged at that moment in robbing a sumpter mule of the larder which these gentlemen were carrying with them and which was well stocked with things to eat. Having made a sack of his greatcoat, he dumped into it all that it would hold and threw it across his ass's back; and then, and only then, did he answer his master's call to come and help get the bachelor out from under the mule. Setting the fellow on his beast once more, they gave him his torch, and Don Quixote told him to follow in the track of his companions and beg their pardon on his behalf for the wrong which he had not been able to avoid doing them.

"And if," said Sancho, "those gentlemen wish to know who the valiant one was who did this to them, your Grace may inform them that he is the famous Don Quixote de la Mancha, otherwise known as the Knight of the Mournful Countenance."

At this the knight inquired of his squire what had led him to call him by such a title at that particular moment.

"I can tell you," said Sancho. "I was looking at you for a time by the light of the torch that poor fellow carried; and truly, your Grace now has the worst-looking countenance that I have ever seen, whether due to exhaustion from this combat or the lack of teeth and grinders, I cannot say."

"It is not that," said Don Quixote; "it is simply that the sage who is to write the history of my exploits must have thought that it would be a good thing for me to take another appellation as all knights of the past have done. Thus one was called the Knight of the Flaming Sword; another the Knight of the Unicorn; one the Knight of Damsels, and one the Knight of the Phoenix; another the Knight of the Griffin; and still another the Knight of Death: and by these names and insignia were they known all the world over. And so, I tell you, it must have been that sage of whom I was speaking who put it into your mind and on your tongue to dub me the Knight of the Mournful Countenance. This title I mean to adopt as my own from now on; and in order that it may better fit me, I propose, as soon as opportunity offers, to have painted on my shield a very sad-looking face."

"There is no necessity of wasting time and money on having a face made for you," said Sancho. "All that your Grace has to do is to uncover your own to those who look at you, and without need of any image or shield they will call you that. This is the truth I speak; for I assure your Grace—not meaning any harm—that hunger and the lack of grinders have given you so ill a countenance that you can very well do without the painted one."

Don Quixote laughed heartily at Sancho's wit, but still he could not give up the idea of calling himself by that name and having a suitable device painted on his buckler or shield just as he had conceived it.

At this point the bachelor prepared to take his departure.[4] "I neglected to warn your Grace," he said, "that you are hereby excommunicated for having laid violent hands on a holy thing: *Iuxta illud, si quis, suadente diablo*, etc." [5]

"I do not understand that Latin of yours," said Don Quixote, "but I

am quite sure that I did not lay my hands on anything; I laid on with
this lance. What is more, I did not realize that I was insulting priests or
sacred things of the Church, which I respect and revere as the good
Catholic and loyal Christian that I am; I thought, rather, that it was
phantoms and monsters from the other world that I was attacking. But,
even so, I cannot but recall what happened to Cid Ruy Díaz when he
broke the chair of the royal ambassador in the presence of his Holiness
the Pope, that day when the worthy Rodrigo de Vivar showed himself
to be a brave and honored knight." [6]

Having listened to this speech, the bachelor went his way without
saying a word in reply.

Don Quixote then wanted to see whether it really was bones they had
in that litter or not; but Sancho would not consent.

"Sir," he said, "your Grace has concluded this adventure in the safest
manner of any yet. But those fellows whom you overcame and routed
may come to realize that it was, after all, only one individual who conquered them; and being thoroughly ashamed of themselves, they may
pluck up courage and return to look for us, in which case they could
give us plenty of trouble. The ass is ready, the mountains near by, and
we are hungry; there is nothing for us to do but to retire as decently as
may be, and as the saying goes, 'To the grave with the dead and the
living to the bread.' " [7]

Urging his ass forward, he begged his master to follow him, and the
latter, deciding that his squire was right, made no reply but fell in behind. After going a short distance they found themselves between two
small mountains, in a broad and hidden valley. Here they dismounted,
and Sancho relieved the donkey of its burden; after which, stretched
upon the green grass and with hunger as a sauce, they breakfasted,
lunched, dined, and supped at one and the same time, satisfying their
stomachs with more than one cold cut which the gentlemen of the
clergy attending the deceased—who seldom stint themselves in this regard—had brought along in their well-stocked larder upon the back of
their sumpter mule.

But they still had one misfortune to endure, which for Sancho was
the worst of all: they had no wine, nor even water, to drink, and so
were harassed by thirst. Whereupon, noting the green young grass of
the meadow round about, he conceived an idea which will be set forth
in the following chapter.

CHAPTER XX . *Of an adventure such as never was seen nor heard of, which was completed by the valorous Don Quixote de la Mancha with less peril than any famous knight in all the world ever incurred in a similar undertaking.*

"IT IS not possible, sir," said Sancho, "that this grass should not betoken the presence near by of some spring or brook that provides it with moisture; and so, it would be a good thing if we were to go a little farther, for I am sure we should be able to find someplace where we might quench this terrible thirst that is consuming us and that, undoubtedly, is more painful to bear than hunger."

This impressed Don Quixote as being good advice; and after they had placed upon the ass what was left of their dinner, he took Rocinante's rein and Sancho took the halter of his beast and they started feeling their way up the meadow, for the night was so dark that they were unable to see anything at all. They had not gone two hundred paces when they heard a roaring sound, which appeared to be that of water falling from great, high cliffs. This cheered them enormously; but as they paused to determine the direction from which it came, another and terrible din fell upon their ears, watering down the satisfaction they had felt at the thought of finding water,[1] especially for Sancho, who was by nature timid and lacking in spirit. What they heard, I am telling you, was the sound of measured blows, together with the rattling of iron chains, accompanied by so furious a thunder of waters as to strike terror in any other heart than that of Don Quixote.

It was night, as has been stated, and they now chanced to reach a cluster of tall trees, whose leaves, stirred by the mild wind that was blowing, rustled with a soft and gentle murmur. The solitude, the place, the darkness, the din of the water, the rustling of the leaves—all this was frightful, horror-inspiring, especially when they found that the blows did not cease, nor did the wind fall asleep or morning come; and added to it all was the fact that they had no idea where they were. Don Quixote, how-

ever, with his own intrepid heart to keep him company, leaped upon
Rocinante's back and, bracing his buckler on his arm, brought his lance
into play.

"Sancho, my friend," he said, "you may know that I was born, by
Heaven's will, in this our age of iron, to revive what is known as the
Golden Age. I am he for whom are reserved the perils, the great exploits, the valiant deeds. I am—I say it again—he who is to revive the
Knights of the Round Table, the Twelve Peers of France, and the
Nine Worthies. I am he who is to cast into oblivion the Platirs, the
Tablantes, the Olivantes, and the Tirants, the Knights of the Sun and
the Belianises, together with the entire throng of famous knights-errant
of times past, by performing in this age in which I live such great and
wonderful feats of arms as shall darken the brightest of their achievements. Note well, my rightful and my loyal squire, the shades of night
that lie about us; this uncanny silence; the low and indistinct rustling of
those trees; the frightful sound made by that water that we came to
seek, which appears to be falling precipitously from the tall mountains
of the moon; those unceasing blows that grieve and wound our ears; all
of which things together, and each one singly, are sufficient to strike
fear, dread, and terror in the breast of Mars himself, not to speak of him
who is not accustomed to such happenings and adventures.

"Well, all these things that I have been describing are for me but the
incentives and awakeners of my courage, causing the heart within my
bosom to burst with the desire of entering upon this adventure, however
difficult it may be. And so, tighten Rocinante's girth a bit if you will,
and God be with you. Wait for me here three days, no longer. If at the
end of that time I have not returned, you may go back to our village;
and then, as a special favor to me, you will go to El Toboso, where you
will tell that incomparable lady, my Dulcinea, how her captive knight
died, undertaking things that would render him worthy of being called
hers."

Hearing his master speak these words, Sancho began weeping as if his
heart would break. "Sir," he said, "I do not know why your Grace is
so bent upon this fearful undertaking. It is night now, no one can see
us, and we can easily turn about and take ourselves out of danger's path,
even though we do not drink for the next three days. Since there is
none here to see us, the fewer will there be to call us cowards. What's
more, I have often heard the curate of our village say in his sermons—
your Grace knows him very well—that whoever goes looking for danger
will perish by it.[2] It is not good to tempt God by entering upon some

monstrous undertaking from which you can escape only by a miracle, and Heaven has performed enough of them for your Grace by saving you from being tossed in a blanket as I was and by bringing you out the victor, safe and free, over all those enemies who were accompanying that corpse.

"And if all this does not suffice to move or soften that hard heart of yours, let it be moved by the thought, the certain knowledge, that no sooner will you have left this spot than I out of fear will yield my soul to any that cares to take it. I have left my native land, my wife and young ones, to come and serve your Grace, believing that by so doing I would better my lot, not make it worse; but as avarice always bursts the bag,[3] so has it torn my hopes to shreds. Just when they are brightest and I seem nearest to obtaining that wretched island, that cursed island, which your Grace so many times has promised me, I perceive that, in place of fulfilling that hope, you are about to go away and leave me in a place like this, so far from any human beings.

"In God's name, sir, do me not this wrong. If your Grace will not wholly desist from this enterprise, at least put it off until morning; for according to that knowledge of the heavens that I acquired as a shepherd, it should not be as much as three hours from now until dawn, seeing that the mouth of the Horn is directly overhead and midnight is in line with the left arm."[4]

"How, Sancho," said Don Quixote, "can you see that line or where the mouth of the Horn or your own head is, when it is so dark and there is not a star in the sky?"

"That," replied Sancho, "is because fear has many eyes and can see things under the earth and much more in the heavens above; and anyway, it stands to reason that daybreak cannot be far off."

"Far off or near," said his master, "it shall not be said of me, either now or at any other time, that tears and entreaties kept me from fulfilling my duties as a knight; and so, Sancho, I beg you to be quiet; for God, who has put it into my heart to undertake this dread adventure such as never before was heard of—God will see to my well-being and will comfort you in your sorrow. The thing for you to do is to tighten Rocinante's girth and remain here, and I shall return soon, either living or dead."

Perceiving his master's firm resolve, and seeing of how little avail were his own tears, advice, and entreaties, Sancho determined to have resort to his ingenuity in compelling him, if he could, to wait until daylight. Accordingly, when he went to tighten Rocinante's girth, he very deftly and without being observed slipped the halter of his ass over the hack's two front feet so that, when Don Quixote started to ride away, he found that his steed was unable to move except by little hops and jumps.

"Ah, sir," Sancho said to his master when he saw that his trick had worked, "Heaven itself, moved by my tears and supplications, has ordained that Rocinante should not stir; and if you stubbornly insist upon spurring and whipping him, you will merely be angering fortune and, so to speak, kicking against the prick."

Don Quixote was truly in despair now; for the more he dug his legs into his horse's flanks the less inclined that animal was to budge; and without noticing that the hack's feet had been bound, the knight decided there was nothing for him to do but be calm and wait until daylight should come or Rocinante should see fit to move; for he was convinced that all this came of something other than his squire's cleverness.

"Since Rocinante will not go," he said, "I am content, Sancho, to wait until dawn shall smile, even though I myself may weep that she is so long in coming."

"There is no occasion for weeping," replied Sancho, "for I will entertain your Grace by telling stories from now until daybreak, unless you care to dismount and lie down to sleep for a little while upon this green grass, as knights-errant are accustomed to do, so that you may be rested when day comes and fit to undertake this unlikely adventure that awaits you."

"Why," said Don Quixote, "do you call upon me to dismount or to sleep? Am I, perchance, one of those knights who take their repose amid dangers? Sleep, then, if you will, for you were born to sleep, or do whatever you like, and I shall do that which best befits my knightly character."

"Sir," said Sancho, "let not your Grace be angry, for I did not mean it in that way."

Coming up to his master, then, he laid both hands on the saddletree in such a manner that he stood embracing Don Quixote's left leg; and he did not stir an inch from there, so great was his fear of those blows which were still to be heard in regular cadence. Don Quixote then remarked that his squire might tell him a story by way of amusing him as he had promised; to which Sancho replied that he would be glad to do so if the fear which that sound inspired in him would only let him.

"But, in spite of all that," he said, "I will try to tell you a story which, if it does not escape me in the telling, and nobody stops me, is one of the best there is; and pay attention, your Grace, for I am about to begin. Let bygones be bygones; and may the good come to all and the evil to him who goes to look for it. For your Grace must know that when the ancients began their fables the beginning was by no means left to the choice of the one who told the tale; instead, they always began with a maxim from Cato Zonzorino,[5] the Roman, who uttered the words that I have quoted, '. . . and the evil to him who goes to look for it,' a saying that fits like the ring on your finger, signifying that your Grace should remain here and not go hunting trouble anywhere else, and that we should return by another road since there is no one to compel us to keep following this one where there are so many frightful things to startle us."

"Go on with your story, Sancho," said Don Quixote, "and as for the road that we are to follow, leave that to me."

"I will tell you, then," continued Sancho, "that in a village of Estremadura there lived a certain goat shepherd—I mean, one who tended goats—and this shepherd or goatherd of my story was named Lope Ruiz; and this Lope Ruiz was in love with a shepherd lass whose name was Torralba, which shepherd lass called Torralba was the daughter of a wealthy cattle-raiser, and this wealthy cattle-raiser—"

"If that is the way you are going to tell your story, Sancho, saying everything over twice, you will not be finished in a couple of days. Tell it in a straightforward manner, like a man of good sense, or otherwise do not tell it at all."

"In my country," said Sancho, "they tell all fables just the way I am telling this one, and I cannot tell it any other way, nor is it right for your Grace to ask me to adopt new customs."

"As you like, then," said Don Quixote, "and since fate has willed that I must listen, proceed with it."

"And so, then, my dear master, as I was saying, this shepherd was in love with Torralba, the shepherd lass, who was sturdy of figure, wild in her ways, and somewhat mannish— I can see yet those little mustaches of hers."

"You knew her, then?" asked Don Quixote.

"I did not know her, but the one who told me the story described her for me so truly and faithfully that, when I go to tell it to another, I could swear and affirm that I have seen her with my own eyes. And so, as days and days went by, the devil, who never sleeps but sweeps everything up into his pile, saw to it that the shepherd's love for the shepherd lass turned into hatred and ill will. The reason for this, according to the gossiping tongues, was that she had given him certain grounds for jealousy, which crossed the line and reached forbidden territory. And as a result of all this, the shepherd hated her from then on, so much, that in order not to have to see her again, he made up his mind to leave his native land and go where his eyes would never behold her. Finding herself thus spurned, La Torralba, who had never loved him before, became enamored of him."

"That is the way with women," said Don Quixote; "they spurn those that care for them and love those that hate them. But go on, Sancho."

"The shepherd then proceeded to do as he had resolved; and, getting together his goats, he set out through the countryside of Estremadura on his way to the kingdom of Portugal. Learning of this, La Torralba set out after him, following him, barefoot, from afar, a shepherd's staff in her hand and a knapsack around her neck, in which, so it is said, she carried a broken mirror, a piece of a comb, and some kind of paint or other for her face; but whatever it was she carried, I am not going to take the trouble to find out. I will merely tell you that the shepherd with his flock had by this time crossed the Guadiana River, which in that season was swollen and almost out of its banks; and at the point where he was, there was neither boat nor bark to be had, nor anyone to ferry him and his goats to the other side; all of which grieved him sorely, for he could now see La Torralba close on his heels and knew that she would be bound to annoy him greatly with her tears and pleas.

"As he was looking about, he saw a fisherman alongside a boat so small that it would hold only one person and a goat, but, nevertheless, he spoke to the man, who agreed to take the shepherd and his flock of three hundred to the opposite bank. The fisherman would climb into the boat and row one of the animals across and then return for another, and he kept this up, rowing across with a goat and coming back, rowing across and coming back— Your Grace must be sure to keep count of the goats that the fisherman rowed across the stream, for if a single one of them escapes your memory, the story is ended and it will not be possible to tell another word of it.

"I will go on, then, and tell you that the landing place on the other side was full of mud and slippery, and it took the fisherman a good while to make the trip each time; but in spite of that, he came back for another goat, and another, and another—"

"Just say he rowed them all across," said Don Quixote; "you need not be coming and going in that manner, or it will take you a year to get them all on the other side."

"How many have gone across up to now?" Sancho demanded.

"How the devil should I know?" replied Don Quixote.

"There, what did I tell you? You should have kept better count. Well, then, by God, the story's ended, for there is no going on with it."

"How can that be?" said the knight. "Is it so essential to know the exact number of goats that if I lose count of one of them you cannot tell the rest of the tale?"

"No, sir, I cannot by any means," said Sancho; "for when I asked your Grace to tell me how many goats had been rowed across and you replied that you did not know, at that very instant everything that I was about to say slipped my memory; and you may take my word for it, it was very good and you would have liked it."

"So," said Don Quixote, "the story is ended, is it?"

"As much ended as my own mother is," Sancho replied.

"Well, then," said Don Quixote, "I can assure you that you have told me one of the most novel fables, stories, or histories that anyone in the world could possibly conceive.[6] And I may add that such a way of telling and ending it has never been nor will be heard of in the course of a lifetime; although I expected nothing else from one with a wit like yours. However, I do not marvel at it, for it is possible that those ceaseless blows we hear have disturbed your understanding."

"Anything may be," said Sancho; "but in the matter of my story, I know that there is nothing more to be told, for it ends where you begin to lose count of the number of goats that have crossed."

"Let it end where it will, and well and good. But come, let us see if Rocinante can carry me now." With this, he applied the spurs once more, and the hack once again gave a start, but without budging from the spot, so well was he shackled.

At this juncture, whether it was the cool of the morning which was coming on, or something laxative he had eaten at supper, or—which is most likely—merely a necessity of nature, Sancho felt the will and desire to do that which no one else could do for him;[7] but so great was the fear that had lodged in his heart that he did not dare stir by so much as the tip of a fingernail from his master's side. It was, however, out of the question not to satisfy the need he felt; and what he did, accordingly, in order to have a little peace, was to remove his right hand which held the back of the saddle, and with this hand he very adroitly and without making any noise unloosed the slip-knot which alone sustained his breeches, thus letting them drop to the ground, where they lay like fetters about his feet; after which, he lifted his shirt and bared his behind, no small one by any means.

Having done this—and he thought it was all he needed to do in order to be rid of his agonizing cramps—he encountered another difficulty: how was he to vent himself without making some noise or sound? Gritting his teeth and huddling his shoulders, he held his breath as best he could; but despite all these precautions, the poor fellow ended by emitting a little sound quite different from the one that had filled him with such fear.

"What noise was that, Sancho?" said Don Quixote.

"I do not know, sir," he replied. "It must be something new; for adventures and misadventures never come singly."

He then tried his luck again and succeeded so well that, without any more noise or disturbance than the last time, he found himself free of the load that had given him so much discomfort. But Don Quixote's sense of smell was quite as keen as his sense of hearing, and Sancho was so close upon him that the fumes rose in almost a direct line, and so it is not surprising if some of them reached the knight's nostrils, whereupon he came to the aid of his nose by compressing it between two fingers.

"It strikes me, Sancho," he said in a somewhat snuffling tone of voice, "that you are very much frightened."

"That I am," replied his squire, "but how does your Grace happen to notice it, now more than ever?"

"Because you smell now more than ever, and it is not of ambergris."

"That may well be," said Sancho, "but I am not to blame; it is rather your Grace, for keeping me up at such hours and putting me through such unaccustomed paces."

"Retire, if you will, three or four paces from here, my friend," said Don Quixote, without taking his fingers from his nose; "and from now on, see to it that you take better care of your person and show more respect for mine. It is my familiarity with you that has bred this contempt."

"I'll wager," said Sancho, "your Grace thinks I have done something with my person that I ought not to have done."

"It only makes it worse to stir it, friend Sancho," Don Quixote answered him.

In talk such as this master and man spent the rest of the night; and when Sancho saw that morning was near he very cautiously removed the fetters from Rocinante and tied up his breeches. Finding himself free, although he was by no means a mettlesome animal, the hack appeared to be in high spirits and began pawing the earth, since—begging his pardon—he was not capable of leaping and prancing. When he beheld his steed in motion, Don Quixote took it for a good sign, a sign that he should begin that dread adventure.

It was light now and things could be clearly seen, and he discovered that they were in a grove of chestnut trees that cast a very deep shade. He was aware, also, that the sound of blows continued, although he could see no cause for it; and so, without any further delay, he dug his spurs into Rocinante and, turning to Sancho to bid him good-by, commanded him to wait three days at the most, as he had told him before. If at the end of that time he had not returned, his squire would know for a certainty that it had pleased God to have him end his life's span in this perilous undertaking.

Once again he reminded Sancho of the mission which the latter was to fulfill by bearing a message on his master's behalf to the lady Dulcinea. As to pay for his services, Sancho was not to let that worry him, as the knight before leaving home had made out his will in which his squire would find himself recompensed in full for all the wages due him in accordance with the time he had served. If, on the other hand, God should bring him, Don Quixote, safe, sound, and unscathed out of this peril, then his faithful servitor might be more than certain of obtaining that promised island. At hearing these sad words from his good master, Sancho again fell to weeping and resolved not to leave him until the final outcome and end of the business.

These tears and this noble resolve on the part of Sancho Panza are duly recorded by the author of the history, who must have been well bred and at the very least an old Christian.[8] Such a display of sentiment somewhat softened his master's heart. Not that Don Quixote showed any weakness, however; on the contrary, hiding his feelings as well as he could, he rode away in the direction from which the noise of water and the sound of blows appeared to be coming, with Sancho following on foot, leading his ass by the halter as usual, for that beast was his constant companion in good fortune or adversity.

When they had gone quite a way through the dense shade of the chestnut trees, they came out upon a little meadow at the foot of some tall cliffs over which poured a huge stream of water. Down below were a number of rude huts which looked more like ruins than houses, and it was from here that the hammering noise which never ceased was coming. Rocinante was frightened by the din of the waters and the sound of the blows, but Don Quixote quieted him and gradually made his way to where the huts stood, commending himself with all his heart to his lady and begging her favor in this dread enterprise; and as he went, he likewise commended himself to God, praying that He would not forget him. Sancho, meanwhile, never left his master's side but kept stretching his neck as far as he could between Rocinante's legs to see if the thing that had caused him so much fear and suspense was at last visible.

They had gone perhaps a hundred yards farther when, upon turning a corner, they discovered the obvious, unmistakable cause of that horrendous and, for them, terror-inspiring noise that all night long had so bewildered and alarmed them. And that cause was—if, O reader! you will not be too disappointed and disgusted—six fulling hammers which with their alternating strokes produced the clangor that resembled the sound of blows.

When Don Quixote saw what it was, he was speechless and remained as if paralyzed from head to foot. Gazing at him, Sancho saw that his head was on his bosom, as if he were abashed. The knight then glanced at his squire and perceived that his cheeks were puffed with laughter as if about to explode, and in spite of the melancholy that possessed him he in turn could not help laughing at the sight. Thus encouraged, Sancho gave in to his mirth and laughed so hard that he had to hold his sides to keep from bursting. He would stop for a while and then begin all over again, any number of times, laughing as hard as he had at first.

Don Quixote was furious at this, especially when he heard his squire saying, as if to mock him, " 'Sancho, my friend, you may know that I was born by Heaven's will, in this our age of iron, to revive what is known as the Golden Age. I am he for whom are reserved the perils, the great exploits, the valiant deeds . . .' " And he went on repeating all the other things that Don Quixote had said the first time they heard those frightening blows.

At seeing himself thus made sport of, the knight was so exceedingly wroth that he raised his lance and let Sancho have a couple of whacks, which, had they been received upon the head instead of across the shoulders, would have freed Don Quixote from the necessity of paying his wages, unless it had been to his heirs. The jest was becoming serious, and Sancho was afraid things might go further. He was very humble now.

"Calm yourself, your Grace," he said. "In God's name, I was only joking."

"Well, you may be joking, but I am not," said Don Quixote. "Come over here, my merry gentleman, I want to ask you a question. Supposing that, in place of fulling hammers, this had really been another dangerous adventure, did not I display the requisite courage for undertaking and carrying it through? Am I obliged, being a gentleman as I am, to recognize and distinguish sounds and know whether they come from fulling hammers or not? Especially when I may never before have laid eyes on such things, as happens to be the case, whereas you, rude bumpkin that you are, were born and brought up among them. But turn these six hammers into six giants and beard me with them one by one, or with all of them together, and if I do not cause them all to turn up their toes, then you may make as much sport of me as you like."

"I shall do so no more, sir," replied Sancho, "for I admit that I carried the joke a little too far. But tell me, your Grace, now that there is peace between us—and may God in the future bring you out of all adventures as safe and sound as He has brought you out of this one—tell me if it was not truly a laughing matter, and a good story as well, that great fright of ours? For I, at least, was afraid, although I am well aware that your Grace does not know what fear is."

"I do not deny," said Don Quixote, "that what happened to us has its comical aspects; but it is best not to tell the story, for not everyone is wise enough to see the point of the thing."

"Well, at any rate," said Sancho, "your Grace saw the point when you pointed your lance at my head—but it fell on my shoulders, thank God, and thanks also to my quickness in dodging it. But never mind, it will all come out in the wash; [9] and I have heard it said, 'He loves you well who makes you weep.' [10] It is the custom of great lords, after they have scolded a servant, to give him a pair of breeches; although I am sure I do not know what they would give him after a good clubbing, unless they happened to be knights-errant, and then perhaps they would give him a few islands or some kingdoms on *terra firma*." [11]

"The dice may so fall," replied Don Quixote, "that everything you say will come true. But let us overlook the past; for you are shrewd enough to know that the first instinctive movements a man makes are not within his control. Be advised of one thing for the future, however: you are to abstain and refrain from conversing with me so much; for in all the books of chivalry that I have read, and they are infinite in number, I have never heard of any squire talking so much to his master as you do to me. The truth is, I look upon it as a great fault, on your part and on mine: on your part because it shows that you have little respect for me; and on mine because I do not make myself more respected.

"There was, for example, Gandalín, squire to Amadis of Gaul, who was count of Firm Island. I have read of him that he never spoke to his master save with cap in hand, with lowered head and body bent double *more turquesco*.[12] Then, what shall we say of Gasabal, squire to Don

Galaor, who was so very silent that, by way of indicating how excellent a thing such taciturnity on his part was, the author of that history, which is as voluminous as it is veracious, sees fit to mention his name only once?

"From all this that I have told you, Sancho, you are to infer that it is necessary that there be a difference between master and man, lord and servant, a knight and his squire. And so, from now on, we must treat each other with more respect and less bantering; for in whatever way I may become annoyed with you, it will be bad for the pitcher.[13] The favors and benefits that I have promised you will all come in due time; and if they should not, your wages at least are safe as I have told you."

"That is all well and good," said Sancho, "but what I should like to know of your Grace is, if by any chance the time for the granting of favors does not come and it is necessary to think of the wages, how much did the squire of a knight-errant earn in those times, and was it reckoned by months, or by days as in the case of bricklayers?"

"I do not think," said Don Quixote, "that the squires of old received wages, but only favors; and if I have provided a wage for you, in the sealed will which I have left at home, it was in view of what might happen; as yet I do not know how chivalry will work out in these calamitous times in which we live, and I do not wish my soul in the other world to have to suffer on account of trifles; for I may tell you, Sancho, that there is no calling anywhere more dangerous than that of adventurer."

"That is the truth," said Sancho, "seeing that the mere sound of fulling hammers can disturb and agitate the heart of so valiant a knightly adventurer as is your Grace. But you may be sure that from now on I will not open my mouth to make light of what concerns your Grace, but will speak only to honor you as my liege lord and master."

"By so doing," replied Don Quixote, "you will live long upon the face of the earth; for after parents, masters are to be respected as if they were the ones that bore us."

CHAPTER XXI. *Which treats of the high and richly rewarded adventure of Mambrino's helmet, together with other things that happened to our invincible knight.*

AT THIS point it began to rain a little, and Sancho suggested that they enter the fulling mill; but Don Quixote had conceived such a dislike for the place by reason of the offensive joke [1] associated with it that he would not hear of their setting foot inside it; and so, turning to the right, they came out into another road like the one they had traveled the day before.

They had not gone far before Don Quixote sighted a man on horseback wearing something on his head that gleamed like gold, and no sooner had he laid eyes upon him than he said to his squire, "It is my opinion, Sancho, that there is no proverb that is not true; for they are all drawn from experience itself, mother of all the sciences, and especially that saying that runs, 'Where one door closes another opens.' By this I mean to say that if, last night, fortune closed the door on what we were seeking by deceiving us with those fulling hammers, she is now opening another upon a better and more assured adventure, and if I do not embark upon that undertaking the fault will be mine, and I shall not be able to blame it upon those hammers or the darkness of night. I tell you this for the reason that, if I am not mistaken, there comes toward us now one who wears upon his head that helmet of Mambrino concerning which, as you know, I have taken a vow."

"But, your Grace," said Sancho, "mark well what I say and even better what you do; for I should not like to have any more fulling hammers fulling and finishing us off and cudgeling our brains."

"To the devil with the fellow!" exclaimed Don Quixote. "What has the helmet to do with fulling mills?"

"I know nothing about that," replied Sancho, "but upon my word, if I were free to talk as I used to, I could give you such reasons that your Grace would see he was mistaken in what he just said."

"How could I be mistaken in what I said, you unbelieving traitor? Tell me, do you not see that knight coming toward us, mounted on a dappled gray steed and with a golden helmet on his head?"

"What I see and perceive," said Sancho, "is a man upon an ass, a gray ass like mine, with something or other on his head that shines."

"Well," said Don Quixote, "that is Mambrino's helmet. Go off to one side and let me meet him singlehanded; and you shall see me end this adventure without wasting a word in parley, and when it is ended, the helmet which I have so greatly desired shall be mine."

"I will take care to go to one side, right enough," said Sancho; "but—I say again—I only pray God that it may turn out to be marjoram and not fulling hammers." [2]

"I have told you, brother," said Don Quixote, "not to think of mentioning those hammers to me again; and if you do, I vow—I need say no more—that I will full your very soul."

Sancho was silent, for he was afraid that his master would carry out this vow which he had hurled at him like a bowling ball.

The truth concerning that helmet and the horse and horseman that Don Quixote had sighted was this: in these parts there were two villages, one so small that it had neither apothecary nor barber, whereas the other had both; and as a consequence, the barber of the larger village served the smaller one, in which, as it happened, there was a sick man who had need of a blood-letting and another individual who needed to have his beard trimmed; and so the barber was on his way now, carrying with him a brass basin, and as it had started to rain and he did not wish to have his hat spoiled (it was probably a new one), he had placed the basin on his head, and since it was very clean it could be seen glittering half a league away. He was riding on an ass, a gray one as Sancho had remarked, and it was all this that had given Don Quixote the impression of a knight, a dappled steed, and a helmet of gold, for he readily fitted all the things that he saw to his own mad, ill-errant [3] thoughts of chivalry.

As he saw the poor fellow whom he took to be a knight approaching, without pausing for any exchange of words he bore down upon him with lowered lance at the best speed that Rocinante could make, with intent to run him through with his pike. As he drew near, without abating his fury in the least, he cried out, "Defend yourself, vile wretch, or else render to me of your own free will that which is so justly my due!"

The barber who, without any thought or fear of what was about to happen, had seen this apparition descending upon him, now had no other recourse by way of protecting himself from the lance blow than to slide down off his ass's back, and he had no more than touched the earth when he was up and running away across the fields faster than the wind, leaving his basin behind him upon the ground. Don Quixote was content with this, observing that the heathenish fellow had been wise in imitating the beaver, which, when it finds itself hard pressed by the hunters, bites and tears off [4] with its teeth that for which it knows it is being pursued. He commanded Sancho to pick up the helmet for him.

"By God," said the squire, taking it in his hands, "if it isn't a very good basin and worth a piece of eight if it's worth a maravedi."

With this, he handed it to his master, and Don Quixote at once placed it on his head, turning it round and round in search of the visor.

"Undoubtedly," he said when he failed to find one, "the pagan to whose measure this helmet was originally made must have had a very large head. The regrettable part of it is, half of it is missing."

Upon hearing the basin called a helmet, Sancho could not help laughing, but mindful of his master's ire, he stopped short.

"What are you laughing at, Sancho?" said Don Quixote.

"I was just thinking what a big pate that pagan had who owned it, for this helmet looks exactly like a barber's basin."

"Do you know what I think, Sancho? I think that this famous piece of that enchanted helmet must by some strange accident have fallen into the hands of someone who did not know, and was incapable of estimating, its worth, and who, seeing that it was of the purest gold and not realizing what he was doing, must have melted down the other half for what he could get for it, while from the remaining portion he fashioned what appears, as you have said, to be a barber's basin. But be that as it may; I recognize its value, and the transformation that it has undergone makes no difference to me; the first village that we come to where there is a blacksmith, I will have it repaired in such a manner that the helmet which the god of smithies made and forged for the god of battles shall not surpass or even come up to it. In the meanwhile, I will wear it the best way I can, for something is better than nothing at all,[5] especially seeing that it will serve quite well to protect me from stones."

"That is," said Sancho, "providing it is not a stone from a slingshot of the kind they let you have in the battle of the two armies, that time they made the sign of the cross on your Grace's grinders and broke the vial which held that blessed potion that made me vomit up my guts."

"I am not greatly grieved over having lost it," said Don Quixote, "for as you know, Sancho, I have the receipt in my memory."

"So have I," replied Sancho, "but if I ever in all my life make it or try it again, may this be my last hour on earth. What is more, I do not expect to have any occasion to use it, for I mean to see to it with all my five senses that I neither wound anybody nor am wounded by anyone else. As to being tossed in a blanket, I say nothing about that. Troubles of that kind are hard to foresee, and if they come, there is nothing to do but shrug your shoulders, hold your breath, shut your eyes, and let yourself go where luck and the blanket take you."

"You are a bad Christian, Sancho," said his master when he heard this, "for you never forget an injury that once has been done you. You should know that it is characteristic of noble and generous hearts to pay no attention to trifles. You have no lame leg, no fractured rib, no broken head to show for it; so why can you not forget that bit of buffoonery? For when you look at it closely, that is all it was: a jest and a little pastime; for had I not regarded it in that light, I should have returned and, in avenging you, should have wrought more damage than those Greeks did who stole Helen of Troy—who, you may be sure, if she had lived in these times or my Dulcinea had lived in those, would not have been so famed for her beauty as she now is." With this, he breathed a sigh and wafted it heavenward.

"Let it pass for a jest," said Sancho, "seeing that it cannot be avenged in earnest; but I know what jest and earnest mean, and I further know that this joke will never slip from my memory any more than it will from my shoulders. But leaving all that aside, tell me, your Grace, what are we to do with this dappled gray steed that looks like a gray-colored ass, which that fellow Martino [6] whom your Grace just routed has left here? For judging by the way he took to his heels, I don't think he ever means to come back for it; and by my beard, but the gray is a good one!"

"It is not my custom," said Don Quixote, "to despoil those whom I conquer, nor is it in accordance with the usages of knighthood to deprive one's enemy of his steed and leave him to go away on foot, unless it be that the victor has lost his own mount in the fray, in which case it is permitted to take that of the vanquished as something that has been won in lawful warfare. And so, Sancho, leave this horse, or ass, or whatever you choose to call him; for as soon as its master sees that we are gone, he will come back for it."

"God knows I'd like to take it," said Sancho, "or at least exchange it for this one of mine, which does not strike me as being a very good one. Surely the laws of knighthood must be pretty strict if they cannot be stretched far enough to permit you to exchange one ass for another. Could I not at least exchange trappings?"

"I am none too certain as to that," replied Don Quixote; "but being in doubt and until I am better informed, I should say that you might exchange them in case of extreme necessity."

"The necessity," said Sancho, "is so extreme that I could not need them more if they were for my own person."

Having been granted permission to do so, he now effected the *mutatio capparum*,[7] trigging his own beast out in great style, in such a manner as to alter its appearance most advantageously. This being done, they made their lunch on what was left over from the spoils of the sumpter mule, drinking water from the brook where the fulling hammers were but without turning their heads to look at them, for they still could not forget the fright which those distasteful objects had given them.

At length, all anger and melancholy gone, they mounted again and without taking any definite direction, as was the custom of knights-errant, they let Rocinante follow his own will, his master's inclinations and those of the ass falling in behind; for the ass followed wherever the hack led, very sociably and affectionately. Proceeding in this manner, they came back to the highway and continued riding along, leaving everything to chance and with no plan whatsoever.

Finally Sancho spoke up and addressed the knight. "Sir," he said, "would your Grace grant me permission to have a word with you? Ever since you gave me that order to be silent, a number of things in my stomach have gone to rot, and I have one now on the tip of my tongue that I do not want to see wasted."

"Say what you have to say," said Don Quixote, "and be brief about it, for there is no pleasure in listening to long speeches."

"Very well, sir," replied Sancho. "I just wanted to tell you that for some days now I have been thinking how little gain or profit there is in your Grace's going in search of adventures in these wasteland and cross-road places; for even if you come out the victor in the most dangerous of them, there is no one to witness them or know about them, and as a result, nothing will ever be heard of them, which is contrary to what your Grace had in mind and what they deserve. And, accordingly, it seems to me that it would be better—saving, always, your Grace's better judgment—for us to go serve some emperor or other great prince who has some war on his hands and in whose service your Grace would have an opportunity to display the valor of your person, the great feats of which you are capable, and your superior understanding. For when the lord we served beheld all this, being obliged to reward each according to his merits, he could not fail to have your Grace's exploits set down in writing, that they might never be forgotten. Of my own I say nothing, for they do not go beyond the bounds of what is becoming in a squire; although I may say this much: that if it were the custom of knighthood to record squirely achievements, I do not think mine would be left out."

"There is something in what you say, Sancho," replied Don Quixote; "but before we come to that, it is necessary for a knight to roam the world in quest of adventures and, so to speak, serve a period of probation, in order that, having brought a number of those adventures to a successful conclusion, he may win such name and fame as will render him well known for his accomplishments by the time he arrives at the court of some great monarch. He must be so well known that, when he enters the gate of the city, all the young lads will follow and surround him, shouting, 'There goes the Knight of the Sun,' or of the Serpent, or whatever insignia it was under which he performed his feats of valor. 'He,' they will say, 'is the one who overcame singlehanded the giant Brocabruno of the Mighty Strength; he it was who freed the Mameluke of Persia of the spell under which he had been for nearly nine hundred years.'

"Thus from mouth to mouth his fame will spread, until at last, aroused by the tumult of the lads and the throng that will have gathered, the king of that realm will appear at the windows of his royal palace, and as soon as he sees the knight, recognizing him by his armor or by the device on his shield, he will be certain to cry, 'What, ho! Up, all ye knights that be in my court and go forth to receive the flower of chivalry who cometh hither.' At this command, they will all come out, and the monarch himself, descending the stair halfway, will welcome the new arrival, giving him a warm embrace and a kiss on the cheek, after which he will conduct him to the apartment of my lady the queen, and in her company the knight will be presented to her daughter, who will be one of the most beautiful and faultless damsels to be met with anywhere in the known world. And then it will come to pass that she will rest her eyes on the knight and he will rest his on her, and each will appear to the other as something that is nearer divine than human; and, without knowing how or why it comes about, they will find themselves caught and entangled in love's inextricable net, with a deep pain in their hearts at not being able to put into words their longings and desires.

"After that, they undoubtedly will take him to some room in the palace that is richly fitted out, and there, having relieved him of his armor, they will bring him a sumptuous scarlet cloak to wear; and if he presented a handsome appearance in his suit of armor, he will be even handsomer in a doublet. When night comes, he will sup with the king, queen, and infanta, and he will never take his eyes off the princess but will steal glances at her without the others seeing him, and she with equal cunning will do the same, for, as I have said, she is a very circumspect young lady. And then, when the tables have been cleared, through the door of the great hall there will at once enter a small and ugly dwarf, followed by a beautiful duenna between two giants, who comes to propose a certain adventure [8] conceived by a wise man of very long ago; and whoever carries it through is to be looked upon as the best knight in the world.

"The king will thereupon command all those present to undertake the adventure, and none will bring it to an end and conclusion except the knight who is their guest. This will greatly add to his fame, and the infanta will be very happy and feel well recompensed for having placed her affections upon so exalted a personage. But the best part of it is, this king or prince or whoever he may be is engaged in a bitter war with another monarch who is quite as powerful as he; and the stranger knight —after a few days spent at court—will then beg his royal host's permission to go serve him in the said war. His Majesty will grant this request with right good grace, and the knight will courteously kiss the king's hand in return for the favor shown him.

"That night, he will take leave of his lady the infanta through the grating of her chamber overlooking the garden where he has already conversed with her many times, the go-between and confidante in the affair being a maid-in-waiting whom the princess greatly trusts. He will sigh and she will swoon, and the damsel will bring water to revive her. He will be very much distressed at this, for morning is near, and for the sake of his lady's honor he would not have them discovered. Finally the infanta will come to herself and will hold out her white hands through the bars to her knight, who will kiss them thousands upon thousands of times, bathing them with his tears.

"It will be arranged between them how they are to keep each other informed as to the good or ill that befalls them, and the princess will entreat him not to remain away any longer than need be. He will give her this promise, with many oaths to bind it, and then he will kiss her hands once more and depart, so deeply moved that he is on the verge of dying. Going to his apartment, he will cast himself down upon his bed, but will be unable to sleep from the pain of parting. In the morning, very early, he will go to bid adieu to the king, queen, and infanta; but after he has paid his respects to the royal pair, he is informed that the princess is indisposed and cannot receive any visitors. The knight will think that she too must be suffering at prospect of their separation, his heart will be transfixed, and it will be all he can do to hide his feelings.

"But the damsel who is the go-between will be there; she will take note of everything and will go to report it all to her mistress, who will receive her with tears. The princess will then tell her maid-in-waiting that one of the things that causes her most sorrow is the fact that she does not know who her knight is, or whether he is of royal lineage or not. The damsel will assure her that so much courtesy, gentleness of bearing, and valor could be displayed only by a grave and royal personage, and with such words as these she will endeavor to assuage her mistress's grief. The princess will then seek to compose herself so as not to make a bad impression upon her parents, and after a couple of days she will appear in public once more.

"Meanwhile, the knight has left for the wars; he conquers the king's enemy, takes many cities, is victorious in many battles, returns to court, meets his lady in the accustomed place, and they agree that he is to ask her father for her hand in payment of his services. The king is unwilling to grant this request, for he does not know who the knight is; but, nevertheless, whether she is carried off or however it happens, she becomes his bride, and her father in the end comes to look upon it as a piece of great good fortune, for he has learned that the knight is the son of the valiant king of some realm or other which I do not think you will find on the map. The king then dies, the infanta inherits the throne, and, in a couple of words, the knight becomes king.[9]

"And here is where the bestowal of favors comes in, as he rewards his squire and all those who have assisted him in rising to so exalted a state. He marries the squire to one of the infanta's damsels, undoubtedly the one who was the go-between in his courting of the princess, and who is the daughter of a very great duke."

"That's what I want, and no mistake about it," said Sancho. "That is what I'm waiting for. All of this, word for word, is bound to happen to your Grace now that you bear the title Knight of the Mournful Countenance."

"Do not doubt it, Sancho," Don Quixote assured him; "for in this very manner and by these very steps of which I have told you, many come, and have come, to be kings and emperors. It only remains to find out what king of the Christians or the pagans is at war and has a beautiful daughter. But there will be time to think of all that; for, as I have said, one must achieve fame elsewhere before repairing to court. There is one other thing: supposing that I find a king with a war and with a beautiful daughter, and supposing that I have won an incredible amount of fame throughout the universe, I do not know how I am going to make myself out to be of royal line or even second cousin to an emperor; for the king will not wish to give me his daughter's hand unless he is first thoroughly satisfied on this point, however much my deeds may merit the honor; and for this reason I fear losing that which my good right arm has so well earned for me. It is true that I am a gentleman property-holder with a country house and estate, and am entitled to an income of five hundred sueldos; [10] and it may further be that the learned scribe who writes my history will so clear up my relationships and ancestry that I shall be found to be the descendant, fifth or sixth in line, of some king.

"For I would have you know, Sancho," he went on, "that there are in this world two kinds of ancestral lines. In the one case, there are those who trace their descent from princes and monarchs whom time has little by little reduced until they come to end in a point like a pyramid upside down; and in the other case, there are those who spring from the lower classes and who go upward, one step after another, until they come to be great lords; the difference being that the former were what they no longer are, while the latter are what they formerly were not. And I may be one of those who, after it has been ascertained that they are of great and famous origin, are accepted for what they are, and the king, my father-in-law, in that case will be content; but should he not be, the infanta will love me so much that, in spite of her father's wishes and even though she definitely knows me to be a water carrier's son, she still will insist upon my being received as a gentleman and her consort. And if everything else fails, then it will come to my abducting and carrying her off wherever I see fit; for time or death must eventually put an end to her parents' wrath."

"It comes to something else as well," said Sancho. "For I am reminded here of what certain wicked ones say: 'Never beg as a favor what you can take by force'; although they might better say: 'An escape from the slaughter is worth more than good men's prayers.' [11] I tell you this because if the king, your Grace's father-in-law, will not condescend to give you my lady the infanta, then, as your Grace says, there is nothing for it but to abduct and carry her off. But the trouble is that until you make your peace and come into the tranquil enjoyment of your kingdom, your poor squire can whistle for his favors—that is, unless the damsel who was the go-between and who is to be his wife accompanies the princess and shares her ill fortune with her until Heaven ordains otherwise; for I take it that his master will give her to him at once as his lawful spouse."

"No one can deny him that," said Don Quixote.

"Well, then," replied Sancho, "if that is so, we have nothing to do but to commend ourselves to God and let fortune take whatever course it will."

"May God fulfill my desires and your needs, Sancho," said Don Quixote; "and let him be vile who looks upon himself as such." [12]

"In God's name, so let him be," said Sancho. "I am an old Christian, and that in itself is enough to make me a count." [13]

"Enough and more than enough for you," said Don Quixote; "and even if you were not, it would make no difference; for once I am king, I can very well make a noble of you without any purchase price or service on your part; and in making you a count, I make a gentleman of you at the same time, and then let them say what they will, upon my word they will have to call you 'my lordship' whether they like it or not."

"And I would lend dignity to the tittle!" [14] said Sancho.

"*Title*, you mean to say, not *tittle*," his master corrected him.

"So be it," said Sancho. "I'd know how to behave myself properly; for there was a time in my life when I was the beadle of a confraternity, and the beadle's gown sat so well upon me that everybody said I ought to be the steward. So what will it be when I put a ducal robe on my back or dress myself out in gold and pearls like one of those foreign counts? I think, myself, that folks will be coming to see me for a hundred leagues around."

"You will cut a fine figure," said Don Quixote, "but it will be necessary for you to shave your beard quite often, for it is so thick and unkempt that unless you use the razor on it every other day at the least, people will be able to see what you are at the distance of a musket shot."

"What more have I to do," said Sancho, "than to hire a barber and keep him in the house? If necessary, I can even have him walk behind me like a nobleman's equerry."

"How do you know," asked Don Quixote, "that noblemen have equerries walking behind them?"

"I will tell you about that," Sancho replied. "Years ago I spent a month near the court, and there I saw a very small gentleman who, they told me, was a very great lord. [15] He was out for a stroll, and there was a man on horseback following him at every turn he took just as if he had been his tail. I asked why it was this man did not join the other one but always rode along behind him, and they replied that he was an equerry and that such was the custom of the nobility. I have known it ever since then, for I have never forgotten it."

"You are right," said Don Quixote, "and you may take your barber with you in the same manner; for all customs did not come into use, nor were they invented, at one and the same time; and so you may be the first count to be followed by his barber, for shaving the beard is a more intimate matter than saddling a horse."

"Just leave the barber to me," said Sancho, "while your Grace sees to becoming a king and making a count of me."

"So shall it be," said Don Quixote; and, raising his eyes, he saw something that will be related in the following chapter.

CHAPTER **XXII**. *Of how Don Quixote freed many unfortunate ones who, much against their will, were being taken where they did not wish to go.*

Cid HAMETE BENENGELI, the Arabic and Manchegan [1] author, in the course of this most grave, high-sounding, minute, delightful, and imaginative history, informs us that, following the remarks that were exchanged between Don Quixote de la Mancha and Sancho Panza, his squire, as related at the end of Chapter XXI, the knight looked up and saw coming toward them down the road which they were following a dozen or so men on foot, strung together by their necks like beads on an iron chain and all of them wearing handcuffs. They were accompanied by two men on horseback and two on foot, the former carrying wheel-lock muskets while the other two were armed with swords and javelins.

"That," said Sancho as soon as he saw them, "is a chain of galley slaves, people on their way to the galleys where by order of the king they are forced to labor."

"What do you mean by 'forced'?" asked Don Quixote. "Is it possible that the king uses force on anyone?"

"I did not say that," replied Sancho. "What I did say was that these are folks who have been condemned for their crimes to forced labor in the galleys for his Majesty the King."

"The short of it is," said the knight, "whichever way you put it, these people are being taken there by force and not of their own free will."

"That is the way it is," said Sancho.

"Well, in that case," said his master, "now is the time for me to fulfill the duties of my calling, which is to right wrongs and come to the aid of the wretched."

"But take note, your Grace," said Sancho, "that justice, that is to say, the king himself, is not using any force upon, or doing any wrong to, people like these, but is merely punishing them for the crimes they have committed."

The chain of galley slaves had come up to them by this time, whereupon Don Quixote very courteously requested the guards to inform him of the reason or reasons why they were conducting these people in such a manner as this. One of the men on horseback then replied that the men were prisoners who had been condemned by his Majesty to serve in the galleys, whither they were bound, and that was all there was to be said about it and all that he, Don Quixote, need know.

"Nevertheless," said the latter, "I should like to inquire of each one of them, individually, the cause of his misfortune." And he went on speaking so very politely in an effort to persuade them to tell him what he wanted to know that the other mounted guard finally said, "Although we have here the record and certificate of sentence of each one of these wretches, we have not the time to get them out and read them to you; and so your Grace may come over and ask the prisoners themselves, and they will tell you if they choose, and you may be sure that they will, for these fellows take a delight in their knavish exploits and in boasting of them afterward."

With this permission, even though he would have done so if it had not been granted him, Don Quixote went up to the chain of prisoners and asked the first whom he encountered what sins had brought him to so sorry a plight. The man replied that it was for being a lover that he found himself in that line.

"For that and nothing more?" said Don Quixote. "And do they, then, send lovers to the galleys? If so, I should have been rowing there long ago."

"But it was not the kind of love that your Grace has in mind," the prisoner went on. "I loved a wash basket full of white linen so well and hugged it so tightly that, if they had not taken it away from me by force, I would never of my own choice have let go of it to this very minute. I was caught in the act, there was no need to torture me, the case was soon disposed of, and they supplied me with a hundred lashes across the shoulders and, in addition, a three-year stretch [2] in the *gurapas*, and that's all there is to tell."

"What are *gurapas?*" asked Don Quixote.

"*Gurapas* are the galleys," replied the prisoner. He was a lad of around twenty-four and stated that he was a native of Piedrahita.

The knight then put the same question to a second man, who appeared to be very downcast and melancholy and did not have a word to say. The first man answered for him.

"This one, sir," he said, "is going as a canary—I mean, as a musician and singer."

"How is that?" Don Quixote wanted to know. "Do musicians and singers go to the galleys too?"

"Yes, sir; and there is nothing worse than singing when you're in trouble."

"On the contrary," said Don Quixote, "I have heard it said that he who sings frightens away his sorrows." [3]

"It is just the opposite," said the prisoner; "for he who sings once weeps all his life long."

"I do not understand," said the knight.

One of the guards then explained. "Sir Knight, with this *non sancta* tribe, to sing when you're in trouble means to confess under torture. [4] This sinner was put to the torture and confessed his crime, which was that of being a *cuatrero*, or cattle thief, and as a result of his confession he was condemned to six years in the galleys in addition to two hundred lashes which he took on his shoulders; and so it is he is always downcast and moody, for the other thieves, those back where he came from and the ones here, mistreat, snub, ridicule, and despise him for having confessed and for not having had the courage to deny his guilt. They are in the habit of saying that the word *no* has the same number of letters as the word *sí*, [5] and that a culprit is in luck when his life or death depends on his own tongue and not that of witnesses or upon evidence; and, in my opinion, they are not very far wrong."

"And I," said Don Quixote, "feel the same way about it." He then went on to a third prisoner and repeated his question.

The fellow answered at once, quite unconcernedly. "I'm going to my ladies, the *gurapas,* for five years, for the lack of five ducats."

"I would gladly give twenty," said Don Quixote, "to get you out of this."

"That," said the prisoner, "reminds me of the man in the middle of the ocean who has money and is dying of hunger because there is no place to buy what he needs. I say this for the reason that if I had had, at the right time, those twenty ducats your Grace is now offering me, I'd have greased the notary's quill and freshened up the attorney's wit with them, and I'd now be living in the middle of Zocodover Square in Toledo instead of being here on this highway coupled like a greyhound. But God is great; patience, and that's enough of it."

Don Quixote went on to a fourth prisoner, a venerable-looking old fellow with a white beard that fell over his bosom. When asked how he came to be there, this one began weeping and made no reply, but a fifth comrade spoke up in his behalf.

"This worthy man," he said, "is on his way to the galleys after having made the usual rounds clad in a robe of state and on horseback." [6]

"That means, I take it," said Sancho, "that he has been put to shame in public."

"That is it," said the prisoner, "and the offense for which he is being punished is that of having been an ear broker, or, better, a body broker. By that I mean to say, in short, that the gentleman is a pimp, and besides, he has his points as a sorcerer."

"If that point had not been thrown in," said Don Quixote, "he would not deserve, for merely being a pimp, to have to row in the galleys, but rather should be the general and give orders there. For the office of pimp is not an indifferent one; it is a function to be performed by persons of discretion and is most necessary in a well-ordered state; it is a profession that should be followed only by the wellborn, and there should, moreover, be a supervisor or examiner as in the case of other offices, and the number of practitioners should be fixed by law as is done with brokers on the exchange. In that way many evils would be averted that arise when this office is filled and this calling practiced by stupid folk and those with little sense, such as silly women and pages or mountebanks with few years and less experience to their credit, who, on the most pressing occasions, when it is necessary to use one's wits, let the crumbs freeze between their hand and their mouth [7] and do not know which is their right hand and which is the left.

"I would go on and give reasons why it is fitting to choose carefully those who are to fulfill so necessary a state function, but this is not the place for it. One of these days I will speak of the matter to someone who is able to do something about it. I will say here only that the pain I felt at seeing those white hairs and this venerable countenance in such a plight, and all for his having been a pimp, has been offset for me by the additional information you have given me, to the effect that he is a sorcerer as well; for I am convinced that there are no sorcerers in the world who can move and compel the will, as some simple-minded persons think, but that our will is free and no herb or charm can force it. All that certain foolish women and cunning tricksters do is to compound a few mixtures and poisons with which they deprive men of their senses while pretending that they have the power to make them loved, although, as I have just said, one cannot affect another's will in that manner." [8]

"That is so," said the worthy old man; "but the truth is, sir, I am not guilty on the sorcery charge. As for being a pimp, that is something I cannot deny. I never thought there was any harm in it, however, my only desire being that everyone should enjoy himself and live in peace and quiet, without any quarrels or troubles. But these good intentions on my part cannot prevent me from going where I do not want to go, to a place from which I do not expect to return; for my years are heavy upon me and an affection of the urine that I have will not give me a moment's rest."

With this, he began weeping once more, and Sancho was so touched by it that he took a four-real piece from his bosom and gave it to him as an act of charity.

Don Quixote then went on and asked another what his offense was. The fellow answered him, not with less, but with much more, briskness than the preceding one had shown.

"I am here," he said, "for the reason that I carried a joke too far with a couple of cousins-german of mine and a couple of others who were not mine, and I ended by jesting with all of them to such an extent that the devil [9] himself would never be able to straighten out the relationship. They proved everything on me, there was no one to show me favor, I had no money, I came near swinging for it, they sentenced me to the galleys for six years, and I accepted the sentence as the punishment that was due me. I am young yet, and if I live long enough, everything will come out all right. If, Sir Knight, your Grace has anything with which to aid these poor creatures that you see before you, God will reward you in Heaven, and we here on earth will make it a point to ask God in our prayers to grant you long life and good health, as long and as good as your amiable presence deserves."

This man was dressed as a student, and one of the guards told Don Quixote that he was a great talker and a very fine Latinist.

Back of these came a man around thirty years of age and of very good appearance, except that when he looked at you his eyes were seen to be a little crossed. He was shackled in a different manner from the others, for he dragged behind him a chain so huge that it was wrapped all around his body, with two rings at the throat, one of which was attached to the chain while the other was fastened to what is known as a keep-friend or friend's foot, from which two irons hung down to his waist, ending in handcuffs secured by a heavy padlock in such a manner that he could neither raise his hands to his mouth nor lower his head to reach his hands.

When Don Quixote asked why this man was so much more heavily chained than the others, the guard replied that it was because he had more crimes against him than all the others put together, and he was so bold and cunning that, even though they had him chained like this, they were by no means sure of him but feared that he might escape from them.

"What crimes could he have committed," asked the knight, "if he has merited a punishment no greater than that of being sent to the galleys?"

"He is being sent there for ten years," replied the guard, "and that is equivalent to civil death. I need tell you no more than that this good man is the famous Ginés de Pasamonte, otherwise known as Ginesillo de Parapilla."

"Señor Commissary," spoke up the prisoner at this point, "go easy there and let us not be so free with names and surnames. My just name is Ginés and not Ginesillo; and Pasamonte, not Parapilla as you make it out to be, is my family name. Let each one mind his own affairs and he will have his hands full."

"Speak a little more respectfully, you big thief, you," said the commissary, "unless you want me to make you be quiet in a way you won't like."

"Man goes as God pleases,[10] that is plain to be seen," replied the galley slave, "but someday someone will know whether my name is Ginesillo de Parapilla or not."

"But, you liar, isn't that what they call you?"

"Yes," said Ginés, "they do call me that; but I'll put a stop to it, or else I'll skin their you-know-what. And you, sir, if you have anything to give us, give it and may God go with you, for I am tired of all this prying into other people's lives. If you want to know anything about my life, know that I am Ginés de Pasamonte whose life story has been written down by these fingers that you see here."

"He speaks the truth," said the commissary, "for he has himself written his story, as big as you please, and has left the book in the prison, having pawned it for two hundred reales."

"And I mean to redeem it," said Ginés, "even if it costs me two hundred ducats."

"Is it as good as that?" inquired Don Quixote.

"It is so good," replied Ginés, "that it will cast into the shade *Lazarillo de Tormes* [11] and all others of that sort that have been or will be written. What I would tell you is that it deals with facts, and facts so interesting and amusing that no lies could equal them."

"And what is the title of the book?" asked Don Quixote.

"The Life of Ginés de Pasamonte."

"Is it finished?"

"How could it be finished," said Ginés, "when my life is not finished as yet? What I have written thus far is an account of what happened to me from the time I was born up to the last time that they sent me to the galleys."

"Then you have been there before?"

"In the service of God and the king I was there four years, and I know what the biscuit and the cowhide are like. I don't mind going very much, for there I will have a chance to finish my book. I still have many things to say, and in the Spanish galleys I shall have all the leisure that I need, though I don't need much, since I know by heart what it is I want to write."

"You seem to be a clever fellow," said Don Quixote.

"And an unfortunate one," said Ginés; "for misfortunes always pursue men of genius."

"They pursue rogues," said the commissary.

"I have told you to go easy, Señor Commissary," said Pasamonte, "for their Lordships did not give you that staff in order that you might mistreat us poor devils with it, but they intended that you should guide and conduct us in accordance with his Majesty's command. Otherwise, by the life of— But enough. It may be that someday the stains made in the inn will come out in the wash. Meanwhile, let everyone hold his tongue, behave well, and speak better, and let us be on our way. We've had enough of this foolishness."

At this point the commissary raised his staff as if to let Pasamonte have it in answer to his threats, but Don Quixote placed himself between them

and begged the officer not to abuse the man; for it was not to be wondered at if one who had his hands so bound should be a trifle free with
his tongue. With this, he turned and addressed them all.

"From all that you have told me, my dearest brothers," he said, "one
thing stands out clearly for me, and that is the fact that, even though it
is a punishment for offenses which you have committed, the penalty you
are about to pay is not greatly to your liking and you are going to the
galleys very much against your own will and desire. It may be that the
lack of spirit which one of you displayed under torture, the lack of
money on the part of another, the lack of influential friends, or, finally,
warped judgment on the part of the magistrate, was the thing that led to
your downfall; and, as a result, justice was not done you. All of which
presents itself to my mind in such a fashion that I am at this moment
engaged in trying to persuade and even force myself to show you what
the purpose was for which Heaven sent me into this world, why it was
it led me to adopt the calling of knighthood which I profess and take the
knightly vow to favor the needy and aid those who are oppressed by the
powerful.

"However, knowing as I do that it is not the part of prudence to do
by foul means what can be accomplished by fair ones, I propose to ask
these gentlemen, your guards, and the commissary to be so good as to
unshackle you and permit you to go in peace. There will be no dearth of
others to serve his Majesty under more propitious circumstances; and it
does not appear to me to be just to make slaves of those whom God
created as free men. What is more, gentlemen of the guard, these poor
fellows have committed no offense against you. Up there, each of us will
have to answer for his own sins; for God in Heaven will not fail to
punish the evil and reward the good; and it is not good for self-respecting
men to be executioners of their fellow-men in something that does not
concern them. And so, I ask this of you, gently and quietly, in order
that, if you comply with my request, I shall have reason to thank you;
and if you do not do so of your own accord, then this lance and this
sword and the valor of my arm shall compel you to do it by force."

"A fine lot of foolishness!" exclaimed the commissary. "So he comes
out at last with this nonsense! He would have us let the prisoners of the
king go free, as if we had any authority to do so or he any right to command it! Be on your way, sir, at once; straighten that basin that you
have on your head, and do not go looking for three feet on a cat." [12]

"You," replied Don Quixote, "are the cat and the rat and the rascal!"

And, saying this, he charged the commissary so quickly that the latter had no chance to defend himself but fell to the ground badly wounded by the lance blow. The other guards were astounded by this unexpected occurrence; but, recovering their self-possession, those on horseback drew their swords,[18] those on foot leveled their javelins, and all bore down on Don Quixote, who stood waiting for them very calmly. Things undoubtedly would have gone badly for him if the galley slaves, seeing an opportunity to gain their freedom, had not succeeded in breaking the chain that linked them together. Such was the confusion that the guards, now running to fall upon the prisoners and now attacking Don Quixote, who in turn was attacking them, accomplished nothing that was of any use.

Sancho for his part aided Ginés de Pasamonte to free himself, and that individual was the first to drop his chains and leap out onto the field, where, attacking the fallen commissary, he took away that officer's sword and musket; and as he stood there, aiming first at one and then at another, though without firing, the plain was soon cleared of guards, for they had taken to their heels, fleeing at once Pasamonte's weapon and the stones which the galley slaves, freed now, were hurling at them. Sancho, meanwhile, was very much disturbed over this unfortunate event, as he felt sure that the fugitives would report the matter to the Holy Brotherhood, which, to the ringing of the alarm bell, would come out to search for the guilty parties. He said as much to his master, telling him that they should leave at once and go into hiding in the near-by mountains.

"That is all very well," said Don Quixote, "but I know what had best be done now." He then summoned all the prisoners, who, running riot, had by this time despoiled the commissary of everything that he had, down to his skin, and as they gathered around to hear what he had to say, he addressed them as follows:

"It is fitting that those who are wellborn should give thanks for the benefits they have received, and one of the sins with which God is most offended is that of ingratitude. I say this, gentlemen, for the reason that you have seen and had manifest proof of what you owe to me; and now that you are free of the yoke which I have removed from about your necks, it is my will and desire that you should set out and proceed to the city of El Toboso and there present yourselves before the lady Dulcinea del Toboso and say to her that her champion, the Knight of the Mournful Countenance, has sent you; and then you will relate to her, point by point, the whole of this famous adventure which has won you your longed-for freedom. Having done that, you may go where you like, and may good luck go with you."

To this Ginés de Pasamonte replied in behalf of all of them, "It is absolutely impossible, your Grace, our liberator, for us to do what you have commanded. We cannot go down the highway all together but must separate and go singly, each in his own direction, endeavoring to hide ourselves in the bowels of the earth in order not to be found by the Holy Brotherhood, which undoubtedly will come out to search for us. What your Grace can do, and it is right that you should do so, is to change this service and toll that you require of us in connection with the lady Dulcinea del Toboso into a certain number of Credos and Hail Marys which we will say for your Grace's intention, as this is something that can be accomplished by day or night, fleeing or resting, in peace or in war. To imagine, on the other hand, that we are going to return to the fleshpots of Egypt, by which I mean, take up our chains again by setting out along the highway for El Toboso, is to believe that it is night now instead of ten o'clock in the morning and is to ask of us something that is the same as asking pears of the elm tree." [14]

"Then by all that's holy!" exclaimed Don Quixote, whose wrath was now aroused, "you, Don Son of a Whore, Don Ginesillo de Parapilla, or whatever your name is, you shall go alone, your tail between your legs and the whole chain on your back."

Pasamonte, who was by no means a long-suffering individual, was by this time convinced that Don Quixote was not quite right in the head, seeing that he had been guilty of such a folly as that of desiring to free them; and so, when he heard himself insulted in this manner, he merely gave the wink to his companions and, going off to one side, began raining so many stones upon the knight that the latter was wholly unable to protect himself with his buckler, while poor Rocinante paid no more attention to the spur than if he had been made of brass. As for Sancho, he took refuge behind his donkey as a protection against the cloud and shower of rocks that was falling on both of them, but Don Quixote was not able to shield himself so well, and there is no telling how many struck his body, with such force as to unhorse and bring him to the ground.

No sooner had he fallen than the student was upon him. Seizing the basin from the knight's head, he struck him three or four blows with it across the shoulders and banged it against the ground an equal number of times until it was fairly shattered to bits. They then stripped Don Quixote of the doublet which he wore over his armor, and would have taken his hose as well, if his greaves had not prevented them from doing so, and made off with Sancho's greatcoat, leaving him naked; after which, dividing the rest of the battle spoils amongst themselves, each of them went his own way, being a good deal more concerned with eluding the dreaded Holy Brotherhood than they were with burdening themselves with a chain or going to present themselves before the lady Dulcinea del Toboso.

They were left alone now—the ass and Rocinante, Sancho and Don Quixote: the ass, crestfallen and pensive, wagging its ears now and then, being under the impression that the hurricane of stones that had raged about them was not yet over; Rocinante, stretched alongside his master, for the hack also had been felled by a stone; Sancho, naked and fearful of the Holy Brotherhood; and Don Quixote, making wry faces at seeing himself so mishandled by those to whom he had done so much good.

CHAPTER XXIII. *Of what happened to the famous Don Quixote in the Sierra Morena, which is one of the rarest adventures related in this true history.*

SEEING himself so mistreated, Don Quixote remarked to his squire, "Always, Sancho, I have heard it said that to do good to boors is to pour water into the sea.[1] Had I believed what you told me, this would not have happened; but it is done now. Patience, and let us be warned from now on."

"If your Grace takes warning," said Sancho, "then I am a Turk; but since you say that all this might have been avoided if you had believed me, why not believe me now and so avoid a worse misfortune? For I must inform you that the Holy Brotherhood does not observe the customs of chivalry; they would not give a couple of maravedis for all the knights-errant that there are—do you know, I think I can already hear their arrows whizzing past my ears."

"You, Sancho," said Don Quixote, "are a natural-born coward; but in order that you may not be able to say that I am obstinate and never

do what you advise, for this once I am going to take your advice and
withdraw to a place where that fury you so dread cannot reach us. Upon
one condition, however: you are never, in life or in death, to say to anyone that I retired and withdrew from this danger out of fear, but only
by way of yielding to your entreaties. If you say anything else, you will
be lying, and from now until then and from then until now I shall give
you the lie, and say that you lie and will lie, every time that you think or
say anything of the sort. Give me no further words; for at the very
thought that I am withdrawing and retiring from some danger, and especially from this present one, which, I admit, does carry with it the
shadow of fear—at the very thought of such a thing, I am all for remaining here and waiting alone, not only for that terrible Holy Brotherhood
of which you are all the time talking, but for the twelve tribes of Israel
and the seven Maccabees and for Castor and Pollux and all the brothers
and brotherhoods that there are in this world."

"Sir," replied Sancho, "to retire is not to flee, nor would remaining here
be an act of prudence on your part. Where danger outweighs hope, wise
men save themselves for the morrow and do not venture all upon a single
day. For you may know that, although I am but an ignorant countryman,
I have a little of what they call good sense. And so, do not repent of having taken my advice, but mount Rocinante if you can, and if you cannot
I will help you, and then follow me. My noodle tells me that we have
more need of feet than we do of hands just now."

Without another word Don Quixote mounted his hack, and with
Sancho leading the way upon his donkey they set out in the direction of
the near-by Sierra Morena, it being Sancho's intention to cross the range
and come out at El Viso or Almodóvar del Campo, where they would
hide for a few days among the crags, in case the Brotherhood came looking for them. He was encouraged in this purpose when he discovered
that the stock of provisions they carried with them upon the ass's back
had emerged safely from the fray with the galley slaves, and this he
looked upon as little less than a miracle in view of the manner in which
they had pillaged and plundered everything else.

[By the time darkness fell [2] they had reached the heart of the highlands,
where Sancho thought it would be a good thing for them to spend the
night and a few days as well, at least as long as their supplies held out.
And so they came to a halt in a dense cork-tree grove between two cliffs;
and it was then that fate took a hand, fate which, according to those who
are not enlightened by the true gospel, directs everything. Fate now

directed and arranged things after its own fashion by ordaining that
Ginés de Pasamonte, the famous rogue and thief who had been freed from
his chains by Don Quixote's mad but kindly whim, should come their
way again. Dreading the Holy Brotherhood, which he had good reason to
fear, Pasamonte, also, had decided to hide out in these mountains, and fate
and his fear brought him to the very same part of the highlands where the
knight and Sancho Panza were.

Arriving while it was light enough to recognize them, he let them fall
asleep; for as evildoers are always ungrateful, necessity prompting them
to misdeeds and with present advantage outweighing future gains, Ginés,
who was neither grateful nor well intentioned, had made up his mind to
steal Sancho Panza's ass, not caring to bother with Rocinante since the
hack could neither be pawned nor sold with profit. Accordingly, while
Sancho slept, he drove the beast off, and by the time daylight came was
too far away to be found.

The dawn brought cheer to the earth but sadness to the heart of Sancho
Panza, who, when he discovered that his gray ass was missing, began
weeping so plaintively that Don Quixote was awakened by the sound.

"O son of my loins, born in my very house," he heard his squire ex-
claiming. "My children's playmate, joy of my wife, envy of my neighbors, solace in my cares, and, finally, half-supporter of my person, since
the twenty-six maravedis that you earned each day met half of my expenses!"

Hearing the weeping and learning the cause, the knight did what he
could to console Sancho. Begging him to be patient, he promised to give
him a letter directing that three out of five ass-colts [3] that he had at home
be turned over to his squire to make up for the loss. Sancho was consoled
by this and, drying his tears and repressing his sobs, thanked his master
for this favor.]

Upon entering the mountains, Don Quixote felt glad at heart, for it
seemed to him that this was a place admirably adapted to the adventures
that he sought. It brought back to mind all the marvelous things which in
similar solitudes, amid surroundings such as these, had happened to
knights-errant of old, and he became so lost in thought and carried away
by his imaginings that he paid no heed to anything else. Nor did Sancho
have any other care—now that it seemed to him they were safe from
harm—than that of satisying his stomach with what remained of the
clerical spoils; and so he came behind his master with all that the ass
carried,[4] emptying the bag and stuffing his paunch at the same time, and

he would not have given a penny for another adventure while he could go along like that.

Glancing up and perceiving that the knight, having come to a halt, was endeavoring to lift with the tip of his lance some bulky object that lay on the ground, he at once hastened to offer his assistance in case it should be needed. He arrived at Don Quixote's side just as the latter was raising the object in question, which proved to be a saddle pad with a valise attached to it, both of them half or wholly rotten and falling to pieces. They weighed so much, however, that it was necessary for Sancho to dismount and take them in his hands. The knight then told him to see what was in the valise. Although it was secured by a chain and padlock, it had so rotted away that its contents were visible through the rents in the side, which revealed four fine cambric shirts and a number of other curious articles made of linen and all very clean, while wrapped in a handkerchief was a small pile of gold crowns.

"Thank Heaven," cried Sancho, "for providing us at last with a profitable adventure!" Looking further, he came upon a memorandum book, richly bound. Don Quixote asked to have this but told his squire to keep the money for himself. Out of gratitude for this favor, Sancho kissed his master's hand; after which he removed the linen and stored it away in the bag with the provisions.

"Do you know, Sancho," said Don Quixote, "it is my opinion—and it cannot be otherwise—that some traveler must have lost his way in these mountains and been set upon by robbers, who must have slain him and then brought his body to this isolated spot to bury it."

"It can't be that," said Sancho, "for if they had been robbers, they would not have left this money behind them."

"That is true," agreed Don Quixote; "and in that case I am sure I cannot guess, nor have I any idea, what all this may mean. But wait a moment. Let us see if in this little memorandum book there may not be something written down that will enable us to make out what we wish to know."

He opened the book and the first thing he found in the way of writing was the rough draft of a sonnet, in a very good hand; and in order that Sancho might hear it, he read it aloud:

> *"Either Love, 'twould seem, lacks sensibility,*
> *Or else 'tis over-cruel, or my poor heart*
> *Is all unequal to its painful part,*
> *Condemned to the direst torment there can be.*
> *If Love is God, why, it is certain He*

> *Knows all—that takes no casuistic art—*
> *And He's not cruel. Where, then, does my grief start,*
> *That grief I cherish so persistently?*
> *To say that it is thou, Phyllis, were wrong;*
> *So much of good and ill cannot abide*
> *In the same body, nor is Heaven to blame.*
> *One thing I know: I am not here for long;*
> *He's a sick man indeed cannot decide*
> *The Nature of his ill or whence it came."*

"There is nothing much to be learned from that ballad," said Sancho, "unless this thread leads to the yarn-ball of the whole matter." [5]

"What thread is that?" asked Don Quixote.

"I thought," said Sancho, "that your Grace said *hilo*." [6]

"No, I did not say *hilo*, but *Fili*," [7] replied Don Quixote. "That is undoubtedly the name of the lady to whom this author addresses his lament; and, upon my word, he must be a very fair poet or else I know nothing about the art." [8]

"So," said Sancho, "your Grace knows something of ballad-making too?"

"More than you think," said Don Quixote. "You will see that I do when you carry a letter, written in verse from beginning to end, to my lady Dulcinea del Toboso. For you must know, Sancho, that all or nearly all knights-errant in ages past were great troubadours and musicians, both these accomplishments, or, better, graces, being characteristic of love-lorn and wandering men of arms, though I must admit that the verses of those knights of old indicate more spirit than rhyming ability."

"Read on, your Grace, until you find something that will throw some light on this matter."

"This," said Don Quixote, turning a page, "is prose and appears to be a letter."

"A regular letter?" asked Sancho.

"The beginning seems to be all about love."

"Well, then, read it aloud, your Grace, for I am very fond of love stories."

"With pleasure," said Don Quixote; and he read the following:

"*Your false promise and my certain misfortune are taking me to a place whence will come to your ears the news of my death. You have rejected me, O ungrateful creature! for one who has more but is not worth more than I. If virtue were esteemed wealth, I should not envy the fortune of others nor weep for my own. That which your beauty raised up your deeds have laid low. By reason of the former I believed you to be an angel, and by reason of the latter I know you to be a woman. Be at peace, you who have sent me to war, and may Heaven grant that the deceits of your husband remain ever hidden, that you may not repent of what you have done, and I take a vengeance that I do not desire.*

"This," said Don Quixote, as he finished reading the letter, "throws even less light on the subject than do the verses, beyond the fact that the one who wrote it was a rejected lover."

Leafing nearly all the way through the little book, he came upon other verses and letters, some of which he was able to read while others he could not. They were filled, all of them, with complaints, laments, misgivings, expressions of joy and sadness, talk of favors granted and a suit rejected. Some were exalted in tone, others mournful. While Don Quixote was going through the book, Sancho was doing the same with the valise; there was not a corner of it, or of the saddle pad, that he did not search, scrutinize, and pry into, not a seam that he did not rip out, not a tuft of wool that he did not unravel, being determined to let nothing escape him from want of care and proper pains, so great was the covetousness that had been awakened in him by the crowns he had discovered, a hundred or more of them all told. And although he found nothing more, he still felt that the tossings in the blanket, the potion that he had drunk, the benediction of the stakes, the mule driver's punches, the loss of his saddlebags, the theft of his greatcoat,[9] and all the hunger, thirst, and weariness that he had known in his good master's service, had been amply repaid by the finding of this treasure.

The Knight of the Mournful Countenance was extremely desirous of knowing who the owner of the valise was; for from the sonnet and the letter, the gold coins and the shirts of such good quality, he conjectured that this must be an important personage, very much in love, who had been led by the disdain his lady showed him and the ill treatment received at her hands to commit some desperate act. But seeing that in this rugged, uninhabitable place there was no one who might be able to give him the information that he wanted, his only concern now was to go on, letting Rocinante as usual choose the road to be followed, with the idea in mind always that by so doing he could not fail to meet with some extraordinary adventure there in those wilds.

As he rode along thinking of these things, he caught sight of a man on top of a small mountain facing him who went leaping from cliff to

cliff and one tuft of underbrush to another with great agility. He had
the appearance of being naked or nearly so, with a thick black beard and
long tangled hair, his feet and lower legs bare, while his thighs were
covered with a pair of trousers which seemed to be of tawny-colored
velvet but which were so ragged that in many places the flesh was visible.
He wore nothing on his head, and although his movements, as has been
stated, were extremely swift, the Knight of the Mournful Countenance
had a chance to observe and make note of all the details mentioned. Although he tried to follow the man, he was not able to do so, for Rocinante
was too weak to traverse such rough ground as that, being, moreover, by
nature slow-paced and phlegmatic.

At once Don Quixote conceived the idea that this must be the owner
of the saddle pad and valise, and he made up his mind that he would
hunt him down even if he had to spend a year in these mountains. And
so he directed Sancho to get down off his donkey [10] and look on one side
of the mountain while he would look on the other, until they should meet,
and in this way it might be that they would be able to come upon the
individual who had fled so hastily from in front of their eyes.

"I could not do that," protested Sancho, "for when I leave your Grace's
side fear assaults me with a thousand different kinds of starts and visions.
And let what I am saying serve as a notice, for from now on I do not
intend to stir an inch from your presence."

"So be it," said the Knight of the Mournful Countenance. "I am very
glad that you wish to avail yourself of my courage, for it shall not fail
you even though your soul fails your body. Follow me closely, then, or
as best you can, and make lanterns of your eyes. Let us circle this ridge,
and perhaps we shall meet the one of whom we had a glimpse and who,
undoubtedly, cannot be any other than the owner of that treasure."

"It would be much better," said Sancho, "not to go looking for him; for
if we do find him and the money turns out to be his, I, of course, will
have to give it back to him; but it would be better, without all this fruit-
less search, for me just to keep it until by some other less meddlesome
and prying means we discover who the true owner is. And who knows,
by that time I may have spent it and the king will then cancel the debt
for me."

"You are wrong about that, Sancho," said Don Quixote; "for since
we already have in advance a well-founded suspicion as to who the real
owner is, we are obliged to seek him out and return the money. If we
do not do this, the strong suspicion that we have of his being the owner
renders us as guilty as if he were. And so, Sancho, do not let our search

for him give you any anxiety, for it will relieve mine if we find him."

So saying, he spurred Rocinante and rode off, followed by Sancho on foot and heavily loaded down, thanks to Ginesillo de Pasamonte.[11] When they had rounded a part of the mountain, they came upon a mule, saddled and bridled, lying dead in a brook and half devoured by dogs and jack-daws; all of which confirmed them in the suspicion that the one who had fled them was the owner of the mule and the saddle pad.

As they stood there looking at the mule they heard a whistle, as of a shepherd tending his flock, and immediately thereafter, on their left hand, there appeared a large number of goats. Behind the flock, on top of the mountain, the figure of the goatherd, a very old man, now appeared. Don Quixote called him to come down where they were. He replied by shouting back at them the question as to what had brought them to this one spot which was almost never trodden by any feet but those of goats or wolves and other wild beasts. Sancho answered him, saying that, if he would come down, they would give him an account of everything.

The goatherd did so, and as he approached Don Quixote, he said, "I'll wager that you are looking at that hack mule that lies dead in that hollow. Upon my word, it's been there for six months now. Tell me, did you meet its owner anywhere?"

"We have met no one," replied Don Quixote. "All that we found was a saddle pad and a small valise not far from here."

"I found it too," said the goatherd, "but I never wanted to pick it up or go near it from fear of some bad luck or other, lest they charge me with having stolen it; for the devil is a sly one, and from under a man's feet things rise up to cause him to stumble and fall without knowing how it comes about."

"That is what I say," Sancho told him. "I also found it and I wouldn't come within a stone's throw of it; I left it there, and there it remains just as it was. I don't want a dog with bells." [12]

"Tell me, my good man," said Don Quixote, "do you know who the owner is?"

"All I know," said the old man, "is that six months ago, more or less, there came to a sheepfold which is some three leagues from here a youth of well-bred manners and appearance, mounted upon that same mule that lies dead there and with the same saddle pad and valise which you say you found and did not touch. He inquired of us which part of these highlands was the most rugged and inaccessible, and we told him that it was this part where we are now; which is indeed the truth, for if you go half a league farther in, you will not be able to find your way out. I am wondering how you two ever came here, seeing that there is no road or footpath that leads to this spot. But as I was saying, the youth upon hearing our answer turned about and made for the site that we had pointed out to him, leaving us all well pleased with the impression which he by his appearance had made upon us, while at the same time we were astonished at his question and the haste with which we had seen him turn toward the mountains and ride away.

"We saw no more of him after that until a few days ago, when without saying a word he fell upon one of our shepherds and began beating and kicking him severely, after which he went up to the ass that carried our supplies and took all the bread and cheese that he found there. Having done this, with amazing swiftness he darted back to his mountain hiding place. When some of us goatherds learned of what had happened, we spent nearly two whole days in looking for him through the most densely wooded part of this region, and at last we found him in the hollow of a thick and sturdy cork tree. He came out and greeted us very mildly, his clothing now in rags and his face burned and scarred by the sun to such an extent that we should scarcely have recognized him if his garments, which were familiar to us even though they were in shreds, had not served to convince us that he was the man we sought.

"His greeting was a courteous one. In a few well-chosen words he told us that we should not marvel at seeing him in this condition, for it was by way of fulfilling a certain penance that had been laid upon him for his many sins. We asked him if he would tell us who he was, but we did not succeed in finding out his name. We also requested him, when he was in need of food, which of course he must have, to let us know where we would find him and we would be only too glad to bring it to him; or if he did not care to do this, he should at least come and ask us for it and not take it by force from the shepherds. He thanked us for our offer, begged forgiveness for the assault he had committed, and promised that from then on he would ask for what he wanted in the name of God, without giving offense to anyone.

"As for his place of abode, he assured us that he had none, save such as chance might offer when night overtook him; and he ended by weeping so bitterly that we who heard him must have been made of stone if we had not wept with him, as we compared the way he looked now with that first sight we had had of him. For, as I have said, he was a very pleasant-mannered youth, and his courtesy and agreeable way of speaking showed him to be a person who was wellborn and well reared. Although we were but countryfolk, his polite way of speaking was such that it was not hard for us to grasp his meaning.

"As he was in the middle of his story, he stopped suddenly and fell silent, fixing his eyes upon the ground for a good long while as we stood there in suspense, waiting to see what the outcome of this fit of abstraction would be. We were more than a little sad as we gazed at him. He would sit there for many minutes, staring down at the earth, his eyes wide open and without batting a lash; and again he would close his eyes, compress his lips, and arch his eyebrows, and we were then sure that some kind of madness had come upon him. He soon convinced us that we were right in thinking this. Rising furiously from the ground to which he had fallen, he attacked the first person he encountered so boldly and in such a rage that if we had not pulled him off, he would have slain his victim with blows and bites. And as he did this he kept shouting, 'Ah, false Fernando! Now, now you shall pay for the wrong you have done me! These hands shall tear out your heart, abode and nesting place of every form of evil, but, above all, of fraud and deceit!' He had more to say, and it was all against Fernando, whom he accused of faithlessness and betrayal.

"With considerable difficulty we forced him to release his hold on our companion, and he then, without saying another word, ran off and hid himself among the brambles and the underbrush, so that it would have been impossible to follow him. This led us to surmise that his madness seized him at intervals, and that someone named Fernando must have done him a very great wrong indeed to have brought him to such a pass; all of which later was shown to be the truth, for he has often come up to the shepherds, sometimes to request them to give him something to eat, and at other times to take it from them by force. When the fit is on him, even though they may offer him food of their own free will, he will not accept it but will attack them with his fists and appropriate it; but when he is in his right senses, he politely and with courteous phrases begs it of them in God's name, thanking them profusely and shedding not a few tears.

"The truth is, gentlemen," the goatherd went on, "that only yesterday I and four other lads, two of them my servants and the other two my friends, made up our minds to keep on looking for him until we found him; and we vowed that when we did find him, we would take him, either of his own free will or by force, to the town of Almodóvar, eight leagues from here, and there would have him given a cure, if there be any cure for his disease, or at least we would find out who he is when he is in his right mind and whether or not he has any relatives that we might notify. This, gentlemen, is all that I can tell you in answer to the question you have asked me. You know now that the owner of those belongings is the same one whom you saw running over the mountains so nimbly and so lightly clad." For Don Quixote had told him of having glimpsed the man.

The knight marveled greatly at what he had just heard and was more eager than ever to learn who the poor madman was, being resolved now to carry out his first intention, which was that of seeking for him all over the mountain without leaving a corner or a cave unsearched until he had found him. Fate, however, arranged matters for him better than he could have hoped or expected, for at that very instant the youth whom he sought emerged from a ravine near where they stood and came toward them, muttering something to himself that could not be understood when one was close upon him, much less from a distance. His costume was such as has been described, except that, as he approached, Don Quixote noticed that the ragged doublet he wore was amberscented,[13] which indicated that a person who wore clothes of such quality could not be of the lowest rank.

As the youth came up, he greeted them in a hoarse, discordant voice, but very courteously. Don Quixote returned his salutation no less politely, and, dismounting from Rocinante, he gently and gracefully went over and embraced the young man, holding him tightly in his arms for some little while, as if he had known him for a long time. The Ragged One of the Sickly Countenance, as we may call him—just as Don Quixote is the Knight of the Mournful Countenance—after permitting himself to be embraced, fell back a step or two and laid his hands upon Don Quixote's shoulders as if to see whether or not he knew him; for it may be that he was no less astonished at beholding the knight's face, figure, and suit of armor than the knight was at seeing him. To make a long story short, the first to speak was the Ragged One, and what he had to say will be set forth in the following pages.

CHAPTER XXIV. *In which is continued the adventure of the Sierra Morena.*

THE history tells us that Don Quixote listened to the Knight of the Mountain most attentively.

"Although I do not know you, sir," the latter went on, "I certainly thank you for the courtesy that you have shown me, and I only wish that I were in a position to repay with something more than good will the kind reception you have accorded me, but fate has given me nothing with which I might suitably requite your favors except the desire to do so."

"My own desire," said Don Quixote, "is to be of service to you, and it was for this reason that I resolved not to leave these highlands until I had found you and learned from your own lips if any remedy was to be found for the sorrow that, from the strange way of life you lead, appears to beset you. I accordingly had meant to leave no stone unturned in searching for you, had a search been necessary. Even though your misfortune might be of that kind that closes the door on any sort of consolation, I would, I thought, weep with you and share your grief in so far as I could. For when one is in trouble, it is consoling to find some person who can feel with one the weight of one's misfortunes.

"But if my good intentions do deserve to be repaid with any of that courtesy that I see you possess in so high a degree, I would beg you, sir, by all in this life that you love or have loved, to tell me who you are and what it is that has brought you to live and die like a brute beast amid these solitudes, for your person and your bearing show that the life you now lead is one that is alien to you. And I further swear, by the order of knighthood which I, though unworthy and a sinner, have received, and by my profession of knight-errant, that if you accede to my request, I will serve you in accordance with those obligations that I have assumed, either by helping you if there is any help to be had, or by weeping with you as I have promised."

The Knight of the Wood, upon hearing the Knight of the Mournful Countenance speak in this manner, could only stare at him long and hard, surveying him from head to foot, and it was not until after he had studied him intently that he replied.

"If you have anything that you can give me to eat," he said, "for the love of God, let me have it, for I have had nothing since yesterday. Give me food, and I will do all that you command, out of gratitude for your good intentions toward me."

Sancho then brought out from his bag, and the shepherd from his pouch, sufficient food to satisfy the Ragged One's hunger. The man ate like one who is stupefied, with no time between mouthfuls, gulping down the victuals rather than swallowing them. Meanwhile, the others watched him, saying nothing. When he had finished, he made signs for them to follow him, which they did. He then led them around the corner of a cliff to a little plot of green not far from there and dropped down upon the grass. The others did the same, and not a word was spoken by any of them until the Ragged One had settled himself to his liking.

"If, gentlemen," he said to them then, "you would like me to tell you briefly how enormous the misfortunes are that I have suffered, you must promise me that you will not interrupt with questions, or in any other manner, the thread of my mournful tale, for the moment you do so it will come to an end."

This remark reminded Don Quixote of the story his squire had told him, when the knight had been unable to remember the number of goats that had crossed the river and the tale had been left hanging in the air. But to come back to the Ragged One—

"If I make this stipulation," the latter continued, "it is for the reason that I desire to relate my misfortunes as briefly as I can, since the telling of them serves only to bring me fresh sorrows; and so, the fewer questions you ask of me the sooner I shall be done, it being understood, of course, that I shall leave out nothing of importance such as you might wish to know."

Don Quixote promised in the name of the others, and with this assurance, the Ragged One began.

"My name is Cardenio, my birthplace one of the finest cities in this province of Andalusia,[1] my lineage noble, my parents rich, my misfortune so great that my kin must have wept and grieved over it, without being able to alleviate it with their wealth; for when it comes to remedying the ills that Heaven sends us, the gifts of fortune are of little avail. In that same country there lived one who was Heaven to me, a Heaven that held all the glory I could desire. Such was the beauty of Luscinda, a damsel noble and rich as I, but more fortunate and with less constancy than was due to such a passion as mine. From my first and tenderest years I had loved, longed for, and adored this Luscinda, and she had cared for me with her simple, innocent, childlike heart. Our parents knew how we felt toward each other and were not disturbed, for they saw that later on our youthful affection must surely lead to marriage, a thing that was altogether fitting in view of the fact that our wealth and lineage were so evenly matched. As we grew older our love grew to such an extent that Luscinda's father felt obliged, out of respect for the conventions, to forbid me his house, thus imitating the example set him by the parents of that Thisbe so celebrated by the poets.

"This denial merely added flame to flame and desire to desire; for even though tongues may be silenced, pens cannot be, and the latter with more freedom than the former can make known to a loved one that which is locked in the heart, since very often the presence of the loved object disturbs the firmest resolution and ties the boldest tongue. Ah, good Heaven, how many letters I wrote her! How many charmingly modest answers did I receive! How many love verses did I compose in which my heart declared and translated its feelings, painted its kindled desires, feasted on its memories, and re-created its passion. In short, seeing myself wasting away like that, my soul consumed with longing to behold her, I determined to go through with what appeared to me to be the best plan for winning the prize that I coveted and deserved: I would ask her father for her hand in lawful wedlock; and this I did. He replied, thanking me for the honor I had shown him by telling him that I should feel honored in receiving such a treasure from him; but he added that, inasmuch as my own father was still alive, it was only right that he and not I should make this request, and if it was not my father's will and pleasure, then Luscinda was not a woman to be taken or given by stealth.

"I thanked him for his kindness, for it seemed to me that he was right, and I felt sure, as I have said, that my father would give his consent. I accordingly lost no time in going to my parent to make my wishes known to him. When I entered the room where he was, I found him with an open letter in his hand, and before I could say a word he began addressing me. 'From this letter, Cardenio,' he said, 'you will see how ready the Duke Ricardo is to do you a favor.' Now, this Duke Ricardo, as you gentlemen should know, is a Grandee of Spain whose estate lies in the best part of this province of Andalusia. I took the letter and read it, and the offer contained in it was so flattering a one that I myself felt my father would have done wrong in not accepting it; for the duke proposed that I should be sent to be the companion, not the servant, of his eldest son, agreeing to see to it that I should be provided for in accordance with that esteem in which he held me. I read the epistle and was silent, especially when I heard my father saying, 'You will be leaving in two days, Cardenio, to do as the duke desires; and I thank God that the way is now being opened for you to attain that which I know should be yours by merit.' To which he added other words of fatherly advice.

"As the time for my departure drew near, I spoke to Luscinda one night and told her all that had happened, and I also had a word with her father, begging him to wait a few days and not dispose of her hand until I could find out what Duke Ricardo wished of me. He promised, and she confirmed it with a thousand oaths and swoons. I then went to the duke's place and was so well received and treated that envy at once began to do its work, the old servants feeling that their master's eagerness to do me favors was to their own detriment. But the one who was most delighted by my arrival was the duke's second son, named Fernando, a gallant lad of gentle breeding, generous and loving by nature, who within a short while became so great a friend of mine that everyone was talking about it. Although the eldest son liked me well enough and was very kind to me, he did not treat me with the extreme show of affection that Fernando did.

"Between friends there is no secret that is not shared, and as my intimacy with Fernando grew into friendship, he told me all that was on his mind, one of his special confidences having to do with a love affair that was giving him some concern. He was enamored of a peasant lass, one of his father's vassals, whose parents were very rich and who was so beautiful, modest, virtuous, and discreet that none could say in which of these virtues she excelled or which outweighed the others. These good qualities on the part of the girl raised Fernando's desires to such a pitch that in order to possess her he determined to give her his word to marry her, since it was impossible to get what he wanted in any other way. I as his friend felt obliged to restrain and dissuade him from doing this, with the best arguments and most striking examples that I could find; and when I saw that my efforts were in vain, I decided to lay the matter before Duke Ricardo, his father.

"Don Fernando, however, being very clever and astute, feared and dreaded this, knowing that as a good servant I was bound to keep nothing hidden that might be prejudicial to the honor of my lord the duke; and, accordingly, by way of distracting and deceiving me, he told me that he could think of no better means of forgetting the beauty that so enslaved him than to absent himself for a few months, and he suggested that the two of us go to my father's house, under the pretext, which he would give to the duke, that he wished to buy a few of the very fine horses that are to be found in my city, which produces the best in the world.

"Upon hearing him say this I was pleased, since even if his resolve had not been so good a one, I still should have looked upon it as one of the most praiseworthy that could be conceived, inasmuch as it would provide me with a fine occasion and opportunity to see my Luscinda once again. With this thought in mind and animated by my own amorous desires, I approved his judgment and urged him to go through with the plan, telling him that he should set about it as soon as possible and assuring him that absence had its effect in spite of the firmest of attachments. But at the very time he told me this story, as I afterward learned, he had already had the peasant girl through a promise of marriage and was only waiting for a chance to reveal it with safety to himself, being fearful of what the duke his father would do when he learned of his son's foolish conduct.

"Now, love with young lads is for the most part nothing more than appetite whose ultimate aim is pleasure, and once that aim has been achieved, love disappears, being unable to pass beyond the bounds assigned it by nature, which on the other hand sets no limit to true love; and so it was that, once Don Fernando had had his way with the peasant lass, his desires were appeased and his ardor cooled, and if he pretended that he wished to go away in order to be cured of his love, it was in reality that he might not have to keep his promise. In any case, the duke having granted his permission and directed me to accompany his son, we came to my city, and Fernando was received by my father in a manner befitting his rank. I then saw Luscinda once more, and although they had never been dead or even deadened, my desires began to live again. To my sorrow, I took Fernando into my confidence, as it seemed to me that, by reason of the great friendship he had shown me, I ought to conceal nothing from him. I praised Luscinda's beauty, grace, and modesty until my words aroused in him the desire to see a young woman adorned with so many good qualities.

"Most unfortunately, I yielded to his wishes and showed her to him one night by the light of a candle at a window where we were accustomed to converse. As she appeared to him in her loose-flowing robe, she at once caused him to forget all the beauties that he had thus far seen. He was struck dumb and stood there in a daze as if he had lost his senses. In brief, as you will see in the course of my story, he had fallen in love with her. His passion, which he hid from me and revealed only to Heaven, was still further inflamed when, as chance would have it, he found one day a letter of hers begging me to ask her father to give her to me in marriage, a letter so modest and discreet and yet so filled with love that upon reading it he assured me that in Luscinda and in her alone were to be found all the grace, beauty, and wit that are divided among the other women of the world.

"As I heard Don Fernando bestowing such well-merited praise upon her, I must confess that I was disturbed and began to fear and distrust him, for not a moment went by without his wishing to speak of her and he would so direct the conversation as to drag her name into it somehow or other. This awakened in me a spark of jealousy, not because I doubted Luscinda's loyalty and virtue, but for the reason that, despite the trust that she inspired, I dreaded what fortune might have in store for me. Don Fernando always contrived to read the notes that I sent her and those that I received from her in reply, under pretense that he greatly enjoyed the wit that each of us displayed. And then it came about that Luscinda asked me for a book of chivalry to read, one of which she was very fond, the *Amadis of Gaul*—"

No sooner did he hear a book of chivalry mentioned than Don Quixote spoke up. "Had your Grace told me," he said, "at the beginning of your story that Señora Luscinda was fond of books of that sort, it would not have been necessary for you to add anything more in order to give me an idea of her superior qualities of mind; for I must say that I should not have found her all that you, sir, have painted her as being if she had lacked the taste for such pleasant reading as that. Consequently, so far as I am concerned, it is not necessary to waste any more words in assuring me of her beauty, worth, and understanding, since merely upon hearing of this preference of hers, I set her down as the most beautiful and modest woman that there is. I could only wish, sir, that along with the *Amadis of Gaul* you had sent her the worthy *Don Rugel of Greece*,[2] for I am sure the lady Luscinda would have liked Daraida and Garaya very much and would have enjoyed the shrewd observations of the shepherd Darinel [3] and those admirable Bucolics of his as sung and recited by himself; but all this can be remedied in time if your Grace will but come with me to my village, for there I can give you more than three hundred books which are the delight of my soul and the solace of my life—but come to think of it, I have not a single one left, thanks to certain evil and envious enchanters who robbed me of them.

"Pardon me, your Grace, if I have broken my promise not to interrupt your story, for in hearing of knights-errant and deeds of chivalry I can no more refrain from speaking of such things than the rays of the sun can help giving heat or those of the moon moisture. And so, forgive me and continue, for that is what matters now."

As Don Quixote was saying all this, Cardenio's head had sunk to his bosom and he gave evidence of being deeply lost in thought. Although the knight twice requested him to go on with his story, he did not raise his head nor utter a word in reply. Finally, however, after a good while, he did so.

"I cannot rid myself of the thought," he said, "nor will anyone in the world ever be able to rid me of it or make me believe anything else— indeed, he would be a blockhead who believed the contrary—no, I am convinced that great villain of an Elisabat was living in adultery with the Queen Madásima—"

"That," replied Don Quixote in high dudgeon, "is not true, I swear it is not!" And he turned upon him angrily as he always did in such cases. "That is pure malice, or, better, a most villainous assertion. The Queen Madásima was an illustrious lady, and it is not to be presumed that a princess of her high birth would commit adultery with a quack. Whoever says that she would lies like a villain himself, and I will give him so to understand, mounted or on foot, armed or unarmed, day or night, as he may prefer—"

Cardenio was now staring attentively at the knight, for his madness had come upon him again and he was in no condition to go on with his story, nor was Don Quixote capable of listening to it, so disgusted was he with what he had just heard regarding Queen Madásima. A strange thing! but he felt impelled to defend her as if she had been his own lady, to such a pass had those unholy books of his brought him. Cardenio, then, being mad as I have said, upon hearing himself called a liar and a villain, along with other epithets of the same sort, and not fancying the jest, picked up a stone that was lying near him and let Don Quixote have such a blow in the chest with it as to lay him flat on his back.

Seeing his master attacked in this fashion, Sancho Panza fell upon the madman with clenched fists, but the Ragged One received him in such a manner, having resort to his own fists, that the squire the next moment was lying at his feet, whereupon he leaped on his ribs and began crushing them with great zest. The goatherd, who sought to defend Sancho, suffered the same fate; and after he had beaten and mauled them all, the mad assailant left them lying there and calmly went away to his hiding place in the mountains.

Furious at having been thus set upon through no fault of his own,

Sancho when he arose ran to take vengeance on the goatherd, saying the shepherd was to blame for not having warned them that this man was subject to fits of madness; for had they known it, they would have been upon their guard and might have been able to protect themselves. The shepherd replied that he had told them this, and if Sancho had not heard it, that was no fault of his. One word led to another until the squire and the goatherd were pulling beards and exchanging such fist blows that if Don Quixote had not made peace between them they would have knocked each other to pieces.

"Leave me alone, your Grace, Sir Knight of the Mournful Countenance," said Sancho as he grappled with the shepherd, "for this one is a countryman like me and has not been dubbed a knight, and so I may take satisfaction for what he has done to me by fighting with him hand to hand like an honest man."

"What you say is true," replied Don Quixote, "but I am sure that he is not in any way to blame for what happened."

Having pacified them, the knight once more inquired of the goatherd if it would be possible to find Cardenio, as he was extremely desirous of hearing the end of the story. The shepherd repeated what he had told him before, to the effect that he was not certain as to the man's place of abode, but if they went about enough in those parts they would not fail to encounter him, whether in his right senses or not.

CHAPTER XXV. *Which treats of the strange things that happened to the valiant Knight of La Mancha in the Sierra Morena and of his imitation of Beltenebros's penance.*

TAKING his leave of the goatherd, Don Quixote once again mounted Rocinante and ordered Sancho, who was now in a very bad humor, to follow him, which the latter did with his donkey.[1] They were gradually making their way into the most rugged part of the mountain, and the squire was dying to have a talk with his master, but he wished the latter to begin the conversation so that he would not have to disobey his command. At last, he was unable to endure the silence any longer.

"Señor Don Quixote," he began, "will your Grace give me your blessing and your permission, for I wish to return home at once to my wife and young ones. I can at least talk to them as much as I like; but to have to go through these lonely places day and night, as your Grace would have me do, without being able to speak when I feel like it, is a living death for me. If fate willed that the animals should talk as they did in Aesop's time, it would not be so bad, for I could then talk to my gray ² about anything that I pleased and forget my troubles. It is a terrible thing, and too much to put up with, to go all your life seeking adventures and get nothing out of it but kicks and blanketings, brickbats and punches, and with all that to have to sew up your mouth and not dare to say what is in your heart, as if you were dumb."

"I know what is the trouble with you," said Don Quixote. "That interdict that I put on your tongue is killing you. Well, just regard it as lifted and say what you like, but with the understanding that it is only for the time it takes us to cross these highlands."

"So be it," said Sancho. "Let me speak now, for God knows what will happen afterward; and so, beginning at once to take advantage of this privilege, let me ask you: what led your Grace to stick up so for that Queen Magimasa or whatever her name was? And what difference did it make whether that abbot ³ was her friend or not? If your Grace had let that pass, seeing that you were not a judge in the matter, I believe the madman would have gone on with his story and we'd have avoided the blow from the stone, the kicks, and more than half a dozen good cuffs."

"Upon my word, Sancho," replied Don Quixote, "if you but knew what an honored and illustrious lady the Queen Madásima was, I am certain you would say that I have a great deal of patience not to smash the mouth from which such blasphemies come. For it is a very great blasphemy to say, or so much as think, that a queen would commit adultery with a surgeon. The truth is, that Master Elisabat of whom the madman spoke was a very prudent man and sound in his judgments, who served the queen as tutor and physician; but to imagine that she was his friend is nonsense and merits severe punishment. And in order to perceive that Cardenio did not know what he was saying, you have but to remember that he was out of his wits when he said it."

"And I say," Sancho insisted, "that it was not for you to make much of the words of one who is mad; for if luck had not favored your Grace and that stone had hit your head instead of your chest, we'd have been in a pretty pickle as a result of standing up for that lady of yours, may God confound her. And what would you wager that Cardenio would not have gone free as being insane?"

"Against the sane and the insane," said Don Quixote, "every knight-errant is obliged to defend the honor of women, especially when they are queens of high rank and dignity such as was Queen Madásima, for whom I have a particular affection by reason of her excellent qualities; for in addition to being comely, she was very prudent, and long-suffering in calamities of which she had many. And the counsels and companionship of Master Elisabat were of great help to her by enabling her to endure her troubles with patience and wisdom. All of which has given the ignorant and ill-intentioned mob an excuse for asserting that she was his mistress. And—I repeat it—all those who say and think so lie, and will lie two hundred times more."

"I neither say nor think it," said Sancho. "Let those that do, eat it with their bread.⁴ Whether they were lovers or not, it is to God that they must give an account. I come from my vineyard, I know nothing. I am not fond of prying into other people's lives. He who buys and lies feels it in his purse. What is more, naked was I born and naked I find myself; I neither win nor lose. Supposing that they were, what's that to me? Many think to find bacon when there are no pegs.⁵ Who can put doors to the open country? Moreover, they said of God—"

"So help me God, Sancho," said Don Quixote, "what are all these absurdities that you are stringing together? What has the subject of which we were speaking to do with those proverbs you are threading? As you value your life, keep quiet; confine yourself to prodding your ass, and do not meddle in what does not concern you. And understand with all your five senses that what I do, have done, and shall do, is the fruit of sound reason and wholly in conformity with the rules of chivalry, with which I am better acquainted than all the professed knights in this world."

"Sir," said Sancho, "is it a good rule of chivalry for us to be wandering lost in these mountains, without road or path, in search of a madman who, when we find him, may undertake to finish what he has begun—and I do not mean his story but your Grace's head and my ribs, by smashing them altogether this time?"

"I tell you once again, Sancho, be quiet; for I will inform you that it is not so much the desire to find a madman that leads me to traverse these regions as it is the hope of accomplishing here an exploit that will win for me perpetual renown and fame throughout the whole of the known world, one that will place the seal on all that there is that can make a knight-errant famous and perfect."

"And is it a very dangerous exploit, that one?" Sancho Panza asked.

"No," replied the Knight of the Mournful Countenance, "it is not—not if the dice fall right for us; but everything will depend on your diligence."

"On my diligence?" said Sancho.

"Yes," said Don Quixote, "for if you return quickly from where I mean to send you, my labors will soon be at an end and my fame will begin to spread. And in order not to keep you any longer in suspense with regard to the meaning of my words, I want you to know, Sancho, that the famous Amadis of Gaul was one of the most perfect of knights-errant. But I am not correct in saying that he was 'one of the'; he was the sole and only one, the very first, the lord of all those in the world in his time. A plague on Don Belianís and all the others who claimed to equal him in anything, for they are wrong, I swear they are! When a painter wishes to become famous, he strives to imitate the works of the most distinctive practitioners of his art; and the same rule holds for all the other arts and crafts that serve as the ornament of states and nations.

"Thus, he who would achieve a reputation for prudence and long-suffering must and does follow in the footsteps of Ulysses; for in describing his character and the hardships that he endured Homer gives us a lively picture of the virtues mentioned. Similarly, Vergil, in the person of Aeneas, portrays for us a dutiful son and the sagacity of a brave and intelligent leader. And these personages, be it noted, are not depicted or revealed to us as they were but as they ought to have been, that they may remain as an example of those qualities for future generations. In this same way, Amadis was the north star, the morning star, the sun of all valiant and enamored knights, and all those of us who fight beneath the banner of love and chivalry should imitate him. This being true, and true it is, I am of the opinion, Sancho my friend, that the knight-errant who most closely models himself upon Amadis will come the nearest to attaining the perfection of chivalry.

"One of the occasions upon which that knight most clearly displayed his prudence, true worth, valor, endurance, firmness of will, and loving devotion was when, having been rejected by the lady Oriana, he retired to do penance on Poor Rock,[6] having changed his name to Beltenebros,[7] one that was certainly significant and suited to the life he had voluntarily chosen. Accordingly, seeing that it is easier for me to imitate him in this than by cleaving giants, beheading serpents, slaying dragons, routing armies, sinking fleets, and undoing enchanters' spells, and seeing, also, that this place where we are is better adapted to such a purpose as the one I have in mind, I feel that I should not let slip the opportunity that now so conveniently offers me its forelock."

"To get down to the purpose," said Sancho, "what is it that your Grace proposes to do in this lonely spot?"

"Have I not told you," replied Don Quixote, "that I mean to imitate Amadis by playing the part of a desperate and raving madman, thus imitating Orlando at the same time, on that occasion when he discovered in a fountain the signs that Angélica the Beautiful had committed a villainy with Medoro, which so grieved him that he went mad, tore up trees, muddied the waters of clear-running springs, slew shepherds, destroyed herds, set fire to huts, tore down houses, dragged mares along after him, and did a hundred thousand other outrageous things that are worthy of eternal renown and record? I grant you, I am not thinking of imitating point by point Roland, or Orlando, or Rotolando—for he went by all three names—in every mad thing that he did, said, and thought; what I shall give, rather, is a rough sketch, containing what appear to me to be the essentials; or it may be I shall content myself with merely imitating Amadis, whose madness did not prompt him to do any damage of that sort but who confined himself to tears and sighs and yet gained as much fame as the best of them."

"It strikes me," said Sancho, "that those knights who did all that had provocation and some cause for such foolish penances, but what reason has your Grace for going mad, what damsel has rejected you, or what signs have you found that lead you to think the lady Dulcinea del Toboso has been up to some foolishness with a Moor or Christian?"

"That," said Don Quixote, "is the point of the thing; that is the beautiful part of it. What thanks does a knight-errant deserve for going mad when he has good cause? The thing is to go out of my head without any occasion for it, thus letting my lady see, if I do this for her in the dry, what I would do in the wet. Moreover, I have occasion enough in the long absence I have endured from the side of her who shall ever be my lady, Dulcinea del Toboso; for you have heard that shepherd Ambrosio saying, 'He who is absent, suffers and fears all evils.' And so, Sancho my friend, do not waste time in advising me to forego so rare, so felicitous, and so unheard of an imitation as this. Mad I am and mad I must be until you return with a letter which I mean to send by you to my lady Dulcinea. If that answer be such as my devotion merits, there will be an end to my madness and my penance; but if the contrary is the case, I shall truly go mad and, being mad, suffer no more. Thus, whatever the manner in which she responds, I shall emerge from the painful struggle in which you leave me, either by enjoying as a sane man the good news you bring me, or, as one who is insane, by ceasing to feel the pain of the bad news.

"But tell me, Sancho, were you careful to preserve Mambrino's helmet? For I saw you pick it up from the ground when that wretch tried to smash it to bits but could not, from which you may see how finely tempered it is."

"God alive, Sir Knight of the Mournful Countenance," said Sancho, "I cannot bear in patience some of the things that your Grace says! Listening to you, I come to think that all you have told me about deeds of chivalry and winning kingdoms and empires and bestowing islands and other favors and dignities is but wind and lies, all buggery or humbuggery, or whatever you choose to call it. For when anyone hears your Grace saying that a barber's basin is Mambrino's helmet, and after four days you still insist that it is, what is he to think except that such a one is out of his mind? I have the basin in my bag, all crushed and dented. I'm taking it home to have it mended so that I can trim my beard into it, if God is only good enough to let me see my wife and children again someday."

"Look, Sancho," said Don Quixote, "by that same God I swear that you have less sense than any squire in the world ever had. How is it possible for you to have accompanied me all this time without coming to perceive that all the things that have to do with knights-errant appear to be mad, foolish, and chimerical, everything being done by contraries? Not that they are so in reality; it is simply that there are always a lot of enchanters going about among us, changing things and giving them a deceitful appearance, directing them as suits their fancy, depending upon whether they wish to favor or destroy us. So, this that appears to you as a barber's basin is for me Mambrino's helmet, and something else again to another person.

"It was a rare bit of foresight on the part of the magician who is on my side to have what really is the helmet appear to all others as a mere basin; for if it were known that it is of so great a worth, everyone would pursue me and endeavor to deprive me of it. On the other hand, thinking that it is no more than what it seems, they do not care to have it, as was shown when that fellow tried to smash it and went off and left it lying on the ground. Believe me, if he had known what it was, he never would have done that. Take good care of it, then, my friend, for I do not need it at present. Indeed, it is my intention to lay aside all this armor and remain naked as when I was born—that is to say, if I decide to take Orlando rather than Amadis as a model in doing my penance." [8]

Conversing in this manner, they reached the foot of a tall mountain, which, standing alone amid a number of surrounding peaks, had almost the appearance of a rock that had been carved out of them. Alongside it flowed a gentle brook, while all about was a meadow so green and luxuriant that it was a delight for the eyes to behold. There were many forest trees and a number of plants and flowers to add to the quiet charm of the scene. And such was the spot which the Knight of the Mournful Countenance was to choose for his penance.

The moment he caught sight of it he cried out in a loud voice, as if he really had lost his senses, "This is the place, O ye heavens! which I select and designate; it is here that I will weep for that misfortune that ye yourselves have brought upon me. This is the place where the fluid from my orbs shall increase the waters of this little brook while my deep and constant sighs shall keep in incessant motion the leaves of these mountain trees, as a sign and testimony of the pain my tortured heart is suffering. O ye rustic deities, whoever ye may be, who make your abode in this uninhabitable place, hear the complaints of this unfortunate lover who, suffering from long absence and a jealous imagination, has come here to voice his laments amid these rugged surroundings and to bemoan the harshness of that fair but thankless creature who is the end and sum of all that humankind may know in the way of beauty!

"And O ye nymphs and dryads too, who are accustomed to dwell in groves and thickets—may the light-footed and lascivious satyrs, who cherish for you an unrequited love, never disturb your sweet repose, but may you join me in weeping for my sorrows, or at least not tire of hearing them! And thou, O Dulcinea del Toboso, day of my night, glory of my sufferings, guide of my every path, star of my fortunes, may Heaven grant thee all thou seekest, and wilt thou look upon the place and state to which absence from thee has brought me and be moved to repay with kindness the debt that is due to my fidelity! Ye trees also, ye solitary trees that from this day forth are to be the companions of my solitude, give me a sign by the gentle murmuring of your leaves that my presence is not displeasing to you! And, finally, thou, my faithful squire, my congenial comrade in prosperity and adversity, remember well what thou seest me do here that thou mayest relate and recite it afterward to the one who is the sole cause of it all."

With these words he dismounted from Rocinante and in a moment had removed saddle and bridle, after which he gave the hack a slap on the rump.

"Freedom," said the knight, "he now gives thee who himself is left without it, O steed as unexcelled in deeds as thou art unfortunate in thy fate! Go where thou wilt, and bear with thee inscribed upon thy forehead this legend: that neither Astolfo's Hippogriff nor the renowned Frontino that cost Bradamante so dear [9] could equal thee in fleetness of foot."

As he saw his master do this, Sancho said, "Good luck to him who has saved us the trouble now of stripping the ass; [10] for upon my word, if the gray had been here, he too would have had a slap on the rump and a few words of praise. I'd never consent to it, however, for there would be no occasion, since there was nothing of the despairing lover about him any more than there was about his master, which I happened to be so long as God willed it. The truth of the matter is, Sir Knight of the Mournful Countenance, if you mean what you say about my departure and your fit of madness, then you'd better saddle Rocinante again so that he can take the gray's place, as that will save me time coming and going. If I go on foot, I cannot tell how long I'll be, for, the short of it is, I'm a very poor walker."

"You may do as you like, Sancho," said Don Quixote. "It is not a bad suggestion that you have made. You will set out three days from now. In the meantime, I want you to see all that I do for her sake and make note of all I say in order that you may be able to tell her of it."

"What more is there for me to see," said Sancho, "than what I've seen already?"

"You do not know what you are talking about," said Don Quixote. "I have yet to rend my garments, scatter my armor about, knock my head against those rocks, and other things of that sort, all of which you must witness."

"For the love of God!" exclaimed Sancho. "I hope your Grace has a care how you go about that head-knocking, for you may come up against such a rock or in such a way that with the very first knock you will put an end to this whole business of your penance. If your Grace feels that it is absolutely necessary to do this, and that you cannot go through with your undertaking without doing it, then it seems to me that, since it is all a matter of pretending and in the nature of a joke, you ought to be satisfied with bumping your head in water or something soft like cotton, and just leave the rest to me; I will tell my lady that your Grace did it against a piece of jutting rock hard as a diamond."

"I thank you for your good intentions, Sancho," said Don Quixote, "but you must know that the things I do are not done in jest but very much in earnest. Otherwise, I should be violating the rules of knighthood, which command that we shall tell no lie whatsoever under pain of suffering the penalty that is meted out for apostasy; and to do one thing in place of another is the same as lying. My head-knockings, therefore, have to be real ones, solid and substantial, with nothing sophistical or imaginary about them. And it will be necessary for you to leave me a little lint to dress my wounds, since fortune would have it that we should be without that balm that we lost."

"It was worse losing the ass," said Sancho, "for with it we lost the lint and all.[11] And I would ask your Grace not to remind me again of that accursed potion; the very mention of it turns my soul, not to speak of my stomach. I also beg of you to regard those three days that you gave me for witnessing your deeds of madness as being past; for, so far as I am concerned, that is the truth; I have seen and judged everything and will tell my lady marvels. Write the letter, then, at once and send me on my way, as I have a great desire to return and rescue your Grace from this purgatory in which I leave you."

"Purgatory you call it, Sancho?" said Don Quixote. "Better say Hell, or even worse, if there is anything worse than that."

"He who is in Hell," said Sancho, "has no retention,[12] so I've heard it said."

"I do not understand what you mean by *retention*," said Don Quixote.

"*Retention*," said Sancho, "means that he who is in Hell never can, and never will, get out. But it will be just the opposite with your Grace, or else my legs will fail me—that is, if I have spurs to put a little life into Rocinante. Just set me down once in El Toboso and in my lady Dulcinea's presence, and I will tell her such things about your Grace's foolishness and madness (it is all one), and all the things you are doing and have done, that, even though I find her harder than a cork tree, I will make her softer than a glove. And then when I have her gentle, honeyed answer, I will come flying back through the air like a witch and snatch your Grace out of this purgatory which seems to you to be a Hell but is not, seeing there is hope of your getting out of it; for as I have just said, those in Hell do not come out, and I do not think your Grace will contradict me on that."

"You speak the truth," said the Knight of the Mournful Countenance, "but how are we going to write the letter?"

"And the order for the ass-colts too," added Sancho.

"All that will be inserted," said Don Quixote, "and since we have no paper, it would be well for us to write it as the ancients did, on the leaves of trees or a few wax tablets; although it would be about as hard to find anything like that now as it would be to procure paper. It would be a good idea, an excellent idea, for me to write it in Cardenio's memorandum book, and then you will take care to have it transcribed on paper, in a fair hand, in the first village where you find a schoolmaster, or, failing that, some sacristan; but do not give it to any notary to be copied, for they write a legal hand that Satan himself would not be able to make out."

"But what is to be done about the signature?" asked Sancho.

"The letters of Amadis were never signed," Don Quixote assured him.

"That is all very well," said the squire, "but that order you are to give me has to be signed, and if it is copied over, they will say the signature is false and I'll not get the ass-colts."

"The order, duly signed, will be in that same little book, and when my niece sees it, she will not give you any trouble about carrying out my instructions. As for the love letter, you will have them put as the signature: 'Yours until death, the Knight of the Mournful Countenance.' It will make little difference if it is in some other person's handwriting, for, as I recall, Dulcinea does not know how to read or write, nor has she ever in all her life seen a letter of mine or anything else that I wrote; for our love has always been platonic and has never gone beyond a modest glance. Even that happened but rarely, since in the course of the dozen years that I have loved her—more than the light of these eyes which the earth will one day devour—I can truthfully swear that I have not seen her four times, and even then, it may be, she did not once perceive that I was looking at her, such is the seclusion and retirement in which her father, Lorenzo Corchuelo, and her mother, Aldonza Nogales, have reared her."

"Aha!" said Sancho, "so the lady Dulcinea del Toboso is Lorenzo Corchuelo's daughter, otherwise known as Aldonza Lorenzo?"

"That is the one," said Don Quixote, "and she deserves to be mistress of the entire universe."

"I know her well," Sancho went on, "and I may tell you that she can toss a bar as well as the lustiest lad in all the village. Long live the Giver of all good things, but she's a sturdy wench, fit as a fiddle and right in the middle of everything that's doing. She can take care of any knight-errant or about to err [13] that has her for a mistress! Son of a whore, what strength she has and what a voice! They tell me that one day she went up into the village belfry to call some lads who were out in the field that belongs to her father, and although they were more than half a league away, they heard her as plainly as if they had been standing at the foot of the tower. And the best of it is, there's nothing prudish about her; she's very friendly with everybody and always laughing and joking. And so, I say to you now, Sir Knight of the Mournful Countenance, that you not only may and ought to play mad for her sake, but you have good reason to despair and go off and hang yourself, and anyone who hears of it will say you did exactly the right thing, even though the devil takes you.

"I'd like to be on my way just to have a look at her again, for it's been a long time since I saw her, and the sun and air do a lot to the complexion of a woman who's all the time working in the field. I must confess the truth, Señor Don Quixote, that up to now I have been laboring under a great mistake; for I thought, right enough, that the lady Dulcinea must be some princess with whom your Grace was smitten, or at least some personage that merited the rich presents which your Grace sent her, such as the Biscayan and the galley slaves, and many others as well, no doubt, for your Grace must have won many victories before I became your squire. But, come to think of it, what is there about Mistress Aldonza Lorenzo—I mean, Mistress Dulcinea del Toboso—that those conquered ones whom your Grace sends to her should bend the knee before her? For at the moment they arrived she may very well have been dressing flax or thrashing in the granary, and they would run away when they saw her and she'd be annoyed by the present."

"Sancho," said Don Quixote, "I have told you many times before that you are much too talkative; and although your wit is very dull, your tongue is all too sharp at times. In order that you may see how foolish you are and how sensible I am, I would have you listen to a brief story which I am about to relate to you. Once upon a time there was a beautiful widow, young, rich, unattached, and, above all, free and easy in her ways, who fell in love with a youthful cropped-headed lay brother [14] of large and sturdy build. When his superior heard of this, he took occasion to speak to the widow one day, giving her a word of brotherly reproof. 'I am astonished, Madam,' he said, 'and not without a good cause, that a woman of your standing, so beautiful and so rich as your Grace is, should be in love with a fellow so coarse, so low, so stupid as is So-and-So, in view of the fact that there are in this institution so many masters, graduates, and theologians from whom your Grace might have her pick as from among so many pears, saying, "This one I like, this one I do not care for." ' She however, answered him with much grace and sprightliness, 'You are mistaken, your Reverence, and very old-fashioned in your ideas, if you think that I have made a bad choice by taking So-and-So, stupid as he may appear to be, since so far as what I want him for is concerned, he knows as much and even more philosophy than Aristotle himself.'

"Similarly, Sancho, as regards my need of Dulcinea del Toboso, she is worth as much to me as any highborn princess on this earth. Not all the poets who praised their ladies under names of their own choosing actually had such mistresses. Do you think that the Amarillises, the Phyllises, the Sylvias, the Dianas, the Galateas, the Filidas, and all the others of whom the books, ballads, barbershops, and theaters are full were in reality flesh-and-blood women who belonged to those that hymned their praises? Certainly not; most of the writers merely invented these creatures to provide them with a subject for their verses in order that they might be taken for lovelorn swains and respected as individuals capable of an amorous passion. And so it is enough for me to think and believe that the good Aldonza Lorenzo is beautiful and modest. So far as her lineage is concerned, that is a matter of small importance; no one is going to look into it by way of conferring on her any robes of nobility, and, as for me, she is the most highborn princess in the world.

"For you should know, Sancho, if you do not know already, that the two things that more than any others incite to love are great beauty and a good name, and these two things are to be found to a consummate degree in Dulcinea; for in beauty none can vie with her, and in good name few can come up to her. But to bring all this to a conclusion: I am content to imagine that what I say is so and that she is neither more nor less than I picture her and would have her be, in comeliness and in high estate. Neither Helen nor Lucretia nor any of the other women of bygone ages, Greek, Latin, or barbarian, can hold a candle to her. And let anyone say what he likes; if for this I am reprehended by the ignorant, I shall not be blamed by men of discernment."

"I agree with all that your Grace says," replied Sancho. "It is true that I am an ass—although I don't know how that word ass happened to slip out, since you do not speak of the rope in the house of a gallows bird. But let us have that letter, and then, God be with you, I am off."

Don Quixote thereupon took out the memorandum book and, going off to one side, proceeded to compose the letter with great deliberation. When he had finished he called Sancho, telling him to listen while he read it to him and to memorize it, in case the original should be lost along the way, as he had reason to fear from the ill luck that seemed to pursue him.

"Just write it two or three times in that book, your Grace," Sancho said, "and then give it to me; for it is nonsense to think I am going to learn it by heart when my memory is so bad that I often forget my own name. But go ahead and read it to me; I'll enjoy hearing it very much, for it ought to be as smooth as if it were all set down in print."

"Listen, then," said Don Quixote. "This is what it says:

DON QUIXOTE'S LETTER TO DULCINEA DEL TOBOSO

SOVEREIGN AND HIGHBORN LADY:

He who is pricked by absence and wounded to the heart, O sweetest Dulcinea del Toboso, wishes thee the health that is not his. If thy beauty despise me, if thy great worth be not for me, if my lot be thy disdain, even though I am sufficiently inured to suffering I hardly shall sustain this affliction which, in addition to being grievous, is lasting in the extreme. My good squire Sancho will tell thee, O beauteous ingrate, my beloved enemy! of the state in which I now find myself on account of thee. Shouldst thou care to succor me, I am thine; if not, do as thou seest fit, for by putting an end to my life I shall pay the price exacted by thy cruelty and mine own desire.

Thine until death.

THE KNIGHT OF THE MOURNFUL COUNTENANCE"

"By the life of my father," exclaimed Sancho when he had heard the letter, "that is the most high-flown thing I ever listened to. Why, damn me, how your Grace does manage to say everything here just the way it should be said, and how well you work that Knight of the Mournful Countenance into the signature! To tell the truth, your Grace is the very devil himself, and there's nothing you don't know."

"In the profession that I follow," replied Don Quixote, "one needs to know everything."

"And now," said Sancho, "if your Grace will put the order for the three ass-colts on this other page and sign it very clearly so that they will recognize your signature when they see it—"

"With pleasure," said Don Quixote. Having written the order, he read it aloud:

*Upon presentation of this first order for ass-colts, mistress my niece,
you will turn over to Sancho Panza, my squire, three of the five that I
left at home and in your Grace's charge. The said three ass-colts to be
delivered in return for three others here received on account; upon
presentation of this order and his receipt they are to be duly turned over
to him as specified.*

Done in the heart of the Sierra Morena on the twenty-second day [15]
of August of this present year.

"That is very good," said Sancho, "and now sign it, your Grace."

"It is not necessary to sign it," said Don Quixote. "All I need do is to
add my flourish, which is the same as a signature and will suffice for three,
and even three hundred, asses."

"I will trust your Grace," said the squire. "And now, let me go saddle
Rocinante, and do you be ready to give me your blessing, for I am thinking of leaving at once without waiting to witness the foolish things that
your Grace has to do; but I will tell her that I saw you do so many of them
that she will not want to hear any more."

"There is one thing at least that I should like to ask of you, Sancho,"
the knight said, "and if I do ask this, it is because it is necessary. I should
like you to see me stripped and performing a couple of dozen acts of madness, which I can get through with in less than half an hour; for having
seen them with your own eyes, you can safely swear to the other things
that you may care to add, and I assure you I mean to do more than you
will be able to relate."

"For the love of God, my master," Sancho replied, "let me not see
your Grace stripped, for I'd feel so sorry that I'd never stop weeping,
and I wept so much for the gray last night that I have no more tears left
to shed. If your Grace wants me to witness some of your insane actions,
please perform them with your clothes on and be brief about it and to
the point. So far as I am concerned, all this is unnecessary; for as I have
told you, it would save time if I were to leave now and I'd be back all
the sooner with the news that your Grace desires and deserves. For if
it is not such as you desire, let the lady Dulcinea be prepared; if she does
not give me a reasonable answer, I solemnly swear I'll have one out of her
stomach with kicks and cuffs. Why should a knight-errant as famous as
is your Grace have to go mad without rhyme or reason for a— Her ladyship had better not force me to say it, or by God I'll speak out and lay
them out by the dozen even though there's no buyer. I am pretty good
at that sort of thing. She doesn't know me very well, or, faith, if she
did, we'd have no trouble in coming to an understanding."

"And faith, Sancho," said Don Quixote, "you appear to me to be no sounder in mind than I am."

"I'm not as crazy as you are," said Sancho; "I've more of a temper, that's all. But leaving all this aside, what is your Grace going to eat until I return? Are you going out, as Cardenio did, and take it away from the shepherds?"

"Do not let that trouble you," said the knight, "for even if I had other food, I should eat nothing but the herbs and fruits with which this meadow and these trees shall provide me. The fine point of my undertaking lies in not eating and in putting up with other hardships of the same sort."

"And, by God," said Sancho, "there's another thing. Do you know what I am afraid of, your Grace? I'm afraid I'll not be able to find my way back to this place once I leave it, it's so out of the way."

"Get your bearings well," said Don Quixote, "and I will try not to stray far from this vicinity. I will also make it a point to go up on those high cliffs to see if I can catch a glimpse of you on your way back. But in order not to miss me and lose yourself, the best thing would be to cut a few branches of the broom plant that is so abundant around here and scatter them along the way at intervals until you come out onto the plain; these will serve you as signs and landmarks, like the clues in Perseus's labyrinth,[16] and will help you to find me when you return."

"I will do that," said Sancho, and cutting a few of the brooms, he asked his master's benediction; after which, each of them shedding not a few tears, he took his departure. Mounting Rocinante—Don Quixote had charged him to take as good care of the steed as he would of his own person—he set out in the direction of the lowlands, scattering the branches at intervals as he had been advised to do. And so he went his way, although the knight still insisted that he wait and watch him perform at least a couple of mad acts. He had not gone a hundred paces when he turned and looked back.

"You know," he said, "I believe your Grace was right. In order to be able to swear without a weight on my conscience, I really ought to see you do at least one mad thing, although your remaining here is mad enough in itself."

"Did I not tell you that?" said Don Quixote. "Wait, Sancho, and you will see me do them before you can say a Credo!"

With this, he hastily slipped off his breeches and, naked from the waist down, leaped into the air a couple of times, falling heels over head and revealing things that caused Sancho to give Rocinante the rein, that he might not have to see them again. The squire was satisfied now; he could swear that his master was quite mad. And so we shall leave him to pursue his journey until his return, which was not to be long delayed.

CHAPTER XXVI. *In which is continued the account of those refinements that Don Quixote practiced in playing the part of a lover on the Sierra Morena.*

BUT to come back to the Knight of the Mournful Countenance and what he did when he found himself alone, the history informs us that after Don Quixote, naked from the waist down and clothed from the waist up, had finished performing those somersaults of his, and after Sancho had departed without waiting to see any more of his master's mad antics, the knight betook himself to the top of a tall cliff and there began turning over in his mind a question which long had been troubling him but for which he had never been able to find a solution: namely, as to whether he should seek to imitate the monstrous things that Orlando did in his fits of madness or, rather, the melancholy actions of Amadis.

"If Orlando," he mused, "was so good and valiant a knight as they all say he was, what is so marvelous about that? After all, he was enchanted and no one could kill him save by running a tenpenny nail through the sole of his foot, and he always wore shoes with seven iron soles, although such wiles did not avail him against Bernardo del Carpio, who understood them very well and strangled him in his arms at Roncesvalles. However, leaving aside the question of his valor, let us consider his loss of reason, for it is certain that he did lose it on account of the evidence that he discovered in the fountain and the news which the shepherd gave him, to the effect that Angélica had slept for more than two siestas with Medoro, a young Moor with curly locks who was Agramante's page.[1] If he was convinced that this was true and that his lady had done him a wrong, it is small wonder that he went mad. But how can I imitate him in his acts of madness unless I have a similar occasion for committing them? I would swear that my Dulcinea del Toboso in all the days of her life has never seen a single Moor, as he is, in his native costume; she is today what she was when her mother bore her, and I should clearly be wronging her if, with any other idea in mind, I were to go mad in the manner of Orlando the Furious.[2]

"On the other hand, I note that Amadis of Gaul, without losing his mind or committing any acts of madness, achieved as much fame as a lover as any other knight; for, seeing himself scorned by his lady Oriana, who commanded him not to appear any more in her presence until she so willed it, what he did, according to the history that we have of him, was to retire to Poor Rock in the company of a hermit, where he had his fill of weeping and commending himself to God until Heaven came to his succor in the midst of his greatest agony and need. And if this be true, and true it is, then why should I go to the trouble of stripping myself stark naked? Why should I injure these trees which have done me no harm or disturb the clear water of these brooks which provide me with a drink when I desire it?

"Long live the memory of Amadis, then, and let him be imitated in so far as may be by Don Quixote de la Mancha, of whom it shall be said, as was said of the other, that if he did not accomplish great things, he died in attempting them. I may not have been scorned or rejected by Dulcinea del Toboso, but it is enough for me, as I have said, to be absent from her. And so, then, to work! Refresh my memory, O Amadis, and teach me how I am to imitate your deeds. I already know that what he did chiefly was to pray and commend himself to God; but what am I to do for a rosary, seeing that I have none with me?"

At this point a thought occurred to him, and, tearing a large strip from the tail of his shirt, which hung down over his buttocks, he made eleven knots in it, one bigger than the others, and this it was that served him as a rosary [3] as long as he was there, during which time he said a round million of Hail Marys. He was not a little put out at the fact that there was no other hermit there to hear his confession and offer him consolation; and so he spent his time walking up and down the little meadow, carving inscriptions on the bark of trees, and writing many verses in the fine sand, all reflective of his melancholy and some of them in praise of Dulcinea; but when he was found there later, the only ones that proved to be legible were the following:

> *Ye trees and shrubs, each plant*
> *In this place that grows,*
> *So tall and green, not scant,*

Do I tire you with my woes
As for my love I pant?
Let not my grief disturb
You, even though it be a
Thing that might perturb.
Don Quixote cannot curb
His tears for Dulcinea
            del Toboso.

Here is the place to which
The lover most loyal far
Hath fled from a beauteous witch,
Under an evil star.
To wander he has an itch;
Love drags him every way,
Which certainly cannot be a
Very good thing, I should say.
Don Quixote his tears doth spray
By the kegful for Dulcinea
            del Toboso.

Seeking adventure he goes
Among the barren rocks;
Cursing his many woes
And fortune's cruel knocks,
He flounders in Love's throes.
Held by no gentle rein,
It must ever be a
Lash that adds to his pain.
Don Quixote, sorrowful swain
Weeps for his Dulcinea
            del Toboso.

Those who came upon the foregoing verses laughed no little at the addition of "del Toboso" to Dulcinea's name; for they assumed that Don Quixote must have thought that unless he added those words the stanza would be unintelligible, which was the fact, as he himself afterward admitted. He wrote many others, as has been said, but only these three could be deciphered in their entirety. Thus it was he spent his days, in sighing and in calling on the fauns and satyrs of these groves, and on the river nymphs and the dolorous and humid Echo, beseeching them to answer him, to hear his prayers and console him; and he also looked for herbs with which to sustain himself until Sancho should return—and if the squire had stayed away for three weeks instead of three days, the Knight of the Mournful Countenance would have worn so altered a look that the mother who bore him would not have recognized him.

But it will be as well to leave him wrapped up in his sighs and verses as we relate what happened to Sancho Panza on his mission. The latter, immediately upon reaching the highroad, had struck out for El Toboso, and the next day he came to the inn where that unfortunate affair of the blanketing had occurred. He no sooner caught sight of it than it seemed to him he was once again flying through the air; and he had no desire to enter, although it was an hour when he might well have done so, for it was dinnertime and he had a great desire to taste something hot, having existed on cold cuts for many days past. Irresistibly, he drew near the tavern, unable to make up his mind whether to enter or not, and as he stood there two persons came out who at once recognized him.

"I say, Señor Licentiate," one of them remarked to the other, "that fellow on the horse there—isn't that Sancho Panza, the one who, so our adventurer's housekeeper told us, went away with her master as his squire?"

"Yes," said the licentiate, "it is, and that is our Don Quixote's horse."

If they knew him so well, it was for the reason that these two were the curate and barber of his own village, the same ones that had scrutinized and passed sentence on the books. As soon as they recognized Sancho and Rocinante, being desirous of having news of Don Quixote, they went up to the squire, the curate calling him by name.

"Friend Sancho Panza," he said, "where is your master?"

Perceiving who they were, Sancho made up his mind not to tell them where he had left the knight or under what circumstances. He accordingly replied that Don Quixote was in a certain place, occupied with a very important matter the nature of which, by the eyes that he had in his head, he could not reveal.

"No, no," said the barber, "that will not do, Sancho Panza. Unless you tell us where he is, we shall imagine, as indeed we do, that you have slain and robbed him, since you come riding on his horse. The truth is, you are going to have to produce the owner of the hack or take the consequences."

"There is no need for you to threaten me," said Sancho. "I am not a man who robs and kills anybody. Let his own fate or the God who made him kill each one. My master is up there in the middle of those mountains doing penance and enjoying himself very much."

And then, all in one breath and without stopping, he proceeded to tell them of the state that Don Quixote was in, the adventures that had happened to him, and how he, Sancho, was at present carrying a letter to the lady Dulcinea del Toboso, who was the daughter of Lorenzo Corchuelo, with whom the knight was hopelessly in love. The pair from the village were greatly astonished at what they heard, for although they were familiar with the nature of their friend's madness, they never ceased to wonder at it. They then asked Sancho to show them the letter, and he informed them that it was written in a memorandum book and that he was to have it transcribed on paper in the first village at which he stopped; whereupon the curate said that he himself would make a fair copy of it. But when Sancho put his hand in his bosom to search for the book he could not find it, and he would not have been able to find it if he had searched until now, for the reason that Don Quixote still had it, the squire having forgotten to ask him for it.

Upon discovering that the book was not there, he turned deadly pale. Hastily feeling all over his person and still not finding it, he plunged both fists into his beard and tore out the half of it and then in rapid succession gave himself half a dozen blows in the face and on the nose until he was fairly dripping with blood. Seeing this, the curate and the barber asked what was the matter with him that he mistreated himself in this manner.

"What is the matter with me?" said Sancho. "I've just lost from one hand to the other, in a moment's time, three ass-colts, and each of them built like a castle."

"How is that?" inquired the barber.

"I've lost the memorandum book," said Sancho, "with the letter for Dulcinea and an order signed by my master directing his niece to turn over to me three ass-colts of the four or five that he has at home."

He then went on to tell them of the loss of the gray ass, whereupon the curate did what he could to console him by telling him that when he returned his master would give him another order and they would have it done on paper this time as was the usage and custom, for those that were made out in memorandum books were never accepted nor complied with. At this, Sancho felt relieved, remarking that the loss of the letter did not worry him greatly since he knew it almost by heart and so they would be able to transcribe it where and when they liked.

"Tell us, then, what was in it," said the barber, "and we will have it copied later."

With this, Sancho began scratching his head and standing first on one foot and then on the other, now staring hard at the ground and now looking up at the sky, in an effort to recall the contents of the note. Finally, after he had gnawed off half the end of one finger as the barber and the curate waited anxiously for him to begin, he turned to them and said, "In God's name, Señor Licentiate, may the devil take me if I can remember it! I know that it began, 'High and sufferable lady—' "

"He would not have said *sufferable*," the barber corrected him; "it must have been *sovereign* lady or something of that sort." [4]

"That's it," said Sancho. "Well, then, unless my memory fails me, it went like this: 'The pierced and wounded one, the sleepless one kisses your Grace's hands, O ungrateful fair one and most unrecognized,' and so on and so forth, all about health and sickness which he was sending her and a rigamarole that ended with 'Yours until death, the Knight of the Mournful Countenance.' "

The village pair were quite pleased with the good memory that Sancho Panza displayed and praised him not a little, asking him to repeat the letter a couple of times so that they themselves might memorize it and be able to copy it out when occasion offered. Repeat it he did, three times, and each time he uttered three thousand other absurdities; after which he went on to tell them other things about his master, but never a word did he say about how he had been tossed in a blanket at this inn which he now refused to enter. He also told how Don Quixote, in case he had a favorable reply from the lady Dulcinea del Toboso, was going to set out to make himself an emperor or at least a monarch, for so they had agreed between them, this being a very easy thing to accomplish in view of his personal worth and the might of his arm; and when he had achieved it, he was to marry off his squire, who would, of course, be a widower by that time, giving him as a wife one of the empress's damsels, the heiress to a large and rich estate on *terra firma*, for he wanted nothing more to do with islands of any kind.

He said all this with so much composure and so little show of judgment, wiping his nose from time to time, that his friends could not but marvel once more as they reflected how very infectious Don Quixote's madness must be to have turned the head of this poor man in such a fashion. They did not care to take the trouble of disabusing Sancho of his errors, for it seemed to them that, as they were doing no harm to his conscience, it was better to leave him his illusions and there would be all the more pleasure in listening to his nonsense. And so they told him that he should pray God for his master's good health, adding that it was a very likely and practicable thing for the knight in the course of time to become an emperor as he said, or at the least an archbishop or some other dignitary of equal rank.

"But, good sirs," said Sancho, "if Fortune should so bring things about that my master should decide upon being an archbishop in place of an emperor, what do archbishops-errant usually give to their squires?"

"They commonly give them," replied the curate, "some simple benefice or curacy, or else they make them a sacristan, which brings them in a sizable fixed income, in addition to the altar fees which are just so much more to the good."

"For that," Sancho reflected, "it will be necessary for the squire not to be married, and he must be able to serve mass, at any rate; and if that is so, poor unfortunate me, for I have a wife and I don't know the first letter of my ABC's! What will become of me if my master takes it into his head to become an archbishop and not an emperor as is the use and custom of knights-errant?"

"Do not let that trouble you, friend Sancho," said the barber, for we will entreat and advise him, even making it a matter of conscience, to decide to be an emperor, as that will be easier for him, since he is more a man of arms than he is a student."

"That's the way it looks to me," said Sancho, "although I can tell you that he has the ability for anything. What I mean to do, for my part, is to pray Our Lord to place him where it will be best for him and where he will be in a position to do me the most favors."

"Spoken like a wise man," said the curate, "and you will be acting like a good Christian. But the thing to be done now is to get your master out of that futile penance which you say he is engaged in performing; and as we think over what we have to do, it would be well for us to enter this inn and have a bite to eat, for it is now dinnertime."

Sancho thereupon told them to go in, saying that he would wait outside, adding that he would give them his reasons later for not wishing to set foot in the tavern. He asked them, however, to bring him out something to eat that was hot and also some barley for Rocinante. They did as he requested, and in a few minutes the barber was back with the food. The curate and his companion then set themselves to thinking how they might achieve the result they desired, and the former hit upon a plan that was very well adapted to Don Quixote's turn of fancy and to the purpose that they had in mind.

That plan, as he outlined it to the barber, was to put on the disguise of a wandering damsel while his friend would make himself up the best

way he could as a squire, and the two of them would then go to Don
Quixote, pretending that it was a maiden in deep affliction and distress
who had come to ask a boon, one which he as a valiant knight-errant
could not refuse her. The boon was to be that he should come with her
wherever she might take him in order to right a wrong which a wicked
knight had done her.

She would further entreat him not to ask her to remove her mask nor
to make any inquiries concerning her affairs until the wrong done by the
wicked knight had been repaired. There was no doubt, the curate
thought, that Don Quixote would do anything they wanted him to when
they put it in this way, and thus they would be able to get him out of
that place and back home, where they would endeavor to see if there was
any remedy to be had for the strange madness that possessed him.

CHAPTER **XXVII**. *How the curate and the
barber carried out their plan, along with other things
worthy of being related in this great history.*

THE curate's plan impressed the barber as not being a bad one at all.
Indeed, it was so good that they at once set about putting it into execution. They asked the landlady for a skirt and a couple of hoods, leaving
in pawn for them the curate's new cassock. The barber then made a great
beard out of a reddish-gray oxtail into which the innkeeper was in the
habit of sticking his comb. When the mistress of the house inquired as
to why they wanted these things, the curate proceeded to describe Don
Quixote's madness to her briefly, explaining that this disguise was necessary in order to get him down off the mountain where he was at present.
At this point it dawned upon the landlord and his wife that the madman
had been their guest, the one who had prepared the balm and whose
squire had been tossed in the blanket; and she then told the curate all
that had happened, not neglecting to mention the incident which Sancho
had taken such pains to pass over in silence.

The short of it is, she dressed the curate up in a way that left nothing to be desired, in a cloth skirt with black velvet stripes as broad as your hand, all gored and flounced, and a bodice of green velvet with white satin trimming, both garments being of the kind that must have been worn in the days of King Wamba.[1] The curate would not consent to their putting a hood on him, but instead donned a quilted linen nightcap, binding his forehead with a strip of black taffeta, while out of another strip he fashioned a mask that served very well to cover his beard and face. He then put on his hat, which was big enough to serve him as an umbrella, and wrapping himself in his cloak he mounted his mule in lady-like fashion, his companion straddled the other beast, and they set out. The barber wore a beard, half red, half white, that fell all the way to his waist, for, as has been said, it was made of the tail of a reddish ox. They took their leave of all those in the inn, not forgetting the good Maritornes, who, sinner that she was, promised to say a rosary that God might grant them success in so arduous and Christian an undertaking as the one upon which they were now embarked.

No sooner had they left the inn, however, than the thought occurred to the priest that it was not right, but an indecent thing, for one of his calling to trig himself out like this, even though much might depend upon it. Accordingly, he asked the barber to change costumes with him, as it was more fitting for the latter to be the damsel in distress while the curate played the squire; in that way the dignity of the cloth would not be profaned to such an extent. He added that if the barber did not agree to this, he was determined to proceed no further and Don Quixote might go to the devil for all he cared.

At this point Sancho came up, and, seeing the two of them dressed in such a manner, he could not keep from laughing. The barber ended by acceding to the curate's wishes, and, changing the plot, the priest went on to school him as to what his words and behavior in Don Quixote's presence should be, in order that they might be able to persuade and compel the knight to come with them and to give up his fondness for the place that he had chosen for his vain and futile penance. The barber replied that he needed no lessons but would carry everything off all right. Meanwhile, he did not care to don his costume until they were near the place where Don Quixote was; and so he folded up the garments, the curate adjusted his beard, and they started off down the road with Sancho Panza as their guide, who was now engaged in telling them about the other madman who had been found upon the mountain, saying nothing, however, of the valise and the treasure it contained; for despite the fact that our young fellow's wits were none too sharp, they were sharp enough where money was concerned.

The next day they came to where Sancho had strewn the branches as a landmark to guide him to the spot where he had left Don Quixote. Recognizing the signs, he told his companions that this was the way into the place and they might put on their costumes if that was what was needed in order to save his master. For they had previously made it clear to him that their going in this manner and dressing in this fashion was of the greatest importance if they were to rescue the knight from the evil way of life that he had chosen; and they strongly charged him not to reveal their identity or let it appear that he knew them. If his master should ask him, as he was bound to do, if he had delivered the letter to Dulcinea, Sancho was to say that, not being able to read or write, she had replied by word of mouth, her message being that her lover was to come to her at once, under pain of her displeasure if he failed to do so. They explained that it meant much for Don Quixote's welfare, and by this means, with what they proposed to say to him, they felt certain that they would be able to bring him to a better life and at once put him on the road to becoming an emperor or a monarch, since no one need fear that he would end as an archbishop.

Sancho listened to it all, taking great pains to fix it in his memory. He was grateful that they intended to advise his master to become an emperor instead of an archbishop, for he still thought that emperors could do more favors for their squires than archbishops-errant could. He also suggested that it would be a good thing for him to go on ahead, hunt up his master, and give him my lady's answer, for it was possible that this would be enough to persuade him to leave and they would not have to go to so much trouble. The squire's advice seemed worth following, and so they decided to wait there until he returned with word of the knight.

Sancho then made his way into the mountain ravines, leaving the curate and the barber in a gully through which there ran a small and gently flowing brook, while other cliffs and a grove of trees that was there cast a cool and pleasing shade. The day on which they arrived at this spot was one in the month of August, which is usually a very hot month in these parts; and the heat and the hour of day—it was three o'clock in the afternoon—combined to render this an inviting spot in which to wait. And then, as they were taking their ease in the shade, they caught the sound of a voice, which, unaccompanied by an instrument of any kind, reached their ears with a sweet and regular cadence. They were quite astonished at hearing so good a singer in a place like this; for though it

is said that in the woods and fields one comes upon shepherds with superlative voices, this is an embellishment of the poets rather than the truth;
and they wondered still more when they discovered that these were not
such verses as rustic herdsmen compose but were, rather, the work of a
city-bred poet. The verses in question were the following, which confirm the truth of what has just been said:

> *What lessens all the good I gain?*
> *Disdain.*
> *What is it augments my agony?*
> *Jealousy.*
> *What tries my patience, keeps me tense?*
> *Absence.*
> *Thus 'tis I'm always in suspense;*
> *No remedy ever do I find,*
> *Since all hope's killed within my mind*
> *By disdain, jealousy, and absence.*
>
> *Who sends this grief, what power above?*
> *Love.*
> *Who at my glory casts a hateful glance?*
> *Chance.*
> *Who consents to my woe without leaven?*
> *Heaven.*
> *And so, I fear, to me 'tis given*
> *To die of this strange malady,*
> *Seeing that there's a conspiracy*
> *Of Love and Chance and highest Heaven.*
>
> *What can diminish my pain of breath?*
> *Death.*
> *What can alter Love's humor strange?*
> *Change.*
> *What can ever cure my sadness?*
> *Madness.*
> *And so, since all of life is badness,*
> *'Tis not wise to seek a cure*
> *When the remedies most sure*
> *Are death and change and utter madness.*

The hour, the season, the solitude, the voice and skill of the singer
aroused admiration in the listeners and brought them contentment as

they waited to see if there was more of the song. When the silence had lasted for some little while, they decided to go out and look for the musician who had given them so much pleasure; but just as they were about to do so, the voice began again, the same one as before, and as they stayed their steps the following sonnet fell upon their ears:

> O sacred Friendship that on lightsome wing,
> Leaving thy counterpart with us below,
> Hast gone to dwell with the blest, amid the glow
> Of Heaven where the saints and angels sing,
> While lending us still thy semblance, signaling
> Thy true self 'neath a veil, thou mayest know
> That what we oft behold is a lying show,
> And from thy good works many evils spring.
> Quit Heaven, then, O Friendship, nor permit
> The hypocrite to don thy livery
> And mock the heart sincere; take back the life
> Thou gavest this shadow, for it is not fit
> To walk the earth; its artful treachery
> Will plunge the world once more in primal strife.

The song ended with a deep sigh, and the two once again waited attentively to see if there would be more; but when they perceived that the music had turned into sobs and mournful cries, they resolved to find out who the saddened singer was whose voice was as marvelous as his moans were lugubrious. They had not gone far when, in rounding the edge of a cliff, they saw before them a man with the same face and figure as Cardenio, according to Sancho Panza's description when he told them the story of the lovelorn swain. This man as they beheld him now was not leaping in the air, but stood with his head on his bosom like one who was deep in thought, and did not raise his eyes to look at them beyond a first glance when they suddenly came upon him.

The curate already knew of Cardenio's misfortune and recognized him from what Sancho had said, and, being a pleasant-spoken man, he now went up to him and with a few brief but well-chosen words endeavored to persuade him to give up this wretched life he was leading, lest by remaining there he lose life itself, which was the greatest misfortune of all. At that moment Cardenio was wholly in his right mind and free of those furious fits that so frequently took him out of himself. Seeing the two dressed in a manner that was so unusual among those who dwelt in these wilds, he could not but wonder somewhat, and he wondered still more when he heard them speaking of his personal affairs as of something that was well known to them; for such was the impression he derived from the curate's words, and he, accordingly, replied as follows:

"I can see plainly enough, gentlemen, whoever you may be, that Heaven, which is careful to succor the good, and the wicked as well very often, without my deserving it has sent to me here in this remote spot, so far from the ways of men, certain persons who with various and forceful reasons have shown me how unreasonable I am in continuing to lead the kind of life that I do, and who would induce me to leave it for a better one. But they do not know what I know, that in escaping from this evil I should but fall into a greater one, and so, they will perhaps take me for a weak-willed individual or one of little sense, and it would be small wonder if they did, for it is plain even to me that thinking about my troubles so intently as I do can lead only to my ruination, and without my being able to avoid it, I come to be like a stone, wholly lacking in consciousness and a proper sense of things.

"I am made aware of this truth when people at times tell me about, or show me, evidence of the things that I have done when that terrible madness rules me, in which case I can do no more than vainly grieve or futilely curse my fate, and by way of excuse can only tell the cause of it all to such as may care to hear it. For those who are sound of mind, when they behold the cause, will not marvel at the effects; if they can offer no remedy, they will at least not blame me, and the repulsion they feel at my waywardness will turn to pity for my woes. And so, if you, my dear sirs, have come here with the same intention as others in the past, before you go any further with your wise reasoning I would have you listen to the story of my misadventures, and perhaps when you have heard it you will spare yourselves the trouble of endeavoring to console a grief that is beyond all consolation."

The curate and the barber, who desired nothing more than to hear from Cardenio's own mouth the cause of his troubles, now begged him to tell them of it, promising him that they would do nothing that he would not want them to do by way of helping or consoling him. At this, the unfortunate gentleman began his pitiful tale with almost the same words and gestures that he had used in speaking to Don Quixote and the goatherd a few days before, when, owing to the dispute over Master Elisabat and the knight's punctiliousness in observing the code of chivalry, the narrative had been left unfinished, as has already been set forth in the course of this history. But this time, as good fortune would have it, the fit held off and gave him an opportunity to tell it to the end. Coming to the incident of the note which Don Fernando had found between the pages of *Amadis of Gaul*, Cardenio said that he could remember it very well and that it went like this:

LUSCINDA TO CARDENIO

Each day I discover in you qualities that persuade and oblige me to esteem you more; and if you would have me fulfill this obligation while leaving my honor intact, you can very easily do so. I have a father who knows you and who loves me well, and he without forcing my inclinations will grant whatever it is right that you should have, if you love me as you say and as I believe you do.

"By this letter I was led to ask for Luscinda's hand in marriage, as I have already told you, and it was by reason of it that she came to be looked upon by Fernando as one of the most discreet and prudent women of her age. It was this letter that gave him the desire to ruin me before my own desires could be gratified. I told Don Fernando that all that Luscinda's father was waiting for was my father's formal request for her, but that I dared not speak to my father about it, being fearful that he would not consent; not that he was unacquainted with her rank, graciousness, virtue, and beauty, for she had enough good qualities to ennoble any other line in Spain; it was simply that he had given me to understand that he did not wish me to marry so soon, until we had seen what Duke Ricardo meant to do for me. Finally, I confessed to my friend that if I had not ventured to tell my father, it was not on account of this difficulty alone, for there were many others that tended to make a coward of me, although I could not rightly say what they were; all I knew was that it seemed to me that I was destined never to attain the object of my desires.

"In reply to all this, Don Fernando told me that he would take it upon himself to speak to my father and have him talk to Luscinda's father. O ambitious Marius! O cruel Catiline! O wicked Sulla! O lying Galalón! [2] O treacherous Vellido! [3] O vengeful Julian! [4] O greedy Judas! O cruel, vengeful, lying traitor! What disservice did this unhappy one do you, he who so openly laid bare to you the contents and inmost secrets of his heart? How did he offend you? What words did he ever say to you, what counsel did he ever give you that were not all intended to augment your honor and advantage? But of what do I complain, poor wretched creature that I am? For it is certain that misfortunes, springing from the course of the stars and coming from on high, fall upon us with such fury and violence that there is no force on earth that can restrain them, no human ingenuity that can forestall them.

"Who would have believed that Don Fernando, a gentleman of illustrious birth and able wit, one who was under obligations to me for my services and who was in a position to take what he wanted in the way of love wherever his fancy might choose to roam—who would have believed that he would stoop so low, as the saying is, as to deprive me of my one ewe lamb which I had not as yet possessed? But let us leave all these considerations aside as being futile and profitless and resume the broken thread of my unfortunate history.

"To continue, then: Finding my presence an obstacle to the carrying out of his treacherous and wicked plan, Don Fernando determined to send me to his elder brother under pretext of asking him for money with which to pay for six horses that he had bought the very day he offered to speak to my father, all of this being a clever ruse on his part, designed solely to get me out of the way in order that he might better be able to put that damnable scheme of his into execution. Could I have foreseen this treason? Could I by any chance have imagined it? Most assuredly not; instead, it was with the greatest pleasure that I understood the errand, being quite happy over the good bargain he had made.

"That night I spoke to Luscinda, telling her of the arrangement with Don Fernando and adding that I now felt confident that our desires, which were right and proper, would be realized. She no more than I suspected Fernando's treason, but urged me to return as speedily as possible since she was convinced that the moment my father spoke to hers the fulfillment of our wishes would be delayed no longer. I do not know why it was, but as she said this her eyes filled with tears and a lump formed in her throat so that she was unable to put into words all the other things that she had to say to me. I was greatly surprised, for I had never seen her in such a mood before. On those occasions when good fortune and my own wits had brought about a meeting, we had always talked gaily and happily, and there had been no tears, sighs, jealousy, fears, or suspicions. At such times, I would thank my stars that Heaven had given her to me for my lady and would extol her beauty and praise her worth and understanding; and she would give me payment in kind by praising in me those qualities that most endeared me to her.

"We would then go on to speak of a hundred thousand trifles and happenings that concerned our neighbors and acquaintances, and the most daring thing I did was to take, almost by force, one of her white hands and raise it to my lips as best I could in those confined quarters, over the low grating that separated us. But on this night, preceding the sad day of my departure, she wept, moaned, and sighed, and then ran off, leaving me deeply bewildered and perturbed, for I still could not recover from my astonishment at seeing so many unwonted and distressing signs of grief and feeling on her part. However, in order not to slay my hopes, I attributed it all to the power of love and the suffering that absence causes in those who care for each other deeply.

"Finally, I set out, downcast and pensive, my heart filled with imaginings and suspicions without my knowing what it was that I suspected or imagined, which in itself was an ill omen of the sorrowful event and misfortune that awaited me. Arriving at my destination, I presented the letter to Don Fernando's brother and was well received, although, much to my disappointment, I was not sent back at once but was ordered to wait for the matter of a week in some place where the duke would not see me, for Fernando had asked his brother to send him a certain sum without their father's knowing anything about it. All this was a treacherous plot on his part, since his brother had sufficient money and there was no need for him to keep me waiting. I was of a mind not to obey the order, as it seemed to me an impossibility to spend so many days of my life away from Luscinda, especially in view of the unhappy state in which I had left her on that last night of which I have told you. Nevertheless, I did obey like a good servant, even though I realized it would have to be at the expense of my own welfare.

"I had not been there four days, however, when a man arrived with a letter for me bearing a superscription which I recognized as that of Luscinda, for the missive proved to be from her. I opened it with fear and trembling, thinking there must be something very wrong indeed that had moved her to write me at a distance, since she seldom wrote when I was near her. Before reading the message I inquired of the man as to who had given it to him and how long he had been on the road, and he informed me that as he chanced to be passing down a city street at midday a very beautiful lady had called to him from a window, her eyes full of tears, and had said to him, 'My brother, if you are a Christian as you appear to be, I beg you to take this letter at once to the place and person, both well known, that are indicated on the back of it and by so doing you will render a great service to Our Lord; and in order that it may not inconvenience you to do so, take what you find in this handkerchief.'

"The man then went on to explain, 'And saying this, she tossed me from the window a handkerchief in which were wrapped up a hundred reales and this gold ring that I hand you now along with the letter that I have already given you; after which, without waiting for any answer, she left the window, but not until she had observed me pick up the letter and the handkerchief and make a sign to her that I would do as she had commanded. And so, seeing that I was being well paid for my trouble in delivering it, and noting by the superscription that it was you, sir, whom I know very well, to whom it was addressed—not to speak of the tears of that beautiful lady and the obligation they laid upon me—I determined not to trust any other person with this communication but to come myself and place it in your hands. And in sixteen hours from the time it was given me, I have made the journey, which as you know is one of eighteen leagues.'

"As the newly arrived and grateful messenger told me all this, I hung on his every word, my legs trembling so that I could hardly stand. When I opened the letter, this was what I found:

"*The promise that Don Fernando gave you to speak to your father and have him speak to mine has been fulfilled by him to his own satisfaction rather than to your advantage. You must know, sir, that he has asked to have me as his wife, and my father, looking upon him as being a more advantageous match than you, has acceded to his request with such alacrity that the marriage is to take place two days from now, with such secrecy and in such privacy that only Heaven and the household servants will be the witnesses. Picture the state that I am in and judge for yourself as to whether it is urgent for you to return, and from the outcome of this affair you will see if I love you dearly or not. Please God that this may reach you before my hands are joined to those of one who knows so little what it means to keep the promise he has made!*

"Such, in brief, were the contents of the note, which caused me to take to the road at once without waiting any longer for the reply or the money which I was supposed to bring back with me; for I now knew that it was not the purchase of horses but his own wayward fancy that had prompted Fernando to send me to his brother. The resentment I felt against him, together with the fear of losing the prize which I had rightfully won through so many years of loving service, gave me wings, so that, almost flying, I reached home the next day, at the very hour when I was accustomed to go and speak to Luscinda. I entered secretly, leaving the mule on which I had come at the house of the good man who had brought me the letter. Fortune for once was kind, and I found

Luscinda at the grating which had been the witness of our love. She recognized me at once and I her, but it was not in the way that we ought to have recognized each other. However, who is there in the world who can flatter himself that he has known and fathomed a woman's confused mind and changeable disposition? [5] No one, certainly.

"As soon as she caught sight of me, Luscinda said, 'Cardenio, you see me in bridal dress. Waiting for me in the great hall at this moment are Don Fernando the traitor, my father the covetous one, and others who shall be the witnesses of my death rather than of my nuptials. Do not be perturbed, my dear, but, rather, try to be present at this sacrifice, and if it cannot be prevented by any words of mine, then this dagger that I have concealed here will forestall more determined violence by putting an end to my life and a beginning to the knowledge that will be yours of the love that I have and always have had for you.'

"Feeling pressed for time, I replied to her hastily and distractedly, 'May your deeds, O lady, make good your words. If you bear a dagger to affirm your honor, I have here a sword to defend you or to slay myself if fate should be against us.' I do not think that she could have heard all that I said, for I became aware that they were calling to her to come quickly as her bridegroom was waiting for her. Thus did the night of my sorrow close in upon me, thus did the sun of my happiness set; the light of my eyes was gone, my mind had lost the power to reason. At first, I could not bring myself to enter the house; indeed, I was not capable of any movement whatsoever; but then, reflecting on what was about to take place and how important my presence might be, I plucked up what courage I could and went in. I was very well acquainted with all the entrances and ways of egress in that house, and in any event, with all the confusion that secretly prevailed there, no one would have noticed me; and so, without being perceived, I contrived to conceal myself in the recess formed by a window in the hall itself, covered by the borders of two tapestries from behind which I could see without being seen and observe everything that went on in the room.

"Who can describe now the dread that was in my heart as I stood there, the thoughts that occurred to me, the things that went through my mind? They were such as cannot be told, and it is as well that they cannot be. I may merely say that the bridegroom entered the room dressed in his ordinary garments, without ornament of any kind. As attendant he had with him a cousin-german of Luscinda's, and there was not a person there from outside the family with the exception of the servants. After a little, Luscinda came out from a dressing-room, accompanied by her mother and her two damsels. She was made up and adorned as befitted her rank and beauty, as for a festive or ceremonial occasion. I had neither the time nor the presence of mind to note the details of her costume, but was conscious only of the colors that she wore, crimson and white,[6] and of the glitter of the gems and jewels on her headdress and all over her robe, which, however, could not vie with the striking beauty of her blond hair, which was such as far to outshine the precious stones and the light from the four torches that flared in the room.

"O memory, mortal foe to my peace of mind! What purpose does it serve to bring before me now the incomparable loveliness of my adored enemy? Would it not be better, O cruel memory, to remind me of, and picture for me, what she then did in order that, moved by so manifest a wrong, I may at least seek to end my life, now that vengeance is no longer mine to take?

"I hope, good sirs, that you will not tire of these digressions that I make, for my sorrow is not one of those that can be related briefly and succinctly, inasmuch as each circumstance appears to me to be worthy of a long discourse."

To this the curate replied that not only were they not tired of listening to him, but all the little things that he had to tell were of great interest to them and deserved not to be passed over in silence but to be narrated as attentively as the main body of the story.

"Well, then," Cardenio went on, "when they were all gathered in the great hall, the curate of the parish entered and, taking the two of them by the hand, performed the required ceremony. As he came to the words 'Do you, Señora Luscinda, take Señor Don Fernando here present to be your lawfully wedded husband as our Holy Mother Church commands?' —at that point I thrust my head and neck all the way out from behind the tapestries and, with deep perturbation of soul, strained my ears for Luscinda's response, feeling that upon her answer depended a death sentence or a grant of life for me. Oh, if then I had but dared to burst forth and cry, 'Ah, Luscinda, Luscinda, look well to what you are doing, think of what you owe to me, and remember that you are mine and cannot belong to another! Remember that if you say yes, my life at that instant will come to an end! Ah, traitorous Don Fernando, robber of my bliss, death of my life, what would you? Reflect that as a Christian you cannot accomplish your desires, for Luscinda is my bride and I her bridegroom!'

"Ah, fool that I am, now that I am far away and out of danger's reach, I keep telling myself that I should have done what I did not do. Now that

I have let him steal my jewel, I can but curse the thief on whom I might have avenged myself had I had the heart for vengeance in place of merely complaining as I do now. In short, I was both a coward and a fool, and it is little wonder if I am now dying a shamed and repentant madman.

"The curate, then, was standing there waiting for Luscinda's response, which was some while in coming; and just as I thought that she was about to take out her dagger to assert her honor or was trying to unloose her tongue to disabuse them and speak some truth that would redound to my advantage, I heard her saying in a weak, fainthearted voice, 'Yes, I do.' Repeating the same words, Don Fernando placed the ring on her finger, and they were bound by an indissoluble knot. The bridegroom then went to kiss his bride, but she with a hand to her heart fell back fainting in her mother's arms. It only remains now for me to tell you the state that I was in as I heard that yes making a mockery of my hopes, proving false Luscinda's words and promises, and rendering impossible for all time to come the attainment of the blessing which I at that moment had lost. I was stunned by it all, left unprotected as it seemed to me by all the heavens, while the earth was my sworn enemy, denying me breath for my sighs, moisture for my tears; it was fire alone that grew in strength until I was wholly aflame with rage and jealousy.

"They were all greatly agitated by Luscinda's fainting fit; and as her mother opened the bride's bodice to give her air, they found there a sealed note which Don Fernando promptly took. When he had read it by the light of the torches, he sat down in a chair with a hand to his cheek, in the attitude of a man who is thinking deeply, paying no attention to what they were doing to revive his bride. Perceiving that the entire household was in confusion, I ventured to slip out. It made little difference to me whether I was seen or not, for, in case I was, I had made up my mind to commit some insane act that would let the world know of the just indignation that burned in my bosom, through the punishment inflicted upon the perfidious Don Fernando and upon the fickle and swooning traitress as well. But my fate, which must have been reserving me, if possible, for still greater ills to come, if there be any such, ordained that at this moment I should have enough and to spare of that wit that I have lacked since then; and accordingly, without seeking to take vengeance on my greatest enemies—all thought of me being so far from their minds, it would have been an easy matter to slay them—I resolved instead to inflict upon myself the suffering that should have been theirs, employing even greater severity, it may be, than I should have shown toward them by killing them, for sudden pain is soon over but that which is marked by long-drawn-out torments always kills without putting an end to life.

"To be brief, departing from that house I returned to the one where I had left the mule. I had the man saddle it for me, and then, without so much as bidding him good-by, I mounted the animal and rode out of the city like another Lot, not daring to turn my face to look back. When I found myself alone in the open country and enveloped in the darkness of night, I was tempted to give vent to my grief without restraint or fear of being heard or recognized, and then it was I raised my voice and loosed my tongue, heaping curses on Luscinda and Don Fernando as if by that means I might obtain satisfaction for the wrong which they had done me. I called her cruel, ungrateful, false, and thankless, but, above all, I upbraided her for covetousness, seeing that my enemy's wealth had closed the eyes of her love and had taken her from me and handed her over to one with whom fortune had dealt more freely and liberally than it had with me.

"Yet even in the midst of this outburst of curses and vituperations I still found excuses for her, telling myself it was no wonder that a young girl reared in seclusion in her parents' house and brought up to obey them always should have seen fit to yield to their choice when they offered her for a husband a gentleman of such high rank and so rich and well bred that not to have readily accepted him would have led others to think either that she was lacking in sound judgment or that she had bestowed her affections somewhere else, a thing which would so have prejudiced her good name and reputation.

"And then again, I said to myself, supposing she had declared me to be her betrothed, they would have seen that she had not chosen so badly that she was not to be forgiven; for before Don Fernando had made his offer of marriage, they themselves, had their desires been tempered with reason, could not have wished a better husband for their daughter than I. And she, before letting herself be placed in that forced and final situation of having to give her hand to another, might very well have said that I had already given her mine, knowing that I would come forward to verify any assertion of this sort that she made. At last I reached the conclusion that little love, small judgment, much ambition, and great worldly longings had led her to forget the words with which she had deceived me and which had served to sustain my own firm hopes and honorable desires.

"Talking to myself in this manner, and deeply agitated, I journeyed all the rest of that night and at dawn found myself in a pass leading into the heart of these highlands. I traveled over the mountains for three days more, with no road or footpath to guide me, until I came to a halt in the meadows that lie on one side of this range, though I cannot tell you which side it is, and there I inquired of some shepherds as to which was the most rugged part of the region. They told me it was where we are now, and so I came here, meaning to end my life; and, upon entering this inhospitable land, my mule fell dead of weariness and hunger, or, I am more inclined to think, in order to be done with so useless a burden as the one he bore. I was left, then, without a mount, worn out, starving, with no one to give me aid and with no thought of seeking it.

"I cannot tell you how long it was I lay stretched out on the ground like that, but at last I arose, feeling no hunger, and found myself in the company of some goatherds, who must have been the ones who had aided me in my distress; for they told me of the condition I was in when they had found me, the nonsensical things I had said, the mad actions I had performed, all of which clearly indicated that I had lost my reason. And I myself since then have become conscious of the fact that I am not always in full possession of it and that it is so weak and decayed that I do a thousand mad things such as rending my garments and shouting at the top of my voice in these solitudes as I curse my fate and vainly repeat the loved name of my fair enemy, all with no other purpose than that of putting an end to my existence through such loudly voiced laments, and then, when I am myself once more, I am so tired and battered that I can barely move.

"My most common habitation is in the hollow of a cork tree large enough to shelter this wretched body. The cowherds and goatherds that frequent these mountains, moved by charity, bring me food, placing it along the paths and cliffs where they think that I may pass and find it; for though my wits may fail me, the necessities of nature teach me what I need in order to sustain the spark of life, awakening in me the desire to seek it and the willingness to accept it. At other times, so they tell me when they find me in my right senses, I go out on the roads and take by force, though they would gladly give it to me, the food which the shepherds are bringing back from the village to their folds.

"Such is the manner in which I spend my wretched life, what is left me of it until Heaven shall see fit to bring it to a close or so order things that I shall no longer remember the beauty of the treacherous Luscinda or the wrong done me by Don Fernando. If it does this without depriving me of life, I will then turn my thoughts to better things; if not, there is nothing left but to pray that it will have mercy on my soul, for I do not feel that I have the ability or the strength to retrieve my body from these straits in which I have placed it of my own volition.

"This, then, O worthy gentlemen, is the bitter story of my misfortunes. Tell me if it is such as could be related with any less feeling than you have seen me display. And do not trouble yourselves with persuading or advising me to take that remedy that reason says may be good for me, for it will do me no more good than the medicine prescribed by a famous physician for a patient who will have none of it. I want no health without Luscinda; and inasmuch as she chooses to be another's when she is or ought to be mine, let my choice be misfortune when it might have been happiness. She with her changeableness would make stable my perdition, and I, by seeking my own ruin, will gratify her wishes, thus serving as an example to those in days to come, of one who alone among men lacked that of which all the wretched have more than enough: that is, the ability to console themselves with the impossibility of any consolation; for this in my case only leads to greater sorrows and sufferings, since I do not believe that there will be an end to my pain even in death."

Here Cardenio brought to a close his long speech and a story as filled with misfortunes as it was with love. The curate was about to offer him a few words of sympathy but stopped short when a voice reached his ears, crying in pitiful accents what will be related in the fourth part of this narrative; for it was at this point that the wise and learned historian, Cid Hemete Benengeli, brought the third part to a conclusion.[7]

CHAPTER XXVIII. *Which treats of the new and pleasing adventure of the curate and the barber on the same mountain.*

MOST happy and most fortunate were those times when that boldest of knights, Don Quixote de la Mancha, came into the world; and it is by reason of his noble resolve to revive and restore to that same world the calling of knight-errantry, so long lost to memory and all but dead, that we now, in this age of ours which is so sadly lacking in merry entertainment, are able to enjoy not only the charm of his veracious history, but also the tales and episodes interpolated in it, which in a manner are no less pleasing, artful, and true than the history itself.

Pursuing, then, its hackled, twisting, winding thread of plot,[1] the work in question goes on to relate that just as the curate was beginning to offer Cardenio certain words of consolation, he heard a voice crying in mournful accents, "O God! Is it possible that I have found a place that may serve as a hidden grave for the burdensome weight of this body which I so unwillingly support? I have indeed, if the solitude that these mountains promise me is not a lie. Ah, unfortunate one that I am! How much more agreeable company do these crags and thickets afford me for my purpose—since here I may cry aloud my woes to Heaven—than would any human being, seeing that there is no one on earth to whom I may look for counsel in my doubts, a comforting answer to my lamentations, or a remedy for the ills that beset me."

Upon hearing and grasping the sense of these words, the curate and his companions rightly decided that the voice came from near by, and they accordingly arose to search for its owner and had not gone twenty paces when, behind a large rock, seated at the foot of an ash tree, they beheld a lad, dressed as a peasant, whose face they could not clearly see at the moment for the reason that his head was bent over as he bathed his feet in the rivulet that flowed there. They came up very quietly, giving no sign of their presence, while he devoted all his attention to what appeared to be two pieces of white crystal embedded among the stones of the brook, rather than feet. Feet they were, however, of a surprising whiteness and beauty, and, belying the lad's garb, they did not seem made to tread clods or follow the plow and the oxen.

Perceiving that the young peasant had not heard them, the curate, who had gone ahead, made signs to the others to crouch down and hide themselves behind some pieces of rock that lay scattered around, and this they all did, watching attentively, meanwhile, the actions of the one by the stream. The latter was clad in a gray-colored double-skirted jacket tightly bound about the waist by a girdle of white cloth, and he also had on breeches and gaiters of gray cloth and a cap of the same material on his head. His gaiters were rolled halfway up his legs, which, it seemed, must surely be of pure alabaster. Having bathed his feet, he took out a towel from beneath his cap and dried them; and in removing his *montera*,[2] he lifted his head, affording the onlookers a glimpse of a face of incomparable beauty.

"That," said Cardenio to the curate, "since it cannot be Luscinda, is no human being but a divine one."

Being now without his cap, the youth shook his head from side to side, and, as he did so, a mass of hair whose brightness the sun might have envied was unloosened and fell down over his shoulders. This told them that the one who had appeared to be a peasant lad was in reality a woman of exquisite loveliness, indeed the most beautiful that two of them had ever beheld, and the same might have been said of Cardenio if he had not looked upon and known Luscinda, for as he afterward observed, only her beauty could compete with that of the creature before them, whose long blond locks not only covered her shoulders, but were so abundant as to conceal the whole of her body with the exception of her feet. For a comb she made use of her two hands, and if her feet in the water had the appearance of crystal, her hands in her hair were like driven snow. All of which filled her beholders with admiration and made them more desirous than ever of knowing who she was.

They accordingly resolved to show themselves, and at the sound which they made upon getting to their feet the lovely lass raised her head and, parting her hair from in front of her eyes with both hands, gazed in their direction. No sooner did she see them than she rose, without pausing to put on her shoes or gather in her flowing locks, and, hastily snatching up something like a bundle of garments that was on the bank beside her, she started to flee in great fear and alarm. She had not gone six paces, however, when, her delicate feet being unused to the rough stones, she sank to the ground; whereupon the three of them ran up to her. The curate was the first to speak.

"Stay, my lady," he said, "whoever you may be, for we whom you see here only wish to be of service to you. There is no reason for you to take to importunate flight like this, for your feet will not suffer it, nor can we consent to it."

To this she replied not a word, being very much astonished and bewildered. They then came closer to her, and the curate, taking her by the hand, went on speaking.

"What your garb denies, lady," he began, "your hair has revealed to us; and we feel sure that the causes cannot have been slight ones that have led you to disguise your beauty in so unworthy a habit and come to so lonely a place as this where it has been our good fortune to find you. If we cannot remedy your griefs, we at least would offer you such comfort as we can; for no sorrow so long as life lasts can be so overwhelming or so far beyond the reach of human aid that the sufferer will refuse to listen to those words of comfort that are uttered with good intentions. And so, dear lady, or dear sir, whichever you prefer, try to overcome the fear which the sight of us has caused you and tell us of your good or evil fortunes, for in all of us together and in each of us individually you will find a sympathetic audience."

While the curate was saying this, the lass in boy's clothing stood as if spellbound, looking first at one and then at another, without moving her lips or saying a word, like a rustic villager who is suddenly shown some curious thing that he has never seen before. But as the priest went on with other arguments to the same effect, she gave a deep sigh and broke her silence at last.

"Inasmuch," she said, "as these mountain wilds have not been able to conceal me, while the sight of my loosened hair renders futile any lie my tongue might tell, it would be vain for me to go on pretending to be what I am not, since if you believed it at all, it would be out of politeness rather than for any other reason. In view of this fact, then, gentlemen, I would say that I thank you for the offer you have made me, which has put me under the obligation of granting your request by telling you all that you may wish to know; although I fear that the story of the misfortunes which I shall relate to you will cause you boredom as well as compassion, seeing that there is no remedy or comfort to be had for them. Nevertheless, I would not have my honor compromised in your sight, for you now know me to be a woman and see me, a young girl, alone here and in this costume, two things that well might drag in the dust any woman's good name. And so, I shall tell you what I would much rather keep secret if I could."

All this was uttered so gracefully and fluently and in so charming a voice that they could not but admire the cleverness as much as they did the beauty of this creature who stood revealed as one of the most entrancing of women. With this, they repeated their offers, begging her to fulfill her promise, and she, without further urging, after first very modestly putting on her shoes and gathering up her hair, seated herself upon a rock with the three about her. Doing her best to restrain her tears, she began the story of her life, in a calm, clear voice.

"In this province of Andalusia there is a village that lies within the domains of a duke, one of those who are known as Grandees of Spain. This duke has two sons: the elder, who is heir to his estate and, apparently, to his good morals as well; and a younger one, who is heir to— I cannot tell you what, unless it be the treasons of Vellido and the lying wiles of Galalón. My own parents are the vassals of this lord, and though of humble antecedents are so rich that if their lineage had been equal to their fortune they would have had nothing left to wish for and I should have had no fear of finding myself in my present plight. For it well may be that my misfortunes spring from theirs in not having been born to the nobility. It is true enough that they are not so lowly born that they need blush for their station in life, but, on the other hand, their rank is not so high that I can rid myself of the thought that it was their humility that brought my troubles upon me.

"They are, in short, plain country people without any admixture of disreputable blood; they are rusty [3] old Christians but so well off that, by reason of their luxurious mode of living, they have come to be known as *hidalgos* and even *caballeros*,[4] although the wealth and nobility that they most prized lay in having me for a daughter. They were fond parents and had no other son or daughter to be their heir, and, as a result, I was one of the most pampered young ladies that ever was. I was the mirror in which they beheld themselves, the staff of their old age, and the object toward which, by the grace of Heaven, all their wishes tended; and their wishes being such worthy ones, my own were in agreement with theirs. And just as I was the mistress of their hearts and minds, so was I of their estate as well. It was through me that they engaged and discharged servants, and it was through my hands that the accounts of the sowing and the harvest passed, of the oil mills, wine presses, herds, flocks, and hives, all the things that a rich farmer like my father might possess— I kept count of them all; I was at once the mistress and the major-domo, all of which duties were performed with such diligence on my part and such satisfaction on the part of my parents that I cannot well describe it to you.

"That portion of the day that was left me after I had dealt with the stewards, overseers, and laborers I devoted to those pursuits that are as proper as they are necessary for young ladies, commonly represented by the needle, the sewing-cushion, and the distaff. And if I occasionally, by way of recreation, forsook these tasks, it was to read some book of devotion or play upon the harp, for experience has taught me that music soothes the troubled mind and brings rest to the weary soul.[5]

"Such, then, was the life that I led in my parents' house. If I have pictured it for you in so great detail, it has not been for purposes of ostentation or by way of impressing upon you the fact that I am wealthy. My object, rather, is to show you how, through no fault of my own, I have fallen from that happy state of which I have told you to the one in which I now find myself. It was a busy life I led but one so cloistered that it can be compared only to that of a convent. It seemed to me I saw no one at all outside the servants; for on those days that I went to early morning mass, accompanied by my mother and the women of the household, I was so veiled and so closely attended that my eyes scarcely beheld more of the ground than that on which I set my feet. Yet for all of that, the eyes of love, or, it would be better to say, dalliance, with which those of the lynx cannot compare, found me out through the persistency of Don Fernando, for that is the name of the duke's younger son of whom I spoke."

The moment he heard Fernando's name mentioned, Cardenio turned pale and began perspiring all over, displaying such signs of deep emotion as to lead the curate and the barber, who were watching him, to fear he was about to have one of those fits that, so they had been told, came over him from time to time. He did nothing more than sweat, however, and sat there quietly, staring hard at the peasant lass, for by now he suspected who she was. Without paying any attention to him, she went on with her story.

"Those eyes of his had had no more than one good glimpse of my face when, as he said afterward, he fell violently in love with me, as his later actions proved. But to bring the tale of my misfortunes to as speedy an end as possible, I will pass over all the means to which Don Fernando had resort in making known his love. He bribed all the servants in the house and gave and offered gifts and favors to my parents. Every day in our street was an occasion for festivity and rejoicing, and at night one could not sleep for the music that was played. The love notes that, without my knowing how, reached my hands were infinite in number and were filled with amorous phrases and declarations. They contained more oaths and promises than they did letters of the alphabet. All of which did not soften me in the least, but, rather, hardened me against him to such an extent that I came to look upon him as my mortal enemy, while all the efforts that he made to win my love had just the opposite effect. It was not that I disliked his courteous intentions or found them excessive; for it gave me a certain satisfaction to be loved and held in such esteem by a gentleman of his illustrious rank. Nor was I annoyed by reading his praises of me in the notes that he sent me, for however ugly we may be, I think we women always enjoy hearing ourselves called beautiful.

"No, it was simply that my sense of propriety was opposed to all this, and my parents, moreover, were constantly advising me against him, as they now very clearly perceived Don Fernando's purpose, and he did not care if all the world knew it. My parents reminded me that my virtue was the sole depository of their honor and good name and urged me to take into consideration the disparity of rank between him and myself, saying that if I did so, I would see that, whatever he might say, he was thinking more of his own pleasure than of my welfare. They added that if I cared to oppose in the slightest degree his unjust claims to my affection, they would marry me at once to anyone I might choose from among the leading families of our village or the neighboring ones, since in view of their wealth and my reputation for virtue, there was no limit to our expectations.

"These assured promises and the truths my parents told me greatly strengthened my resolution, and I never said a word in reply to Don Fernando that might have afforded him the remotest hope of attaining his desire. This reserved attitude on my part, which he must have mistaken for flirtatiousness, merely served to whet his lascivious appetite; for that is the only name that I can give to the feeling that he showed for me, since if it had been anything else, you would not be hearing of it now, as there would be no occasion for telling you of it.

"Finally, he learned that my parents were about to arrange another match by way of putting an end to his hopes of possessing me, or at least were going to have me more carefully watched over in the future, and it was this news or suspicion that led him to commit the act which I shall now relate. One night, being alone in my room, with the doors well locked and only my maid for company—for I feared that in some way, though I did not know how, my virtue might be endangered—I suddenly found him, in spite of all my modesty and precautions, standing before me there in the silence and seclusion of my chamber. The sight of him so perturbed me that I could not take my eyes off him and my tongue was tied.

"I was so frightened that I could not even cry out, and I do not believe that he would have permitted me to do so; for he at once came up to me and, taking me in his arms—as I have told you, I did not have the strength or presence of mind to defend myself—he began to say all sorts of things to me, making lies appear to be the truth in a manner that I should not have believed possible. And what is more, the traitor even managed a few tears and sighs by way of making his words sound plausible. As a result, poor young thing that I was, alone with my attendants who had had little experience in such cases as this, I came somehow to accept his falsehoods as the truth, although it was nothing more than a kindly compassion that his tearful protestations aroused in me.

"And so, when my first start of surprise was over, I began to recover somewhat of my self-possession and with more spirit than I should have believed myself capable of showing, I spoke to him.

" 'Sir,' I said,[6] 'if instead of being in your arms as I am at this moment I were in the grasp of a fierce lion and my liberation depended upon my saying or doing something which would prejudice my virtue, that thing would be as impossible for me as it is to undo that which has already been. Though your arms may hold me like this, my soul is firmly attached to worthy desires very different from yours, as you shall see if you endeavor by force to put your own into effect. I am your vassal, but I am not your slave, and your nobility of blood does not, and should not, give you the right to despise and dishonor my humble origins. As a peasant girl of the countryside I have as much self-respect as do you, a lordly gentleman. With me neither force nor your wealth nor any words that you may utter to deceive me nor all your sighs and tears shall be of any avail in softening my resolve.

" 'If I were to find any of these qualities [7] I have mentioned in the one whom my parents gave me for a husband, I would adjust my will to his and never go beyond the bounds of his wishes; and thus my honor would be left me even though my desires were not gratified, and I would give him freely that which you, sir, now seek to take so forcibly. I have told you all this in order that you may know that he who is not my husband never will obtain anything from me.'

" 'If that,' replied the faithless gentleman, 'is all that is troubling you, my loveliest Dorotea' "—for such was the name the unfortunate one bore—" 'then look, I give you my hand and promise to be yours, and Heaven itself from which nothing is hidden shall be my witness as well as that image of Our Lady that you have there.' "

When Cardenio heard the name Dorotea he was once more deeply agitated, for it appeared to him to confirm the opinion he had held from the start, but he did not wish to interrupt the story whose end, he felt almost certain, he already knew.

"So, Dorotea is your name, lady?" was all he said. "I know another of whom the same story is told and whose misfortunes, it may be, equal your own. But continue. When the time comes, I may tell you some things that will astonish you as much as they will excite your pity."

Listening attentively to what Cardenio had to say and studying at the same time his strange manner and shabby attire, Dorotea begged him if he knew anything else concerning her to tell her at once. For if Fortune had left her any blessing at all, it was that of being able to bear any calamity that might overtake her, inasmuch as, so it seemed to her, nothing could increase in the slightest degree the weight of suffering that she already carried.

"Lady," replied Cardenio, "I should not let the opportunity pass to tell you what I think if I felt that my suspicions had any basis in fact, but up to now there is nothing to show that they do have, and so it is not important that you should know of them."

"Be that as it may," said Dorotea, "and to go on with my story: Picking up a holy image that was in the room, Don Fernando took it to be the witness of our troth. With highly persuasive arguments and the most unusual oaths, he gave me his word that he would be my husband; although, before he said this, I warned him that he should take good care as to what he was doing and think of what his father would say of his being married to a peasant girl who was his vassal. I added that he should not let my beauty, such as it was, blind him, as it would not be a sufficient excuse for his error, and that if he really loved me he ought to let my fate take its course in accordance with my station in life, for marriages in which the parties were so unevenly matched never made for happiness, nor did the glow with which they began ever last for long.

"All this I told him, and many other things besides which I do not recall; but nothing that I might say could dissuade him from his purpose, since he who has no intention of paying does not quibble over the bargain. At this point, I thought things over, saying to myself, 'I certainly shall not be the first one to rise from a lowly estate to a high one by way of matrimony, nor will Don Fernando be the first whom beauty or, what is surely the better word, a blind passion has led to take a companion unsuited to his lofty rank. Accordingly, seeing that I am setting no new custom or fashion, it would be well to accept this honor that fate offers me even though the affection that he displays toward me lasts no longer than the achievement of his desires; for when all is said, I shall still be his wife before God. If I repel him with scorn, I can see that, fair means failing him, he is of a mind to use force, and then I shall be left dishonored and without excuse in the mind of anyone who did not know how blamelessly I came to be in such a position as this. For what could ever bring my parents to believe that this gentleman had thus come into my chamber without my consent?'

"To turn over all these questions and answers in my mind was the work of a moment. But it was, above all, Don Fernando's oaths, the witnesses to whom he appealed, the tears he shed, and, finally, his high-bred manner, which, accompanied by so many manifestations of true love, well might have won over any heart, even one as free and shy as mine—it was these things that inclined me to what, without my realizing it at the time, was to be my ruin. I summoned my maid in order that she might be an earthly witness to go with the heavenly ones he had invoked. Don Fernando then began reiterating and confirming his previous oaths, calling upon yet more saints and invoking a thousand future curses upon himself in case he did not fulfill his promises. Once again his eyes brimmed with tears and his sighs grew in volume as he clasped me still more tightly in his arms which had never let go of me. As a consequence of all this and of my maid's leaving the room at that moment, I ceased to be a maid and he became a traitor and a faithless wretch.

"The day that followed the night of my dishonor did not come as quickly, I imagine, as Don Fernando would have liked; for once appetite has had its fill, the dominant impulse is to hasten away from the place where it has found satisfaction. By this I mean to say that he was in great haste to leave me, and through the cleverness of my maid, who was the one who had admitted him in the first place, he slipped out into the street before it was yet dawn. Upon bidding me farewell, he swore again, though not with so much earnestness and vehemence, that I might be assured of his good faith and that all his vows were stanch and true. By way of confirming what he said, he took from his finger a costly ring and put it upon my hand.

"With this, he departed and I was left neither sad nor happy. That is to say, I was pensive and bewildered, almost beside myself with what had just happened, and I either did not have the spirit or I forgot to scold my maid for the treachery of which she had been guilty by closeting Don Fernando with me; for the truth is, I could not as yet make up my mind as to whether what had befallen me was good or bad. I had told Don Fernando as he left that he might visit me on other nights by the same means that he had employed on this occasion, until such time as he should see fit to make it public, since I now belonged to him. With the exception of the following night, however, he came no more, and for a month and longer I was unable to catch a glimpse of him either in the street or in church. Vainly, I wore myself out waiting for some word, for I knew that he was in the town and that most days he went hunting, this being a sport of which he was very fond.

"Those days, those hours, I well remember, were sad and wretched ones for me. It was then that I began to doubt and disbelieve in Don Fernando's good faith, and it was then, also, that my maid had from me those words of reproof for her bold act that she had not heard before. I recall that it was all I could do to restrain my tears and maintain the

composure of my countenance that I might not give my parents an excuse for inquiring as to the cause of my unhappiness, and the result was
that I had to invent lies to tell them. But the time came when considerations of this sort and all thoughts of honor were abandoned, for as my
patience gave out my secret thoughts became known. The occasion was
the news that came, within a short while, of Don Fernando's marriage to
an exceedingly beautiful maiden in a near-by city, the daughter of
parents who enjoyed some rank, though she was not so rich that by reason
of her dowry she might have looked forward to such a match as this.
They tell me that her name was Luscinda and that at her wedding certain
things happened that are truly cause for wonderment."

Upon hearing Luscinda's name, Cardenio did no more than shrug his
shoulders, bite his lips, and arch his brows as a double stream of tears
poured from his eyes. Dorotea, however, did not for this reason break off
her story.

"When this news reached my ears," she went on, "in place of my
heart's being congealed, the rage and desire for vengeance that was
kindled in it was so great that it was all I could do to keep from running
out into the street and crying aloud the perfidy and treason of which he
had been guilty toward me. The only thing that stayed my wrath was
the plan that came to me then, one that I put into execution that very
night. The plan in question was to don this costume which I now have
on and which was given me by one of those *zagales*,[8] as they are called
in peasant homes. He was a servant of my father's, and I had told him all
that had happened and had asked him to come with me to the city where
I had heard that my enemy was. After reproving me for my bold scheme
of which he sternly disapproved, he nevertheless, when he saw how bent
I was upon carrying it out, offered to accompany me—to the end of the
world as he assured me. I at once put into a pillowcase a woman's dress
and a few pieces of jewelry along with a little money in order that I might
be prepared for any eventuality; and that night when all was still, without saying anything to my treacherous maid, I left my home, and in
the company of the servant lad and my many thoughts I set out on foot
for the city, borne on the wings of desire as it were, being anxious, if
not to prevent what was already done, at least to demand of Don
Fernando how in all conscience he could have done it.

"I arrived at my destination in two days and a half, and, entering the
city, I inquired at once for the home of Luscinda's parents. The first person to whom I put the question told me more than I sought to know.
Pointing out the house, he informed me of all that had occurred at the

marriage of the daughter, a thing so well known throughout the town that people formed in groups on the street to discuss it. It seemed that, after the ceremony had been performed and Luscinda had given him her promise to be his bride, she had been seized with a violent fainting fit, and when he had opened her bodice to give her air he had found there a letter in her handwriting in which she stated and declared that she could not be his bride for the reason that she belonged to Cardenio—the name, so the man assured me, of a leading gentleman of that same city—adding that if she had said yes to Fernando, it was to avoid having to disobey her parents.

"In short, as the story was told to me, the letter made plain her intention to kill herself following her marriage and went on to set forth the reasons why she was taking her life. All of which, they say, was confirmed by a dagger that they found somewhere or other on her person. In view of this, Don Fernando could not but feel that she had mocked and belittled him, and, accordingly, before she had been revived from her faint, he fell upon her and endeavored to stab her to death and would have done so if the parents and others present had not prevented him. It was further stated that Don Fernando went away at once and that Luscinda did not recover from her fit until the next day, when she informed her parents that she was in reality the bride of that Cardenio whom I have mentioned.

"Another thing: they say that Cardenio was present at the wedding and that upon seeing Luscinda given to another as a bride, something he had never thought would happen, he had flung himself out of the city in desperation, leaving behind him a note in which he spoke of the wrong that she had done him and announced his intention of going where people would never see him again. All this, as I say, was well known throughout the town and everyone was talking of it, and they talked still more when it was learned that she was not to be found either in her father's house or anywhere in the city, and that as a consequence her parents were frantic, not knowing what measures to take.

"These circumstances of which I had just learned gave me fresh hope, for it seemed to me better not to have found Don Fernando at all than to have found him married, as this meant that the door might not yet be wholly closed upon my chance for happiness. It might be that Heaven had placed this obstacle in the way of a second match as a means of bringing him to realize his obligations to the first one, and perhaps now he would come to reflect that he was, after all, a Christian and owed more consideration to his soul than to mundane matters.

"All these things I turned over in my mind, consoling myself without achieving consolation, pretending that I cherished certain faint and distant hopes of sustaining the life that I now abhor. Being in the city, then, and not knowing what to do since Don Fernando was not there, I chanced to hear a public crier who was promising a large reward to anyone that found me and was giving my age and a description of the clothes I wore. The crier went on to say that I had been taken from the home of my parents by the lad who was with me, a thing that cut me to the quick when I saw how low my reputation had sunk. It was not enough to tarnish my good name by reporting my flight, but they must add with whom I had fled, a person so low of station and so unworthy of my affections. Upon hearing the crier, I left the city immediately, along with my servant, who was already giving signs of wavering in the faith and loyalty that he had promised me, and that same night we entered this mountain fastness, being very much afraid of being discovered.

"But, as the saying is, one evil calls to another, and the end of one trouble is usually the beginning of a greater one. That was the way it was with me; for my servant, who up to that time had been loyal and dependable, upon finding himself with me in this lonely spot, moved more by his own vileness than by my beauty, sought to take advantage of the opportunity which, as he saw it, was offered him by these solitudes. With no shame and less fear of God or respect for me, he made advances to me, and when I replied to his disgraceful proposals with well-merited words of scorn, he left off the entreaties which he had at first employed and began to use force.

"But Heaven is just and seldom or never fails to regard and favor good intentions; and so, with the little strength that I had and no great amount of effort, I managed to push him over a precipice, where I left him, whether dead or alive I do not know. After which, with greater swiftness than I would have thought possible in my weariness and fright, I made my way into the heart of these mountains with no other thought, no other plan, than that of hiding myself here from my father and those whom he had sent out to look for me.

"I cannot tell you how many months ago it was that, animated by this desire, I came here. I ended by meeting a herdsman who took me as his servant to a place in the very heart of these mountains, where I have worked up to now as a shepherd, striving always to stay out in the meadows in order that they might not catch a glimpse of this hair of mine, which you, through no intention on your part, have chanced to discover. However, all my care and ingenuity were in vain, for my master found out that I was not a lad, whereupon there was born in him the same evil passion as in my servant; and inasmuch as fate does not invariably provide a remedy along with a misfortune, I now found no cliff or ravine where I might fling him down as I had done in the other instance. Accordingly, I decided that it would be better to leave him and hide myself once more in this rugged place than to risk trying my strength or force of arguments.

"And so, as I say, I came back here to look for a spot where, with nothing to prevent me, I might beseech Heaven to take pity on my woes and either give me the intelligence and the luck to escape them or else let me lay down my life amid these wastes, leaving no memory of one who, through no fault of hers, has given occasion for talk and gossip in her own and other provinces."

CHAPTER XXIX. *Which treats of the amusing artifice and means employed in extricating our enamored knight from the extremely harsh penance he had inflicted upon himself.*

"AND that, sirs, is the true story of my tragedy. Look now and judge if the sighs to which you listened, the words you heard, the tears that you saw starting from my eyes, might not well have been more in number. When you shall have considered the nature of my disgrace, you will see how vain is all consolation, how impossible is any kind of remedy. All that I ask—a thing that you can and should do—is that you advise me where I may spend the rest of my life without suffering from this deadly fear I have of being found by those who are searching for me. For even though the great love that my parents have for me is assurance that I shall be well received by them, so great is the shame that lays hold of me at the mere thought of appearing in their presence in so different a guise than what they expect, that I regard it as better to banish myself from their sight forever than to look them in the face with the thought that they are beholding my own countenance robbed of that decency that they had a right to expect of me."

Saying this, she fell silent, her visage taking on a hue that showed clearly enough the deep shame and feeling of her soul. The faces of those who listened to her, meanwhile, were filled as much with pity as with wonderment at her troubles, and although the curate was ready to console and counsel her, it was Cardenio who first addressed her.

"The short of it is, lady," he said, "that you are the beauteous Dorotea, only daughter of the rich Clenardo."

Dorotea was astonished at hearing her father's name mentioned, especially by so unprepossessing a person as this; for we have already spoken of the shabby manner in which Cardenio was clothed.

"And who are you, my brother, who thus know my father's name? For I up to now, unless my memory fails me, in all the course of my unhappy story have not mentioned it once."

"I," replied Cardenio, "am that luckless one whom, you tell me, Luscinda claimed for her bridegroom. I am the unfortunate Cardenio, who have been brought to the plight in which you now see me by the evil designs of the same one who is responsible for your being where you are. You behold me now, ragged, half-naked, lacking all human comfort, and, what is worse, lacking in reason as well, of which none is left me save when it pleases Heaven to restore it to me for a brief while. I, Dorotea, am he who was present when Don Fernando committed those wrongs, who waited to hear the yes uttered by his bride, Luscinda. I am he who did not have the courage to wait and see what came of her swoon or what resulted from the letter that was found in her bosom, for my soul did not have the power of suffering to endure so many misfortunes all at once. And so, I lost my patience and quit the house, leaving a letter with my host which I asked him to place in Luscinda's hands.

"After that, I came to these solitudes with the intention of spending the rest of my life here, a life which I hated as if it had been my mortal enemy. Fate, however, was not minded to end my existence, being content to deprive me of my reason, possibly with the object of preserving me for the good fortune of meeting you. If what you have told us is true, as I believe it is, it may be that Heaven has planned a better outcome for our calamities than we think. For since Luscinda, being mine as she openly declared herself to be, cannot marry Don Fernando, and Don Fernando, being yours, cannot marry her, we have a right to hope that Heaven will restore to us that which is ours, seeing that it still exists and has not been alienated or destroyed.

"And since we do have this comfort, not born of an exceedingly remote hope nor founded on the hallucinations of our own minds, I beg of you, lady, to adopt another resolution, letting your virtuous thoughts dwell upon it, as I myself mean to do: namely, to become used to looking forward to better times to come; for I swear to you by the faith of a gentleman and a Christian not to desert you until I see you possessed of Don Fernando. If words will not bring him to recognize his obligations to you, then I will make use of that privilege which my rank as a gentleman gives me and will justly challenge him, calling upon him to give an account of the wrong he has done you, without taking thought of those that I have suffered at his hands and which I shall leave to Heaven to avenge while I here on earth see to righting yours."

By the time that Cardenio finished speaking Dorotea had ceased to wonder at his appearance and, not knowing how to thank him for so great an offer, wished to take his feet and kiss them, but he would not consent. The licentiate replied for both of them, expressing approval of the fine sentiments that Cardenio had voiced, and then he begged, advised, and sought to persuade them to accompany him to his village where he could supply them with the things they lacked and where they could plan how to set about looking for Don Fernando and how to get Dorotea back to her parents, while making such other arrangements as might be necessary.

Cardenio and Dorotea accepted his offer with thanks, and the barber, who had been taking it all in without saying a word, now made a pleasing little speech, declaring his willingness as the curate had done to help them in any way in which he could best be of service. He also informed them what it was that had brought him and his companion to this place, and told them of Don Quixote's strange madness and how they were waiting for the latter's squire who had gone to look for him. Then it was that Cardenio recalled as in a dream the struggle he had had with the knight, and he related the incident to the others, although he no longer remembered what had occasioned the quarrel.

At this moment they heard a shout which the curate and the barber recognized as coming from Sancho Panza, who, not finding the pair where he had left them, was now calling to them at the top of his lungs. They thereupon went forward to meet him, and when they made inquiries concerning Don Quixote, he told them how he had found him clad only in his shirt, very lean, jaundiced-looking, near-dead with hunger, and sighing constantly for his lady Dulcinea. Sancho had told his master that Dulcinea had commanded him to leave this place and come to El Toboso where she was awaiting him, but the knight had replied that he was determined not to appear before his beauteous one until he should have performed such exploits as would render him deserving of her grace. And if all this kept up, the squire added, there was a danger that the poor man would never become an emperor as was his bounden duty, nor even so much as an archbishop, which was the very least that he ought to expect. And so, they must all put their heads together to see what could be done to get him away from there.

The licentiate replied by assuring Sancho that there was no cause for uneasiness, for they would rescue the knight whether he liked it or not. He then revealed to Cardenio and Dorotea the plan they had formed, by which they hoped, in any event, to be able to induce Don Quixote to return home with them. She thereupon remarked that she could play the part of the damsel in distress better than the barber; and what was more, she had with her the garments that would enable her to give a most lifelike semblance to the role. All they needed to do was to leave it all to her and she would see to everything that was necessary to the carrying out of their plan; for she had read many books of chivalry and was familiar with the mode of speech that was employed by afflicted maidens when they sought a boon of knights-errant.

"Well, then," said the curate, "it only remains for us to put our scheme into execution. Fortune is undoubtedly favoring you,[1] seeing that it has so unexpectedly opened the door for your relief, and by doing so it has at the same time facilitated our present task."

Dorotea then took from her pillowcase a skirt made of a certain rich woolen material and a *mantellina* [2] of elegant green cloth, and from a small box she drew forth a necklace and other jewels, and within a moment's time she was adorned as befitted a rich young lady of high estate. All these things and others too, she told them, she had brought with her from home in case of emergency, but up to then she had had no occasion to use them. They were all extremely pleased with her grace and beauty and highbred appearance, which led them to reflect that Don Fernando must have been a man of very little discernment to have cast aside such charms as these.

The one who admired her most of all, however, was Sancho Panza, for it seemed to him, which was indeed the truth, that he had never in all the days of his life beheld so ravishing a creature. He accordingly with great eagerness now inquired of the curate who this beautiful woman might be and what she was doing in these parts.

"This lovely lady, Sancho, my brother," replied the curate, "and let no one tell you otherwise, is heiress in the direct male line to the great kingdom of Micomicon,[3] and she comes here in search of your master to ask a favor of him, which is that he right the injury or wrong which a wicked giant has done her. By reason of the fame as a worthy knight which your master enjoys throughout the known world, this princess has journeyed all the way from Guinea to seek him out." [4]

"Happy search and happy find!" exclaimed Sancho upon hearing this. "And still more so if my master is fortunate enough to right the wrong and redress the injury by slaying that son of a whore of a giant that your Grace is speaking about. Slay him he will if he meets him and the giant is not a phantom, for against phantoms he can do nothing whatsoever. But there is one thing among others, Señor Licentiate, that I would ask of your Grace. In order that my master may not take it into his head to be an archbishop, which is what I am afraid of, I would have your Grace advise him to marry this princess and in that way it would be impossible for him to be ordained, and he would get his empire and I'd get my wish. For I have studied it all out very thoroughly and have come to the conclusion that it would not be a good thing for me if he took holy orders, since I, being married, am of no use to the Church, and it would be an endless business for me with my wife and children to set about trying to obtain a dispensation so that I could hold a benefice. And so, everything depends upon my master's marrying this lady—for as yet I am unacquainted with her Grace and cannot call her by name."

"Her name," said the curate," is Princess Micomicona, for inasmuch as her realm is Micomicon, it could not be anything else."

"I do not doubt that," replied Sancho, "for I have known many who took their name and title from the place where they were born, calling themselves Pedro of Alcalá, Juan of Úbeda, Diego of Valladolid, and so forth, and they must have this same custom in Guinea, that of calling queens after their kingdoms."

"Yes," agreed the curate, "that is the way it is. And as to marrying off your master, I will do all that lies within my power."

Sancho was as pleased with this as the curate was astonished at his simplicity. The priest could not but marvel still at the extent to which the master's mad whims had laid hold of his man's imagination, for there was no doubt that Panza had fully convinced himself that Don Quixote was going to be an emperor.

By this time Dorotea had seated herself upon the curate's mule and the barber had put on his oxtail beard, and they now directed Sancho to lead them to the place where the knight was, after first warning him to give no sign that he knew either the licentiate or his companion, since his master's becoming an emperor depended upon their not being recognized. However, neither Cardenio nor the curate wished to accompany them, the former fearing that Don Quixote would be reminded of their quarrel, while the latter felt that his presence was not called for as yet. They accordingly let the others go on ahead while they followed slowly on foot. The curate in the meantime had not failed to advise Dorotea as to how she was to conduct herself, but she replied that they should not worry about that, for she would do everything precisely as it should be done in accordance with the rules and descriptions in the books of chivalry.

They had gone about three-quarters of a league when they came upon Don Quixote amid a confused cluster of rocks. He was clothed now but did not have on his armor; and as soon as Dorotea had caught sight of him and had been assured that it was he, she applied the whip to her palfrey [5] and hastened toward him, followed by the well-bearded barber. As she drew near to where the knight stood, her squire leaped down from his mule and, taking her in his arms, assisted her to alight, which she did very gracefully. She then fell upon her knees in front of Don Quixote, and, though he did his best to lift her to her feet, she remained kneeling and addressed him in the following manner:

"I shall not rise from this spot, O brave and doughty knight, until you out of your courtesy and kindness shall have granted me a boon, one which will redound to your own honor and glory and which will be of advantage to the most grievously wronged and disconsolate maiden that ever the sun has looked upon. If your immortal fame is indeed borne out by the valor of your strong right arm, then you are bound to show favor to the hapless one who, brought here by the fragrance that attaches to your name of great renown, has come from distant lands to seek a remedy for her woes."

"I shall not answer you a word, beauteous lady," said Don Quixote, "nor will I hear anything more of your business until you rise."

"That, sir, I will not do," responded the afflicted damsel, "unless you first, out of your courtesy, grant me the boon I seek."

"I grant and bestow it," said the knight, "providing that it does no hurt or detriment to my king, my country, and the one who holds the key to the freedom of my heart."

"It shall not be to the hurt or detriment of any of those you mention, my good sir," was the grieving maiden's answer.

Sancho Panza then came up and whispered very softly in his master's ear, "Your Grace may very well grant her the boon she asks, for it is nothing at all: just killing a big giant, and she who asks it is the highborn Princess Micomicona, queen of the great kingdom of Micomicon, in Ethiopia."

"No matter who she may be," said Don Quixote, "I shall do my duty and follow the dictates of my conscience in accordance with the calling that I profess." And, turning to the damsel, he added, "Rise, most beautiful one; I grant you the boon you seek."

"What I ask, then," said the damsel, "is this: that your magnanimous person deign to accompany me at once to the place to which I shall conduct you, and that you further promise me not to concern yourself with any other adventure or request until you shall have taken vengeance on a traitor who, in defiance of all laws human and divine, has usurped my kingdom."

"I tell you again that I grant it," said the knight. "And so, lady, you may now lay aside the melancholy that oppresses you and let your fainting hope recover new strength and courage; for by the aid of God and my good arm you shall soon see your kingdom restored to you and shall sit once again on the throne of your great and ancient realm in spite of all the knaves who would forbid it. To work, then; for it is the common saying that there is danger in delay." [6]

The distressed lady stubbornly insisted upon kissing his hands, but Don Quixote, who in every respect was the courteous and obliging gentleman, would by no means consent to this. Instead, he made her rise and then embraced her with great affability and politeness. He thereupon ordered Sancho to see to Rocinante's girths at once and bring him his suit of armor, which was hanging like a trophy from the bough of a tree. The squire did as he had been commanded. Having taken down the armor, he helped his master on with it, and then, seeing his steed in readiness and himself in battle harness, Don Quixote spoke.

"Let us go," he said, "in the name of God, that we may succor this great lady."

The barber was still on his knees, doing his best to keep from laughing and to prevent his beard from falling off, for if that had happened they would not have been able to carry out their clever scheme. Upon hearing the boon granted and perceiving that Don Quixote was so ready to embark upon the enterprise, he arose and took his lady's other hand and between the two of them they helped her on the mule. The knight then mounted Rocinante and the barber his own beast, while Sancho came along on foot, which led him to think once more of the gray ass whose loss he now felt worse than ever, although he bore it all very cheerfully, being convinced that his master was on the road to becoming an emperor very soon; for there was no doubt that he would marry this princess and become at the very least king of Micomicon. The only thing that troubled Sancho was that the kingdom in question was in the land of the blacks, and his vassals accordingly would all be Negroes. But for this he at once thought of a good remedy.

"Does it make any difference to me if they are black?" he said to himself. "What more do I have to do than take a boatload of them to Spain and sell them for ready cash, and with the money buy some title or office and live at ease all the rest of my life? That is to say, unless I'm asleep and am not clever or shrewd enough to make the most of things and sell thirty or ten thousand vassals in the twinkling of an eye! By God, but I'd make them fly, the little with the big, or do the best I could at it; I'd turn the blacks into white or yellow men! But come, I'm making a fool of myself!" [7]

Occupied with these thoughts, he went along so contentedly that he forgot all about his annoyance at having to travel on foot.

Observing all this from behind a thicket, Cardenio and the curate did not know just how to set about joining the others, but the priest, who was a great schemer, at once thought up a means by which they could accomplish what they desired. Taking out a pair of scissors that he carried with him in a sheath, he very skillfully trimmed Cardenio's beard and then threw over his companion's shoulders a drab-colored cape that he wore, giving him in addition a black coat, while he himself remained in breeches and doublet; all of which so altered the young man's appearance that he would not have recognized his own image in a mirror. While they were thus engaged in disguising themselves, the others had gone on ahead, but they had little difficulty in reaching the highroad before Don Quixote and his party did, for owing to the brambles and the rough places it was impossible to make as good time mounted as on foot. They therewith took up their position on the plain at the entrance to the mountain passes, and as soon as Don Quixote and his companions appeared, the curate began staring at the knight from afar, making signs as if he recognized him. After he had stood gazing at him in this fashion for a little while, he went up to him with open arms.

"Why bless me!" he exclaimed, "what a fortunate thing that I should here encounter the mirror of chivalry, my good countryman, Don Quixote de la Mancha, the flower and cream of nobility, friend and protector of those in distress, the very quintessence of knight-errantry!"

Saying this, he embraced the knight's left knee. Startled at the man's words and behavior, Don Quixote studied him attentively for a moment or so and then, recognizing him at last and being very much taken aback at seeing him there, made a great effort to dismount. The curate, however, would not permit him to do so.

"But allow me, Señor Licentiate," Don Quixote protested. "It is not fitting that I should remain mounted while a reverend person like your Grace is on foot."

"To that," replied the curate, "I can by no means give my consent. Let your Excellency remain on horseback since it was on horseback that you accomplished the greatest exploits and adventures that this age of ours has known. As for me, unworthy priest that I am, it will be enough if I may ride the crupper of one of the mules belonging to these gentlefolk who are of your company—that is to say, if there is no objection to it. If you grant this, it will seem to me that I go mounted on the steed Pegasus, or upon the zebra, or else upon the charger that the famous Moor Muzaraque rode, the same Muzaraque who to this day lies enchanted beneath the great slope of Zulema, not far distant from the great Complutum." [8]

"That, Señor Licentiate, is something to which I in turn cannot agree," said Don Quixote. "I am sure that my lady the princess will do me the favor of commanding her squire to yield you his saddle upon the mule, and he can ride the beast's crupper if she will allow it."

"She will, I am sure," said the princess; "and as to commanding my squire, that will not be necessary, for he is so courteous and urbane that he would never think of letting a churchman go on foot while he himself was in the saddle."

"Indeed, I would not," said the barber. And, dismounting at once, he offered his seat to the curate, who accepted it without much urging.

The unfortunate thing was, however, that just as the barber was settling himself upon the crupper, the mule—which was one of those that are for hire, that is to say, a bad one—raised its hind quarters in the air and gave a couple of kicks which, had he received them in the head or chest, would have caused Master Nicholas to curse himself for ever having come in search of Don Quixote. As it was, the shock was such that he was thrown to the ground, and at the same time his beard, to which he was able to give little thought, fell off. Finding himself without it, he could think of nothing better to do than cover his face with both hands and moan that his grinders had been knocked out.

Seeing that heap of beard lying there, far from the squire's face but without any sign of jawbone or blood, Don Quixote cried out, "By the living God, this is a miracle! His beard has been knocked off and torn away from his face as cleanly as if he had deliberately shaved it off."

The curate, seeing that his scheme was in danger of being discovered, ran over and, snatching up the beard, took it over to where Master Nicholas still lay. Drawing the barber's head down to his chest, he quickly attached the oxtail once more, muttering certain words as he did so which he said were a psalm that was appropriate to the sticking-on of beards, as they would see for themselves. Then he stepped aside, and there was the squire as well bearded and sound of limb as he had been before. Don Quixote was tremendously impressed by this and begged the curate, when he had time, to teach him that psalm, since it must be possessed of virtues beyond the one just demonstrated, it being obvious that when beards are torn off the flesh must remain raw and bleeding, but there was nothing like that in the present instance. The psalm, then, must be good for something more than beards.

"That it is," said the curate; and he promised to teach it to him at the first opportunity.

It was agreed upon among them that for the present the curate should mount the mule and that he should take turns with Cardenio and the barber until they reached the inn, a distance of some two leagues from there.[9] There were, then, three of them in the saddle, namely, Don Quixote, the princess, and the priest, while the other three walked along beside them.

As they started out, the knight turned to the damsel. "My lady," he said, "will your Highness be so good as to lead the way?"

Before she could reply, the licentiate spoke up. "Toward what kingdom does your Ladyship mean to guide us? Is it by any chance the realm of Micomicon? I take it that it is, or I know little of kingdoms."

She, being well schooled in everything, understood that she was supposed to answer yes, and so she said, "Yes, sir, my road lies toward that realm."

"If that is so," said the curate, "then we shall have to pass through my village, and from there your Grace will take the highway to Cartagena, where with good fortune you will be able to embark; and if you have a fair wind and a calm sea without squalls, in less than nine years you should come within sight of the great Meona—I mean Meotides—lake,[10] which is only a little more than a hundred days' journey from your Highness's kingdom."

"Your Grace is mistaken," she replied, "for it is not yet two years since

I left there; and although the truth is that I never had good weather, nevertheless I am here to behold that which I so greatly desired: Señor Don Quixote de la Mancha, whose fame, reaching my ears the moment I set foot in Spain, has induced me to seek him out, commend myself to his courtesy, and entrust my cause to the might of his invincible arm."

"That will be enough!" said Don Quixote. "Let me hear no more words of praise! For I am opposed to any kind of adulation, and even though this be no fawning, such talk for all of that offends my chaste ears. But one thing I may tell you, my lady: whether my arm is or is not possessed of might, it shall be employed in your service until I yield my life in your behalf. But, leaving all this for the time being, I should like to ask the Señor Licentiate what it is that brings him to these parts, alone, unaccompanied even by servants, and so lightly clad that I am really amazed by it."

"I can answer that in a few words," said the curate. "I may inform your Grace that I and Master Nicholas, our friend and barber, were on our way to Seville to collect a certain sum of money which a relative of mine who went to the Indies many years ago had sent me. It was not so small a sum at that, since it came to more than seventy thousand pieces of eight duly assayed, which is something. And as we were passing through this region yesterday we were set upon by four highwaymen who stripped us of everything down to our beards, and, as a result, the barber had to put on a false one. Even this young man here," and he pointed to Cardenio, "they so mistreated that you would not recognize him.

"And the best part of it is," the curate went on, "it is a matter of common rumor around here that those who set upon us were certain galley slaves who, so they tell me, had been freed on this very spot by a man so valiant that, in spite of the commissary and the guards, he was able to turn them all loose. He must undoubtedly have been out of his mind, or else he must be as great a villain as they, some soulless creature without a conscience; for one might as well think of turning the wolf loose among the sheep, the fox among the hens, the fly in the honey,[11] as to seek to defraud justice and go against the king, his natural liege lord, for this was indeed an act against his Majesty's just commandments. I tell you, that one has cheated the gallows of their feet, has aroused the Holy Brotherhood which for many years had been quiet, and, finally, has committed an act for which he well may lose his soul while his body gains nothing by it."

Sancho had told the curate and the barber about the adventure of the galley slaves and the glory that his master had achieved thereby; and the priest now thought that he would allude to it by way of seeing what Don Quixote would say or do. The knight changed color at every word and did not dare to tell them that he was the one who had freed those worthy folk.

"And they," continued the curate, "were the ones who robbed us. May God in His mercy pardon him who kept them from the punishment they deserved."

CHAPTER XXX. *Which treats of the fair Dorotea's ready wit and other matters very pleasant and amusing.*

THE curate had scarcely finished speaking when Sancho addressed him.

"Faith, Señor Licentiate," he said, "the one who performed that deed was my master. Not that I didn't warn him beforehand and advise him to look to what he was doing, it being a sin to free them, for they were all of them the greatest rogues that ever were."

"Blockhead!" cried Don Quixote upon hearing this. "It is not the business of knights-errant to stop and ascertain as to whether the afflicted and oppressed whom they encounter going along the road in chains like that are in such straits by reason of their crimes or as a result of misfortunes that they have suffered. The only thing that does concern them is to aid those individuals as persons in distress, with an eye to their sufferings and not to their villainies. I chanced to meet with a rosary, or string, of poor wretches and merely did for them that which my religion demands of me. As for the rest, that is no affair of mine. And whoever thinks ill of it—saving the dignity of your holy office and your respected person, Señor Licentiate—I will simply say that he knows little of the laws of chivalry and lies like an ill-begotten son of a whore. All of which I will make plain to him, to the fullest extent, with my sword."

Having said this, he settled himself in the stirrups and pulled down his morion; for the barber's basin, which to him was Mambrino's helmet, he carried hanging from the saddletree in front of him until such time as he could have the damage repaired that the galley slaves had done to it. Then Dorotea, who was a very discerning and witty young lady, perceiving the mad character of Don Quixote's fancies and noting that all the others with the exception of Sancho were making sport of him, decided that she would have her share of the fun; and observing how annoyed he was, she now spoke to him.

"Sir Knight," she said, "I would remind your Grace of the boon that you have promised me, and of the stipulation that you are not to engage in any other adventure however urgent it may be. And so, let your Grace calm that breast of yours, for had the Señor Licentiate known that it was by your unconquered arm those prisoners were liberated, he would have taken three stitches in his lip or would have bit his tongue three times before he would have spoken a disrespectful word of your Grace."

"That I would, I swear it," said the curate, "and I would even have lopped off a mustache."

"I will be silent, my lady," Don Quixote assured her. "I will repress the just wrath that has arisen in my bosom and will go along quietly and peacefully until I shall have rendered you the boon that I have promised. But in return for this good will on my part, I beg you, if it will not trouble you too much, to tell me what the nature of your grievance is and who, how many, and of what sort are the persons of whom I am to demand full satisfaction and upon whom I am to wreak an utter vengeance."

"That I will gladly do," replied Dorotea, "if it will not tire you to listen to my griefs and misfortunes."

"It most certainly will not, my lady," said Don Quixote.

"Very well, then," continued Dorotea, "pay attention, kind sirs."

As she said this, Cardenio and the barber came up alongside her, for they were curious to see how her ready wit would serve her in making up her story; and Sancho likewise drew near, though he was as much deceived by her as was his master. Having straightened herself in the saddle, she coughed a little and indulged in a few other mannerisms by way of gaining time and then with an easy grace began her narrative.

"In the first place, I would have your Worships know that I am called—" At this point she paused for a moment, for she had forgotten the name which the curate had bestowed upon her. He, however, seeing what her trouble was, promptly came to her rescue.

"It is no wonder, my lady," he said, "if your Highness in relating your

misfortunes should become confused and embarrassed; for they are of the
kind that very frequently deprive those who suffer them of their
memory, so that they are unable even to remember their own names. That
is what has happened to your exalted Ladyship, who has forgotten that
she is the Princess Micomicona, legitimate heiress to the great kingdom
of Micomicon; but with this reminder, your Highness will readily be
able to recall all that she may desire to tell us."

"That is true enough," said the damsel. "And from now on, I do not
believe that I shall require any more prompting but shall be able to bring
this true story of mine safely into port. To continue, then: The king my
father bore the name Tinacrio the Wise, being very learned in what is
known as the art of magic. It was through this science that he learned that
my mother, the queen Jaramilla, was to die before he did and that he himself shortly after would pass from this life, leaving me bereaved of father
and mother alike. He said, however, that this did not cause him so much
anxiety as did the certain knowledge of what a monstrous giant, the lord
of a great island near our kingdom who was called Pandafilando of the
Frowning Look, was to do when he heard that I was left an orphan. This
giant was so called for the reason that, so it was asserted, though his eyes
were straight enough, he always squinted as if cross-eyed by way of giving himself a malignant appearance and striking fear and terror in those
who beheld him.

"But as I was saying: My father knew that this giant, upon learning
that I was an orphan, was to overrun my kingdom with a powerful army
and drive me out of it, without leaving me so much as a tiny village where
I might take refuge. The only thing that could save me from all this ruin
and misfortune was for me to consent to marry him, but my father pre-
dicted that I would never agree to so unsuitable a match, and in this he
was quite right, for I never would have entertained the thought of taking
this or any other giant for a husband, however powerful and lawless he
might be.

"My father also said that when, following his death, I saw my realm
being overrun by Pandafilando, I should not wait to put myself upon the
defensive, since that would be sheer self-destruction, but that, if I would
avoid the slaughter of my good and loyal vassals, I should leave the kingdom free and open to him, since it would be impossible to defend myself
against his diabolic strength. What I rather must do was to take a few
attendants and set out for Spain, where I would find relief for my troubles
in the person of a certain knight-errant, whose fame at that time extended

throughout the whole of our country and whose name, unless my memory plays me false, was Azote or Don Gigote—"

"Don Quixote it should be, lady," Sancho Panzo corrected her, "otherwise known as the Knight of the Mournful Countenance."

"Yes, that is it," said Dorotea. "My father told me more: that this knight was to be tall, with a lean face, and that on his right side, under his left shoulder, or somewhere thereabouts, he was to have a brown mole with a few hairs around it resembling bristles."

Upon hearing this, Don Quixote said to his squire, "Come here, Sancho, my son, and help me undress, for I wish to see if I am the knight that wise king meant when he made that prophecy."

"But why undress, your Grace?" asked Dorotea.

"To see if I have the mole that your father spoke of," Don Quixote replied.

"There is no need of your Grace's doing that," said Sancho, "for I happen to know that you have a mole with those markings in the middle of your backbone, which is the sign of a strong man."

"That will suffice," said Dorotea. "With friends, one does not look into little things, and whether it is on his shoulder or his backbone does not greatly matter; it is enough that he has it wherever it may be, seeing that it is all of the same flesh. There is no doubt that my father was right in everything, and I was right in throwing myself on the mercy of Don Quixote. I know that he is the one my father meant, for the signs of his face are in accord with the high repute which this knight enjoys not only in Spain but throughout La Mancha. Indeed, I had barely disembarked at Osuna when I heard of all his many exploits, and my heart at once told me that he was the one I had come to seek."

"But, my lady," said Don Quixote, "how is it that your Grace disembarked at Osuna when it is not a seaport?"

Before she could reply, the curate took a hand in the matter. "What the princess must mean," he said, "is that after she had disembarked at Málaga, the first place that she had news of your Grace was in Osuna."

"Yes, that is what I meant to say," said Dorotea.

"That is all natural enough," remarked the priest. "And now, if your Highness will continue—"

"There is nothing more to add, except that, in the end, fate has been kind to me and I have found Señor Don Quixote. As a consequence, I already account and look upon myself as the queen and liege lady of all my realm, since he out of his courtesy and splendid bounty has promised to grant me the boon of going with me wherever I may take him, and that will be nowhere else than to the place where he may confront Pandafilando of the Frowning Look, in order that he may slay him and restore to me those domains that the giant has so unjustly usurped. And all this is bound to come about, for my good father, Tinacrio the Wise, has prophesied it; and he also said, and put it down in writing, in Chaldean or Greek characters which I am unable to read, that if this knight, after having beheaded the giant, wished to marry me, I was to give myself at once, with not the slightest demurring, to be his legitimate bride, and I was to yield him possession of my kingdom along with that of my person."

"What do you think of that, friend Sancho?" said Don Quixote at this point. "Do you hear what is happening? What did I tell you? Just look, we already have a kingdom to rule over and a queen to wed."

"You're right, I'll swear you are," said Sancho, "and he's a whoring rascal who wouldn't slit that Señor Pandahilado's windpipe and marry her! Why, just see how homely she is! I only wish the fleas in my bed were like that!"

Saying this, he gave a couple of leaps in the air with a great show of satisfaction and then ran up to take the reins of Dorotea's mule; forcing her to come to a halt, he fell upon his knees before her, begging her to let him have her hands to kiss as a sign that he took her to be his queen and mistress. Who would not have had a good laugh over it all, at beholding the master's madness and his servant's simple-mindedness? Dorotea let him kiss her hand and promised to make him a great lord of her realm, whenever Heaven should be so kind as to let her recover and enjoy it. And Sancho thanked her for these favors in words that set them all to laughing once more.

"That, gentlemen," continued the princess, "is my story. It only remains for me to tell you that of the many subjects whom I brought along there is left me only this well-bearded squire, for all the others were drowned in a great storm which overtook us within sight of port. He and I by a miracle managed to reach land upon a couple of planks; but, for that matter, my entire life is at once a miracle and a mystery, as you will have observed. If in telling my story I have in any respect been too prolix or not as accurate as I should have been, the blame must be ascribed to the circumstance which the curate mentioned at the beginning: the tendency of constant and extraordinary troubles to deprive those who suffer them of their memory."

"They shall not deprive me of mine, O highborn and worthy lady!"

said Don Quixote. "And it makes no difference how many I shall have
to endure in serving you nor how great and unheard of they may be. And
so, once again I confirm the boon I promised you and swear to go with
you to the end of the world until I find myself face to face with that
fierce enemy of yours. God helping me, and my own good arm, I mean
to cut off his head with the edge of this—I cannot say good sword, thanks
to Ginés de Pasamonte who carried mine away with him." [1] (This was
uttered between his teeth.) "And after I have cut it off," he went on,
"and have placed you in peaceful possession of your country, it will then
be for you to make such disposition of your person as you may desire;
for so long as my memory is occupied, my will held captive, and my mind
enslaved by a certain lady—I say no more—it is out of the question for me
to think of marrying anyone, even the Phoenix herself."

This last remark on the part of his master, to the effect that he did not
wish to marry, displeased Sancho very much, and it was with a great deal
of annoyance that he now spoke to the knight.

"Señor Don Quixote," he exclaimed, "I swear and vow that you are not
in your right senses! How can your Grace hesitate about marrying so
highborn a princess? Do you think that fortune is going to offer you
behind every stone such a piece of luck as this? Is my lady Dulcinea more
beautiful, perchance? No, indeed, not by a half; and I will even say that
she does not come up to the shoe of the one you see in front of you. A
fine chance I have of getting that earldom I'm waiting for if your Grace
goes around looking for tidbits at the bottom of the ocean.[2] Marry, then,
marry, in Satan's name, and take this kingdom which is falling into your
hands with no effort on your part;[3] and then, when you are king, make
me a marquis or the governor of a province, and to the devil with all the
rest."

Unable to endure such blasphemies against his lady Dulcinea, Don
Quixote raised his lance and, without saying a word to Sancho or giving
him a warning of any kind, he let him have a couple of thwacks which
sent him sprawling on the ground; and if Dorotea had not cried out to
him to desist, the knight undoubtedly would have finished off his squire
then and there.

"Do you think, base lout," he said after a while, "that you can always
be meddling in my affairs and that you can do anything you like and
I will forgive you? If so, excommunicated knave, for that undoubtedly
is what you are, think it no longer, now that you have set your tongue
to wagging against the peerless Dulcinea! Do you not know, clodhopper,
drudge, scoundrel, that if it were not for the valor she infuses into my

arm, I should not have the strength to kill a flea? Tell me, rascal with a viper's tongue, what do you think it was that won this kingdom and cut off that giant's head and made you a marquis—for I regard all this as a thing settled and accomplished—unless it was Dulcinea's own valor making use of my arm merely as the instrument for the achievement of her own enterprises? She fights and conquers in my person, and I live and breathe and have my life and being in her. O knavish son of a whoring mother, how ungrateful you are! You see yourself raised from the dust of the earth to be a titled lord, and all this you repay by speaking ill of your benefactress!"

Sancho was not so badly stunned that he did not hear all his master was saying, and, scrambling to his feet with some agility, he ran and stood behind Dorotea's palfrey and from there answered the knight.

"Tell me this, sir," he said. "If your Grace is bent upon not marrying this great princess, then it is clear that the kingdom will not be yours, and if that is the case, what favors will you be in a position to do me? That is just what I am complaining about. Let your Grace marry this queen once and for all, now that we have her here as if she had been rained down from Heaven, and afterward you can go back to my lady Dulcinea. After all, there must have been kings in this world who kept concubines. So far as beauty is concerned, I'm not saying anything about that. To tell you the truth, I like them both, although I have never seen the lady Dulcinea."

"What do you mean, you have never seen her, blasphemous traitor?" said Don Quixote. "Did you not just bring me a message from her?"

"What I mean," replied Sancho, "is that I did not have a good look at her. That is to say, I did not have a chance to take particular note of her beauty and her good features, point by point, but in the bulk I liked her well enough."

"Then I forgive you," said Don Quixote, "and pardon me for having lost my temper, for it is not in the power of men to control their first impulses."

"I can see that," said Sancho. "My first impulse is always the desire to speak, and I cannot keep from saying for once at least whatever is on the tip of my tongue."

"Nevertheless," his master admonished him, "be careful of your words, Sancho; for the pitcher that goes to the well too often—I need say no more." [4]

"Ah, well," replied his squire, "God's in his Heaven and sees all our tricks, and He will be the judge of who is the greater sinner: I in not speaking as I should, or you in doing what you should not do."

"Let's have no more of this!" cried Dorotea. "Sancho, run over and kiss your master's hand and beg his pardon, and from now on be more careful of whom you praise and whom you vituperate, and do not be speaking ill of that lady Tobosa, whom I do not know but whose servant I am. Meanwhile, trust in God to raise you to that condition where you may live like a prince."

Hanging his head, Sancho then came up and asked for his master's hand, and Don Quixote extended it with great dignity and composure. After the squire had kissed it, the knight gave him his blessing and then suggested that they go on a little way together as he had something to ask him and some very important matters to discuss with him.

Sancho complied with this request, and when they were some little distance in advance of the others, Don Quixote said to him, "Since you returned, I have not had the time nor the opportunity to question you with regard to many of the details connected with your mission and the answer that you brought back with you; and now that fortune does provide the time and the place, do not deny me the pleasure that you can give me with such good news."

"Ask whatever you will, your Grace," said Sancho, "and I will find my way out of everything as well as I found my way in. But I beg your Grace not to be so revengeful after this."

"Why do you say that, Sancho?"

"I say it," he replied, "because those blows you gave me just now were more for the quarrel that the devil got us into the other night than for anything that I said against my lady Dulcinea, whom I love and reverence as I would a relic—not that I mean to say she is one; I was merely thinking of her as something belonging to your Grace."

"Upon your life, Sancho," said Don Quixote, "let us not go back to that subject, for it is one that causes me annoyance. I have pardoned you for it once, and you know the saying—'Fresh sin, fresh penance.' " [5]

[As they were proceeding in this manner, they saw coming down the road toward them a man mounted upon an ass, who, as he drew near, appeared to them to be a gypsy. But Sancho Panza, whose heart and soul were stirred every time he caught sight of a donkey, had no sooner laid eyes on the fellow than he recognized him as Ginés de Pasamonte, and in this case the gypsy served as the thread that led him to the yarn-ball of his stolen gray, for it was indeed the gray upon which Pasamonte was riding. That worthy, in order to dispose of the ass and avoid being identified, had got himself up in gypsy costume, for he knew how to speak their language and many others as if they had been his native tongue.

As soon as Sancho had seen and recognized him, he called out at the top of his voice, "Hey, Ginesillo, you thief! Release my jewel, my treasure, my life, the beast on which I take my rest. Flee, you whoring knave; begone, you robber, and leave me that which is not yours!"

All these words and insults were quite unnecessary, for at the first sound of Sancho's voice Ginés had leaped down and, trotting, or, better, running, away, had soon left them all behind. Sancho then went up to the gray and threw his arms around it.

"How have you been, old friend," he said, "joy of my life, apple of my eye?" With this, he kissed and caressed it as if it had been a person, the ass standing quietly all the while, submitting without a word to this show of affection. The others now came up and congratulated him on the recovery of the beast, especially Don Quixote, who assured him that he would not for this reason annul the order for the three ass-colts, for which Sancho thanked him very much.]

As the two [6] went along conversing in this manner, the curate remarked to Dorotea that she had shown a great deal of cleverness in the telling of her story as well as in keeping it so short and preserving so close a resemblance to the books of chivalry. She replied that she had often found entertainment in reading those books; but, unfortunately, she was unfamiliar with the various provinces and seaports and so had said, quite at random, that she had landed at Osuna.

"I suspected as much," said the curate, "and for that reason I came to your assistance by saying what I did, which smoothed everything over. But is it not a strange thing to see how readily this unfortunate gentleman believes all these falsehoods and inventions, simply because they are in the style and manner of those absurd tales?"

"It is indeed," said Cardenio, "so rare and unheard of a thing that if anyone desired to invent and fabricate it, in the form of fiction, I do not know if there would be any mind that would be equal to the task."

"But there is another aspect of the matter," the curate went on. "Outside of the nonsense that he talks where his madness is concerned, if some other subject comes up he will discuss it most intelligently and will reason everything out very calmly and clearly; and, accordingly, unless the topic of chivalry is mentioned, no one would ever take him to be anything other than a man of very sound sense."

While this conversation was in progress, Don Quixote was saying to Sancho, "Friend Sancho, let us make up our quarrel. And now, laying aside all rancor and irritation, tell me how and when it was you found Dulcinea. What was she doing? What did you say to her and what did she reply? What was the expression on her face when she read my letter? Who copied it out for you? Tell me all this and everything else that seems to you worth knowing or asking about or concerning which I might be curious, neither adding anything nor telling me anything that is not true merely to please me; and be sure that you do not shorten the story and thereby deprive me of any of it."

"Sir," replied Sancho, "if I am to tell the truth, the letter was not copied for me by anyone, for I did not have it with me."

"That is true enough," said Don Quixote, "for a couple of days after you had left I found the memorandum book in which I had written it out and was very much grieved about it, not knowing what you would do when you found you did not have it, though I felt sure you would return for it."

"That is what I'd have done," said Sancho, "if I hadn't learned it by heart while your Grace was reading it to me, so that I was able to recite it to a sacristan who copied it all down for me, point by point. And he said that in the course of his life he had read many a letter of excommunication but never a pretty one like that."

"And do you still remember it, Sancho?" Don Quixote asked.

"No, sir, I do not; for as soon as I had said it over to him, seeing that I had no further need of remembering it, I proceeded to forget it. If there is anything I do recall, it is that business about the sufferable—I mean, sovereign—lady, and the ending, 'Yours until death, the Knight of the Mournful Countenance.' And between those two I put in 'my soul,' 'my life,' and 'light of my eyes,' more than three hundred times."

CHAPTER XXXI. *Of the delectable conversation that took place between Don Quixote and Sancho Panza, his squire, together with other events.*

"ALL this does not displease me," said Don Quixote. "You may continue. What was my beauteous queen engaged in doing when you arrived? Surely you must have found her stringing pearls or embroidering some device in gold thread for this her captive knight."

"No," replied Sancho, "I did not. I found her winnowing two fanegas [1] of wheat in the stable yard of her house."

"If that is so," said Don Quixote, "then you may be sure that those grains of wheat were so many pearls when her fingers touched them. And did you observe, my friend, if the wheat was fine and white or of the ordinary spring-sown variety?"

"It was neither," Sancho informed him; "it was the reddish kind."

"Then I assure you," the knight insisted, "that without a doubt, when winnowed by her hands, it made the finest of white bread. But go on. When you gave her my letter, did she kiss it? Did she place it on her head [2] or accord it any ceremony such as it deserved? If not, what was it that she did?"

"When I went to give it to her," said Sancho, "she was busy swinging the sieve, with a good part of the wheat in it, from side to side. 'Lay it on that sack,' she said to me. 'I'll not have time to read it until I have finished sifting all that there is here.'"

"Discreet lady!" said Don Quixote. "That was in order that she might take her time in reading it and revel in it. Continue, Sancho. While she was thus occupied, what words passed between you? Did she ask after me? And what did you say in reply? Come, tell me all and do not leave the smallest part of it in the inkwell." [3]

"She asked me nothing," said Sancho, "but I told her how your Grace, in her service, was doing penance naked from the waist up, living in these mountains like a wild animal, sleeping on the ground, without eating bread off a tablecloth or combing your beard, and weeping and cursing over your unhappy fate."

"That was wrong to say that I was cursing my unhappy fate; the truth is, I bless it and shall do so all the days of my life, for having rendered me worthy of loving so highborn a lady as Dulcinea del Toboso."

"She is so high," said Sancho, "that she tops me by more than a hand's breadth."

"How do you come to know that, Sancho? Did you measure with her?"

"I measured in this way. When I went to help her lift a sack of wheat onto a mule's back, we stood so close alongside each other that I could see she was the taller by more than a good-sized palm."

"That may be true," said Don Quixote, "though her height is accompanied and set off by a thousand million spiritual graces! You will not deny one thing, Sancho: that when you come near her you are conscious of a Sabaean odor, an aromatic fragrance, an indescribable and pleasing something for which I can find no name? What I mean is, an exhalation or emanation, as if one were in the shop of some exquisite glovemaker."

"All I can tell you," said Sancho, "is that I did notice a sort of mannish smell about her—it must have been because she was working so hard and all in a sweat."

"No," said Don Quixote, "it could not have been that. You must have been suffering from a cold in the head, or else it was yourself that you were smelling; for I well know what the fragrance of that rose among thorns is like—that lily of the field, that bit of diluted amber."

"You may be right," said Sancho, "for very often that same smell comes from me that I then thought was coming from her Grace, the lady Dulcinea. There's nothing surprising in that, for one devil's like another, you know."

"Very well, then," continued Don Quixote, "she has finished sifting her wheat and sent it to the mill. What did she do when she read the letter?"

"She did not read it; for, as I have told you, she does not know how to read or write. Instead, she tore it up into small pieces, saying she did not want anyone else to see it and have her private affairs known in the village. It was enough what I had told her about the love your Grace has for her and the extraordinary penance you are doing for her sake. Finally, she said to tell your Grace that she kissed your hands and that she would rather see you than write to you. And she further begged and commanded you, upon receipt of this message, to leave off your foolishness, come out of these woods, and set out at once for El Toboso before something worse happened to you, for she was very anxious for a sight of your Grace. She had a good laugh when I told her that your Grace was known as the Knight of the Mournful Countenance. I asked her if the Biscayan that we met a long while ago had been there, and she told me that he had been and that he was a very fine man. I also asked after the galley slaves, but she said she had seen nothing of any of them as yet."

"All goes very well up to now," said Don Quixote. "But tell me, what jewel was it that she gave you when you took your leave, in return for the news of me that you had brought her? For it is the usage and ancient custom among knights- and ladies-errant to present to the squires, damsels, or dwarfs who bring them word of their mistresses or their champions some costly gem as a guerdon and token of appreciation of the message they have received."

"That may all be true," said Sancho, "and I think it is a very good custom myself; but that must have been in times past, for nowadays all that they commonly give you is a little bread and cheese, which is what I had from my lady Dulcinea. She handed it to me over the wall of the stable yard as I was leaving, and that it might be still more of a token, it was cheese made from sheep's milk."

"She is extremely generous," observed Don Quixote, "and if she did not give you a golden jewel, it was undoubtedly because she did not have one at hand, for sleeves are good after Easter.⁴ I shall see her and everything will be taken care of. But do you know what astonishes me, Sancho? I think you must have gone and returned through the air, for it has taken you less than three days to make the journey from here to El Toboso and back, a distance of more than thirty leagues. Which leads me to think that the wise necromancer who watches over my affairs and is a friend of mine—for there must be someone of that sort or else I should not be a real knight-errant—I think he must have aided you without your knowing it. For there are cases in which one of those magicians will snatch up a knight-errant as he lies sleeping in his bed and, without his knowing how or in what manner it was done, the next morning that knight will find himself thousands of leagues away from where he was the evening before.

"If it were not for this, knights-errant would not be able to succor one another when in peril as they are in the habit of doing all the time. For it may happen that one of them is fighting in the mountains of Armenia with some dragon or other fierce monster or with another knight, and he is having the worst of the battle and is at the point of death when suddenly, just as he least expects it, there appears over his head upon a cloud or a chariot of fire another knight, a friend of his, who a short while before was in England and who has now come to aid him and save him from death; and that same evening he is back at his lodgings having a pleasant dinner, although from one place to the other is a distance of two or three thousand leagues. All this is done through the wisdom and ingenuity of those skilled enchanters who watch over valiant knights. And so, friend Sancho, it is not hard for me to believe that you have gone from here to El Toboso and back in so short a space of time, for, as I have said, some wise magician must have carried you through the air without your knowing it."

"That may be," said Sancho, "for 'pon my word, if Rocinante didn't go as if he had been a gypsy's donkey with quicksilver in his ears!" [5]

"Quicksilver indeed!" exclaimed Don Quixote; "and a legion of devils besides, for they are folk who can travel and cause others to travel without growing weary, whenever the fancy takes them. But, putting all this aside, what do you think I should do now about going to see my lady as she has commanded? On the one hand, I am obligated to obey her command, and on the other, this is rendered impossible by the promise I have given to the princess who accompanies us, and the law of knighthood requires that I should keep my word before satisfying my own inclinations. I am wearied and harassed with longing to see my lady, yet my pledged word and the glory to be won in this undertaking calls to me and spurs me on.

"What I plan to do, accordingly, is to go with all haste to where this giant is, and then, after I have cut off his head and restored the princess to the peaceful possession of her throne, I shall return at once to see the light that illuminates my senses, giving her such excuses for my delay that she will come to be glad of it, inasmuch as it all redounds to her greater fame and glory. All that I have ever achieved or shall achieve by force of arms in this life is due to the favor she bestows upon me and the fact that I am hers."

"Ah," cried Sancho, "what a sad muddle your Grace's brains are in! For tell me, sir, do you mean to go all that way for nothing and let slip the chance of making so rich and important a match as this, where the bride's dowry is a kingdom? A kingdom which in all truth, I have heard them say, is more than twenty thousand leagues around, which abounds in all the things that are necessary to support human life, and which, in short, is greater than Portugal and Castile combined. For the love of God, do not talk like that, but be ashamed of what you have just said. Pardon me and take my advice, which is that you get married in the first village where you find a curate; or, for that matter, here is our own licentiate, who would do a first-rate job. Believe me, I am old enough to be giving advice, and this that I now give you is very pat; for a small bird in the hand is worth more than a vulture on the wing,[6] and he who has the good and chooses the bad, let the good that he longs for not come to him."[7]

"See here, Sancho," said Don Quixote, "if the reason for your advising me to marry is that you wish me, when I have slain the giant, to become a king at once so that I shall be in a position to grant you the favors I have promised, I may inform you that without marrying I can very easily gratify your desires; for before going into battle I shall lay down the condition that, in case I come out victorious, whether I marry or not, they are to give me a part of the kingdom which I may bestow upon whomsoever I see fit, and to whom should I give it if not to you?"

"That is fair enough," said Sancho, "but let your Grace see to it that my part is on the seacoast, so that, if I don't like the life there, I can take ship with my Negro vassals and do with them what I have said. Meanwhile, your Grace should not be seeing my lady Dulcinea just now, but should rather go and kill the giant and have done with this business; for, by God, it strikes me there's great honor and profit in it."

"You are quite right about that, Sancho, and I shall take your advice so far as going with the princess before I see Dulcinea is concerned. And I would impress upon you that you are to say nothing to anyone, including those who come with us, regarding the subject that we have just been discussing; for Dulcinea is of so retiring a disposition that she would not have her thoughts known, and it is not for me or any other to reveal them."

"Well, then," said Sancho, "how comes it that your Grace sends all those whom you conquer by the might of your arm to present themselves before my lady Dulcinea, this being as good as a signature to the effect that you are lovers? And since those that go there have to kneel before her and say that they come from your Grace to yield obedience to her, how can the thoughts of the two of you be kept hidden?"

"Oh, what a simple-minded fool you are!" exclaimed Don Quixote. "Can you not see that all this redounds to her greater praise? For you must know that in accordance with our rules of chivalry it is a great honor for a lady to have many knights-errant who serve her and whose thoughts never go beyond rendering her homage for her own sake, with no expectation of any reward for their many and praiseworthy endeavors other than that of being accepted as her champions."

"That," observed Sancho, "is the kind of love I have heard the preacher say we ought to give to Our Lord, for Himself alone, without being moved by any hope of eternal glory or fear of Hell; but, for my part, I prefer to love and serve Him for what He can do for me."

"May the devil take the bumpkin!" cried Don Quixote. "What a wit you show at times; one would think you had been a student."

"But, on my word," said Sancho, "I cannot even read."

At this point Master Nicholas called out to them to wait a while as the others wished to pause at a little roadside spring for a drink. Don Quixote accordingly came to a halt, and Sancho was by no means displeased with this, for he was tired by now of telling so many lies and was afraid that his master would catch him up, the truth being that, while he knew that Dulcinea was a peasant girl of El Toboso, he had never in his life laid eyes upon her.

Cardenio in the meantime had put on the clothes that Dorotea had worn when they found her. Though they were none too good, they were much better than the ones he took off. They then dismounted beside the spring, and with the food that the curate had procured at the inn, while it was not much, they all contrived to satisfy their hunger. As they were engaged in their repast, a lad came along the highway and, after studying them all attentively, ran over to Don Quixote and clasped him around the legs, weeping copiously.

"Ah sir! Do you not know me, your Grace? Look at me well, for I am the lad Andrés that your Grace freed from the oak tree to which he was bound."

The knight then recognized him and, taking him by the hand, he turned to the others and said, "In order that your Worships may see how important it is to have knights-errant in the world to right the wrongs and injuries done by the insolent and evil beings who inhabit it, you may know that some while ago, as I was passing through a wood, I heard certain pitiful cries and moans as from one who was afflicted and in distress. I then, as was my duty, went to the place from which the cries appeared to come, and there I found, bound to an oak tree, this lad who now stands before you. I am heartily glad that he is with us now, for he will be my witness that I do not lie in anything I say. He was, as I said, bound to that tree while a peasant who, I later learned, was his master lashed him unmercifully with the reins of his mare. The moment I saw this, I asked the man what was the reason for the flogging, and the lout replied that he was whipping the boy because he was his servant and had been guilty of certain acts of carelessness that indicated he was a thief rather than a dunce. At this, however, the lad spoke up and said, 'Sir, he is whipping me because I asked for my wages and for no other reason.' The master then made some excuses or other which, if I heard them, I did not accept as valid.

"The short of it was, I compelled the peasant to release the boy and made him promise to take him home and pay him every real of what he owed him, and perfumed into the bargain.[8] Is not that all true, Andrés, my son? Did you not note how imperiously I commanded him to do that and with what humility he promised to carry out all my orders and instructions? Speak up and tell these ladies and gentlemen, clearly and in a straightforward manner, just what happened; for I would have them see and be convinced that I was right when I said that it is very useful to have knights-errant going up and down the highroads."

"All that your Grace has said is very true," the lad replied, "but the end of the matter was quite different from what you think."

"What do you mean by saying that it was quite different?" Don Quixote demanded. "Did not the peasant pay you?"

"He not only did not pay me," said the boy, "but the moment your Grace had left the wood and we were alone, he tied me to that same tree again and gave me so many fresh lashes that I was like St. Bartholomew when they had done flaying him. And at each stroke he made some jest or gibe about how he had fooled you, so funny that I would have laughed myself if the pain had not been so great. In short, he mishandled me to such an extent that I have been in a hospital up to now with the cuts that wicked lout gave me. For all of which your Grace is to blame. If you had gone your way and had not come where you were not called nor meddled in the affairs of others, my master would have been satisfied with giving me one or two dozen lashes and then would have untied me and paid me what he owed me. But your Grace roused his anger by insulting him so unreasonably and calling him all those names, and since he could not avenge himself on you, the moment we were alone the storm burst on me, and, as a result, I do not think I shall ever be a man again as long as I live."

"My mistake," said Don Quixote, "was in going off and leaving you like that. I should not have left until I had seen you paid; for I ought to have known from long experience that there is no peasant who keeps his word if he finds that it is not in his interest to do so. But you remember, Andrés, I swore that if he did not pay you I would come looking for him, and would find him even though he were hidden in the belly of the whale."

"That you did," said Andrés, "but it was of no use."

"Well, we will see now whether it is of use or not," said Don Quixote. And, saying this, he hastily arose and ordered Sancho to put the bridle on Rocinante, for the hack had been grazing while they were eating. Dorotea then asked him what he proposed to do, and he replied that he meant to go look for the peasant and chastise him for his behavior, and he also intended to make him pay Andrés to the last maravedi, notwithstanding and in spite of all the clodhoppers in the world. She thereupon reminded him that in accordance with his promise he could not embark upon any enterprise until he had finished the undertaking with which she had charged him. After all, she added, he knew this better than anyone else and should restrain the fury in his bosom until he had returned from her realm.

"That is true," Don Quixote agreed. "As you say, lady, Andrés will have to be patient until I come back; but I hereby swear and promise him anew that I will not desist until I have avenged him and seen him paid."

"I do not believe in those oaths," said Andrés. "What I need now is enough to take me to Seville; I would rather have that than all the vengeance in the world. So, if you have here anything to eat that I can take with me, let me have it; and God be with your Grace and all knights-errant, and may they be as errant with themselves as they have been with me."

Sancho then produced a bit of bread and cheese and gave it to the lad.

"Take it, brother Andrés," he said, "for we all have a share in your troubles."

"Why, what share is yours?" Andrés asked.

"This portion of bread and cheese. God knows whether I am going to need it or not, for I may tell you, my friend, that the squires of knights-errant are greatly subject to hunger and misfortune and other things that are better felt than put into words."

Andrés accepted the food and, seeing that no one offered him anything else, lowered his head and, as the saying goes, took the road in hand. But, before leaving, he turned to Don Quixote.

"For the love of God, Sir Knight-errant," he said, "if ever again you meet me, even though they are hacking me to bits, do not aid or succor me but let me bear it, for no misfortune could be so great as that which comes of being helped by you. May God curse you and all the knights-errant that were ever born into this world!"

Don Quixote was about to arise and follow him, but the lad started running so swiftly that no one thought of trying to overtake him. The knight was exceedingly crestfallen over the story Andrés had told, and the others had to do their best to keep from laughing so as not to discomfit him entirely.

CHAPTER XXXII. *Which treats of what befell Don Quixote and all his company at the inn.*

HAVING had a good meal, they saddled their animals and set out once more, and nothing worthy of note happened until the following day, when they arrived at the inn, the place that Sancho Panza so feared and dreaded. He did not wish to enter, but there was no escape for him. When they saw Don Quixote and his squire approaching, the innkeeper and his wife, their daughter, and Maritornes came out to receive them most cordially. As for the knight, he greeted his hosts with great dignity and condescension, remarking to them that they should prepare him a better bed than the one he had had the last time. To this the landlady replied that if he paid better than he did the other time, she would give him one fit for a prince. He assured her that he would, and so they made a fairly comfortable pallet for him in the same garret where he had slept before; and as he was very much shaken up and weary in mind as well as body, he went to bed at once.

No sooner had the door closed upon him than the landlady fell upon the barber and seized him by the beard.

"By the sign of the holy cross!" she cried, "you are not going to make use of my tail as a beard any longer. Give it back to me at once. It is a shame the way that thing of my husband's is all the time on the floor— I mean the comb that I used to stick into that pretty tail of mine."

She tugged and tugged, but the barber would not give up until the licentiate told him to let her have it, as there was no further need to make use of that device. Instead, he should show himself in his own person and tell Don Quixote that after the galley-slave robbers had despoiled him, he had fled to this inn; and should the knight inquire after the princess's squire, they would tell him that she had sent the man on ahead to advise her subjects that she was on the way and was bringing with her one who would liberate them all. Upon hearing this, the barber readily enough let the landlady have her tail, and at the same time they returned all the other objects they had borrowed in connection with their scheme to rescue Don Quixote. All those of the inn were very much struck with Dorotea's beauty and the shepherd Cardenio's fine figure; and the curate then directed them to lay out whatever they had to eat, and the landlord, hoping to be better paid this time, set before them a very decent meal. Don Quixote all this while was still asleep, and they deemed it best not to awaken him, as slumber would do him more good than food just now.

At the dinner table, at which were present the landlord, his wife, his daughter, Maritornes, and all the guests, the subject of discussion was Don Quixote's strange madness and the state in which they had found him. The landlady told them of the incident between the knight and the carter, and then, looking around to see if Sancho was there and perceiving that he was not, she went on to describe for them the blanketing that the squire had received, a story that afforded them no little amusement. When the curate made the observation that it was books of chivalry that had unbalanced Don Quixote's mind, the innkeeper took exception to this statement.

"I do not know," he said, "how that can be; for, to tell the truth, so far as I can see, there is no better reading in the world. I myself have two or three of them along with some manuscripts, and they have been the very breath of life not only to me, but to many others as well. For in harvest time the reapers gather here in large numbers on feast days, and there are always some among them who can read. One of them will take a book in his hands and thirty or more of us will crowd around and listen to him with so much pleasure that we lose a thousand gray hairs. For my own part at least, I can say that when I hear of the terrible and furious blows the knights exchange with one another, I feel like dealing a few myself, and could sit there hearing of them day and night."

"That," said the landlady, "suits me well enough; for I never have a moment's peace in the house except when you are listening to them. Then you are so absorbed that you forget for once to scold."

"That is the truth," said Maritornes; "and I give you my word, I also like to hear about those things, for they are very pretty, especially when they tell about some lady or other being embraced by her knight under the orange trees while a duenna keeps watch over them, and she herself is dying of envy and fright. I say that all that is better than honey."

"And what do you think, young lady?" said the curate, addressing the innkeeper's daughter.

"I really cannot tell you, sir," she replied. "Although I do not understand them, I get a great deal of pleasure out of listening to them. The only thing is, I do not like those blows that my father speaks of; I prefer the laments which the knights utter when absent from their lady loves and which sometimes make me weep from sympathy."

"Well, young lady," said Dorotea, "would you console them if it was for you that they wept?"

"I do not know what I should do," the girl answered. "All I know is that some of those ladies are so cruel that they call their knights tigers and lions and a thousand other nasty things like that. Good Lord! I don't know what kind of creatures they can be, without soul or conscience, if they cannot give a decent man so much as a glance but leave him to die or go mad. I don't see how they can be such prudes. If it is their honor they are thinking about, let them marry, for that is all the poor knights desire."

"Be quiet, child!" said the landlady. "You appear to know too much about such things, and it is not good for young girls to know or talk so much."

"This gentleman asked me," said the lass, "and I could not refuse to answer him."

"That will do," said the curate. "And now, mine host, if you will bring out those books of yours, I should like to have a look at them."

"With pleasure," replied the innkeeper. And, going into his room, he came back with an old valise held closed by a small chain. When it was opened it was found to contain three large books and a number of manuscripts in a very good hand. The first book that the curate inspected was *Don Cirongilio of Thrace.* Another was *Felixmarte of Hircania,* and there was also the *History of the Great Captain Gonzalo Hernández de Córdoba, with the Life of Diego García de Paredes.*[1] As soon as he had read the first two titles, the priest turned to the barber and said, "What we need here now is our friend's housekeeper and niece."

"No, we do not need them," said the barber. "I am quite capable of carrying these books out into the stable yard or over to the hearth, for, in truth, there is a very good fire burning there."

"What!" said the innkeeper; "is your Grace going to burn more books?"[2]

"No more," said the curate, "than these two: the *Don Cirongilio* and the *Felixmarte.*"

"Are these books of mine, then, heretics or phlegmatics that you should wish to burn them?" the landlord wanted to know.

"*Schismatics*, you mean, friend," the barber corrected him, "not *phlegmatics*."

"Be that as it may," said their host, "but if you are bent on burning any, let it be this one about the Great Captain and this other about Diego García, for I would rather see my own child sent to the flames than any of the rest of them."

"But, my brother," the curate remonstrated with him, "those two books are full of lies, foolishness, and nonsense, whereas this one about the Great Captain is a true history and has the deeds of Gonzalo Hernández de Córdoba, who by his many and mighty exploits deserves to be known as the Great Captain to all the world. And this Diego García de Paredes was a leading knight, a native of the city of Trujillo in Estremadura, a most valiant soldier and one endowed with such natural strength that with the finger of one hand he could stop a mill wheel turning at full speed. On one occasion, armed with a large two-handed broadsword,[3] he took up his post at the entrance to a bridge and prevented a large army from crossing. These and other feats he performed, and he writes of them with the modesty of a knight who is his own chronicler; but if some other free and dispassionate author had recorded them, they would have cast into oblivion the deeds of all the Hectors, Achilles', and Rolands."

"Go tell that to my father!" exclaimed the innkeeper. "What is there so astonishing about stopping a mill wheel? By God, your Grace should read what Felixmarte of Hircania did,[4] who with a single backward stroke cut five giants in two around the middle, as if they had been made of horse beans like the little friars that children fashion for themselves. Another time he attacked a huge and powerful army, with more than one million six hundred thousand soldiers all armed from head to foot, and he put them to rout like a flock of sheep.

"And then, what have you to say of the worthy Don Cirongilio of Thrace, a sturdy and courageous knight as you will see from that book. For it tells there how, as he was sailing on a river, a fiery serpent arose from the water, and as soon as he saw it he fell upon it, straddled its scaly back, and, grasping its throat in both his hands, choked it with such force that the serpent, perceiving that it was being throttled, had no choice but to sink to the bottom of the river, carrying with it the knight, who would not let go his hold? And, down there, he found himself among palaces and gardens so pretty that they were a marvel to behold; and then the snake turned into an old man who told him such things as were never heard before. Ah, sir, say no more! If you were to hear that one, you would be beside yourself with joy. And a couple of figs for that Great Captain and for that Diego García that you talk about!"

As she listened to this, Dorotea whispered to Cardenio, "Our host could almost play a second to Don Quixote."

"Yes, it would seem so," replied Cardenio, "for, according to all indications, he holds it as certain that everything happened exactly as it is set down in those books, and the barefooted friars themselves would never convince him of the contrary."

"See here, brother," the curate went on, "there never was in this world a Felixmarte of Hircania or a Don Cirongilio of Thrace, nor any such knights as those mentioned in the books of chivalry. It is all a fiction, a story made up by idle minds for the purpose you speak of: whiling the time away, which is what those reapers of yours do when they read them; for I swear to you once more, there never were such knights, such exploits, or such nonsensical happenings."

"Give that bone to another dog!" said the innkeeper. "As if I didn't know how much is five and where the shoe pinches me! And do not think you can feed me pap, for, by God, I am nobody's fool. A fine thing, your Grace's trying to make me believe that all these good books say is nothing but lies and foolishness, when they are printed with the license of the Royal Council! Do you mean to tell me they are the kind of folk who would consent to the printing of a lot of stories that are not true, with all those battles and enchantments and other things that are enough to drive a person crazy?"

"I have told you, my friend," the curate replied, "that this is done simply to amuse your idle hours. Just as in well-ordered states there are games of chess, handball, and billiards to amuse those that do not desire, are not obliged, or are unable to work, so do they consent to the printing and distribution of such books as these, in the belief—and they are right in so believing—that there is no one so ignorant that he would take any of them to be a veracious history. If this were the proper occasion and my listeners so desired, I might say something about the qualities which books of chivalry should possess in order to be good ones and such as would be to the profit of certain readers and would please their taste as well. However, I trust the time will come when I shall be able to communicate my ideas to someone who is in a position to remedy the situation. In the meanwhile, mine host, remember what I say. And now, take your books and make up your mind as to whether they are true or false. Much good may they do you, and, please God you do not go lame on the same foot as your guest Don Quixote."

"That I shall not," replied the innkeeper. "I could never be so mad as to turn knight-errant, for I am aware that the customs of those days when famous knights roamed the world no longer prevail today."

In the midst of this conversation Sancho Panza had entered the room. He was very downcast and bewildered when he heard them say that there were no more knights-errant and that the books of chivalry were full of lies and nonsense, and he secretly made up his mind that he would wait and see how this expedition of his master's turned out; if the result did not come up to expectations, he would part company with the knight and return to his wife and young ones and his accustomed toil.

The landlord was about to remove the valise with the books it contained when the curate stopped him. "Wait," said the latter, "I want to see what papers those are that are written in so fine a hand."

Their host then took out the manuscript and gave it to them to read, whereupon they saw that it was on eight sheets, with a title in large letters at the top of the first one which read: *Story of the One Who Was Too Curious for His Own Good*. Having glanced over three or four lines, the curate remarked, "The title of this certainly impresses me as being an excellent one, and I should very much like to read the tale itself."

"Very well," replied the innkeeper, "your Reverence may do so; for I may tell you that certain of my guests who have read it have greatly enjoyed it and have earnestly begged me to let them have it, but I would not give it to them, thinking that I would return it to the one who forgetfully went away and left the valise here with these books and papers in it; for its owner may well come back for it sometime, and although I should not like to part with them, upon my word, I shall restore them to him, for although I am an innkeeper, I am also a Christian."

"You are quite right in that, my friend," said the curate, "However, if the story pleases me, you must let me copy it."

"I shall be glad to do so," the landlord assured him.

While the two were conversing, Cardenio had picked up the story and begun reading it. He liked it as well as had the curate, whom he now begged to read it aloud in order that all might hear it.

"I should not mind reading it," said the priest, "if it were not that it would be better to spend our time sleeping."

"I shall have my fill of rest," said Dorotea, "in passing the time away by listening to some story; for my mind is not as yet sufficiently calm to permit me to sleep when I ought to do so."

"In that case," said the curate, "I will read it, if only out of curiosity, and we may find some enjoyment in it."

Master Nicholas and Sancho now joined in urging him, and, seeing that it would give so much pleasure to all of them as well as to himself, he said, "Very well, then. Pay attention, all of you. This is the way the story begins."

CHAPTER XXXIII. *In which is related the "Story of the One Who Was Too Curious for His Own Good."*

IN FLORENCE, a rich and famous city of Italy, in the province of Tuscany, there lived two gentlemen named Anselmo and Lotario. They were wealthy and of high station and were so closely bound together in ties of friendship that all who knew them commonly referred to them as "the two friends." They were bachelor lads of the same age and habits, which in itself was enough to explain the bond of affection between them. It is true that Anselmo was somewhat more inclined to amorous pastimes than was Lotario, the latter being very fond of the hunt, but when occasion offered, the one would leave off his own pursuits to devote himself to those favored by the other, and in this manner their inclinations kept pace better than the best-regulated clock.

Anselmo was greatly enamored of a certain beautiful and wellborn maiden of the same city. Her parents were so worthy, and she herself so estimable, that the youth, upon the advice of his friend, without whom he did nothing, made up his mind to ask for her hand in marriage. This plan he put into execution, with Lotario as his emissary, who concluded the business so satisfactorily that the suitor soon found himself in possession of that which he desired, while Camila was so happy at having him for a husband that she never ceased giving thanks to Heaven and to Lotario who had been the means of bringing her so much happiness.

The first days of marriage commonly being given over to merrymaking, Lotario continued to frequent his friend's house as was his wont, doing all in his power to honor him and help make the occasion a joyful one. But when the wedding days were over and congratulatory visits became less frequent, he was careful not to go so often; for it seemed to him, as it must to all men of good sense, that one should not continue visiting the homes of married friends with the same frequency as in their bachelor days. Good and true friendship neither can nor should be at all suspect; but, nevertheless, the honor of a married man is so delicate a matter that even blood brothers may give offense, to say nothing of those who are no more than friends.

Anselmo noted all this and was greatly put out, telling Lotario that if he had known that his marriage was to come between them in such a manner, he would never have gone through with it. Seeing that when they were single they had been so intimate as to win for themselves the pleasing epithet of "the two friends," he would not consent to so famous and agreeable an association as theirs being sacrificed for no other reason than that of a conventional circumspectness. He therefore entreated him, if such a manner of speaking was permissible between them, to resume his old place as master of his friend's household, coming and going as he liked. Camila, he added, had no other will or pleasure than his own, and when she had learned how fond the two were of each other, she had not known what to think of such coldness on Lotario's part.

To this and all the other things that Anselmo had to say in an effort to persuade him to resume his former habits, Lotario replied so wisely and discreetly that his friend was quite satisfied of his good intentions; and so they made an arrangement to the effect that two days a week and on feast days Lotario was to dine at Anselmo's house. Nevertheless, the former was determined to observe this agreement only insofar as it did not conflict with his friend's honor, whose reputation he valued more than he did his own. He maintained, and rightly, that the man to whom Heaven had given a beautiful wife should exercise as much care as to the friends he brought home with him as he did with regard to his wife's feminine acquaintances—for while it may be difficult to arrange a clandestine meeting in the market place, in church, at public festivals, or in connection with private visits to religious shrines (and husbands cannot always forbid their wives such opportunities), these things are readily managed in the house of a trusted female friend or relative.[1]

Lotario was also in the habit of saying that every married man should have some friend of his own sex who would call his attention to any negligence on his part; for it frequently happens that a husband who is very much in love with his wife either does not warn her or, in order not to annoy her, says nothing to her whatever about doing or not doing certain things, although his own honor or loss of reputation depends upon her conduct; whereas, if advised by a friend, he may easily set everything to rights. But where is so true a friend to be found, one so loyal and discreet as Lotario would have him be? I cannot tell you, certainly; for only he was of that sort, zealously and painstakingly watching over Anselmo's honor so that the wandering and malicious gaze of the idle throng might not find occasion for scandal in seeing a young gentleman as rich, well-born, and attractive as he frequenting the house of a woman as beautiful as Camila. Even though her modesty and worth might put a bridle on every gossiping tongue, he nonetheless did not wish to cast even the shadow of doubt upon her good repute or that of his friend; and for this reason, on most of the days when he was supposed to go there, he occupied himself with other matters which he pretended were unavoidable. As a consequence, a good part of the time was spent in complaints on the one side and excuses on the other.

And so it came about one day, as they were strolling in a meadow outside the city, that Anselmo said to Lotario, "You may think, my friend, that in return for the favors God has shown me by giving me such parents as mine and bestowing upon me with no stinting hand what are commonly known as the gifts of nature as well as those of fortune, I should never be able to thank Him enough, not to speak of what He has done for me by giving me you as a friend and Camila for my wife, two blessings which I esteem, if not at their full worth, as much as I am able. Yet with all these advantages, which are commonly all that men require to live happily, I lead the most boring and fretful existence of any man in this universe. For some time now I have been wearied and oppressed by a desire so strange, so out of the ordinary, that I marvel at myself. I blame and scold myself for it when I am alone and endeavor to silence it and conceal it from my own thoughts, but I have no more succeeded in keeping it a secret than if I had deliberately set out to tell everyone about it. And since it has to come out, I would entrust it to your safekeeping; for I am confident that by this means and through your readiness as a true friend to do what you can to help me, the joy I derive from your kind offices will be as intense as the unhappiness which my madness has caused me."

Lotario did not know what to think of Anselmo's speech, nor did he have any idea as to what the object of this long and ominous preamble was. Though he did his best to imagine what the desire could be that so harassed his friend, his guesses were far from the truth, and by way of relieving the anxiety which this uncertainty caused him, he remarked to his companion that to adopt so roundabout a way of revealing one's most secret thoughts was to commit a grievous offense against a friendship as deep as theirs. If Anselmo would but tell him his troubles, he felt sure that he would be able to give him some advice that would help him in allaying them or in taking such action as was necessary to remedy matters.

"That is the truth," replied Anselmo, "and so, in all confidence, I will inform you, friend Lotario, that the thing that so tortures me is the desire to know whether or not my wife Camila is as good and perfect as I think she is, for this is a truth that I cannot accept until the quality of her virtue is proved to me in the same manner that fire brings out the purity of gold. For it is my opinion, my friend, that a woman is virtuous only in the degree to which she is tempted and resists temptation, and that she alone is strong who does not yield to promises, gifts, tears, and the constant wooing of importunate suitors. What thanks does a woman deserve for being good if no one urges her to be bad? What wonder if she is reserved and timid who has no opportunity to abandon herself, and who, moreover, knows that her husband will slay her for the first false move that he discovers on her part? Accordingly, she who is virtuous out of fear and lack of occasion is one whom I cannot esteem as I do her who is solicited and beset and still emerges with the crown of victory.

"For this reason," he continued, "and many others which I could give you by way of verifying and confirming the opinion I have just expressed, I desire that my wife Camila meet this test and go through the fire of seeing herself longed for and sought after by one who is of sufficient worth to offer her his affections. If she comes out of this battle, as I am convinced she will, bearing the victor's palm, I shall consider myself the happiest man alive. I shall be able to say that my cup runneth over and that I have had the good fortune to come upon that virtuous woman of whom the Wise Man has asked, 'Who can find her?' [2] And if things should turn out contrary to my expectations, then I shall have the satisfaction of knowing the truth and shall bear without complaining the pain which so costly an experience will naturally cause me.

"Inasmuch as nothing you may say will dissuade me from carrying out my plan, I would have you, friend Lotario, consent to be the instrument for putting it into execution. I will provide you with the opportunity and will see that none of the conditions are lacking for paying suit to a woman who is respectable, honored, reserved, and without inclination to let her fancies roam. What leads me, among other things, to entrust you with so

arduous an undertaking is the consideration that, in case Camila is overcome, you will not carry your conquest too far, but, instead, you will
regard as done that which out of respect for me you will leave undone.
Thus I shall be offended only by her intent, and the injury that I suffer
will remain shrouded in your virtuous silence, which I know to be eternal
as that of death itself. And so, if you would have me enjoy what may
properly be called life, from now on you will enter into amorous battle,
and neither lukewarmly nor slothfully, but with all the earnestness and
diligence that I so greatly desire and with that trustworthiness of which
our friendship assures me."

Such were the words that Anselmo spoke to Lotario. The latter listened
to them all most attentively and, beyond the remarks he had already
made, did not open his lips until his friend had finished. When he perceived that the speech was ended, he gazed at him for a good while as if
at some strange and amazing object that he had never before seen before.

"I cannot persuade myself, friend Anselmo," he said at last, "that you
are not jesting in what you have just told me. If I were convinced that
you are in earnest, I would never have permitted you to go so far but
would have put an end to all this talk by refusing to listen to you. Surely,
either I do not know you, or you do not know me. But that cannot be;
for I am well aware that you are Anselmo, and you are conscious of the
fact that I am Lotario. Unfortunately, however, I cannot regard you as
the Anselmo that used to be, and you likewise must have thought that
I am no longer the Lotario of old. For the things that you have said to
me are not those that my friend Anselmo would say, nor are the things
you ask of me such as you would ask of the Lotario that you know. True
friends, as the poet has said, will prove and make use of each other *usque
ad aras*, which is to say, they will not put their friendship to the test in
a manner that is contrary to God's will. If this was the way a pagan [3] felt
about it, how much stronger should be the feeling of a Christian, who
knows that divine friendship must not be sacrificed for that which exists
between human beings? And if the time does come when a man goes so
far as to lay aside the respect he owes to Heaven, it will not be for little
things of slight importance, but only those that concern the very life
and honor of his earthly friend.

"Tell me, then, Anselmo," Lotario went on, "which of these—your
life or your honor—is now imperiled that I at risk to myself should oblige
you by doing a thing so detestable as that which you ask of me? Neither
of them, certainly. What you are demanding of me is, rather, as I understand it, that I seek and endeavor to deprive you, and myself at the same

time, of both honor and life. For if I take away your honor, it goes without saying that I am also robbing you of life, since the man without honor is in worse plight than a dead man; and if I am to be the instrument, as you would have me be, of bringing so great a misfortune upon you, shall I not then remain a dishonored and hence a lifeless man? Hear me out, friend Anselmo, and be so patient as not to answer me until I have finished telling you all I think of this wish of yours. There will be time later for me to hear what you have to say in reply."

"With pleasure," was Anselmo's response. "Say whatever you like."

"It seems to me that you are reasoning now as the Moors always do, who cannot be brought to see the error inherent in their sect, through citations from Holy Writ; nor are they to be moved by intellectual speculation or arguments based upon the articles of faith, but they demand palpable examples, readily understood and demonstrable, and such as admit of undeniable and indubitable mathematical proof, as when they say, 'If equals are subtracted from equals, the remainders are equal.' If they do not understand this from words, as indeed they do not, it has to be shown them with the hands and placed before their eyes, and with all this no one could ever succeed in persuading them of the truths of my holy religion.[4] And this same mode of reasoning I am going to have to use with you; for the desire that has been born in you is so mistaken and utterly unreasonable a one that it appears to me a waste of time to endeavor to bring you to an understanding of your simple-mindedness— for the present I will call it by no other name than that. I am inclined to leave you to your folly, as a punishment for having conceived such a wish, but the friendship that I have for you will not permit me to deal with you so harshly, nor will it consent to my deserting you in this imminent danger of self-destruction that now obviously threatens you.

"In order that you may see clearly how the matter stands, answer me this, Anselmo. Did you not tell me that I am to pay court to a woman of reserve, bring my persuasive wiles to bear upon a respectable matron, make advances to one who is not looking for anything of that sort, and offer my attentions to a lady who is noted for her prudence? Yes, that is precisely what you told me. Well, then, if you know that you have such a wife, reserved, respected, prudent, and retiring, what is it that you seek? And if you are convinced that she will emerge the victor from all my assaults, as she undoubtedly will, what better titles do you think to bestow upon her than those that she already possesses? Or is it that you do not believe her to be what you say she is, or that you do not realize what you are asking? If you doubt her virtue, why trouble to test it?

Why not treat her as guilty and take what action you may see fit? If, on the other hand, she is as good as you are convinced she is, it is a futile proceeding to put that truth to the trial since in the end you will be left with the same opinion that you held before.

"It is therefore obvious that to undertake things from which harm rather than good is likely to come is a senseless and foolhardy act, especially when one is not forced or compelled to do so, and when the madness that lies in such a course of conduct is evident from afar. Difficult feats are attempted for the love of God or the world's praise or for both. It is saints who undertake the former as they strive to live an angelic life in human bodies, while they who seek the respect of the world are those who traverse great bodies of water and visit many climes and strange peoples in order to obtain what are known as fortune's favors. And, finally, those deeds that are performed for God and man alike are the work of valiant soldiers who, the moment they sight a breach in the opposite wall no bigger than a cannon ball can make, cast aside all fear and, with no word or thought of the manifest danger that threatens them but borne on the wings of their desire to defend their faith, their nation, and their king, hurl themselves intrepidly into the midst of a thousand deaths that await them at the hands of the enemy. Such are the deeds that men commonly attempt for the reason that there are honor, glory, and profit in them, despite the accompanying hardships and perils.

"But this undertaking of yours, as you explain it to me, has for object neither the glory of God, fortune's favors, nor worldly fame; for, supposing that the outcome is such as you desire, you will be neither happier nor richer nor more honored than you are at present; while if the result is not what you hope for, you will find yourself in the greatest misery that can be imagined, and there will be no comfort in the thought that none knows of your misfortune, as the fact that you yourself know it will be the greatest of afflictions.

"By way of confirming the truth of this, I should like to recite to you a stanza by the poet Luigi Tansillo which occurs at the end of the first part of his *St. Peter's Tears.*[5] It runs like this:

> *Then Peter's sorrow and his shame did grow*
> *As the day dawned and morning drew on apace,*
> *And although none was there to see or know,*
> *He was himself aware of his disgrace;*
> *For with the magnanimous heart 'tis ever so:*
> *Its own self-knowledge nothing can efface.*

Though only Heaven and earth behold its shame,
It still will never cease itself to blame.

"Thus, you will not be able to shun your grief by keeping it secret, but, rather, you will weep endlessly—if not tears from the eyes, tears of blood from the heart of the kind that simple-souled doctor wept of whom our poet tells us, who submitted to the test of the cup,[6] something that the more prudent Rinaldo declined to do. Granted that this is poetic fiction, it nonetheless contains certain secrets of morality that are worthy of being noted, understood, and imitated. Moreover, by what I am about to say you will be brought to see the great mistake that you would be making if you carried out your plan.

"Tell me, Anselmo, supposing that Heaven or good fortune had made you the master and lawful owner of a very fine diamond to whose quality and purity all the lapidaries who had seen it had testified, stating in unison their common opinion that in quality, purity, and fineness it was the best that nature could produce in the way of such a stone; and supposing, further, that you yourself believed all this to be true, without knowing anything that would cause you to believe otherwise, would it be right for you to wish to take that diamond and place it between a hammer and an anvil and there by force of blows and strength of arm endeavor to see whether or not it was as hard and fine as they had said it was? And supposing that you went through with this and the stone withstood so foolish a test, would you thereby be adding anything to its worth and the esteem in which it was held? Whereas, if it should break, a thing that could happen, would not all be lost? It would indeed; for certainly its owner would be looked upon by everyone as a man of little sense.

"Well, then, friend Anselmo, you must realize that Camila is a very fine diamond, both in your own estimation and in that of others, and there is no sense in placing her in a situation where she may be broken; for even though she remain whole, she will not then be of greater worth than she is now; and if she should weaken and not hold out, you must take into consideration that from that time forth you would have to do without her, and with what good reason you would reproach yourself for having been the cause of her ruination and your own as well. Remember that there is no jewel in all this world of so great worth as a wife who is chaste and respected, and that the honor of women lies wholly in the good opinion which others have of them; and since you know how excellent your own wife's reputation is, why do you seek to cast doubt upon that truth? Bear in mind, my friend, that woman is an imperfect creature, and we should not put stumbling blocks in her way where she may trip and fall; rather, we should remove them and clear her path of all obstacles, so that, without any hindrances, she may run swiftly on toward the goal of that perfection that she lacks, which lies in the attainment of virtue.

"The naturalists tell us that the ermine is a small animal with a very white skin and that hunters when they wish to track it down make use of the following artifice: knowing the places where it passes, they block them off with mud, and then, rousing the little beast, they drive it toward those places; but the ermine, as soon as it comes to the mud, stops and lets itself be captured rather than go through the mire and lose or sully its whiteness, which it values more than it does its liberty or its life. Now, the chaste and respected woman is an ermine, and the virtue of modesty is something that is whiter and purer than snow, but he who would not have her lose it but keep and preserve it must adopt with her a different course than that which the ermine hunters employ. He must not put before her the mire of presents and the attentions of importunate suitors; for perhaps—and, indeed, there is no perhaps about it—she will not be possessed of sufficient virtue and native strength to enable her to tread under foot and pass over these obstacles, for which reason it is necessary to remove them and instead place before her the purity of virtue and the beauty that lies in a woman's good name.

"The good woman is like a crystal mirror, shining and clear but likely to be dimmed and darkened by any breath that touches her. The respectable woman has to be treated as one does relics: she is to be adored, not touched. She is to be guarded and cherished, like a fine garden full of roses and other flowers whose master permits no one to enter and handle the blooms—it is enough to enjoy their beauty and fragrance from afar, through an iron grating.

"Finally, I should like to quote you some verses that I happen to remember. I heard them in a modern comedy, and they appear to me to have a bearing on the subject we are now discussing. One wise old man was advising another, who had a young daughter, to take the girl, shut her up, and watch over her carefully, and among other reasons he gave the following:

> *Woman is made of glass,*
> *But do not the trouble take*
> *To see if she will break,*
> *For anything may come to pass.*

> *She is easy to shatter;*
> *And so, then, be not rash*
> *Or you the glass may smash,*
> *But mending's another matter.*
> *This truth all men will tell,*
> *For 'tis known everywhere:*
> *If in this world are Danaës fair,*
> *There are showers of gold as well.*[1]

"What I have said to you so far, Anselmo, has been with reference to yourself; it is time now that you should hear something of my part in the matter. If I seem to you to be speaking at too great length, forgive me. This labyrinth in which you have become involved and from which you would have me extricate you makes it necessary. You look upon me as a friend, and yet you would take away my honor, which is a thing contrary to all friendship; and, what is more, you wish me to rob you of yours at the same time. That you would deprive me of mine is obvious; for when Camila sees me paying suit to her as you ask me to do, she will certainly take me for a man without honor and of evil intentions, since I shall be undertaking to accomplish something that is entirely out of keeping with my character and the obligations of friendship. And that you would have me deprive you of yours is equally clear; for when I press my attentions upon her, she will think that I have discovered something frivolous about her that has emboldened me to reveal my evil desires, and she will then look upon herself as dishonored, and inasmuch as she belongs to you, her dishonor will be your own.

"All this explains what commonly happens with the husband of an adulterous wife. He may be in no wise to blame for her straying from the path of duty; indeed, he may not even be aware of it. Owing to his carelessness and lack of precautions, it may not have been within his power to prevent the unfortunate occurrence; but, nevertheless, he is called by a low, vile name, and to a certain extent those who are aware of his wife's misbehavior look upon him with contempt rather than with pity, even though they can see that his misfortune is not due to any fault of his own but to the waywardness of his faithless spouse.

"But I should like to tell you why it is that the husband of an erring wife is with good reason looked down upon even though he knows nothing of her misdeeds and has been in no way to blame, having given her no cause or provocation for what she did. And please do not become bored with listening to me, for all that I say is for your own good. When

God created our first male parent in the earthly paradise, the Holy Scripture tells us that, having put him to sleep, He took a rib from Adam's left side and out of it fashioned our mother Eve; and when Adam awoke and saw her, he said, 'This is flesh of my flesh and bone of my bone.' And God said, 'Therefore shall a man leave his father and his mother, and they shall be one flesh.' [8] Then it was that the holy sacrament of marriage was instituted, with bonds that are only to be put asunder by death. And this miraculous sacrament is possessed of such force and virtue that it does indeed make one and the same flesh of two different persons; and it does even more in the case of the happily married, for although they have two separate souls, they have but a single will.

"From this it follows that, the woman's flesh being one with that of her husband, the stains and blemishes that she incurs are reflected upon his flesh, even though, as has been said, he has given no occasion for her sinning. For just as a pain in the foot or in any other member is felt by the body as a whole (being all of the same flesh), and the head feels the pain in the ankle though it has not caused it, so the husband, by the fact of being one with her, shares in his wife's dishonor. For, since all worldly honors and disgraces are born of flesh and blood, and those of the erring wife are of this sort, it is inevitable that the husband should bear his part of them and be looked upon as dishonored whether or not he is aware of it.

"Consider, then, Anselmo, the risk you are running in thus disturbing that tranquillity in which your good wife spends her days. Think well before, out of vain and ill-advised curiosity, you seek to stir up the passions that are now slumbering in your chaste wife's bosom. Remember that what you stand to gain is little, and that what you will lose is so much that words fail me and I shall not even try to express it. If all that I have said is not sufficient to dissuade you from your unworthy purpose, then you will have to look for another to be the instrument of your dishonor and undoing, for I have no intention of being that instrument though I lose your friendship, which is the greatest loss that I can conceive."

With these words the virtuous and prudent Lotario fell silent. As for Anselmo, he was confused and thoughful and for some little while did not speak.

"Friend Lotario," he said at last, "you have seen how attentively I have listened to all you had to say to me, and your arguments, examples, and comparisons have shown me how wise you are and how fine and true a friend. I further perceive and admit that if I follow my own inclinations instead of your advice, I shall be fleeing the good and running after the evil. Granting this, however, you must take into consideration that I am suffering from that infirmity which some women have who are seized with the desire to eat earth, plaster, charcoal, and still worse things that are disgusting enough to look at and even more so to eat. In my case, it is necessary to employ a degree of artifice in curing me, and this can readily be done, but only if you begin, even though lukewarmly and in a feigned manner, to make advances to Camila, who will not be so susceptible that her virtue will be overthrown at the first encounter. With this beginning I will be content, and you will have done your duty by me as a friend, not only by giving me life but by persuading me not to part with my honor.

"This," Anselmo continued, "you are obliged to do for one reason only. Being resolved as I am to carry out this test, you surely cannot consent to my revealing my foolishness to another person, since I should thereby be risking that honor that you would have me keep. And if your honor does not appear in the proper light to Camila while you are pressing your suit, that makes little or no difference, since very soon, when we see that she is all that we expect of her, you will be in a position to tell her the whole truth concerning our scheme and your standing with her will be what it was before. As you are in reality risking so little and are offering me so much contentment by risking it, I trust you will not refuse me even if more serious obstacles should arise; for, as I have said, when you shall have made no more than a beginning, I will regard the point at issue as having been conclusively settled."

Seeing Anselmo's resolute attitude and not having any more examples to cite him or any more arguments to present as to why he should refrain from putting his resolve into effect—especially when he heard him threaten to confide to another his ill-omened scheme—Lotario, by way of avoiding a greater evil, decided to give in to him and do what he asked, with the object and intention of guiding the affair in such a manner that, without Camila's affections being altered in the least, his friend at the same time should be satisfied. He accordingly told him now that he should not communicate his plan to anyone else, as he, Lotario, would take charge of the matter and would begin to act upon this decision as soon as was desired.

Anselmo thereupon embraced him tenderly and affectionately, thanking his friend for the offer as if it had been some great favor, and it was agreed between them that they would begin carrying out the plan the very next day. Anselmo was to provide the opportunity for Lotario and Camila to be alone together, and he was also to furnish the money and jewels that were to be offered her. He advised Lotario to arrange for serenades and compose verses in her praise. If this was too much trouble, he would write the verses himself. And Lotario assented to it all, but with a different purpose in view than Anselmo thought.

Having settled the matter, they returned to Anselmo's house, where they found Camila dutifully and anxiously awaiting her husband, for he was later that day than was his wont. Lotario then went to his own home, being as troubled in mind as Anselmo was satisfied, for he did not know just what course to follow by way of extricating himself from this unpleasant business. That night, however, he thought of a means by which he could deceive Anselmo without offending Camila; and the following day he went to dine at his friend's house and was well received by the mistress, who entertained him most cordially since she knew the high esteem in which her husband held him.

When dinner was over and the cloth had been removed, Anselmo remarked that he had some urgent business to attend to but would return in an hour and a half, and in the meanwhile Lotario might stay with Camila. The latter begged her husband not to go, and their guest offered to keep him company, but he declined this offer and instead insisted that Lotario wait for him there as he had a matter of great importance to discuss with him, and at the same time he directed Camila not to leave Lotario alone until he returned. In short, he feigned it all so cleverly, making his absence appear necessary, that no one would have suspected it was but pretense. When he had gone, Camila and Lotario were left alone at the table, for the household servants were all engaged in having their own meal. And so it was that the husband's friend found himself in the amorous lists just as the husband had desired, with an enemy in front of him who by her beauty alone well might conquer an entire company of armed knights. Is it any wonder if Lotario was afraid?

What he now did was to lean his elbow upon the arm of his chair and rest his cheek upon his hand; and then, begging Camila's pardon for the discourtesy, he observed that he would like to take a little nap until Anselmo came back. She replied that he would be more comfortable in the drawing-room than in a chair and suggested that he go in there to sleep, but he did not care to do this. Instead, he remained sleeping there; and when Anselmo came in and found his friend dozing and Camila in her room, he thought that he had been away so long as to have given the pair time for talk and a little sleep besides, and was impatient for Lotario to awake so that he might take him outside and question him as to the result of his venture.

It all happened as he desired. Lotario awoke and the two then left the house together and he was able to put the questions which he was so anxious to ask. Lotario replied that he had not thought it a good thing to reveal the whole of his design the first time, and so he had done no more than praise Camila's beauty, assuring her that in all the city there was none other so lovely and discreet. This had seemed to him a good beginning, by way of winning her favor and disposing her to listen to him with pleasure on another occasion. In this he was employing the same stratagem that the devil makes use of when he wishes to deceive someone who is on the watch for him: what the Prince of Darkness does in such a case is to transform himself into an angel of light by putting on a good appearance; it is only at the end that he reveals himself and achieves his purpose, providing his ruse has not been discovered in the beginning. Anselmo was well pleased and declared that every day he would provide the same opportunity. He would not leave the house, however, but would find something at which to busy himself so that Camila would not come to learn of his scheme.

Many days then went by, and Lotario, without saying a word to Camila, kept reporting to Anselmo that he had talked with her but had never been able to obtain from her the least show of consent to anything that was dishonorable; she had afforded him no sign or shadow of hope, but had threatened that if he did not abandon his evil suggestions she would have to tell her husband about him.

"That is well," said Anselmo. "So far Camila has held out against words; it is necessary for us to see now how well she can resist deeds. Tomorrow I will give you two thousand gold crowns to offer or present to her, and as many more to buy jewels with which to tempt her; for women, particularly those that are beautiful, and however chaste they may be, are very fond of being sprucely attired, and if she resists this temptation, I shall be satisfied and will give you no more trouble." Lotario replied that, having entered upon this undertaking, he meant to go through with it, although he was certain that he would come out of it weary and vanquished. The next day he was forced to accept the four thousand crowns, and with them four thousand crowns' worth of embarrassment, for he was unable to think of any fresh lie to give his friend. Finally, he made up his mind that he would tell him that Camila had stood as firm against gifts and promises as she had against words, and there was no need of going to any further trouble since all this was time wasted. But fate, which directs things after its own fashion, was to ordain otherwise.

Having left Lotario and Camila alone together as on other occasions, Anselmo this time shut himself in a room and began listening and spying through a keyhole, only to discover that in more than half an hour the pair had not exchanged a single word, nor would they do so if they were to remain there for a hundred years. It was then he realized that all his friend had told him about Camila's replies was falsehood and fiction. By way of seeing if this was so, he came out of the room and, calling Lotario to one side, asked him what news there was and inquired as to Camila's state of mind. Lotario replied that he did not care to go on with this business, for she had answered him so harshly and angrily that he had not had the courage to say anything more to her.

"Ha!" exclaimed Anselmo, "Lotario! Lotario! How ill you have repaid the debt of friendship that you owe me and the confidence that I have reposed in you! I have been watching through this keyhole, and you did not say a single word to Camila, from which I gather that you have yet to utter your first ones. If that is the case, and it undoubtedly is, why have you deceived me? Why have you so ingeniously sought to deprive me of the means by which I might achieve my desire?"

Anselmo said no more, but he had already said enough to leave Lotario feeling confused and abashed. The latter upon being caught in a lie took it as a point of honor and swore to his friend that from that moment he would assume the responsibility of satisfying him and would lie to him no more, as he would see if he chose to spy upon them again. It would not be necessary, however, to resort to that, since what he proposed to do by way of gratifying him would remove all suspicion of laxity on his part. Anselmo took him at his word and, in order to afford him a safer opportunity and one less subject to surprise, he decided to absent himself from home for a week and go visit another friend who lived in a village not far from the city. And by way of presenting Camila with a more plausible excuse for his departure, he arranged with the friend in question to send him a pressing invitation.

Ah, unfortunate and ill-advised Anselmo! What is it that you are doing? What is it you are plotting? What do you seek to bring about? Behold what you are doing to yourself: plotting your own dishonor and bringing about your own ruin. Your wife Camila is a good woman, and you are in quiet and tranquil possession of her. There is none to disturb your happiness, her thoughts do not go beyond the walls of her home, you are her Heaven on earth, the object of her desires, the fulfillment of all that she could wish for, the measure of her will which she in every respect adjusts to yours and to the will of Heaven. If, then, the mine of her honor, beauty, modesty, and reserve yields you without any labor on your part all the wealth that it holds and that you could want, why do you wish to go deeper into the earth and seek out new veins of new and unheard-of treasure at the risk of bringing everything down, since when all is said it is supported only on the weak props of her frail nature? Bear in mind that when a man seeks the impossible, it is only just that the possible be denied him. But a poet has put it better when he says:

> *Life in death I implore,*
> *In sickness health I would see,*
> *In prison I would be free,*
> *In the closed room I ask a door,*
> *In the traitor loyalty.*
> *From my fate I never should*
> *Hope for anything that's good;*
> *And since the impossible I would find,*
> *Fate and Heaven have combined,*
> *And I could not have the possible if I would.*

The next day Anselmo set out for the village, having told Camila that during the time he was absent Lotario would come to look after the house and dine with her and that she was to take care to treat him as she would himself. She was pained at her husband's instructions as any discreet and modest wife would have been and reminded him that it was not well that anyone else should occupy his seat at table. If the reason for his doing this was that he had no confidence in her ability to direct the household, let him try her this once and he would see from experience that she was equal to greater tasks. Anselmo replied that he would have it so, and there was nothing for her to do but bow her head and obey. She promised him that she would do as he had ordered even though it was against her wishes.

And so Anselmo departed, and the next day Lotario came to the house, where he was received by Camila in modest and friendly fashion. But she never permitted him to see her alone, for she was always surrounded by her male and female servants, being closely attended, in particular, by her maid named Leonela, of whom she was very fond for the reason that the two of them had grown up together in the home of Camila's parents, and when she married Anselmo, she had brought the girl with her. During the first three days Lotario said nothing to her, although he might have done so when the cloth was removed and the servants in accordance with their mistress's orders went to make their own repast with as much haste as possible. She had even ordered Leonela to eat first in order that she might not have to leave her side, but the maid had her mind upon other things more to her taste and, needing the time and opportunity for her own concerns, did not always obey her mistress on this point, with the result that the pair were left alone as if they had deliberately sent her out of the room.

Camila's modest appearance, it is true, the serious look on her face, and her quiet and assured bearing, were such as to put a bridle on Lotario's tongue, but in the end her many virtues by the silence that they thus imposed were to prove harmful to both of them; for if his tongue was still, his thoughts were given free play and he had a chance to observe one by one all of her many fine qualities, her charms of mind and body, which were enough to inspire love in a marble statue, not to speak of a human heart. In place of conversing with her, he spent the time thinking how worthy she was of being loved, and this consideration began little by little to impair the respect that he had for Anselmo. A thousand times he felt an impulse to leave the city and go where his friend would never see him again and he would never see Camila, but the pleasure he found in gazing upon her prevented this and kept him there. Struggling with himself, he made an effort to reject and not to feel the happiness which the sight of her gave him.

When alone, he would indulge in self-reproaches for his folly, calling himself a bad friend and a bad Christian. He would argue the matter in his mind, making comparisons between himself and Anselmo, and he always reached the same concluson: to the effect that Anselmo's madness and rashness outweighed his own treachery, and if he could find an excuse before God as in the eyes of men for what he now thought of doing, then he need fear no punishment for his offense.

The short of it is that Camila's beauty and virtue, together with the opportunity which the foolish husband had placed in his hands, had proved too much for Lotario's loyalty as a friend. Unable to think of anything but her toward whom his affections were inclined, after Anselmo had been gone for three days, during which time he had waged a continuous battle in an effort to hold out against his own desires, he began making love to Camila so violently and in such amorous terms that she did not know what to do and could only rise and go to her room without giving him a single word in reply. This stern demeanor on her part, however, was not enough to discourage in Lotario the hope that is always born along with love. Instead, he was more bent than ever upon winning her.

As for Camila, this was a side of Lotario's character that she had never glimpsed nor suspected, and she was at a loss as to what course to adopt. It seemed to her that it was not safe nor the proper thing to give him an opportunity to speak to her again; and, accordingly, she resolved to send one of her menservants that very night with a note to Anselmo, a note that read as follows.

CHAPTER XXXIV. *In which is continued the "Story of the One Who Was Too Curious for His Own Good."*

*I*t is commonly said that an army does not present a good appearance *without its general nor a castle without its castellan, but in my opinion the young married woman without her husband creates an even worse impression unless there is a good reason for it. I find myself so badly off without you and so incapable of enduring your absence that unless you come quickly I shall seek refuge in my parents' house, even though I leave your own without a guardian. For the guardian that you left me, if he still deserves that title, I think is concerned rather with his own pleasure than with your interests; but since you are a discerning person, I shall say no more, nor is it fitting that I should.*

Upon receiving this letter Anselmo thought that Lotario must have begun the undertaking and that Camila had responded as he would have wished. Being extremely happy over this news, he wrote his wife that she should by no means leave his house as he would return very shortly. Camila was greatly astonished at such a reply, which threw her into greater confusion than ever, since now she dared not remain in her own home nor go to that of her parents; for if she remained, she would be imperiling her virtue, and if she went, she would be disobeying her husband's express command.

Finally, she chose what was for her the worse of two possible courses by deciding to stay; and she further resolved that she would not shun Lotario's company, since she did not wish to occasion talk among the servants. She was sorry now that she had written her husband, for she was afraid he would think that Lotario had perceived in her some evidence of frivolity which had caused him to forget the decorum that he should have preserved. Confident, however, of her own virtuous conduct and good intentions, she made up her mind to put her trust in God and to offer a silent resistance to all of Lotario's pleas. In the meanwhile, she would say nothing more to her husband in order not to involve him in any quarrel or unpleasantness.

She even thought of how she might be able to excuse his friend's conduct in explaining things to him, when he should ask what had led her to write that letter. These thoughts of hers were honorable enough, but they were not of much help or to the point as she sat listening to Lotario the next day. He was now wooing her so ardently that her firmness was already beginning to waver and her virtue had to come to the aid of her eyes lest they give some sign of the amorous compassion that his words and tears had awakened in her bosom. Lotario noted all this and became more ardent than ever.

It seemed to him that he must take advantage of the opportunity afforded him by Anselmo's absence by pressing the siege of this fortress, and so he proceeded to attack her self-conceit with praises of her beauty; for there is nothing that more quickly lays low and levels the castled towers of lovely women's vanity than vanity itself on the tongue of adulation. In brief, he most diligently undermined the rock of her integrity with such devices that, even had she been made of bronze, she must have fallen to earth. He wept, entreated, promised, flattered, importuned, and pretended with such a show of real feeling that he ended by overcoming Camila's reserve and winning the victory that he least expected and most desired.

Camila surrendered, yes, Camila fell. Was it to be wondered at if friendship in Lotario's case could not keep its footing? Here we have an example which shows us clearly that the passion of love is to be conquered only by fleeing it. There is none may grapple with so powerful an enemy, for divine strength is needed to subdue its human power. Leonela alone knew of her mistress's weakness, the two false friends and new lovers being unable to conceal it from her. Lotario did not wish to tell Camila of Anselmo's purpose nor how the latter had provided the opportunity for him to reach this point, as he did not want her to underrate his love or derive the impression that it was purely by chance and unthinkingly that he had paid court to her.

Anselmo returned to his home a few days later but failed to perceive what was lacking there: namely, the thing that he had treated so lightly yet had treasured most. He then went to call upon Lotario and found him at his house. The two embraced and Anselmo at once asked for the news that meant life or death to him.

"The only news that I can give you, friend Anselmo," said Lotario, "is that you have a wife who is worthy to serve as the crowning example of all good women. The words that I spoke were borne away on the wind, my offerings were disdained, my gifts not accepted, while the feigned tears that I shed she regarded as a very enlivening jest. In a few words: just as Camila is the emblem of all beauty, so is she the treasure-house of modesty, good deportment, matronly reserve, and all the virtues that can render a respectable woman praiseworthy and happy. So, take your money, my friend. You see that I still have it, for I had no need of touching it, as Camila's integrity is something that is not to be laid low by gifts and promises.

"Be content now, Anselmo," he went on, "and do not seek for any further proof. Having passed dryshod over the sea of those doubts and suspicions that may be, and commonly are, held of women, do not think of embarking once again upon an ocean of fresh troubles or seek with another pilot to test the strength and seaworthiness of the good ship which Heaven has given you as your lot that you may cross the waters of this world. Rather, you should consider that you are now safely in port and should cast out the anchor of good sense, letting things be as they are until you are called upon to pay the debt that no human being however noble is dispensed from paying."

Anselmo was very happy at hearing Lotario's words and believed them as if they had been uttered by an oracle. Nevertheless, he begged him, if only out of curiosity and for the sake of amusement, not to abandon the undertaking, though he need not press his suit with as much fervor as he had shown up to now. All that he asked of him was that he write some verses in praise of Camila, alluding to her under the name of Chloris; for he would give Camila to understand that their friend was smitten with a lady on whom he had bestowed that name—this, in order that he might be able to praise her with that respect that was due to her virtue. If Lotario did not care to take the trouble to compose the verses, he himself would do so.

"That will not be necessary," said Lotario, "for the Muses are not such enemies of mine that they do not pay me a visit now and then in the course of the year. So, go ahead and tell Camila that story about my amours, and if my verses are not all that the subject deserves, they will at least be the best that I can produce."

Such, then, was the agreement reached between the one who was too curious and his treacherous friend; after which, returning to his own house, Anselmo asked Camila the question which she wondered that he had not asked before: as to what the occasion was for her having written the letter that she had sent him. Her answer was that it had seemed to her that Lotario was gazing at her a little more freely than when he, Anselmo, had been at home, but in this she had found that she was mistaken and was convinced that it had been her imagination, for now Lotario shunned her and avoided being alone with her. Her husband thereupon assured her that she might feel safe so far as any suspicion of that sort was concerned, for he happened to know that his friend was in love with a young lady in the city of very prominent family whose praises he was in the habit of singing under the name of Chloris; and even if this were not the case, their great friendship and Lotario's loyalty left nothing to fear.

Had not Camila previously been informed by her lover that his passion for Chloris was a feigned one and that he had merely told Anselmo this in order to be able to write an occasional poem to herself, she undoubtedly would have been desperately jealous; but, being forewarned, she was not taken by surprise and gave no sign of uneasiness. Another day, the three of them being together at table, Anselmo asked Lotario to recite for them some of the verses he had composed for his beloved Chloris; for since Camila did not know the young lady, he might feel free to do so.

"Even if she did know her," said Lotario, "I should make no effort at concealment; for when a poet praises his lady's beauty and calls her cruel, he does not thereby cast any reflection upon her good name. However, be that as it may, I will tell you that yesterday I did a sonnet on Chloris's ingratitude, which runs like this:

SONNET [1]

In the silence of the night when gentle sleep
Holds all the world beneath its soothing spell,
'Tis then that I am ever wont to tell
My many woes, the sorry score I keep
For Heaven and for Chloris. When the sun doth peep
From the rosy portals of the east, my hell
Begins once more, the plaint I know so well,
The broken words, the sighs—I can but weep.
And when from his burning, star-girdled midday throne

The sun sends down his rays to warm the earth,
My moans are doubled 'mid a flood of tears.
The night returns, and still the mournful drone
Continues. Sorrow is of little worth
When Heaven is deaf and Chloris hath no ears."

Camila was well pleased with the sonnet, but Anselmo liked it even better. He praised it, remarking that the lady was exceedingly cruel not to show her appreciation of so much sincerity as was there expressed.

"Does that mean," said Camila, "that all poets who are in love are sincere in what they say and always speak the truth?"

"As poets," replied Lotario, "they may go beyond the truth, but as lovers they fall far short of it."

"That," Anselmo agreed, "is undoubtedly so." For he wished to support what his friend had to say in order to lend it weight with Camila. She, however, was as unconcerned with her husband's design as she was deeply in love with Lotario; and so, taking a pleasure in anything that had to do with the latter and knowing well that she herself was the object of his desires and poems and was the real Chloris, she asked him if he did not have another sonnet or bit of verse that he could recite to them.

"Yes, I have," said Lotario, "but I do not think it is as good as the other one, or perhaps I should say it is no worse. In any event, you may judge for yourselves, for here it is:

SONNET [2]

I'm dying, that I know—believest thou me?
Dost not believe thou wouldst behold me dead
Here at thy feet, cruel one, uncomforted,
Before I should repent of loving thee?
When I to oblivion shall go and see
Life, fame, and fortune, all I valued, fled,
Open then my bosom, look how I have bled,
And find thine image carved in mimicry.
This relic will I guard 'gainst the harsh fate
That I to mine own obstinacy owe,
Which thy severity doth but increase.
The sailor on darkened seas must needs await
His doom when no pole star there is to show
Where lies the way unto some port's release."

Anselmo praised this sonnet as he had the preceding one, and so went on adding link after link to the chain by which he was binding himself and assuring his own dishonor; for the more Lotario dishonored him, the more he held that he was being honored. As a consequence, each step that Camila descended toward the depths of scorn she mounted one, in the opinion of her husband, toward those heights of virtue and good repute that he wished her to attain. On a certain occasion, finding herself alone with her maid, Camila unburdened herself to the waiting woman.

"Friend Leonela," she said, "I am ashamed to see how cheaply I have held myself that I did not compel Lotario to purchase by an expenditure of time that complete possession of my will and affections that I so quickly yielded him. I fear that he will see only haste and frivolity on my part [3] without taking into consideration the irresistible pressure that he brought to bear upon me."

"Do not let that worry you, my lady," replied Leonela; "it does not diminish the value of the thing given to give it at once, providing it is a good thing and worthy of being esteemed. Indeed, there is a saying that he who gives quickly gives twice."

"And there is also a saying," Camila reminded her, "that what costs little is valued less." [4]

"That does not apply to you," observed Leonela, "for love, I have heard it said, sometimes flies and sometimes walks; it sometimes runs and sometimes loiters; some it chills and others it inflames; it wounds some and slays others. The course of its desires begins and ends at one and the same point. In the morning it lays siege to a fortress and by night the besieged will have surrendered, for there is no force that can withstand it. And since this is so, why then are you astonished or what do you fear upon seeing that the same thing has happened with you and Lotario, love having taken my master's absence as the means of overcoming us? [5] For it was essential that love's labor be accomplished within that time, before Anselmo should return and by his presence compel it to remain uncompleted. Love has no better minister to carry out his designs than opportunity, of which he makes use in all his undertakings, particularly at the beginning. All this I know very well, and more from experience than from hearsay. I will tell you all about it someday, my lady, for I too am made of flesh and my blood is young.

"What is more, my lady Camila," she went on, "you did not yield and give yourself so quickly, before you had seen in Lotario's eyes, in his words and sighs and in his gifts and promises, his whole soul laid bare, revealing all those virtues that render him worthy of being loved. This

being so, do not trouble your thoughts with all these finical scruples and
imaginings, but be assured that Lotario esteems you as you do him, and
be content and satisfied with knowing that if you have fallen into the
amorous net, it is one of worth and valor who has caught you in it, one
who not only has the four S's that they say all true lovers ought to have,
but a whole alphabet. If you do not believe me, just listen and I will
repeat it for you. As I see it, it goes like this: Amiable, Bountiful, Courteous, Devoted, Enamored, Faithful, Gallant, Honorable, Illustrious,
Loyal, Manly, Noble, Open, Princely, Qualified, Rich, and the S's that I
have mentioned. And then, Trusty, Veracious—the X does not suit him,
being too harsh a letter. The Y has already been given, and Z is for Zealous
of your honor." [6]

Camila had to laugh at these ABC's and decided that her waiting woman
was more experienced in affairs of the heart than she admitted. Leonela
now confessed as much by telling of an affair she was having with a wellborn youth of that same city. Her mistress was alarmed at this, fearing
that her own honor would thus be endangered, and inquired as to whether
the matter had gone beyond mere words, to which the maid, with little
shame and much effrontery, replied that it had; for there is no doubt
that the careless conduct of ladies renders their maids shameless, and the
latter, when they see their mistresses stumble, think nothing of limping
themselves, nor do they care who knows it.

All that Camila could do was to beg the girl to say nothing to the one
who was supposed to be her lover, but to regard all such matters as
strictly private in order that they might not come to the attention of
either Anselmo or Lotario. Leonela assured her that she would do this,
but she carried out her promise in such a manner as to make certain that
Camila's fears of losing her reputation would be justified. For the brazen
and dishonorable creature, upon seeing that her lady's conduct was not
what it should be, had the audacity to bring her lover into the house,
being confident her mistress, even though she might see him, would not
dare say anything.

For one of the punishments that ladies must suffer for their sins is that
of becoming the slaves of their own servants. This was what happened
with Camila, who found herself obliged to cover up the immodesty and
baseness of her serving woman. Although she more than once saw that
Leonela was entertaining her gallant in a room of the house, she not only
dared not reprove her, but even helped her conceal him and did all she
could to keep her husband from catching a glimpse of him. She was
unable, however, to prevent Lotario from seeing him as the man was

stealing away at daybreak one morning. Not knowing who he was, Lotario thought at first that he must be an apparition of some sort, but when he saw him muffling himself in his cloak and taking great pains not to be observed, he at once had another idea which would have been the ruination of them all if Camila had not set things to rights.

It did not occur to him that this man whom he had seen leaving Anselmo's house at so untimely an hour had gone there to meet Leonela; as a matter of fact, he had forgotten that such a person existed. He believed, rather, that Camila, just as she had been light and easy with him, was now playing the same game with another. For there is yet another penalty that the erring woman must pay for her sin, and that is, to have her honor mistrusted even by the one to whom, upon his urgent entreaties and persuasions, she has given herself, for he is convinced that she will yield all the more readily to others, and so he will give unquestioning credence to any suspicion of this sort that occurs to him.

For what Lotario did at this point there would seem to be no other explanation than that he had lost his good sense entirely. He forgot all the words of wisdom that he had spoken on the subject, nor did he pause to consider what was proper or reasonable under the circumstances. Moved only by a blind impatience inspired by the jealous rage that gnawed at his entrails, he was dying to avenge himself on Camila, who had not offended him in the slightest; and, accordingly, without more ado, he hastened to the master of the house before the latter had risen.

"I want you to know, Anselmo," he said, "that for some time now I have been struggling with myself, trying to force myself to tell you that which it is neither possible nor right that I should any longer withhold from you. And so, I will inform you that the fortress that was Camila has already fallen and is now wholly at my disposition. If I have delayed in telling you this truth, it was in order that I might see if it was merely some passing whim on her part, or if, possibly, she was doing it to test those protestations of love that, with your permission, I had begun to offer her. I feel, moreover, that if she were all that she ought to be and all that we both thought she was, that she would already have told you of my advances. However, seeing that she has waited so long, I know now that the promises she made me were true when she told me that, the next time you were absent from home, she would talk to me in that closet where your jewels are kept." And it was true that Camila was in the habit of conversing with him there.

"I should not wish you," he continued, "to rush out at once and take some vengeance or other, for as yet the sin has been committed only by intent, and it is possible that between now and the time for carrying it out Camila's intention will change and repentance will spring up in its place. And as you have always wholly or in part followed my advice in the past, so be guided by it now in order that, without any mistake but with cautious deliberation, you may be able to decide upon the best course to follow. Pretend that you are going away for two or three days as you have done on other occasions, and arrange to hide in your closet, for the tapestries and other things there will make it easy for you to conceal yourself. You will then be able to see with your own eyes, and I with mine, what Camila's purpose is; and if it be an evil one, which is to be feared rather than expected, you may with silence, wisdom, and discretion exact punishment for the wrong done you."

Anselmo was amazed, bewildered, astounded at what Lotario had just told him. The news came at a time when he least expected to hear it, for he believed that Camila had already come out victorious in his friend's feigned assaults and he was beginning to revel in her glorious triumph. He was silent for some time, staring hard at the ground without batting an eyelash.

"Lotario," he said at last, "you have acted as I expected you to, in view of our friendship, and I will follow your advice in everything. Do as you see fit, and guard this secret as you know it should be guarded under circumstances as unlooked for as these."

Lotario promised that he would do so, but as he left Anselmo he began wholly to repent having said what he did, perceiving that he had been very foolish in what he had done, since he might have avenged himself upon Camila in some less cruel and dishonorable a fashion. He cursed his lack of sense and condemned the hasty impulse upon which he had acted, without knowing what means to adopt to undo the wrong or how he could fairly find a way out of it all. He finally made up his mind to tell Camila everything, and as it was not hard to find an opportunity for doing so, he sought her out that very day.

She was alone when he came upon her, and as soon as she saw that she might speak to him freely, she said, "Friend Lotario, I must tell you that there is something that pains me until it seems my heart will burst, and it will be a wonder if it does not. Leonela's shamelessness has reached such a point that every night she closets herself with a gallant here in this house and stays with him until daybreak, at great cost to my reputation, inasmuch as anyone seeing him leave my house at so unaccustomed an hour well might form his own opinion of the matter. What annoys me most is that I cannot punish nor scold her, for the fact that she is acquainted with our relationship puts a bridle on my tongue by way of silencing hers, and I very much fear that something unfortunate may come of all this."

When Camila first began speaking, Lotario had believed this to be an artifice on her part with the object of making him think that the man he had seen leaving was Leonela's lover and not her own; but her tears, her very real suffering, and her pleas to him to help her, ended by convincing him of the truth of what she said, and this at the same time completed his confusion and feeling of remorse. He nonetheless told her not to worry, that he would see to putting a stop to Leonela's insolence. At the same time he informed her of what he had said to Anselmo in his jealous rage and how they had arranged for her husband to hide in the closet that he might there see plainly how disloyal she was to him. He implored her forgiveness for this act of madness on his part and her advice as to what he should do to get out of the intricate labyrinth in which, through his impetuosity, he had become involved.

Camila was alarmed and very angry at what Lotario had told her and proceeded to scold him most sensibly, reproving him for his evil thoughts and for the wicked and foolish resolution that he had adopted. But woman naturally has keener wits than man, for good and evil, although they may fail her when it is a question of reasoning things out logically; and so it was that Camila at once found the means of remedying what appeared to be an irremediable situation, by telling Lotario he should see to it that Anselmo hid himself in the closet the next day as he had planned, as she meant to make good use of his presence there so that from then on they would be able to enjoy each other's company without fear of being taken by surprise. Without revealing to her lover all that was in her mind, she directed him to be sure to come when Leonela called him, after Anselmo was safely hidden away, and to reply to anything that she said to him exactly as he would have done if he had not known that her husband was listening. Lotario, however, insisted that she explain to him more fully just what it was that she intended to do in order that he might be able to act with greater certainty and take such precautions as were necessary.

"I assure you," said Camila, "that there are no precautions to take; all that you have to do is to answer the questions that I put to you." She would not give him any further account of her plan, for although it appeared to her to be an excellent one, she feared that he might not care to follow it and would start looking for another that would not be so good.

Lotario then took his departure, and the next day Anselmo, acting upon the excuse that he had to go to the village where his friend lived, left the house and returned to take up his hiding place, which he was able to do without any inconvenience, for Camila and Leonela made it easy for him. His feelings as he concealed himself behind the draperies may be imagined: they were those of a man who expected to see the entrails of his honor laid bare before his eyes and who was about to lose that supreme good that he had thought he possessed in his beloved Camila. Having made certain that Anselmo was there, Camila and Leonela now entered the closet, and no sooner had she set foot in the room than the former gave a deep sigh.

"Ah, Leonela, my friend!" she exclaimed, "before I do something of which I will say nothing to you lest you seek to prevent it, would it not be better for you to take Anselmo's dagger which I asked you to procure for me and run it through this infamous bosom of mine? But no, do not do that; for there is no reason why I should suffer the penalty for another's fault. First of all, I should like to know what it was that Lotario's bold and shameless eyes beheld in me that caused him thus rashly to reveal to me a passion as evil as that which he has disclosed, in contempt of his friend's honor and my own. Go to that window, Leonela, and call down to him; for without any doubt he is there in the street, waiting to carry out his wicked intentions. But my own intentions, as cruel as they are honorable, shall be carried out first."

"Ah, my lady!" replied the crafty Leonela, who had been well schooled in her part, "what is it that you mean to do with that dagger? Are you perchance thinking of taking your own life or Lotario's? Whatever it is, it will result in the loss of your good name and reputation. It would be better for you to say nothing of the wrong that has been done you; rather, you should see to it that this evil man does not enter our house and find us alone. Consider, my lady: we are weak women and he is a man, strong and determined, and, coming as he does, blindly and passionately bent upon that foul design of his, he may well put it into execution before you can carry out yours, and may do that which in your eyes would be worse than if he were to slay you. A plague on my master for having given this shameless fellow the upper hand in his household! But supposing, my lady, that you kill him, for such I think is your intention, what shall we do with the body?"

"What shall we do with it, my friend?" replied Camila. "Why, we shall leave it for Anselmo to bury; for he should regard it as no task at all to put the betrayer of his good name underground. Go, then, and call him; for every moment that I delay taking the vengeance that is due my wrong appears to me an offense against that loyalty that I owe to my husband."

Anselmo was listening to all this, and at each word that Camila spoke his thoughts underwent a change. When he heard that she was resolved to kill Lotario, his impulse was to come out and reveal his presence and prevent such a deed, but, wishing to see what the outcome of her noble and virtuous determination would be, he restrained himself, thinking that he would be able to appear in time to stop her. At this point she was seized with a violent fainting fit and threw herself upon a near-by couch, as Leonela began weeping bitterly. "Ah, woe is me!" she exclaimed, "how unfortunate I am that the world's flower of virtue, the crowning example of chastity for all good wives, should be dying here in my arms!" She went on uttering other similar lamentations, and anyone hearing her would have thought that she was the most loyal and woebegone lady's maid that ever was, while her mistress was another and persecuted Penelope.

Camila, however, was not long in recovering from her swoon. "Leonela," she said, as she regained consciousness once more, "why do you not go call that most disloyal 7 friend to his friend that ever the sun shone upon or the night covered with its darkness? Go, run, hasten, make speed, lest the fire of my wrath burn itself out with delay and the just vengeance that I hope for be consumed in threats and curses!"

"That I will, my lady," said Leonela, "but first give me the dagger that you may not do something while I am gone that will cause all those who love you to weep for the rest of their lives."

"You may rest assured, friend Leonela, that I shall do nothing of the kind; for however rash and foolish I may appear to you to be in thus defending my honor, I am not like Lucretia, of whom it is said that she slew herself without being guilty of any fault whatsoever and without first having slain the one who was the cause of her dishonor. I shall die if needs be, but only after I have had revenge and satisfaction from him who is responsible for my being in this state where I must weep over audacious proposals for which I can in no wise be held accountable."

It required much urging before Leonela could be persuaded to call Lotario, but finally she left the room, and while she was gone Camila went on talking to herself.

"God help me! Would it not have been better to send Lotario away as I have done many times before than to give him the opportunity as I am doing now to look upon me as evil and unchaste, even for the brief space of time that it takes to undeceive him? It would have been better, no doubt, but then I should not have had my vengeance, nor would my husband's honor have been satisfied if Lotario had been allowed to wash his hands of the matter and escape so easily from this situation into which his own wicked impulses have led him. Let the traitor pay with his life for his lewd desires. Let the world know if it must that Camila not only preserved her loyalty to her husband, but avenged herself on the one who had dared offend him.

"But after all, I imagine it would have been better to give Anselmo an account of everything that has happened; yet I informed him of it in the letter that I wrote to him while he was in the village, and it is my opinion that if he did not at once hasten back to remedy the wrong of which I told him, it must have been because, being so pure-minded and trusting, he would not or could not believe that so stanch a friend could ever think of thus dishonoring him. Indeed, I could not believe it myself for a long while, nor should I ever have done so if Lotario's insolence had not been carried to the point where his open gifts and lavish promises and constant tears made it all too plain. But why do I let myself run on like this? Does a noble resolve, perchance, stand in need of any counsels? No, certainly not. Away, traitorous thoughts! Come, vengeance! Let the false one approach and enter, let him die and end it all, and then come what may! Pure I came to him whom Heaven gave me as my own, and pure I will leave him; nay, more, I will leave him bathed in my own chaste blood and in the impure blood of one who in all the world has been the greatest betrayer of friendship that ever was."

As she said this, she paced up and down the room with the dagger unsheathed, swaying and staggering and making such wild gestures that she appeared to be out of her mind, and one would have taken her for some desperate ruffian rather than a woman who had been gently bred and reared. Anselmo watched her from behind the tapestries where he had hidden and was vastly astonished by it all. It seemed to him that what he had seen and heard was sufficient answer to the worst suspicions he had entertained, and he would have been well enough pleased if Lotario had not come now, fearing as he did some sudden untoward event. He was about to come out and embrace his wife and tell her the whole story but stopped short when he saw Leonela returning, leading Lotario by the hand. The moment she saw the latter, Camila took the dagger and with it drew a long line across the floor.

"Lotario," she said, "mark well what I tell you. If by any chance you are so bold as to cross this line that you see here, or even come up to it, the instant I see you intend to do so I shall pierce my bosom with this dagger that I hold in my hand. Before you utter a single word in reply, I would have you listen to a few words that I have to say to you, and afterward you may make such answer as you like. In the first place, Lotario, I would ask you if you know my husband, Anselmo, and what opinion you hold of him. And in the second place, I would likewise inquire if you know me. Answer me this, clearly and plainly and without stopping to think for long what you are going to say, for the questions I have put to you are simple enough."

Lotario was not so dull-witted but that, when Camila told him to have Anselmo hide there, he had at once surmised what she meant to do, and he was now so clever and prompt in helping her carry out her plan that the lie came to seem the truest truth.

"I did not think, beauteous Camila," he answered her, "that you were sending for me to question me about things so foreign to the purpose for which I come here. If you are doing this merely to defer the promised favor, you might have put it off still longer, for an ardent desire is most painful when the hope of its being fulfilled is nearest to realization. However, in order that you may not be able to say that I have not answered your questions, I will tell you that your husband Anselmo and I have known each other since our tenderest years. I need not tell you further what you already know concerning the friendship between us, merely by way of bearing witness [8] against the wrong that love compels me to do to my friend—love, the most powerful excuse that can be offered for greater misdeeds than this. Yes, I know you well and you are as much mine as his; for I can assure you that, if it were not so, I would not for any lesser reward have gone against that which I owe to myself and to the holy laws of true friendship, now broken and violated by me through the work of an enemy no less powerful than love itself."

"If you admit this," replied Camila, "O mortal enemy of all that justly deserves to be loved, how then do you have the countenance to appear before one whom you know to be the mirror in which Anselmo beholds himself, who should be in turn the glass in which you see the unjustifiable injury that you have done him. But, alas, I now realize that it must have been some frivolity on my part that caused you to show so little self-respect. I will not call it immodesty, since it was in no way deliberate but must have been due to that careless attitude into which women sometimes inadvertently fall when they think that there is no occasion for reserve. If this be not so, then tell me, O traitor, when did I respond to your entreaties with any word or sign that might have awakened in you the shadowy hope of being able to accomplish your infamous desires?

When were your amorous pleadings not repelled and reprehended? When did they not meet with stern, harsh words from me? When were your many promises believed, your still more lavish gifts accepted?

"Nevertheless," she continued, "inasmuch as it seems to me that no one could persevere for so long in a purpose of this sort if he were not sustained by a hope of some kind, I must seek to attribute to myself the blame for your impudence, since no doubt some careless act of mine has all this time been giving you ground for hope. And so, it is my intention to punish myself and assume the penalty that you deserve. And as I would have you see that, being so cruel toward myself, I could not but be the same toward you, I have brought you here to witness the sacrifice that I am about to make to the offended honor of my so honored husband, to whom you have done the greatest wrong that was in your power, while I as well have wronged him by failing to avoid the occasion, if any, that I have given you by appearing to encourage and sanction your designs.

"I will say again that the suspicion I have that some bit of carelessness on my part has engendered in you this mad passion is the thing that most harasses me, and it is this negligence that I desire to punish with my own hands; for if another were to be my executioner, my fault would perhaps become more widely known. Before I do this, however, I mean to slay even in death and take with me one who will satisfy the desire and hope of vengeance that I cherish; for there where I go, wherever it may be, I shall see a disinterested and unyielding justice inflicted upon him who has placed me in my present plight."

Saying this, with incredible strength and swiftness she fell upon Lotario with the unsheathed dagger, with so evident an intention of burying it in his bosom that he was half in doubt as to whether it was a false show or she really meant to do as she said. In any event, he had to employ all his own strength and dexterity to prevent her from stabbing him; for she was so very lifelike in acting out this strange drama of conjugal fidelity [9] that, by way of lending it the color of truth, she even wished to stain it with her own blood.

Seeing that she could not come at Lotario,[10] or pretending that she was unable to, she said, "Since fate is unwilling to satisfy wholly my just desire, it at least is not so powerful as to keep me from satisfying it in part."

With a great effort she freed the hand with the dagger which Lotario held and, directing its point to a place where it would not inflict a deep wound, she plunged it into her left side near the shoulder and then fell to the floor as if in a faint. Leonela and Lotario were dumbfounded by this unexpected turn of events, and as they beheld Camila lying stretched out there and bathed in her own blood, they were uncertain as to whether the act was real or feigned. Terrified and breathless, Lotario ran up and withdrew the dagger, and when he saw the small wound it had made he was greatly relieved and once more was led to admire the sagacity, prudence, and extreme cleverness of the beauteous Camila. By way of carrying out his own part, he then began to lament long and loudly over her body, as though she were already dead, heaping curses not only upon himself but upon the one who had placed him in such a position. And as he knew that his friend Anselmo was listening, he said things that caused the latter to feel much more pity for him than for Camila, who was supposed to be dead.

Leonela then took her mistress in her arms and laid her upon the couch, begging Lotario to go seek some trustworthy person to care for her wound. At the same time she asked his advice as to what they should tell Anselmo if by chance he should return before it was healed. He replied that they might say whatever they liked, as he was in no condition to give advice that would be of any value. All he could tell her was to try to stop the bleeding. As for himself, he was going where no one would ever see him again. And then, with a great show of grief and feeling, he left the house; and as soon as he was alone and safely out of sight, he began crossing himself any number of times as he marveled at Camila's ingenuity and the telling manner in which Leonela played her part. Anselmo, he reflected, would surely be convinced that he had a second Portia for a wife, and he was eager to be alone with him in order that they together might celebrate this mixture of falsehood and truth dissimulated in a fashion that never could be imagined.

Leonela stopped the flow of her mistress's blood as he had directed, there being no more of it than was necessary to lend credence to the fiction, and, having bathed the wound with a little wine, she bandaged it as well as she could, meanwhile keeping up such a flow of words as would have sufficed to convince Anselmo, if the ones already spoken had not done so, that he had in Camila a model of virtue.

Mingled with Leonela's words were those of her mistress, who reproached herself for being a coward and lacking in courage, which had failed her at the time she most needed it—the courage to take her life, which was so abhorrent to her. She asked her waiting woman's advice as to whether or not she should tell her beloved husband of all that had happened, and Leonela counseled against this since it would put him under the obligation of revenging himself upon Lotario, which he could do only at great risk to himself. It was the duty of a good wife not to involve her husband in quarrels over her, but rather to remove the occasion for such disputes. Camila replied that this advice impressed her as being very good and she would follow it; but, in any case, they must begin to think of something to tell Anselmo concerning the cause of this wound, which he could not help seeing. To this the maid answered that she was incapable of telling a lie even in jest.

"Well, then, my sister," said Camila, "how do you expect me to tell one, who should not dare invent or keep up a falsehood if my life depended on it? And so, the best thing will be to tell him the naked truth in order that he may not catch us in a lie."

"Do not trouble yourself, my lady," said Leonela. "Between now and tomorrow morning I will think up something that we can tell him; and possibly, the wound being where it is, it may be kept covered so that he will not see it, and Heaven will be thus pleased to favor our just and honorable intentions. In the meantime, calm yourself and try not to appear so excited, for it is not well that my master should find you in this state of agitation. Just leave it to my care and God's, for He always looks after the desires of the righteous."

Anselmo had most attentively watched and listened to this tragedy involving the death of his own honor which had been performed with such marvelous and effective realism that the actors appeared to have been transformed into the very parts they played. He was eager for night to come so that he might have an opportunity to leave the house and go see his good friend Lotario that they might rejoice together over the precious pearl he had found in thus establishing beyond a doubt the virtue of his wife. Mistress and maid were at pains to provide him with an opportunity to leave, and, taking advantage of it, he went at once to seek Lotario. It would be quite impossible to describe the affectionate embraces that he gave him when they met, the many things he said out of the happiness of his heart, or the praises that he bestowed on Camila. Lotario listened to it all without being able to give any sign of joy, for he kept remembering what a deceived man his friend was and how unjustly he had wronged him. Although Anselmo saw that Lotario was not in good spirits, he believed the reason was that he had left Camila wounded and felt that he was to blame.

Anselmo accordingly told him, among other things, that he should not worry about what had happened to her, since her wound undoubtedly was a slight one, seeing that she and Leonela had agreed to conceal it.

This being so, there was nothing to fear, but henceforth he should be glad and rejoice with his friend, who, through his capable mediation, now found himself raised to the greatest heights of happiness that could be desired, with no other ambition than that of spending his time in composing verses in Camila's honor such as would preserve her name for all the ages to come. Lotario praised this good intention and promised to do his part in helping to erect so illustrious a monument.

Thus did Anselmo remain the most delightfully deceived man that could possibly be found anywhere in the world. He himself led home by the hand the one who had wrought the destruction of his good name, in the belief that he was bringing with him one who had exalted it. As for Camila, she received her husband's friend with a wry look but a smiling heart. This deception lasted for a number of months until, at a turn of fortune's wheel, the guilty relationship that had been so artfully concealed finally became known and Anselmo paid with his life for his ill-advised curiosity.

CHAPTER XXXV. *In which the "Story of the One Who Was Too Curious for His Own Good" is brought to a close, and in which is related the fierce and monstrous battle that Don Quixote waged with certain skins of red wine.*

THE reading of the story was nearly completed when from the garret where Don Quixote was taking his repose Sancho Panza burst forth in great excitement, shouting, "Come quick, sirs, and help my master, for he is in the thick of the most stubborn and fiercest battle that ever my eyes beheld! By the living God but he gave that giant who is the enemy of my lady, the Princess Micomicona, such a slash that he cut his head off all the way around as if it had been a turnip!"

"What are you talking about, brother?" asked the curate as he paused in his reading. "Have you gone out of your head, Sancho? How in the

devil could what you say be true when the giant is two thousand leagues
from here?"

At this point there came a loud noise from the upper room and Don
Quixote could be heard crying, "Hold, robber, scoundrel, knave! I have
you now, and your scimitar will not avail you!" And then it sounded as
if he were giving great slashes at the wall.

"Don't stop to listen," said Sancho, "but go on in and stop the fight
or else help my master; although, come to think of it, that will not be
necessary, for there is no doubt whatever that the giant is already dead
by this time and is now giving an account to God of his past life and evil
ways. I myself saw the blood running all over the floor and his head cut
off and lying to one side, and it was big as a wineskin."

"May they slay me!" cried the innkeeper at this point. "I'll bet Don
Quixote or Don Devil has been slashing at one of those skins full of
red wine that are at the head of his bed, and it must have been the wine
spilling over the floor that looked like blood to this good man."

He then made his way to the garret, followed by all the rest of them,
and there they found Don Quixote in the strangest costume imaginable.
He was clad in his shirt, which was not long enough in front to cover
his thighs completely and was about six fingers shorter behind. His legs
were very long, lean, and hairy and anything but clean. On his head he
had a little greasy red cap that belonged to the innkeeper, and around
his left arm he had rolled a red blanket—an object against which Sancho,
for reasons of his own, had a special grudge—while in his right hand he
held an unsheathed sword with which he was laying about him in every
direction, and all the time he kept talking to himself as if he were really
fighting with some giant. The best part of it was that he had his eyes shut,
for he was still asleep and dreaming that he was doing battle with the
giant, the adventure which he was about to undertake having so worked
upon his imagination that he fancied in his dream that he had already
reached the kingdom of Micomicon and was engaged in a struggle with
his enemy.

Under this illusion he had given the skins so many thrusts, believing
them to be the giant, that the entire room was filled with wine. Seeing
what his guest had done, the landlord was so angry that he fell upon Don
Quixote with clenched fists and began pommeling him so hard that if
Cardenio and the curate had not pulled him off, he would soon have
concluded the war with the giant. But in spite of it all they did not succeed in awakening the poor gentleman until the barber had brought a
large pot of cold water from the well and they had dashed its contents

over the knight, who then regained consciousness but not sufficiently to be able to realize what had happened.

Seeing how scantily and thinly he was clad, Dorotea would not come in to witness the encounter between her champion and his adversary; and Sancho, meanwhile, was looking all over the floor for the giant's head, which he was unable to find.

"I knew all along," he said, "that everything about this house was under a spell. The other time, in this very room where I am now, they gave me any number of cuffs and blows without my knowing from where they came, for I was never able to see anyone doing it; and now I can't find that head though I saw it chopped off with my own eyes, with the blood spurting from his body as from a fountain."

"What blood and what fountain, enemy of God and his saints?" cried the innkeeper. "Can't you see, you brigand, that the blood and fountain you are talking about are nothing other than these skins that have been punctured and the red wine from them that is flowing all over the room —and I only wish I saw the soul of him who pierced them swimming in Hell!"

"I know nothing about that," said Sancho. "All I know is that, if I don't find that head, it will be my bad luck to see my earldom melting away like salt in water."

For Sancho awake was worse than his master asleep, such had been the effect of the promises Don Quixote had made him. The innkeeper was in despair at seeing this lack of concern on the part of the squire and the deviltry wrought by the knight, and he swore that it was not going to be like the last time, when they had left without paying. This time the privileges of knighthood would not let either one or the other of them off, but they would have to reimburse him even for the cost of the plugs to patch up the punctured skins. The curate all this while was holding Don Quixote's hands, and the knight, thinking that the exploit had been accomplished and that he was now in the presence of the Princess Micomicona, dropped to his knees in front of the priest.

"O exalted and famous lady," he said, "your Highness from this day forth may live assured against any harm this lowborn creature could have done you; and I too am now free of the promise I gave you, since with the help of Almighty God and the favor of her in whom I live and breathe, I have so thoroughly [1] fulfilled it."

"There!" exclaimed Sancho upon hearing this, "what did I tell you? You see I was not drunk after all. Just look how my master has salted down that giant! You can depend on the bulls,[2] and my earldom is certain."

Who would not have laughed at hearing the nonsense the two of them talked, master and man? And laugh they all did with the exception of mine host, who was roundly cursing himself. At last, however, with no little effort, the barber, Cardenio, and the curate managed to get Don Quixote back into bed, and he at once fell asleep with every appearance of being utterly exhausted. Leaving him there, they then went down to the gateway of the inn to console Sancho Panza for not having found the giant's head; but they had a good deal more on their hands when it came to placating the landlord, who was in a rage over the sudden death of his wineskins. The landlady, for her part, was screaming and carrying on at a great rate.

"It was an evil moment and an unlucky hour," she shouted, "when that knight-errant entered my house. I had never laid eyes on him before, but he cost me dearly. The last time it was the price of a lodging, a dinner, a bed, and straw and barley, for himself, his squire, a hack, and an ass. He said he was a knightly adventurer—may God give him and all the adventurers in this world nothing but misadventures!—and for that reason was obliged to pay nothing, since that was the way it was written down in the tariff code of knight-errantry. And now, on account of him, this other gentleman comes along and carries off my tail and gives it back to me with more than two cuartillos'[3] worth of damage done to it, all stripped of its hair and of no further use for my husband's purpose. And as the finishing touch to everything, he punctures my wineskins and spills my wine—if I could only see his blood spilled instead! But let him not think he'll be able to do the same thing this time! By my father's bones and my mother's ghost, he's going to pay me every cuarto [4] that he owes me or my name is not what it is and I am not my parents' daughter!"

The innkeeper's wife had all this and many other things to say, for she was very angry indeed, and her slavey, the worthy Maritornes, joined in the scolding. The daughter, however, was silent and merely smiled quietly to herself from time to time. The curate finally settled matters by promising to make good the loss to the best of his ability. He agreed to pay them for the wineskins and the wine and especially for the damage done to that tail of which they were forever talking. Dorotea, meanwhile, was comforting Sancho Panza by telling him that, the moment it was definitely established that his master had cut off the giant's head and she had come into peaceful possession of her kingdom, she would bestow upon him the finest earldom that it contained. Sancho felt better upon hearing this and assured the princess that he had seen the giant's head, adding by way of further identification that the monster had a beard that came all the way down to his waist, and if he was not to be seen at the moment, it was for the reason that everything that happened in that house was directed by an enchanter, as he himself had found to be the case the other time that he had stopped there. Dorotea said that she believed this to be true, but that he should not let it worry him, as things would come out all right in the end and he would have whatever he wished.

When they had all quieted down, the curate suggested that they finish reading the story, for there was still a little of it left. Cardenio, Dorotea, and the others thereupon begged him to continue, and by reason of the pleasure that he as well as they derived from it, he went on with the tale, as follows:

As a result of it all, Anselmo was so convinced of Camila's virtue that he went on living a happy and carefree life, while she was deliberately cool toward Lotario in order that her husband might think her feeling for his friend was the opposite of what it was. By way of confirming this impression, Lotario begged permission not to come to the house, since it was plain to be seen that his visits were an annoyance to Camila; but Anselmo, thoroughly deluded, would by no means hear of this, and thus in a thousand ways he became the creator of his own dishonor in place of what he took to be his happiness.

In the meantime, Leonela was so elated at finding herself free to carry on her amours [5] that she came to think of nothing else and gave free rein to her passion, being confident that her mistress would afford her concealment and even show her how to manage the affair with little fear of discovery. Finally, one night Anselmo heard footsteps in her room, and when he sought to enter to find out who was there, he found the door held against him, a circumstance that made him all the more determined to open it. Open it he did by main force and entered just in time to see a man leaping from the window to the street.

He was about to follow in an effort to overtake him or see if he could recognize him but was prevented from doing either by Leonela, who threw her arms about him as she cried, "Calm yourself, my master. Do not excite yourself and go running after the one who just leaped from that window, for he belongs to me; in fact, he is my husband."

Anselmo was unwilling to believe this and, blind with rage, drew a dagger and threatened to stab Leonela, assuring her that he would kill her if she did not tell him the truth. She was so frightened that she did not know what she was saying and could only stammer, "Do not kill me, master, for I can tell you things that are more important than you can imagine."

"Tell me, then," said Anselmo. "If you do not, you are a dead woman."

"It would be impossible for me to do so now," she replied. "I am so excited that I cannot think. Give me until tomorrow morning, and then you will learn from me something that will astonish you. Meanwhile, you may rest assured that the one who left by way of this window is a young man of this city who has promised to marry me."

Anselmo was mollified by this and consented to grant her the time for which she asked. It did not occur to him that he would hear anything against Camila, for he felt perfectly sure of her virtue; and so he went away and left Leonela locked in the room, telling her that she would not come out until he had heard her story. He then went to inform Camila of all that had passed between him and her waiting woman and how the latter had promised to reveal to him some things of very great importance. As to whether his wife was alarmed or not by all this, there is no need of our saying. A terrible fear came over her, for she really believed—and she had good reason to believe it—that Leonela meant to tell Anselmo everything that she knew concerning his wife's disloyalty.

As a result, she did not have the courage to wait and see if her suspicion was false or not, but that very night, as soon as she thought her husband had gone to sleep, she got together the best jewels that she had and a little money and, slipping out unnoticed, made her way to Lotario's house. There she told him all that had happened and begged him to put her in hiding or go with her to some place where Anselmo would not find them. But he was greatly confused by it all and could not give her a single word in reply, nor was he able to make up his mind as to what should be done.

At last he decided to take her to a convent the prioress of which was his sister; and this he did, with her consent and with all the haste that the situation called for, after which he at once left the city without notifying anyone of his departure.

When dawn came, Anselmo was so eager to hear what Leonela had to tell him that he did not even notice that Camila was missing from beside him, but arose and went to where he had left the maid locked in her room. Opening the door, he went in but found no Leonela there. All that he did find was some sheets knotted to the window, an obvious indication that she had let herself down and made her escape. Very much disappointed, he returned to tell Camila, and when he failed to discover her in bed or anywhere in the house, he was truly dumfounded. He made inquiries of all the servants but none could give him any explanation.

As he was looking for her, he chanced to see her jewel boxes lying open and noted that most of the gems were missing from them. Then it was that he began to realize the nature of his misfortune, of which Leonela was not the cause; and without waiting to complete his toilet, he sadly and pensively went to seek his friend Lotario that he might tell him of his sorrow. Lotario, however, was not at home, and his servants said that he had not been there all night long but had left the house with all the money that he had. At this point Anselmo began to feel as if he were losing his mind, and to crown it all, when he returned to his own house, he found it utterly deserted, with all the many servants, male and female, gone. He did not know what to think or say nor what to do; his reason seemed to be deserting him, little by little. As he contemplated his situation, he had an instant view of himself as a man without a wife, without a friend, without servants, left wholly unprotected as it seemed to him by Heaven—above all, left without honor; for in the loss of Camila he saw his own ruination.

Finally, after a considerable length of time, he resolved to go to the village where his friend lived and where he himself had been while this great misfortune was in the making. Locking the doors of his house, he mounted his horse and with fainting heart took to the road. He had gone barely halfway when, harassed by his thoughts, he found it necessary to dismount and tie his steed to a tree, at the foot of which he threw himself down with many piteous and mournful sighs, and there he remained until nightfall, when he saw a horseman coming along the road from the direction of the city. Having greeted the man, he inquired of him what the news in Florence was.

" 'Tis the strangest I have heard in many a day," the citizen replied; "for they are now saying openly that Lotario, that great friend of the rich Anselmo who lived at San Giovanni, last night carried off Camila, the wife of Anselmo, who likewise is missing. All this was learned from a maid of Camila's who was found by the watch last night as she was lowering herself by a sheet from a window of the house. The truth is, no one rightly knows just what did happen, but the whole city is astonished over it, since no one would ever have expected such a thing in view of the great and close friendship that existed between the men, a friendship so strong that the pair were commonly called 'the two friends.' "

"Is it by any chance known," asked Anselmo, "what road Lotario and Camila took?"

"There is not so much as a trace of them," said the citizen, "although the governor has instituted a most thorough search."

"God go with you, sir," said Anselmo.

"God be with you," responded the citizen as he rode away.

With such overwhelming news as this, Anselmo was not only near to losing his mind but to ending his life as well. He arose and mounted his horse as best he could and made his way to the house of his friend, who had not yet learned of his misfortune but who, when he saw him arriving in this state, looking so pale, haggard, and worn, realized at once that his guest must be laboring under some deep sorrow. Anselmo at once asked if he might go to bed and requested them to provide him with writing materials. They did so and then left him alone, for he would have it that way and even directed them to bar the door. When they were gone, he began once more to think about the misfortune that had befallen him, which weighed upon his mind to such an extent that he perceived clearly enough that his end was drawing near.[6] Desiring to leave some record as to the cause of his strange death, he thereupon started to write, but before he had finished setting down all that he wished to say, his breath failed him and he died a victim of the grief which his ill-advised curiosity had brought upon him.

When the master of the house saw that it was growing late and Anselmo had not yet called, he decided to enter the room and see if his guest's indisposition had grown worse. He found him there, lying on his face, half of his body in the bed and the other half upon the writing-table over which he had been leaning. The paper with the writing on it was spread out in front of him, and he still held the pen in his hand. His host first called to him, and when he did not answer, he took him by the hand and found that it was cold, and then he knew that his friend was dead. He was astounded and deeply dismayed by this and at once summoned the members of his household to come and witness Anselmo's sad end. Finally he read the paper, which he recognized as being in the dead man's handwriting. It contained the following words:

A foolish and ill-advised desire has robbed me of my life. If the news of my death should reach Camila's ears, let her know that I forgive her; for she was under no obligation to perform miracles and I had no right to ask them of her. Thus, I was the creator of my own dishonor, and there is no reason why

That was as far as Anselmo had gone with his last note; for it was plain that at this point, before he had finished what he had to say, death had overtaken him. His parents were notified the following day by the one in whose house he had breathed his last. They already knew of their son's misfortune, and they knew as well of the convent where Camila lay, almost on the verge of accompanying her husband on his inevitable last journey, owing not to grief over the news of his death but to sorrow over the word she had received of her lover's departure. And they say that, although she had been left a widow, she did not care to leave the monastery, nor, on the other hand, to adopt the calling of a nun—at least not until, some while afterward, news came that Lotario had been killed in a recent battle between Monsieur de Lautrec and the Great Captain, Gonzalo Hernández de Córdoba in the kingdom of Naples: [7] for it appears that her lover had tardily repented. Upon learning of this, Camila forthwith took the veil and died within a short while of sorrow and melancholy. And such was the end of all of them, the end that came of so foolish a beginning.

"I like this tale well enough," remarked the curate, "but I cannot persuade myself that it is true. If it is pure invention, then the author is to blame; for I cannot imagine a husband so foolish as to make such a costly experiment as Anselmo did. If it were the case of a gallant and his mistress, that might do, but as between a husband and wife it is lacking in plausibility. As to the method of telling the story, I have no fault to find with that."

CHAPTER XXXVI. *Which treats of other extraordinary events that occurred at the inn.*

JUST at that moment the landlord, who was standing in the gateway of the inn, cried out, "Here comes a fine lot of guests for you; if they stop here, we well may sing *Gaudeamus*."

"What kind of folk are they?" asked Cardenio.

"They are four men," replied the innkeeper, "riding high in the saddle and short in the stirrup,[1] with lances and bucklers and black masks, and with them is a woman clad in white; she is riding on a sidesaddle and her face, also, is veiled; and there are two servants on foot."

"Are they very near?" inquired the curate.

"So near," said the landlord, "that they are arriving now."

Upon hearing this, Dorotea covered her face and Cardenio went into the room where Don Quixote was, and they had barely had time to do this when all those persons whom the innkeeper had described came trooping into the hostelry. The four on horseback, who had the look and manner of the wellborn, at once dismounted and went over to assist the lady to alight. One of them then took her in his arms and seated her in the chair that stood beside the entrance to the room where Cardenio was hidden. During all this time neither she nor her companions had removed their masks nor had they uttered a single word. The only sound to be heard was the deep sigh that the lady gave as she let her arms drop to her side like one who was ill and faint. The two servants, meanwhile, had taken the horses out to the stable.

Having watched all this, the curate, being desirous of knowing who these people were who came in such a costume and preserved such a silence, went over to where the servants were and asked one of them for the information that he wished.

"Upon my word, sir, I can't tell you," the youth replied. "All I know is that they appear to be very important people, especially the one who, as you saw, just took the lady in his arms. My reason for saying this is that all the others show him respect and do only what he orders and commands."

"And the lady, who is she?"

"That also is something that I do not know; for all along the way I did not have a glimpse of her face. It is true, I heard her sigh many times, and once in a while she would moan as if she were about to give up the ghost. It is no wonder, however, if we do not know any more about them than what I have told you, for my companion and I have not been with them more than a couple of days. We met them on the highway and they begged and persuaded us to come with them as far as Andalusia, promising to pay us very well."

"And have you heard any of them called by name?" the curate persisted.

"No indeed," said the lad. "They all go along so silently that it is really amazing. You can hear nothing but the sighs and sobs of the poor lady, which make us sorry for her, and we feel quite certain that, wherever it is she is being taken, it is against her will. So far as can be gathered from the habit she wears, she is a nun or, what is more likely, is about to become one; and it may be that it is against her will that she is entering a convent, which is the reason why she seems so sad."

"That may all be true," said the curate; and, leaving the servants, he returned to where Dorotea was. She, having heard the veiled lady sigh, moved by a natural compassion now went up and spoke to her.

"What is it that is troubling you, my lady?" she said. "If it is anything that women by their knowledge and experience can remedy, I herewith gladly offer you my services."

The poor woman said nothing, and although the offer was repeated, more earnestly than ever, she still remained silent, until the masked gentleman whom the servant had said the rest of them obeyed came over and addressed Dorotea.

"Do not tire yourself, lady," he said, "by making any offers of assistance to this woman, for it is her custom to show no thanks for any favor that is done her; so do not seek to get an answer from her, unless you wish to hear some lie from her mouth."

"I have never told a lie," declared the one who up to that point had been silent. "Rather, it is because I have been so truthful and without any lying propensities that I am now placed in this unfortunate situation. I call upon you yourself to be my witness, for it is the simple truth I speak that has made you out a purveyor of falsehoods and a liar."

Cardenio heard these words as clearly and distinctly as if he had been standing beside the one who spoke them, for there was only the door of Don Quixote's room between them; and he at once gave a shout and cried, "My God! What is this I hear? What voice is this that reaches my ears?"

Very much startled, the lady turned her head, and, not seeing who it was that had uttered this cry, she arose and was about to enter the other room, but the gentleman stopped her, refusing to allow her to move a step. As a result of the stir and excitement the lady's veil now fell down, revealing a face of incomparable, truly marvelous beauty, though pale and frightened in appearance, with a pair of eyes that kept searching all around wherever their gaze could reach, with so much anxiety that it seemed as if their owner were out of her senses. Dorotea and all the others who beheld her were deeply moved by all this, though they did not understand the reason for it. The gentleman all the while was grasping her firmly by the shoulders and was so occupied in doing so that he was unable to lift a hand to prevent his own mask from falling off, as it did a moment later.

Dorotea, who was standing there with her arms about the lady, now looked up and saw that the gentleman was none other than her own husband, Don Fernando. No sooner was she aware of his identity than, giving vent to a prolonged and mournful cry that appeared to come from the very depths of her being, she fell back in a faint; and if the barber had not been there to catch her in his arms, she would have fallen to the floor.

The curate then came over to remove her veil and throw water on her face, and as soon as he saw her features Don Fernando recognized her even as he held the other woman in his arms, and at the sight of her his own face turned deathly pale. He could not, however, release his hold on Luscinda, who was struggling to free herself from his grasp, she and Cardenio having recognized each other by their voices. For Cardenio also had heard the cry that Dorotea gave as she fainted, and believing it to be his Luscinda, he had rushed out terror-stricken. The first thing he saw was Don Fernando with Luscinda in his arms, and Fernando now recognized him, while the three of them—Luscinda, Cardenio, and Dorotea—remained silent and bewildered, scarcely knowing what had happened. They all gazed at one another without saying a word: Dorotea at Don Fernando, Fernando at Cardenio, Cardenio at Luscinda, and Luscinda at Cardenio. Luscinda was the first to break the silence, by addressing Fernando in the following manner:

"Let me go, Señor Don Fernando, for the sake of what you owe to yourself, seeing that nothing else can prevail upon you to do so. Leave me here to cling to the wall of which I am the ivy, to the support from which neither your importunities nor your threats nor your promises nor your gifts can separate me. Take note how Heaven, by unaccustomed paths that are dark to us, has placed before me my true husband. You know well, by a thousand costly experiences, that only death would ever suffice to efface him from my memory. Let this plain declaration, then, lead you, since you can do nothing else, to turn your love into wrath, your affection into spite, that you may do away with my life which I will gladly render here in the presence of my husband; and perhaps, seeing me die in this manner, he will be satisfied that I have kept faith with him to the very end."

Dorotea, who had by now fully recovered from her fainting fit, had listened closely to all that Luscinda had to say, and the latter's words told her clearly who the speaker was. Perceiving that Don Fernando would not let his victim go nor give her any answer, she now summoned all the strength she could and, rising, went over and dropped to her knees at Fernando's feet.

"If, my lord," she began, "the rays of that sun in eclipse that you hold in your arms had not blinded your eyes, you would have seen that the unfortunate creature (so long as you will have it so) who now kneels at your feet is none other than the ill-starred Dorotea. I am that humble peasant girl whom you, out of graciousness or for your own pleasure, saw fit to lift to the height where she might call herself yours. I am she who, locked within the bounds of virtue, lived a happy life until, in response to your importunities and what appeared to be your proper and sincerely intended declarations of love, she opened the gates of her modesty and delivered to you the keys of her heart, a gift so ill appreciated that I now of necessity find myself in my present position and behold you under such circumstances as these.

"But, nevertheless, I would not have you think that it is my shame that has brought me here; it is only my feeling of sorrow at seeing myself forgotten by you. You insisted upon my being yours, and in such a way that, though you would have it otherwise now, you still cannot help being mine. Reflect on this, my lord: may not the incomparable affection that I bear you compensate for the beauty and nobility of birth for which you would leave me? You cannot belong to the lovely Luscinda for you belong to me, and she cannot be yours for she belongs to Cardenio. If you will think it over, you will see that it will be easier to bring yourself to love one who adores you than to force one to love you who now abhors you. You played upon my innocence and sought to undermine my virtue. You were not unaware of my station in life, and you well know how I gave myself to you wholly, so that you cannot say that you were deceived.

"If all this is so, and it is, and if you are a Christian as you are a gentleman, then why by all these subterfuges do you delay making me happy in the end as you did in the beginning? And if you would not have me for what I am, which is your true and lawful wife, at least show me enough affection to take me as your slave; for merely by being in your possession, I shall look upon myself as happy and fortunate. Do not, by leaving me unprotected, permit my shame to be the subject of gossip in the street. Do not inflict so wretched an old age upon my parents, for they do not deserve such treatment in view of the faithful services which they as vassals have always rendered to you and yours. And if you think your blood will be contaminated by mingling with mine, remember that there is little or no nobility in this world that has not traveled the same road, and that in the case of illustrious lineages it is not the woman's blood that counts. What is more, true nobility consists in virtue, and if you show a lack of this by denying me what is so justly my due, then I shall have shown myself in the end to be more noble than you.

"In short, my lord, when all is said, I would have you know that I am your wife, whether you like it or not. Your own words are my witnesses, which cannot be lying ones if you pride yourself on that nobility for the lack of which I am despicable in your sight. I have your signed pledge,[2] and Heaven also, which you called upon to witness the vows you made, will bear me out. Failing all this, your own conscience should raise its voice amid your merrymaking and remind you of this truth I have just spoken, thus disturbing your hours of greatest happiness and contentment."

These and other words were spoken by the woebegone Dorotea with such feeling and so many tears that even those who accompanied Don Fernando and all the others present wept with her. Fernando listened without making any reply until she had finished, whereupon she began sighing and sobbing so passionately that it would have been a heart of bronze that would not have melted at such a show of grief. Luscinda gazed at her with no less sympathy for her suffering than admiration for her wit and beauty, and she would have gone up to her and uttered a few words of consolation if Don Fernando's arms had not restrained her, for he still clasped her tightly. Greatly astonished and confused by it all, he stared fixedly at Dorotea for a good while and then, opening his arms, he let Luscinda go.

"You have conquered, O beauteous Dorotea," he said, "you have conquered. No one could have the heart to deny so many truths as you have uttered."

Luscinda, when Don Fernando released his hold of her, was so faint that she would have fallen; but, as it happened, Cardenio, in order to avoid being recognized, was standing behind his former friend, and now, casting aside all fear and risking everything, he came forward to support the one he loved.

"If merciful Heaven," he said, as he took her in his embrace, "is pleased to let you have a little rest at last, O my loyal, steadfast, and beautiful lady, I do not think you will find a safer haven than in these arms that now receive you as they did of old, when fortune willed that I might call you mine."

At these words, Luscinda gazed at Cardenio. She had begun to recognize him by the sound of his voice, and now, being assured by the sight of her eyes that it was indeed he, she forgot all about decorum and, flinging her arms around his neck, laid her cheek against his.

"Yes, my lord," she said, "you are the true master of this your captive one, even though an adverse fate should once more intervene and once again threaten this life which is sustained by yours."

It was a strange sight for Don Fernando and all the bystanders as they stood marveling at so extraordinary an occurrence. It seemed to Dorotea that Fernando changed color and made a gesture as if he meant to avenge himself upon Cardenio, for she saw him put a hand to his sword; and no sooner did this thought enter her mind than she threw her arms about his knees, kissing them and holding him fast so that he could not move as her tears all the while continued to flow.

"What is it that you think of doing in this unforeseen situation, O sole refuge that I have?" she cried. "Here at your feet is your own wife and she whom you would have for wife is in her husband's arms. Do you think that it would be well or even possible for you to undo that which Heaven has done or seek to take as your own one who, in spite of every obstacle, confirmed in her loyalty and stanchness of purpose, there before your eyes is now bathing with her loving tears the face and bosom of her cherished mate? In God's name and for your own sake I beg and entreat you not to let this open manifestation of their love increase your ire, but rather let it diminish your wrath so that these two lovers, quietly and in peace and without any interference on your part, may spend together the rest of the time that Heaven allots them. In this way you will be displaying the generosity that your noble and illustrious bosom harbors, and the world will see that reason with you is stronger than passion."

Cardenio had stood with his arm about Luscinda all the time that Dorotea was speaking. He did not take his eyes off Don Fernando, for he was resolved that, if his erstwhile friend made any move in his direction, he would actively defend himself to the best of his ability against any and all who might attack him, even though it cost him his life; but at that moment Don Fernando's companions and the curate, the barber, and all the others present, not forgetting the worthy Sancho Panza, came up and surrounded the irate lover, imploring him to have regard to Dorotea's tears, and if what she had said was true, and they believed that it undoubtedly was, not to permit her to be cheated of what she had every right to expect. Let him reflect that it was not by mere chance, as it might seem, but rather by a special providence of Heaven, that they had all been brought together in a place where they would never have thought they would meet. Let him remember also, the curate admonished him, that only death could part Luscinda and Cardenio, and that even though the edge of a sword were to come between them, they still would regard their end as a most happy one. In cases like this for which there was no remedy, it was the part of practical wisdom, by exerting an effort and overcoming one's inclinations, to show oneself generous-hearted; and so he ought of his own accord to permit this pair to enjoy the blessing which Heaven had conferred upon them.

Let him, moreover, but cast an eye on Dorotea's beauty and he would see that few if any could equal, much less excel, her. And in addition to her beauty, there was her meekness and the very great love she had for him. Above all, let him bear in mind that if he prided himself upon being a gentleman and a Christian, he could not do anything else but keep the promise he had made, and, keeping it, he would at the same time be fulfilling his duty to God and would win the approval of all right-minded folk, who would realize and admit that it is the prerogative of beauty, even though in humble guise, to be elevated to any height whatsoever when accompanied by modesty, and without any hint of detriment to the one who places it upon an equal footing with himself. What was more, no one was to be blamed for following the strong dictates of passion when there was no taint of sin involved.

The others then added their arguments, so many of them and such forceful ones that Don Fernando's manly heart could not hold out against them; for he, after all, was of noble blood. He thereupon relented and let himself be vanquished by the truth, which he could not deny however much he might have wished to do so; and as a sign that he had surrendered and yielded to their good advice, he now stooped and embraced Dorotea.

"Rise, my lady," he said to her, "for it is not fitting that she whom I hold in my heart should be kneeling at my feet. If up to now I have given no evidence of the truth of what I am saying, it may be that Heaven has ordered it so in order that, beholding the steadfast love that you have for me, I may be able to cherish you as you deserve. All that I ask is that you do not reprehend me for the ill I have done you and for my very great neglect, since the same cause and force that moved me to accept you as mine likewise impelled me to struggle against being yours. If you would perceive the truth of this, turn your eyes and see how happy Luscinda is, and in those eyes you will find an excuse for all my erring ways. And since she has found and attained that which she desired, and

I have found in you all that I need, may she spend many tranquil and happy years with her Cardenio, and I pray that Heaven grant the same boon to Dorotea and me."

Saying this, he turned and embraced her, laying his face against hers with so tender a display of feeling that it was all he could do to keep from weeping as the indubitable sign of his love and repentance. The rest of them, however, were not so successful in this regard, and Luscinda, Cardenio, and nearly all those present began shedding so many tears, by reason of their own happiness or that of others, that it was as if some grave misfortune had befallen them. Even Sancho Panza wept, although, as he said afterward, it was only at finding that Dorotea was not as he had thought Queen Micomicona, of whom he expected so many favors. It took them all some time to recover from their emotion and astonishment, and then Cardenio and Luscinda fell on their knees before Don Fernando, thanking him so courteously for the favor he had bestowed upon them that he did not know what to say in reply but raised them up and embraced them most graciously and affectionately.

He then inquired of Dorotea how she came to be in this place so far from her home, and she very briefly and clearly related all that she had previously told Cardenio, at which Don Fernando and his companions were so pleased that they wished the tale had been longer, such was her skill as a storyteller. When she had finished, Fernando informed them of what had happened to him in the city, after he had found in Luscinda's bodice the note in which she declared that she was Cardenio's bride and could not be his. He stated that he would have liked to kill her, and would have done so if her parents had not prevented him. He then had left the house in an angry and disgruntled mood, being determined to avenge himself as soon as he had a better opportunity. The next day he heard that Luscinda had disappeared from her parents' home and that no one knew where she had gone. After some months he had learned that she was in a convent, having expressed a desire to spend the rest of her days there if she could not be with Cardenio.

Upon receiving this news, he had chosen three gentlemen companions and had gone to the place where she was but had not spoken with her since he feared that, if they knew he was there, a closer watch would be kept in the convent. He accordingly had waited for a day when the porter's lodge was open, and then, leaving two of them to guard the gate, he and the other one had gone in to look for Luscinda, whom they found in a cloister, in conversation with a nun. Carrying her off without ceremony, they had taken her to another place where they could provide themselves with the things they needed for carrying out their plan. All of which they had been able to do in safety, owing to the fact that the convent was in the open country, at some little distance from the town.

He added that as soon as Luscinda saw that she was in their power, she had fainted away, and that all she had done after recovering from her swoon was to weep and sigh without uttering a single word. And thus, with silence and her tears for company, they had reached this inn, which for him was like attaining Heaven itself, where all the misadventures of earth are at an end.

CHAPTER XXXVII. *Wherein is continued the story of the famous Princess Micomicona, along with other droll adventures.*

IT WAS with no little sorrow in his heart that Sancho listened to all this, for he could see his hopes of a title going up in smoke and disappearing as the lovely Princess Micomicona turned into Dorotea, and the giant into Don Fernando, while his master was sleeping peacefully, wholly unconcerned with what was happening. As for Dorotea, she could not be sure that the happiness she possessed was not a dream, and Cardenio and Luscinda felt the same way. Don Fernando, meanwhile, was giving thanks to Heaven for having taken him out of that intricate labyrinth in which he had been wandering at the imminent risk of losing at once his good name and his soul. In short, all those in the inn were quite pleased and satisfied with the fortunate outcome of so complicated and desperate an affair.

It was the curate who, as a man of wisdom, made it all clear to them, congratulating each in turn on the good fortune he had achieved. But the one who was the happiest and most jubilant of all was the landlady by reason of the promise that Cardenio and the curate had made her to the effect that they would pay with interest for all the damage wrought by Don Quixote. Sancho alone, as has been said, was wretched, sad, and dejected, and it was with a melancholy air that he went in to speak to his master, who had just awakened.

"Sir Mournful Countenance," he said, "your Grace may as well go on sleeping. In fact, you may sleep as much as you like, without troubling to kill any giant or restore the princess to her kingdom, for it is all done and settled now."

"That I can well believe," replied Don Quixote, "for I have just had the most monstrous and terrible battle with that giant that ever I hope to have in all the days of my life; and with one back-thrust—whack!—I laid his head on the ground, and the blood ran in rivulets, like water, all over the earth."

"Like red wine, your Grace might better say," Sancho corrected him; "for I would have your Grace know, if you do not know it already, that the dead giant is a punctured wineskin and the blood was six arrobas ¹ of *vino tinto* that it held in its belly, and the head you chopped off is the whore who mothered me, and may the devil take it all!"

"What is this you are saying, you lunatic?" cried Don Quixote. "Are you in your right senses?"

"If your Grace will rise," said Sancho, "you will see the fine mess you have made and what we are going to have to pay for it all. And you will also see your queen converted into a lady in private life, by the name of Dorotea, along with other things that will astonish you if you can get them through your head."

"I should not wonder at anything of the sort," said Don Quixote, "for, if you remember, the last time we were here I told you that everything that happened in this place was the work of an enchanter, and so it would not be surprising if this were also."

"I could believe all that," said Sancho, "if my blanketing had been like that, but it wasn't; it was real and true. I saw the landlord, who is here right now, holding one end of the blanket and tossing me up to the sky as lustily and heartily as you please and laughing fit to burst all the while. When it comes to recognizing persons, so far as I'm concerned, and I'm only a poor sinner, there's no enchantment about it but only a lot of bruises and bad luck."

"Well, then," said Don Quixote, "God will set everything to rights. Come help me dress so that I can go out, for I wish to see what has happened and view these transformations that you are talking about."

Sancho helped him on with his clothes; and, in the meantime, the curate was telling Don Fernando and the others of the knight's strange madness and the stratagem they had employed to get him off Poor Rock, where he imagined that he was doing penance for his lady's sake. He repeated at the same time nearly all the adventures that Sancho had related, at which they were considerably astonished and laughed a good deal; for this seemed to them to be, as it did to all who heard of it, the weirdest sort of insanity that could ever lay hold of a disordered intellect. The curate added that, inasmuch as Dorotea's good fortune prevented their going on with their plan, they would have to find and invent another one in order to get him back to his native heath. Cardenio then offered to continue what they had begun, saying that Luscinda would be able to take Dorotea's part very well.

"No," said Don Fernando, "that will not be necessary, for I wish Dorotea to continue with it. The village where this good gentleman lives is not far from here, and I shall be happy to see something done for his malady."

"It is more than two days' journey," said the curate.[2]

"Even if it were more, I should be glad to make it in so worthy a cause."

At that moment Don Quixote came out in full panoply, with Mambrino's helmet, still dented, on his head and his buckler on his arm, and with his tree bough or lance serving him as a staff. Don Fernando and the others were amazed by his strange appearance: his lean and jaundiced-looking face, half a league long; his fantastic assortment of arms; his dignified bearing; and they all remained silent to see what he would have to say as he, very calmly and gravely, turned to the comely Dorotea.

"I am informed by my squire, lovely lady," he said, "that your Highness's very being has been undone and annihilated, and that from the queen and great dame that you used to be you have been transformed into an ordinary damsel. If this has been done on the order of that royal necromancer, your father, because he feared I would not give you the aid you need and which I owe you, I will say that he did not and does not know half the mass [3] and was little versed in the annals of chivalry; for if he had read and meditated upon them attentively, and for as long a time as I have, he would have found that other knights less famous than I were constantly achieving more difficult undertakings. After all, it is no great thing to slay a little giant, however insolent he may be. As a matter of fact, it is not many hours since I was in his presence and— I shall say no more, lest you think I am lying. But time, which brings all things to light, will tell the tale when least we think to hear it."

"That was a couple of wineskins you were fighting, not a giant," said the innkeeper at this point; but Don Fernando ordered him to be still and not interrupt Don Quixote in any way.

The knight then continued, "I was about to say, in short, highborn and disinherited lady, that if it was for the reason I have mentioned that your father worked this metamorphosis in your person, do not be misled by it; for there is no peril on this earth where my sword will not open a path; and with that sword I will shortly bring your enemy's head to earth and place upon yours the crown of your realm."

Pausing here, Don Quixote waited for the princess to answer him, and she, knowing Don Fernando's determination to go through with the deception until they had the knight back in his village, now replied with much gravity and ease of manner, "Whoever it was that told you, valiant Knight of the Mournful Countenance, that my being had been changed and transformed, was not speaking the truth. It is true that certain fortunate circumstances that have given me more than I could have wished for have worked a change of a sort in me; but I have not for that reason ceased to be the person that I was before, and I still have the same intention that I always did of availing myself of the might of your valiant and invulnerable arm.[4] And so, my dear sir, I beg you to be so good as to honor once more the father who begot me, and I trust that you will look upon him as a wise and foreseeing man, since with his science he found so ready and reliable a means of aiding me in my trouble. For I am convinced that if it had not been for you, sir, I should never have had the good fortune that is now mine, and in this I speak the veriest truth, as most of these worthy folk who are present can testify. It only remains for us to set out tomorrow morning, since we could not travel far today. As for the rest, I trust in God and in your own valiant heart for a happy outcome."

Thus spoke the clever Dorotea. Upon hearing her words, Don Quixote was very angry and, turning to his squire, he said, "I tell you right now, my little Sancho, that you are the greatest little rascal in all Spain. Vagabond thief, did you not inform me a moment ago that this princess had been turned into a damsel by the name of Dorotea, and that the giant's head which I am sure I cut off was that of the whoring mother that bore you, along with other nonsense that threw me into the greatest confusion I have ever known in all the days of my life? I swear"—and here he gazed heavenward and ground his teeth—"I have a mind to do something to you that will put salt in the pate of all the lying squires of knights-errant that there are in this world, from this time forth!"

"Calm yourself, my master," said Sancho. "It may be that I was deceived in what I took to be the transformation of my lady, the Princess Micomicona; but as to the giant's head, or, at any rate, the puncturing of the skins and the fact that the blood was red wine, I was not wrong in that, by the living God! For the wounded skins are still there at the head of your Grace's bed, and the red wine has made a lake of the room. If you don't believe it, you will see when you go to fry the eggs.[5] By that I mean, when the landlord presents your Grace with the score for all the damage you did. Otherwise, if my lady the queen is as she always was, I rejoice in my heart, for it concerns me as much as any neighbor's son."

"Once again, Sancho," said Don Quixote, "I tell you that you are a fool, and, begging your pardon, that will do."

"That will do," said Don Fernando, "and let us hear no more of it. And since my lady the princess has said that we travel tomorrow, seeing that today is far gone, so be it. The evening we may spend in pleasant conversation as we wait for tomorrow to come, when we will all accompany Señor Don Quixote, as we desire to be witnesses of the valorous and unheard-of exploits that he is to perform in the course of this great enterprise that he has undertaken."

"It is I who will serve and accompany you," replied Don Quixote. "I thank your Grace very much for the good opinion that you hold of me, and I shall endeavor to live up to it or it shall cost me my life—or even more than my life, if such a thing be possible."

Many courteous words and compliments were exchanged between the two of them; but they all fell silent as a traveler entered the inn, one who from his attire appeared to be a Christian recently returned from the land of the Moors. He had on a short-skirted coat made out of blue cloth, with half-sleeves and without a collar. His breeches were of the same shade and material, and he had a blue cap on his head. On his feet were date-colored buskins, and slung across his breast from a shoulder strap was a Moorish cutlass. Behind him, mounted upon an ass, came a woman dressed after the manner of the Moors. Her face was covered and she wore a little brocaded cap on her head and a mantle that fell from her shoulders to her feet. The man, who was a little more than forty years of age, had a robust and graceful figure, a somewhat swarthy complexion, long mustaches, and a well-tended beard. In short, if he had been well clad, one would have said from his appearance that he was a person of birth and breeding.

Upon entering the inn, he asked for a room and, when told that there was none to be had, seemed to be very much put out. Going up to the Moorish-looking woman, he took her in his arms and assisted her to dismount, as Luscinda, Dorotea, the landlady, her daughter, and Maritornes all gathered around, attracted by the novelty of her costume, which was of a kind they had never seen before. Being always gracious, courteous, and discerning, Dorotea perceived that the woman as well as the man was vexed at not being able to obtain a lodging, and she accordingly sought to console her.

"Do not be too much disturbed, my lady," she said, "by the lack of accommodations that you find here, for that is the usual thing in roadside taverns; but if you would like to share our lodgings"—and she nodded at Luscinda—"you will perhaps say that in the course of your journey you have found others that were not so good."

The veiled lady made no reply to this but merely rose from where she was sitting and, crossing her hands upon her bosom, bowed her head and bent her body from the waist down by way of thanks. From her silence, they decided that she must undoubtedly be a Moor and unable to speak a Christian tongue.

At that moment, the captive,[6] who had been busied with other matters, returned; and, seeing all the womenfolk gathered about his companion while she made no reply, he said, "Ladies, this damsel understands very little of my language, nor does she know how to speak any tongue other than that of her native land, and it is for this reason that she does not and cannot answer your questions."

"We have not asked her anything," said Luscinda. "We have merely offered to share with her our company and our lodgings, where we will provide her with all the comforts that we can; for we are under obligations to be of service to all strangers in need, especially when they happen to be women."

"On her behalf and on mine, my lady," the captive replied, "I kiss your hand and esteem very highly, as I ought, this proffered favor, which, coming from persons such as your appearance shows you to be and under such circumstances, is indeed a great one."

"Tell me, sir," said Dorotea, "is this lady a Christian or a Moor? For her costume and her silence lead us to believe that she is what we would rather she was not."

"A Moor she is in costume and in body, but in her soul she is thoroughly Christian, for she has a very great desire to be one."

"Then she has not been baptized?" inquired Luscinda.

"There has been no opportunity for that," replied the captive. "Since leaving Algiers, which is her fatherland, there has been up to now no near peril of death such as would render it obligatory to baptize her at once, before she had first learned all the ceremonies that our Holy Mother Church enjoins. But God willing, the rite will soon be administered to her with the solemnity that befits the quality of her person, which is more than her garb or my own would indicate."

Upon hearing this, they were all eager to learn who the captive and the Moorish damsel were, but no one cared to ask just then, as it seemed that at that moment they ought rather to be seeking to make them comfortable than to be questioning them about their past lives. Dorotea took the girl by the hand and led her over to a seat beside her, requesting that she remove her veil. The damsel looked at the captive as though inquiring what they were saying and what she should do, and he thereupon explained to her in Arabic that they wished her to uncover her countenance. This she now did, revealing a face of such rare loveliness that Dorotea and Luscinda each thought her more beautiful than the other, while all the bystanders agreed that if there was anyone who could equal those two, it was the Moorish lady, and there were some, even, who maintained that she held a slight advantage. And inasmuch as it is beauty's gracious prerogative to win the heart and arouse good will, the entire company from then on manifested a desire to serve the lovely Moor and do her favors.

When Don Fernando asked what her name was, the captive replied that it was Lela Zoraida; and as soon as she heard this, having divined what the Christian had asked, she spoke up hastily, with much vexation and spirit.

"No, not Zoraida," she cried, "Maria, Maria!" thus giving them to understand that her name was Maria and not Zoraida.

These words and the deep earnestness with which the Moorish damsel had uttered them caused more than one tear to be shed by some of the listeners, especially the women, since women by nature are tender-hearted and sympathetic. Luscinda embraced her most affectionately.

"Yes, yes," she said, "Maria, Maria!" To which the damsel replied, "Yes, yes, Maria; Zoraida *macange*" [7]—by which expression she meant to say *no*.

Night was now coming on, and by order of Don Fernando's companions the landlord had set about preparing with all care and diligence the best supper that he could give them. When the time came, they all sat down at a long table of the kind to be found in servants' quarters, for there was neither a round table nor a square one to be found in the hostelry. They gave Don Quixote the place of honor at the head of the table, though he was for refusing it at first; and he insisted that the Princess Micomicona take the place by his side, as he was her protector.

Luscinda and Zoraida then seated themselves, and opposite them were Don Fernando and Cardenio. Then came the captive and the other gentlemen, while the curate and the barber had places alongside the ladies. And thus they supped in great good humor, which was increased when they saw the knight stop eating and begin to speak; for he was now moved by an impulse similiar to that which had led him to hold forth at such length when he was having supper with the goatherds.

"Truly, ladies and gentlemen," he began, "when you stop to think of it, those who follow the calling of knight-errantry behold some marvelous and unheard-of things. By way of example, let me ask you: what living being is there in all the world who, coming through the gateway of the castle at this moment and seeing us as we are, would take or believe us to be what we are? Who would say that this lady at my side is the great queen who is known to all of us, or that I am the famous Knight of the Mournful Countenance? No, there is no doubt that this profession and employment excels all others that men have invented, and it is all the more to be esteemed by reason of the greater perils to which it is subject.

"Away with those who would tell you that letters have the advantage over arms. I will tell them, whoever they may be, they know not of what they speak. For the reason that such persons commonly give, the one upon which they base their arguments, is that the labors of the mind exceed those of the body and the profession of arms is a physical one exclusively, a common laborer's trade as it were, for which nothing more than a sturdy frame is needed. What they fail to take into consideration is the fact that in the profession that is known to us who follow it as that of arms, there are included many acts of fortitude that require for their execution a high degree of intelligence. Does not a warrior who is charged with leading an army or defending a besieged city work with his mind as well as his body? How otherwise, by physical strength alone, would he be able to divine the intentions of the enemy, his plans and stratagems and the obstacles to be overcome, since all these things call for mental activity in which the body plays no part?

"It being true, then, that the profession of arms as well as that of letters has need of mind, let us see whose mind does the greater amount of work, that of the warrior or that of the man of letters.[8] This may be seen from the end and goal that each has in view; for that intention is to be most esteemed that has for its end the noblest object. The end and goal of letters is—I am not here speaking of divine learning whose purpose is to lead souls heavenward, since with an end so endless as that no other can be compared—what I have in mind, rather, is human knowledge,

whose object is to administer distributive justice and give to each that
which is his and see that good laws are observed—such an end and goal
is assuredly a generous and a lofty one and deserving of high praise, but
not such praise as should be bestowed upon the warrior's purpose, for
here the objective is peace, which is the greatest blessing that men can
wish for in this life.

"For the first good news that mankind and the world received was that
which the angels brought on the night that was our day: 'Glory to God
in the highest, and on earth peace, good will toward men.' [9] And the
salutation which the great Master of Heaven and earth taught his chosen
disciples to use when they entered any dwelling was, 'Peace be to this
house.' [10] And another time he said to them, 'Peace I leave with you, my
peace I give unto you, peace be with you.' [11] It was as a jewel and a
precious gift given and left by such a hand, a jewel without which there
can be no blessing whatsoever either in Heaven or on the earth. This
peace is the true end of war, and for 'war' you may substitute 'arms.' Accepting, then, this truth that the end of war is peace, let us turn now to
the physical hardships of the scholar and those of the man of arms and see
which are the greater."

This speech of Don Quixote's was delivered in such a manner and
couched in such excellent terms that it was quite impossible for the moment for any of those who heard him to take him for a madman. Indeed,
most of them being gentlemen to whom arms were a natural appurte-
nance, they listened to him with right good will as he continued speaking.

"I will begin by saying that the student's chief hardship is poverty—
not that they are all poor, but by way of putting the case in the strongest
possible terms—and when the word poverty has been uttered, it seems
to me there is nothing more to be said of their misfortune. For he who
is poor has nothing that is good. He must suffer his destitution under
various forms: hunger, cold, nakedness, and all of them combined. But,
still, his poverty is not so great that he does not eat some time, even
though it be a little later than usual and even though he must feed on
the leftovers of the rich. His greatest wretchedness lies in what they call
'going for soup,' [12] but still he will not fail to find some other's brazier or
hearth which, if it does not warm him, at least will temper the cold. And,
finally, of a night, they sleep beneath a roof. I shall not go into any further details, such as their lack of shirts and not too many shoes, their
thin and threadbare garments, or the pleasure with which they gorge
themselves when luck affords them a banquet of some sort.

"By this path, then, which I have described, a rough and difficult one, stumbling here, falling there, raising themselves up and falling once more, they finally obtain their degree. And then, after all this, how many of them have we seen who, having passed through these Syrtes,[13] between these Scyllas and Charybdises, as if borne on the favoring wings of fortune—how many of them, I say, have we seen later ruling and governing the world from a chair, their hunger turned into satiety, their cold into comfort, their nakedness into courtly attire, their sleep on a mat into repose on damask and fine linen, all of which is the justly merited reward of their virtue. But contrasted and compared with the hardships of the warrior, theirs fall far short of those that he endures, as I shall now show."

CHAPTER **XXXVIII**. *Which treats of the curious discourse that Don Quixote delivered on the subject of arms and letters.*[1]

CONTINUING his discourse, Don Quixote spoke as follows:

"Since in the case of the student we began with poverty and the things that go with it, let us see if the soldier is any better off in this regard. We shall find that he is the poorest of the poor, being dependent upon his wretched pay, which comes late or never, or upon such booty as he can amass with his own hands, to the grave peril of his life and conscience. At times his nakedness is such that a slashed doublet serves him at once as shirt and uniform; and in midwinter, in the open country, it is his habit to protect himself against the inclemencies of the heavens with nothing more than the breath from his mouth, which, inasmuch as it emerges from an empty place, must obviously, contrary to all the laws of nature, come out cold. True, he looks forward to the coming of night that he may find a respite from all these discomforts in the bed that awaits him, which, unless it is through some fault of his own, will never offend by being too narrow; for he may measure out upon the earth as many feet as he likes for his couch and then may toss and turn in it to his heart's content, without fear of the sheets slipping off.

"Comes then the day and hour when he is to take his professional degree; comes then the day of battle; and then it is they place upon his head a doctor's cap made of lint, by way of healing the wound inflicted by some bullet that may have passed through his temple or left him mutilated in an arm or a leg. And if this does not happen and a merciful Heaven keeps and preserves him safe and sound, he still may be as poor as he was before and must go through more engagements and more battles and come out victorious from them all before he has some chance of improving his fortunes. Miracles of that sort, however, are very seldom seen.

"But tell me, gentlemen, if you have ever given it a thought, by how far do those who have prospered in war fall short of those who have perished in it? You undoubtedly will reply that there is no comparison, that the dead are innumerable while those who have lived and thrived can be represented by some number less than a thousand. All of which is just the opposite of what happens with scholars, for, by means of skirts, to say nothing of sleeves, the latter all find a way of supporting themselves.[2] Thus it is evident that, although the soldier's work is far harder, his reward is far less. To this the answer may be made that it is easier to reward two thousand scholars than thirty thousand soldiers, for upon the former may be bestowed such posts as must of necessity be allotted to men of their calling, whereas if the latter are to be given any compensation at all, it can only be out of the property of the master they serve. But this objection merely strengthens my argument.

"However, let us leave all this to one side, for it is a labyrinth from which it is difficult to find one's way out, and, instead, let us turn to the question of the pre-eminence of arms over letters, one that up to now has not been settled, so many are the arguments put forth by either side. In addition to those that I have mentioned, letters say that without their help arms cannot support themselves, for war also has its laws to which it is subject and which fall within the domain of scholars. To this arms will reply that without them laws cannot be maintained, since it is by force of arms that states are defended, kingdoms preserved, cities guarded, highways rendered safe, and the seas rid of corsairs; and, finally, if it were not for them, states, kingdoms, monarchies, cities, highroads by sea and land would be subjected to the oppression and confusion that war brings with it, so long as it lasts and is free to make use of its privileges and powers. And it is a well-known fact that what costs most is and ought to be most highly valued.

"For anyone to attain eminence in letters costs time, loss of sleep, hunger, nakedness, headaches, indigestion, and other things that go with them, some of which I have already mentioned. But to become a good soldier costs all that the student has to pay and in so much higher a degree that there is no comparison, for such a one at every step runs the risk of losing his life. And what fear of want and poverty that can affect and harass the student is comparable to that fear which the soldier knows as he stands guard in some ravelin or bastion, knowing that the enemy is running a mine toward the place where he stands, and unable under any circumstances whatsoever to leave his post and flee the danger that so imminently threatens him? All that he can do is to notify his captain of what is happening in order that a countermine may be laid; and, meanwhile, he must remain there, fearing and expecting that he will suddenly fly up to the clouds without wings or descend into the lower depths against his will.

"And if this appears to be a small risk to run, let us see if it is equaled or exceeded when two galleys clash and lock prows in the middle of the ocean, leaving the soldier no more standing room than a couple of feet on the plank of the spur-beam. In such a case, he sees in front of him as many ministers of death as there are enemy cannon pointed at him, at no greater distance from his body than the length of a lance, and he further perceives that at the first false step he will go down to visit the depths of Neptune's bosom; yet, nevertheless, with intrepid heart, sustained by the sense of honor that incites him, he will make himself a target for the musketry and will endeavor to cross that narrow passageway to the enemy's ship. And the most marvelous thing of all is that one has no sooner fallen, never to rise again until the end of the world, than another steps forward to take his place, and if he too falls into the sea that hostilely awaits him, another and yet another will follow without any pause between their deaths, the whole constituting the greatest exhibition of valor and daring that is to be found in all the hazardous annals of warfare.

"Happy were the blessed ages that were free of those devilish instruments of artillery, whose inventor, I feel certain, is now in Hell paying the penalty for his diabolic device—a device by means of which an infamous and cowardly arm may take the life of a valiant knight, without his knowing how or from where the blow fell, when amid that courage and fire that is kindled in the breasts of the brave suddenly there comes a random bullet, fired it may be by someone who fled in terror at the flash of his own accursed machine and who thus in an instant cuts off and brings to an end the projects and the life of one who deserved to live for ages to come.

"And so, from this point of view, I could almost say that it grieves my soul that I should have taken up the profession of knight-errant in an age so detestable as this one in which we now live.[3] For, although no danger strikes terror in my bosom, I do fear that powder and lead may deprive me of the opportunity to make myself famous and renowned, by the might of my arm and the edge of my sword, throughout the whole of the known world. But Heaven's will be done. If I succeed in carrying out my design, I shall be all the more honored for it, inasmuch as I shall have confronted greater perils than the knights-errant of old ever did."

All this long discourse was delivered by Don Quixote as the others were having their supper; and he was so occupied with talking that he forgot to raise a single bite of food to his mouth, although Sancho reminded him a number of times that it would be better to eat now and say what he had to say afterward. Those who heard him were moved to fresh pity at seeing a man, who to all appearances was perfectly sensible and able to discuss any other topic quite rationally, so hopelessly lost whenever the subject of chivalry came up, for that was his dark, pitch-black obsession. The curate assured him there was much reason in what he had said on the warrior's behalf, and that, although he himself was a man of letters and a university graduate, he was of the same opinion.

When supper was over, they took the tablecloth away, and while the landlady, her daughter, and Maritornes were busy preparing Don Quixote's garret so that the ladies, as had been decided, might have it to themselves for the night, Don Fernando asked the captive to tell them the story of his life, which must be a tale quite out of the ordinary and one well-worth hearing, if they were to judge from the hints he had dropped when he arrived with Zoraida. The captive replied that he would be glad to do as requested, adding that he was afraid his story would not give them the pleasure they hoped for, but in order to comply with their wishes he would tell it anyway. The curate and all the others thanked him for this, and they too begged him to begin. In response to their insistence, he remarked that so much urging was unnecessary where a mere command would suffice.

"And so, then, your Worships, pay attention and you shall hear a true tale which possibly cannot be matched by those fictitious ones that are composed with such cunning craftsmanship."

As he said this, they all settled themselves in their places and a deep silence fell; and, seeing that they were quietly waiting to hear what he had to say, he began speaking in a calm and pleasant voice.

CHAPTER XXXIX. *In which the captive narrates the events of his life.*

"IT WAS in a village in the mountains of León that the line of which I come had its beginnings, a family more favored by nature than by fortune, although amid the poverty that prevailed in that region my father had the reputation of being a rich man and indeed might have been one, had he displayed the same skill in conserving his property that he did in squandering it. His inclination to liberal spending came from his having been a soldier in his youth, for that is a school in which the miser becomes generous and the generous becomes prodigal; if there are some soldiers that are parsimonious, they may be said to be freaks such as are rarely to be met with.

"My father went beyond the bounds of liberality and came close to prodigality, which is not a profitable thing for a married man with children to bring up who are to succeed him and carry on his name. He had three of them, all of them males and of an age to decide upon their calling in life. Accordingly, when he saw that, as he put it, there was no use in his trying to overcome his natural propensity, he made up his mind to rid himself of the instrument and cause of his lavish spending; in other words, he would get rid of his property, for without his fortune Alexander himself would have appeared in straitened circumstances. And so, calling the three of us together one day and closeting himself alone with us, he proceeded to address us somewhat in the following manner: [1]

" 'My sons, there is no need of my telling you that I have your welfare at heart; it is enough to know and state that you are my sons. On the other hand, the fact that I am unable to control myself when it comes to preserving your estate may well give you a contrary impression. For this reason, in order that you may be assured from now on that I love you

as a father should and have no desire to ruin you as a stepfather might,
I have decided to do for you something that I have long had in mind and
to which I have given the most mature consideration. You are of an age
to enter upon your professions in life, or at least to choose the ones which,
when you are older, will bring you profit and honor.

" 'What I have thought of doing is to divide my estate into four parts,
three of which I will turn over to you so that each has that which is his by
right, while the fourth part I will retain for my own livelihood and support for the rest of the time that Heaven shall be pleased to grant me.
But after each of you has had his due share of the property, I would have
you follow one of the courses that I shall indicate. We have here in Spain
a proverb which to my mind is a very true one, as indeed they all are,
being wise maxims drawn from long experience. This one runs, "The
Church, the sea, or the Royal Household," [2] which in plainer language is
equivalent to saying, "He who would make the most of himself and
become a rich man, let him become a churchman, or go to sea and be a
merchant, or enter the service of kings in their palaces." For there is another saying, "Better a king's crumb than a lord's favor." '

" 'I tell you this because it is my wish that one of you follow the profession of letters, that another go into trade, and that the third serve his king
as a soldier, seeing that it is a difficult thing to obtain service in his household; for if the military life does not bring much wealth, it does confer
fame and high esteem. Within a week, I will give you your shares in
money, without defrauding you of a single penny, as you shall see in due
course. Tell me, then, if you feel inclined to follow my advice and precepts in relation to what I have suggested.'

"He then called upon me as the eldest to answer; and after having told
him that he ought not to rid himself of his property in that manner but
should spend as much of it as he wished, since we were young and able
to make our own way, I ended by assuring him that I would do as he
desired, my own choice being to follow the profession of arms and thus
serve God and my king. My second brother, having made a similar
declaration, announced his intention of going to the Indies and investing
his share in commerce. The youngest one, and in my opinion the wisest,
said that he preferred to enter the Church or to go to Salamanca to complete the course of study that he had already begun.

"When we had made our choice of callings, my father embraced us
all, and within the brief space of time mentioned he carried out his
promise by giving each of us his share, which as I remember amounted to
three thousand ducats in currency; for an uncle of ours had purchased

the estate and paid for it in cash in order to keep it in the family. On that same day the three of us took leave of our goodhearted father; but inasmuch as it seemed to me an inhuman thing for him to be left with so little money in his old age, I prevailed upon him to take two of my three thousand ducats, since the remainder would be sufficient to meet my wants as a soldier. Moved by my example, my two brothers each gave him a thousand, so that he had in all four thousand, plus the three thousand which, as it appeared, his share of the estate was worth; for he did not care to dispose of his portion but preferred to keep it in land.

"And so, then, as I was saying, we took our leave of him and of our uncle, not without much feeling and many tears on the part of all. They charged us to let them know, whenever it was possible for us to do so, as to how we were faring and whether we were meeting with prosperity or adversity, and we promised them that we would. When he had embraced us and given us his benediction, we all departed, one setting out for Salamanca, another for Seville, while I made for Alicante, where I had heard there was a Genoese craft taking on a cargo of wool for that city.

"It is now twenty-two years since I left my father's house, and although in the course of that time I have written a number of letters, I have had no word either of him or of my brothers. As to my own experiences during those years, I shall relate them for you briefly. Embarking at Alicante, I had a fair voyage to Genoa, and from there I went on to Milan, where I fitted myself out with arms and a few accessories. For it was my intention to take service in the Piedmont, and I was already on my way to Alessandria della Paglia when I heard that the great Duke of Alva was starting for Flanders.[3] I then changed my plan and, joining his army, served with him in the three campaigns that he waged. I was present at the deaths of the Counts of Egmont and Hoorne and rose to the rank of ensign under a famous captain of Guadalajara, Diego de Urbina by name.[4] After I had been in Flanders for some while, news came of the league which his Holiness, Pope Pius V of blessed memory, had formed with Venice and Spain against the common enemy, the Turk, who about that time had taken, with his fleet, the famous island of Cyprus, which was then under the rule of the Venetians. This was a serious loss and one truly to be deplored.

"It was known for a fact that the commanding general of this league was to be his Most Serene Highness, John of Austria, brother of our good King Philip, and there was much talk of the great and warlike preparations that he was making. I was deeply stirred by all this and felt a desire to take part in the coming campaign; and although I had prospects and almost certain promises of being promoted to captain where I then served, on the first occasion that offered, I chose to leave all this and return to Italy. And as it happened, John of Austria had just arrived in Genoa on his way to Naples to join the Venetian fleet, as he afterward did at Messina.[5]

"In short, I may tell you that I was soon taking part in that most fortunate campaign,[6] having already been made a captain of infantry, an honor that I owed to my good fortune rather than to my merits. And on that day that was so happy a one for all Christendom, since it revealed to all the nations of the world the error under which they had been laboring in believing that the Turks were invincible at sea—on that day, I repeat, in which the haughty Ottoman pride was shattered, among all the happy ones that were there (and those Christians that died were even happier than those that remained alive and victorious), I alone was wretched; for in place of a naval crown such as I might have hoped for had it been in Roman times, I found myself on the night that followed that famous day with chains on my feet and manacles on my hands.

"The way in which it came about was this: El Uchali,[7] King of Algiers, a bold and successful corsair, had attacked and captured the flagship of Malta, on which only three knights were left alive and those three badly wounded; whereupon the ship of Giovanni Andrea,[8] on which I and my company were stationed, came to its assistance. Doing what was customary under the circumstances, I leaped aboard the enemy galley, which, by veering off from the attacking vessel, prevented my men from following me. Thus I was alone among the enemy, who so greatly outnumbered me that any hope of resistance was vain; and the short of it is, after I had been badly wounded, they captured me. As you know, gentlemen, El Uchali and all his fleet made their escape, so that I was left a prisoner in his hands; and that is the reason why it was that only I was miserable among so many who were happy, and a captive among so many who were free. For there were fifteen thousand Christians slaving at the oars in the Turkish fleet who that day obtained their liberty.

"They took me to Constantinople, where the Grand Turk Selim made my master commander at sea for having done his duty in battle so well and displayed his bravery by carrying off the standard of the Order of Malta. The following year, which was '72, I was in Navarino, rowing in the flagship with the three lanterns,[9] and there I saw and noted how the opportunity was lost for capturing the entire Turkish fleet in the harbor;

for all the sailors and Janizaries were convinced that they would be attacked while in port and had their clothing and their *passamaques,* or shoes, in readiness in order that they might be able to flee overland without waiting to give combat, so great was the fear that our fleet inspired in them. But Heaven ordained otherwise, not because of any fault or carelessness on the part of our commander, but as a punishment for the sins of Christendom, since it is God's will that we should have with us always the agents of his wrath.

"The upshot of it was, El Uchali withdrew to Modon, which is an island near Navarino, and there, disembarking his men, he proceeded to fortify the mouth of the harbor, after which he waited quietly until John retired. On this voyage one of the galleys, called the *Prize,* whose captain was a son of the famous corsair Barbarossa, was captured by the Neapolitan craft known as the *She-Wolf,* commanded by that thunderbolt of war, that father to his men, the fortunate and never-vanquished captain, Don Alvaro de Bazán, Marquis of Santa Cruz.

"I must not omit telling you what took place in connection with this capture. Barbarossa's son was so cruel and treated his captives so badly that the moment the rowers saw the *She-Wolf* bearing down and gaining upon them, they all at one and the same time dropped their oars and seized the captain, who was standing upon the gangway platform, urging them to row faster. Laying hold of him, they passed him on from bench to bench and from poop to prow, and so bit and chewed him that before he had gone much farther than the ship's mast his soul had already gone to Hell. Such, as I have said, was the cruelty with which he treated them and the hatred that they had for him.

"We then returned to Constantinople, and the next year, which was '73, we learned how John had captured Tunis, driven the Turks out of that kingdom, and placed Muley Hamet on the throne, thus cutting short the hopes that Muley Hamida, bravest and cruelest Moor in all the world, had of returning to rule there. The Great Turk felt this loss very keenly and, having resort to the cunning which all those of his line possess, he made peace with the Venetians, who desired it much more than he did; and the following year, in '74, he attacked the Goleta [10] and the Fort near Tunis which John had left in a state of semi-completion.

"During all this time I was at the oar, with no hope whatever of gaining my freedom. At least I had no hope of ransom, for I was determined not to write the news of my misfortune to my father. Both the Goleta and the Fort finally fell, for in front of them were massed seventy-five thousand Turkish regulars, while the number of Moors and Arabs from all over Africa was in excess of four hundred thousand; and this enormous force was equipped with so many munitions and engines of war and accompanied by so many sappers that the latter might readily have buried both their objectives under handfuls of earth.

"The Goleta, which had previously been looked upon as inexpugnable, was the first to succumb; and if it was lost, this was not the fault of its defenders, who did all that they should and could have done. It was rather due to the fact that, as experience showed, it was easy to throw up entrenchments in the desert sand; for water was commonly found there at a depth of two palms, but the Turks went down for a depth of two varas [11] without striking any, and as a result, piling their sandbags one on top of another, they were able to raise ramparts so high that they could command the walls of the fort and fire upon them as from a bastion, so that it was impossible to make a stand or put up a defense.

"It was the common opinion that our men did wrong in shutting themselves up in the Goleta instead of waiting for the enemy in the open, along the landing place; but those who say this speak from a distance and with little experience in such matters. If in the Goleta and the Fort there were barely seven thousand soldiers in all, how could so small a force, no matter how courageous, hope to sally forth onto the open plain and hold its own against so numerous an opposing one? And how could such a force fail to be lost unless reinforcements were sent to it, especially when surrounded by enemies that were not only so many in number and so determined, but that were fighting on their own soil?

"It seemed to many, and to me as well, that Heaven was doing Spain a special favor by mercifully permitting the destruction of that source and lair of so many woes, that glutton, sponge, and waster responsible for the profitless spending of an infinite amount of money which served no other cause than that of preserving the memory of its capture by the invincible Charles V—as if, to sustain that memory, which is and shall be eternal, those stones were necessary. The Fort likewise fell, but the Turks had to win it inch by inch, for the soldiers who defended it fought so stoutly and bravely that they slew more than twenty-five thousand of the enemy in the course of twenty-two general assaults. Of the three hundred of them that were taken prisoners, not one was without a wound, which is clear proof of their valor and determination and the ability with which they had defended and held their posts.

"A small fort or tower that stood in the middle of the lagoon also conditionally surrendered. It was under the command of a gentleman and famous soldier of Valencia, Don Juan Zanoguerra. Among those captured was Don Pedro Puertocarrero, commandant of the Goleta, who had done all that he could to defend his fort and felt the loss of it so keenly that he died of grief on the way to Constantinople, where his captors were taking him. Yet another was Gabriele Serbelloni, a Milanese gentleman, a great engineer and a very brave soldier.

"In the defense of these two strongholds there died many noteworthy persons, among whom was Pagano Doria, a knight of the Order of St. John, a man of generous disposition as was shown by the extreme liberality with which he treated his brother, the famous Giovanni Andrea Doria; and the saddest part of it all was that he died at the hands of some Arabs to whom, when he saw that the Fort was lost, he had entrusted himself when they offered to conduct him, disguised in Moorish costume, to Tabarca, a small coastal fort or station held by the Genoese, who there ply the trade of coral fishing. The Arabs cut off his head and took it to the commander of the Turkish fleet, who thereupon proved the truth of our Castilian proverb that asserts that 'although the treason may be acceptable, the traitor is abhorred'; for it is said that the general in question ordered those who had brought him this present to be hanged because they had not delivered their victim alive.

"Among the Christians in the Fort was one named Don Pedro de Aguilar, a native of some village in Andalusia, I cannot tell you which one; he had been an ensign and was looked upon as a most capable soldier, and in addition, he was a man of rare intellectual attainments, being especially gifted in what is known as poetry. I speak of him for the reason that fate brought him to my galley and my bench, since we were both slaves to the same master; and before we left port this gentleman composed two sonnets in the manner of epitaphs, one to the Goleta and the other to the Fort. As a matter of fact, I mean to recite them for you, for I know them by heart, and I do not think they will bore you, but quite the reverse."

When the captive mentioned Don Pedro de Aguilar's name, Don Fernando glanced at his companions and all three of them smiled; and when he came to read the sonnets, one of them interrupted him.

"Before your Grace goes any further," he said, "I beg you to tell me what became of that Pedro de Aguilar of whom you speak."

"All I know," replied the captive, "is that at the end of the two years he spent in Constantinople he disguised himself as an Albanian and made his escape in the company of a Greek spy. I cannot tell you if he succeeded in regaining his liberty or not, but it is my belief that he did, for a year later I saw the Greek in Constantinople but was unable to ask him what the outcome of their journey had been."

"I can tell you that," replied the gentleman, "for this Don Pedro is my brother and at this moment is in our village, in sound health, rich, married, and the father of three children." [12]

"Thanks be to God," said the captive, "for all His mercies; for in my opinion there is no happiness on earth that can equal that of recovering one's lost liberty."

"What is more," the gentleman went on, "I am familiar with those sonnets that my brother composed."

"Recite them, then, your Grace," said the captive, "for you will be able to do so better than I."

"With pleasure," said the gentleman; and he proceeded to recite the one on the Goleta, which was as follows:

CHAPTER XL. *In which the captive's story is continued.*

SONNET

Blest souls that have been freed of mortal guise
And by reason of your good deeds here below,
The noble exploits that ye have to show,
Have gone to a better home there in the skies,
How often 'mid the heat of battle cries
Have ye spilt the blood of many a doughty foe
As, staining sand and sea, ye did overthrow
The wicked in their pride, O high emprise!
'Twas life not valor failed the weary arm,
And even as ye died ye well might claim
The victory, thus wrested from defeat.
Ye fell, 'tis true, and suffered mortal harm
Between the blade and wall, yet still your fame
Lives on and rises to the glory seat.

"That is the way I remember it also," remarked the captive.

"And the one on the Fort," said the gentleman, "runs like this, if I am not mistaken."

SONNET

Out of the sterile earth, this rubble heap,
These tumbled ruins that now strew the ground,
Three thousand souls a better home have found;
Three thousand soldiers that once here did sleep
Have gone above, their guerdon fair to reap.
It was in vain their valor did abound;
Few and exhausted, suffering many a wound,
They gave their lives their honor bright to keep.
This bit of earth has ever been the haunt
Of mournful memories beyond man's count,
Both now and in the ages long since past;
But no more worthy souls can Heaven vaunt
Amongst the many that from this spot did mount
Than these brave ones that are Heaven's own at last.

The sonnets were not displeasing, and the captive was happy over the news of his comrade which he had received. He then went on with his story.

"Well, then, the Goleta and the Fort having fallen, the Turks ordered the former stronghold dismantled, there being nothing left of the Fort to raze; and in order to accomplish the task more speedily and with less labor, they mined three-quarters of it, but by no device could they succeed in blowing up what appeared to be the weakest part, namely the old walls. On the other hand, all that remained of the new fortifications that the Little Friar [1] had built was brought to the ground with the greatest of ease.

"Finally, the victorious fleet returned in triumph to Constantinople, and a few months afterward my master, El Uchali, died, the one who was known as 'Uchali Fartax,' which in the Turkish tongue means 'scurvy renegade'; for that is what he was, and it is the custom of the Turks to bestow names that signify some fault or virtue. This is for the reason that they have only four surnames altogether, which apply to those descended from the Ottoman line; [2] the others, as I started to say, take their names and surnames from bodily defects or moral characteristics. And this Scurvy One, being a slave of the Grand Seignior's, had slaved at the oar for fourteen years, being then more than thirty-

four years of age when he turned renegade. The way it came about
was this: as he was rowing one day a Turk had dealt him a blow, and
in order to be revenged on the fellow he renounced his faith. After
that, his valor proved to be so outstanding that he did not have to
resort to the usual underhanded ways and means by which the Great
Turk's favorites rise at court, but was made king of Algiers and later
commander at sea, which is the office that is third in rank in that seigniory.

"El Uchali was a Calabrian by birth and a man of moral principle who
treated his captives with great humanity. He came to have three thousand of them, and after his death they were divided in accordance with
the provisions of his will between the Grand Seignior (who is heir to
all who die and who shares with the offspring left by the deceased)
and his renegades. I fell to a Venetian renegade who, as a cabin boy
aboard a ship, had been captured by Uchali. His master grew so fond
of him that the youth became his prime favorite, and he also came to
be the cruelest one of his kind that was ever seen. His name was Hassan
Aga,[3] and, amassing great wealth, he rose to be king of Algiers. I accompanied him there from Constantinople and was somewhat pleased
at being so near to Spain. Not that I intended to write to anyone there
concerning my misfortunes; but I wished to see if fortune would be
more favorable to me here than it had been in Turkey, where I had
unsuccessfully essayed a thousand different means of escape. In Algiers
I thought to find other ways of attaining what I desired; for never once
did the hope leave me of achieving my freedom; and when my plottings and schemings did not come up to expectations and my attempts
were unsuccessful, I did not at once abandon myself to despair but
began to look for or invent some fresh hope to sustain me, however
faint and weak it might be.[4]

"In this way I managed to keep myself alive, shut up in a prison or
house which the Turks call a bagnio, in which they confine their Christian captives, both those of the king and those belonging to certain
private individuals, and also those that are referred to as being *del
Almacen*, that is to say, captives that belong to the Council and serve
the city in public works and other employment. It is very difficult for
these last to obtain their freedom, for inasmuch as they are held in common and have no individual for a master, there is no one with whom to
treat regarding their ransom even where they have the means for purchasing their liberation. In these bagnios, as I have said, they are accustomed to place captives belonging to certain private citizens of the
town, chiefly the ones that are to be ransomed, since there they may

keep them in safety and leisure. For the king's captives do not go out to labor with the rest of the galley crew, unless their ransom be late in coming, in which case, by way of inducing them to write for it more urgently, they put them to work and send them to gather wood with the others, which is no small task.

"I, then, was one of this group; for when they discovered that I was a captain, although I told them that I had no fortune and few prospects, they nevertheless insisted upon placing me among those gentlemen and others who were waiting for ransom. They put a chain upon me, but more as a mark of my status than in order to keep me from escaping; and thus I spent my days in that bagnio along with many important personages who had been designated and were being held for the purpose I have mentioned. And although we were at times harassed by hunger and the want of clothing, nothing distressed us so much as what we almost constantly saw and heard of the cruelties, such as never before were heard of or seen, which my master practiced upon the Christians. Each day he hanged his man, impaled one, cut off the ear of another; and all this with so little excuse, or with none at all, that the Turks had to admit he did it simply to be doing it, inasmuch as their natural bent toward the entire human race is a homicidal one.

"The only person who made out well with him was a Spanish soldier by the name of Saavedra,[5] for although this man had done things which will remain in the memory of that people for years to come, and all by way of obtaining his liberty, yet the Moor never dealt him a blow nor ordered him flogged; as a matter of fact, he never even gave him so much as a harsh word. And for the least of the many things that Saavedra did, we were all afraid that he would be impaled, and he himself feared it more than once. If time permitted, which unfortunately it does not, I could tell you here and now something of that soldier's exploits which would interest and amaze you much more than my own story.

"To continue: Overlooking the courtyard of our prison were the windows of a wealthy Moor of high rank. These, as is usually the case, more nearly resembled peepholes and were, moreover, covered with very thick and tightly drawn blinds. It happened, then, that one day I and three companions were on the prison terrace, amusing ourselves by seeing how far we could leap with our chains on; and, since we were alone, all the rest of the Christians having gone out to labor, I chanced to raise my eyes, when through one of those closed windows

I saw a reed appear with a piece of linen cloth attached to the end of it, and it was moving and waving as if signaling for us to come and take it. As we stood gazing up at it, one of those who was with me went over and placed himself directly beneath the reed to see if it would be released or what would happen; but the moment he did so, it was raised and moved from side to side as if someone were saying no by shaking the head. The Christian then came back, and at once it was lowered again and the person above began making exactly the same motions with it as before. Another of my companions repeated the performance, and the same thing happened with him. And a third man had a similar experience.

"Seeing this, I could not resist the temptation to try my luck, and as soon as I was beneath the reed, it was dropped. It fell at my feet there in the bagnio, and I immediately hastened to untie the linen cloth, whereupon I found knotted in it ten cianis, which are gold coins of base alloy in use among the Moors, each being worth ten reales in our money.[6] I need not tell you how happy I was over this windfall, and my happiness was equaled by my wonder as to how it had come to us, and to me in particular, since the unwillingness of the donor to release the reed to anyone other than me showed clearly that I was the one for whom the favor was intended. Taking the welcome money, I broke the reed and went back to the terrace, where I once more gazed up at the window. Then it was I saw a very white hand emerge, which opened and closed very quickly; and by this we understood or were led to imagine that it was some woman who lived in that house who had shown us this act of kindness. By way of thanking her, we salaamed after the fashion of the Moors, which is done by bowing the head, bending the body at the waist, and crossing the arms upon the bosom.

"Shortly afterward, through the same window, there came a little cross made of reeds, only to be at once withdrawn. This strengthened us in the belief that some Christian woman must be a captive in that house, and that it was she who had done us the favor; but the whiteness of the hand and the Moorish bracelets of which we had caught a glimpse inclined us to think otherwise, although we fancied that it might be some fair renegade, for such women are commonly taken as lawful wives by their masters, who are glad to do this, since they esteem them more highly than those of their own race.

"In all our discussions about the matter, however, we were very far from the truth; but from that time forth we were solely concerned with looking up at that window from which the reed had appeared, as if it had been our north star. Two weeks went by in which we had no further sight of it, nor of the hand, nor any signal whatsoever. And although during that time we did our best to find out who lived in the house and if there was any renegade Christian woman in it, we found no one who could tell us any more about the matter than that the house belonged to a rich and prominent Moor by the name of Hadji Morato, a former alcaide of La Pata, which is a very important office with them.

"But just as we had given up hope of a second rain of cianis, we unexpectedly saw the reed appear again with another knotted cloth on the end of it, a thicker one this time. This happened at an hour when the bagnio was all but deserted, as it had been on the previous occasion, and we made the same test, each of the others in turn going to stand beneath the window before I did, but it was only when I came up that the reed was released and dropped. I undid the knot and found forty Spanish gold crowns and a message written in Arabic with the sign of the cross beneath it. I kissed the cross, took the crowns, and returned to the terrace, where we all again salaamed. Then the hand appeared once more, and I made signs that we would read the message, after which the window was closed. We were at once pleased and bewildered by what had occurred, and as none of us understood Arabic, great was our curiosity to know what the message contained, and greater still our difficulty in finding someone who could read it for us.

"Finally, I decided to take a certain renegade into my confidence. He was a native of Murcia who professed to be a good friend of mine and who had promised to keep any secret that I might entrust to him; for it is the custom of some renegades, when they intend to return to Christian territory, to carry about with them testimonials of one sort or another from important captives to the effect that So-and-So is a good man, has always shown kindness to Christians, and is anxious to flee at the first opportunity that offers. There are those who procure these certificates with a proper object in mind, and there are others who cunningly misemploy them in case of need. The latter, when they go to commit depredations on Christian soil, if perchance they are lost or captured, will produce their affidavits as evidence of the purpose for which they came: namely, that of remaining in a Christian land; and they will assert that it was for this reason they joined the Turks. In such a manner they escape the immediate consequences of their act and are reconciled with the Church before it can punish them; and then, as soon as they are able to do so, they return to Barbary to become what they were before. But, as has been said, there are others who make honest use of these certificates and actually do remain with their coreligionists.

"It was one of these renegades who was my friend. He had testimonials from all of us in which we expressed our confidence in him as forcefully as we could, and if the Moors had found him with these papers on his person, they would have burned him alive. He was known to be well versed in Arabic, being able not only to speak it but to write it as well. And so, before I unbosomed myself to him, I asked him to read the message for me, telling him that I had accidentally come upon it in a hole in my cell. He opened it and studied it for some little time, muttering to himself all the while. I asked him if he understood it, and he assured me that he did, very well, and that if I wished him to give it to me word for word, I should provide him with pen and ink, as he could do it better that way. We gave him what he asked for, and he translated the message little by little. When he had finished he said, 'You will find set down here in Spanish absolutely everything that is written on this paper; and you are to remember that where it says Lela Marien, that means Our Lady the Virgin Mary.'

"Following is the message as he had transcribed it:

"*When I was young, my father had a slave girl who taught me the Christian zala* [7] *in my language, and she also told me many things about Lela Marien. The Christian woman died, and I know that she did not go to the fire but is with Allah, for twice afterward I saw her and she told me to make my way to the land of the Christians to see Lela Marien, who loved me a great deal. I do not know how to do so. I have seen many Christians from this window, and only you have seemed to me to be a gentleman. I am very young and beautiful and have much money to take with me. See if you can arrange for us to go, and there you may be my husband if you wish. If you do not wish it so, it will not matter to me, for Lela Marien will provide someone to marry me. I myself have written this; have a care as to whom you give it to read; do not trust any Moor, for they are all treacherous. I am deeply concerned lest you show this to someone, for if my father knew of it, he would cast me into a well and cover me with stones. On the reed I shall put a thread. Attach your reply to it, and in case you have no one who can write Arabic for you, tell me by means of signs and Lela*

Marien will make me understand. May She and Allah and this cross
protect you. The cross I kiss many times, as the Christian slave woman
bade me.

"You can imagine, gentle folk, how astonished and pleased we were
by the contents of this message. Indeed, we showed our feelings so
openly that the renegade realized it was not by chance that this paper
had been found but that it was in reality addressed to one of our number. He accordingly now asked us if his suspicions were true, telling us
that we should confide everything to him, as he would be willing to
risk his life for our freedom. Saying this, he brought forth from his
bosom a metal crucifix and with many tears swore by the God whom
that image represented and in whom he, though a wicked sinner, still
fully and faithfully believed, that he would loyally guard all the secrets we might see fit to reveal to him; for he felt—indeed, he was
almost certain—that through the one who had written that message
he and all of us would be able to gain our freedom and it would be
possible for him to fulfill his dearest wish, that of returning to the
bosom of Holy Mother Church, from which like a rotten limb he had
been severed and separated through ignorance and sin.

"So many tears did the renegade shed, and so many signs of repentance did he show, that we all of us unanimously consented and
agreed to tell him the truth of the matter; and so we proceeded to give
him an account of everything, keeping nothing hidden. We pointed out
to him the little window through which the reed had appeared, and
he then and there made note of the house and announced his intention of taking special pains to find out who lived in it. We also decided that it would be well to reply to the Moorish damsel's note, and,
seeing that we had someone there who was capable of doing this, the
renegade at once wrote out the words that I dictated to him, which were
exactly as I shall give them to you; for nothing of any importance that
happened to me in the course of this adventure has slipped my memory,
nor shall it escape me as long as I live. This was the reply that we sent
to the Moorish lady:

"*May the true Allah protect you, my lady, and that blessed Mary who*
is the true Mother of God and who has put it in your heart to go to
the land of the Christians, because she loves you well. Pray to her to
show you how you may carry out her command, for she is well dis-
posed and will assuredly do so. Do not fail to write and advise me of
your plans, and I will always let you have an answer. The great Allah

has given us a Christian captive who knows how to read and write your language, as you can plainly see from this message. Thus, with nothing to fear, we shall be able to know your wishes. You say that if you go to the land of the Christians, you will be my wife, and I as a good Christian promise you that you shall be, and you know that Christians keep their promises better than Moors. May Allah and Mary His Mother watch over you, my lady.

"Having written and sealed this message, I waited two days until the bagnio was deserted as usual, and then I went out to my accustomed place on the terrace to see if the reed would appear, which it did very shortly. As soon as I caught sight of it, although I could not see who was letting it down, I held up the paper as a sign the person above should attach the thread. This had already been done, however, and I now fastened the paper to it, and shortly thereafter our star once more made its appearance with the white banner of peace in the form of a little bundle. It fell at my feet, and, upon picking it up, I found in the cloth all sorts of gold and silver coins, more than fifty crowns, which more than fifty times doubled our happiness and strengthened our hope of obtaining our liberty.

"That same night our renegade came back and told us what he had learned. The one who lived in that house was the same Moor whose name, Hadji Morato, had been mentioned to us. He was enormously rich and had one daughter, the only heir to all his wealth; and it was the general opinion in the city that she was the most beautiful woman in Barbary. Many of the viceroys who came there had sought her hand in marriage, but she had been unwilling to wed; and it was also known that she had had a female slave who was a Christian and who was now dead. All of which bore out what was said in the note. We then took counsel with the renegade as to what we should do in order to rescue the Moorish damsel and make our escape to the land of Christians, and it was finally agreed that we should wait until we had further word from Zoraida, which was the name of the one who now wishes to be known as Maria. For we saw plainly enough that she and no other would be able to provide a way out of all these difficulties. When we had reached this decision, the renegade told us not to worry, that he would set us at liberty or lose his life in the attempt.

"For four days the bagnio was full of people, and as a result the reed did not appear, but at the end of that period, when the place was once more empty, the bundle was again let down, so pregnant-looking as to promise a very happy birth. The reed and the cloth descended to me, and I found in the latter a message and a hundred gold crowns, with no other money whatsoever. The renegade being present, we gave him the note to read inside our cell, and he translated it for us as follows:

"Sir, I do not know how to arrange for us to go to Spain, nor has Lela Marien told me, although I have asked it of her. The thing that can be done is for me to give you for this venture much money in gold. Ransom yourself and your friends with it, and let one of you go ahead to the land of the Christians, purchase a boat there, and return for the others. He will find me in my father's garden, which is at the Babazón gate,[8] *near the seashore. I expect to be there all this summer with my father and my servants. You will be able to take me away from there by night and carry me to the boat with nothing to fear. And remember that you are to be my husband, or I shall ask Mary to punish you. If you can trust no one to go for the boat, ransom yourself and go; for I know that you are more trustworthy than any other, being a gentleman and a Christian. Make it a point to become familiar with the garden; and, meanwhile, when I see you out for a stroll, I shall know that the bagnio is empty and will give you much money. Allah protect you, my lord.*

"Such were the contents of the second note; and when all had heard it read, each offered to be the ransomed one, promising to go and return with all haste; and I myself made the same offer. But the renegade opposed all this, saying he would by no means consent for anyone to go free until we all went together; for experience had taught him that men when freed were lax about keeping the word they had given in captivity. He added that many times certain important captives had had recourse to this expedient and had ransomed one of their number to go to Valencia or Majorca, providing him with sufficient money to fit out a boat and return for them, but he had never come back. For, the renegade observed, liberty recovered and the dread of losing it again would erase from their memories all the obligations that there are. By way of showing us the truth of this statement, he briefly related for us what had recently happened to some Christian gentlemen, one of the strangest cases that had ever been heard of in those parts where the most astonishing and terrifying things are all the time occurring.

"In short, he told us that what we could and should do was to give him the ransom money intended for one of us Christians, and he would buy a boat there in Algiers under pretext of turning merchant and trading with Tetuan and along the coast in that region. Being a ship's mas-

ter, it would be easy for him to hit upon a way of rescuing us from the
bagnio and putting us all aboard, especially if the Moorish lady, as she
said, was to provide the money for ransoming the entire lot of us. As
free men, it would be the easiest thing in the world to embark, even
at midday. The greatest obstacle lay in the fact that the Moors would
not permit any renegade to buy or own a boat, unless it was a vessel
to go on pillaging expeditions; for they feared that if he purchased
a small one, especially if he was a Spaniard, he merely wanted it for
the purpose of escaping to Christian territory. He, our friend, could
readily overcome this difficulty, however, by taking a Tagarin Moor [9]
into partnership with him in the purchase of the boat and the profits
to be derived from it, and under cover of this arrangement he could
become master of the craft; and with that he regarded the rest of it
as something already accomplished.

"Although it seemed to me and to my comrades that it would have
been better to send to Majorca for the boat as the Moorish lady had
suggested, we did not dare oppose him, being fearful that if we did not
do as he said he would reveal our plans and put us in danger of losing
our lives when our dealings with Zoraida were discovered, for whose
life we would all have given our own. We accordingly determined to
leave the matter in the hands of God and in those of the renegade, and
we therewith replied to Zoraida that we would do all that she had
counseled us, since the advice she had given us was as good as if it had
come from Lela Marien herself, adding that it remained for her to
decide as to whether the project was to be postponed or put into execution at once. I also, once more, made an offer to marry her. And
so it came about that the next day, when there was no one in the
bagnio, she on various occasions by means of the reed and the cloth
conveyed to us two thousand gold crowns and a message in which she
informed us that on the next *Jumá*, that is to say, Friday, she was leaving for her father's summer place and that before she left she would give
us more money. In case this was not enough, we were to let her know
and we might have anything we asked for; for her father had so much
that he would never miss it, and, what was more, she held the keys to
everything.

"We at once gave the renegade fifteen hundred crowns with which
to buy the boat, while I took eight hundred to procure my own ransom,
giving the money to a merchant of Valencia who was in Algiers at the
time and who had the king release me on the promise that, when the
next boat arrived from home, he would pay the ransom fee; for if he

were to pay it at once, the king might suspect that the funds had been in Algiers for some time and that the merchant for his own profit had kept the matter secret. Moreover, my master was so captious that I on no account dared pay him immediately. And so, on the Thursday before the Friday that the beauteous Zoraida had fixed as the day for going to her father's summer place, she gave us another thousand crowns, at the same time advising us of her departure and requesting me, in case I was ransomed, to make myself acquainted with the site or, in any event, to seek to procure an opportunity for going there to see her. I replied in a few words that I would do this, urging her to be sure and commend us to Lela Marien by making use of all those prayers that the slave woman had taught her.

"When this had been done, it was arranged that my three companions likewise should be ransomed, so that they would be able to leave the bagnio; since if they saw me set at liberty while they remained behind, despite the fact that there was sufficient money to ransom them, they might create a disturbance and the devil might put it into their heads to do something that would injure Zoraida. It was true that, in view of their rank, I could feel reasonably safe in this regard, but, nevertheless, I did not wish to imperil the undertaking, and so I had them released at the same time as myself, paying over all the money to the merchant in order that he might with confidence and security pledge his word, although we never once divulged to him our secret plan, as there would have been too much danger in doing so."

CHAPTER XLI. *In which the captive's story is still further continued.*

"A FORTNIGHT had not gone by before our renegade had bought a boat capable of carrying more than thirty persons; and by way of rendering the project safer and allaying suspicion, he made a voyage, as he had suggested, to a place called Shershel which is thirty leagues from Algiers in the direction of Oran [1] and which does a large trade in dried figs. Two or three times he did this in the company of the Tagarin Moor I have mentioned; for *Tagarinos* is the name given in Barbary to the Moors of Aragon, while those of Granada are called *Mudéjares;* but in the kingdom of Fez the *Mudéjares* are termed *Elches,* and they are the ones whom that king chiefly employs in war.

"To go on with my story, then: Each time that he passed with his boat he anchored in a cove that was not two crossbow shots from the house where Zoraida was waiting, and there, with the two little Moors that served him as oarsmen, he would deliberately station himself, either to say his prayers or by way of acting out the part he was later to perform in earnest. Thus, he would go to Zoraida's garden and beg fruit, and her father would give it to him without recognizing him. As he told me afterward, he would have liked to have a word with Zoraida herself so he could tell her he was there on my orders to bear her off to the land of the Christians and at the same time urge her to feel safe and happy.

"This, however, was impossible, for Moorish ladies do not permit themselves to be seen by any of their own race or by any Turk unless their husband or father so commands them. With Christian captives, on the other hand, they are allowed to converse and have dealings to a rather surprising extent. For my part, I was just as glad that he had not spoken to her, for she might have been disturbed to find her plan being discussed by renegades.

"But God in any case had ordained otherwise, and our renegade did not have an opportunity of gratifying his laudable desire. Seeing how safely he was able to go to Shershel and return and anchor where he chose, and perceiving that the Tagarin, his companion, was wholly compliant with his wishes and that all that was needed now was a few Christians to man the oars, he told me to look about for some that I might take with me in addition to those that were being ransomed and to engage them for the following Friday, which was the date he had set for our departure. I accordingly spoke to a dozen Spaniards, all of them powerful rowers. They were chosen from among those that were best in a position to leave the city, and it was no small task finding so many of them at that particular moment, since there were then twenty ships at sea and they had taken all the available oarsmen.

"I should not have been able to find them if it had not been that their master that summer was not going on a cruise but was occupied with completing the construction of a galiot which he had on the stocks. All that I told these men was that the next Friday afternoon they should steal out one by one and wait for me in the vicinity of Hadji Morato's garden. I gave these directions to each one separately, instructing them that if they saw any other Christians in the neighborhood, all they were to say to them was that I had ordered them to stay there until I came.

"Having attended to this, I had something else to do that was still more important, and that was to let Zoraida know how far our plans had progressed in order that she might be forewarned and not be caught off guard if we suddenly decided to abduct her before, as she would think, the Christian's boat would have had time to return. I therefore resolved to go to the garden and see if I could speak with her; so on a day before my departure I went there under pretense of gathering a few herbs, and the first person I encountered was her father, who addressed me in the language that throughout Barbary and even in Constantinople is in use between captives and Moors, and which is neither Moorish nor Castilian nor the tongue of any other nation, but a mixture of all of them by means of which we manage to understand one another. It was in this language that he asked me who I was and what I was doing in his garden. I replied that I was Arnaut Mami's [2] slave—because I knew for a certainty that Arnaut Mami was a very great friend of his—and that I was looking for herbs to make him a salad. He then inquired as to whether I was a ransomed man or not and what price my master wanted for me.

"As I was thus engaged in answering his questionings, the lovely Zoraida came out of the garden house. She had caught sight of me some while before; and since Moorish women, as I have said, are not at all prudish about showing themselves to Christians and do not avoid their company, she thought nothing of coming up to where her father stood conversing with me. In fact, when her father saw her slowly approaching, he called to her to come. It would be too much for me to undertake to describe for you now the great beauty, the air of gentle breeding, the rich and elegant attire with which my beloved Zoraida presented herself to my gaze. I shall merely tell you that more pearls hung from her comely throat, her ears, her hair than she has hairs on her head. On her feet, which, as is the custom, were bare, she wore two *carcajes*—for that is what they call bracelets for the ankles in the Moorish tongue—made of purest gold and set with many diamonds whose value, as she told me afterward, her father estimated at ten thousand doblas,[3] while those upon her wrist were worth fully as much as the others.

"The pearls also were numerous, for the way that Moorish women have of displaying their magnificence is by decking themselves out in this manner.[4] And so it is you find more pearls of one kind or another among the Moors than all the other nations combined have to show, and Zoraida's father was reputed to have an abundance of them and the best that there were in Algiers. In addition, he had more than two hundred thousand Spanish crowns, and the fair one I now call mine was mistress of all this wealth.

"If you would form an idea of how beautiful she was in her prosperous days and when so adorned, you have but to observe how much of beauty is left her now after all that she has suffered. For it is a well-known fact that the beauty of some women has its day and season and is diminished or heightened by accidental causes. It is, moreover, a natural thing that the passions of the mind should add to or detract from it, and most often they destroy it utterly. What I am trying to say is that, as she came toward me that day, she impressed me as being, both in herself and in her adornments, the most dazzling creature that I had ever seen, and when I thought of all that I owed to her, it seemed to me that I had before me a goddess from Heaven who had come to earth for my delight and comfort.

"As she came up, her father told her in their language that I was the captive of his friend, Arnaut Mami, and that I had come to look for a salad. She gave me her hand and, in that admixture of tongues that I have described, asked me if I was a gentleman and why it was I had not been ransomed. I replied that I already had been, and that from the price paid she could see the esteem in which my master held me, for the sum of one thousand five hundred soltanis [5] had been put up for me. To which she answered, 'In truth, had you been my father's slave, I would not have permitted him to let you go for twice as much, for you Christians always lie in everything you say and make yourselves out to be poor in order to cheat the Moors.'

" 'That may be, lady,' I said, 'but I dealt truthfully with my master, as I do and shall do with everybody in this world.'

" 'And when are you going?' Zoraida asked.

" 'Tomorrow, I expect; for there is a vessel here from France that sets sail then and I intend to go on it.'

" 'Would it not be better,' said Zoraida, 'to wait for one from Spain, seeing that the French are not your friends?'

" 'No,' I told her, 'although if I were certain that a ship from Spain was on the way, I would wait for it. It is more likely, however, that I shall go tomorrow, for the desire I have to see my native land and my loved ones is such that I cannot bear to wait for another opportunity, even though a better one, if it be late in coming.'

" 'You no doubt have a wife in your own country,' she said, 'and I suppose you are anxious to see her.'

" 'No,' I assured her, 'I am not married, but I have promised to wed as soon as I return.'

" 'And is the lady to whom you have given this promise beautiful?'

" 'She is so beautiful,' I replied, 'that by way of praising her and telling the simple truth, I will say that she very much resembles you.'

"Her father laughed heartily at this. 'In Allah's name, Christian,' he said, 'she must be beautiful indeed if she is like my daughter, who is the most beautiful in all this realm. If you do not believe me, look at her well and tell me if I do not speak the truth.'

"Throughout the greater part of this conversation, Zoraida's father acted as our interpreter, being the more adept at languages; for while she spoke the bastard tongue that, as I have said, is in use there, she expressed her meaning by signs rather than by words.

"As we were discussing these and other subjects, a Moor came running up, crying in a loud voice that four Turks had leaped the garden railing or wall and were picking the fruit although it was not yet ripe. Both the old man and Zoraida were alarmed at this; for the fear that the Moors have of the Turks is a common and, so to speak, an instinctive thing. They are especially afraid of Turkish soldiers, who treat their Moorish subjects more haughtily, insolently, and cruelly than if the latter were their slaves.

"Zoraida's father then said to her, 'Daughter, retire to the house and shut yourself in while I speak to these dogs. As for you, Christian, gather your herbs and go in peace, and may Allah bring you safely to your own country.'

"I bowed, and he went away to look for the Turks, leaving me alone with Zoraida, who made as if to go back into the house as her father had commanded her. He had no sooner disappeared among the garden trees, however, than she, her eyes brimming with tears, turned to me and said, '*Tameji*, Christian, *tameji?*' [6] Which means, 'Are you going, Christian, are you going?'

"And I answered her, 'Yes, lady, but under no condition without you. Wait for me next *Jumá*, and do not be frightened when you see us, for we are surely going to the land of the Christians.'

"I said this in such a way that she understood everything very well; and, throwing her arm about my neck, she began with faltering step to walk toward the house. But as luck would have it—and it would have been very unlucky indeed for us if Heaven had not ordered it otherwise—as we were going along in this manner, her father, who was coming back from his encounter with the Turks, caught sight of us, and we knew that he had seen us and had seen her arm about me. But Zoraida, cleverly on her guard, did not remove her arm; instead, she clung to me more than ever and laid her head upon my bosom, swaying at the knees a little and giving every evidence of having fainted, while I pretended to be supporting her against my will. The old man ran up to us and, seeing his daughter in this condition, asked her what the matter was.

" 'Undoubtedly,' he said, when he received no reply, 'it was those dogs coming into the garden that did this to her.' And, taking her off my bosom, he pressed her to his own, as she, her eyes not yet dry from her tears, sighed deeply and said, '*Ameji*, Christian, *ameji!*' [7]

" 'It is not necessary, my daughter, for the Christian to go,' her father said. 'He has done you no harm, and the Turks have left. There is no cause for you to be frightened, for nothing is going to hurt you, since the Turks at my request have gone back to where they belong.'

" 'It is true, sir, as you have said,' I told him, 'that they have given her a fright; but since she says for me to go, I would not cause her any annoyance; and so, peace be with you, and with your permission I will return to this garden for herbs, if I find it necessary, for my master says there are no better ones for salad than those that grow here.'

" 'Come back for all that you need,' replied Hadji Morato. 'My daughter does not say this because you or any of the other Christians annoy her. She either meant that the Turks should go, not you, or else that it was time you were looking for your herbs.'

"With this, I at once took my leave of both of them, and Zoraida, who appeared to be suffering deeply, went away with her father, while I, under pretense of gathering my salad, was able to roam the garden at will. I carefully noted the entrances and exits, the means they used to secure the house, and everything that might facilitate our plan; after which, I went to give an account of what had happened to the renegade and my companions. In the meanwhile, I looked forward to the time when I should be able to enjoy undisturbed the boon which fate had bestowed upon me in the person of the beauteous and charming Zoraida.

"Time went by, and at length the day came that meant so much to us. With all of us following the plan which, after many long discussions and the most careful consideration, we had decided upon, we met with the success that we longed for. On the next Friday after the day on which I had spoken to Zoraida in the garden, our renegade at nightfall anchored his boat almost directly opposite the house where she was, the Christians who were to man the oars having been notified in advance that they might hide themselves in various places round about. As they waited for me, they were all of them anxious and elated, eager to board the vessel on which their gaze was fixed; for they were unaware of the arrangement with the renegade and thought that they would have to gain their freedom by force of arm, through slaying the Moors who were on the boat.

"Accordingly, as soon as I and my companions showed ourselves, those who were in hiding sighted us and came up. This was at an hour when the gates of the city were closed, and in the whole of the country-side not a soul was to be seen. When we were all together, we discussed the question as to whether it would be better to go first for Zoraida or to make prisoners of the Moorish oarsmen. Before we had reached a decision, our renegade arrived and asked us what was the cause of our delay, for it was now time, all the Moors being off guard and most of them asleep. I told him why we were hesitating, and he replied that the most important thing was to capture the vessel first of all, which could be done very easily and with no danger whatever, and after that we could go for Zoraida. We all agreed with him, and so, without waiting any longer and with him as our guide, we went to the vessel, where he was the first to leap aboard. Laying a hand on his cutlass, he cried in the Moorish tongue, 'None of you stir from here or it will cost you your lives!'

"By this time nearly all the Christians were aboard; and the Moors, who were possessed of little courage, upon hearing their captain address them in this manner, were thoroughly terrified. None of them dared reach for his weapons, and for that matter, they had few if any; and so, without saying a word, they let themselves be shackled by the Christians, who accomplished this very quickly, threatening them that if they raised any kind of outcry they would all die by the knife.

"When this had been achieved, with half our number remaining behind to guard the prisoners, the rest of us, again with the renegade as our guide, made our way to Hadji Morato's garden; and it was our good fortune that, as we went to try the gate, it swung open as readily as if it had not been locked. We then, very quietly and saying nothing, went on to the house without our presence being discovered by anyone.

Zoraida, fairest of the fair, was waiting for us at a window, and as soon as she heard the sound of people below, she asked in a low voice if we were *Nizarani*, that is to say, Christians. I answered in the affirmative, saying that she should come down. Recognizing me, she did not hesitate for a moment, but without a word she came down instantly and, opening the door, appeared there in the sight of all, so beautiful and so richly clad that I cannot possibly tell you how she looked.

"As soon as I saw her, I took one of her hands and began kissing it, and the renegade and my two comrades did the same, while the others, being unacquainted with the circumstances, followed our example, since it seemed to them that we were merely recognizing and thanking her as the lady who was responsible for our going free. The renegade asked in Moorish if her father was in the house, and she replied that he was sleeping.

" 'Then it will be necessary to wake him,' he said, 'for we must take him with us and everything of value that there is in this beautiful summer place.'

" 'No,' she answered, 'you must by no means lay hands on my father. In this house there is nothing for you save that which I bring with me, and it is enough to make you all rich and happy. Wait a moment and you will see.'

"She then went back into the house, saying she would return at once and bidding us meanwhile not to make any noise. I took this opportunity of asking the renegade what had passed between them, and when he told me, I made it clear to him that under no condition was he to go beyond Zoraida's wishes. She now reappeared with a small trunk filled with gold crowns, so heavy that she could hardly carry it. At that instant, unfortunately, her father awoke and, hearing a noise in the garden, came to the window and looked out. Recognizing us all as Christians, he began bawling at the top of his lungs in Arabic, 'Christians! Christians! Thieves! Thieves!' This frightened us very much and threw us into confusion; but the renegade, perceiving the danger we were in and how important it was to go through with our undertaking before being detected, ran up as fast as he could to where Hadji Morato was, being accompanied by some of the rest of us. As for myself I did not dare leave Zoraida unprotected, for she, half fainting, had fallen in my arms.

"In brief, those who went up handled the matter so expeditiously that in a moment they were back, bringing with them Hadji Morato, his hands bound and with a napkin over his mouth so that he could not speak a word—and they threatened him that if he tried to speak it would cost him his life. When his daughter saw him, she put her hands over her eyes, and her father in turn was horrified at sight of her, not knowing that she had placed herself in our hands of her own free will. But it was essential now for us to be on our way, and so we hastily but with due care boarded the ship, where those that we had left behind were waiting for us, fearful that some untoward accident had befallen us.

"It was a little after two in the morning by the time we were all on the vessel. They then untied Hadji Morato's hands and removed the napkin from his mouth, but the renegade again warned him not to say anything or they would kill him. As the old man looked at his daughter, he began sighing mournfully, especially when he saw her held tightly in my embrace, and when he observed that she did not struggle, protest, or attempt to escape me; but he nonetheless remained silent lest they carry out the renegade's threat.

"Finding herself on the boat now and perceiving that we were about to row away while her father and the other Moors remained bound, Zoraida spoke to the renegade, requesting him to do her the favor of releasing the prisoners, particularly her father, as she would rather cast herself into the sea than have a parent who loved her so dearly carried away captive in front of her eyes and through her fault. The renegade repeated to me what she had said, and, for my part, I was quite willing. He, however, replied that this was not the wise thing to do, for the reason that, if they were left behind, they would alarm the entire city and countryside, whereupon some fast-sailing craft would put out in pursuit of us and so comb the sea and land that there would be no possibility of our escaping. What we might do, he added, was to give them their freedom as soon as we set foot on Christian soil. We all agreed to this, and when the matter was explained to Zoraida, along with the reasons why we could not comply with her wishes, she also was satisfied. And then, gladly and silently, cheerfully and with alacrity, each one of our powerful rowers took up his oar, as, commending ourselves with all our hearts to God, we set out on our voyage to the island of Majorca, which is the nearest Christian territory.

"However, inasmuch as the tramontane wind [8] was blowing a little and the sea was a bit rough, it was impossible for us to follow the route to Majorca, and we were compelled to hug the coast in the direction of Oran. This worried us considerably, for we feared that we would be discovered from the town of Shershel, which is about seventy miles from Algiers. And we also were afraid that we might encounter in those waters one of the galiots that commonly ply the coast with merchandise of Tetuán, although each of us secretly felt that if we did meet with a merchant vessel of that sort, providing it was not a cruiser, we not only should not be captured but, rather, should be able to come into possession of a craft in which we could more safely complete our voyage. In the meantime, as we were sailing along, Zoraida buried her face in my hands in order not to see her father, and I could hear her calling on Lela Marien to come to our aid.

"We must have gone a good thirty miles when dawn came, and we found ourselves at a distance of something like three musket shots off land. The shore was deserted, and we saw no one who might descry us, but, nevertheless, by rowing as hard as we could we put out a little more to the open sea, which was now somewhat calmer. When we were about two leagues from the coast, the order was given to row by turns so that we could have a bite to eat, the ship being well stocked with food; but those at the oars said it was not yet time for them to take a rest—the others might eat, but they themselves did not wish on any account to relax their efforts. We were starting to do as they had suggested when a strong wind came up, which obliged us to leave off rowing and set sail at once for Oran, that being the only course left us. All this was done very quickly, and with the sail we made more than eight miles an hour, with no fear other than that of falling in with a vessel that was out cruising.

"We gave the Moorish rowers some food, and the renegade consoled them by telling them they were not captives but would be given their freedom at the first opportunity. He said the same to Zoraida's father, who replied, 'If you promised me anything else, O Christian, I might believe it and hope for it by reason of the generous treatment you have accorded me, but when it comes to setting me free, do not think that I am so simple-minded as to put any credence in that; for you would never have incurred the risk of depriving me of my liberty only to restore it to me so freely, especially since you know who I am and the profit you may derive from releasing me. Indeed, if you wish to name the sum, I hereby offer you whatever you ask for me and for this unfortunate daughter of mine, or for her alone, for she is the greater and better part of my soul.'

"As he said this, he began weeping so bitterly that we were all moved to compassion, and Zoraida could not resist stealing a glance at him. When she saw him weeping, she was so touched that she rose from my feet and went over to embrace him, and as she laid her cheek against his the two of them shed so many tears that a number of us could not but join them in their weeping. But when her father perceived that she was in festive attire and decked out in all her jewels, he spoke to her in their own language.

" 'How does it come, my daughter,' he said, 'that last night, at dusk, before this terrible thing happened to us, I saw you clad in ordinary household garb; and now, without your having had time to dress, and without my having brought you any good news to celebrate by thus adorning and bedecking your person, I nonetheless behold you wearing the best garments with which I was able to provide you when fortune smiled upon us? Answer me this, for I am even more astonished and bewildered by it than I am by this misfortune that has come to us.'

The renegade informed us of all that the Moor had said to his daughter, who did not utter a word in reply. And when the old man saw, over at one side of the boat, the small trunk in which she was in the habit of keeping her jewels, he was more bewildered than ever; for he knew very well that he had not brought it to the summer place but had left it in Algiers. He thereupon asked her how the trunk had come into our hands and what was inside it; and then the renegade, without giving Zoraida time to answer, spoke up.

" 'You need not trouble, sir, to ask your daughter Zoraida so many questions, for I can give you one answer that will serve for all. I would have you know that she is a Christian, and that it is she who has filed our chains for us and set us free from our captivity. She goes of her own free will and, I fancy, is as happy about it as one who emerges from darkness into light, from death into life, or from the pains of hell into glory everlasting.'

" 'Is it true, my daughter, what this man says?' asked the Moor.

" 'It is,' said Zoraida.

" 'So you are a Christian,' said the old man, 'and it is you who have placed your father in the hands of his enemies?'

" 'As to my being a Christian,' she told him, 'that is true enough, but it is not true that I am responsible for your being in this situation; for I never had any desire to leave you or to do you harm, but only to do good to myself.'

" 'And what good have you done yourself, daughter?'

" 'Put that question,' she said, 'to Lela Marien, for she can tell you better than I.'

"No sooner had he heard this than the Moor, with an incredibly swift movement, hurled himself head foremost into the sea; and he would undoubtedly have drowned if the long and cumbersome robe that he wore had not tended to bear him up. Zoraida screamed for someone to rescue him, whereupon we all ran forward and, seizing him by his robe, hauled him in, half drowned and unconscious, at which his daughter was so distressed that she wept over him as bitterly and mournfully as if he were already dead. We turned him face downward and he disgorged much water, and after a couple of hours he was himself once more.

"Meanwhile, the wind had changed and we had to make for land, exerting all our strength at the oars in order not to be driven ashore. Luck was with us, and we were able to put into a cove alongside a promontory or cape which the Moors call *Cava Rumia*,[9] signifying in our language 'the wicked Christian woman'; for it is a tradition among them that La Cava, through whom Spain was lost, is buried in that spot, *'cava'* in their tongue meaning 'bad woman,' while *'rumia'* is 'Christian.' They regard it as bad luck to be compelled to drop anchor there, and they never do so unless it is absolutely necessary. But for us it was not the 'bad woman's' shelter; rather, it was a haven in distress, as the sea was now raging.

"Stationing our sentinels on land and never once relinquishing the oars, we ate what the renegade had provided and prayed to God and Our Lady with all our hearts that they would favor and aid us in order that we might bring to a happy conclusion an undertaking that had begun so propitiously. Upon Zoraida's request, the order was given to set her father and all the other Moors ashore, for her tender heart could not bear to see her father thus bound and her fellow countrymen held prisoners in front of her very eyes. We promised her that this should be done as soon as it came time for us to depart; for we ran no risk by leaving them in this deserted place. Our prayers were not in vain; for, Heaven favoring us, the wind changed and the sea grew calm, inviting us to resume with cheerful hearts the voyage that we had begun.

"We then unbound the Moors and, one by one, set them on land, at which they were greatly astonished; but when it came to disembarking Zoraida's father, who had by now completely recovered his senses, he gave us a piece of his mind.

"'Why do you think, Christians,' he said, 'that this wicked female is happy at your giving me my liberty? Do you imagine that it is out of filial affection? Assuredly not. It is only because my presence is an impediment to the carrying out of her base designs. And do not think that what has led her to change her religion is a belief that yours is better than ours; it is because she knows that in your country immodesty is more freely practiced than in ours.'

"As her father spoke, another Christian and I held Zoraida's arms that she might not be tempted to some foolish act. The old man now turned upon her.

" 'O infamous and ill-advised maiden! Where do you think you are going, so blindly and foolishly, with these dogs, our natural enemies? Cursed be the hour in which I begot you, and cursed all the luxury in which I have reared you!'

"Seeing that he was likely to go on in this way for some while, I hastened to put him ashore; and from there he kept on shouting at us, pursuing us with his curses and lamentations as he implored Mohammed to pray to Allah that we be destroyed, confounded, and brought to an end. And when, having set sail, we could no longer hear his words, we could still see his gestures, could see him plucking out his beard, tearing his hair, and rolling on the ground. At one point he raised his voice to such a pitch that we could make out what he said.

" 'Return, my beloved daughter, return to land, and I will forgive you everything. Give those men the money that is yours and come back to comfort your brokenhearted father, who, if you leave him now, will leave his bones on these deserted sands.'

"Zoraida heard all this and was deeply grieved by it. Weeping, she could only say to him in reply, 'O my father, may it please Allah that Lela Marien, who has been the cause of my turning Christian, console you in your sorrow! Allah well knows that I could have done nothing other than what I did. These Christians are in no wise to blame, for even had I not wished to come with them, even had I chosen to remain at home, it would have been impossible, so eagerly did my soul urge me to do that which to me seems as good, my dear father, as it seems evil to you.'

"When she said this, her father could no longer hear her, for we had lost him from view; and so, while I comforted Zoraida, we all of us turned our attention to the voyage, as we now had a wind so favorable that we firmly expected to be off the coast of Spain by dawn the next day.

"Blessings, however, are almost never unmixed with some evil that, without our having foreseen it, comes to disturb them. It may have been simply our misfortune, or it may have been those curses that the Moor had heaped upon his daughter (for a curse of that kind is always to be dreaded, whatever the father may be like), but, in any event, our luck now changed. We were on the high seas, and the night was a little more than three hours gone. We were proceeding at full sail with the oars lashed, since the wind had relieved us of the necessity of using them, when by the light of the moon, which was shining brightly, we sighted alongside us a square-rigged vessel with all sails set that was luffing a little and standing across our course.[10] It was so close upon us that we had to strike sail in order not to run foul of her, while they swung their prow about to give us room to pass.

"They now came to the ship's rail to ask us who we were, from where we came, and where we were going. When these questions were put to us in French, our renegade said, 'Let no one answer, for they are undoubtedly French pirates who plunder everything in sight.' As a result of this warning, no one said a word in reply. We were a little ahead, and the other vessel was lying to leeward, when suddenly they fired two pieces of artillery, both of them, as it seemed, loaded with chain-shot; for with one they cut our mast in half and brought both mast and sail down into the sea, while the other cannon, discharged at the same moment, sent a shot into the middle of our craft, laying it wide open but doing no further damage to it. As we saw ourselves sinking, we began crying out for help, imploring those on the other ship to come to our aid as we were filling with water. They then struck their own sails, and, lowering a skiff or boat, as many as a dozen Frenchmen, all well armed, with matchlocks and matches lighted, came alongside us. When they saw how few we were and how our craft was going down, they took us in, telling us that this had come about through our discourtesy in not answering them.

"Our renegade, then, without anyone's seeing what he did, took the trunk containing Zoraida's wealth and dumped it into the sea. To make a long story short, we all went aboard with the Frenchmen, who, after they had learned everything they wished to know about us, proceeded to despoil us of all that we possessed as if we had been their deadly enemies. They even took Zoraida's anklets, but this did not grieve me as much as it did her. What I feared more was that, having deprived her of her exceedingly rich and precious gems, they would go on to steal that jewel that was worth more than all the others and which she most esteemed. Their desires, however, did not go beyond money, in which regard they were insatiable in their covetousness. They would even have taken the garments their captives wore if these had been of any use to them. Some of them were for wrapping us all in a sail and tossing us into the sea; for it was their intention, by passing themselves off as Bretons, to put in at certain Spanish ports, and if they brought us in alive they would be punished when the theft was discovered.

"But the captain, who was the one who had despoiled my beloved Zoraida, said that he was content with the prize that he had and did not wish to stop at any port in Spain. Instead, he preferred to slip through the Strait of Gibraltar at night, or any way he could, and go on to La Rochelle, the port from which he had put out. Accordingly, they agreed to let us take their small boat and all that we needed for the brief voyage that remained for us. This they did the next day, within sight of the Spanish coast, a sight that caused us wholly to forget all our sufferings and hardships, which were as if they had never been, so great is the joy that comes from recovering one's lost freedom.

"It may have been around midday when they put us in the boat, giving us two kegs of water and some biscuit. And as the lovely Zoraida went to embark, the captain, moved by some sympathetic impulse or other, gave her as many as twenty gold crowns and would not permit his men to take from her those same garments that she is now wearing. As we entered the small boat, we thanked them for their kindness, our manner being one of gratitude rather than indignation, and they then put out to sea, making for the Strait, while we, needing no other compass than the land that lay ahead of us, bent to the oars so lustily that by sundown we were, as we thought, near enough to be able to reach it before the night was far gone.

"But as there was no moon and the sky was darkened over and we were ignorant of our exact whereabouts, it did not seem wise to attempt a landing, although many of us thought that we should do so, saying that it would be better to run ashore even if it were on some rocks, far from any inhabited place, since in that way we would assure ourselves against the very likely danger of Tetuán corsairs, who at night are in Barbary and by morning off the coast of Spain, where they commonly take some prize and then return to sleep in their own houses. There were a number of conflicting suggestions, but the one that was finally adopted was that we should gradually draw near the shore and, if the sea was calm enough to permit it, land wherever we were able.

"This was the plan followed, and shortly before midnight we came to the foot of an enormous and very high mountain that was not so near the sea but that it afforded a convenient space for a landing. We ran up on the sand and leaped ashore, kissing the ground on which we stood and shedding many joyful tears as we gave thanks to God, Our

Lord, for the incomparable blessing that He had conferred upon us. Removing the provisions from the boat, we drew it ashore and then went a long way up the mountain; for even here we could not feel in our hearts or bring ourselves to believe that the land beneath our feet was Christian soil. The sun, it seemed to me, came up more slowly than we could have wished, and in the meanwhile we had climbed the entire mountainside in an effort to see if we could discover any village or even a few shepherds' huts; but however much we strained our eyes, we were able to descry no village, no human being, no path, no road.

"Nevertheless, we determined to keep on and go farther inland, since surely we could not fail to come upon someone who could give us our bearings. What distressed me more than anything else was seeing Zoraida go on foot over this rough country; for though I once tried carrying her on my shoulders, my weariness wearied her more than she was rested by her repose, and so she would not again consent to my making the exertion but went along very cheerfully and patiently, her hand in mine. We had gone, I imagine, a little less than a quarter of a league when there reached our ears the sound of a little bell, which showed plainly that we must be near some flock or herd, and as we all gazed about us attentively to see if we could discern any, we saw at the foot of a cork tree a young shepherd who very calmly and unconcernedly was engaged in whittling a stick with his knife.

"We called to him, and he, raising his head, got to his feet very nimbly. As we afterward learned, the first persons that he caught sight of among us were the renegade and Zoraida, and seeing them in Moorish costume, he thought that all Barbary must have descended upon him. Dashing with amazing swiftness into a near-by wood, he began raising a terrible din as he shouted, 'Moors! Moors! The Moors have landed! Moors! Moors! To arms! To arms!'

"We were quite perplexed by all this, not knowing what to do; but, reflecting that the shepherd's cries would arouse the countryside and that the mounted coast guard would soon be along to find out what the trouble was, we decided that the renegade should take off his Turkish clothes and put on a captive's jacket, which one of us now gave him though he himself was left with only his shirt. And then, commending ourselves to God, we proceeded along the same path that the shepherd had taken, expecting that the guard would be upon us at any moment. In this we were not wrong, for two hours had not gone by when, as we were coming out of a thicket onto a plain, we caught sight of all of fifty horsemen coming toward us at top speed.

"As soon as we saw them, we stopped and watched them, and they, when they came up and found, in place of the Moors they were seeking, a handful of poor Christians, were very much surprised. One of them asked if it was we who had caused the shepherd to sound the call to arms. 'Yes,' I replied, and was about to go on and tell him our story, who we were and from whence we came, when one of our number happened to recognize the horseman who had put the question and, without giving me a chance to reply, spoke up and said, 'Thanks be to God, sirs, for having brought us into such good hands; for unless I am mistaken, this region where we now are is in the neighborhood of Vélez Málaga—unless all the years of my captivity have so deprived me of my memory that I cannot recall that you, sir, who have just asked us our names, are Pedro de Bustamente, my uncle.'

"The Christian captive had no sooner said this than the horseman dismounted and came up to embrace the young fellow. 'My dearest nephew!' he cried. 'I recognize you now. I and my sister—your mother —and all your relatives who are still alive have wept for you as dead, and now it appears that God has been pleased to prolong their lives that they might have the pleasure of seeing you again. We had heard that you were in Algiers, but from the look of your garments and those of all this company I realize that you have been miraculously liberated.'

" 'That,' replied the young man, 'is the truth, and there will be time to tell you all about it.'

"As soon as the guardsmen realized that we were Christian captives, they dismounted, and each then offered us his own horse to carry us to the city of Vélez Málaga, which was a league and a half from there. We told them where we had left the boat, and some of them went back to get it and take it to the town. Others mounted behind us on the cruppers, Zoraida going with the young man's uncle.

"The entire town came out to receive us, for someone had ridden ahead and told them of our coming. They were not the kind of folk to be astonished at seeing captives free or Moors held prisoner, being quite accustomed to such a sight. What they rather marveled at was Zoraida's beauty. Despite the fact that she was weary from the journey, she looked her loveliest at that moment, so joyful was she at finding herself on Christian soil with nothing to fear any longer. Happiness had put so much color into her face that—unless it can be that my love for her deceived me—I shall venture to say that there never was a more beautiful creature in all this world, none that I have ever seen, at any rate.

"We went directly to the church to thank God for his mercy; and as soon as Zoraida entered the portals, she remarked that there were faces there that resembled that of Lela Marien. We informed her that these were images of the Virgin, and the renegade to the best of his ability then went on to explain what their meaning was and how she might worship them as if each were the same Lela Marien who had spoken to her. Being possessed of a good, clear mind, she understood all this very readily. After that, they took us to various houses in the town, and the Christian who had come with us brought the renegade, Zoraida, and me to the home of his parents, who were people in moderately comfortable circumstances and who entertained us with as great a show of affection as they did their own son.

"We were in Vélez for six days, at the end of which time the renegade, having ascertained what he had to do, departed for Granada in order that, through the mediation of the Holy Inquisition, he might be restored to the sacred bosom of the Church. Each of the other liberated Christians went his own way, Zoraida and I being left with no other means than the crowns which the French captain had courteously given her. With them I purchased the beast on which she now rides; and with me serving her up to now as father and squire, not as husband, we are at present on our way to see if my own father is still alive or if one of my brothers has prospered to a greater extent than I.

"Seeing that Heaven has seen fit to give her to me as my companion, I can imagine no other fortune, however good, that might come to me which I should hold to be of greater worth. The patience with which she endures the hardships that poverty brings with it, and her desire to become a Christian, are such as to fill me with admiration and induce me to serve her all my life long. My happiness, however, at knowing that I am hers and she is mine is marred by the fact that I am at a loss where to find a nook in my own country in which to shelter her. For it may be that time and death have wrought such changes in the life and fortunes of my father and my brothers that, if they should not be there, I shall hardly find anyone who is acquainted with me.

"Gentle folk, that is all there is to my story. As to whether it be a pleasing and a curious one, that is for you in your good judgment to decide. For my own part, I may say that I should like to have told it more briefly, although, as it is, the fear of tiring you has led me to omit a number of incidents."

CHAPTER XLII . *Which treats of further happenings at the inn and other things worthy of being known.*

WITH these words the captive was silent, whereupon Don Fernando addressed him.

"Most assuredly, Captain," he said, "your manner of relating this extraordinary adventure has been equal to the novelty and unusual character of the subject matter. Your story is a strange one indeed, filled with incidents such as cause those who hear it to marvel greatly. We have enjoyed listening to it so much that we should be glad if you were to begin it all over again, even though tomorrow should find us still taken up with the same tale."

Cardenio and all the others then spoke in turn, offering to serve the captain in any way that they possibly could, and their words were so warm and sincere that he was quite touched by these expressions of good will. Don Fernando in particular told him that if he wished to come back with him, he would have the marquis, his brother, act as godfather at Zoraida's baptism, while on his own part he would be glad to fit him out so that he would be able to return to his own province with the dignity and outward appearance that befitted his rank. For all these generous offers the captain thanked them most courteously, although he would not accept any of them.

Night was now coming on, and just as darkness fell a coach accompanied by a number of men on horseback drew up at the inn; but when the newcomers asked for a lodging, the innkeeper's wife replied that there was not a hand's breadth of space in the hostelry that was not occupied.

"That being the case," said one of the mounted attendants who had ridden into the courtyard, "room must be found for his Lordship the judge."

Upon hearing this, the landlady was all aflutter. "Sir," she said, "the truth of the matter is that I have no beds; but if his Lordship carries one with him, as I have no doubt he does, let him come in, and welcome, for my husband and I will be glad to give up our room to accommodate him."

"That will do very well," said the squire.

At that moment there descended from the coach an individual whose garb plainly indicated the office and rank he held; for his long robe with the ruffled sleeves showed him to be a judge, as his servant had said. By his hand he led a damsel who looked to be around sixteen years of age. She was in traveling attire and was so beautiful, well bred, and elegant in appearance that all who beheld her were struck with admiration. Indeed, had they not seen Dorotea and Luscinda and Zoraida, who were now inside the inn, they would have regarded this maiden's loveliness as being of a sort that was hard to find.

Don Quixote was there when the judge and the young lady came in, and as soon as he saw them, he said to his Lordship, "Your Grace may enter and take your ease in this castle; for though it is but poor and lacking in conveniences, there is no poverty or inconvenience in the world that cannot provide accommodation for arms and letters, especially when arms and letters have beauty for their guide and leader, as letters, represented by your Grace, have in this charming damsel, for whom not only should castle gates be thrown wide open, but cliffs should rend themselves and mountains divide and bow low to give her welcome. Enter, your Grace, I say again, into this paradise; for here will be found stars and suns to keep company with the Heaven that your Grace brings with you. Here you will find the bravest of the brave and the fairest of the fair, both arms and beauty at their highest point of excellence."

The judge was astonished by this speech of Don Quixote's and stared at him very hard, being no less amazed by the knight's appearance than by his words; and he was still further surprised when he beheld Luscinda, Dorotea, and Zoraida, who, having heard of the arrival of the new guests and having been told by the landlady how beautiful the damsel was, had come out to see and welcome the young lady. Don Fernando, Cardenio, and the curate greeted the judge in a manner that was at once more intelligible and more urbane, while the beautiful ladies of the inn were doing the honors to his fair companion; but with it all, his Lordship was not a little bewildered as he made his entrance.

He could see that they were all persons of quality, but he was wholly at a loss to account for the figure, face, and bearing of Don Quixote. When the polite exchange of greetings was over and the question of accommodations had been discussed, it was finally decided that the previous arrangement was to stand and that all the women should sleep together in the garret already mentioned, while the men should remain outside as a kind of guard for them. The judge was well pleased that the damsel who accompanied him and who was his daughter was to be lodged with the other ladies, and she accepted with right good grace. And so, sharing between them what the landlord could provide and his Lordship had brought with him in the way of beds, they made out that night better than they expected.

The moment he laid eyes upon the judge, the captive's [1] heart had given a bound, for something told him that this was his own brother. He accordingly now inquired of one of the attendants what his Lordship's name was and from what province he came. The servant replied that his master was the licentiate Juan Pérez de Viedma and that he had heard it said that he was from a village in the mountains of León. This information together with what he had seen of the man was enough to convince the captive that the new arrival was indeed his brother, the one who upon their father's urging had chosen the profession of letters.[2] Very happy and excited, he called Don Fernando, Cardenio, and the curate to one side and explained the situation to them, assuring them that he was certain he was right.

The attendant had further stated that his Lordship was on his way to the Indies, having been appointed a judge of the High Tribunal [3] of Mexico. The damsel accompanying him was his daughter, whose mother had died in childbirth, leaving her husband very rich through the dowry that came to him with the girl. And the captive was now asking advice as to the best way in which to reveal his identity and how he might first find out if his brother, seeing him poor like this, would be ashamed of him or would receive him warmly and affectionately.

"Leave that to me," said the curate; "although, Señor Capitán, there is no reason to think that you will not be well received, as the worth and wisdom of which your brother's bearing shows him to be possessed do not indicate that he would be arrogant or unfeeling or would be incapable of making due allowance for the reverses of fortune."

"Nevertheless," said the captain, "I should like to make myself known to him, not suddenly, but in a roundabout way."

"You may take my word for it," said the curate, "that I shall handle it in such a manner that we shall all be satisfied."

At this point supper was served [4] and the entire company sat down at table, with the exception of the captive, and the ladies, who were supping by themselves in the other room. It was in the middle of the meal that the curate spoke to the judge.

"Your Lordship," he began, "I had a comrade in Constantinople, where I was a captive for a number of years, who bore the same name that your Grace does. He was one of the bravest soldiers and captains to be found in the whole of the Spanish infantry. But he was quite as unfortunate as he was valiant and daring."

"And what, sir, was the name of this captain?" the judge asked.

"His name," replied the curate, "was Ruy Pérez de Viedma, and he was a native of some village in the mountains of León. He told me a story about his father and his brothers which, if I had not known him to be so truthful a man, I should have taken to be one of those tales that old women tell by the fireside in wintertime. According to what he said, his father had divided his property among his three sons and had given them a certain piece of advice that was better than any Cato ever gave.[5] And I may say that the choice my comrade made of going to the wars proved to be so fortunate a one that within a few years, by reason of his worth and courage and with nothing to aid him save his own merits, he rose to be an infantry captain and was well on his way to becoming a corps commander. Fortune, however, did not favor him; for just as it appeared to smile upon him, he lost everything by losing his liberty on that glorious day when so many recovered their freedom, at the battle of Lepanto. I lost mine at the Goleta, and after each of us had gone through a series of adventures, we met in Constantinople. From there he went to Algiers, where one of the strangest things in the world happened to him."

The curate then went on and briefly related the story of Zoraida and the captive, to all of which the judge gave such a "hearing" as he never before had accorded to any case before him.[6] The narrator did not go beyond the point where the French had despoiled the Christians on the boat, but he dwelt upon the poverty and extreme want in which his comrade and the lovely Moor had found themselves, adding that he had not been able to learn how they had come out, whether they had reached Spain or had been carried off to France.[7]

The captain, who was standing a little to one side, was listening to all the curate said and at the same time was watching his brother's every movement. Perceiving that the story was ended, his Lordship heaved a deep sigh and his eyes filled with tears as he said, "O sir, if you only realized what news you have brought me and what it means to me. It means so much that, in spite of all my reasoned efforts at self-control, the tears start from my eyes! This brave captain of whom you speak is my elder brother, who, being hardier and endowed with loftier ambitions than those that I and my younger brother cherished, chose the honorable and worthy calling of arms, which was one of the three paths in life that our father pointed out to us, as your comrade told you in relating what seemed to you to be a fairy tale. I chose the profession of law, and God and my own faithful application have brought me to the position in which you see me now. My younger brother is in Peru and is so rich that, with what he has sent back to my father and to me, he has well repaid the portion of the estate that he took with him and in addition has furnished my father with the means of gratifying fully his generous inclinations, while I too have been enabled to pursue my studies, lead a more self-respecting life, and attain my present station.

"My father is still living, though he is dying [8] to hear from his eldest son and prays God unceasingly not to close his eyes in death until in life they have rested on him once again. At all of this I cannot but wonder, for my brother is extremely sensible and I cannot understand why, in all his troubles and afflictions or in prosperity, he should have neglected to let his father have some word of him; for if any of us had known where he was and the straits he was in, it would not have been necessary to wait for the miracle of the reed in order to obtain his ransom. But what distresses me now is the uncertainty as to whether those Frenchmen will have let him go free or whether they may have murdered him by way of covering up their robbery.

"As a result of it all, I shall continue my journey, not with that satisfaction with which I began it, but filled with melancholy and sadness. O my dear brother, if I but knew where you are now, I would go seek you and free you of your sufferings, however much of suffering it meant for me! Oh, to bring word to our aged father that you are still alive, even though you might be in the most deeply hidden dungeon of Barbary! For my father's riches, my own, and those of my brother would speedily get you out! O beauteous and generous-hearted Zoraida, if I could but repay you for what you have done for my brother! If I could but be present at the rebirth of your soul, and at your wedding, which would give us all so much pleasure!"

The judge went on talking in this manner, for he was deeply moved by the news of his brother which he had received, and all the listeners joined in showing the sympathy that they had for him in his sorrow.

And then the curate, seeing that he had achieved his purpose and fulfilled the captain's wish, arose from the table and went to the room where Zoraida was; for he had no desire to prolong their mood of sadness. Taking her by the hand, he came back, followed by Luscinda, Dorotea, and the judge's daughter. The captain was waiting to see what he was going to do, when the priest came over and with his other hand took that of Zoraida's husband-to-be; after which, with one of them on either side of him, he walked over to where the judge and the other gentlemen were.

"Dry your tears, my lord," he said, "and let your heart's desire be gratified; for you have here in front of you your worthy brother and your equally worthy sister-in-law. He whom you see here is Captain Viedma, and this is the lovely Moor who was so kind to him. The Frenchmen of whom I told you are responsible for their being in this poverty-stricken state, which will afford you an opportunity of exercising the generosity of heart that we know is yours."

The captain then ran over to embrace his brother, who placed both hands upon his chest and held him off in order that he might have a good look at him; but when he finally recognized him, he clasped him so tightly and shed so many tears of joy and affection that most of those present also wept. The words which the two brothers exchanged, the feelings they displayed, were such, I think, as could hardly be imagined, much less described. There and then, each gave the other an account of his life during the past years, providing the best of examples of what good friends two brothers can be. The judge embraced Zoraida, putting all that he had at her disposal, after which he had his daughter embrace her, and the beautiful Christian and the loveliest of Moors once more brought tears to the eyes of all.

Don Quixote stood there all the while observing these happenings most attentively but saying not a word, for he associated them all with his chimerical fancies that had to do with knight-errantry. It was agreed that the captain and Zoraida should return with his brother to Seville, where they would advise his father that he had been set free and found, so that the old man might be able to come to the wedding and baptism, since it was not possible for the judge to defer his journey, as he had just heard that within a month a fleet was leaving Seville for New Spain and it would be a very great inconvenience if he missed sailing with it.

In short, they were all happy and joyful over the fortunate outcome of the captive's adventure; and as the night was now nearly two-thirds gone, they decided to retire and get what rest they could. Don Quixote offered to stand guard over the castle lest they be attacked by some giant or wandering rogue of evil intent who might be covetous of the great treasure of feminine beauty within these walls. Those who knew him thanked him for this and gave the judge an account of the knight's strange fancies, which afforded him considerable amusement.

Sancho Panza alone was fretting over their delay in retiring, but he was the one that ended by making himself the most comfortable of all, for he simply threw himself down on the trappings of his ass, though he was to pay for this dearly a little later, as will be told further on.

The ladies, then, having retired to their room while the others accommodated themselves as best they could, Don Quixote left the inn and went outside to stand sentinel as he had promised to do. And so it was that, shortly before daylight, the womenfolk heard a voice so sweet and musical that they were compelled to pay heed to it, especially Dorotea, who was lying there awake while Doña Clara de Viedma, the judge's daughter, slumbered by her side. None of them could imagine who the person was who sang so well without the accompaniment of any instrument. At times the singing appeared to come from the courtyard, at other times from the stable; and as they were straining their ears and wondering about it, Cardenio came to the door of their room.

"Those of you who are not asleep," he said, "should listen, and you will hear the voice of a mule driver who sings most charmingly."

"We hear it, sir," replied Dorotea. And with this Cardenio went away. She then gave all her attention to the song, the words of which were the following.

CHAPTER XLIII. *In which is related the pleasing story of the muleteer, with other strange events that took place at the inn.*

> "Love's mariner am I,
> Sailing Love's own deep sea,
> Bereft of hope, forlorn;
> No haven waits for me.
>   And yet, my course I steer
> By a bright and gleaming star
> Palinurus [1] never sighted—
> I behold its light afar.
>   I know not whither it leads;
> No other thought have I
> Than to fix my soul's gaze upon it,
> Let all the rest go by.
>   A maiden reserve uncalled for,
> An unheard of modesty:
> These the dark clouds that cover
> My star of ecstasy.
>   O star so bright and gleaming,
> I tell thee with bated breath:
> To lose forever the sight of thee
> Would surely be my death." [2]

As the singer reached this point, it occurred to Dorotea that it would not be right to let Clara sleep through it all and miss hearing so fine a voice, and so, shaking her from side to side, she roused her from her slumbers.

"Forgive me for waking you, my child," she said. "I do it because I wish you to hear the best singing that you have ever heard in all your life, it may be."

Clara awoke, sleepy-eyed, without understanding at first what Dorotea was saying to her. She accordingly asked her to repeat what she had said, which Dorotea did, and she was then all ears. She had barely heard a couple of lines, however, as the singer went on with his ballad, when she was seized with a strange trembling, as if she were suffering from a sudden and severe attack of quartan fever.

"Ah, my dearest lady!" she exclaimed as she clung to Dorotea, "why did you wake me? The greatest boon that fortune could bestow upon me would be to keep my eyes and ears closed so that I might not see nor hear that hapless musician!"

"What are you saying, child? Why, they tell me that the one who is doing that singing is a mule driver."

"No," replied Clara, "that is not so. He is lord of many places,[3] and the place that he so securely holds in my heart shall never be taken from him for all eternity, unless he would have it so."

Dorotea was greatly surprised at hearing the girl express such sentiments as these, which so belied her years.

"You speak, Señora Clara," she said, "in such a way that I cannot understand you. Tell me more, and explain what you mean by the places which that musician, whose voice so disturbs you, holds, including the place in your heart. But do not tell me anything just now; for I would not forego, by listening to you, the pleasure I derive from that song. I think he is beginning again, with new words and a new air."

"Let him, in Heaven's name," said Clara. And in order not to hear him, she put both hands to her ears, at which Dorotea was more astonished than ever. The latter, meanwhile, was listening closely as the singer continued:

> "*Thou sweetest hope I know,*
> *Through impassable thickets thou dost wend thy way,*
> *Straight on dost go*
> *To the end thou hast set thyself. Let not dismay*
> *Come near when thou dost see*
> *How Death walks every step along with thee.*
>
> *The faint of heart ne'er gain*
> *The hard won victory, the triumph dear;*
> *The slothful ne'er attain*
> *That happiness they seek, nor those who fear*
> *To come to grips with Chance*
> *That they their fortune may thereby enhance.*
>
> *Love sells his favors high,*
> *But that is only just. What better gold*
> *Could anyone supply*

Than that which bears his stamp of worth untold?
For it would surely seem,
What costs but little is of small esteem.

   A lover's persistency
At times achieves the impossible, and thus
In all consistency
I take Love's way, of all most arduous.
   But still my heart is stout:
That I shall win my Heaven, I do not doubt." [4]

With this the song stopped and the girl once more began sobbing, all of which kindled her companion's desire to know what lay behind a song so sweet and tears so bitter. Dorotea thereupon asked her what it was she had been going to tell her a while ago. Being afraid that Luscinda would hear what she had to say, Clara then threw her arms about the older woman and clasped her tightly, putting her mouth close to the other's ear to avoid being overheard.

"That singer, dear lady," she began, "is a gentleman's son, a native of the kingdom of Aragon. His father, who is lord of two villages, has a house opposite my father's in the capital. And although we had curtains to our windows in winter and blinds in summer, this gentleman, who was engaged in pursuing his studies, in some way or other had a glimpse of me, whether it was in church or somewhere else I cannot say. The short of it is, he fell in love with me, and gave me to understand as much from the windows of his own house, with so many tears and gestures that I could not but believe him. I even fell in love with him, without knowing what it was he wanted of me. Among the signs that he made to me was one that consisted in clasping one of his hands in the other, thus indicating that he wished to marry me; and while I was very happy over this, being alone and motherless I had no one with whom to talk it over, and the result was, I let matters stand as they were and gave him but small encouragement. The most that I did, when my father and his were away from home, was to raise the curtain or the blind a little so that he might have a good look at me, which made him so happy that he acted as if he were going mad.

"The time came for my father to leave, and the young man learned of it, though not from me, since I had had no opportunity to tell him. He then fell ill, and I believe that it was due to grief; and so it was that, on the day we left, I was not even able to see him from afar and say good-by to him with my eyes. But after we had traveled for a couple of days, as we were entering a wayside tavern one day's journey from here, I saw him standing at the gateway of the inn clad as a muleteer and looking the part so thoroughly that, had I not carried an image of him in my heart, it would have been impossible to recognize him. But I did recognize him and was at once astonished and overjoyed, and he would occasionally steal a glance at me; but he always keeps out of my father's way when he crosses my path on the road or at the inns where we stop. Since I know who he is, I feel very bad when I reflect that for love of me he has come all this way on foot, and wherever he goes my eyes follow him.

"I do not know what his purpose is in coming, nor how he has been able to slip away from his father, who is extremely fond of him, since he has no other heir and his son is fully deserving of his affection, as your Grace will perceive when you have had a sight of him. Another thing I can tell you is that he himself makes up those songs that he sings, for I have heard it said that he is a very fine student and also a poet. What is more, every time that I see him and hear him sing, I tremble all over and am terribly upset, for I am afraid that my father will recognize him and learn of our love. I have never spoken a word to him in my life, yet I love him so dearly that I cannot live without him. And that, my dear lady, is all that I can tell you about this musician whose voice has given you so much pleasure, and which alone should be enough to assure you that he is no muleteer as you say, but the lord of hearts and towns, as I have told you."

"Say no more, Doña Clara." For Dorotea had interrupted her; and, giving her a thousand kisses, she repeated, "Say no more, but wait until tomorrow comes, when I hope to God I shall be able to arrange this affair of yours so that it may have the happy ending that so innocent a beginning deserves."

"Ah, Señora!" cried Doña Clara, "what end can I hope for when his father is so rich and important a personage that it would seem I could not even be a servant much less a wife to his son? And as to marrying without my own father's knowledge, I would not do that for anything in the world. All I ask is that this young man leave me and return home, and perhaps with not seeing him and the great distance between us, my pain will be somewhat alleviated, although I dare say this remedy that I suggest would not do me much good. I do not know how in the name of Satan this came about or how this love found its way into our hearts, seeing that we are both so young; for we are really about the same age, and I am not yet sixteen but shall be on next St. Michael's day, my father tells me."

Dorotea could not help smiling as she heard Doña Clara talking so much like a child.

"Let us get some rest, Señora," she said, "for if I am not mistaken, morning will soon be here, and then everything will be all right or I shall be greatly disappointed."

With this they settled down for what remained of the night, and all the inn was wrapped in silence, the only ones not asleep being the inn-keeper's daughter and Maritornes the slavey, who, familiar with Don Quixote's whimsies and knowing that he was outside clad in his armor and on horseback, standing guard, decided to play some kind of prac-tical joke on him, or at least to have a little amusement by listening to his nonsense. Now, as it happened, there was not a window in the house that looked out over the fields, but only an opening in a straw-loft through which they used to throw out the straw. At this opening the two demi-damsels now stationed themselves. They could see Don Quixote in the saddle and leaning on his pike as he every now and then heaved such deep and mournful sighs that it seemed each one would tear his heart out; and they could also hear him talking to himself in a gentle, soft, and loving tone of voice.

"O my lady Dulcinea del Toboso," he was saying, "supreme model and ultimate goal of all beauty and discretion, treasury of grace, de-pository of virtue; in short, the ideal of all that is worth while, honor-able, and delectable in this world! And what would thy Grace be doing now? Art thou perchance thinking of thy captive knight who, merely to serve thee and carry out thy wishes, hath seen fit to expose himself to all these perils? Give me some word of her, O luminary of the three faces! [5] It may be that out of envy of her face thou lookest upon her even now as she paces some gallery of her sumptuous palace, or as, lean-ing from a balcony, she considers how, without detriment to her modesty and exalted rank, she may assuage the torment that this griev-ing heart of mine endures for her sake. Does she think of the glory that should compensate me for my sufferings, the repose that should be mine after all my exertions, or, in brief, what life should be bestowed upon this my death, what reward I should have for my services?

"And thou, O Sun, who must even now be harnessing thy steeds that dawn may soon come and thou mayest emerge to behold my mis-tress, I beg thee when thou dost see her to greet her for me. But have a care that, when thou dost see and greet her, thou dost not kiss her face; for I shall be more jealous of thee than wast thou of that swift-footed and ungrateful one that caused thee so to run and sweat over the plains of Thessaly and the banks of the Peneus—I do not rightly recall just where it was that thou didst run in thine amorous and jealous rage on that occasion." [6]

Don Quixote had gone as far as this with his lugubrious monologue when the innkeeper's daughter began signaling to him.[7] "Good sir," she called to him softly, "come over here, if your Grace is pleased to do so."

At this signal and the sound of her voice, Don Quixote raised his head, and by the light of the moon, which was then shining in all its brightness, he perceived that someone was summoning him from the opening in the loft, which to him appeared to be a window—a window with a gilded grating of the kind that a magnificent castle ought to have, for such he took the inn to be. And then, instantly, it occurred to his insane imagination that, as on a previous occasion, the daughter of the lord of this castle, overcome with love of him, was seeking to make a conquest. With this thought in mind and desiring not to be discourteous or unfeeling, he turned Rocinante and rode up to the opening where the two lasses were.

"It is a pity, lovely lady," he said as soon as he caught sight of them, "that thou shouldst have let thy affections roam where they can never be requited in a manner that befits thy great worth and high estate; but for this thou shouldst not blame this wretched knight-errant, for love hath rendered it impossible for him to yield his will to any other than her whom, the moment he beheld her, he made the absolute mistress of his heart. Forgive me, then, good lady, and withdraw into thy chamber, and do not display thy feeling for me any further, that I may not once more have to show myself ungrateful. If there is any other way, outside of love itself, in which I may gratify that love thou hast for me, thou hast but to ask it and I swear to thee by that sweet and absent enemy of mine that I will incontinently do thy bidding, even though the boon thou seekest be a lock of Medusa's serpent hair or the rays of the sun itself stoppered in a vial."

"My mistress has need of nothing of that sort," said Maritornes at this point.

"Then, discreet matron," replied Don Quixote, "what is it that she needs?"

"Merely one of your shapely hands," said Maritornes, "that she may vent upon it the consuming passion that has brought her to this loop-hole, at so great a risk to her honor that, if her father were to hear of it, the least slice of her that he would take would be her ear."

"I should like to see him do that!" said the knight. "Let him beware if he does not want to meet the most disastrous end of any father in this world for having laid hands upon the delicate members of his lovesick daughter."

Having no doubt that Don Quixote would offer his hand as she had asked of him, Maritornes at once began thinking what she would do now; and, climbing down from the opening, she went out to the stable and took the halter of Sancho Panza's ass, returning with it quickly just as the knight was getting to his feet on Rocinante's saddle in order to be able to reach the gilded window-rail where, so he imagined, the brokenhearted damsel was.

"Lady," he was saying, "take this hand, or better, this avenger of the world's evildoers. The hand of no other woman has ever touched it, not even that of her who holds entire possession of my body. I extend it to thee, not that thou shouldst kiss it, but that thou mayest study the contexture of the sinews, the network of the muscles, the breadth and spaciousness of the veins, from which thou canst deduce how great must be the might of the arm that supports such a hand."

"That we shall soon see," said Maritornes. And, making a slip-knot in the halter, she put it over his wrist; then, getting down from the opening, she tied the other end to the bolt on the door of the loft.

"But it seems to me," said Don Quixote, as he felt the rope grating on his wrist, "that thy Grace is scraping rather than caressing my hand. Do not treat it so harshly, for it is not to blame for my unresponsive will. It is not right that thou shouldst wreak all thy vengeance upon so small a part, for remember that one who loves well should not avenge herself in a manner so ill."

But there was no one to hear these words; for as soon as Maritornes had attached the halter, she and the other girl left, fit to burst with laughing, and they left Don Quixote tied in such a way that it was impossible for him to free himself. As has been said, he was standing on Rocinante's back and his entire arm was through the opening while his wrist was fastened to the bolt on the door; and he was very much afraid that if Rocinante should swerve to one side or the other, he would remain hanging there. For this reason, he dared not make the slightest movement, although Rocinante stood so quietly and patiently that he might have been expected not to stir for a century to come.

Finally, seeing that he was caught in this manner and the ladies
had departed, the knight began imagining that all this was a kind of enchantment, like the last time when, in this very castle, that enchanted
Moor of a carter had given him such a mauling. He now cursed himself for his lack of judgment and sound sense in having ventured to set
foot there a second time after having fared so badly before; for it was
generally accepted by knights-errant that, when they had essayed an
adventure and had not succeeded in it, this meant that it was not for
them but for others, and there was no necessity of trying again. Meanwhile, he kept pulling on his arm to see if he could loosen it, but it was
well tied and all his efforts were in vain. It is true, he pulled very
gently, lest Rocinante should move; but, in any event, he was unable
to seat himself in the saddle, and there was nothing for it but to remain
standing or wrench his hand off.

Then it was that he longed for the sword of Amadis, against which
no enchantment whatever could prevail. Then it was that he cursed
his ill fortune, exaggerating the loss which the world would suffer while
he was held there under a spell, for he had no doubt that this was the
case. Then he remembered once again his beloved Dulcinea del Toboso,
and then too it was that he called for his good squire, Sancho Panza,
who, lying stretched out on the packsaddle of his ass and dead to the
world, was unmindful even of the mother who bore him. Then it was
that he called upon the wise Lirgandeo and Alquife [8] to aid him, beseeching also his good friend Urganda to succor him. And then,
at last, morning found him so despairing and bewildered that he brayed
like a bull; for he had no hope that with the coming of day his sufferings would be ended; rather, he believed that, as a result of the magician's spell, they would be eternal. This belief was strengthened in him
when he observed that Rocinante never so much as stirred. And so he
was convinced that he and his steed would have to remain there in
that condition, without eating, drinking, or sleeping, until the evil influence of the stars had waned or until another, more skillful enchanter
came to disenchant him.

In this, however, he was greatly deceived; for it was no sooner
daylight than four fully accoutered horsemen, their firelocks across
their saddlebows, drew up at the inn. Finding the gateway closed, they
pounded lustily upon it; and when he saw and heard this, even in his
present position, Don Quixote did not fail to play the sentinel.

"Knights," he said to them, "or squires, or whoever you may be,
you have no right to knock at the gates of this castle; for you should

know that at such an hour those inside are asleep, or are not in the habit of throwing open the fortress until the sun is fully up. Withdraw, then, and wait for day, and we shall then see whether or not it is fitting that they open for you."

"What the devil kind of fortress or castle is this," asked one of them, "that we are obliged to stand on such ceremony? If you are the innkeeper, have them open the gate for us. We are travelers who desire no more than to give some barley to our horses and go on, for we are in a hurry."

"Do I impress you, gentlemen, as having the appearance of an innkeeper?" was Don Quixote's answer.

"I do not know what appearance you have," replied the man. "But I know that you are talking nonsense when you refer to this inn as a castle."

"A castle it is," Don Quixote insisted, "and one of the best in all this province. And there are those within who have held a scepter in their hands and have worn a crown upon their heads."

"It would have been better the other way around," said the traveler: "the scepter on the head and the crown in the hand; but it may be there is some company of actors inside, for they very often have those crowns and scepters that you are talking about, and I cannot believe that in a small tavern like this, where you cannot hear a sound, any persons would be lodged who are entitled to them in real life."

"You know little of the ways of the world," replied Don Quixote, "seeing that you are ignorant of the things that happen in connection with knight-errantry."

The companions of the one who asked the questions were by this time tired of the conversation between him and the knight, and they again began pounding so furiously that the innkeeper and all the others awoke and the landlord arose to inquire who was knocking. At that moment one of the horsemen's mounts came up to smell Rocinante as the hack, sad and melancholy, with his ears drooping, stood there motionless, supporting his well-stretched master's weight; and being, when all is said, only flesh and blood though he appeared to be of wood, Rocinante could not but weaken and in turn smell the one that had come to court him. In doing this, he moved ever so little, and at once Don Quixote's feet slipped from the saddle and he would have fallen to the ground if his arm had not been held fast, a circumstance which caused him so much pain that he thought his wrist would be cut off or his arm torn from his body. For he was left hanging so near the ground that he could touch the earth with the tips of his toes, which was all the worse for him since, being conscious of how little he lacked of being able to plant his feet firmly, he wore himself out by stretching himself as far as he could in an attempt to accomplish this. He was like those who, suffering the strappado and placed in the position of touch-without-touching, merely add to their pain by the effort they make to stretch their bodies, in the vain hope that with a little more straining they will be able to find solid footing.[9]

CHAPTER XLIV. *In which are continued the unheard-of adventures at the inn.*

DON QUIXOTE by now was bawling so loudly that the landlord, very much alarmed, ran out and threw open the gate to see what the matter was, while those outside were equally curious. Maritornes also had been awakened by the shouts, and, suspecting what the cause of it all was, she hastened to the straw-loft without anyone's seeing her and unfastened the halter by which Don Quixote was supported, whereupon he at once dropped to the ground as the innkeeper and the travelers looked on. Coming up to him, they asked why he was shouting in that manner; but he without saying a word removed the rope from his wrist, rose to his feet, mounted Rocinante, braced his buckler on his arm, fixed his lance, and, retiring down the field for some little distance, came back at a half-gallop.

"If there be anyone," he cried, "who says that I deserved to have this spell put upon me, providing the Princess Micomicona grant me permission to do so, I hereby give him the lie; I defy him and challenge him to single combat."

The new arrivals were amazed by Don Quixote's words, but the landlord explained matters to them by telling them who the knight was, adding that they were to pay no attention to him as he was out of his mind. They then inquired of him if a lad about fifteen years of age and dressed as a muleteer had stopped at the inn, the description they gave being one that fitted Doña Clara's lover; to which he replied that there were so many guests that he had not noticed the lad they mentioned. One of the travelers, however, had caught sight of the judge's equipage.

"He is undoubtedly here," he said, "for this is the coach that he is following. One of us will stay at the gate and the others will go in and look for him; and it would be well, also, to ride around the side of the inn to make sure he does not get away over the stable-yard wall."

"We will see to that," was the reply.

Two of them then went in while one remained at the gate and a fourth man rode to the back. The landlord, meanwhile, was unable to guess why they were making so thorough a search, although he believed they must be after that youth whose description they had given him. The sun was now up, and for this reason as well as on account of the uproar that Don Quixote had created, they were all awake and stirring, especially Doña Clara and Dorotea, neither of whom had slept much that night, the one being too excited by the near-presence of her lover, while the other was eager to see what he looked like.

When he perceived that none of the four travelers was paying the slightest attention to him nor would answer his challenge, Don Quixote was ready to die with rage and spite; and had he found by the ordinances of chivalry that a knight-errant could lawfully assume and undertake any other enterprise than the one for which he had given his word of honor, until his pledge had been fulfilled, he would have attacked them all and compelled them to answer him whether they wished to or not. As it was, he felt that he could not do this until he should have restored Micomicona's kingdom to her. In the meanwhile, he must keep silent, remain quietly where he was, and wait to see what the result of the horsemen's search would be.

One of them had by this time come upon the youth sleeping beside a mule driver, not dreaming that anyone was looking for him, much less that his whereabouts had been discovered.

"Well, Don Luis," said the man, taking him by the arm, "that garb you wear is certainly becoming to you, and the bed in which you sleep goes well with the luxury in which your mother reared you."

Rubbing his sleep-filled eyes, the youth stared for a moment at the one who had hold of him. Then he recognized him as a servant of his father's, which gave him such a shock that for some while he was not able to say a word.

"There is nothing for you to do now, Don Luis," the man went on, "but to come along quietly and return home, unless your Grace desires to be the death of your father and my lord, for no less than that is to be expected as a result of his grief over your absence."

"But," said Don Luis, "how did my father know that I had taken this road and in this disguise?"

"It was a student," the servant replied, "to whom you had revealed your plans who told him of them, for he was moved to pity when he saw how your father was suffering. And so, my lord dispatched four of us to look for you, and we are all here now at your service, happier than you can imagine at the thought that we shall speedily return and restore you to the gaze of him who so longs to see you."

"That," said Don Luis, "shall be as I decide or as Heaven may ordain."

"What is there for Heaven to ordain or you to decide, beyond your consenting to come with us, since there is no other possible course?"

This entire conversation was heard by the mule driver at Don Luis' side; and, rising from where he lay, he went to inform Don Fernando, Cardenio, and the others of what had happened, for they were by now up and fully clothed. The muleteer told them how the man had addressed the lad as "Don" and what they had said to each other, with the servant urging the youth to return home while the latter was unwilling to do so. When they learned of this and recalled what a fine voice Heaven had bestowed upon the young fellow, they were all of them eager to know more about him, and even to help him should an attempt be made to use force with him. They accordingly hastened out to where the two stood talking and arguing.

Dorotea at this point came out of her room, followed by Doña Clara, who was trembling all over. Calling Cardenio to one side, she related to him briefly the story of the musician and his love, and he in turn described how the father's servants had come looking for the lad. He kept his voice low, but not so low that Clara failed to hear what he said, and she was so beside herself that she would have fallen in a faint had not her friend supported her. Cardenio then advised Dorotea to go back to the room, saying that he would take care of everything, and this they now did.

All four of the servants were inside the inn, standing around Don Luis and endeavoring to persuade him that, without a moment's hesitation, he should return to console his father. His answer was that he could by no means do this until he had settled a matter on which his life, his honor, and his soul depended. The servants thereupon grew more insistent, impressing upon him that on no account would they go back without him, and that they meant to take him whether he liked it or not.

"That you will not do," said Don Luis, "unless you take me back dead; although whatever way you took me, there would be no life in me."

By this time all those in the hostelry were gathered around listening to the argument, including Cardenio, Don Fernando and his companions, the judge, the curate, the barber, and Don Quixote; for the knight deemed there was no further necessity of his guarding the castle. Knowing the youth's story, Cardenio asked the men why it was they wished to take this boy away against his will.

"Because," one of them said, "we wish to restore life to his father who, on account of this young gentleman's absence, is on the verge of losing it."

At this Don Luis spoke up for himself. "There is no necessity," he told them, "of going into my affairs here. I am a free being and shall return if it pleases me; if it does not, none of you is going to compel me."

"Reason should compel your Grace," the man went on, "and if reason does not suffice to persuade you, it is sufficient to persuade us to do what we came to do and what it is our duty to do."

It was now the judge's turn. "Let us hear what is at the bottom of all this," he said.

"Sir," replied the man, who recognized him as a neighbor, "does not your Lordship recognize this young gentleman, your neighbor's son, who has thus run away from his father's house in a guise that so ill befits his station, as your Grace may see for yourself?"

The judge studied the youth more attentively and, when he saw who it was, gave him an embrace. "What child's play is this, Don Luis," he asked him. "What motive could have been powerful enough to prevail upon you to come clad in this manner that is so unbecoming to you?"

At this the lad's eyes filled with tears and he was unable to make any reply. The judge then requested the four servants to be calm, assuring them that it would all be settled properly; after which, taking Don Luis by the hand, he led him off to one side and inquired of him what the reason was for his presence there.

While these and other questions were being asked and answered, a loud shouting was heard at the gateway of the inn. What had happened was this: two guests who had been lodged there that night, observing that everyone was occupied with questioning the four travelers, had attempted to leave without paying what they owed; but the innkeeper, who was more attentive to his own business than to that of others, had waylaid them as they went out the gate and was demanding that they pay the score. His language to them was such that they were led to reply to him with their fists, and they were laying it on so heavily that the poor landlord had to cry out for help. His wife and daughter looked about for someone to aid him, but the only person whose attention was not taken up was Don Quixote; so the innkeeper's daughter addressed herself to him.

"Sir Knight," she said, "by the power that God has reposed in you, I beg you to succor my poor father. There are two wicked men out there who are beating him to a pulp."

"Lovely damsel," was the knight's measured and phlegmatic response, "your request is at this moment out of place, for I am prevented from entering upon any other adventure until I shall have fulfilled my word and brought to a conclusion the one upon which I am at present embarked. What I may do, however, in order to serve you is this: run and tell your father to sustain this combat as best he may and in no wise to allow himself to be vanquished while I go beg permission of the Princess Micomicona to succor him in his distress. If she but grant me that permission, you may rest assured that I will rescue him."

"Sinner that I am!" exclaimed Maritornes when she heard this, "before your Grace obtains the permission you speak of, my master will be in the other world."

"I beg you, lady," replied Don Quixote, "to give me leave to obtain it. Once I have the princess's consent, it will make little difference if your father is in the other world, for I will have him out of it in spite of all that the world in question can do; or, at the least, I will take such vengeance on those who have sent him there that you will be more than moderately satisfied."

Saying no more, he went over and dropped to his knees in front of Dorotea, imploring her in the language of knight-errantry that her Highness be pleased to grant him permission to aid and succor the castellan of that castle, who was in grave peril. The princess gave her consent readily enough, and he then, bracing his buckler and grasping his sword, ran out to the gate of the inn, where the two guests were still mistreating the landlord. But as he came up, he stopped short as if perplexed, although Maritornes and the landlady kept urging him to help their master and husband, asking him why he hesitated.

"If I hesitate," said Don Quixote, "it is for the reason that it is not permitted me to lay hand to sword against those of the rank of squire;

but go call my own squire, Sancho, for me, for it appertains to him to undertake this defense and vengeance."

All this took place at the gateway of the inn, where many most effective blows and punches were being exchanged to the great detriment of the landlord as the wrath of Maritornes and of the landlady and her daughter increased; for they were now in despair over Don Quixote's cowardice and the beating that was being administered to their master, husband, and father.

But let us leave him there; for there will surely be someone to succor him; or, if not, let him bear it and hold his peace who is rash enough to attempt more than his strength will warrant. Let us, rather, fall back some fifty paces and see what was Don Luis' reply to the judge. It will be recalled that we left them conversing to one side, with his Lordship inquiring of the lad why he had come on foot and so vilely clad. At this, the youth wrung his hands, indicating that some great sorrow lay upon his heart.

"My dear sir," he said, his tears flowing freely. "I can tell you no more than this: that from the moment Heaven willed, through our being neighbors, that I should lay eyes upon Doña Clara, your daughter and my lady, I have made her the mistress of my will, and if your will, O true father of mine, is no obstacle, I would make her my wife this very day. For her sake it was that I left my father's house, and for her I donned this attire in order to be able to follow her wherever she went, even as the arrow seeks the target or the mariner the north star. She knows nothing more of my desires than what she may have learned from seeing me, on a number of occasions and from afar, weeping for love of her. You, sir, are acquainted with the wealth and noble lineage of my parents, and you also know that I am their only heir. If these be sufficient qualifications to lead you to risk making me perfectly happy, then accept me at once as your son; for if my father, having other plans of his own, should not approve of this blessing I have sought out for myself, time still is more potent than the human will when it comes to undoing and altering things."

Having said this, the lovelorn boy was silent, and the judge upon hearing it was at once astonished, agreeably surprised, and filled with uncertainty. He was surprised by the skillful manner in which Don Luis had declared himself, and uncertain as to the course that he as a father should pursue in so sudden and unlooked-for a situation. The only answer he could make was that the young man should put his mind at rest for the present and meanwhile arrange with his servants not to take him back that day, in order that there might be time to consider what was the best for all concerned. Don Luis insisted upon kissing his hands and even bathed them with his tears, a sight that might have melted a heart of marble, to say nothing of that of the judge, whose worldly wisdom told him how advantageous such a marriage would be to his daughter, although, if it were possible, he preferred to see it consummated with the consent of Don Luis' father, who, as he knew, was looking for a titled match for his son.

By this time the two guests out at the gate had made their peace with the innkeeper and, owing to Don Quixote's mild and persuasive reasoning rather than to any threats on his part, they had paid all that was asked of them. As for Don Luis' servants, they were waiting for him to finish his conversation with the judge and make up his mind what he was going to do, when at that moment—so the devil, who never sleeps, would have it—the very same barber from whom Don Quixote had taken Mambrino's helmet and Sancho the trappings for his ass, came up to the inn. The said barber, as he was leading his beast out to the stable, chanced to catch sight of Sancho Panza, who was engaged in tinkering with his packsaddle, and the instant that he saw him he recognized him.

"Hah! Sir Thief," he cried, "I have you now! Give me back my basin and my packsaddle and all the other things you stole from me."

Sancho, being unexpectedly assailed in this manner and hearing himself called such names, with one hand laid hold of the packsaddle and with the other dealt the barber such a blow that he drenched his teeth in blood. The barber, however, did not for this reason let go his prize in the form of the packsaddle, but began shouting so loud that everybody in the place came running out to see what was the cause of all the uproar and the fighting.

"Here, in the name of the king's justice!" he screamed. "Not satisfied with taking my property, he wants to kill me, this robber, this highway bandit!"

"You lie," said Sancho. "I am not a bandit. My master Don Quixote won those spoils in honorable warfare."

The knight was standing by while this was going on and was greatly pleased to see how well his squire could both defend himself and take the offensive. From that time forth, he was to look upon him as a man of mettle, and he resolved in his heart that upon the first occasion that offered he would have him dubbed a knight, for he felt sure that the order of knighthood might worthily be bestowed upon him. The barber, meanwhile, was running on.

"Gentlemen," he was saying, "this packsaddle is mine, as surely as I owe it to God to die someday. I know it as well as if I had given birth to it. And there is my donkey in the stable; he will not let me lie. If you don't believe me, try it on him, and if it doesn't fit him perfectly, then I'm a rogue. What is more, the same day that he took the packsaddle he also robbed me of a brass basin which I had not yet broken in and which was worth all of a crown."

At this point Don Quixote, unable to contain himself any longer, stepped between the two and parted them, and then, picking up the packsaddle, he placed it upon the ground where all could see it that it might lie there until the truth was established.

"In order," he said, "that your Worships may behold plainly and clearly the error into which this worthy squire has fallen, you have but to observe that he calls a basin that which was, is, and shall be Mambrino's helmet, a trophy won by me in honorable warfare and of which I took lawful and rightful possession! As for the packsaddle, I have nothing to do with that. All I can say is that my squire, Sancho, begged permission of me to strip the mount belonging to this conquered coward of its trappings. To this I consented, and he did so. As to how those trappings came to be converted into a packsaddle, I can give no explanation other than the usual one: namely, that such transformations frequently occur in connection with the practice of chivalry. And by way of confirming all this, run, Sancho my lad, and bring me that helmet which this good man says is a basin."

"Good Lord!" exclaimed Sancho, "if that is all the proof we have that what your Grace says is true, then that basin is just as much Malino's [1] helmet as this good man's trappings are a packsaddle."

"Do what I command you," said Don Quixote; "for surely everything in this castle cannot be controlled by enchantments."

Sancho went for the basin and returned with it, and as soon as Don Quixote saw it he took it up in his hands.

"Your Worships," he said, "can see what cheek this squire has to say that this is a basin and not the helmet of which I have told you. I swear by the calling of knighthood which I follow that this is the same one I took from him and that I have neither added anything to nor subtracted anything from it."

"There can be no doubt of that," remarked Sancho at this point;

"for from the time my master won it until the present he has fought but one battle in it, and that was when he freed those poor unfortunate ones that were going along in chains; and if it had not been for this basin-helmet, it would have gone hard with him that time, for there were certainly enough stones thrown."

CHAPTER XLV. *In which the dispute over Mambrino's helmet and the packsaddle is finally settled, with other events that in all truth occurred.*

"WELL, gentlemen," said the barber, "and what do your Worships think of that which these fine fellows have to say, who still insist that this is not a basin but a helmet?"

"And if anyone states the contrary," maintained Don Quixote, "I will have him know that he lies, if he be a knight, and if he be a squire, that he lies a thousand times."

Our own barber, who had witnessed all this and who was well acquainted with Don Quixote's fancies, now decided to fall in with them and carry the joke a little further so that they might all have a good laugh.

"Master barber," he said, addressing the other one, "or whoever you may be, I may inform you that I also am of your profession and have held a license for more than twenty years, being quite familiar with each and every tool that a barber uses. And in my youth I was a soldier for some little while, and I likewise know what a helmet is, and a morion, and a closed helmet, along with other things having to do with a soldier's life. And I can tell you—standing always to be corrected by those of better judgment—that the piece we have before us here, which that worthy gentleman holds in his hands, is as far from being a barber's basin as white is from black or truth from falsehood; and I further assert that it is a helmet, though not a whole one."

"No, certainly not," agreed Don Quixote, "for half of it is missing, that is to say, the beaver."

"That is right," said the curate, who had already divined the intentions of his friend the barber.

Cardenio and Don Fernando and his companions confirmed this; and even the judge, had he not been so preoccupied with Don Luis' affair, would have helped carry on the jest, but, as it was, the weighty matters that he had on his mind prevented him from giving his attention to such trifles.

"God help me!" cried the barber of whom they were making sport. "Is it possible that so many worthy folk can say that this is not a basin but a helmet? It is enough to astonish an entire university, however learned it may be. But enough; if this basin is a helmet, then this saddlebag must be a horse's trappings, as this gentleman has just stated."

"It looks to me like a saddlebag," Don Quixote admitted, "but as I have said, it is something that does not concern me."

"As to whether it be a saddlebag or a horse's trappings," said the curate, "Don Quixote has but to give us his opinion, for in matters pertaining to chivalry, I and all these gentlemen bow to him."

"In God's name, my good folk," said Don Quixote, "so many strange things have happened in this castle on the two occasions that I have tarried here that I should not venture to give a positive reply to a question regarding anything that is in it, for it is my belief that all that takes place within its confines is the result of magic. The first time that I was here, there was an enchanted Moor who gave me a great deal of trouble, while Sancho did not make out any too well with some of his followers. And then, last night, I was strung up by this arm for nearly two hours without knowing how or why I came to be in such straits. And so, in a matter as far from clear as the present one, if I were to undertake to give an opinion, I should run the risk of rendering a rash decision. As to the charge that this is a basin and not a helmet, I have already answered that, but when it comes to declaring whether that is a saddlebag or a horse's trappings, I shall not venture to make any definite statement but shall leave it to your Worships' own good judgment. It may be that, inasmuch as you have not been dubbed knights as I have been, your Worships will not be subject to the enchantments of this place and, accordingly, your judgment being unimpaired, will be able to form an impression of things in this castle as they really and truly are and not as they appear to me to be."

"There is no doubt," said Don Fernando in reply to this, "that Don Quixote has put the case very well and that the decision rests with us; and in order that we may proceed upon firm ground, I will take the secret votes of these gentlemen and will announce the result plainly and fully."

To those acquainted with Don Quixote's mad whims, all this was very amusing indeed, but to the rest it seemed utter nonsense. This was especially true of Don Luis' four servants, and of their master as well, so far as that was concerned; besides whom there were three other travelers who had just arrived at the inn and who had the appearance of being patrolmen of the Holy Brotherhood, as in fact they were. The one, however, who was the most desperately bewildered of all was the barber, whose basin, there in front of his eyes, had turned into Mambrino's helmet, and whose packsaddle, also, he had not the slightest doubt, was due to turn into the rich caparison of a steed. The others, meanwhile, were laughing heartily as Don Fernando went around collecting the votes, whispering in the ear of each and asking him to give his private opinion as to whether the treasure over which there was so much dispute was a packsaddle or equine trappings.

Having obtained the votes of all those who knew Don Quixote, he turned to the barber and said, "The truth of the matter is, my good man, I am tired of gathering all these opinions; for there is not a one to whom I have put the question who has not assured me that it is nonsense to say that this is the packsaddle of an ass, when it is plain to be seen that it is the caparison of a horse and of a thoroughbred horse at that. And so there is nothing for you to do but yield, since in spite of you and your ass it is in fact a horse's trappings, and you have presented and proved your case very badly."

"May I forfeit my interest in Heaven!" cried the poor barber,[1] "if your Worships are not all mistaken. As my soul must appear before God, so does this appear to me to be a saddlebag; but 'laws go—'[2] I say no more; and I am not drunk, for I am fasting this morning—unless it be from sin."

These stupid remarks on the part of the barber aroused no less laughter than did Don Quixote's foolish talk; and it was now the knight's turn.

"There is nothing more to be done here," he announced, "except for each to take that which is his, and may St. Peter bless him to whom God has given it."

One of Don Luis' servants was the next to speak. "Unless this is a deliberate joke," he said, "I cannot believe that men of such good sense as all of those present are, or appear to be, would be so bold as to state and maintain that this is not a basin nor that a packsaddle; but inasmuch as I perceive that they do state and maintain it, I cannot but believe that there is some mystery behind their insistence upon something that is so contrary to what truth and experience teaches. For I swear"—and swear he did, a good round oath—"that all the people now living in the world will never convince me that this is not a barber's basin, and that, the packsaddle of an ass."

"It might be a she-ass," remarked the curate.

"It's all the same," said the servant. "That's not the point. The point is whether this is or, as your Graces say, is not a packsaddle."

Hearing this, one of the troopers who had come in and had been listening to the argument cried out angrily, "That is as much a packsaddle as my father is my father, and he who says anything else must be drunk."

"You lie like a peasant knave!" replied Don Quixote. And, raising his pike, which he never let out of his hands, he aimed such a blow at the trooper's head that if the officer had not dodged, it would have left him stretched out on the ground. The pike as it struck the ground was shattered to bits; whereupon the other officers, seeing their companion assaulted in this manner, cried out for help in the name of the Holy Brotherhood. The innkeeper, who was one of the band, at once ran to get his staff of office and his sword and, returning, took his place alongside his comrades. Don Luis' servants surrounded their master that he might not escape amid the excitement; and the barber, perceiving that the household was turned upside down, once more seized his packsaddle as Sancho did the same.

Drawing his sword, Don Quixote attacked the officers, while Don Luis cried to his servants to release him and go to the aid of the knight and of Cardenio and Don Fernando, both of whom were lending their support. The curate shouted, the landlady screamed, her daughter wailed, Maritornes wept, Dorotea was dumfounded, Luscinda terrified, and Doña Clara ready to faint. The barber cudgeled Sancho, and Sancho mauled the barber. Don Luis, when one of his servants seized his arm to keep him from running away, gave the fellow a punch that bloodied his mouth, and the judge came to the lad's defense. Don Fernando had a trooper down and was kicking him vigorously, and the innkeeper was again raising his voice to call for help for the Holy Brotherhood. In short, the entire hostelry was filled with shouts, cries, screams, with tumult, terror, and confusion, with sword slashes, fisticuffs, cudgelings, kickings, bloodshed, and mishaps of every sort. And in the midst of all this hubbub and labyrinthine chaos, Don Quixote came to imagine that he had been plunged headlong into the discord of Agramante's camp.[3]

"Hold, all of you!" he suddenly cried in a voice that rocked the inn like thunder. "Sheathe your swords, be calm, and hear me as you value your lives!"

At this mighty sound they all stopped short.

"Did I not tell you, gentlemen," he went on, "that this castle was enchanted and that it must be inhabited by some legion of devils? In confirmation of which, I would have you note how the strife that marked the camp of Agramante has been transferred and repeated here in front of your very eyes. Look you how here they fight for the sword, there for the horse, over there for the eagle, and there for the helmet. We are all engaged in fighting one another without knowing why. Come, then, your Lordship the judge and your Reverence the curate; let one of you take the part of King Agramante and the other that of King Sobrino, and make peace between us. For it is a very great shame for so many persons of high rank as are gathered here to be killing one another over causes so trifling."

The officers of the Brotherhood, who did not understand what Don Quixote was talking about, but who did know that they were being mishandled by Don Fernando, Cardenio, and their companions, were of no mind to calm themselves. The barber, however, was; for in the course of the fray both his beard and his packsaddle had suffered considerably. As for Sancho, he obeyed, as a good servant does, his master's slightest command, while Don Luis' four men likewise were quiet, seeing how little they had gained by not being so. The innkeeper alone was insisting that he had to punish the insolence of that madman who was all the time throwing his place into an uproar. But at last the tumult died down, the packsaddle remained a caparison and the basin a helmet until the Day of Judgment, and the inn was still a castle in Don Quixote's imagination.

When order had finally been restored and all of them, upon the persuasion of the curate and the judge, had become friends once more, Don Luis' servants began insisting that he go with them at once. While the lad went off to one side to discuss the matter with them, the judge took counsel with Fernando, Cardenio, and the curate as to what was to be done in the case, informing them of what Don Luis had told him. In the end, it was agreed that Fernando should reveal his identity to the men and say that it was his pleasure that their master should come with him to Andalusia, where his brother the marquis would show him the honor that was due to one of his rank; for it was plain to be seen that Don Luis had no intention of returning to his father just now, even though they hacked him to bits. Accordingly, when the four of them learned who Don Fernando was and saw how their master felt about it, they decided that three of their number should go back to inform the lad's father of how matters stood, while the fourth should remain to wait upon Don Luis, with the understanding that he was not to leave him until they returned or until it was known what the father's orders were.

In this manner, then, through the prestige of Agramante and the wisdom of King Sobrino, all the fighting at cross-purposes was finally quelled; but with this, the enemy of peace and concord, seeing himself thus despised and made sport of, and perceiving how little he had gained by setting them all against one another, resolved to try his hand once again by stirring up more strife and tumult.

As it happened, the officers of the Brotherhood had quieted down upon learning the rank of those with whom they were fighting and had been glad enough to retire from the fray, since it seemed to them that, whatever the outcome, they were bound to get the worst of it. One of them, however, the one who had been beaten and trampled by Don Fernando, chanced to remember that among the warrants he carried for the arrest of certain offenders was a writ for Don Quixote, whom the Holy Brotherhood had been instructed to apprehend on the charge of having freed the galley slaves, just as Sancho had rightly feared. An idea having come to him now, he wished to satisfy himself as to whether the knight answered the description that he had of him; and, taking a parchment out of his bosom, he found the document he was looking for and then began reading it slowly (for he was not a good reader), glancing up at every word to see if Don Quixote's features corresponded with those set down in the writ. Deciding that this was undoubtedly his man, he then took the parchment in his left hand and with his right seized Don Quixote by the collar so forcefully that he nearly choked him.

"Help for the Holy Brotherhood!" he cried in a loud voice. "And in order that you may see that I ask it in earnest, you have but to read this warrant where it is set forth that this highwayman is to be arrested."

The curate took the warrant and saw that what the officer said was true and that the description did indeed fit Don Quixote. But the knight, finding himself thus manhandled by this knavish boor, grew exceedingly angry and, with every bone in his body creaking, he seized the officer's throat with all the strength he could muster and would have choked the life out of him if the other troopers had not come to their comrade's rescue. The landlord, who was bound to render help to other members of the fraternity, now came running up, while his wife, believing her husband was again about to become involved in a fight, raised her voice and began screaming, in which she was at once joined by Maritornes and her daughter as all three of them called on Heaven and the others present to lend their aid.

"Good Lord!" cried Sancho, when he saw what was happening, "it is true what my master says about this castle being enchanted, for it is impossible to live an hour in peace here."

Don Fernando then separated the patrolman and Don Quixote, each of them being glad enough to have the other's firm grip released, on his jacket collar in the one case and on his throat in the other instance. The officers did not, however, for this reason give up their demand for the knight's arrest but insisted that the others help bind and deliver him into the hands of the law and thereby render a service to their king and to the Holy Brotherhood, in whose name they once more sought aid and assistance in effecting the capture of this highway bandit.

Don Quixote smiled as he heard these words. When he spoke, it was very calmly. "Come, now," he said, "you vile and lowborn wretches, do you call him a highwayman who gives freedom to those in chains, succors those who are in distress, lifts up the fallen, and brings aid to the needy? Ah, infamous rabble, by reason of your low and filthy minds you do not deserve that Heaven should reveal to you the true worth of knight-errantry and your own sin and ignorance when you fail to reverence the shadow, not to speak of the presence, of any knight-errant whatsoever! Come, come, you are a band of robbers, not of officers, footpads of the highway with the license of the Holy Brotherhood. Tell me, who was the ignorant one who signed that warrant for the arrest of such a knight as I am? Who is so ignorant as not to know that knights-errant are beyond all jurisdiction, their only law their swords, while their charter is their mettle and their will is their decrees?

"Who, I ask it again, is the stupid one who does not know that there are no letters-patent of nobility that confer such privileges and exemptions as those that a knight-errant acquires the day he is dubbed a knight and devotes himself to the rigorous duties of his calling? When did such a knight ever pay poll-tax, excise, queen's pattens, king's levies, toll, or ferry? What tailor ever took payment for the clothes he made for him? What castellan who received him in his castle ever made him pay his score? What king would not seat him at his board? What damsel but did love him, being ready to yield herself wholly to his will and pleasure? And, finally, what knight-errant was there ever, or ever will be in this world, without the mettle to deal singlehanded four hundred sturdy blows to any four hundred officers of the Holy Brotherhood that come his way?"

CHAPTER XLVI. *Wherein is concluded the notable adventure of the troopers, together with an account of the great ferocity of our good knight, Don Quixote.*

EVEN as Don Quixote spoke, the curate was endeavoring to convince the officers that the knight was not in his right mind, as they should be able to see from what he said and did, and that, accordingly, they ought to let the matter drop, since even though they did arrest him and take him away, they would only have to turn him loose again as being a madman. To which the one who held the warrant replied that it was not for him to judge Don Quixote's sanity but rather to carry out the orders of his superior, adding that once he had made the arrest, they might let him go three hundred times over if they chose.

"Nevertheless," said the curate, "for this once you are not going to take him, nor will he permit himself to be taken unless I miss my guess."

The short of it is, the curate was so very persuasive, and Don Quixote so very mad in his actions, that the troopers would have been even madder than he was had they not recognized his want of wit. And so they thought it best to allow themselves to be pacified and even to act as peacemakers between the barber and Sancho Panza, who were still engaged in a heated quarrel. As the representatives of the law they proceeded to arbitrate the dispute and did it in such a manner that both parties were, if not wholly, at least somewhat satisfied; for they exchanged the packsaddles but not the girths nor the headstalls. As for Mambrino's helmet, the curate quietly, and without Don Quixote's knowledge, gave the barber eight reales for it, obtaining from him a receipt with the understanding that he was to make no more mistaken demands, for the present or for all time to come, Amen.

These two disputes, which were the most important ones, having been settled, it remained for the three of Don Luis' servants to consent to take their departure while the fourth remained to accompany his master wherever Don Fernando might conduct him. And now that good luck and better fortune had begun to shatter lances and remove obstacles in favor of the lovers and the brave ones of the inn, fate appeared bent upon bringing everything to a happy conclusion; for the servants proved amenable to all that Don Luis asked of them, which gave Doña Clara so much satisfaction that none could look upon her face without being aware of the joy that was in her heart.

As for Zoraida, although she did not thoroughly comprehend all the happenings she witnessed, she nonetheless became sad or joyful to fit the mood of each of the others, and especially that of her beloved Spaniard on whom her eyes and heart were ever fixed. The landlord, in the meanwhile, had not failed to observe [1] the gift which the curate had made to the barber by way of recompense, and he now asked Don Quixote to pay for his lodging and also to reimburse him for the wine skins and the wine that had been spilled, swearing that neither Rocinante nor Sancho's ass [2] would leave the place until he had had the last penny that was due him. The curate, however, set everything to rights, and Don Fernando paid what was owing, with the judge very kindly offering to do the same. In this fashion peace was made between them all and quiet reigned, the inn no longer presenting the discordant aspect of Agramante's camp, as Don Quixote had put it, but rather suggesting the calm and tranquillity of the time of Octavianus.[3] And for this, all were agreed that thanks were to be given to the curate for his great eloquence and good will and to Don Fernando for his incomparable liberality.

Finding himself at last free and disembarrassed of all these disputes, those of his squire as well as his own, Don Quixote reflected that it would be a good thing to continue with the journey he had begun and bring to a conclusion the great adventure for which he had been called and chosen. With this firm resolve, he went and knelt before Dorotea, who would not permit him to say a word until he had risen, which he, to comply with her wishes, then did.

"Lovely lady," he said, "it is a common proverb that diligence is the mother of good fortune, and experience has shown in many and grave instances how the faithful application of the one engaged in it may bring to a successful close a doubtful undertaking. But in no case is this truth more apparent than in war, where swiftness and decision forestall the plans of the enemy and carry off the victory before he has had a chance to put himself upon the defensive. All this I say to you, O highborn and highly esteemed lady, for the reason that our stay in this castle appears to me to be a profitless one and may even result in very great harm to us as we shall someday discover. For who knows but that your enemy, the giant, through hidden spies who are ever at work, has already learned that I am coming to destroy him and is already fortifying himself in some inexpugnable castle or fortress against which all my efforts and the might of my tireless arm will avail me little? And so, my lady, let us with a show of diligence on our own part anticipate his designs by setting out at once in quest of that good fortune which your Highness desires and is only prevented from enjoying by my delay in confronting your foe."

The knight said no more but waited very composedly for the beauteous infanta's response; and she, with highbred manner that suited Don Quixote's own speech and bearing, thereupon spoke as follows:

"I thank you, Sir Knight, for the eagerness you have shown to aid me in my distress, as appertains to the calling of one whose duty it is to succor the orphan and the needy; and I pray to Heaven that your and my desire be fulfilled, so that you may see that there are women in this world who are capable of gratitude. As to what you say concerning our departure, let it be at once, for I have no will other than yours. Dispose of me as you may wish and deem best; for she who once has placed in your hands the defense of her person and the restoration of her royal holdings should not desire anything that is contrary to what you in your wisdom may ordain."

"Then let it be in the hands of God," said Don Quixote; "for when a lady [4] humbles herself to me, I would not lose the opportunity to raise her up and set her on her ancestral throne. Let us depart at once; the danger that lies in delay lends spurs to my eagerness to take the road. And seeing that Heaven hath not created nor Hell seen anyone who could frighten or make a coward of me, saddle Rocinante, Sancho, and harness your ass and the queen's palfrey, and let us bid farewell to the castellan and these gentlefolk and go hence immediately."

Sancho, who was taking all this in, wagged his head from side to side. "Ah, master, master," he said, "there's more mischief in the little village than you hear talked of, [5] begging the pardon of all good folks."

"What mischief could there be, you bumpkin, in any village or in all the cities of the world that could possibly harm my good name?"

"If your Grace is going to be angry," replied Sancho, "I shall keep still and leave unsaid that which I feel obliged to say and which a good servant ought to say to his master."

"Say whatever you like," Don Quixote told him, "for your words do not frighten me. When you are afraid, you are being yourself, and when I am not afraid, I am being the person that I am."

"That," said Sancho, "is not what I am talking about. I merely meant to tell you that I know it to be a fact that this lady who claims to be queen of the great kingdom of Micomicon is no more a queen than my mother is; for if she was what she says, she would not be rubbing noses with a certain one who is here, every time you turn your head, and behind every door."

Dorotea's face turned red at Sancho's words; for it was true that her husband, Don Fernando, when the others were not looking, had claimed with his lips a part of the reward that his affection merited, and Sancho, happening to espy them, had thought that such free and easy manners were more becoming in a courtesan than in a great and mighty queen. As a result, she did not know what reply to make, but let him run on.

"I tell you this, my master," he was saying, "for a very good reason. If after we have roamed the highways and the byways and spent bad days and worse nights, the one who is having his sport here in this inn is to come and gather the fruit of our labors, then I do not see why I should be in any hurry to saddle Rocinante, put the packsaddle on the ass, and get the palfrey ready; for it would be better if we stayed here and let every wench mind her spinning [6] while we go to dinner."

Heaven help me, what a rage was Don Quixote's when he heard these disrespectful words from his squire! So great was it that his eyes darted fire, as with stuttering, stammering tongue he turned on Sancho.

"O knavish lout!" he cried, "O villainous, insolent, ignorant, foul-mouthed, loose-tongued backbiter and slanderer! How dare you utter such words in my presence and that of these ladies? How dare you let such immodest and shameless thoughts enter that muddled head of yours? Go from my presence, O monstrous deformity of nature, depository of lies, storehouse of deceits, granary of villainies, inventor of iniquities, publisher of absurdities, and enemy of that respect that is due to royal personages! Begone and do not appear before me again under pain of my wrath!"

As he said this, Don Quixote arched his brows, puffed out his cheeks, glared all around him, and stamped on the ground with his right foot as hard as he could as a manifestation of the pent-up rage within him. Sancho was so intimidated and terrified by the knight's furious words and bearing that he would have been glad if at that instant the earth had opened beneath his feet and swallowed him up. He did not know what to do and was about to turn his back and leave the presence of his irate master when the clever-minded Dorotea, who by this time understood very well Don Quixote's whims, took a hand in the matter.

"Sir Knight of the Mournful Countenance," she began by way of appeasing his anger, "be not wroth at the foolish things your squire has just said. It may be that he has some reason for saying them, for his good sense and Christian conscience are such that he is not to be suspected of bearing false witness against anyone. And hence we are to believe, and indeed there is no doubt about it, since everything in this castle happens by way of enchantment as you yourself have stated, Sir Knight —we are to believe that Sancho must have been led by diabolic means to see that which he says he beheld and which is so great an offense to my honor."

"I swear by almighty God!" exclaimed Don Quixote at this point, "that your Highness has hit upon it, and that some evil vision must have appeared before this sinner of a Sancho that caused him to see what it would have been impossible to behold through any other means than those of magic; for I am well acquainted with the poor fellow's simplicity and goodheartedness, and I know that he would not willingly be guilty of slander."

"So it is and so it shall be," said Don Fernando; "and for that reason, Sir Don Quixote, your Grace ought to pardon him and restore him to the bosom of your favor, *sicut erat in principio*—as he was before such visions as these had deprived him of his senses."

The knight agreed to this, and the curate went in search of Sancho, who came back very humbly and, falling on his knees, asked for his master's hand to kiss, a request that was granted him.

"And now, Sancho my son," said Don Quixote as he gave him his blessing, "you will realize that it is true what I have told you so many times, that everything in this castle is under a magic spell."

"I can well believe it," said Sancho, "that is, everything except that business with the blanket, which happened in the ordinary way."

"Do not think that," said Don Quixote, "for if such were the case,

I should have avenged you, and should do so even now; but it was not possible then, and it is not possible now, to exact any vengeance for the wrong that was done you."

They all immediately wanted to know what this affair of the blanket was, and the innkeeper gave them the story in all its details, describing how Sancho had gone flying up in the air, at which they laughed not a little. The victim of the blanketing would have been quite as angry as they were amused, if Don Quixote had not once more assured him that it was all magic. His simple-mindedness, however, never reached the point where he could be brought to believe that it was not an established fact and the purest, unadulterated truth that he had indeed been tossed in a blanket by flesh-and-blood beings rather than by phantoms that he had dreamed or conjured up in his imagination as his master believed and maintained.

Two days had now gone by since all this illustrious company was gathered in the inn, and it seemed to them all that it was high time to be on their way. It was accordingly agreed that, without putting Dorotea and Don Fernando to the trouble of accompanying Don Quixote to his native village, under pretext of liberating the Queen Micomicona, the curate and the barber instead should take the knight with them as they had suggested, and once they had got him safely home, they would see what could be done about curing his madness. With this object in view, they proceeded to arrange with an ox-cart driver who chanced to be passing that way to bear their friend off in the following manner: first, they constructed a kind of cage with wooden bars, capable of holding him comfortably; after which, Don Fernando and his companions, along with Don Luis' servants, the troopers, and the landlord, all of them acting under the curate's direction, covered their faces and disguised themselves in one fashion or another so that Don Quixote would not recognize them as his acquaintances of the inn.

Having done this, they very quietly entered the room where he lay sleeping and resting from his recent frays, wholly unsuspecting of anything of this sort. Going up to him, they seized him firmly and bound him hand and foot, so that when he awoke with a start, he was unable to move or do anything except marvel at finding himself surrounded by so many strange faces. As a result, his disordered mind at once began to fancy that all these figures were phantoms of that enchanted castle and that he himself, without a doubt, was under a magic spell, seeing that he could not move nor defend himself. All of which was just as the curate, the originator of this scheme, had planned it.

Sancho alone of all those present was at once in his right mind and proper character, and while he was near to being as mad as his master, he did not fail to recognize these disguised figures; but he did not dare open his mouth until he saw what the outcome of this assault and capture would be. As for Don Quixote, he said not a word, for he too was waiting to see what was going to happen to him further. What happened was: they took him to the cage and shut him in it, nailing the bars so firmly that they could not easily be broken down.

As they lifted him on their shoulders and bore him from the room, there was heard an awe-inspiring voice—as much so as the barber (not he of the packsaddle but the other one) could make it.

"O Knight of the Mournful Countenance, be not grieved by the prison in which thou goest, for it is a fitting thing in order that thou mayest the sooner bring to a conclusion the adventure to which thy great courage hath impelled thee. That shall be when the raging Manchegan lion [7] and the white Tobosan dove shall have been made one, after they shall have bowed their proud necks to the gentle yoke of matrimony. And from this mating, of a kind that never was before, shall come forth into the light of this world brave whelps which shall emulate the ravening claws of their valiant sire. And this shall be ere the pursuer of the fleeing nymph in his swift and natural course shall twice have visited the luminous signs.

"And thou, O noblest and most obedient squire that ever girded on a sword, wore a beard on his face, or had a nose to smell with! be thou not dismayed nor unhappy at thus beholding the flower of knight-errantry borne away in front of your very eyes; for soon, if it be pleasing to Him who fashioned this world, thou shalt see thyself raised to so sublime a height that thou shalt not know thyself, nor shalt thou be defrauded of all the promises which thy good master hath made thee. And be assured on the part of the wise Mentironiana [8] that thou shalt be paid thy wages, as thou shalt see in due course. Do thou, then, continue to follow in the footsteps of this valiant and enchanted knight; for it behooves thee to go whither both of you are bound. It is not permitted me to say more; and so, may God be with thee, for I now return to the place that I well know."

As he concluded this prophecy, the barber raised and lowered his voice with so intense an emotional effect that even those who knew it to be a jest almost believed that it was the truth they heard. Don Quixote was greatly consoled by these predictions, for he at once grasped their purport, to the effect that he was to be united in holy and lawful bonds of matrimony with his beloved Dulcinea del Toboso, from whose fortunate loins should come forth whelps that were his sons, to the perpetual glory of La Mancha. Thoroughly imbued with this belief, he heaved a deep sigh and, lifting up his voice, he spoke as follows:

"O thou, whoever thou art, who hast prophesied all these blessings for me! I implore thee on my behalf to ask the wise enchanter who hath these things in his charge not to allow me to perish in this captivity in which they now bear me away before I shall have seen fulfilled all the joyful and incomparable promises that have just been made me. Let this be granted me and I shall glory in the sufferings of my prison house, my chains will be light indeed, and this bed upon which they lay me will be, not a hard-fought battlefield, but a soft and happy nuptial couch. As for the consolation that has been offered to Sancho Panza, my squire, I can only say that I rely upon his goodness and integrity, trusting him never to leave me in good fortune or in bad. And if by his or my own ill luck I should not be able to give him the island or some equivalent fief as I have promised, at least his wages shall not be forfeited; for in my will, which is already drawn up, I have declared that which is to be his, not in proportion to his many and faithful services, but in accordance with my means."

At this Sancho bowed most respectfully and kissed both his master's hands, it being impossible for him to kiss but one of them as they were tied together. Then those phantom figures put the cage upon their shoulders and carried it out and placed it on the ox-cart.

CHAPTER XLVII. *Of the strange manner in which a spell was laid on Don Quixote de la Mancha,*[1] *together with other remarkable occurrences.*

WHEN Don Quixote found himself caged in this manner and placed upon the cart, he spoke as follows:

"Many very grave histories have I read of knights-errant, but never have I read, seen, or heard of enchanted knights being borne away in this fashion and at the slow pace that these lazy animals seem likely to provide; for it is the custom to spirit them through the air, with marvelous speed, wrapped in some dark, dense cloud or upon a chariot of fire or some hippogriff or other similar beast. But that they should now be taking me upon an ox-cart, Heaven help me, that is something I cannot understand![2] However, it may be that chivalry and the art of magic in this our time must follow another path than the one it did in days gone by. And it may also be that, inasmuch as I am a new knight in this world, the first to revive the forgotten calling of knightly adventurers, they may likewise have invented other means of enchantment and other ways of carrying off the enchanted. What do you think of it, Sancho, my son?"

"I don't know what I think," replied Sancho, "not being as well read as is your Grace in the writings of errantry. But for all of that, I'd venture to swear and affirm that those apparitions are not altogether Catholic."[3]

"Catholic? My father!" said Don Quixote. "How can they be Catholic if they are all demons who have assumed fantastic shapes in order to do this thing and put me in this condition? If you would ascertain the truth, you have but to touch and feel them and you will perceive that they have none but an airy body and consist only of appearances."

"By God, sir," Sancho answered him, "I've already touched them, and that devil you see bustling along there is as plump as can be and it's real flesh that's on him; and there is something else about him that is very different from what I have heard tell of demons, for they say that they all stink of sulphur and other evil smells, but you can scent the amber on this one half a league away."

He was speaking of Don Fernando, who as a gentleman must of necessity give off the odor that Sancho had mentioned.

"You need not marvel at that, friend Sancho," said Don Quixote; "for I would have you know that the devils are very wise, and while they bear odors with them, they themselves smell of nothing, since, being spirits, they can emit no scent whatsoever, or if they do smell, it is not of anything pleasant but rather something evil and fetid. The reason for this is that, wherever they may be, they bring with them Hell itself and can receive no manner of comfort in their torments; and inasmuch as a pleasing fragrance is something that gives delight and happiness, it is obviously impossible for them to be possessed of such a thing. Accordingly, if this devil appears to you to smell of amber, either you are mistaken or he is trying to deceive you so that you will not take him to be a devil."

As this conversation occurred between master and man, Don Fernando and Cardenio began to fear that Sancho would discover the entire plot, for he had already gone a long way toward doing so. They therefore decided to hasten their departure and, calling the landlord to one side, they directed him to saddle Rocinante and put the packsaddle on Sancho's ass, which he did very quickly. The curate, meanwhile, had arranged with the troopers to accompany them as far as the village, promising to pay them so much a day. Cardenio then hung the buckler on one side of the saddletree and the basin on the other and made signs to Sancho to mount his ass and take Rocinante's rein, while the two troopers[4] with their muskets were placed one on either side of the cart. Before that vehicle could get under way, however, the landlady, her daughter, and Maritornes came running out to say good-by to Don Quixote, shedding feigned tears of sorrow over his plight.

"Do not weep, my good ladies," he now said to them, "for all these misfortunes are such as go with the calling that I profess; indeed, if they did not befall me, I should not look upon myself as a famous knight-errant. Such things never happen to knights of little name and reputation for the reason that no one in the world gives them a thought. With the valiant ones it is otherwise, for many princes and many other knights envy them their virtue and their valor and are bent upon destroying the worthy by foul means. But in spite of all this, virtue is omnipotent and, notwithstanding all the necromancy that Zoroaster, first inventor of the art,[5] ever knew, will emerge triumphant from every peril and bestow light on the world as does the sun in the heavens.

Forgive me, fair ladies, if, without meaning to do so, I have given you any offense, for I would not willingly and knowingly offend anyone. Pray, then, to God to rescue me from this captivity in which some enchanter of evil intent has placed me; and when I am free, I will by no means forget the favors which you in this castle have shown me, but will acknowledge, requite, and reward them as they deserve."

While the ladies of the castle were conversing with Don Quixote, the curate and the barber were taking their leave of Don Fernando and his companions, the captain and his brother, and all those happy damsels, particularly Dorotea and Luscinda. They all embraced one another and agreed to keep in touch by letter, Don Fernando telling the curate where to write to inform him of the outcome of Don Quixote's case, as nothing would give him more pleasure than this. For his part, Fernando promised to send back any news that might be of interest pertaining to his marriage as well as Zoraida's baptism, the upshot of Don Luis' affair, and Luscinda's return home. The curate gave his assurance that he would comply most faithfully with all that was asked of him, and then, with another exchange of embraces, they renewed their promises all over again.

The innkeeper at this point came up to the curate and handed him some papers, saying he had found them in the lining of the trunk where the *Story of the One Who Was Too Curious for His Own Good* had been discovered; and, seeing that their owner had not returned for them, he told the priest to take them all, as he himself did not know how to read and so did not care to keep them. The curate thanked him and, opening the manuscript at once, he saw that the title was *The Story of Riconete and Cortadillo*,[6] from which he gathered that it was a work of fiction; and since *The One Who Was Too Curious* had afforded such pleasant reading, he assumed that this must also be an interesting tale, as there was a possibility that they were by the same author, and so he kept it with the intention of reading it later when he had an opportunity.

He then mounted his horse and the barber did the same, both wearing their masks in order not to be recognized by Don Quixote; whereupon the entire party fell in, alongside and behind the ox-cart, in the following formation: first came the cart, driven by its owner; at the sides were the two officers of the Holy Brotherhood with their muskets, as has been stated; Sancho Panza then followed on his ass, leading Rocinante; and bringing up the rear were the curate and the barber upon their sturdy mules, their faces covered in the manner described as they solemnly rode along, suiting their pace to that of the oxen. Seated in the cage was Don Quixote, who with his hands bound and his feet stretched out, leaned patiently back against the bars, preserving a silence so complete that it seemed he was not a flesh-and-blood being but rather a stone statue.

They had proceeded thus slowly and silently for a matter of two leagues when they came to a valley which impressed the carter as being a good place to rest and feed his oxen, and he suggested to the curate that they halt there. The barber, however, spoke up and said that he thought they should go a little farther because he knew of a valley beyond a near-by slope where there was more and much better grass than was to be found here. And so, having decided to take his advice, they set out again.

Turning his head, the curate now saw six or seven horsemen, all of them well equipped and accoutered, riding up behind them. The cavalcade was soon upon them, for these men rode, not as those who must accommodate their pace to the sluggish gait of oxen, but rather as those do who go mounted on canons' mules, spurred by the desire to reach the inn as soon as possible for their noontide repose, for the hostelry was already in sight half a league away. In such manner did the ones who made haste overtake the ones who were compelled to lag. There was a courteous exchange of greetings, and then one of the newcomers, who was, as a matter of fact, a canon of Toledo and the superior of the others, upon beholding the slow and solemn ox-cart procession—the troopers, Sancho, Rocinante, the curate and the barber, and finally Don Quixote caged and imprisoned—could not refrain from asking what the purpose was in transporting the man in such a fashion, although he had already assumed from a sight of the officers' insignia that the fellow must be some villainous highwayman or other criminal who came under the jurisdiction of the Holy Brotherhood.

"Sir," replied one of the troopers to whom he had put the question, "he himself will have to answer that, for we do not know."

Hearing this, Don Quixote addressed the canon's party. "Gentlemen," he said, "are your Worships by any chance versed and skilled in what pertains to knight-errantry? For if you are, I can tell you of my misfortunes; but if you are not, there is no reason why I should put myself to the trouble."

In the meantime, seeing the travelers engaged in conversation with Don Quixote de la Mancha, the curate and the barber had come forward that they might answer the questions in such a way that their artifice would not be discovered.

"In truth, my brother," said the canon, for it was to him that the knight had directed his remarks, "I know more about books of chivalry than I do about Villalpando's *Compendium;* [7] and so, if that is the only thing that stands in the way, you may freely tell me anything that you desire."

"So be it, then, in Heaven's name," replied Don Quixote. "Sir," he went on, "I would inform you that I am being carried away enchanted in this cage as a result of the envy and deceit of wicked magicians; for virtue is more persecuted by the wicked than loved by the good. A knight-errant am I, and not one of those whom fame never thought of immortalizing in her annals. I am, rather, of that number who, in spite of the envy of which I have spoken, in spite of all the Magi that Persia has spawned, all the Brahmans that India has produced, all the gymnosophists [8] that have come out of Ethiopia, are destined to leave their names in the temple of immortality that they may serve as examples and as models for ages to come, wherein knights-errant may behold the paths they have to follow if it be their desire to attain the highest peak and pinnacle of honor in their pursuit of the calling of arms."

"Don Quixote de la Mancha speaks the truth," the curate put in, "when he tells you that he goes enchanted upon this cart, not through any fault or sin of his own, but owing to the ill will of those whom virtue annoys and valor angers. This, sir, is the Knight of the Mournful Countenance, whose name you may have heard upon occasion and whose brave deeds and great exploits shall be recorded in enduring bronze and eternal marble, no matter how tirelessly envy may seek to obscure them and malice endeavor to keep them hidden."

When the canon heard both the prisoner and the one who walked free beside him speak in this manner, he was ready to cross himself from astonishment and could not believe his own ears, while all his companions were equally amazed. Then it was that Sancho Panza, who had drawn near to listen to their talk, put the finishing touch on it all.

"Well, sirs," he said, "whether or not you like what I am going to say, the fact is that my master, Don Quixote, is no more enchanted than my mother, for he has all his senses about him and eats and drinks and attends to his necessities like the rest of us, just as he did yesterday before they put him in this cage. This being so, how would you have me believe that he is enchanted? For I have heard many people say that those that are under a magic spell neither eat nor sleep nor speak whereas my master, if you do not take him in hand, will do more talking than thirty lawyers."

Turning, then, to look the curate in the face, he went on, "Ah, Señor Curate! Señor Curate! So, your Grace thought I didn't know you and that I would not guess what the purpose of these new enchantments is? Well, then, I can tell you that I recognize you no matter how much you cover your face and that I know what you are up to no matter how cleverly and deceitfully you attempt to hide it. In short, where envy reigns virtue cannot live, nor generosity where there is miserliness. Devil take it all, if it wasn't for your Reverence, my master would be getting married to the Princess Micomicona right now and I would be a count at the very least, since I could expect no less from my kind-hearted master, him of the Mournful Countenance, after all that I have done for him. But now I see that it is true what they say hereabouts, that fortune's wheel turns faster than that of a mill,[9] and those that yesterday were up on top today are down on the ground.

"It grieves me to think about my wife and children, who rightly expect to see their father and husband returning home and coming through the door as governor or viceroy of some island or kingdom, and instead they will see him coming in as a stable boy. All this that I am saying to you, Señor Curate, is by way of urging your Paternity to have a conscience and not treat my master so badly as you are doing; for look well to it that God in the other life does not ask you to account for holding Señor Don Quixote a prisoner like this, and hold you responsible for all the good my master might have done and the aid he might have given others during all this time."

"Trim those lamps for me!"[10] cried the barber at this point. "So you, Sancho, are of the same confraternity as your master, are you? Good lord, but I'm beginning to think you ought to be in the cage there with him, for you're as much bewitched as he is when it comes to the subject of chivalry! It was an evil day for you when your brains became impregnated with all those promises that he made you and you got that island into your head that you've so set your heart on."

"I'm not pregnant by anybody," declared Sancho, "nor am I the man to let myself be put in that condition by any king that ever lived. I may be poor, but I'm an old Christian and I don't owe anyone anything. If I want islands, there are others who want worse things. Each one is the son of his own works, and being a man I may come to be pope,[11] not to speak of being governor of an island; for my master may win so many that there will not be people enough to give them to. Sir Barber, you had better watch what you say, for there is some difference between Peter and Peter.[12] I say this because we all know one another and it won't do to throw false dice with me. And as for my master's being enchanted, God knows the truth, so leave it as it is, for it is better not to stir it."

The barber did not care to answer Sancho for fear that the latter in his simple-mindedness would reveal what he and the curate were trying so hard to conceal. It was the same consideration that led the curate to suggest to the canon that they ride on a little way ahead, where he would explain to him the mystery of the man in the cage along with other things that would interest him. The canon accompanied by his servants accordingly did so and listened most attentively to all that was told him regarding Don Quixote's life, his madness, and his habits, along with a brief account of the beginning and cause of his derangement, the course of events which had led up to his being placed in that cage, and the plan they had for taking him back home to see if some remedy could be found for the form of insanity from which he suffered. Both the canon and his attendants marveled afresh at this strange history, and when it was finished, the churchman voiced his view of the matter.

"Truly, Señor Curate," he said, "it is my opinion that those so-called books of chivalry are harmful to the well-being of the state. And while it is true that, out of idle curiosity and a false sense of pleasure, I have read the beginning of nearly all that have been printed, I have never been able to read any of them from beginning to end, for it seems to me that they are all more or less the same and one is worth about as much as another. As I see it, this species of writing and composition is in the same class with what are called Milesian fables,[13] which are non-sensical tales designed solely to amuse and not to instruct, in which respect they are unlike those apologues which afford entertainment and instruction at one and the same time. Granting, even, that the chief purpose of such works is to amuse, I do not see how it can be achieved when they are so full of monstrous nonsense.

"For that beauty which the soul conceives," he went on, "must come from the beauty and harmony that it beholds or contemplates in those things that are presented to it by sight or by the imagination, and nothing that is ugly or inharmonious can give us any pleasure whatsoever. Well, then, I ask you, what beauty can there be, or what proportion of parts with the whole or of the whole with its parts, in a book or fable in which a seventeen-year-old lad slashes a giant tall as a tower and cuts him in half as if he were a sugar-pastry? And when they go to depict a battle scene for us, although we may have been told that there are a million fighting men on the enemy's side, nevertheless, let the hero of the book be against them and of necessity, whether we like it or not, we have to believe that the knight in question carried off the victory single-handed, by virtue of his mighty arm.

"Then, what shall we say of the readiness with which a hereditary queen or empress throws herself into the arms of an unknown knight-errant? Could any person, save one with a barbarous and uncultivated mind, find pleasure in reading that a great tower filled with knights goes sailing over the sea like a ship with a favoring wind and is tonight in Lombardy and tomorrow morning in the land of Prester John of the Indies,[14] or in other domains such as Ptolemy never discovered and Marco Polo never laid eyes on? And if you should answer me by saying that those who write such books offer them to us as fiction and hence are not obliged to observe the fine points of the truth, I should reply that the falsehood is all the greater when it appears in the guise of truth, and that as fiction, the more it contains of the pleasing [15] and the possible the more it delights us.

"For in works of fiction there should be a mating between the plot and the reader's intelligence. They should be so written that the impossible is made to appear possible, things hard to believe being smoothed over and the mind held in suspense in such a manner as to create surprise and astonishment while at the same time they divert and entertain so that admiration and pleasure go hand in hand. But these are things which he cannot accomplish who flees verisimilitude and the imitation of nature, qualities that go to constitute perfection in the art of writing.

"Never," concluded the canon, "have I seen any book of chivalry that held the body of a story completely with all its members so that the middle was consistent with the beginning and the end with the beginning and the middle. Rather, they are made up of so many disparate members that it would seem the author's intention was to create a chimera or a monster rather than a well-proportioned figure. In addition to all this, they are crude in style, unconvincing in the exploits that they relate, lascivious in the love affairs that they portray, uncouth in their efforts at courtliness, prolix in their descriptions of battles, absurd in their dialogue, nonsensical in their accounts of journeyings, and, finally, destitute of anything that resembles art; for which reason it is they deserve to be banished from the Christian state as not being of public utility."

The curate had listened to all this very closely, for the canon impressed him as being a man of sound understanding who was right in what he said. He now told him that he was of the same opinion and, having a grudge against such works, had burned all those that Don Quixote possessed, of which there were a great many. He then went on to relate how he had gone through all the books in the knight's library, mentioning those that he had condemned to the flames and those that he had let live, at which the canon laughed not a little.

But for all the harsh things that he had said of such books, the canon added, he had found one good thing about them, and that was the chance they afforded for a good mind to display its true worth, for they offered a broad and spacious field over which the author's pen might run without impediment, describing shipwrecks, tempests, battles, and encounters; depicting a valiant captain with all the qualities requisite to such a character, showing him as prudent, capable of anticipating the stratagems of the enemy, an eloquent orator in persuading or dissuading his soldiers, exhibiting a ripened wisdom in council, quick in making decisions, and as brave when it came to biding his time as he was in the attack; the author could relate now a lamentable and tragic event and now some joyful and unexpected occurrence; he could picture here a lovely lady, modest, discreet, and reserved, and there a Christian knight, gentle and brave, setting a lawless, barbarous braggart over against a prince, courtly, valorous, and benign, letting us see at once the loyalty and devotion of the vassals and the greatness and generosity of their lords.

The author might further show himself to be an astrologer, an excellent cosmographer, a musician, a student of statecraft, or even upon occasion, if he chose, a necromancer. He might take as his theme the astuteness of Ulysses, the filial piety of Aeneas, the bravery of Achilles, the woes of Hector, the treasons of Sinon,[16] the friendship of Euryalus,[17] the liberality of Alexander, the valor of Caesar, the clemency and truthfulness of Trajan, the fidelity of Zopyrus,[18] the prudence of Cato—in short, all those attributes that go to make an illustrious man perfect, as shown sometimes in a single individual and other times as shared among many. All of which being done in an easy-flowing style, with a skilled inventiveness that draws insofar as possible upon the truth of things, the result would surely be a web woven of beautiful and variegated threads,[19] one which when completed would exhibit such a perfected beauty of form as to attain the most worth-while goal of all writing, which as I have said is at once to instruct and to entertain. These books, indeed, by their very nature, provided the author with an unlimited field in which

to try his hand at the epic, lyric, tragic, and comic genres and depict in
turn all the moods that are represented by these most sweet and pleasing
branches of poetry and oratory; for the epic may be written in prose as
well as in verse.

CHAPTER XLVIII. *In which the canon continues his discourse on the subject of books of chivalry, with other matters worthy of his intelligence.*

"IT IS as your Grace has said, Señor Canon," remarked the curate,
"and for that reason they are all the more deserving of reprehension who
up to now have composed such books without giving any thought to
good taste or the rules of art by which they might have been guided
and thereby have rendered themselves as famous in prose as the two
princes of Greek and Latin poetry are in verse."

"However that may be," replied the canon, "I myself was once
tempted to write a book of chivalry, observing all the points that I have
mentioned; and if I am to confess the truth, I have more than a hundred
sheets already written. By way of putting them to the test and seeing
if they were as good as I thought they were, I have submitted them to
certain individuals who are passionately fond of this type of reading.
Some of these persons were wise and learned, while others were ignorant, being concerned solely with the pleasure they derive from listening to nonsense, but all of them were warmly appreciative of my effort.
I did not go on, however, for it seemed to me, on the one hand, that I
was engaged in doing something that was foreign to my profession, and,
on the other hand, the foolish impressed me as being more numerous
than the wise; and while the praise of the discerning few offsets [1] the
scorn of the unknowing many, I still did not care to subject myself to
the confused judgment of that vapid public to which the reading of
such works is for the most part confined.

"But what did most to stay my hand and even caused me to give up
all thought of finishing what I had begun was an argument that I put to

myself, drawn from the comedies that are now being performed. It ran as follows: All of these pieces, or the greater part of them at any rate, whether purely fictitious or historical in character, are obviously non-sensical, without head or tail, yet the public takes pleasure in witnessing them and regards them as worthy productions, though they are far from good. And the authors who compose them and the actors who perform them tell us that plays have to be of this sort, since the public wants precisely that kind of thing and nothing else, whereas those pieces that have a plot and develop the story in an artistic fashion will appeal only to a handful of intelligent persons who are able to understand them, while all the others will fail to perceive the art that is in them. This being so, they—the authors and actors—prefer to gain their bread with the many rather than subsist on the good opinion of the few. In which case, my book, after I should have scorched my eyebrows in an attempt to observe the precepts I have mentioned, would meet with the same fate as other works of merit, and I should end up by being the tailor of Campillo.[2]

"Although I have a number of times endeavored to persuade the actors [3] that they are wrong in the view they hold, and that they would attract more people and win more fame for themselves by producing comedies that follow the rules of art than they do by performing in these silly ones, they are so firmly set in their opinion that no amount of reasoning or evidence will convince them that they are wrong. I remember saying to one of the stubborn fellows once upon a time: 'Do you not recall that, only a few years ago, there were three tragedies put upon the boards here in Spain, written by a famous poet of this realm, which were so pleasing as to arouse the admiration and hold the interest of all who heard them, the simple as well as the wise, the general public as well as the select few, and which brought in more money to the performers—these three alone—than thirty of the best that up to then had been produced?'

" 'You mean, of course,' the author [4] replied, 'the *Isabella*, the *Phyllis*, and the *Alexandra*?' [5]

" 'Yes,' I said, 'those are the ones of which I am speaking; and see if they do not well observe the rules of art, and if, superior creations that they are, they are not still pleasing to everyone. The fault therefore lies not with the public that asks for silly pieces, but with those who do not know how to put on anything else. The *Ingratitude Avenged* was not nonsense; neither was the *Numantia*, nor *The Merchant Lover*, and certainly not *The Fair and Favoring Enemy*; [6] and the same might be said of others composed by intelligent poets, to their own fame and renown and the profit of those who put on the plays.'

"I had other things to say along the same line, which left him, I thought, a bit embarrassed but by no means sufficiently convinced to give up his erroneous opinion."

"Señor Canon," said the curate, "by touching upon this subject you have awakened an old grudge of mine against the comedies of today, one that is equal to that which I hold against books of chivalry. For, according to Tully, a comedy should be a mirror of human life, an example of manners, and an image of the truth; [7] yet those that we see now are mirrors of nonsense, examples of foolishness, and images of lasciviousness. In connection with the subject of which we are speaking, what could be more absurd than for a character to appear as an infant in Act I, Scene 1, and in the following scene step out as a full-bearded man? What more out of place than to depict for us an old man parading his valor, a youth who plays the cringing coward, an eloquent lackey, a page wise in giving counsel, a king turned porter, or a princess serving as a kitchen wench?

"And what shall I say of the attention that is paid to the element of time in connection with the action that is represented? I may merely tell you that I have witnessed a comedy in which the first act takes place in Europe, the second in Asia, and the third in Africa—and if there had been a fourth act, the scene would have been laid in America and thus they would have encompassed the four quarters of the globe. If fidelity to life be the principal object which a comedy should have in view, how is it possible for the most mediocre intelligence to find any satisfaction in one where the action is supposed to take place in the time of King Pepin or Charlemagne, yet which has for its leading character the Emperor Heraclius entering Jerusalem with the Holy Cross and recovering the Holy Sepulcher like Godefroi de Bouillon, when there is a vast stretch of time between the two monarchs? Or in one which, essentially fictitious, makes a pretense at historical accuracy by mingling odds and ends of various events that happened to different persons at different times, and this with no attempt at verisimilitude but with obvious errors that are utterly inexcusable? And the sad part of it is, there are ignorant ones who say that this is the perfect thing and all the rest is affectation.

"And then, coming to religious dramas, what do we find? How many false miracles do their authors invent, how many apocryphal and erroneous incidents, with the wonders worked by one saint attributed to another! And even in those comedies that deal with human themes they dare to introduce miracles without rhyme or reason, merely because they think that such a scenic effect,[8] as they term it, will fit in well and serve to attract the ignorant, who will come to see the play and marvel at it. All of which is prejudicial to the truth, tending to corrupt history and cast opprobrium upon the Spanish genius; for those foreigners [9] that scrupulously observe the rules of comedy are led to look upon us as unschooled barbarians by reason of the absurdity and nonsense to be found in the productions of our theater.

"Nor is it a sufficient excuse for all this to say that the principal object which well-ordered states have in view in permitting the public performance of comedies is to provide the community with a little harmless recreation now and then and thus divert those evil impulses that idleness is wont to breed. It may be said that this end is attained by any comedy, good or bad, and that there is no necessity of laying down laws to govern the composition and performance of such pieces, since, as I have said, the same object is achieved by any kind of play. To this I would reply that it is, beyond any comparison, better achieved by good plays than by the other kind.

"For when he has witnessed a comedy that is well and artfully constructed, the spectator will come out laughing at its humor, enlightened by the truths it contained, marveling at the various incidents, rendered wiser by the arguments, made more wary by the snares he has seen depicted, and more prudent by the examples afforded him; he will leave the theater hating vice and in love with virtue; such are the effects that a good comedy has upon the mind of the listener, however boorish and dull-witted he may be. Nothing, in short, is more impossible than that the play that contains all these qualities should fail to provide more entertainment, satisfaction, and pleasure than the one lacking in them, as is the case with the majority of those that are at present to be viewed.

"It is not the dramatic poets who are to blame for this state of affairs; for many of them are fully conscious of their faults and know very well what ought to be done. But inasmuch as comedies have become salable commodities, the poets in question will tell us, and in this they are right, that their plays will not be bought unless they are after the accepted pattern, and, accordingly, the author seeks to adapt himself to what the actor who is to pay him for his work requires of him. That this is so may be seen from the countless number of comedies composed by one of the most fertile minds in this realm, plays so full of brilliancy and grace, marked by such polished versification, admirable dialogue, and profound wisdom, and, finally, so full of eloquence and so elevated in style, that his fame has gone out to all the world; and yet, owing to the necessity he has been under of having to adapt them to the taste of the players, not all his productions have attained that degree of perfection that is to be desired.[10]

"Still others compose their pieces without giving a thought to what they are doing; and, as a result, after the performance, the actors have to take to their heels and flee for fear of being punished, as they oftentimes have been, for having put something on the stage that was offensive to a certain monarch or that cast aspersions on some noble house. But all these improprieties would cease, and with them many others that I do not mention, if there were at court some wise and intelligent person to examine all the comedies before they are put on, not only those that are to be performed in the capital but those that are to be produced in other parts of Spain as well,[11] and without the approval, seal, and signature of that individual no local officer of the crown should permit any comedy to be staged. Under such a system, the performers would be at pains to forward their plays to the capital for inspection and then would be able to act in them with safety, while the authors, knowing that their works would have to pass a rigorous and intelligent censorship and being fearful of offending, would devote more care and attention to them, and as a consequence would produce good comedies, thus achieving in a felicitous manner the objectives for which they strive: the entertainment of the people and, at the same time, the furthering of the reputation of Spanish dramatists and of the interest and security of the performers, the necessity of punishing the latter having been removed.

"And if they were to charge some other person, or this same one, with the task of examining the newly published books of chivalry, we then undoubtedly should have some that would be possessed of that perfection that your Grace has described, works that would enrich our language with a pleasing and precious store of eloquence; and the luster of the older books would be dimmed by the light of these newer ones, whose purpose is to provide an innocent pastime, not for the idle alone, but even for the busiest of men. For it is not possible for the bow to be always bent, nor can weak human nature be sustained without legitimate recreation of some sort."

The canon and the curate had reached this point in their colloquy when the barber came up and spoke to the latter.

"Here, Señor Licentiate," he said, "is the place of which I was telling you; it is a good spot in which to take our noontide rest, and there is fresh and abundant pasturage for the oxen."

"It looks to me as if it would do very well," replied the curate.

When the canon was told of their intentions, he expressed a desire to make the halt with them, being attracted by the charming prospect which the valley afforded. He also wished to enjoy more of the curate's conversation, for he had become quite fond of him, and to hear of Don Quixote's exploits in greater detail. He accordingly ordered some of his servants to go to the inn, which was not far away, and bring back enough for them all to eat, as he meant to rest there in the valley that afternoon; to which one of them replied that the sumpter mule, which ought by this time to have reached the inn, carried sufficient provisions so that they would not have to procure anything from the hostelry except barley.

"In that case," said the canon, "lead all our mounts there and bring back the mule."

While this was going on, Sancho decided to take advantage of the opportunity to speak to his master without the constant presence of the curate and the barber, whom he looked upon with suspicion.

"Master," he said, going up to the cage, "I want to get a load off my conscience by telling you what goes on in connection with your enchantment. The truth of the matter is that those two with their faces covered are the curate of our village and the barber, and it is my belief that they have plotted to carry you off like this out of pure spite, because your Grace is so far ahead of them in famous deeds. If this is so, then it follows that you are not under a spell at all but have been hoodwinked and made a fool of. Just to prove this, I'd like to ask you one thing, and if you answer me as I think you will have to, then you'll be able to lay your hand on what's wrong and will see that you are not enchanted but simply out of your head."

"Ask me whatever you like, Sancho my son," replied Don Quixote, "and I will give you an answer that will satisfy you on every point. As to what you say about those who accompany us being the curate and the barber, our fellow townsmen whom we know very well, that is who they may appear to you to be, but you are not by any manner of means to believe that that is what they really and truly are. What you are rather to understand is that if they have, as you say, this appearance in your eyes, it must be for the reason that those who have put this spell upon me have seen fit to assume that form and likeness; for it is easy enough for enchanters to take whatever form they like, and so they must have assumed the appearance of our friends expressly for the purpose of leading you to think what you do, thus involving you in a labyrinth of fancies from which you would not succeed in extricating yourself even though you had the cord of Theseus.

"They also doubtless had another purpose, that of causing me to waver in my mind, so that I should not be able to form a conjecture as to the source of this wrong that is done me. For, if on the one hand you tell me it is the barber and the curate of our village who accompany us, and on the other hand I find myself shut up in a cage, knowing full well that no human but only a superhuman power could have put me behind these bars, what would you have me say to you or what would you have me think except that my enchantment, in view of the manner in which it has been accomplished, is like none that I have ever read about in all the histories that treat of knights-errant who have been laid under a spell? And so you may set your mind at rest as to the suspicions that you have voiced, for those two are no more what you say they are than I am a Turk. But you said that you had something to ask me; speak, then, and I will answer you, though you keep on asking until tomorrow morning."

"May Our Lady help me!" cried Sancho in a loud voice. "Is it possible your Grace is so thick-headed and so lacking in brains that you cannot see that I am telling you the simple truth when I say that malice has more to do than magic with your being in this plight? But since that is the way matters stand, I'd like to prove to you beyond a doubt that there is no magic about it. And now, tell me, as you would have God rescue you from this torment, and as you hope to find yourself in the arms of my lady Dulcinea when you least expect it—"

"Stop conjuring me," said Don Quixote, "and ask what you like. I have already told you that I will answer you point by point."

"What I ask is this," Sancho went on, "and what I would have you tell me, without adding anything to it or leaving anything out, but in all truthfulness, as you would expect it to be told, and as it is told, by all those who like your Grace follow the calling of arms, under the title of knights-errant—"

"I have said that I will tell you no lies," replied Don Quixote. "Go ahead and finish your question; for in truth you weary me, Sancho, with all these solemn oaths, adjurations, and precautions."

"I am sure," said Sancho, "that my master is kindhearted and truthful; and so, because it has a bearing on what we are talking about, I would ask your Grace, speaking with all due respect, if by any chance, since you have been in that cage and, as it seems to you, under a spell, you have felt the need of doing a major or a minor,[12] as the saying goes."

"I do not understand what you mean by 'doing a major or a minor,' Sancho. Speak more plainly if you wish me to give you a direct answer."

"Is it possible that your Grace doesn't know what 'a major or a minor' is? Why, lads in school are weaned on it. What I mean to say is, have you felt like doing that which can't be put off?"

"Ah, I understand you, Sancho! Yes, many times; and for that matter, right now. Get me out of this, or all will not be as clean here as it ought to be!"

CHAPTER XLIX. *Of the shrewd conversation that Sancho Panza had with his master, Don Quixote.*

"Ha!" cried Sancho, "I have you there! That is what I wanted with all my life and soul to know! Come now, sir, can you deny the common saying around here when a person is out of sorts: 'I don't know what's the matter with So-and-So; he neither eats nor drinks nor sleeps nor gives you a sensible answer to any question that you ask him; he must be bewitched?' From which we are to gather that while those that do not do any of these things or attend to those duties of nature that I have mentioned are under a spell, the ones like your Grace, on the other hand, who feel a desire to do them, who eat and drink what is set before them and answer all questions, are not enchanted."

"You speak the truth, Sancho," replied Don Quixote, "but as I have told you before there are many ways of being enchanted, and it may be that the fashion has changed with the course of time and that today those who are in such a plight do everything that I do, although formerly such was not the case. So, there is no use arguing against custom or drawing inferences as you are doing. I know for a certainty that I am the victim of an enchanter, and that is all I need to know to set my conscience at rest, for it would hurt me sorely if I thought that, without being enchanted, I had slothfully and like a coward permitted myself to be put into this cage, thus cheating the wretched and the needy who at this very moment may be in great distress for want of my aid and protection."

"But for all of that," said Sancho, "I still insist it would be better, in order to satisfy yourself completely, if your Grace would try to get out of that jail. I promise to do everything I can to help you out of it and see if you can mount Rocinante once more, for he looks so sad and melancholy, I think he must be enchanted too. When you've done that, you can try your luck at seeking more adventures, and if they don't turn out well, there will be plenty of time for us to come back to the jail; in which case I promise you, as the law says a good and faithful squire should do, that I will shut myself up with your Grace, if by any chance your Grace should be so unlucky or I so foolish as not to be able to go through with what I've told you."

"I am willing to do anything you say, brother Sancho," Don Quixote assured him; "and when you find an opportunity to set me free, I will obey you in everything; but you will see, Sancho, that you are wrong in your explanation of my misfortune."

Conversing in this manner, knight-errant and errant squire arrived at the place where the curate, the canon, and the barber, who had already dismounted, were awaiting them. The carter then unyoked his oxen to let them graze in that pleasant pasturage, whose cool green proved alluring to persons not only as bewitched as Don Quixote but as shrewd and wide awake as his squire. The latter now begged the curate to allow his master to leave the cage for a little while, since otherwise it would not remain as clean as decency required in the case of such a knight.

The curate understood what he meant and told him that he would gladly grant his request, if it was not that he feared his master, once set at liberty, would be up to his old tricks and go off someplace where no one would ever see him again.

"I will answer for that," replied Sancho.

"And I for everything," said the canon, "especially if he but give me his word as a knight that he will not leave us against our will."

"I give it," answered Don Quixote, who had been listening to it all. "In any event, one who is enchanted as I am is not at liberty to do what he likes with his person, for the one who put the spell upon him may very well prevent him from stirring from a certain place for three whole centuries, and if he were to flee, he would be brought back flying."

He went on to say that, this being so, they might as well release him, as it was to the advantage of all of them; for, he protested, if they did not do so, he would not be able to avoid offending their sense of smell, unless they kept their distance from him.

The canon thereupon took the knight's hand, although it was bound to the other one, and, upon receiving his word and solemn promise, they let him out of the cage, which made him immeasurably happy. The first thing he did was to stretch his entire body, and then he went over to Rocinante and slapped him on the rump.

"O flower and mirror of steeds," he said, "I still trust in God and His blessed Mother that we shall both soon have our desire: you with your master on your back and I astride you, in pursuit of that calling for which God sent me into the world."

Having said this, he went off with Sancho to a remote spot, and when he came back he was greatly relieved and more desirous than ever of putting his squire's scheme into execution. Gazing at him, the canon could not but be struck by the strange nature of his madness and was astonished at the extremely sensible manner in which the knight talked and answered questions, losing his stirrups, so to speak, only when the subject of chivalry was mentioned. And so, as they all sat around on the green grass waiting for the meal which the canon had ordered, the churchman addressed him, saying:

"Is it possible, my good sir, that those disgusting books of chivalry which your Grace has read in your idle hours have had such an effect upon you as to turn your head, causing you to believe that you are being carried away under a magic spell and other things of that sort that are as far from being true as truth itself is from falsehood? How is it possible for any human mind to believe that there ever existed in this world all that infinite number of Amadises, or all that multitude of famous knights—all the emperors of Trebizond, all the Felixmartes of Hircania, all the palfreys, errant damsels, serpents, monsters, giants, all the adventures such as never before were heard of, all the battles and fearful encounters, all the splendid costumes, lovelorn princesses, squires turned into counts, facetious dwarfs, gallantries, warrior ladies—in short, all the absurdities to be found in the romances of chivalry?

"For myself, I can say that when I read such books without stopping to think how mendacious and frivolous they are, they do give me a certain pleasure; but when I reflect upon their real character, I fling the best of them against the wall and would even toss them into the fire if there happened to be one at hand; for they are deserving of the same punishment as cheats and impostors, who are beyond the pale of human nature, or as the founders of new sects and new ways of life, for leading the ignorant public to believe and regard as the truth all the nonsense that they contain.

"And these audacious works even upset the minds of intelligent and wellborn gentlemen like your Grace, as is plainly to be seen from the things that you have done, which have finally made it necessary to lock you up in a cage and convey you upon an ox-cart like some lion or tiger that is being taken from place to place to be exhibited for money. Ah, Señor Don Quixote, have mercy upon yourself, return to the bosom of common sense, and wisely make use of the many gifts with which Heaven has seen fit to endow you by applying your fertile mind to reading of another sort such as will be better for your conscience and for your good name as well.

"If, however, carried away by your natural inclination, you feel that you must read of knightly exploits, then turn to the Book of Judges in the Holy Scriptures, for there you will find great deeds recorded, and as true as they are valiant. Lusitania had a Viriatus,[1] Rome a Caesar, Carthage a Hannibal, Greece an Alexander, Castile a Count Fernán González, Valencia a Cid, Andalusia a Gonzalo Hernández, Estremadura a Diego García de Paredes, Jerez a Garci Pérez de Vargas, Toledo a Garcilaso, Seville a Manuel de León;[2] and in perusing the account of their feats of valor the loftiest intellect will find instruction and entertainment, diversion, and cause for wonderment. Here, my dear Señor Don Quixote, is reading matter worthy of your intelligence and which will leave you versed in history, in love with virtue, schooled in goodness of heart, and improved in manners and morals; it will render you valiant but not rash, prudent but not a coward; and all this to the honor of God and the fame of La Mancha, which, so I am informed, is your Grace's native province."

Don Quixote was all attention as the canon spoke, and when he saw that he had finished, after gazing at him for some little while, he replied as follows:

"It appears to me, my dear sir, that the purpose of your Grace's remarks is to lead me to believe that there have never been knights-errant in the world and that all the books of chivalry are false, lying, harmful, and lacking in public usefulness. You further imply that I have done wrong in reading them, worse in believing them, and worst of all in imitating them by setting out to follow the extremely arduous profession of errantry in accordance with the precepts to be found in such works. You would tell me that the world has never seen an Amadis, either of Gaul or of Greece, nor any of the other knights with whose names those books are filled."

"You have stated the case exactly," said the canon.

"Your Grace," said Don Quixote, "also went on to assert that such books had done me much harm, having turned my head and landed me in a cage, and that it would be better to mend my ways, change my reading matter, and turn my attention to other writings that are more truthful, pleasing, and edifying."

"That is right," said the canon.

"Whereas I," continued the knight, "find that it is your Grace who have had your head turned and have been bewitched. For to utter such blasphemies as your Grace has done against something that all the world knows to be true, by denying that it exists, is an offense deserving of the same punishment that your Grace says ought to be meted out to those books that so annoy you when you read them. For to endeavor to persuade anyone that Amadis never lived, nor any of the other knightly adventurers that fill the history books, is the same as trying to make him believe that the sun does not shine, that ice is not cold, or that the earth does not bear fruit. For who could ever be clever enough to convince another person that the story of the Princess Florípes and Guy of Burgundy is not true? And there is the story of Fierabrás and the bridge of Mantible,[3] which happened in the time of Charlemagne, and which I swear is as true as when I say it is daylight at this moment.

"But if all this is a lie, then it must be that there was no Hector nor Achilles nor Trojan War nor Twelve Peers of France nor King Arthur of England who to this day goes about in the form of a raven and is expected to reappear in his kingdom at any time. Similarly, they are so bold as to tell us that the history of Guarino Mesquino [4] is false as well as that of the quest of the Holy Grail, and that the love of Tristan and Queen Yseult is a fabrication, as is that of Guinevere and Lancelot, even though there are persons who can recall having seen Dame Quintañona,[5] who was the best cupbearer to be met with in all Britain. So true is this that I can remember how my grandmother on my father's side used to say to me, when she saw a lady in a venerable hood, 'That one, my grandson, looks just like Dame Quintañona.' From which I infer that she must have known her or at least have seen some portrait of her.

"And, then, who would deny the truth of the story of Pierres and the beautiful Magalona, seeing that to this very day, in the royal armory, one may behold the pin—a little bigger than a cart-pole—with which

the valiant Pierres guided his wooden horse through the air, while alongside it is Babieca's saddle? And at Roncesvalles there is Roland's horn of
the size of a beam.[6] From which it is to be inferred that the Twelve
Peers and Pierres and the Cid and other similar knights did of a truth
exist,

> *Of whom it is folks say,*
> *They to adventures go.*

"Furthermore, let them tell me whether or not it is true that there was
a brave Lusitanian knight-errant by the name of Juan de Merlo, who
went to Burgundy and in the city of Arras fought with the famous lord
of Charny called Monsieur Pierre, and afterward in the city of Basle
with Monsieur Henri de Remestan, emerging victorious from both encounters, with great fame and honor.[7] And what of the adventures and
challenges of those brave Spaniards, Pedro Barba and Gutierre Quijada
(from whom I am descended in the direct male line), who—likewise in
Burgundy—fought and overcame the sons of the Count of St. Paul? [8]
Let them tell me, also, that Don Fernando de Guevara did not go to
Germany in quest of adventures, where he engaged in combat with
Messire George, a knight of the Duke of Austria's line.[9] Let them tell
me that the joustings of Suero de Quiñones of the *Paso* were but a
hoax,[10] or the emprises of Monsieur Louis de Faux against the Castilian
knight, Gonzalo de Guzmán,[11] along with many other exploits performed by Christian knights of this and other realms, all of them so
true and authentic that, I say it once more, he who would deny them
is lacking in all reason and sound judgment."

The canon as he listened was amazed at the manner in which Don
Quixote jumbled truth and falsehood and also at the knowledge he
possessed of everything touching upon and pertaining to those feats of
knight-errantry of which he was so fond.

"Señor Don Quixote," he now answered him, "I cannot deny that
there is some truth in what your Grace has said, especially insofar
as pertains to Spanish knights-errant. I am willing to grant you that
there were Twelve Peers of France, although I cannot admit that all
the things that the Archbishop of Turpin has written of them are
true; [12] for the truth of the matter is, they were knights chosen by
the king of France, being called Peers to signify that they were equal
in worth, rank, and valor (or at least they were supposed to be, whether
they were or not). They constituted something like a religious order,
resembling the present ones of Santiago and Calatrava, in which it is

presumed that all those that take the vows are gentlemen, brave, worthy, and wellborn; and just as we speak of a Knight of St. John or a Knight of Alcántara, so in those days they would refer to someone as being a Knight of the Twelve Peers, for the reason that twelve equals were chosen for that military order.[13]

"That there was a Cid, and a Bernardo del Carpio [14] as well, there can be no doubt, but that they performed the feats attributed to them, I very much doubt. As to the Count Pierres' pin with which he guided his steed and which your Grace claims to have seen alongside Babieca's saddle in the royal armory, I must confess that I am either so stupid or so shortsighted that, although I have seen the former I have never laid eyes on the latter, even though it be as big as your Grace says it is."

"Yet there is not the slightest doubt that it is there, for all of that," replied Don Quixote, "and what is more, they say that it is encased in a cowhide sheath to keep it from rusting."

"That may all very well be," said the canon, "but I assure you by the holy orders which I have received that I cannot recall having seen it. But even assuming that it is there, that is no reason why I should believe the stories of all those Amadises and all the multitude of other knights that we read about; nor is it any reason why a man like your Grace, so worthy and respected and endowed with so fine a mind, should permit himself to believe that all the mad things described in those nonsensical books of chivalry are true."

CHAPTER L. *Of the weighty argument which took place between Don Quixote and the canon.*

"THAT," replied Don Quixote, "is a fine thing to say! Do you mean to tell me that those books that have been printed with a royal license and with the approval of the ones to whom they have been submitted and which are read with general enjoyment and praised by young and old alike, by rich and poor, the learned and the ignorant, the gentry and the plain people—in brief, by all sorts of persons of every

condition and walk in life—do you mean to tell me that they are but
lies? Do they not have every appearance of being true? Do they not
tell us who the father, mother, relatives of these knights were, the name
of the country from which they came, their age, the feats that they
performed, point by point and day by day, and the places where all
these events occurred? Your Grace had best be silent and not utter such
a blasphemy; for let me give you a bit of advice, which is something
that, as a sensible man, I ought to do: if you do not believe me, read
them for yourself and you will see what pleasure you will derive from
them.

"Tell me: could there be anything more fascinating than to see before us, right here and now, so to speak, a lake of bubbling pitch, with
a host of snakes, serpents, lizards, and all sorts of fierce and terrifying
animals swimming about in it, while from the middle of it there comes
as mournful a voice as ever was heard, saying, 'Thou, O knight, whoever thou mayest be, who standest gazing upon this dreadful lake, if
thou wouldst attain the boon that lieth covered beneath these dark
waters, show then thy valor and thy stout heart by leaping into the
midst of this black and burning liquid; for if thou dost not, thou shalt
not be held worthy of looking upon the mighty marvels locked and
contained in the seven castles of the seven fays that are situated beneath its ebony expanse.' And no sooner does the knight hear that aw-
ful voice than, without taking any further thought or pausing to consider the peril involved, he plunges into that seething lagoon, burdened
with the full weight of his armor and commending his soul to God and
Our Lady.

"And then, not knowing where he is or what the outcome is to be,
he suddenly finds himself amidst flowering meadows to which the
Elysian fields cannot compare. It seems to him that the heavens there
are more transparent, while the sun is brighter than he has ever known
it to be. His eyes behold a charming grove composed of leafy trees
whose greenery is a joy to the sight, while his ears are delighted by the
sweet and untaught song of an infinite number of little brilliant-hued
birds, flying in and out through the interweaving branches. Here he
discovers a brook whose clear-running waters, which have the appearance of molten glass, glide along over a bed of fine sand and white pebbles, giving the impression of sifted gold and the purest of pearls. Over
there he sees an artfully wrought fountain of varicolored jasper and
smooth marble; and there another of rustic design, with tiny clam shells

and the twisted white and yellow houses of the snail arranged in a well-ordered disorder, mingled with bits of gleaming crystal and counterfeit emeralds, the whole forming a work in which art, imitating nature, would seem to have outdone the latter.

"In yet another place, his gaze unexpectedly comes to rest upon a strong-built castle or showy palace, with walls of solid gold, diamond turrets, and gates of jacinth—in short, of such marvelous construction that, though the materials of which it is built are nothing less than diamonds, carbuncles, rubies, pearls, gold, and emeralds, the workmanship in itself is of greater worth. But there is more to come. Having beheld all this, he now descries, trooping out of the castle gate, a goodly number of damsels so richly and festively attired that if I were to undertake to describe their costumes as the histories do, I should never be done with it.

"And the one who appears to be the leader of them all now extends her hand to the bold knight who has cast himself into the boiling lake and, without saying a word, conducts him into the splendid palace or castle, where she makes him strip until he is as bare as when his mother bore him, and then bathes him in lukewarm water, after which she anoints him all over with sweet-smelling unguents and clothes him in a shirt of finest sendal, all odorous and perfumed, as another maid tosses a mantle over his shoulders, one which at the very least, so they say, must be worth as much as a city and even more.

"And how pleasing it is when, after all this, we are told how they take him to another chamber, a great hall, where he finds the tables all laid in a manner that fills him with amazement. What must be his feelings as he sees them pouring over his hands water that has been distilled from amber and fragrant flowers? As they seat him upon a chair of marble? As all those damsels serve him in a deep and impressive silence? As they bring him a great variety of dishes so tastefully garnished that, tempted as his appetite may be, he is at a loss as to which he should reach for first? As he listens to the music that is played all the while, not knowing from whence it comes or who the musician may be? And then, when the repast is over and the tables have been cleared, as the knight leans back in his chair, picking his teeth, it may be, as is his custom, there enters unexpectedly through the doorway of the great hall a damsel far more beautiful than any of the others; and, seating herself at his side, she begins telling him to whom it is that castle belongs and how she is being held in it under a magic spell, along with other things that astonish him and amaze the one who reads his history. What, I ask you again, could be more charming than all this?

"I do not care to elaborate upon this point any further; from the examples I have cited it may be gathered that no matter what part of what history of a knight-errant one reads, it is bound to give pleasure and arouse wonderment. If, your Grace, you will believe me and, as I have said, read these books for yourself, you will see how they drive away melancholy and make you feel better in case you are out of sorts. As for myself, I may say that, since becoming a knight-errant, I am brave, polite, liberal, well-bred, generous, courteous, bold, gentle, patient, and long-suffering when it comes to enduring hardships, imprisonment, and enchantments; and although it was only a short while ago that I was shut up in a cage as a madman, I still expect, through the valor of my arm, with Heaven favoring and fortune not opposing, to find myself within a few days king of some realm or other where I may be able to display the gratitude and liberality that is in my heart.

"For take my word for it, sir, he who is poor cannot exhibit those virtues to anyone, no matter in how high a degree he may be possessed of them; and gratitude that consists only in the will to show it is a dead thing, just as is faith without works. For this reason it is, I wish that fortune would speedily provide me with the opportunity of becoming an emperor in order that I might make manifest the virtues of my heart by doing good to my friends and especially to this poor fellow, Sancho Panza, my squire, who is the best little man in the world; I should like to reward him by conferring upon him an earldom, which I promised him long ago. The only thing is I do not know if he has the ability to govern it."

These last words were no sooner out of his mouth than Sancho broke in upon his master. "Just you see to it that I get that earldom, Señor Don Quixote," he said, "the one you promised me and which I have been waiting for all this time, and I give you my word that I'll be able to govern it all right; and if I should fail, I've heard them say that there are men in this world who rent such estates from their lords, giving them so much a year, while they themselves take over the government, in which case all the lord has to do is to stretch out his legs and enjoy his income without worrying about anything else. That's what I'll do. I'll not haggle over a penny here and a penny there. I'll get rid of all the bother and live like a duke on what's coming to me."

"What you are speaking of, brother Sancho," said the canon, "is the matter of revenues; but the lord of a great estate also has to administer justice, and it is this that calls for ability and sound judgment and, above all, a right intention on his part in ascertaining the truth; for if this be lacking in the beginning, the middle and the end will always be wrong, whence it is that God is inclined to favor the simple when their hearts are in the right place and to frustrate the clever designs of the wicked."

"I don't understand those philosophies," replied Sancho. "All I know is that once I have that earldom, I'll be able to rule it; for I have a soul like anybody else and a body like the rest of them, and I'll be as much a king in my state as the others are in theirs. And when I'm king, I'll do as I please, and doing as I please, I'll be satisfied; and when you're satisfied, there's nothing more to be desired, so bring it on. God be with you and we shall see, as one blind man said to another."

"That is not a bad philosophy, as you call it, Sancho," observed the canon, "but there still remains much to be said on this subject of earldoms."

"I do not know what more there is to be said," Don Quixote answered him.[1] "I am guided simply by the example of the great Amadis of Gaul, who made his squire count of Firm Island;[2] and so, I, without any conscientious scruples, may make a count of Sancho Panza, who is one of the best squires that a knight-errant ever had."

The canon was astonished at Don Quixote's well-reasoned nonsense, at the vivid manner in which he had described the Knight of the Lake's adventure, and at the impression which the deliberate falsehoods contained in his books had made upon him; and he likewise marveled at the simple-mindedness of Sancho, who so eagerly longed to obtain that earldom that his master had promised him.

At this point the canon's servants, who had been to the inn for the sumpter mule, returned; and, spreading a carpet upon the green grass of the meadow, they sat down in the shade of some trees and made their repast there, in order, as we have said, that the carter might take advantage of the spot. As they were engaged in eating, they suddenly heard a loud noise and the sound of a small bell, which came from among some brambles and dense undergrowth near by, and at the same instant they saw coming out of the thicket a beautiful nanny-goat, its skin all speckled with black, white, and brown spots. Behind it came a goatherd, shouting at it, with such language as his kind customarily use and calling upon it to stop and come back to the fold. The fugitive goat, however, thoroughly frightened, ran up to where they were sitting, as if asking protection of them, followed by the goatherd, who, seizing it by the horns, spoke to it as if it had been capable of understanding.

"Ah, Spotty! Spotty!" he cried, "what a wild one you are! How comes it that you go limping around these days? What wolves have frightened you, my daughter? Won't you tell me what it is, my beauty? What else can it be than that you are a female and hence naturally restless? What ails you, anyway, and all those that you take after? Come back, come back, my dear; you may not be quite so happy there, but at least you'll be safer in the fold, along with your companions. For if you, who ought to watch over and lead them, go wandering off so aimlessly, what is to become of them?"

They were all quite amused by the goatherd's words, especially the canon. "As you live, brother," he said, "calm yourself a little and do not be in such haste to return this goat to the fold; for, seeing that she is a female, as you say, she must follow her natural bent no matter how much you try to stop her. Have a bite with us and take a drink; that will cool your anger and give the goat a chance to rest at the same time."

He therewith presented him with some cold loin of rabbit on the end of a knife and handed him a glass of wine. The goatherd accepted it with thanks, drank the wine, and grew calmer.

"I hope," he said, "that your Worships will not take me for a simpleton because I spoke the way I did to this animal; the truth of the matter is, there is a certain mystery behind the words I spoke. I may be a countryman, but I know how to treat both men and beasts."

"That I can well believe," said the curate, "for I know from experience that the woods breed men of learning and that many a philosopher is to be found in a shepherd's hut."

"At least, sir," replied the goatherd, "they shelter men who have some knowledge of life. And in order that you may be convinced of the truth of this and grasp it thoroughly, even though I may appear to speak without being invited, I should like you, gentlemen, if it will not tire you, to listen closely as I tell you a story which will confirm what this gentleman"—pointing to the curate—"and I myself have just been saying."

Don Quixote then spoke up. "Inasmuch," he said, "as this appears to me to savor somewhat of a knightly adventure, I for my part will gladly listen to you, brother, and so will all these other gentlemen; for they are extremely intelligent and fond of hearing new and strange things that astonish, divert, and entertain the mind as I am sure your story will. Begin, then, my friend, for we are all listening."

"I take back my stakes," [3] declared Sancho. "I'm going down to that brook that I see over there, with this pastry, and stuff myself for three whole days. I have heard my master Don Quixote say that a knight-errant's squire ought to eat all he can when he has the chance; for, likely as not, they will be getting into some wood or other and will not be able to find their way out for a week, and if his belly is not full or his saddlebags well stocked, he may remain there, as very often happens, dead as a mummy."

"In that you are right, Sancho," said Don Quixote. "Go wherever you like and eat as much as you like, for I have had my fill and it is only left for me to give my soul a little reflection as I shall do by listening to this good man's story."

"And we will all do the same," said the canon.

He then requested the goatherd to begin the tale that he had promised them; whereupon the man gave the animal a couple of slaps on the side, saying to it, "Lie down here beside me, Spotty; there will be time later for us to return to the fold." It seemed that the goat understood, for as soon as her master had said this she stretched out beside him very tranquilly, gazing up into his face as if to give him to understand that she was listening for the story he was about to tell. He then began as follows.

CHAPTER LI. *Which treats of the story the goatherd told to all those who were bearing off Don Quixote.*

"THREE leagues from this valley there is a village which, although it is a small one, is one of the richest to be found in all these parts. In it there lived a farmer who was highly respected, and while it is a common thing for the well-to-do to be treated with respect, he was held in even greater esteem for his virtue than for the wealth that he had acquired. But what made him happier than anything else, as he himself put it, was the possession of a daughter of such rare and exceeding beauty, grace, wit, and modesty, that any who knew and looked upon her could not but be astonished at the lavish gifts with which Heaven and nature had endowed her.

"She had been beautiful as a small child and had grown more so with the years until by the time she reached the age of sixteen she was the loveliest of creatures and her fame had begun to spread to the neighboring villages—what am I saying? to the far away cities—and had even reached the halls of royalty and the ears of persons of every class, who came from all around to behold her as if she had been some rare and curious thing or some miracle-working image.

"Her father watched over her and she watched over herself; for there are no locks, guards, or bolts that afford better protection to a maiden than does her own modesty. His wealth and her beauty led many of the villagers and others from distant parts to seek her hand in marriage, but, having so precious a jewel to dispose of, he was wholly unable to make up his mind as to which of her countless suitors he should give her. I was one of the many who were in love with her, and I had great hopes of being successful, since her father knew me as a native of the same village and I was of pure stock and in the flower of youth and in addition was very well off in this world's goods while my qualities of mind left nothing to be desired.

"But there was another suitor of the village possessing these same qualifications, and this caused the father to weigh his choice and hold it in suspense, since it seemed to him that either of us would be a good match for his daughter. By way of ridding himself of his perplexity, he resolved to speak to Leandra, for that was the name of the wealthy lass who had brought me to a state of misery. He accordingly told his beloved child that, inasmuch as we were equals in what we had to offer, he would leave the matter of choosing between us to her own good pleasure—a procedure that deserves to be imitated by all parents with children to whom they wish to give a start in life. I do not mean that the latter should be permitted to choose that which is evil and vile; what I am saying is that the good things should be set before them and from these they should make their own choice. I do not know which of us Leandra chose, but I do know that her father put us off with vague words, on the ground that the girl was so young, words that neither bound him to anything nor constituted an outright dismissal for us.

"My rival's name was Anselmo and mine is Eugenio; I tell you this to acquaint you with the characters in this tragedy, the end of which is not yet, although it is clearly bound to be disastrous.

"At this time there came to our village a certain Vicente de la Rosa, son of a poor peasant who lived there. Vicente had been a soldier in Italy and elsewhere, having been taken away when a lad of about twelve by a captain who chanced to be passing through the place with his company; and now, here he was back again, twelve years later, dressed in a soldier's gaudy uniform covered with any number of glass trinkets and fine steel chains. Today he would put on one uniform and tomorrow another, but all of them flimsy and showy, of little weight and less worth. The peasants, who are naturally malicious and, when time hangs heavy on their hands, can be malice itself, were quick to observe all this. They made an inventory of his jewelry and other finery piece by piece and discovered that he had, altogether, three uniforms of different colors with stockings and garters to match, but with these he effected so many combinations that, had they not counted them, they would have sworn that he had displayed more than ten different suits and more than a score of feathered bonnets. And do not think that, in enumerating the garments that he wore, I am straying from the point, for they have a considerable part to play in the story.

"He used to seat himself upon a bench that stood beneath a large poplar tree in the public square of our village, and there he would keep us all gaping as we listened to the story of the feats he had performed. There was no country on earth that he had not visited, no battle in which he had not taken part, and he had slain a greater number of Moors than there are in Morocco and Tunis put together. He had also been engaged in more singlehanded combats than Garcilaso,[1] Diego García de Paredes, and a thousand other knights whom he mentioned, and had emerged victorious from all of them without having lost a single drop of blood. What was more, he showed us the scars of wounds, and although they were so faint that we could not make them out, he gave us to understand that they were from gunshot and that he had received them in various battles and skirmishes. And to cap it all, he, with an unheard-of arrogance, addressed his equals, even those that he knew well, with the condescendingly formal pronoun *vos*, remarking that his father was his own good arm, his deeds his pedigree, and that by reason of being a soldier he owed nothing to the king himself.

"In addition to these arrogant attitudes, he was something of a musician and used to strum the guitar in such a way as to make it speak, according to some. His accomplishments did not stop here, however, for he was also a bit of a poet and would compose a ballad a league and a half long on any trifling event that occurred in the village.

"This soldier, then, whom I have described for you, this Vicente de la Rosa, this braggart, this gallant, this musician, this poet, was seen and admired by Leandra many times from the window of her house overlooking the square. She was charmed by the tinsel and glitter of his uniforms and by his ballads, for he gave away a score of copies of each one that he composed, and she had heard of his exploits as he himself had narrated them. The result was that finally—the devil must have had a hand in it—she came to fall in love with him before he had thought of paying court to her; and since no love affair runs more smoothly than the one in which the lady is enamored, Leandra and Vicente readily came to an understanding, and before any of her numerous suitors so much as suspected her plan, she had carried it through by leaving her father's house (she had no mother) and running away with the soldier, who came out of this undertaking more triumphantly than he had out of all the others of which he boasted.

"The entire village and all those who heard the news were very much shocked by it; I was dumfounded, Anselmo was thunderstruck, her father was deeply grieved, her relatives angry and ashamed, the law was invoked, and the officers of the Brotherhood held themselves in readiness. A thorough search was made of the highways, woods, and all the surrounding territory, and at the end of three days they found the wayward Leandra in a mountain cave, naked save for her chemise and without the large sum of money and extremely valuable jewels with which she had left home. Bringing her back to her grief-stricken father, they questioned her as to what had happened, and she freely confessed that Vicente de la Rosa had deceived her by promising that, if she would leave her father's house, he would marry her and take her to the richest and most luxurious city in all the world, which was Naples. Deluded by his words, she had foolishly believed him and, having robbed her father, had handed everything over to her lover on the night that she disappeared. He then had borne her away to a rugged mountain and there had shut her up in that cave where they had found her. She further told how the soldier, without depriving her of her honor, had robbed her of all her other possessions, after which he had gone off and left her alone, a circumstance that filled all who heard it with fresh amazement.

"It was hard for us to believe in the young fellow's continence, but she asserted it so emphatically that it did much to console the disconsolate father, who gave no thought to his material losses, seeing that his daughter had been left him with the one jewel which, once it is lost, is gone beyond hope of recovery. On the very day that Leandra returned, he removed her from our sight and took her to a convent in a near-by city, trusting that time would repair somewhat the damage to her reputation. The girl's youth served to excuse her for her fault, at least with those who had no interest in branding her as good or bad; but those who were aware of her excellent mind and sound judgment did not attribute her sin to ignorance, but rather to forwardness and the natural inclination of women, which for the most part is toward flightiness and irresponsibility.

"With Leandra shut away, Anselmo's eyes were blind, or at least had nothing to look upon that gave him any happiness, and my own also were in darkness, without a ray of light to guide them to anything that was pleasurable. With her absence our sadness grew, our patience became exhausted, and we cursed the soldier's fancy uniforms and railed at the carelessness of Leandra's father in not having kept a better watch upon her. Finally, the two of us decided to leave the village and come to this valley, and here, pasturing a large number of sheep which are his and a numerous herd of goats which are mine, we spend our lives amid the trees, giving vent to our sorrow as we sing together the praises of the fair Leandra and upbraid her for her fickleness, or go about, each by himself, sighing and sending up our complaints to Heaven.

"Imitating our example, a number of Leandra's other suitors have come to these inhospitable mountains, to practice the same mode of life as we. There are so many of them, indeed, that it would seem that this place has been converted into a pastoral Arcadia, being full of shepherds and sheepfolds, and there is no spot where the name of the beauteous Leandra is not heard. One curses her, calling her capricious, fickle, and immodest. Another condemns her as a woman of light and easy manners. One absolves and pardons, and another judges and reviles her. One hymns her beauty, another dwells on her bad qualities. In short, they all abuse her and all of them adore her, and their madness is carried to such a point that there are some even who complain of her scorn who had never had a word with her, while others moan and suffer all the rage and pangs of jealousy, although she never gave anyone cause to be jealous, for, as I have said, her misstep was known before we learned of her passion. And so, there is no cavity among the rocks, no brookside, no leafy shade where you will not find some shepherd lifting his voice to bewail his lot. Wherever there is an echo, it repeats the name of Leandra. The mountains resound with

'Leandra'; 'Leandra' murmur the brooks; and Leandra it is who holds us all under an agonizing spell, hoping without hope and fearing without knowing what it is we dread.

"Among all these foolish beings, the one who shows most and least sense is my rival Anselmo. Having so many other things of which he might complain, he laments only the fact that Leandra is far away, and to the sound of a rebec, which he plays admirably well, he goes about singing verses that display his fine abilities as a poet. As for me, I follow an easier and, as it seems to me, a wiser course, which consists in berating women for their frivolity, their inconstancy, their double dealing, their unkept promises, their broken troth, and, lastly, the want of sense they show in selecting the one upon whom they see fit to settle their affections. And there, gentlemen, you have the explanation of the words I used in addressing this goat as I came up to you; for, inasmuch as she is a female, I have little respect for her, even though she is the best of all my flock.

"Such is the story that I promised to tell you. If I have been tedious in the way I told it, that does not mean that I shall be slow in serving you. My hut is near by, and in it I have fresh milk and some cheese that you will like very much, along with ripe fruit that is no less pleasing to the eye than it is to the taste."

CHAPTER LII. *Of the quarrel that Don Quixote had with the goatherd, together with the rare adventure of the penitents, which the knight by the sweat of his brow brought to a happy conclusion.*

ALL those who had listened to it were greatly pleased with the goatherd's story, especially the canon, who was more than usually interested in noting the manner in which it had been told. Far from being a mere rustic herdsman, the narrator seemed rather a cultured city dweller; and the canon accordingly remarked that the curate had been quite right in saying that the mountain groves bred men of learning. They all now offered their services to Eugenio, and Don Quixote was the most generous of any in this regard.

"Most assuredly, brother goatherd," he said, "if it were possible for me to undertake any adventure just now, I would set out at once to aid you and would take Leandra out of that convent, where she is undoubtedly being held against her will, in spite of the abbess and all the others who might try to prevent me, after which I would place her in your hands to do with as you liked, with due respect, however, for the laws of chivalry, which command that no violence be offered to any damsel. But I trust in God, Our Lord, that the power of one malicious enchanter is not so great that another magician may not prove still more powerful, and then I promise you my favor and my aid, as my calling obliges me to do, since it is none other than that of succoring the weak and those who are in distress."

The goatherd stared at him, observing in some astonishment the knight's unprepossessing appearance.

"Sir," he said, turning to the barber who sat beside him, "who is this man who looks so strange and talks in this way?"

"Who should it be," the barber replied, "if not the famous Don Quixote de la Mancha, righter of wrongs, avenger of injustices, protector of damsels, terror of giants, and champion of battles?"

"That," said the goatherd, "sounds to me like the sort of thing you read of in books of chivalry, where they do all those things that your Grace has mentioned in connection with this man. But if you ask me, either your Grace is joking or this worthy gentleman must have a number of rooms to let inside his head."

"You are the greatest villain that ever was!" cried Don Quixote when he heard this. "It is you who are the empty one; I am fuller than the bitch that bore you ever was." Saying this, he snatched up a loaf of bread that was lying beside him and hurled it straight in the goatherd's face with such force as to flatten the man's nose. Upon finding himself thus mistreated in earnest, Eugenio, who did not understand this kind of joke, forgot all about the carpet, the tablecloth, and the other diners and leaped upon Don Quixote. Seizing him by the throat with both hands, he would no doubt have strangled him if Sancho Panza, who now came running up, had not grasped him by the shoulders and flung him backward over the table, smashing plates and cups and spilling and scattering all the food and drink that was there. Thus freed of his assailant, Don Quixote then threw himself upon the shepherd, who, with bleeding face and very much battered by Sancho's feet, was creeping about on his hands and knees in search of a table knife with which to exact a sanguinary vengeance, a purpose which the canon and the curate prevented him from carrying out. The barber, however, so contrived it that the goatherd came down on top of his opponent, upon whom he now showered so many blows that the poor knight's countenance was soon as bloody as his own.

As all this went on, the canon and the curate were laughing fit to burst, the troopers were dancing with glee, and they all hissed on the pair as men do at a dog fight. Sancho Panza alone was in despair, being unable to free himself of one of the canon's servants who held him back from going to his master's aid. And then, just as they were all enjoying themselves hugely, with the exception of the two who were mauling each other, the note of a trumpet fell upon their ears, a sound so mournful that it caused them all to turn their heads in the direction from which it came. The one who was most excited by it was Don Quixote; who, very much against his will and more than a little bruised, was lying pinned beneath the goatherd.

"Brother Demon," he now said to the shepherd, "for you could not possibly be anything but a demon, seeing that you have shown a strength and valor greater than mine, I request you to call a truce for no more than an hour; for the doleful sound of that trumpet that we hear seems to me to be some new adventure that is calling me."

Tired of mauling and being mauled, the goatherd let him up at once. As he rose to his feet and turned his head in the direction of the sound, Don Quixote then saw, coming down the slope of a hill, a large number of persons clad in white after the fashion of penitents; for, as it happened, the clouds that year had denied their moisture to the earth, and in all the villages of that district processions for prayer and penance were being organized with the purpose of beseeching God to have mercy and send rain. With this object in view, the good folk from a near-by town were making a pilgrimage to a devout hermit who dwelt on these slopes. Upon beholding the strange costumes that the penitents wore, without pausing to think how many times he had seen them before, Don Quixote imagined that this must be some adventure or other, and that it was for him alone as a knight-errant to undertake it. He was strengthened in this belief by the sight of a covered image that they bore, as it seemed to him this must be some highborn lady whom these scoundrelly and discourteous brigands were forcibly carrying off; and no sooner did this idea occur to him than he made for Rocinante, who was grazing not far away.

Taking the bridle and his buckler from off the saddletree, he had the bridle adjusted in no time, and then, asking Sancho for his sword, he climbed into the saddle, braced his shield upon his arm, and cried out to those present, "And now, valorous company, you shall see how important it is to have in the world those who follow the profession of knight-errantry. You have but to watch how I shall set at liberty that worthy lady who there goes captive, and then you may tell me whether or not such knights are to be esteemed."

As he said this, he dug his legs into Rocinante's flanks, since he had no spurs, and at a fast trot (for nowhere in this veracious history are we ever told that the hack ran full speed) he bore down on the penitents in spite of all that the canon, the curate, and the barber could do to restrain him—their efforts were as vain as were the pleadings of his squire.

"Where are you bound for, Señor Don Quixote?" Sancho called after him. "What evil spirits in your bosom spur you on to go against our Catholic faith? Plague take me, can't you see that's a procession of penitents and that lady they're carrying on the litter is the most blessed image of the Immaculate Virgin? Look well what you're doing, my master, for this time it may be said that you really do not know."

His exertions were in vain, however, for his master was so bent upon having it out with the sheeted figures and freeing the lady clad in mourning that he did not hear a word, nor would he have turned back if he had, though the king himself might have commanded it. Having reached the procession, he reined in Rocinante, who by this time was wanting a little rest, and in a hoarse, excited voice he shouted, "You who go there with your faces covered, out of shame, it may be, listen well to what I have to say to you."

The first to come to a halt were those who carried the image; and then one of the four clerics who were intoning the litanies, upon beholding Don Quixote's weird figure, his bony nag, and other amusing appurtenances, spoke up in reply.

"Brother, if you have something to say to us, say it quickly, for these brethren are engaged in macerating their flesh, and we cannot stop to hear anything, nor is it fitting that we should, unless it is capable of being said in a couple of words."

"I will say it to you in one word," Don Quixote answered, "and that word is the following: 'Set free at once that lovely lady whose tears and mournful countenance show plainly that you are carrying her away against her will and that you have done her some shameful wrong. I will not consent to your going one step farther until you shall have given her the freedom that should be hers.' "

Hearing these words, they all thought that Don Quixote must be some madman or other and began laughing heartily; but their laughter proved to be gunpowder to his wrath, and without saying another word he drew his sword and fell upon the litter. One of those who bore the image, leaving his share of the burden to his companions, then sallied forth to meet the knight, flourishing a forked stick that he used to support the Virgin while he was resting; and upon this stick he now received a mighty slash that Don Quixote dealt him, one that shattered it in two, but with the piece about a third long that remained in his hand he came down on the shoulder of his opponent's sword arm, left unprotected by the buckler, with so much force that the poor fellow sank to the ground sorely battered and bruised.

Sancho Panza, who was puffing along close behind his master, upon seeing him fall cried out to the attacker not to deal another blow, as this was an unfortunate knight who was under a magic spell but who had never in all the days of his life done any harm to anyone. But the thing that stopped the rustic was not Sancho's words; it was, rather, the sight of Don Quixote lying there without moving hand or foot. And so, thinking that he had killed him, he hastily girded up his tunic and took to his heels across the countryside like a deer.

By this time all of Don Quixote's companions had come running up to where he lay; and the penitents, when they observed this, and especially when they caught sight of the officers of the Brotherhood with their crossbows,[1] at once rallied around the image, where they raised their hoods and grasped their whips [2] as the priests raised their tapers aloft in expectation of an assault; for they were resolved to defend themselves and even, if possible, to take the offensive against their assailants, but, as luck would have it, things turned out better than they had hoped. Sancho, meanwhile, believing Don Quixote to be dead, had flung himself across his master's body and was weeping and wailing in the most lugubrious and, at the same time, the most laughable fashion that could be imagined; and the curate had discovered among those who marched in the procession another curate whom he knew, their recognition of each other serving to allay the fears of all parties concerned. The first curate then gave the second a very brief account of who Don

Quixote was, whereupon all the penitents came up to see if the poor knight was dead. And as they did so, they heard Sancho Panza speaking with tears in his eyes.

"O flower of chivalry," he was saying, "the course of whose well-spent years has been brought to an end by a single blow of a club! O honor of your line, honor and glory of all La Mancha and of all the world, which, with you absent from it, will be full of evildoers who will not fear being punished for their deeds! O master more generous than all the Alexanders, who after only eight months of service presented me with the best island that the sea washes and surrounds! Humble with the proud, haughty with the humble, brave in facing dangers, long-suffering under outrages, in love without reason, imitator of the good, scourge of the wicked, enemy of the mean—in a word, a knight-errant, which is all there is to say." [3]

At the sound of Sancho's cries and moans, Don Quixote revived, and the first thing he said was, "He who lives apart from thee, O fairest Dulcinea, is subject to greater woes than those I now endure. Friend Sancho, help me onto that enchanted cart, as I am in no condition to sit in Rocinante's saddle with this shoulder of mine knocked to pieces the way it is."

"That I will gladly do, my master," replied Sancho, "and we will go back to my village in the company of these gentlemen who are concerned for your welfare, and there we will arrange for another sally and one, let us hope, that will bring us more profit and fame than this one has."

"Well spoken, Sancho," said Don Quixote, "for it will be an act of great prudence to wait until the present evil influence of the stars has passed."

The canon, the curate. and the barber all assured him that he would be wise in doing this; and so, much amused by Sancho Panza's simplicity, they placed Don Quixote upon the cart as before, while the procession of penitents re-formed and continued on its way. The goatherd took leave of all of them, and the curate paid the troopers what was coming to them, since they did not wish to go any farther. The canon requested the priest to inform him of the outcome of Don Quixote's madness, as to whether it yielded to treatment or not; and with this he begged permission to resume his journey. In short, the party broke up and separated, leaving only the curate and the barber, Don Quixote and Panza, and the good Rocinante, who looked upon everything that he had seen with the same resignation as his master.

Yoking his oxen, the carter made the knight comfortable upon a bale of hay, and then at his customary slow pace proceeded to follow the road that the curate directed him to take. At the end of six days they reached Don Quixote's village, making their entrance at noon of a Sunday, when the square was filled with a crowd of people through which the cart had to pass.

They all came running to see who it was, and when they recognized their townsman, they were vastly astonished. One lad sped to bring the news to the knight's housekeeper and his niece, telling them that their master had returned lean and jaundiced and lying stretched out upon a bale of hay on an ox-cart. It was pitiful to hear the good ladies' screams, to behold the way in which they beat their breasts, and to listen to the curses which they once more heaped upon those damnable books of chivalry, and this demonstration increased as they saw Don Quixote coming through the doorway.

At news of the knight's return, Sancho Panza's wife had hurried to the scene, for she had some while since learned that her husband had accompanied him as his squire; and now, as soon as she laid eyes upon her man, the first question she asked was if all was well with the ass, to which Sancho replied that the beast was better off than his master.

"Thank God," she exclaimed, "for all his blessings! But tell me now, my dear, what have you brought me from all your squirings? A new cloak to wear? Or shoes for the young ones?"

"I've brought you nothing of the sort, good wife," said Sancho, "but other things of greater value and importance."

"I'm glad to hear that," she replied. "Show me those things of greater value and importance, my dear. I'd like a sight of them just to cheer this heart of mine which has been so sad and unhappy all the centuries that you've been gone."

"I will show them to you at home, wife," said Sancho. "For the present be satisfied that if, God willing, we set out on another journey in search of adventures, you will see me in no time a count or the governor of an island, and not one of those around here, but the best that is to be had."

"I hope to Heaven it's true, my husband, for we certainly need it. But tell me, what is all this about islands? I don't understand."

"Honey," replied Sancho, "is not for the mouth of an ass.[4] You will find out in good time, woman; and you're going to be surprised to hear yourself called 'my Ladyship' by all your vassals."

"What's this you are saying, Sancho, about ladyships, islands, and vassals?" Juana Panza insisted on knowing—for such was the name of Sancho's wife, although they were not blood relatives, it being the custom in La Mancha for wives to take their husbands' surnames.

"Do not be in such a hurry to know all this, Juana," he said. "It is enough that I am telling you the truth. Sew up your mouth, then; for all I will say, in passing, is that there is nothing in the world that is more pleasant than being a respected man, squire to a knight-errant who goes in search of adventures. It is true that most of the adventures you meet with do not come out the way you'd like them to, for ninety-nine out of a hundred will prove to be all twisted and crosswise. I know that from experience, for I've come out of some of them blanketed and out of others beaten to a pulp. But, all the same, it's a fine thing to go along waiting for what will happen next, crossing mountains, making your way through woods, climbing over cliffs, visiting castles, and putting up at inns free of charge, and the devil take the maravedi that is to pay."

Such was the conversation that took place between Sancho Panza and Juana Panza, his wife, as Don Quixote's housekeeper and niece were taking him in, stripping him, and stretching him out on his old-time bed. He gazed at them blankly, being unable to make out where he was. The curate charged the niece to take great care to see that her uncle was comfortable and to keep close watch over him so that he would not slip away from them another time. He then told them of what it had been necessary to do in order to get him home, at which they once more screamed to Heaven and began cursing the books of chivalry all over again, praying God to plunge the authors of such lying nonsense into the center of the bottomless pit. In short, they scarcely knew what to do, for they were very much afraid that their master and uncle would give them the slip once more, the moment he was a little better, and it turned out just the way they feared it might.

But the author of this history, although he has made a most thorough and diligent search, has been unable to come upon any account—at least none based on authentic sources—of the deeds performed by Don Quixote on his third sally. There is only the tradition, handed down in La Mancha, to the effect that in the course of this third expedition he went to Saragossa, where he was present at some famous tourneys that were held in that city and where he met with adventures such as befitted his valor and sound judgment. As regards his last days and his death, the present writer was unable to come upon any record whatsoever, nor would he have known anything at all about it if it had not been for an old physician who had in his possession a lead box which, so he said, had been found in the crumbling foundation of a very old hermitage that was being rebuilt. In this box were discovered certain writings on parchment, consisting of Castilian verses in Gothic characters, which had much to say of the beauty of Dulcinea del Toboso, of Rocinante's figure, Sancho Panza's loyalty, and the burial of Don Quixote himself, along with various epitaphs and elegies having to do with his life and habits.

Those verses that could be plainly read and made out were the following, as set down here by the author of this new and matchless history, who, in return for all the enormous labor that it has cost him to compile this book and all the research amid the archives of La Mancha, only asks of his readers that they give it the same credence that the discerning do to those books of chivalry that are so popular in the world today. Let them but do this, and he will regard himself as having been well repaid. And he will then endeavor to search out and bring to light others which, if not so true, will at least be equal to the present one in the matter of invention and the diversion they afford.

The first words written on the parchment that was found in the leaden box were these:

*The academicians of Argamasilla,*⁵ *a village of La Mancha, on the life and death of the valorous Don Quixote de la Mancha,* HOC SCRIPSERUNT.

Monicongo,⁶ academician of Argamasilla, for Don Quixote's tomb:

EPITAPH

The scatterbrain who was fair La Mancha's pride
And brought her more spoils than Jason brought to Crete;
The wit like a weathercock, pointed so neat,
That would have better been on the blunter side;
The arm whose might was celebrated wide—
From Cathay to Gaeta ran its fame so fleet;
Muse most horrendous, with wisdom most replete
That e'er her verses did to bronze confide;
He who left the Amadises behind him far,
Resting upon his love and gallantry;
Who held the Galaors to be but drab;
Whose calm the Belianises could not mar;
Who on Rocinante rode for chivalry:
Such the one now lies beneath this frigid slab.

Paniaguado,[7] academician of Argamasilla, *in laudem Dulcineae del Toboso:*

SONNET

She whom you here behold, with the chubby face,
With the high bosom and the vigorous mien,
Is the beauteous Dulcinea, Toboso's queen.
The great Quixote loved her regal grace,
And for her sake it was that he did trace
The slopes of the black Sierra, the famed demesne
Of Montiel's fields and the alluring green
Of Aranjuez' plain, on foot, with weary pace.
'Twas Rocinante's fault! O unkind star
Of this Manchegan lady and this bold
Knight-errant: she in the flower of her youth
Saw her beauty fade in death as he roamed far;
And though his fame in marble has been told,
He had to flee from love, spite, man's untruth.

Caprichoso,[8] a most learned academician of Argamasilla, in praise of Rocinante, steed of Don Quixote de la Mancha:

SONNET[9]

Upon the haughty adamantine throne,[10]
Which Mars with bloody footprints doth defile,
The mad Manchegan bravely all the while
Unfurls his standard with a strength unknown,
Hangs up his arms, the steel of finest tone
That shatters, rends, and razes with his bile.
Undreamed of prowess! Art invents a style
For the new paladin she calls her own.
If Gaul of its Amadis is justly proud,
Whose brave descendants brought triumph to Greece,
A thousand triumphs and a fame widespread,
Today it is Quixote the unbowed
Whom Bellona crowns there where the wars ne'er cease;
And proudest of all, La Mancha rears its head.
His fame shall live when others long are dead;
For Baiardo, Brigliador [11] did not exceed
In valor Rocinante, that gallant steed.

Burlador,[12] academician of Argamasilla, on Sancho Panza:

SONNET

Sancho Panza is this one with body small,
But big in valor, miracle how strange!
The simplest-minded squire that e'er did range
This world of ours, believe me one and all.
He'd have been a count if this age's biting gall
Had not prevented him; he could not change
The spite of men that gnawed them like a mange,
Pursuing even a donkey to its stall.
Upon the ass he went, if I'm not wrong,
Meekest of squires behind the very meek
And faithful Rocinante, and his lord.
Oh, the vain hopes we cherish all life long!
Thinking at last to find the rest we seek,
But shadow, smoke, and dreams are our reward.

Cachidiablo,[13] academician of Argamasilla, on Don Quixote's tomb:

EPITAPH [14]

Below there rests the knight,
Ill-errant, battered, sore,
Whom Rocinante bore
On his wanderings, left and right.
Sancho Panza, if you inquire,
Lies also within this span,
The most faithful little man
E'er followed the trade of squire.

Tiquitoc,[15] academician of Argamasilla, for Dulcinea del Toboso's tomb:

EPITAPH

Here Dulcinea doth lie,
Who was plump and high of bust;
Now she is ashes and dust,
For horrid death passed by.

> *She was of noble race,*
> *Truly a highbred dame,*
> *The great Don Quixote's flame*
> *And the glory of this place.*

Such were the verses that could be made out. The others, being worm-eaten, were turned over to an academician that he might decipher their meaning by conjecture. It is reported that he has done so, at the cost of much labor and many sleepless nights, and that it is his purpose to publish them, which leads us to hope that we may be given an account of Don Quixote's third sally.

> *Forse altri canterá con miglior plettro.*[16]

NOTES

Translator's Introduction

1. Aubrey F. G. Bell, *Cervantes* (Norman: University of Oklahoma Press, 1947). For two distinguished articles called forth by this book see "Knight-Errant from La Mancha, Anniversary Reflections on Don Quixote and the Literary Magic of His Creator," by T. R. Ybarra, *The New York Times Book Review*, August 17, 1947, p. 1; and "The Laughter and Sanity of Don Quixote; This Year Marks the 400th Anniversary of a Genius, Cervantes," by Bertram D. Wolfe, *The New York Herald Tribune Weekly Book Review*, August 17, 1947, pp. 1–2. Mr. Ybarra is himself the author of one of the best biographical-interpretative studies, entitled *Cervantes* (New York: Albert and Charles Boni, 1931).

2. See the article by Aubrey Bell, "The Wisdom of Don Quixote," *Books Abroad,* Summer 1947, pp. 259–63.

3. Ibid.

4. See the beginning of Chapter LXXIV, Part II.

5. Aubrey Bell is of the opinion that every one should read *Don Quixote* "not less than three times in his or her life," in youth, middle age, and old age. (*Cervantes*, p. ix.)

6. One thinks of Lang's Homer, Childs' *Beowulf.*

7. *Paradise Lost* is another classic on which the dust has for some time been gathering; but T. S. Eliot has recently called for a return to Milton (whom Ezra Pound violently condemns), and this may have its effects upon the intellectuals at least.

8. Bell makes the point that Cervantes in reality brought the Spanish Renaissance to the people of Spain, serving as a mediator between the culture of the elite and the great popular audience. (See the opening chapter of his book, "Cervantes and the Renaissance.")

9. On Cervantes and the art of fiction, consult *Five Masters, A Study in Imitations of the Novel,* by Joseph Wood Krutch (New York: Jonathan Cape and Harrison Smith, 1930).

10. Himself a native of the province, Rodríguez Marín was the first to stress the heavy Andalusian element in Cervantes' work. See his brochures, *Cervantes en Andalucía* (Seville, 1905), and *El Andalucismo y el Cordobesismo de Miguel de Cervantes* (Madrid, 1915). In the notes to his edition of the *Don Quixote* he is constantly pointing out traces of this influence. It was while serving as a tax collector that Cervantes became familiar with the speech and customs of the Andalusians, just as Rabelais while residing at Fontenay-le-Comte absorbed the idiom and the folklore of Poitou. On this, see what I have to say in my introduction to *The Portable Rabelais* (New York: Viking Press, 1946), p. 21.

11. His article cited in note 1.

12. Two of these appeared in Lisbon and one in Valencia early in 1605.

13. The first French translation of the *Don Quixote* was César Oudin's version, Paris, 1616. Pahsch Basteln von der Sohle's partial German version was published at Cöthen in 1621, and Lorenzo Franciosini's Italian rendering appeared at Venice in 1621.

14. For English-language versions see the Bibliography following this Introduction.

15. See the Introduction to Ormsby's translation of *Don Quixote.*

16. Filleau de Saint-Martin's *Histoire de l'Admirable Don Quichotte de la Manche,* in four volumes, was first published at Paris, 1677–78. It ran through numerous editions down to the 1890's. His *Continuation* appeared in 1713. In this latter work he has Don Quixote recover from his illness at the end of Part II and resume his adventures.

17. This will be referred to simply as the Motteux version from now on.

18. See the Bibliography. For convenient reference, Lockhart's notes, including his translation of numerous ballads, will be found in the two-volume revised edition of Motteux's *Don Quixote* published in Bohn's Popular Library (London: G. Bell & Sons, 1913). It is Ozell's revision of Motteux, with a notable Introduction by Herschel Brickell, that appears in the Modern Library edition (New York, 1930).

19. As Ormsby remarks, Motteux could hardly be worse than Phillips. Ticknor may be said to have damned Motteux with faint praise. See the constrained apology for the use of the Motteux version, by E. Bell, in the Editor's Preface to the Bohn's Popular Library edition cited in the preceding note.

20. In this respect Motteux is far from being an Urquhart, whose version of Rabelais he completed. When Urquhart expands upon his author he gives us a piece of English that is worth reading for its own sake, whereas Peter Anthony only becomes all the more dull and offensive. (He was a Frenchman by birth, who came to England in his midtwenties and afterward wrote in the language of that country.) It is well to bear in mind the admonition given to the Moorish translator in Part I, Chapter IX: "Add nothing and subtract nothing."

21. The works referred to are Edmund Gayton's *Festivous Notes on the History and Adventures of the Renowned Don Quixote, Pleasant Notes upon Don Quixote* (London, 1654); and Edward Ward's *The Life and Notable Adventures of that Renown'd Knight, Don Quixote de la Mancha, Merrily Translated into Hudibrastick Verse* (London, 1711-12). Gayton was an Oxford don.

22. He will be referred to as Jarvis hereafter.

23. See Pope's "Epistle to Jervas."

24. For example, E. Bell (see note 19 above) finds the Jarvis version "more precise but dull and spiritless," while in his view Motteux is "the best representative" of the "expressive language that Steele, Defoe, and Fielding used."

25. Jarvis has been worked over, touched up, by later editors in an effort to make him more readable, but, as Ormsby notes, they have only detracted from his chief merit, which is his fidelity to the original—the revisions obviously were made without reference to the Spanish text.

26. Ormsby: "A literary imposture of remarkable impudence."

27. Miss Smirke's version was compiled to accompany the engravings of her brother, Robert Smirke, R. A. Ormsby calls it "a patchwork version made out of previous translations," while E. Bell terms it "a careful revision of Jarvis's translation." On the title-page of the first three editions it is described as "translated from the Spanish," but in the fourth and last printing (New York: D. Appleton & Company, 1855) it is frankly announced as "a revised translation based on those of Motteux, Jarvis, and Smollett." In connection with the Smirke plates, see *Illustrations for Don Quixote, Engraved by C. Warren, F. Engleheart, R. Golding, I. Scott, A. Smith, and S. Noble, from Designs by Robert Smirke* (London, 1811?).

28. It may be observed in passing that the four translators cited by Professor Rudolph Schevill in the notes to his Spanish edition of the *Don Quixote* are Oudin, Franciosini, Ludwig Tieck, and Ormsby. (On Tieck and the importance of his German version see the Bibliography following.) It is the Ormsby translation of *Don Quixote* that was selected by Fitzmaurice-Kelly for Volumes III-VI of his seven-volume edition in English of *The Complete Works of Miguel de Cervantes Saavedra* (Glasgow, 1901-1903); and Robinson Smith in the Introduction to his new edition of 1932 pays tribute to his predecessor.

29. This despite the locutions that have been dropped from general usage.

30. In Part II, Chapter XXVI, this saying is put into the mouth of Master Pedro, the puppet showman, who is addressing his apprentice; in Part II, Chapter XLIII, it is Don Quixote who utters the aphorism.

31. See the valuable dissertation of Margaret J. Bates, *"Discreción" in the Works of Cervantes* (Washington: Catholic University of America Press, 1945). Dr. Bates here takes one word that has a large number of fine shadings and shows how important it is not only for the interpretation of Cervantes'

text but for an understanding of his view of life as well. For an interesting discussion of the problems of the Cervantes translator the reader may refer to the essay by F. B. Franz Biedermann, *Don Quichotte et la Tâche de Ses Traducteurs* (Paris, 1837); this is a treatise based upon the work of the French translator Louis Viardot.

32. Unfortunately, this edition has for some while been out of print. In his Cervantes bibliography (see note 63) Professor Grismer indicates there is some question as to the date of the first edition of the Smith version.

33. See Ormsby's note, Part II, Chapter vi, of his translation.

34. Part II, Chapter iii.

35. For these works see the Bibliography.

36. In *La Lengua de Cervantes* Cejador has done for the creator of Don Quixote what M. Lazare Sainéan in *La Langue de Rabelais* (Paris, 1923) was to do a little later for the author of the *Gargantua* and *Pantagruel*.

37. Of the University of California.

38. The first two volumes, published in 1914, contain *La Galatea* and *Persiles y Sigismunda;* these were followed by six volumes of *Comedias y Entremeses,* 1915–22; the *Viaje del Parnaso* and the *Poesías Sueltas* (one volume each), 1922; three volumes of the *Novelas Ejemplares,* 1922–25; and, finally, Schevill's *Don Quixote,* the four volumes of which appeared in 1928, 1931, 1935, and 1941. Announced for future publication are a *Reseña Sucinta de la Vida de Cervantes* and an alphabetic index to the notes.

39. Such emendations, for instance, as are to be found in the edition of Juan Eugenio Hartzenbusch (1863), an editor whom Ormsby often follows. Hartzenbusch performed a valuable service by calling attention to the textual differences between the first and later editions, pointing out that these were not due to corrections made by the author; but he then proceeded to emend the first-edition text upon the basis of what he believed Cervantes "must have" written. Numerous examples of this will be found in the notes to the present translation.

40. See the editor's "Prólogo" to Tomo I of Schevill's *Don Quixote.*

41. See Chapter xxiii and note 2.

42. On this subject see Cortejón's brochure, *¿Corrigió Cervantes alguna de las ediciones del Don Quixote impresas por Juan de la Cuesta?* (Barcelona, 1907).

43. Compare Ormsby's remarks in the Introduction to his *Don Quixote.*

44. Duffield, Ormsby, and Watts all retain "ingenious" and the spelling "Quixote."

45. See Part I, Chapters xii–xiv.

46. This is the form that Cervantes regularly employs in place of the modern *Usted,* which, however, occurs in the *novela* of uncertain authorship, *La Tia Fingida.*

47. "Your Worship" is somewhat foreign to American ears. "Your Grace" has the advantage of being literal and the disadvantage of being commonly associated with a personage of ducal or archiepiscopal rank.

48. Here, the Schevill text has been used as a guide from which I have freely departed when there was reason for doing so.

49. An example of the kind of sentence that comes near to being the despair of any translator will be found in Part II, Chapter 1 (Schevill, Tomo III, pp. 45–46): "*Ya no ay ninguno que saliendo deste bosque entre en aquella montaña, y de alli, pise vna esteril y desierta playa del mar, las mas vezes proceloso y alterado; y hallando en ella y en su orilla vn pequeño batel sin remos, vela, mastil, ni xarcia alguna, con intrepido coraçon se arroge en el, entregandose a las implacables olas del mar profundo, que ya le suben al cielo y ya le baxan al abismo, y el, puesto el pecho a la incontrastable borrasca, quando menos se cata, se halla tres mil y mas leguas distante del lugar donde se embarco; y saltando en tierra remota y no conocida le suceden cosas dignas de estar escritas, no en pergaminos, sino en bronces.*" Yet this is beautiful Castilian, with a classic dignity that puts one in mind of certain passages in Vergil. And it will be observed how that terseness within the sentence of which I have spoken is achieved. Not infrequently Cervantes is so very terse as to recall the famous *"Veni, vidi, vici"* attributed to Caesar, as in the closing lines of Chapter iii, Part II: "*. . . tuuo el bachiller el em-*

bite, quedose, añadiose al ordinario vn par de pichones, tratose en la mesa de cauallerias, siguiole el humor Carrasco, acabose el banquete, durmieron la siesta, boluio Sancho y renouose la platica passada."

50. There is good precedent for this among the great Elizabethan translators: compare the practice of Philemon Holland in his translation of Livy; see F. O. Matthiessen's *Translation, An Elizabethan Art* (Cambridge: Harvard University Press, 1931), pp. 185–86.

51. Two examples at random: Part II, Chapter LX (Schevill, Tomo IV, p. 267): *Mandoselos boluer al punto Roque Guinart, y, mandando poner los suyos en ala, mandó traer alli delante . . ."* (the verb *mandar* used three times in two lines); and Part II, Chapter LXVI (Schevill, Tomo IV, p. 331): *". . . vn vezino deste lugar, tan gordo que pesa onze arrobas, dessafió a correr a otro su vezino, que no pesa mas que cinco. Fue le condicion que auian de correr vna carrera de cien pasos con pesos iguales, y, auiendole preguntado al dessafiador como se auia de igualar el peso, dixo que el dessaffiado, que pesa cinco arrobas, se pusiesse seis de hierro a cuestas . . ."* (note the repetition of *pesar—peso*, five times in six lines of text!).

52. Occasionally the synonyms have the effect of the rhetorical figure known as hendiadys, while the verbs may have an adjectival shading.

53. See the *Journey to Parnassus, Translated into English Tercets with Preface and Illustrative Notes,* by James Y. Gibson (London, 1883).

54. See *The Poetry of the "Don Quixote" of Don Miguel de Cervantes Saavedra* (London, 1887). I have not looked at the Gibson version while making this translation.

55. Compare M. Eloi Johanneau's Variorum edition of Rabelais.

56. See the Bibliography. The edition by the Spanish Royal Academy had appeared the year before (1780).

57. To suit his fancy, he even changed the title of the work to *Historia del Famoso Cavallero Don Quixote de la Mancha (History of the Famous Knight,* etc.).

58. See Appendix III to Ormsby's translation, "Bibliography of 'Don Quixote.' "

59. This is essentially the stress of Rodríguez Marín. An annotator like Robinson Smith, on the other hand, is in the Bowle tradition.

60. See the introduction to the Rodríguez Marín edition in the Clásicos Castellanos series (see Bibliography).

61. See *Sancho Panza's Proverbs and Others Which Occur in Don Quixote; with a Literal English Translation, Notes, and an Introduction,* by U. R. Burke (London, 1872; third edition, 1892). Also, by the same hand, *Spanish Salt, A Collection of All the Proverbs Which Are to Be Found in Don Quixote* (London, 1877).

62. See the Bibliography under "Commentators and Lexicographers."

63. Raymond L. Grismer, *Cervantes: A Bibliography: Books, Essays, Articles, and Other Studies on the Life of Cervantes, His Works, and His Imitators* (New York: H. W. Wilson, 1946). See also, *Cervantes, A Tentative Bibliography of His Works and of the Biographical and Critical Material Concerning Him,* by Jeremiah D. M. Ford and Ruth Lansing (Cambridge: Harvard University Press, 1931).

A Note On the Author

1. For scholarly summaries of what is known about Cervantes the reader may be referred to the following works: *Cervantes,* by William J. Entwhistle (Oxford: Clarendon Press, 1940); *Cervantes,* by Rudolph Schevill (New York: Duffield & Company [Master Spirits of Literature series], 1919); *Miguel de Cervantes Saavedra: A Memoir,* by James Fitzmaurice-Kelly (Oxford: Clarendon Press, 1913); and *Two Essays* (I: "Don Quixote"), by William Paton Kerr (Glasgow: J. Maclehose and Sons, 1918).

2. It is in thinking of him as an old soldier that we are best able to understand Cervantes' psychology, his attitude on many questions. He is essentially an ardent patriot, a fervent Catholic, an impecunious *hidalgo*, and a life-battered man of letters.

3. What may be a description of the author's own Italian journeyings, resembling those of the ordinary tourist, will be found in the story "Man of Glass" (*El Licenciado Vidriera*) in the *Exemplary Novels*.

4. This is not to be taken as a literal account of Cervantes' experiences, but it is basically autobiographic.

5. In 1581, for example, he is in the service of the King as a messenger and in May and June of that year visits Tomar (Portugal), Oran, and Cartagena.

6. These were the *Numancia* and the *Pictures of Algiers* (*El Trato de Argel*). They were first printed in 1784, from newly discovered manuscript copies. On one occasion Cervantes is to be found contracting with a theatrical manager for six comedies at fifty ducats (about thirty dollars) each. When he published his dramatic works, in 1615, he entitled the volume *Eight Comedies and Eight Interludes, Original and Never Performed* (*Ocho Comedias y Ocho Entremeses Nuevos y Nunca Representados*). See the recent fine translation of the *Interludes* by S. Griswold Morley (Princeton: Princeton University Press, 1948).

7. See especially the *novela* "Rinconete and Cortadillo." Some of this argot is also to be found in *Don Quixote*, in such an episode, for example, as the freeing of the galley slaves (Part I, Chapter XXII). On the legend concerning the composition of Part I in prison, see the Prologue to Part I, note 1.

8. Valladolid was then the capital.

9. He may have been living in retirement at Esquivias, possibly at Valladolid.

10. "In any genre," says Lionel Trilling, "it may happen that the first great example contains the whole potentiality of the genre. It has been said that all philosophy is a footnote to Plato. It can be said that all prose fiction is a variation on the theme of *Don Quixote*. Cervantes sets for the novel the problem of

appearance and reality . . ." See Trilling's essay on "Manners and the Novel," *The Kenyon Review*, Winter 1948.

11. See Part II, Chapter III. In the following chapter we are told that Cid Hamete (the supposed author of *Don Quixote*) is "more interested in the profit that may come to him from it than in any praise it may earn him." See also Part II, Chapter LXII, where another author says: "I do not write books to win fame in this world . . . it is money that I seek, for without it a good reputation is not worth a cent." I for one cannot accept the view put forth by Professor Joaquín Casalduero, to the effect that Cervantes had from the start, deliberately and carefully, plotted out a masterpiece of baroque art. See the paper by Casalduero, "The Composition of *Don Quixote*," in *Cervantes Across the Centuries, A Quadricentennial Volume*, edited by Angel Flores and M. J. Benardete (New York: The Dryden Press, 1947) pp. 56–93. Both the internal and the external evidence seems to me to be against it. Whatever else he may or may not have been, the author of *Don Quixote* was not an ivory tower dweller. (The Flores-Benardete collection, by the way, affords a good cross section of present day Cervantes scholarship and is the only one of its kind available in English.)

12. The idea was not original with Cervantes. In 1597 it had formed the subject of a dramatic piece of inferior quality, the *Entremés de los Romances* (*Interlude of the Ballads*, that is, the ballads of chivalry), the authorship of which is unknown—one critic has attempted to assign it to Cervantes himself. And in the fourteenth century the Italian novelist Franco Sacchetti had created a character whose adventures resemble those of the Knight of La Mancha.

13. In his *Five Masters: A Study in the Mutations of the Novel* (New York: Jonathan Cape & Harrison Smith, 1930), Joseph Wood Krutch compares certain aspects of Cervantes' thinking with the philosophy of "As If"; and in Part II, Chapter XXII, Don Quixote makes a statement that sounds as if it

were directly out of Sartre: "God knows whether or not there is a Dulcinea in this world . . . I contemplate her as she needs must be" ("*como conviene que sea*"). Today it is Kierkegaard and Sartre and the Existentialists. In Cervantes' time it was Augustine and Plato—Plato versus Aristotle.

14. See the essay by Frank, "The Career of the Hero," in *Cervantes Across the Centuries* (*op. cit.*, pp. 183–94).

15. Judging from what Cervantes has to say about publishers, one suspects that they may not always have been honest with him in their dealings.

16. It was formerly believed that the *Persiles* was written during the period under consideration here, but Professor Mack Singleton has put forward the somewhat heretical idea that it was a work of Cervantes' youth which he resurrected as he lay dying in order to provide a little revenue for his family. See Singleton's paper: "The 'Persiles' Mystery," in *Cervantes Across the Centuries* (*op. cit.*, pp. 256–63).

17. For some time the belief was current that Cervantes and Shakespeare had died on the same day; but the latter's death occurred on April 23 (Old Style).

NOTES

Part One

PROLOGUE

1. In the biographical sketch of Cervantes prefixed to his translation of the *Don Quixote*, John Ormsby writes: "The words in the preface to the First Part of 'Don Quixote' are generally held to be conclusive that he conceived the idea of the book, and wrote the beginning of it at least, in a prison, and that he may have done so is extremely likely. At the same time it should be borne in mind that they contain no assertion to that effect, and may mean nothing more than that this brain-child of his was begotten under circumstances as depressing as prison life. If we accept them literally, the prison may well have been that in which he was confined for nearly three months at Seville." A recent biographer, Mariano Tomás (*The Life and Misadventures of*

Miguel de Cervantes, translated from the Spanish by Warre B. Wells [Boston: Houghton Mifflin, 1934], pp. 160–161) states: "When . . . Miguel de Cervantes was released from the prison of Seville . . . he also carried with him . . . the first part of *The Ingenious Knight, Don Quixote de la Mancha.*"

2. In its original form, this proverb reads: "*Al rey mando*—I give orders to the king"; compare "An Englishman's house is his castle."

3. From a fable, *De cane et lupo*, of the twelfth-century Walther [Gualterus] Anglicus. Compare Aesop and La Fontaine.

4. Horace, *Odes*, 1, iv, 13–14.

5. For the first of these biblical quotations, see Matthew 5:44 and Luke 6: 27, 35. For the second, Matthew 15:19 and Mark 7:21.

6. These lines are from Ovid's *Tristia*, I, ix, 5–6; the Cato referred to is Dionysius Cato, author of the *Disticha de Moribus*, a verse treatise on morals and manners widely used as a school text in the Renaissance era.

7. Reference here is to the valley of Elah, mentioned in I. Samuel 17:2; in the Vulgate, Elah is rendered as Terebinthus.

8. Noted thief of classical mythology, giant son of Vulcan, who dwelt on Mount Aventinus and disturbed the entire region round about with his depredations; he stole the cattle of Geryon from Hercules and was slain by him; see Ovid's *Fasti*, I, 543 ff., Vergil's *Aeneid*, VIII, 190 ff., and other Latin writers.

9. Allusion to the *Epistolae Familiares* (1539–45) of Antonio de Guevara. Orsmby finds this "a touch after Swift's heart."

10. Leon the Hebrew (died in 1520) was the author of the *Dialoghi d'Amore*, published in 1535.

11. The *Amor de Dios* of Cristóbal de Fonseca was published in 1594.

12. See Chapter II following and note 2.

PREFATORY VERSES

1. These pieces are burlesques on the laudatory poems which customarily prefaced the books that appeared in Cervantes' day. They are not to be taken as serious poetry. Urganda is a personage in the *Amadis of Gaul*, Lobeira's famous romance of chivalry (see Part I, Chapter VI). She in a manner combines the traits of Morgan the Fay, Vivien, and Merlin, the connotation here being that of "magic," which the author, in the original Spanish, playfully endeavors to suggest by means of a most unusual verse form. The epithet "*Desconocida*" (rendered as "Unknown") refers to Urganda's manifold disguises or transformations—"the Unrecognized." As for the verse form in question, it is a ten-line stanza with the rhyme scheme abbaaccddc; but its peculiarity consists in lopping off the final syllable of the last word in each verse, throwing the assonantal rhyme on the penultimate vowel. Thus:

> De un noble hidalgo manche—
> contarás las aventu—

a quien ociosas lectu—
trastornaron las cabe—

This passage from the beginning of the third stanza will serve to show how it is done. (It will be noted that the lopped-off syllables may or may not rhyme.) The invention of this form was commonly attributed to Cervantes, though it does him no great credit, but it probably was used before his time. It is one that in reality cannot be imitated in English, and there would seem to be little point in making the attempt. Accordingly, in this first piece I have ignored the lopped-line technique, but in two short ones later on in which it is again employed I have tried to give some idea of it.

2. Cervantes' patron; see the dedication of Part I.

3. Of La Mancha.

4. This is seen as a dig at Lope de Vega, whose portrait in a couple of early volumes of his work had beneath it a heraldic shield.

5. Alvaro (Alvarez) de Luna, Constable of Castile and favorite of John II, lost the royal favor and was beheaded at Valladolid in 1450.

6. Allusion to the Spanish captivity of Francis I of France, Charles V's prisoner.

7. Allusion to Juan Latino, Negro slave of the Duke of Sesa, who was made professor of Latin and Rhetoric at the University of Granada, a post that he held for sixty years.

8. This sonnet has reference to Don Quixote's penance in the Sierra Morena as narrated in Part I, Chapters xxv ff.

9. See Part I, Chapter xxv and note 6.

10. See Part I, Chapter I and note 4.

11. Heroine of the *Amadis of Gaul*.

12. Oriana's castle near London.

13. The lady's reputation had suffered from the too frequent visits which Amadis paid to her castle.

14. Reference has been seen to the author himself or to Lope de Vega.

15. The *buzcorona* consisted in cuffing a person over the head as he bent to kiss another's hand.

16. "Donoso" signifies gay, witty, or graceful. "Interlarded" is for "*entreverado*"—literally, "intermingled." On the verse form, see note 1 preceding. For the reader's convenience, the last word of each line has been given in full

in parentheses, which is not done in the original. The imitation is by no means an exact one, since in the Spanish it is not merely the final consonant or consonant and unaccented final vowel that is omitted but an entire syllable that is normally pronounced.

17. The allusion is not clear. No such character as Villadiego the Silent is to be met with in the comedy *Celestina*, referred to a few lines farther on.

18. *Celestina, or the Tragicomedy of Calisto and Melibaea*, by Fernando Rojas, published in 1499.

19. Babieca was the Cid's famous mount.

20. Hero of *Lazarillo de Tormes*, the well-known *novela* by Diego Hurtado de Mendoza. In this picaresque tale, Lazarillo steals his blind master's wine by means of a straw. Another allusion to the work will be found in Part I, Chapter XXII.

21. These sonnets are very inferior productions, and the first one, in particular, is so muddled at the end as to make little or no sense; it is only by adopting, as I have done here, Hartzenbusch's suggested emendation that one is able to extract a satisfactory meaning from the closing lines.

22. Orlando was one of the Twelve Peers (see Part I, Chapters VI and XLIX); there is, of course, a play on Peer and peer.

23. Angelica was Orlando's love who threw him over for Medoro; see Part I, Chapter X, and elsewhere following.

24. Hero of the romance *Knight of the Sun, Mirror of Princes and Knights (Caballero del Febo, Espejo de Principes y Caballeros)*, by Diego Ortuñez de Calahorra and Marcos Martínez, first printed at Saragossa in 1562.

25. Either an invented name or a printer's error for Solinan, a knight mentioned in the *Amadis of Gaul*.

26. The Cid's famous steed.

27. The name Rocinante is from *"rocin,"* a "hack."

CHAPTER I

1. In the past this village has been identified as Argamasilla de Alba, in La Mancha, and a legend grew up to the effect that Cervantes had been imprisoned there and hence had a grudge against the place "the name of which I have no desire to recall." Thus, Ormsby, in his biographical sketch of Cervantes, states emphatically: "That Argamasilla is Don Quixote's village does not admit of a doubt," and he goes on to point out that it is the only village in the region ("except perhaps its near neighbor Tomelloso") that satisfies the topographical exigencies of the narrative. More recent researches, however, have shown that down to the beginning of the seventeenth century there was no jail in Argamasilla and that Cervantes, in all probability, was never there. In the introduction to his edition of Ludwig Tieck's German version of *Don Quixote* (Strassburg, 1905, 1911), Wolfgang von Wurzbach compares this legend to the fiction of the Arabic "author" of the tale, Cid Hamete Benengeli. In his spurious continuation of *Don Quixote*, Alonso Fernández de Avellaneda named Argamasilla as the village in question, but it is more likely that Cervantes had no particular one in mind.

2. The phrase in the original, *"duelos y quebrantos,"* has given commentators and translators no end of trouble, and its meaning still remains uncertain (see the extended note in Schevill and Bonilla's edition of the *Obras Completas*, Vol. 15, *Don Quixote*, Tomo I, pp. 431–36). It does not seem to have occurred in literature before Cervantes, who was probably drawing upon the popular speech. It seems to have been a mixture of the scraps of fowl and pork, etc., which it was permissible to eat on Saturday, a day of semi-abstinence. Oudin in his French translation of 1614 rendered the expression as *"des oeufs et du lard,"* and Franciosini in his Italian version (1621) has *"frittate rognose,"* which he explains in a marginal note as being *"presciutto fritto con huova."* In other words, bacon and eggs, or ham and eggs, which Rodríguez Marín accepts as a good translation. Jarvis translates as "pains and breakings" and in his notes describes the dish as an "amlet" (omelet). Motteux: "griefs and groans on Saturdays." All in all, "scraps" appears to be the best, or at any rate the safest, rendering in English.

3. Feliciano de Silva was the author of the *Chronicle of Don Florisel de Niquea*, published in 1532, 1536, and

1551. The first passage quoted immediately below is from this work; the second is from Torquemada's *Olivante de Laura* (1564).

4. Reference is to the *History of Don Belianís of Greece*, by Jerónimo Fernández (1547).

5. Sigüenza was one of the "minor universities" (*universidades menores*), and a good deal of fun was poked at its graduates.

6. Protagonist of the ninth book of the *Amadis* series.

7. One of the principal personages in Boiardo's *Orlando Innamorato*.

8. Galalón (Ganelon) was the traitor of the Charlemagne legend.

9. The *real de vellón* was a coin worth about five cents. The cuarto, or four-maravedi piece, was the eighth part of a real.

10. "All skin and bones." The expression is common in classic literature; it will be found in Plautus and elsewhere. Gonela was an Italian jester in the service of the Duke of Ferrara (1450–1470).

11. In Spanish, *rocín*.

12. Quixote (*quijote*) literally means the piece of armor that protects the thigh. Quijada and Quesada were distinguished family names.

CHAPTER II

1. "*Armas blancas*" is properly "blank armor," but Don Quixote takes "*blancas*" in its literal sense—"white."

2. The Campo de Montiel was the scene of the battle, in 1369, in which Peter the Cruel was defeated by his brother Henry.

3. On Puerto Lápice and the windmills, see Chapters VIII and IX following.

4. Ormsby: "The particular *venta* [inn] . . . in this and the next chapter is said to be the Venta de Quesada, about two and a half leagues north of Manzanares, on the Madrid and Seville road. The house itself was burned down about a century ago, and has been rebuilt, but the yard at the back with its draw-well and stone trough are said to remain as they were in his [Cervantes'] day."

5. The sense of "*sanos de Castilla*" appears to be "thieves in disguise" (gypsy argot). "*Castellano*" means both "Castilian" and "a castellan."

6. These verses and the two quoted above are from an old ballad, "Moriana en un Castillo," possibly dating from the fourteenth century.

7. A parody of the opening lines of the ballad of Lancelot of the Lake. See Chapter XIII and note 2.

8. The first edition reads "*alzada la visera*"—"with his visor raised," but in that case, as commentators have pointed out, Don Quixote would have had no trouble in feeding himself. Hartzenbusch first emended "*visera*" to read "*babera*" ("beaver"), an emendation which Ormsby adopted, but later he decided that the correct reading was "*atada la visera*"—"with the visor fastened," and with this Fitzmaurice-Kelly agrees. Rodríguez Marín states that "*alzada la visera*" is obviously an error, though he does not suggest an emendation of his own. I have followed Hartzenbusch and Fitzmaurice-Kelly.

CHAPTER III

1. Percheles was the name of the place outside Málaga where fish were dried and sold; Isles of Riarán was the name of a disreputable suburb of the same city. The District of Seville was an open space on the river side of the town, near the Plaza de Toros, where fairs, etc., were held. The Olivera of Valencia was a small plaza in the center of the city. The Rondilla of Granada is said to have been in the Albaycin quarter. The Horse Fountain of Cordova refers to a section on the south side of the town that took its name from a stone horse standing over a fountain. The other expressions are self-explanatory. All these localities are said to have been the haunts of rogues and thieves.

2. This clause ("*como que era otra cosa de más importancia*") is none too clear.

3. An old plaza in Toledo.

CHAPTER IV

1. The barber was also the surgeon.

2. The word "*haldudo*" means "fullskirted."

3. A proverbial expression.

4. The sense of "perfumed" is "completely," "to perfection."

5. An obscure oath.

6. Alcarria was a sparsely populated region in the upper valley of the Tagus.

Estremadura was a province noted for its backwardness.

7. A proverb.

8. Civet, a favored perfume, was imported in cotton packing.

9. Another proverb. Guadarrama was known for its spindles.

CHAPTER V

1. Cervantes is here confusing two old ballads. According to the story, Carloto (or Charlot), Charlemagne's son, sought to kill Baldwin that he might marry his widow. Sorely wounded, Baldwin was found and succored by his uncle, the Marquis of Mantua.

2. The love of the Moor Abindarráez and the beautiful Jarifa (or Xarifa) was a favorite theme with Moorish and Christian minstrels and was incorporated by Jorge de Montemayor, referred to a few lines further on, in the second edition of his *Diana*.

3. See the following chapter and note 17.

CHAPTER VI

1. Fifth book of the Amadis of Gaul series, published in 1521.

2. Work by Feliciano de Silva (1535), ninth book of the Amadis series.

3. Work by Antonio de Torquemada (1564). The *Garden of Flowers* (1575) was translated into English in 1600 as *The Spanish Mandeville*.

4. Work by Lenchor Ortega de Ubeda (1556).

5. Fourth book of the Palmerin series (1533).

6. The first part of *The Knight of the Cross*, by an unknown hand, appeared in 1543; the second part, by Pedro de Luxan, in 1563.

7. Published in four parts, at Seville, 1533–50, one of the most popular of the Carolingian romances.

8. The *Fables* of Turpin (1527) belong to the Carolingian cycle. He was a monk of Saint-Denis and Bishop of Reims (mentioned by Rabelais). In *The Mirror of Chivalry* he is constantly cited for his veracity, and the Italian writers Ariosto, Boiardo, and Pulci speak of him as "Turpin who never lies in any place."

9. Matteo Maria Boiardo, fifteenth-century author of the *Orlando Innamorato*.

10. As a token of respect.

11. Allusion to Ariosto's Spanish translator, Gerónimo Jiménez de Urrea, whose version was published at Antwerp in 1549.

12. The works referred to are the *History of the Deeds of Bernardo del Carpio*, by Agustín Alonso of Salamanca (Toledo, 1585), and *The Famous Battle of Roncesvalles* by Francisco Garrido de Villena (Valencia, 1555).

13. The *Palmerin de Oliva* (Salamanca, 1511), of uncertain authorship, was the first of the Palmerin cycle. The first Spanish edition of the *Palmerin of England* appeared in 1547, translated from the first Portuguese edition (1544?). See W. E. Purser, *Palmerin of England* (London, 1904).

14. See Chapter I, note 4.

15. This clause provided that when a person overseas was sued or indicted he might have a certain allowance of time in which to put in an appearance.

16. This work, by Johannot Martorell and Johan de Galba, was first published in the Catalan language at Valencia in 1490; a Castilian version appeared at Valladolid in 1511.

17. Jorge de Montemayor died in 1561, in which year the second edition of his *Diana* appeared (the date of the first is uncertain). Gil Polo's continuation was published at Valencia in 1564. This was the first and best of the Spanish pastoral romances. See H. A. Rennert, *The Spanish Pastoral Romances* (Philadelphia: University of Pennsylvania Press, 1912; originally published at Baltimore in 1892 by the Modern Language Association).

18. Published at Barcelona in 1573.

19. *The Shepherd of Iberia* is by Bernardo de la Vega (Seville, 1591); *The Nymphs and Shepherds of Henares*, by Bernardo González de Bovadilla, was published at Alcalá de Henares in 1587; *The Disenchantments of Jealousy*, by Bartolmé López de Enciso appeared at Madrid in 1586.

20. This pastoral by Luis Gálvez de Montalvo of Guadalajara was published at Madrid in 1582.

21. Work by Pedro de Padilla (Madrid, 1580).

22. López de Maldonado's *Cancionero* appeared at Madrid in 1586.

23. A proverb.

24. According to Ormsby, this "shows pretty clearly that until *Don Quixote* had made the author's name known, the *Galatea* had remained unnoticed."

25. There were three editions of the *Araucana*: Madrid, 1569, 1578, and 1590. The *Austriada* (Madrid, 1584) deals with John of Austria. The *Monserrate*, by the dramatist Virués (Madrid, 1588) gave M. G. Lewis the inspiration for his famous novel *The Monk*.

26. The work referred to is the *Angélica* of Luis Barahona de Soto (Madrid, 1586).

27. In connection with this chapter and the works mentioned in it, see Esther B. Sylvia, "Don Quixote's Library," *More Books, The Bulletin of the Boston Public Library*, April 1940, pp. 135-52.

CHAPTER VII

1. Reference to the *Carolea* of Gerónimo Sempere (1560), dealing with the victories of Charles V and the *León of Spain* of Pedro de la Vezilla, a poem on the history of the city of León.

2. No work by this title is known. Luis de Avila was the author of a prose commentary on the wars with the German Protestants.

3. Frestón was a magician; he was reputed to be the author of the *Belianís of Greece*.

4. A proverb.

5. Sancho's wife appears under various names.

CHAPTER VIII

1. That is, "the Pounder."

2. The Biscayans, or Basques, were supposed to speak broken Spanish. One characteristic of their speech was the use of the second person for the first. This can be brought out in English only if one is using the "thou" form. Thus Ormsby renders this passage: ". . . by the God that made me, unless thou quittest coach, slayest thee as art here a Biscayan." Like Motteux, I have represented this idiosyncrasy of dialect by substituting the objective for the nominative case—"me kill you."

3. A play on the double meaning of *"caballero"*—"knight" and "gentleman."

4. The proverbial expression is "carry the cat to the water"—*"llevar el gato al agua."* The Biscayan inverts the saying.

5. The allusion is to the *Amadis of Gaul*. The expression is one used at the beginning of a fray. Agrajes is a bellicose personage in that romance.

6. This device of breaking off the tale between one part of a work and the following one is common in the romances of chivalry.

7. Reference here is to the four-part division of the first volume of *Don Quixote*, a division which the author ignored when he came to publish the second volume. The first part originally ended here.

CHAPTER IX

1. Reference is to the Hebrew language.

2. Two arrobas would be about fifty pounds; two fanegas, a little over three bushels.

3. That is, "Paunch and Shanks."

CHAPTER X

1. A tribunal, dating from the thirteenth century, for dealing with crimes on the highway and in the open countryside.

2. Play on the words *"homecidio"* and *"omecillo"*; the phrase *"no catar omecillo a ninguno"* means "not to bear ill will, or a grudge, toward anyone."

3. Allusion to Boiardo's *Orlando*; it was, however, not Sacripante, but another personage, Dardinel, who paid so dearly for the helmet of Mambrino, the Moorish king. Another allusion to the *Orlando* occurs a few paragraphs further on ("men of arms that came to Albraca to win the fair Angelica").

4. An imaginary realm.

5. In the *Amadis of Gaul* Firm Island is the promised land for the faithful squires of knights-errant.

CHAPTER XI

1. Reference to the *noria*, a machine with buckets attached used in irrigation.

2. The verse form here is trochaic tetrameter with assonant rhymes in the second and fourth lines, a variety of rhyme which is impossible to imitate in English but which in Spanish with its stressed vowels is adapted to singing. The ballad has accordingly been rendered with ordinary rhymes.

CHAPTER XII

1. Reference to the *autos*, or allegorical religious dramas.

2. Play on *sarna*, the itch, and Sarah, Abraham's wife. "Older than the itch" is a proverb of ancient lineage.

3. Ormsby: "Though Cervantes tries to observe dramatic propriety by making Pedro blunder, in the end he puts into his mouth language as fine and words as long as Don Quixote's."

4. Literally, "which had the sun on one side [one cheek] and the moon on the other." Compare Part II, Chapter XLVIII.

CHAPTER XIII

1. The name Quintañona is Spanish, meaning a woman with a hundredweight (*quintal*) of years, i.e., a centenarian.

2. These lines are from the ballad that was parodied in Chapter II preceding. The ballad will be found in the *Cancionero de Romances* (Antwerp, n.d.) and in Agustín Durán's *Romancero General* (Madrid: 1849-51), No. 352.

3. The *Felixmarte of Hircania* has been referred to in Chapter VI preceding as *Florismarte of Hircania* (see note 4 there).

4. The lines are translated from the *Orlando Furioso*, XXIV, 57.

5. The word *"Gachupin"* literally means a Spaniard living in or returned from the colonies.

CHAPTER XIV

1. This poem in the original is marked by an intricacy of structure (interwoven rhymes, etc.) that cannot be imitated in English. The rhyme scheme of the sixteen-line stanza is abcabccdbbdeefef.

2. Envied as the bird that witnessed the crucifixion.

3. The Tagus River.

4. The Guadalquivir River.

CHAPTER XV

1. Yanguas was a district in the north of Castile. In the first edition there is a confusion in the text between Yanguesans and Galicians.

2. Untranslatable word play on *"feo Blas"* ("ugly Blas") and *"Fierabrás"*;

on Fierabrás's balm see Chapter X preceding.

3. Another pun that cannot be rendered literally, a play on *"sin costas"*—"without (court) costs," and *"sin costillas"*—"without ribs." Ormsby translates it: ". . . that my beast should have come off scot-free while we come out scotched."

4. The Greek city of Thebes.

CHAPTER XVI

1. The knight muttered his lady's name "between his teeth" as he went into the fray; see Chapter XIII preceding.

2. In the sense of "star-lit" (compare Ormsby); that is, with crevices in the roof through which the light of the stars could enter. The phrase has troubled translators. Shelton omits it; Jarvis renders it as "illustrious"; Motteux has "wretched apartment."

3. The work bearing the title *The Chronicle of the Noble Knights Tablante de Ricamonte and Jofre, Son of Count Donason*, etc., was published at Toledo in 1531; there is a copy in the British Museum. It is by an unknown hand. A later version is attributed to one Nuño Garay. Count Tomillas was a character in the *novela* entitled *Story of Enrique de Oliva, King of Jerusalem, Emperor of Constantinople* (Seville, 1498).

4. Allusion to a children's tale that is part of the European folklore heritage. (See Schevill and Rodríguez Marín.)

5. The highway police; see Chapter X preceding, note 1.

CHAPTER XVII

1. The phrase is from the beginning of one of the old ballads of the Cid.

2. Coin worth about a sixth of a maravedi.

3. The wool carders of Segovia were famous throughout Spain. On the Horse Fountain of Cordova, see Chapter III preceding, note 1. Fair of Seville was the name given to a low quarter of that city.

CHAPTER XVIII

1. "Ceca" (literally, "a mint") was the name given to a part of the Mosque of Cordova. A proverbial expression corresponding to our "from pillar to post."

2. The reference here is not to Amadis of Gaul but to Amadis of Greece.

3. The participle *"cuajada"* means "curdled," which Ormsby renders as "churned up." Clemencín substitutes *"causada"*—"caused."

4. Ormsby: "Suero de Quiñones, hero of the *Paso Honroso* at Orbiga in 1434, used to fight against the Moors with his arm bare."

5. The sense is either "trail my fortune" or "my fortune creeps." There may be a double meaning. The asparagus plant would suggest the latter interpretation.

6. As has been noted, the Betis (Baetis) is the present Guadalquivir River.

7. Granada is on the Genil River.

8. Tartessus was an ancient maritime city of Spain.

9. Jerez (Xerez), near Cadiz, is noted for its sherry wines; our word "sherry" is derived from the name.

10. River flowing down from the Cantabrian Mountains and emptying into the Douro River below Valladolid.

11. This river of Spain and Portugal, emptying into the Atlantic, flows underground for a part of its course.

12. The primary meaning of the word *"peladilla"* is "a sugar almond"; secondary meaning, "a small pebble." Ormsby: "Here came a sugar-plum from the brook."

13. *"Almendra"* is literally an almond.

14. Dr. Andrés Laguna translated Dioscorides with copious notes in 1570.

15. A proverb.

16. The original reads "I will send to the devil flock and shepherd's crook (*hato y garabato*)."

CHAPTER XIX

1. Allusion to the story of Mambrino's helmet; see Chapter x preceding and note 3. Malandrino (*"malandrín"*—"rascal") is a play on Mambrino.

2. *"Encamisados,"* that is, those wearing shirts (*camisas*) over their armor as in a *camisado*, or night attack.

3. There is a word play here on *"derecho"*—"right" or "straight," and *"tuerto"*—"wrong" or "crooked."

4. There is a confused text at this point in some of the editions; I have

followed the first edition. The latter part of the chapter in Ormsby is badly jumbled.

5. "Moreover, if any, persuaded of the devil . . ."

6. Reference to a ballad of which Lockhart has a version. See Sylvanus Griswold Morley's *Spanish Ballads* (New York: Henry Holt, 1911), pp. 118 ff.

7. A proverb; literally, "The dead man to the grave, the living to the loaf."

CHAPTER XX

1. The original has *"les aguó el contento del agua."*

2. A proverb.

3. A proverb.

4. The Horn is the constellation of Ursa Minor, with a curved shape somewhat like a hunting-horn. In this method of telling the time of night by the stars, the arms were extended in the form of a cross and the hour was indicated by the position of the Horn in relation to the arms.

5. Cato Censorino, or Cato the Censor; Sancho believes the name to be derived from *"zonzo"*—"a blockhead."

6. The story that Sancho undertakes to tell is an old one, probably of Oriental origin. It will be found in the Italian collection, *Cento Novelle Antiche*, and there are also Latin and Provençal versions.

7. Compare Swift's *Gulliver's Travels*, Part II, Chapter i: "I was pressed to do more than one thing which another could not do for me."

8. As distinguished from a Moorish or Jewish convert, or "new Christian."

9. *"Todo saldrá en la colada."* We have the proverb today.

10. A proverb.

11. Compare the reference to Firm Island a little further on; see also Chapter x preceding, note 5.

12. "Turkish fashion."

13. Tag of a proverb: "Whether the pitcher hits the stone or the stone the pitcher, it will be bad for the pitcher."

CHAPTER XXI

1. The reading of the first edition, *"pesada burla,"* has been followed here. A later edition has *"pasada"* in place of *"pesada,"* which has led some translators

'o render the phrase as "the late joke," "the late jest," etc.

2. Allusion to a proverb: "Please God that it be marjoram and not turn out to be caraway."

3. The original is "*malandantes*," meaning "unfortunate"; but there is a slight play on "*caballero andante*"— "knight-errant."

4. Earlier translators have "cuts off," in accordance with a later reading, "*corta*"; but the first edition has "*harta*," an obvious misprint for "*harpa*," from "*harpar (arpar)*"—"to tear" or "claw." This example and the one given in note 1 above will serve to show how a careful study of the original edition will provide the modern translator with a more accurate text as a whole, even though the variant in a particular case will often make little difference so far as the English-language reader is concerned.

5. A proverb.

6. Sancho means Mambrino.

7. Literally, a changing of hoods. Reference is seen to a seasonal change of hoods on the part of cardinals as provided for in an ecclesiastical manual which Professor Schevill discovered in the Central Library of Zurich: *Sacrarvm Ceremoniarvm, sive ritvvm ecclesiasticorvm Sanctae Romanae Ecclesiae, libri tres,* etc. (Rome, 1560). John S. Nainfa, S.S., in his *Costume of Prelates of the Catholic Church* (Baltimore, 1900), has a passage concerning a change of bishops' hoods, applicable also to cardinals.

8. Hartzenbusch, always free with his corrections of the author's text, would substitute "enigma" or "prophecy" for "adventure," and "explain" for "carry through (*acabar*)."

9. Ormsby: "Cervantes gives here an admirable epitome, and without any extravagant caricature, of a typical romance of chivalry. For every incident there is ample authority in the romances." John Gibson Lockhart, notes to the Motteux translation: "The reader of romance does not need to be told how faithfully Don Quixote . . . has abridged the main story of many a ponderous folio. The imaginary career of glory which he unfolds before the eyes of Sancho is paralleled almost *ad literatim* in the romance of Sir Degore.

. . . The conclusion of Belianís is almost exactly the same sort of adventure."

10. There is some question as to what is meant by this "*vengar quinientos sueldos.*" According to the *Dictionary of the Academy,* the verb "*devengar*" signifies "to acquire the right to some . . . compensation by reason of labor performed, services rendered, or other qualifications." Others have seen an allusion to an old Castilian law providing damages of five hundred sueldos as compensation for injury to person or property. In any event, whatever its source, the gentleman of La Mancha's income was not a large one by modern standards, seeing that the sueldo was worth anywhere from one to three cents.

11. Two proverbs.

12. A proverb.

13. A proverb.

14. For the play on "*litado*" and "*dictado*," Ormsby's rendering has been adopted.

15. Ormsby: "No doubt Pedro Tallez Girón, third Duke of Osuna, afterward Viceroy in Sicily and Naples; 'a little man but of great fame and fortunes . . .'"

CHAPTER XXII

1. Of La Mancha.

2. The first edition reading is "*tres precisos de gurapas*"; a later edition has "*tres años*"—"three years."

3. A proverb.

4. It is interesting to compare the term "sing" in our American underworld of today. The one who "sang" was as unpopular then as now. There are numerous specimens of rogues' dialect in this chapter and indeed throughout the pages of *Don Quixote.* "*Gurapas*" is one example.

5. A proverb.

6. Allusion to the ceremony of public flogging.

7. Proverbial expression.

8. This does not appear to agree with Don Quixote's belief in enchanters and their spells, but he is here speaking, apparently, of love sorcerers.

9. The first edition has "*no ay diablo*"; later editions have "*sumista*" in place of "*diablo*," rendered by Motteux

as "casuist" and by Ormsby as "accountant."

10. A proverb.

11. Reference to the famous work by Diego Hurtado de Mendoza, one of the classics of Spanish literature.

12. The proverb properly reads: "Do not go looking for five feet on a cat."

13. At the beginning of the chapter it was stated that the two men on horseback carried muskets.

14. A proverb.

CHAPTER XXIII

1. A proverb.

2. The passage beginning here and ending a few paragraphs below with the words ". . . he thanked his master for this favor" is not found in the first edition but is given in the second. Professor Schevill says: "We shall never know (in the author's own words) 'if the historian made a mistake' or if it was 'carelessness on the part of the printer.' I believe that Cervantes, upon completing [the first edition] wished to introduce the incident of the theft and for that purpose wrote an [additional] sheet, leaving it with the manuscript, and then forgot the additions and the changes they necessitated. Obviously, the printer did not know what to do with the loose leaf and introduced it later, while the text of [the second edition] was on the press." (Translated from Schevill's note in Spanish.) This will explain why, later in the chapter, the author speaks of Sancho as still having his ass, while still further on he again alludes to the theft. As the text originally stood, the episode of the galley slaves and the one related here all occurred on the same day, which was too much action for so short a space of time. That was doubtless why Cervantes desired to insert an interlude. Ormsby, in the latter part of the chapter, rather bungles the matter by tampering with the text in order to cover the discrepancy. Compare Part II, Chapters III, IV, and XXVII.

3. The word "pollinos"—"ass-colts," missing in the original, has been supplied by the translator.

4. Ormsby has: "with what Dapple used to carry."

5. A proverb previously quoted: "The thread leads to the ball of yarn." "Thread" here has the sense of "clue."

6. That is, "thread."

7. That is, "Phyllis."

8. Cervantes seems to have thought well of this sonnet of his, as he later inserted it in one of his comedies, La Casa de los Celos y Selvas de Ardenia.

9. It will be noted that the theft of the ass is not mentioned here.

10. The ass is present again.

11. This passage is not found until the third edition. The edition of Brussels reads ". . . Sancho on foot, consoled for the loss of his donkey by the promise of the three ass-colts . . ." The thief's two names are here confused.

12. Proverbial expression.

13 Ormsby says: "This is the explanation commonly given of the phrase 'de ambar,' and it is true that scented doublets were in fashion in the sixteenth century; but it seems somewhat improbable that a tattered doublet which had been for six months exposed to all weathers would have retained sufficient perfume to be detected."

CHAPTER XXIV

1. Clemencín believes that Cervantes wrote "in this province of Andalusia" for the reason that the interlocutors were actually in that province at the time; but Schevill remarks that "it is also possible that Cervantes had written this story and (then) interpolated it without altering these details introduced while the author himself was in Andalusia." (Translated from Schevill's Spanish note.)

2. Allusion to the eleventh book (third and fourth parts) of the Amadis.

3. The shepherd Darinel has been mentioned in Chapter VI preceding.

CHAPTER XXV

1. Ormsby, still trying to cover the textual discrepancy, has "bade Sancho follow him, which he, having no ass, did very discontentedly."

2. Ormsby: "could talk to Rocinante" (!).

3. Sancho confuses the name Elisabad with "abad"—an "abbot."

4. The squire here begins a barrage of proverbs.

5. That is, no pegs on which to hang the bacon.

6. Poor Rock (Peña Pobre) was so named because those who sojourned

there lived in extreme poverty; Clemencín suggests that it was Mont St. Michel,
but Ormsby thinks the island of Jersey
would be a better identification.

7. The sense of the name Beltenebros
is "darkly fair."

8. It is at this point that the editor
Hartzenbusch introduces the episode of
the theft of the ass.

9. The Hippogriff was the winged
horse on which Astolfo went to seek
news of Orlando. Frontino was the
steed of Bradamante's lover, Ruggiero.

10. This is the first reference in the
first edition to the theft.

11. "According to this passage, the
gray was lost *with the lint and all;* but
the lint was kept in the saddlebags
which were left in the innkeeper's possession; that Ginés stole the packsaddle
along with the beast appears more likely
than the *ad hoc* explanation later given
(Part II, Chapter IV), where it is related
that Ginés stole only the ass, leaving
Sancho seated upon the packsaddle suspended on four stakes." (Translated
from Schevill's Spanish note.)

12. Sancho means, of course, redemption.

13. Freely for *"caballero andante, o
por andar."*

14. Reference to the lay brothers who
acted as servants in schools and con-
vents and who wore their hair cropped
short but without the tonsure.

15. Reading of the first and second
editions; the third edition has "twenty-
seventh of August."

16. The first three editions have Perseus; the edition of Brussels has Theseus.
Schevill prefers to leave the reading
Perseus, believing that it may have been
in the original manuscript as the result
of a mistake on the part of the author.

CHAPTER XXVI

1. The allusions here are to the *Or-
lando Furioso:* Medoro, however, was
Dardinel's page, not Agramante's (XVIII,
166); and it was Ferrau, not Orlando
(Roland), who had the seven iron soles
(XII, 48).

2. That is, in Italian, Orlando Furioso.

3. The second and third editions and
the edition of Brussels have another
reading: "And for a rosary he made use

of the galls of a cork tree, putting them
together to form a string of ten beads."
This is the reading that Motteux and
some of the other translators have followed; Ormsby has the one given here.

4. The word play on *"sobajada,"*
"sobrehumana" (omitted in my rendering), and *"soberana"* is in reality untranslatable.

CHAPTER XXVII

1. Wamba was a king of the Gothic
line in the Iberian peninsula (672–680).

2. Galalón, previously mentioned
(Chapter I), was the traitor of Roncesvalles.

3. Vellido (or Bellido) Dolfos was
the murderer of Don Sancho, King of
Castile.

4. The story of Count Julian is well
known (Southey has treated it in English). His betrayal of Spain to the
Moors is related in an old ballad, "En
Ceupta está Julián," which Lockhart
has translated.

5. This, of course, is an old, old
theme. Compare Vergil (*Aeneid*, IV,
569): *"varium et mutabile semper/
femina,"* or the popular grand opera
aria "La Donna è mobile." One thinks
also of Francis I's saying: *"Femme sou-
vent varie."*

6. The colors crimson and white signified joy and happiness, and sometimes,
apparently, cruelty and innocence.

7. Part III ends here in the first edition.

CHAPTER XXVIII

1. The image is that of a ball of yarn
being wound.

2. The *montera* was a cloth cap worn
by peasants.

3. The adjective *"rancio"* literally
means "rancid"; its secondary meaning
is, anything that has been kept for a
long time—such as wine or bacon—and
so has acquired the flavor of age.

4. The *hidalgo* (literally, "son of a
somebody") was a gentleman by birth,
the *caballero* one by social position.

5. This saying was a commonplace
among Spanish writers of the Golden
Age. On the effects of music in purify-
ing the passions, Schevill suggests a
comparison with the section on music
in Aristotle's *Politics*. And, of course,

there is Shakespeare's "Music hath charms . . ."

6. The Motteux version in this passage strays widely from the text.

7. It is not too clear to what Dorotea is referring.

8. The *zagal* was a shepherd or swain.

CHAPTER XXIX

1. The first three Spanish editions have: ". . . *la buena suerte se muestra en favor mio*"—"is favoring me." The edition of Brussels and some modern ones have "*nuestro*"—"is favoring us," in place of "*mio*"; but if "*mio*" is not correct, Schevill prefers the reading "*vuestro*"—"is favoring you," which is the one that I have followed here. Ormsby has "in our favor"; Motteux, as frequently, slurs the passage.

2. A variety of mantilla.

3. Needless to say, an imaginary kingdom.

4. The edition of Brussels and that of the Spanish Academy (1780) punctuate the passage to read: "throughout the known parts of Guinea."

5. A palfrey ("*su palafrén*") is usually a horse, commonly a saddle horse for ladies, and Dorotea is mounted on a mule.

6. A proverb.

7. Literally, "Come, I am sucking my finger."

8. The reference is to Alcalá de Henares, Cervantes' birthplace. Rodríguez Marín: "The Zulema slope is a large hill to the southeast of Alcalá de Henares, on which was situated the Complutum of Ptolomeus." Complutum was the Latin name of the town.

9. Ormsby substitutes the reading "three leagues." He remarks: "The original says 'two leagues,' but the context shows it must have been at least thrice as far."

10. Bowle notes that this is reminiscent of a passage in *La Angélica* of Luis Barahona de Soto, Canto VIII: "*La gran laguna Meótide*"—"the great Meotides Lake," etc. Clemencín identifies Lake Meotis as the "gulf of the Black Sea into which the River Don or Tanais empties."

11. Two commentators, Clemencín and Hartzenbusch, point out that this would be worse on the fly than on the honey. Hartzenbusch substitutes "the bear."

CHAPTER XXX

1. The author has not previously referred to this incident.

2. Proverbial expression denoting an impossibility or something beyond one's reach: "*pedir cotufas en el golfo.*"

3. The first edition reads "*que se le viene a las manos de vobis, vobis*"; but Schevill remarks that the Latin "*vobis*" is out of place in Sancho's mouth and that Cervantes doubtless wrote "*bóbilis, bóbilis*" (meaning "easily," "without effort"), the mistake being one on the part of the compositor when the passage was dictated to him. This is borne out by the fact that the phrase "*bóbilis, bóbilis*" occurs later on, in Part II, Chapter LXXI.

4. The proverb runs: "The pitcher that goes to the well too often leaves either its handle or its spout behind."

5. A proverb. The bracketed passage that follows is not found in the first edition but occurs in the second La Cuesta edition of 1605.

6. That is, Don Quixote and Sancho. The passage goes on from the point at which the preceding one was introduced.

CHAPTER XXXI

1. A fanega is equivalent to 1.6 bushels.

2. As a token of reverence; the expression has occurred before.

3. A proverbial expression which the author has previously employed.

4. The sense is: "A good thing (gift) is good in any season." Ormsby cites the Scottish proverb: "A Yule feast may be done at Pasch." Rodríguez Marín points out that sleeves were originally given as presents and hence came to signify a gift.

5. Gypsy dealers were in the habit of putting quicksilver in the ears of a beast for sale, by way of quickening its pace.

6. Motteux gives the version: "A bird in hand is worth two in the bush."

7. Sancho misquotes the proverb, which runs: "He who has the good and chooses the bad, let him not complain of the bad that comes to him."

8. See Chapter IV and note 4.

CHAPTER XXXII

1. The *Don Cirongilio of Thrace*, in four books, by Bernardo de Vargas, was published at Seville in 1545. Copies are preserved in the Biblioteca Nacional of Madrid and the British Museum. The *Felixmarte of Hircania* has been referred to as *Florismarte of Hircania* (see Chapter VI, note 4). The *History of the Great Captain Gonzalo Hernández de Córdoba y Aguilar, with the Life of the Knight D. García de Paredes* was published at Seville in 1580 and 1582; there are copies in the British Museum and the library of the Hispanic Society. This is a later account based upon the *Chronicle Entitled the Two Conquests of the Kingdom of Naples* (Saragossa, 1559), copies of which are to be found in the Biblioteca Nacional and the library of the Hispanic Society. Gonzalo was the general in command against the Moors at Granada and the French at Naples. García de Paredes was his comrade-in-arms in both campaigns.

2. I follow here the reading of the first, second, and third editions, "more books," instead of "my books," the reading of the edition of Brussels which has been adopted by other translators. In Chapter XXVII preceding, the curate tells the innkeeper and his wife of Don Quixote's madness and may have mentioned the burning of the knight's books.

3. The *montante* was a broadsword with large *quillons*, requiring two hands to wield it.

4. I follow the readings of Hartzenbusch and Schevill, in place of "what I have read of Felixmarte of Hircania."

CHAPTER XXXIII

1. Schevill remarks that similar views of women are to be found in many of Cervantes' contemporaries. This was, as a matter of fact, a prolongation of the attitude toward the sex that was held at the close of the Middle Ages. Compare the "*Querelle des femmes*," or argument over the "woman question," among French writers of the sixteenth century, e.g., Rabelais. Ormsby observes that "among the scenes of the Italian and Spanish tales of intrigue the church plays a leading part." "Private visits to religious shrines" is a rendering of the Spanish "*estaciones*" and refers to "attendance at church for private devotion at other hours than those of the celebration of the mass." (Ormsby)

2. Proverbs 31:10: "Who can find a virtuous woman? for her price is far above rubies."

3. Allusion to Pericles in Plutarch's *On False Shame*.

4. I follow the reading of the first two editions, instead of the later one, "our holy religion."

5. *Le Lagrime de San Pietro* by Luigi Tansillo (1510–1568).

6. The cup was supposed to be a magic one. If the wife of the one who drank from it was unfaithful, it would spill. There is a confusion here of two stories in the *Orlando Furioso*, XLIII.

7. Reference to the well-known classic myth which tells how Zeus visited Danaë in her prison tower in the form of a shower of gold.

8. Genesis 2:24: "Therefore shall a man leave his father and his mother, and shall cleave unto his wife: and they shall be one flesh." Lotario omits the central clause.

CHAPTER XXXIV

1. This sonnet, like the one in Chapter XXIII preceding, will be found in Cervantes' play *The House of Jealousy*.

2. Commentators have seen these sonnets as "isolated compositions," having nothing to do with the text. Schevill believes that the author composed them years before and simply inserted them in the *Don Quixote*.

3. This follows the reading of the first edition: "*ha de estimar mi presteza o ligereza*"; later editions have "*desestimar*" (Ormsby: "will think ill of my pliancy or lightness"). As will be seen, "*estimar*" makes sense.

4. Two proverbs.

5. Reading of the early editions is "*rendirnos*"; modern editions have "*de rendiros*"—"of overcoming you." As Schevill points out, the reference well may be to both Camila and Leonela.

6. The "four S's" were *Sabio* (knowing); *Solo* (single-hearted); *Solicito* (diligent); *Segreto* (secret). It goes without saying that this "alphabet" cannot be rendered with anything more than an approach to literalness.

7. The first edition has *"más leal"*—"most loyal"; later ones have *"más desleal"*—"most disloyal."

8. This is the reading of all the earliest editions: *"por me hazer testigo"*; the edition of the Academy (1780) has: *"por no hacerme testigo"*—"in order not to bear witness."

9. Reading of the early Spanish editions is *"fealdad"*; the edition of Brussels and certain modern ones have *"falsedad"*—"conjugal faithlessness."

10. First edition reads *"no podia aber a Lotario"*; edition of Brussels: *"no podia herir"*—"could not wound."

CHAPTER XXXV

1. The first edition reads *"tambien la he cumplido"*; the emendation of Pellicer and later editors, *"tan bien,"* has been followed here.

2. *"Ciertos son los toros"*—allusion to the sport of bull-fighting. Ormsby has: "There's no doubt about the bulls," and explains the saying as "expressive probably of popular anxiety on the eve of a bull-fight." Motteux and Jarvis have: "Here are the bulls," Lockhart's explanation being: "In allusion to the joy of the mob in Spain when they see the bulls coming." In connection with the battle of the wineskins, Lockhart draws attention to the well-known story in Apuleius's *The Golden Ass.*

3. The cuartillo was one fourth of a real.

4. The cuarto was a coin worth four maravedis.

5. The text of the first two editions is confused at this point: *"qualificada no de con sus amores,"* which does not make sense. As Schevill notes, something apparently has been inadvertently dropped. It has seemed best to follow a later emendation: *"calificada en sus amores"* (third edition), or *"cualificada con sus amores"* (edition of Brussels).

6. A later edition has the reading: "perceived clearly enough by the mortal symptoms that he felt . . ."

7. Odet de Foix, Sieur de Lautrec, was Marshal of France under Francis I. On the Great Captain, see Chapter XXXII, note 1. Reference here apparently is to the battle of Cerignola (1503) in which the Spaniards won a victory over the French that resulted in the loss to Louis XII of the kingdom of Naples.

CHAPTER XXXVI

1. The fashion of riding known as *"a la jineta,"* in which the stirrups are high and the horseman is compelled to bend his legs.

2. The original has *"la firma que hiziste"*; but Ormsby notes: "Don Fernando did not sign any paper, but gave Dorothea a ring"; he translates: "the pledge which thou didst give me."

CHAPTER XXXVII

1. The arroba was equivalent to 4.26 gallons; the amount of spilled wine represented here is, accordingly, about twenty-five and a half gallons.

2. The words "said the curate" are supplied by the edition of Brussels.

3. Proverbial expression.

4. The first two editions have: *"vuestro . . . inuenerable braço"*—"your unvenerable arm." The third edition and the edition of Brussels read: *"inuencible"*—"invincible," and the Academy edition accepts this emendation. Hartzenbusch and Rodríguez Marín would read: *"inuulnerable"*—"invulnerable." This last appears to be the most logical reading, although Schevill thinks the "unvenerable" may not have been an error but a witticism on Dorotea's part, which seems unlikely in view of the serious tone that she consistently maintains in addressing Don Quixote.

5. A proverb.

6. In referring to the "captive," the author is running ahead of the story.

7. *"Macange"* (ma-kan-shi) is an emphatic negative in popular Arabic.

8. *"Letrado"*: reference here, in particular, to the student of jurisprudence.

9. Luke 2:14.

10. Luke 10:5.

11. John 14:27.

12. That is, going to the monasteries where soup was given out to the poor.

13. Syrtis was the name given by the ancients to sandbars in the sea, especially off the northern coast of Africa.

CHAPTER XXXVIII

1. Schevill observes that "this discussion of the subject of arms and letters

has its roots in the ancient literature and comes to be a commonplace with authors of the sixteenth century." (Translated from the Spanish note.) Among other works, the reader may be referred to Castiglione's *The Courtier*.

2. Motteux appears to have the sense here when he translates "either by hook or by crook." Clemencín gives the meaning as "in one way or another." Ormsby says: "Another explanation is that by skirts (*faldas*) regular salary is meant, and by sleeves (*mangas*) douceurs, perquisites, and the like."

3. It may be of interest to compare Rabelais' treatment of this theme in his *Gargantua*. The Chevalier Bayard stood for the type of chivalry or knighthood to which the introduction of artillery put an end.

CHAPTER XXXIX

1. Schevill points out that this tale of the father sending his three sons out into the world to choose their careers is a common one in the folk literature of Europe. To each the father gives good advice and his blessing and sometimes a talisman to guard him against harm. "It is possible that Cervantes, influenced by the proverb, 'Church or sea or Royal Household,' took the formula of the father and his three sons and found in the saying an indication of what the careers were to be." (From the Spanish note.)

2. This proverb is found in Lope de Vega; a variant reads: "Three things cause a man to prosper: learning and the sea and the royal household."

3. The Duke arrived at Brussels on August 22, 1567, with ten thousand men.

4. Cervantes had served in Diego de Urbina's company. See J. Fitzmaurice-Kelly, *Miguel de Cervantes Saavedra* (London: Chapman and Hall, 1917), pp. 42 ff.

5. Schevill notes that it is possible Cervantes entered this port on September 2, 1571.

6. The campaign of Lepanto in which Cervantes took part. The battle of Lepanto occurred on October 7, 1571. Compare the allusion in the Prologue to Part II.

7. Proper form: Aluch Ali.

8. Giovanni Andrea Doria (died in 1606), nephew of the great Andrea Doria, Genoese naval commander.

9. Motteux has: "in the flag-galley *The Three Beacons*"; but the "*capitana de los tres fanales*" refers to the three lanterns that were the sign of the admiral's ship.

10. Fort at the entrance to the lagoon of Tunis.

11. The vara is a variable measure, equal to about 2.8 feet.

12. Pedro de Aguilar's *Memoirs* were published at Madrid in 1875.

CHAPTER XL

1. Nickname of Jacome Palearo, who served under Charles V and Philip II.

2. Schevill: Cervantes here may possibly be alluding to the sovereigns who from 1360 to 1603 occupied the Turkish throne: Murad, Bayazid, Mohammed, and Selim or Suleiman.

3. The reference should be to Hassan Pacha.

4. Ormsby: "The story of the captive, it is needless to say, is not the story of Cervantes himself, but it is colored throughout by his own experiences, and he himself speaks in the person of the captive."

5. The author is referring to himself. The story of Cervantes' captivity is told in the work by Diego de Haedo, *Topography and General History of Algiers*, etc., published at Valladolid in 1612.

6. The cianí was worth a little more than six pesetas.

7. The term means "salaam," or form of worship.

8. South gate of Algiers.

9. A *Tagarino* was a Moor who lived among Christians. See the chapter following.

CHAPTER XLI

1. Motteux has: "to the eastward of Algiers towards Oran"; but Oran is west of Algiers. Ormsby has: "twenty leagues from Algiers." The original is: "*treynta leguas*"—"thirty leagues."

2. It was Arnaut Mami who captured the ship on which Cervantes and his brother were returning to Spain.

3. The dobla was a gold coin worth around ten pesetas. It is not to be confused with the doblón, or doubloon,

worth twice as much. Ormsby has: "ten thousand doubloons."

4. The original is: "*de ricas perlas y aljófar*," the *aljófar* being a small pearl of irregular shape. Ormsby has: "rich pearls and seed-pearls."

5. The soltani was a Turkish coin equivalent to about nine pesetas.

6. The first edition has the form "*Amexi?*" Schevill believes this was what the author wrote, and adds: "It is not likely that Cervantes wrote such words correctly, and I do not care to emend the copy." (From the Spanish note.)

7. Which means, "Go, Christian, go!"

8. Literally, the wind from the other side of the mountains (the Alps); generally equivalent to north wind.

9. "La Cava" is the name given in ballads to Florinda, daughter of Count Julian (see Chapter XXVII preceding, note 4), who is said to have been seduced by King Rodrigo. Ormsby: "Cervantes gives the popular name by which the spot is known. Properly, it is 'Kuba Rumia,' 'the Christian's tomb'; that being the name given to the curious circular structure about which there has been so much discussion among French archaeologists."

10. I have followed Ormsby here as his rendering appears to be the only possible one for the nautical terms involved.

CHAPTER XLII

1. In the present chapter this person is sometimes referred to as "the captain," at other times as "the captive."

2. Here, as before, "letters" refers to jurisprudence.

3. The Audiencia.

4. The author apparently forgets that most of them had previously had supper.

5. See the Prologue to Part I, note 6.

6. A play on the word for "judge": "*oidor*," literally, "hearer."

7. If the curate did not know whether they had reached Spain or not, how could he have known of the attack by the French pirates?

8. Rodríguez Marín would alter the punctuation here to make this passage read: "my father still lives dying, with the desire," etc. Schevill rejects this emendation.

CHAPTER XLIII

1. Palinurus was the pilot of Aeneas: ". . . *surgit Palinurus, et . . . sidera cuncta notat tacito labentia caelo*"; see the *Aeneid*, III, 513–515.

2. In the original, this ballad has double assonant rhymes in the second and fourth lines of each stanza; no imitation of this has been attempted here. Ormsby does attempt it and the result is an interesting version.

3. There is a play here in the word "*lugar*," which sometimes means "place" and sometimes "town" or "village." Compare below: "lord of hearts and towns."

4. This ballad is said to have been set to music by Don Salvadore Luis, in 1591, fourteen years before the *Don Quixote* appeared; Schevill cites in this connection the four-volume *History of Spanish Music* by M. Soriano Fuertes, published in 1855–59.

5. Allusion to Diana; see Vergil's *Aeneid*, IV, 511: "*Tria virginis ora Dianae*."

6. The reference is to Daphne. Schevill notes the frequency of this allusion in Cervantes; see his *Ovid and the Renaissance in Spain* (Berkeley: University of California Press, 1913), p. 184. Compare Pliny's *Natural History*, IV, 8.

7. The Spanish verb here—"*cecear*" —is untranslatable; it literally means the sort of sound that Andalusians make in pronouncing the sibilant *ce*.

8. Lirgandeo was the tutor and chronicler of the Knight of the Sun. Alquife was the chronicler of the Knight of the Flaming Sword, Amadis of Greece. For Urganda, see the prefatory verses, note 1.

9. An inconsistency has been seen here, since if Don Quixote had been tied as tightly as we were told, how could his feet have come so near the ground? As Ormsby observes, the simple explanation is that "Cervantes never gave a thought to the matter."

CHAPTER XLIV

1. Reading of the first edition; other editions have Mambrino.

CHAPTER XLV

1. The first three editions have "*sobrebarbero*," which, it has been suggested, may possibly mean "supernu-

merary barber." Certain modern editions have "*pobre barbero*," or "poor barber," the reading that has been adopted here. The edition of Brussels has "*dixo el barbero burlado*"—"said the barber who was being made sport of."

2. A proverb: "Laws go as kings like."

3. Agramante and King Sobrino are personages in Ariosto's *Orlando Furioso*. For the incident referred to here, see Cantos xiv and xxvii.

CHAPTER XLVI

1. Pellicer's reading has been followed here: "*no se le passó por alto*," in place of that of the first and second editions: "*se le pagó por alto*."

2. "Aside from the mention of the 'trappings' of the ass (Chapter xlii) and of the 'halter' and the 'packsaddle' (Chapter xliv), this is the first allusion since the beast was found to the existence of Sancho's gray; from which I am inclined to think that the account of the finding of it was interpolated hastily and inopportunely in Chapter xxx, thus leaving fifteen chapters in which no mention whatever is made of its presence." (From Schevill's Spanish note.)

3. Augustus Caesar—the Augustan Age.

4. I follow here the first edition reading, "*vna señora*." Schevill is inclined to adopt the emendation of the edition of Brussels, "*vuestra señoria*"—"your Ladyship."

5. A proverb.

6. A proverb.

7. The early editions all have "*león manchado*"—"spotted lion"; but later editors have adopted the reading "*manchego*"—"Manchegan," or "of La Mancha."

8. From "*mentir*"—"to lie."

CHAPTER XLVII

1. The chapter heading in the original is not quite accurate. Ormsby: "Of the Strange Manner in Which Don Quixote of La Mancha Was Carried Away Enchanted."

2. It was considered an utter disgrace for a knight to ride in such a vehicle. Schevill draws attention to a similar incident in the French *nouvelle* of the fifteenth century, *Lancelot du Lac*.

3. Motteux substitutes "orthodox" for "Catholic."

4. We have previously been told (Chapter xlv preceding) that the officers were three in number.

5. In Covarrubias's *Tesoro de la lengua castellana* (cited by Schevill) it is stated that Zoroaster, "King of the Bactrians, was the first inventor of the magic art."

6. Allusion to Cervantes' own work, of course; the third of the *Exemplary Novels*, published (later) in 1613.

7. The work referred to is the *Suma de las Súmulas*, a treatise on logic by the theologian Gaspar Carillo de Villalpando, published at Alcalá in 1557.

8. The gymnosophists were Hindu philosophers who led a hermit existence, practiced mysticism and asceticism, and wore little clothing. Alexander the Great found them in India upon his arrival there.

9. A proverb.

10. Proverbial expression.

11. A proverb.

12. A proverb.

13. The aesthetic ideas expressed by Cervantes here were more or less current in his day. See J. C. Dunlop, *History of Prose Fiction* (London, 1906; first edition, 1888), Vol. I, pp. 10 ff.; on Cervantes, see Vol. II, pp. 313-23.

14. Prester John was a legendary Christian priest and king who in the Middle Ages and early Renaissance was believed to reign over a country in the Far East, his realm being later identified with Abyssinia. He is mentioned in Rabelais and other sixteenth-century writers.

15. The original reads "*quanto tiene más de lo dudoso y possible*"—literally, "the more it contains of the doubtful and the possible," the word "doubtful" being here understood in the sense of "probable." But Schevill points out that Cervantes does not elsewhere employ "*dudoso*" in this sense. It accordingly seems best to adopt Hartzenbusch's emendation: "*gustoso*"—"pleasing." The "*dudoso*" was probably a typesetter's error.

16. Sinon was the Greek soldier who persuaded the Trojans to drag the wooden horse into their city.

17. Euryalus, in Vergil's *Aeneid*, was the faithful friend of Nisus.

18. Zopyrus was a Persian nobleman who mutilated himself and thereby helped to conquer Babylon; a celebrated general of Darius Hystaspis, he is mentioned in Herodotus (III, 153) and Justinus (I, 10 ff.).

19. The original has "*varios y hermosos lazos*"—literally, "variegated and beautiful knots"; but the reading of modern editions, "*lizos*"—"threads," seems preferable.

CHAPTER XLVIII

1. The original reads "*puesto que es mejor ser loado de los pocos sabios que burlado de los muchos necios*"—literally, "better to be praised by the discerning few than scoffed at by the unknowing many." The word "*burlado*" has given commentators and translators some little trouble, since it does not appear to make sense. Hartzenbusch suggests substituting "*vitoreado*"—"acclaimed." Ormsby reads "*alabado*" and translates "better to be praised by the wise few than applauded by the foolish many." But the translation given above will perhaps solve the difficulty.

2. The original has "*sastre del cantillo*," which is meaningless. El Campillo was the name of a number of places in Spain. The proverb ran: "*El sastre del Campillo, que cosia de balde y ponia el hilo*"—"The tailor of El Campillo who threaded his needle and stitched for nothing." There were other versions, such as "The tailor of the crossroads," etc. *The Tailor of El Campillo* was the title of plays by Belmonte and Candamo and of a *novela* by Santos.

3. The third edition has "*autores*"—"authors."

4. The edition of Brussels has "actor."

5. These plays are by Lupercio Leonardo de Argensola. See Otis Howard Green's *The Life and Works of Lupercio Leonardo de Argensola* (Philadelphia. University of Pennsylvania Press, 1927).

6. *Ingratitude Avenged* (*La Ingratitud Vengada*) is by Lope de Vega; the *Numantia* (*Numancia*) is Cervantes' own piece; *The Merchant Lover* (*El Mercader Amante*) is the work of Gaspar Aguilar; and *The Fair and Favoring Enemy* (*La Enemiga Favorable*) is from the pen of Francisco Agustín Tárrega.

7. What Cicero said was: "*Comoedia*

est imitatio vitae, speculum consuetudinis, imago veritatis"—"Comedy is an imitation of life, a mirror of manners, and an image of the truth." The words are quoted by Lope de Vega in his *New Art of Making Comedies* (*Arte Nuevo de Hacer Comedias*).

8. "*Apariencia.*"

9. There has been considerable discussion as to whom Cervantes meant by these "foreigners." Literary historians will tell us that the theater in both France and Italy at this time was in a state of decadence, and as Ormsby remarks, the English certainly did not "scrupulously observe" the rules of comedy. Schevill believes that the author, carried away by his desire to criticize the type of comedy produced in Spain, may have been thinking, rather, of certain poetic manuals and treatises such as were commonly discussed (possibly years before) by those associated with the playhouse.

10. The author referred to is Lope de Vega. This chapter had a good deal to do with the bitter feeling against Cervantes on the part of Lope and his followers. Lope himself, however, in his *New Art of Making Comedies*, gives expression to practically the same cynical views that are here under attack. Later, in the second act of his play, *The Fortunate Procurer* (*El Rufián Dichoso*), Cervantes recanted the opinions set forth in this passage.

11. This proposal is characterized by Professor Schevill as a "reactionary doctrine" which would have rendered impossible the creation of a national and popular theater, and the same commentator further describes it as a "feeble imitation" of Plato's views as expounded in the seventh book of *The Republic*. Plato wrote: "The magistrate will appoint censors to judge the compositions [of the poet] and see to it that they do not stray from the eternal types or laws of the beautiful, but shall tend to preserve the power and prestige of constituted authority, of tradition, and of ancient customs, in songs, games, ceremonies, sacrifices, spectacles, and all that pertains to the giving of pleasure. Otherwise, the citizens will readily fall in with dangerous novelties of a more serious nature." Plato was frequently cited in the Renaissance by those who

favored a censorship. "These pages of *Don Quixote,*" says Schevill, "lead us to believe that Cervantes, regarding the novelties of the school of Lope as dangerous, had to take refuge in Plato's doctrine of censorship, applying it to comedy in such a manner that only those pieces of which the author of Don Quixote approved would be performed." (From the Spanish note.)

12. The Spanish is "*hazer aguas menores o mayores.*" "Major or minor" is a common American euphemism and seems appropriate here.

CHAPTER XLIX

1. Viriatus, celebrated leader of the Lusitanians in the war against the Romans, is mentioned by Livy and other historians.

2. Don Manuel Ponce de León, knight of the time of Ferdinand and Isabella, whose name occurs in ballads relating to the siege of Granada, is the hero who figures in the incident of the glove in Schiller's poem, "Der Handschuh"; compare Leigh Hunt's "The Glove and the Lions" and Browning's "The Glove." He is mentioned again in Part II, Chapter XVII. Count Fernán González was a tenth-century knight of Castile. On Gonzalo Hernández (Fernández) and Diego García de Paredes, see Chapter XXXII preceding and note 1. Garci Pérez de Vargas is another ballad hero, but it would appear that the author is referring to Diego Pérez de Vargas, known as "the Pounder" (see Chapter VIII preceding and note 1). Garcilaso was a famous soldier of Ferdinand and Isabella.

3. The Princess Florípes was the sister of Fierabrás and wife of Guy of Burgundy, Charlemagne's nephew. The bridge of Mantible was defended by a huge giant, Galafre, supported by Turks, and was taken by Charlemagne with the aid of Fierabrás. The incident is related in the Charlemagne chronicle.

4. Guarino Mesquino was the hero of an Italian romance of the Charlemagne cycle which had been translated into Spanish.

5. Queen Guinevere's waiting woman; see Chapter XVI preceding.

6. The story of Pierres and Magalona is a twelfth-century Provençal romance by Bernardo Treviez which had been translated into Spanish. Babieca was the Cid's steed. On Roncesvalles, see Chapter VI preceding and note 12.

7. Juan de Merlo (Melo) was a fifteenth-century knight of Portuguese descent, born in Castile in the reign of John II. At the tournament of Arras, held under the auspices of Philip, Duke of Burgundy, he overthrew Pierre de Brecemont, Sieur de Charny, and at Basle he vanquished the famous German knight, Heinrich von Rabenstein (Henri de Remestan). The original has "*Mosen Pierres*" and "*Mosen Enrique de Remestan,*" the "*Mosen*" (rendered as "Monsieur") being a shortened form of "*mio señor,*" my lord, and a common Aragonian prefix corresponding to the Castilian "Don."

8. Allusion to a tournament held at St. Omer in Burgundy, in 1435, at which Gutierre Quijada, Lord of Villagracia, jousted with Pierre, Sieur de Haburdin, natural son of the Comte de St. Paul. Barba was Quijada's friend who was prevented by illness from taking part in the tourney. The stories in this passage were possibly taken by Cervantes from the *Chronicle of King John II.* (Schevill)

9. Another knight of the reign of John II.

10. Suero de Quiñones was one of ten knights who in 1434 undertook to hold the bridge of Orbiga, near Astorga, against all comers for thirty days, a feat of great renown in the later Middle Ages and that came to be known as the "*Paso Honroso,*" or "Passage of Honor."

11. These knights, also, are mentioned in the *Chronicle of King John II.* Louis de Faux was a knight of Navarre.

12. On Turpin, see Chapter VI preceding and note 8.

13. The title "Knight of the Twelve Peers" mentioned here is an imaginary one.

14. See Chapter VI preceding and note 12.

CHAPTER L

1. At this point the third edition has an inserted passage for which there is no authority.

2. The promised land of squires; see Chapter X and note 5.

3. Expression used by gamblers.

CHAPTER LI

1. The original has "Garcia y Luna," apparently an erratum. Hartzenbusch's emendation has been adopted.

CHAPTER LII

1. Previously we were told that they were armed with muskets.

2. With which they were flagellating themselves.

3. This speech of Sancho's seems somewhat out of character—for example, the reference to "the Alexanders"—but it is to be presumed that by this time he has picked up some of his master's phraseology as well as ideas.

4. A proverb.

5. Don Quixote's village, "the name of which I have no desire to recall." (See Chapter 1, note 1.)

6. The sense of the word is manikin, a puppet or ridiculous figure (compare the modern Spanish *"monigote,"* from *"monachus,"* "a monk").

7. The name signifies a parasite or hanger-on.

8. The meaning is whimsical, crotchety.

9. This "sonnet," it will be noted, is of seventeen lines, the rhyme scheme of the sestet and final tercet being cdecdeeff.

10. This is the reading of the original —*"trono"*; the second and third editions and the edition of Brussels have *"tronco"*—literally, "trunk," which Hartzenbusch rejects, but which may have reference to a "trophy" instead of a "throne."

11. In the *Orlando Furioso*, Brigliador was Orlando's horse and Baiardo was Rinaldo's.

12. The name means jester.

13. Signifying hobgoblin.

14. In this and the following piece the rhyme scheme, in place of the one followed here, is abbaabba.

15. The name is onomatopoeic.

16. This line from the *Orlando Furioso* (xxx, 16) is wrongly given in the first edition: *"Forsi altro canterá con miglior plectio."* This is the end of the original Part IV.

PART TWO

The Ingenious Gentleman

DON QUIXOTE

DE LA MANCHA

PART TWO: CONTENTS

Certificate of Price

I, Hernando de Vallejo, scrivener of the Chamber of our master the King, in behalf of those who reside in his Council, do hereby certify that, those lords having seen a book which was composed by Miguel de Cervantes Saavedra, entitled *Don Quixote de la Mancha, Second Part*, the said book having been printed by his Majesty's license, they have estimated the value of each sheet at four maravedis, and inasmuch as the book contains seventy-three sheets, the value of the paper in it amounts to two-hundred-ninety-two maravedis; and they have commanded that this certificate of price be placed in the front of each volume of the said book, in order that it may be known and understood what is to be asked and received for it, the price in no wise to exceed this amount, as is plainly set forth in the original edict and decree upon this subject, which I am charged with enforcing and to which I do hereby refer; and upon the order of the said lords of the Council and at the request of the said Miguel de Cervantes, I do give this certificate in Madrid, on the twenty-first day of the month of October of the year one-thousand-six-hundred-and-fifteen.

HERNANDO DE VALLEJO

Certificate of Errata

I HAVE seen this book entitled *Second Part of Don Quixote de la Mancha*, composed by Miguel de Cervantes Saavedra, and there is in it nothing worthy of note that does not correspond to the original. Given in Madrid, on the twenty-first day of October, one-thousand-six-hundred-and-fifteen.

THE LICENTIATE FRANCISCO MURCIA DE LA LLANA

Approbation

By COMMISSION and order of the lords of the Council, I have had submitted to me the book referred to in this memorandum. It does not contain anything contrary to the faith or good morals, but rather offers much wholesome entertainment intermingled with much moral philosophy. A license may be granted for the printing of it.

In Madrid, on the fifth of November, one-thousand-six-hundred-and-fifteen.

DOCTOR GUTIERRE DE CETINA

Approbation

By COMMISSION and order of the lords of the Council, I have seen *The Second Part of Don Quixote de la Mancha*, by Miguel de Cervantes Saavedra. It does not contain anything against our Catholic faith or good morals, but rather offers much decent recreation and harmless amusement such as the ancients looked upon as being of utility to their States, seeing that even the Lacedaemonians reared a statue to Laughter while the Thessalians had festivals devoted to that god, as Pausanias (cited by Bosio, *De Signis Eccles.*, Book II, Chapter 10) informs us.[1] For laughter inspires and revives weary minds and melancholy spirits, as Tully notes in the first book of his *De Legibus*, and the poet as well when he says: *"Interpone tuis interdum gaudia curis."* [2] That is what the author does, by mingling jest with earnest, the pleasing with the profitable, and the moral with the facetious, dissimulating under the bait of wit the hook of reprehension. All this in pursuance of his professed aim, which is that of driving out the books of chivalry, from whose contagious and baleful influence he has done much to cleanse these realms through the employment of his fine and cunning wit. It is a work such as befits his great talent, being the honor and glory of our nation and the object of admiration and envy on the part of other peoples. Such is my humble opinion. In Madrid, on the seventeenth of March, 1615.

MAESTRO JOSEPH DE VALDIVIELSO

Approbation

BY COMMISSION of Dr. Gutierre de Cetina, vicar-general of this city of Madrid, his Majesty's capital, I have seen this book, the second part of the *Ingenious Gentleman, Don Quixote de la Mancha*, by Miguel de Cervantes Saavedra, and have found in it nothing unworthy of a zealous Christian nor anything that is opposed to decency, the setting of a good example, or the moral virtues. On the contrary, it contains much erudition and profitable reading in worthy pursuance of its aim, which is that of extirpating the vain and lying books of chivalry, whose contagious influence is far too widespread. It is likewise commendable by reason of the smoothness of the Castilian tongue as employed therein, which is here not adulterated with any tiresome and studied affectations such as are rightly abhorred by the wise. Moreover, in the correction of vices the author in the course of his astute reasoning observes so wisely the laws of Christian reprehension that the one who is infected with the disease which he sets out to cure will unsuspectingly and with pleasure drink the sweet and savory medicine that is thus provided, with no feeling whatsoever of surfeit or of loathing, and will in this manner come to hate his own particular vice. All of which, the combining of pleasure and reproof, is an exceedingly difficult thing to accomplish.

There have been many who, not knowing how to mingle the useful with the pleasing in the right proportions, have had all their toil and pains for nothing; and being incapable of imitating Diogenes the learned philosopher, they have audaciously, not to say licentiously and stupidly, endeavored to imitate the cynic by having resort to slander and inventing cases that never occurred in order to enlarge upon the vice which they would so sternly reprove. Such as these may even discover new ways of pursuing the said vice and thus become the teachers of it rather than its censors. As a result, they render themselves odious to those of sound understanding and lose their reputation, if they ever had any, with the public, while the vices which they have so brazenly and imprudently undertaken to correct are left more deeply rooted than before. Not all abscesses yield to the cautery, but some are much better treated by mild and soothing medicines through the application of which the discreet and skilled physician finally succeeds in curing them, with far more satisfactory consequences, frequently, than are to be attained through the use of such stern measures as the iron.

Quite different has been the effect produced by the writings of Miguel de Cervantes upon our own nation and upon foreign ones as well. For even as they would wish to behold a miracle, so do the men of other lands desire to lay eyes upon the author of those books that, by reason of their circumspection and propriety as well as their urbanity and other pleasing qualities, have met with general applause in Spain, France, Italy, Germany, and Flanders.[3]

I can truthfully certify that on the twenty-fifth of February of this year 1615, that most illustrious gentleman Don Bernardo de Sandoval y Rojas, Cardinal Archbishop of Toledo and my lord, having gone to repay the visit of the French ambassador (who had come to treat of things having to do with marriages between the royal house of his country and that of Spain), a number of the French knights who accompanied the ambassador and who were as courteous as they were intelligent and fond of good literature, came to me and other chaplains of my lord the Cardinal to make inquiries concerning the most worth-while books then current. We thereupon fell to discussing those that I was at the time engaged in censoring, and no sooner had they heard the name of Miguel de Cervantes than they at once began speaking most enthusiastically of the high esteem in which his works were held not only in France but in neighboring kingdoms. They mentioned in particular the *Galatea*, the first part of which one of them could almost repeat from memory, and the *Novelas*. So fervent, indeed, was their praise, that I offered to take them to see the author of those works, an invitation which they eagerly accepted. They went on to question me in great detail regarding his age, his profession, his rank and worldly state, and I was obliged to inform them that he was an old soldier and an impoverished gentleman, whereupon one of them replied to me most gravely, "How comes it Spain does not see to it that such a man is maintained in luxury out of the public treasury?"

One of the others then made this astute observation. "If," he said, "it is necessity that obliges him to write, then God grant that he never be possessed of abundance, in order that, while poor himself, he may continue to enrich all the world." [4]

I realize that, as a censor's report, this document is somewhat long, and some will say that it borders on flattery, but the truth that I have here briefly stated should be sufficient to relieve the critic of suspicion and me of all concern; for today it is the custom to flatter only the one that is able to stuff the maw of the flatterer, who, even though he speak affectedly, falsely, and in jest, none the less expects to be rewarded in earnest. In Madrid, on the twenty-seventh of February, one-thousand-six-hundred-and-fifteen.

THE LICENTIATE MÁRQUEZ TORRES [5]

Royal Privilege

INASMUCH as we have been informed by you, Miguel de Cervantes Saavedra, that you have composed *The Second Part of Don Quixote de la Mancha,* with a copy of which you have presented us; and inasmuch as this is a storybook that is both pleasing and decorous and one that has cost you much labor and study, and you have besought us to command that a license be granted for the printing of it, along with a Privilege for twenty years or such time as we in our good grace may see fit; and inasmuch as the said book has been duly scrutinized by the members of our Council in accordance with our decree upon the subject, it has been decided that we should grant you this our scroll for the said purpose, the which we do right willingly.

With this object in view, we do hereby grant you, or the person whom you shall employ and none other, for the time and space of ten years current from the date of this our scroll, license and authority to print and sell the said book, herein above-mentioned. And for the present, we grant license and authority to any printer of our realms whom you may name to print the said book for the space of time herein provided, from the original copy as seen by our Council and signed at the end with his flourish by Hernando de Vallejo, our scrivener of the Chamber, and one of those resident therein. And it is further provided that, before the book is placed on sale, you shall bring it before them, together with the said original, in order that they may see if the printed text is in conformity with the aforesaid original; or you shall take public oath that the said printing has been seen and corrected by the reader appointed by us.

And the said printer who shall print the said book shall not print the beginning nor the first sheet thereof, nor deliver more than a single book along with the original to the author and person who pays the cost of the printing, or any other person whomsoever, until, first and foremost, the said book shall have been corrected and its price fixed by the members of our Council. Only when this shall have been done and under no other circumstances may the beginning and the first sheet be printed. And in the front of the said book shall be placed this our license and approbation, together with the certificate of price and the errata, nor shall you or any other person sell the book until the above provisions have been complied with, under pain of incurring those penalties provided for in the aforesaid decree and the laws of our realm having to do with this matter.

It is further provided that, during the said space of time no person may without your permission print or sell the said book, and whosoever shall so print or sell it shall lose whatever copies of it he may have in his possession along with the type and the forms, and shall in addition incur the penalty of a fine of fifty thousand maravedis for each offense, one third of the said fine to go to our Chamber, one third to the judge who shall sentence him, and the remaining third to the plaintiff.

And we do further command the members of our Council, the Judges and Magistrates of our Courts, the Justices and Bailiffs of our Household and Court Chancelleries, and all other magistrates of all the cities, towns, and villages within our realm and seignories, each one in his own jurisdiction, both those that now are and those that henceforth shall be, to observe and comply with the provisions of this our scroll which we by our grace do hereby grant you, and we forbid them to go contrary to it or neglect to fulfill it in any manner whatsoever, under pain of our disfavor and a fine of ten thousand maravedis for our Chamber.

Given in Madrid, on the thirtieth day of the month of March, one-thousand-six-hundred-and-fifteen.

I, THE KING

By command of our master, the King,

PEDRO DE CONTRERAS

Prologue

TO THE READER [1]

GOD bless me, gentle or, it may be, plebeian reader, how eagerly you must be awaiting this prologue, thinking to find in it vengeful scoldings and vituperations directed against the author of the second Don Quixote—I mean the one who, so it is said, was begotten in Tordesillas and born in Tarragona.[2] The truth is, however, that I am not going to be able to satisfy you in this regard; for granting that injuries are capable of awakening wrath in the humblest of bosoms, my own must be an exception to the rule. You would, perhaps, have me call him an ass, a crackbrain, and an upstart, but it is not my intention so to chastise him for his sin. Let him eat it with his bread and have done with it.[3]

What I cannot but resent is the fact that he describes me as being old and one-handed, as if it were in my power to make time stand still for me, or as if I had lost my hand in some tavern instead of upon the greatest occasion that the past or present has ever known or the future may ever hope to see.[4] If my wounds are not resplendent in the eyes of the chance beholder, they are at least highly thought of by those who know where they were received. The soldier who lies dead in battle has a more impressive mien than the one who by flight attains his liberty. So strongly do I feel about this that even if it were possible to work a miracle in my case, I still would rather have taken part in that prodigious battle than be today free of my wounds without having been there. The scars that the soldier has to show on face and breast are stars that guide others to the Heaven of honor, inspiring them with a longing for well-merited praise. What is more, it may be noted that one does not write with gray hairs but with his understanding, which usually grows better with the years.

I likewise resent his calling me envious; and as though I were some ignorant person, he goes on to explain to me what is meant by envy; when the truth of the matter is that of the two kinds,[5] I am acquainted only with that which is holy, noble, and right-intentioned. And this being so, as indeed it is, it is not likely that I should attack any priest, above all, one that is a familiar of the Holy Office.[6] If he made this statement, as it appears that he did, on behalf of a certain person, then he is utterly mistaken; for the person in question is one whose genius I hold in veneration and whose works I admire, as well as his constant industry and powers of application. But when all is said, I wish to thank this gentlemanly author for observing that my *Novels* are more satirical than exemplary, while admitting at the same time that they are good;[7] for they could not be good unless they had in them a little of everything.

You will likely tell me that I am being too restrained and over-modest, but it is my belief that affliction is not to be heaped upon the afflicted, and this gentleman must be suffering greatly, seeing that he does not dare to come out into the open and show himself by the light of day, but must conceal his name and dissemble his place of origin, as if he had been guilty of some treason or act of lese majesty. If you by chance should come to know him, tell him on my behalf that I do not hold it against him; for I know what temptations the devil has to offer, one of the greatest of which consists in putting it into a man's head that he can write a book and have it printed and thereby achieve as much fame as he does money and acquire as much money as he does fame; in confirmation of which I would have you, in your own witty and charming manner, tell him this tale.

There was in Seville a certain madman whose madness assumed one of the drollest forms that ever was seen in this world. Taking a hollow reed sharpened at one end, he would catch a dog in the street or somewhere else; and, holding one of the animal's legs with his foot and raising the other with his hand, he would fix his reed as best he could in a certain part, after which he would blow the dog up, round as a ball. When he had it in this condition he would give it a couple of slaps on the belly and let it go, remarking to the bystanders, of whom there were always plenty, "Do your Worships think, then, that it is so easy a thing to inflate a dog?" So you might ask, "Does your Grace think that it is so easy a thing to write a book?" And if this story does not set well with him, here is another one, dear reader, that you may tell him. This one, also, is about a madman and a dog.

The madman in this instance lived in Cordova. He was in the habit of carrying on his head a marble slab or stone of considerable weight, and when he met some stray cur he would go up alongside it and drop the weight full upon it, and the dog in a rage, barking and howling, would then scurry off down three whole streets without stopping. Now, it happened that among the dogs that he treated in this fashion was one belonging to a capmaker, who was very fond of the beast. Going up to it as usual, the madman let the stone fall on its head, whereupon the animal set up a great yowling, and its owner, hearing its moans and seeing what had been done to it, promptly snatched up a measuring rod and fell upon the dog's assailant, flaying him until there was not a sound bone left in the fellow's body; and with each blow that he gave him he cried, "You dog! You thief! Treat my greyhound like that, would you? You brute, couldn't you see it was a greyhound?" And repeating the word "greyhound"[8] over and over, he sent the madman away beaten to a pulp.

Profiting by the lesson that had been taught him, the fellow disappeared and was not seen in public for more than a month, at the end of which time he returned, up to his old tricks and with a heavier stone than ever on his head. He would go up to a dog and stare at it, long and hard, and without daring to drop his stone, would say, "This is a greyhound; beware." And so with all the dogs that he encountered: whether they were mastiffs or curs, he would assert that they were greyhounds and let them go unharmed.

The same thing possibly may happen to our historian; it may be that he will not again venture to let fall the weight of his wit in the form of books which, being bad ones, are harder than rocks.

As for the threat he has made to the effect that through his book he will deprive me of the profits on my own,[9] you may tell him that I do not give a rap. Quoting from the famous interlude, *La Perendenga*,[10] I will say to him in reply, "Long live my master, the Four-and-twenty,[11] and Christ be with us all." Long live the great Count of Lemos, whose Christian spirit and well-known liberality have kept me on my feet despite all the blows an unkind fate has dealt me. Long life to his Eminence of Toledo, the supremely charitable Don Bernardo de Sandoval y Rojas. Even though there were no printing presses in all the world, or such as there are should print more books directed against me than there are letters in the verses of *Mingo Revulgo*,[12] what would it matter to me? These two princes, without any cringing flattery or adulation on my part but solely out of their own goodness of heart, have taken it upon themselves to grant me their favor and protection, in which respect I consider myself richer and more fortunate than if by ordinary means I had attained the peak of prosperity. The poor man may keep his honor, but not the vicious one. Poverty may cast a cloud over nobility but cannot wholly obscure it. Virtue of itself gives off a certain light, even though it be through the chinks and crevices and despite the obstacles of adversity, and so comes to be esteemed and as a consequence favored by high and noble minds.

Tell him no more than this, nor do I have anything more to say to you, except to ask you to bear in mind that this *Second Part of Don Quixote,* which I herewith present to you, is cut from the same cloth and by the same craftsman as Part I. In this book I give you Don Quixote continued and, finally, dead and buried, in order that no one may dare testify any further concerning him, for there has been quite enough evidence as it is. It is sufficient that a reputable individual should have chronicled these ingenious acts of madness once and for all, without going into the matter again; for an abundance even of good things causes them to be little esteemed, while scarcity may lend a certain worth to those that are bad.

I almost forgot to tell you that you may look forward to the *Persiles,* on which I am now putting the finishing touches, as well as Part Second of the *Galatea.*

To the Count of Lemos [1]

WHEN, some days ago, I sent your Excellency my *Comedies,* printed before being performed, I stated, if I remember rightly, that Don Quixote was then engaged in putting on his spurs to go kiss your Excellency's hands; and I may now add that he has put them on and has set out. If he arrives, it is my belief that I shall have been of some service to your Excellency; for I am being strongly urged on all sides to send him forth by way of getting rid of the loathing and nausea occasioned by another *Don Quixote* who, disguising himself under the name of Part Second, has been wandering about the world. The one who has shown himself most eager in this regard is the Emperor of China, who about a month ago dispatched to me by courier a letter written in the Chinese language, in which he requested or, more properly speaking, implored, me to send the Knight to him, since he wished to found a college where the Castilian tongue should be read and he desired that the book to be used should be the story of Don Quixote. At the same time he informed me that I was to be the rector of this college.[2]

I thereupon asked the bearer of the message if His Majesty had given him anything toward defraying my expenses, and the reply was that he had not even thought of it.

"Well, then, brother," I said to him, "you may go back to that China of yours at ten o'clock, at twenty, or whatever time it was that you were sent; for I am not in good enough health to undertake so long a voyage. Moreover, in addition to being ill, I am without money, and emperor for emperor, monarch for monarch, in Naples I have the great Count of Lemos, who, without all those college titles and rectorships, still supports, protects, and favors me beyond anything that I could desire."

With this, I sent him away, and I myself now take my leave by offering to your Excellency *The Trials of Persilis and Sigismunda,* a work which, *Deo volente,* I shall bring to a close within the next four months. It ought to be the worst or the best that has been written in our language—I am referring, of course, to books designed for entertainment. As a matter of fact, I repent having said "the worst," for according to the opinion of my friends it should be extremely good.

May your Excellency come back to us in that state of health in which all wish to see you. Persiles will be there to kiss your hands and I your feet, as your Excellency's humble servant that I am.

From Madrid, on the last day of October, one-thousand-six-hundred-fifteen.

Your Excellency's servant,

MIGUEL DE CERVANTES SAAVEDRA

The Ingenious Gentleman

DON QUIXOTE

DE LA MANCHA

Part Two

CHAPTER I. *Of the conversation which the curate and the barber had with Don Quixote concerning his malady.*

I

N THE second part of this history, dealing with Don Quixote's third sally, Cid Hamete Benengeli tells us that the curate and the barber went nearly a month without seeing their friend, in order not to remind him of what had happened. But they did not for this reason leave off visiting the niece and housekeeper, whom they urged to treat the knight with the greatest of care by seeing to it that he had comforting things to eat and such as would be good for his heart and for his brain as well, the latter being to all appearances the seat of his trouble and the cause of all his misfortunes. The women replied that this was what they were doing, and would continue to do, with a right good will and most attentively; for they had noticed that the master of the house at moments seemed to be in full possession of his senses.

The curate and the barber were well pleased at hearing this, and concluded that they had done the wise thing in having Don Quixote borne away in an ox-cart, as has been related in the last chapter of the First Part of this great and painstaking chronicle. They accordingly determined to visit him and see for themselves what improvement he had made, although they believed it to be all but impossible that he could be any better. They agreed that they would not bring up any subject that had to do with knight-errantry, as they did not wish to run the risk of reopening a wound that was still so sore.

When the pair came to pay their visit, they found their host seated upon the bed, clad in a green baize waistcoat and a red Toledo cap, and looking as withered and dried up as an Egyptian mummy. He received them very well and, when they made inquiries regarding his health, discussed with them this and other matters of a personal nature most sensibly and in words that were very well chosen. In the course of their conversation they came to touch upon what is known as statecraft and forms of government, correcting this abuse, condemning that one, reforming one custom and banishing another, with each of the three setting himself up as a new lawgiver, a modern Lycurgus or newly fledged Solon. In this manner they proceeded to remodel the State, as if they had placed it in a forge and had drawn out something quite different from what they had put in. And all the while Don Quixote displayed such good sound sense in connection with whatever topic was broached as to lead the two examiners to feel that he must undoubtedly be fully recovered and in his right mind.

The niece and housekeeper were present at this conversation and could not thank God enough when they saw how clear-headed their master apparently was. It was then that the curate changed his mind about not bringing up anything that had to do with chivalry; for he wished to make the test complete and assure himself as to whether the knight's recovery was real or not. And so, speaking of one thing and another, he came to relate various items of news that had just been received from the capital, including a report to the effect that it was looked upon as a certainty that the Turk was bearing down with a powerful fleet, although nothing was known of his plans as yet, nor where so great a storm as this would break, but as a result all Christendom was stirred by that feeling of dread that almost every year summons us to take up arms, and his Majesty had seen to fortifying the coasts of Naples and Sicily and the island of Malta.

"His Majesty," remarked Don Quixote, "has acted like a most prudent warrior in providing for the safety of his dominions while there is yet time, in order that the enemy may not take him unawares; but if he were to follow my advice, I should counsel him to adopt a measure which I am sure is far from his thoughts at the present moment."

"Poor Don Quixote," said the curate to himself when he heard this, "may God help you; for it looks to me as if you have fallen from the high cliff of madness into the abyss of simple-mindedness."

The same thought had occurred to the barber, who now asked the knight what this measure was that in his opinion should be adopted, adding that perhaps it was one that would have to be added to the long list of impertinent suggestions of the kind commonly offered to princes.

"My suggestion, Master Shaver," replied Don Quixote, "is not an impertinent one but is very much to the point."

"That is not what I meant," said the barber, "but experience has shown that all or most of the expedients that are proposed to his Majesty are either impossible or nonsensical, or else would be detrimental to king and kingdom."

"But mine," Don Quixote insisted, "is not impossible nor is it nonsensical, but rather is the easiest, the most reasonable, the readiest, and most expeditious scheme that anyone could devise."

"It takes your Grace a long time to tell it," observed the curate.

"I do not care to tell it to you here and now," said the knight, "and, the first thing tomorrow morning, have it reach the ears of my lords, the councilors, so that some other person may carry off the reward and win the thanks that are rightly due me."

"For my part," the barber assured him, "I give you my word, here and before God, that I will say nothing of what your Grace may tell me, to king, rook, or earthly man.[1] That, by the way, is an oath I picked up from the ballad about the curate who, in the prelude, tells the king of the thief who had robbed him of a hundred doblas [2] and his fast-pacing mule." [3]

"I know nothing about such stories," said Don Quixote, "but I do know that the oath is a good one by reason of the faith that I have in this worthy man, our master barber."

"And even if he were not what you take him to be," the curate went on, "I would go bond and put in an appearance for him, to the effect that in this case he will be as silent as a mute, under pain of any sentence that might be pronounced upon him."

"And who will go your Grace's bond?" Don Quixote asked the priest.

"My profession," was the curate's reply, "which consists in keeping secrets."

"Then, damn it, sir!" exclaimed the knight, "what more need his Majesty do than command by public proclamation that all the knights-errant at present wandering over Spain shall assemble in the capital on a given day? Even if no more than half a dozen came, there well might be one among them who alone would be able to overthrow the Turk's mighty power. Pay attention, your Worships, and listen closely to what I am about to say. Is it by any chance an unheard-of thing for a single knight-errant to rout an army of two hundred thousand men, as if they all had but one throat or were made of sugar paste? Tell me, how many stories do we have that are filled with such marvels? If only, alas for me (I do not care to speak for any other), the famous Don Belianís were alive today, or any of the countless other descendants of Amadis of Gaul! Let one of these but confront the Turk, and my word, they would have the best of him. But God will look after his people and will provide someone who, if not so brave as the knights of old, will not be inferior to them in the matter of courage. God knows what I mean. I need say no more."

"Oh, dear," wailed the niece at this point, "may they slay me if my master doesn't want to go back to being a knight-errant!"

"A knight-errant I shall live and die," said Don Quixote, "and let the Turk come or go as he will, with all the strength he can muster. Again I say to you, God understands."

The barber now spoke up. "I beg your Worships to grant me permission to relate to you briefly something that happened in Seville. It is a story that is made for the present occasion, which is why I should like to tell it."

Don Quixote gave his consent, and the curate and the others prepared to lend him their attention.

"In the madhouse of Seville," he began, "was a certain individual who had been placed there by his relatives, as being out of his mind. He was a graduate of Osuna, in canon law; but it was the opinion of most people that even if he had been of Salamanca, he would have been mad all the same. After a few years of seclusion, this man took it into his head that he had been wholly cured, and, being so convinced, he wrote to the archbishop, begging that prelate, earnestly and in well-chosen words, to have him released from the misery in which he was living, since he had now recovered his lost reason, even though his family, which was enjoying his share of the estate, insisted upon keeping him there; for contrary to the truth of the matter, they would make him out to be a madman until his dying day.

"Impressed by the many well and sensibly written letters he had received from the man, the archbishop sent one of his chaplains to find out from the superintendent of the madhouse if what the licentiate had written was true or not. The chaplain was further directed to converse with the patient and if he found him to be sane, he was to take him out and set him at liberty. Following these instructions, he was informed by the superintendent that the man was as mad as ever, and that while he very frequently spoke like a person of great intelligence, he would suddenly burst out with so many absurdities that they more than made up, in quantity and in quality, for all the sensible things he had previously said, as was readily to be seen by talking with him. This the chaplain resolved to do, and, sitting down with the patient, he carried on a conversation with him for more than an hour, during all of which time the madman did not make one incoherent or foolish remark but appeared to be so rational in everything he said that his visitor was compelled to believe him sane.

"Among other things, the man stated that the superintendent had it in for him, being motivated by a desire not to lose the gifts that the relatives made him for saying that his ward was still insane with lucid intervals. The greatest misfortune that he had to contend with, the poor fellow added, was his large estate, since it was for the purpose of enjoying his wealth that his enemies belied and cast doubts upon the grace which Our Lord had shown him by turning him from a beast into a man once more. In short, he spoke in such a way as to make the superintendent's conduct seem highly suspicious, while his relatives were made out to be covetous and heartless creatures; all of which was uttered with such a show of reason that the chaplain made up his mind to take the man with him that the archbishop might see him and come at the truth of this business.

"With this worthy intention, he asked the superintendent to send for the clothes which the licentiate had worn when he entered the place, whereupon that official once more begged him to look well to what he was doing, as there was not the slightest doubt that the patient was still mad; but all these cautions and warnings were lost upon the chaplain, who was bent upon having the man released. Seeing that it was the archbishop's orders, the superintendent complied, and they then brought the licentiate his clothes, which were new and very presentable. When the latter saw himself dressed like one in his right senses and rid of his madman's garments, he begged the chaplain to be so kind as to permit him to take leave of his fellow patients. The chaplain consented, remarking that he would like to go along and see the others who were confined in

the institution. They accordingly went upstairs, accompanied by some of
those who were present, and came to a cell where one who was raving
mad was lodged, though at that moment he was calm and quiet.

" 'Brother,' the licentiate said to him, 'think if there is anything that I
can do for you. I am going home, God in His infinite goodness and mercy,
and through no merit of my own, having seen fit to restore my reason
to me. I am now cured and sane, since where the power of God is concerned, nothing is impossible. You must have a great hope and confidence
in Him, who, just as He has restored me to my former state, will do the
same for you if you trust in Him. I will make it a point to send you some
good things to eat, and be sure that you do eat them; for as one who has
gone through it, I may tell you that in my opinion all our madness comes
from having our stomachs empty and our brains full of air. Pluck up your
courage, then. Despondency in misfortune only impairs the health and
brings death all the sooner.'

"Everything the licentiate said was heard by another madman in a cell
across the way, and, rising from an old mat where he had been lying
stark naked, this man now cried out in a loud voice, demanding to know
who it was that was going away cured and sane.

" 'It is I, brother,' the licentiate replied. 'I am leaving you. There is
no longer any need of my remaining here, thanks be to Heaven for having shown me this mercy.'

" 'Mind what you are saying, licentiate,' the other warned him, 'and do
not let the devil deceive you. You had best not stir a foot but stay where
you are and save yourself the trouble of coming back.'

" 'I know that I am all right,' was the reply, 'and that it will not be
necessary for me to do the stations again.' *

" 'You are all right, are you?' said the madman across the way. 'We
shall see as to that. May God go with you; but I swear to you, in the
name of Jupiter whose majesty I represent on earth, that for this one
sin which Seville today is committing by releasing you from this place
as if you were cured, I shall have to inflict such a punishment upon it
as will be remembered throughout all the ages to come. Amen. Do you
not know, miserable little licentiate, that I can do this, seeing that, as I
have said, I am Jupiter the Thunderer and hold in my hands the fiery
bolts with which I am accustomed to threaten the world and by means
of which I can destroy it? There is, however, only one way in which
I wish to punish this ignorant town, and that is by not raining upon it
or anywhere in the entire district and vicinity for three whole years,
beginning with the day and moment when this threat is made. You free,

cured, in your right senses, and I a madman, sickly minded and confined?
I would no more think of sending rain than I would of hanging myself.'

"The bystanders all listened attentively to the madman's words and
cries. Then our licentiate turned to the chaplain and seized his hands.
'Do not be disturbed, your Grace,' he pleaded, 'and pay no attention to
what this fellow says. If he is Jupiter and will not rain, then I who am
Neptune, father and god of the waters, will do so any time that I feel
like it or whenever it may be necessary.'

" 'For all of that, Sir Neptune,' the chaplain answered him, 'it would
be as well not to annoy Sir Jupiter. Stay here, your Grace, and another
day, when we have more time and it is more convenient, we will return
for you.'

"The superintendent and the others laughed at this, and the chaplain
was greatly embarrassed. They then undressed the licentiate, and he remained where he was, and that is the end of the story."

"If that is the tale, Master Barber," said Don Quixote, "what did you
mean by saying that it was made for the present occasion, for which
reason you could not refrain from telling it? Ah, Master Shaver, Master
Shaver, how blind is he who cannot see through a sieve! Is your Grace
not aware that comparisons of mind with mind, valor with valor, beauty
with beauty, birth with birth, are invariably odious and ill received? I,
Master Barber, am not Neptune, god of the waters, nor would I have anyone take me for a wise man when I am not wise. My sole endeavor is to
bring the world to realize the mistake it is making in failing to revive
that happiest of times when the order of knight-errantry was in the field.
But this degenerate age of ours does not deserve to enjoy so great a blessing as that which former ages knew, when wandering men of arms took
upon themselves the defense of realms, the protection of damsels, the succor of orphans, the punishment of the proud, and the rewarding of the
humble.

"The knights of the present time, for the most part, are accompanied
by the rustling of damasks, brocades, and other rich stuffs that they wear,
rather than by the rattling of coats of mail. There is none that sleeps in
the field, exposed to the inclemency of the heavens and fully armed from
head to foot. There is none who, as they say, snatches forty winks without taking foot from stirrup, merely leaning on his lance. There is none
who, sallying forth from a wood, will go up onto yonder mountain, and
from there come down to tread the barren and deserted shore beside a
sea that is almost always angry and tempest-tossed; or who, finding upon
the beach a small craft, without oars, sail, mast, or rigging of any kind,

will leap into it with intrepid heart and entrust himself to the implacable waves of the stormy deep, waves that now mount heavenward and now drag him down into the abyss. Such a one, breasting the irresistible tempest, may find himself more than three thousand miles from the place where he embarked; in which case, bounding ashore upon the soil of a remote and unknown land, he will meet with such adventures as are worthy of being recorded, not upon parchment, but in bronze.

"Today, sloth triumphs over diligence, idleness and ease over exertion, vice over virtue, arrogance over valor, and theory over practice of the warrior's art. Tell me, if you will, who was more virtuous or more valiant than the famous Amadis of Gaul? Who more prudent than Palmerin of England? Who more gracious and reasonable than Tirant lo Blanch? Who was more the courtier than Lisuarte of Greece? Who was more slashed or slashing than Don Belianís? Who more intrepid than Perión of Gaul? Or who more forward in facing danger than Felixmarte of Hircania? Who was more sincere than Esplandián? More daring than Don Cirongilio of Thrace? Who was braver than Rodamonte? Wiser than King Sobrino? Bolder than Rinaldo? More invincible than Orlando? Who was more gallant and courteous than Ruggiero, from whom the present dukes of Ferrara are descended, according to Turpin in his *Cosmography?* [5]

"All these and many others whom I could mention, Señor Curate, were knights-errant, the light and glory of chivalry. It is these, or such as these, that I would have carry out my plan, in which case his majesty would be well served and would save himself much expense, while the Turk would be left tearing out his beard. For this reason, I do not propose to remain at home,[6] even though the chaplain does not take me out; and if Jupiter, as the barber has said, does not choose to rain, then I am here to do so whenever it pleases me. I say this in order that Master Basin may know that I understand him."

"Really, Señor Don Quixote," said the barber, "I did not mean it in that way. So help me God, my intentions were of the best, and your Grace ought not to take offense."

"Whether I take offense or not," replied Don Quixote, "is for me to decide."

With this, the curate took a hand in the conversation. "I have hardly said a word up to now, but there is one little doubt that gnaws and pecks at my conscience and that comes from what Don Quixote has just told us."

"You may go as far as you like, Señor Curate," said Don Quixote

"Feel perfectly free to state your doubt, for it is not pleasant to have something on one's conscience."

"Well, then, with your permission," the curate continued, "I will say that my doubt arises from the fact that I am unable to persuade myself by any manner of means that all the many knights-errant your Grace has mentioned were in reality flesh-and-blood beings who actually lived in this world. I rather fancy that it is all fiction, fables, and lies, a lot of dreams related by men just awakened from sleep, or, better, still half asleep."

"That," declared Don Quixote, "is another error into which many have fallen who do not believe that such knights ever existed; and I many times, with various persons and on various occasions, have endeavored to bring this all too common mistake to the light of truth. Sometimes I have not succeeded in my purpose, but other times, sustained upon the shoulders of the truth, I have been more fortunate. For the truth is so clear that I can almost assure you that I saw with my own eyes Amadis of Gaul. He was a tall man, of fair complexion and with a beard which, though black, was quite handsome. His countenance was half mild, half stern; his words were few, but he was slow to anger and quick to lay aside his wrath. And just as I have depicted Amadis for you, so I might go on, I think, to portray and describe [7] all the other knights-errant in all the storybooks of the world. For I feel sure that they were what the histories make them out to have been, and from the exploits that they performed and the kind of men they were it would be possible, with the aid of a little sound philosophy, to reconstruct their features, their complexions, and their stature."

"How big, Señor Don Quixote, was the giant Morgante as your Grace conceives him?" the barber asked.

"On this subject of giants," replied the knight, "opinions differ as to whether or not there ever were any in this world: but the Holy Scriptures, which do not depart from the truth by one iota, show us plainly that giants did exist, when they tell us the story of that big Philistine of a Goliath, who was seven cubits and a half in height, which is a very great size. [8] Moreover, in the island of Sicily they have found thigh and shoulder bones so large that they must have belonged to giants as tall as towers. [9] It is a matter of simple geometry. But for all of this, I should not be able to state with any certainty what Morgante's size was, although I imagine that he was not exceedingly tall, since I find in that history where special mention is made of his exploits [10] that he very frequently slept under a roof, and inasmuch as he found houses that were large enough to accommodate him, he could not have been too big after all."

"I agree with you," said the curate. And merely for the pleasure of listening to such utter nonsense, he went on to ask Don Quixote what he thought the countenances of Rinaldo of Montalbán, Don Orlando, and the other Twelve Peers of France must have been like, seeing that they were all knights-errant.

"Concerning Rinaldo," Don Quixote answered him, "I would venture to say that he had a broad face, a ruddy complexion, and twinkling, rather prominent eyes, and that he was punctilious, extremely choleric, and a friend of robbers and those beyond the pale of the law. As to Roldán, or Rotolando, or Orlando—for the histories give him all these names—I am of the opinion, indeed I would assert, that he was of medium stature, broad-shouldered, somewhat bowlegged, red-bearded, with a hairy body and a threatening expression, a man of few words, but very courteous and well bred."

"If Orlando," observed the curate, "had no more of a gentlemanly appearance than that, I do not wonder that the lady Angélica the Fair should have disdained him or that she should have left him for that downy-faced young Moor who was so gay, so sprightly, and so witty. It seems to me she did wisely in preferring the softness of Medora to Orlando's ruggedness."

"That Angélica," replied the knight, "was a giddy damsel, flighty and capricious, and filled the world with her whims as much as with the fame of her beauty. She spurned a thousand gentlemen of wit and valor and was satisfied with a smooth-faced pageling with no other wealth or claim to fame than his reputation for gratitude, due to the affection that he showed his friend.[11] The great poet who sang of her beauty, the famous Ariosto, either did not dare or did not wish to relate what happened to this lady following her disgraceful surrender, but her adventures could not have been any too edifying, and it is with these lines that the bard takes his leave of her:

> *How she received the scepter of Cathay,*
> *Another with better plectrum will sing someday.*[12]

There can be no doubt that this was a kind of prophecy; for poets are also called *vates*, which means 'diviners.' The truth of this is plainly to be seen in the fact that a famous Andalusian poet wept for her and sang of her tears, while another famous and exceptional one of Castile hymned her beauty." [13]

"But tell me, Señor Don Quixote," said the barber, "among all the poets who have praised her, has there been none to compose a satire on this Lady Angélica?"

"I can well believe," replied Don Quixote, "that if Sacripante or Orlando had been poets, they would have given the damsel a dressing-down; for when poets have been scorned and rejected by their ladies, whether the ladies in question be real or imaginary [14]—in short, when they have been spurned by those whom they have chosen to be the mistresses of their affection—it is natural for them to seek to avenge themselves by means of satires and libels, although, to be sure, this is something that is unworthy of generous hearts; but up to now I have not come upon any defamatory verses directed at the Lady Angélica, who set the world on end." [15]

"That is very strange," said the curate.

At that moment they heard the housekeeper and the niece, who had left the room a while ago, shouting at someone in the courtyard, and they all ran out to see what the uproar was about.

CHAPTER II. *Which treats of the notable quarrel that Sancho Panza had with Don Quixote's niece and housekeeper, along with other droll happenings.*

THE history tells us that the cries which Don Quixote, the curate, and the barber heard came from the niece and the housekeeper. They were shouting at Sancho Panza, who was struggling to get in to see the knight, while they were doing their best to keep him out.

"What is this vagabond doing here? Home with you, brother; for you and no one else are the one who puts these foolish notions into my master's head; it is you who lure him away to go wandering over the countryside."

"You devil's housekeeper, you!" exclaimed Sancho. "The one who has foolish notions put in his head and is lured away is I and not your master. He has taken me all over this world; and you do not know the half of it. It was through a trick that he persuaded me to leave home, by promising me an island which I am still waiting to see."

"May you choke on your cursed islands, Sancho, you wretch!" the niece replied. "What are islands anyway? Are they something to eat, glutton that you are?"

"No," replied Sancho, "they are not something to eat, but something to govern and rule over and better than four cities [1] or four judgeships at court."

"Well, in spite of all that," said the housekeeper, "you are not coming in here, you bag of mischief. Go govern that weedpatch of yours and let us hear no more talk of islands or drylands or what have you." [2]

The curate and the barber greatly enjoyed listening to the conversation of these three; but Don Quixote, fearing that Sancho would talk too much, blurt out a lot of mischievous nonsense, and touch upon certain subjects that would not redound to his master's credit, now called his squire over to him and at the same time ordered the other two to hold their tongues and let the unwelcome visitor come in. Sancho entered the house as the curate and the barber took their leave. They were in despair over Don Quixote's state of mind, for they could not help perceiving how firmly fixed his hallucinations were and how imbued he was with those foolish ideas of his about knight-errantry.

"You will see, my friend," remarked the curate, "our gentleman will be off again one of these days when we least expect it."

"I have not the slightest doubt of that," replied the barber. "But I do not wonder so much at the knight's madness as I do at the simple-mindedness of his squire, who believes so firmly in that island that no matter what you did to disillusion him, you would never be able to get it out of his head. Such at least is my opinion."

"God help them," said the curate, "and let us keep a close watch to see what comes of all this falderal about knight and squire. It would seem they had both been turned out from the same mold and that the madness of the master without the foolishness of the man would not be worth a penny."

"You are right," agreed the barber, "and I would give a good deal to know what the two of them are talking about at this moment."

"I feel certain," replied the curate, "that the niece or the housekeeper will tell us all about it afterward, for it is not like them to fail to listen."

In the meanwhile Don Quixote had shut himself up in his room with Sancho.

"It grieves me very much, Sancho," he began as soon as they were alone, "to hear you saying that it was I who took you away from your cottage. You know very well that I did not remain in my own house. We sallied forth and rode away together, and together we wandered here and there. We shared the same fortune and the same fate, and if they blanketed you once, they flayed me a hundred times, that is the only advantage that I have over you."

"That is as it should be," Sancho told him, "for, according to what your Grace says, misfortunes are better suited to knights-errant than to their squires."

"That is where you are wrong, Sancho," replied the knight, "in accordance with the proverb '*Quando caput dolet*,' etc."

"I understand no other language than my own," said Sancho.

"I mean," said Don Quixote, "that when the head suffers, all the other members suffer also. Being your master and lord, I am your head, and you, being my servant, are a part of me; and so it is that the evil which affects me must likewise affect you and your pain must be my own."

"It may be so," Sancho answered, "but I know that when they were blanketing me, as a member, my head was on the other side of the wall, watching me fly through the air, without feeling any pain whatever. And it does seem to me that if the members are obliged to suffer with the head, the head ought to suffer with them."

"Do you mean to stand there and tell me, Sancho, that I felt nothing when they were tossing you in the blanket? You must not say or think such a thing as that, for I felt more pain in my mind than you did in your body. However, let us put all this to one side; for there will be time enough later for us to consider this point and reach a conclusion. Rather, Sancho my friend, tell me, what are they saying about me here in the village? What opinion do the people have of me, and what do the gentry think, the *hidalgos* and the *caballeros*? ³ What do they say of my valor, of my exploits, of my courtesy? What kind of talk is there about my having undertaken to restore to the world the forgotten order of chivalry? In brief, Sancho, I would have you tell me everything that you have heard on this subject; and this you are to do without adding to the good or keeping back any of the bad; for it is fitting that loyal vassals should tell the truth to their lords, just as it is, without magnifying it out of adulation or diminishing it out of a feeling of false respect. I may tell you, Sancho, that if the naked truth could only reach the ears of princes, stripped of the garments of flattery, the times would be quite different from what they are and other eras would be known as the age of iron, not ours, which indeed I hold to be a golden epoch among those of the

modern world. Give heed to this advice, Sancho, in order that you may
be able to answer my questions intelligently and faithfully and tell me
what you know to be the truth about these things."

"That I will do right willingly, my master," Sancho replied, "on condition that your Grace will not be angry at what I tell you, seeing that you
would have me give it to you stark naked, without putting any other
clothes on it than those in which it came to me."

"Of course I shall not be angry," said Don Quixote. "You may speak
freely, Sancho, without any beating around the bush."

"Well, in the first place, the common people look upon your Grace as
an utter madman and me as no less a fool. The *hidalgos* are saying that,
not content with being a gentleman, you have had to put a 'Don' in front
of your name [4] and at a bound have made yourself into a *caballero*,
with four vinestocks, a couple of acres [5] of land, and one tatter in
front and another behind. The *caballeros,* on the other hand, do not
relish having the *hidalgos* set up in opposition to them, especially those
gentlemen who perform the duties of a squire by polishing their own
shoes and darning their black stockings with green silk."

"That," said the knight, "has nothing to do with me, since I always go
well dressed and never in patches. Ragged I well may be, but rather from
the wear and tear of armor than of time." [6]

"So far as your Grace's valor is concerned," Sancho went on, "your
courtesy, exploits, and undertaking, there are different opinions. Some
say: 'Crazy but amusing'; others: 'Brave but unfortunate'; others still:
'Courteous but meddlesome'; and they go on clacking their tongues about
this thing and that until there is not a whole bone left in your Grace's
body or in mine."

"Look you, Sancho," replied his master, "wherever virtue exists in an
outstanding degree, it is always persecuted. Few or none of the famous
men of the past have escaped without being slandered by the malicious.
Julius Caesar, a most courageous, wise, and valiant captain, was charged
with ambition and with being none too clean either in his dress or in his
morals. Alexander, whose deeds won him the title of Great, was reported
to be somewhat of a drunkard. Hercules—he of the many labors—if we
are to believe what they say of him, was lascivious and inclined to
effeminacy. Of Don Galaor, brother of Amadis of Gaul, it was whispered
about that he was far too quarrelsome, while Amadis himself was called a
whiner. So you see, Sancho, when good men have been traduced in this
fashion, what they say about me may be overlooked, if it is no more
than what you have told me."

"Body of my father!" exclaimed Sancho, "but there's the rub."

"What?" Don Quixote asked. "Is there more then?"

"That there is," said Sancho. "The tail is yet to be skinned.[7] All so far has been tarts and fancy cakes;[8] but if your Grace really wants to know what they are saying, I can bring you here at once one who will tell you everything, without leaving out the least particle of it. Bartolomé Carrasco's son came home last night. He has been studying at Salamanca and has just been made a bachelor. When I went to welcome him, he told me that the story of your Grace has already been put into a book called *The Ingenious Gentleman, Don Quixote de la Mancha*. And he says they mention me in it, under my own name, Sancho Panza, and the lady Dulcinea del Toboso as well, along with things that happened to us when we were alone together. I had to cross myself, for I could not help wondering how the one who wrote all those things down could have come to know about them."

"I can assure you, Sancho," said Don Quixote, "that the author of our history must be some wise enchanter; for nothing that they choose to write about is hidden from those who practice that art."

"What do you mean by saying he was an enchanter?" Sancho asked. "Why, the bachelor Sansón Carrasco—which is the name of the man I was telling you of—says that the one who wrote the story is called Cid Hamete Berenjena."

"That," said Don Quixote, "is a Moorish name."

"It may be," replied Sancho; "for I have generally heard it said that the Moors are great lovers of eggplant."[9]

"You must have made some mistake," said the knight, "regarding the surname of this Cid, a title which in Arabic means 'Señor.' "

"Maybe I did," replied Sancho; "but if your Grace would like me to bring the man here, I will go for him in a jiffy."

"It would give me much pleasure, my friend," said Don Quixote, "for I am astonished by what you have told me and shall not eat a mouthful that sets well on my stomach until I have learned all about it."

"Very well, then," said Sancho, "I will go fetch him." And, leaving his master, he went out to look for the bachelor. He returned with him a short while later, and the three of them then had a most amusing conversation.

CHAPTER III. *Of the laughable conversation that took place between Don Quixote, Sancho Panza, and the bachelor Sansón Carrasco.*

DON QUIXOTE remained in a thoughtful mood as he waited for the bachelor Carrasco, from whom he hoped to hear the news as to how he had been put into a book, as Sancho had said. He could not bring himself to believe that any such history existed, since the blood of the enemies he had slain was not yet dry on the blade of his sword; and here they were trying to tell him that his high deeds of chivalry were already circulating in printed form.[1] But, for that matter, he imagined that some sage, either friend or enemy, must have seen to the printing of them through the art of magic. If the chronicler was a friend, he must have undertaken the task in order to magnify and exalt Don Quixote's exploits above the most notable ones achieved by knights-errant of old. If an enemy, his purpose would have been to make them out as nothing at all, by debasing them below the meanest acts ever recorded of any mean squire. The only thing was, the knight reflected, the exploits of squires never were set down in writing. If it was true that such a history existed, being about a knight-errant, then it must be eloquent and lofty in tone, a splendid and distinguished piece of work and veracious in its details.

This consoled him somewhat, although he was a bit put out at the thought that the author was a Moor, if the appellation "Cid" was to be taken as an indication, and from the Moors you could never hope for any word of truth,[2] seeing that they are all of them cheats, forgers, and schemers. He feared lest his love should not have been treated with becoming modesty but rather in a way that would reflect upon the virtue of his lady Dulcinea del Toboso. He hoped that his fidelity had been made clear, and the respect he had always shown her, and that something had been said as to how he had spurned queens, empresses, and damsels of every rank while keeping a rein upon those impulses that are natural to a man. He was still wrapped up in these and many other similar thoughts when Sancho returned with Carrasco.

Don Quixote received the bachelor very amiably. The latter, although his name was Sansón, or Samson, was not very big so far as bodily size went, but he was a great joker, with a sallow complexion and a ready wit. He was going on twenty-four and had a round face, a snub nose, and a large mouth, all of which showed him to be of a mischievous disposition and fond of jests and witticisms. This became apparent when, as soon as he saw Don Quixote, he fell upon his knees and addressed the knight as follows:

"O mighty Don Quixote de la Mancha, give me your hands; for by the habit of St. Peter that I wear [3]—though I have received but the first four orders—your Grace is one of the most famous knights-errant that ever have been or ever will be anywhere on this earth. Blessings upon Cid Hamete Benengeli who wrote down the history of your great achievements, and upon that curious-minded one who was at pains to have it translated from the Arabic into our Castilian vulgate for the universal entertainment of the people."

Don Quixote bade him rise. "Is it true, then," he asked, "that there is a book about me and that it was some Moorish sage who composed it?"

"By way of showing you how true it is," replied Sansón, "I may tell you that it is my belief that there are in existence today more than twelve thousand copies of that history. If you do not believe me, you have but to make inquiries in Portugal, Barcelona, and Valencia, where editions have been brought out, and there is even a report to the effect that one edition was printed at Antwerp.[4] In short, I feel certain that there will soon not be a nation that does not know it or a language into which it has not been translated."

"One of the things," remarked Don Quixote, "that should give most satisfaction to a virtuous and eminent man is to see his good name spread abroad during his own lifetime, by means of the printing press, through translations into the languages of the various peoples. I have said 'good name,' for if he has any other kind, his fate is worse than death."

"If it is a matter of good name and good reputation," said the bachelor, "your Grace bears off the palm from all the knights-errant in the world; for the Moor in his tongue and the Christian in his have most vividly depicted your Grace's gallantry, your courage in facing dangers, your patience in adversity and suffering, whether the suffering be due to wounds or to misfortunes of another sort, and your virtue and continence in love, in connection with that platonic relationship that exists between your Grace and my lady Doña Dulcinea del Toboso."

At this point Sancho spoke up. "Never in my life," he said, "have I heard my lady Dulcinea called 'Doña,' but only 'la Señora Dulcinea del Toboso'; so on that point, already, the history is wrong."

"That is not important," said Carrasco.

"No, certainly not," Don Quixote agreed. "But tell me, Señor Bachelor, what adventures of mine as set down in this book have made the deepest impression?"

"As to that," the bachelor answered, "opinions differ, for it is a matter of individual taste. There are some who are very fond of the adventure of the windmills—those windmills which to your Grace appeared to be so many Briareuses and giants. Others like the episode at the fulling mill. One relishes the story of the two armies which took on the appearance of droves of sheep, while another fancies the tale of the dead man whom they were taking to Segovia for burial. One will assert that the freeing of the galley slaves is the best of all, and yet another will maintain that nothing can come up to the Benedictine giants and the encounter with the valiant Biscayan."

Again Sancho interrupted him. "Tell me, Señor Bachelor," he said, "does the book say anything about the adventure with the Yanguesans, that time our good Rocinante took it into his head to go looking for tidbits in the sea?"

"The sage," replied Sansón, "has left nothing in the inkwell. He has told everything and to the point, even to the capers which the worthy Sancho cut as they tossed him in the blanket."

"I cut no capers in the blanket," objected Sancho, "but I did in the air, and more than I liked."

"I imagine," said Don Quixote, "that there is no history in the world, dealing with humankind, that does not have its ups and downs, and this is particularly true of those that have to do with deeds of chivalry, for they can never be filled with happy incidents alone."

"Nevertheless," the bachelor went on, "there are some who have read the book who say that they would have been glad if the authors had forgotten a few of the innumerable cudgelings which Señor Don Quixote received in the course of his various encounters." [5]

"But that is where the truth of the story comes in," Sancho protested.

"For all of that," observed Don Quixote, "they might well have said nothing about them; for there is no need of recording those events that do not alter the veracity of the chronicle, when they tend only to lessen the reader's respect for the hero. You may be sure that Aeneas was not as pious as Vergil would have us believe, nor was Ulysses as wise as Homer depicts him."

"That is true enough," replied Sansón, "but it is one thing to write as a poet and another as a historian. The former may narrate or sing of things not as they were but as they should have been; the latter must describe them not as they should have been but as they were, without adding to or detracting from the truth in any degree whatsoever."

"Well," said Sancho, "if this Moorish gentleman is bent upon telling the truth, I have no doubt that among my master's thrashings my own will be found; for they never took the measure of his Grace's shoulders without measuring my whole body. But I don't wonder at that; for as my master himself says, when there's an ache in the head the members have to share it."

"You are a sly fox, Sancho," said Don Quixote. "My word, but you can remember things well enough when you choose to do so!"

"Even if I wanted to forget the whacks they gave me," Sancho answered him, "the welts on my ribs wouldn't let me, for they are still fresh."

"Be quiet, Sancho," his master admonished him, "and do not interrupt the bachelor. I beg him to go on and tell me what is said of me in this book."

"And what it says about me, too," put in Sancho, "for I have heard that I am one of the main presonages in it—"

"*Personages*, not *presonages*, Sancho my friend," said Sansón.

"So we have another one who catches you up on everything you say," was Sancho's retort. "If we go on at this rate, we'll never be through in a lifetime."

"May God put a curse on *my* life," the bachelor told him, "if you are not the second most important person in the story; and there are some who would rather listen to you talk than to anyone else in the book. It is true, there are those who say that you are too gullible in believing it to be the truth that you could become the governor of that island that was offered you by Señor Don Quixote, here present."

"There is still sun on the top of the wall,"[6] said Don Quixote, "and when Sancho is a little older, with the experience that the years bring, he will be wiser and better fitted to be a governor than he is at the present time."

"By God, master," said Sancho, "the island that I couldn't govern right now I'd never be able to govern if I lived to be as old as Methuselah. The trouble is, I don't know where that island we are talking about is located; it is not due to any lack of noddle on my part."

"Leave it to God, Sancho," was Don Quixote's advice, "and everything will come out all right, perhaps even better than you think; for not a leaf on the tree stirs except by His will."

"Yes," said Sansón, "if it be God's will, Sancho will not lack a thousand islands to govern, not to speak of one island alone."

"I have seen governors around here," said Sancho, "that are not to be compared to the sole of my shoe, and yet they call them 'your Lordship' and serve them on silver plate."

"Those are not the same kind of governors," Sansón informed him. "Their task is a good deal easier. The ones that govern islands must at least know grammar."

"I could make out well enough with the *gram*," replied Sancho, "but with the *mar*[7] I want nothing to do, for I don't understand it at all. But leaving this business of the governorship in God's hands—for He will send me wherever I can best serve Him—I will tell you, Señor Bachelor Sansón Carrasco, that I am very much pleased that the author of the history should have spoken of me in such a way as does not offend me; for, upon the word of a faithful squire, if he had said anything about me that was not becoming to an old Christian, the deaf would have heard of it."

"That would be to work miracles," said Sansón.

"Miracles or no miracles," was the answer, "let everyone take care as to what he says or writes about people and not be setting down the first thing that pops into his head."

"One of the faults that is found with the book," continued the bachelor, "is that the author has inserted in it a story entitled *The One Who Was Too Curious for His Own Good*. It is not that the story in itself is a bad one or badly written; it is simply that it is out of place there, having nothing to do with the story of his Grace, Señor Don Quixote."

"I will bet you," said Sancho, "that the son of a dog has mixed the cabbages with the baskets."[8]

"And I will say right now," declared Don Quixote, "that the author of this book was not a sage but some ignorant prattler who at haphazard and without any method set about the writing of it, being content to let things turn out as they might. In the same manner, Orbaneja, the painter of Ubeda, when asked what he was painting would reply, 'Whatever it turns out to be.'[9] Sometimes it would be a cock, in which case he would have to write alongside it, in Gothic letters, 'This is a cock.' And so it must be with my story, which will need a commentary to make it understandable."

"No," replied Sansón, "that it will not; for it is so clearly written that none can fail to understand it. Little children leaf through it, young people read it, adults appreciate it, and the aged sing its praises. In short, it is so thumbed and read and so well known to persons of every walk in life that no sooner do folks see some skinny nag than they at once cry, 'There goes Rocinante!' Those that like it best of all are the pages; for there is no lord's antechamber where a *Don Quixote* is not to be found. If one lays it down, another will pick it up; one will pounce upon it, and another will beg for it. It affords the pleasantest and least harmful reading of any book that has been published up to now. In the whole of it there is not to be found an indecent word or a thought that is other than Catholic." [10]

"To write in any other manner," observed Don Quixote, "would be to write lies and not the truth. Those historians who make use of falsehoods ought to be burned like the makers of counterfeit money. I do not know what could have led the author to introduce stories and episodes that are foreign to the subject matter when he had so much to write about in describing my adventures. He must, undoubtedly, have been inspired by the old saying, 'With straw or with hay . . .' [11] For, in truth, all he had to do was to record my thoughts, my sighs, my tears, my lofty purposes, and my undertakings, and he would have had a volume bigger or at least as big as that which the works of El Tostado [12] would make. To sum the matter up, Señor Bachelor, it is my opinion that, in composing histories or books of any sort, a great deal of judgment and ripe understanding is called for. To say and write witty and amusing things is the mark of great genius. The cleverest character in a comedy is the clown, since he who would make himself out to be a simpleton cannot be one. History is a near-sacred thing, for it must be true, and where the truth is, there is God. And yet there are those who compose books and toss them out into the world as if they were no more than fritters."

"There is no book so bad," opined the bachelor, "that there is not some good in it." [13]

"Doubtless that is so," replied Don Quixote, "but it very often happens that those who have won in advance a great and well-deserved reputation for their writings, lose it in whole or in part when they give their works to the printer."

"The reason for it," said Sansón, "is that, printed works being read at leisure, their faults are the more readily apparent, and the greater the reputation of the author the more closely are they scrutinized. Men famous for their genius, great poets, illustrious historians, are almost always envied by those who take a special delight in criticizing the writings of others without having produced anything of their own."

"That is not to be wondered at," said Don Quixote, "for there are many theologians who are not good enough for the pulpit but who are very good indeed when it comes to detecting the faults or excesses of those who preach."

"All of this is very true, Señor Don Quixote," replied Carrasco, "but, all the same, I could wish that these self-appointed censors were a bit more forbearing and less hypercritical; I wish they would pay a little less attention to the spots on the bright sun of the work that occasions their fault-finding. For if *aliquando bonus dormitat Homerus*,[14] let them consider how much of his time he spent awake, shedding the light of his genius with a minimum of shade. It well may be that what to them seems a flaw is but one of those moles which sometimes add to the beauty of a face. In any event, I insist that he who has a book printed runs a very great risk, inasmuch as it is an utter impossibility to write it in such a manner that it will please all who read it."

"This book about me must have pleased very few," remarked Don Quixote.

"Quite the contrary," said Sansón, "for just as *stultorum infinitus est numerus*,[15] so the number of those who have enjoyed this history is likewise infinite. Some, to be sure, have complained of the author's forgetfulness, seeing that he neglected to make it plain who the thief was who stole Sancho's gray; [16] for it is not stated there, but merely implied, that the ass was stolen; and, a little further on, we find the knight mounted on the same beast, although it has not made its reappearance in the story. They also say that the author forgot to tell us what Sancho did with those hundred crowns that he found in the valise on the Sierra Morena, as nothing more is said of them and there are many who would like to know how he disposed of the money or how he spent it. This is one of the serious omissons to be found in the work."

To this Sancho replied, "I, Señor Sansón, do not feel like giving any account or accounting just now; for I feel a little weak in my stomach, and if I don't do something about it by taking a few swigs of the old stuff, I'll be sitting on St. Lucy's thorn.[17] I have some of it at home, and my old woman is waiting for me. After I've had my dinner, I'll come back and answer any questions your Grace or anybody else wants to ask me, whether it's about the loss of the ass or the spending of the hundred crowns."

And without waiting for a reply or saying another word, he went on home. Don Quixote urged the bachelor to stay and take potluck with him,[18] and Sansón accepted the invitation and remained. In addition to the knight's ordinary fare, they had a couple of pigeons, and at table their talk was of chivalry and feats of arms. Carrasco was careful to humor his host, and when the meal was over they took their siesta. Then Sancho returned and their previous conversation was resumed.

CHAPTER IV. *Wherein Sancho Panza answers the bachelor's questions and removes his doubts, together with other events that are worthy of being known and set down.*

RETURNING to Don Quixote's house, Sancho began where they had left off.

"Señor Sansón has said that he would like to know who it was that stole my ass and how and when it was done. In answer to that, I can tell him that it was the same night that we went up onto the Sierra Morena, to get away from the Holy Brotherhood. It was after the adventure of the galley slaves and that of the dead man that they were taking to Segovia. My master and I had gone into a thicket; and there, with him leaning on his lance and me seated on my gray and the both of us bruised and tired from the scuffles we had been through, we dozed off and slept as if we had had four feather beds beneath us. As for me, I was so dead to the world that whoever it was that came along was able to put four stakes under the four sides of my packsaddle and leave me sitting astraddle of it while he took my gray out from under me without my knowing anything about it."

"That," said Sansón, "is an easy thing to do and has been done before. It happened to Sacripante when, at the siege of Albraca, the famous thief known as Brunello, employing the same device, took the horse out from between the knight's legs."[1]

"Well," Sancho went on, "morning came, and when I went to stretch myself the stakes gave way and I took a mighty tumble. I looked around for the ass and could not see it, and then the tears came to my eyes and I set up such a howling that if the author of the book did not put it in, then he left out something very good. After I don't know how many days, going along with her Ladyship, the Princess Micomicona, I caught sight of Ginés de Pasamonte coming down the road dressed like a gypsy and mounted on my beast—he was that big rogue and trickster that my master and I freed from the galley slaves' chain."

"That is not where the error lies," replied Sansón, "but rather in the fact that before the ass turns up again the author has Sancho riding on it."

"I don't know what answer to give you," said Sancho, "except that the one who wrote the story must have made a mistake, or else it must be due to carelessness on the part of the printer."

"No doubt that is it," said Sansón, "but what became of the hundred crowns? Did they vanish into thin air?"

"I spent them on myself and on my wife and young ones, and that is why it is she puts up with my wanderings along the highways and by-ways in the service of my master Don Quixote; for if after all that time I had come home without my gray or a penny to my name, I would have had one devil of a welcome. If there is anything else you would like to know about me, here I am, ready to answer in person to the king himself, and it is nobody's business whether I took it or did not take it, whether I spent it or didn't spend it. If all the whacks they gave me on those journeys had to be paid for in money, even if they valued them only at four maravedis apiece, another hundred crowns would not be enough to pay for the half of them. Let every man look after himself and not be trying to make out that white is black and black is white; for each one is as God made him, and a good deal worse a lot of times."

"I shall make it a point," said Carrasco, "to remind the author that if he has another edition printed, he is by no means to forget what the good Sancho has told us, which I am sure will greatly improve the book." [2]

"Are there any other corrections to be made in this work?" Don Quixote inquired.

"There probably are," the bachelor replied, "but the ones we have mentioned are the most important."

"And does the author by any chance promise a second part?"

"Yes, he does," said Sansón, "but he states that he has not yet come upon it, nor does he know in whose possession it is, and accordingly there is a doubt as to whether it will appear or not. Indeed, there is some question as to whether a second part is desirable. There are those who say, 'Sequels are never good,' while others assert, 'Enough has been written already about Don Quixote.' But certain ones who are more jovially inclined and not of so morose a disposition will tell you, 'Let us have more of these Quixotic adventures; let Don Quixote lay on and Sancho talk, and, come what may, we shall be satisfied.' "

"And how does the author feel about it?"

"If he finds the history he is looking for so diligently," said Sansón, "he will send it to the printer at once, being more interested in the profit that may come to him from it than in any praise it may earn him."

Sancho now put in his word. "So, he is interested in money, is he? Then it will be a wonder if he doesn't botch the job, for it will be nothing but hurry, hurry, hurry, as at the tailor's on Easter Eve, and work done in haste is never done as it should be. Let that Moorish gentleman, or whoever he is, pay attention, and my master and I will supply him with enough stuff,[3] ready at hand, in the way of adventures and other happenings, to make not only one second part but a hundred of them. The good man thinks, no doubt, that we are asleep here in the straw, but let him hold up our hoofs to be shod and he will see which foot is the lame one. All I have to say is that if my master would take my advice, we would be in the field this minute, avenging outrages and righting wrongs as is the use and custom of good knights-errant."

No sooner had Sancho said this than they heard the whinnying of Rocinante, which Don Quixote took to be a very good omen; and he resolved then and there that they would sally forth again within the next three or four days. Announcing his intention to Carrasco, he asked the bachelor to advise him as to what direction he should take; whereupon Sansón replied that in his opinion the knight ought to head for the kingdom of Aragon and the city of Saragossa, as they were to have some ceremonious joustings there very shortly, in honor of the feast of St. George,[4] in which tournament Don Quixote might win a renown above that of all the knights of Aragon, who in turn would be sure to vanquish all others in the world. Sansón went on to praise his host's highly praiseworthy and valiant undertaking, but warned him to be a little more careful in confronting dangers, since his life was not his own but belonged to all those who had need of his succor and protection in the misfortunes that befell them.

"That is what I don't like about it, Señor Sansón," said Sancho. "My master will attack a hundred armed men just like a greedy boy falling on a half-dozen melons. Body of the world,[5] Señor Bachelor, but there is a time to attack and a time to retreat! Everything is not 'Santiago, and close in upon them, Spain!'[6] For I have heard it said—and I think my master himself was the one who said it—that true bravery lies somewhere in between being a coward and being foolhardy; and, for this reason, I would not have him run away when there is not good reason for it, nor have him attack when the odds are all against him. But, above everything else, I want to warn him that if he is going to take me with him, it will have to be on condition that he does all the fighting, it being understood that all I am to do is to look after his person and see to keeping him clean and comfortable. When it comes to that, I will be at his beck and call; but to look for me to lay hand to sword, even against the most rascally villains of hatchet and hood, is a waste of thinking.

"I do not expect, Señor Sansón," he continued, "to win fame as a fighting man, but only as the best and most loyal squire that ever served a knight-errant; and if my master Don Quixote, as a reward for my many faithful services, sees fit to give me some island of all those that his Grace says are to be had, I will accept it as a great favor; but if he does not give it to me, well, I was born like everyone else, and a man should depend on no one but God, and what is more, my bread will taste as good, and it may be even better, without a governorship than if I was a governor. How do I know that in connection with governments the devil has not prepared some trap for me where I may stumble and fall and knock my grinders out? Sancho was born and Sancho expects to die; but, for all of that, if without much risk or trouble on my part Heaven should provide me with an island, fair and square, I am not such a fool as to refuse it. For they also have a saying, 'When they offer you a heifer, come running with a halter,' and, 'When good luck comes along, open the door and let it in.' "[7]

"Spoken like a professor, brother Sancho," said Carrasco. "Put your trust in God and in Señor Don Quixote, and your master will see to it that you are provided with a kingdom and no mere island."

"More or less, it is all the same to me," replied Sancho. "I may tell you, Señor Carrasco, that my master would not be tossing that kingdom he is going to give me into a sack that was full of holes. I have taken my own pulse, and I find that I am man enough to rule over realms and govern islands, and I have already told him as much any number of times."

"But see here, Sancho," said the bachelor, "manners change when honors come,[8] and it may be that when you get to be governor you will not know the mother who bore you."

"That may be true of those that were born in the mallows,[9] but not of one like me with the fat of an old Christian four fingers deep on his soul. Do I look to you like the kind of man who would be ungrateful to anyone?"

"God's will be done," said Don Quixote. "We can tell better when the governorship comes, and it seems to me I can see it already."

Having said this, he turned to the bachelor and inquired if that gentleman was a poet. If so, would he do him the favor of composing some farewell verses for my lady Dulcinea del Toboso, each line to begin with a letter of her name, so that when the poem was complete those letters would spell out the name. Carrasco replied that, although he was not one of the famous poets of Spain—of whom, he said, there were but three and a half altogether [10]—he would not fail to do as Don Quixote had requested, although he found the task rather difficult, seeing that there were seventeen letters to be accounted for; if he made four stanzas of four lines each, there would be one letter left over, while if he employed one of those five-line stanzas known as *décimas* or *redondillas*, he would be three letters short.[11] Nevertheless, he would try, some way or other, to drop a letter in order that he might get the name Dulcinea del Toboso into a set of four-line stanzas.

"You must manage it somehow," said Don Quixote; "for if the name is not plainly to be made out, no woman would believe that the verses were written expressly for her."

This point having been settled, it was decided that the knight's departure should be one week from that day. The bachelor was charged to keep it secret, especially from the curate and Master Nicholas, and from the niece and housekeeper as well, in order that they might not prevent the carrying out of this commendable and valorous undertaking. Carrasco gave his promise and took his leave, and as he did so he urged Don Quixote to keep him informed, whenever the opportunity presented itself, of any good or ill fortune that might come to master and man. Thus they parted, and Sancho went away to make the necessary preparations for the expedition.

CHAPTER V. *Of the shrewd and droll remarks that passed between Sancho Panza and his wife, Teresa Panza, with other matters of a pleasant nature that deserve to be recorded.*

AS HE comes to set down this fifth chapter of our history, the translator desires to make it plain that he looks upon it as apocryphal, since in it Sancho Panza speaks in a manner that does not appear to go with his limited intelligence and indulges in such subtle observations that it is quite impossible to conceive of his saying the things attributed to him. However, the translator in question did not wish to leave his task unfinished; and the narrative is accordingly herewith resumed.

As Sancho approached his house, he was feeling so happy and so gay that his wife could tell it at the distance of a crossbow shot.

"What do you bring with you, friend Sancho," she asked, "that makes you so merry?"

"Wife," he replied, "if it was God's will, I'd be glad not to be as happy as I am."

"I don't understand you, husband," said she. "I don't know what you mean by wishing you were not as happy as you are. I may be a fool, but I fail to see how you can find pleasure in not having it."

"Look here, Teresa," said Sancho, "I am happy because I have made up my mind to go back to serving my master Don Quixote, who wants to go out a third time in search of adventures, and I mean to go with him. It is necessity that leads me to do this, and then, too, I like to think that I may be able to come upon another hundred crowns to take the place of those we've spent, although, naturally, it makes me sad to have to leave you and the young ones. If God would only let me eat my bread at home, dryshod, without dragging me through the byways and crossroads—and it would not cost Him anything, all He has to do is will it— it goes without saying that my happiness would be more solid and lasting than it is, whereas now it is mixed up with my sorrow at leaving you.

That is what I meant when I said that I'd be glad if, God willing, I was not so happy."

"Listen to me, Sancho," his wife replied. "Ever since you joined up with a knight-errant, you've been talking in such a roundabout way that there's no understanding you."

"It is enough, wife, if God understands me; for He understands every-thing, and that is good enough for me. And I want to warn you, sister, that you are to keep an eye on the gray these next few days so that he will be in condition to take up arms. Give him double rations, and look after the packsaddle and the other harness, for it's not to a wedding that we're bound; we're out to roam the world and play give and take with giants, dragons, and other monsters. We'll be hearing hissings and roar-ings and bellowings and howlings. But all that would be lavender if we didn't have to count upon meeting with Yanguesans and enchanted Moors."

"I know well, my husband," said Teresa, "that the squires of knights-errant have to earn the bread they eat, and so I will keep on praying to Our Lord to get you out of all this hard luck."

"I can tell you one thing, wife," said Sancho, "that if I did not expect to see myself the governor of an island before long, I would die right here and now."

"No, not that, my husband," Teresa protested. "Let the hen live even though she may have the pip,[1] and in the same way you should go on living and to the devil with all the governorships in the world. Without a governorship you came out of your mother's belly, without a governor-ship you've lived up to now, and without a governorship you will go, or they will carry you, to your grave when God so wills. There are plenty of folk in this world who manage to get along without being governors, yet they do not for that reason give up but are still numbered among the living. The best sauce in the world is hunger,[2] and since this is something they never lack, the poor always have an appetite. But look, Sancho, if by any chance you do fall in with a governorship, don't forget me and your children. Remember that little Sancho is already turned fifteen, and it is only right that he should go to school, if his uncle, the abbot, means to have him trained for the Church. Remember, too, that your daughter, Mari-Sancha, would not drop dead if we married her off; for I have my suspicions that she is as anxious for a husband as you are to be a governor, and, when all is said and done, a daughter badly married is better than one well kept outside of marriage."

"I promise you, wife," replied Sancho, "that if God only sees to it that I get hold of any kind of an island at all, I will get Mari-Sancha a husband so high up in the world that no one will be able to come near her without calling her 'my Ladyship.' "

"No, Sancho," said his wife. "Marry her to someone who is her equal; that's the best way. If you take her out of wooden shoes and put her into pattens, if you take her out of her gray flannel petticoat and put her into silken hoop skirts, if you stop saying 'thou' to her and change her from 'Marica' into 'Doña So-and-So' and 'my lady,' then the poor girl will not know where she is and every step she takes she will be making a thousand blunders and showing the thread of the coarse homespun stuff she's made of."

"Be quiet, foolish woman," said Sancho. "All she will need is two or three years to get used to it, and, after that, dignity and fine manners will fit her like a glove; and if not, what does it matter? Let her be 'your Ladyship' and come what may."

"Better keep to your own station, Sancho," Teresa admonished him, "and not be trying to lift yourself up to a higher one. Remember the old saying, 'Wipe the nose of your neighbor's son and take him into your house.' [3] It would be a fine thing, wouldn't it, to have our Maria married to some great count or high and mighty gentleman who every time he happened to feel like it would call her an upstart, a clodhopper's daughter, a country wench who ought to be at the spinning wheel. No, as I live, my husband, it was not for this that I brought up my daughter! You bring home the money, Sancho, and leave the marrying of her to me. There is Lope Tocho, Juan Tocho's boy. He's a strong, healthy lad and we know him well, and I can see he rather likes our lass. He's our kind, and she'll be making no mistake in marrying him. That way, we'll be able to keep an eye on her, and we'll all be together, parents and children, grandchildren, sons-in-law and daughters-in-law, and peace and God's blessing will be upon us. So don't go marrying her off in those courts and grand palaces where she will be a stranger to others and to herself."

"Why, you stupid creature!" exclaimed Sancho. "You wife of Barabbas! [4] What do you mean by trying to keep me from marrying my daughter to someone who will give me grandchildren that will be called 'your Lordship' and 'your Ladyship'? Look, Teresa, I have always heard the old folks say that the one that doesn't know how to make the most of luck when it comes his way has no business complaining if it passes him by. And now that luck is knocking at our door, we don't want to shut it out. Let us go with the favoring breeze that fills our sail." (It was this way of speaking, and what Sancho has to say a little further on, that led the translator of the history to remark that he looked upon this chapter as apocryphal.)

"Can't you see, you ninny," Sancho went on, "what a fine thing it will be for me to fall into some nice governorship or other that will help us get our feet out of the mud? Just let me find the husband I choose for Mari-Sancha, and you'll see how they'll be calling you 'Doña Teresa Panza,' and you will sit in church on a rug and cushions and fancy drapes in spite of the highborn ladies of the village. But no, you'd better stay the way you are, neither bigger nor smaller, like a figure on a tapestry, and we'll say no more about it. Little Sancha is going to be a countess, no matter what you think." [5]

"Husband," said Teresa, "are you sure you know what you are talking about? For I am very much afraid that if my daughter becomes a countess it will be her ruination. You can do what you like, you can make a duchess or a princess of her, but I want to tell you it will be without my will or consent. I always did believe in equality, brother, and I can't bear to see people put on airs without any reason for it. Teresa was the name they gave me when I was baptized, without any tags, or strings, or trimmings; there were no 'Dons' or 'Doñas' in my family. My father's name was Cascajo. As your wife, I am now called Teresa Panza, though by rights I should be known as Teresa Cascajo. But kings go where the laws would have them go,[6] and the name I have is good enough for me without their putting a 'Doña' on top of it and making it so heavy I can't carry it. I don't want to give people a chance to talk when they see me dressed like a countess or a governor's wife and have them saying, 'Just see the airs that hog-feeder [7] puts on, will you? Only yesterday she was spinning flax and went to mass with the tail of her petticoat over her head in place of a mantle, and today she goes in hoops, with her brooches and her nose in the air, as if we didn't know her!'

"If God lets me keep my six or seven senses, or whatever number it is that I have, I don't propose to give them a chance to see me in such a predicament. You, brother, go ahead and govern your island and strut all you like, but I tell you in the name of my sainted mother that neither my daughter nor I is going to stir one step from our village. The respectable woman has a broken leg and stays at home, and to be busy at something is a feast day for the maid that is virtuous.[8] Go, then, to look for adventures with that Don Quixote of yours, and leave us to our misadventures; for God will make things better for us if we deserve it. I'm sure I don't know," she added, "who made him a 'Don,' for neither his father nor his grandfather was one before him."

"I do declare," said Sancho, "you must have a devil in you. God help you, wife, but what a lot of things you have strung together so that there's no making head nor tail of any of them! What do the name Cascajo and brooches and proverbs and haughty airs have to do with what I'm saying? Look here, you foolish, ignorant woman—for I have a right to call you that, seeing you won't listen to reason but run away from good fortune. If I had said that my daughter was to throw herself from a tower or go wandering about the world as the Infanta Doña Uracca threatened to do,[9] you would be right in not agreeing with me; but when I want to put a 'Doña' or a 'ladyship' on her back and in the blink of an eye take her out of the stubble and seat her on a dais under a canopy or on a divan with more velvet cushions [10] than the Almohades of Morocco had Moors in their family tree, why won't you give your consent and let me have it my way?"

"Do you want to know why, husband?" Teresa asked him. "It's on account of the proverb that says, 'He who covers you discovers you.' To the poor, people give only a passing glance, but the rich man holds their gaze; and if he was poor once upon a time, then it is that the whispering and the evil gossip and the spitework begin, for the slanderers in these streets are as thick as a swarm of bees."

"Pay attention, Teresa," said Sancho, "and listen to what I am about to tell you. It may be that you have never heard it in all the days of your life. I am not speaking for myself but am giving you the opinions of the reverend father who preached in this village during Lent, the last time. If I remember rightly, he said that all present things which our eyes behold make much more of an impression on us and remain better fixed in our memories than things that are past." (These remarks of Sancho's are another reason for the translator's saying what he did about the apocryphal character of this chapter, since they are beyond the mental capacity of the squire.) "Hence it is that when we see some person richly dressed and making a fine appearance, accompanied by a retinue of servants, we feel compelled to respect him, even though our memory at the moment may remind us of some lowly condition in which we had previously seen him. That condition, whether due to poverty or humble birth, being a thing of the past, does not exist, since the only thing that is real to us is what we have before our eyes. And—these were the padre's very words—if the one that fortune has thus raised up out of the depths to the height of prosperity is well bred, generous, and courteous toward all and does not seek to vie with those that come of an old and noble line, then you may depend upon it, Teresa, there will be no one to remember what he was, but instead they will respect him for what he is, unless it be the envious, for no good fortune is safe against them."

"I do not understand you, husband," replied Teresa. "Do as you like and don't be addling my brains with your flowery speeches. If you have revolved to do what you say—"

"You mean *resolved*, wife, not *revolved*."

"Don't dispute my word," said Teresa. "I talk the way God would have me talk without beating around the bush. What I say is, if you are determined to be a governor, take your son Sancho with you so that you can teach him how to govern also; for it is a good thing for sons to learn and follow their father's trade."

"As soon as I have a government," said Sancho, "I will send for him posthaste. I will send you some money too; for there are always plenty of people to lend it to governors that do not have it. And I want you to dress him up in such a way as to hide what he is and make him look like what he is not."

"You send the money," Teresa replied, "and I'll see to that." [11]

"So, then, it's understood, is it, that our daughter is to be a countess?"

"The day that I see her a countess," was Teresa's answer, "I'll feel that I am laying her in her grave. But I tell you again: do as you like; for we women are born with the obligation of obeying our husbands, however stupid they may be."

Saying this, she began weeping in earnest, as though she already saw her Sanchica dead and buried. Sancho consoled her by assuring her that, while he might have to make his daughter a countess, he would put off doing so as long as he could. Thus ended the conversation, and Sancho went back to see Don Quixote to make arrangements for their departure.

CHAPTER VI. *Of what took place between Don Quixote and his niece and housekeeper, which is one of the most important chapters in the entire history.*

WHILE Sancho Panza and his wife, Teresa Cascajo, were engaged in the irrelevant conversation that has just been reported, Don Quixote's niece and housekeeper were by no means idle, for they could tell by any number of signs that their uncle and master was about to slip away a third time and return to what they looked upon as being his ill-errant conception of knighthood. They accordingly strove in every way possible to get so evil a thought out of his mind, but all this was like preaching in the desert or hammering cold iron.

"In truth, my master," the housekeeper said to him in the course of their many talks on the subject, "if you do not make up your mind to stay quietly at home and stop wandering over mountains and valleys like a lost soul, seeking what I am told are called adventures but which I call misfortunes, there will be nothing for me to do but raise my voice to God and the king, as loud as I can, so that they may do something about it."

"My good woman," replied Don Quixote, "what answer God will make to your complaints, or his Majesty either, for that matter, I am sure I do not know. But I do know that if I were king, I would not trouble to reply to all the innumerable and foolish petitions presented to me every day. One of the greatest of the many trials kings have to endure is that of being obliged to listen to everybody and give everyone some kind of answer, and I do not care to add my troubles to the burden that his Majesty has to bear."

"Tell us one thing," said the housekeeper, "are there no knights at his Majesty's court?"

"There are, and many of them; and it is right and proper that there should be, to set off the greatness of princes and show forth the majesty of royal power."

"Well, then," persisted the housekeeper, "could not your Grace be one of those who, without stirring a foot, serve their lord and king at court?"

"Look, my friend," said Don Quixote, "not all knights can be courtiers, nor can all courtiers be, nor should they be, knights-errant. There have to be all kinds in this world, and even though we may all be knights, there is a great deal of difference between us. For the courtiers, without leaving their rooms or the threshold of the court, may travel all over the earth merely by looking at a map; it does not cost them anything and they do not suffer heat or cold, hunger or thirst. But those of us who are real knights-errant, we take the measure of the entire globe with our feet, beneath the sun of day and in the cold of night, out in the open and exposed to all the inclemencies of the weather. We know our enemies not from pictures but as they really are, and we attack them on every occasion and under no matter what conditions of combat. We pay no attention to the childish rules that are supposed to govern knightly duels; we are not concerned as to whether one has a longer lance or sword than the other or may carry upon him holy relics or some secret contrivance; we do not worry about the proper placing of the combatants with regard to the sun [1] nor any of the other ceremonious usages of this sort that commonly prevail in man-to-man encounters, with which you are unfamiliar but which I know well.

"And let me tell you something else. The good knight-errant, even though he may behold ten giants with heads that not merely touch but rise above the clouds; and even though each of these giants may have two tallest towers for legs while his arms resemble the masts of huge and powerful ships; even though each may have eyes that are like great mill wheels and that glow more brightly than any glass furnace—in spite of all this, he is not to be in the least frightened but with highborn mien and intrepid heart is to give them battle and if possible vanquish and destroy them in a moment's time. And this, though they bear armor made of the shells of a certain fish that are said to be harder than diamonds, and in place of swords carry keen-edged blades of Damascus steel or clubs studded with spikes of the same material such as I have more than once seen. I tell you all this, my good woman, in order that you may perceive what a difference there is between knights; and it would be well if there were no prince who did not more esteem this second, or, rather, first, variety of knight-errant. For the history books tell us that some of the latter have been the salvation not of one kingdom alone but of many."

"Ah, sir!" cried the niece at this point, "your Grace must remember that all this you are saying about knights-errant is a fable and a lie. And as for those history books, if they are not to be burned, they ought all to wear the *sambenito* [2] or some other sign to show how infamous they are and how they corrupt good manners."

"By the God who sustains me!" exclaimed Don Quixote, "if you were not my flesh-and-blood niece, being the daughter of my own sister, I would so punish you for the blasphemy you have uttered that all the world would hear about it. How comes it that a lass who barely knows how to handle a dozen lace bobbins should set her tongue to wagging and presume to criticize these knightly histories? What would my lord Amadis say if he could hear such a thing? To be sure, he would pardon you, since he was the most humble and courteous knight of his age, and was, moreover, a great protector of damsels. But there are others who might have heard you, and in that case it would not have gone so well with you. For they were not all courteous and circumspect; some of them were the most unmannerly of rascals.

"By no means all of those that call themselves knights, or gentlemen, [3] are what they pretend to be. Some are of pure gold, others are a base alloy. They all look the part, but not all can stand the touchstone of truth. Some there are of low degree who split themselves trying to appear gentlemanly. On the other hand, there are those of high station who, one would wager, were dying to be mistaken for their inferiors. The former pull themselves up through ambition or by reason of their merits, while the latter debase themselves by slothfulness or vice. And a good deal of wisdom is required to distinguish between these two kinds of gentlemen who are alike in name but whose conduct is so different."

"So help me God, uncle," said the niece, "your Grace knows so much that in a pinch you could get right up in the pulpit or go out and start preaching in the streets. And yet, to think that you could be so blind and foolish as to try to make out that you are a hero when you are really an old man, that you are strong when you are sick, that you are able to straighten out the wrongs of the world when you yourself are bent with age, and, above all, that you are a knight; for, while the real gentry [4] may become knights, the poor never can."

"There is much in what you say, my niece," replied Don Quixote. "I could tell you things having to do with family trees that would astonish you; but since I do not wish to mix the human with the divine, I shall not mention them. You see, my friends—and pay attention to what I say—so far as family is concerned, all the people in this world may be divided into four classes: those who from humble beginnings have grown and expanded until they have attained a pinnacle of greatness; those who were great to begin with and who have since consistently maintained their original state; those who have arrived at a pyramidal point, having progressively diminished and consumed the greatness that was theirs at the start until, like the point of the pyramid with respect to its base or foundation, they have come to be nothing at all; and, finally, there is the vast majority who had neither a good start nor a subsequent history that was in any way out of the ordinary and who accordingly will have a nameless end, like the ordinary plebeian stock.

"Of the first group, who rose from humble origins to a greatness which they continue to maintain, the House of Ottoman may serve as an example; for it was founded by a lowly shepherd and later attained the heights which we now see it occupying. Of the second class, those who have maintained their original greatness without adding to or detracting from it, I may cite the case of many princes who have been content to remain peacefully within the confines of their kingdoms. As for those that began great only to taper away in a point, there are thousands of examples. For all the Pharaohs and Ptolemies of Egypt, the Caesars of Rome, and the countless drove (if I may employ that word) of princes, monarchs, and lords, of Medes, Persians, Greeks, and barbarians—all these royal and noble lines have ended in the point of nothingness, both they and their founders, and today it would be impossible to find a single one of their descendants, or if one did come upon any of them, they would be in some low and humble station. Of the plebeians I have nothing to say, except that they serve to increase the number of the living without any other claim to fame, since they have achieved no form of greatness that entitles them to praise.

"My reason for telling you all this, my innocent ones, is that you may see how much confusion exists with regard to the subject of family descent. They alone impress us as being great and illustrious that show themselves to be virtuous, rich, and generous. I say this for the reason that the great man who was also vicious would be no more than an outstanding example of vice, and the rich man who was not generous would be but a miserly beggar. What brings happiness to the possessor of wealth is not the having but the spending of it, and by that I mean, spending it well and not simply to gratify his own whims. The gentleman who is poor, however, has no other means of proving that he is a gentleman than by following the path of virtue, by being affable, well bred, courteous and polite, and prompt to do favors for others; he will not be proud and haughty or a backbiter, and, above all, he will be charitable. With the two maravedis that he gives with a cheerful heart to the poor he will show himself to be as generous as the one who distributes alms to the ringing of a bell, and no one who sees him adorned with the virtues that I have mentioned, even though he may not know him, will fail to regard him as coming of good stock. It would be a wonder if it were not so, for praise has ever been the reward of virtue, and those who are virtuous are bound to be commended.

"There are two paths, my daughters, by which men may succeed in becoming rich and honored. One is that of letters, the other that of arms. For my part, I am more inclined to the latter than to the former. Indeed, so strong is my inclination that it would seem that I must have been born under the influence of the planet Mars. And so I am practically compelled to follow that path, and I shall keep to it in spite of all the world. It is useless for you to wear yourselves out trying to persuade me not to do what Heaven wills, fate ordains, reason asks, and, above all, my own will desires. Knowing as I do all the innumerable hardships that go with knight-errantry, I also know the infinite number of good things that are to be attained by it. I am aware that the path of virtue is a straight and narrow one, while that of vice is a broad and spacious highway. I realize that the ends and goals are different in the two cases, the highroad of vice leading to death, while virtue's narrow, thorny trail conducts us to life, and not a life that has a mortal close, but life everlasting. As our great Castilian poet has put it:

> *This is the rugged path, the toilsome way*
> *That leads to immortality's fair heights,*
> *Which none e'er reach who from that path do stray."* [5]

"Oh, dear me!" said the niece, "my master is a poet, too. He knows everything and can do everything. I'll bet that if he chose to turn mason he could build a house as easily as he could a birdcage."

"I can tell you one thing, niece," replied Don Quixote, "that if my mind were not so wholly occupied with thoughts of chivalry, there is nothing that I could not do, no trinket that I could not turn out with my own hands, especially birdcages and toothpicks."

At that moment there was a knock at the door, and when they asked who was there, Sancho replied that it was he. No sooner did the housekeeper hear this than she ran and hid herself, so great was her abhorrence of the squire. The niece opened the door and Don Quixote came forward to meet the visitor with open arms, after which the two of them shut themselves up in the knight's room where they had another conversation that was in no way surpassed by their previous one.

CHAPTER VII. *Of what passed between Don Quixote and his squire, with other very famous incidents.*

SEEING her master and Sancho Panza closeted together, the housekeeper at once suspected what they were up to. Feeling certain that as a result of their consultation they would resolve to sally forth a third time, she snatched up her mantle and, full of anxiety and deeply distressed, went out to look for the bachelor Sansón Carrasco; for it seemed to her that, being a well-spoken young man and a new acquaintance of Don Quixote's, he might be able to persuade the knight to give up so insane an undertaking. She found the bachelor walking up and down the patio of his house, and the moment she caught sight of him she ran up to him and fell on her knees in front of him, sweating all over and giving every evidence of affliction. Carrasco was surprised to see her so upset and grief-stricken.

"What is the meaning of this, Mistress Housekeeper?" he asked. "What has happened to cause you to appear so heartbroken?"

"It is nothing, Señor Sansón," she replied, "except that my master is breaking out again, there's no doubt of that."

"Breaking out where, Señora? Has he burst any part of his body?"

"No," said she, "it's through the door of his madness that he's bursting. I mean to say, my dear Señor Bachelor, that he wants to leave home again, which will be the third time, to go roaming the world and looking for what he calls ventures, though for the life of me I can't see why he gives them that name.[1] The first time he came home to us slung over the back of an ass and nearly clubbed to death. The second time it was in an oxcart, locked in a cage, where he said he had been put through some magic spell or other, and such a sorry-looking sight he was that the mother who bore him would not have recognized him. He was lean and yellow and his eyes were deep-sunken in his head, and in order to bring him around again to something of his old self I had to use more than six hundred eggs, as God knows, and all the world and my hens as well, for they wouldn't let me lie."

"I can well believe," the bachelor assured her, "that those hens of yours are so good, so fat, and so well brought up that they would not say one thing in place of another even if they burst. In short, Mistress Housekeeper, nothing has happened except what you fear that Señor Don Quixote may do?"

"Nothing else," she said.

"Well, then," he told her, "don't worry, but go on home and prepare me a warm breakfast, and on the way you might repeat St. Apollonia's prayer, if you happen to know it. I will be with you shortly, and you shall see miracles."

"Ah, poor me!" said the housekeeper, "so it's St. Apollonia's prayer that I should be saying, is it? That would be all right if my master had the toothache,[2] but his trouble is not in his teeth but in his brains."

"I know what I am talking about, Mistress Housekeeper; so run along and do not dispute my word, for, as you know, I am a bachelor of Salamanca and that means the best there is."[3]

With this, the housekeeper returned home and Carrasco went to hunt up the curate and make certain arrangements with him which will be duly narrated when the time comes.

When they were shut up together, Don Quixote and Sancho had a conversation which the historian has very minutely and truthfully reported.

"Sir," began Sancho, "I have reduced my wife to let me go with your Grace wherever you choose to take me."

"*Induced*, you mean to say, Sancho, not *reduced*."

"Once or twice before, if I remember rightly," said Sancho, "I have begged your Grace not to correct my words so long as you understand what I mean by them. When you don't understand, all you have to do is to say, 'Sancho, I don't know what the devil you mean'; and then, if I don't make myself plain, you can go ahead and correct me all you want to. You know how focile I am."

"I fail to understand you right now, Sancho," said Don Quixote, "for I'm sure I don't know what you mean when you say, 'I am so *focile*.'"

"So *focile*," replied Sancho, "means, 'I am so much that way.'"

"I understand you less than ever," said his master.

"Well, if you can't make it out," answered the squire, "I don't know what to say to you. That's the best I can do, so help me God."

"Ah! I get it. What you mean to say is that you are so *docile*, easygoing, and tractable that you will accept whatever I say to you and follow my teachings."

"I will bet you," said Sancho, "that you understood what I meant all the time and just wanted to mix me up so that you could hear me make a lot more blunders."

"You may be right," replied Don Quixote, "but tell me, exactly what was it that Teresa said?"

"She said that I should get everything down in black and white with your Grace, to let papers talk and beards be still,[4] since he who binds does not wrangle,[5] and one 'take' is worth a couple of 'I'll give you's.'[6] And I can tell you that a woman's advice is of little worth and he who won't take it is a fool."[7]

"And so say I," observed Don Quixote. "Go on, friend Sancho, you are in rare form today."[8]

"The fact of the matter is, as your Grace well knows," continued Sancho, "we are all of us subject to death, we are here today and gone tomorrow, and the lamb goes as soon as the sheep,[9] and no one can promise himself more hours of life in this world than God may see fit to give him, for death is deaf, and when it comes to knock at the door of our life it is always in a hurry, and neither prayers nor force nor scepters nor miters can hold it back, all of which is a matter of common talk and knowledge and we hear it from the pulpit right along."

"That is all very true," said Don Quixote, "but I can't see what you are getting at."

"What I am getting at," replied Sancho, "is that your Grace ought to give me a fixed wage to be paid to me every month during the time that I am in your service, out of your estate. I don't like to depend on favors that come late or never and may not be what you expect—God help me where those that I am expecting are concerned. The short of it is, I'd like to know what I am earning, however much or little it may be; for a hen will set on one egg, and many littles make a much, and so long as something's gained nothing's lost.[10] If it should turn out to be true—which I neither believe nor expect—that your Grace is going to give me that island you promised me, I am not so ungrateful nor would I go so far as to say that you shouldn't take what the income from the island amounts to out of my wages on a *pro cata* basis."

"Friend Sancho," remarked Don Quixote, "a cat may sometimes be as good as a rat."

"I get you," was Sancho's answer. "I'll bet you that what I should have said was *pro rata* and not *pro cata*, but it makes no difference, since your Grace understood me anyway."

"I understand you so well," said Don Quixote, "that I can read you like a book. I know what the bull's-eye is you're shooting at with all those proverbs of yours. Look, Sancho, I should be glad to give you a fixed wage if I could find in the histories of knights-errant any instance that would afford me the slightest hint as to what their squires used to receive by the month or by the year. I have read all or most of those histories, and I cannot recall any knight who paid his squire such a wage. Rather, they all served for the favors that came to them; and when they least expected it, if things had gone well with their masters, they would find themselves rewarded with an island or something else that amounted to the same thing, or at the least they would have a title and a seigniory.

"If for the sake of these hopes and inducements, Sancho," the knight went on, "you choose to return to my service, well and good; but you are wasting your time if you think that I am going to violate and unhinge the ancient customs of chivalry. And so, my good Sancho, go back home and tell your Teresa how I feel about it, and if she and you are willing to depend upon my favors, *bene quidem,* and if not, we will be as good friends as we were before; for if there is no lack of food in the pigeon house, it will not lack pigeons.[11] And remember, my son, a good hope is better than a bad holding,[12] and a good complaint better than bad pay.[13] If I speak in this manner, Sancho, it is to show you that I, too, can scatter proverbs like showers. In conclusion, I would say to you that if you do not choose to come with me on these terms and take the same chance that I do, may God keep you and make you a saint, for I shall not fail to find other squires who will be more obedient, more diligent, and not so stupid or so talkative as you."

When Sancho saw how firmly resolved his master was on this point, the heavens darkened over for him and the wings of his heart drooped; for he had felt certain that Don Quixote would not go without him for anything in the world. He was very much astonished and was still lost in thought when Sansón Carrasco, accompanied by the housekeeper and the niece,[14] entered the room; for the womenfolk wished to hear the arguments which the bachelor would employ in persuading their master not to go back to seeking adventures. Sansón, that famous wag, now came forward and embraced Don Quixote as he had done on the previous occasion, and, raising his voice, he addressed him as follows:

"O flower of knight-errantry, O shining light of the profession of arms, O honor and mirror of the Spanish nation! May it please Almighty God in His infinite power that the person or persons who would prevent or impede your third sally never find their way out of the labyrinth of their schemings nor ever succeed in accomplishing what they most desire."

Turning then to the housekeeper, he went on, "Mistress Housekeeper, you may just as well leave off saying St. Apollonia's prayer; for I now realize that it has been definitely determined by the spheres that Don Quixote shall carry out his new and lofty undertakings, and I should be laying a great burden upon my conscience if I did not urge and entreat this knight to keep his good right arm and valiant spirit curbed and confined no longer, since by his tarrying here he is cheating the wronged of their rights, orphans of his protection, damsels of the honor he might save for them, widows of the favors he might bestow upon them, and wives of the support with which he might provide them, along with other things of the sort that have to do with, appertain to, and are the proper appurtenances of, the order of knight-errantry. Come, then, my dear Señor Don Quixote, so handsome and so brave, let it be today rather than tomorrow that your Grace and Highness takes the road, and if anything be lacking for the carrying out of your plan, here am I to supply the need. My person and my fortune are at your disposal, and, if needs be, I will even serve your Magnificence as squire. Indeed, I should count myself most fortunate in being allowed to do so."

At this point Don Quixote spoke up. "Did not I tell you, Sancho," he said, "that I would have no trouble in finding squires? Look who is now offering to serve me. None other than the distinguished bachelor, Sansón Carrasco, the darling and perpetual delight of the Salamancan schools. He is sound in body, agile-limbed, and discreet, and can stand heat as well as cold, hunger as well as thirst. In brief, he has all the qualifications that are required of a squire to a knight-errant. But Heaven forbid that, to gratify my own inclinations, I should shatter this pillar of letters and vase of learning and cut down this towering palm of the fine and liberal arts. Let this new Samson remain in his own country, bringing honor to it and at the same time to the gray hairs of his aged parents. As for me, I shall make out with any squire that comes along, seeing that Sancho does not deign to come with me."

"I do deign to come," Sancho protested. He was deeply moved and his eyes were filled with tears. "It shall not be said of me, my master," he went on, "that 'once the bread is eaten, the company breaks up.'[15] I do not come of ungrateful stock; for all the world, and especially my village, knows who the Panzas were, and I am descended from them. What's more, I know from the many kind things you have done and the kind words you have spoken how much your Grace desires to show me favor. If I seem to have haggled a bit over my wages, that was to please my wife. When she undertakes to get you to do something, there's no mallet that drives in the hoops of a cask the way she drives you until you've done it. But, after all, a man has to be a man and a woman a woman; and, seeing that I'm a man wherever I am, which there's no denying, I mean to be one in my own house as well, whatever anybody says. So, then, there is nothing more to be done except for your Grace to draw up your will, with a codicil that can't be provoked, and we will set out at once. That way, Señor Sansón will not have to suffer any more, for he says his conscience is nagging at him to persuade your Grace to sally out into the world a third time. And I offer to serve your Grace faithfully and loyally, as well and better than all the squires that have served knights-errant in times past or present."

The bachelor was amazed at Sancho Panza's way of talking; for, although he had read the First Part of the history, he never would have believed that the squire was as droll as he was depicted there. But as he now heard him speaking of a will and codicil that could not be *provoked* (in place of *revoked*), he was convinced of the truth of it all and came to the conclusion that this was one of the greatest simpletons of the age. Never before in the world, he told himself, had the like been seen of such a pair of madmen as this master and his servant.

In the end, Don Quixote and Sancho embraced and were friends once more; and with the advice and approval of the great Carrasco, who for the present was their oracle, they set the date for their departure at three days from then, which would give them time enough to make the necessary preparations and look for a closed helmet, as Don Quixote insisted that he must by all means have one to take with him. Sansón offered to see to this, saying a friend of his had such a piece and would not refuse it to him, although, to be sure, it was not bright and clean as polished steel ought to be but was covered with rust and mildew.

The curses which the two women, the housekeeper and the niece, heaped upon the bachelor's head were innumerable. They tore their hair, clawed their faces, and, like the hired mourners of old, set up such a wailing over their master's departure that one would have thought it was his death they were lamenting. In thus persuading the knight to sally forth again, Sansón had a plan in mind which the history relates further on. All that he did was on the advice of the curate and the barber, with whom he had previously discussed the matter.

The short of it is, in the course of those three days Don Quixote and Sancho provided themselves with what they thought was necessary, and, the squire having pacified his wife and the knight having calmed his niece and housekeeper, the two of them set out at nightfall for El Toboso, without being seen by anyone except the bachelor, who expressed a desire to accompany them for a distance of half a league from the village. Don Quixote was mounted upon his good Rocinante and Sancho upon his ancient gray, his saddlebags stuffed with certain victuals and his pocket with money which his master had given him for whatever might come up. Sansón gave the knight a farewell embrace, urging him to send back word of the good or ill fortune that the pair met with, in order that he, Carrasco, as the laws of friendship demanded, might rejoice over the former or grieve over the latter. Don Quixote promised that he would do so, and the bachelor thereupon returned to the village while the other two took the highway for the great city of El Toboso.

CHAPTER VIII. *Wherein is related what happened to Don Quixote as he went to see his lady, Dulcinea del Toboso.*

"BLESSED be the mighty Allah!" exclaims Hamete Benengeli at the beginning of this eighth chapter; and he repeats it three times: "Blessed be Allah!" He goes on to tell us that the reason for the benediction is his thankfulness at seeing Don Quixote and Sancho together once more, and he wishes the readers of this pleasant chronicle to feel that the exploits and the drolleries of the knight and his squire really start at this point. Let them forget, he says, the chivalrous deeds which the Ingenious Gentleman has performed in the past and fix their eyes, rather, on those that are to come and that have their beginning here and now on the El Toboso highway just as the others began on the plains of Montiel. It surely is not much to ask in return for all he promises, and so he continues as follows:

No sooner had Sansón left Don Quixote and Sancho alone than Rocinante began neighing and the gray started sighing, which both knight and squire took to be a very good sign and most fortunate omen, even though, if the truth must be told, the sighings and brayings of the ass exceeded the whinnyings of the hack, which led Sancho to infer that his own good fortune was destined to surpass and overtop that of his master, in making which assumption it may be that he was relying upon some system of judicial astrology with which he chanced to be familiar, though the history is silent on this point. All that is known is that, when he stumbled or fell, he was heard to say that he wished he had not come out of the house, since nothing was to be had from it but a torn shoe or a set of broken ribs, and in this, fool that he was, he was not far wrong.

"Friend Sancho," remarked Don Quixote, "night is descending upon us and it is becoming so dark that we shall not be able to reach El Toboso while it is yet daylight; but I am determined to go there before embarking upon another adventure, for there it is that I shall receive the blessing and kind consent of my peerless Dulcinea, with whose favor I feel assured of bringing to a happy conclusion every dangerous undertaking, since nothing in this life inspires more valor in knights-errant than the knowledge that they are favored by their ladies."

"I can believe that," replied Sancho, "but if I am not mistaken, your Grace may have a hard time seeing or talking to her, at least in any place where she could give you her blessing, unless she was to toss it over the wall of the stable yard where I saw her the last time, when I took her the letter with the news about the mad and foolish things your Grace was doing in the heart of the Sierra Morena."

"And did you fancy that was a stable-yard wall," said Don Quixote, "where or at which you beheld that grace and beauty that never can be praised enough? It must have been in the gallery, corridor, or portico, or whatever you call it, of some rich and royal palace."

"That may all be true," said Sancho, "but it looked like a wall to me, if my memory serves me right."

"Nevertheless, Sancho, we are going there," Don Quixote insisted; "for so long as I see her, it is all the same to me whether it be over a wall, at a window, or through the chinks in a door or the railing of a garden. Let but one ray of the sun of her beauty fall upon these eyes and it shall illuminate my understanding and fortify my heart to such a degree that I shall be matchless and without an equal in wisdom and in valor."

"To tell you the truth," said Sancho, "when I saw the lady Dulcinea del Toboso's sun, it was not bright enough to shed rays of any kind. This must have been due to the fact that, as I told you, she was winnowing wheat at the time, and this raised a lot of dust which came before her face like a cloud and darkened it."

"What!" cried Don Quixote, "do you still persist, Sancho, in saying, thinking, and believing that my lady Dulcinea was winnowing wheat, when you know that this is a task and occupation that is at variance with everything that persons of high distinction do and are supposed to do, seeing that they are constituted and reserved for other employments and avocations such as make manifest their rank at the distance of a bow-shot? I can see, O Sancho, that you have forgotten those verses of our poet in which he describes for us the labors performed, up there in their crystal dwellings, by the four nymphs that rose from their beloved Tagus and set themselves down in a verdant meadow to embroider those rich tapestries, of which the bard tells us, that were all worked and woven of gold and silk and pearls.[1]

"My lady, when you saw her, must have been busied at a similar task. The only thing is that some evil enchanter must be envious of me, since all things that give me pleasure he at once changes into shapes that are not their own. This leads me to fear that the history of my exploits, which they tell me has been printed, may be the work of some magician who is my enemy, in which case he would have set down one thing in place of another and, mingling a thousand lies with a little truth, would doubt-less have amused himself by relating many things that have nothing to do with the true sequence of events. O envy, thou root of endless evils, thou cankerworm of the virtues! All the other vices, Sancho, have in them some element of pleasure, but envy brings with it only vexation, bitterness, and rage."

"That is what I say too," replied Sancho, "and I think that in this legend or history of our deeds which the bachelor Carrasco says he has seen, my honor must have been knocked around and dragged up and down in the mud;[2] they must have swept the streets with it. And yet, I give you my word as an honest man, I have never spoken ill of any en-chanter, nor do I have so many worldly goods that anybody would envy me. It is true, I am somewhat sly, and I have certain marks of the rogue, but it is all covered over with the great cloak of my simplicity, which is always natural and never artificial; and if I had no other virtue than that of believing, as I always have believed, firmly and truly in God and in all that the holy Roman Catholic Church holds and believes, as well as that of being, as I am, a mortal enemy of the Jews, the historians ought to have mercy on me and treat me well in their writings. But let them say what they will, naked was I born and naked I find myself, and so I neither lose nor gain; and although I see myself being put into a book and going through the world from hand to hand, I still don't care a fig; let them say anything about me that they like."

"That reminds me, Sancho," said Don Quixote, "of what happened to a famous poet of these days who, having composed a malicious satire against all the court ladies,[3] failed to mention in it a particular lady as to whose standing there was some question. When she saw that she was not on the list with the others, she complained to the poet, demanding to know what he had seen in her that had caused him to leave her out. She further insisted that he add a sequel to his satire and put her in it, or, otherwise, let him beware of the consequences. The poet did so, making her out to be the kind of woman of whom duennas do not speak, and she was satisfied with the fame he bestowed upon her even though it was infamy. Then there is the story they tell of the shepherd who set fire and burned down the famous temple of Diana, accounted one of the seven wonders of the world, simply in order that his name might be remembered for centuries to come. And although it was commanded that no one should mention his name either by word of mouth or in writing, so that his ambition might not be fulfilled, it is nevertheless known that he was called Erostratus.

"Much the same thing happened in the case of the great emperor, Charles V, and a certain gentleman in Rome. The emperor was desirous of seeing the famous temple of the Rotunda, which in antiquity was known as the temple of all the gods [4] and today is more appropriately named All Saints'. Of all the pagan edifices in Rome, this is the one that comes nearest to being preserved in its entirety, and it constitutes a fitting tribute to the grandeur and magnificence of those who built it. It is constructed in the shape of a half-orange and is very large and well lighted, the only illumination being afforded by a window, or, better, a rounded skylight at the top, and it was from this point of vantage that the emperor surveyed the building. At his side was a Roman gentleman who explained to him all the beauties and fine points of the huge and intricate structure with its memorable architecture.

"As they made their way down from the skylight, the gentleman turned to the emperor and said, 'A thousand times, your Sacred Majesty, I had a desire to throw my arms about your Majesty and cast myself down from that dome in order that my fame might be eternal in this world.'

" 'I thank you,' the emperor replied, 'for not having yielded to so wicked an impulse. From now on, I shall see to it that you have no further opportunity to put your loyalty to the test. I accordingly command you not to speak to me or enter my presence again.' And with these words he made him a handsome gift.

"What I mean to say, Sancho, is that the desire of achieving fame is a powerful incentive. What do you think it was that threw Horatius down from the bridge, clad in full armor, into the depths of the Tiber? What was it burned Mutius's arm and hand? What was it that impelled Curtius to hurl himself into the deep and flaming abyss that yawned in the middle of the city of Rome? What was it led Julius Caesar to cross the Rubicon in spite of all the auguries which had warned against it? To come down to more modern times, what was it, in the New World, that scuttled and beached the ships and cut off those valiant Spaniards led by the most courtier-like Cortés?[5] All these and other great deeds of various sorts are, were, and shall continue to be a manifestation of the mortal desire for fame as a reward for notable achievements that confer upon man a portion of immortality. We Christians, Catholics, and knights-errant, on the other hand, are more concerned with the glory that, in ages to come, shall be eternal in the ethereal and celestial regions than we are with the vanity of that fame that is to be won in this present and finite time; for however long such fame may endure, it needs must finally end with the world itself, the close of which has been foreordained.

"And so, Sancho, our deeds should not exceed those limits set by the Christian religion which we profess. In confronting giants, it is the sin of pride that we slay, even as we combat envy with generosity and goodness of heart; anger, with equanimity and a calm bearing; gluttony and an overfondness for sleep, by eating little when we do eat and by keeping long vigils; lust and lewdness, with the loyalty that we show to those whom we have made the mistresses of our affections; and sloth, by going everywhere in the world in search of opportunities that may and do make of us famous knights as well as better Christians.[6] You behold here, Sancho, the means by which one may attain the highest praise that the right sort of fame brings with it."

"I have understood very well," Sancho told him, "all that your Grace has said up to now; but still there is one doubtful point I happened to think of that I wish your Grace would dissolve for me."

"*Solve* is what you mean to say, Sancho," replied Don Quixote. "Speak out, and I will answer you as best I can."

"Tell me, then, sir," Sancho went on, "those Julys [7] or Augusts, and all those knights you mentioned that were always up and doing, seeing that they are dead, where are they now?"

"The heathen ones," said Don Quixote, "are undoubtedly in Hell; the Christians, if they were good Christians, are either in purgatory or in Heaven."

"That is all very well," said Sancho, "but what I want to know is this: do the tombs where the bodies of those great lords are preserved have silver lamps in front of them, and are the walls of their chapels decorated with crutches, shrouds, locks of hair, legs, and eyes made of wax? Or, if not, what kind of decorations do they have?"

"The pagan sepulchers," Don Quixote answered him, "were for the most part sumptuous temples. Julius Caesar's ashes, for example, were placed upon a stone pyramid of enormous size which in the Rome of to-day is known as St. Peter's Needle. The Emperor Hadrian's burial place was a castle as big as a good-sized town and was called the Moles Adriani, which at the present time is St. Angelo's Castle. The Queen Artemisia buried her husband in a tomb that was reckoned one of the seven wonders of the world. But none of the many pagan tombs was adorned with shrouds or offerings and tokens such as you commonly see where saints are buried."

"I am coming to that," said Sancho. "And now, tell me, which is the greater thing, to bring a dead man to life or to kill a giant?"

"The answer to that question is easy," replied Don Quixote. "To bring the dead to life, of course."

"Ah," said Sancho, "that is where I have you. Then the fame of those who resurrect the dead, who give sight to the blind, who heal cripples and bring health to the sick, and who have burning lamps in front of their tombs while their chapels are filled with kneeling worshipers who have come to adore their relics—will not their fame, both in this world and in the world to come, be a better one than that which all the heathen emperors and knights-errant that ever were have left or shall ever leave behind them?"

"I am willing to grant you that also," Don Quixote admitted.

"Well, then," continued Sancho, "seeing that this fame, these favors, these privileges, or whatever you call them, belong to the bodies and relics of the saints, who, with the approval and permission of our Holy Mother Church, have lamps, candles, shrouds, crutches, paintings, locks of hair, eyes, legs, and what not, to spread their Christian fame and make the worshipers more devout; and seeing that kings are in the habit of taking the bodies of saints, or saints' relics, upon their backs, while they kiss the bits of bone and use them to decorate and enrich their chapels and their favorite altars—"

"What are you getting at, Sancho, with all this you are saying?" Don Quixote asked.

"What I mean," said Sancho, "is that we ought to become saints, and that way we'd have the fame we are after all the sooner. You may know, sir, that yesterday or day before yesterday—in a manner of speaking, for it was only a short while ago—they canonized or beatified two little barefoot friars,[8] and it is now considered a great piece of luck to be able to kiss and touch the iron chains with which they girt and tormented their bodies. Those chains, so it is said, are more venerated than is Orlando's sword in the armory of our lord the king, God save him. And so, my dear sir, it is better to be a humble little barefoot friar, whatever the order he belongs to, than a brave knight-errant. With God, a couple of dozen penances will get you more than two thousand lance thrusts, whether they be given to giants, dragons, or other monsters."

"I agree with all that," said Don Quixote, "but we cannot all be friars, and there are many paths by which God takes His own to Heaven. Chivalry is a religion in itself, and there are sainted knights in glory."

"Yes," said Sancho, "but I have heard that there are more friars in Heaven than there are knights-errant."

"That," Don Quixote explained, "is for the reason that the number of religious is greater than the number of knights."

"There are many errant ones," observed Sancho.

"Many," his master assented, "but few that deserve the name of knight."

In talk of this kind they spent that night and the following day, without anything happening to them worthy of note, at which Don Quixote was not a little put out. On the day after that, at sunset, they sighted the great city of El Toboso. The knight was elated, but Sancho was downcast, for he did not know where Dulcinea lived nor had he ever in his life laid eyes upon her any more than his master had. As a result, each of them was uneasy in his mind, the one being anxious to behold her while the other was worried because he had not already seen her. Sancho could not imagine what he was going to do when his master should send him into the town; but Don Quixote finally decided that they would wait until nightfall to make their entrance, and in the meanwhile they tarried amid some oak trees that grew round about. When the time came, they made their way into the streets of El Toboso, where the things that happened to them were really something.[9]

CHAPTER IX. *A chapter in which is related what will be found set forth in it.*

It was midnight on the hour,[1] a little more or less, when Don Quixote and Sancho left the wood [2] and entered the city of El Toboso. The town was wrapped in a peaceful silence, for all the good people were asleep, or were stretching a leg, as the saying goes.[3] The night was not wholly dark, though Sancho wished it had been, as that might have provided an excuse for his inability to find his way. Nothing was to be heard anywhere but the barking of dogs, which deafened Don Quixote's ears and troubled his squire's heart. Now and then an ass would bray, pigs would grunt, a cat would miaul, and these various noises grew in volume with the silence. All of which the lovelorn knight took to be an ill omen, but he nonetheless adhered to his purpose.

"Sancho, my son," he cried, "lead the way to Dulcinea's palace; it may be that we shall find her awake."

"Body of the sun!" cried Sancho, "to what palace should I lead you? When I saw her Highness, she was in a very small house."

"Then," replied Don Quixote, "she must merely have retired to some small apartment of her castle, to amuse herself in solitude with her damsels, as is the custom of highborn ladies and princesses."

"Sir," said Sancho, "seeing that, in spite of anything I say, your Grace will have it that my lady Dulcinea's house is a castle, are we likely at this hour to find the gate open? And would it be right for us to go knocking at the gate in order to arouse them so that they can let us in, thus creating an uproar and disturbing everybody? Do you think, by any chance, that we are going to the house where our concubines live, as those who keep such women do, who come and call out and go in at any time, however late it may be?"

"First of all," said Don Quixote, "let us find out where the palace is, and then, Sancho, I will tell you what we should do. Look you, either my eyes deceive me or that huge dark bulk that we see yonder must be it."

"Then lead the way, your Grace, for it may be you are right. But, though I see it with my eyes and touch it with my hands, I will believe it is a palace just as soon as I would that it is now day."

Don Quixote accordingly led on, and when they had gone some two hundred paces they came up to the dark object and saw that it was a great tower, and then they realized that this was not a palace but the principal church of the town. "It's the church we've lighted on," the knight remarked to Sancho.

"So I see," replied the squire, "and please God we don't light upon our graves as well. It's not a good sign to be wandering in cemeteries at this hour of the night; and what's more, I told your Grace, if I remember rightly, that this lady's house would be up a blind alley."

"May God curse you, you fool!" cried his master, "and when did you ever hear of castles and royal palaces being built in blind alleys?"

"Sir," was Sancho's answer, "every land has its own customs,[4] and it may be that the custom here in El Toboso is to put up their palaces and other great buildings in alleyways. And so I beg your Grace to let me look through these streets and lanes, and in some nook or corner I may come upon this palace, though I'd like to see it eaten by dogs right now for leading us on such a wild goose chase."

"I wish, Sancho," said Don Quixote, "that you would show some respect in speaking of those things that pertain to my lady. Let us keep the feast and be merry and not throw the rope after the bucket."[5]

"I will control myself," said Sancho, "but how can I be patient when your Grace expects me, though I only saw our mistress's house once, to remember it always, and to find her in the middle of the night when your Grace, who must have seen her thousands of times, is unable to do so?"

"Sancho," said Don Quixote, "you will drive me to despair. Look, you heretic, have I not told you any number of times that I have never in all the days of my life laid eyes upon the peerless Dulcinea, that I have never crossed the threshold of her palace but am enamored of her only by hearsay, as she is famous far and wide for her beauty and her wit?"

"I hear you say it now," replied Sancho, "and I may tell you that if your Grace has never seen her, neither have I."

"But that cannot be," said Don Quixote, "or at any rate you have told me that you saw her winnowing wheat, that time you brought me back the answer to the letter that I sent to her by you."

"Pay no attention to that, sir, for I would have you know that it was also by hearsay that I saw her and brought her answer to you. I could no more tell you who the lady Dulcinea is than I could strike the sky with my fist."

"Sancho, Sancho," said Don Quixote, "there is a time for jesting and a time when jests are out of place. Just because I tell you that I have never seen nor spoken to the lady of my heart is no reason why you should say the same thing when you know it is not true."

As they were engaged in this conversation, they saw a man coming toward them with a team of mules hitched to a plow, which made a loud noise as it scraped along the ground. They assumed that he must be some farmer up before daybreak and on his way to the field, and this proved to be the case. The farmer was singing the ballad that runs:

> *The day of Roncesvalles was a dismal day for you,*
> *Ye men of France . . .*[6]

"May they slay me, Sancho," said Don Quixote when he heard it, "if anything good is going to come of this night. Do you hear what that rustic is singing?"

"Yes, I hear it," replied Sancho, "but what has the pursuit of Roncesvalles to do with the business that we have in hand? It would be all the same if it was the ballad of Calainos."[7]

At this point the farmer came up to them, and Don Quixote proceeded to question him. "Can you tell me, my good friend," he asked, "and may God prosper you, where in this vicinity is the palace of the peerless princess Doña Dulcinea del Toboso?"

"Señor," the lad answered, "I am a stranger here. I have been in this town only a few days, in the service of a rich farmer whose fields I plow. In that house across the way the curate and the sacristan live, and either one of them can tell your Grace what you wish to know about this princess, for they have a list of all the good folk of El Toboso. But, for my part, I never saw any princess whatever anywhere in the entire city. There are many ladies of high rank, it is true, and each may be a princess in her own house."

"Then the one that I am inquiring about must be among them, my friend," said Don Quixote.

"It may be so," replied the lad, "and God be with you, for there comes the dawn." And, lashing his mules, he did not wait to be questioned any further.

Seeing the unhappy state of mind his master was in, Sancho now spoke to him. "Sir," he said, "it will soon be daylight, and it will not do for the sun to find us here in the street. It would be better for us to go outside the town and for your Grace to hide yourself in some near-by forest. I will then come back and look in every corner for my lady's house, castle, or palace. It will be too bad if I do not find it, and when I do I will speak to her Grace and tell her how your Worship is waiting for her to arrange for you to come and see her without damage to her honor and good name."

"Sancho," said Don Quixote, "you have uttered a thousand sentences within the compass of a few words. I thank you for the advice you have given me and I accept it with right good grace. Come, my son, let us go look for a place where I may hide; after which, as you say, you will come back to look for and to see and talk with my lady, from whose discretion and courtesy I expect favors that will be more than miraculous."

Sancho was in furious haste to get his master out of the town so that the knight would not discover the lie that had been told him regarding Dulcinea's answer which his squire had brought back to the Sierra Morena. They set out at once, and at a distance of two miles from the city they found a forest or wood where Don Quixote might hide himself while Sancho returned to talk to Dulcinea, in the course of which embassy things happened to the messenger that call for fresh attention and belief.

CHAPTER X. *Wherein is related the ingenuity that Sancho displayed by laying a spell upon the lady Dulcinea, with other events as outlandish as they are true.*

WHEN the author of this great history comes to relate the events set forth in the present chapter, he remarks that he would prefer to pass over them in silence, as he fears that he will not be believed. For Don Quixote's madness here reaches a point beyond which the imagination cannot go, and even exceeds that point by a couple of bowshots. Nevertheless, in spite of such fear and misgiving, the historian has written down the events in question just as they happened, without adding to the chronicle in any way or holding back one particle of the truth, being in the end wholly unconcerned with the objections that might be raised by those who would make him out to be a liar. And in doing so he was right; for while the truth may run thin, it never breaks, and always rises above falsehood as oil does above water.[1]

The history, then, goes on to state that, after he had hidden himself in the wood, forest, or oak grove near El Toboso, Don Quixote ordered Sancho to return to the city and not to appear in his master's presence again until he should first have spoken in person to the lady Dulcinea and begged her to be pleased to grant her captive knight a glimpse of her, that she might bestow her blessing upon him, which would enable him to hope for a most fortunate conclusion to all his difficult enterprises and undertakings. Taking upon himself this task that had been assigned him, the squire promised to bring back as fair a reply as he had on the previous occasion.

"Go, my son," Don Quixote said to him, "and do not let yourself be dazed by the light from that sun of beauty that you go to seek. Ah, happy are you above all the squires in the world! Be sure to remember, and do not let it slip your mind, just how she receives you. Note whether she changes color while you are giving her my message and if she is restless and perturbed upon hearing my name. It may be that you will find her seated in sumptuous and royal state, in which case she will perhaps fall back upon a cushion; or if she be standing, see if she rests first upon one foot and then upon the other. Observe if she repeats two or three times the answer she gives you and if her mood varies from mildness to austerity, from the harsh to the amorous. She may raise a hand to her hair to smooth it back, though it be not disordered.

"In short, my son, note her every action and movement. If you report to me faithfully all these things, I shall be able to make out the hidden secret of her heart and discover how she feels with regard to my love; for I may tell you, Sancho, if you do not know it already, that among lovers exterior signs of this sort are the most reliable couriers that there are, bringing news of what goes on inside the heart. Go, then, my friend and may a better fortune than mine be your guide. May you be more successful than I dare hope in this fearful and bitter solitude in which you leave me."

"I go," said Sancho, "and I will return shortly. In the meantime, my master, cheer up that little heart of yours; for right now you must have one no bigger than a hazelnut. Remember what they say, that a stout heart breaks bad luck, and where there is no bacon there are no pegs. And they also say that when you least expect it the hare leaps out.[2] I tell you this for the reason that, if we did not find my lady's palace or castle last night, now that it is day I expect to come upon it when I'm not looking for it; and once I've found it, leave it to me to deal with her."

"I must say, Sancho," replied Don Quixote, "that your proverbs always come in very pat no matter what it is we are talking about. May God give me luck and grant me that which I desire."

With this, Sancho turned his back on his master and, lashing his donkey, rode off, leaving the knight seated in the saddle, his feet in the stirrups, and leaning on his lance. We, too, shall leave Don Quixote there, full of sad and troubled thoughts, as we accompany his squire, who was quite as pensive and troubled as he. As soon as he was out of the wood, Sancho turned his head and looked back, and, perceiving that he was by this time out of sight, he dismounted from his ass and sat down at the foot of a tree, where he began talking to himself, as follows:

"Look here, brother Sancho, supposing that you tell us where your Grace is going. Is it to hunt for some ass that has strayed? No, certainly not. Then, what *are* you hunting for? I am going to hunt for a princess, nothing more nor less than that, and in her I am to find the sun of beauty and all the heavens combined. And where do you think you are going to find all this, Sancho? Where? In the great city of El Toboso. Well and good; and who sent you to look for her? The famous knight, Don Quixote de la Mancha, who rights wrongs and gives food to the thirsty and drink to the hungry. That is all very well; but do you know where her house is, Sancho? My master says it will be some royal palace or proud castle. And have you ever laid eyes upon her by any chance? Neither I nor my master has ever seen her. And supposing the people of El Toboso knew that you were here luring their princesses and disturbing their ladies, don't you think it would be only right and proper if they came and clubbed your ribs without leaving a whole bone in your body? And, to tell the truth, they would be right, if you did not take into account that I am sent here under orders and that

A messenger you are, my friend,
No blame belongs to you.[3]

But don't put your trust in that, Sancho, for the Manchegan folks are as hot-tempered as they are honest and will not put up with anything from anybody. God help you if they get wind of you, for it will mean bad luck. Out with you, villain! Let the bolt fall![4] Am I to go looking for a cat with three feet just to please another?[5] Hunting for Dulcinea in El Toboso is like trying to find Marica in Rávena or a bachelor in Salamanca.[6] It was the devil, it was the devil himself and nobody else, that got me into this."

Such was Sancho's soliloquy. It had led him to no conclusion thus far, and so he continued:

"Well, there is a remedy for everything except death, beneath whose yoke we all have to pass, however heavy it may weigh upon us, when life draws to a close. I have seen by a thousand signs that this master of mine is a madman who ought to be in a cell, yet I am not behind him in that respect, seeing that I am foolish enough to follow and serve him. That is certainly the case if there's any truth in the old saying, 'Tell me what company you keep and I'll tell you who you are,' or that other one, 'Not with whom you are bred but with whom you are fed.' [7] And seeing that he is a madman, and that he is there can be no doubt—so mad that he takes one thing for another, white for black and black for white, like the time when he insisted the windmills were giants and the monks' mules were dromedaries, and the flocks of sheep were enemy armies, and other things of the same sort—seeing that this is so, it will not be hard to make him believe that the first farm girl I fall in with around here is the lady Dulcinea. If he doesn't believe it, I'll swear to it; and if he swears that it isn't so, I'll swear right back at him; and if he insists, I'll insist more than he does, so that, come what may, I'll always have my quoit on the peg. If I keep it up like that, I'll bring him around to the point where he won't be sending me on any more such errands as this, when he sees how little comes of it. Or maybe, and I imagine that this will more likely be the case, he will think that one of those wicked enchanters, who, he says, have it in for him, has changed her form just to spite and harm him."

These reflections greatly calmed Sancho Panza's mind and led him to look upon his business as already accomplished. He accordingly remained where he was until the afternoon, in order that Don Quixote might think he had had time to go to El Toboso and return. Everything went off so well with him that when he arose to mount his gray again, he saw coming toward him from the direction of the city three peasant lasses astride three ass-colts or fillies—the author is not specific on this point, but it seems more likely that they were she-asses, on which village girls commonly ride. However, it is of no great importance and there is no reason why we should stop to verify so trifling a detail.

The short of the matter is, as soon as Sancho saw the lasses he hastened to where Don Quixote was, only to find the knight sighing and uttering a thousand amorous laments.

"What is it, Sancho, my friend? Am I to be able to mark this day with a white stone or a black one?"

"It would be better," replied Sancho, "if your Grace marked it with red ocher like the lists on the professors' chairs,[8] so that all could see it very plainly."

"That means, I take it," said Don Quixote, "that you bring good news."

"Good news it is," replied Sancho. "All your Grace has to do is to put spur to Rocinante and ride out into the open, and there you will see the lady Dulcinea del Toboso in person, who with two of her damsels has come to pay her respects to your Grace."

"Good Lord, Sancho my friend, what is this you are telling me? Take care that you do not deceive me or try to relieve with false joy my very real sadness."

"And what would I get by deceiving your Grace," Sancho wanted to know, "when you will soon enough discover for yourself whether I am speaking the truth or not? Come quickly, sir, and you will see the princess, our mistress, clad and adorned as befits one of her quality. She and her damsels are all one blaze of gold, pearls, diamonds, rubies, and brocade cloth with more than ten borders.[9] Their hair falling loose over their shoulders are so many sunbeams playing with the wind. And, what is more, they come mounted upon three piebald cackneys,[10] the finest you ever saw."

"*Hackneys*, you mean to say, Sancho."

"*Hackneys* or *cackneys*, it makes very little difference," replied Sancho. "No matter what their mounts, they are the finest ladies you could wish for, especially the Princess Dulcinea, my lady, who stuns your senses."

"Come, Sancho, my son," said Don Quixote, "let us go. As a reward for the news you bring me, as good as it is unexpected, I promise you the best spoils that I win in my first adventure; and in case this is not enough to satisfy you, I will send you the colts which my three mares will give me this year—as you know, they are now out on the village common and are about to foal."

"I will take the colts," said Sancho, "for the spoils from that first adventure are rather uncertain."

At this point they emerged from the wood close to where the three village lasses were. Gazing up and down the highway that led to El Toboso, Don Quixote was completely bewildered, since all he could see was these country maidens. He then asked Sancho if the princess and her damsels had left the city or were, perhaps, waiting there.

"What do you mean?" said Sancho. "Are your Grace's eyes in the back of your head that you cannot see that those are the ones coming there, as bright and shining as the sun itself at midday?"

"I see nothing," declared Don Quixote, "except three farm girls on three jackasses."

"Then God deliver me from the devil!" exclaimed Sancho. "Is it possible that those three hackneys, or whatever you call them, white as the driven snow, look like jackasses to your Grace? By the living God, I would tear out this beard of mine if that were true!"

"But I tell you, friend Sancho, it is as true that those are jackasses, or she-asses, as it is that I am Don Quixote and you Sancho Panza. At least, that is the way they look to me."

"Be quiet, sir," Sancho admonished him, "you must not say such a thing as that. Open those eyes of yours and come do reverence to the lady of your affections, for she draws near."

Saying this, he rode on to meet the village maids and, slipping down off his donkey, seized one of their beasts by the halter and fell on his knees in front of its rider.

"O queen and princess and duchess of beauty," he said, "may your Highness and Majesty be pleased to receive and show favor to your captive knight, who stands there as if turned to marble, overwhelmed and breathless at finding himself in your magnificent presence. I am Sancho Panza, his squire, and he is the world-weary knight Don Quixote, otherwise known as the Knight of the Mournful Countenance."

By this time Don Quixote was down on his knees beside Sancho. His eyes were fairly starting from their sockets and there was a deeply troubled look in them as he stared up at the one whom Sancho had called queen and lady; all that he could see in her was a village wench, and not a very pretty one at that, for she was round-faced and snub-nosed. He was astounded and perplexed and did not dare open his mouth. The girls were also very much astonished to behold these two men, so different in appearance, kneeling in front of one of them so that she could not pass. It was this one who most ungraciously broke the silence.

"Get out of my way," she said peevishly, "and let me pass. And bad luck go with you. For we are in a hurry."

"O princess and universal lady of El Toboso!" cried Sancho. "How can your magnanimous heart fail to melt as you behold kneeling before your sublimated presence the one who is the very pillar and support of knight-errantry?" [11]

Hearing this, one of the others spoke up. "Whoa, there, she-ass of my father!" she said. "Wait until I curry you down.[12] Just look at the small-fry gentry, will you, who've come to make sport of us country girls!

Just as if we couldn't give them tit for tat. Be on your way and get out of ours, if you know what's good for you."

"Arise, Sancho," said Don Quixote, "for I perceive that fortune has not had her fill of evil done to me but has taken possession of all the roads by which some happiness may come to what little soul is left within me. And thou, who art all that could be desired, the sum of human gentleness and sole remedy for this afflicted heart that doth adore thee! The malign enchanter who doth persecute me hath placed clouds and cataracts upon my eyes, and for them and them alone hath transformed thy peerless beauty into the face of a lowly peasant maid; and I can only hope that he has not likewise changed my face into that of some monster by way of rendering it abhorrent in thy sight. But for all of that, hesitate not to gaze upon me tenderly and lovingly, beholding in this act of submission as I kneel before thee a tribute to thy metamorphosed beauty from this humbly worshiping heart of mine."

"Just listen to him run on, will you? My grandmother!" cried the lass. "Enough of such gibberish. We'll thank you to let us go our way."

Sancho fell back and let her pass, being very thankful to get out of it so easily.

No sooner did she find herself free than the girl who was supposed to have Dulcinea's face began spurring her "cackney" with a spike on the end of a long stick that she carried with her, whereupon the beast set off at top speed across the meadow. Feeling the prick, which appeared to annoy it more than was ordinarily the case, the ass started cutting such capers that the lady Dulcinea was thrown to the ground. When he saw this, Don Quixote hastened to lift her up while Sancho busied himself with tightening the girths and adjusting the packsaddle, which had slipped down under the animal's belly. This having been accomplished, Don Quixote was about to take his enchanted lady in his arms to place her upon the she-ass when the girl saved him the trouble by jumping up from the ground, stepping back a few paces, and taking a run for it. Placing both hands upon the crupper of the ass, she landed more lightly than a falcon upon the packsaddle and remained sitting there astride it like a man.

"In the name of Roque!" [13] exclaimed Sancho, "our lady is like a lanner, only lighter, and can teach the cleverest Cordovan or Mexican how to mount. She cleared the back of the saddle in one jump, and without any spurs she makes her hackney run like a zebra, and her damsels are not far behind, for they all of them go like the wind."

This was the truth. Seeing Dulcinea in the saddle, the other two prodded their beasts and followed her on the run, without so much as turning their heads to look back for a distance of half a league. Don Quixote stood gazing after them, and when they were no longer visible he turned to Sancho and spoke.

"Sancho," he said, "you can see now, can you not, how the enchanters hate me? And just see how far they carry their malice and the grudge they bear me, since they would deprive me of the happiness I might derive from a sight of my mistress. The truth of the matter is, I was born to be an example of misfortune and to be the target and mark at which the arrows of ill luck are aimed and directed. I would further call your attention, Sancho, to the fact that, not content with merely transforming my Dulcinea, they must change her into a figure as low and repulsive as that village girl, robbing her at the same time of that which is so characteristic of highborn ladies, namely, their pleasing scent, which comes from always being among amber and flowers. For I would have you know, Sancho, that when Dulcinea leaped upon her hackney as you call it (though I must say, it seemed to me more like a she-ass), the odor that she gave off was one of raw garlic that made my head swim and poisoned my heart."

"O you scum!" cried Sancho. "O wretched and evil-minded enchanters! If I could but see you strung up by the gills like sardines on a reed! Great is your wisdom, great is your power, and greater yet the harm you do! [14] Was it not enough, O villainous ones, to have changed the pearls of my lady's eyes into cork galls [15] and her hair of purest gold into the bristles of a red ox's tail? No, you had to change all of her features from good to ill, and even alter her smell, since had you not done so we might have discovered what lay concealed beneath that ugly bark. And yet, to tell the truth, I never noticed her ugliness but only her beauty, which was set off to perfection by a mole that she had on her right lip— it resembled a mustache, being surrounded by seven or eight red hairs of more than a palm in length."

"As a rule," observed Don Quixote, "moles on the face correspond to those on the body, and Dulcinea must accordingly have one of the same sort on the flat of her thigh, on the same side as the other. But hairs of the length you mentioned are very long for moles."

"Well, all I can tell you," answered Sancho, "is that there they were as big as life."

"I believe you, friend," said Don Quixote, "for everything pertaining to Dulcinea is by nature perfect and well finished, and so, if she had a hundred moles of the kind you have described, upon her they would not be moles but resplendent moons and stars. But tell me one thing, Sancho: that thing that looked to me like a packsaddle which you were adjusting, was it a flat saddle or a sidesaddle?"

"It was neither one nor the other," replied Sancho, "but a *jineta*,[16] with a field-covering so rich that it must have been worth half a kingdom."

"Oh, if I could but have seen all that, Sancho! I tell you again, and I will tell you a thousand times, that I am the most unfortunate of men."

It was all that the rogue of a Sancho could do to keep from laughing as he listened to this foolish talk on the part of his master, who had been so ingeniously deceived. Finally, after much other talk had passed between them, they mounted their beasts once more and took the road for Saragossa, hoping to arrive there in time for a certain important feast that is celebrated in that illustrious city every year. Before they reached their destination, however, many strange and noteworthy things were to happen to them that deserve to be set down and read, as will be seen further on.

CHAPTER XI. *Of the strange adventure that befell the valiant Don Quixote in connection with the cart or wagon of the Parliament of Death.*

CONTINUING on his way, Don Quixote was deeply dejected as he thought of the cruel joke which the enchanters had played upon him by transforming his lady Dulcinea into the ugly form of the village girl, nor could he imagine any means of restoring her to her original shape. He was so absorbed in these reflections that, without noticing it, he let go Rocinante's rein, and that animal, taking advantage of the freedom granted him, now paused at every step to feed upon the abundant green grass that covered the plain. It was Sancho who awakened the knight from his daydreams.

"Sir," he said, "sorrows are made not for beasts but for men, but if men feel them too much they become beasts. Your Grace ought to pull yourself together and pick up Rocinante's rein; you ought to wake up

and cheer up and show that gallant spirit that knights-errant are supposed
to have. What the devil is this, anyway? What kind of weakness is it?
Are we here or in France? Let Satan carry off all the Dulcineas in the
world; the welfare of a single knight means more than all the spells and
transformations on this earth."

"Hush, Sancho," replied Don Quixote, in not too wan a voice,[1] "hush,
I say, and do not be uttering blasphemies against that enchanted lady,
seeing that I alone am to blame for her misfortunes, which are due to
the envy that the wicked ones bear me."

"That is what I say," agreed Sancho. "Who saw her once and saw her
now, his heart would surely weep, I vow."[2]

"You, Sancho, may well say that," was Don Quixote's response, "for
you beheld her in all the fullness of her beauty; the spell did not go so far
as to disturb *your* sight or conceal her loveliness from you; it was solely
against me and these eyes of mine that the force of its venom was
directed. And yet, Sancho, there is one thing that occurs to me. It would
seem that you have not well described her; for, unless my memory serves
me wrong, you said that she had eyes like pearls, and eyes of that sort
are more characteristic of the sea bream than they are of a lady. Dulcinea's eyes must be green emeralds, large and luscious, with two rainbows for brows. Take those pearls from her eyes and bestow them upon
her teeth, for undoubtedly, Sancho, you must have mistaken the former
for the latter."

"That may be," said Sancho, "for her beauty disturbed me as much
as her ugliness did your Grace. But let us leave it to God, for he knows
all that is to happen in this vale of tears, in this evil world of ours, where
you scarcely find anything that does not have in it some mixture of
wickedness, deceit, and villainy. But there is one thing, my master, that
worries me most of all: what is your Grace going to do when you have
overcome some giant or knight and wish to send him to present himself
before the beautiful Dulcinea? Where is that poor giant or wretched
knight going to find her? I can see them now, wandering like a lot of nit-
wits through the streets of El Toboso looking for my lady. Even if they
were to meet her in the middle of the street, they wouldn't know her
from my father."

"It may be, Sancho," said Don Quixote, "that the spell will not prevent
them from recognizing her as it does me. But we shall see as to that after
we shall have dispatched one or two of them to seek her out; for I shall
command them to return and give me an account of what happened."

"I must say," replied Sancho, "that your Grace has spoken very much

to the point, and by this means we shall be able to find out what we wish
to know. And since it is only to your Grace that her beauty is hidden,
the misfortune is more yours than hers. So long as the lady Dulcinea has
health and happiness, we will make the best of it and go on seeking adventures, leaving it to time to work a cure, for he is the best doctor for
this and other greater ills."

Don Quixote was about to make a reply but was interrupted by the
sight of a cart crossing the highway, filled with the most varied and
weird assortment of persons and figures that could be imagined. He who
drove the mules and served as carter was an ugly demon, and the vehicle
was open to the heavens and had neither awning nor framework of
branches on which to stretch it.[3] The first figure that Don Quixote beheld
was that of Death himself, with a human countenance. Next came an
angel with large and painted wings. At one side was an emperor with
what appeared to be a gold crown on his head, and at Death's feet was the
god called Cupid, without a bandage over his eyes but with his bow, his
quiver, and his arrows. There was also a knight in full armor, except that
he had no morion or helmet but instead wore a hat decked with varicolored plumes.

Such a sight as this, coming as it did so unexpectedly, somewhat
startled Don Quixote and struck fear in Sancho's heart, but the knight
was at once cheered by the thought that this must be some new and
perilous adventure, and with a mind disposed to confront any danger
he stepped in front of the cart and called out in a loud and threatening
voice, "O carter, coachman, demon, or whoever you may be! Tell me
at once who you are and whither you are bound and who the persons
are whom you carry with you in that wagonette, which looks more to
me like Charon's bark than the kind of conveyance in common use."

Stopping the wagon, the demon gave him a most civil reply. "Sir," he
said, "we are strolling players of Angulo el Malo's company.[4] This morning, which marks the octave of Corpus Christi, we have performed a
theatrical piece in the village which lies beyond that hill yonder. It was
a play called *The Parliament of Death*,[5] and we have to give it this afternoon in another village which you can see from here. Since the distance
is so short, and in order to save ourselves the trouble of undressing and
dressing again, we are traveling in the garments that we wear on the
stage. That youth there is Death, the other is an Angel. That woman,
who is the author's wife, takes the part of a Queen. This one is a Soldier,
that one an Emperor, and I am a Devil—in fact, I am one of the principal
characters in the play, for I take the leading roles in this company. If

there is anything else your Grace would like to know concerning us, you have but to ask me and I will answer you very precisely; for, being a demon, I am capable of anything."

"Upon the word of a knight-errant," said Don Quixote, "when I first saw this wagon, I thought that some great adventure must be awaiting me, but I perceive now that one must actually touch with his hands what appears to the eye if he is to avoid being deceived. God go with you, my good people; be off to your festival; and if I can serve you in any way, I will gladly do so, for as a lad I was very fond of masks and in my youth my eyes were fixed upon the stage."

Now, fate would have it that as they were engaged in this conversation one of the company should come up, dressed in a mummer's costume, with many bells and with three cow's bladders on the end of a stick. Approaching Don Quixote, the clown began brandishing his stick, beating the ground with the bladders, and leaping high in the air to the jingling accompaniment of his bells. This terrifying apparition so frightened Rocinante that, without his master's being able to restrain him, the hack took the bit in his teeth and started off on a run across the plain, more swiftly than one would ever have thought possible, viewing the bones of his anatomy. Perceiving that his master was in danger of being thrown, Sancho leaped from his gray and ran with all haste to help him; but by the time he reached the spot both horse and rider were on the ground, which was the way it usually ended whenever Rocinante showed any signs of life.

No sooner had Sancho quitted his mount to go to Don Quixote's assistance than the dancing demon of the bladders jumped upon the gray's back and began beating it with them. Frightened by the sound rather than pained by the blows, the animal promptly started off at full speed over the countryside, in the direction of the village where the festival was to be held. As he witnessed his donkey's flight and his master's fall, Sancho was at a loss as to which case merited his attention first; but inasmuch as he was a good squire and a good servant, love of his master prevailed in the end over affection for his beast. Nevertheless, as he saw the bladders rising in the air and coming down on the donkey's flanks, he experienced all the throes and terrors of death; he would rather have had those blows fall upon his eyeballs than upon the least hair of his gray's tail. He was still troubled and perplexed as he reached the spot where Don Quixote lay, in a good deal worse plight than was to his liking.

"Sir," he said as he helped his master up on Rocinante's back, "the Devil's run off with the gray."

"What devil?" asked Don Quixote.

"The one with the bladders."

"Then I will recover it for you," said the knight, "though it be shut up with him in the deepest and darkest dungeons of Hell. Follow me, Sancho, for the wagon proceeds at a slow pace and its mules will make up for the loss of your gray."

"There is no need to go to all that trouble, sir," replied Sancho. "Your Grace may calm himself; for if I am not mistaken, the Devil has turned the gray loose and the beast is coming back to its old haunts."

This proved to be the truth; for, having taken a fall with the donkey in imitation of Don Quixote and Rocinante, the Devil had made off on foot toward the village, leaving the ass free to return to its owner.

"But I still think," said Don Quixote, "that it would be well to punish the discourtesy of that demon by taking it out on one of those in the wagon, even though it be the Emperor himself."

"Put that out of your mind, your Grace," Sancho urged him. "You had best take my advice, which is never to meddle with players, for they are a favored lot. I knew one of them who was up for two murders, yet he went scot free. Your Grace must be aware that, being merry folk whose business it is to amuse, they are liked by everybody and everyone protects, aids, and esteems them. This is especially true when they happen to belong to a royal company with a king's patent.[6] In that case, you might think that all or most of them were lords, from the clothes they wear and the manners they affect."

"Nonetheless," said Don Quixote, "I am not going to let that player demon go away boasting, even if the whole human race is on his side." Saying this, he returned to the wagon, which by this time was very near the town. "Stop!" he cried. "Wait, you merry, clowning crew! I'll teach you how to behave toward the beasts that serve as mounts to the squires of knights-errant."

Don Quixote was shouting so loudly that those in the wagon were able to hear and make out what he said; and, judging from the knight's words what his intentions were, the figure of Death leaped down, followed by the Emperor, the carter-Devil, and the Angel, nor did the Queen or the god Cupid stay behind. Arming themselves with pebbles, they formed in line and waited to receive Don Quixote with their missiles. The latter, seeing them drawn up in this gallant formation, their arms uplifted and ready to let fly a powerful volley, drew in Rocinante's rein and fell to thinking what would be the best way of attacking them with the least danger to his person. At this point Sancho came up and, perceiving that his master was about to fall upon the well-formed squadron, began remonstrating with him.

"It would be the height of madness," he said, "to undertake such a thing. Bear in mind, your Grace, that against brook-sop,[7] and plenty of it in this case, there is no defensive armor in the world except to hide yourself under a brass bell. Remember, too, that it is foolhardiness rather than valor for one man singlehanded to attack an army when Death is on the other side, when emperors are fighting there in person, and when the enemy has both good and fallen angels to aid him. And if this cannot lead you to be calm, it should interest you to know that, for a certainty, that among all those facing you, though they appear to be kings, princes, and emperors, there is not one knight-errant."

"Ah," said Don Quixote, "you have hit upon something there, Sancho, something that can and should sway me from my resolve. For, as I have told you many times, I ought not to draw sword against one who has not been dubbed a knight. It is for you, Sancho, if you so desire, to avenge the wrong that has been done to your gray, and I will cheer you on and help you with sound advice."

"There is no reason," replied Sancho, "why I should take vengeance on anyone; for it is not for good Christians to avenge the wrongs that are done them. I will arrange with my ass to leave everything to me, and my advice to him will be to live out peaceably the days that Heaven has allotted to him."

"Since that is your resolve, my good Sancho, my wise Sancho, my sincere and Christian Sancho, let us leave these phantoms and go back to seeking better and more legitimate adventures; for I can see this country is such that we cannot fail to meet with many most miraculous ones."

With this the knight turned his steed, Sancho made for his own mount, and Death with the whole of his flying squadron returned to the wagon, after which they continued on their way.

Such was the happy ending of this bold adventure of the wagon of Death, thanks to the wise counsel which Sancho Panza gave his master, who the very next day fell in with another enamored and erring knight, an episode quite as thrilling as the one that has just been related.

CHAPTER XII. *Of the strange adventure that befell the valiant Don Quixote with the fearless Knight of the Mirrors.*

THE night following the encounter with Death was spent by Don Quixote and his squire beneath some tall and shady trees, the knight having been persuaded to eat a little from the stock of provisions carried by the gray.

"Sir," said Sancho, in the course of their repast, "how foolish I'd have been if I had chosen the spoils from your Grace's first adventure rather than the foals from the three mares. Truly, truly, a sparrow in the hand is worth more than a vulture on the wing." [1]

"And yet, Sancho," replied Don Quixote, "if you had but let me attack them as I wished to do, you would at least have had as spoils the Empress's gold crown and Cupid's painted wings; for I should have taken them whether or no and placed them in your hands."

"The crowns and scepters of stage emperors," remarked Sancho, "were never known to be of pure gold; they are always of tinsel or tinplate."

"That is the truth," said Don Quixote, "for it is only right that the accessories of a drama should be fictitious and not real, like the play itself. Speaking of that, Sancho, I would have you look kindly upon the art of the theater and, as a consequence, upon those who write the pieces and perform in them, for they all render a service of great value to the State by holding up a mirror for us at each step that we take, wherein we may observe, vividly depicted, all the varied aspects of human life; and I may add that there is nothing that shows us more clearly, by similitude, what we are and what we ought to be than do plays and players.

"Tell me, have you not seen some comedy in which kings, emperors, pontiffs, knights, ladies, and numerous other characters are introduced? One plays the ruffian, another the cheat, this one a merchant and that one a soldier, while yet another is the fool who is not so foolish as he appears, and still another the one of whom love has made a fool. Yet when the play is over and they have taken off their players' garments, all the actors are once more equal."

"Yes," replied Sancho, "I have seen all that."

"Well," continued Don Quixote, "the same thing happens in the comedy that we call life,[2] where some play the part of emperors, others that of pontiffs—in short, all the characters that a drama may have—but when it is all over, that is to say, when life is done, death takes from each the garb that differentiates him, and all at last are equal in the grave."

"It is a fine comparison," Sancho admitted, "though not so new but that I have heard it many times before. It reminds me of that other one, about the game of chess. So long as the game lasts, each piece has its special qualities, but when it is over they are all mixed and jumbled together and put into a bag, which is to the chess pieces what the grave is to life."[3]

"Every day, Sancho," said Don Quixote, "you are becoming less stupid and more sensible."[4]

"It must be that some of your Grace's good sense is sticking to me," was Sancho's answer. "I am like a piece of land that of itself is dry and barren, but if you scatter manure over it and cultivate it, it will bear good fruit. By this I mean to say that your Grace's conversation is the manure that has been cast upon the barren land of my dry wit; the time that I spend in your service, associating with you, does the cultivating; and as a result of it all, I hope to bring forth blessed fruits by not departing, slipping, or sliding, from those paths of good breeding which your Grace has marked out for me in my parched understanding."

Don Quixote had to laugh at this affected speech of Sancho's, but he could not help perceiving that what the squire had said about his improvement was true enough; for every now and then the servant would speak in a manner that astonished his master. It must be admitted, however, that most of the time when he tried to use fine language, he would tumble from the mountain of his simple-mindedness into the abyss of his ignorance. It was when he was quoting old saws and sayings, whether or not they had anything to do with the subject under discussion, that he was at his best, displaying upon such occasions a prodigious memory, as will already have been seen and noted in the course of this history.

With such talk as this they spent a good part of the night. Then Sancho felt a desire to draw down the curtains of his eyes, as he was in the habit of saying when he wished to sleep, and, unsaddling his mount, he turned him loose to graze at will on the abundant grass. If he did not remove Rocinante's saddle, this was due to his master's express command; for when they had taken the field and were not sleeping under a roof, the hack was under no circumstances to be stripped. This was in accordance with an old and established custom which knights-errant faithfully observed: the bridle and saddlebow might be removed, but beware of touching the saddle itself! Guided by this precept, Sancho now gave Rocinante the same freedom that the ass enjoyed.

The close friendship that existed between the two animals was a most unusual one, so remarkable indeed that it has become a tradition handed down from father to son, and the author of this veracious chronicle even wrote a number of special chapters on the subject, although, in order to preserve the decency and decorum that are fitting in so heroic an account, he chose to omit them in the final version. But he forgets himself once in a while and goes on to tell us how the two beasts when they were together would hasten to scratch each other, and how, when they were tired and their bellies were full, Rocinante would lay his long neck over that of the ass—it extended more than half a yard on the other side—and the pair would then stand there gazing pensively at the ground for as much as three whole days at a time, or at least until someone came for them or hunger compelled them to seek nourishment.

I may tell you that I have heard it said that the author of this history, in one of his writings, has compared the friendship of Rocinante and the gray to that of Nisus and Euryalus and that of Pylades and Orestes; [5] and if this be true, it shows for the edification of all what great friends these two peace-loving animals were, and should be enough to make men ashamed, who are so inept at preserving friendship with one another. For this reason it has been said:

> There is no friend for friend,
> Reeds to lances turn . . .[6]

And there was the other poet who sang:

> Between friend and friend the bug . . .[7]

Let no one think that the author has gone out of his way in comparing the friendship of animals with that of men; for human beings have received valuable lessons from the beasts and have learned many important things from them. From the stork they have learned the use of clysters; the dog has taught them the salutary effects of vomiting as well as a lesson in gratitude; the cranes have taught them vigilance, the ants foresight, the elephants modesty, and the horse loyalty.[8]

Sancho had at last fallen asleep at the foot of a cork tree, while Don Quixote was slumbering beneath a sturdy oak. Very little time had passed when the knight was awakened by a noise behind him, and, starting up, he began looking about him and listening to see if he could make out where it came from. Then he caught sight of two men on horseback, one of whom, slipping down from the saddle, said to the other, "Dismount, my friend, and unbridle the horses; for there seems to be plenty of grass around here for them and sufficient silence and solitude for my amorous thoughts."

Saying this, he stretched himself out on the ground, and as he flung himself down the armor that he wore made such a noise that Don Quixote knew at once, for a certainty, that he must be a knight-errant. Going over to Sancho, who was still sleeping, he shook him by the arm and with no little effort managed to get him awake.

"Brother Sancho," he said to him in a low voice, "we have an adventure on our hands."

"God give us a good one," said Sancho. "And where, my master, may her Ladyship, Mistress Adventure, be?"

"Where, Sancho?" replied Don Quixote. "Turn your eyes and look, and you will see stretched out over there a knight-errant who, so far as I can make out, is not any too happy; for I saw him fling himself from his horse to the ground with a certain show of despondency, and as he fell his armor rattled."

"Well," said Sancho, "and how does your Grace make this out to be an adventure?"

"I would not say," the knight answered him, "that this is an adventure in itself, but rather the beginning of one, for that is the way they start. But listen; he seems to be tuning a lute or guitar, and from the way he is spitting and clearing his throat he must be getting ready to sing something."

"Faith, so he is," said Sancho. "He must be some lovesick knight."

"There are no knights-errant that are not lovesick," Don Quixote informed him. "Let us listen to him, and the thread of his song will lead us to the yarn-ball of his thoughts; [9] for out of the abundance of the heart the mouth speaketh." [10]

Sancho would have liked to reply to his master, but the voice of the Knight of the Wood, which was neither very good nor very bad, kept him from it; and as the two of them listened attentively, [11] they heard the following:

SONNET

Show me, O lady, the pattern of thy will,
That mine may take that very form and shape;
For my will in thine own I fain would drape,
Each slightest wish of thine I would fulfill.

> *If thou wouldst have me silence this dread ill*
> *Of which I'm dying now, prepare the crape!*
> *Or if I must another manner ape,*
> *Then let Love's self display his rhyming skill.*
> *Of opposites I am made, that's manifest:*
> *In part soft wax, in part hard-diamond fire;*
> *Yet to Love's laws my heart I do adjust,*
> *And, hard or soft, I offer thee this breast:*
> *Print or engrave there what thou may'st desire,*
> *And I'll preserve it in eternal trust.*[12]

With an *Ay!* that appeared to be wrung from the very depths of his heart, the Knight of the Wood brought his song to a close, and then after a brief pause began speaking in a grief-stricken voice that was piteous to hear.

"O most beautiful and most ungrateful woman in all the world!" he cried, "how is it possible, O most serene Casildea de Vandalia, for you to permit this captive knight of yours to waste away and perish in constant wanderings, amid rude toils and bitter hardships? Is it not enough that I have compelled all the knights of Navarre, all those of León, all the Tartessians [13] and Castilians, and, finally, all those of La Mancha, to confess that there is no beauty anywhere that can rival yours?"

"That is not so!" cried Don Quixote at this point. "I am of La Mancha, and I have never confessed, I never could nor would confess a thing so prejudicial to the beauty of my lady.[14] The knight whom you see there, Sancho, is raving; but let us listen and perhaps he will tell us more."

"That he will," replied Sancho, "for at the rate he is carrying on, he is good for a month at a stretch."

This did not prove to be the case, however; for when the Knight of the Wood heard voices near him, he cut short his lamentations and rose to his feet.

"Who goes there?" he called in a loud but courteous tone. "What kind of people are you? Are you, perchance, numbered among the happy or among the afflicted?"

"Among the afflicted," was Don Quixote's response.

"Then come to me," said the one of the Wood, "and, in doing so, know that you come to sorrow's self and the very essence of affliction."

Upon receiving so gentle and courteous an answer, Don Quixote and Sancho as well went over to him, whereupon the sorrowing one took the Manchegan's arm.

"Sit down here, Sir Knight," he continued, "for in order to know that you are one of those who follow the profession of knight-errantry, it is enough for me to have found you in this place where solitude and serenity keep you company, such a spot being the natural bed and proper dwelling of wandering men of arms."

"A knight I am," replied Don Quixote, "and of the profession that you mention; and though sorrows, troubles, and misfortunes have made my heart their abode, this does not mean that compassion for the woes of others has been banished from it. From your song a while ago I gather that your misfortunes are due to love—the love you bear that ungrateful fair one whom you named in your lamentations."

As they conversed in this manner, they sat together upon the hard earth, very peaceably and companionably, as if at daybreak they were not going to break each other's heads.

"Sir Knight," inquired the one of the Wood, "are you by any chance in love?"

"By mischance I am," said Don Quixote, "although the ills that come from well-placed affection should be looked upon as favors rather than as misfortunes."

"That is the truth," the Knight of the Wood agreed, "if it were not that the loved one's scorn disturbs our reason and understanding; for when it is excessive scorn appears as vengeance."

"I was never scorned by my lady," said Don Quixote.

"No, certainly not," said Sancho, who was standing near by, "for my lady is gentle as a ewe lamb and soft as butter."

"Is he your squire?" asked the one of the Wood.

"He is," replied Don Quixote.

"I never saw a squire," said the one of the Wood, "who dared to speak while his master was talking. At least, there is mine over there; he is as big as your father, and it cannot be proved that he has ever opened his lips while I was conversing."

"Well, upon my word," said Sancho, "I have spoken, and I will speak in front of any other as good—but never mind; it only makes it worse to stir it." [15]

The Knight of the Wood's squire now seized Sancho's arm. "Come along," he said, "let the two of us go where we can talk all we like, squire fashion, and leave these gentlemen our masters to come to lance blows as they tell each other the story of their loves; for you may rest assured, daybreak will find them still at it."

"Let us, by all means," said Sancho, "and I will tell your Grace who

I am, so that you may be able to see for yourself whether or not I am to be numbered among the dozen most talkative squires."

With this, the pair went off to one side, and there then took place between them a conversation that was as droll as the one between their masters was solemn.

CHAPTER XIII . *In which is continued the adventure of the Knight of the Wood,*[1] *together with the shrewd, highly original, and amicable conversation that took place between the two squires.*

THE knights and the squires had now separated, the latter to tell their life stories, the former to talk of their loves; but the history first relates the conversation of the servants and then goes on to report that of the masters. We are told that, after they had gone some little distance from where the others were, the one who served the Knight of the Wood began speaking to Sancho as follows:

"It is a hard life that we lead and live, *Señor mio,* those of us who are squires to knights-errant. It is certainly true that we eat our bread in the sweat of our faces,[2] which is one of the curses that God put upon our first parents."

"It might also be said," added Sancho, "that we eat it in the chill of our bodies, for who endures more heat and cold than we wretched ones who wait upon these wandering men of arms? It would not be so bad if we did eat once in a while, for troubles are less where there is bread;[3] but as it is, we sometimes go for a day or two without breaking our fast, unless we feed on the wind that blows."

"But all this," said the other, "may very well be put up with, by reason of the hope we have of being rewarded; for if a knight is not too unlucky, his squire after a little while will find himself the governor of some fine island or prosperous earldom."

"I," replied Sancho, "have told my master that I would be satisfied with the governorship of an island, and he is so noble and so generous that he has promised it to me on many different occasions."

"In return for my services," said the Squire of the Wood, "I'd be content with a canonry. My master has already appointed me to one—and what a canonry!"

"Then he must be a churchly knight," said Sancho, "and in a position to grant favors of that sort to his faithful squire; but mine is a layman, pure and simple, although, as I recall, certain shrewd and, as I see it, scheming persons did advise him to try to become an archbishop. However, he did not want to be anything but an emperor. And there I was, all the time trembling for fear he would take it into his head to enter the Church, since I was not educated enough to hold any benefices. For I may as well tell your Grace that, though I look like a man, I am no more than a beast where holy orders are concerned."

"That is where you are making a mistake," the Squire of the Wood assured him. "Not all island governments are desirable. Some of them are misshapen bits of land, some are poor, others are gloomy, and, in short, the best of them lays a heavy burden of care and trouble upon the shoulders of the unfortunate one to whose lot it falls. It would be far better if we who follow this cursed trade were to go back to our homes and there engage in pleasanter occupations, such as hunting or fishing, for example; for where is there in this world a squire so poor that he does not have a hack, a couple of greyhounds, and a fishing rod to provide him with sport in his own village?"

"I don't lack any of those," replied Sancho. "It is true, I have no hack, but I do have an ass that is worth twice as much as my master's horse. God send me a bad Easter, and let it be the next one that comes, if I would make a trade, even though he gave me four fanegas⁴ of barley to boot. Your Grace will laugh at the price I put on my gray—for that is the color of the beast. As to greyhounds, I shan't want for them, as there are plenty and to spare in my village. And, anyway, there is more pleasure in hunting when someone else pays for it."

"Really and truly, Sir Squire," said the one of the Wood, "I have made up my mind and resolved to have no more to do with the mad whims of these knights; I intend to retire to my village and bring up my little ones—I have three of them, and they are like oriental pearls."

"I have two of them," said Sancho, "that might be presented to the Pope in person, especially one of my girls that I am bringing up to be a countess, God willing, in spite of what her mother says."

"And how old is this young lady that is destined to be a countess?"

"Fifteen," replied Sancho, "or a couple of years more or less. But she is tall as a lance, fresh as an April morning, and strong as a porter."

"Those," remarked the one of the Wood, "are qualifications that fit her to be not merely a countess but a nymph of the verdant wildwood. O whore's daughter of a whore! What strength the she-rogue must have!"

Sancho was a bit put out by this. "She is not a whore," he said, "nor was her mother before her, nor will either of them ever be, please God, so long as I live. And you might speak more courteously. For one who has been brought up among knights-errant, who are the soul of courtesy, those words are not very becoming."

"Oh, how little your Grace knows about compliments, Sir Squire!" the one of the Wood exclaimed. "Are you not aware that when some knight gives a good lance thrust to the bull in the plaza, or when a person does anything remarkably well, it is the custom for the crowd to cry out, 'Well done, whoreson rascal!' and that what appears to be vituperation in such a case is in reality high praise? Sir, I would bid you disown those sons or daughters who do nothing to cause such praise to be bestowed upon their parents."

"I would indeed disown them if they didn't," replied Sancho, "and so your Grace may go ahead and call me, my children, and my wife all the whores in the world if you like, for everything that they say and do deserves the very highest praise. And in order that I may see them all again, I pray God to deliver me from mortal sin, or, what amounts to the same thing, from this dangerous calling of squire, seeing that I have fallen into it a second time, decoyed and deceived by a purse of a hundred ducats that I found one day in the heart of the Sierra Morena. The devil is always holding up a bag full of doubloons in front of my eyes, here, there—no, not here, but there—everywhere, until it seems to me at every step I take that I am touching it with my hand, hugging it, carrying it off home with me, investing it, drawing an income from it, and living on it like a prince. And while I am thinking such thoughts, all the hardships I have to put up with serving this crackbrained master of mine, who is more of a madman than a knight, seem to me light and easy to bear."

"That," observed the Squire of the Wood, "is why it is they say that avarice bursts the bag.[5] But, speaking of madmen, there is no greater one in all this world than my master; for he is one of those of whom it is said, 'The cares of others kill the ass.'[6] Because another knight has lost his senses, he has to play mad too and go hunting for that which, when he finds it, may fly up in his snout."

"Is he in love, maybe?"

"Yes, with a certain Casildea de Vandalia, the rawest [7] and best-roasted lady to be found anywhere on earth; but her rawness is not the foot he limps on, for he has other and greater schemes rumbling in his bowels, as you will hear tell before many hours have gone by."

"There is no road so smooth," said Sancho, "that it does not have some hole or rut to make you stumble. In other houses they cook horse beans, in mine they boil them by the kettleful.[8] Madness has more companions and attendants than good sense does. But if it is true what they say, that company in trouble brings relief, I may take comfort from your Grace, since you serve a master as foolish as my own."

"Foolish but brave," the one of the Wood corrected him, "and more of a rogue than anything else."

"That is not true of my master," replied Sancho. "I can assure you there is nothing of the rogue about him; he is as open and aboveboard as a wine pitcher and would not harm anyone but does good to all. There is no malice in his make-up, and a child could make him believe it was night at midday. For that very reason I love him with all my heart and cannot bring myself to leave him, no matter how many foolish things he does." [9]

"But, nevertheless, good sir and brother," said the Squire of the Wood, "with the blind leading the blind, both are in danger of falling into the pit. It would be better for us to get out of all this as quickly as we can and return to our old haunts; for those that go seeking adventures do not always find good ones."

Sancho kept clearing his throat from time to time, and his saliva seemed rather viscous and dry; seeing which, the woodland squire said to him, "It looks to me as if we have been talking so much that our tongues are cleaving to our palates, but I have a loosener over there, hanging from the bow of my saddle, and a pretty good one it is." With this, he got up and went over to his horse and came back a moment later with a big flask of wine and a meat pie half a yard in diameter. This is no exaggeration, for the pasty in question was made of a hutch-rabbit of such a size that Sancho took it to be a goat, or at the very least a kid.

"And are you in the habit of carrying this with you, Señor?" he asked.

"What do you think?" replied the other. "Am I by any chance one of your wool-and-water squires? [10] I carry better rations on the flanks of my horse than a general does when he takes the field."

Sancho ate without any urging, gulping down mouthfuls that were like the knots on a tether,[11] as they sat there in the dark.

"You are a squire of the right sort," he said, "loyal and true, and you live in grand style as shown by this feast, which I would almost say was produced by magic. You are not like me, poor wretch, who have in my saddlebags only a morsel of cheese so hard you could crack a giant's skull with it, three or four dozen carob beans, and a few nuts. For this I have my master to thank, who believes in observing the rule that knights-errant should nourish and sustain themselves on nothing but dried fruits and the herbs of the field."

"Upon my word, brother," said the other squire, "my stomach was not made for thistles, wild pears, and woodland herbs. Let our masters observe those knightly laws and traditions and eat what their rules prescribe; I carry a hamper of food and a flask on my saddlebow, whether they like it or not. And speaking of that flask, how I love it! There is scarcely a minute in the day that I'm not hugging and kissing it, over and over again."

As he said this, he placed the wine bag in Sancho's hands, who put it to his mouth, threw his head back, and sat there gazing up at the stars for a quarter of an hour.[12] Then, when he had finished drinking, he let his head loll on one side and heaved a deep sigh.

"The whoreson rascal!" he exclaimed, "that's a fine vintage for you!"

"There!" cried the Squire of the Wood, as he heard the epithet Sancho had used, "do you see how you have praised this wine by calling it 'whoreson'?"

"I grant you," replied Sancho, "that it is no insult to call anyone a son of a whore so long as you really do mean to praise him. But tell me, sir, in the name of what you love most, is this the wine of Ciudad Real?"[13]

"What a winetaster you are! It comes from nowhere else, and it's a few years old, at that."

"Leave it to me," said Sancho, "and never fear, I'll show you how much I know about it. Would you believe me, Sir Squire, I have such a great natural instinct in this matter of wines that I have but to smell a vintage and I will tell you the country where it was grown, from what kind of grapes, what it tastes like, and how good it is, and everything that has to do with it. There is nothing so unusual about this, however, seeing that on my father's side were two of the best winetasters La Mancha has known in many a year, in proof of which, listen to the story of what happened to them.

"The two were given a sample of wine from a certain vat and asked to state its condition and quality and determine whether it was good or bad. One of them tasted it with the tip of his tongue while the other merely brought it up to his nose. The first man said that it tasted of iron, the second that it smelled of Cordovan leather. The owner insisted that the vat was clean and that there could be nothing in the wine to give it a flavor of leather or of iron, but, nevertheless, the two famous wine-tasters stood their ground. Time went by, and when they came to clean out the vat they found in it a small key attached to a leather strap.[14] And so your Grace may see for yourself whether or not one who comes of that kind of stock has a right to give his opinion in such cases."

"And for that very reason," said the Squire of the Wood, "I maintain that we ought to stop going about in search of adventures. Seeing that we have loaves, let us not go looking for cakes, but return to our cottages, for God will find us there if He so wills."

"I mean to stay with my master," Sancho replied, "until he reaches Saragossa, but after that we will come to an understanding."

The short of the matter is, the two worthy squires talked so much and drank so much that sleep had to tie their tongues and moderate their thirst, since to quench the latter was impossible. Clinging to the wine flask, which was almost empty by now, and with half-chewed morsels of food in their mouths, they both slept peacefully; and we shall leave them there as we go on to relate what took place between the Knight of the Wood and the Knight of the Mournful Countenance.

CHAPTER XIV. *Wherein is continued the adventure of the Knight of the Wood.*

IN THE course of the long conversation that took place between Don Quixote and the Knight of the Wood, the history informs us that the latter addressed the following remarks to the Manchegan:

"In short, Sir Knight, I would have you know that my destiny, or, more properly speaking, my own free choice, has led me to fall in love with the peerless Casildea de Vandalia. I call her peerless for the reason that she has no equal as regards either her bodily proportions or her very great beauty. This Casildea, then, of whom I am telling you, repaid my worthy affections and honorable intentions by forcing me, as Hercules was forced by his stepmother, to incur many and diverse perils; and each time as I overcame one of them she would promise me that with the next one I should have that which I desired; but instead my labors have continued, forming a chain whose links I am no longer able to count, nor can I say which will be the last one, that shall mark the beginning of the realization of my hopes.

"One time she sent me forth to challenge that famous giantess of Seville, known as La Giralda, who is as strong and brave as if made of brass, and who without moving from the spot where she stands is the most changeable and fickle woman in the world.[1] I came, I saw, I conquered her. I made her stand still and point in one direction only, and for more than a week nothing but north winds blew. Then, there was that other time when Casildea sent me to lift those ancient stones, the mighty Bulls of Guisando,[2] an enterprise that had better have been entrusted to porters than to knights. On another occasion she commanded me to hurl myself down into the Cabra chasm [3]—an unheard-of and terribly dangerous undertaking—and bring her back a detailed account of what lay concealed in that deep and gloomy pit. I rendered La Giralda motionless, I lifted the Bulls of Guisando, and I threw myself into the abyss and brought to light what was hidden in its depths; yet my hopes are dead—how dead!—while her commands and her scorn are as lively as can be.

"Finally, she commanded me to ride through all the provinces of Spain and compel all the knights-errant whom I met with to confess that she is the most beautiful woman now living and that I am the most enamored man of arms that is to be found anywhere in the world. In fulfillment of this behest I have already traveled over the greater part of these realms and have vanquished many knights who have dared to contradict me. But the one whom I am proudest to have overcome in single combat is that famous gentleman, Don Quixote de la Mancha; for I made him confess that my Casildea is more beautiful than his Dulcinea, and by achieving such a conquest I reckon that I have conquered all the others on the face of the earth, seeing that this same Don Quixote had himself routed them. Accordingly, when I vanquished him, his fame, glory, and honor passed over and were transferred to my person.

> The brighter is the conquered one's lost crown,
> The greater is the conqueror's renown.[4]

Thus, the innumerable exploits of the said Don Quixote are now set down to my account and are indeed my own."

Don Quixote was astounded as he listened to the Knight of the Wood, and was about to tell him any number of times that he lied; the words were on the tip of his tongue, but he held them back as best he could, thinking that he would bring the other to confess with his own lips that what he had said was a lie. And so it was quite calmly that he now replied to him.

"Sir Knight," he began, "as to the assertion that your Grace has conquered most of the knights-errant in Spain and even in all the world, I have nothing to say, but that you have vanquished Don Quixote de la Mancha, I am inclined to doubt. It may be that it was someone else who resembled him, although there are very few that do."

"What do you mean?" replied the one of the Wood. "I swear by the heavens above that I did fight with Don Quixote and that I overcame him and forced him to yield. He is a tall man, with a dried-up face, long, lean legs, graying hair, an eagle-like nose somewhat hooked, and a big, black, drooping mustache. He takes the field under the name of the Knight of the Mournful Countenance, he has for squire a peasant named Sancho Panza, and he rides a famous steed called Rocinante. Lastly, the lady of his heart is a certain Dulcinea del Toboso, once upon a time known as Aldonza Lorenzo, just as my own lady, whose name is Casildea and who is an Andalusian by birth, is called by me Casildea de Vandalia. If all this is not sufficient to show that I speak the truth, here is my sword which shall make incredulity itself believe."

"Calm yourself, Sir Knight," replied Don Quixote, "and listen to what I have to say to you. You must know that this Don Quixote of whom you speak is the best friend that I have in the world, so great a friend that I may say that I feel toward him as I do toward my own self; and from all that you have told me, the very definite and accurate details that you have given me, I cannot doubt that he is the one whom you have conquered. On the other hand, the sight of my eyes and the touch of my hands assure me that he could not possibly be the one, unless some enchanter who is his enemy—for he has many, and one in particular who delights in persecuting him—may have assumed the knight's form and then permitted himself to be routed, by way of defrauding Don Quixote of the fame which his high deeds of chivalry have earned for him throughout the known world. To show you how true this may be, I will inform you that not more than a couple of days ago those same enemy magicians transformed the figure and person of the beauteous Dulcinea del Toboso into a low and mean village lass, and it is possible that they have done something of the same sort to the knight who is her lover. And if all this does not suffice to convince you of the truth of what I say, here is Don Quixote himself who will maintain it by force of arms, on foot or on horseback, or in any way you like."

Saying this, he rose and laid hold of his sword, and waited to see what the Knight of the Wood's decision would be. That worthy now replied in a voice as calm as the one Don Quixote had used.

"Pledges," he said, "do not distress one who is sure of his ability to pay.[5] He who was able to overcome you when you were transformed, Señor Don Quixote, may hope to bring you to your knees when you are your own proper self. But inasmuch as it is not fitting that knights should perform their feats of arms in the darkness, like ruffians and highwaymen, let us wait until it is day in order that the sun may behold what we do. And the condition governing our encounter shall be that the one who is vanquished must submit to the will of his conqueror and perform all those things that are commanded of him, provided they are such as are in keeping with the state of knighthood."

"With that condition and understanding," said Don Quixote, "I shall be satisfied."

With this, they went off to where their squires were, only to find them snoring away as hard as when sleep had first overtaken them. Awakening the pair, they ordered them to look to the horses; for as soon as the sun was up the two knights meant to stage an arduous and bloody single-handed combat. At this news Sancho was astonished and terrified, since, as a result of what the other squire had told him of the Knight of the Wood's prowess, he was led to fear for his master's safety. Nevertheless, he and his friend now went to seek the mounts without saying a word, and they found the animals all together, for by this time the two horses and the ass had smelled one another out. On the way the Squire of the Wood turned to Sancho and addressed him as follows:

"I must inform you, brother, that it is the custom of the fighters of Andalusia, when they are godfathers in any combat, not to remain idly by, with folded hands, while their godsons fight it out. I tell you this by way of warning you that while our masters are settling matters, we, too, shall have to come to blows and hack each other to bits."

"That custom, Sir Squire," replied Sancho, "may be all very well among the fighters and ruffians that you mention, but with the squires of knights-errant it is not to be thought of. At least, I have never heard my master speak of any such custom, and he knows all the laws of chivalry by heart. But granting that it is true and that there is a law which states in so many words that squires must fight while their masters do, I have no intention of obeying it but rather will pay whatever penalty is laid on peaceable-minded ones like myself, for I am sure it cannot be more than a couple of pounds of wax,⁶ and that would be less expensive than the lint which it would take to heal my head—I can already see it split in two. What's more, it's out of the question for me to fight since I have no sword nor did I ever in my life carry one."

"That," said the one of the Wood, "is something that is easily remedied. I have here two linen bags of the same size. You take one and I'll take the other and we will fight that way, on equal terms."

"So be it, by all means," said Sancho, "for that will simply knock the dust out of us without wounding us."

"But that's not the way it's to be," said the other squire. "Inside the bags, to keep the wind from blowing them away, we will put a half-dozen nice smooth pebbles of the same weight, and so we'll be able to give each other a good pounding without doing ourselves any real harm or damage."

"Body of my father!" cried Sancho, "just look, will you, at the marten and sable and wads of carded cotton that he's stuffing into those bags so that we won't get our heads cracked or our bones crushed to a pulp. But I am telling you, *Señor mio,* that even though you fill them with silken pellets, I don't mean to fight. Let our masters fight and make the best of it, but as for us, let us drink and live; for time will see to ending our lives without any help on our part by way of bringing them to a close before they have reached their proper season and fall from ripeness."

"Nevertheless," replied the Squire of the Wood, "fight we must, if only for half an hour."

"No," Sancho insisted, "that I will not do. I will not be so impolite or so ungrateful as to pick any quarrel however slight with one whose food and drink I've shared. And, moreover, who in the devil could bring himself to fight in cold blood, when he's not angry or vexed in any way?"

"I can take care of that, right enough," said the one of the Wood. "Before we begin, I will come up to your Grace as nicely as you please and give you three or four punches that will stretch you out at my feet; and that will surely be enough to awaken your anger, even though it's sleeping sounder than a dormouse."

"And I," said Sancho, "have another idea that's every bit as good as yours. I will take a big club, and before your Grace has had a chance to awaken my anger I will put yours to sleep with such mighty whacks that if it wakes at all it will be in the other world; for it is known there that I am not the man to let my face be mussed by anyone, and let each look out for the arrow.[7] But the best thing to do would be to leave each one's anger to its slumbers, for no one knows the heart of any other, he who comes for wool may go back shorn,[8] and God bless peace and curse all strife. If a hunted cat when surrounded and cornered turns into a lion,[9] God knows what I who am a man might not become. And so from this time forth I am warning you, Sir Squire, that all the harm and damage that may result from our quarrel will be upon your head."

"Very well," the one of the Wood replied, "God will send the dawn and we shall make out somehow."

At that moment gay-colored birds of all sorts began warbling in the trees and with their merry and varied songs appeared to be greeting and welcoming the fresh-dawning day, which already at the gates and on the balconies of the east was revealing its beautiful face as it shook out from its hair an infinite number of liquid pearls. Bathed in this gentle moisture, the grass seemed to shed a pearly spray, the willows distilled a savory manna, the fountains laughed, the brooks murmured, the woods were glad, and the meadows put on their finest raiment. The first thing that Sancho Panza beheld, as soon as it was light enough to tell one object from another, was the Squire of the Wood's nose, which was so big as to cast into the shade all the rest of his body. In addition to being of enormous size, it is said to have been hooked in the middle and all covered with warts of a mulberry hue, like eggplant; it hung down for a couple of inches below his mouth, and the size, color, warts, and shape of this organ gave his face so ugly an appearance that Sancho began trembling hand and foot like a child with convulsions and made up his mind then and there that he would take a couple of hundred punches before he would let his anger be awakened to the point where he would fight with this monster.

Don Quixote in the meanwhile was surveying his opponent, who had already adjusted and closed his helmet so that it was impossible to make out what he looked like. It was apparent, however, that he was not very tall and was stockily built. Over his armor he wore a coat of some kind or other made of what appeared to be the finest cloth of gold, all bespangled with glittering mirrors that resembled little moons and that gave him a most gallant and festive air, while above his helmet were a large number of waving plumes, green, white, and yellow in color. His lance, which was leaning against a tree, was very long and stout and had a steel point of more than a palm in length. Don Quixote took all this in, and from what he observed concluded that his opponent must be of tremendous strength, but he was not for this reason filled with fear as

Sancho Panza was. Rather, he proceeded to address the Knight of the Mirrors, quite boldly and in a highbred manner.

"Sir Knight," he said, "if in your eagerness to fight you have not lost your courtesy, I would beg you to be so good as to raise your visor a little in order that I may see if your face is as handsome as your trappings."

"Whether you come out of this emprise the victor or the vanquished, Sir Knight," he of the Mirrors replied, "there will be ample time and opportunity for you to have a sight of me. If I do not now gratify your desire, it is because it seems to me that I should be doing a very great wrong to the beauteous Casildea de Vandalia by wasting the time it would take me to raise my visor before having forced you to confess that I am right in my contention, with which you are well acquainted."

"Well, then," said Don Quixote, "while we are mounting our steeds you might at least inform me if I am that knight of La Mancha whom you say you conquered."

"To that our answer," [10] said he of the Mirrors, "is that you are as like the knight I overcame as one egg is like another; but since you assert that you are persecuted by enchanters, I should not venture to state positively that you are the one in question."

"All of which," said Don Quixote, "is sufficient to convince me that you are laboring under a misapprehension; but in order to relieve you of it once and for all, let them bring our steeds, and in less time than you would spend in lifting your visor, if God, my lady, and my arm give me strength, I will see your face and you shall see that I am not the vanquished knight you take me to be."

With this, they cut short their conversation and mounted, and, turning Rocinante around, Don Quixote began measuring off the proper length of field for a run against his opponent as he of the Mirrors did the same. But the Knight of La Mancha had not gone twenty paces when he heard his adversary calling to him, whereupon each of them turned halfway and he of the Mirrors spoke.

"I must remind you, Sir Knight," he said, "of the condition under which we fight, which is that the vanquished, as I have said before, shall place himself wholly at the disposition of the victor."

"I am aware of that," replied Don Quixote, "not forgetting the provision that the behest laid upon the vanquished shall not exceed the bounds of chivalry."

"Agreed," said the Knight of the Mirrors.

At that moment Don Quixote caught sight of the other squire's weird nose and was as greatly astonished by it as Sancho had been. Indeed, he took the fellow for some monster, or some new kind of human being wholly unlike those that people this world. As he saw his master riding away down the field preparatory to the tilt, Sancho was alarmed; for he did not like to be left alone with the big-nosed individual, fearing that one powerful swipe of that protuberance against his own nose would end the battle so far as he was concerned and he would be lying stretched out on the ground, from fear if not from the force of the blow.

He accordingly ran after the knight, clinging to one of Rocinante's stirrup straps, and when he thought it was time for Don Quixote to whirl about and bear down upon his opponent, he called to him and said, "*Señor mio*, I beg your Grace, before you turn for the charge, to help me up into that cork tree yonder where I can watch the encounter which your Grace is going to have with this knight better than I can from the ground and in a way that is much more to my liking."

"I rather think, Sancho," said Don Quixote, "that what you wish to do is to mount a platform where you can see the bulls without any danger to yourself."

"The truth of the matter is," Sancho admitted, "the monstrous nose on that squire has given me such a fright that I don't dare stay near him."

"It is indeed of such a sort," his master assured him, "that if I were not the person I am, I myself should be frightened. And so, come, I will help you up."

While Don Quixote tarried to see Sancho ensconced in the cork tree, the Knight of the Mirrors measured as much ground as seemed to him necessary and then, assuming that his adversary had done the same, without waiting for sound of trumpet or any other signal, he wheeled his horse, which was no swifter nor any more impressive-looking than Rocinante, and bore down upon his enemy at a mild trot; but when he saw that the Manchegan was busy helping his squire, he reined in his mount and came to a stop midway in his course, for which his horse was extremely grateful, being no longer able to stir a single step. To Don Quixote, on the other hand, it seemed as if his enemy was flying, and digging his spurs with all his might into Rocinante's lean flanks he caused that animal to run a bit for the first and only time, according to the history, for on all other occasions a simple trot had represented his utmost speed. And so it was that, with an unheard-of fury, the Knight of the Mournful Countenance came down upon the Knight of the Mirrors as the latter sat there sinking his spurs all the way up to the buttons [11] without being able to persuade his horse to budge a single inch from the spot where he had come to a sudden standstill.

It was at this fortunate moment, while his adversary was in such a predicament, that Don Quixote fell upon him, quite unmindful of the fact that the other knight was having trouble with his mount and either was unable or did not have time to put his lance at rest. The upshot of it was, he encountered him with such force that, much against his will, the Knight of the Mirrors went rolling over his horse's flanks and tumbled to the ground, where as a result of his terrific fall he lay as if dead, without moving hand or foot.

No sooner did Sancho perceive what had happened than he slipped down from the cork tree and ran up as fast as he could to where his master was. Dismounting from Rocinante, Don Quixote now stood over the Knight of the Mirrors, and undoing the helmet straps to see if the man was dead, or to give him air in case he was alive, he beheld—who can say what he beheld without creating astonishment, wonder, and amazement in those who hear the tale? The history tells us that it was the very countenance, form, aspect, physiognomy, effigy, and image of the bachelor Sansón Carrasco!

"Come, Sancho," he cried in a loud voice, "and see what is to be seen but is not to be believed. Hasten, my son, and learn what magic can do and how great is the power of wizards and enchanters."

Sancho came, and the moment his eyes fell on the bachelor Carrasco's face he began crossing and blessing himself a countless number of times. Meanwhile, the overthrown knight gave no signs of life.

"If you ask me, master," said Sancho, "I would say that the best thing for your Grace to do is to run his sword down the mouth of this one who appears to be the bachelor Carrasco; maybe by so doing you would be killing one of your enemies, the enchanters."

"That is not a bad idea," replied Don Quixote, "for the fewer enemies the better." [12] And, drawing his sword, he was about to act upon Sancho's advice and counsel when the Knight of the Mirrors' squire came up to them, now minus the nose which had made him so ugly.

"Look well what you are doing, Don Quixote!" he cried. "The one who lies there at your feet is your Grace's friend, the bachelor Sansón Carrasco, and I am his squire."

"And where is your nose?" inquired Sancho, who was surprised to see him without that deformity.

"Here in my pocket," was the reply. And, thrusting his hand into his coat, he drew out a nose of varnished pasteboard of the make that has been described. Studying him more and more closely, Sancho finally exclaimed, in a voice that was filled with amazement, "Holy Mary preserve me! And is this not my neighbor and crony, Tomé Cecial?"

"That is who I am!" replied the de-nosed squire, "your good friend Tomé Cecial, Sancho Panza. I will tell you presently of the means and snares and falsehoods that brought me here. But, for the present, I beg and entreat your master not to lay hands on, mistreat, wound, or slay the Knight of the Mirrors whom he now has at his feet; for without any doubt it is the rash and ill-advised bachelor Sansón Carrasco, our fellow villager." [13]

The Knight of the Mirrors now recovered consciousness, and, seeing this, Don Quixote at once placed the naked point of his sword above the face of the vanquished one.

"Dead you are, knight," he said, "unless you confess that the peerless Dulcinea del Toboso is more beautiful than your Casildea de Vandalia. And what is more, you will have to promise that, should you survive this encounter and the fall you have had, you will go to the city of El Toboso and present yourself to her in my behalf, that she may do with you as she may see fit. And in case she leaves you free to follow your own will, you are to return to seek me out—the trail of my exploits will serve as a guide to bring you wherever I may be—and tell me all that has taken place between you and her. These conditions are in conformity with those that we arranged before our combat and they do not go beyond the bounds of knight-errantry."

"I confess," said the fallen knight, "that the tattered and filthy shoe of the lady Dulcinea del Toboso is of greater worth than the badly combed if clean beard of Casildea, and I promise to go to her presence and return to yours and to give you a complete and detailed account concerning anything you may wish to know."

"Another thing," added Don Quixote, "that you will have to confess and believe is that the knight you conquered was not and could not have been Don Quixote de la Mancha, but was some other that resembled him, just as I am convinced that you, though you appear to be the bachelor Sansón Carrasco, are another person in his form and likeness who has been put here by my enemies to induce me to restrain and moderate the impetuosity of my wrath and make a gentle use of my glorious victory."

"I confess, think, and feel as you feel, think, and believe," replied the lamed knight. "Permit me to rise, I beg of you, if the jolt I received in my fall will let me do so, for I am in very bad shape."

Don Quixote and Tomé Cecial the squire now helped him to his feet. As for Sancho, he could not take his eyes off Tomé but kept asking him one question after another, and although the answers he received afforded clear enough proof that the man was really his fellow townsman, the fear that had been aroused in him by his master's words—about the enchanters' having transformed the Knight of the Mirrors into the bachelor Sansón Carrasco—prevented him from believing the truth that was apparent to his eyes. The short of it is, both master and servant were left with this delusion as the other ill-errant knight and his squire, in no pleasant state of mind, took their departure with the object of looking for some village where they might be able to apply poultices and splints to the bachelor's battered ribs.

Don Quixote and Sancho then resumed their journey along the road to Saragossa, and here for the time being the history leaves them in order to give an account of who the Knight of the Mirrors and his long-nosed squire really were.

<hr />

CHAPTER XV. *Wherein is told and revealed who the Knight of the Mirrors and his squire were.*

DON QUIXOTE went off very happy, self-satisfied, and vainglorious at having achieved a victory over so valiant a knight as he imagined the one of the Mirrors to be, from whose knightly word he hoped to learn whether or not the spell which had been put upon his lady was still in effect; for, unless he chose to forfeit his honor, the vanquished contender must of necessity return and give an account of what had happened in the course of his interview with her. But Don Quixote was of one mind, the Knight of the Mirrors of another,[1] for, as has been stated, the latter's only thought at the moment was to find some village where plasters were available.

The history goes on to state that when the bachelor Sansón Carrasco advised Don Quixote to resume his feats of chivalry, after having desisted from them for a while, this action was taken as the result of a conference which he had held with the curate and the barber as to the means to be adopted in persuading the knight to remain quietly at home and cease agitating himself over his unfortunate adventures. It had been Carrasco's suggestion, to which they had unanimously agreed, that they let Don Quixote sally forth, since it appeared to be impossible to prevent his doing so, and that Sansón should then take to the road as a knight-errant and pick a quarrel and do battle with him. There would be no difficulty about finding a pretext, and then the bachelor knight would overcome him (which was looked upon as easy of accomplishment), having first entered into a pact to the effect that the vanquished should remain at the mercy and bidding of his conqueror. The behest in this case was to be that the fallen one should return to his village and home and not leave it for the space of two years or until further orders were given him, it being a certainty that, once having been overcome, Don Quixote would fulfill the agreement, in order not to contravene or fail to obey the laws of chivalry. And it was possible that in the course of his seclusion he would forget his fancies, or they would at least have an opportunity to seek some suitable cure for his madness.

Sansón agreed to undertake this, and Tomé Cecial, Sancho's friend and neighbor, a merry but featherbrained chap, offered to go along as squire. Sansón then proceeded to arm himself in the manner that has been described, while Tomé disguised his nose with the aforementioned mask so that his crony would not recognize him when they met. Thus equipped, they followed the same route as Don Quixote and had almost caught up with him by the time he had the adventure with the Cart of Death. They finally overtook him in the wood, where those events occurred with which the attentive reader is already familiar; and if it had not been for the knight's extraordinary fancies, which led him to believe that the bachelor was not the bachelor, the said bachelor might have been prevented from ever attaining his degree of licentiate, as a result of having found no nests where he thought to find birds.[2]

Seeing how ill they had succeeded in their undertaking and what an end they had reached, Tomé Cecial now addressed his master.

"Surely, Señor Sansón Carrasco," he said, "we have had our deserts. It is easy enough to plan and embark upon an enterprise, but most of the time it's hard to get out of it. Don Quixote is a madman and we are sane, yet he goes away sound and laughing while your Grace is left here, battered and sorrowful. I wish you would tell me now who is the crazier: the one who is so because he cannot help it, or he who turns crazy of his own free will?"

"The difference between the two," replied Sansón, "lies in this: that the one who cannot help being crazy will be so always, whereas the one who is a madman by choice can leave off being one whenever he so desires."

"Well," said Tomé Cecial, "since that is the way it is, and since I chose to be crazy when I became your Grace's squire, by the same reasoning I now choose to stop being insane and to return to my home."

"That is your affair," said Sansón, "but to imagine that I am going back before I have given Don Quixote a good thrashing is senseless; and what will urge me on now is not any desire to see him recover his wits, but rather a thirst for vengeance; for with the terrible pain that I have in my ribs, you can't expect me to feel very charitable."

Conversing in this manner they kept on until they reached a village where it was their luck to find a bonesetter to take care of poor Sansón. Tomé Cecial then left him and returned home, while the bachelor meditated plans for revenge. The history has more to say of him in due time, but for the present it goes on to make merry with Don Quixote.

CHAPTER XVI. *Of what happened to Don Quixote upon his meeting with a prudent gentleman of La Mancha.*

WITH that feeling of happiness and vainglorious self-satisfaction that has been mentioned, Don Quixote continued on his way, imagining himself to be, as a result of the victory he had just achieved, the most valiant knight-errant of the age. Whatever adventures might befall him from then on he regarded as already accomplished and brought to a fortunate conclusion. He thought little now of enchanters and enchantments and was unmindful of the innumerable beatings he had received in the course of his knightly wanderings, of the volley of pebbles that had knocked out half his teeth, of the ungratefulness of the galley slaves and the audacity of the Yanguesans whose poles had fallen upon his body like rain. In short, he told himself, if he could but find the means, manner, or way of freeing his lady Dulcinea of the spell that had been put upon her, he would not envy the greatest good fortune that the most fortunate of knights-errant in ages past had ever by any possibility attained. He was still wholly wrapped up in these thoughts when Sancho spoke to him.

"Isn't it strange, sir, that I can still see in front of my eyes the huge and monstrous nose of my old crony, Tomé Cecial?"

"And do you by any chance believe, Sancho, that the Knight of the Mirrors was the bachelor Sansón Carrasco and that his squire was your friend Tomé?"

"I don't know what to say to that," replied Sancho. "All I know is that the things he told me about my home, my wife and young ones, could not have come from anybody else; and the face, too, once you took the nose away, was the same as Tomé Cecial's, which I have seen many times in our village, right next door to my own house, and the tone of voice was the same also."

"Let us reason the matter out, Sancho," said Don Quixote. "Look at it this way: how can it be thought that the bachelor Sansón Carrasco would come as a knight-errant, equipped with offensive and defensive armor, to contend with me? Am I, perchance, his enemy? Have I given him any occasion to cherish a grudge against me? Am I a rival of his? Or can it be jealousy of the fame I have acquired that has led him to take up the profession of arms?"

"Well, then, sir," Sancho answered him, "how are we to explain the fact that the knight was so like the bachelor and his squire like my friend? And if this was a magic spell, as your Grace has said, was there no other pair in the world whose likeness they might have taken?"

"It is all a scheme and a plot," replied Don Quixote, "on the part of those wicked magicians who are persecuting me and who, foreseeing that I would be the victor in the combat, saw to it that the conquered knight should display the face of my friend the bachelor, so that the affection which I bear him would come between my fallen enemy and the edge of my sword and might of my arm, to temper the righteous indignation of my heart. In that way, he who had sought by falsehood and deceits to take my life, would be left to go on living. As proof of all this, Sancho, experience, which neither lies nor deceives, has already taught you how easy it is for enchanters to change one countenance into another, making the beautiful ugly and the ugly beautiful. It was not two days ago that you beheld the peerless Dulcinea's beauty and elegance in its entirety and natural form. while I saw only the repulsive features of a low and ignorant peasant girl with cataracts over her eyes and a foul smell in her mouth.[1] And if the perverse enchanter was bold enough to effect so vile a transformation as this, there is certainly no cause for wonderment at what he has done in the case of Sansón Carrasco and your friend, all by way of snatching my glorious victory out of my hands. But in spite of it all, I find consolation in the fact that, whatever the shape he may have chosen to assume, I have laid my enemy low."

"God knows what the truth of it all may be," was Sancho's comment. Knowing as he did that Dulcinea's transformation had been due to his own scheming and plotting, he was not taken in by his master's delusions. He was at a loss for a reply, however, lest he say something that would reveal his own trickery.

As they were carrying on this conversation, they were overtaken by a man who, following the same road, was coming along behind them. He was mounted on a handsome flea-bitten mare and wore a hooded greatcoat of fine green cloth trimmed in tawny velvet and a cap of the same material,[2] while the trappings of his steed, which was accoutered for the field, were green and mulberry in hue, his saddle being of the *jineta* mode.[3] From his broad green and gold shoulder strap there dangled a Moorish cutlass, and his half-boots were of the same make as the baldric. His spurs were not gilded but were covered with highly polished green lacquer, so that, harmonizing as they did with the rest of his apparel, they seemed more appropriate than if they had been of purest gold. As he came up, he greeted the pair courteously and, spurring his mare, was about to ride on past when Don Quixote called to him.

"Gallant sir," he said, "if your Grace is going our way and is not in a hurry, it would be a favor to us if we might travel together."

"The truth is," replied the stranger, "I should not have ridden past you if I had not been afraid that the company of my mare would excite your horse."

"In that case, sir," Sancho spoke up, "you may as well rein in, for this horse of ours is the most virtuous and well mannered of any that there is. Never on such an occasion has he done anything that was not right—the only time he did misbehave, my master and I suffered for it aplenty. And so, I say again, your Grace may slow up if you like; for even if you offered him your mare on a couple of platters, he'd never try to mount her."

With this, the other traveler drew rein, being greatly astonished at Don Quixote's face and figure. For the knight was now riding along without his helmet, which was carried by Sancho like a piece of luggage on the back of his gray, in front of the packsaddle. If the green-clad gentleman stared hard at his new-found companion, the latter returned his gaze with an even greater intensity. He impressed Don Quixote as being a man of good judgment, around fifty years of age, with hair that was slightly graying and an aquiline nose, while the expression of his countenance was half humorous, half serious. In short, both his person and his accouterments indicated that he was an individual of some worth.

As for the man in green's impression of Don Quixote de la Mancha, he was thinking that he had never before seen any human being that resembled this one. He could not but marvel at the knight's long neck,[4] his tall frame, and the leanness and the sallowness of his face, as well as his armor and his grave bearing, the whole constituting a sight such as had not been seen for many a day in those parts. Don Quixote in turn was quite conscious of the attentiveness with which the traveler was studying him and could tell from the man's astonished look how curious he was; and so, being very courteous and fond of pleasing everyone, he proceeded to anticipate any questions that might be asked him.

"I am aware," he said, "that my appearance must strike your Grace as being very strange and out of the ordinary, and for that reason I am not surprised at your wonderment. But your Grace will cease to wonder when I tell you, as I am telling you now, that I am a knight, one of those

Of whom it is folks say,
They to adventures go.[5]

I have left my native heath, mortgaged my estate, given up my comfortable life, and cast myself into fortune's arms for her to do with me what she will. It has been my desire to revive a knight-errantry that is now dead, and for some time past, stumbling here and falling there, now throwing myself down headlong and then rising up once more, I have been able in good part to carry out my design by succoring widows, protecting damsels, and aiding the fallen, the orphans, and the young, all of which is the proper and natural duty of knights-errant. As a result, owing to my many valiant and Christian exploits, I have been deemed worthy of visiting in printed form nearly all the nations of the world. Thirty thousand copies of my history have been published, and, unless Heaven forbid, they will print thirty million of them.[6]

"In short, to put it all into a few words, or even one, I will tell you that I am Don Quixote de la Mancha, otherwise known as the Knight of the Mournful Countenance. Granted that self-praise is degrading, there still are times when I must praise myself, that is to say, when there is no one else present to speak in my behalf. And so, good sir, neither this steed nor this lance nor this buckler nor this squire of mine, nor all the armor that I wear and arms I carry, nor the sallowness of my complexion, nor my leanness and gauntness,[7] should any longer astonish you, now that you know who I am and what the profession is that I follow."

Having thus spoken, Don Quixote fell silent, and the man in green was so slow in replying that it seemed as if he was at a loss for words. Finally, however, after a considerable while, he brought himself to the point of speaking.

"You were correct, Sir Knight," he said, "about my astonishment and my curiosity, but you have not succeeded in removing the wonderment that the sight of you has aroused in me. You say that, knowing who you are, I should not wonder any more, but such is not the case, for I am now more amazed than ever. How can it be that there are knights-errant in the world today and that histories of them are actually printed? I find it hard to convince myself that at the present time there is anyone on earth who goes about aiding widows, protecting damsels, defending the honor of wives, and succoring orphans, and I should never have believed it had I not beheld your Grace with my own eyes. Thank Heaven for that book that your Grace tells me has been published concerning your true and exalted deeds of chivalry, as it should cast into oblivion all the innumerable stories of fictitious knights-errant with which the world is filled, greatly to the detriment of good morals and the prejudice and discredit of legitimate histories."

"As to whether the stories of knights-errant are fictitious or not," observed Don Quixote, "there is much that remains to be said."

"Why," replied the gentleman in green, "is there anyone who can doubt that such tales are false?"

"I doubt it," was the knight's answer, "but let the matter rest there. If our journey lasts long enough, I trust with God's help to be able to show your Grace that you are wrong in going along with those who hold it to be a certainty that they are not true."

From this last remark the traveler was led to suspect that Don Quixote must be some kind of crackbrain, and he was waiting for him to confirm the impression by further observations of the same sort; but before they could get off on another subject, the knight, seeing that he had given an account of his own station in life, turned to the stranger and politely inquired who his companion might be.

"I, Sir Knight of the Mournful Countenance," replied the one in the green-colored greatcoat, "am a gentleman, and a native of the village where, please God, we are going to dine today. I am more than moderately rich, and my name is Don Diego de Miranda. I spend my life with my wife and children and with my friends. My occupations are hunting and fishing, though I keep neither falcon nor hounds but only a tame partridge [8] and a bold ferret or two. I am the owner of about six dozen books, some of them in Spanish, others in Latin, including both histories and devotional works. As for books of chivalry, they have not as yet crossed the threshold of my door. My own preference is for profane rather than devotional writings, such as afford an innocent amusement, charming us by their style and arousing and holding our interest by their inventiveness, although I must say there are very few of that sort to be found in Spain.

"Sometimes," the man in green continued, "I dine with my friends and neighbors, and I often invite them to my house. My meals are wholesome and well prepared and there is always plenty to eat. I do not care for gossip, nor will I permit it in my presence. I am not lynx-eyed and do not pry into the lives and doings of others. I hear mass every day and share my substance with the poor, but make no parade of my good works lest hypocrisy and vainglory, those enemies that so imperceptibly take possession of the most modest heart, should find their way into mine. I try to make peace between those who are at strife. I am the devoted servant of Our Lady, and my trust is in the infinite mercy of God Our Savior."

Sancho had listened most attentively to the gentleman's account of his mode of life, and inasmuch as it seemed to him that this was a good and holy way to live and that the one who followed such a pattern ought to be able to work miracles, he now jumped down from his gray's back and, running over to seize the stranger's right stirrup, began kissing the feet of the man in green with a show of devotion that bordered on tears.

"Why are you doing that, brother?" the gentleman asked him. "What is the meaning of these kisses?"

"Let me kiss your feet," Sancho insisted, "for if I am not mistaken, your Grace is the first saint riding *jineta* fashion [9] that I have seen in all the days of my life."

"I am not a saint," the gentleman assured him, "but a great sinner. It is you, brother, who are the saint; for you must be a good man, judging by the simplicity of heart that you show."

Sancho then went back to his packsaddle, having evoked a laugh from the depths of his master's melancholy and given Don Diego fresh cause for astonishment.

Don Quixote thereupon inquired of the newcomer how many children he had, remarking as he did so that the ancient philosophers, who were without a true knowledge of God, believed that mankind's greatest good lay in the gifts of nature, in those of fortune, and in having many friends and many and worthy sons.

"I, Señor Don Quixote," replied the gentleman, "have a son without whom I should, perhaps, be happier than I am. It is not that he is bad, but rather that he is not as good as I should like him to be. He is eighteen years old, and for six of those years he has been at Salamanca studying the Greek and Latin languages. When I desired him to pass on to other branches of learning, I found him so immersed in the science of Poetry (if it can be called such) that it was not possible to interest him in the Law, which I wanted him to study, nor in Theology, the queen of them all. My wish was that he might be an honor to his family; for in this age in which we are living our monarchs are in the habit of highly rewarding those forms of learning that are good and virtuous, since learning without virtue is like pearls on a dunghill. But he spends the whole day trying to decide whether such and such a verse of Homer's *Iliad* is well conceived or not, whether or not Martial is immodest in a certain epigram, whether certain lines of Vergil are to be understood in this way or in that. In short, he spends all his time with the books written by those poets whom I have mentioned and with those of Horace, Persius, Juvenal, and Tibullus. As for our own moderns,[10] he sets little store by them, and yet, for all his disdain of Spanish poetry, he is at this moment racking his brains in an effort to compose a gloss on a quatrain that was sent him from Salamanca and which, I fancy, is for some literary tournament." [11]

To all this Don Quixote made the following answer:

"Children, sir, are out of their parents' bowels and so are to be loved whether they be good or bad, just as we love those that gave us life. It is for parents to bring up their offspring, from the time they are infants, in the paths of virtue, good breeding, proper conduct, and Christian morality, in order that, when they are grown, they may be a staff to the old age of the ones that bore them and an honor to their own posterity. As to compelling them to study a particular branch of learning, I am not so sure as to that, though there may be no harm in trying to persuade them to do so. But where there is no need to study *pane lucrando*—where Heaven has provided them with parents that can supply their daily bread —I should be in favor of permitting them to follow that course to which they are most inclined; and although poetry may be more pleasurable than useful, it is not one of those pursuits that bring dishonor upon those who engage in them.

"Poetry in my opinion, my dear sir," he went on, "is a young and tender maid of surpassing beauty, who has many other damsels (that is to say, the other disciplines) whose duty it is to bedeck, embellish, and adorn her. She may call upon all of them for service, and all of them in turn depend upon her nod. She is not one to be rudely handled, nor dragged through the streets, nor exposed at street corners, in the market place, or in the private nooks of palaces. She is fashioned through an alchemy of such power that he who knows how to make use of it will be able to convert her into the purest gold of inestimable price. Possessing her, he must keep her within bounds and not permit her to run wild in bawdy satires or soulless sonnets. She is not to be put up for sale in any manner, unless it be in the form of heroic poems, pity-inspiring tragedies, or pleasing and ingenious comedies. Let mountebanks keep hands off her, and the ignorant mob as well, which is incapable of recognizing or appreciating the treasures that are locked within her. And do not think, sir, that I apply that term 'mob' solely to plebeians and those of low estate; for anyone who is ignorant, whether he be lord or prince, may, and should, be included in the vulgar herd.

"But," Don Quixote continued, "he who possesses the gift of poetry and who makes the use of it that I have indicated, shall become famous and his name shall be honored among all the civilized nations of the world. You have stated, sir, that your son does not greatly care for poetry written in our Spanish tongue, and in that I am inclined to think he is somewhat mistaken. My reason for saying so is this: the great Homer did not write in Latin, for the reason that he was a Greek, and Vergil did not write in Greek since he was a Latin. In a word, all the poets of antiquity wrote in the language which they had imbibed with their mother's milk and did not go searching after foreign ones to express their loftiest conceptions. This being so, it would be well if the same custom were to be adopted by all nations, the German poet being no longer looked down upon because he writes in German, nor the Castilian or the Basque for employing his native speech.

"As for your son, I fancy, sir, that his quarrel is not so much with Spanish poetry as with those poets who have no other tongue or discipline at their command such as would help to awaken their natural gift; and yet, here, too, he may be wrong. There is an opinion, and a true one, to the effect that 'the poet is born,' [12] that is to say, it is as a poet that he comes forth from his mother's womb, and with the propensity that has been bestowed upon him by Heaven, without study or artifice, he produces those compositions that attest the truth of the line: '*Est deus in nobis*,' etc.[13] I further maintain that the born poet who is aided by art will have a great advantage over the one who by art alone would become a poet, the reason being that art does not go beyond, but merely perfects, nature; and so it is that, by combining nature with art and art with nature, the finished poet is produced.

"In conclusion, then, my dear sir, my advice to you would be to let your son go where his star beckons him; for being a good student as he must be, and having already successfully mounted the first step on the stairway of learning, which is that of languages, he will be able to continue of his own accord to the very peak of humane letters, an accomplishment that is altogether becoming in a gentleman, one that adorns, honors, and distinguishes him as much as the miter does the bishop or his flowing robe the learned jurisconsult. Your Grace well may reprove your son, should he compose satires that reflect upon the honor of other persons; in that case, punish him and tear them up. But should he compose discourses in the manner of Horace, in which he reprehends vice in general as that poet so elegantly does, then praise him by all means; for it is permitted the poet to write verses in which he inveighs against envy and the other vices as well, and to lash out at the vicious without, however, designating any particular individual. On the other hand, there are poets who for the sake of uttering something malicious would run the risk of being banished to the shores of Pontus.[14]

"If the poet be chaste where his own manners are concerned, he will likewise be modest in his verses, for the pen is the tongue of the mind, and whatever thoughts are engendered there are bound to appear in his writings. When kings and princes behold the marvelous art of poetry as practiced by prudent, virtuous, and serious-minded subjects of their realm, they honor, esteem, and reward those persons and crown them with the leaves of the tree that is never struck by lightning [15]—as if to show that those who are crowned and adorned with such wreaths are not to be assailed by anyone."

The gentleman in the green-colored greatcoat was vastly astonished by this speech of Don Quixote's and was rapidly altering the opinion he had previously held, to the effect that his companion was but a crackbrain. In the middle of the long discourse, which was not greatly to his liking, Sancho had left the highway to go seek a little milk from some shepherds who were draining the udders of their ewes near by. Extremely well pleased with the knight's sound sense and excellent reasoning, the gentleman was about to resume the conversation when, raising his head, Don Quixote caught sight of a cart flying royal flags that was coming toward them down the road and, thinking it must be a fresh adventure, began calling to Sancho in a loud voice to bring him his helmet. Whereupon Sancho hastily left the shepherds and spurred his gray until he was once more alongside his master, who was now about to encounter a dreadful and bewildering ordeal.

CHAPTER XVII. *Wherein Don Quixote's unimaginable courage reaches its highest point, together with the adventure of the lions and its happy ending.*

THE history relates that, when Don Quixote called to Sancho to bring him his helmet,[1] the squire was busy buying some curds from the shepherds and, flustered by his master's great haste, did not know what to do with them or how to carry them. Having already paid for the curds, he did not care to lose them, and so he decided to put them into the headpiece, and, acting upon this happy inspiration, he returned to see what was wanted of him.

"Give me that helmet," said the knight; "for either I know little about adventures or here is one where I am going to need my armor."

Upon hearing this, the gentleman in the green-colored greatcoat looked around in all directions but could see nothing except the cart that was approaching them, decked out with two or three flags which indicated that the vehicle in question must be conveying his Majesty's property. He remarked as much to Don Quixote, but the latter paid no attention, for he was always convinced that whatever happened to him meant adventures and more adventures.

"Forewarned is forearmed," [2] he said. "I lose nothing by being prepared, knowing as I do that I have enemies both visible and invisible and cannot tell when or where or in what form they will attack me."

Turning to Sancho, he asked for his helmet again, and as there was no time to shake out the curds, the squire had to hand it to him as it was. Don Quixote took it and, without noticing what was in it, hastily clapped it on his head; and forthwith, as a result of the pressure on the curds, the whey began running down all over his face and beard, at which he was very much startled.

"What is this, Sancho?" he cried. "I think my head must be softening or my brains melting, or else I am sweating from head to foot. If sweat it be, I assure you it is not from fear, though I can well believe that the adventure which now awaits me is a terrible one indeed. Give me something with which to wipe my face, if you have anything, for this perspiration is so abundant that it blinds me."

Sancho said nothing but gave him a cloth and at the same time gave thanks to God that his master had not discovered what the trouble was. Don Quixote wiped his face and then took off his helmet to see what it was that made his head feel so cool. Catching sight of that watery white mass, he lifted it to his nose and smelled it.

"By the life of my lady Dulcinea del Toboso!" he exclaimed. "Those are curds that you have put there, you treacherous, brazen, ill-mannered squire!"

To this Sancho replied, very calmly and with a straight face, "If they are curds, give them to me, your Grace, so that I can eat them. But no, let the devil eat them, for he must be the one who did it. Do you think I would be so bold as to soil your Grace's helmet? Upon my word, master, by the understanding that God has given me, I, too, must have enchanters who are persecuting me as your Grace's creature and one of his members, and they are the ones who put that filthy mess there to make you lose your patience and your temper and cause you to whack my ribs as you are in the habit of doing. Well, this time, I must say, they have missed the mark; for I trust my master's good sense to tell him that I have neither curds nor milk nor anything of the kind, and if I did have, I'd put it in my stomach and not in that helmet."

"That may very well be," said Don Quixote.

Don Diego was observing all this and was more astonished than ever, especially when, after he had wiped his head, face, beard, and helmet, Don Quixote once more donned the piece of armor and, settling himself in the stirrups, proceeded to adjust his sword and fix his lance.

"Come what may, here I stand, ready to take on Satan himself in person!" shouted the knight.

The cart with the flags had come up to them by this time, accompanied only by a driver riding one of the mules and a man seated up in front.

"Where are you going, brothers?" Don Quixote called out as he placed himself in the path of the cart. "What conveyance is this, what do you carry in it, and what is the meaning of those flags?"

"The cart is mine," replied the driver, "and in it are two fierce lions in cages which the governor of Oran is sending to court as a present for his Majesty. The flags are those of our lord the King, as a sign that his property goes here." [3]

"And are the lions large?" inquired Don Quixote.

It was the man sitting at the door of the cage who answered him. "The largest," he said, "that ever were sent from Africa to Spain. I am the lionkeeper and I have brought back others, but never any like these. They are male and female. The male is in this first cage, the female in the one behind. They are hungry right now, for they have had nothing to eat today; and so we'd be obliged if your Grace would get out of the way, for we must hasten on to the place where we are to feed them."

"Lion whelps against me?" said Don Quixote with a slight smile. "Lion whelps against me? And at such an hour? Then, by God, those gentlemen who sent them shall see whether I am the man to be frightened by lions. Get down, my good fellow, and since you are the lionkeeper, open the cages and turn those beasts out for me; and in the middle of this plain I will teach them who Don Quixote de la Mancha is, notwithstanding and in spite of the enchanters who are responsible for their being here."

"So," said the gentleman to himself as he heard this, "our worthy knight has revealed himself. It must indeed be true that the curds have softened his skull and mellowed his brains."

At this point Sancho approached him. "For God's sake, sir," he said, "do something to keep my master from fighting those lions. For if he does, they're going to tear us all to bits."

"Is your master, then, so insane," the gentleman asked, "that you fear and believe he means to tackle those fierce animals?"

"It is not that he is insane," replied Sancho, "but, rather, foolhardy."

"Very well," said the gentleman, "I will put a stop to it." And going up to Don Quixote, who was still urging the lionkeeper to open the cages, he said, "Sir Knight, knights-errant should undertake only those adventures that afford some hope of a successful outcome, not those that are utterly hopeless to begin with; for valor when it turns to temerity has in it more of madness than of bravery. Moreover, these lions have no thought of attacking your Grace but are a present to his Majesty, and it would not be well to detain them or interfere with their journey."

"My dear sir," answered Don Quixote, "you had best go mind your tame partridge and that bold ferret of yours and let each one attend to his own business. This is my affair, and I know whether these gentlemen, the lions, have come to attack me or not." He then turned to the lion-keeper. "I swear, Sir Rascal, if you do not open those cages at once, I'll pin you to the cart with this lance!"

Perceiving how determined the armed phantom was, the driver now spoke up. "Good sir," he said, "will your Grace please be so kind as to let me unhitch the mules and take them to a safe place before you turn those lions loose? For if they kill them for me, I am ruined for life, since the mules and cart are all the property I own."

"O man of little faith!" said Don Quixote. "Get down and unhitch your mules if you like, but you will soon see that it was quite unnecessary and that you might have spared yourself the trouble."

The driver did so, in great haste, as the lionkeeper began shouting, "I want you all to witness that I am being compelled against my will to open the cages and turn the lions out, and I further warn this gentleman that he will be responsible for all the harm and damage the beasts may do, plus my wages and my fees. You other gentlemen take cover before I open the doors; I am sure they will not do any harm to me."

Once more Don Diego sought to persuade his companion not to commit such an act of madness, as it was tempting God to undertake anything so foolish as that; but Don Quixote's only answer was that he knew what he was doing. And when the gentleman in green insisted that he was sure the knight was laboring under a delusion and ought to consider the matter well, the latter cut him short.

"Well, then, sir," he said, "if your Grace does not care to be a spectator at what you believe is going to turn out to be a tragedy, all you have to do is to spur your flea-bitten mare and seek safety."

Hearing this, Sancho with tears in his eyes again begged him to give up the undertaking, in comparison with which the adventure of the windmills and the dreadful one at the fulling mills—indeed, all the exploits his master had ever in the course of his life undertaken—were but bread and cakes.

"Look, sir," Sancho went on, "there is no enchantment here nor anything of the sort. Through the bars and chinks of that cage I have seen a real lion's claw, and judging by the size of it, the lion that it belongs to is bigger than a mountain."

"Fear, at any rate," said Don Quixote, "will make him look bigger to you than half the world. Retire, Sancho, and leave me, and if I die here, you know our ancient pact: you are to repair to Dulcinea—I say no more."

To this he added other remarks that took away any hope they had that he might not go through with his insane plan. The gentleman in the green-colored greatcoat was of a mind to resist him but saw that he was no match for the knight in the matter of arms. Then, too, it did not seem to him the part of wisdom to fight it out with a madman; for Don Quixote now impressed him as being quite mad in every way. Accordingly, while the knight was repeating his threats to the lionkeeper, Don Diego spurred his mare, Sancho his gray, and the driver his mules, all of them seeking to put as great a distance as possible between themselves and the cart before the lions broke loose.

Sancho already was bewailing his master's death, which he was convinced was bound to come from the lions' claws, and at the same time he cursed his fate and called it an unlucky hour in which he had taken it into his head to serve such a one. But despite his tears and lamentations, he did not leave off thrashing his gray in an effort to leave the cart behind them. When the lionkeeper saw that those who had fled were a good distance away, he once more entreated and warned Don Quixote as he had warned and entreated him before, but the answer he received was that he might save his breath as it would do him no good and he had best hurry and obey. In the space of time that it took the keeper to open the first cage, Don Quixote considered the question as to whether it would be well to give battle on foot or on horseback. He finally decided that he would do better on foot, as he feared that Rocinante would become frightened at sight of the lions; and so, leaping down from his horse, he fixed his lance, braced his buckler, and drew his sword, and then advanced with marvelous daring and great resoluteness until he stood directly in front of the cart, meanwhile commending himself to God with all his heart and then to his lady Dulcinea.

Upon reaching this point, the reader should know, the author of our veracious history indulges in the following exclamatory passage: "O great-souled Don Quixote de la Mancha, thou whose courage is beyond all praise, mirror wherein all the valiant of the world may behold themselves, a new and second Don Manuel de León,[4] once the glory and the honor of Spanish knighthood! With what words shall I relate thy terrifying exploit, how render it credible to the ages that are to come? What eulogies do not belong to thee of right, even though they consist of hyperbole piled upon hyperbole? On foot and singlehanded, intrepid and with greathearted valor, armed but with a sword, and not one of the keen-edged Little Dog make,[5] and with a shield that was not of gleaming and polished steel, thou didst stand and wait for the two fiercest lions that ever the African forests bred! Thy deeds shall be thy praise, O valorous Manchegan; I leave them to speak for thee, since words fail me with which to extol them."

Here the author leaves off his exclamations and resumes the thread of the story.

Seeing Don Quixote posed there before him and perceiving that, unless he wished to incur the bold knight's indignation there was nothing for him to do but release the male lion, the keeper now opened the first cage, and it could be seen at once how extraordinarily big and horribly ugly the beast was. The first thing the recumbent animal did was to turn round, put out a claw, and stretch himself all over. Then he opened his mouth and yawned very slowly, after which he put out a tongue that was nearly two palms in length and with it licked the dust out of his eyes and washed his face. Having done this, he stuck his head outside the cage and gazed about him in all directions. His eyes were now like live coals and his appearance and demeanor were such as to strike terror in temerity itself. But Don Quixote merely stared at him attentively, waiting for him to descend from the cart so that they could come to grips, for the knight was determined to hack the brute to pieces, such was the extent of his unheard-of madness.

The lion, however, proved to be courteous rather than arrogant and was in no mood for childish bravado. After having gazed first in one direction and then in another, as has been said, he turned his back and presented his hind parts to Don Quixote and then very calmly and peaceably lay down and stretched himself out once more in his cage. At this, Don Quixote ordered the keeper to stir him up with a stick in order to irritate him and drive him out.

"That I will not do," the keeper replied, "for if I stir him, I will be the first one he will tear to bits. Be satisfied with what you have already accomplished, Sir Knight, which leaves nothing more to be said on the score of valor, and do not go tempting your fortune a second time. The door was open and the lion could have gone out if he had chosen; since he has not done so up to now, that means he will stay where he is all day long. Your Grace's stoutheartedness has been well established; for no brave fighter, as I see it, is obliged to do more than challenge his enemy and wait for him in the field; his adversary, if he does not come, is the one who is disgraced and the one who awaits him gains the crown of victory."

"That is the truth," said Don Quixote. "Shut the door, my friend, and bear me witness as best you can with regard to what you have seen me do here. I would have you certify: that you opened the door for the lion, that I waited for him and he did not come out, that I continued to wait and still he stayed there, and finally went back and lay down. I am under no further obligation. Away with enchantments, and God uphold the right, the truth, and true chivalry! So close the door, as I have told you, while I signal to the fugitives in order that they who were not present may hear of this exploit from your lips."[6]

The keeper did as he was commanded, and Don Quixote, taking the cloth with which he had dried his face after the rain of curds, fastened it to the point of his lance and began summoning the runaways, who, all in a body with the gentleman in green bringing up the rear,[7] were still fleeing and turning around to look back at every step. Sancho was the first to see the white cloth.

"May they slay me," he said, "if my master hasn't conquered those fierce beasts, for he's calling to us."

They all stopped and made sure that the one who was doing the signaling was indeed Don Quixote, and then, losing some of their fear, they little by little made their way back to a point where they could distinctly hear what the knight was saying. At last they returned to the cart, and as they drew near Don Quixote spoke to the driver.

"You may come back, brother, hitch your mules, and continue your journey. And you, Sancho, may give each of them two gold crowns to recompense them for the delay they have suffered on my account."

"That I will, right enough," said Sancho. "But what has become of the lions? Are they dead or alive?"

The keeper thereupon, in leisurely fashion and in full detail, proceeded to tell them how the encounter had ended, taking pains to stress to the best of his ability the valor displayed by Don Quixote, at sight of whom the lion had been so cowed that he was unwilling to leave his cage, though the door had been left open quite a while. The fellow went on to state that the knight had wanted him to stir the lion up and force him out, but had finally been convinced that this would be tempting God and so, much to his displeasure and against his will, had permitted the door to be closed.

"What do you think of that, Sancho?" asked Don Quixote. "Are there any spells that can withstand true gallantry? The enchanters may take my luck away, but to deprive me of my strength and courage is an impossibility."

Sancho then bestowed the crowns, the driver hitched his mules, and the lionkeeper kissed Don Quixote's hands for the favor received, promising that, when he reached the court, he would relate this brave exploit to the king himself.

"In that case," replied Don Quixote, "if his Majesty by any chance should inquire who it was that performed it, you are to say that it was the Knight of the Lions; for that is the name by which I wish to be known from now on, thus changing, exchanging, altering, and converting the one I have previously borne, that of Knight of the Mournful Countenance; in which respect I am but following the old custom of knights-errant, who changed their names whenever they liked or found it convenient to do so." [8]

With this, the cart continued on its way, and Don Quixote, Sancho, and the gentleman in the green-colored greatcoat likewise resumed their journey. During all this time Don Diego de Miranda had not uttered a word but was wholly taken up with observing what Don Quixote did and listening to what he had to say. The knight impressed him as being a crazy sane man and an insane one on the verge of sanity. The gentleman did not happen to be familiar with the first part of our history, but if he had read it he would have ceased to wonder at such talk and conduct, for he would then have known what kind of madness this was. Remaining as he did in ignorance of his companion's malady, he took him now for a sensible individual and now for a madman, since what Don Quixote said was coherent, elegantly phrased, and to the point, whereas his actions were nonsensical, foolhardy, and downright silly. What greater madness could there be, Don Diego asked himself, than to don a helmet filled with curds and then persuade oneself that enchanters were softening one's cranium? What could be more rashly absurd than to wish to fight lions by sheer strength alone? He was roused from these thoughts, this inward soliloquy, by the sound of Don Quixote's voice.

"Undoubtedly, Señor Don Diego de Miranda, your Grace must take me for a fool and a madman, am I not right? And it would be small wonder if such were the case, seeing that my deeds give evidence of nothing else. But, nevertheless, I would advise your Grace that I am neither so mad nor so lacking in wit as I must appear to you to be. A gaily caparisoned knight giving a fortunate lance thrust to a fierce bull in the middle of a great square makes a pleasing appearance in the eyes of his king. The same is true of a knight clad in shining armor as he paces the lists in front of the ladies in some joyous tournament. It is true of all those knights who, by means of military exercises or what appear to be such, divert and entertain and, if one may say so, honor the courts of princes. But the best showing of all is made by a knight-errant who, traversing deserts and solitudes, crossroads, forests, and mountains, goes seeking dangerous adventures with the intention of bringing them to a happy and successful conclusion, and solely for the purpose of winning a glorious and enduring renown.

"More impressive, I repeat, is the knight-errant succoring a widow in some unpopulated place than a courtly man of arms making love to a damsel in the city. All knights have their special callings: let the courtier wait upon the ladies and lend luster by his liveries to his sovereign's palace; let him nourish impoverished gentlemen with the splendid fare of his table; let him give tourneys and show himself truly great, generous, and magnificent and a good Christian above all, thus fulfilling his particular obligations. But the knight-errant's case is different.

"Let the latter seek out the nooks and corners of the world; let him enter into the most intricate of labyrinths; let him attempt the impossible at every step; let him endure on desolate highlands the burning rays of the midsummer sun and in winter the harsh inclemencies of wind and frost; let no lions inspire him with fear, no monsters frighten him, no dragons terrify him, for to seek them out, attack them, and conquer them all is his chief and legitimate occupation. Accordingly, I whose lot it is to be numbered among the knights-errant cannot fail to attempt anything that appears to me to fall within the scope of my duties, just as I attacked those lions a while ago even though I knew it to be an exceedingly rash thing to do, for that was a matter that directly concerned me.

"For I well know the meaning of valor: namely, a virtue that lies between the two extremes of cowardice on the one hand and temerity on the other. It is, nonetheless, better for the brave man to carry his bravery to the point of rashness than for him to sink into cowardice. Even as it is easier for the prodigal to become a generous man than it is for the miser, so is it easier for the foolhardy to become truly brave than it is for the coward to attain valor. And in this matter of adventures, you may believe me, Señor Don Diego, it is better to lose by a card too many than a card too few,[9] and 'Such and such a knight is temerarious and overbold' sounds better to the ear than 'That knight is timid and a coward.' "

"I must assure you, Señor Don Quixote," replied Don Diego, "that everything your Grace has said and done will stand the test of reason; and it is my opinion that if the laws and ordinances of knight-errantry were to be lost, they would be found again in your Grace's bosom, which is their depository and storehouse. But it is growing late; let us hasten to my village and my home, where your Grace shall rest from your recent exertions; for if the body is not tired the spirit may be, and that sometimes results in bodily fatigue."

"I accept your offer as a great favor and an honor, Señor Don Diego," was the knight's reply. And, by spurring their mounts more than they had up to then, they arrived at the village around two in the afternoon and came to the house that was occupied by Don Diego, whom Don Quixote had dubbed the Knight of the Green-colored Greatcoat.

CHAPTER **XVIII**. *Of what happened to Don Quixote in the castle or house of the Knight of the Green-colored Greatcoat, along with other extraordinary things.*

DON QUIXOTE found Don Diego de Miranda's house to be a rambling one of the village type, with the gentleman's coat of arms in rough-hewn stone over the street door and with the storehouse in the patio and the cellar under the entryway. In the cellar were many wine jars, which, by reason of the fact that they came from El Toboso, served to revive the knight's memories of his enchanted and transformed Dulcinea; and without regard to what he was saying or the others present, he exclaimed:

> *O treasures sweet, now saddening to the sight,*
> *Ye once were pleasing when God willed it so.*[1]

O ye Tobosan jars that have brought to mind my sweetest treasure and my greatest grief!"

Among those who heard this was the student poet, Don Diego's son, who with his mother had come out to welcome the guest. Both mother and son were astonished at the knight's strange appearance as he dismounted from Rocinante and, with a great show of courtesy, asked to kiss the lady's hands.

"Señora," said Don Diego, "I would have you receive with your customary kindness Señor Don Quixote de la Mancha, who stands before you here, a knight-errant and the bravest and wisest that there is in all the world."

The lady, whose name was Doña Cristina, was most courteous and affable in her greetings, and Don Quixote at once, with many polite and suitable protestations of regard, put himself at her service. Practically the same exchange of courtesies occurred between Don Quixote and the student, who, upon hearing the knight speak, took him for a sensible and sharp-witted person.

Here, the author goes on to give a minute description of Don Diego's house, describing everything which such an abode, that of a rich gentleman farmer, might be expected to contain. But the translator of the history appears to have passed over these and other similar details in silence, since they did not fit in with the chief purpose of the chronicle, the value of which lies in its truthfulness rather than in wearisome digressions.

They conducted Don Quixote into one of the rooms, and there Sancho proceeded to remove his master's armor, leaving him in his Walloon breeches and chamois-skin doublet, which was all stained with rust. He wore a falling-band collar after the student fashion, without starch or lace, his half-boots[2] were date-colored and his shoes waxed.[3] His trusty sword hung from a shoulder strap made of sea-wolf's hide, for it is said that he had suffered for many years from a kidney ailment.[4] He then donned a cloak of good gray cloth, but not before he had doused his head and face with five or six buckets of water (there is some difference of opinion as to the exact number)—yet the water still remained whey-colored, thanks to Sancho's greediness in purchasing those damnable curds that had made his master's face so white.[5]

Attired in the manner described and with a gallant and sprightly air, Don Quixote now entered another room, where the student was waiting to entertain him while the table was being laid; for Doña Cristina wished to show that she possessed the means and the ability to set a proper board for those who came to her house, and especially so distinguished a guest as this one. While Don Quixote was taking off his armor, Don Lorenzo (for that was the name of Don Diego's son) had put a question to his father.

"Sir," he had asked, "what are we to make of this gentleman whom you have brought home with you? My mother and I are quite astonished by his name, his appearance, and his calling himself a knight-errant."

"I do not know what to say in answer to that, my son," Don Diego replied. "I can only tell you that I have seen him do things that lead one to believe he is the greatest madman in the world, yet his conversation is so sensible that it belies and causes one to forget his actions. But speak to him yourself and sound him out.[6] You are a discerning young man; form your own opinion, then, as to how wise or foolish he may be; although, to tell you the truth, I am inclined to regard him as insane rather than sane."

Don Lorenzo had then gone in to converse with Don Quixote, as we have said, and in the course of their talk the knight remarked to him, "Your Grace's father, Señor Don Diego de Miranda, has told me of your rare ability and intellectual capacity, and, what interests me most of all, has informed me that you are a great poet."

"A poet I may be," replied Don Lorenzo, "but by no means a great one. The truth is, I am rather fond of poetry and of reading the good poets, but I do not deserve the title which my father has given me."

"I like your humility," said Don Quixote, "for there is no poet who is not arrogant and who does not think he is the greatest there is."

"There is no rule without an exception," Don Lorenzo reminded him. "There may be some who are poets without knowing it."

"Very few," was Don Quixote's answer. "But tell me, what are those verses that your Grace is working on at the present time, and which, according to your father, have rendered you rather restless and distracted? If it is a matter of glosses, I know something about that sort of thing and should enjoy hearing them. If by chance they are for some literary tournament, your Grace should strive to carry off the second prize, for the first is always awarded as a favor to someone of high rank, the second goes to the one who merits first place, and thus the third is in reality second, while the first, by this reckoning, would be third, after the manner of the licentiate degrees that are conferred in the universities. But for all of that, the first prize carries with it a great distinction."[7]

"Up to now," Don Lorenzo thought to himself, "I cannot take you for a madman; but let's go on." And, speaking aloud, he said, "It would appear that your Grace has attended the schools; what branches have you studied?"

"Knight-errantry," said Don Quixote, "which is the equal of poetry and even a fraction of an inch or so above it."

"That," said the young man, "is a branch of learning with which I am unfamiliar. This is the first time I have heard of it."

"It is a discipline," the knight went on to explain, "that comprises within itself all or most of the others in existence. For the one who professes it has to be skilled in jurisprudence; he must be versed in the laws of justice and equity in order to be able to give each that which is his by right. He must be a theologian in order that, whenever it is asked of him, he may give a clear and logical reason for his Christian faith. He must be a physician, and above all a herbalist, so that when he finds himself in a desert or some desolate spot he will know what plants possess the property of healing wounds, for a knight-errant cannot be looking at every step for someone to treat his injuries. He must be an astronomer in order that he may know from the stars how far the night has advanced, what part of the world he is in, and in what clime. He must have a knowledge of mathematics, for he will have need of it at every turn.

"But," continued Don Quixote, "leaving aside the fact that he should be adorned with all the theological and cardinal virtues, and coming down to details, I would say that he must be able to swim like Nicolao the Fish, as the story has it.[8] He must know how to shoe a horse and repair his saddle and his bridle. And to return to higher matters, he must keep faith with God and with his lady. He must be chaste in his thoughts, decorous in words, and must show himself generous in good works, valiant in his deeds, long-suffering under hardships, charitable toward the needy. And, lastly, he must uphold the truth though it cost him his life to defend it.

"All these qualities, great and small," he concluded, "go to make up a good knight-errant. Judge, then, Señor Don Lorenzo, as to whether this be a contemptible science which the knight-errant has to study, learn, and practice, or whether it may not rather be compared to the most elevated branches that are taught in the schools."

"If that is so," replied Don Lorenzo, "I would say that this science excels all the others."

"If what is so?" inquired Don Quixote.

"What I mean," Don Lorenzo continued, "is that I doubt that there have been or are today any knights-errant, and adorned with all those virtues."

"What I am about to say now," remarked Don Quixote, "I have said many times before. The majority of people in this world are of the opinion that knights-errant never existed; and it is my belief that if Heaven does not miraculously reveal the truth to them, by showing them that there once were such knights and that they are still to be met with today, then all one's labors are in vain, as experience has many times taught me. I do not care to take the time here to disabuse your Grace of this error which you share with so many others. Rather, I mean to pray Heaven to deliver you from it and to make clear to you how profit-able and necessary to the world knights-errant have been in ages past, and how useful they would be at the present time if the custom were still maintained. But today, owing to the state of sin in which we live, idle-ness and sloth, gluttony and luxury, rule triumphant."

"Now our guest is breaking out on us," thought Don Lorenzo; "but all the same, he is a most unusual kind of madman, and I'd be a dull-witted fool myself if I did not admit it."

At this point they were called to dinner and their conversation came to an end. Don Diego took occasion to ask his son what he had made out regarding their guest's state of mind.

"His madness," replied the young man, "is a scrawl, and all the doctors and clever scribes in the world would not be able to decipher it. He is a streaked madman, full of lucid intervals."

They then sat down at the table, and the meal fully bore out what Diego had said upon the highway concerning his manner of entertaining those whom he invited to his home. It was well served, abundant, and appetizing; but what pleased Don Quixote more than anything else was the marvelous silence that prevailed throughout the house, a silence which was like that of a Carthusian monastery. When the cloth had finally been removed and grace had been said and they had washed their hands, Don Quixote earnestly requested Don Lorenzo to recite the verses that were intended for the literary tournament. To this the youth replied that, inasmuch as he did not wish to appear to be one of those poets who when asked to read their verses refuse to do so but who vomit them forth when they are not asked,[9] he would consent.

"I will let you hear my gloss," he said; "but I do not expect it to win any prize, for I composed it solely to exercise my ingenuity."

"A friend of mine," observed Don Quixote, "a man of intelligence, is of the opinion that the writing of poetic glosses is a waste of energy, and the reason he gave me was this: that the gloss almost never can come up to the text but very often or most of the time goes beyond the meaning and intention of the original lines. And, moreover, he added, the rules govern-ing this form of composition are too strict; they do not permit of inter-rogations or any 'said he' or 'I will say'; they do not allow verbs to be turned into nouns or the general sense and construction of the passage to be altered, along with other restrictions by which those who write glosses are bound, as your Grace must know."

"Really, Señor Don Quixote," said Don Lorenzo, "I wish I could trip your Grace up now and then, but I cannot, for you slip through my fingers like an eel."

"I do not understand," said Don Quixote, "what your Grace means by that."

"I will explain myself later," replied the young man, "but for the present I would have your Grace listen attentively to the original verses and the gloss.[10] They run like this:

> *Oh, could my 'was' an 'is' become,*
> *I'd wait no more for 'it shall be';*
> *or could I the future now but see,*
> *and not this present, dour and glum.*

GLOSS

> *All things must pass away at last,*
> *and so, the blessing that was mine,*
> *fair Fortune's gift, it also pass'd,*
> *ne'er to return, though I repine;*
> *my skies are wholly overcast.*
> *Long hast thou seen me at thy feet,*
> *O Fortune fickle, Fortune fleet;*
> *but make me happy once again*
> *and I'd forget my present pain,*
> *could but my 'was' and 'is' now meet.*

> *No other pleasure do I crave,*
> *no other palm or warrior's prize,*
> *such triumph as befits the brave;*
> *all that I ask: those happier skies*
> *to which my memory is a slave.*
> *Would'st thou but give this gift to me,*
> *O Fortune, then perchance I'd see*
> *this fire of mine—O priceless boon!—*
> *consume me less, and if 'twere soon,*
> *I'd wait no more for 'it shall be.'*

> *Impossible the thing I ask,*
> *since Time, once gone, none can recall;*
> *for to accomplish such a task,*
> *no power on earth but is too small.*

No more beneath those skies I'll bask.
Swift doth he come and swiftly flee,
nor doth return, light-footed he!
and well I know it is not right
to seek to stay Time in his flight;
turn past to present—futile plea!

My life is anxious, filled with gloom;
and living thus 'twixt hope and fear,
is naught but death's familiar doom;
better to lie upon my bier
and seek the door to pain's dark room.
It seemeth me, it would be sweet
to end it now, thus life to cheat;
but living long and living longer,
the fear within grows ever stronger
of that dread 'shall be' I must greet."

As Don Lorenzo finished reading his gloss, Don Quixote rose to his feet and seized the young man's right hand. Raising his voice until he was almost shouting, he said, "By the highest heavens, O noble youth, you are the best poet on the face of the earth and ought to be crowned with laurel, not by Cyprus or by Gaeta, as a certain rhymester—Heaven forgive him!—said,[11] but by the Academies of Athens, if they were still in existence, and by those that now flourish at Paris, Bologna, and Salamanca. If the judges rob you of the first prize, may Phoebus, please Heaven, pierce them with his arrows, and may the Muses never cross the thresholds of their houses! Read me, sir, if you will, some of your verses in other forms, for I desire to have a complete impression of your admirable talent."

Is there any need to say that Don Lorenzo enjoyed hearing himself praised by Don Quixote even though he looked upon him as a madman? O power of flattery, how broad and far-reaching are the bounds of your pleasant jurisdiction! The youth proved the truth of this and acceded to the knight's request by reading the following sonnet, based upon the story or fable of Pyramus and Thisbe:

SONNET

"The beauteous maiden now bursts through the wall,
she who in Pyramus's gallant breast
hath left a gaping wound. Love cannot rest

but, leaving Cyprus, comes to see it all.
Silence there speaks, there is no word or call;
the language of the heart alone is best
for the fulfillment of Love's fond behest,
and he all obstacles doth soon forestall.
Desire grows, rashly the amorous maid,
seeking her pleasure, hastens to her death.
Ah, what a tale is here for hearts that strive!
Two lovers dying by a single blade
to find a common grave, and yet the breath
of memory doth keep them still alive." [12]

"Blessed be God!" cried Don Quixote when he had heard this composition. "Thank Him that among the infinite number of consumed poets [13] I have found one consummate bard, in your person, my dear sir; for the skill you display in the sonnet you have just read is enough to convince me of that."

For four days Don Quixote was entertained most royally in Don Diego's house, at the end of which time he asked permission to take his departure, saying that while he was deeply grateful for the kind and courteous treatment he had received, he did not think it a good thing for a knight-errant to spend many hours taking his ease and being entertained if he meant to fulfill the duties of his calling by seeking adventures, which he had been told were plentiful around there. He added that he intended to pass the time in those parts until the day came for the tournament at Saragossa, which was really his destination. Meanwhile, he planned to make his way into the Cave of Montesinos [14] of which so many marvelous stories had been told in that region, and he also meant to look into the true source and headwaters of the seven lakes that are commonly known as the Lakes of Ruidera.

Don Diego and his son assured their guest that this was a highly laudable enterprise, and they urged that he take with him out of their house and possessions anything that he might desire, as they could do no less in view of his personal worth and the honorable profession that he followed. The day set for his departure came at last, a happy one for Don Quixote but sad and bitter for Sancho Panza, who was making out very nicely with all the good things that Don Diego's household afforded and was loath to go back to the hunger of forest and desert and the short rations of his ill-stocked saddlebag, which he now proceeded to fill and stuff with whatever seemed to him most necessary.

As they went to leave, Don Quixote turned to Don Lorenzo. "I do not know," he said, "if I have told you this before or not, but, if so, I will tell you again: that if you wish to spare yourself toil and trouble in attaining the inaccessible summit of the temple of fame, you have but to turn aside from the somewhat narrow path of poetry and take the still narrower one of knight-errantry, but wide enough for all of that to make you an emperor in the twinkling of an eye."

With these words Don Quixote closed the case so far as convicting himself of madness was concerned, and this impression was still further confirmed when he went on to say, "God knows, Señor Don Lorenzo, I should like to have taken you along with me,[15] in order to teach you how to spare the humble and trample the proud under foot,[16] these being virtues that go with my profession; but since neither your youth nor your praiseworthy pursuits will admit of this, I shall content myself with advising your Grace that you may become a famous poet provided you are guided more by the opinion of others than by your own; for there is no father or mother whose children look ugly to them, and this illusion is even more common with respect to the children of our brain."

Once more father and son marveled at the mixture of nonsense and wisdom that Don Quixote talked, as well as at the pertinacity he displayed in going through with his unfortunate adventures in spite of everything, for such was the end and aim of his desires. And so, with a fresh exchange of courtesies and offers of service and with the kind permission of the lady of the castle,[17] Don Quixote and Sancho took their leave, the one mounted on Rocinante, the other on his donkey.

CHAPTER **XIX**. *Wherein is related the adventure of the enamored shepherd, with other truly amusing incidents.*

DON QUIXOTE had gone some little way from Don Diego's village when he encountered what appeared to be a couple of priests or students accompanied by a couple of peasants, the party being mounted upon four animals of the ass variety. One of the students carried, wrapped up in a piece of buckram that served as a portmanteau, a small supply of linen [1] and two pairs of coarse ribbed stockings,[2] as nearly as could be made out. The other had only a pair of fencing foils with their buttons. As for the peasants, they were laden down with other things and were apparently taking them back to their village from some large city where they had purchased them.

Both the students and the peasants were as astonished as all persons were when they beheld Don Quixote for the first time, and were consumed with curiosity to know who this man was who looked so different from other men. The knight greeted them and, upon learning that they were going in the same direction as himself, offered them his company, begging them, however, to slacken their pace a bit as their young she-asses traveled faster than his horse. And then, to oblige them, he told them in a few words who he was and acquainted them with his calling and profession, that of a knight-errant who went seeking adventures in all parts of the world. He informed them that his right name was Don Quixote de la Mancha but that he was known as the Knight of the Lions. All of which was Greek, or at any rate gibberish, to the peasants but not to the students, who at once realized that Don Quixote must be weak in the head but who nonetheless looked upon him with admiration and respect.

"If, Sir Knight," one of them said to him, "your Grace is not bound for any place in particular, seeing that such is not the custom of knights-errant, you would do well to come with us and see one of the finest and richest weddings that up to this day has ever been celebrated in La Mancha or for many miles around."

Don Quixote thereupon inquired if it was the marriage of some prince that he was describing in such terms as these.

"No," replied the student, "it is that of a farmer and a farmer's daughter. He is the richest man in all this region, and she the fairest maid that ever was seen; and the ceremony, which is to be held in a meadow adjoining the town where the bride lives, is to be marked by a pomp that is out of the ordinary. By reason of her surpassing beauty, the bride is known as Quiteria the Fair, and the bridegroom as Camacho the Rich. She is eighteen years of age and he is twenty-two, and they are well matched, although certain prying ones, who know all the pedigrees in the world by heart, will tell you that the beauteous Quiteria's family tree is better than Camacho's. That, however, is something that is readily overlooked these days, for wealth can solder many a crack.

"However this may be," the student continued, "this man Camacho is one who spares no expense, and he has taken it into his head to screen and roof the entire meadow with branches, in such a manner that the sun, if it wishes to visit the green grass with which the ground is covered, will have a hard time doing so. There are also to be dances, not only sword-dances but bell-dances as well; for in his town there are some who are very adept at ringing and jingling the chimes. I shall not speak of the clog-dancers,[3] except to say that they will be there in large numbers. But none of the things I have mentioned nor many others I have neglected to mention will do more to make this a memorable occasion than will the actions of the despairing Basilio, if he behaves as I expect him to. This Basilio is a youth of the same village as Quiteria and lives next door to her parents. Love accordingly took advantage of this fact to revive for the world the forgotten romance of Pyramus and Thisbe; for Basilio became enamored of Quiteria from his earliest years, and she in turn gave him innumerable signs of affection, until the relationship between the two of them came to be the talk of the town.

"As the pair grew up, Quiteria's father decided to forbid Basilio the run of the house which the lad had previously enjoyed, and by way of relieving himself of fear and suspicion, he ordered his daughter to marry the wealthy Camacho, since it did not seem well for her to wed Basilio, whose fortune did not equal his native gifts; for to tell the truth without prejudice, he is the cleverest young fellow that we have, expert at throwing the bar, the finest of wrestlers, and a great ball player; he runs like a deer, leaps better than a goat, and bowls over the ninepins as if by magic; he sings like a lark and can make a guitar speak, and, above all, he handles a sword with the best of them."

"By reason of those accomplishments alone," remarked Don Quixote, "the lad deserves to wed not merely the fair Quiteria, but Queen Guinevere herself, if she were alive today, and this in spite of Lancelot and all those who might try to prevent it."

"Tell that to my wife," said Sancho Panza, who up to then had been listening in silence, "for she insists that each one should marry his equal, according to the old saying, 'Every ewe to her mate.'[4] I'd like to see the good Basilio—for I'm taking a liking to him already—marry this lady Quiteria, and eternal blessings—no, I mean just the opposite—on all those that would keep true lovers apart."

"If all those who love each other were to marry," said Don Quixote, "that would deprive parents of the right to decide with whom and when their children should wed.[5] If it were left to daughters to choose their husbands, one would take her father's servant and another some stranger she had seen going down the street who had impressed her as being gallant and haughty, even though he might in reality be nothing more than a rake and a bully. For love and natural inclination readily blind those eyes of the mind that are so necessary in making life's important decisions; and when it comes to choosing a mate there is an especial danger of going astray, and great caution and the grace of Heaven are needed if one is to be guided aright. Before one sets out upon a long journey, he will, if he is prudent, seek some dependable and agreeable companion to accompany him. Why, then, should he not do the same who must travel all his life long toward the destination of death and whose companion must be ever with him, in the bed, at table, wherever he may go, which is the relation of wife to husband?

"The companionship of one's own wife," Don Quixote went on, "is not an article of merchandise that, once bought, may be returned, bartered, or exchanged; for this is an unbreakable bond that lasts as long as life endures, a noose that, once placed upon the neck, turns into a Gordian knot which cannot be undone until death comes to cut it. I could say much more upon this subject if I were not so anxious to hear whether or not the Señor Licentiate has more to tell us regarding the story of Basilio."

To this, the student, bachelor, or, as Don Quixote had called him, the licentiate made the following reply:

"I have told you all there is, except that from the moment Basilio learned that the fair Quiteria was to wed Camacho the Rich, he was never again seen to smile or heard to utter a rational word but has remained sad and pensive and goes about talking to himself in a way that clearly shows he has lost his senses. He eats little and sleeps little. His diet is fruits, and as for sleep, if he sleeps at all, it is in the open, upon the hard earth like a brute beast. From time to time he will look up at the heavens, and again he will fasten his gaze upon the ground, with such an air of abstraction that he appears to be no more than a clothed statue whose draperies are stirred by the wind. In short, he gives evidence of being so heart-stricken that all of us who know him fear that when the fair Quiteria says 'yes' tomorrow, it will be his death sentence."

"God will do better than that," said Sancho. "God gives the wound and He will give the medicine.⁶ No one knows what is to come; from now until tomorrow is a long time, and at any hour or minute the house may fall. I have seen it rain while the sun was shining. Many a one goes to bed healthy at night and the next day cannot move. Tell me one thing: can anyone boast that he has driven a spoke into fortune's wheel? No, certainly not; and between a woman's 'yes' and her 'no' I wouldn't venture to put a pinpoint, for it couldn't be done. Tell me that Quiteria loves Basilio with all her heart, and I'll give him a bag of good luck; for love, so I've heard folks say, looks through spectacles that make copper seem gold, poverty riches, and a pair of bleary eyes like a couple of pearls."

"What are you trying to get at, Sancho, curses on you?" said Don Quixote. "When you start stringing together proverbs and sayings, Judas himself couldn't stop you, and I wish he would carry you off. Tell me, stupid creature, what do you know of spokes or wheels or anything else?"

"Oh," replied Sancho, "if you don't understand me, then it's no wonder that my sayings are taken for nonsense. But no matter; I understand myself, and I know there is not much foolishness in what I've just said. The trouble is, my master, your Grace is too crickety of everything I say and do."

"*Critical,* you mean," said Don Quixote, "not *crickety,* you corrupter of good language, may God confound you!"

"Don't be cross with me, your Grace. You know that I was not brought up at court, nor have I studied at Salamanca, that I should know whether I am adding or dropping a letter now and then. Why, God help me, it's not fair to expect a man from Sayago to speak like one from Toledo,[7] and there are Toledans who do not make so good a job of it when it comes to polished talk."

"That is true," said the licentiate; "those that are brought up in the Tanneries and the Zocodover[8] cannot talk as well as those that spend practically the entire day in the Cathedral cloisters,[9] yet they are all Toledans. For language that is pure, correct, clear, and refined one must look to men of courtly taste, even though they may have been born in Majadahonda.[10] I speak of *taste,* for there are many who do not possess that quality, yet it is the grammar of good speech when accompanied by practice. I, gentlemen, for my sins,[11] have studied canon law at Salamanca and pride myself somewhat on being able to express my meaning plainly and intelligibly."

"If you did not pride yourself more on being able to handle those foils you carry than you do on skill with your tongue," the other student put in, "you would have been first among the licentiates instead of at the tail end as you were."

"See here, bachelor," replied the licentiate, "you are as mistaken as can be if you think that dexterity with the sword is a vain accomplishment."

"It is no mere opinion on my part," said Corchuelo (for that was the other student's name),[12] "but the established truth. If you would have me prove it to you by experience, this is your opportunity. You have swords with you, and I have a steady hand and a strong right arm; and aided by my courage, of which I have not a little, they will force you to confess that I am in the right. Get down and look to your stance, your circles, and your angles; make the most of your science, for I hope to make you see stars at midday with my rude and recently acquired swordsmanship, in which, next to God, I put my trust that the man is yet to be born who can compel me to turn my back and whom I cannot make give ground."

"As to whether you turn your back or not is no concern of mine," [13] replied the one who prided himself on his skill, "for it well may be that where you set your foot down for the first time, there they will dig your grave; that is to say, you will be lying there dead as a result of your contempt for the art of fencing."

"We shall see as to that," said Corchuelo. And, dismounting with great alacrity and in a towering rage, he drew one of the swords which the licentiate carried.

At that instant Don Quixote spoke up. "No," he said, "that is not the way it is to be. I propose to act as fencing master here and judge this much debated question." With these words he too dismounted and, lance in hand, took up his position in the middle of the road just as the licentiate with easy grace of feet and body bore down upon Corchuelo, who similarly advanced to meet his adversary with fire darting from his eyes, as the saying goes. Meanwhile, the two peasants who accompanied the students, sitting there upon their donkeys, provided the audience for the tragedy. The slashes, thrusts, down-strokes, back-strokes, and double-handed blows that Corchuelo dealt came thicker than liver [14] or hail. He attacked like a lion whose temper has been roused, but only to meet with a tap on the mouth from the button of the licentiate's sword that stopped him short in the middle of his furious onslaught and forced him to kiss the blade as if it had been a relic, though not with that degree of devotion that ought to be, and commonly is, shown to relics.

To make a long story short, the licentiate tore off, one by one, all the buttons of a short cassock which Corchuelo wore and ripped the skirt into shreds until it looked like a cuttlefish's tail. Twice he knocked off his adversary's hat and wore him out to such an extent that at last, in despair, anger, and rage, the bachelor seized his sword by the hilt and sent it sailing through the air with such force that one of the peasants, who happened to be a notary and who went after it, later made a deposition to the effect that it had landed nearly three quarters of a league away,[15] a statement which serves, and has served, to show how very true it is that brute strength is overcome by skill.

Corchuelo now sat down, for he was exhausted, and at this point Sancho came up to him.

"Upon my word, Señor Bachelor," he said, "if your Grace will take my advice, you won't challenge anyone to a fencing match from now on but will only wrestle or toss the bar. You are young and have the strength for that sort of thing, but I have heard it said that these experts,[16] as they call them, can run the point of a sword though the eye of a needle."

"I am satisfied," replied Corchuelo, "to have fallen off my donkey,[17] and am glad that experience has shown me how far I was from the truth."

Getting to his feet, he embraced the licentiate, and they were as good friends as they had been before. Not caring to wait for the notary who had gone after the sword, since it appeared that it would take him some little while, they then decided to ride on in order that they might arrive in good time at the village where Quiteria lived, of which they all were natives.[18] For the balance of their journey the licentiate held forth on the advantages of the art of swordsmanship, so convincingly and with so many mathematical proofs and demonstrations that every man of them was persuaded of the excellence of this science and Corchuelo gave up the opinion he had so stubbornly held.

Night had fallen, but before they reached the town it appeared to all of them as though the sky were filled with numberless gleaming stars. At the same time they could hear the mingled and pleasing notes that came from various musical instruments such as flutes, tabors, psalteries, rustic pipes, tambourines, and timbrels. And as they came nearer they perceived that the trees of an arcade of branches that had been erected at the entrance to the village [19] were all filled with lights which were motionless in the gentle breeze then blowing that did not even stir the leaves. It was the musicians who were providing the merriment for the wedding party as they went in little groups through the pleasant grounds, some of them dancing, others singing, and all of them playing upon one or another of the instruments mentioned. In brief, it seemed as if mirth were running wild over the meadow and happiness were gamboling there.

Many other persons were occupied in raising platforms from which people might watch the performances and dances that were to be given there the following day by way of solemnizing the marriage of the rich Camacho and the obsequies of Basilio. Don Quixote was unwilling to enter the village, although the peasant [20] and the bachelor urged him to do so. The excuse he gave, an all-sufficient one as he saw it, was that it was the custom of knights-errant to sleep in the fields and forests rather than in towns, even though the shelter offered them might be a gilded roof. He accordingly turned off the road a little way, much to the displeasure of Sancho, who remembered the good lodgings he had had in Don Diego's castle or house.

CHAPTER XX. *Wherein is contained an account of the wedding of Camacho the Rich* [1] *and of what happened to Basilio the Poor.*

SCARCELY had the fair Aurora given the glowing Phoebus an opportunity to dry the liquid pearls upon her golden locks with the warmth of his rays when Don Quixote, shaking off all sloth from his limbs, rose to his feet and called to his squire Sancho, who was still snoring. As he stood gazing down upon him and before awakening him, the knight uttered the following soliloquy:

"Blessed art thou above all those upon the face of the earth, seeing that, without envying or being envied by any person, thou canst sleep so calmly, with no enchanters or spells to trouble or alarm thee! Thou sleepest,[2] I repeat, and I will say it a hundred times, without any jealous thoughts of thy lady to keep thee awake, with no concern as to how thou art going to pay the debts thou owest or provide food on the morrow for thyself and thy needy little family. Ambition doth not disturb thee nor this world's empty show; thou thinkest only of that beast of thine, having placed upon my shoulders the burden of thine own support, that counterweight that nature and custom have decreed masters should bear. The servant sleeps and the master keeps watch, thinking how he is to feed him, improve his lot, and do him favors. When the sky turns brazen and withholds from the earth its fitting dew, it is the master not the servant who is distressed, it is he who suffers, since he it is who must support amid sterility and hunger the one who hath served him faithfully in fertility and abundance."

To all this Sancho made no reply, for the very good reason that he was asleep, nor would he have awaked as quickly as he did if Don Quixote had not prodded him with the butt of his lance. He finally did rouse himself, however, sleepy-eyed and lazy, and turned his face around in all directions.

"If I am not mistaken," he said, "there is a steam and smell coming from around that arcade that is more like that of broiled rashers than it is like jonquils [3] or thyme. Faith, and a wedding that begins with such a smell ought to be all right; there should be plenty to eat."

"That will be enough from you, glutton," said Don Quixote. "Come, we are going to those nuptials to see what the rejected suitor, Basilio, will do."

"Let him do what he likes," replied Sancho. "He's a poor man, and yet he is bent on marrying Quiteria. He hasn't a cuarto [4] to his name, and yet he'd put his head in the clouds to look for a bride. Is that all he wants? My word, master, but I think the poor should be content with what comes their way and not go looking for tidbits at the bottom of the sea! [5] I will bet you an arm that Camacho could bury Basilio under the reales that he has; and if this is so, as it must be, then Quiteria would be a fool to give up the jewels and finery that Camacho must have given her (for he is well able to give them to her) and choose instead Basilio's bar-throwing and sword-juggling. For a good toss of the bar or a neat feint with the sword they won't give you a pint of wine at the tavern. Let Count Dirlos [6] have those graces and accomplishments that are not salable,[7] but when the same graces go with someone who has plenty of money, then so help me if they're not as pretty as can be. Upon a good foundation you can raise a good building, and the best foundation in the world is cash."

"For God's sake, Sancho," Don Quixote broke in, "have done with your harangue; for I am of the opinion that if you were to be permitted to finish what you are every minute beginning, you would never have time for sleeping but would waste it all in talking."

"If your Grace had a good memory," said Sancho, "you would recall that one of the articles of our agreement before we left home this last time was that I was to be allowed to say whatever I wanted to, so long as it was not against my neighbor or disrespectful to you, and it seems to me I've kept my part of the bargain so far as that article is concerned."

"I do not recall any such article as that," said Don Quixote, "and even if what you say is true, I want you to be quiet and come along; for those instruments that we heard last night are beginning to make the valleys ring with merriment once more, and the nuptials will undoubtedly be celebrated in the cool of the morning and not in the heat of the day."

Sancho did as his master had commanded, and when he had saddled Rocinante and placed the saddlebag upon his gray, the two of them mounted and, at a slow pace, made their way into the arcade. The first thing that met Sancho's gaze was a steer spitted entire upon an elm tree, and upon the fire for roasting it was a small mountain of logs, while round about were six stew-pots, but not fashioned like ordinary ones, for they were in reality half-sized wine jars and each of them big enough to hold a slaughterhouse. These pots swallowed up and concealed in their insides whole sheep as if they had been pigeons; and there was a countless number of hares, already skinned, and plucked hens, which had been hung up on the trees until the time came for burying them in the pots, and a multitude of birds and much game of various sorts had similarly been suspended from the boughs so that the air might keep them cool.

Sancho counted more than sixty wine bags, each holding more than two arrobas [8] and all of them, as later became evident, filled with the best of vintages. There were stacks of the whitest bread, resembling piles of wheat on the threshing floor, and a wall of cheeses arranged like a latticed brickwork. The oil was contained in two caldrons larger than those in a dyer's shop and was used for frying fritters, which when done were taken out with two powerful shovels and dropped into another caldron, of prepared honey, that stood near by. There were more than fifty cooks altogether, male and female, and all were neat-appearing, busy, and cheerful. Sewed inside the steer's big belly, twelve delicate little suckling pigs gave it flavor and tenderness. The various kinds of spices seemed to have been bought not by the pound but by the arroba, and all of them were open to view in a huge chest. In a few words, it was a country-style wedding but with enough provisions to feed an army.

Sancho Panza looked everything over, studied it closely, and was delighted with what he saw. It was the stew-pots first of all that completely won his affections, and he would most gladly have helped himself to a fair-sized dish of their contents. Then the wine bags claimed his attention, and, lastly, the fruit of the frying pan, if such pompous caldrons as those could be termed frying pans. Finally, unable to bear it or to control himself any longer, he went up to one of the bustling cooks and politely but hungrily begged permission to dip a piece of bread in one of the pots.

"Brother," the cook replied, "this is not a day when hunger has any rights here, thanks to the rich Camacho. Get down and look about for a ladle and skim off a hen or two, and much good may it do you."

"I don't see any," said Sancho.

"Wait a minute," said the cook. "Sinner that I am, how helpless you are!" And taking a pail he dipped it into one of the jars and brought up three hens and a couple of geese. "Eat my friend, and break your fast on these skimmings until dinnertime comes."

"But I have no place to put it," said Sancho.

"Then," replied the cook, "take spoon and all and thank Camacho and his happiness for it."

While Sancho was thus engaged, Don Quixote was watching a group of about a dozen peasants who had entered the enclosure from one end. They were mounted upon very handsome mares fitted out with rich and showy field trappings and many bells, and all of them were attired in their holiday best. In regular file, they ran their mounts up and down the meadow, not once but a number of times, shouting jubilantly, "Long live Camacho and Quiteria, he as rich as she is fair, and she the fairest in the world!"

"Quite evidently," thought Don Quixote, "they have not seen my Dulcinea del Toboso, or they would be a little more restrained in their praise of that Quiteria of theirs."

Shortly afterward many and varied sets of dancers made their entrance from different sides of the arcade. Among them was a band of sword-dancers, made up of some twenty-four lads of gallant and dashing mien, all of them clad in the finest and whitest of linen and wearing fine silk kerchiefs embroidered in various hues. One of those upon the mares inquired of the sprightly youth who led the group if any of the dancers had been wounded.

"Not as yet, thank God," was the reply. "We are all sound and whole." And with this he and his companions began to execute any number of complicated maneuvers, with so many evolutions and such skill that, although Don Quixote was used to witnessing such dances, he thought he had never seen any to equal this. He also was pleased by another group that came in, consisting of very beautiful young girls, apparently between the ages of fourteen and eighteen. They had on dresses of palm-leaf green and some of them had their hair braided while others wore it loose-flowing, but their locks in every case were of a golden shade that rivaled the sun, and their heads were decked with garlands of jessamine, roses, amaranth, and honeysuckle. They were led by a venerable old man and an aged matron who, however, were more active and nimble than might have been expected of them, considering their years. The maidens were accompanied by the notes of a Zamora bagpipe, and, with modest gaze and light-treading feet, they proved to be the very best of dancers.

The next dance was an artistic one, of the sort known as "talking dances." It was performed by eight nymphs. There were two rows of them, one being headed by Cupid, the other by Worldly Wealth.[9] The winged god of love carried his bow and arrows and his quiver, while the other figure was richly attired in gold and silk of many colors. On the back of each of Cupid's followers was a white parchment with the bearer's name written upon it in large letters. Poetry was the first one's name, the second was Wit, the third one Birth, and the fourth Valor. Worldly Wealth's attendants were similarly identified, the first being Liberality, the second Bounty, the third Treasure, and the fourth Pacific Possession. The nymphs were preceded by a wooden castle drawn by four savages appareled in ivy and green-dyed hemp [10] and looking so lifelike that Sancho was almost frightened by them. On the front and each of the other sides of the structure was the inscription: "Castle of Wise Discretion." Accompanying this group were four skillful musicians playing upon the tabor and the flute, and Cupid thereupon began his dance. Having executed a couple of turns, he raised his eyes and drew his bow against a maiden who stood upon the battlements of the castle, addressing her in this manner:

> "*The God of love behold in me,*
> *mighty on land and in the air,*
> *and on the broad and tossing sea;*
> *great is my power everywhere,*
> *e'en though in Hell's dread pit it be.*
> *Fear is a thing I never knew,*
> *all that I wish must needs come true,*
> *howe'er impossible it seem;*
> *for my will and word are still supreme,*
> *I command, enjoin, forbid, subdue.*"

Having recited the foregoing stanza, he let fly an arrow at the top of the castle and retired. Worldly Wealth then performed a figure or two and, when the tabors had ceased, spoke as follows:

> *"More powerful I than Love's fair face,*
> *though Love himself is now my guide,*
> *for I am of the finest race*
> *that on this earth did e'er abide,*
> *far famed and great in every place.*
>   *Wealth is my name, I bring delight,*
> *but few know how to use me right,*
> *and to do without me is harder still.*
> *Such as I am, I bend my will*
> *To serve you ever, day and night."*

As Worldly Wealth stepped back, Poetry came forward and, having done the customary figures, gazed up at the maid on the battlements and recited these verses:

> *"With many a fancy and conceit,*
> *that charming goddess, Poesy,*
> *in measures lofty and discreet,*
> *lady, her soul doth send to thee,*
> *wrapped in a myriad sonnets neat.*
>   *Oh, do not let me importune;*
> *but accept my homage, and thou right soon,*
> *the envy of a host of eyes,*
> *shalt be borne upward to the skies,*
> *beyond the very rim of the moon."*

Poetry then withdrew and, from the side of Worldly Wealth, Liberality advanced and proceeded to declaim:

> *"What men call liberality*
> *consists in giving without excess:*
> *no weak-willed prodigality;*
> *no grudging hand or miserliness:*
> *such the giver's law in totality.*
>   *Howe'er, by way of enriching thee,*
> *I today shall more prodigal be;*
> *for though 'tis a vice, 'tis a goodly one*
> *when from loving heart 'tis done,*
> *which in the giving itself doth see."*

In this manner all the figures from the two groups came forward and retired, each executing her steps and repeating her verses, some of which were polished while others were mere burlesque; but although Don

Quixote had an exceptional memory, the stanzas quoted are all that he was able to recall. The dancers now mingled together, weaving in and out with an easy and pleasing grace. As Cupid went past the castle he let fly his darts, and Worldly Wealth broke gilded pellets against it.

Finally, after they had danced a good while, Worldly Wealth took out a large purse, made of the skin of a striped cat and seemingly full of money, and hurled it at the castle with such force that the walls fell apart and came tumbling down, leaving the maiden exposed and with no protection whatsoever; following which, he and his followers advanced and cast a huge gold chain about the damsel's neck as if to subdue her and take her captive. Seeing this, Cupid and his band made a show of freeing her, all to the accompaniment of tabors and in the form of a dance. It was the savages who made peace between them and with great dexterity set the walls of the castle up once more. The maiden then took her place in it as before, and thus the dance ended to the great satisfaction of the spectators.

Don Quixote inquired of one of the nymphs who it was that had composed and arranged the performance and was told that a certain cleric of the town who had a neat gift for that sort of thing was responsible for it.

"I will wager," said the knight, "that the bachelor or cleric in question is a better friend of Camacho's than he is of Basilio's and that he must have more of the satirist in him than he has of the vesper spirit, for in this dance he has well portrayed the youth's accomplishments and the other's wealth."

Sancho Panza, who was listening, now spoke up. "The king is my cock," [11] he said. "I stick to Camacho."

"It is plain to be seen, Sancho," said Don Quixote, "that you are one of the rabble who cry 'Long live the conqueror!' "

"I don't know what I am," replied Sancho. "All I know is that from Basilio's stew-pots I'll never get such elegant skimmings as I have had from Camacho's." With this, he showed his master the pail filled with geese and hens, and, taking one of the fowls, he began to devour it with a hearty zest and great good humor.

"Basilio," he exclaimed, "is out of luck with his accomplishments! [12] A man is worth as much as he has and has as much as he is worth. [13] There are two kinds of people in this world, my grandmother used to say: the Have's and the Have-not's, [14] and she stuck to the Have's. And today, Señor Don Quixote, people are more interested in having than in knowing. [15] An ass covered with gold makes a better impression than a horse with a packsaddle. And so I tell you again, I'm sticking to Camacho, whose pots hold plenty of geese and hens, hares and rabbits; but if any-thing of Basilio's comes to hand, or even to foot, it will be no better than wine slop."

"Have you finished your speech, Sancho?" asked Don Quixote.

"I'll have to finish it, seeing that your Grace takes offense at it; but if it wasn't for that, I'd have my work cut out for me for three days to come."

"I hope to God," said Don Quixote, "that I see you struck dumb before I die."

"At the rate we're going," replied Sancho, "I'll be chewing clay before your Grace dies, and then maybe I'll be so dumb that I'll not have a word to say until the end of the world, or at least not until Judgment Day."

"Even if that should happen, Sancho," said Don Quixote, "you could never make up with your silence for all the talking you have done, are doing, and will do in the course of your life. It stands to reason that I shall die before you do, and so I never hope to see you dumb, not even when you are drinking or sleeping, which is the most I can say."

"In good faith, sir," said Sancho, "there's no trusting that one with no flesh on her bones who eats lamb as well as mutton, for I've heard our curate say that she treads both the tall towers of kings and the humble cottages of the poor.[16] The lady is powerful but not finical or squeamish; she devours everything that comes her way and fills her saddlebags with people of every sort, of every age and station. She is not one of those reapers who take a siesta; she works at all hours and mows down the withered grass and the green alike. She doesn't seem to chew her food but gulps down anything that is set in front of her, for she is as hungry as a dog that never has its fill; and although she has no belly, you would think she had the dropsy, so thirsty is she to drink the lives of all who live as one might drink from a jug of cold water."

"Stop where you are, Sancho," said Don Quixote, "and don't risk a fall. For, really, what you have said about death, in your own rustic way, might have come from the mouth of a good preacher. I tell you, Sancho, if you had [17] as much judgment as you have mother wit, you might take a pulpit in hand and go through this world delivering fine sermons."

"He preaches well who lives well," was Sancho's answer. "That's all the theology I know."

"And all you need to know," said his master. "But what I cannot make out is this: the fear of God, they tell us, is the beginning of wisdom, yet you are more afraid of a lizard than you are of Him."

"Sir," replied Sancho, "your Grace would do well to judge your own deeds of chivalry and not go meddling with the fears or bravery of other people. I'm as God-fearing a man as any neighbor's son; so will your Grace please let me finish these skimmings, for all the rest is idle talk and we'll have to answer for it in the life to come."

Saying this, he once more attacked his pail with so hearty an appetite as to awaken Don Quixote's, who no doubt would have helped him out had he not been prevented from doing so by a circumstance which must be related further on.

CHAPTER XXI. *In which Camacho's wedding is continued, with other delightful incidents.*

As Don Quixote and Sancho were engaged in the conversation that has been related in the preceding chapter, they heard loud shouts and a great din created by those on the mares, who now rode forward with welcoming cries to receive the bride and groom. The bridal pair were accompanied by a large number of musical instruments and pageants of various kinds, as well as by the priest, the relatives of both parties, and all the most distinguished gentry of the neighboring villages, in holiday garb.

"My word!" exclaimed Sancho when he caught sight of the bride. "She's not dressed like any farmer's daughter but rather like some fine lady of the court. Damn me if those medals [1] she's wearing aren't of rich coral, and that palm-green cloth of Cuenca is thirty-pile velvet! [2] And look at that white linen trimming—I'll swear it's satin! and those jet rings that she has on her hands, may I never have any luck if they're not gold, and fine gold at that, and set with pearls white as a milk curd, every one of them worth an eye of your head! Oh, the whoreson wench! What hair she has, if it's her own; I never in all my life saw any that was longer or brighter colored. Just see her shape and the way she carries herself and then try to tell me that she doesn't remind you of a palm tree loaded down with clusters of dates, for that is just what those trinkets are like that she has hanging from her hair and neck. Upon my soul, she's an up-and-coming lass and fit to pass the banks of Flanders." [3]

Don Quixote had to laugh at these rustic praises which Sancho was bestowing upon the bride; but it nonetheless seemed to him that, with the exception of his own lady, Dulcinea del Toboso, he had never beheld so fair a creature. [4] The beauteous Quiteria was a trifle pale, however, owing no doubt to the bad night she had spent, as is always the case with brides busied with preparations on the eve of their wedding day. The members of the bridal party made their way to a theater on one side of the meadow, decked out with carpets and boughs, where they were to plight their troth and watch the dances and the pageants; but just as they reached the place they heard someone behind them shouting in a loud voice, "Wait a moment, you who are as inconsiderate as you are hasty!"

At the sound of these words, all turned their heads and saw that the speaker was a man attired in what appeared to be a large loose-fitting black coat with flame-colored patches. Upon his head, as they presently perceived, was a wreath of funereal cypress, and in his hands he carried a long staff. As he drew nearer they all recognized him as the gallant Basilio and waited anxiously to see what would come of his words and cries, for they feared that some misfortune would result from his appearance there at such a time. He was exhausted and breathless as he arrived; and, taking his staff, which had a steel point on the end of it, he planted it in the ground in front of the betrothed pair. His face was pale and his eyes were fixed on the bride as he addressed her in a hoarse and trembling voice.

"Well do you know, O heartless Quiteria," he said, "that in accordance with the holy law which we acknowledge you cannot take a husband so long as I am alive; nor are you ignorant of the fact that, hoping time and diligence would improve my fortune, I never failed to observe that respect that was due your honor. But you, turning your back on all that you owe to my true love, would surrender what is rightfully mine to another, whose riches serve to bring him not merely prosperity but the greatest happiness there is. And now, to crown his happiness—not that I think he deserves it, but because Heaven has seen fit to bestow it upon him—I with my own hands will do away with the obstacle that might interfere with it, by removing myself from between you. Long live the rich Camacho! May he spend many long and happy years with the heartless Quiteria! As for the poor Basilio, let him die, seeing that his poverty has clipped the wings of his own happiness and has brought him to the grave!"

Saying this, he seized the staff which he had driven into the ground, and they could then see that it served as a sheath to a fairly long rapier that had been hidden in it. With what might be termed the hilt still planted in the earth, he swiftly, coolly, and resolutely threw himself upon it, and a moment later the crimson point and half the steel blade could be seen protruding from his back, as he lay there transfixed by his own weapon and bathed in blood.

His friends at once came running up to aid him, for they were grief-stricken at his sad fate. Dismounting from Rocinante, Don Quixote took him in his arms and found that he had not yet expired. They were about to withdraw the rapier, but the priest who was present was of the opinion that they should not do so until the dying man had confessed, since the removal of the blade would mean his immediate death. At this point Basilio revived somewhat.

"O cruel Quiteria," he said in a weak and sorrowing voice, "if in this last and fatal moment you would but give me your hand in marriage, I then might hope that my rash act would find pardon, since through it I had achieved the blessing of being yours."

Upon hearing this, the priest told Basilio that he should be thinking of the welfare of his soul rather than of his bodily pleasures and should beg God in all earnestness to forgive him his sins and the rash act he had committed. Basilio's reply was that he would by no manner of means confess himself unless Quiteria first became his bride as only that happiness would give him the will and strength to do it. Don Quixote then took a hand by loudly declaring that the wounded man's request was only just and reasonable and, moreover, very easy to comply with, and that Señor Camacho would be as much honored by marrying the brave Basilio's widow as he would be if he were to receive Señora Quiteria directly from her father.

"In this case," he explained, "it is merely a matter of saying 'yes' and no consequence will follow, for the marriage bed will be the grave."

Camacho was listening to it all and was very much bewildered and confused, not knowing what to say or do; but Basilio's friends were so insistent that he give his consent for Quiteria to marry his rival, in order that the latter's soul might not be lost as it quitted this life in desperation, that he was moved and even compelled to say that she might do so if she wished, adding that he would be satisfied since it only meant putting off for a moment the fulfillment of his desires. All then crowded around Quiteria and with tears, prayers, and convincing reasons endeavored to persuade her to give her hand to poor Basilio; but she, harder than marble and more imperturbable than any statue, appeared unable or unwilling to utter a single word in reply, nor would she have answered at all had not the priest told her that she must make up her mind quickly, as Basilio was at the point of death [5] and this was no time for hesitation.

Then the fair Quiteria, speechless still but now deeply disturbed and, as it seemed, sad and regretful, came up to where Basilio lay with eyes upturned, his breath coming in short, quick gasps as he muttered his loved one's name—to all appearances he was dying like a heathen and not like a Christian. Kneeling beside him, she indicated by signs, not by words, that she wished to take his hand, and at this Basilio opened his eyes and gazed at her with a fixed stare.

"O Quiteria," he said, "you have relented at last when your pity can serve only as a dagger to deprive me of life, since I have not the strength to enjoy the supreme happiness you bestow by choosing me as yours, nor am I able to mitigate this pain which is so rapidly closing my eyes in the dread shadow of death. What I ask of you, O fatal star of mine! is that this handclasp you offer be no mere act of compliance on your part nor intended to deceive me afresh; instead, I would have you state and confess that it is of your own free will and without coercion that you take me to be your lawful husband; for there is no reason why, at such a time as this, you should trifle with me or lie to one who has always dealt so honestly with you."

As he uttered these words he grew weaker and weaker, and all the bystanders feared that each sinking spell would be his last. Overcome with shame, the modest Quiteria now took his right hand in hers.

"Nothing," she assured him, "could force me to do a thing that was against my will; and so, as freely as possible, I give you my hand as your lawfully wedded wife and take your own in return, providing that you too are acting in accordance with your own free choice and not merely because your mind has been deranged as a result of this calamity which your rash deed has brought upon you."

"My mind," replied Basilio, "is not deranged, nor is my thinking confused, and so, with that power of lucid reasoning with which Heaven has seen fit to endow me, I do hereby give myself to be your husband."

"And I," said Quiteria, "will be your wife, whether you live many years or they carry you now from my arms to the grave."

"That young fellow," remarked Sancho Panza at this point, "talks a lot to be so badly wounded. They should make him stop this love-making and attend to his soul; for so far as I can make out, if it is leaving his body, it has got no farther than his tongue." [6]

As the pair continued to hold hands, the priest, moved to tears, gave them his benediction; and no sooner had he done so than Basilio nimbly leaped to his feet and, with an unheard-of brazenness, drew the rapier from his body which had served as its sheath. The bystanders were dumfounded, and some of the more simple-minded and less inquisitive among them began shouting at the top of their voices, "A miracle! A miracle!"

"No miracle," said Basilio, "but a trick." [7]

Astounded and bewildered, the priest ran up and, putting out both hands to examine the wound, discovered that the blade had passed, not through Basilio's flesh and ribs, but through a hollow iron tube filled with blood which he had placed there, the blood, as was afterward learned, having been especially prepared so that it would not congeal.

The short of it was, the priest, Camacho, and all the others found that they had been tricked and made sport of. As for the bride, she did not appear to be resentful. Indeed, when some were heard to say that, having been accomplished through fraud, the marriage would not be valid, she promptly spoke up and stated that she confirmed it anew; from which all present derived the impression that the whole thing had been arranged between the two of them. Camacho and his supporters, on the other hand, were so angry that they proceeded to take vengeance into their own hands. Unsheathing their swords, and there were many of them, they fell upon Basilio, but nearly as many blades were drawn with equal promptness in his defense.

Taking the lead on horseback, with his lance braced upon his arm and well protected by his shield, Don Quixote then made them all give way, while Sancho, who never did care for such doings, retired to the pots from which he had had such pleasant skimmings, this being for him a sacred place and one for which a proper respect was to be shown.

"Hold, gentlemen, hold!" cried Don Quixote. "It is not reasonable to take vengeance for the wrongs done us by love. Remember that love and war are one and the same thing; and just as in war it is permissible to use wiles and stratagems to overcome the enemy, so in amorous contests those deceptions that are employed in order to attain the desired object are looked upon as proper, providing they are not to the detriment or dishonor of the lady who is sought. Basilio and Quiteria belong to each other by favorable and just decree of Heaven. Camacho is rich and may buy his pleasure when, where, and as it suits him. Basilio has but this ewe lamb, and no one, however powerful he may be, is going to take it away from him. What therefore God hath joined together, let not man put asunder; [8] and whoever shall attempt it will first have to pass the point of this lance."

As he said this, he brandished his weapon with such strength and skill as to frighten all those that did not know him. The effect upon Camacho was to fasten his thoughts intently upon the scorn that Quiteria had shown him, and he accordingly determined to efface her at once from his memory and was ready to listen to the persuasions of the priest, who was a prudent, well-meaning individual. The upshot of it all was, Camacho and his followers became calm and peaceful and put their swords back in their scabbards; for all were now inclined to place the blame upon Quiteria's fickleness rather than Basilio's wiles, the spurned bridegroom reasoning that if she had loved his rival before marriage, she would go on loving him after she was wed, and he would do better to thank Heaven for having taken her from him than for giving her to him.

Camacho and those in his train being thus pacified and consoled, Basilio and his friends likewise quieted down; and by way of showing that he harbored no ill will for the trick that had been played on him, the host expressed a desire that the festivities should continue just as if the marriage were to take place. This, however, proved inacceptable to Basilio, his bride, and their attendants, and they now went off to the village where the groom lived. For the poor, if they be virtuous and discreet, have those who follow, honor, and defend them, just as the rich have those who accompany and flatter them. [9] They took Don Quixote along, for they regarded him as a man of valor, with hair on his chest. [10] Sancho alone was heartsick when he saw that he would not be able to wait for Camacho's splendid feast and entertainment, which lasted until nightfall; and thus, it was in deep dejection that he followed his master and Basilio's party, leaving behind him the flesh-pots of Egypt though he bore them with him in his soul, the few skimmings that remained in his pail representing for him the glory and abundance of the good cheer he had lost. In this manner, grief-stricken and pensive though for once not hungry, he plodded along in Rocinante's foot-tracks without dismounting from his gray.

CHAPTER XXII . *Wherein is related the great adventure of the Cave of Montesinos in the heart of La Mancha, which the valiant Don Quixote brought to a triumphant conclusion.*

MANY and great were the attentions that the newly married pair showered upon Don Quixote, for they felt under obligations to him for having shown his readiness to defend their cause. They were as much pleased by his wisdom as by his bravery and looked upon him as a Cid in the matter of arms and a Cicero in eloquence. The worthy Sancho enjoyed himself for three whole days at their expense, and in the course of that time it was learned that Basilio's pretense at wounding himself had been a scheme of his own and not a plot between him and the fair Quiteria, and he had expected it to turn out precisely as it did. He admitted, however, that he had confided his plan in part to a few of his friends who might assist him in carrying out the deception.

"Deception," observed Don Quixote, "is not the word where aims are virtuous." And he went on to point out that the marriage of lovers is an excellent purpose to be achieved, reminding them, however, that love has no greater enemy than hunger and constant want; for love is all joy, happiness, and contentment when the lover is in possession of the object of his affections, and want and poverty thereby become his open and relentless foes. All this was said in an effort to induce Señor Basilio to give up the practice of his accomplishments, since even though they brought him fame they would bring in no money, and to devote his attention instead to the acquisition of a fortune by legitimate means and his own industry; for those who are prudent and persevering always find a way.

The poor man who is a man of honor (if such a thing is possible) has a jewel when he has a beautiful wife, and when she leaves him, his honor at the same time departs and is slain. The woman who is beautiful and virtuous and whose husband is pure deserves to be crowned with laurels and garlands of victory. Her beauty in itself attracts the desires of all who look upon and know it, and royal eagles and birds of lofty flight swoop down on it as if it were an alluring bait; and when such loveliness is accompanied by want and straitened circumstances, it is then assailed by ravens, kites, and other birds of prey, and she who can stand firm against such an onslaught may well be called her husband's crown.[1]

"Let me remind you, prudent Basilio," Don Quixote continued, "of something which some wise man or other has said. It was his opinion that there was only one good woman in all the world, and his advice was for each man to bring himself to believe that this woman was his wife, and in that way he might live happily. I myself am not married, nor have I ever thought of marrying up to now,[2] but for all that, I should not hesitate to advise anyone who might ask me as to the proper method of looking for a woman of the sort one would want to have as his wife. First of all, he should look at her reputation rather than at her dowry, for a good name is something to be won, not alone by being good, but by appearing good in the eyes of others, and loose manners in public do more harm to a woman's honor than secret sins. If you bring a good woman into your house, it should be an easy matter to keep her so and even to improve her virtue, but if you bring a bad one, you will have a hard time of it correcting her, since it is not very feasible to pass from one extreme to another. I do not say that it is impossible, but I hold it to be difficult."

Listening to all this, Sancho was talking to himself. "This master of mine, when I say something that has some pith and body to it, is in the habit of telling me that I ought to take a pulpit in hand and go through this world preaching fine sermons; and I will say of him that when he begins stringing sayings together and giving advice, he not only could take a pulpit in hand, but two of them by each finger and go through the market places talking his head off.[3] The devil take you for a knight-errant, what a lot of things you know! I thought in my heart that he knew only those things that had to do with chivalry, but he has a finger in everything and is always putting in his spoonful."

He had muttered this loud enough [4] for his master to hear.

"What are you mumbling about, Sancho?" Don Quixote asked him.

"I am not mumbling anything," Sancho replied. "I was only telling myself that I wish I had heard what your Grace said just now before I was married. In that case I might be saying, 'The ox that's loose licks himself well.' " [5]

"Is your Teresa so bad as all that?"

"She's not bad, but she's not good, at least not as good as I could wish."

"It is wrong of you, Sancho," said Don Quixote, "to be speaking ill of your wife, who after all is the mother of your children."

"We're even, then," was the answer, "for she also speaks ill of me whenever she happens to feel like it, especially when she is jealous. Satan himself couldn't put up with her then."

At length, when three days had gone by, during which time they had been feasted and entertained like royalty, Don Quixote asked the swordsman-licentiate to provide him with a guide who would conduct him to the Cave of Montesinos, as he had a great desire to enter it and see with his own eyes if the marvelous tales they told of it throughout that region were true or not. The bachelor replied that he would acquaint him with a first cousin of his, a notable student and very fond of reading books of chivalry, who would be delighted to conduct him to the mouth of the said cave and show him the Lakes of Ruidera, which were famous throughout La Mancha and all Spain as well. He assured the knight that the youth would be found to be entertaining company, since he knew enough to write books of his own, books that were printed and dedicated to princes.

The cousin finally arrived leading an ass in foal, with a pack-saddle covered by a striped carpet or sackcloth; and Sancho thereupon proceeded to saddle Rocinante and get his gray ready, taking care to stuff his saddlebags to keep company with those the newcomer had brought with him. Being thus well provisioned, they commended themselves to God and, taking leave of all present, set out along the road that led to the celebrated cave.

On the way, Don Quixote inquired of the cousin what his pursuits were, his profession, and his studies. To this their companion replied that his profession was that of humanist, adding that his pursuits and studies had to do with composing books for the printers, all of them of great public utility and very entertaining. One of them, he stated, was entitled *The Book of Liveries*, in which were depicted seven hundred and three different liveries with their colors, mottoes, and ciphers, from which the gentlemen of the court might pick and choose the ones that suited them best for their feasts and revels without having to go begging for them from anyone or, as the saying has it, straining their wits to procure the costumes adapted to their purpose.

"For," he went on to say, "I provide the jealous, the scorned, the forgotten, the far-absent, with the garb that they should have and that becomes them very well. I have another book which I am going to call *Metamorphoses, or the Spanish Ovid*, an original and extraordinary work, for in it, imitating Ovid in burlesque style, I show who Giralda of Seville and the Angel of the Magdalena were, and I further identify the Vecinguerra Conduit of Cordova, the Bulls of Guisando, the Sierra Morena, and the Legitanos and Lavapies Fountains of Madrid, not forgetting El Piojo, the Caño Dorado, and La Priora,[6] together with the allegories, metaphors, and versions associated with them, and all in such a manner as to interest, amuse, and instruct the reader at one and the same time.

"I have another book which I call *Supplement to Virgilius Polydorus.*[7] It treats of the invention of things and is a very scholarly work and one that cost me much study. In it I set forth in a pleasing style, with due proof and explanation, certain things of great moment that Polydorus neglected to mention. He forgot to tell us who was the first man in the world to have a cold in the head, or the first to take unctions for the French disease,[8] all of which I bring out most accurately, citing the authority of more than twenty-five authors. From this your Grace may see how well I have labored and may judge for yourself as to whether or not such a work should be useful to everyone."

Sancho, who had been listening very attentively to what the cousin had to say, now put in his word. "Tell me, sir, and may God guide your hand well in the printing of your books, tell me if you can, seeing that you know everything, who was the first man that ever scratched his head? For my part, I believe it must have been Father Adam."

"So it would have been," replied the cousin, "seeing there is no doubt that Adam had a head with hair on it, and being the first man, he would have scratched it some time or other."

"That is what I think," said Sancho. "But tell me something else: who was the first tumbler [9] in the world?"

"Really, brother," said the cousin, "I cannot determine that just now, not until I have given it some study. I will look into it as soon as I go back to where I keep my books and will let you know the next time we see each other again; for this is not going to be the last time."

"Then look here, sir," said Sancho, "you needn't go to the trouble, for I have hit upon the answer to my question. I can tell you that the first tumbler was Lucifer when they cast him out of Heaven and he came tumbling down into Hell."

"Right you are, friend," said the cousin.

"Sancho," said Don Quixote, "that question and answer are not your own; you've heard them somewhere."

"Hush, master," replied Sancho. "Upon my word, if I started asking foolish questions and giving silly answers, I'd be at it from now until tomorrow morning. When it comes to that, I don't need any help from my neighbors."

"You have spoken more wisely than you know, Sancho," declared Don Quixote; "for there are some who wear themselves out in learning and verifying things which, after they have been mastered, are not worth a rap so far as mind or memory goes."

With this and other pleasing talk they spent the day, and when night came found lodgings in a little village which, as the cousin informed Don Quixote, was not more than a couple of leagues from the Cave of Montesinos; and their guide took occasion to remind the knight that if he was resolved to make the descent, he would have to find ropes with which to lower himself into the depths. To this Don Quixote's answer was that even if it was as deep as Hell, he proposed to see the bottom of it; and so they bought nearly a hundred fathoms of rope, and the following day, at two o'clock in the afternoon, they reached the cave, the mouth of which is broad and spacious, but clogged with boxthorn, wild fig trees, shrubs, and brambles, so dense and tangled an undergrowth as wholly to cover over and conceal the entrance. All three of them then dismounted, and Sancho and the cousin bound Don Quixote very stoutly with the ropes.

"Look well what you do, master," said Sancho as they were girdling him. "Don't go burying yourself alive or get yourself caught so you will hang there like a bottle that has been let down into the well to cool. If you ask me, I would say it is none of your Grace's affair to be prying into this cave, which must be worse than a dungeon."

"Keep on tying and keep still," Don Quixote admonished him. "It is just such an undertaking as this, Sancho, that is reserved for me." [10]

The guide then addressed him. "Señor Don Quixote," he said, "I beg your Grace to view thoroughly and inspect with a hundred eyes what you find down there; who knows, maybe it will be something that I can put in my book on *Transformations*."

"Leave the tambourine," Sancho advised him, "to the one who knows how to play it." [11]

By this time they had finished tying Don Quixote, passing the rope over his doublet, not over his battle harness.

"It was careless of us," said the knight, "not to have provided ourselves with a cattle bell to attach to the rope at my side so that you might be able to tell from the sound of it whether I was still descending and still alive. However, there is nothing for it now. I am in God's hands and may He be my guide."

He knelt and prayed to Heaven in a low voice, imploring God to aid him and grant him success in this adventure, which impressed him as being a rare and dangerous one. Then he raised his voice:

"O lady who dost inspire my every deed and action, O most illustrious and peerless Dulcinea del Toboso! If it be possible for the prayers and entreaties of this thy fortunate lover to reach thine ears, I do beseech thee to hear them. What I ask of thee is nothing other than thy favor and protection, of which I so greatly stand in need at this moment. I am now about to sink, to hurl and plunge myself into the abyss that yawns before me here, simply in order that the world may know that there is nothing, however impossible it may seem, that I will not undertake and accomplish, provided only I have thy favor."

Having said this, he went up to the chasm [12] and perceived that if he was to make a descent he would first have to clear an entrance by force of arm or by hacking away the underbrush; and accordingly, taking his sword, he began cutting and felling the brambles at the mouth of the cave, the noise of which caused a very great number of crows and jackdaws to fly out. There were so many of these birds and such was their velocity that they knocked Don Quixote down, and had he been as much of a believer in augury as he was a good Catholic Christian, he would have taken this as an ill omen and would have declined to bury himself in such a place as that. Finally, he arose and, seeing that no more crows or other night birds were emerging, such as the bats that flew out with the crows, he allowed himself to be lowered into the depths of the horrendous cavern, with Sancho and the cousin letting out the rope as the squire bestowed his benediction and crossed himself an endless number of times.

"May God be your guide," exclaimed Sancho, "and the Rock of France,[13] along with the Trinity of Gaeta,[14] O flower, cream, and skimming of knights-errant! There you go, daredevil of the earth,[15] heart of steel, arms of brass! Once more, may God be your guide and bring you back safe, sound, and without a scratch to the light of this world which you are leaving to bury yourself in that darkness that you go to seek!"

The cousin, meanwhile, was offering up practically the same prayers. Don Quixote then went on down, calling for them to give him rope and more rope, and they let it out for him little by little. By the time they could no longer hear his voice, which came out of the cave as through a pipe, they had let him have the entire hundred fathoms, all the rope there was, and were of a mind to pull him up again. They decided, however, to wait for half an hour, and then they once more began hauling in the line, with no effort whatever, for they could feel no weight on the other end, which led them to think that Don Quixote must have remained behind. Believing this to be the case, Sancho began weeping bitterly and started pulling with all his might in order to learn the truth of the matter; but when they had come to a little more than eighty fathoms, as it seemed to them, they once more felt a tug, which made them very happy indeed. Finally, at ten fathoms, they could see Don Quixote quite distinctly, and as he caught sight of him, Sancho cried out, "Welcome, master, we are glad to see you again. We thought you had stayed down there to found a family."

But Don Quixote said not a word in reply, and when they had him all the way up they saw that his eyes were closed and that, to all appearances, he was sound asleep. They laid him on the ground and untied him, but even this did not wake him. It was not until they had turned him over first on one side and then on the other and had given him a thorough shaking and mauling that, after a considerable length of time, he at last regained consciousness, stretching himself as if he had been roused from a profound slumber and gazing about him with a bewildered look.

"God forgive you, friends," he said, "you have taken me away from the most delightful existence mortal ever knew and the pleasantest sight human eyes ever rested upon. Now truly do I begin to understand how it is that all the pleasures of this life pass away like a shadow or a dream or wither like the flower of the field.[16] O unfortunate Montesinos! O sorely wounded Durandarte! O unhappy Belerma! O tearful Guadiana! And you, hapless daughters of Ruidera, who in your waters display the tears your eyes once wept!"[17]

The cousin and Sancho listened attentively to Don Quixote's words, which appeared to have been uttered in great pain, as though drawn from his entrails. They thereupon begged him to tell them the meaning of it all and what it was he had seen in that Hell he had visited.

"Hell do you call it?" said Don Quixote. "Do not call it that, for it does not deserve the name, as you shall see."

He then asked them to give him something to eat, as he was exceedingly hungry; and so they spread the cousin's sackcloth upon the green grass and laid out what fare the saddlebags could afford, and, sitting down together like the three good friends and companions that they were, they proceeded to make a meal of it, combining lunch and supper. When the sackcloth had been removed, Don Quixote de la Mancha spoke.

"Let no one arise," he said, "but both of you listen most attentively to what I have to say."

CHAPTER **XXIII**. *Of the amazing things which the incomparable Don Quixote told of having seen in the deep Cave of Montesinos, an adventure the grandeur and impossible nature of which have caused it to be regarded as apocryphal.*

IT WAS around four in the afternoon when the subdued light and tempered rays of the sun, which was now covered over with clouds, afforded Don Quixote an opportunity to tell his two illustrious listeners, without undue heat or weariness, what it was he had seen in the Cave of Montesinos. He began in the following manner:

"At a depth corresponding to the height of twelve or fourteen men, on the right-hand side of this dungeon, there is a concave recess capable of containing a large cart with its mules. A small light filters into it through distant chinks or crevices in the surface of the earth; and I caught sight of this nook just at a time when I was feeling tired and vexed at finding myself dangling from a rope in that manner as I descended into those dark regions without any certain knowledge as to where I was going. And so I decided to enter the recess and rest a little. I called to you, asking you not to give out any more rope until I told you to do so, but you must not have heard me. Accordingly, I gathered it in as you sent it to me and, making a coil or pile of it, I seated myself upon it, meanwhile thinking what I should have to do in order to let myself all the way down to the bottom, as I now had no one to hold me up.

"As I sat there lost in thought and deeply perplexed, suddenly and without my doing anything to bring it about a profound sleep fell upon me; and then, all unexpectedly and not knowing how it happened, I awoke and found myself in the midst of the most beautiful, pleasant, and delightful meadow that nature could create or the most fertile imagination could conceive. Opening my eyes, I rubbed them and discovered that I was not sleeping but really awake. Nevertheless, I felt my head and bosom to make sure it was I who was there and not some empty and deceptive phantom. And my sense of touch and feeling and the coherence of my thoughts were sufficient to assure me that I was the same then and there that I am here and now.

"It was at that moment that my eyes fell upon a sumptuous royal palace or castle, the walls and battlements of which appeared to be built of clear, transparent crystal. The two wings of the main gate were suddenly thrown open, and there emerged and came toward me a venerable old man clad in a hooded cloak of mulberry-colored stuff that swept the ground. Around his head and his bosom was a collegiate green satin sash, and on his head a black Milanese bonnet. His beard was snow-white and fell below his waist, and he carried no arms whatever, nothing but a rosary which he held in his hand, a string on which the beads were larger than fair-sized walnuts, every tenth one being as big as an ordinary ostrich egg. His bearing, his stride, the gravity of his demeanor, and his stately presence, each in itself and all of them together, filled me with wonder and astonishment. Upon reaching my side, the first thing he did was to give me a close embrace.

" 'It is a long time,' he said, 'O valiant knight, Don Quixote de la Mancha, that we in these enchanted solitudes have been waiting for a sight of you, that you might go back and inform the world of what lies locked and concealed in the depths of this cave which you have entered, the so-called Cave of Montesinos, an exploit solely reserved for your invincible heart and stupendous courage. Come with me, most illustrious sir, and I will show you the hidden marvels of this transparent castle of which I am the governor and perpetual guardian; for I am Montesinos himself, after whom the cave is named.'

"No sooner had he informed me that he was Montesinos than I asked him if the story was true that was told in the world above, to the effect that with a small dagger he had cut out the heart of his great friend Durandarte and had borne it to the lady Belerma as his friend at the point of death had requested him to do. He replied that it was all true except the part about the dagger, for it was not a dagger, nor was it small, but a burnished poniard sharper than an awl."

"It must have been such a poniard," said Sancho at this point, "as that of Ramón de Hoces of Seville." [1]

"I cannot say as to that," replied Don Quixote, "for Ramón de Hoces lived only yesterday and the battle of Roncesvalles, where this unfortunate affair occurred, was many years ago; and, in any case, it does not alter in any way the truth and substance of the tale."

"That is right," said the cousin. "Continue, Señor Don Quixote, for I am listening to your Grace with the greatest of pleasure."

"And mine in relating the story is no less," Don Quixote assured him. "And so, as I am saying, the venerable Montesinos took me into the crystal palace, where, in a low room that was made entirely of alabaster and very cool, I beheld a tomb fashioned out of marble with masterly craftsmanship, and upon it lay a knight stretched at full length. He was not a bronze knight, nor one of marble or of jasper, as you see on other tombs; he was of actual flesh and bone. His right hand, which seemed to me somewhat hairy and sinewy, a sign that its owner had been possessed of great strength—his right hand lay upon his heart; and before I could ask any questions, Montesinos, seeing how amazed I was, went on to explain.

" 'This,' he said, 'is my friend Durandarte, flower and mirror of the brave and enamored knights of his age. Merlin, that French enchanter, who they say was the devil's own son,[2] holds him here under a spell as he does me and many other knights and ladies. How or why he did it to us, no one knows; but time will tell, and it is my belief that the time is not far off. What astonishes me is the fact that it is as certain that Durandarte died in my arms as it is that it is now day; and there is likewise no doubt that after his death I took out his heart with my own hands. It weighed all of two pounds; for according to the naturalists he who has a large heart is endowed with greater valor than he who has a small one.[3] And if it is true, then, that this knight really died, how is it that he still sighs and laments from time to time as though he were alive?'

"As Montesinos said this, the wretched Durandarte cried out in a loud voice:

'O my cousin Montesinos!
the last request I made of thee

was that when I should be lying
cold in death, thou wouldst favor me
by bearing this my captive heart
to fair Belerma where'er she be,
and ripping it from out my bosom
with knife or dagger, set it free.' [4]

"Hearing these words, the venerable Montesinos knelt before the unfortunate knight and addressed him with tears in his eyes. 'Long since, O dearest cousin, Señor Durandarte, I did what you requested of me on that bitter day when we lost you. I took out your heart as well as I could, without leaving the smallest particle of it in your breast. I cleaned it with a lace handkerchief and set out for France with it, having first laid you in the bosom of the earth with enough tears to wash my hands of the blood that stained them after they had been in your entrails. What is more, beloved cousin, at the first village I came to after leaving Roncesvalles I put a little salt upon your heart so that it would not have an unpleasant odor but would remain, if not fresh, at least well preserved when I came to present it to the lady Belerma.

" 'That lady, like you and me and Guadiana your squire and the duenna Ruidera and her seven daughters and two nieces and many others among your friends and acquaintances, has been held here many a year through Merlin's magic art; and although more than five hundred years have passed, not a one of us has died. The only ones that are missing are Ruidera, her daughters and her nieces, for Merlin would seem to have taken pity on their tears and has transformed them into an equal number of lakes which today, in the world of the living and the province of La Mancha, are known as the Lakes of Ruidera.[5] Seven of them belong to the King of Spain, and the two nieces to the knights of a very holy order called the Order of St. John.[6]

" 'As for Guadiana, your squire, weeping for your sad fate, he was transformed into a river of the same name. When he came to the surface and beheld the sun of that other heaven, he was so grieved at thought of leaving you that he plunged down into the bowels of the earth once more; but inasmuch as he must needs yield to his natural current, he rises again from time to time where men and the sun may see him.[7] The said lakes supply him with their waters, and with these and many others that reach him he enters Portugal with great pomp. But, for all of that, wherever he goes he is still sad and melancholy and does not pride himself upon breeding dainty fish of the kind that are sought after, but only coarse ones lacking in flavor, quite different from those of the Tagus with its golden sands.

" 'All this, O cousin, I have told you many times; and since you do not answer me, I am led to think that you do not believe me, or it may be you do not hear, all of which pains me, God only knows how much. But now I have some news to give you which, if it does not assuage your grief, will not add to it in any way. Know that here in your presence—you have but to open your eyes and you will see him—is that great knight of whom the wise Merlin prophesied so many things, I mean the famous Don Quixote de la Mancha, who once again and to better advantage than in past ages has undertaken to revive in this present age the long-forgotten profession of knight-errantry. It may be that, thanks to his favor and mediation, we shall be disenchanted; for great exploits are reserved for great men.' [8]

" 'And even if it be not so,' replied the wretched Durandarte in a low, faint voice, 'and even if it be not so, O cousin, I say to you: patience, and shuffle.' [9] And, turning on his side, he relapsed into his accustomed silence without uttering another word.

"At that moment a great outcry was heard, accompanied by the sound of weeping, profound sighs, and anguished sobs; and I turned my head and saw, through the crystal walls, a procession of exceedingly lovely damsels passing through another chamber. There were two rows of them, and they were all clad in mourning with white turbans on their heads after the Turkish fashion. At the end of the procession came a lady, as was to be seen from her dignified appearance, who wore a flowing white veil so long that it touched the ground. Her turban was twice as large as the largest of the others, her eyebrows were so close together that they met, her nose was somewhat flat and her mouth wide, but her lips were red; her teeth, when she displayed them, were seen to be few and uneven but white as peeled almonds. In her hands she carried a fine piece of cloth, and wrapped in it, so far as could be made out, was a mummified heart, all dried and withered.

"Montesinos informed me that all these people in the procession were the attendants of Durandarte and Belerma who had been enchanted along with their master and mistress, and that the last one, with the heart in her hands, was the lady Belerma herself, who with her damsels was accustomed to parade like this four days a week, singing, or rather weeping, dirges over the heart and body of his unfortunate cousin. He added that in case she impressed me as being somewhat ugly, or at any rate not as beautiful as report would have it, this was due to the bad nights and worse days that she spent as an enchanted being, as I could see for myself from the circles under her eyes and her sickly hue.

" 'And do not think,' continued Montesinos, 'that her sallowness and those circles are due to an affliction that is common to women at a certain period of the month, for it has been many months and even years since she has had that experience. It is, rather, the grief that she feels in her heart for that other heart she holds in her hands, which but serves to bring back to memory and revive the misfortune that befell her ill-starred lover. If it were not for that, even the great Dulcinea del Toboso, so famous in these parts and throughout the world, would scarcely equal her in beauty, grace, and dashing manner.'

" 'Hold there, Señor Don Montesinos!' said I at this point. 'Your Grace should tell your story in the proper way for, as you know, all comparisons are odious.[10] There is no reason for comparing anybody with anybody. The peerless Dulcinea del Toboso is who she is and has been, and let the matter rest there.'

" 'Señor Don Quixote,' he replied to me, 'forgive me, your Grace. I confess that I was wrong in saying that Señora Dulcinea could scarcely equal Señora Belerma; for by some means or other I have learned that your Grace is her knight, and that is enough to make me bite my tongue out before comparing her with anything but Heaven itself.'

"And so the great Montesinos having given me this satisfaction, my heart recovered from the shock it had received when I heard my lady mentioned in the same breath with his."

"But," said Sancho, "I still can't help wondering why your Grace didn't jump on the old fellow and kick his bones to a pulp and pull his beard until there wasn't a hair left in it."

"No, friend Sancho," replied Don Quixote, "it would not have been right for me to do that, for we are all of us obliged to respect the aged, even though they be knights, and especially when they are under a magic spell. But I can tell you that we came off even in all the other questions and answers that passed between us."

The cousin now put in a word. "I do not understand, Señor Don Quixote," he said, "how your Grace in the short time you were down there could have seen so many things and done so much talking."

"How long has it been since I went down?" asked Don Quixote.

"A little more than an hour," Sancho told him.

"That cannot be," said the knight, "for night fell and day dawned, and it was day and night three times altogether; so that, according to my count, it was three whole days that I spent in those remote regions that are hidden from our sight."

"My master," averred Sancho, "must be speaking the truth; for since all the things that happened to him came about through magic, who knows? what seemed to us an hour may have been three days and nights for him."

"That is right," said Don Quixote.

"And did your Grace eat in all that time?" the cousin inquired.

"Not a mouthful," replied Don Quixote, "nor did I feel the least bit hungry."

"Then, those that are enchanted do not eat?" the student persisted.

"They neither eat nor are they subject to the major excretions," was Don Quixote's answer, "although it is believed that their nails, beard, and hair continue to grow."

"And do they sleep by any chance?" asked Sancho.

"No, certainly not," said Don Quixote, "or, at least, during the three days I was with them, none of them shut an eye, and the same was true of me."

"The proverb, 'Tell me what company you keep and I'll tell you what you are,' [11] fits in here," observed Sancho. "Seeing your Grace has been keeping company with the bewitched, who fast and stay awake, it is small wonder if you didn't sleep either while you were with them. But forgive me, master, if I tell you that God—I was about to say the devil—may take me if I believe a word of your Grace's story."

"How is that?" asked the cousin. "Do you mean to say that Señor Don Quixote is lying? Why, even if he wished to, he had no opportunity to imagine and invent such a lot of falsehoods."

"I do not think that my master is lying," said Sancho.

"Well, then, what do you think?" Don Quixote wanted to know.

"I think," replied Sancho, "that Merlin or those enchanters that laid a spell on the whole crew you say you saw and talked with down there have put into your noddle or your memory all this rigmarole that you've been telling us, and all that remains to be told."

"Such a thing could be," said Don Quixote, "but it is not so in this case; for I have simply told you what I saw with my own eyes and felt with my own hands. Montesinos showed me countless other marvelous things which I will relate to you in due time and at leisure in the course of our journey, for this is not the place to speak of them. But what will you say when I tell you he pointed out to me three peasant lasses who were gamboling and disporting themselves like goats in those lovely meadows; and no sooner did I see them than I recognized one of them as being the peerless Dulcinea del Toboso and the other two as the same girls who had come with her and with whom we spoke upon the El Toboso road.

"I asked Montesinos if he knew them and he replied that he did not, but that he thought they must be some highborn ladies with a spell upon them. He added that they had arrived but a few days ago, which to me was not surprising in view of the fact that many other ladies of the present time as well as of past ages were to be found there in various strange and enchanted shapes, among whom he said he recognized Queen Guinevere and her duenna Quintañona, she who poured the wine for Lancelot 'when from Britain he came.' " [12]

As he heard his master say this, Sancho Panza thought he would lose his mind or die of laughing. Knowing as he did the truth respecting Dulcinea's supposed enchantment, since he himself had been the enchanter and the concoctor of the evidence, he now was convinced beyond a doubt that the knight was out of his senses and wholly mad.

"It was an evil hour, my dear master," he said, "a worse season, and a sad day when your Grace went down into the other world, and an unlucky moment when you met that Señor Montesinos, who has sent you back to us like this. You would have been better off if you had stayed up here, with all your wits about you as God gave them to you, speaking in proverbs and giving advice at every step of the way, in place of telling us the most foolish stories that could be imagined."

"Knowing you as I do, Sancho," said Don Quixote, "I take no account of your words."

"Nor I of your Grace's," was the reply, "even though you beat me or kill me for those I have already spoken or those that I mean to speak, unless you correct and mend your own. But tell me, seeing that we are now at peace: how or by what sign did you recognize the lady who is our mistress? Did you speak to her, and if so, what did you say and what did she answer you?"

"I recognized her," said Don Quixote, "by the fact that she wore the same clothes that she did when you first made me acquainted with her. I spoke to her, but she did not answer a word; she merely turned her back on me and fled so swiftly that a bolt from a crossbow would not have overtaken her. I was for following her and should have done so had not Montesinos advised me not to waste my strength as it would be in vain; and, moreover, the hour had come for me to leave the cavern. He further assured me that, in the course of time, he would let me know how he and Belerma and Durandarte and all the others who were there had been disenchanted. What gave me the most pain, however, of all the things that I saw and observed, was this. Even as Montesinos was speaking, one of the damsels who accompanied the hapless Dulcinea came up to me from one side, without my having noticed her, and, her eyes brimming with tears, addressed me in a low and troubled voice.

" 'My lady Dulcinea del Toboso,' she said, 'kisses your Grace's hand and implores your Grace to do her the favor of informing her how you are; and being in great want, she also begs your Grace in all earnestness to be so good as to lend her, upon this new dimity petticoat that I am wearing, half a dozen reales or whatever your Grace may have upon you, and she gives you her word that she will pay them back just as soon as she can.'

"I was astonished to receive such a message as this, and, turning to Señor Montesinos, I asked him, 'Is it possible, sir, for the highborn who have been enchanted to suffer want?' To which he made the following reply:

" 'Believe me, your Grace, Señor Don Quixote de la Mancha, this thing that is called want is to be found everywhere; it extends to and reaches all persons and does not even spare the enchanted; and since the lady Dulcinea del Toboso has sent you a request for those six reales and has offered you good security, there is nothing to be done, as I see it, but to give them to her, for she must undoubtedly be hard pressed.'

" 'Security I will not take,' I told him, 'nor can I give her what she asks, for I have only four reales on me.'

"With this, I handed the coins to the damsel—they were the ones that you let me have the other day to bestow as alms upon the poor that I might meet with along the road.

" 'Tell your lady, my dear,' I said, 'that her sufferings weigh upon my heart, and that I only wish I were a Fugger [13] that I might cure them. And you may inform her, further, that there can be no such thing as health for me so long as I am deprived of the pleasure of seeing her and enjoying her discreet conversation. Tell her, also, that I most earnestly beg her Grace to permit herself to be seen and addressed by her captive servant and world-weary knight, and that when she least expects it she will hear that I have taken an oath and made a vow similar to that of the Marquis of Mantua, who swore to avenge his nephew, Baldwin, that time he found him expiring in the heart of the mountains,[14] his vow being not to eat bread off a cloth, along with other trifling stipulations which he added, until vengeance had been had. For I mean to take no rest but to roam the seven parts of the world more faithfully than did the prince Dom Pedro of Portugal [15] until I shall have freed her from this spell.'

" 'All this and more you owe my lady,' was the damsel's answer; and, taking the four reales, in place of dropping a curtsy she cut a caper, leaping more than two yards into the air."

"Holy God!" cried Sancho as Don Quixote reached this point of his story. "Can it be that there are in this world enchanters of such power that they have changed my master's good sense into such madness as this? O master, master! in God's name, think what you are doing, look to your Grace's honor, and do not go believing all this nonsense that has turned your head and left you short of wit."

"It is because you love me, Sancho, that you talk that way," said Don Quixote. "Since you are not experienced in worldly matters, everything that is a little difficult seems to you impossible; but, as I said before, I will tell you more later on of what I saw down there, and you shall hear things that will compel you to believe that what I have already told you is the truth and admits of neither question nor reply."

CHAPTER **XXIV**. *Wherein are related a thousand trifling matters as inconsequential as they are necessary to the proper understanding of this great history.*

HE WHO translated this great history from the original manuscript left by its author, Cid Hamete Benengeli, states that when he came to the chapter dealing with the adventure in the Cave of Montesinos, he found in the margin, in Hamete's own handwriting, these words:

"I cannot bring myself to believe that everything set down in the preceding chapter actually happened to the valiant Don Quixote. The reason is that all the adventures that have taken place up to now have been both possible and likely seeming, but as for this one of the cave,

I see no way in which I can accept it as true, as it is so far beyond the bounds of reason. On the other hand, it is impossible for me to believe that Don Quixote lied, since he is the truest gentleman and noblest knight of his age and would not utter a falsehood if he were to be shot through with arrows; and, furthermore, I must take into account that he related the story in great detail and that in so brief a space of time as that he could not have fabricated such a farrago of nonsense. Accordingly, I would state that if the episode has the appearance of being apocryphal, the fault is not mine, and so, without asserting that it is either false or true, I write it down. You, wise reader, may decide for yourself; for I cannot, nor am I obliged, to do any more. It is definitely reported, however, that at the time of his death he retracted what he had said, confessing that he had invented the incident because it seemed to him to fit in well with those adventures that he had read of in his storybooks."

After that, the chronicle continues.

The cousin was astonished at Sancho's boldness and his master's patience and concluded that the good humor which the knight displayed on that occasion came from the happiness he felt at having seen his lady Dulcinea del Toboso, even though she was enchanted. Otherwise, Sancho deserved a clubbing for the things he had said, for he had certainly been rather impudent. It was to the knight that the student now addressed himself.

"I, Señor Don Quixote de la Mancha," he said, "look upon this journey I have made with you as having been exceedingly worth while, since from it I have gained four things. In the first place, I have made your Grace's acquaintance, which I hold to be a great good fortune. In the second place, I have learned what lies hidden in this Cave of Montesinos and have heard of the mutations of Guadiana and of the Lakes of Ruidera, all of which will stand me in good stead in connection with my *Spanish Ovid* which I now have under way.

"Thirdly, I have discovered something about the antiquity of playing cards; [1] for so far as I was able to gather from Durandarte's words as your Grace quoted them, they must have been in use in the time of the Emperor Charlemagne. After Montesinos had been talking to him for some time, Durandarte awoke and said, 'Patience, and shuffle.' He could not have learned to speak in that manner after he had been enchanted, but only before the spell had been put upon him, that is to say, in France and in Charlemagne's time. And the verification of this point will come in very pat in another book which I am composing, called *Supplement to Virgilius Polydorus on the Invention of Antiquities;* for I believe that in his book he forgot to say anything about cards, and so, if I put it in mine, it will be of very great importance, especially when I am able to cite so distinguished and unimpeachable an authority as Señor Durandarte.

"And fourthly," he concluded, "I have established for a certainty what the source of the Guadiana River is, which up to now has not been known."

"Your Grace is right," said Don Quixote, "but what I should like to know is, if by God's favor they grant you a license to print those books, which I doubt, to whom do you propose to dedicate them?"

"There are lords and grandees in Spain," replied the cousin, "to whom they can be dedicated."

"Not many of them," said Don Quixote. "Not that they do not deserve such a tribute, but because they do not care to accept it, as they do not wish to feel obliged to give the authors the reward that is obviously due them for their courtesy and their pains. But I know a prince who could more than make up for the others—by how much more I should not venture to say, lest perchance I should arouse envy in more than one noble bosom.[2] But let us leave this subject for a more convenient time and see what we can do about finding a lodging for the night."

"Not far from here," said the cousin, "is a hermitage, and the hermit who makes his dwelling there is said to have been a soldier and is reputed to be a good Christian, and, moreover, he is very wise and charitable. Adjoining the hermitage is a little house which he has put up at his own expense, and, although small, it is large enough to accommodate guests."

"Does that hermit you are speaking of by any chance keep hens?" Sancho asked.

"Few hermits are without them," said Don Quixote; "for those of today are not like the ones that dwelt in the deserts of Egypt, who clothed themselves in palm leaves and lived on the roots of the earth. And do not think that by praising the latter I am disparaging the former. What I mean to say is that the penances they do now cannot compare in rigor and harshness with those performed in olden times. This is not to say that they are not all of them good men, for I look upon them as such; and if worst comes to worst, the hypocrite who pretends to be good does less harm than the flagrant sinner."

While they were engaged in this conversation, they saw approaching them a man on foot, walking along swiftly and beating a mule that was laden down with lances and halberds. As he came up to them, he greeted them and was about to pass on when Don Quixote spoke to him.

"Hold, my good man," said the knight. "You seem to be in more of a hurry than your mule."

"I cannot stop, sir," the man replied, "for the arms that you see here are to be used tomorrow and I cannot afford to lose any time. *Adiós.* But in case you would like to know more about the matter, I intend to put up tonight at the inn that is just beyond the hermitage, and if you happen to be going the same way you will find me there, where I will tell you marvels. And so, once more, *adiós.*"

With this he prodded his mule so hard that Don Quixote did not have a chance to ask him what kind of marvels he meant. Being more than a little curious and never able to rest when there was something new to be learned, the knight decided that they would set out at once and spend the night at the inn without stopping at the hermitage which the cousin had suggested as their lodging; and, mounting once more, they all three made straight for the hostelry (where they arrived a little before nightfall). The cousin, on the way,[3] had proposed to Don Quixote that they go up to the hermitage and have a drink, and no sooner did Sancho Panza hear this than he turned his gray's head in that direction, followed by Don Quixote and the student. But Sancho's bad luck would seem to have ordained that the hermit should not be at home, as they were informed by a feminine sub-hermit.[4] When they asked her for a little of the best, she replied that her master did not have any, but if they cared for some of the cheap water [5] she would give it to them with great pleasure.

"If I found any pleasure in water," replied Sancho, "there are wells along the road where I could have satisfied my thirst. Ah, that wedding of Camacho's and all the good things they had in Don Diego's house, how I miss you!"

They then left the hermitage and spurred toward the inn, and had gone but a short distance when they overtook a youth who was walking along leisurely in front of them. He had a sword over his shoulder, and attached to it was a bundle, consisting apparently of his clothes, in all likelihood his trousers or breeches, a cloak, and a shirt or two. He was dressed in a short velvet jacket that was shiny as satin in spots, his shirt was showing, his stockings were of silk, and his shoes were of the square-toed variety in use at court.[6] He was around eighteen or nineteen years of age, with a merry countenance and a seemingly agile body, and he was singing short-meter ballads [7] as he went along, to while away the tedium of his journey. He had just finished a song which the cousin proceeded to memorize and which went like this:

> My purse is lean, so to war I go;
> If I had money, more sense I'd show.

Don Quixote was the first to address the youth. "Your Grace is traveling very lightly, gallant sir," he said. "Whither are you bound, may we ask, if it be your pleasure to tell us?"

"My traveling so lightly," the young fellow answered him, "is to be explained by the heat and by my poverty, and as to where I am going, I am off to war."

"What do you mean by poverty?" asked Don Quixote. "The heat I can understand."

"Sir," the youth replied, "I carry in this bundle a few pairs of velvet breeches to go with this jacket. If I wear them out along the way, I'll have no decent clothes when I reach the city, and I have no money with which to buy others. For that reason, as well as to keep myself cool, I am traveling in this manner until I overtake some companies of infantry that are not twelve leagues from here. I intend to enlist, and there will be no lack of baggage trains in which to travel from then on until we reach the port of embarkation, which they say is to be Cartagena. I would rather have the king for a master and serve him in war than wait on some pauper at court."

"And does not your Grace have any allowance?" inquired the cousin.

"If I had served some grandee of Spain or other highly placed personage," said the youth, "you may be sure that I'd have one. That is what comes of having a good master: from the servants' hall you may rise to be a lieutenant or a captain or get a good pension; but it was always my luck to be attached to some upstart or fortune-hunter where the keep and wages were so wretchedly slim that by the time you paid for the starching of a collar, half of it would be gone, and it would be a miracle indeed if a luckless page was ever able to lay by anything."

"But tell me, friend, upon your life," said Don Quixote, "is it possible that during all the years of your service you have not been able to acquire a livery?"

"Yes," replied the page, "they gave me two suits of livery; but just as they take away the habit from a novice who leaves an order before making his vows, and give him back his own clothes, so did my masters return mine to me; for as soon as their business at court was finished, they went home, taking with them the liveries which they had given their servants merely for purposes of show."

"What *spilorceria!* [8] as the Italians would say," exclaimed Don Quixote. "But for all that, you are to be congratulated on having left the court with so worthy an object in view; for there is nothing on earth more honorable or useful than, first of all, to serve God, and, after that, one's king and rightful lord. This is especially true of the profession of arms, by which more honor if not more wealth is to be attained than by following that of letters, as I have said many times.[9] Granting it is true that letters have founded more great houses than have arms, nevertheless, arms have somewhat of an advantage over letters, being accompanied by a certain splendor with which nothing else can compare. Be sure that you remember what I am about to say to you now, as it will be of great profit and comfort to you under hardship: do not let your mind dwell upon the adversities that may befall you, for the worst of them is death, and if it be a good death, the best fate of all is to die.

"When they asked Julius Caesar, that valiant Roman emperor, what the best death was, he replied: that which comes unexpectedly, suddenly, without having been foreseen; and although he spoke as a pagan who did not know the true God, yet from the point of view of human feeling he was right. Supposing that they kill you in the first skirmish or encounter, or that you are struck down by a cannon ball, blown up by a mine, what does it matter? You die, and that is the end of it. According to Terence, the soldier who dies in battle is more to be admired than the one who lives and seeks safety in flight,[10] and the good soldier achieves fame through obedience to his captain and others in command.

"Remember, my son, that to a soldier the smell of gunpowder is more pleasing than that of civet, and if old age comes upon you while you are still engaged in that honorable calling, even though you be full of wounds and maimed and crippled, at least it will not find you bereft of honor of a kind that poverty cannot diminish. What is more, provisions are now being made for giving aid and relief to old and disabled soldiers; for it is not right to treat them after the manner of certain persons who, when their aged blacks can be of no further use to them, turn the poor creatures out of the house under pretense of freeing them, only to make them the slaves of hunger from which death alone can liberate them. For the present, I do not care to say anything more to you, except that you should get up on the crupper of my **steed** and accompany me to the inn where you will sup with me; and **tomorrow** you shall go your way and may God speed you in accordance with the worthiness of your intentions."

The page did not accept the invitation to mount behind Don Quixote, but he did consent to have supper with him; all of which led Sancho to indulge in a few reflections.

"God help you, what a master!" he thought to himself. "Is it possible that a man who can say as many wise things as you have just said could have told the nonsensical and impossible tale that you did of the Cave of Montesinos? Well, well, we shall see."

They had reached the inn by now, just as night was falling, and Sancho was pleased to see that his master took it for a real inn this time and not for a castle as was his wont. As soon as they entered, Don Quixote inquired of the landlord if the man with the lances and halberds was there and was informed that the fellow was in the stable looking after his mule. The cousin [11] and Sancho therefore proceeded to follow his example, seeing to it that Rocinante had the best stall and manger in the place.

CHAPTER XXV. *Wherein is set down the braying adventure and the droll one of the puppet master, along with the memorable divinations of the divining ape.*

DON QUIXOTE'S bread would not bake,[1] as the saying goes, until he had heard the marvels which the man conveying the arms had promised to relate to him, and he accordingly went out to look for the fellow where the innkeeper had said that he was to be found. Coming upon him there, the knight urged him by all means to give him an immediate answer to the question which he had asked of him upon the highway.

"Not so fast," said the man. "My tale of wonders is not one that can be told standing up; but if you will wait, my good sir, until I have finished bedding down my beast, you shall hear things that will astonish you."

"Don't let that detain you," said Don Quixote. "I'll lend you a hand." And so he did, by sifting out the barley and cleaning the manger, an act of humility which made the man feel obliged to tell the knight with good grace all that he wished to know. And so, seating himself upon a bench with Don Quixote beside him and with the cousin, the page, Sancho Panza, and the innkeeper as senate and audience, the one of the lances and halberds began his story in the following manner:

"Your Worships must know that in a village four leagues and a half from this inn there lives an alderman [2] who, through the scheming and trickery of a servant girl of his, came to lose an ass, and although he searched everywhere for it he was unable to find it. A couple of weeks or so, according to report, had gone by when, as he was standing one day in the public square, another alderman accosted him. 'Reward me for bringing you good news,[3] friend,' the other man said, 'your ass has shown up.'

" 'That I will, and gladly,' replied the owner of the ass, 'but tell me, where was he found?'

" 'In the woods,' was the answer. 'I saw him this morning, without a packsaddle or harness of any kind and so lean-looking that it was really pitiful. I wanted to drive him home for you, but he is already so wild and shy that everytime I went up to him he would run away into the thickest part of the forest. If you like, we will both go back and hunt for him. Just let me put this she-ass in the stable and I'll be with you in a moment.'

" 'You will be doing me a great favor,' said the owner of the ass that was lost, 'and I will try to pay you back in the same coin.'

"All those that know the truth of the matter," the man who was conveying the weapons went on, "tell the story in the same way that I am telling it to you, with all these details. In short, the two aldermen set out for the forest, on foot and arm in arm, but when they came to the place where they thought the ass would be, they discovered no trace of him, nor were they able, however much they searched, to find him anywhere around.

"Whereupon the alderman who had had a glimpse of the beast said to the other one, 'See here, my friend, I've just thought of a plan that will undoubtedly enable us to discover this animal even though he has hidden himself in the bowels of the earth, not to speak of the forest. As it happens, I know how to bray marvelously well, and if you are at all good at it, then regard the thing as accomplished.'

" 'Do I know how to bray?' said the other. 'By God, when it comes to that, I won't take second place to anybody, not even to the asses themselves.'

" 'We shall see as to that presently,' said the second alderman. 'It is my plan for you to take one side of the woods and I the other in such a way as to make a complete circuit; and every so often you will bray and I will bray, and the ass cannot fail to hear and answer us if he is in this forest at all.'

" 'I assure you, my friend,' replied the owner of the beast, 'your plan is an excellent one and worthy of your great intellect.'

"They then separated as they had agreed to do, and as it happened, they both brayed at practically the same moment, and each deceived by the other came running up, thinking that the ass had put in an appearance.

" 'Is it possible, my friend,' said the one who had lost the animal, 'that it was not my ass that brayed?'

" 'No,' said the other, 'it was I.'

" 'Well, in that case,' said the owner, 'there is not the slightest difference between you and an ass so far as braying is concerned, for I never in my life heard anything that sounded more like it.'

" 'That compliment,' replied the one who had thought up the plot, 'is one that is better suited to you than to me, my friend, for by the God that made me, you can give a couple of brays by way of odds to the best and most skillful brayer in the world. Your voice is deep, the tone sustained, the time and pitch are excellent, and the cadenzas are magnificent.⁴ The short of it is, I yield you the palm and banner for this rare accomplishment.'

" 'In that case,' said the owner of the ass, 'I am going to have a little higher opinion of myself from now on, in the belief that I know something, seeing that I possess at least one talent. Although I thought that I brayed very well, I never knew I was as good as all that.'

" 'And I will further assert,' said the second alderman, 'that there are rare gifts going to waste in this world for the reason that those who possess them do not know how to make proper use of them.'

" 'Ours,' replied his friend, 'cannot be of much use save in cases like the present one; but please God it may aid us here.'

"Following this conversation, they parted once more and went back to their braying, but they continued to mistake each other for the ass and meet again. Finally, they hit upon a countersign to distinguish themselves from the donkey: it was agreed that each should bray twice in succession; and in this manner, repeating their calls at every step they took, they made the circuit of the entire wood, but the ass did not answer them or give any sign of his presence. Indeed, how could the poor unfortunate beast have done so? For at last they found him in the thick of the forest, devoured by wolves.

" 'I wondered why he did not answer,' said his owner, 'for if he had not been dead, he would surely have brayed when he heard us, or he would not have been an ass. However, in exchange for having heard you bray so prettily, my friend, I count all the trouble I have had in looking for him as worth my while, even though I find him like this.'

" 'After you, my friend,' [5] the other replied. 'If the abbot sings well, the acolyte is not far behind.' [6]

"Hoarse and disappointed, they then returned to their village, where they told their friends, neighbors, and acquaintances all that had happened as they were searching for the ass, each one extolling the other's skill at braying; all of which was rumored about and discussed in the neighboring hamlets. Now, the devil as you know never sleeps but is fond of sowing and spreading discord and resentments everywhere, carrying gossip on the wind and creating quarrels out of nothing; and the devil it was who ordained and saw to it that the people of the other villages, when they met someone from ours, should promptly start braying, as if they were throwing up to us the accomplishment of our aldermen. Then the small lads took to it, and that was worse than all Hell itself. Thus the braying spread from one town to another, until now the natives of our village are well known and stand out as much as blacks do from whites; and the sorry joke has been carried so far that the victims have on many occasions sallied forth in an armed band and well-formed squadron to give battle to the ones who mock them, and neither king nor rook, fear nor shame, can remedy matters.

"Tomorrow or the day after," the speaker concluded, "I think the people of my village—that is to say, the brayers—mean to take the field against another town which is two leagues from ours and which is one of those that persecute us most. And in order that they may go forth well prepared, I am taking them those lances and halberds that you saw. These are the marvelous things I was going to tell you about, and if you do not think they are wonderful, I don't know any others."

With these words the good man finished his story, and at that moment there came through the gate of the inn a man all clad in chamois skin, hose, breeches, and a doublet.

"Have you a lodging, mine host?" he asked. "Here comes the divining ape and the spectacle of the freeing of Melisendra."

"Body of so-and-so," exclaimed the innkeeper, "if it isn't Master Pedro! We're going to have a fine night of it."

(I neglected to mention that the said Master Pedro had a patch of green taffeta over one eye and the whole side of his face, showing that something ailed it.)

"Your Grace is very welcome, Señor Master Pedro," said the landlord, "but where are the ape and the show? I don't see them."

"They are near at hand," replied the chamois-clad arrival. "I came on ahead to find out if you could put us up."

"I'd turn out the Duke of Alva himself to make room for you," the innkeeper assured him. "Bring on the show, for there are those in the inn tonight that will pay to see it and to watch that ape's clever tricks."

"Very well," said the one with the patch. "I will lower my price and will consider myself well paid if I make expenses. I'll go back now and bring on the cart." And, with this, he left the inn.

Don Quixote then inquired of the innkeeper who Master Pedro was and asked, also, concerning the show and the ape.

"This man," replied the landlord, "is a puppet master [7] who for a long time now has been roaming this Mancha de Aragon region,[8] giving a performance that shows the freeing of Melisendra by the famous Don Gaiferos,[9] which is one of the most interesting and best-staged stories that has been seen in this part of the kingdom for many a year. In addition, he carries with him one of the cleverest apes that you ever saw; indeed, you cannot imagine his like among men, for if you ask him anything, after listening carefully to what you say, he will jump up on his master's shoulder and whisper the answer in his ear, and then Master Pedro will announce it. He can tell you a good deal more about past events than he can about those that are to come, and although he does not always hit the truth, in most cases he does not miss it, until we are forced to think that he has the devil in him.

"He gets two reales for every question if the ape answers it—I mean, if his master does after the ape has whispered it to him. And, as a result, it is believed that Master Pedro is a very rich man. He is a 'gallant man,' as they say in Italy, and a 'good companion,' [10] and leads the finest kind of life; he talks more than six men, and drinks more than a dozen, all at the expense of his tongue, his ape, and his puppet show."

At this point Master Pedro returned, bringing with him in a cart his puppet theater and a big tailless ape with hindquarters that were as bare as a piece of felt. It was not a vicious-looking animal, however.

"Sir Diviner," said Don Quixote the moment he caught sight of the beast, "can your Grace tell me what fish we are going to catch [11] and how we are going to make out? See, here are my two reales." And he ordered Sancho to give the coins to Master Pedro, who replied in the ape's behalf.

"Señor," he said, "this animal does not answer any questions concerning things that are to come, but he knows something concerning the past and more or less about the present."

"Pshaw!" [12] exclaimed Sancho. "I wouldn't give a penny to be told my past, since who can know it better than I? It would be foolish to pay you for that. But since he knows the present also, here are my two reales, and let this Sir Ape of Apes [13] tell me what my wife, Teresa Panza, is doing right now and how she is amusing herself."

Master Pedro, however, declined to take the money. "I accept no fees in advance," he said; "you can pay me when the service has been rendered." Saying this, he slapped his left shoulder a couple of times, and with a single bound the ape was there and with his mouth close to his master's ear began chattering his teeth very rapidly. Having kept this up for the time it takes to say a Credo, he gave another leap and was back on the ground once more. In great haste Pedro then ran over and threw himself upon his knees before Don Quixote, embracing the knight's legs.

"I embrace these legs as I would the columns of Hercules, O illustrious reviver of the now-forgotten profession of knight-errantry, O Don Quixote de la Mancha, thou who canst never be praised enough, bringer of courage to the faint of heart, support of those that are about to fall, arm of the fallen, staff and counsel of all the unfortunate!"

Upon hearing these words, Don Quixote was astounded, Sancho was amazed, the cousin was staggered, the page was astonished, the man from the braying town was dumfounded, the landlord was bewildered, and all present were filled with wonder.

"And thou, O worthy Sancho Panza," the puppet master went on, "the best squire to the best knight in the world, be of good cheer, for your good wife Teresa is well and at this moment is engaged in hackling a pound of flax. What is more, she has at her left hand a jug with a broken spout that holds a good sip of wine to cheer her at her work."

"That I can very well believe," said Sancho, "and if it wasn't that she is so jealous, I wouldn't change her for the giantess Andandona,[14] who, according to my master, was all you could ask for in the way of a woman. My Teresa is one of those that won't deprive themselves of anything though their heirs may have to pay for it."

"Well, all I have to say," observed Don Quixote, "is that he who reads much and travels far, sees much and learns a great deal. For what could ever have led me to believe that there are apes in this world that can divine things as I have seen this one do with my own eyes? I am that same Don Quixote de la Mancha this animal has mentioned, though he has gone a bit too far in his praise of me. But whatever sort of man I may be, I thank Heaven that it has endowed me with a tender and compassionate heart, always inclined to do good to all and evil to none."

"If I had money," said the page, "I would ask Señor Ape what is going to happen to me in the course of my wanderings."

Master Pedro by this time had risen from his position at Don Quixote's feet. "I have told you," he said to the page, "that this little beast does not answer questions about the future; if he did, it would make no difference whether you had money or not. In order to be of service to Don Quixote here present, I am willing to sacrifice all profits; and now, because I have promised to do so [15] and in order to afford him pleasure, I should like to set up my show and provide amusement for all those that are in the house, at no cost whatsoever."

Delighted at this, the landlord pointed out a place where the puppet theater might be erected, and Master Pedro at once began his preparations. Don Quixote, meanwhile, was not wholly satisfied with the performance that had just been given; for it did not seem to him quite proper that an ape should be able to divine either past or present things. And so, while the puppet master was getting his show ready, the knight retired with Sancho to a corner of the stable where no one could hear them.

"Look, Sancho," he said, "I have given considerable thought to the extraordinary ability this ape displays, and it is my personal opinion that Master Pedro, his owner, must have a pact with the devil, either tacit or express."

"If the pack is express [16] and from the devil," said Sancho, "then it must undoubtedly be a dirty one; but of what use are such packs as that to Master Pedro?"

"You don't understand me, Sancho. What I mean to say is, he must have made some bargain with the devil for Satan to put this power into the ape so that he, Master Pedro, can earn a living by it; and then, when he is rich, he will give the devil his soul, which is the thing that this enemy of mankind is after. I was led to believe this when I learned that the animal answers only questions about the past or the present, for that is as far as the devil's knowledge extends; he does not know what is to be, but can only guess at it and not always rightly, since it is for God alone to know all times and seasons, and for Him there is no past or future but only the present.

"This being true, and true it is," the knight continued, "I wonder that they have not denounced him to the Holy Office so that he might be questioned and forced to confess from whom it is he derives that power of divination. For it is certain that this ape is no astrologer; neither he nor his master set up, nor do they know how to set up, those figures that are known as judiciary,[17] now so popular in Spain that there is not a wench or a page or a cobbler that does not presume to try his or her hand at them just as readily as one would pick up from the ground a knave from a deck of cards, thus bringing to nought with their lies and ignorance the marvelous truths of science. I know a lady who asked one of these figure-makers if a little lap dog she had was going to have pups and how many of them and what color they would be; to which Sir Astrologer, after he had made his calculations, replied that the bitch would have a litter of three, one green, one flesh-colored, and one striped, provided she was covered between ten and eleven o'clock, in the morning or at night, and on a Monday or a Saturday. But what happened was, the bitch died of overeating two days later, and as a result, Sir Horoscope-caster, like most of his kind, continued to be looked upon as being most expert in the matter of planetary science."

"But, nevertheless," said Sancho, "I wish you would have Master Pedro ask his ape if what happened to your Grace in the Cave of Montesinos is true or not; for, begging your Grace's pardon, it is my opinion that it was all humbug and lies, or else it was something that you dreamed."

"That may be," admitted Don Quixote. "In any event, I will act upon your advice, though I have my scruples about doing so."

Master Pedro now came up to look for Don Quixote and tell him that everything was in order for the show and that his Grace should come see it as it was worth his while. The knight thereupon told the puppet master what was on his mind and requested him to ask the ape if certain things that had taken place in the Cave of Montesinos were true or if they were but dreams, as it seemed to him they were partly true and partly imaginary. Without a word in reply, Master Pedro went back and got his ape and put it down in front of Don Quixote and Sancho.

"Look, Sir Ape," he said, "this gentleman would like to know if certain things that happened in a cave known as the Cave of Montesinos are true or false." He then gave the accustomed signal, and the animal jumped up on his left shoulder and to all appearances began speaking in his ear.

"The ape," announced Master Pedro, "says that the things your Grace saw or experienced down there are in part false and in part credible, and that is all he can tell you. He says that if your Grace wishes to know more, he will answer any questions you have to ask him next Friday, as his power has left him for the present and will not return until then."

"Didn't I tell you, my master," said Sancho, "that I couldn't believe all those happenings in the cave that your Grace told us about were true, or even the half of them?"

"Time will tell, Sancho," was Don Quixote's reply; "for time, the discoverer of all things, never fails to bring them to the light of the sun even though they be hidden in the bosom of the earth. But enough of this. Let us go see the good Master Pedro's show, for I fancy there is going to be something novel about it."

"What do you mean, something?" said the puppet master. "This spectacle of mine has sixty thousand novelties to offer. I assure you, Señor Don Quixote, it is one of the things best worth seeing that are to be found in the world today; but *operibus credite, et non verbis,*[18] and now, fall to! for it is growing late and we have much to do and say and show."

Don Quixote and Sancho did as they had been requested and went to the place where the puppet theater had been set up. It was uncovered and surrounded on all sides by lighted wax tapers, which made it look very bright and gay. Since he was the one who had to manipulate the puppets, Master Pedro took his place in the rear, while out in front, to act as interpreter, stood a lad who was his servant. It was the interpreter's business to explain the mysteries of the performance, and he had a rod with which he pointed to the figures as they came out. When all those in the house had taken their places in front of the stage, some of them standing, and with Don Quixote, Sancho, the page, and the cousin in the best seats, the interpreter began speaking. As to what he had to say, that will be heard and seen by the one who reads or listens to the chapter that is to follow.

CHAPTER XXVI. *Wherein is continued the droll adventure of the puppet master, with other things that are truly quite good.*

The Tyrians and Trojans were silent all,[1] by which I mean to say that all those watching the show were hanging on the lips of the one who announced its marvels, when of a sudden, from behind the scene, there came the sound of drums and trumpets with much artillery firing. This lasted but a short while, and then the lad raised his voice and spoke.

"This true story,"[2] he said, "which your Worships are about to witness, is taken word for word from the French chronicles and Spanish ballads that you hear in the mouths of people everywhere, even the young ones in the street. It tells how Señor Don Gaiferos freed his wife, Melisendra, who was held captive by the Moors in Spain, in the city of Sansueña, for that was the name then given to what is now known as Saragossa. Here your Worships may see Don Gaiferos playing at backgammon, as in the song:

> *At backgammon playing is Don Gaiferos,*
> *Melisendra's already forgotten now.*[3]

And that personage whom you see there, with a crown on his head and a scepter in his hand, is the Emperor Charlemagne, Melisendra's supposed father, who, angered by his son-in-law's idleness and unconcern, comes to chide him. Observe how vehemently and earnestly he does it. You would think he was going to give him half a dozen raps with his scepter, and there are some authors who say that he did let him have it, and properly.

"After making a long speech on how his son-in-law is imperiling his honor by not endeavoring to procure his wife's release, Charlemagne, according to the ballad, addresses these words to him:

> *Enough I have said; see to it.*[4]

Your Worships will observe how the emperor turns his back on Don Gaiferos and leaves him fretting and fuming. Impatiently and in a towering rage, Gaiferos flings the draughtboard far from him; he hastily asks for his armor and begs his cousin, Don Orlando, to lend him his sword, Durindana.[5] Orlando refuses to do this but offers his company in the difficult undertaking. The valiant Gaiferos, however, in his anger will not accept it, saying that he is well able to save his wife single-handed though she were hidden away at the center of the earth. He then goes to don his armor and set out on his journey.

"Notice, your Worships, the eyes on the bull you see there, which is supposed to be one of those of the palace at Saragossa, today known as the Aljafería. That lady who appears upon the balcony, dressed in the Moorish fashion, is the peerless Melisendra, who from that vantage point often gazes out upon the road that leads from France, for this is the way she consoles herself in her captivity, by thinking of Paris and of her husband. Note, also, the strange thing that is about to happen now, the like of which has never been seen before, it may be. Behold that Moor who silently and stealthily, a finger on his mouth, creeps up behind her. Next, he gives her a kiss full on the lips, and she cannot wait to spit it out as she wipes her mouth with the white sleeve of her smock. Hear her moans; watch her as she tears her hair, as if it were to blame for the wrong that has been done her.

"That stately looking Moor you see in that corridor is King Marsilio of Sansueña.[6] He has witnessed the other Moor's insolence, and although the man is a kinsman and a great favorite of his, he has him arrested at once and orders that he be given two hundred lashes as he is borne through the streets in accordance with the custom of the city,

with criers in front
and rods of justice behind.[7]

You will note how quickly they carry out the sentence, though the offense has barely been committed; for with the Moors there are no indictments, warrants, and similar processes as there are with us."

"Child, child," said Don Quixote in a loud voice at this point, "keep to the straight line of your story and do not go off on curves and tangents; for a great deal of proof is required in such cases."

From behind the scenes Master Pedro also spoke up. "Boy," he said, "don't try any flourishes but do as this gentleman says, that is the safest way. Stick to your plain song and don't try any counterpoint melodies, for they are likely to break down from being overfine."

"I will do so," replied the lad; and then he went on, "This figure on horseback, wearing a Gascon cloak, is Don Gaiferos himself, and this is his wife, who has now been avenged for the enamored Moor's bold affront. With calmer mien she has taken her place on the balcony of the tower, from which she speaks to her husband, believing him to be some traveler, and holds a long conversation with him:

> If to France you go, Sir Knight,
> Ask for Gaiferos,[8]

as the ballad has it. I will not repeat it all, since prolixity begets disgust. It is enough for you to observe how Don Gaiferos makes himself known, and how Melisendra by her happy manner shows that she has recognized him. We now see her lowering herself from the balcony to take her place upon the crupper of her worthy consort's steed—but ah! the unfortunate one! The edge of her petticoat has caught on one of the iron railings and she is left hanging in the air, unable to reach the ground.

"But see how merciful Heaven sends aid when it is needed most. Don Gaiferos now comes up and, without minding whether or not he tears the rich petticoat, he brings her down by main force and then in a trice lifts her onto his horse, seating her astride like a man and bidding her put her arms around him so that she will not fall, for the Señora Melisendra is not used to riding in that manner.[9] See, too, how the steed neighs, as a sign that he is proud to bear such a burden of valor and beauty in the persons of his master and mistress. See how they wheel and leave the city behind them and joyfully take the road for Paris. Go in peace, O true and peerless lovers; may you find safety in your beloved fatherland, and may fortune place no obstacle in the way of your happy journey. May the eyes of your friends and kinsfolk rest upon you as you spend in peace and tranquillity the remaining days of your life—and let them be as many as those of Nestor!"

Here, once again, Master Pedro raised his voice. "Speak plainly, lad, and don't indulge in any flights. All affectation is bad."

The interpreter made no reply to this, but continued as follows:

"There was no want of idle eyes of the kind that see everything; and, seeing Melisendra descend from the balcony and mount her husband's horse, these persons notified King Marsilio, who at once ordered the call to arms to be sounded. Observe with what haste they go about it. The entire city is now drowned in the sound of bells, pealing from the towers of all the mosques."

At this point Don Quixote interrupted him. "No," he said, "that won't do. In this matter of the bells Master Pedro is far from accurate, for bells are not in use among the Moors; instead, they employ kettledrums and a kind of flute somewhat like our flageolet. So, you can see that this business of bells ringing in Sansueña is beyond a doubt a great piece of nonsense."

Hearing this, Master Pedro stopped ringing the bells. "Don't be looking for trifles, Señor Don Quixote," he said, "or expect things to be impossibly perfect. Are not a thousand comedies performed almost every day that are full of inaccuracies and absurdities, yet they run their course and are received not only with applause but with admiration and all the rest? Go on, boy, and let him talk; for so long as I fill my wallet, it makes no difference if there are as many inaccuracies in my show as there are motes in the sun." [10]

"You have spoken the truth," was Don Quixote's reply.

With this, the lad resumed his commentary. "And now, just see the glittering cavalcade that is leaving the city in pursuit of the Catholic lovers; [11] listen to all the trumpets and flutes, the drums and tabors. I fear me they are going to overtake them and bring them back tied to the tail of their own horse, which would be a dreadful sight to behold."

Upon seeing such a lot of Moors and hearing such a din, Don Quixote thought that it would be a good thing for him to aid the fugitives; and, rising to his feet, he cried out, "Never as long as I live and in my presence will I permit such violence to be done to so famous a knight and so bold a lover as Don Gaiferos. Halt, lowborn rabble; cease your pursuit and persecution, or otherwise ye shall do battle with me!"

With these words he drew his sword, and in one bound was beside the stage; and then with accelerated and unheard-of fury he began slashing at the Moorish puppets, knocking some of them over, beheading others, crippling this one, mangling that one. Among the many blows he dealt was one downward stroke that, if Master Pedro had not ducked and crouched, would have sliced off his head more easily than if it had been made of almond paste.

"Stop, Señor Don Quixote!" cried Master Pedro. "Those are not real Moors that your Grace is knocking over, maiming, and killing, but pasteboard figures. Sinner that I am, if you haven't destroyed and ruined all the property I own!"

But this was not sufficient to halt the rain of cuts and slashes, downstrokes, back-strokes, and doublehanded blows that Don Quixote was dealing. The short of the matter is, in less time than it takes to say two Credos he had knocked the entire theater to the ground and had slashed to bits all its fixtures and its puppets, King Marsilio being badly wounded while the Emperor Charlemagne had both his head and his crown split in two. The audience, meanwhile, had been thrown into confusion; the ape fled over the roof of the inn, the cousin was frightened, the page was intimidated, and even Sancho Panza was terrified, for, as he swore upon his word when the tempest was over, he had never seen his master in such a towering passion.

When the destruction of the theater had been completed, Don Quixote calmed down a bit. "I only wish," he said, "that I had here before me right now those who do not or will not see how useful knights-errant are to the world. Just think, if I had not been present, what would have become of the worthy Don Gaiferos and the beauteous Melisendra? You may be sure that those dogs would have overtaken them by this time and would have committed some outrage upon them. And so I say to you: Long live knight-errantry over all living things on the face of this earth!"

"Let it live, and welcome," said Master Pedro in a sickly voice, "and let me die, since I am so unfortunate that I can say with the king, Don Rodrigo:

> *Yesterday I was lord of Spain,*
> *And today I do not have a tower left*
> *That I can call my own.*[12]

Not half an hour ago, nay, not half a minute ago, I was lord of kings and emperors; my stables were filled with countless horses and my trunks and bags with any number of gala costumes; and now I am but a poor beggar, ruined and destitute. Above all, I have lost my ape; for I give you my word, my teeth will sweat before I get him back, and all owing to the ill-advised wrath of this Sir Knight. I have heard it said of him that he protects orphans, sets wrongs to right, and performs other acts of charity; but in my case alone he has failed to manifest his generous intentions, blessed be the highest heavens! I can well believe that he is the Knight of the Mournful Countenance, seeing he has so disfigured mine!"

Sancho Panza was quite touched by the puppet master's words. "Don't cry, Master Pedro," he begged him; "don't carry on like that, you break my heart. For I can tell you that my master, Don Quixote, is so Catholic and scrupulous a Christian that if he can be brought to see he has done you any wrong, he will own up to it, and what's more, he will want to pay you for all the damage he has caused you and a good deal over and above it."

"If Señor Don Quixote," replied the puppet master, "will but pay me for some small part of my fixtures which he has destroyed, I will be satisfied and his Grace will have a clear conscience; for one cannot be saved who holds the property of another against its owner's will without making restitution."

"That is true enough," said Don Quixote, "but up to now I am not aware that I hold anything of yours, Master Pedro."

"How is that?" replied the showman. "Those remains lying there on the hard and barren ground, what was it scattered and annihilated them if not the invincible strength of that mighty arm? Whose puppets were those if not mine? And how else did I make my living?"

"I am now coming to believe," said Don Quixote, "that I was right in thinking, as I often have, that the enchanters who persecute me merely place figures like these in front of my eyes and then change and transform them as they like. In all earnestness, gentlemen, I can assure you that everything that took place here seemed to me very real indeed, and Melisendra, Don Gaiferos, Marsilio, and Charlemagne were all their flesh-and-blood selves. That was why I became so angry. In order to fulfill the duties of my profession as knight-errant, I wished to aid and favor the fugitives, and with this in mind I did what you saw me do. If it came out wrong, it is not my fault but that of my wicked persecutors; but, nevertheless, I willingly sentence myself to pay the costs of my error, even though it did not proceed from malice. Reckon up what I owe you, Master Pedro, for those figures I have destroyed, and I will reimburse you in good Castilian currency."

Master Pedro bowed. "I expected no less," he said, "of so rare a Christian as the valiant Don Quixote de la Mancha, the true friend and protector of all needy vagabonds. Mine host here and the great Sancho shall act as arbiters between your Grace and me and they shall appraise the value, or likely value, of the properties destroyed."

Both the landlord and Sancho agreed to act in this capacity, and Master Pedro then picked up off the ground King Marsilio of Saragossa, minus his head.

"You can see," he said, "how impossible it is to restore this king to his former state; and so, it seems to me, saving your better judgment, that for his death, demise, and final end I should have four and a half reales."

"Proceed," said Don Quixote.

"As for this one who is split open from top to bottom," Master Pedro went on, taking in his hands the late Emperor Charlemagne, "it would not be too much if I were to ask five reales and a quarter."

"That's no small sum," said Sancho.

"Nor is it very much," replied the innkeeper.

"Give him the whole five and a quarter," said Don Quixote. "The sum total of this memorable disaster does not hang on a quarter more or less. And please be quick about it, Master Pedro, for it is suppertime and I feel the stirrings of hunger."

"This figure," continued Master Pedro, "without a nose and with one eye missing, is that of the beauteous Melisendra; and for it I ask, and I think I am right in doing so, two reales and twelve maravedis."

"The devil," said Don Quixote, "must have a hand in it if Melisendra and her husband have not reached the French border, at the very least, by this time, for the horse they rode on seemed to me to fly rather than gallop; and so there is no need to try to sell me the cat for the hare [13] by showing me here a Melisendra without any nose when she is now, if things went right, stretched out at her ease and enjoying herself with her husband in France. God help everyone to his own, Master Pedro. Let us deal plainly and with honest intent. You may continue."

Master Pedro perceived that Don Quixote's wits were wandering and that he was beginning to harp on the old chord again, but he was not disposed to let him off so easily.

"This cannot be Melisendra after all," he said; "it must be one of the damsels that waited upon her; and if you will give me sixty maravedis for her, I will consider myself well paid."

In this manner he went on putting a price on each of the puppets that had been destroyed, and after these estimates had been adjusted by the two arbiters to the satisfacion of both parties, it was found that the total came to forty reales and three quarters, and Sancho promptly handed over this sum; whereupon Master Pedro asked for two reales more for the trouble of catching the ape.

"Give them to him, Sancho," said Don Quixote, "not for catching the ape, but for getting the she-ape by the tail. [14] And I would further give two hundred right now to anyone who could assure me that Melisendra and Don Gaiferos are safe in France with their own people."

"No one can tell you that better than my ape," said Master Pedro, "but there's no devil that could catch him now, although I fancy lonesomeness and hunger will force him to come looking for me tonight, and God will bring another day, and we shall see what we shall see."

The storm centering around the puppet theater having finally subsided, they all sat down to eat their supper in peace and good companionship, and all at Don Quixote's expense, for he was extremely generous. Before daybreak the one who was conveying the lances and halberds took his departure, and shortly after sunup the cousin and the page came to bid Don Quixote good-by, as the former was returning home, while the latter wished to be upon his way; and to help the soldier out the knight made him a present of twelve reales. Not caring to engage in any further arguments with the one of the Mournful Countenance, whom he knew very well, Master Pedro was up before the sun, and, having caught his ape and gathered up what was left of his show, he too was off to seek adventures.

As for the innkeeper, to whom Don Quixote was a stranger, he was equally astonished at his guest's madness and his liberality. Sancho, upon his master's orders, paid very generously for their lodgings, and, having said farewell, they left the inn around eight in the morning and took to the road once more. Here we shall leave them, as it is necessary to do so in order to clear up certain other matters that are pertinent to this famous history.

CHAPTER XXVII. *Wherein is set forth who Master Pedro and his ape were, with the misfortune that befell Don Quixote in the braying adventure, which did not end as he had hoped and expected it would.*

CID HAMETE, the chronicler of this great history, begins the present chapter with these words: "I swear as a Catholic Christian"; which leads his translator to remark that, being a Moor as he undoubtedly was, the author merely meant that, just as a Catholic Christian when he takes an oath swears, or is supposed to swear, to tell the truth in all that he says, so in what he himself has to set down about Don Quixote he will adhere to the truth just as if he were taking such a Christian oath, especially when it comes to explaining who Master Pedro was, as well as that ape of his whose divinations had astonished all the towns and villages in those parts.

He then goes on to say that whoever has read the first part of this story will very well remember Ginés de Pasamonte, who was one of the galley slaves that Don Quixote freed in the Sierra Morena,[1] a favor for which he received poor thanks and worse payment at the hands of that vicious, low-life crew. This Ginés de Pasamonte, whom Don Quixote insisted upon calling Ginesillo de Parapilla, was the one who stole Sancho's ass, although, through a fault of the printers, there was no explanation as to how or when the theft was committed,[2] a circumstance which has led many to attribute a typographical blunder to bad memory on the part of the author. But the short of the matter is, Ginés did steal the gray by creeping up on the sleeping Sancho Panza and making use of the stratagem that Brunello employed when he stole the horse from between Sacripante's legs at Albraca,[3] and Sancho afterward recovered his beast as has been related.[4]

This fellow Ginés, then, fearful of being brought to justice for his innumerable crimes and villainies, which were so many and so great that he himself composed a big book about them, had made up his mind to go over into the kingdom of Aragon;[5] and there, covering his left eye with a patch, he had taken to the trade of puppet master, for he was exceedingly skillful at this, and at the art of juggling as well. He accordingly had purchased the ape of some freed Christians coming from Barbary and had taught it to jump on his shoulder when he made a certain sign, and whisper, or pretend to whisper, in his ear. Before entering a village with his show he would make inquiries in the neighboring one, or of the person who could best give him the information, as to what special events had occurred there and which individuals were involved, and he would then commit to memory the facts he had thus gathered.

Upon arrival, he would first put on his puppet show, which now had to do with one story and now with another, but all of them lively, merry, and familiar to his audience. When the performance was over, he would introduce his ape and extol the cleverness of the animal, which was able to divine anything past or present but which possessed no skill so far as the future was concerned. For each question answered he charged two reales, but he would sometimes make a reduction, depending upon the attitude which he sensed in his listeners. Occasionally he would come to a house where people lived that he knew something about, and even though they asked him nothing, not caring to pay for it, he would signal to his ape and assert that the beast had told him such and such things that fitted in perfectly with the facts of the case. By this means he acquired an extraordinary reputation and everyone ran after him. At other times he would give so crafty an answer that it was bound to suit the question; and inasmuch as no one pressed him to explain how his ape did it, he made monkeys of them all and filled his pouch.

Thus, the moment he entered the inn he recognized Don Quixote and Sancho, and so it was easy to astonish them both and all those present. But it would have cost him dearly had the knight dropped his hand a little more that time he cut off King Marsilio's head and destroyed all his cavalry, as told in the preceding chapter.

So much for Master Pedro and his ape. Returning now to Don Quixote de la Mancha, I may state that after having sallied forth from the inn, he resolved to take a look at the banks of the Ebro and the surrounding region before entering the city of Saragossa, for there was still plenty of time to spare between then and the day of the tournament. With this purpose in mind he continued his journey for a couple of days without anything happening to him that is worthy of being set down in writing. On the third day, as he was ascending a hill, he heard a great din of drums, trumpets, and musket fire. At first he thought it must be some regiment of soldiers that was passing that way, and in order to have a sight of them he spurred Rocinante and hastened to the top of the hill, at the foot of which on the other side he could see what appeared to be more than two hundred men armed with various kinds of weapons, such as lances, crossbows, truncheons, halberds, pikes, a few muskets, and many bucklers.

Coming down the slope, he drew near enough to see their banners plainly and make out their colors and devices. He noted in particular one of white satin, mounted upon a standard, upon which was painted a very lifelike ass, resembling a Sardinian pony,[6] with its head reared, its mouth open, and its tongue out, in the posture and seeming act of braying, while round about it in large letters were these verses:

> *They did not bray in vain,*
> *Those judges twain.*

From which Don Quixote surmised that these must be the people from the braying town, and he remarked as much to Sancho, informing him at the same time what was inscribed on the banner. He further observed that the one who had told them of this affair in the first place had been wrong in stating that it was a couple of aldermen who had done the braying, since according to those verses they were officers of justice.[7]

"Sir," said Sancho Panza in reply, "you need not let that trouble you, for it may be that the aldermen who did the braying in the course of time have come to be justices of the peace of their village, and so it is all right to call them by either title, especially since it makes no difference so far as the truth of the story is concerned whether the brayers were one or the other, so long as bray they did, and a judge can bray just as well as an alderman."

In short, they perceived that one town had come out to do battle with the other which had jeered at it more than was right or neighborly. Don Quixote now went up to them, not without some misgivings on the part of Sancho, who never liked to get mixed up in such affrays. Those who were drawn up in squadron formation opened ranks to receive him, for they thought he was someone on their side, and with considerable dash and self-composure the knight rode up to where the standard was. There, all the leaders of the army gathered around to stare at him, for they were as astonished as everyone was when they beheld him for the first time. Seeing them gazing at him so attentively, before anyone had spoken or asked him a single question, he chose to be the first to break the silence by raising his voice and addressing them in this manner:

"Good sirs, I would beg you as earnestly as I can not to interrupt what I am about to say to you unless you disagree with it or find that it wearies you. If that should happen, you have but to raise a hand and I will put a seal upon my mouth and a gag upon my tongue."

They all thereupon informed him that he might say whatever he liked and they would be very glad to listen to it; and with this permission, he continued.

"I, my dear sirs, am a knight-errant, whose profession is that of arms and whose business it is to lend aid and favor to all those that stand in need of it. Some days ago I learned of your unfortunate plight and am aware of the reason that has led you to take up arms and avenge yourselves upon your enemies. Having thought the matter over a great many times, I find that according to the rules of honor you are mistaken in thinking that you have been insulted, for no one individual can insult an entire community unless, not knowing who is guilty of some act of treason, he defies it as a body. Of this we have an example in Don Diego Ordóñez de Lara, who, ignorant of the fact that Vellido Dolfos alone was guilty of slaying his king, challenged them all, laying upon them all the burden of answering for the crime and exacting vengeance accordingly.[8] It is true that Don Diego went a little too far, indeed he went very much beyond the rules governing a challenge; it was not proper for him to defy the dead, nor the waters, nor the loaves of bread,[9] nor those as yet unborn, with all the other details that he set forth. But let that pass; for when anger is spawned, the tongue has no father, governor, or bridle to control it.

"This being true, that no single person can insult a kingdom, province, city, state, or entire town, it plainly follows that there is no excuse for seeking to avenge such an insult since it really is not one. A fine thing it would be if the inhabitants of the Clocktown [10] were to be constantly falling out with everyone who called them by that name; and the same goes for those known as the Scullions, Eggplant-growers, Whalers, and Soapmen,[11] and those to whom other appellations are applied such as are prevalent in the mouths of children and the common people! It would be a pretty state of affairs, surely, if these distinguished communities were all the time to go about seeking vengeance and making sackbuts of their swords over every misunderstanding however slight a one it might be!

"No, no, God forbid! There are four conditions under which prudent men and well-ordered states may take up arms, draw their swords, and risk their persons, lives, and fortunes.[12] The first is in order to defend the Catholic faith; the second, to defend their lives, which is in accordance with natural and divine law; the third, to defend their family honor and possessions; the fourth, to serve their king in a just war; and if we care to add a fifth, which may be included under the second, to defend their native land.[13]

"To these five justifications for war, which may be looked upon as the principal ones, other causes may be added that are right and reasonable and that make it a duty to resort to arms. But to go to war over trifles and things that, in place of constituting an insult, are in reality laughable and amusing, would appear to be the act of one who is lacking in sound sense. Moreover, to take an unjust revenge—and there can be no just vengeance—runs directly counter to the holy law that we observe, which teaches us to do good to our enemies and love those that hate us,[14] a commandment which may seem to be rather a difficult one to keep but which is so only for those that think less of God than they do of the world and more of the flesh than of the spirit. For Jesus Christ, who is God and true man and our legislator, who neither lies nor could lie, has said that His yoke is easy and His burden light,[15] and

He would not lay upon us any commandment that was impossible to fulfill. And so, my dear sirs, your Worships are bound by human and divine laws to desist."

"May the devil take me," said Sancho to himself, "if my master's not a tologian, and if not, he's as like one as one egg is like another."

Don Quixote took a breath and, seeing that they were all keeping silent, was about to continue with his sermon, and would have done so had not Sancho taken advantage of the pause to display his own wit.

"My master, Don Quixote de la Mancha," he began, "who formerly was known as the Knight of the Mournful Countenance and who now is called the Knight of the Lions, is a very learned gentleman who knows both Latin and his mother tongue like a bachelor and in everything that he does and advises others to do acts like the best kind of soldier. He has all the laws and ordinances of what they call combat at his fingertips; and so there is nothing to do but be guided by what he says, and let it be on my head if you make any mistake in doing that. He has told you that it is foolish to lose your temper just because you hear someone braying. Why, I can remember that when I was a lad I brayed every time I happened to feel like it without anyone's trying to stop me, and I did it so nicely and properly that all the asses in the village answered me; yet I did not for that reason cease to be the son of my parents, who were most respectable folks. And though I was envied for this accomplishment by a number of the gentry, I didn't give two cents for it myself.[16] And so that you can see that it's the truth I'm telling you, just wait and listen. It's like swimming, once you learn it you never forget it."

And, with this, putting his hands to his nose, he began braying so lustily that all the neighboring valleys echoed with the sound. One of those who was standing near him, thinking that he was making sport of them, raised a staff that he held in his hand and brought it down with such force that Sancho dropped helplessly to the ground. Seeing his squire thus mishandled, Don Quixote, lance in hand, then attacked the one who had dealt the blow; but so many thrust themselves in his way that he was unable to chastise the aggressor, and since a rain of stones was falling upon him and innumerable crossbows and muskets were aimed at him, he turned Rocinante's head and at the best gallop he could manage fled from their midst, meanwhile praying to God with all his heart to deliver him from this peril. He feared at every step that some arrow might pierce his back and come out through his bosom, and he was constantly drawing in his breath to make sure it had not failed him.

The members of the squadron, however, were satisfied to see him take flight like this and did not fire upon him. As for Sancho, as soon as he had somewhat recovered his senses, they placed him upon his mount and permitted him to follow his master. He was in no condition to guide the beast, but the gray went along in Rocinante's foot-tracks as he could not bear to be separated from his companion for a single moment. When he was a good distance away, Don Quixote turned his head and, perceiving that Sancho was coming and that no one was in pursuit, stopped to wait for him. The squadron from the braying town remained there until nightfall, and then, since their enemies had not come out to join battle with them, they returned to their village in very high spirits; and had they been familiar with the custom of the ancient Greeks, they would have erected a monument upon that spot.

CHAPTER **XXVIII**. *Of things that, Benengeli says, the reader will come to know if he reads attentively.*

WHEN the brave man flees, it means that treachery has been uncovered, and it is the part of the wise to save themselves for better occasions.

This truth was brought out in the case of Don Quixote, who, having aroused the fury of the townspeople and the ill will and indignation of the squadron, showed his heels and, without thought of Sancho or the danger in which he was leaving him, put as much distance between himself and the enemy as he deemed necessary in order to assure his own safety. Sancho followed, slung across his ass in the manner that has been described. He finally came up, in full possession of his wits by this time, and as he did so he slid from the gray's back to Rocinante's feet, all battered and bruised and in a sorrowful plight. Don Quixote

then dismounted to examine his squire's wounds and, finding him sound
from head to foot, addressed him angrily enough.

"An evil hour it was, Sancho," he said, "when you learned how to
bray! Where did you ever hear that it was a good thing to mention the
rope in the house of the hanged man? [1] What counterpoint can braying
music have except that of cudgels? You may give thanks to God, Sancho,
that they made the sign of the cross on you just now with a club and
not with a cutlass."

"I'm in no condition to answer," replied Sancho, "for it seems to me
that I'm talking through my shoulders. Let's mount and get away from
here. I'll not bray any more, but I can't help remarking [2] that knights-
errant appear to run away and leave their faithful squires in the hands
of the enemy to be pounded like privet or like wheat in the hopper."

"He who retires," said Don Quixote, "does not flee. I would have you
know, Sancho, that valor not based upon prudence can only be termed
temerity, and the triumphs of the foolhardy are to be attributed to good
luck rather than to courage. I admit that I retired, but not that I fled;
and in this I have merely followed the example of many brave men
who have saved themselves for a more propitious time. The histories
are full of such instances, but as it would do you no good to refer you
to them, I shall spare myself the trouble for the present."

Sancho by now was once more on his gray's back, having been helped
up by Don Quixote, who then mounted Rocinante; and, riding slowly
along, they made for a grove that was visible about a quarter of a league
away. Every so often Sancho would heave a deep sigh or moan as if in
pain, and when his master asked him what the cause of it was, he replied
that he ached all over, from the base of his spine to the nape of his
neck, and it was nearly driving him crazy.

"The reason for that," remarked Don Quixote, "is undoubtedly the
fact that the club they used was a long one and caught you all the way
down your back where those aching parts are located; and if it had
gone any farther down, you would ache still more."

"By God," exclaimed Sancho, "your Grace has taken a great load off
my mind and made everything as clear as can be! Body of me! Is the
cause of my pain such a mystery that it is necessary to explain to me that
I ache wherever the club reached me? If it was my ankles hurting me,
there might be some sense in trying to find out what caused it, but to
tell me that I'm sore because they beat me is not much in the way of a
discovery. On my word, master of mine, the misfortune of another
hangs by a hair, [3] and I am every day discovering how little I have to

hope for from keeping company with your Grace. This time you have let them club me. Another time, or a hundred times more, it will be the old story of the blanketings and other foolish pranks all over again; and if up to now I've had it only across the shoulders, I'll be getting it later straight in the eyes.

"I'd do a lot better," he went on, "if I wasn't a numbskull who will never do anything well as long as he lives—I'd do a lot better, I say, by going home to my wife and young ones, to support and bring them up on whatever God may see fit to give me, instead of trailing after your Grace along roads that lead nowhere and highways and byways that don't deserve the name, with little to drink and less to eat. And as for sleeping! Pace off seven feet of earth, brother squire, and if you want any more than that, take another seven; the dish is in your hands,[4] help yourself; so stretch out to your heart's content, and welcome. I'd like to see the one who started this knight-errantry business burned to ashes, or at least the first man who was willing to be a squire to such fools as all the knights-errant of times past must have been. As to those of the present day, I say nothing, for since your Grace is one of them, I must respect them; and what's more, your Grace knows a little more than the devil when it comes to talking and thinking."

"I would like to lay a good wager with you, Sancho," said Don Quixote, "that since you have been running on like this with no one to stop you, you don't feel an ache in your entire body. Talk on, my son; say anything that comes to your mind or to the tip of your tongue; for if it will relieve your pain, I will gladly put up with the annoyance which your impudence causes me. If you are so anxious to go home to your wife and children, God forbid that I should stop you. You have my money; reckon up how long it has been since we left our village this third time [5] and what your wages should be each month, and then pay yourself out of hand."

"When I worked for Tomé Carrasco," [6] replied Sancho, "father of the bachelor Sansón Carrasco, your Grace's acquaintance, I earned two ducats a month and my board; but with your Grace, I can't say what it should be, for your Grace knows that the squire to a knight-errant does more work than a farmer's helper. The work in the fields may be hard, but at the worst, when night comes we have our *olla* and a bed to sleep in—and that's something I haven't had since I've been serving your Grace, except for the brief time we spent at Don Diego de Miranda's house, and the feast I had on the skimmings that I took from Camacho's pots, and the bed and what I had to drink at Basilio's.

All the rest of the time I've slept on the hard earth, under the open sky, in what they call the inclemencies of the weather. I've kept myself alive on scraps of cheese and crusts of bread; and as for drinking, it has been water from the brooks or springs in the bypaths that we traveled."

"I admit," said Don Quixote, "that everything you say, Sancho, is the truth. How much more do you think I should give you than what you had from Tomé Carrasco?"

"As I see it," said Sancho, "if your Grace would give me a couple of reales more for each month, I could consider myself well paid. That is to say, so far as my wages go, for the work I've done. But seeing that you gave me your word and solemn promise to make me the governor of an island, it would only be fair for your Grace to add another six reales, making thirty altogether."

"Very well," Don Quixote agreed, "it is now twenty-five days since we left our village; so reckon it up, Sancho, on the basis of the wage you think you ought to have, and see how much it is I owe you; and then, as I have said, you can pay yourself by your own hand."

"O body of me!" cried Sancho, "your Grace is very wrong in this reckoning; for so far as the island is concerned, we have to count from the day your Grace promised it to me down to the present hour."

"Well," said Don Quixote, "and how long has it been since I made you the promise?"

"If I'm not mistaken," replied Sancho, "it must be more than twenty years and three days, more or less."

At this Don Quixote slapped his forehead with his hand and burst into a hearty laugh.

"Why," he said, "with my wanderings in the Sierra and all the rest barely two months have gone by. And are you trying to tell me, Sancho, that it was twenty years ago I promised you that island? I am convinced now that you would take all the money I have as your wages; and if such is the case and that is what you want, I hereby give it to you; it is yours from now on, and much good may it do you. In order to be rid of so faithless a squire, I shall be content to remain a pauper, without a penny to my name. But tell me, you perverter of the laws of chivalry and the rules that govern squires, where have you ever heard of a squire who made such terms with his lord: 'You must give me so much a month for serving you?' Plunge, O rogue, scoundrel, monster—plunge, I say, into the *mare magnum* of their histories; and if you find one single squire who ever said or thought of saying such a thing as you have just said, I would have you nail it to my forehead and in addition give me four resounding slaps in the face.

"Turn, then, the reins, or better, the halter of your ass, and go back to your home; for you are not going one step farther with me. O bread ungratefully received! O promises ill bestowed! O man who has more of the beast in him than of the human! So you are leaving me now, are you, just when I was about to elevate you to a position in life where, no matter what your wife might say, people would address you as your Lordship? So you are leaving me just when I had firmly resolved to make you governor of the best island in the world? In short, as you have said before, honey is not for the ass's mouth.[7] An ass you are and an ass you will be to your dying day, for I think that day will come before you ever realize that you are a stupid beast."

Sancho stared hard at Don Quixote as the knight heaped these insults upon him and was so smitten with remorse that the tears came to his eyes.

"Master," he said in a weak and sorrowing voice, "I will grant you that all I lack is a tail and I would be an ass; and if your Grace wants to put one on me, I'll look upon it as well placed and will serve you as a beast of burden all the days of my life that are left me. Forgive me, your Grace; have mercy on my foolishness. Remember that I know little, and if I talk much, that is due to weakness rather than to malice. But he who sins and mends his ways, commends himself to God." [8]

"I should have been surprised, Sancho," said his master, "if in the course of your speech you had not rung in some proverb. Very well, I forgive you, on condition that you do mend your ways and that from now on you do not think so much of your own interests. Rather, you should take heart, be of good cheer, pluck up courage, and trust me to fulfill my promises. Fulfillment may be late in coming, but that does not mean that it is impossible."

Sancho assured him that he would do so, contriving somehow to draw strength from weakness. By this time they had reached the grove, and Don Quixote now sat down at the foot of an elm and Sancho at the foot of a beech (for trees of this sort and others like them always have feet but no hands). Sancho spent an uncomfortable night, his aches returning with the evening dew. Don Quixote as always was deep in reveries; but, in spite of everything, the two of them had some sleep and at sunup resumed their journey toward the banks of the famous Ebro, where they had an experience that is related in the chapter to follow.

CHAPTER XXIX. *Of the famous adventure of the enchanted bark.*

By the stages described or undescribed, two days [1] after leaving the grove Don Quixote and Sancho reached the River Ebro, the sight of which afforded the knight great pleasure as he beheld the charm of its banks and gazed upon its clear and abundant, gently flowing waters, which had the appearance of liquid crystal. It was a sight that brought back a thousand fond memories, reminding him in particular of the things he had viewed in the Cave of Montesinos; for although Master Pedro's ape had said that a part of those things were true and the rest were lies, he was inclined to regard them all as true rather than false, whereas for Sancho they were all lies from beginning to end.

As they were going along the bank in this manner, they came upon a small boat without oars or rigging of any kind that was lying at the water's edge, being moored to the trunk of a tree. Don Quixote looked around in all directions, and, seeing no one, he without more ado dismounted from Rocinante and ordered Sancho to get down off the ass and tie both animals very securely to an elm or a willow that stood near by. When Sancho wanted to know the reason for all this, his master answered him as follows:

"I may tell you, Sancho, that the bark you see there is plainly and unmistakably calling and inviting me to enter it and proceed in it to give succor to some knight or other highborn personage who stands in need of my assistance and who must be in dire straits indeed; for that is the way it is in the books of chivalry, in the stories where enchanters figure and speak. When one knight is in some difficulty from which he can be freed only by the hand of another knight, though they be two or three thousand leagues distant from each other, or even more, the enchanters will either snatch him up in a cloud or provide a bark for him, and in less than the wink of an eye they will carry him through the air or over the sea, wherever it is they wish to take him and where his aid is needed. And this bark, O Sancho! is placed here for the same purpose. I am as certain of that as I am that it is now day, and so, before this day passes, tie Rocinante and the gray together, and then let it be in

God's hand to guide us, for I would not refrain from embarking though barefooted friars should beg me to do so."

"If that is the way it is," replied Sancho, "and your Grace must be getting into this kind of foolishness (if I may call it that) at every turn, there's nothing for me to do but bow my head and obey; for, as the old saying goes, 'Do what your master bids you and sit with him at table.' [2] But, for all that, just to get it off my conscience, I want to warn your Grace that this boat doesn't look to me as if it belonged to any enchanters but to some fishermen; for you catch the best shad in the world in this river."

Sancho said this as he was tying the beasts. It grieved him deeply to have to leave them to the tender mercies of the enchanters, but Don Quixote assured him that he need not worry about their going uncared for, as the one who was taking them on so long a journey, into such far longitudes, would see to it that they were fed.

"I don't know anything about logitudes," [3] said Sancho, "nor did I ever hear such a word in all my born days."

"*Longitude*," Don Quixote explained, "is an expression that is used in referring to distance. But it is no wonder that you do not understand, seeing you are not obliged to know Latin, like some who think they know it but are in reality ignorant of it."

"I have them tied," Sancho informed him. "What do we do now?"

"What do we do?" replied Don Quixote. "We cross ourselves and weigh anchor; by which I mean, we climb aboard and cut the moorings by which this bark is fastened."

With this, he leaped into the boat, followed by Sancho, and severed the rope that held it. The bark then began drifting slowly away from the bank, and when Sancho found himself some two yards out in the river, he started trembling all over, fearing that he was lost. What pained him most of all was the braying of the ass and the sight of Rocinante struggling to get loose.

"The gray," he said to his master, "is heartbroken because we are leaving him, and Rocinante wants to get free so he can plunge in after us. Peace be with you, O dearly beloved creatures! May the madness that takes us from you be turned into sound sense and bring us back to you once more!"

As he said this, he began weeping so bitterly that Don Quixote became angry.

"What are you afraid of, cowardly one? Why those tears, you butter-heart? Who is pursuing or attacking you, O man with the soul of a tame mouse? What do you lack, O beggar in the very midst of plenty? Are you perchance tramping barefoot over the Riphaean Mountains [4] in place of being seated like an archduke on a bench as you drift with the gentle current of this pleasant river, from which we shall soon come out upon the broad expanse of the ocean? But we must surely be on the sea by now; indeed, we must have gone seven or eight hundred leagues, and if I but had an astrolabe with which to take the latitude of the pole, I should be able to tell you exactly how far we have traveled. Either I know little about it or we already have passed, or soon shall pass, the equinoctial line which lies between the two opposite poles at an equal distance from each."

"And when we get to that lane [5] your Grace is speaking of," said Sancho, "how far shall we have gone?"

"Very far," said Don Quixote, "for of the three hundred and sixty degrees on the terraqueous globe, according to the computation of Ptolemy, the greatest known cosmographer, we shall have traversed half that number in arriving at the line I have mentioned."

"By God," exclaimed Sancho, "if it isn't a nice sort of person your Grace produces to witness what you say—a tall hoggifer [6] with a *me* or something or other on the end of his name!"

Don Quixote had to laugh at what his squire had contrived to make out of Ptolemy the cosmographer.

"I may inform you, Sancho," he continued, "that one of the ways the Spaniards who embark at Cadiz for the East Indies have of telling when they have passed that equinoctial line is this: if the lice die upon every man aboard so that not a one is to be found anywhere even though they offer its weight in gold for it, then they know they are past the line; and so, Sancho, just run your hand over your thigh and if you come on anything that's alive, it will remove all doubt, but if you find nothing, then we have made the crossing." [7]

"I don't believe a word of it," declared Sancho, "but, nevertheless, I will do as your Grace bids me, although I must say I don't know why we have to make all these experiments, for I can see with my own eyes that we're not five yards away from the bank, nor have we dropped two yards below the spot where the animals stand; for Rocinante and the ass are still there where we left them, and if you take a fixed point as I am doing now, then, I swear, we're not moving any faster than an ant's pace."

"Make the test that I asked you to, Sancho," said Don Quixote, "and do not be bothering your head with anything else; for you know nothing of colures, lines, parallels, zodiacs, ecliptics, poles, solstices, equinoxes, planets, signs, and points of the compass, these being the units of which the celestial and terrestrial spheres are composed. If you knew all these things, or even a part of them, you would clearly perceive what parallels we have crossed, what zodiacal signs we have seen, and what constellations we have left, and are now leaving, behind us. But I tell you again: feel and hunt, for I am certain that you are cleaner than a smooth white sheet of paper."

Sancho did so and, having run his hand gently all the way down to the inside of his left knee, he looked up at his master and said, "Either the test is a false one or we're not within many leagues of where your Grace says we are."

"How is that?" said Don Quixote. "Did you find something?"

"Yes, a number of somethings," [8] said Sancho. And, shaking his fingers, he dipped his entire hand in the river, down which the bark was gently drifting without being moved by any occult intelligence or invisible enchanter but merely by the current itself, which was there flowing along very smoothly.

At that moment they descried some big watermills moored in the middle of the river, and no sooner did Don Quixote catch sight of them than he called out to Sancho in a loud voice, "Do you see that, my friend? There is the city, castle, or fortress where they must be holding some knight in captivity, or some sorely wronged queen, infanta, or princess, to rescue whom I am being brought there."

"What the devil city, fortress, or castle is your Grace talking about?" said Sancho. "Can't you see, master, that those are nothing but watermills on the river, where they grind corn?"

"Be quiet, Sancho," Don Quixote admonished him, "for though they may appear to be watermills, they are not. I have already explained to you how enchanters change and transform things from their natural shape. I do not mean that they actually change them from one shape to another, but they appear to do so, as experience has taught us in connection with the transformation of Dulcinea, sole refuge of my hopes."

By this time the bark was in midstream and was not moving as gently as it had been up to then. The millers, seeing this boat coming down the river and perceiving that it was about to be sucked in by the millwheels, came running out in all haste to stop it. Many of them carried poles, and, as their faces and their clothes were covered with flour, they presented a sinister appearance.

"Devils of men!" they cried out, "where are you going? Do you come in desperation to drown yourselves or be battered to pieces by those wheels?"

"Did I not tell you, Sancho," said Don Quixote, "that we had come to a place where I would have to display the might of my arm? Look at those rogues and scoundrels who have sallied forth to meet me! Look at those monsters who would oppose me! Behold the hideous countenances with which they think to frighten us! You shall soon see, you villains!" And then, standing up in the boat and shouting at the top of his voice, he began hurling threats at the millers: "Lowborn and ill-advised rabble, set free and restore to liberty the person whom you hold in durance vile in that fortress or prison, whether that person be of high or low degree, whatever his station or walk in life; for I am Don Quixote de la Mancha, otherwise known as the Knight of the Lions, for whom it is reserved, by order of the highest heavens, to bring this adventure to a fortunate conclusion!"

Saying this, he drew his sword and began brandishing it in the air by way of intimidating the millers, who, hearing but not understanding these nonsensical remarks, now fell to with their poles to prevent the bark from entering the millrace, as it was on the verge of doing. Sancho, meanwhile, had dropped to his knees and was devoutly praying to Heaven to deliver him from so manifest a peril; and thanks to the quick work of the millers, his prayer was granted. By the aid of their poles they succeeded in stopping the boat, but not without upsetting it and throwing Don Quixote and Sancho into the water. Luckily for the former, he could swim like a duck, but the weight of his armor twice dragged him under, and if it had not been for the millers who dived in and hauled them both out, it would have been the fall of Troy for the two of them.

As soon as they had been brought to land, drenched to the skin but hardly suffering from thirst, Sancho again fell on his knees, clasped his hands, turned his eyes heavenward, and made a long and fervent prayer in which he besought God to deliver him, from that day forth, from his master's rash designs and undertakings. While he was thus engaged, the fishermen who owned the boat, which had been hacked to pieces by the millwheels, came up and, seeing what had been done to their property, fell upon Sancho and stripped him of his clothing, demanding at the same time that Don Quixote make good their loss. The knight was not in the least perturbed by this, but with a calm manner, as if nothing whatever had happened, informed the millers and the fishermen that he would be very glad to pay for the boat on condition that they would deliver up to him, free and unharmed, the person or persons whom they were holding in durance in that castle.

"What persons and what castle are you talking about, you fool?" one of the millers answered him. "Do you by any chance, want to carry off those who come to grind corn in these mills?"

"That will do," said Don Quixote to himself. "It would be preaching in the desert to attempt by entreaties to induce this rabble to perform any worthy deed. In the course of this adventure two powerful enchanters must have clashed, and one has undone what the other proposed to do. God help us all, this world is nothing but schemes and plots, all working at cross-purposes. I can do no more."

Raising his voice, he continued speaking as he gazed at the mills. "Friends," he said, "whoever ye may be who are locked within these prison walls, forgive me. It is my misfortune and yours that I am unable to rescue you from your dire peril. This emprise must doubtless be reserved for some other knight." [9]

Having said this, he came to an understanding with the fishermen and paid them fifty reales for their boat, which Sancho handed over with a very ill grace. "A couple of more boat rides [10] like this," he said, "and we'll have sunk our entire capital."

Both fishermen and millers were filled with wonder at beholding these two figures, so different to all appearances from the common run of men. Unable to make out what Don Quixote was driving at with his speeches and his questions, they decided that the pair were crazy and went back to their tasks, the millers to their mills and the fishermen to their shacks. Don Quixote and Sancho then returned to their beasts and the life of beasts that they led, and thus ended the adventure of the enchanted bark.

CHAPTER XXX. *Of what befell Don Quixote upon meeting with a beautiful huntress.*

THE knight and his squire were in a bad humor and more than a little downcast as they returned to their beasts. This was especially true of Sancho, for anything that touched their supply of money touched his heart, and when any of it was taken from him it was as if he were being deprived of the apple of his eye. And so, without saying a word, they mounted and rode away from the banks of the famous river. While Don Quixote was immersed in thoughts of love, Sancho was thinking of the worldly advancement that had been promised him. It all seemed to him very far away now; for while he may have been a simpleton, he could not help perceiving that all or most of his master's actions were quite mad, and he began casting about in his mind for some occasion that one day would afford him an opportunity to slip away and return home without getting into any arguments or so much as saying good-by. Fortune, however, had something better in store for him.

The next day, as they emerged from a wood at sunset, Don Quixote looked out over a green meadow, at the far end of which he could see a group of people. Drawing closer, he saw that it was a hawking party, and upon coming nearer still he perceived among the company a fine lady seated upon a gleaming white palfrey or hackney caparisoned in green and with a silver sidesaddle.[1] The lady was in green also, and so richly clad that she appeared to be elegance itself. On her left hand she bore a hawk, which to Don Quixote signified that she must be some great dame and the mistress of the party, which proved to be the case.

"Run, Sancho, my lad," he said, "and inform that lady of the palfrey and the hawk that I, the Knight of the Lions, humbly salute her great beauty,[2] and if her Highness will grant me permission, I will come and kiss her hands in person and serve her as my strength may enable me and her Highness may command. Take care how you address her, Sancho, and see that you do not mingle any of your proverbs with the message."

"Why say that to me?" replied Sancho. "I'm no mingler! This is not the first time in my life that I've carried messages to high and mighty ladies!"

"With the exception of the one you carried to the lady Dulcinea," said Don Quixote, "I do not know of any other, at least not since you have been in my service."

"That is the truth," Sancho admitted, "but he who can pay doesn't worry about pledges,[3] and in the house where there's plenty supper is soon on the table.[4] By that I mean to say, you don't need to tell me or warn me of anything, for I'm equal to anything and know a little of everything."

"I believe that, Sancho," his master assured him, "and so good luck and Godspeed."

Forcing his mount out of its usual pace, Sancho hastened to where the beautiful huntress sat, and there, slipping down off his gray and kneeling before her, he spoke as follows:

"Beautiful lady, the knight you see there, known as the Knight of the Lions, is my master and I am a squire of his, Sancho Panza by name. This same Knight of the Lions, who not long ago was called the Knight of the Mournful Countenance, has sent me to beg your Highness to be pleased to grant him permission, with your full approval and consent, to come and fulfill his desire, which I believe to be none other than that of serving your Highness's exalted beauty.[5] If your Ladyship sees fit to bestow this permission, it will be to her advantage, and he will be most happy to receive so distinguished a favor." [6]

"Most certainly, good squire," replied the lady, "you have conveyed the message with all the formalities that are required in such a case. Rise from the ground; for it is not fitting that the squire to so great a Knight as is he of the Mournful Countenance (of whom we have already heard a great deal) should remain on his knees. Rise, friend, and say to your master that he is welcome to my own services, and those of my husband the duke, in a country house that we have not far from here."

As Sancho rose, he was as much impressed by the good lady's beauty as by her high breeding and her courtesy, and he was particularly surprised that she should have heard of his master, the Knight of the Mournful Countenance—if she had not referred to him as the Knight of the Lions, that must be due to the fact that he had but recently assumed the appellation. The duchess (whose full title he did not know) now went on speaking to him.

"Tell me, brother squire," she said, "is not your master the one concerning whom they have printed a story called *The Ingenious Gentleman, Don Quixote de la Mancha,* and who has as lady of his heart a certain Dulcinea del Toboso?"

"He is the same, my lady," replied Sancho, "and I am that squire of his that figures, or is supposed to figure, in the story, the one named Sancho Panza—that is to say, unless they changed me in the cradle—I mean, in the press."

"I am very happy to hear all this," said the duchess. "Go, brother Sancho, and tell your master that he will be most welcome at my estate, as I can think of nothing that would give me greater pleasure."

With so gracious an answer as this to convey, Sancho hastened back in high spirits to his master, to whom he repeated everything that the great lady had said to him, extolling her beauty to the heavens in his own rustic way and dwelling upon her gentle demeanor and her courtesy. Don Quixote at once drew himself up in the saddle, settled himself firmly in the stirrups, adjusted his visor, put spurs to Rocinante, and with a graceful ease of manner rode forward to kiss the duchess's hands. In the meantime, as Don Quixote was approaching, the duchess had summoned her husband and told him of the message, and inasmuch as they had read the first part of this story and were familiar with the knight's nonsensical whims, they were both delighted and extremely eager to make his acquaintance. As they waited for him, they decided that they would humor him in every way and fall in with everything he said, and that as long as he stayed with them they would treat him as a knight-errant, with all the customary ceremonies as described in the books of chivalry; for they had read those books and were very fond of them.[7]

Don Quixote then rode up with his visor raised, and as he went to dismount, Sancho came alongside to hold his stirrup for him; but unfortunately, as he descended from his gray, the squire caught his foot in one of the ropes of his packsaddle in such a manner that he could not get it loose and was left hanging there with his face and bosom on the ground. Now, Don Quixote was not used to dismounting without his stirrup being held, and, thinking that Sancho was already there to see to it, he threw himself off with a lurch, bringing with him Rocinante's saddle, which must have been poorly fastened, and, as a result, both he and the saddle came tumbling to the earth. Needless to say, he was very much ashamed and could only mutter curses between his teeth at the unfortunate Sancho, who still had his feet in the stocks.

The duke thereupon ordered his huntsmen to assist the knight and squire, and they proceeded to lift Don Quixote, who was greatly shaken by his fall but who nonetheless, limping along as best he could, now came forward to kneel before the noble pair. The duke, however, would by no means consent to this, but, dismounting from his own steed, advanced to meet and embrace his guest.

"Sir Knight of the Mournful Countenance," he said, "I deeply regret that the first time you set foot in my domains you should have met with so unfortunate an accident, but the carelessness of squires is often the cause of worse ones."

"Whatever might have happened to me, valorous prince," was Don Quixote's reply, "could not possibly have been evil, even though I had fallen all the way to the depths of the bottomless pit; for the great honor of meeting you would have raised me up and delivered me. My squire, God curse him, is better at loosening his impudent tongue than he is at tightening a saddle girth so that it will stay. But in whatever state I may be, fallen or erect, on foot or on horseback, I shall always be at your service and that of my lady the duchess, your worthy consort, beauty's deserving queen and sovereign princess of courtesy."

"Be careful what you say, Señor Don Quixote de la Mancha," the duke advised him, "for where my lady Doña Dulcinea del Toboso is, other beauties are not to be praised."

Sancho Panza, who by this time had been freed of the noose, was standing close by, and before his master could answer, he spoke up. "It cannot be denied," he said; "indeed, it is to be maintained, that my lady Dulcinea del Toboso is very beautiful; but the hare jumps where you least expect it,[8] and I have heard folks say that what is called nature is like a potter who makes vessels out of clay: he who makes one beautiful jar can make two, three, or a hundred. I say that because, on my word, my lady the duchess is not one whit behind my mistress."

At this, Don Quixote turned to the duchess. "Your Highness," he said to her, "can well imagine that no knight-errant in the world ever had a more talkative or droller squire than I have, and he will prove to you that I speak the truth if your exalted Highness be pleased to accept my services for a few days."

"If the worthy Sancho is droll," replied the duchess, "that is a very good thing, for it shows that he is possessed of sound sense. As your Grace is aware, Señor Don Quixote, drollery and wit do not go with a dull mind and so, since Sancho is both droll and witty, I shall regard him from now on as a shrewd fellow."

"And a talkative one," added Don Quixote.

"So much the better," said the duke; "for many drolleries cannot be expressed in a few words. But come, great Knight of the Mournful Countenance, let us not waste our time talking."

"Knight of the Lions, your Highness should say," Sancho reminded him. "There is no Knight of the Mournful Countenance any more, nor of any kind of Countenance." [9]

"Of the Lions let it be," the duke went on. "What I started to say was that Sir Knight of the Lions should come to a castle of mine that is hard by, where he will be accorded the reception that is justly due to so exalted a personage, such a reception as the duchess and I are accustomed to give to all knights-errant who arrive there."

Sancho lost no time in saddling Rocinante, seeing to it this time that the girths were properly fastened, and they then set out for the castle, with the duke mounted upon a handsome steed and the duchess in between them, the lady having requested Sancho to ride with her, as she took a great delight in listening to his witticisms. Sancho required no urging, and, riding in the center of the group, he made a fourth in the conversation, all to the vast enjoyment of the titled pair, who were only too happy to receive in their castle such a knight-errant and his arrant squire.[10]

CHAPTER XXXI. *Which treats of many and great things.*

SANCHO was supremely happy at finding himself, as he thought, in the good graces of the duchess, for he expected the same kind of treatment in her castle that he had received in Don Diego's house and at Basilio's place. Fond of good living always, he never failed to take opportunity by the forelock and enjoy a feast whenever he could.

The history then goes on to relate that before they reached the country house or castle the duke went on ahead and gave orders to all his servants as to how they were to treat Don Quixote. Accordingly, the moment the knight arrived at the castle gates in the company of the duchess, two lackeys or equerries came out clad from head to foot in what are known as morning robes of finest crimson satin, and, taking the guest in their arms before he had seen or heard them, they said to him, "Your Highness should go and help the duchess to dismount." He started to do as they had suggested, and there followed an elaborate exchange of courtesies regarding the matter, with the duchess insisting that she would descend only in the arms of the duke, since she did not deem it proper to impose so useless a burden on so distinguished a knight; and in the end she had her way and the duke came out to help her down.

They then entered a large patio, and as they did so two beautiful maidens threw over Don Quixote's shoulders a great cloak of sumptuous scarlet cloth, and upon the instant all the galleries of the courtyard were filled with male and female servants of the noble pair, crying loudly, "Welcome, O flower and cream of knight-errantry." And all or most of them spilled vials of scented water upon the knight and the duke and duchess. All of which greatly astonished Don Quixote; indeed, it may be said that this was the first time that he really and wholly believed himself to be a true knight-errant and not a fanciful one, for here he was being treated in the very same manner as knights-errant in ages past, according to the storybooks he had read.

Dismounting from his gray, Sancho contrived to keep close to the duchess and entered the castle with her, although it hurt his conscience a bit to leave the ass alone like that. There he encountered a dignified duenna who with the other womenfolk had come out to receive their mistress, and he took occasion to say to her in a low voice, "Señora González, or whatever your name may be—"

"Doña Rodríguez de Grijalba is my name," the duenna replied. "What is your pleasure, brother?"

"I would have your Grace do me the favor," said Sancho, "of going out to the castle gate, where you will find a gray ass of mine. Will your Grace be pleased to have them put him in the stable, or else put him there yourself, for the poor beast is a little timid and simply can't bear being alone."

"If the master is as wise as the man," replied the duenna, "we're in for it. Be off with you, brother! You and the one who brought you here can go to blazes! As for your ass, the ladies of this household are not used to work of that sort."

"Well," said Sancho, "the truth is, I've heard my master, who is a wizard when it comes to stories—I've heard him say of Lancelot:

> *When from Britain he came,*
> *ladies took care of him,*
> *duennas looked after his hack.*[1]

And so far as that ass of mine is concerned, I wouldn't exchange him for that hack of Sir Lancelot's."

"Brother," said the duenna, "if you are a jester [2] save your jokes for those that appreciate them and will pay you for them, for you'll get nothing out of me but a fig." [3]

"It will be a ripe one at least," was Sancho's answer, "for if years are trumps, you won't lose the game for want of a point." [4]

"Son of a whore!" cried the duenna, who was now very angry. "How old I am is a matter between me and God and no business of yours, you garlic-stuffed rascal!"

She had raised her voice to such a pitch that the duchess heard her; and the lady of the castle, upon turning her head and seeing her waiting woman so excited, with her eyes all aflame, thereupon wished to know who it was with whom she was quarreling.

"This fine fellow here," replied the duenna. "He has been urging me to go out and stable an ass of his that is standing at the castle gate; and he tells me by way of precedent that somewhere or other some ladies took care of a certain Lancelot in that fashion and some duennas looked after his horse. What's more, for good measure, he called me an old woman."

"I should consider that the greatest insult that anyone could offer me," said the duchess and, turning to the squire, she went on, "I must advise you, friend Sancho, that Doña Rodríguez is very young, and if she wears a hood, it is merely to lend her dignity and because it is the custom and not on account of her years."

"May all the years that are left to me be bad ones," said Sancho, "if I meant it that way. What I was trying to say was that I am very fond of my beast and I thought I could not entrust him to a more kind-hearted person than Doña Rodríguez."

Don Quixote, who had been listening all the while, now put in a word. "Is this the place, Sancho," he asked, "for such talk as that?"

"Sir," replied Sancho, "everyone must say what he has to say wherever he may be. I happened to think of my gray, and so I spoke of him. If it had been in the stable that I thought of him, I'd have spoken of him there."

"Sancho," said the duke, "is quite right about that and is not to be blamed for anything. The gray shall have all he wants to eat and Sancho need not worry; the ass will receive the same good treatment as his owner."

Following this conversation, which was very amusing to all of them except Don Quixote, they ascended the stairs to the floor above, and there they took the knight into a chamber richly adorned with cloth of gold and brocade, where six damsels, acting as his pages, proceeded to disarm him. They had all been well instructed by the duke and duchess as to what they were to say and do and how they were to behave toward Don Quixote so that he would have reason to believe he was being treated as a knight-errant. With his armor off, their guest stood there in his tight-fitting breeches and chamois-skin doublet, tall, lean, lanky, with cheeks that appeared to be kissing each other on the inside of his mouth. In short, he presented such an appearance that, if the damsels waiting on him had not done their best to restrain themselves —this being one of the definite orders their master and mistress had given them—they would have burst with laughing.

They then wanted to strip him so that they could put a shirt on him, but he refused to consent to this, saying that modesty was as becoming as valor in knights-errant. Instead, he directed them to give the shirt to Sancho, and shutting himself up in a room where there was a sumptuous bed, he undressed himself and put on the garment.

"Tell me, you old simpleton turned buffoon," he said upon finding himself alone with Sancho, "do you think it was right to insult so venerable a duenna and one so worthy of respect as that one? Was that any time to be thinking of your gray? Are these the kind of people to let beasts suffer when they treat their owners so royally? For God's sake, Sancho, restrain yourself and do not be showing your fiber so that they can see of what coarse, clownish stuff you are made. Bear in mind, sinner that you are, that the more respectable and well bred his servants are, the more is the master honored, and one of the great advantages that princes have over other men is that they are waited upon by those who are as good as themselves.

"Do you not know," he continued, "small-minded creature that you are and unfortunate man that I am, that if they perceive you to be a boor and a clown they will take me for an impostor, for some swindler or other? No, no, friend Sancho, that is a stumbling block you should avoid; for whoever falls into the way of being a prattler for the amusement of others, the first time he trips will end as a wretched buffoon. Put a bridle on your tongue, then; think over and ruminate on your words before they leave your mouth, remembering that we have now reached the point where, by God's help and the might of my arm, we shall come forth greatly bettered in fame and fortune."

Sancho earnestly promised to do as his master had commanded and keep his mouth closed, vowing that he would bite his tongue out before he uttered a word that was not in place and well considered. The knight could set his mind at ease on one point: no one would ever know through him, Sancho, who they were. Don Quixote then put on his clothes, strapped on his baldric and his sword, threw a scarlet cloak over his shoulders, and donned a cloth cap [5] which the damsels had given him; and dressed in this manner he descended to the great hall, where he found the maidens drawn up in two equal rows to present him with what was needed for washing his hands, all of which was done with many curtsies and great ceremony.

Twelve pages, [6] accompanied by the seneschal, next made their appearance to bring him to the dinner, as his hosts were awaiting him. Placing him in their midst, they conducted him with truly regal pomp into another room where a rich table was laid with four places only. The duke and duchess came to the door to receive him, and with them was a solemn-faced ecclesiastic, one of those who rule over noble households and who, not having been born to the nobility themselves, are unable to instruct their charges in the proper behavior. He was one of those who would measure the greatness of great men by their own narrow minds, one of those who, desirous of inculcating economy, merely succeed in making misers. [7] Such a one, I repeat, must have been the grave-appearing churchman who now came forward with the lord and lady of the castle to greet Don Quixote. There were innumerable compliments on either side, after which, the knight walking between his host and hostess, they went to take their places at the table.

The duke invited Don Quixote to take the head of the table and insisted upon it so strongly that, although the knight at first declined, there was nothing to do but yield. The ecclesiastic took the seat opposite, while the duke and duchess sat at the sides. Sancho, meanwhile, was watching all this in open-mouthed amazement, unable to believe his eyes as he saw the honor that was being shown his master by these noble personages; and as he observed the ceremonies that marked the dinner and heard the duke begging Don Quixote to take the place of honor, he could not refrain from speaking up.

"If your Worships will grant me permission," he said, "I will tell you a story concerning something that happened in my village. It has to do with this matter of seats."

No sooner did he hear these words than Don Quixote began trembling, for he thought that undoubtedly his squire was going to give utterance to some absurdity. Sancho saw the look on his face and understood it.

"You needn't fear, master," he assured him, "I'm not going to disobey you or say anything that's not to the point. I haven't forgotten the advice your Grace gave me a while ago about speaking much or little, well or ill."

"I remember nothing about it," replied Don Quixote. "Say what you like, so long as you say it quickly."

"What I am about to tell you," Sancho went on, "is the truth, and my master here present will not let me lie."

"So far as I am concerned, Sancho," said Don Quixote, "you can lie all you want to and I shan't stop you; but watch your words, that's all."

"I've considered and reconsidered them," was the answer, "and the bell-ringer's in a safe place,[8] as you will see."

"It would be a good thing," remarked Don Quixote, "if your Highnesses would have them throw this fool out, for he will talk all kinds of nonsense."

"By the life of the duke," exclaimed the duchess, "I am not going to part with Sancho for a moment. I am extremely fond of him, for I know him to be very discreet."

"And may your days be discreet, your Holiness,"[9] said Sancho, "in return for the good opinion you have of me, even if I don't deserve it. But the story I want to tell you is this. There was a gentleman of my village, a very rich and important one, seeing that he came of the Alamos of Medina del Campo and was married to Doña Mencia de Quiñones, who was the daughter of Don Alonso de Marañon, a knight of the Order of Santiago who was drowned at Herradura, the same one who was the cause of that quarrel in our town some years ago in which my master, Don Quixote, was mixed up, so I've heard them say, and Tomasillo the scapegrace, son of Balbastro the blacksmith, who was wounded—isn't all that the truth, my master? Speak up, on your life, so that these good people will not take me for a lying prattler."

"Up to now," said the ecclesiastic, "I have taken you for a prattler rather than a liar, but I cannot say what I shall take you for later on."

"You cite so many witnesses, Sancho," said Don Quixote, "and go into so much circumstantial detail that I am forced to admit you must be telling the truth; but get on with your story and cut it short, for at the rate you are going you will not be finished in a couple of days."

"He is not to cut it short on my account," said the duchess. "Rather, let him tell it in his own way, even if it takes him six days, for they would be the best I ever spent in my life."

"Well, then, as I was saying, good people," continued Sancho, "this certain gentleman—I know him as well as I do my own hands, for from my house to his it is not a crossbow shot—this gentleman invited a farmer, who was poor but respected—"

"Get on, brother," said the churchman at this point, "or otherwise you will not be through with your story until you get to the other world."

"I'll stop a little this side of halfway, please God," replied Sancho. "And so, as I was saying, this farmer, coming to the house of this gentleman I was telling you of who had invited him—God rest his soul, for he is dead now and what's more, they say he died the death of an angel—I wasn't there, having gone down to Tembleque for the harvest at that time—"

"On your life, son," said the churchman, "hurry back from Tembleque [10] and finish your story without stopping to bury the gentleman, unless you want more funerals on your hands."

"Well, then," Sancho went on, "it so happened that as the two of them sat down at the table—it seems to me I can see them now plainer than ever—"

The duke and duchess were delighted at the churchman's annoyance, occasioned by Sancho's prolixity and digressions in the telling of his story, but Don Quixote was consumed with rage.

"As I was saying," Sancho rambled on, "just as the two of them were about to sit down to eat, the farmer began insisting that the gentleman should take the head of the table and the gentleman insisted that the farmer should take it, saying that in his house his orders had to be obeyed; but the farmer, who had been well brought up and was proud of his manners, would not hear of it until the gentleman, becoming quite angry, laid both hands on the farmer's shoulders and forced him into the place, saying, 'Sit down, you stupid ass, for wherever I sit will be the head of the table to you.' That is my story, and to tell the truth, I don't think it's out of place here." [11]

Don Quixote turned a thousand colors that mottled his brown face until it took on the appearance of jasper. The duke and duchess had to conceal their laughter so as not to add to his embarrassment, for they had seen through Sancho's maliciousness; and in order to change the subject and prevent his squire from running on in this manner, the duchess now inquired of the knight what news he had had of the lady Dulcinea and asked if he had made her a present lately of any more giants or evildoers, as he must surely have vanquished a great many of them.

"Lady," he replied, "my misfortunes, though they had a beginning, will never have an end. Giants I have conquered and rascals and scoundrels I have sent her, but where are they to find her if she is under a magic spell and has been turned into the homeliest peasant lass that could be imagined?"

"I don't know about that," said Sancho Panza. "To me she seemed the most beautiful creature in the world. At least, when it comes to nimbleness and frisking, she won't give in to a tumbler. My word, Duchess, she leaps from the ground onto the back of a she-ass as if she were a cat."

"Have you seen her, Sancho, since she has been enchanted?" the duke asked.

"Have I seen her!" exclaimed Sancho. "Who in the devil was it but me that first thought up this enchantment business! She's as much enchanted as my father."

The ecclesiastic, upon hearing this talk of giants, rogues, and enchanters, decided that their guest must be none other than Don Quixote de la Mancha whose story the duke was always reading—he had reproved him for it many times, telling him it was nonsensical to waste his time on such nonsense—and now, becoming convinced that his suspicions were correct, he turned to the duke and addressed him angrily.

"Your Excellency, *Señor mío*," he said, "will have to give an account to the Lord for what this good man does. This Don Quixote, or Don Simpleton, or whatever his name is, surely cannot be such a dunce as your Excellency would make him out to be by thus lending encouragement to his foolish carryings-on." Addressing himself, then, to Don Quixote, he continued, "And as for you, addlepate, who ever put it into your head that you are a knight-errant who conquers giants and captures malefactors? I say to you: go your way and Heaven be with you; return to your home, see to bringing up your children if you have any, look after your property, and stop wandering about the world like a gaping ninny, making a laughingstock of yourself in the eyes of all, whether they know you or not. Where in the name of goodness [12] did you ever come upon any knights-errant living or dead? Where are there giants in Spain, or bandits in La Mancha, or enchanted Dulcineas, or any of the other silly things they tell about in connection with you?"

Don Quixote listened very attentively to what the reverend gentleman had to say, and when he saw that the speaker had finished, disregarding the presence of the duke and duchess he sprang to his feet with an angry and excited look on his face, and said— But his answer deserves a chapter to itself.

CHAPTER **XXXII.** *Concerning the answer which Don Quixote gave to his reprover, with other incidents, some serious and some amusing.*

As Don Quixote rose from his seat, he was trembling from head to foot like a man with an overdose of mercury, and he spoke in a hurried, agitated voice.

"The place and presence in which I stand," he began, "and the respect I have always had for your Reverence's profession, tie and bind the hands of my just wrath. For this reason, and because I am aware that the weapons of men in gowns [1] are the same as those of a woman— namely, the tongue—I shall employ that same weapon in doing battle with your Reverence, from whom one might have looked for good counsel rather than infamous abuse. Reprehension that is righteous and well meant should be administered in a different way and calls for other arguments. By reproving me in public and so rudely, you have exceeded all proper bounds; for Christian reprehension should be based upon mildness not upon asperity, nor is it right, knowing nothing of the sin you are censuring, to call the sinner straightaway a simpleton and a fool.

"Otherwise," he went on, "tell me, your Reverence, what manifestation of foolishness have you discerned in me that leads you thus to vituperate and condemn me and order me to return home, look after the management of my affairs, and care for my wife and children, when you do not even know whether or not I have a house or family? Is nothing more required than to make your way by hook or crook into other people's houses to rule over their masters, and that, perhaps, after having been brought up in some poverty-stricken seminary [2] and having seen no more of the world than was to be found within a radius of twenty or thirty leagues? Is such a one suddenly to take it upon himself to lay down the law for chivalry and pass judgment on knights-errant? Is it, perchance, a vain occupation or a waste of time to wander over the earth, seeking not the pleasures of this life but those hardships by which the virtuous may mount to the seat of immortality? [3] If true gentlemen or great lords of high and noble station were to call me a fool I should take it as an irreparable insult, but for the opinion of mere bookworms who have never entered upon or trod the paths of chivalry I would not give a penny. A knight I am and a knight I shall die, if it be pleasing to Almighty God.

"Some men," the knight concluded, "take the broad field of ambition,[4] others the road of low and servile adulation; some choose the way of hypocrisy and deception, and others still that of religion; but, as for me, led on by my star, I follow the narrow path of knight-errantry, and in the exercise of that profession I despise wealth but not honor. I have undone wrongs, righted grievances, chastised the insolent, overcome giants, and trampled monsters under foot. I am enamored, for the very good reason that knights-errant must be. I am not, however, one of those vicious lovers, but, rather, chaste and platonic. My intention is always a worthy one: that of doing good to all and harm to none. As to whether a man with such a purpose and who puts it into execution deserves to be called a simpleton, that is for your Highnesses to say, O excellent Duke and Duchess."

"By God," exclaimed Sancho, "that's good! Say no more, master mine, in your own behalf, for there's nothing more in the world to be said, thought, or insisted upon.[5] So far as that goes, seeing that this gentleman denies, as he has denied, that there are or have been knights-errant in the world, is it any wonder if he doesn't know what he's talking about?"

"Brother," said the ecclesiastic, "are you by any chance that Sancho Panza to whom, so they tell me, his master has promised an island?"

"I am," replied Sancho, "and I am one who deserves it as well as any other. I am one of those of whom it is said, 'Keep good company and you'll be one of them,' [6] and, 'Not with whom you are bred but with whom you are fed,' [7] and, 'Who leans against a good tree is covered by a goodly shade.' [8] I've leaned against a good master, it's many months now that I've been going about with him, and, God willing, I'll be just such another as he is. Long life to him and long life to me, and may he never lack empires to rule and may I always have islands to govern."

"Have them you certainly shall, friend Sancho," said the duke at this point; "for in the name of Señor Don Quixote, I hereby confer upon you the government of an island that I happen to possess, and one of no small importance."

"Get down on your knees, Sancho," said Don Quixote, "and kiss his Excellency's feet for the favor he has done you."

Sancho did as he was bidden and when he saw this, the ecclesiastic rose from the table in a temper.

"By the habit that I wear," he said, "I feel like saying that your Excellency is as much of a crackbrain as these sinners. It is not surprising that they are mad when those who are sane applaud their madness. Let your Excellency stay with them if you like, but as long as they are in this house I shall remain in mine and shall ask to be excused from reproving that which I cannot remedy."

And without uttering another word or eating another bite, he left the room, despite the entreaties of the duke and duchess. The duke, in fact, did not say much, as he was laughing too hard at the churchman's uncalled-for anger.

"Sir Knight of the Lions," he said to Don Quixote when he had finally stopped laughing. "Your Grace has answered him so well that there is no further satisfaction to be sought. While this may appear to be an affront, it is not so in reality; for, as your Grace knows, ecclesiastics, like women, can give no offense."

"That is true," agreed Don Quixote, "and the reason for it is that he who is not to be offended cannot offend another. Women, children, and churchmen, since they cannot protect themselves, even though they may be wronged cannot be insulted; for between an offense and an insult there is this difference, as your Excellency is aware: the insult comes from one who can and does sustain it; an offense may come from any quarter, with no insult attached to it. Let us take an example. A man is standing unsuspectingly in the street when ten armed ruffians come up and start beating him. He draws his sword and does his duty, but his opponents are too many for him and he cannot carry out his intention, which is that of avenging himself. This man is offended but not insulted. Or let us take another case. A man is standing with his back turned when another comes up and strikes him and then flees. He pursues his assailant but is unable to overtake him; and so we may say that the one who was struck received an offense but no insult, since the insult has to be sustained.

"On the other hand,," continued the knight, "if the one who struck him, even though he did it by stealth, should lay hand to his sword and face it out with his enemy, the latter would then be both offended and insulted at one and the same time; he would be insulted for the reason that the one who dealt the blow did not turn tail but stood and backed it up. And so, in accordance with the laws of the accursed duel, I may have been offended but not insulted; for neither women nor children can maintain an affront, nor can they flee or stand their ground, and the same is true of those who are in the Church, since these three classes of people lack both offensive and defensive arms and, though they are naturally obliged to defend themselves, should offend no one.

"I said a moment ago," Don Quixote went on, "that I might have been offended, but now I say no, by no manner of means; for he who cannot receive an insult is still less capable of giving one; and for this reason I ought not to resent, nor do I resent, what this good man said to me. My only regret is that he did not wait a while so that I might have shown him how wrong he is in thinking and saying that there are not and never have been any knights-errant in this world. Had Amadis heard him, or any one of that knight's innumerable progeny, it would not have been well for his Reverence."

"That I can surely swear to," said Sancho. "He would have given him a slash that would have laid him open from top to bottom like a pomegranate or an overripe melon. They were not the fellows to put up with jokes like that! Faith, and if Rinaldo de Montalbán [9] had heard the little man he'd have rapped him over the mouth so hard his Reverence wouldn't have had anything more to say for three whole years. He'd better not get mixed up with them or he'll see how he comes out!"

The duchess nearly died laughing as she listened to Sancho. In her opinion he was even droller and more insane than his master, and there were many at that time who would have agreed with her. Finally, Don Quixote quieted down and the meal was finished; and as they removed the cloth, four damsels appeared, one with a silver basin, one with a jug likewise of silver, a third with the finest of white towels over her shoulder, while the fourth, whose arms were bare to the elbow, carried in her white hands (for white they assuredly were) a rounded cake of Neapolitan soap.[10] The one with the basin then came up with a graceful, free, and easy manner and held the vessel under Don Quixote's beard. The knight did not say a word, being quite astonished at such a ceremony, but thinking it must be the custom of that region to wash the beard in place of the hands, he stretched his whiskers out as far as he could, and at that very moment the damsel with the jug began to pour and the one with the soap started scrubbing most energetically, raising snowflakes out of the lather that covered not only the beard of the obedient knight but his entire face, compelling him to keep his eyes closed.

The duke and duchess, who were wholly unprepared for all this, waited to see what the outcome of these extraordinary ablutions would be. The barber damsel, when she had her victim a palm's breadth deep in lather, pretended that the water had run out and ordered the maid with the jug to go fetch some more while Don Quixote remained like that, the weirdest and most laughable-looking figure that could be imagined. All those present, and there were many of them, stared at him, at his neck half a yard long and uncommonly brown, his closed eyes, and his beard full of soap, and it was all they could do to keep from laughing outright. As for the damsels who had thought up the joke, they kept their gaze lowered, not daring to look up at their master and mistress, who were torn between laughter and anger and did not know what to do, whether to punish the girls for their boldness or reward them for the pleasure of seeing Don Quixote in this plight.

At last the girl with the jug came back and they finished bathing the knight, after which they brought in towels and cleaned and dried him very matter-of-factly. Having done this, all four of them made deep bows, and curtsied and were about to withdraw when the duke, who did not wish Don Quixote to discover the jest, called to them and said, "Come and wash me too, and be sure there is plenty of water."

The girl, being sharp-witted, promptly placed the basin in front of the duke as she had done with Don Quixote, and with the same energy and thoroughness they proceeded to bathe and lather him. Then, with more curtsies, they all went away and it was afterward learned that the duke had sworn that if they had not bathed him in the same manner as they had the knight, he would have punished them for their impudence, but, as it was, they had cleverly made amends.

"So help me God!" muttered Sancho to himself as he watched this ceremonious bathing. "Could it be the custom in this country to wash squires' beards as well as knights'? For, by God and 'pon my soul, I have need of it. And if they gave me a shave as well, I'd take it as an extra favor."

"What are you mumbling about, Sancho?" the duchess inquired.

"I was just saying to myself that in the courts of other princes, so I've heard tell, when they take the cloth away they bring water for the hands but not lye for the beard. For that reason, it's good to live a long time so that you'll see a lot of things.[11] They also say that he who has a long life has to go through much trouble,[12] though I'd call it pleasure, not trouble, to have a bath like that."

"Do not let it worry you, friend Sancho," said the duchess, "for I will have my damsels bathe you and they will even put you in the tub if necessary."

"I'll be satisfied with the beard," replied Sancho, "for the present at least. As for the future, God knows what is to be."

"Seneschal," called the duchess, "see that the good Sancho has whatever he asks for, and carry out his wishes in every respect."

The seneschal replied that he was wholly at Señor Sancho's service, and with this he went off to eat, taking the squire with him, while the duke and duchess and Don Quixote were left at the table talking of many and various things, but all of them having to do with the profession of arms and the calling of knight-errantry. The duchess then requested her guest, since he appeared to have so good a memory, to describe for her the features of the beautiful Dulcinea del Toboso, who, if what fame had trumpeted abroad concerning her loveliness was true, must surely be the fairest creature in the world and even in all La Mancha. Upon hearing this, Don Quixote heaved a sigh.

"If," he said, "I could but take my heart out and lay it before your Highness's eyes, upon a plate here on this table, I should be able to spare my tongue the trouble of telling what is scarcely to be conceived; for in my heart your Excellency would see her fully portrayed. After all, why should I undertake to describe and depict, point by point and feature by feature, the beauty of the peerless Dulcinea? That is a task that should be laid upon other shoulders than mine, being one worthy of the brushes of Parrhasius, Timanthes, and Apelles and of the chisel of Lysippus;[13] artists such as they should preserve that beauty in pictures, in marble, and in bronze, and a Ciceronian and Demosthene eloquence are called for to eulogize it."

"What does Demosthene mean, Señor Don Quixote?"[14] asked the duchess. "That is a word I never heard in all my life."

"Demosthene eloquence," Don Quixote explained, "is equivalent to saying the eloquence of Demosthenes, just as Ciceronian means of Cicero, for they were the two greatest orators in the world."

"That is right," said the duke. "Your mind must have been wandering," he added, speaking to the duchess, "or you would not have asked such a question. But, for all of that, it would give us a very great pleasure if Señor Don Quixote would portray her for us; for I am sure that, even though it be the merest outline or sketch, she will emerge in such a manner as to arouse envy in the fairest of ladies."

"I should most certainly do so," said Don Quixote, "if it were not that the misfortune that befell her a short while ago, of a kind to be wept over rather than described, had blurred my mental image of her. For I must inform your Highnesses that, some days past, when I went to kiss her hand and to receive her blessing, her approval, and her permission for this third sally of mine, I found her quite a different being from the one I sought. I found her under a magic spell, converted from a princess into a peasant girl, from a beautiful creature into an ugly one, from an angel into a devil, from a fragrant-scented being into a foul-smelling wench, from a fine-garbed, dignified lady into a rustic clown, leaping in the air—in short, from Dulcinea del Toboso into a Sayago country woman." [15]

"God save us!" cried the duke in a loud voice at this juncture. "Who is it could have done such a wrong to the world? Who could have deprived it of that beauty that rendered it joyful, that grace that charmed it, and that modesty that so redounded to its credit?"

"Who?" Don Quixote repeated. "Who could it have been except some malign enchanter of the many envious ones who persecute me? That cursed race of beings was born into the world to darken it, to frustrate the achievements of the virtuous and exalt those of the wicked. These enchanters have persecuted, are persecuting, and will continue to persecute me until they shall have sunk me and my high deeds of chivalry into the deep pit of oblivion. They seek to harm and wound me where they know I am most vulnerable, for to take away his lady from a knight-errant is to rob him of the eyes with which he sees, the sun that lights him, and the sustenance that is his life. I have said many times before and I will say it again, that the knight-errant without a lady is like the tree without leaves, a building without a foundation, or a shadow without the body that casts it."

"There is no more to be said on the subject," observed the duchess; "but, nevertheless, if we are to believe the tale about Señor Don Quixote that was recently published in these parts and that won the praise of all—we are to gather from this tale, if I remember rightly, that your Grace has never seen the lady Dulcinea, that there is, in fact, no such lady in existence, or, rather, that she is a purely fanciful one, created in your Grace's own mind, whom you have endowed with all the charms and perfections that you chose to give her."

"That," replied Don Quixote, "is a long story. God knows whether or not there is a Dulcinea in this world or if she is a fanciful creation. This is not one of those cases where you can prove a thing conclusively. I have not begotten or given birth to my lady, although I contemplate her as she needs must be, seeing that she is a damsel who possesses all those qualities that may render her famous in all parts of the world, such as: a flawless beauty; dignity without haughtiness; a tenderness that is never immodest; a graciousness due to courtesy and a courtesy that comes from good breeding; and, finally, a highborn lineage, for beauty is more resplendent and more nearly perfect in those of lofty extraction than in creatures of a humbler origin."

"True enough," said the duke, "but if Señor Don Quixote will permit me, after having read the story of his exploits I am compelled to remind him that it is stated there that, granted there is a Dulcinea in or out of El Toboso, and granted that she is as supremely beautiful as your Grace has depicted her, she still cannot compare in the matter of ancestry with the Orianas, the Alastrajareas, the Madásimas,[16] or others of that sort with whose names the histories that your Grace knows so well are filled."

"As to that," Don Quixote answered, "I can say only that Dulcinea is the daughter of her works,[17] that virtues shed luster upon the bloodstream, and that a person of low degree who is possessed of them is more to be esteemed than the vicious one who has risen to high station.[18] Moreover, Dulcinea has qualities that well may bring her to a crown and scepter; for a woman who is at once beautiful and virtuous may by her merits come to work miracles, and has locked within her, potentially if not actually, a higher fortune than the one she knows."

"I must remark," said the duchess, "that in everything your Grace tells us you proceed with leaden foot and plummet in hand, as the saying is.[19] As for myself, I shall continue to believe and shall see to it that all in my household do the same—even my lord the duke if necessary —that there is a Dulcinea now living in El Toboso, and that she is beautiful and highborn, a lady worthy of being served by such a knight as Señor Don Quixote, which is the highest praise I can bestow upon her. But, for all of that, there is still some small doubt in my mind, and here I hold a grudge against Sancho Panza; for the story that I have mentioned states that when Sancho brought the lady Dulcinea a message from your Grace, he found her winnowing a bag of wheat, and red wheat at that, a circumstance that leads me to question her exalted lineage." [20]

"My lady," replied Don Quixote, "your Highness should know that all or most of the things that happen to me are beyond the common experience of other knights-errant, being brought about either through the inscrutable will of the fates or through the malice of some envious enchanter. For it is a known fact that all or most of the famous knights-errant either had a special gift that was proof against enchantment or else had flesh that was impenetrable so that they could not be wounded. There was, for example, Orlando, one of the Twelve Peers of France, of whom it is related that he could be wounded only in the sole of his left foot, and with no other weapon whatever than a large pin; and so when Bernardo del Carpio slew him at Roncesvalles,[21] upon perceiving that he could not reach him with his sword, he was compelled to lift him from the ground and strangle him, thus recalling the manner in which Hercules disposed of Antaeus, the ferocious giant who, they say, was Earth's own son.

"By this," he went on, "I mean to infer that I may possibly possess some gift of this sort. Not the gift of invulnerability, however, since experience has frequently taught me that my flesh is tender and by no means impenetrable; nor am I proof against enchantment, having, before now, found myself thrust into a cage,[22] a thing which all the world combined could never have accomplished except through the power of magic. But inasmuch as I succeeded in freeing myself from that spell, I am of the opinion that no one will henceforth be able to hurt me. Accordingly, those enchanters, seeing they can no longer lay their evil hands upon my person, are avenging themselves upon the object that I most love and would deprive me of life by mistreating Dulcinea, in whom I have my being.

"What I think is that when my squire brought her my message, those same enchanters transformed her into a country wench and set her at so low a task as is that of winnowing wheat. But I have already said that the wheat in question was not red, nor was it wheat, but oriental pearls; and, in proof of this, I may inform your Highnesses that when I came to El Toboso not long ago, I was able to find Dulcinea's palace; and the very next day Sancho, my squire, beheld her in her proper form, which is the most beautiful of any on earth, while to me she appeared as a coarse and ugly peasant girl and very rude in her speech, though she herself is the soul of propriety. And seeing that I am not enchanted and, it stands to reason, cannot be, she must be the one who has suffered this injury and has been thus altered, changed, and transformed. That is to say, my enemies through her have had their revenge on me, and it is on account of her that I live amid ceaseless tears until I shall once more have beheld her in her pristine state.

"All this," continued Don Quixote, "I have told you in order that no one may believe what Sancho says about Dulcinea's winnowing or sifting grain; for if they altered her in my sight, it is no wonder if they transformed her for him. Dulcinea is illustrious and wellborn and comes from one of those noble lines such as are to be met with in El Toboso,[23] where they are numerous, ancient, and respected; and, without a doubt, much of the credit for the esteem in which these houses are held must go to her, on account of whom her town will be as famous and renowned as Troy was on account of Helen or Spain by reason of Cava,[24] and with an even better title to fame.

"On the other hand, I would have your Highnesses know that Sancho Panza is one of the drollest squires that ever served a knight-errant. He is so sharp in his simple-mindedness that one may derive no little amusement from trying to determine whether he is in reality simple or sharp-witted. He has in him a certain malicious streak that seems to indicate he is a rogue, and from his blundering you would take him for a dunce. He doubts everything and believes everything, and just as I think he is about to tumble headlong, owing to some stupidity, he will come up with some witticism or other that sends him skyward in my estimation. The short of the matter is, I would not exchange him for another squire even though they threw in a city to boot.

"And so I am in some doubt as to whether it would be a good thing to entrust him with that governorship that your Highness has done him the favor of bestowing on him; although it is true that I discern in him a certain aptitude for governing, and with a little brushing-up of his wits he might make out as well with any government whatsoever as a king with his taxes.[25] Especially since we know from long experience that neither much ability nor much learning is necessary in order to be a governor; for there are a hundred hereabouts who are barely able to read and who yet acquit themselves of their task like so many ger-falcons.[26] The main thing is for them to be possessed of good intentions and a desire to do the right thing always, for they will never lack those who can advise and direct them in what they have to do, just as those who are knights and not scholars pass judgment with the aid of an assessor. My advice to him would be to take no bribe and sur-render no right,[27] and there are a few other little points I have in mind that I can bring up when the time comes and that will be useful to Sancho and of benefit to the island he is to govern."

The duke, the duchess, and Don Quixote had reached this point in their conversation when they heard the sound of many voices and a great uproar in the palace, and of a sudden Sancho burst into the room in a rage, with a straining cloth under his chin for a bib, followed by a large number of lads, or, more precisely, scullions and other kitchen help. One of the pursuers carried a small trough filled with a liquid that, from its color and unclean appearance, was clearly seen to be dish-water, and he kept insisting on placing the receptacle under Sancho's beard while one of his companions sought to give the squire a bath.

"What is this, brothers?" the duchess demanded. "What is this? What are you trying to do to this good man? Do you not know that he has just been appointed a governor?"

"The gentleman does not want to let us bathe him," replied the barber-scullion, "as is the custom and as we bathed my lord the duke, and his own master."

"Yes," said Sancho wrathfully, "I do want to be bathed, but with cleaner towels, clearer suds,[28] and hands that are not so dirty. There is not so much difference between my master and me that they should bathe him with angel water[29] and me with these damnable suds! The customs of countries and of princely palaces are good so long as they do not cause hardship, but the custom of bathing as in use here is worse than the rule of the flagellants. My beard is clean and does not need to be freshened up in that way, and I will say, with all due respect, that if anyone tries to wash me or touches a hair of my head, I mean, of my beard, I'll give him a punch that will leave my fist buried in his skull; for, in my opinion, cirimonies[30] and soapings such as these are more of a joke than they are the kind of treatment that should be shown to a guest."

The duchess nearly died with laughter as she saw how very angry Sancho was and listened to his words; but Don Quixote was not greatly amused at seeing his squire in such a plight, with the dirty towel about him and surrounded by the pranksters from the kitchen. And so, making a profound obeisance to the duke and duchess, as if begging their permission to speak, the knight turned and addressed the rowdies in these words:

"I say there, you gentlemen,[31] leave this young man alone and go back where you came from, or anywhere else that you please. My squire is as clean as any other, and he likes those troughs of yours no better than he does slim, narrow-mouthed wine jars;[32] so take my advice and leave him alone, for neither he nor I is fond of jests."

At this point Sancho took the words out of his mouth.

"Let them come on," he said, "and try their jokes on this bumpkin. It's as likely I'll stand for them as it is that it is now night.[33] Let them bring a comb or whatever they like and curry this beard of mine, and if they bring out of it anything that's not clean, I'll let them give me a fool's haircut." [34]

"Sancho Panza," said the duchess, laughing still, "is right in everything he has said or will say. He is clean and, as he has told us, has no need of a bath; so, if our custom is not pleasing to him, let him do as he likes. What is more, you ministers of cleanliness have been entirely too careless and remiss, perhaps I should say audacious, in bringing such a person as this, with such a beard, a wooden trough and dishclouts in place of a basin and jugs of purest gold and towels of Holland linen. In short, you are ill behaved and ill bred and, knaves that you are, cannot refrain from showing the grudge you harbor against the squires of knights-errant."

The impudent servants and even the seneschal who had come with them believed that the duchess was speaking in earnest. They now removed the straining cloth from around Sancho's neck and, more than a little embarrassed and out of countenance, went away and left him there; whereupon, seeing himself delivered from what he looked upon as a supreme peril, the squire ran over and fell on his knees in front of the duchess.

"From great ladies great favors are to be expected," he said, "but in order to repay the one your Highness has shown me, I can only wish that I could be dubbed a knight-errant so that I could spend all the days of my life in serving your exalted Ladyship. I am a peasant, Sancho Panza by name, I am married and the father of a family, and I serve as a squire. If in any of these respects I can be of service to your Highness, I shall hesitate less in obeying than your Ladyship in commanding."

"It is quite apparent, Sancho," replied the duchess, "that you have studied in the school of courtesy itself; by that I mean to say, that you have been nourished at the bosom of Señor Don Quixote, who is the very cream of courtesy and flower of ceremony—or cirimony, as you yourself would say.[35] Well may such a master and man fare, the one being the north pole of knight-errantry while the other is the star of squirely fidelity! Arise, friend Sancho, that I may repay your courtesy by having my lord the duke fulfill as soon as possible the promise of a governorship that he has made you."

This ended their conversation. Don Quixote now went off to take his siesta, and the duchess requested Sancho, in case he was not too sleepy, to spend the afternoon with her and her damsels in a very cool apartment that they had. He replied that, although it was true that he liked to take a nap of four or five hours in the summertime, in order to be of service to her Excellency he would strive with all his might to go without sleep that day and in obedience to her command would come to her chambers. The duke, meanwhile, gave fresh orders to the effect that Don Quixote was to be treated as a knight-errant in every way, without departing one jot from the formalities that, according to the storybooks, were observed in the case of knights of old.

CHAPTER XXXIII. *Of the delightful conversation which the duchess and her waiting women had with Sancho Panza, worth reading and worth noting.*

THE history goes on to relate that Sancho did not take his siesta but, by way of keeping his word, came in to see the duchess before he had scarcely done eating. As she was very fond of listening to him, she insisted on his sitting down beside her on a low chair. Merely out of good breeding, Sancho declined at first, but the duchess made matters right by telling him that he should sit as a governor and talk as a squire, since in either capacity he deserved nothing less than the seat of Cid Ruy Díaz, the Campeador himself.[1] Shrugging his shoulders, Sancho obeyed and sat down, and all the damsels and duennas then gathered around him and, preserving a deep silence, waited to hear what he might have to say. It was the duchess, however, who was the first to speak.

"Now that we are alone," she said, "with no one to hear us, I should like the Señor Governor to resolve certain doubts that I have, growing out of the story of the great Don Quixote that has already been printed. For one thing, inasmuch as the worthy Sancho never saw Dulcinea, I mean the lady Dulcinea del Toboso, and never brought her Don Quixote's letter, which was left in the memorandum book on the Sierra Morena,[2] how did he dare make up the answer and that tale about her winnowing wheat, a hoax and a falsehood so detrimental to the reputation of the peerless Dulcinea, and so unbecoming to the character of a good and faithful squire?"

Sancho listened to these words without making any reply whatsoever. Instead, he rose from his chair and, with his back bent and a finger on his lips, went all around the room lifting the draperies. Having done this, he came back and sat down again. It was only then that he broke his silence.

"My lady," he began, "now that I have seen that there are no eavesdroppers but only the bystanders to hear what is said, I will answer your question and any other that you may wish to ask me. In the first place, I must tell you that I look upon my master Don Quixote as stark mad, even though at times he says things that to me and all those who listen to him seem so wise and directed in such a straight rut that Satan himself could not do any better. But, for all of that, there is not the slightest doubt in my mind that he's cracked. Well, then, having this in my noddle, I can venture to make him believe things that don't make head nor tail, like that business of the answer to his letter, and that other that only happened six or eight days ago and so is not in the story yet, by which I mean, the enchantment of my lady, Doña Dulcinea; for though I gave him to understand that she was under a spell, there's no more truth in it than over the hills of Ubeda." [3]

The duchess then asked him to tell her about the hoax having to do with the enchantment, and he narrated the incident just as it had happened, at which his audience was not a little amused. The duchess then resumed the conversation.

"As a result of what the worthy Sancho has told me," she said, "there arises a question in my mind, a certain whispering in my ear which says: if Don Quixote is crazy, weak-minded, crackbrained, and Sancho his squire knows it and still continues to serve him and to cling to the empty promises his master has made him, he must undoubtedly be the more foolish and the more insane of the two; and if this is the case, my lady the Duchess, as I am sure it is, you are bound to be reproached for having given him an island to govern; for if he cannot govern himself, how can he govern others?"

"By God, lady," said Sancho, "you've spoken straight to the point; but go ahead, your Highness, and say whatever you like, as plain as you like, for I know it to be the truth. I know that if I had good sense I'd have left my master long ago. But this is my luck, my misfortune, and I can't help following him. We're from the same village, I've eaten his bread, I like him very much, he's generous to me,[4] he gave me his ass-colts, and, above all, I'm loyal; and so it's impossible for anything to separate us except the pick and spade.[5] And if your Highness doesn't want to give me that island that you promised me, well, I didn't have it when God made me, and it may be that your not giving it to me will be all the better for my conscience.

"I may be a fool," he went on, "but I know what is meant by the saying, 'To her harm the ant grew wings.'[6] It may be that Sancho the squire will go to Heaven sooner than Sancho the governor. They make as good bread here as in France, and at night all cats are gray. He is hard up who hasn't broken his fast by two in the afternoon, and there's no stomach that's bigger than another by the breadth of your palm, and you can fill it with straw or hay, as the saying goes. The little birds of the field have God for their provider, and four yards of Cuenca frieze keep you warmer than four of Segovia broadcloth.[7] Once we have left this world and gone down under the earth, the prince travels by as narrow a path as the day laborer, and the pope's body takes up no more feet of earth than does the sacristan's,[8] even though one is higher than the other; for, when we go to the grave, we all make ourselves as small as we can, or they do it for us whether we like it or not, and then it's good night all.

"And so I will say once again that if your Ladyship doesn't care to give me that island because I'm a fool, then like a wise man I'll not let it worry me. I've heard it said that behind the cross stands the devil, and all is not gold that glitters.[9] The peasant Wamba[10] was taken from behind the oxen, the plows, and the yokes to be king of Spain, and Rodrigo[11] was taken from among his brocades, pastimes, and riches to be devoured by serpents, if the old ballads do not lie."

"Of course they do not lie!" exclaimed the duenna Doña Rodríguez, who was one of the listeners. "Why, there is a ballad that tells how they put King Rodrigo while he was still alive into a tomb full of toads, snakes, and lizards, and two days later he cried out from inside the tomb in a low, pain-stricken voice:

> *They are eating me now, they are eating me now,*
> *There where I most have sinned.*[12]

And according to that, this gentleman is quite right in saying he would rather be a peasant than a king if he is to be eaten by reptiles in the end."

The duchess could not help laughing at the simplicity of her duenna, nor could she get over her astonishment as she listened to Sancho and his proverbs. She now addressed herself to him.

"The worthy Sancho well knows," she said, "that once a knight makes a promise he strives to fulfill it though it cost him his life. The duke, my lord and husband, though not of the errant variety, is nonetheless a knight, and he accordingly will keep his word with regard to that island he promised despite the envy and malice of others. Let Sancho be of good courage, for when he least expects it he will find himself on some island throne, in the seat of authority, and he will then take over the government, that he may exchange it for another of triple brocade.[13] The charge that I would lay upon him is this: that he look well to the manner in which he governs his vassals, in view of the fact that they all are loyal and wellborn."

"As to this business of governing them well," said Sancho, "there's no need of charging me to do that, for I am by nature kindhearted and charitable toward the poor. You don't steal the bread from one who kneads and bakes,[14] and, faith, they'd better not throw false dice with me. I'm an old dog and know all about *tus, tus*.[15] I can get the dust out of my eyes when the time comes, and there are no specks in front of them, either. I know where the shoe pinches me.[16] I say this by way of letting you know that the good will find in me a support and a refuge and the bad will not get a foothold. As I see it, in this matter of governments, everything depends on the kind of start you make; and it may be that after I've been governor for a couple of weeks, I'll have my hand in and will be better at the job than at work in the fields, which I was brought up to do."

"You are right, Sancho," the duchess assured him, "for no one is born educated, and bishops are made out of men, not out of stones. But to return to the subject of which we were speaking a short while ago, the lady Dulcinea's enchantment. I hold it to be certain and thoroughly established that Sancho's idea of hoaxing his master and making him think that the peasant girl was Dulcinea, and of leading him to believe that if he did not recognize her it must be because she was under a magic spell—I maintain that all this was indeed the invention of one of those enchanters that persecute Don Quixote; for, in all seriousness, I know from good authority that the country maid who leaped upon the she-ass was Dulcinea del Toboso, and that the worthy Sancho, thinking he is the deceiver, is in reality the deceived.

"There is no more reason to doubt the truth of this than there is to doubt anything simply because we have not seen it with our own eyes. I would inform Señor Sancho Panza that we also have enchanters here, friendly ones, who tell us what goes on in the world, plainly and simply, without any plotting or scheming; and, believe me, Sancho, that sportive lass was and is Dulcinea del Toboso, who is as much enchanted as the mother that bore her,[17] and when we are least expecting it we shall behold her in her proper form, and then Sancho will be freed of the misapprehension under which he is laboring."

"That may all very well be," said Sancho Panza, "and now I am ready to believe what my master told me he saw in the Cave of Montesinos. He says that when he saw the lady Dulcinea del Toboso there, she was wearing the same clothes that I told him I had seen her wearing when I enchanted her for my own pleasure. But it must be just the other way around, as you say, my lady; for it is not to be, and cannot be, supposed that one who is no brighter than I am should have been able to concoct so clever a trick in a moment's time, nor do I think my master is so mad that my weak and feeble persuasion could bring him to believe a thing that is so beyond the bounds of reason. But your Ladyship must not on this account look upon me as a mischief-maker, since a stupid fellow like me cannot be expected to see through the evil designs of those wicked enchanters. I made all that up simply in order to escape a scolding from my master, Señor Don Quixote, and not with any intention of harming him, and if it has come out just the opposite way from what I intended, God's in his Heaven and He judges our hearts."

"That is true," said the duchess, "but tell me, Sancho, what is all this about the Cave of Montesinos? I should like to hear it."

Sancho then related the adventure point by point as it has been set down here.

"From this episode," remarked the duchess when he had finished, "one may infer that, since the great Don Quixote says he saw down there the same peasant girl that Sancho encountered on the El Toboso road, she must undoubtedly be Dulcinea, and that means that there are some very clever and meddlesome enchanters at work around here."

"That is what I say," replied Sancho Panza, "and if my lady Dulcinea del Toboso is enchanted, so much the worse for her; I'm not going to pick a quarrel with my master's enemies, who must be many and wicked. The truth is that the one I saw was a peasant lass and that was what I took her to be and set her down for; and if Dulcinea it was, that is not to be held against me, nor should I take the consequences. But they have to be after me at every step with Sancho said this and Sancho did that, Sancho here and Sancho there—just as if Sancho was nobody at all, instead of being that same Sancho Panza that is now going about the world in books, according to what Sansón Carrasco told me, and he at least is a bachelor of Salamanca, and people like him can't lie, unless the fancy happens to take them or they find it very convenient to do so. There's no reason for anybody's falling out with me, for I have a fine reputation, and I've heard my master say that a good name is worth more than great riches;[18] so, stick me into this governorship and you'll see marvels. He who has been a good squire will make a good governor."

"All that the worthy Sancho has just said," remarked the duchess, "is out of Cato's maxims[19] or, at the least, drawn from the very entrails of Miguel Verino himself, who *florentibus occidit annis*.[20] In short, speaking after his own manner, under a bad cloak you commonly find a good drinker."[21]

"Well, to tell you the truth, lady," replied Sancho, "I never in my life have drunk from malice, though it well may be that I have from thirst, for there's nothing of the hypocrite in me. I drink when I feel like it, and even when I don't feel like it, if they offer it to me, so as not to appear strait-laced or ill bred. If a friend drinks to your health, you'd have to have a heart of marble, wouldn't you, not to raise your glass with his? But though I put on my shoes I never get them dirty.[22] And, anyhow, the squires of knights-errant commonly drink water, for they are always going through forests, woods, and meadows, and over mountains and cliffs, without finding a paltry drop of wine, though they'd be willing to give one of their eyes for it."

"I believe all that," the duchess answered him, "but, for now, let Sancho go and take his rest and later we will talk of all these things at greater length and will make arrangements to stick Sancho into that governorship, as he himself would put it, as soon as possible."

Sancho once more kissed the duchess's hand and begged her to do him the favor of seeing that his gray was well cared for, as it was the light of his eye.

"What gray is that?" inquired the duchess.

"That ass of mine," replied Sancho. "So that I won't have to mention him by that name, I'm in the habit of calling him 'the gray.' When I first came into the castle, I asked this lady duenna to look after him, and she was as angry about it as if I had said she was old or ugly, though it ought to be more fitting and proper for duennas to feed the beasts in the stable than to pose in halls of state. There was a certain gentleman in my village—Heaven help me, how he had it in for those ladies!"

"He must have been some clown or other," said Doña Rodríguez. "If he had been a gentleman and wellborn, he would have placed them in his estimation higher than the horns of the moon."

"Come now," said the duchess, "that will do for the present. Be quiet, Doña Rodríguez, and let Señor Panza rest easy and leave the care of his gray to me. Seeing that the ass is his precious jewel, I will put it on the apple of my eye."

"He will do well enough in the stable," said Sancho, "since neither he nor I is worthy of being on the apple of your Highness's eye for a single moment, and I would as soon stab myself as consent to it; for although my master says that in the matter of courtesies it is better to lose by a card too many than a card too few,[23] when it comes to beastly and asinine civilities,[24] we must be careful to steer a middle course."

"Take him along with you to your government, Sancho," said the duchess. "There you'll be able to feast him as much as you like, and you can even pension him off so that he will not have to work any more."

"Do not think, my lady the Duchess," replied Sancho, "that there would be anything so strange in that. I have seen more than one ass go up to a government, and so it would be nothing new if I took mine with me."

The duchess was more delighted than ever with Sancho's amusing conversation, and, having packed him off to bed, she went to tell the duke of what had happened. Between the two of them they arranged to play a famous joke upon Don Quixote, in true knightly style; and, in fact, they carried out a number of jests of that sort which are the best adventures to be met with in this great history.

CHAPTER XXXIV. *Which relates how they found the way of disenchanting the peerless Dulcinea del Toboso, one of the most famous adventures in this book.*

GREAT was the pleasure which the duke and duchess found in the conversation of Don Quixote and Sancho Panza, and being more anxious than ever to play a few jokes upon them that would have all the appearance of adventures, they decided to take what the knight had told them concerning the Cave of Montesinos [1] as their starting point in perpetrating a hoax that should be truly out of the ordinary. What astonished the duchess most of all was Sancho's vast simplicity; for he had come to believe it to be the gospel truth that Dulcinea had been enchanted, though he himself had plotted the whole business.

And so, a week later, having instructed the servants in everything that was expected of them, they proceeded to take Don Quixote on a hunting expedition with as large a retinue of huntsmen and beaters as might have accompanied a crowned monarch. They presented their guest with a hunting suit, and Sancho with another of the finest green cloth, but the knight declined the garment, saying that he would soon be returning to the arduous life of a man of arms and did not wish to carry with him a wardrobe or luggage of any sort. Sancho, however, accepted the gift, meaning to sell it at the first opportunity.

When the appointed day arrived, Don Quixote donned his armor and Sancho trigged himself out; and, mounted on his gray, from which he was unwilling to part despite the fact that they had provided him with a horse, the squire took his place among the troop of beaters. The duchess rode forth in splendid attire, and out of pure courtesy the knight held her palfrey's rein though the duke protested that he should not do so. At length they came to a wood between two very high mountains, and here they took up their various posts and hiding places and spread out along the paths; and then, when all was in readiness, the hunt began, accompanied by such a din of shouting voices, barking dogs, and blaring horns that they could not hear one another speak. With a sharp-pointed javelin in her hands, the duchess dismounted and posted herself where she knew the boars were in the habit of passing. The duke and Don Quixote did the same, stationing themselves at her side, but Sancho remained behind, seated upon his gray, which he did not care to leave unprotected lest some misfortune should befall it. No sooner were they in position, with the many servants drawn up in a line, than they saw coming toward them, hotly pursued by the hounds and followed by the hunters, a huge boar, gnashing his teeth, grinding his tusks, and scattering foam from his mouth; and immediately upon catching sight of the beast, Don Quixote braced his shield, drew his sword, and went forward to meet it. The duke, armed with a spear, followed the knight's example; and as for the duchess, she would have left them all behind had not her husband restrained her; but Sancho, frightened by the animal's fierce mien, left his gray to shift for itself and ran as fast as his legs would carry him.

Trying in vain to scramble up a tall oak, the unfortunate squire was caught on a branch midway, and as he was struggling to reach the top the bough broke and he fell, only to be hooked by another snag and left hanging there, unable to reach the ground. Finding himself in this plight and perceiving that his green hunting coat was ripping, and, moreover, being afraid that if the boar came that way it might succeed in getting at him, he began screaming so loudly and calling for help so earnestly that all those who heard him without being able to see him thought he must surely be in the teeth of some wild beast.

Finally the boar fell, pierced by the many spears that were thrust in his way; and it was then that Don Quixote, who had heard and recognized Sancho's cries, turned his head and beheld his squire hanging head downward from the oak, with the gray standing close by, for it had been unwilling to forsake its owner in his calamity. (And here Cid Hamete goes on to observe that he seldom saw Sancho Panza without the ass or the ass without Sancho Panza, such was the friendship and loyalty that existed between them.) The knight came up and freed the captive, who, as soon as he was safe on the ground once more, looked at the rent in his hunting coat. It pained him deeply, for that garment was like an ancestral estate to him.

In the meantime, they had slung the mighty boar across the back of a mule and, covering it with branches of rosemary and myrtle, they brought it as the spoils of victory to some large field tents that had been set up in the middle of the wood. Here they found the tables laid and a meal prepared, so sumptuous and so plentiful that it was easy to see the rank and magnificence of the one who had provided it.

"If we had been hunting hares or small birds," remarked Sancho to the duchess as he showed her the rents in his hunting suit, "my coat would never have been in this state. I'm sure I don't know what pleasure there is in waiting for an animal that will be the death of you if he reaches you with one of his tusks. I remember hearing an old song that goes like this:

> *By the bears be thou eaten*
> *as was Favila the famed.*"

"He was a Gothic king," said Don Quixote, "who went out hunting and was eaten by a bear." [2]

"That is what I was saying," replied Sancho, "and I would not have kings and princes put themselves in such danger in exchange for a pleasure which, as I see it, ought not to be one, since it consists in killing an animal that has done no harm whatever."

"That is where you are wrong, Sancho," said the duke, "for the hunting of big game is an exercise that is more becoming in kings and princes, and more necessary to them, than any other. It is an image of war; [3] in it will be found stratagems, wiles, and ambuscades for the purpose of overcoming the enemy in safety; the hunter must endure the greatest cold and the most intolerable heat and must forego ease and sleep, while at the same time his bodily strength is increased, his limbs rendered supple. In short, it is an exercise that harms no one and gives pleasure to many. And the best thing about it is that it is not a diversion for everyone as are other field sports, with the exception of hawking, which also is only for kings and great lords. And so, Sancho, you would do well to change your mind and take up hunting when you become a governor. You will see how worth-while it is." [4]

"Not I," said Sancho. "The worthy governor has broken his leg and cannot leave the house. [5] It would be a fine thing, wouldn't it, if when people went to the trouble of coming to see him on business he was always out in the woods having a good time? That way, the government would go to pot. My word, sir, hunting and such like amusements are for loafers rather than for governors. I mean to amuse myself by playing a game of brag [6] at Eastertime and bowling a little on Sundays and feast days, but hunting doesn't agree with either my constitution or my conscience."

"Please God it may be so, Sancho, for it is a long way from saying to doing." [7]

"Be that as it may," replied Sancho, "pledges don't bother a good paymaster,[8] God's help is worth more than getting up early,[9] and it's the tripes that carry the feet, not feet the tripes.[10] What I mean to say is, that if God helps me and I do what I ought to do with the right intentions, I'll undoubtedly make out better at governing than a gerfalcon. Otherwise, let them put a finger in my mouth and see whether I bite or not."

"May God and all his saints curse you, accursed Sancho!" exclaimed Don Quixote. "As I have said many times before, will the day ever come when I shall hear you talk plainly and coherently without all those proverbs of yours? My lord and lady, your Highnesses had best leave this fool alone, for he will grind your souls between, not two, but a thousand old saws, which he will drag in with as much rhyme and reason as I hope God gives him health—or me, for that matter, if I am foolish enough to listen to them."

"Sancho's proverbs," observed the duchess, "granting that they exceed in number those of the Greek Commander,[11] are not for that reason to be less esteemed on account of their brevity. For my own part, I can say that they give me greater pleasure than others, even when those others are more timely and to the point."

Conversing on such subjects as these, they left the tent and returned to the wood to visit some of the hiding places that had been set up, and thus the day quickly passed and night came, but a night not as bright and tranquil as was to have been expected at that season, for it was midsummer. There was a kind of haze in the air that was a great help to the duke and duchess in carrying out what they had in mind. A little after twilight, just as night was falling, it seemed of a sudden as if the entire wood was on fire; and a moment later, here, there, and everywhere, a countless number of trumpets and other martial instruments were heard, as if many troops of cavalry were passing by, and the light of the fire and those warlike sounds all but blinded and deafened the eyes and ears of the onlookers, and, indeed, of all those that were in the wood.

Then were heard innumerable cries of the kind the Moors give when joining battle,[12] mingled with the blare of trumpets and bugles, the roll of drums, the sound of fifes, all at one and the same time, creating so furious and continuous a din that he could have had no senses who would not have lost them as a result of all this uproar. The duke was astounded, the duchess was amazed, Don Quixote was astonished, Sancho Panza was trembling all over, and even they who knew what the cause of it was were frightened. In the midst of their fear, silence fell upon them as a postilion dressed like a demon passed in front of them, playing upon a huge hollow horn that served him as a bugle and that gave forth a hoarse and terrifying sound.

"Ho, there, brother courier!" cried the duke. "Who are you, where are you going, and what army is that which appears to be passing through this wood?"

"I am the devil," replied the courier in a horrendous voice. "I come to seek Don Quixote de la Mancha. Those whom you see here are six troops of enchanters who are bringing with them in a triumphal car the peerless Dulcinea del Toboso. She is under a magic spell and is accompanied by the gallant Frenchman, Montesinos. They come to inform Don Quixote as to how she, the said lady, may be disenchanted."

"If you are a devil as you say and as your appearance shows you to be, you would have recognized Don Quixote de la Mancha, for he stands here before you."

"In God's name and upon my conscience," said the devil, "I did not take a good look at him. I have so much on my mind that I am forgetting the chief thing for which I came."

"There is no doubt about it," said Sancho, "this demon must be a good man and a good Christian, for if he wasn't, he wouldn't swear by God and his conscience. For my part, I'm convinced now that there are good people even in Hell."

Then, without dismounting, the demon fastened his gaze upon Don Quixote. "O Knight of the Lions," he said, "for I can see you between their claws at this very moment, it is that ill-starred but valiant knight, Montesinos, who has sent me to you to inform you that you should wait for him in whatever place you chance to be, as he is bringing with him the one who is known as Dulcinea del Toboso in order that he may show you what you must do to disenchant her. And since I came for no more than that, I need tarry no longer. May demons like me be with you, and good angels with these gentle folk."

Saying this, he blew upon that monstrous horn of his and turned his back and went away without waiting for an answer from anyone.

They were more astonished than ever now, especially Sancho and Don Quixote: Sancho at seeing how, in spite of the truth, they would have it that Dulcinea was enchanted;[13] while Don Quixote was unable to make up his mind as to whether what had happened to him in the Cave of Montesinos was real or not. He was immersed in these thoughts when the duke spoke to him.

"Does your Grace intend to wait, Señor Don Quixote?"

"Why not?" was the reply. "I will wait here, strong and intrepid, though all Hell should come to attack me."

"If I see another devil or hear another horn like that last one," said Sancho, "I will wait here about as much as I would in Flanders."

Night had closed in by now, and many lights could be seen darting through the wood, just as those fiery exhalations of the earth that appear to us to be shooting stars are to be descried flitting across the sky. At the same time there came a frightening rumble, like that caused by the solid wheels of ox-carts, the strident and constant creaking of which is said to put the wolves and bears to flight if there happen to be any along the way.[14] And this tempest of sound was still further increased when it was discovered that on all four sides of the wood were what really seemed to be four encounters or battles, going on simultaneously: on one side, the dread thunder of artillery; on another, a heavy musket fire. The shouts of the combatants apparently came from close at hand as the battle cry of the Moors rose again in the distance.

In short, the bugles, horns, clarions, trumpets, drums, artillery, muskets, and, above all, that terrifying rumble of wagon wheels created so horrible a tumult that Don Quixote had to summon all his courage in order to endure it. Sancho fell in a faint on the duchess's skirt and she, letting him lie there, ordered them to throw water on his face. This was done, and he came to himself again just as one of the carts with the creaking wheels reached the spot. It was drawn by four sluggish oxen, all of them covered with black trappings. On each of the oxen's horns was a lighted wax taper, and on the bed of the cart was an elevated seat on which sat a venerable old man with a beard that was whiter than snow itself and so long that it fell below his waist. He was clad in a robe of black buckram; for, as the cart was brilliantly lighted, it was easy to see and make out everything that was in it. The oxen were led by two demons, also dressed in buckram, whose faces were so ugly that, once having had a glimpse of them, Sancho shut his eyes that he might not have to look at them a second time.

As the cart came up the old man rose from his seat and cried in a loud voice, "I am Lirgandeo the magician."

And the cart passed on, without his saying another word. It was followed by another of the same sort, and here, too, there was an old man seated upon a throne, who, ordering them to halt the vehicle, cried in a voice that was no less portentous than that of the one who had gone before, "I am the sage Alquife, great friend of Urganda the Unknown." [15] And he, like the other, went his way.

A third cart now passed; but in this case the one who was seated on the throne was not an old man but a large robust fellow with an evil-looking countenance, who, as he reached the spot, rose as the others had done.

"I," he announced in a voice that was hoarser and more devilish than those of his predecessors, "I am Archelaus, mortal enemy of Amadis of Gaul and all his kin." And with these words he was gone.

When they were a short distance away the three carts came to a stop and the monotonous rumble of their wheels was heard no more. Then there came another sound, not a noise this time, but a soothing melody, at which Sancho was greatly relieved, since he took it to be a good sign. He remarked as much to the duchess, from whose side he had not stirred one step.

"Lady," he said, "where there is music there cannot be anything evil."

"Or where there is light and brightness," replied the duchess.

"Fire gives light," said Sancho, "and brightness may come from bonfires, as we see from those all around us, which yet may burn us; but music is always a sign of feasting and merrymaking."

"That remains to be seen," said Don Quixote, who had been listening to all that was said. And he spoke truly, as will be clear from the following chapter.

CHAPTER XXXV. *Wherein is continued the information that Don Quixote received concerning Dulcinea's disenchantment, with other astonishing incidents.*

To THE sound of the pleasing strains they saw coming toward them a cart, one of the kind known as triumphal chariots, drawn by six gray mules with white linen trappings, and on each of them rode a penitent, likewise clad in white, with a lighted wax taper in his hand. This car or chariot was twice, and even three times, as big as those that had gone before, and on top and along the sides of it stood twelve other penitents, in snow-white garb and with their tapers. It was an astonishing and at the same time an awe-inspiring sight. Seated upon an elevated throne was a nymph who wore countless cloth-of-silver veils, all of them glittering with a countless number of embroidered gold spangles, which gave her, if not a sumptuous, at least a showy appearance. Her face was covered with a fine, transparent sendal, the warp of which did not prevent the features of a most beautiful maiden from being discovered. In the light of the many tapers her comeliness was revealed, and her age as well; she was apparently not older than twenty nor younger than seventeen.

Beside the maiden was a figure wearing what is known as a robe of state, which fell all the way down to its feet, while its head was covered with a black veil. When the cart was directly opposite Don Quixote and the ducal pair, the music of the flageolets ceased, and then that of the flutes and harps on the car; whereupon the figure rose up, parted her robe, and, removing the veil from her face, disclosed for all to see the ugly, fleshless form of Death itself, which startled Don Quixote, filled Sancho with terror, and even made the duke and duchess a little afraid. Having risen to its feet, this living Death, in a somewhat sleepy voice and with a tongue that was not quite awake, began reciting the following verses :

> "*Merlin am I, who, so the histories say,*
> *had the devil for a sire (it is a lie*
> *that with the course of time hath stronger grown).*
> *The prince of magic, monarch and archivist*
> *of Zoroastric science, with unfriendly gaze*
> *I view the ages and the centuries*
> *that would conceal the deeds of high emprise*
> *of brave and errant knights, toward whom I bear*
> *a great affection, always, and esteem.*
> *For granted that enchanters and their kind—*
> *sages, magicians, call them what you will—*
> *are mostly hard of heart, of temper stern,*
> *my own heart's soft and tender, loving-kind,*
> *and fond of doing good to one and all.*
>
> *In Pluto's murky pit I was absorbed*
> *in contemplation of the mystic shape*
> *of geometric figures, when there came a voice,*
> *the grief-filled voice of the ever beauteous*

Dulcinea del Toboso without peer.
'Twas then I learned of her enchantment foul
and heard how she had been vilely transformed
from highbred lady into rustic wench.
My pity was aroused, I turned the leaves
of a hundred thousand books of demonic art,
then wrapped my spirit in the frightful shell
of this grisly skeleton and hied me here
to announce the remedy that must be had
for such a sorrow, such a dreadful wrong.
    O thou, the pride and glory of all that wear
the knightly coat of adamantine steel,
O beacon-light, north star, pathfinder, guide
of all that would forsake the downy couch
and numbing sleep for the unbearable toil
of bloody combat and a warrior's life!
Be thou forever praised, O valiant one,
O Don Quixote, wise as thou art brave,
La Mancha's splendor and of Spain the star!
To thee I say that if the peerless maid,
Dulcinea del Toboso, is to be restored
to the state that once was hers, it needs must be
that thy squire Sancho on his bared behind,
those sturdy buttocks, must consent to take
three thousand lashes and three hundred more,
and well laid on, that they may sting and smart;
for those that are the authors of her woe
have thus resolved, and that is why I've come.
This, gentles, is the word I bring to you."

"For Heaven's sake!" cried Sancho, "I'd just as soon give myself three stabs as three thousand lashes. To the devil with that kind of disenchanting! I don't see what my backside has to do with it. By God, if Señor Merlin hasn't found any other way of taking the spell off the lady Dulcinea del Toboso, she can go to her grave that way!"

"What!" exclaimed Don Quixote. "I myself will take you, Don Clown stuffed with garlic, and bind you to a tree, naked as when your mother bore you, and I will give you not three thousand three hundred but six thousand six hundred, and so well laid on that you will not be rid of them though you rub yourself as many times as you have been sentenced to have lashes. And say not a word in reply or I will snatch your heart out."

"No," said Merlin when he heard this, "it cannot be that way; for the lashes that the worthy Sancho is to receive must be inflicted of his own free will and not by force. It may be done at any time he chooses, there is no time limit set; but should he wish to spare himself half the pain of this flogging, he may do so by permitting the strokes to be given by the hand of another, even though it be a somewhat weighty hand."

"Neither the hand of another nor my own hand nor weighty nor weighable," [2] replied Sancho. "No one is going to lay a hand on me. Am I, by any chance, the one that bore the lady Dulcinea del Toboso that my backside should pay for the sins of her eyes? My master, yes, seeing that he's a part of her—for he is always calling her 'my life, my soul,' his 'sustenance and support'—he may, and ought, to flog himself on her account and do everything that is necessary to disenchant her, but as for me, *abernuncio!*" [3]

No sooner had Sancho finished saying this than the silver-clad nymph who accompanied Merlin's ghost stood up and, casting aside her thin veil, disclosed what seemed to all of them a most beautiful face. With a masculine assurance and a voice that was not precisely feminine, she then began speaking directly to Sancho Panza.

"O wretched squire," she cried, "soul of a pitcher,[4] heart of a cork tree, with entrails of flint and pebbles! If, brazen thief, they ordered you to hurl yourself down from a tall tower to the earth below; if they asked you, enemy of the human race, to swallow a dozen toads, two lizards, and three snakes; if they wished you to slay your wife and young ones with a deadly, keen-bladed scimitar—if any of these things were required of you, it would be no wonder if you were squeamish and loath to comply with such commands. But to make so much of three thousand three hundred lashes, when every charity schoolboy,[5] poor lad, receives as many every month, is enough to amaze and confound the bowels of compassion in all those who hear of such a thing or who may come to know of it in the course of time.

"O miserable, hardhearted animal!" she went on, "turn those red-owl's eyes of yours—turn them, I say, upon mine, which have been compared to gleaming stars, and you will behold the tears flowing in rivulets, making furrows, tracks, and bypaths in the fair fields of my cheeks. Does it not move you, O crafty, ill-intentioned monster, that the flower of my youth (for I am still in my teens, being a little under

twenty) should thus be consumed and wither away beneath the rude
bark of a country wench? If I do not appear in such a shape at this moment, that is owing to the special favor which Señor Merlin, here present,
has done me, with the sole thought that my beauty might soften your
heart. For the tears of a lovely woman in affliction have power to turn
stony cliffs into cotton and tigers into ewe lambs. Lay on, then, lay
on, O untamed beast! Flay that coarse hide of yours; rouse that energy
that you possess but that inclines you only to eat and eat again; and set
at liberty my own smooth flesh, my loving disposition, my beautiful
face. If for my sake you will not relent or come to reason, do so for
that poor knight at your side—I mean, your master. I can see his heart
right now, it is stuck in his throat not ten fingers from his lips and only
awaits your yielding or unyielding reply to leap forth from his mouth
or go back to his stomach."

At this point, Don Quixote felt his throat and turned to the duke.
"By God, sir," he said, "Dulcinea has spoken the truth. My heart *is*
stuck in my throat, like a crossbow nut."

"What do you say to that, Sancho?" asked the duchess.

"I say, my lady," he answered her, "just what I have said: so far as
lashes are concerned, *abernuncio!*"

"*Abrenuncio,* you mean to say, Sancho," the duke corrected him.

"Let me alone, your Highness," replied the squire. "I'm in no humor
for fine points just now and can't be bothered by a letter more or less.
Those lashes that they are to give me or that I have to give myself have
got me so upset that I don't know what I'm saying or doing. But what
I'd like the lady to tell me—my lady Dulcinea del Toboso—is where she
learned that way of asking for a favor. She comes to ask me to lay my
flesh open, and she calls me a soul of a pitcher and an untamed beast
and a string of other foul names that the devil himself wouldn't stand for.
Am I made of brass, do you think? What difference is it to me whether
she's disenchanted or not? Does she come bringing me a hamper of fine
linen, shirts, handkerchiefs, socks—even if I don't wear 'em—in order
to soften me? No, nothing but abuse heaped upon abuse, although she
knows that old saying in these parts, 'An ass laden with gold goes lightly
up the mountain,' and, 'Gifts break rocks,' and, 'Pray to God and ply
the hammer,' [6] and, 'One "take" is better than two "I'll give you's." ' [7]

"And now," continued Sancho, "my master, who ought to stroke my
neck and pet me until I turn to wool and carded cotton, says that if he
gets hold of me he'll tie me naked to a tree and give me double the number of lashes. You kindhearted people ought to bear in mind that it's

not merely a squire but a governor that you're asking to have flogged, just as if it was 'Have a drink with your cherries.' [8] Let them learn, plague take it! Let them learn, I say, how to ask for something in the right way and show they had some bringing-up. They should know that there is a time for everything,[9] and people are not always in a good humor. Here I am, feeling so bad I'm fit to burst at seeing my green coat torn, and they come around asking me to flog myself of my own free will, when I feel as much like doing that as I do like becoming an Indian chief." [10]

"Well, the fact is, friend Sancho," said the duke, "that unless you become softer than a ripe fig, you are not going to have that governorship. It would be a fine thing for me to send to my islanders a cruel governor, with bowels of stone, who would not yield to the tears of damsels in distress or the entreaties of ancient, wise, and powerful enchanters and magicians. The short of it is, Sancho, either you whip yourself, let them whip you, or give up all idea of being governor."

"Sir," replied Sancho, "can't they give me a couple of days to think it over and decide what is best for me to do?"

"By no manner of means," said Merlin. "This matter must be settled here, on the instant, and on this very spot: either Dulcinea goes back to the Cave of Montesinos and her former peasant-girl state, or else she will be conveyed as she is to the Elysian fields, there to wait until the requisite number of lash strokes has been administered."

"Come, good Sancho," said the duchess, "pluck up your courage and show a proper appreciation of your master Don Quixote's bread that you have eaten; for we are all obligated to serve him and gratify his wishes, by reason of his generous nature and high deeds of chivalry. And so, my son, consent to this flogging, let the devil go to the devil, and leave fear to little minds; for, as you well know, a stout heart breaks bad luck." [11]

To this Sancho replied with the following foolish question, addressed to Merlin. "Señor Merlin, will your Grace tell me this: after the devil came running up here to hand my master a message from Señor Montesinos, requesting him to wait here as he, Montesinos, was coming to arrange for Señora Dulcinea del Toboso's disenchantment, what happened, anyway? Up to now we've seen nothing of Montesinos or any of his likes."

To which Merlin's answer was, "The devil, friend Sancho, is an ignorant wretch and a great scoundrel. I sent him to your master with a message, not from Montesinos, but from me; for Montesinos is still in his cave, expecting, or better, waiting for, his disenchantment, for there is still the tail to be skinned.[12] If he owes you anything or you have any business with him, I'll fetch him for you and set him down wherever you say; but for the present the thing to do is for you to consent to this penance, which, I can assure you, will be very good for your soul as well as your body: for your soul on account of the charitable impulse that leads you to submit to it; and for your body because, as I happen to know, you are of a sanguine disposition and a little blood-letting will do you no harm."

"There are a lot of doctors in this world," remarked Sancho. "Even the enchanters are doctors now. But since you all urge me to do it, though I can't see it myself, I am willing to give myself those three thousand three hundred lashes, on condition that I can lay them on whenever I feel like it, without any limit on the days or the time. I'll try to get out of debt as soon as possible, however, so that the world may enjoy the beauty of my lady, Doña Dulcinea del Toboso; for it appears that, contrary to what I thought, she really is beautiful after all. Another condition must be that I am not to be obliged to draw blood with that penance, and if some of the strokes happen to be fly-swatters,[13] they are to be counted just the same. And here's another item: if I should make a miscount, Señor Merlin, who knows everything, is to keep track of them and tell me if I'm giving myself too few or too many."

"It will not be necessary for me to stop you from giving yourself too many," said Merlin, "for when you have reached the proper number, the lady Dulcinea will be immediately disenchanted, and she will be so grateful that she will come to seek out the worthy Sancho and thank and reward him for his good work. So you do not need to worry about too many or too few, since Heaven will not permit me to cheat anyone out of so much as a hair of his head."

"Well, then," said Sancho, "it's in God's hands. I accept my hard luck—I mean, I consent to the penance with the conditions that have been laid down."

No sooner had he said this than the clarions struck up once more, accompanied by a great firing of muskets, and Don Quixote threw his arms about Sancho's neck, giving him a thousand kisses on the forehead and on the cheeks. The duke and duchess and all the bystanders showed that they were very pleased, and as the cart got under way once more the beauteous Dulcinea bowed to the ducal pair and dropped a low curtsy to Sancho.

With this, the merry-smiling dawn hastened her coming, the little flowers in the fields lifted their heads, and the liquid crystal of the brooks, murmuring over their white and gray pebbles, went to pay tribute to the waiting rivers. The earth was joyous, the sky unclouded, the air limpid, the light serene, and each of these things in itself and all of them together showed that the day which was treading on the skirts of morning was to be bright and clear. Satisfied with the results of the chase and with having carried out their intention so cleverly and successfully, the duke and duchess now returned to their castle with the object of following up the jest which had thus been begun, as there was no serious occupation that gave them greater pleasure than this.

CHAPTER **XXXVI**. *Wherein is related the weird and never-before-imagined adventure of the Distressed Duenna, otherwise known as the Countess Trifaldi, together with a letter that Sancho Panza wrote to his wife, Teresa Panza.*

THE duke had a major-domo who was of a very jovial and playful disposition, and he it was who had impersonated Merlin and made all the arrangements for the adventure that has just been described; he had also composed the verses and had seen to having a page take the part of Dulcinea. And so he now, with the assistance of his lord and lady, proceeded to contrive an episode of the strangest and drollest sort that could be imagined.

The duchess inquired of Sancho the next day if he had as yet begun his penitential task which had to be performed in order to obtain Dulcinea's disenchantment, and he replied in the affirmative, saying that the night before he had given himself five lashes. When she wished to know what he had given them with, he informed her that he had made use of his hand.

"That," she said, "is slapping rather than flogging yourself, and it is my belief that the wise Merlin will not be satisfied with such soft measures. It will be necessary for the worthy Sancho to make himself a scourge with prickles or employ a cat-o'-nine-tails—something that can be felt—for learning enters with blood,[1] and the liberty of so great a lady as is Dulcinea is not to be granted for so small a price. Mark you, Sancho, works of charity that are performed lukewarmly and halfheartedly are of no merit but are, indeed, worthless." [2]

"If your Ladyship," replied Sancho, "will give me some proper kind of strap or scourge, I will lay on with it, so long as it doesn't hurt too much; for I would have you know that, though I am a countryman, my flesh is more like cotton than it is like matweed, and it would not be a good thing for me to ruin myself for another's gain."

"So be it," said the duchess. "I will give you tomorrow a scourge that will suit you nicely, one that will accommodate itself to your tender flesh like a sister."

"Lady of my soul," Sancho said to her at this point, "I would have your Highness know that I have a letter written to my wife, Teresa Panza, giving her an account of everything that has happened since I left her. I have it here in my bosom; all it lacks is an address. I would have your learned Highness read it, for it seems to me to be in true governor style, I mean, the way governors ought to write."

"And who composed it for you?" inquired the duchess.

"I composed it myself, sinner that I am," replied Sancho.

"And did you write it out yourself?"

"That I did not, for I can neither read nor write, though I can sign my name."

"Let us have a look at it," said the duchess. "I am certain that it shows the quantity and quality of your wit."

Sancho drew out an unsealed letter and handed it to her. It read as follows:

SANCHO PANZA'S LETTER
TO TERESA PANZA, HIS WIFE

Though they gave me many good lashes, I went mounted like a fine gentleman;[3] if I have got a good government, it is costing me a good flogging. You will not understand this for the present, my Teresa, but later you will hear all about it. I want you to know, Teresa, that I have made up my mind you are to go in a coach; that is how you ought to go, for any other way of traveling is but creeping on all fours. You are a governor's wife now; see that no one treads on your heels! [4] I am sending you here a green hunting suit that my lady the duchess gave me; you can alter it so that it will make a petticoat and bodice for our daughter.

Don Quixote, my master, according to what I hear in these parts, is a madman with good sense, and a crackbrain who amuses people, and I don't lag behind him. We have been in the cave of Montesinos, and Merlin the magician has laid hold of me for the disenchantment of Dulcinea del Toboso, who down our way is known as Aldonza Lorenzo. With three thousand three hundred lashes minus five that I have to give myself, she will be as much disenchanted as the mother that bore her. Do not say anything about this to anyone; for if you show your privates to other people, some will say they are white and others will make them out to be black. [5]

In a few days from now I will be setting out for my government, where I go with a great desire to make money, which they tell me is the case with all new governors. I will see how things are and will let you know whether you are to come and be with me or not. The gray is well and sends you his warm regards. I don't mean to part with him even though they take me away to be Grand Turk. My lady the duchess kisses your hand a thousand times, so you must return it with two thousand; for, as my master says, there is nothing that costs less or comes cheaper than good manners. God has not seen fit to provide me with another valise containing eight hundred crowns as He did some time ago, but don't let that worry you, Teresa mine, for the bell-ringer's in a safe place, [6] and so far as the government is concerned, it will all come out in the wash. [7] The only thing is, I am told that after I once try it I'll be eating my hands off for it, [8] and if that is the case, it will not come so cheap after all, though, to be sure, the maimed and the crippled have their benefice [9] in the alms that they beg. And so, one way or another, you are going to be a rich woman and a lucky one. God give you luck the best way He can and keep me to serve you. From this castle, the twentieth of July 1614.

Your husband, the governor,

SANCHO PANZA

"In a couple of respects," said the duchess, when she had finished reading the letter, "the worthy governor goes a little astray. In the first place, he states that this governorship was bestowed upon him in return for the strokes that he is to give himself, when he knows very well—and he cannot deny it—that my lord the duke had promised it to him before that flogging was ever thought of. And in the second place, he shows himself to be too covetous; I would not have him be a gold-seeker,[10] for avarice bursts the bag,[11] and where there is an avaricious governor there is ungoverned justice."

"I don't mean it that way," said Sancho, "but if your Highness thinks that the letter is not what it should be, there is nothing to do but tear it up and write another, which may be an even worse one if it's left to my gumption."

"No, no," protested the duchess, "this one is very good, and I wish the duke to see it."

With this, they repaired to a garden where they were to dine that day, and the duchess showed Sancho's letter to the duke, who was exceedingly amused by it. When they had finished their repast and the cloth had been removed, they found entertainment for a while in listening to the squire's delightful conversation; and then, of a sudden, the melancholy notes of a fife and the hoarse, discordant roll of a drum fell upon their ears. They were all startled by this martial air which was at the same time so dull and mournful-sounding, especially Don Quixote, who was so excited he could not remain seated. As for Sancho, there is nothing to be said except that fear took him to his accustomed refuge, at the duchess's side or on the edge of her skirts; for, without any exaggeration, that sound was a most depressing one.

As they waited in suspense, they saw coming toward them through the garden two men clad in mourning robes so long and flowing that they trailed upon the ground; and these two were beating large drums, which were likewise covered in black. At their side came the fife player, a pitch-black figure like the others, and the three of them were followed by an individual of gigantic size, wrapped rather than clad in a gown that was the blackest of all, with a skirt of enormous dimensions. Over his gown this personage wore a wide baldric of the same hue, from which dangled a huge scimitar, with black scabbard and trimmings. His face was covered with a dark veil through which could be glimpsed a very long snow-white beard. He strode forward to the sound of the drums with the utmost dignity and composure; and the effect of it all—his size, his bearing, his somber appearance, and his retinue— was to fill with amazement those who beheld him without knowing who he was.

Clad in this manner and with the slow and measured pace that has been described, the figure in black came up and knelt before the duke, who with the others was standing to receive him. The duke, however, would not permit him to speak until he had risen. The monstrous scarecrow did so, and as he rose he cast aside the veil from his face, revealing the most terrifyingly long, white, and bushy beard that human eyes had ever seen. He then brought forth from the depths of his broad, capacious chest a grave and sonorous voice, and, fixing his eyes upon the duke, he began speaking:

"All-highest and mighty lord, I am called Trifaldín [12] of the White Beard, squire to the Countess Trifaldi, otherwise known as the Distressed Duenna, on whose behalf I bring your Highness a message. She beseeches your Magnificence to be pleased to grant her authority and permission to come in person and tell you of her plight, which is one of the strangest, most astonishing cases that could be conceived, even by those who are most familiar with the afflictions of this world. To begin with, she would know if that valiant and never-conquered knight, Don Quixote de la Mancha, is in this castle; for she has come on foot to seek him, without once breaking her fast, all the way from the kingdom of Candaya [13] to this your realm, a thing which may and deserves to be looked upon as a miracle, or else as something due to the power of magic. She is now at the gate of this fortress or country-seat and only awaits your pleasure that she may enter. I have spoken." [14]

The speaker coughed and stroked his beard from top to bottom with both hands as he calmly waited for the duke's reply.

"Squire Trifaldín of the White Beard," said the duke, "it is now many days since we heard of the plight of my lady, the Countess Trifaldi, whom the enchanters have caused to be known as the Distressed Duenna. You may bid her enter, O marvelous squire, and you may inform her that the valiant knight, Don Quixote de la Mancha, is indeed here, in view of whose generous disposition you may safely promise her all aid and protection; and you may further say to her that if my own assistance should be needed, it will not be lacking, for that is no more than my duty as a knight requires of me, a knight being bound to show favor to all women, and especially to widowed dames who have been wronged and are in distress as her Ladyship appears to be."

Hearing these words, Trifaldín bent one knee to the ground; and then, making a sign for the fife player and the drummers to strike up, he left the garden at the same slow and solemn pace with which he had entered it.

They all wondered at his presence and composure, and, turning to Don Quixote, the duke said, "O famous knight, when all is done the shades of malice and of ignorance cannot cover over or obscure the light of valor or of virtue. What leads me to say this is the fact that it is barely a week that your Excellency has been in this castle, yet already the unhappy and the afflicted are coming from far and out-of-the-way lands to seek you; and they come not in coaches of state or upon drome-daries, but on foot and fasting, being confident that they will find in that exceeding brave arm of yours the remedy for all their woes and troubles, thanks to your great exploits which are famed throughout the known world."

"I only wish, Señor Duke," replied Don Quixote, "that it were pos-sible for that blessed priest I had at my table not long ago to be here now, the one who was so ill-humored toward knights-errant and held such a grudge against them. I should like him to see with his own eyes whether or not knights-errant are needed in this world. He would at least be able to perceive, and at first hand, that those who are suffering extraordinary afflictions, those who are prey to some tremendous sor-row, do not come for a remedy to the houses of the learned, nor to the village sacristan, nor to the gentleman who never has set foot beyond the bounds of his village, nor to the idling courtier who is more inter-ested in news that he may talk about and pass on to others than he is in performing deeds and exploits which others may relate and set down in writing. It is, rather, in the persons of knights-errant that relief for the afflicted, succor for those in need, protection for damsels, and con-solation for widows are to be found. I thank Heaven with all my heart that such a knight am I, and any hardship or misfortune that may come to me in the exercise of so honorable a profession I look upon as well worth while. Let this dame come and ask what she may; I will set her at liberty through the strength that lies in my arm and in the undaunted resolution of my stout heart."

CHAPTER XXXVII. *In which is continued the famous adventure of the Distressed Duenna.*

THE duke and duchess were greatly pleased to see how Don Quixote had fallen in with their plan; and then Sancho spoke up.

"I hope," he said, "that this lady duenna will not put anything in the way of my getting that government that has been promised me; for I have heard a Toledo apothecary, who talked like a linnet, say that whenever duennas were mixed up in something, nothing good could come of it. God help me, but how he did have it in for them, that apothecary! From which my conclusion is that, since all duennas, no matter what their station or walk in life, are busybodies and nuisances, what must they be like when they are distressed, as they say this Countess Three Skirts,[1] or Three Tails, is? For in my country skirts and tails, tails and skirts, it's all one and the same thing."

"Be quiet, friend Sancho," said Don Quixote; "for, seeing that this lady, the duenna, comes from distant lands to seek me, she cannot be one of those that the apothecary had in mind; especially since she is a countess, for when countesses serve as duennas, that means that they wait upon queens and empresses, but in their own houses they are great ladies themselves with other duennas to act as their servants."

Doña Rodríguez, who was among those present, now put in her word. "My lady the Duchess," she said, "has in her service duennas who might well have been countesses, if fate had so willed it. However, laws go as kings like,[2] and let no one speak ill of duennas, particularly those elderly maiden ones; for although I am not one myself, I can see the advantage which a maiden duenna has over a widow, but he who clipped us kept the scissors."[3]

"For all of that," said Sancho, "when it comes to duennas, there's so much to be clipped, according to what my barber[4] tells me, that it would be better not to stir the rice even though it sticks."[5]

"Squires," observed Doña Rodríguez, "are enemies of ours; and since they haunt the antechambers and keep an eye on us every minute when they're not saying their prayers, which is often enough, they spend their time whispering about us, digging up our bones, and burying our reputations. But I can inform these walking logs that we mean to go on living in spite of them, and in great houses at that, even though we die of hunger and cover our flesh, whether delicate or not, with a black mourning robe, just as one covers over and conceals a dunghill with a carpet on procession day. Faith, and if it were permitted me and time allowed, I would prove not only to those present but to all the world that there is no virtue that is not to be found embodied in a duenna."

"I think," said the duchess, "that my good Doña Rodríguez is quite right; but she will have to wait for another time to fight her battle and that of the other duennas, to refute the ill opinion that is held of them by that wicked apothecary, and to root out the prejudice against them in the great Sancho Panza's breast."

But Sancho had an answer for her. "Ever since I had a whiff of that governorship," he said, "I'm through with the notions of a squire and don't give a wild fig for all the duennas that there are."

And so the duenna dispute would have continued had they not heard the sound of the fife and drums once more, which told them that the Distressed Duenna was entering the garden. The duchess thereupon inquired of the duke if it would be the proper thing to go out to meet her, seeing that she was a countess and an important personage.

"So far as her being a countess is concerned," remarked Sancho before the duke had a chance to reply, "I am all for your Highnesses going out to meet her, but regarding her as a duenna, I'm of the opinion that you should not stir a step."

"Who asked you to meddle in this, Sancho?" Don Quixote wanted to know.

"Who, sir?" answered Sancho. "I meddle of my own accord, and well I may, as a squire who has learned the forms of courtesy in your Grace's own school, you being the most courteous and best-bred knight that there is in all the world of courtliness. And in these matters, as I've heard your Grace say, as much is lost by a card too many as a card too few,[6] and to the good listener few words."[7]

"Sancho is right," said the duke. "We will see what this countess is like, and we shall then be able to measure out to her the courtesy that is her due."

At this point the fife and drums entered as they had before. And it is here that the author ended this brief chapter to begin another continuing the same adventure, which is one of the most notable to be found in the history.

FOLLOWING the musicians who produced those mournful strains, as many as a dozen duennas began filing into the garden. There were two rows of them, and they were all clad in wide-flowing widow's weeds, apparently made of milled serge.[1] They also wore white hoods of the thinnest cotton cloth,[2] and so long that only the hems of their robes could be seen. Behind these ladies came the Countess Trifaldi with her squire, Trifaldín of the White Beard, leading her by the hand. Her garment was of unnapped baize; and had it been napped, each tuft would have stood out like one of those big Martos chickpeas.[3] The tail or skirt, or whatever you choose to call it, was a three-pointed one and was borne by three pages, likewise in mourning, who with their mistress formed a beautiful mathematical figure with three acute angles.

This led all the beholders to the conclusion that it must be on account of those three points that she was known as the Countess Trifaldi, as one might say: the Countess of the Three Skirts, an opinion that is supported by Benengeli, who asserts that the lady's right name was the Countess Lobuna and that she was so called on account of the many wolves[4] in her country. If they had been foxes instead of wolves, she would have been called the Countess Zorruna,[5] it being the custom in those parts for the nobility to derive their names from the thing or things that were most abundant in their domains. And so this particular countess, in honor of the new fashion in skirts that she had adopted, ceased to be Lobuna and became Trifaldi.

The twelve duennas and the lady came on at processional pace, their faces covered with black veils which were not transparent like Trifaldín's but so heavy as to afford no glimpse of anything beneath them. As soon as the little band had made its entrance, the duke and duchess and Don Quixote rose to their feet, and all the others did the same as they watched the slowly moving procession. The duennas then halted and opened ranks, and the Distressed One advanced, still without letting go of Trifaldín's hand. Seeing this, the ducal pair and the knight stepped forward a dozen paces or so to receive their guest and she, dropping to her knees, thereupon addressed them in a voice that was hoarse and rough rather than fine and delicate.

"May your Highnesses be pleased not to show such courtesy to their manservant—I mean, their handmaiden [6]—for I am too stricken with grief to be able to make a fitting reply, owing to the strange, unheard-of misfortune that has borne away my wits—I know not whither, but it must be very far indeed, seeing that the longer I look for them the farther I am from finding them."

"He would truly be a witless one, Lady Countess," replied the duke, "who from a sight of your person did not at once discern your great worth, which merits the cream of courtesy and the flower of well-bred ceremony." And, taking her by the hand, he conducted her to a seat beside the duchess, who received her with the utmost graciousness.

Don Quixote, meanwhile, was silent, but Sancho was dying to glimpse Trifaldi's face and those of some of her duennas. This, however, was out of the question until the ladies themselves, of their own free will, should choose to disclose their features. A silence having fallen upon all of them, they waited to see who would be the first to break it. It proved to be the Distressed Duenna, with these words:

"O most powerful lord, most beautiful lady, and most discreet by-standers, I am confident that my indescribable woe will meet with a reception no less dispassionate than generous and sympathetic in your valiant breasts; for it is such as to melt marble, soften diamonds, and mollify the most steel-hardened hearts this world can show. But ere it is made public in your hearing,[7] I would have you inform me if there be present in your midst, your group, or company, that knight immaculatissimus, Don Quixote de la Manchissima, and Panza, his squirissimus." [8]

At this point Sancho spoke up before anyone else had a chance to reply. "Panza," he said, "is here, and Don Quixotissimus as well; and so, Distressedissima Duennissima, you may say whatever you pleasissimus, for we are all readissimus and preparedissimus to be of servissimus to you."

Don Quixote then arose and, addressing the Distressed Duenna, spoke as follows:

"If your woe, O grief-stricken lady, admits of any hope of remedy through the valor and strength of arm of any knight-errant, here are my arm and my courage which, though weak and insufficient, are wholly

at your service. I am Don Quixote de la Mancha, whose business it is
to succor all those who need my aid; and this being the case, as indeed
it is, my lady, there is no need of your appealing to our benevolence or
seeking to compose preambles; rather, you should tell us your troubles
plainly and without any circumlocution, for you have here listeners
who, if they cannot give you any help, will lend you at least a sympathetic ear."

Hearing these words, the Distressed Duenna threw herself at Don
Quixote's feet and sought to embrace them. "O invincible knight," she
cried, "I cast myself down before these feet and legs as before the very
bases and pillars of knight-errantry. If I would kiss thy feet, it is because all the remedy for my misfortune hangs and depends upon the
steps that they may take, O valiant and errant one whose true exploits
leave far behind and eclipse the fabled ones of the Amadises, the Esplan-
dians, and the Belianises!"

Turning then to Sancho Panza, she took his hands and continued, "O
thou most loyal squire that ever served a knight-errant, either in the present age or in times past, thou whose goodness is longer than the beard
of Trifaldín, my companion, here present! Well mayest thou pride
thyself upon the fact that in serving Don Quixote thou art figuratively
serving all that host of knights who have borne arms in this world. I
conjure thee, by all that thou owest to thine own goodness and loyalty,
kindly to intercede for me with thy master that he may show favor to
this humblest and most unfortunate of countesses."

"So far as my goodness is concerned, your Ladyship," replied Sancho,
"it makes little difference to me whether or not it is as long as your
squire's beard; what matters is that my soul should have a good beard
and mustache when it comes to leave this world; for whiskers here
below I don't give a rap.[9] But without all this flattery and all this begging on your part, I will ask my master to favor and help your Grace in
any way he can—he likes me, and, what's more, he has need of me just
now in connection with a certain matter. So your Grace may go ahead
and unpack your troubles and tell us all about them, leaving the rest
of it to us, for we understand one another very well."

The duke and duchess were bursting with laughter at all this, for it
was they who had planned the adventure; and they congratulated themselves upon the clever acting of La Trifaldi, who, as she resumed her
seat, continued speaking.

"The famous kingdom of Candaya,"[10] she said, "which lies between
great Trapobana[11] and the Southern Sea, two leagues beyond Cape

Cómorin,[12] had for its sovereign Queen Doña Maguncia, widow of King Archipiela, her lord and husband, and from their union sprang the Infanta Antonomasia,[13] heiress to the realm. The said Infanta Antonomasia grew up and was reared under my tutelage and direction, for I was her mother's oldest and ranking duenna. By the time she had reached the age of fourteen, her beauty was so perfect that nature's self could not have improved upon it in any particular, nor is it to be supposed that her mind was that of a child. She was, in fact, as intelligent as she was lovely, and with her loveliness there was nothing in this world to compare; and this is still true, unless it be that those envious sisters, the hardhearted Parcae, have severed her life thread; but that I cannot believe, for Heaven would never permit so great a wrong to be done to earth as would be the case if this unripe cluster from the fairest of vineyards were to be plucked before its season.

"Endowed with such beauty as this, which my halting tongue cannot fittingly praise, she was loved by princes, both native and foreign; and in addition to these, there was a certain private gentleman at the court who, trusting in his youth and elegance, his many graces and accomplishments, and his ready and pleasing wit, dared to raise his eyes to this heaven of pulchritude. For—if I am not boring you—I would have your Highnesses know that he played the guitar in such a way as to make it talk, and he was also a poet and a great dancer and could make a birdcage so well that, if worst came to worst, he might have earned his living in that fashion;[14] and these are accomplishments sufficient to lay low a mountain, not to speak of a tender maid.

"However, all his cleverness and grace of manner would have been of little or no avail when it came to reducing the fortress of my young mistress's heart had not the impudent rascal first taken the precaution of subduing me, her guardian. Scoundrel and heartless vagabond that he was, he strove to win my good will and induce me to comply with his wishes, so that I, faithless warden, would hand him over the keys to the castle which it was my duty to guard. The short of the matter is, he flattered me and won me over with the gift of this or that little trinket; but what really brought about my downfall was some verses that I heard him singing one night through a street railing. If I remember rightly, they went like this:

> *From that sweet enemy of mine*
> *is born a woe that wounds my heart,*
> *and what adds torment to its smart:*
> *I must keep silent, make no sign.*[15]

The words of the song were as pearls to me, and the singer's voice sweet as sugar sirup; and ever since then, in view of the evil into which I have fallen through these and other similar verses, I have been led to reflect that poets ought to be banished from well-ordered states, as Plato advised,[16] at least those that write amorous poetry, not couplets after the manner of 'The Marquis of Mantua,'[17] which are the delight of women and children and bring tears to their eyes, but poems containing sharp-pointed conceits[18] that pierce the heart like soft thorns and, like the lightning, wound it while leaving the body sound and clothed.

"Another time he sang:

> *Come, Death, so well disguised that I*
> *thy nearing presence may not feel,*
> *lest Life should once more on me steal,*
> *when I find how sweet it is to die.*[19]

There were other stanzas and refrains of the same sort, which cast a spell over you when they are sung and hold you fascinated as you read them. And when they condescend to compose a poem of the kind that was once very popular in Candaya and that went by the name of *seguidilla*[20]—ah! then it is that hearts frolic and laughter bursts forth, while the body grows restless and all the senses finally turn to quicksilver. And so I say, my lord and lady, that such troubadours as these should rightfully be banished to the Lizard Islands.[21]

"Yet they, after all, are not to blame, but rather those simple-minded ones that praise them and the foolish girls who believe them. And had I been the good duenna that I ought to have been, I should not have allowed myself to be moved by such labored conceits, nor should I have believed that the poet was speaking the truth when he declared, 'I live dying, burn in ice, tremble in the fire, hope without hope, go and stay,' along with other contradictory conceptions of this sort with which their writings are filled. And when they come to promise the Phoenix of Arabia, the crown of Ariadne, the horses of the Sun, the pearls of the South, the gold of Tibar, and the balsam of Panchaia[22]—it is then that they really let their pens go, seeing that it costs them little to make a promise they never dream of fulfilling.

"But I am permitting myself to wander. Poor me! What folly, what madness, is it that leads me to dwell on the faults of others when there is so much to be said regarding my own? Ah, I was luckless once again! It was not the verses that overcame me but my own simplicity; it was not the music that softened me but my own levity. It was my great ignorance and want of caution that opened the road and cleared the path that Don Clavijo was to tread—for that is the name of the gentleman in question. With me as go-between, he made his way not once but many times into the apartment of my deceived Antonomasia (deceived not by him, but by me). He did this as her true husband; for, though I am a sinner, I otherwise would never have consented even to his touching the edge of her shoe soles. No, no, nothing like that; marriage comes before anything else whenever I have such a business in hand! The only trouble in the present instance was that they were so unequal in rank, Don Clavijo being a mere private gentleman while the Infanta Antonomasia was, as I have said, the heiress to the kingdom.

"For some time this entanglement remained a secret, carefully concealed by the precautions that I took, until I perceived that a certain swelling of Antonomasia's belly was bound to reveal it shortly. Frightened by this, we held a consultation and decided that, before the affair came to light, Don Calvijo should appear before the Vicar and ask for Antonomasia's hand in marriage, by virtue of a written promise to marry him which she had made under my dictation and which was so bindingly worded that not even Samson with all his strength would ever have been able to break it. The proper steps were accordingly taken; the Vicar was shown the agreement and, after hearing her confession, committed her to the house and custody of a highly respectable bailiff."

At this point Sancho put in a word. "So," he said, "in Candaya, too, they have court bailiffs, poets, and *seguidillas*. I swear, the world is the same all over! But hurry up, Señora Trifaldi, for it's getting late and I'm dying to hear the end of this long story."

"I will do so," replied the countess.

CHAPTER XXXIX . *In which La Trifaldi goes on with her wondrous and memorable story.*

EVERY word that Sancho uttered delighted the duchess and drove Don Quixote to despair. The latter now ordered his squire to hold his tongue, and the Distressed One then resumed her tale.

"After many questions and answers, with the infanta always standing her ground, never varying from her original declaration, the Vicar finally decided in favor of Don Clavijo and gave the princess to him as his lawful wife, at which the queen, Doña Maguncia, the infanta's mother, was so grieved that within three days' time we had buried her."

"She died, no doubt," put in Sancho.

"Obviously," replied Trifaldín. "In Candaya we do not bury people alive, only the dead ones."

"I, Sir Squire," Sancho answered him, "have seen them, before now, bury a person who had no more than fainted, in the belief that he was dead; and it seems to me that Queen Maguncia ought to have fainted rather than died, for in this life there are so many things that come out all right in the end that she ought not to have felt so bad over the foolish thing the infanta did. If the young lady had married some page or other household servant as many others have done, or so I've heard tell, there'd have been no repairing the damage; but for her to have married such a fine gentleman as you say this one is—well, while it may have been a piece of foolishness, it was not so big a one as you seem to think. For, according to the rules laid down by my master, who is here present and will not let me lie, just as they make bishops out of men of learning, so may knights, especially if they be errant ones, become kings and emperors."

"Right you are, Sancho," said Don Quixote. "A knight-errant, if he has two fingers' worth of luck, has it in his power to become the greatest lord on earth. But let the Distressed Lady go on with her story; for I have an idea that she has yet to tell us the bitter part of this tale that up to now has been a pleasing one."

"What is to come is indeed bitter," replied the countess; "so bitter that by comparison the colocynth is sweet and the oleander savory. The queen, then, died—she did not faint—and we buried her; and no sooner had we covered her with earth and said the last farewell when, *quis talia fando temperet a lacrimis?* [1] over the queen's grave there appeared, mounted upon a wooden horse, Malambruno, Maguncia's first cousin, who is not merely a cruel being but an enchanter as well. In order to punish Don Clavijo for his rashness and avenge his cousin's death, and also out of spite over Antonomasia's stubbornness, Malambruno thereupon, by the exercise of his magic arts, proceeded to cast a spell upon the two of them and left them there upon the grave itself, the infanta having been transformed into a female ape while her lover had become a crocodile made of some unknown metal, with a pillar, also of metal, standing between them, bearing an inscription in Syriac characters that, translated into the Candayan, and now into the Castilian, read as follows:

" 'These two rash lovers shall not regain their former shape until the valiant Manchegan shall come to meet me in singlehanded encounter, since it is for his great valor alone that the fates have reserved this unheard-of adventure.' [2]

"Saying this, he drew forth from its scabbard an enormous broad-bladed scimitar and, seizing me by the hair, pretended that he was going to slash my throat and cut off my head. I was so frightened and distressed that my voice stuck in my throat, but, nevertheless, I forced myself to exert what strength I had, and in a trembling, sorrow-filled voice I pleaded with him so long and in such a way as to lead him to suspend execution of so rigorous a sentence. Finally he had them bring before him all the palace duennas, who are the ladies that you see here; and, after having spoken in exaggerated terms of our offense, holding them all guilty where I alone was to blame, and railing against duennas in general and their evil schemes and plottings, he went on to say that he did not choose to inflict a capital punishment upon us but preferred a more long-drawn-out penalty such as would leave us in a perpetual state of civil [3] death.

"At the very moment, the very instant, that he said this, we felt the pores of our faces opening, as if our countenances were being pricked all over with needle points, and when we put our hands up to see what the trouble was, we found ourselves in the condition in which you see us now."

With this, the Distressed One and all the other duennas raised their veils, revealing faces covered with heavy beards, some red, some black, some white, and some grizzled, at sight of which the duke and duchess feigned astonishment, while Don Quixote and Sancho were truly astounded and all the others present were filled with wonder.

"Such was the punishment," continued La Trifaldi, "which that malign scoundrel, Malambruno, meted out to us, by covering our soft white faces with these coarse bristles. Oh, would to Heaven that he had cut off our heads with that monstrous scimitar of his in place of dimming the light of our countenances with these wool-combings that cover them! For, gentle folk, if we stop to consider the matter—and I wish my eyes could weep like fountains as an accompaniment to what I am about to say; but, alas, I have brooded so long upon our woes and have already wept so many oceans of brine that these orbs are now as dry as beards of wheat, and so I must tell it without tears—as I was saying, then, where is a bearded duenna to go, what father or mother will take pity on her, who will aid her? For even if she have a smooth face, one that has been martyred by a countless variety of cosmetics, it is hard enough to find someone to care for her; and what will happen when she discloses a visage that is like a wood or a thicket? O ye duennas, companions of mine, it was indeed an unlucky moment, an unfortunate hour, when our parents did beget us!"

As she said this, she seemed about to swoon away.

CHAPTER XL. *Of things relating and pertaining to this adventure and this memorable history.*

REALLY and truly, all those who enjoy such histories as this one ought to be grateful to Cid Hamete, its original author, for the pains he has taken in setting forth every detail of it, leaving out nothing, however slight, but making everything very clear and plain. He describes thoughts, reveals fancies, answers unasked questions,[1] clears up doubts, and settles arguments. In short, he satisfies on every minutest point the curiosity of the most curious. O author celebrated above all others! O fortunate Don Quixote! O famous Dulcinea! O droll Sancho Panza! May all of you together and each of you separately live for unnumbered centuries, for the delight and general pastime of your fellowmen!

The history then goes on to inform us that as soon as he saw the Distressed One in a swoon, Sancho Panza spoke up. "By the faith of an honest man," he exclaimed, "and the souls of all the Panzas that have gone before me, I swear that I have never seen nor heard of such an adventure as this, nor has my master ever thought up such a one or told me of anything like it. A thousand devils take you, Malambruno—not that I mean to curse you—for the enchanter and the giant that you are! Couldn't you have found any other kind of punishment for these lady sinners that you had to put beards on them? Wouldn't it have been better for them if you had slit their noses down the middle, even if, as a result of it, they did sniffle when they talked? And I'll bet they do not even have the price of a shave!" [2]

"That is the truth, sir," replied one of the twelve, "we have not the money for that purpose, and some of us accordingly have resorted to the use of sticking plasters; by applying them to our faces and pulling them off with a jerk, we are left as smooth and bare as the bottom of a stone mortar.[3] It is true that we have in Candaya women who go from house to house, removing hair, trimming eyebrows, and making cosmetics,[4] but we, my lady's duennas, never would admit them to our presence, as they have about them the third-rate odor of women who have come down in the world.[5] And so, if Señor Don Quixote does not lend us help, we shall carry these beards to our graves."

"I will pluck out my own beard," said Don Quixote, "in the land of the Moors, if I do not do something about those that you wear."

At this juncture La Trifaldi recovered from her swoon. "The echo of that promise, O valiant knight," she said, "has reached my ears even as I lay in a faint; it is, indeed, the thing that has enabled me to recover my senses. And so I beg you once more, O renowned errant and indomitable lord, let your gracious promise be converted into deeds."

"It will be no fault of mine if there is any delay," was Don Quixote's answer. "Tell me, lady, what it is I have to do, for my stout heart is ready and at your service."

"As it happens," said the Distressed One, "the distance from here to the kingdom of Candaya, if one goes by land, is five thousand leagues, a couple more or less, but if one goes by air and in a straight line, it is three thousand two hundred twenty-seven. I must further inform you of what Malambruno told me: that whenever fate should provide me with a knight who would seek to free me, he himself would send a mount much better and less skittish than those that are to be had for hire; [6] for the mount in question is none other than that same wooden horse upon which the valiant Pierres carried off the beauteous Magalona.[7] This steed is guided by means of a peg that he has in his forehead, which serves as a bridle, and he goes through the air at such a speed that it seems as if the very devils themselves must be carrying him.

"This horse," she went on, "according to ancient tradition, was created by Merlin the Sage. He lent him to his friend, Pierres, who upon his back made long journeys and, as I have said, bore off the fair Magalona, leaving all those that beheld them from the earth gaping with astonishment. He never permitted anyone to make use of the steed unless it was someone he dearly loved or who paid him dearly, and no mortal that we know of, save the great Pierres, has mounted him from that day to this. Malambruno, through his arts, contrived to get possession of him and employs him in the journeys which he is all the time making here and there throughout the world. He is here today and tomorrow in France, and the next day in Potosí and the best of it is, this horse neither eats nor sleeps nor does he have to be shod. Without wings, he ambles through the air so smoothly that his rider can carry a cup full of water in his hand without spilling a single drop; for which reason it was, the fair Magalona was very fond of riding him."

"When it comes to smooth ambling," said Sancho at this point, "give me my gray. He doesn't go through the air, but on the ground I'll back him against all comers."

They all had a good laugh, and then the Distressed One continued, "And this horse that I am telling you of, if Malambruno is of a mind to put an end to our sufferings, will be here in our presence within half an hour after night has fallen; for such, he told me, was to be the sign by which I should know that I had found the champion I was seeking. As soon as I had found him, the mount was to be sent to me with all speed."

"And how many can ride him?" Sancho inquired.

"Two persons," was the reply, "one on the saddle and the other on the crupper. Usually those two persons are a knight and his squire, unless some maiden is being carried off."

"And what is this horse's name?"

"His name," said the Distressed One, "is not that of Bellerophon's horse, which was called Pegasus; nor is it Bucephalus, like that of Alexander the Great's steed; nor Brigliador, as Orlando's mount was known; nor Bayard, after that of Rinaldo of Montalbán; nor Frontino, after that of Ruggiero; nor Bootes or Peritoa, which, they say, were the names of the horses of the Sun; nor is he called Orelia, after the horse on which the unfortunate Rodrigo, last king of the Goths, rode into battle where he lost his life and kingdom."

"I will bet you," said Sancho, "seeing they haven't given him any of the famous names of well-known horses, they never thought of naming him after my master's Rocinante either, though when it comes to an all-around mount, he has it over all those that you have mentioned."

"That is true enough," replied the bearded countess, "but the name that he does have fits him very well; for he is called Clavileño the Swift, due to his being made of wood with a peg in his forehead [8] and the speed at which he travels. And thus, so far as his name goes, he may very well compete with the famous Rocinante."

"I don't mind the name," said Sancho, "but what kind of bridle or halter do you use to control him?"

"I have told you," said La Trifaldi, "that the knight who rides him directs him this way or that by turning the peg. It may be through the air or skimming, one might say sweeping, the earth, or else he may take that middle course that is to be sought out and adhered to in all well-regulated actions." [9]

"That I should like to see," said Sancho, "but to think for one minute that I'm going to mount him, either in the saddle or on the crupper, is to ask pears of the elm tree.[10] A fine thing that would be! Why, it is all I can do to hold on to my gray, seated on a packsaddle that is softer than silk itself; and now they'd have me straddle a wooden crupper without a pad or cushion of any kind! By Heaven, I don't intend to bruise myself to get rid of anyone's beard; let each one shave himself the best way he can, I don't mean to accompany my master on any long journey like that. And, anyhow, I can't help as much with the shaving of those beards as I can with the disenchanting of my lady Dulcinea."

"Yes, you can, my friend," said La Trifaldi. "Indeed, without your presence I do not think we shall be able to accomplish anything."

"In the king's name," cried Sancho, "what have squires to do with the adventures of their masters? Are they to get all the fame for what they accomplish while we do all the work? Body of me! If the historians would only say, 'Such and such a knight brought such and such an adventure to a successful conclusion, with the aid of So-and-So, his squire, without whom it would have been impossible—' But no, they simply write down, 'Don Paralipomenon of the Three Stars accomplished the adventure of the six monsters,' without so much as mentioning the squire, who was present all the time, just as if he didn't exist! And so, ladies and gentlemen, I tell you once more: my master may go alone if he likes, and much good may it do him, but I am going to stay right here, in the company of my lady the duchess; and it may be that when he comes back he will find the lady Dulcinea's affair greatly advanced, for in my leisure moments I mean to give myself a batch of lashes without a hair to cover me." [11]

"Nevertheless," said the duchess, "you will have to go along if necessary, my worthy Sancho; for these are good people that ask it of you, and besides, the faces of these ladies must not remain in such a condition and all on account of your foolish fears. It would indeed be a pity if that were to happen."

"In the king's name again!" exclaimed Sancho. "If he was asked to do this for some modest, retiring damsels or charity girls, a man might venture to put himself to a little trouble; but to ask him to suffer in order to rid duennas of their beards—devil take it, no! I'd rather see them all with beards, from the highest to the lowest and from the most prudish to the most simpering of the lot."

"You certainly have it in for duennas, Sancho, my friend," remarked the duchess. "You seem to be very much of the same opinion as that Toledo apothecary, but, upon my word, you are wrong. There are in my household some most excellent ladies of this sort, and here is Doña Rodríguez, who will not permit me to say anything else."

"Your Excellency may say what you like," replied Rodríguez, "for God knows the truth of every matter, and good or bad, bearded or smooth-faced, we are our mothers' daughters just like other women, and it was God who sent us into this world. He knows why He did so, and I cling to His mercy and not to anybody's beard."

"Well, Señora Rodríguez," said Don Quixote, "and Señora Trifaldi and company, I trust to Heaven to look with favoring eye upon your woes. As for Sancho, he will do as I bid him. Let Clavileño come that I may meet Malambruno face to face; for I can assure you that no razors would shave you ladies as easily as my sword will shave Malambruno's head from his shoulders. God may suffer the wicked for a time but not forever."

"Ah," exclaimed the Distressed One, "may all the stars of the celestial regions gaze down upon you, O valiant knight; may they infuse your heart with courage and prosper your undertaking, that you may be the shield and protector of the downtrodden and much maligned race of duennas, which is abominated by apothecaries, slandered by squires, and made sport of by pages. Woe to the wench who in the flower of her youth would not sooner become a nun than one of us! Ah, how unfortunate we are! Even though we be descended in direct male line from Trojan Hector himself, our mistresses never fail to address us with a *vos* if they think that will make them queens! [12] O giant Malambruno, you may be an enchanter but you keep your promises most faithfully. Send us now the unequaled Clavileño, that our misfortunes may come to an end; for if the hot weather sets in and our beards are with us still, we shall be in a very bad way."

This was said with such feeling as to bring tears from the eyes of all the bystanders, and even from Sancho, who resolved in his heart that he would accompany his master to the end of the world, if it had to be done in order to remove the wool from those venerable countenances.

CHAPTER XLI. *Of the coming of Clavileño, with the conclusion of this long-drawn-out adventure.*

NIGHT came on, and with it the appointed moment at which the famous steed, Clavileño, was to arrive. Don Quixote was uneasy over the animal's delay in making an appearance; for it seemed to him that, if Malambruno was slow in sending the mount, it must mean either that the adventure was reserved for some other knight, or that the enchanter did not dare come forth to engage in single combat. These thoughts were running through his mind, when, lo and behold! four wild men clad in green ivy [1] entered the garden, bearing upon their shoulders a great wooden horse. Having deposited it upon the ground, one of the savages addressed the company.

"Let him who has the courage," he said, "mount this contrivance."

"I am not going to mount," said Sancho, "for I have not the courage, nor am I a knight."

"And let his squire, if he has one," the wild man went on, "seat himself upon the crupper, putting his trust in the valiant Malambruno, for he need fear no other sword or wile of any sort.[2] There is nothing to do but give a twist to this peg on the horse's neck [3] and he will carry them through the air to where Malambruno waits. But lest the great altitude should cause them dizziness, they must cover their eyes until they hear him neigh, which will be the sign that they have reached the end of their journey."

Saying this, they gracefully retired the way they had come, leaving Clavileño behind them. The moment she caught sight of the horse, the Distressed One turned to Don Quixote and, on the verge of tears, said to him, "O valiant knight, the promises of Malambruno are to be depended upon, the steed is here, our beards are growing; and each one of us, by every hair in those same beards, herewith beseeches you to shave and shear us, to accomplish which you have but to mount this horse, along with your squire, and make a happy beginning of your new journey."

"That I will do, Señora Countess Trifaldi," said Don Quixote, "and with right good will. I will not even lose time by looking for a cushion or putting on my spurs, so great is my desire to see you, my lady, and all the other duennas clean-shaven as you should be."

"That I will not do," declared Sancho, "good will or ill will, it makes no difference. If this shaving business can be accomplished only by my getting up on the crupper, my master can very well look for another squire to go with him, and these ladies can find some other way of making their faces smooth again. I am no wizard to go flying through the air like that. What will my islanders say when they hear that their governor is going out for a stroll on the winds? And there's something else: seeing that it is three thousand odd leagues from here to Candaya, if the horse should tire or the giant become vexed, it would take us half a dozen years to get back again, and there won't be isle or islander [4] in the world that will know who I am. It's a common saying that there's danger in delay, and when they offer you a heifer, run with the halter.[5] Begging the pardon of these ladies' beards, St. Peter is very well off in Rome.[6] By which I mean to say, I'm very well off in this house where everyone treats me so well, and whose master, I hope, is going to be so good as to make me a governor."

"Friend Sancho," said the duke, "the island that I promised you is not a movable one, nor is it likely to fly away; it has roots so deeply sunken in the bowels of the earth that it is not to be torn up or so much as budged by a few stout pulls. What is more, you know as well as I do that there is no office of any importance that is not obtained through some sort of bribe, great or small; and what I ask in exchange for this governorship is that you accompany your master, Don Quixote, so that he may be able to bring this memorable adventure to a conclusion. And whether you come back mounted on Clavileño, with all the speed that is to be expected of him, or whether contrary fortune brings you back as a pilgrim, on foot, going from inn to inn, whenever you do return you will find your island where you left it and your islanders with the same desire of having you for their governor that they always had, nor will I have changed my mind on the subject. And so, Señor Sancho, do not doubt the truth of what I tell you, for that would be to do me a grievous wrong when I am so eager to be of service to you."

"Sir," replied Sancho, "you need say no more. I am but a poor squire and do not know how to return such courtesy in the proper way. Let my master mount, then, cover my eyes, pray God for my soul, and tell me if, when we are away up there on high, it is all right for me to call upon Our Lord and ask the angels to protect me."

"You may pray to God or anyone you like, Sancho," said Trifaldi; "for although Malambruno is an enchanter, he is a Christian and very sagacious and circumspect in the practice of his art, taking care not to meddle with other people's concerns."

"Well, then," said Sancho, "God help me, and the Holy Trinity of Gaeta!" [7]

"Since the memorable adventure of the fulling mills," observed Don Quixote, "I have never seen Sancho so frightened as he is now; and if I were as much given to omens as others are, his pusillanimity would shake my own courage a bit. However— Come here, Sancho; with the permission of these ladies and gentlemen I should like to have a couple of words with you."

With this, he led the squire to one side, among some of the garden trees, and there, taking both of his hands, spoke to him as follows:

"You are aware, brother Sancho, of the long journey that awaits us. God knows when we shall return or how much leisure it will allow us; and so I wish you would retire to your room as if you were seeking something that is needed for the road, and there in a twinkling pay something on account toward those three thousand three hundred lashes that you are supposed to give yourself, even if it be no more than five hundred for the present. It will be just so many of them out of the way, and a thing well begun is half done." [8]

"By God," exclaimed Sancho, "your Grace must be out of your mind! As the saying has it, you see me pregnant and you want me a virgin. Here, I'm supposed to go seated on a bare board and you'd have me skin my backside before I start! No, no, your Grace is all wrong. Let us go now and see to shaving those duennas, and when we come back, I give you my word, I'll make such haste to fulfill my obligation that your Grace will be more than satisfied. That is all I have to say."

"Well, my good Sancho," replied Don Quixote, "I shall console myself with that promise; and I believe you will keep it, too, for while you may be a simpleton, you are really a trusty fellow."

"I'm not rusty," said Sancho, "only sunburned; [9] but even if I was a little of each, I'd still keep my word."

With this, they came back to mount Clavileño; and as they did so Don

Quixote said, "Cover your eyes, Sancho, and take your place; for he who is sending us to such far lands cannot be doing it merely to deceive us, inasmuch as there would be little glory for him in thus tricking those who had put their trust in him. And even though everything should go contrary to what I expect, the honor of having undertaken such an exploit is such as no malice could dim."

"Let us go, sir," Sancho answered him, "for the beards and tears of these ladies are more than my heart can bear, and I shall not eat a bite that agrees with me until I have seen them smooth-faced as they were before. Mount, then, your Grace, but be sure to blindfold yourself. If I am to ride the crupper, it is plain that the one in the saddle must be the first to mount."

"That is true enough," Don Quixote agreed. And, taking a handkerchief from his pocket, he asked the Distressed One to cover his eyes very carefully; but no sooner had this been done than he uncovered them.

"If I remember rightly," he said, "I have read something in Vergil about that Trojan Palladium,[10] which was a wooden horse that the Greeks offered to the goddess Pallas, and which, being pregnant with armed knights, was later the ruination of Troy. For this reason, I think it would be a good thing to see what Clavileño has in his belly."

"There is no need of that," said the Distressed One. "I will vouch for him. I know that Malambruno is in no wise treacherous or malicious; and, accordingly, Señor Don Quixote, your Grace may mount without any hesitancy whatsoever, and may it be on my head if anything happens to you."

The knight felt that anything he might say regarding his safety would but cast doubt upon his valor; and so, without any further argument, he mounted Clavileño. Trying the peg, he discovered that it turned very easily; and as he sat there, with no stirrups and his legs hanging down, he looked like nothing so much as a figure in some Roman triumph, painted or woven upon a Flemish tapestry. Against his will and little by little, Sancho climbed up and made himself as comfortable as he could on the crupper, which he found to be quite hard; whereupon he asked the duke if it would not be possible to provide him with a pillow or cushion, even though they had to take one from the couch of my lady the duchess or from some page's bed; for the flanks of this horse seemed to him more like marble than they did like wood.

At this point Trifaldi spoke up, saying that Clavileño would not endure any kind of trappings and that the best thing for the squire to do was to sit sideways so that he would not feel the hardness so much. Sancho did as she advised, and, bidding them farewell, he let his eyes be bandaged. He promptly removed the cloth, however, and, gazing tenderly and tearfully at all those in the garden, begged them to aid him in his present trouble with plenty of Hail Marys and Our Fathers,[11] so that God might provide someone to do the same for them when they should find themselves in such straits.

"Thief," exclaimed Don Quixote, "are you by any chance on the gallows or at death's door that you resort to such entreaties? Are you not, soulless and cowardly creature, in the very spot that the beauteous Magalona occupied and from which she descended, not to her grave, but to become queen of France,[12] unless the histories lie? And I here at your side, am I not on a par with the brave Pierres, who sat in this same saddle where I now sit? Cover your eyes, you spiritless animal, cover them I say, and do not give voice to your fears, at least not in my presence."

"Let them go ahead and blindfold me," said Sancho; "but since you won't allow me to commend myself or be commended to God, is it any wonder if I'm afraid we may be going to some region of devils [13] who will make off with us to Peralvillo?" [14]

When their eyes had been covered and Don Quixote had settled himself to his satisfaction, the knight tried the peg, and no sooner had he laid hands upon it than the duennas and all the others there present began calling out to them, "God guide you, valiant knight! God be with you, intrepid squire! Now, now, you are going through the air, swifter than a dart! Already those below are gazing up at you in astonishment! Try not to sway so much, brave Sancho; see to it that you do not fall, for your fall would be worse than that of the rash youth who sought to drive the chariot of his father, the Sun!"

Sancho, meanwhile, was clinging tightly to his master, with his arms about him. "Señor," he asked, "what do they mean by saying that we are riding so high when their voices can reach us just as plainly as if they were right alongside us?"

"Think nothing of that, Sancho," said the knight, "for such flights as these are out of the ordinary course of events, and at a distance of a thousand leagues you can still see and hear anything you like. And do not squeeze me so much or you will throw me off. There is really no reason for you to be disturbed or frightened, for I can swear that in all the days of my life I never had an easier-going mount. It is as if we never stirred from one spot. Banish all fear, my friend, for the truth is, everything is going as it should and we have the wind to our poop."

"So we do," replied Sancho. "On this side it's as strong as if they were blowing on me with a thousand pairs of bellows."

This was the truth, for a number of large bellows were producing the breeze in question. The whole adventure had been so thoroughly planned by the duke and duchess and their major-domo that not a single essential detail was lacking to make it perfect.

"Without any doubt, Sancho," remarked Don Quixote as he felt the puff, "we must have reached the second aerial region, where the snow and hail are produced; it is in the third region that the thunder and lightning are engendered, and if we keep on ascending at this rate, we shall soon be in the region of fire. I do not know how to control the peg to keep us from mounting so high that the flames will scorch us."

Even as he said this they felt a warmth upon their faces, which came from pieces of tow, easy to ignite and to extinguish, suspended from the end of a reed held at some distance from them.

"May they slay me," said Sancho, "if we're not already in that fiery place, or somewhere very near it, for a good part of my beard is singed already. I've a mind, master, to take a peep and see where we are."

"Don't do that," Don Quixote advised him. "Remember that true story they tell about the licentiate Torralba,[15] whom the devils carried through the air upon a reed, with his eyes shut; in twelve hours' time he arrived in Rome and dismounted at Torre di Nona, which is a street in that city,[16] where he witnessed the rioting, the assault, and the death of Bourbon; [17] and by the next morning he was back in Madrid to give an account of all he had seen. He himself stated that as he was sailing through the air the devil ordered him to open his eyes, which he did, only to discover he was so near the body of the moon that, as it seemed to him, he could put out his hand and take hold of it, and he did not dare look down at the earth or it would have made him dizzy.

"And so, Sancho," the knight concluded, "there is no good reason why we should uncover our eyes, since he who has us in charge will take care of us. It may be that we are merely gaining altitude in order to swoop down upon the kingdom of Candaya as the saker or the falcon does upon the heron, that he may be able to seize the bird no matter how high it may soar.[18] And although it seems to us that it has not been a half hour since we left the garden, believe me, we must have gone a very long way."

"I do not know as to that," said Sancho. "All I can say is that if that Señora Magallanes [19] or Magalona found any pleasure in riding this crupper, she couldn't have had very tender flesh."

The entire conversation of the two brave horsemen was heard by the duke and duchess, who were extremely amused by it; and, wishing to put a finishing touch to this extraordinary and well-planned adventure, they now set fire to Clavileño's tail with some bits of tow, whereupon the horse, which was filled with detonating rockets, at once blew up with a loud noise, hurling Don Quixote and Sancho Panza to the ground half scorched.

By this time the entire band of bearded ladies, La Trifaldi and all the others, had disappeared from the garden, and those that remained lay stretched out on the ground as if unconscious. The knight and his squire rose, rather the worse for wear, and, glancing about them in all directions, were very much astonished to find themselves back in the same garden from which they had started, with all those people prostrate on the earth. And their wonder grew as, at one side of the garden, they caught sight of a long lance that had been thrust into the ground, with a smooth white parchment hanging from it by two silken cords. Upon the parchment, written in large gilt letters, was the following inscription:

The renowned knight, Don Quixote de la Mancha, merely by undertaking it, has finished and concluded the adventure of the Countess Trifaldi, otherwise known as the Distressed Duenna. Malambruno is satisfied in every way,[20] the faces of the duennas are once more smooth and clean, King Clavijo and Queen Antonomasia have been restored to their former state, and as soon as the squirely flogging shall have been completed, the white dove shall be free of the annoying gerfalcons that persecute it and shall return to the arms of its beloved mate. For it is so ordered by Merlin the Sage, proto-enchanter of enchanters.

Having read the inscription, Don Quixote understood clearly that it had reference to the disenchantment of Dulcinea; and, giving thanks to Heaven with all his heart that he had been able to achieve so great a deed at so little peril, thus restoring to the venerable but no longer visible duennas their former countenances, he went over to where the duke and duchess lay, still in a state of unconsciousness.

"Ah, my worthy lord," he said, taking the duke's hand, "be of good cheer—be of good cheer, for it is all over now! The adventure is finished and no harm done, as the inscription on that post yonder plainly shows."

Little by little, like one coming out of a deep slumber, the duke recovered his senses, and the same was true of the duchess and all the others there in the garden who had fallen to the ground; and they all gave such evidence of wonder and astonishment as almost to convince any-one who saw them that the thing they pretended so cleverly by way of jest had actually happened to them. The duke read the inscription with half-closed eyes and then threw open his arms to embrace Don Quixote, assuring him that he was the best knight ever seen in any age.

Sancho in the meantime was gazing about in search of the Distressed One, for he wished to see what she looked like without her beard and whether or not she was as beautiful as her gallant exterior appeared to indicate; but they told him that as soon as Clavileño had dropped to the earth in flames, the entire band of duennas, and Trifaldi with them, had disappeared, but that they were already clean-shaven, without a sign of hair on their faces. The duchess then inquired of him how he had made out on the long journey.

"Señora," replied Sancho, "as we were flying through the region of fire, or so my master told me, I wanted to uncover my eyes a little, but when I asked him if I might do so, he would not let me. However, I have a little bit of curiosity in my make-up and always want to know anything that is forbidden me; and so, very quietly and without anyone's seeing me, I lifted the handkerchief ever so little, close to my nose, and looked down at the earth. It seemed as if the whole earth was no bigger than a grain of mustard and the people walking about on it were a little larger than hazelnuts. You can see from that how high up we must have been."

"Friend Sancho," said the duchess, "you had better mind what you are saying. From what you tell me, you did not see the earth at all, but only the people on it; for if the earth itself was like a grain of mustard and each person on it like a hazelnut, then, obviously, one man would have covered the entire earth."

"That is true," Sancho admitted, "but I had a peep at it from one side and saw it all."

"Look here, Sancho," said the duchess, "with a side peep like that you don't see the whole of anything you are looking at."

"I don't know anything about that way of looking at things," the squire answered her, "but I do think your Ladyship ought to bear in mind that we were flying by enchantment, and it was by enchantment that I was able to see the whole earth and all the people on it, no matter which way I looked. And if your Highness doesn't believe me, neither will you believe me when I tell you that, having uncovered my face all the way to the eyebrows, I found myself so close to the sky that there was not a palm-and-a-half's distance between it and me; and a mighty big place it is, my lady, I can tell you that! Then we went through the region where the seven little she-goats [21] are, and, seeing that as a lad I had been a goatherd in my country, the minute I laid eyes on them I felt like getting down and playing with them a bit, and if I hadn't done so I think I would have burst. And so, what do I do? Without saying anything to my master or anybody else, I slip down off Clavileño as quietly as you please and for three-quarters of an hour I have a good time with those goats, which are like gillyflowers,[22] and all the time Clavileño doesn't stir from the spot."

"And while the worthy Sancho was playing with the goats," said the duke, "how did Señor Don Quixote amuse himself?"

It was the knight himself who answered this question. "Since all these things," he said, "all these happenings, are outside the natural order, it is not surprising that Sancho should say what he does. As for myself, I can only state that I looked neither upward nor downward, nor did I behold either the sky or the earth or the sea or the sandy shore. It is true, I was aware that I was passing through the aerial region and was close upon the region of fire; but that we went any farther than that I cannot believe; and inasmuch as the fiery region lies between the heaven where the moon is and the outmost portion of the aerial one, we could not have come to the heaven where the seven young she-goats are, of which Sancho speaks, without being burned, and since we were not burned, either Sancho is lying or Sancho is dreaming."

"I am neither lying nor dreaming," replied Sancho. "If you don't believe me, ask me to describe those goats for you, and you will see whether I'm telling the truth or not."

"Do describe them for us, Sancho," said the duchess.

"Two of them are green, two are flesh-colored, two are blue, and one is a mixture."

"That," said the duke, "is a new kind of goat. Here in our earthly region we do not have such shades—I mean, goats of such hues."

"Naturally," said Sancho, "there is a difference between heavenly goats and earthly ones."

"Tell me, Sancho," continued the duke, "did you see any he-goat among them?"

"No, sir," was the answer, "and I've heard tell that none ever passed the horns of the moon."

They did not care to question him any further regarding his journey, for they perceived that he was in a mood to go rambling all over the heavens, giving them news of everything that went on there without ever having stirred from the garden. In brief, this was the end of the adventure of the Distressed Duenna, one that provided amusement for the duke and duchess all the rest of their lives. As for Sancho, he had something to talk about for ages, if he lived so long.

Don Quixote now came up to him, to whisper in his ear. "Sancho," he said, "if you want us to believe what you saw in Heaven, then you must believe me when I tell you what I saw in the Cave of Montesinos. I need say no more."

CHAPTER XLII. *Of the advice which Don Quixote gave Sancho Panza before the latter set out to govern his island, with other well-considered matters.*

THE duke and duchess were so well pleased with the successful and amusing outcome of the adventure of the Distressed One that they made up their minds to continue with the jest, seeing what a suitable subject they had when it came to accepting the imaginary for the real. Accordingly, having instructed their servants and vassals as to how to behave toward Sancho in the governorship of his promised island, they informed the squire the next day (which was the one following Clavileño's flight) that he was to make ready to go and assume his gubernatorial duties, as his islanders were waiting for him as for the showers of May. Sancho made a low bow.

"Ever since I dropped down from Heaven," he said, "ever since I looked at the earth from up there and saw how little it is, I am not as anxious to be a governor as I was once upon a time. What greatness is there in ruling over a grain of mustard, or imperial dignity and power in governing half a dozen human beings the size of hazelnuts? For there did not seem to me to be any more than that. If your Lordship would be pleased to give me a little bit of Heaven, even if it was no more than half a league, I'd rather have it than the biggest island in the world."

"See here, friend Sancho," replied the duke, "I cannot give anyone a bit of Heaven, even if it were a piece no bigger than your fingernail.

It is reserved for God alone to grant such grace and favors as that. What I can give, I do give you; and that is an island, perfect in every respect, tight and well proportioned and exceedingly fertile, where, if you know how to make use of your opportunities, you may contrive to gain Heaven's riches along with those of earth."

"Very well, then," said Sancho, "let the island come, and I'll do my best to be such a governor that, in spite of all the rascals, I'll go straight to Heaven. It's not out of greed that I want to quit my humble station or better myself; it is because I wish to see what it's like to be a governor." [1]

"Once you try it, Sancho," the duke warned him, "you will be eating your hands off after it,[2] so sweet a thing it is to give orders and be obeyed. You may be sure that when your master gets to be an emperor —as he undoubtedly will, the way things are going for him now— no one will be able to take that office away from him without a struggle, and he will be sick at heart over all the time he lost in not being one."

"Sir," said Sancho, "in my opinion, it is a good thing to be the one to give the orders, if only to a herd of cattle."

"Let them bury me with you, Sancho," said the duke, "if you do not know everything, and I only hope you will be such a governor as your wit seems to promise. But let us leave the matter there. Remember, it is tomorrow that you go to assume the governorship of your island, and this afternoon they will fit you out with the proper apparel and all the other things needed for your departure."

"Let them clothe me any way they like," replied the squire, "for however I go dressed, I'll still be Sancho Panza."

"That is true enough," agreed the duke, "but clothes must be suited to one's rank or dignity. It would not be well, for example, for a jurisconsult to wear the garb of a soldier, or a soldier that of a priest. You, Sancho, will go clad partly as a man of learning and partly as a captain, for in the island that I am bestowing on you arms and letters are equally necessary."

"I don't know much about letters," said Sancho; "in fact, I don't even know my ABC's; but to be a good governor, it's enough for me to be able to remember the Christus.[3] As to arms, I'll handle those that they give me till I drop, and God help me from then on."

"With so good a memory as that," observed the duke, "Sancho cannot go wrong."

At this point Don Quixote came up and, upon hearing that Sancho was to leave so soon for his government, with the duke's permission, took him by the hand and led him to his room, with the intention of advising him as to how he was to conduct himself in office. Having entered the room and closed the door, he almost forced Sancho to sit down beside him, and then, very calmly, he began speaking as follows:

"Sancho, my friend, I thank Heaven with all my heart that good Fortune should have come your way before I have met with her. I had counted upon my luck to enable me to pay you for your services, but here am I at the beginning of my adventures while you, ahead of time and contrary to all reasonable expectation, are seeing your desires fulfilled. Some there be that count upon bribery, importunity, begging, early rising, entreaties, and pertinacity, and still do not attain what they seek; and then some other will come along and, without knowing the why or wherefore of it all, will find himself in the place and office that so many covet. Here it is that the common saying fits in well, to the effect that there is good luck and bad luck in all the strivings of men. You to my mind are beyond any doubt a blockhead, you neither rise with the sun nor keep nightly vigil, you are not industrious, and yet, as a result of the mere breath of knight-errantry that has been breathed upon you, you find yourself without more ado the governor of an island, as if it were nothing at all.

"I say all this, Sancho, in order that you may not attribute to your own merits the favor you have received. Rather, you should give thanks to Heaven for its beneficence, and, after that, to the great profession of knight-errantry for the potentialities inherent in it. Having, then, disposed your heart to believe what I have said to you, be attentive, my son, to this your Cato,[4] who would counsel you and be the guiding star that leads you to a safe harbor as you set forth upon the storm-tossed sea [5] that is now about to engulf you; for office and high trusts are nothing other than a deep abyss of trouble and confusion.

"First of all, my son, you are to fear God; for therein lies wisdom,[6] and, being wise, you cannot go astray in anything. And in the second place, you are to bear in mind who you are and seek to know yourself, which is the most difficult knowledge to acquire that can be imagined. Knowing yourself, you will not be puffed up, like the frog that sought to make himself as big as the ox.[7] Do this, and the memory of the fact that you once herded pigs in your own country will come to serve as the ugly feet to the tail of your folly." [8]

"That is true," said Sancho, "but it was when I was a lad. Afterward, as a young fellow, it was geese, not pigs, that I guarded. But I can't see what all this has to do with the case. Not all those that govern come from the race of kings."

"You are right," replied Don Quixote, "and for that very reason those who are not of noble origin should be suave and mild in fulfilling the grave duties of their office. In this way they will be able to free themselves of that malicious gossiping to which no station in life is immune. Look to humility for your lineage, Sancho, and do not be ashamed to say that you come of peasant stock, for when it is seen that you do not blush for it, no one will try to make you do so. Pride yourself more on being a good man and humble than on being a haughty sinner. The number of persons of lowly birth who have gone up to the highest pontifical and imperial posts is beyond counting; by way of proving the truth of this, I could give you so many examples that it would tire you to listen to them.

"Remember, Sancho, that if you employ virtue as your means and pride yourself on virtuous deeds, you will have no cause to envy the means possessed by princes and noble lords; [9] for blood is inherited but virtue is acquired,[10] and virtue by itself alone has a worth that blood does not have. This being the case, as indeed it is, if perchance one of your relatives should come to your island to visit you, do not neglect or offend him, but rather receive, welcome, and entertain him. By so doing, you will be pleasing Heaven, which does not like anyone to despise what it hath wrought, and at the same time you will be acting in accordance with the laws of your own better nature.

"Should you bring your wife to be with you—and it is not well for those in government to be long without their womenfolk—teach and instruct her and smooth down her native roughness; for all that a wise governor may acquire, a foolish and boorish wife may well squander and lose for him. In case you become a widower (a thing that may happen), by virtue of your office look for a better consort. Do not take one to serve you merely as a hook and fishing rod or as a friar's hood for the receiving of alms; [11] for, of a truth I tell you, all that the judge's wife receives her husband will have to account for on Judgment Day, when he will have to make in death a fourfold payment for things that in life meant nothing to him.

"Never be guided by arbitrary law, which finds favor only with the ignorant who plume themselves on their cleverness. Let the tears of the poor find more compassion in you, but not more justice, than the testimony of the rich. Seek to uncover the truth amid the promises and gifts of the man of wealth as amid the sobs and pleadings of the poverty-stricken. When it is a question of equity, do not bring all the rigor of the law to bear upon the delinquent, for the fame of the stern judge is no greater than that of the merciful one. If the rod of justice is to be bent, let it not be by the weight of a gift but by that of mercy. When you come to judge the case of someone who is your enemy, put aside all thought of the wrong he has done you and think only of the truth. Let not passion blind you where another's rights are concerned, for the mistakes you make will be irremediable, or only to be remedied at the expense of your good name and fortune.

"If some beautiful woman come to you seeking justice, take your eyes from her tears, listen not to her moans, but consider slowly and deliberately the substance of her petition, unless you would have your reason drowned in her weeping and your integrity swept away by her sighs. Abuse not by words the one upon whom punishment must be inflicted; for the pain of the punishment itself is enough without the addition of insults. When a guilty man comes under your jurisdiction, remember that he is but a wretched creature, subject to the inclinations of our depraved human nature, and insofar as you may be able to do so without wrong to the other side, show yourself clement and merciful; for while the attributes of God are all equal, that of mercy shines brighter in our eyes than does that of justice.

"If you observe these rules and precepts, Sancho, your days will be long, your fame will be eternal, rewards will be heaped upon you, indescribable happiness shall be yours, you will be able to marry off your children as you like, your children and your grandchildren will have titles to their names, you will live in peace with all men, and in your last days death will come to you amid a ripe and tranquil old age, and the gentle, loving hands of your great-grandchildren will tenderly close your eyes.

"What I have said to you thus far has been in the nature of instructions for the adornment of your soul. Listen now to those that will serve you where your body is concerned."

CHAPTER XLIII. *Of the further advice which Don Quixote gave to Sancho Panza.*

WHO, upon listening to the foregoing speech of Don Quixote's, would not have taken him for a very wise person, one whose wisdom was exceeded only by his integrity? It has frequently been remarked in the course of this great history that it was only when he came to touch upon the subject of chivalry that the knight talked nonsense and that when any other topic was under discussion he showed himself to be possessed of a clear-seeing, unfettered mind, the result being that his deeds were all the time contradicting his own best judgment and his judgment his deeds. And so, in the course of these further instructions that he gave Sancho, marked by a lively play of fancy, he carried to a high pitch both his good sense and his folly.

Sancho listened to it all most attentively, seeking to commit to memory the counsels thus given him, as if to preserve them for future use that he might make a success of his governorship.

"As to your own person, Sancho, and the mode of ruling your household," Don Quixote continued, "the first thing to bear in mind is that you must be neat-appearing. Remember to trim your nails, and do not let them grow as some do who in their ignorance have been led to believe that long fingernails make the hands look beautiful, just as if that growth, that excrescence, that they neglect to cut were really a nail and not rather the claw of a lizard-catching kestrel.[1] This, I may tell you, is a filthy and unnatural abuse. Another thing, Sancho: do not go with your girdle loosened and your garments slack; for slovenly attire is the sign of a disorderly mind, unless such carelessness is deliberate, as is believed to have been the case with Julius Caesar.[2]

"Be sure to ascertain very carefully just what the revenues of your office are, and, if they suffice for the purpose, provide your servants with respectable and serviceable, rather than showy and brilliant, liveries. And what is more, divide the liveries between your servants and the poor; by which I mean to say: if you have three pages to clothe, see that you clothe three of the poor also, and in that way you will have pages both in Heaven and on earth. This is a new mode of bestowing liveries and one that is beyond the conception of the vainglorious.

"Eat neither garlic nor onions that your breath may not betray your rustic origin.[3] Walk slowly and speak with deliberation, but not in such a manner as to give the impression that you are listening to yourself; for all affectation is bad.[4] Eat sparingly during the day and have a light supper,[5] for it is in the workshop of the stomach that the health of the entire body is forged. Be temperate in your drinking, remembering that he who imbibes too much wine keeps neither secret nor promise. And take care, Sancho, not to roll your food from one cheek to the other or to eruct in front of anyone."

"I don't know what you mean by *eruct*," said the squire.

"To *eruct*, Sancho, is the same as to belch, which is one of the most unpleasant words in our Castilian tongue, although an expressive one.[6] For this reason, those that are careful of their choice of language, in place of 'belch' and 'belchings,' say 'eruct' and 'eructations.' If someone fails to understand these terms, it makes little difference; in the course of time they will come to be readily understood and thus the language will be enriched, for it is determined by popular usage." [7]

"In truth, sir," said Sancho, "that is one bit of advice that I mean to remember: not to belch; for I do it very often."

"Eruct, Sancho, not belch," Don Quixote corrected him.

"Eruct I will say from now on," replied Sancho; "I give you my word, I won't forget."

"Also, Sancho, you must not introduce such a host of proverbs into your conversation; for although proverbs are concise maxims, you very often drag them in by the hair of the head, with the result that they sound more like nonsense than wisdom."

"That is something only God can remedy," said Sancho; "for I know more old sayings than would fill a book, and when I start to speak they all come rushing into my mouth at once, fighting with one another to get out, and so, what happens is, my tongue throws out the first ones it gets hold of, whether or not they are to the point. But I'll remember after this to use the ones that are suited to the dignity of my office; for in the house where there is plenty supper is soon on the table,[8] and he who binds does not wrangle,[9] and the bell-ringer's in a safe place,[10] and keeping and giving call for brains." [11]

"That's it, Sancho!" cried Don Quixote. "Go on threading and stringing and coupling your proverbs, there is no one to stop you! My mother whips me and I keep right on.[12] I have just done telling you that you should avoid proverbs, and here in a moment you have let go with a

whole litany of them that, so far as what we are talking about is concerned, are over the hills of Ubeda.[13] Mind you, Sancho, I do not say that
a proverb aptly brought in is not all right, but when you overload your
speech with them and string them together helter-skelter, it makes your
conversation dull and vulgar.

"But to continue: When you mount your horse, do not throw the
weight of your body against the back of the saddle nor ride with your
legs held stiffly, straight out in front of you or away from the horse's
belly; and, on the other hand, do not sit so limply that it will seem as if
you were astride your gray. The way they ride makes gentlemen of
some and grooms of others.

"Observe moderation in the matter of sleep, for he who is not up with
the sun does not make the most of the day. Bear in mind, Sancho, that
diligence is the mother of good fortune,[14] and sloth, its contrary, never
yet achieved anything worth while.

"There is one more piece of advice which I should like to give you,
and—although it does not have to do with the care of your person—I
wish you would be sure to remember it, as I think it will be no less useful
to you than the counsels I have already imparted to you. It is this: that
you never become involved in a discussion of family trees, at least not
when it is a matter of comparing one with another; for, of necessity, one
of the two will have to be better than the other, and you will be hated
by those whose lineage you have disparaged, while those whose ancestry
you have exalted will in no wise reward you.

"As for your dress, you should wear full-length hose, a long jacket,
and a cloak that is a little longer still; and by all means eschew Grecian
wide-breeches, for they are becoming neither to gentlemen nor to governors.

"For the present, that is all that I think of, Sancho, in the way of advice. As time goes on and the occasion arises, I will send you further
instructions if you will take care to keep me informed of the state of
your affairs."

"Sir," replied Sancho, "I can see very plainly that all the things your
Grace has said to me are good, holy, and profitable, but of what use
are they going to be if I do not remember a single one of them? True,
what you told me about not letting my nails grow and about marrying
again if I have a chance will not slip out of my noddle; but as for all
that other mess of hash, I don't remember, nor will I remember, any
more of it than I do of last year's clouds. And so you will have to put
it down in writing for me. While I may not be able to read or write, I

will give it to my confessor so that he can run over it with me and hammer it into my head whenever necessary."

"Ah, sinner that I am!" exclaimed Don Quixote. "How bad it looks for governors not to be able to read and write! For I would have you know, Sancho, that when a man cannot read or is left-handed, it points to one of two things: either he comes of exceedingly mean parentage, or else he himself is of so wayward a disposition that good companionship and good training are wasted upon him. That is a grave shortcoming on your part, and for that reason I would have you at least learn to sign your name."

"I can sign my name well enough," said Sancho. "When I was steward of the confraternity in my village I learned to make certain letters such as they use in marking bundles and which, so they told me, spelled out my name. And, anyway, I can always pretend that my right hand is crippled and have someone else sign for me; for there's a remedy for everything except death,[15] and, seeing that I'm in command and hold the rod, I can do anything I like. 'He whose father is a judge—' you know.[16] And I'll be a governor, which is higher than a judge; so come on and see! Let them make fun of me and slander me; let them come for wool and go back shorn.[17] For whom God loves, his house knows it,[18] and the silly sayings of the rich pass for maxims in this world.[19] Being a governor, I'll be rich, and I mean to be generous at the same time; and that way no one will find any fault with me. Only make yourself some honey and the flies will come to suck you, as much as you have so much are you worth,[20] as my grandmother used to say, and there's no way of getting even with a man of means." [21]

"May God curse you, Sancho!" cried Don Quixote at this point. "May sixty thousand devils carry you off, and your proverbs with you! For an hour now you have been stringing them, and every one is a torture to me. I can assure you that these sayings of yours will one day bring you to the gallows; on account of them your vassals will take the government away from you, or else there will be conspiracies among them. Tell me, where do you find them all, you ignorant lout, or how do you manage to apply them? If I utter one and apply it properly, I have to sweat and labor as if I were digging a ditch."

"In God's name, master," replied Sancho, "you are complaining over very little. Why should you be vexed if I make use of my own property, seeing that I have no other—no other wealth except sayings and more sayings? Here are four that have just popped into my head, as pat to the purpose as could be, or like pears in a basket; but I'm not going to repeat them, for to keep silence well is called *Sancho*." [22]

"That Sancho is not you," said Don Quixote, "for not only do you not know how to keep silent, but you are a mischievous prattler in the bargain. Nevertheless, I am curious to know what the four sayings are that you have just remembered and that fit in so aptly here; for I have been ransacking my own memory—and it is a good one—and none of the sort have occurred to me."

"What better could you ask for," said Sancho, "than these: 'Never put your thumbs between two of your back grinders'; [23] and 'To "Get out of my house" and "What do you want with my wife?" there is no answer'; and 'Whether the pitcher hits the stone or the stone the pitcher, it will be bad for the pitcher,' [24] all of which fit to a hair? Let no one fall out with his governor or with the one who is in command or he will be sorry for it in the end, like him who puts his thumb between his grinders, whether they be back teeth or not, so long as they are grinders that's all that matters. And to whatever the governor may say there's no answer to be made, any more than there is to 'Get out of my house' or 'What do you want with my wife?' As for the stone and the pitcher, a blind man could see that. And so it is that he who sees the mote in another's eye should see the beam in his own, [25] that it may not be said of him, 'The dead woman was frightened at the one with her throat cut'; [26] for your Grace is well aware that the fool knows more in his own house than the wise man in the house of another." [27]

"That is not true, Sancho," said Don Quixote, "for the fool knows nothing, in his own house or in the house of another, for the reason that upon a foundation of folly no edifice of wisdom can be reared. But let us leave the matter there. If you make a bad governor, the fault will be yours and mine will be the shame, but I find consolation in the thought that I have done my duty in thus earnestly advising you, with all the wisdom at my command; in this way am I released from my obligation and my promise. May God guide you, Sancho, and govern you in your government, and may He deliver me from the fear I have that you are going to turn the whole island upside down, a thing that I might prevent by revealing to the duke what you are, telling him that your fat little person is nothing other than a bag stuffed with proverbs and mischief."

"Sir," replied Sancho, "if your Grace is of the opinion that I am not fitted for this governorship, I give it up here and now; for I am more concerned for the black-of-the-nail of my soul than for my entire body. As plain Sancho, I can make out just as well on bread and onions as I can as governor on partridges and capons. When it comes to that, all are equal when they are asleep, the great and the small, the poor and the rich; and if your Grace will stop to think, you will remember that you alone were the one who put me up to being a governor, for I know no more about governing islands than a buzzard does, and if I thought for a minute that in order to be a governor the devil would have to carry me off, then I would rather go to Heaven as Sancho than go to Hell as a governor."

"So help me God, Sancho," said Don Quixote, "if only by reason of these last words that you have spoken, I hold you fit to be the governor of a thousand islands. You have by nature a good disposition without which no knowledge is worth anything. Commend yourself to God, then, and try not to lose sight of your main purpose; by which I mean, that you should make it your unswerving aim to do the right thing in all matters that come up for your judgment, for Heaven always favors good intentions. And now, let us go to dinner, for I think our hosts are waiting for us."

CHAPTER XLIV. *How Sancho Panza was taken away to be governor, and the strange adventure that befell Don Quixote in the castle.*

THEY say that in the original version of the history it is stated that the interpreter did not translate the present chapter as Cid Hamete had written it,[1] owing to a kind of grudge that the Moor had against himself for having undertaken a story so dry and limited in scope as is this one of Don Quixote. For it seemed to him he was always having to speak of the knight and of Sancho, without being able to indulge in digressions of a more serious and entertaining nature. He remarked that to go on like this, pen in hand, with his mind fixed upon a single subject and having to speak through the mouths of a few persons only, was for him an intolerable and unprofitable drudgery.

By way of relieving the monotony, in the first part of the work he had employed the artifice of introducing a few *novelas,* such as the *Story of the One Who Was Too Curious for His Own Good* and *The Captive's Story,*[2] tales that, so to speak, had nothing to do with the narrative proper, the other portions being concerned with things that had happened to Don Quixote himself, such as could not be omitted.[3] He also felt, he tells us, that many readers, carried away by the interest attaching to the knight's exploits, would be inclined to pass over these novelettes either hastily or with boredom, thereby failing to note the fine craftsmanship they exhibited, which, however, would be plainly evident when they should be published by themselves instead of appearing as mere adjuncts to Don Quixote's madness and Sancho's foolishness.

Accordingly, in this second part it was not his intention to insert any more tales of that kind, whether separate or interwoven with the narrative as a whole, but rather only a few episodes that resembled them, arising naturally out of the course of events; and even with these he meant to be sparing, employing as few words as possible in the telling. He goes on to say that, while thus confining himself closely within the narrow limits of the plot, he wishes it understood that he has sufficient ability and intelligence to take the entire universe for his theme if he so desired and he asks that his labors be not looked down upon, but that he be given credit not for what he writes, but for what he has refrained from writing.

He then goes on with the story by saying that, on the afternoon of the day on which he had given the oral advice to Sancho,[4] Don Quixote presented him with a written copy of what he had said to him, that the squire might look for someone to read it to him. Scarcely had he done so when Sancho lost the document and it found its way into the hands of the duke, who communicated its contents to the duchess, whereupon they both marveled once again at the knight's folly and good sense. And with the object of carrying on the jest, they sent Sancho that same afternoon, with a large retinue, to the place that for him was to be his island.[5]

Now, it happened that the one who was in charge of Sancho and his train was a major-domo of the duke's, a fellow with a keen sense of humor who was at the same time very discreet (for there can be no humor where there is not discretion). He it was who had played the part of the Countess Trifaldi so amusingly, as has been related, and so was well suited for his present role. In addition, he had been thoroughly instructed by his lord and lady as to how he was to behave toward the squire, and as a result everything went off marvelously well.

The moment Sancho laid eyes upon the major-domo, he had a vision of La Trifaldi. "Sir," he said, turning to his master, "may the devil take me right here and now, as a righteous man and a believer,[6] if your Grace is not going to have to admit that the face on that steward is the Distressed One's very own."

Don Quixote gazed at the man attentively. "There is no reason why the devil should take you, Sancho," he replied, "either as a righteous man or as a believer—I don't know what you mean by that—for, while the Distressed One's face is that of the major-domo, the major-domo's countenance is not that of the Distressed One, for if such were the case it would imply too great a contradiction. However, this is not the time for going into all that, as it would involve us in an endless labyrinth. Believe me, friend, we must pray Our Lord most earnestly to deliver us from the wiles of wizards and enchanters."

"It is no joke, master," said Sancho, "for a while ago I heard him speak, and it was like La Trifaldi's voice sounding in my ears. Very well, I'll keep silent; but from now on I intend to be on my guard to see if I can discover any other sign that will tell me whether I am right or wrong in what I suspect."

"That you should do, Sancho," agreed Don Quixote, "and you must keep me advised of all that you discover in regard to this matter and of everything that happens to you in connection with your government."

Finally Sancho and his train set out. He was dressed like a man of the law, and over all wore a tawny-hued, wide-flaring greatcoat of watered camlet, with a cap of the same material.[7] He was mounted upon a mule, his saddle being of the high-backed short-stirrup variety,[8] and behind him, by order of the duke, came the gray, decked out in brilliant[9] silken trappings and such ornaments as are suited to an ass. Sancho every now and then would turn his head to look back at the beast, being so glad of the animal's company that he would not have changed places with the emperor of Germany.

Upon taking his leave of the duke and duchess, he kissed their hands and received the blessing which his master bestowed upon him. Don Quixote was in tears, and he himself was blubbering.

And now, gentle reader, let the worthy Sancho go in peace and good luck go with him. You may expect two bushels[10] of laughter when you hear how he deported himself in office. Meanwhile, listen to what happened to his master that same night, and if it does not make you laugh, it will at least cause you to part your lips in an apelike grin; for Don Quixote's adventures are to be greeted either with astonishment or with mirth.

As soon as Sancho had gone, the story continues, Don Quixote felt his loneliness [11] so keenly that, if it had been possible for him to have done so, he would have revoked his squire's commission and had his government taken away from him. Seeing how melancholy the knight was, the duchess inquired the cause of his sadness, observing that if it was Sancho's absence, there were squires, duennas, and damsels a-plenty in her household who would serve the guest to his entire satisfaction.

"It is true, my lady," replied Don Quixote, "that I miss Sancho, but that is not the chief reason that I seem so sad. Of the many offers that your Excellency has made me, I choose and accept but one: the good will with which they are made. As for the rest, I beg your Excellency to consent to my waiting upon myself, in my own chamber."

"Really, Señor Don Quixote," said the duchess, "I could not think of that. Four of my damsels, lovely as flowers, shall be at your service."

"For me," said Don Quixote, "they will not be as flowers, but rather as thorns that pierce my soul, and neither they nor any like them shall enter my chamber any more than they would fly.[12] If your Highness would do me yet another favor, though I deserve none, permit me to serve myself as I prefer behind closed doors; for I would place a wall between my desires and my virtue. It is a habit of mine, and I do not wish to abandon it by reason of the generosity that your Highness would show me. The short of the matter is, I will sleep with my clothes on before I will consent to anyone's undressing me."

"Say no more, say no more, Señor Don Quixote," the duchess begged him. "I promise you I will give orders that not so much as a fly, not to speak of a maiden, shall enter your room. I am not the one to impair the decency of Don Quixote de la Mancha; for it appears to me that of his many virtues the one that shines forth most clearly is that of modesty. Let your Grace dress and undress alone, as and when you like; there will be no one to hinder you. Within this chamber you will find those vessels that are necessary for one who sleeps behind locked doors, and you will not have to open the door to satisfy any call of nature. May the great Dulcinea del Toboso live a thousand ages, and may her fame be extended all over the surface of the globe, seeing that she has merited the love of so valiant and so chaste a knight; and may a kind Heaven put it into the heart of Sancho Panza, our governor, to have done soon with his penance, that the world may once more enjoy the beauty of so exalted a lady."

"Your Highness," replied Don Quixote, "has spoken as befits the person that she is; for worthy ladies never take upon their lips the name of any who is bad,[13] and Dulcinea will be more fortunate and better known throughout the world by reason of your Highness's praise than she would be as a result of the eulogies of the most eloquent tongues on earth."

"Very well, then, Señor Don Quixote," said the duchess, "the supper hour has come and the duke must be waiting for us. Let us go to supper, your Grace, after which you may retire early; for the journey from Candaya yesterday was not a short one and must have tired you somewhat."

"I do not feel in the least tired, my lady," Don Quixote assured her. "I will venture to give your Excellency my oath that never in my life have I mounted a beast that was easier riding or better paced than Clavileño, and I do not understand what could have induced Malambruno to do away with so swift and gentle a steed by burning it the way he did, as if it were nothing at all."

"I fancy," said the duchess, "that he must have repented of the harm he had done to La Trifaldi and her companions, and to other persons as well, and of the misdeeds which, as a wizard and enchanter, he must have committed, and, as a consequence, he wished to have done with all the instruments of his art, chief among which was Clavileño, the one that bore him, a restless wanderer, from land to land. And so he burned it, and by its ashes and the inscription that was set up in the form of a trophy the valor of the great Don Quixote de la Mancha remains established for all time to come."

Once more Don Quixote thanked the duchess; and, after he had supped, he retired to his room alone, declining to permit any servant to enter with him, so greatly did he fear an occasion that might move or compel him to part with that decency and modesty that he preserved in honor of his lady Dulcinea; for he had ever in mind the virtue displayed by Amadis, flower and mirror of knight-errantry. Having locked his door, he proceeded to undress by the light of two wax candles; and as he went to take off his stockings—O disaster that never should have befallen such a person as this!—there burst from him, not sighs or anything of an indelicate nature, but up to two dozen stitches in one of his stockings, which now had the appearance of a piece of lattice work.

The worthy gentleman was deeply grieved over it and would have given an ounce of silver then and there for half a dram of green silk—since the hose that he wore were green.

Here Benengeli, as he goes on writing, exclaims:

"O poverty! poverty! I know not what could have led that great Cordovan poet to call thee a 'holy, unappreciated gift.' [14] I, though a Moor, know well, through the intercourse I have had with Christians, that holiness consists in charity, humility, faith, obedience, and poverty; but, for all of that, I assert that he must indeed be possessed of much godliness who can be content with being poor, unless it be that kind of poverty of which one of their greatest saints was speaking when he said, 'Possess all things as though ye possessed them not.' [15] That is what is known as poverty of spirit. But there is another kind of poverty, and it is of thee I speak. Why dost thou love to dog the steps of gentlemen and the wellborn rather than those of other folk? Why dost thou oblige them to go with patched shoes,[16] while some of the buttons on their doublets are of silk, others of hair, and others still of glass? Why must their ruffs be all wrinkled instead of being properly crimped with an iron?" (From this may be seen how ancient is the use of starch and of crimped ruffs as well.)

"How wretched," continues Benengeli, "is he who comes of good family who must all the time be pampering his honor! Eating badly behind closed doors, he plays the hypocrite when he steps out into the street with a toothpick in his mouth although he has had no cause to clean his teeth.[17] Poor wretch, I say, so worried about his honor that he fancies the patch on his shoe can be seen a league away and who is concerned over the sweat stains on his hat, his threadbare cloak, and his empty stomach, imagining that they must all be equally visible!"

Don Quixote was led to reflect on all this as he surveyed the burst threads in his stockings; but he was relieved to notice that Sancho had left behind him a pair of traveling boots, and he resolved to wear these the next day. He finally went to bed, moody and heavyhearted, owing as much to Sancho's absence as to the irreparable damage done to his hose, which he would even have been willing to patch with thread of another color, one of the greatest signs of poverty that a gentleman can exhibit in the course of his long-drawn-out and threadbare existence. He put out the candles, but it was warm and he could not sleep. Rising from his bed, he partly opened a grated window that looked out on a beautiful garden, and as he did so he became aware of people walking and talking down below. He listened attentively, and as the speakers raised their voices somewhat, he overheard the following conversation:

"Do not urge me to sing, Emerencia, for you know that ever since that stranger entered this castle and my eyes beheld him, I cannot sing but only weep. Moreover, my lady sleeps rather lightly, and I would not have her find us here for all the wealth in the world. And even if she did not awake but slept on, my song would be in vain if this new Aeneas who has come here only to scorn me should likewise be deep in slumber and fail to lend a listening ear."

"Give no heed to that, my dear Altisidora," a voice replied. "There is no doubt that the duchess and all those in the house are sleeping now, all save the lord of your heart and the awakener of your soul; for I heard him opening the window of his room a moment ago, and that must mean that he is awake. Sing, my poor dear, low and softly, to the sound of your harp, and if the duchess should hear us, we will blame it on the heat of the night."

"That is not the point, Emerencia," said Altisidora. "I do not wish that my song should lay bare my soul and that I should be taken for a light and frivolous maid by those who know nothing of the mighty power of love. But, come what will, shame on the cheek is better than an ache in the heart." [18]

There came then the sound of an instrument very gently touched, hearing which Don Quixote was deeply moved; for at that moment all the innumerable adventures of a like sort, at windows, gratings, and in gardens, to the accompaniment of serenades, love-making, and fainting fits, that he had read of in those vapid books of chivalry of his, came back to mind. He at once fancied that one of the duchess's waiting women must be enamored of him but was compelled by her modesty to conceal her passion. He feared that he would yield to temptation, but took a firm resolve not to permit himself to be overcome; and, commending himself with all his heart and soul to his lady Dulcinea del Toboso, he decided that he would listen to the music, giving as a token of his presence a feigned sneeze, which pleased the maidens very much, since their one desire was for him to hear them. And then, having tuned her harp and run her fingers over it, Altisidora began the following ballad: [19]

> *O thou above who in thy bed,*
> *'Tween sheets of linen fine,*
> *With outstretched legs dost sleep all night,*
> *Ah, 'tis for thee I pine!*

O thou, La Mancha's bravest knight,
The purest, when all is told,
Thy virtue and thy noble worth
Outweigh Arabia's gold!

Then, hear the plaint of gentle maid
Aweary with desire,
Who in the light of thy twin orbs
Doth feel her heart catch fire.

Seeking adventures, thou dost roam,
To others bringing woe;
Wounds thou dost deal, deniest balm:
No mercy wouldst thou show.

Tell me, O valiant-hearted youth—
God prosper thine emprise!—
Wast born 'mid Jaca's barren crags
Or 'neath the Libyan skies? [20]

And was it serpents suckled thee?
Thy nurses, who were they,
In forest wild, dark mountain cave,
Amongst the beasts of prey?

Ah, well may Dulcinea boast,
The plump and sturdy lass,
That she a tiger fierce hath tamed
And doth all maids surpass.

For this, her fame shall spread abroad
From Jarama to Henares,
From Pisuerga to Arlanza,
From the Tagus to Manzanares. [21]

How gladly would I change with her,
Give a petticoat to boot,
My gayest one with golden fringe,
To win my hapless suit.

Oh, to be clasped within thine arms
Or sit beside thy bed,
Fondly caress thee with my hand,
And scratch thy scurvy head!

But I am asking far too much,
Ah, no, it is not meet;

Most humbly I should be content
Playing with thy feet.

What coifs I'd bring thee, wert thou mine,
And silver slippers, too,
And damask breeches, Holland capes:
With gifts like these I'd woo! [22]

What finest pearls of gallnut size;
Unrivaled they would be
Thus, each "La Sola" [23] *would be called*
For want of company.

Then, gaze not from Tarpeian rock
Upon this kindling blaze.
Manchegan Nero, spare thy wrath
Ere it my heart doth raze.

I'm but a child, a virgin young,
Just three months past fourteen;
By God and on my soul I swear,
'Tis all of life I've seen.

I am not lame, I do not limp,
I'm whole of limb and sound;
My lily locks [24] *thou may'st perceive,*
Go trailing on the ground.

My mouth is wide, my nose is flat,
These faults I'll not deny,
But topaz teeth my beauty save,
Exalt it to the sky.

My voice thou knowest to be sweet,
If thou dost hear me now;
My build is middling, a little less,
It is not bad, I vow.

And these and all my other charms
Thy quiver hath won for thee.
Altisidora is my name;
This house is home to me.

Here the sorely wounded Altisidora brought her song to a close, and it was then that Don Quixote, object of her wooing, began to be perturbed. Heaving a deep sigh, he exclaimed to himself, "Oh, why must

I be so unfortunate a knight that no damsel who looks upon me can help falling in love with me! Why must it be the misfortune of the peerless Dulcinea del Toboso not to be left in peace to enjoy my incomparable fidelity! What would you of her, O queens! Empresses, why do you persecute her! Why do you pursue her, O maids of fourteen and fifteen years of age! Leave, oh, leave the wretched one to rejoice in her triumph and to glory in the lot that Love has bestowed upon her by rendering her my heart and delivering to her my very soul! Listen, enamored ones: to Dulcinea alone I am a doughy paste, but to all other females I am made of flint. To her I am honey, aloes to you. For me, Dulcinea alone is beautiful, prudent, modest, elegant, and wellborn, and all the rest are ugly, stupid, frivolous, and of ignoble lineage. Nature sent me into the world to belong to her and none other. Then, weep or sing, Altisidora; let that Madam [25] on whose account they belabored me in the castle of the enchanted Moor [26] continue to despair; I still must be Dulcinea's, boiled or roasted,[27] and I shall remain clean, well bred, and chaste in spite of all the witching powers on the face of the earth."

With this, he banged the window shut and, gloomy and out of sorts as if some dire misfortune had befallen him, went to bed. There we shall leave him for the present; for the great Sancho Panza, now about to enter upon his famous governorship, is beckoning to us.

CHAPTER XLV. *Of how the great Sancho took possession of his island and of the way in which he began to govern.*

O PERPETUAL discoverer of the antipodes, great taper of the world, eye of the heavens, sweet shaker of the water-coolers,[1] Thymbraeus [2] here, Phoebus there, archer in one place, in another a physician, father of poetry, inventor of music, thou who dost ever rise and, though appearing to do so, dost never set! [3] 'Tis thee, O Sun, by whose aid man doth beget man,[4] 'tis thee whom I beseech to favor and enlighten my darkened intellect that I may be able to give an absolutely exact account of the government of the great Sancho Panza; for without thee I feel lukewarm, fainthearted, and confused.

To continue, then: Sancho with all his train arrived at a village of around a thousand inhabitants, one of the best in the duke's domains.[5] They informed him that it was called Barataria Island, either because the real name of the village was Baratario, or by reason of the *barato* [6] which had led to the government being bestowed upon him. As they reached the town, which had a wall around it, the officers of the municipality came out to meet them, the bells rang, and all the townspeople evidenced their satisfaction. With much pomp they conducted him to the cathedral to give thanks to God, and then, with a few mock ceremonies, they handed over to him the keys of the city, acknowledging him to be the island's perpetual governor.

The new governor's apparel, his beard, and his little fat figure astonished all those who were not in on the joke, and even those who were, and they were many. Finally, upon leaving the church, they took him to the judge's chair and seated him in it, and the duke's major-domo then addressed him.

"Sir Governor," he said, "it is an ancient and obligatory custom in this famous island for the one who comes to take possession of it to answer a question that is put to him, one that shall be somewhat difficult and intricate, so that from his answer the people may be able to form an idea of their ruler's intelligence and judge for themselves as to whether they should hail his coming with joy or look upon it with sorrow."

All the time the major-domo was saying this, Sancho was gazing steadily at some large letters inscribed upon the wall facing him, and inasmuch as he did not know how to read, he asked what they were.

"Sir," was the reply, "that inscription is a notation of the day upon which your Lordship took possession of this island. It reads: 'On this day—such and such a day of such and such a year—Don Sancho Panza took over the government of this island and many years may he enjoy it.'"

"And who is it that they call 'Don Sancho Panza'?" asked Sancho.

"Your Lordship," the major-domo answered, "for no other Panza has set foot here except the one who is seated in that chair."

"Well, then, brother," said Sancho, "I will let you know that there has never been any 'Don' in my family. Plain Sancho Panza they call me, and Sancho was my father's name before me, and my grandfather's before him; they all were Panzas, without any 'Dons' or 'Doñas' tacked on.[7] In this island, I imagine, there must be more 'Dons' than there are stones. But enough of that; God knows what I mean. It may be, if my government lasts four days, I'll weed them all out; for there are so many of them they must be as troublesome as gnats.[8] Go ahead with your question, Señor Major-domo, and I'll reply the best way I can, whether the people are sorry or not."

At this moment there came into the court two men, one dressed like a peasant, the other like a tailor, for this latter held in his hands a pair of shears.

"Sir Governor," said the tailor, "I and this peasant have come before your Grace to have you settle a difference between us. Yesterday this good man entered my shop—for, begging the pardon of those present,[9] I am a licensed tailor, God be praised—and, putting a piece of cloth in my hands, he asked me, 'Señor, is there enough here to make me a cap?' Feeling the cloth, I told him there was. He must have supposed—as I supposed, and I supposed right—that I undoubtedly meant to make away with a part of the material, being led to think so by his own maliciousness and the bad opinion that people have of tailors. He then asked me to look and see if there would be enough for two. Guessing what was in his mind, I said yes; whereupon he, persisting in his damnable first intention, went on adding cap after cap, with me saying, yes, yes, until we were up to five caps in all. Just a while ago he came to call for them and I gave them to him, but he doesn't want to pay me for my labor but insists I should pay *him* or give him back his cloth."

"Is all this true, brother?" inquired Sancho.

"Yes, sir," replied the man, "but will your Grace please have him show the five caps that he made for me?"

"I'll be glad to," said the tailor. And, with this, he at once brought his hand out from under his cloak, displaying the five caps upon his four fingers and thumb. "There they are, and I swear by God and my conscience there's not a scrap of cloth left; I am willing to submit my work to the inspectors of the trade."

All those present had a laugh over the number of caps and the novel character of this lawsuit. As for Sancho, he considered the matter for a while and then said, "It appears to me that in this case there is no need of lengthy arguments; all that is called for is the judgment of an honest man. And so my decision is that the tailor shall lose his work and the peasant his cloth, and the caps shall go to the prisoners in the jail,[10] and let us hear no more about it."

If the decision in the case of the cattle-driver's purse [11] had aroused the admiration of the bystanders, this one provoked them to laughter; but the governor's orders were nonetheless carried out. Two old men were the next to present themselves before him, one of whom carried a reed by way of staff. It was the one without a staff who was the first to speak.

"My lord," he began, "some days ago I lent this good man ten gold crowns by way of service duly rendered,[12] on condition that he should repay me upon demand. A long time went by without my demanding payment, for the reason that I did not wish to cause him an even greater hardship than that which he was suffering when he sought the loan. However, when I saw that he was making no effort to pay me, I asked him for the money, not once but many times, and he not only failed to reimburse me, he even refused to do so, saying I had never let him take the ten crowns in question. I have no witnesses of the loan, and naturally there are none of the payment since no payment was made. Accordingly, I would have your Grace put him under oath, and if he swears that he did pay me, then I will cancel the debt, here and before God." [13]

"What do you say to that, old man with the staff?" Sancho asked.

"My lord," replied the old man, "I admit that he lent them to me; but your Grace may lower that rod,[14] for, seeing that he has had me put under oath, I will also swear that I paid him back, really and truly."

The governor lowered the rod that he held, and in the meanwhile the old man who had spoken handed his staff over to the other one while he took the oath, as if he found it in his way. Then, placing his hand upon the cross of the rod, he once more affirmed that it was true that he had borrowed the ten crowns that were being demanded of him but that he had paid them back into the other's hand, the only thing being that the other old man did not appear to realize it but was all the time asking for his money. In view of this, the great governor then asked the creditor what he had to say in reply to his adversary's statement; whereupon the old fellow who now held the staff replied that his debtor must undoubtedly be speaking the truth, as he knew him to be a worthy man and a good Christian. The one who had lent the crowns added that he must surely have forgotten how and when they had been repaid and that from that time forth he would never ask his adversary for anything.

The debtor thereupon took back his staff and, with bowed head, left the court. When he saw the defendant leaving in this manner, without saying another word, and when he perceived how resigned the plaintiff was, Sancho dropped his chin to his bosom and, placing the forefinger of his right hand in turn upon his eyebrows and his nose, remained lost in thought for a short while. Then he raised his head and ordered them to call back the old man with the staff who had already left.

They did so, and as soon as Sancho saw him, he said, "Good man, give me that staff. I have need of it."

"Gladly," replied the old man. "Here it is, my lord." And he placed it in the governor's hand.

Sancho took it and handed it to the other old man, remarking, "Go in peace, for you are now repaid."

"Repaid, my lord? And is this reed worth ten gold crowns?"

"Yes," said the governor, "it is; or if it is not, then I am the biggest blockhead in the world. We will see right now whether or not I have it in me to govern an entire kingdom."

With this, he ordered that the reed be broken and laid open there in the sight of all, and in the heart of it they found the ten gold crowns. They were all greatly astonished at this, looking upon their governor as another Solomon. When they inquired of him how he knew that the crowns were there, he replied that it had come to him when he saw the old man hand the staff to his adversary while he was taking an oath to the effect that he had really and truly paid his creditor, and then, when he was through, had heard him ask for it back again. From which it was to be deduced that, even when those who governed were simpletons, God sometimes guided them in their judgments. Moreover, he had heard the curate of his village tell of another case like this one,[15] and if it was a question of not forgetting what he had need to remember, there was not another memory like his own in all the island.

The short of the matter is, one old man went off crestfallen, the other with his money in hand, while those present continued to marvel at the thing. As for him whose duty it was to record Sancho's words, deeds, and movements, he could not make up his mind as to whether he should take the new governor for a fool or set him down as a wise man.

When this case had been concluded, there came into the court a woman holding on tightly to a man who was dressed like a rich drover.

"Justice, Señor Governor! Justice!" she cried, "and if I don't find it on earth, I'll go look for it in Heaven! Beloved Governor, this evil man caught me in the middle of a field and made use of my body as if it had been some filthy rag. Ah, poor me! he has taken from me that which I had guarded more than twenty-three years, defending it alike against Moors and Christians, foreigners and native-born. I was always hard as corkwood, keeping myself as pure as a salamander in the flames or wool among the brambles, and now this fine fellow comes along and handles me with clean hands!"

"It remains to be seen," said Sancho, "whether this gallant has clean hands or not." And, turning to the man, he ordered him to reply to the complaint which the woman had made against him.

The defendant was in a state of confusion. "Good sirs," he answered, "I am but a poor dealer in hogs. This morning I left the village to sell—begging your pardon [16]—four pigs, and what with taxes and cheating they took away from me practically all that they came to. As I was returning home, I fell in with this good dame, and the devil, who likes to jumble everything, saw to it that we were yoked together. I paid her quite enough, but she, dissatisfied, laid hold of me and would not let me go until she had dragged me here. She says that I forced her, but she lies by the oath that I am taking or am ready to take. And that is the whole truth, every particle of it."

The governor asked the man if he had any silver coins with him, and the drover replied that he had some twenty ducats in a purse that was hidden in his bosom. Sancho then directed him to take the purse out and hand it over to the plaintiff, which the drover did, trembling all the while. The woman took it and, with many curtsies to all present, offered a prayer to God for the life and health of the Señor Governor who thus looked after damsels and orphans in distress. With this, she left the court, grasping the purse with both hands, but not until she first had looked to see if the coins in it were of silver. No sooner was she gone than Sancho turned to the drover, who, with eyes and heart following the purse, was on the verge of tears.

"My good man," he said, "go after that woman, take the purse away from her whether she is willing to give it up or not, and come back here with it."

He was not talking to a fool or a deaf man, for the drover was off at once like a streak of lightning, to carry out the order that had been given him. The bystanders, meanwhile, waited eagerly to see what the outcome of this case would be. Within a short while the pair returned, engaged in more of a struggle than before; she had her petticoat up with the purse in the lap of it while he strove to take it from her. This was not possible, however, so stoutly did she defend herself.

"Justice!" she was crying, "God's justice and the world's justice, too! Behold, Señor Governor, how bold and shameless this ruffian is. In the center of the town and middle of the street he tried to take away from me the purse which your Grace had ordered him to give me!"

"And did he take it?" asked the governor.

"Take it?" replied the woman. "I'd give up my life sooner than I would the purse. A fine young thing I'd be! They'll have to throw other rats in my face! [17] Hammers and pincers, mallets and chisels, would not be enough to get it out of my clutches, nor even a lion's claws. They'd take the soul from out my body before they'd do that!"

"She's right," said the man. "I give up. I admit I haven't the strength to take it away from her." And he let go his hold.

Sancho then addressed the woman. "Let us have a look at that purse, my respectable and valiant one," he said. She gave it to him and he then handed it back to the man, saying, as he did so, to the one who had been forced and who had not been forced, "Sister, if you had shown the same or even half the courage and valor in defending your body that you have in protecting the purse, the might of Hercules would not have been sufficient to overcome you. Be on your way, in God's name, and bad luck to you, and do not show yourself again in this entire island or for six leagues around, under pain of two hundred lashes. Go, then, I say, you shameless, cheating hussy! Be off with you!" [18]

Frightened by this, the woman left with her head down, very much disgruntled.

"My good man," said Sancho to the defendant, "return to your village with your money and may God go with you; and hereafter, if you do not want to lose your purse, see to it that you do not take it into your head to yoke with anyone."

Mumbling his thanks, the man departed, and the spectators once again expressed their astonishment at the wise decisions made by their new governor. All of which the chronicler duly noted down, to be forwarded to the duke who was eagerly awaiting his report. And here, let us leave the worthy Sancho; for his master, greatly excited by Altisidora's music, urgently claims our attention.

CHAPTER XLVI. *Of Don Quixote's bell-and-cat fright in the course of the enamored Altisidora's wooing.*

WE LEFT the great Don Quixote lost in revery as a result of the enamored damsel Altisidora's serenade. Upon going to bed, he found that his thoughts were like fleas: they would not let him sleep nor give him a moment's rest, and mingled with his amorous fancies were the torn stitches in his stockings. But Time, which is swift-footed and knows no obstacle, came riding on the hours, and very soon it was morning. As soon as he saw that it was daylight, being by no means slothful, the knight quitted his downy couch and proceeded to dress himself, donning his chamois-skin suit and drawing on his traveling boots to hide the rents in his hose. Over all he threw his scarlet cloak and, placing upon his head a cap of green velvet trimmed in silver, he strapped on his baldric and his good keen-bladed sword and then picked up a large rosary that he always carried and with a solemn strut set out for the anteroom where the duke and duchess, already dressed, appeared to be expecting him.

As he made his way down a corridor he came upon Altisidora and the other maiden who was her friend, and the moment the enamored one laid eyes upon him, she promptly fainted. Her companion caught her and at once began undoing her bosom, and when Don Quixote saw this, he went over to them.

"I know," he said, "what causes such attacks as that."

"I do not understand it," replied the friend, "for Altisidora is the healthiest damsel in this household. I have never heard her so much as utter an *Ay!* in all the time that I have known her. Bad luck to all the knights-errants in this world if they are all of them so ungrateful! Go away, Señor Don Quixote, for this poor girl will not come to herself as long as your Grace stands there."

"Lady," said Don Quixote, "I wish you would have them put a lute in my chamber this evening, and I will console the unfortunate lass as best I can; for when love is in its first stages, a prompt disillusionment is recognized as the most efficacious remedy."

With this, he went his way in order that his presence might not be noted by any passers-by; and he was no sooner out of sight than the swooning Altisidora recovered her senses.

"We shall have to place that lute there for him," she said, "for if Don Quixote means to give us a serenade, it ought not to be bad, coming from him."

They then went to inform the duchess of what had happened, telling her that the knight wished a lute. Their mistress was delighted with the idea and at once arranged with the duke and her waiting women to play a joke upon their guest, one that should be more amusing than harmful. With this in mind, they looked forward eagerly to the night, which was as quick in coming as the day, a day spent by the ducal pair in pleasing conversation with Don Quixote.

It was on this day that the duchess really and truly dispatched one of her pages—the one who in the wood had impersonated the enchanted figure of Dulcinea—to Teresa Panza with the letter that her husband had written her, and also with the bundle of clothes that Sancho had left to be sent to her, the servant being duly charged to bring back a full account of all that happened.[1]

The arrangements having been made, when Don Quixote retired to his room at eleven o'clock he found there a guitar.[2] He first tried it out, then opened the window, and, perceiving that there was someone in the garden, once more ran his hands over the frets, tuning the instrument as well as he could. Having done this, he spat and cleared his throat and in a voice that was a little hoarse but well modulated began singing the following ballad, which he had composed that very day:[3]

> Love is mighty, love is powerful,
> Wrecks the heart without redress,
> And with maids the tool he uses
> Commonly is idleness.

> Let them sew, do household labor,
> Busied always they should be:
> Such the antidote most certain
> 'Gainst Love's envenomed malady.

> Damsels modest and retiring,
> Who to marriage do aspire,
> Have their virtue for their dowry,
> Highest praise they could desire.

Courtiers and knightly errants
With the wanton take their ease,
But to the good their troth is plighted,
For modesty doth ever please.

There are loves that start with morning,
As between guests at an inn,
But they quickly end at sunset—
Ended ere they scarce begin.

Here today and gone tomorrow,
Love of that kind doth impart
Little lasting joy or pleasure,
Leaves no imprint on the heart.

Painting laid upon a painting
Makes a very sorry show;
Where one beauty holds the canvas,
None other can subdue its glow.

On my own heart is engraven
Dulcinea's image fair,
And there's naught that can erase it,
'Twill be always printed there.

Loyalty's the thing most valued
In the one who loves and sighs;
It is this that doth work wonders,
Raising him up to the skies.

Don Quixote had come to this point in his song, with the duke and duchess, Altisidora, and nearly all the household listening, when suddenly from a gallery directly above his window they let down a rope to which were attached more than a hundred bells, and then they emptied a large bag filled with cats that had bells of a smaller size fastened to their tails. And so great was the din of the bells and so loud the squalling of the felines that even though the duke and duchess were the ones who had thought up the joke, they still were startled by it all. As for Don Quixote, he was quaking with fear. As luck would have it, two or three of the cats came in through the window of his room, darting from side to side, and it was as though a legion [4] of devils had been let loose there. As they ran about seeking a means of escape, they put out the candles that were burning in the chamber. In the meantime, those above kept hauling up and letting down the rope, while the majority of the castle inmates, being unaware of what was going on, were left gasping with astonishment.

Getting to his feet, Don Quixote drew his sword and started slashing at the window grating as he shouted, "Away with you, malign enchanters! Out with you, witching rabble! Know that I am Don Quixote de la Mancha, against whom your evil intentions are of no avail!"

Turning on the cats that were rushing around the room, he made many thrusts at them, but they dashed for the window and leaped out —all except one, which, upon finding itself thus belabored by Don Quixote's sword, sprang at his face and seized his nose with its claws and teeth, causing him to cry out with pain at the top of his voice. When they heard this, the duke and duchess, who suspected what the trouble was, ran to his room and opened the door with their master key, only to behold the poor knight struggling with all the strength that he had to pull the cat away from his face.

As they entered the chamber with lights in their hands, they had a full view of the unequal combat; but when the duke came forward to part the two, Don Quixote called to him, "Let no one take him away from me! Leave me to fight this demon, this wizard, this enchanter hand to hand. I will show him who Don Quixote de la Mancha is!"

The cat, however, only growled and held on; but the duke finally pulled it off and tossed it out the window. Don Quixote's face was perforated like a sieve and his nose was not in very good shape; yet for all of that, he was very much displeased that they had not permitted him to finish the hard-fought battle with that scoundrelly enchanter. They then sent for some oil of Hypericum,⁵ and Altisidora herself, with her fair white hands, applied bandages to all his wounds.

As she did so, she said to him in a low voice, "All these misfortunes have befallen you, hardhearted knight, as a punishment for your stubborn cruelty. I hope to God that Sancho, your squire, forgets to flog himself so that your beloved Dulcinea may never be released from her spell and you may never enjoy her or go with her to the marriage bed, at least not so long as I, who adore you, am still among the living."

To all this Don Quixote replied not a word. He merely heaved a deep sigh and stretched out on his bed, after which he thanked his hosts for their kindness, not because he had been afraid of that witching bell-decked feline rabble, but because he was grateful to them for their good intentions in coming to his aid. Leaving him to calm himself, the

duke and duchess thereupon took their departure, worried not a little
over the unfortunate outcome of the jest; for they had not thought
that this adventure would prove so painful and costly a one to the
knight. It did cost him five days in bed, where he had yet another, more
pleasant than the one just described, which the historian does not care
to relate at this time since he wishes to hurry back to Sancho Panza,
who all the while was going ahead with his government most diligently
and in a way that was very amusing.

CHAPTER XLVII. *Wherein is continued the account of how Sancho Panza deported himself in his government.*

THE history goes on to relate how they conducted Sancho from
the court to a sumptuous palace, where, in a great hall, a royal and
truly magnificent board was spread. He entered to the sound of flageolets, and four pages came forward to present him with water that he
might wash his hands, which he did in a most dignified manner. As the
music ceased, he took the seat at the head of the table, that being the
only one there was, since no other place had been laid. An individual
with a whalebone wand in his hand, who later turned out to be a physician, then stationed himself at Sancho's side, after which they lifted up
a fine white cloth, revealing an assortment of fruit and many other
edibles of various sorts.

One who appeared to be a student said grace as a page put a lace bib
under the governor's chin and another who performed the functions
of a butler set a dish of fruit in front of him. No sooner had he taken
a bite, however, than the personage at his side touched the plate with
the wand and it was instantly removed. The butler thereupon presented
a dish containing other food, but before Sancho had had a chance to taste
it—indeed, before it had so much as come within his reach—the wand
had been laid upon it and a page had withdrawn it as swiftly as the other

attendant had borne away the fruit. Astonished at this, the governor looked around at all the others present and demanded to know if this meal was supposed to be eaten by sleight of hand.[1]

"Señor Governor," replied the man with the wand, "one may eat here only in accordance with the usage and custom in other islands where there are governors. I, sir, am a physician and am paid to serve the rulers of this particular island. I am far more attentive to their health than I am to my own, and study night and day to become acquainted with my patient's constitution in order to be able to cure him when he falls sick. My chief duty is to be present at his dinners and suppers and permit him to eat only what is good for him while depriving him of anything that may do harm or injury to his stomach.[2] Thus I had them remove that dish of fruit for the reason that it contained too much moisture, and I had them do the same with the other dish because it was too hot and filled with spices that tend to increase the thirst. For he who drinks much slays and consumes that radical moisture wherein life consists." [3]

"Well, then," said Sancho, "that dish of roast partridges over there, which appears to be very properly seasoned, surely will not hurt me."

"Ah," was the physician's answer, "so long as I live my lord the governor shall not partake of those."

"And why not?" asked Sancho.

"For the reason that our master, Hippocrates, lodestar and luminary of the science of medicine, in one of his aphorisms has stated: '*Omnis saturatio mala, perdicis autem pessima*,' which is to say, 'All surfeit is bad, but a surfeit of partridges is the worst of all.' " [4]

"If that be true," said Sancho, "will the Señor Doctor kindly see what dishes there are on this table that will do me the most good and the least harm and then let me eat them without any more tapping; for by the life of the governor, and may God let me enjoy it, I'm dying of hunger, and in spite of the Señor Doctor and all that he may say, to deny me food is to take my life and not to prolong it."

"Your Grace is right, my Lord Governor," replied the physician. "And so, I may tell you that in my opinion you should not eat of those stewed rabbits, for it is a furry kind of food.[5] And that veal—if it were not roasted and pickled, you might try it, but as it is, there can be no question of your doing so."

"Take that big dish," said Sancho, "that I see smoking down there —it looks to me like an olla-podrida;[6] and, considering all the different things that go to make it up, I can't fail to hit upon something that will be tasty and at the same time good for me."

"*Absit*," declared the doctor. "Let us put far from us any such evil thought as that. There is nothing in the world that affords less nourishment than an olla-podrida. Save them for canons, university rectors, or peasant weddings. Its presence is out of place on the tables of governors, where all should be delicacy and refinement. The reason for this is that always, everywhere and by everybody, simple medicines are more esteemed than are the compounded ones, since in the case of the former it is impossible to make a mistake whereas with the others one may readily do so by altering the proportion of the ingredients. In my opinion, what my Lord Governor should eat at the present time is a hundred wafers [7] and a few thin slices of quince marmalade, which will be good for the stomach and an aid to digestion."

Upon hearing this, Sancho leaned back in his chair and, staring hard at the doctor, asked him what his name was and where he had studied.

"I, my Lord Governor, am Doctor Pedro Recio de Agüero, native of the village of Tirteafuera,[8] which is on the right-hand side going from Caracuel to Almodóvar del Campo, and I hold the degree of doctor from the University of Osuna." [9]

Sancho was greatly incensed by now. "Very well, let the Señor Doctor Pedro Recio de Mal-Agüero, graduate of Osuna and native of Tirteafuera, a village which is on the right-hand side as we come from Caracuel to Almodóvar del Campo—let him get out of here at once; for, if he does not, I swear by the sun that I will take a club and by making use of it, starting with him, will see to it that there is not a doctor left in this whole island, or, at any rate, none of those that I look upon as being ignorant. As for the wise, prudent, and learned ones, I will honor them as divine beings.[10] And so I say once more, let Pedro Recio be gone or I will take this chair in which I am sitting and break it over his head; and if I am called into court for it, I will clear myself by saying that I did God a service by slaying a bad physician and a public executioner. Either give me something to eat or take back your government; a trade that does not feed the one who practices it is not worth two beans."

The doctor was terrified when he saw how wrathful the governor was and would have made a Tirteafuera [11] of that room if at that moment the sound of a post horn had not been heard in the street. Going over to the window, the butler turned and said, "A courier from the duke, my lord; he must bring some message of importance." The courier entered, covered with sweat and very much agitated, and, drawing a paper from his bosom, he handed it to the major-domo, who read aloud the superscription, which ran as follows:

TO DON SANCHO PANZA, GOVERNOR OF THE ISLAND OF
BARATARIA, TO BE DELIVERED INTO HIS HANDS OR THOSE
OF HIS SECRETARY.

"Who here is my secretary?" inquired Sancho when he heard this.

"I, my lord," one of those present spoke up, "for I know how to read and write and I am a Biscayan." [12]

"With what you have just added," remarked Sancho, "you could well be secretary to the emperor himself. Open that paper and see what it says."

The newly fledged [13] secretary did so and, having perused the contents of the letter, announced that the matter was one to be discussed in private. Sancho thereupon ordered them to clear the hall, and when the doctor and all the others with the exception of the major-domo and the butler had gone, the secretary proceeded to read the communication:

It has come to my knowledge, Señor Don Sancho Panza, that certain enemies of mine and of the island are planning to launch a furious assault upon it one of these nights, and it will accordingly be necessary for you to keep a watch and be on the alert in order not to be taken unawares. I have further learned through trustworthy scouts that four persons have entered your village in disguise with the object of taking your life, for the reason that they fear your great ability. Keep your eyes open, observe closely all who come up to speak to you, and eat nothing that is offered you. I will send aid to you if I see that you are in trouble. Meanwhile, in all instances, you are to do the thing that is to be expected of your good judgment.

From this village, the 16th of August, at four o'clock in the morning. Your friend,

THE DUKE.

Sancho was astonished, and so, apparently, were the others. "The thing to be done now," said the governor, "and it must be done at once, is to throw Doctor Recio into jail; for if anybody is out to kill me, he must be the one, and he means to do it by slow starvation, which is the worst kind of death." [14]

"Moreover," said the butler, "it is my opinion that your Grace should not eat any of the food that is on this table, for it was a donation from some nuns, and, as the saying goes, behind the cross lurks the devil." [15]

"I do not deny it," replied Sancho, "and so for the present give me a slice of bread and three or four pounds of grapes; there can be no poison in that. The truth of the matter is, I cannot go on without eating. If we are to be ready for those battles that threaten us, we must be well nourished; for it is the tripes that carry the heart and not the other way around.[16] As for you, my secretary, reply to my lord, the duke, and tell him that I will carry out his orders exactly as he gives them. And say to my lady the duchess that I kiss her hands and beg her to send a special messenger with the letter and bundle for my wife, Teresa Panza, as that will be a great favor to me, and I will do all in my power to serve her in any way that I can. While you are about it, you may also put in a kiss of the hands for my master, Don Quixote de la Mancha, that he may see that I am grateful for his bread which I have eaten. As a good secretary and a good Biscayan, you may add whatever you like and is most to the point. And now take away this cloth and give me something to eat and I'll be ready for all the spies, murderers, and enchanters that may descend on me or on this island of mine."

A page now came in. "There is a farmer outside who would like a word with your Lordship on a matter of business. He says it is very important."

"It is strange about these people who come to see me on business," said Sancho. "Is it possible they are so foolish as not to see that this is no time for things of that sort? We governors, we judges, are we not flesh-and-blood beings? Are we not to be allowed the time that is necessary for taking a little rest—unless they would have us made of blocks of marble? By God and upon my conscience, if this government of mine holds out (and I have a feeling that it won't), I'll have more than one of these fellows who come on business hauled up short. For the present, show this good man in, but make sure first that he is not one of those spies or killers that are after me."

"No, sir," replied the page, "I do not think he is; for he appears to be a simple soul,[17] and either I miss my guess or he's as good as good bread."[18]

"There is nothing to be afraid of," added the major-domo, "for we are all here."

"Butler," said Sancho, "would it be possible, now that Doctor Recio is no longer with us, for me to eat something with a little body and substance to it, even if it is only a slice of bread and an onion?"

"Tonight at supper," the butler informed him, "your Lordship will be fully compensated for what was lacking at dinner."

"God grant it may be so," was Sancho's answer.

At this point the farmer appeared. He made a very favorable impression; for it could be seen from a thousand leagues away that he was a worthy man and a good soul.

"Who is the governor here?" was the first thing he asked.

"Who would it be," said the secretary, "if not the one who occupies that seat?"

"Then, I humble myself in his presence," said the man; and, dropping to his knees, he sought to kiss the governor's hand, but Sancho would not permit it. Instead, he bade him rise and state what he wanted. The petitioner did so.

"Sir," he began, "I am a farmer, a native of Miguelturra, a village two leagues distant from Ciudad Real."

"I see we have another Tirteafuera," observed Sancho. "Say what you have to say, brother; for I will say to you that I know Miguelturra very well, as it is not very far from my town."

"Well, then, sir," continued the farmer, "this is the case that I would lay before you. By the grace of God I was married, in the peace and with the blessing of the Holy Roman Catholic Church. I have two sons who are students. The younger is studying to be a bachelor and the older one to be a licentiate. I am a widower. My wife died, or, more properly speaking, a stupid doctor killed her by giving her a purge when she was pregnant. If it had pleased God to let the child be born and it had been a boy, I would have had him study to be a doctor so that he would not be jealous of his brothers, the licentiate and the bachelor."

"And in the same way," put in Sancho, "if your wife had not died or been killed, you would not now be a widower?"

"No, sir, of course not," replied the farmer.

"Well," said Sancho, "we are coming along; but hurry, brother, for it is nearer bedtime than business time."

"I will inform you," the farmer went on, "that this son of mine who is studying to be a bachelor has fallen in love with a lass in the same town by the name of Clara Perlerina, daughter of Andrés Perlerino, another farmer and a very rich one. That name, I may tell you, is not one that has been handed down for generations but is due to the fact that all the members of this family are paralytics, and by way of improving on it they call them Perlerines.[19]

"If the truth be told, this lass is like an oriental pearl or a flower of the field only when you look at her from the right-hand side; from the left-hand, not so much so, for on that side one eye is missing which she lost when she had the smallpox. The pockmarks on her face are many and large, but those who are fond of her will assert that those are not scars at all but graves where the hearts of her lovers lie buried. She is so neat that, in order not to dirty her face, she carries her nose turned up, as they say, so that it looks as if it were running away from her mouth. But, with all this, she is very good-looking. Her mouth is wide, and if it were not that ten or a dozen front teeth and grinders are missing, she might pass as one of the comeliest of maidens.

"Of her lips I shall say nothing, for they are so thin and delicate that, if it were the custom to use lips for such a purpose, one might wind them in a skein. Their color is different from that which is commonly seen, and the effect is marvelous: they are speckled with blue, green, and an eggplant hue— But pardon me, Sir Governor, for painting in such detail one who, when all is said, is destined to be my daughter. I love her and to me she is not bad-looking." [20]

"Do all the painting you like," said Sancho. "I'm enjoying it, and if I had only had my dinner, I wouldn't ask for a better dessert than this portrait of yours."

"That," replied the farmer, "is something which I have yet to serve, [21] but we will get to it in due time. I can only assure you, sir, that if I could but paint for you her tall figure and her bodily charms, you would find cause for astonishment; but this cannot be, for the reason that she is so bent and stooped that her knees touch her mouth, yet it is plain to be seen that if she could draw herself erect her head would scrape the roof. She would long since have given her hand to my bachelor son if she had been able to stretch it out, but it happens to be shrunken; nevertheless, you can tell from her broad, furrowed nails how elegant and shapely it is."

"That will do, brother," said Sancho. "You may consider that you have painted her from head to foot. What is it you want now? Come to the point without all this beating around the bush and all these odds and ends that you are tagging on to the story."

"What I desire, sir," the farmer went on, "is for your Grace to give me a letter of recommendation to her father, asking him to be so good as to let this marriage take place. We are not badly matched in the matter of worldly fortune or gifts of nature; for, to tell you the truth, Sir Governor, my son is bewitched, and there is not a day that the evil spirits do not torment him three or four times. Once he fell into the fire, and as a result his face is as shriveled as a bit of parchment. His eyes, too, are somewhat watery. But he has the disposition of an angel, and if it wasn't for his always flaying and punching himself with his fist, he'd be a saint."

"Is there anything else you would like, my good man?" Sancho inquired.

"There is," replied the farmer, "though I hesitate to mention it. But come, come, in any case I cannot let it go on rotting in my bosom. Sir, I would have your Grace give me from three to six hundred ducats to help make up my bachelor son's dowry, by which I mean, to help him set up housekeeping; for, after all, they must live by themselves, without being subjected to the meddling of their families."

"Think it over well," said Sancho, "and see if there is anything else. Don't be bashful but speak right out."

"No, I am quite sure there isn't."

No sooner did the man say this than the governor rose to his feet and picked up the chair in which he had been sitting.

"I swear, Don Country Bumpkin!" he cried, "if you don't get out of my sight at once, you unmannerly lout, and go hide yourself somewhere, I'll take this chair and lay your head wide open! Son of a whore, rascal, devil's painter! Is this any time to come asking me for six hundred ducats? Where would I get them, you stinking cur? And if I did have them, why should I give them to a crafty dunce like you? What is Miguelturra or the whole Perlerines family to me? Away with you, or by the life of the duke, my lord, I'll do what I said! I don't think you are from Miguelturra at all; you are some scoundrel that Hell has sent here to tempt me! Tell me, you wretch: I've not had the government a day and a half yet, and where do you expect me to lay hands on six hundred ducats?"

The butler motioned to the farmer to leave the room, which he did, hanging his head, for the fellow was obviously afraid that the governor would carry out his angry threat. (The rogue knew how to play his part very well.) But let us leave Sancho with his anger, and peace to them all, while we return to Don Quixote, who, when we last saw him, had his face treated and bandaged as a result of the cat wounds, from which he was not cured in a week's time. Meanwhile, during that week, something happened to him one day which Cid Hamete promises to relate with that truth and exactitude that mark every detail, however small, of this great history.

CHAPTER XLVIII. *Of what happened to Don Quixote and Doña Rodríguez, duenna to the duchess, with other events worthy of record and of eternal remembrance.*

THE badly wounded Don Quixote was exceedingly melancholy and dejected, with his bandaged face which bore the marks not of God's hand [1] but of the claws of a cat, this being one of the misfortunes that are the accompaniment of knight-errantry. For six days he did not go out in public; and one night as he lay wide awake, thinking of all his troubles and of how Altisidora was pursuing him, he heard the door of his room being opened with a key, and at once he leaped to the conclusion that the enamored maiden must be coming to make an assault upon his virtue and cause him to waver in that fidelity that he owed to his lady, Dulcinea del Toboso.

"No!" he cried aloud, convinced of the truth of his imaginings, "for the sake of the greatest beauty on earth I shall not cease to adore the one who is stamped and engraved upon my heart of hearts, who is hidden away in the depths of my bowels! O lady mine, thou may'st be transformed now into an ungainly [2] peasant lass and now into a nymph of the gilded Tagus, weaving tapestries of gold and silk.[3] Merlin or Montesinos may hold thee captive where they will; but wherever it may be, thou art mine; and wherever I may be, I am thine."

Even as he finished saying this the door opened, and he immediately stood up in the bed, wrapped from head to foot in a yellow satin coverlet, with a nightcap on his head and with his face and mustaches swathed in bandages—his face by reason of the scratches and his mustaches to keep them from drooping and falling down—all of which gave him the most extraordinary and fantastic appearance that could possibly be conceived. Watchfully he kept his eyes fastened on the door, expecting to see Altisidora enter, in tears and ready to yield herself; but, instead, he beheld a most dignified duenna in a long, white-bordered veil, so long that it enveloped her entire body like a cloak all the way down to her feet. In her left hand she carried a half-burned candle, while with her right hand she shaded it to keep the light out of her eyes, which were concealed behind a pair of huge spectacles. She came treading softly and cautiously.

Don Quixote gazed upon her from his watchtower and, noting her garb and the silence which she was careful to maintain, decided that it must be some witch or sorceress who had come in this guise to do him harm, and he began crossing himself with great fervor. The apparition, meanwhile, was drawing nearer, and when it reached the middle of the room it raised its eyes and let them rest upon the knight as he stood there furiously making the sign of the cross. If he was terrified at the sight of such a figure as this, the specter in turn was equally frightened by the tall yellow form in the coverlet with a face muffled in bandages.

"Jesus!" screamed the visitor. "What is this I see?" And she gave such a start that the candle fell from her hands, leaving the room in darkness. With this, she turned her back and made for the door, but in her terror tripped over her skirt and came down to the floor with a tremendous thud.

Don Quixote was very much alarmed. "O phantom," he said, "or whatever thou art, I conjure thee to tell me who thou art and what it is that thou desirest of me. If thou beest a soul in torment, speak out, and I will do for thee all that lies within my power; for I am a Catholic Christian and like to do good to everyone. It was with this purpose in view that I took up the profession of knight-errantry, a calling that extends even to the helping of souls in purgatory."

The bewildered duenna, upon hearing herself conjured in this manner, was able to judge of Don Quixote's fear from the fright which she herself felt.

"Señor Don Quixote," she said, "if that, perchance, is who you are, I am no ghost nor apparition nor soul out of purgatory as your Grace must have thought. I am Doña Rodríguez, maid of honor to my lady the duchess, and I come to you with one of those wrongs that your Grace is in the habit of redressing."

"Tell me one thing, Señora Doña Rodríguez," said the knight, "has your Grace perhaps come here as a go-between? For I would have you know that I am not at the disposal of anyone, thanks to the peerless beauty of my lady Dulcinea del Toboso. In short, if you but put aside all love messages, you may go back to light your candle and return, and we will then discuss whatever it is that you would have me do, with the exception, as I have said, of any kind of amorous dalliance."

"*I* carry love messages, my good sir?" replied the duenna. "Little does your Grace know me. I am not so old as to indulge in such child's play as that. What's more, praise God, my soul is still in the flesh and I have all my teeth and grinders in my mouth, save for a few which I lost owing to the colds that are so common in this land of Aragon. If your Grace will wait a moment, I will go light my candle and will be back in an instant to relate my woes to the one who is capable of remedying those of all the world."

And without giving him time to answer she went out the door, leaving Don Quixote in a thoughtful mood as he quietly waited for her to return. Then, of a sudden, a thousand suspicions assailed him regarding this new adventure, which impressed him as being ill fashioned and worse conceived, since it placed him in danger of having to break his plighted troth to his lady.

"Who knows," he said to himself, "but that the devil, who is subtle and cunning, may be trying to deceive me now with a duenna, which is something he has not been able to accomplish with empresses, queens, marchionesses, or countesses? I have often heard it said by the wise that, if he has his way, he will give you a flat-nosed female rather than one with a Roman nose any time.[4] May it not be that this solitude, this silence, and the opportunity that is afforded me, will awaken my sleeping desires and lead me, at the end of my life's span, to fall where I never before have stumbled? In such cases it is better to flee than to stand one's ground and give battle.

"But surely," he went on, "I cannot be in my right mind to be saying and thinking such nonsense as this! It is impossible that a tall, lank, white-hooded duenna in spectacles should arouse a lascivious thought in the bosom of the most graceless wretch in this world. Is there a duenna on this earth who is fair of body? Is there a duenna in the world who is not meddlesome, wrinkled, and prudish? Away with you, then, the whole duenna crew, seeing that ye serve no human pleasure! Oh, how right that lady was of whom it is said that she kept two stuffed duennas, with their spectacles and cushions, at the far end of her reception hall, just as if they were sitting there at work on their embroidery, and those figurines conferred as much respectability upon the room as if they had been real flesh-and-blood matrons!"

Saying this, he flung himself out of bed with the intention of bolting the door and not permitting Señora Rodríguez to enter again; but, just as he was about to do so, that lady returned with a lighted white wax candle, and when she saw Don Quixote at close hand, wrapped in the coverlet, with his bandages, nightcap, and all, she was once more afraid.

"Am I safe, Sir Knight?" she asked, falling back a step or two. "For I do not look upon it as very decent on your part to have left your bed."

"Lady," replied Don Quixote, "that is a question which I well might ask of you. In fact, I do ask you if I am safe from being attacked and raped."

"Of whom do you demand this assurance, Sir Knight, and of whom are you thinking when you ask it?"

"I ask it of you," said Don Quixote, "and it is you that I have in mind; for I am not made of marble nor you of brass. This is not ten o'clock in the morning but midnight, or a little later than that, I fancy, and we are in a room that is more closed in and secret than that cave must have been where the bold and faithless Aeneas enjoyed the beauty of tender-hearted Dido. But give me your hand, lady, for I ask no greater security than my own modesty and continence and such as is afforded me by that most venerable headdress." [5]

With this, he kissed his own right hand and took hold of hers, which she extended to him with the same degree of ceremony.

(Here, Cid Hamete inserts a parenthesis in which he swears by Mohammed that to have seen the two walking hand and hand like this from the door to the bed he would have given the better of the two cloaks that he had.)

Finally Don Quixote went back to bed while Doña Rodríguez remained seated in a chair some distance away. She was still holding her candle and wearing her spectacles. He then huddled down and covered himself until only his face was visible; and when they both were settled, he broke the silence.

"Now, my lady Doña Rodríguez," he said, "your Grace may unburden herself. Tell me everything that is in your anguished heart and grieving bowels. You shall be heard with chaste ears and succored with deeds of compassion."

"That I can well believe," replied the duenna, "for so Christian a response as the one you have given me was the only thing to be expected of your kind and charming self. I will tell you, then, Señor Don Quixote, that although your Grace sees me here seated in this chair, in the heart of the kingdom of Aragon, wearing the attire of an old worn-out duenna, I am in reality a native of Asturias on the Oviedo side,[6] and I come of a family that is related to many of the best in that province. But owing to my own ill luck and the negligence of my parents, who somehow or other lost their fortune at an early date, I was brought to the

court of Madrid, where, for the sake of security and in order to prevent greater misfortunes, I was placed as a seamstress with a lady of
rank—and I may inform your Grace that when it comes to any kind of
needlework, no one in all my life has ever surpassed me. My parents left
me there in service and returned to their own country; and a few years
later they went to Heaven, in all probability, for they were very good
Catholic Christians. I thus became an orphan dependent upon the miserable wage and paltry favors which servant girls in a palace customarily
receive.

"Then it was, without my having given him any occasion for doing
so, that a squire in that household fell in love with me. He was a man
well along in years, bearded and personable, and, above all, he was as
much a gentleman as the king himself, for he was a highlander.[7] We were
not able to keep our love so secret but that it came to the notice of
my mistress, who without more ado had us married in the peace and
with the blessing of the Holy Roman Catholic Church. Of that marriage
a daughter was born, to put an end to my good fortune if I ever had
any. True, I did not succumb in childbed, which I passed through safely
and in season; but my husband died shortly afterward of a shock that he
had—if there were time to tell you of it, I am sure your Grace would
marvel at it."

At this point she began weeping bitterly. "Pardon me, Señor Don
Quixote," she said, "if I am unable to control myself; every time that I
think of my poor unfortunate husband, my eyes brim with tears. God
bless me, how dignified he used to look as he rode along carrying my
mistress behind him on the crupper of a jet-black mule! For in those
days they did not have coaches and chairs [8] as they tell me they do now,
but ladies rode behind their squires in the manner I have mentioned.

"This much at least I must tell you, in order that you may see how
well bred and punctilious my worthy husband was. As he was entering the Calle de Santiago in Madrid, which is a rather narrow street, a
judge of the court with two constables in front of him was coming
out of it. As soon as my good squire saw the judge, he turned the mule
and made as if to accompany the magistrate, but my lady, who was on
the crupper, whispered to him, 'What are you doing, you wretch?
Don't you know that I am here?' The judge, being a courteous gentleman, reined in his horse and said, 'Continue on your way, sir; it is I
who should accompany my lady, Doña Casilda'—for that was my mistress's name. My husband, however, cap in hand, insisted on going
with the judge; and when she saw this, my mistress, vexed and angry,

drew out a big pin—a bodkin, I think it was—from her needlecase and stuck it into my husband's back so forcefully that he gave a loud scream and fell writhing to the ground, bringing my lady with him.

"Her two lackeys came running to lift her up and the judge and his bailiffs did the same. The Guadalajara Gate [9] was in a hubbub—I am referring to the idlers there. My mistress returned home on foot while my husband hurried to the barber's,[10] saying that his intestines had been pierced. His courtesy became the talk of the town, to such an extent that small boys ran after him in the street. For this reason and because he was somewhat shortsighted my lady dismissed him, and this in my opinion was what brought on his death.[11] I was left a widow with no one to protect me and with a daughter to care for who was growing in beauty like the foam of the sea.

"At last, as a result of my reputation as a seamstress, my lady the duchess, who had recently been married to my lord the duke, offered to bring me with her to this kingdom of Aragon, and my daughter as well, who, as time went by, grew up to be one of the most accomplished young ladies to be found anywhere: she sings like a lark; she is like fancy itself as she goes through the stately movements of the court dances, while in the dances of the people she trips it like a mad woman; [12] she reads and writes like a schoolmaster and does sums like a miser. Of the neatness of her person I say nothing: running water is not cleaner than she. She must be now, if I remember rightly, sixteen years, five months, and three days old—a day more or less.

"But to get on with my story: The son of a very rich farmer, in a village not far from here that belongs to my lord the duke, fell in love with her. How it happened I do not know, but they came together and, under promise of marrying her, he made a fool of my daughter and now is unwilling to keep his word. My lord the duke is aware of this, for I have complained to him not one but many times, imploring him to order that farmer's son to marry her, but he turns a deaf ear [13] and scarcely listens to me. The reason is that the young deceiver's father is so rich; he lends the duke money and goes security for his debts from time to time, and so my lord does not wish to offend him or give him trouble of any sort.

"What I would ask of you, then, my good sir, is that you take it upon yourself to undo this wrong, either by entreaties or by force of arms; for everyone says that you were born into the world for that purpose: to redress grievances and protect the wretched. Let your Grace bear in mind that my daughter is an orphan; think of her youth, her charm, and all those accomplishments of which I have told you. For I swear to God and upon my conscience that of all the damsels that my lady has in attendance upon her, there is not one that comes up to the sole of my daughter's shoe. Take that one whom they call Altisidora and who is regarded as the sprightliest and gayest of the lot: in comparison with my daughter she is two leagues and more away. For, my dear sir, I may remind you that all is not gold that glitters. In this girl Altisidora there is more of presumption than of beauty and more of sprightliness than of modesty. What is more, she is none too healthy. Her breath is so bad that one cannot bear to be near her for a moment, and even my lady the duchess—but I must be silent, for as the saying goes, walls have ears."

"Upon my life, Señora Doña Rodríguez," said Don Quixote, "what ails my lady the duchess?"

"Seeing that you adjure me in this manner," replied the duenna, "I can do no more than answer you in all truthfulness. You are aware, Señor Don Quixote, of my lady's beauty: that complexion of hers which is like a smooth-polished sword; those cheeks of milk and carmine, one of which is like the sun while the other resembles the moon;[14] that lightsome step with which she barely skims the ground. From all of this would it not seem that she radiates health wherever she goes? But I would have your Grace know, she may first of all thank God for it, and in the second place she may be grateful for two issues that she has, one in each leg, through which are discharged all the evil humors of which the doctors say she is full."[15]

"Holy Mary!" exclaimed Don Quixote, "and is it possible that my lady the duchess has drains of that sort? I should not have believed it if the barefoot friars had told me, but seeing that it is Señora Doña Rodríguez who so informs me, then it must be so. But such issues and in such places ought not to drain off humors, but, rather, liquid amber. Truly, now, I am beginning to be convinced that this matter of opening issues is important for the health."

No sooner had Don Quixote said this than the door of the room was thrown open with a loud bang. Doña Rodríguez was so startled that she again let the candle fall, and the room became as dark as a wolf's mouth, as the saying has it. Then the poor duenna felt a pair of hands closing about her throat so tightly that she could not even croak, while another person without saying a word, lifted her petticoats and, with what appeared to be a slipper, began giving her such a spanking that it was piteous to behold. Don Quixote, indeed, felt pity for her, but for all of that he did not stir from his bed. Not knowing what the meaning of it was, he lay there quietly, fearful lest his turn should come next. His fears were justified. Having given the duenna (who did not dare cry out) a thorough drubbing, the silent executioners fell upon the knight. Stripping the sheet and coverlet from him, they pinched him so hard and fast that there was nothing for him to do but defend himself with his fists; all of which took place in a silence that was truly astonishing.

The battle lasted for something like half an hour, at the end of which time the phantom figures departed. Pulling down her skirts and bemoaning her ill fortune, Doña Rodríguez went out the door without a word to Don Quixote. Here we shall leave him to his solitude, sorely pinched, bewildered, and downcast, wondering who the perverse enchanter could be who had placed him in such a predicament. All this, however, will be told in due time. Sancho Panza is calling us now, and the proper arrangement of this history demands that we give him our attention.

CHAPTER XLIX. Of what happened to Sancho Panza as he made the rounds of his island.

WE LEFT the great governor angry and out of sorts with the roguish farmer-painter, who, put up to it by the major-domo and the major-domo in turn by the duke, had been making sport of him. Sancho, nonetheless, though he may have been but a simpleton, a stupid boor, contrived to hold his own against them all. He now addressed himself to those present, including Doctor Recio, who had returned to the room as soon as the business of the duke's confidential letter was out of the way.

"By this time," he said, "I see plainly that judges and governors ought to be made of brass so that they might not have to listen to those who come to petition them and who insist that they be heard and their business disposed of, no matter what the time or season. And if the poor judge does not hear them and attend to their requests, either because he is unable to do so or because it is not the time set aside for audiences, then they at once begin to curse and slander him, gnawing at his bones and even assailing his family tree. O silly petitioner, foolish petitioner, do not be in such haste as that, but wait for the proper occasion and opportunity. Come neither at mealtime nor at bedtime, for judges are of flesh and blood and must satisfy the needs of nature. All except me, that is to say; for thanks to the Señor Doctor Pedro Recio Tirteafuera, who stands before me here, I cannot satisfy my natural need of eating. He would have me die of hunger, and to this form of death he gives the name of life—may God give him and all his stripe that kind of life, say I, and the same goes for all bad doctors, while the good one merits palms and laurels."

All those who were acquainted with Sancho Panza were astonished at hearing him use such elegant language and did not know to what to attribute it unless it was that offices carrying grave responsibilities sharpened the wits of some men while in the case of others the effect was merely stupefying. Doctor Pedro Recio Agüero of Tirteafuera finally promised that the governor should have his supper that night even though it might be in violation of all the aphorisms of Hippocrates,[1] and with this Sancho was content. He waited eagerly for night and the supper hour to come, and although it seemed to him that time was standing still, the hour so longed for arrived at last. They then served him a dish of beef and onions with a few boiled calves' feet that were rather stale. He fell to, however, more heartily than if they had set before him francolins from Milan, Roman pheasants, veal of Sorrento, partridges from Moron, or geese from Lavajos.

"See here, Señor Doctor," he said in the course of the meal, "from now on you needn't bother to give me dainty dishes or anything special as it would only unhinge my stomach, which is used to goat's meat, beef, bacon, hung beef, turnips, and onions. If I am given other victuals of the kind they serve in palaces, my stomach will turn squeamish and I'll sometimes be sick. What the butler may do is this: he may serve me what are known as ollas-podridas (for the more rotten they are, the better they smell).[2] He may put whatever he likes into them, so long as it is something good to eat, and I will thank him for it, and pay him for it, too, someday. But don't let anyone try to play any jokes on me, for either we are or we are not, and so let us all live together and eat our food in peace and good fellowship. When God sends the dawn, it is daylight for all.[3] I mean to govern this island without giving up a right or taking a bribe.[4] Let everyone keep his eyes open and look out for the arrow.[5] For I would have you know that the devil's in Cantillana,[6] and if they give me cause for it, they're going to see marvels. Make yourself into honey and the flies will eat you!"[7]

"Señor Governor," replied the butler, "there is certainly much truth in what you have said, and I promise you in the name of all the inhabitants of this island that they will serve your Grace faithfully, willingly, and affectionately; for the mild way in which you have begun to govern affords them no excuse for doing or thinking anything that would be a disservice to your Grace."

"That I can believe," said Sancho, "since they would be fools to think or do anything of the sort. Once more I say to you: see to feeding me and my gray; that is the important thing and most to the point. When the time comes, we will make the rounds. It is my intention to rid this island of all kinds of trash, of all good-for-nothing loafers and vagabonds; for I would have you know, my friends, that the lazy and idle are to a state what drones are to a hive, which eat the honey that the worker bees have made. I propose to aid the farmer, to preserve the privileges of gentlemen, to reward the virtuous, and, above all, to respect religion and to honor those in holy orders.[8] What do you think of that, my friends? Is there something in what I say or not?"

"There is so much in what your Grace says," the major-domo assured him, "that I am indeed astonished to hear a man wholly unlettered, as I believe your Grace to be, uttering so many wise maxims and observations, all of which is quite contrary to what was expected of your Grace's intelligence by those who sent us and by us who came here with you. Each day new things are seen in this world, jests are turned into earnest and the jesters are mocked."

Night came, and the governor had his supper with permission of the Señor Doctor Recio.[9] They then prepared to make the rounds, and Sancho set out accompanied by the major-domo, the secretary, the butler, a chronicler whose duty it was to record his deeds, and a number of bailiffs and notaries, enough to form a fair-sized squadron. In the midst of them all walked Sancho with his staff of office in hand, as fine a sight as one could wish to see. They had traversed but a few streets of the town when they heard the noise of clashing swords. Upon hastening to the spot, they found only two men, who, when they saw the authorities approaching, at once ceased fighting.

"Help, in God's name and the King's!" cried one of the swordsmen.

"Does one here have to put up with being openly robbed and set upon in the middle of the street?"

"Be quiet, my good fellow," said Sancho, "and tell me what is the cause of this quarrel; for I am the governor."

The other man now spoke up. "Señor Governor," he said, "I will tell you, very briefly. Your Grace should know that in that gambling house directly across the way this man has just won, God knows how, more than a thousand reales. I was present at the time and judged more than one doubtful point in his favor, very much against the dictates of my conscience, after which he made off with what he had won. I had expected him to give me a crown or so out of his winnings,[10] such being the custom where gentlemen of my rank look on to see whether the play is fair or foul and to support those who are actually losers and thus prevent brawls. He, however, pocketed his money and left the house, and, angered at this, I followed him.

"Very civilly and courteously I asked him to let me have at least eight reales, as he knows me to be a respectable individual and one without employment or income, my parents having given me no profession and left me no property. But Cacus is not a bigger thief nor Andradilla [11] a worse sharper than this rogue. He would not part with more than four reales, from which, Señor Governor, you may see how little shame and conscience he has! But, in faith, if your Grace had not arrived when you did, I would have made him disgorge those winnings of his and he'd have learned how to balance the scales." [12]

"What have you to say to that?" Sancho inquired of the first swordsman.

The other replied that all his antagonist had said was true, adding that he had felt that four reales was enough, since he very often gave the man money, and those who expect gratuities [13] from players ought to be polite and accept with a cheerful countenance whatever is offered them, without making any demands on the winners unless they know for a certainty that the latter's gains are ill gotten. There was, he pointed out, no better proof that he was an honest man, and not a thief as his accuser had stated, than the fact that he had at first refused to give anything; for sharpers always have to pay tribute to the onlookers who are acquainted with them.

"That is true," observed the major-domo; "and now, my Lord Governor, it is for your Grace to decide what is to be done with these men."

"What is to be done with them," said Sancho, "is this: you, the winner, whether you won by fair, foul, or indifferent means, will immediately pay this bully a hundred reales, and you will disburse thirty more for the poor prisoners. As for you who have neither occupation nor source of income but roam about with nothing to do, you will take those hundred reales and before tomorrow night will leave this island under sentence of banishment for ten years. If you violate that sentence, you will serve the remainder of it in the life to come, for I will hang you on a gibbet, or the public executioner, at any rate, will do it for me. And not a word from either of you or I will let you feel the weight of my hand."

The one man thereupon paid over the money and went on home, and the other, who received it, promptly left the island.

"Either I am not good for much," remarked Sancho when it was all over, "or I will do away with these gambling houses, for it seems to me that much harm comes from them."

"This one, at least," said one of the notaries, "your Grace will not be able to do away with, for it is kept by a very important personage, and what he loses in the course of the year is beyond all comparison more than what he makes by the cards. Against other houses, of less importance, your Grace may take action, and they are the ones that do the most harm and conceal the most flagrant abuses. In the houses of gentlemen of rank and of noblemen, notorious sharpers do not dare to play their tricks; and, seeing that gambling has now become a common vice, it is better that it be done there than in the home of some artisan,[14] where they catch a poor fellow in the small hours of the morning and skin him alive."

"I can see, notary," replied Sancho, "that there is much to be said as to that."

A constable now came up, grasping a youth by the arm. "My Lord Governor," he said, "this young man was coming toward us, and as soon as he caught sight of the officers of the law he started running like a deer, a sign that he must be an evildoer of some sort. I set out after him, and if it had not been that he stumbled and fell, I'd never have overtaken him."

"Why were you running away, my man?" asked Sancho.

"Sir," replied the youth, "it was to avoid answering all the questions that the officers put to you."

"What is your trade?"

"A weaver."

"And what do you weave?"

"Lance points, with your Grace's kind permission."

"So, you are being funny with me, are you? You pride yourself on being a great joker, I suppose? Very well. And where were you bound for just now?"

"To take the air."

"And where do you take the air in this island?"

"Where it blows."

"Good enough; you answer very much to the point; you're a clever young man. But please note that I am the air, and I am blowing on your poop right now and sending you to jail. Ho, there, take him away; I'll see that he sleeps without any air tonight."

"By God!" exclaimed the youth, "your Grace can no more make me sleep in jail than you can make me a king!"

"And why can't I?" Sancho demanded. "Do you mean to tell me it is not in my power to have you arrested or set free whenever I like?"

"However much power your Grace may have," said the youth, "it is not enough to make me sleep in jail."

"You think not?" said Sancho. "Take him away at once that he may see with his own eyes how mistaken he is; and it will do no good for the jailer to be generous with him, for a consideration, for I will fine him two thousand ducats if he lets this fellow stir a step out of prison tonight."

"All that is laughable," said the youth. "The fact of the matter is, there are not enough people in this world to make me sleep there."

"Tell me, you devil," said Sancho, "do you have some angel who is going to get you out, who will take off the irons that I am going to order them to put on you?"

"Ah, now, Señor Governor," replied the youth with great vivacity, "let us talk sense and come to the point. Let us suppose that your Grace orders me taken off to jail and that they put me in irons and chains and throw me into a dungeon, and let us further suppose that you threaten the jailer with a heavy fine if he does not carry out his orders but lets me out—in spite of all this, if I do not wish to sleep but choose to remain awake all night without closing an eyelid, will your Grace be able, with all your power, to make me do so?"

"No, certainly not," said the secretary. "The fellow is right."

"That is all very well," said Sancho, "so long as you stay awake merely because it is your pleasure to do so and not in opposition to my will."

"Oh," replied the youth, "nothing like that, sir. Not for one moment."

"Well, then," said Sancho, "God be with you. Go to your house and may He give you a good sleep, for I would not deprive you of it. But I would advise you from now on not to make light of those in authority or you may fall in with someone who will bring the joke down on your skull."

The youth went away, and the governor continued on his rounds and a short while later two more constables came up with a man in custody.

"Señor Governor," one of them said, "this person who appears to be a man is in reality a woman, and not an ugly one at that, who goes dressed in men's clothing."

Two or three lanterns were lifted, and by their light was revealed the face of a girl who appeared to be about sixteen years old or a little more. Her hair, lovely as a thousand pearls, was caught up in a small net of gold and green silk. Surveying her from head to foot, they perceived that she had on red silk stockings and white taffeta garters with a border of gold and seed pearls; her breeches were of green-colored cloth of gold and her jacket [15] was of the same material, beneath which she wore a doublet of the finest gold-and-white texture, while her shoes, which were those of a man, were white. She carried no sword at her side, but, instead, an extremely ornate dagger, and on her fingers were many rings of good quality. In short, the young woman made a very favorable impression upon all of them, but none of those who beheld her were acquainted with her, and the natives of the town said they could not imagine who she could be. Most astonished of all were the ones who were supposed to be playing the joke upon Sancho, or who knew about it, as this incident and encounter had not been arranged by them, and they were, accordingly, left in some perplexity and waited to see what the outcome would be.

Sancho, taken aback by the girl's beauty, inquired of her who she was, where she was going, and what had induced her to assume that costume.

"Sir," she replied, keeping her eyes fixed upon the ground and exhibiting an embarrassment that bespoke a high degree of modesty, "I cannot tell you in public of something which it is important to me to have kept secret. But there is one thing I should like you to understand: I am not a thief nor criminal of any sort, but an unfortunate maiden who by force of jealousy has been led to violate that decorum that is modesty's due."

"My Lord Governor," said the major-domo when he heard this, "have the people stand back in order that this lady may say what she has to say with less embarrassment."

The governor gave the order, and they all fell back with the exception of the major-domo, the butler, and the secretary. Seeing that they were alone, the girl then went on with her story.

"I, gentlemen, am the daughter of Pedro Pérez Mazorca, a wool farmer of this town who comes very often to my father's house."

"That will not do, Señora," said the major-domo, "for I know Pedro Pérez very well and he has no child, either son or daughter. What is more, you say that he is your father and then you add that he is in the habit of coming to see your father."

"I had noticed that," remarked Sancho.

"I am so confused just now, gentlemen, that I do not know what I am saying," was the young woman's answer. "The truth is that I am the daughter of Don Diego de la Llana, whom you all must know."

"That is better," said the major-domo. "I am acquainted with Diego de la Llana and know him to be a wealthy gentleman of some prominence. I also know that he has a son and a daughter, and that since he became a widower no one in this town can boast of having seen the daughter's face; he keeps her so shut away that not even the sun can behold her, and yet, for all of that, report has it that she is exceedingly beautiful."

"That is the truth," replied the maiden, "and I am that daughter. As to whether the report of my beauty is true or not, gentlemen, you may judge for yourselves."

She now began weeping bitterly, and, seeing this, the secretary turned to the butler and whispered in his ear, "Without a doubt, something serious must have happened to this poor maid or one of her station would not leave her home and go wandering about the streets at such an hour and in such a costume."

"True enough," replied the butler; "your suspicion is confirmed by her tears."

Sancho consoled her as best he could, begging her to have no hesitancy about telling them what the trouble was, as they would all most earnestly endeavor to help her in every possible way.

"Gentlemen," she said, "the fact of the matter is that my father has kept me shut up for ten years now, ever since they laid my mother in the earth. In our house, mass is said in a sumptuous chapel; and in all that time I have seen but the sun in the heavens by day and the moon and stars by night. I do not know what streets, public squares, or churches are, nor even what men are like, outside of my father and a brother of mine and Pedro Pérez, the wool farmer, who frequently comes to visit us—it was for that reason that I took it into my head to say that he was my father, in order to avoid having to name my real one. This confinement—I am not allowed to leave the house even to go to church—has made me very unhappy for many days and months. I wanted to see the world, or at least the town where I was born, for it seemed to me that this wish did not run counter to that decorum that wellborn maidens ought to observe.

"When I heard them talking of bullfights, jousting with reeds,[16] and play-acting, I asked my brother, who is a year older than I, to tell me what these things were, together with many others which I had not seen, and he explained them to me as well as he could, and all this only kindled my desire to see for myself. But, to cut short the story of my downfall, I may tell you that I begged and entreated my brother— oh, that I had never done so!" And once again she began weeping.

"Continue, Señora," the major-domo said to her. "Go ahead and tell us what happened; for we are all in suspense at hearing what you have to say and seeing your tears."

"There is not much left to tell, though I have many tears that remain to be shed, for that is the payment one must always make for such misplaced desires as mine."

The butler's heart was deeply touched by the maiden's beauty, and he now lifted his lantern for another look at her. It appeared to him that those were not tears, but, rather, seed pearls or meadow dew, and he even went so far as to compare them to the pearls of the Orient. He could only hope that her misfortunes were not as great as her weeping and her sighs would seem to indicate. The governor for his part was becoming impatient over the way in which the girl dragged out her story and urged her not to keep them any longer in suspense as it was growing late and they had yet to cover a good deal of the town.

With broken sobs and half-sighs, she went on, "My misfortune is that I asked my brother to dress me up like a man in one of his suits and to take me out some night to see the town while our father was asleep. I insisted so strongly that he finally agreed to humor me, and so I put on his clothes and he dressed in mine—for he has no hair on his face and looks like a very pretty girl—and tonight, about an hour ago, we left the house and, led on by a youthful and foolish impulse, roamed the entire town. Just as we had made up our minds to return home, we saw coming toward us a large group of people, and my brother said to me, 'Sister, that must be the watch; pick up your feet and put wings on them and follow me as fast as you can, for if they should recognize us, it would be a bad business.' Saying this, he turned his back and started to fly rather than run; but I was so frightened that I had not gone more than six paces when I fell, and then the officer of justice who has brought me before you came, and I find myself put to shame before all these people as a bad and willful girl."

"So, then, young lady," said Sancho, "no other misfortune than this has befallen you, and it was not jealousy, after all, that drove you from your home, as you told us at the beginning of your story."

"No, nothing has happened to me, and it was not jealousy that drove me away, but only a desire to see the world, which did not go any further than seeing the streets of this town."

The truth of what she had said was now confirmed by the arrival of constables with her brother, one of them having overtaken the lad as he ran away from his sister. He had on nothing but a skirt of rich material and a short blue damask cloak with a fine-gold border; he had no bonnet on his head nor adornment of any kind other than his blond curly hair, which resembled golden ringlets. The governor, major-domo, and butler then took the youth to one side and, being out of earshot of his sister, asked him why he had donned that disguise. He was no less ashamed and embarrassed than the young woman had been and told the same story they had heard from her, much to the delight of the enamored butler.

"Young lady and gentleman," the governor said to them, "this was certainly a very childish thing to do, and there was no occasion for all those tears and sighs in telling us of so rash an escapade. All you needed to say was, 'We are So-and-So and So-and-So, and we wandered away from our parents' home merely out of curiosity and with no other purpose in view.' Your story could have ended then and there, without all this weeping and wailing and carrying-on."

"That is so," replied the maiden, "but your Worships must realize that I was so excited I was unable to control myself."

"There is no harm done," said Sancho. "Come, we will take you back to your father's house, and it may be that he will not have noticed your absence. After this, do not be such children or so anxious to see the world; for the respected damsel has a broken leg and stays at home,[17] a woman and a hen by gadding about are soon lost,[18] and she who is eager to see is also anxious to be seen.[19] I say no more."

The young man thanked the governor for the favor of escorting them to their home, which was not far away, and they all set out. When they arrived there the lad threw a pebble against a grating, and in a

moment a woman servant who was waiting for them came down and let
the pair in. All the members of the governor's party were astonished at
the grace and beauty of the two young people and marveled at their
desire to see the world by night without, however, going beyond the
confines of the town. All this they attributed to their extreme youth.

As for the butler, his heart was transfixed, and he at once resolved
that he would ask the girl's father for her hand in marriage the very
next day, feeling certain that he would not meet with a refusal, in view
of the fact that he was a servant of the duke. And Sancho for his part
began forming plans for marrying the young man to his daughter,
Sanchica, and determined to carry out his scheme in due season, since,
he reflected, no prospective husband would decline a governor's daughter.

With this, their rounds for that night came to an end, and two days
later the government as well, all the governor's plans being overthrown
and swept away, as will be seen further on.

CHAPTER L. *Wherein is set forth who the
enchanters and executioners were who spanked the
duenna and pinched and scratched Don Quixote, together with what happened to the page who carried
the letter to Teresa Panza,*[1] *Sancho Panza's wife.*

CID HAMETE, that most painstaking investigator of the minute
details of this true history, tells us that as Doña Rodríguez left her own
apartment to go to Don Quixote's, another matron who was her room-
mate observed her movements; and inasmuch as all duennas are eager
to know, hear, and smell out things, this one proceeded to follow her
so quietly that the worthy Rodríguez was unaware of the fact. As soon
as the second duenna saw the first one enter the guest's chamber, true
to the tattling character of her kind she at once hastened to inform my
lady the duchess that Doña Rodríguez and the knight were closeted to-

gether, and the duchess in turn told the duke, begging his permission
to go with Altisidora and find out what it was her serving woman
wanted of Don Quixote.

The duke gave his consent, and the two women then tiptoed along
very cautiously to the door of the knight's room and took up a position near by where they could hear all that was said. As the duchess
listened to Doña Rodríguez making public property of her mistress's
ailments,[2] she was unable to bear it, and Altisidora felt the same way
about it, and so, filled with rage and thirsting for vengeance, they burst
into the chamber, where they spanked the duenna and punished Don
Quixote in the manner that has already been described; for insults
offered to the beauty and pretensions of women invariably arouse in
them a mighty wrath and kindle a passion for revenge. The duchess
gave an account of the affair to the duke, who was very much amused
by it; and then by way of continuing the jest and having still further
sport with the knight, she summoned the page who had impersonated
Dulcinea in the little comedy having to do with that lady's disenchantment—a matter which Sancho had entirely forgotten, being so busy
with his government. The page was now dispatched to Teresa Panza,
Sancho's wife, with her husband's letter and another which the duchess
had written, and with a large string of valuable coral beads as a present.[3]

The history goes on to say that the page was very keen-witted and
anxious to be of service to his lord and lady, and that he set out right
willingly for Sancho's village. Just before entering it he saw a number
of women washing clothes in a brook,[4] and, going up to them, he inquired if they could tell him whether or not a woman by the name of
Teresa Panza lived there, wife of one Sancho Panza, squire to a knight
known as Don Quixote de la Mancha. In response to this question, a
young lass stood up.

"Teresa Panza is my mother," she said, "the Sancho you speak of is
my father, and that knight is our master."

"Come, then, young lady," said the page, "and take me to your
mother; for I bring a letter and a present from your father."

"That I will gladly do, my good sir," replied the girl, who appeared
to be around fourteen years of age. Leaving the clothes that she was
washing with one of her companions and without putting anything on
her head or feet, for she was barelegged and her hair was hanging down,
she leaped in front of the page's mount and said, "Come with me, your
Grace. Our house is on the edge of the village and my mother is there,

very much worried because she has had no news of my father for a long time."

"Well," said the page, "I am bringing her some, and such good news that she may well thank God for it."

With the girl leaping, running, and skipping, they reached the village, but before going into the house she called from the doorway, "Come out, Mother Teresa, come out, come out; here is a gentleman with letters and other things from my father."

At these words Teresa Panza appeared, spinning a bundle of flax. She was clad in a gray skirt so short that it seemed they had "cut it to her shame," [5] with a bodice of the same color and a chemise. She was not so very old, although she was obviously past forty; but she was strong of body, robust and vigorous, with a nutbrown complexion.

"What is it, daughter? Who is this gentleman?" she asked as she saw the page on horseback.

"A servant of my lady Doña Teresa Panza," replied the page. With this, he dismounted and went to kneel before Teresa with great humility. "Give me your hands, my lady Doña Teresa," he said, "as the lawful wedded wife of Señor Don Sancho Panza, rightful governor of the island of Barataria."

"Ah, my good sir," she said, "be off with you. Don't do that; for I am no palace lady but a poor peasant woman, daughter of a clodhopper and wife of a squire-errant and not of any governor."

"Your Grace," the page insisted, "is the most worthy wife of an arch-worthy governor, as proof of which I hand your Grace this letter and this present." And he forthwith took out of his pocket a string of coral beads with golden clasps.

"This letter," he said, placing the beads about her neck, "is from my Lord Governor and the other one and the necklace are from my lady the duchess, who has sent me to you."

Teresa was quite overcome by it all, and her daughter as well. "May they slay me," said the lass, "if our master Don Quixote is not at the bottom of this; he must have given father that government or earldom that he promised him so many times."

"That is right," said the page. "Thanks to Señor Don Quixote, Señor Sancho is now governor of the island of Barataria, as you will see from this letter."

"Read it for me, noble sir," said Teresa, "for although I know how to spin, I cannot read a mite."

"Nor I," added Sanchica; "but wait here a moment and I will go call someone who will read it for us, even though it be the curate himself or the bachelor, Sansón Carrasco. They will be very glad to come and hear news of my father."

"There is no need to call anyone," said the page. "I may not know how to spin, but I can read, and I will tell you what it says." He proceeded to do so, reading Sancho's letter in its entirety, which, since it has already been given in these pages, need not be set down here again. Then he took out the other one, from the duchess, the contents of which were as follows:

Friend Teresa: Your husband Sancho's sterling qualities, his upright character, and his ability have made me feel impelled to ask my own husband, the duke, to give him an island out of the many in my lord's possession. I have received word that he, Sancho, is governing like a gerfalcon,[6] a thing which I am very glad to hear, and my lord, the duke, also. I thank Heaven most heartily that I made no mistake in choosing him for such a post; for I would have my lady Teresa know that it is extremely hard to find a good governor in this world, but God grant that I do as well as Sancho is doing now.

I send you herewith, my dear, a string of coral beads with gold clasps, and could only wish that they were oriental pearls. However, he who gives you a bone would not see you dead.[7] The time will come when we shall meet and become acquainted, but God only knows what is to be. Remember me to Sanchica, your daughter, and tell her for me that she should hold herself in readiness, for I mean to make a good match for her when she least expects it.

They tell me that in your village you have some large acorns. Send me a couple of dozen or so of them and I shall prize them greatly as coming from you. Write me at length, telling me of your health and how you are doing; and if you stand in need of anything, you have but to open your mouth and you shall have your wish.[8]

From this place. Your loving friend,

THE DUCHESS.

"Ah!" exclaimed Teresa when she had heard the letter, "and what a kind lady it is, how plain and humble! Let me be buried with [9] such ladies as that and not with the *hidalgas* you find in this town, who think that because they are ladies the wind should not touch them, who when they go to church put on as many airs as if they were queens, and who think that they are disgraced if they so much as look at a countrywoman. You can see how goodhearted she is. For all that she's a duchess, she calls me her friend and treats me like an equal—and may I see her equal to the tallest belfry in La Mancha!

"As for the acorns, my good sir, I will send her ladyship a peck [10] of them, and such big ones that people well may come to see them as a show and wonder at them. And now, for the present, Sanchica, entertain this gentleman, look after his horse, get some eggs from the stable, slice plenty of bacon, and give him a meal fit for a prince; [11] for the good news he brings and the good face on him deserve the best there is. In the meanwhile, I'll run out and tell the neighbor women about our good luck, and the father curate and Master Nicholas the barber, for they always have been such good friends of your father's."

"I will do as you say, mother," said Sanchica, "but you must give me half of that string of beads; for I don't think my lady the duchess would have been so stupid as to send them all to you."

"They are all for you, daughter," replied Teresa, "but let me wear them around my neck for a few days, for it seems as if they really gladdened my heart."

"You will be glad, too," said the page, "when you see the bundle that is in this portmanteau; for it contains a suit of the finest cloth, which the governor wore only one day to the hunt and which he now sends to Señora Sanchica."

"May he live a thousand years," said Sanchica, "and the one who brings it no less, and even two thousand if needs be."

Teresa then left the house with the letters and with the beads about her neck, strumming upon the former with her fingers as if they had been a tambourine. Falling in by chance with the curate and Sansón Carrasco, she began doing a dance as she cried, "Faith, and we are no poor relations now! We've got a little government! Let the finest lady there is meddle with me and I'll set her down as an upstart!"

"What's all this, Teresa Panza? Why are you acting like mad, and what papers are those you have there?"

"Those are letters from duchesses and governors, if you call that madness, and these beads that I have about my neck are of finest coral, with Ave Marias and Pater Nosters of beaten gold, and I am a governor's wife!"

"God help us, Teresa, but we don't understand you. We can't make out what you are talking about."

"There, see for yourselves," she said, and handed them the letters. The curate read them aloud as Sansón Carrasco listened, and the two of them then gazed at each other as if dumfounded. The bachelor asked who had brought the letters, and she replied by saying that they should come home with her and meet the messenger, a young man fine as gold [12] who had brought her another present worth even more than this one. The curate took the beads from her neck and looked at them again and again, and, having made sure that they were really valuable, he was more astonished than ever.

"By the habit that I wear," he declared, "I do not know what to say or think about these letters and presents. On the one hand, I can perceive by touching them the fineness of these coral beads, and, on the other hand, I read here that a duchess is sending to ask for two dozen acorns."

"Make sense out of that for me if you can," said Carrasco. "But come along, let's go see the one who brought this letter; he may be able to throw some light upon the mystery."

They did so, and Teresa returned with them. They found the page sifting a little barley for his horse and Sanchica cutting a slice of bacon to be fried with the eggs for the page's dinner. Both of them were pleased by the young man's bearing and fine apparel, and after a courteous exchange of greetings Sansón requested him to give them what news he had of Don Quixote, and of Sancho Panza as well. He added that they had read the letters from Sancho and my lady the duchess but were still puzzled, being unable to make out what was meant by Sancho's government, especially the reference to an island, seeing that all or most of the islands in the Mediterranean belonged to his Majesty.

"As to Señor Sancho Panza's being a governor," replied the page, "there can be no doubt. As to whether his government consists of an island or not, is no concern of mine. It is sufficient to state that it is a town of more than a thousand inhabitants. With regard to the acorns, I may say that my lady the duchess is so modest and unassuming that she not only would ask a peasant woman for such a gift as that, but has even been known to send to a neighbor of hers to ask for the loan of a comb. For I would have your Worships know that the ladies of Aragon, however highborn they may be, are not so haughty and punctilious as are those of Castile, and are in the habit of treating people with greater informality."

In the midst of their conversation Sanchica came out, her skirt filled with eggs.

"Tell me, sir," she asked of the page, "does my father by any chance wear trunk-hose since he became a governor?"

"I never noticed, but I imagine so."

"Oh, my God! What a sight it must be, my father in tights! Isn't it strange, ever since I was born I have wanted to see him dressed like that?"

"As things are going now," replied the page, "you will see it if you live long enough. By God, if his government lasts him two more months, he'll be going about in a traveler's hood." [13]

It was plain to the curate and the bachelor that the page was speaking in jest, but the fine quality of the beads and of the hunting suit that Sancho had sent (Teresa had already shown them the garment) seemed to contradict this impression. Meanwhile, they had a good laugh over the wish that Sanchica had expressed, and they laughed still more as Teresa went on to say, "Señor Curate, I wish you would find out if there is anyone going to Madrid or Toledo who could buy me a hoop skirt, the best there is and in the latest fashion; for I certainly mean to be as much of an honor as I can to my husband in his government, that I do, and if I get my pride up I intend to go to court and set up a coach like all the other ladies, for she who is the wife of a governor may very well keep one."

"And why shouldn't you, mother!" cried Sanchica. "Would to God it was today instead of tomorrow, even though they said, when they saw me seated in the coach with my mother, 'Just look at that little nobody, that garlic-eater's daughter, how she rides around at her ease as if she were a female pope!' But let them tramp in the mud and let me go in my carriage, with my feet off the ground. Bad luck[14] to all the gossips in the world. So long as I go warm, let the people laugh! [15] Am I right, mother?"

"Indeed you are, my daughter," replied Teresa. "My good Sancho prophesied all this luck and even better, and you'll see, my child, I'll not stop until I've become a countess. For luck is all in the way you begin; as I've heard your father say many times—and he's the father of proverbs as well—when they offer you a heifer, run with the halter,[16] and when they offer you a government, take it; when they give you an earldom, grab it, and when they say *tus, tus* [17] to you with some nice present, snap at it. It would be just as if you were to go on sleeping and not answer when fortune and good luck stand knocking at the door of your house!"

"And what do I care," added Sanchica, "if somebody or other says, when they see me holding my head up like a fine lady, 'The dog saw himself in hempen breeches,' [18] and so forth?"

Listening to this, the curate was led to remark, "I cannot help believing that every member of the Panza family was born with a bagful of proverbs inside him; I never saw one that did not spill them at all hours and on every occasion."

"That is the truth," said the page, "for the Lord Governor Sancho goes around quoting them at every turn, and even though they may not be to the point, they are very amusing, and my lady the duchess and the duke praise them highly."

"Then, my dear sir," said the bachelor, "you still maintain, do you, that all this about Sancho's government is the truth, and that there really is a duchess in this world who sends him presents and writes to him? As for us, we have handled the presents and read the letters, but still are not convinced and are inclined to think, rather, that this is something that has to do with our fellow townsman Don Quixote. He believes that everything is done by enchantment; and I might say that I should like to touch and feel your Grace to see if you are a ghostly ambassador or a flesh-and-blood being."

"Gentlemen," replied the page, "with regard to myself I only know that I am a real messenger and that Señor Sancho Panza is indeed a governor; I know that my lord and lady, the duke and duchess, are in a position to give, and have given him this government, and I have heard that the same Sancho Panza is deporting himself in it most valiantly. As to whether or not there is any enchantment in it, that is something for your Worships to argue. I swear by my parents, who are still living and whom I dearly love, that this is all I know about it."

"It may very well be," said the bachelor, "but *dubitat Augustinus*." [19]

"Let him doubt who will," said the page. "The truth is as I have told it to you, and truth always rises above a lie as oil above water. [20] *Operibus credite, et non verbis;* [21] let one of you come with me, and he shall see with his own eyes what he will not believe with his ears."

"I am the one who should make that journey," said Sanchica. "Take me with you, sir, on the crupper of your hack; I'll be very glad to go see my father."

"Governors' daughters," replied the page, "do not travel the highways alone, but only when escorted by carriages and litters and a large number of servants."

"In God's name," said Sanchica, "I can go just as well mounted on a she-ass as in a coach! What a dainty creature you must think I am!"

"Be quiet, girl," said Teresa, "you don't know what you are saying. This gentleman is quite right. Different times, different manners. [22] When my husband was Sancho, I was Sancha; and now that he's a governor, I am Señora—I don't know if there is anything in what I am saying or not."

"Señora Teresa is saying more than she realizes," remarked the page; "but give me something to eat and let me be on my way, for I intend to return this evening."

"Your Grace," said the curate, "will partake of my frugal fare; [23] for Señora Teresa is more willing than able when it comes to serving such a guest as you."

The page at first declined, but finally had to yield for the sake of his own well-being; and the curate then gladly bore him off in order that he might question him at length regarding Don Quixote and his exploits. The bachelor offered to write the replies for Teresa to the letters she had received, but she would not have him meddling in her affairs, since she looked upon him as being something of a practical joker. Instead, she gave a cake and a couple of eggs to a young acolyte, who copied out two epistles for her, one addressed to her husband and the other to the duchess, which she herself had composed and which are not the worst to be met with in this great history, as will be seen further on.

CHAPTER LI. *Of the course of Sancho Panza's government, with other entertaining matters of a similar nature.*

DAY dawned following the night on which the governor had made his rounds. That night had been a sleepless one for the butler, his mind being occupied with the beautiful face and general attractiveness of the disguised maiden. As for the major-domo, he had spent the remaining hours until daylight in writing to his lord and lady, giving them an account of all that Sancho had done and said, for he was equally astonished by the governor's actions and by his speech, finding in both an admixture of wisdom and simple-mindedness.

The lord governor finally arose and, on orders of Doctor Pedro Recio, made a breakfast on a bit of preserves and four draughts of cold water, though he would rather have had a slice of bread and a cluster of grapes. However, seeing there was no help for it, he made the best of things, with sorrowing heart and a weary stomach, Pedro Recio having given him to understand that a light diet of dainty food was the one best suited to individuals in positions of command and in offices entailing grave responsibility where one had need not so much of bodily strength as of mental faculties. As a result of this sophistry, Sancho suffered hunger to such an extent that in his heart he was led to curse the government and the one who had bestowed it upon him.

Nevertheless, in spite of his hunger and fortified only by the preserves he had eaten, he undertook to sit in judgment that day; and the first matter that came before him was a problem [1] propounded by a foreigner in the presence of the major-domo and the other attendants.

"My lord," he began, "there was a large river that separated two districts of one and the same seignorial domain—and let your Grace pay attention, for the matter is an important one and somewhat difficult of solution. To continue then: Over this river there was a bridge, and at one end of it stood a gallows with what resembled a court of justice, where four judges commonly sat to see to the enforcement of a law decreed by the lord of the river, of the bridge, and of the seignory. That law was the following: 'Anyone who crosses this river shall first take oath as to whither he is bound and why. If he swears to the truth, he shall be permitted to pass; but if he tells a falsehood, he shall die without hope of pardon on the gallows that has been set up there.' Once this law and the rigorous conditions it laid down had been promulgated, there were many who told the truth and whom the judges permitted to pass freely enough. And then it happened that one day, when they came to administer the oath to a certain man, he swore and affirmed that his destination was to die upon the gallows which they had erected and that he had no other purpose in view.

"The judges held a consultation. 'If,' they said, 'we let this man pass, without hindrance, then he has perjured himself and according to the law should be put to death; but he swore that he came to die upon that scaffold, and if we hang him that will have been the truth, and in accordance with the same law he should go free.' [2] And now, my Lord Governor, we should like to have your Grace's opinion as to what the judges should do with the man; for up to now they have been very doubtful and perplexed, and, having heard of your Grace's keen understanding and great intellect, they have sent me to beseech your Grace on their behalf to tell them what you think regarding this intricate and puzzling question."

"Certainly," said Sancho, "those judges who sent you to me might have spared themselves the trouble, for I am a fellow who has in him more of the dull than of the sharp; but, nevertheless, let me hear the case once more and it may be that I'll hit upon something."

The one who had propounded the question then repeated it over and over again.

"It seems to me," said Sancho at last, "that I can settle the matter very shortly. This man swore that he was going to die upon the gallows, and if he does, he swore to the truth and the law says he should be freed and permitted to cross the bridge; but if they do not hang him, he swore falsely and according to the same law ought to be hanged."

"My Lord Governor has stated it correctly," said the messenger; "so far as a complete understanding of the case is concerned, there is no room for any further doubt or questioning."

"Well, then," said Sancho, "my opinion is this: that part of the man that swore to the truth should be permitted to pass and that part of him that lied should be hanged, and thus the letter of the law will be carried out."

"But, my Lord Governor," replied the one who had put the question, "it would be necessary to divide the man into two halves, the lying half and the truthful half, and if he were so divided it would kill him and the law would in no wise be fulfilled, whereas it is essential that its express provisions be carried out."

"See here, my good sir," said Sancho, "either I am a blockhead or this man you speak of deserves to die as much as he deserves to live and cross the bridge; for if the truth saves him, the lie equally condemns him. And this being the case, as indeed it is, it is my opinion that you should go back and tell those gentlemen who sent you to me that, since there is as much reason for acquitting as for condemning him, they ought to let him go free, as it is always more praiseworthy to do good than to do harm. I would give you this decision over my signature if I knew how to sign my name;[3] and in saying what I do I am not speaking on my own account but am remembering one of the many pieces of advice which my master Don Quixote gave me the night before I came here to be governor of this island. When justice was in doubt, he said, I was to lean to the side of mercy; and I thank God that I happened to recollect it just now, for it fits this case as if made for it."

"So it does," agreed the major-domo, "and it is my belief that Lycurgus himself, who gave laws to the Lacedaemonians, could not have handed down a better decision than that which our great Panza has rendered us. Court is now over for this morning," he added, "and I will give orders that my Lord Governor be served a meal that is very much to his taste."

"That is all I ask," said Sancho, "that you be fair with me. See to it that I eat, and then let it rain cases and problems and I'll make quick work of them." [4]

The major-domo kept his word, it being against his conscience to starve to death so wise a governor as this; and, in any event, he expected to have done with him that night by playing the final joke upon him in accordance with the instructions of his lord and lady. Accordingly, after Sancho had eaten for once in violation of all the rules and aphorisms of the Doctor Tirteafuera, as soon as the cloth had been removed a messenger entered with a letter from Don Quixote addressed to the governor. Sancho ordered the secretary to cast an eye over it and, if it contained nothing that should be kept secret, to read it aloud.

The secretary obeyed. "It may very well be read aloud," he said after he had glanced at it, "for what Señor Don Quixote has here written to your Grace deserves to be engraved in letters of gold. You shall hear for yourself:

LETTER OF DON QUIXOTE DE LA MANCHA TO SANCHO PANZA,
GOVERNOR OF THE ISLAND OF BARATARIA

Whereas, friend Sancho, I had expected to hear news of your indolence and follies, I hear, instead, of the wisdom you have displayed, and for this I give special thanks to Heaven, which raises the poor up from the dungheap [5] and makes wise men out of fools. They tell me that you govern like a man, but that as a man you are as humble as any beast of the field. In this connection, I would have you note, Sancho, that it very often behooves those in positions of authority to resist the natural humility of their hearts, and it is indeed necessary for them to do so; for the attire of one who is in a post of grave responsibility should be conformable to his station and not limited by his own humble tastes. Dress well; a stick properly clothed no longer has the appearance of a stick. [6] By this I do not mean that you should deck yourself out with trinkets and showy raiment, or that, being a judge, you should dress like a soldier; rather, the garb should be suited to the office, provided always that it is neat and well made.

In order to win the good will of the people that you govern, there are two things, among others, that you must do: one is to act in a well-bred manner toward every one (this I have told you before); and the other is to see that there is an abundance of food, since nothing weighs more heavily upon the hearts of the poor than hunger and want.

Do not issue many decrees, and when you do, see to it that they are good ones and, above all, that they are observed and fulfilled, for decrees that are not observed are as none at all but, rather, convey the impression that the prince who had the wisdom and authority requisite for issuing them has not had the power to enforce them, and laws that merely hold a threat without being put into execution are like the log that was king of the frogs: at first he frightened them, but in time they came to despise him and mounted upon him.[7]

Be a father to virtue and a stepfather to vice. Be not always strict nor always lenient but observe a middle course between these two extremes, for therein lies wisdom. Visit the prisons, slaughter houses, and public squares, for the presence of the governor in such places is a matter of great importance: it comforts the prisoners, who hope to be speedily released; it is a bugbear to the butchers, who for once give fair weight; and it terrifies the market women for the same reason. Do not show yourself, even though perchance you may be (and I do not think you are) either covetous, a woman-chaser, or a glutton; for when the people and those with whom you have to deal come to know your weakness, they will train their batteries upon you at that point until they have brought you down to the depths of perdition.

Go over time and again, consider and reconsider, the advice and instructions that I gave you in writing before you set out from here for your government; if you follow these counsels you will find in them a ready aid in those labors and difficulties that governors encounter at every turn. Write to your lord and lady by way of showing them that you are grateful; for ingratitude is the daughter of pride and one of the greatest of known sins, and the person who is ungrateful to his benefactors shows clearly that he would be ungrateful to God as well, who has conferred and continues to confer so many blessings upon him.

My lady the duchess sent a special messenger with your suit and another present to your wife, Teresa Panza, and we are expecting an answer at any moment. I have been a trifle indisposed as the result of a certain scratching that was of no great benefit to my nose, but it was in reality nothing at all. If there are enchanters who mistreat me, there are also those that defend me. Let me know as to whether the major-domo who is with you had anything to do with the business of La Trifaldi as you suspected. Keep me informed of everything that happens to you, since the distance is so short and, moreover, I am thinking of giving up very soon this idle life that I lead here, as I was not born for it. I have been asked to undertake a certain business that may bring me into disfavor with my lord and lady; but although this gives me no little concern, it really means nothing to me, for, when all is said and done, I must fulfill the duties of my profession rather than think of their pleasure, in accordance with the saying, "*Amicus Plato, sed magis amica veritas.*" [8] If I quote Latin to you, it is because I assume that since becoming a governor you will have learned it. I commend you to God, and may He keep you from becoming an object of pity to anyone.

Your friend,

DON QUIXOTE DE LA MANCHA.

Sancho listened to the letter very attentively, and it was praised by all who heard it for the wisdom it contained. The governor then rose from the table and, summoning his secretary, shut himself up in his room, for he wished to answer his master Don Quixote without delay. He instructed the secretary to write down what was dictated to him, without adding anything to it or leaving out anything, and the following is the letter that he composed:

I have been so very busy that I have not had time to scratch my head or even trim my nails, which is the reason why I wear them so long, God help me. I tell you this, my dear master, so that your Grace may not be surprised that I have not let you know sooner how well or ill I am making out in this government, where I am suffering more hunger than the two of us did when we roamed the forests and desert places together.

My lord the duke wrote to me the other day, advising me that certain spies had come to my island to assassinate me, but up to now the only one I have discovered is a doctor in this town who is hired to kill all the governors that come here. He is Doctor Pedro Recio, a native of Tirteafuera, and from his name [9] your Grace may judge as to whether or not I have reason to fear dying at his hands. This doctor that I am telling you about says that he himself does not cure diseases when they come but aims to prevent them from coming, and the medicine that he gives you is diet and more diet until he has you down to your bare bones—just as if leanness wasn't worse than fever. The short of it is, he is starving me to death and I'm dying of disappointment; for when I came here as governor, I expected to have my meals hot and my drinks cool and to sleep in comfort between sheets of Holland linen, on feather beds, and instead I find that I have to do penance like a hermit. I do not like it at all, and in the end I imagine the devil will take me.

So far, I have not laid hands on any dues or accepted any bribes,[10] and I do not know what to think of it; for they tell me that the governors who come to this island usually have plenty of money which has been given them or lent them by the people of the town, and I understand that this is the custom not only here but with governors in general.

Last night, in making the rounds, I fell in with a very pretty girl dressed like a boy, in the company of her brother who was in woman's clothes. My butler has fallen in love with the lass and has his mind set on having her for his wife, or so he says, and I have picked the lad for my son-in-law. Today we are going to take the matter up with the father of the pair, who is a certain Diego de la Llana, an old Christian and as fine a gentleman as anyone could wish.

I am in the habit of visiting the market places as your Grace recommends, and yesterday I came upon a hucksteress selling hazelnuts and found that she had mixed with a fanega [11] of fresh ones an equal measure of empty, rotten nuts. I confiscated them all for the charity school children, who know well enough how to tell one kind from the other, and sentenced her to stay away from the market place for a couple of weeks. My action was heartily approved; for I may tell your Grace that there is no one in this town with a worse reputation than these market women; they are all said to be bold and shameless creatures without a conscience, and I can well believe it from what I have seen of them in other places.[12]

I am very glad to hear that my lady the duchess has written to my wife, Teresa Panza, and has sent her the present, and I will try to show my gratitude at the proper time. I would have your Grace kiss her hands for me and tell her that she has not thrown me into any sack with a hole in it, as she will see from the outcome. I hope your Grace will not have any quarrel with my lord and lady, for if you fall out with them, it is plain to be seen that it will do me harm. And it would be contrary to the advice you yourself have given me for you to be ungrateful to those who have shown you so many favors and have treated you so royally in their castle.

That business of the scratching I do not understand, but I imagine it must be the work of those wicked enchanters that are always tormenting your Grace, and I'll hear all about it when we meet again. I'd like to send your Grace some present or other, but I don't know what it would be unless it was some of those very curious clyster pipes to be worked with bladders that they make in this island. However, if my office holds out, I'll try to send you something, one way or another.[13] If my wife, Teresa Panza, should write to me, please pay the postage and send the letter on to me, as I am very anxious to hear how my wife and young ones are doing at home. And so, may God free your Grace from those evil-minded enchanters and see me through with my government, safe and sound—though this I am inclined to doubt, for I think I'll rather leave it and my life behind me at one and the same time, the way Doctor Pedro Recio is treating me.

Your Grace's servant,

SANCHO PANZA, THE GOVERNOR.

The secretary sealed the letter and dispatched it by courier at once; and then the practical jokers put their heads together and began planning how they would dispatch Sancho from his governorship. That afternoon was spent by him in drawing up a number of ordinances for the proper administration of what he took to be his island. He decreed that there were to be no peddlers of provisions in the state, and that wine might be imported from any region whatever so long as its place of origin was declared in order that a price might be put upon it according to its reputation for quality and the esteem in which it was held, while anyone who watered wine or put a false name on it was to pay for it with his life. He reduced the cost of all shoes and stockings, but especially of shoes, as it seemed to him that the prices being charged for them were exorbitant. He put a tax on servants' wages, which were out of all proportion to the service rendered.[14] He prescribed an extremely heavy fine for those who sang lewd and lascivious songs, either by night or by day, and ordained that no blind man should go about singing verses [15] having to do with miracles unless he could produce trustworthy evidence that the miracles had actually occurred; for it was his opinion that most of the events that formed the burden of their lays were trumped up, to the detriment of the truly miraculous ones.[16]

He created and appointed a bailiff for the poor, not for the purpose of harassing them but to make an investigation of their real status, since many a thief or drunkard of sound body goes about as a make-believe cripple or displaying false sores. In brief, he ordered things so wisely that to this day his decrees are preserved in that town, under the title of *The Constitutions of the Great Governor, Sancho Panza.*

CHAPTER LII. *Wherein is related the adventure of the second distressed, or afflicted, duenna, otherwise known as Doña Rodríguez.*

CID HAMETE tells us that, being now healed of his scratches, Don Quixote came to the conclusion that the life he was leading in that castle was wholly contrary to the order of chivalry that he professed; and he accordingly resolved to ask permission of the duke and duchess to set out for Saragossa, where the festival was near at hand in which he hoped to win the suit of armor that was the prize in such tournaments. He was sitting at table with the ducal pair one day and was just about to carry out his intention and beg their leave when all of a sudden there came through the doorway two women (as they afterward turned out to be), clad in mourning from head to foot. Going over to Don Quixote, one of them threw herself full-length at his feet, pressing her lips to them and uttering moans so deep, so sad, and so heart-rending as to throw all those who heard and beheld her into a state of confusion.

Although the duke and duchess thought that this must be some joke which their servants were playing on the knight, they nonetheless were puzzled and uncertain as they saw how earnestly the woman sighed, moaned, and wept. Finally, taking pity upon her, Don Quixote raised her up and made her remove the veil and mantle that covered her weeping face. As she did so, she revealed—something they had never expected to see!—the countenance of Doña Rodríguez, the duenna of the household, while the other lady in mourning proved to be her daughter, the one who had been deceived by the rich farmer's son. All who knew the duenna were astonished, and my lord and lady more than any, for, although they looked upon her as a weak and pliant creature, they had not thought her capable of acts of madness. At length she turned to her master and mistress and addressed them.

"Will your Excellencies," she said, "be so kind as to permit me a word with this knight, seeing that it is necessary if I am to get myself well out of a predicament in which the impudence of an evil-intentioned boor has placed me?"

The duke gave her the permission she sought, telling her that she might say whatever she liked; and she then fastened her gaze upon Don Quixote.

"Some time ago, O valiant knight," she said, "I gave you an account of the unjust and treacherous manner in which a certain heartless peasant had treated my dearly beloved daughter, the unfortunate maid who stands here before you now, and you promised me at that time that you would espouse her cause and right the wrong that had been done her. But now word has reached me that you are planning to leave this castle in search of such adventures as God may fittingly provide, and ere you take to the road I would beg of you to challenge this impudent yokel and compel him to marry my daughter, for before they first came together he promised her that he would make her his wife. To expect my lord the duke to see justice done is to ask pears of the elm tree,[1] due to reasons which I have already set forth to your Grace in private. And now, may God grant you health, and as for us, may He not forsake us."

To this speech Don Quixote replied with a grave and solemn demeanor. "Worthy duenna," he said, "moderate your tears, or better, dry them up and spare those sighs as well; for I am taking it upon myself to redress the wrong that has been done your daughter, who would have been better off if she had not been so ready to believe the promises of lovers, promises that are lightly made but extremely burdensome when it comes to fulfilling them. With the permission of my lord the duke, I will set out at once in search of this unfeeling youth; I will find and challenge him, and, if he refuses to keep his word, I will surely slay him. The principal object of my calling is to spare the humble and chastise the haughty, to succor the wretched and destroy the oppressor."

"Your Grace," said the duke, "need not go to the trouble of seeking out this rustic of whom the worthy duenna is complaining, nor need you ask my permission to challenge him; I accept the challenge in his behalf and will see that he is duly informed of the fact and that he comes here, to this my castle, to answer and accept in person. I will afford you both fair play, observing all the customary and rightful conditions and seeing that justice is done to each as is the duty of all those princes who offer an open field to combatants who come to fight within the bounds of their dominions."

"Very well," replied Don Quixote, "with this assurance and with your Highness's kind permission, I declare that from now on I renounce my status as a gentleman in order to put myself upon a level with the lowborn culprit and make it possible for him as my equal to do battle with me. And even though he be absent, I hereby challenge and defy him by reason of the wrong that he has done in deceiving this poor maiden, who was a virgin and now, through his fault, no longer is. I maintain that he has either to keep the promise that he gave her or die on the field of combat."

With this, he drew off one of his gloves and threw it down in the middle of the room. The duke at once picked it up, saying again that he accepted the challenge in the name of his vassal. He then fixed the time for the duel at six days hence, the place to be the courtyard of the castle and the weapons those customarily employed by knights: the lance and buckler and coat of mail and all the other accessories, without any trickery, cheating, or charms of any sort,[2] the said weapons and armor to be viewed and passed upon by the judges of the contest.

"But first of all," he added, "it is necessary that this worthy duenna and this unfortunate maiden place their cause entirely in the hands of Don Quixote, for otherwise there is nothing to be done and the challenge cannot be put into effect."

"I hereby do so," said the duenna.

"I, too," said the daughter, who was all in tears and very much ashamed of her sorry plight.

These arrangements having been made and the duke having determined what was to be done in the matter, the pair in mourning took their leave; and the duchess gave orders that from then on they were to be treated not as her servants but as ladies in trouble who had come to her house to seek justice. They were, accordingly, given a room apart and were waited upon as if they had been strangers, to the considerable astonishment of the other servants, who wondered where the folly and impudence of Doña Rodríguez and her ill-errant daughter [3] would stop.

At this point, by way of adding the finishing touch to the meal and bringing it to a pleasant close, lo and behold, that same page who had carried the letters and presents to Teresa Panza, wife of Sancho Panza, the governor, now entered the room. The duke and duchess were very glad to see him, being anxious to hear what had happened to him in the course of his journey; but in response to a question from them he replied that he could not make his report in the presence of so many people or in a few words, and so he suggested that they leave it for another time, when they would be alone, and in the meanwhile amuse themselves by listening to the letters that he had brought back with him. With this, he took out the two letters and handed them to the duchess. One of them bore the superscription: "Letter for My Lady the Duchess So-and-So, of I Don't Know Where," while the other was directed "To My Husband, Sancho Panza, Governor of the Island of Barataria, and May God Prosper Him Longer Than He Does Me."

The duchess's bread would not bake, as the saying goes, until she had read the one that was addressed to her. She opened it and glanced at its contents, and then, seeing that it was proper to do so, she read it aloud for the duke and the others to hear:

TERESA PANZA'S LETTER TO THE DUCHESS

The letter that your Highness wrote me, my lady, gave me great pleasure and was very welcome indeed.[4] The string of coral beads is very fine, and I can say the same of my husband's hunting suit. This whole village is happy to know that you have made my husband, Sancho, a governor, although nobody believes it, especially the curate, and Master Nicholas the barber, and Sansón Carrasco the bachelor; but that makes no difference to me, for so long as it is true, and I am sure that it is, they may all say what they like—to tell the truth, I would not have believed it myself if it had not been for the beads and the suit. In this town everybody thinks my husband is a numskull, fit only for governing a flock of goats, and cannot imagine what other kind of government he would be good for. May the Lord's will be done, and may God direct him in the right path for the best interests of his children.

I, my dear lady, with your Grace's permission, have made up my mind to take advantage of this fine day[5] by coming to court where I may stretch out in a coach and cause a thousand who are already jealous of me to burst their eyeballs. And so I beg your Excellency to order my husband to send me a little money, and let it be quite a little, for expenses are heavy at court, with a loaf of bread costing a real and meat thirty maravedis a pound,[6] which is really frightful. If he does not want me to come, have him let me know at once, for my feet are itching to be off. My women friends and neighbors tell me that if I and my daughter cut a figure and make a fine show at court, my husband will come to be better known on account of me than I will be on account of him. For, of course, there will be many who will ask, 'Who are those ladies in that coach yonder?' And one of my servants will answer, 'The wife and daughter of Sancho Panza, governor of the island of Barataria.' And that way, people will learn who Sancho is, I'll be well thought of, and to Rome for everything.[7]

I am sorry as sorry can be that this year they have gathered no acorns here, but for all of that I am sending your Highness about half a peck; I myself went to the woods to gather them, one by one, but I couldn't find any that were bigger than these—I only wish they were as big as ostrich eggs.

Don't forget to write to me, your Mightiness,[8] and I will be sure to answer, letting you know how I am and whatever news there is in this village, where I remain, praying Our Lord to keep your Highness and not be unmindful of me. My daughter Sancha and my son [9] kiss your Grace's hands.

She who would rather see your Ladyship than write to you,

Your servant,

TERESA PANZA.

They were all very much pleased with this letter, especially the ducal pair; and the duchess then asked Don Quixote if he thought it would be right to open the one addressed to the governor, as she fancied it must be a very good one. The knight replied that she might do so if it gave her pleasure, and they found that it read as follows:

TERESA PANZA'S LETTER TO SANCHO PANZA,
HER HUSBAND

I received your letter, my dear Sancho, and I swear as a Catholic Christian that I was within two fingers' breadth of going mad with joy. Listen, brother, when I heard you were a governor, I was so happy I thought I would drop dead; for you know what they say: that sudden joy can kill you just as well as a great sorrow. As for your daughter, Sanchica, she let her water go from pure delight. There before me was the suit that you sent me and the beads from my lady the duchess, for my neck, and there in my hand were the letters with the messenger standing beside me; and yet, in spite of all that, I fancied that what I saw and touched must be a dream, since who would ever think that a goatherd would come to be governor of islands?

But you know, my dear, what my mother used to say: that you had to live a long time to see a lot. I tell you this because I expect to see more if I live longer. I don't mean to stop until I see you a farmer of revenues or tax collector; for while the devil carries off those that abuse such offices,[10] still they always hold and handle money. My lady the duchess will tell you how anxious I am to come to court; think it over and let me know how you feel about it. I will try to be an honor to you by going in a coach.

The curate, the barber, the bachelor, and even the sacristan cannot believe that you are a governor and say it is all some kind of humbug or enchantment like everything that concerns your master, Don Quixote; and Sansón says they are coming to look for you as they mean to get that government out of your head and the madness out of Don Quixote's noddle, but I only laugh and look at my string of beads and go on planning the dress that I am going to make for our daughter out of your suit. I sent some acorns to my lady the duchess and wish they had been of gold. Send me a few strings of pearls if they have any in that island.

The news of this village is that Berrueca has married off her daughter to a good-for-nothing painter who came here looking for anything that offered. The council gave him an order to paint his Majesty's arms over the door of the town hall. His price was two ducats, which they paid him in advance; he worked for a week and at the end of that time had done nothing, saying that he could not bring himself to paint trifling things of that sort. He paid them back the money but got himself a wife by passing himself off as a good workman. The truth is, he has now laid down the brush and taken up the spade and goes to the field like a gentleman.

Pedro de Lobo's son has taken orders and the tonsure, with the intention of becoming a priest. Minguilla, Mingo Silvato's granddaughter found it out and is suing him for promise to marry her, and the evil tongues will have it that she is pregnant by him, although he stoutly denies it.

There are no olives this year, nor is there a drop of vinegar to be had in all the town. A company of soldiers passed this way, taking with them three village girls; I would rather not tell you who they are, for it may be they will come back and will not fail to find those who will marry them with all their faults, for better or for worse. Sanchica is making bone-lace [11] and earns eight maravedis [12] a day, clear, which she puts into a money box toward household furnishings; but now that you are a governor, you will give her a dowry without her having to work. The fountain in the public square dried up and lightning struck the pillory (it would suit me if that was where it always hit).

I am waiting for an answer to this letter that I may know what you think about my coming to court. And so, may God give you a longer life than He does me, or at least as long a one since I would not want to leave you without me in this world.

Your wife,

TERESA PANZA.

These letters were praised, laughed over, relished, and admired; and then, as if to put the seal on everything, the courier arrived with the one that Sancho had written to Don Quixote. This also was read aloud and led them to doubt that the squire was as simple-minded as they had taken him to be. The duchess then retired that she might hear from the page what had happened in Sancho's village. He gave her a full account, leaving out no slightest detail, and delivered to her the acorns together with a cheese which Teresa assured him was very good, being better than those of Tronchón.[13] The duchess received it with great pleasure; and we shall leave her there as we go on to relate how the rule of the great Sancho Panza, flower and mirror of all island governors, came to an end.

CHAPTER LIII. *Of the troublous end and conclusion of Sancho Panza's government.*

TO IMAGINE that things in this life are always to remain as they are is to indulge in an idle dream. It would appear, rather, that everything moves in a circle, that is to say, around and around:[1] spring follows summer, summer the harvest season, harvest autumn, autumn winter, and winter spring;[2] and thus does time continue to turn like a never-ceasing wheel. Human life alone hastens onward to its end, swifter than time's self[3] and without hope of renewal, unless it be in that other life that has no bounds. So sayeth Cid Hamete, the Mohammedan phi-

losopher; for many who have lacked the light of faith, being guided
solely by the illumination that nature affords them, have yet attained
to a comprehension of the swiftness and instability of this present
existence and the eternal duration of the one we hope for. Our author,
however, is here thinking of the speed with which Sancho's government
was overthrown and brought to a close, and, so to speak, sent up in smoke
and shadow.

On the night of the seventh day after assuming his governorship
Sancho was lying in bed, sated not with bread or with wine but with
sitting in judgment, giving opinions, enacting statutes, and issuing decrees. In spite of his hunger, sleep was beginning to close his eyelids
when of a sudden he heard a great noise of bells and shouting as if the
whole island were sinking. He sat up in bed and strained his ears to
see if he could make out what the cause of such an uproar could be,
but in vain, for the sound of countless drums and trumpets was now
added to the din and he was more bewildered than ever and was filled
with fear and trembling. Getting to his feet, he put on a pair of slippers
on account of the dampness of the floor but did not stop for a dressing
gown or anything of the sort. As he dashed out the door of his room, he
saw coming toward him down the corridor more than a score of persons carrying lighted torches and unsheathed swords.

"To arms! To arms, Lord Governor!" they cried. "An enemy host
has invaded the island and we are lost unless your wit and valor can
save us." And, keeping up the furious din all the while, they came to
where Sancho stood, dazed and terrified by what he saw and heard.

"Arm at once, your Lordship," one of them said to him, "unless you
choose to be lost, and the whole island with you."

"What have I to do with arming?" replied Sancho. "Or what do I
know about fighting? [4] Better leave such things as that to my master
Don Quixote, who will settle everything in the blink of an eye and
save us all. Sinner that I am, God help me, I understand nothing about
these squabbles."

"Ah! my Lord Governor," said another, "what kind of faintheartd-
ness is this? Arm, your Grace; we bring you arms, both offensive and
defensive. Arm, and go out into the public square; be our leader and our
captain as is your duty, seeing that you are the governor."

"Arm me, then, for Heaven's sake," said Sancho.

They at once produced two large shields which they had brought
with them and put them on him over his shirt, one in front and the other
behind, permitting him to don no other garment. Through holes that

they had made for the purpose they drew his arms and then proceeded to bind him very firmly with pieces of rope in such a manner as to leave him walled in and boarded up straight as a spindle so that he could not bend his knees or stir a single step. They then handed him a lance, on which he leaned to keep from falling, and when they had him in this condition they bade him lead them on and inspire them all with courage, assuring him that he was their north pole, their lantern,[5] and their morning star who would bring this business to a successful conclusion.

"And how am I going to lead on, unlucky creature that I am," said Sancho, "when these boards that cut into my flesh are bound so tight I can't even move my kneecaps? What you are going to have to do is, pick me up in your arms and set me down, crosswise or on my feet, in some passageway, and I'll guarantee to hold it either with this lance or with my body."

"Come, my Lord Governor," said one of them, "it is fear rather than the boards that keeps you from moving. Have done with it and bestir yourself, for it is late and the enemy's numbers are increasing, the shouting grows louder, and the danger is pressing."

As a result of these exhortations and reproaches the poor governor did his best to move, whereupon he fell down to the floor with such a thud that they thought surely he must have broken himself to pieces. He lay there like a tortoise in its shell, or a side of bacon between two troughs, or a boat lying bottom upward on the beach; nor did the jokers feel any compassion for him as they saw him in that plight, but extinguishing their torches they began shouting louder than ever, renewing the cry "To arms! To arms!" with great vigor as they trampled over poor Sancho, slashing so furiously at the shields that covered him that, if he had not drawn his head in, the luckless governor would have been in a very bad way indeed. As it was, huddled into that narrow space, he sweat and sweat again as he prayed God with all his heart to deliver him from this peril. Some stumbled over him, others fell upon him, and one of them stood upon him for a good while, as if he had been in a watchtower issuing orders to an army.

"Over this way, our men!" he cried in a stentorian voice. "Here's where the enemy is charging in full force! Hold that breach! Close that gate! Block those ladders! [6] Bring on the pitch and resin and the boiling oil! Barricade the streets with feather beds!" In brief, he shouted most ardently for every variety of engine, implement, or contrivance that is used in war and in defending a city against an assault.

As he heard and suffered all this, Sancho, thoroughly mauled and trampled, said to himself, "Oh, if it would only please the Lord to let them go ahead and take this island and let me die or else free me from this torment!" Heaven granted his prayer, and when he least expected it there came a cry, "Victory! Victory! The enemy is beaten and is falling back! Ho, my Lord Governor, rise! Come and rejoice with us and divide the spoils won by the might of that invincible arm."

"Lift me up," said the sorely battered Sancho in a sickly voice. And when they had helped him to his feet, he went on, "The enemy that I have conquered you can nail to my forehead. I don't want to divide any spoils. All I ask is that some friend of mine, if I have any, give me a drink of wine, for I am parched; and let him wipe the sweat from me, as I am dripping wet." [7]

They wiped him off and brought him some wine, unbound the shields, and seated him upon the bed, and then he promptly fainted away as a result of all the fear and excitement and the harsh treatment he had undergone. Those who had perpetrated the joke were now sorry that they had carried it so far and they were relieved when Sancho came to himself again. He asked what time it was and was informed that it was already daylight; and then, without saying another word, he started dressing himself amid a profound silence as they all watched and waited to see why he should be in such a hurry to put his clothes on. At length, when he was fully clad, he little by little (for he was too stiff and sore to walk fast) made his way out to the stable, followed by all those present; and there he went up to the gray, embraced it, and gave it a kiss on the forehead, not without tears in his eyes.

"Come, comrade and friend," he said, "partner in all my troubles and hardships. When I was with you, I had no other care than that of mending your harness and feeding that little carcass of yours. Those for me were the happy hours, days, and years; but since leaving you and mounting the towers of ambition and pride, a thousand troubles, a thousand torments, and four thousand worries have entered my soul."

Even as he said this he was adjusting the packsaddle, without a word from any of the bystanders. He then with great pain and difficulty climbed up onto the gray's back and, addressing the major-domo, the secretary, the butler, Doctor Pedro Recio, and all the others, he spoke as follows:

"Clear the way, gentlemen, and let me go back to my old freedom. Let me go look for my past life so that I may be resurrected from this present death. I was not born to be a governor or to defend islands

and cities from enemies that would attack them. I know more about
plowing and digging and pruning vines than I do about laws or the
protection of islands and kingdoms. St. Peter is well enough off in
Rome; [8] by which I mean that each one should follow the trade to which
he was born. In my hand a sickle is better than a governor's scepter.
I'd rather have my fill of *gazpacho* [9] than have to put up with a miserable,
meddling doctor who kills me with hunger. I'd rather stretch out in
the shade of an oak in summer and in winter wrap myself in a double
sheepskin jacket and enjoy my freedom than go to bed between sheets
of Holland linen and dress myself in sables and be no freer than a governor is.

"And so, your Worships, God be with you. Tell my lord the duke
that naked was I born and naked I find myself, and so I neither win
nor lose.[10] By this I mean that I came into this government without a
penny and I leave it without one, which is just the opposite of what
generally happens with the governors of other islands. Fall back, then,
and let me pass; I must get myself poulticed, for I think that all my
ribs are smashed, thanks to the enemies that trampled me last night."

"You must not do that, my Lord Governor," said Doctor Recio. "I
will give your Grace a potion that will soon make you as sound and
vigorous as ever; and as for your meals, I promise your Grace to do
better, by permitting you to eat abundantly of anything you desire."

"You speak too late," said Sancho. "I'd as soon turn Turk as stay
here. These jokes won't do a second time. By God, I would no more
keep this government or take another, even though they handed it to
me between two platters, than I would fly to Heaven without wings. I
come of Panza stock, and they are a stubborn lot; if they say odds,
then odds it must be even though it may be evens, and this in spite of
all the world. In this stable I leave behind me the ant's wings [11] that lifted
me in the air so that the swifts and other birds might eat me; let's come
back to earth and walk with our feet once more, and if they're not shod
in pinked Cordovan leather, they'll not lack coarse hempen sandals.
Every ewe to her mate,[12] and let no one stretch his leg beyond the sheet.[13]
And so, once again, let me pass, for it is growing late."

To this the major-domo replied, "My Lord Governor, we will
gladly permit your Grace to leave, even though it grieves us very much
to lose you, as your wit and Christian conduct have endeared you to us.
But it is a well-known fact that every governor, before he departs from
the place where he has been governing, must first render an accounting,
and your Grace should do the same for the ten days [14] that you have

been in office, and then you may go and the peace of God go with you."

"No one," said Sancho, "can demand that of me, unless it is someone that my lord the duke has appointed, and I am on my way now to see the duke and will give him an exact account. And, in any case, seeing that I leave here naked, there is no other proof needed to show that I have governed like an angel."

"By God, if the great Sancho isn't right!" exclaimed Doctor Recio. "I am of the opinion that we should let him go, for the duke will be delighted to see him."

They all agreed to this and allowed Sancho to depart, having first offered to provide him with company and anything that he needed in the way of comfort or conveniences for the journey. He replied that all he wanted was a little barley for his gray and half a cheese and half a loaf of bread for himself, adding that since the distance was so short there was no necessity for him to carry any more or better provisions than that. They all embraced him then, and he, weeping, embraced them all in turn after which he rode away, leaving them filled with admiration at the words he had spoken and at the firmness and wisdom of his resolve.

CHAPTER LIV. *Which treats of matters having to do with this history and none other.*

THE duke and duchess resolved to go ahead with the challenge which Don Quixote, for reasons already set forth, had given their vassal; and inasmuch as the young man was in Flanders, whither he had fled to escape having Doña Rodríguez for a mother-in-law, they decided to substitute for him a Gascon lackey by the name of Tosilos, whom they first instructed very carefully in all that he had to do.

A couple of days later the duke informed his guest that in four days' time the opponent would come to present himself on the field of combat, armed as a knight, and would there maintain that the damsel had lied by half a beard, and even by a beard,[1] if she asserted that he had promised to marry her. Don Quixote was very much pleased with the news and promised himself that he would do wonders in this instance; for he looked upon it as a great good fortune that he should have an opportunity to show his hosts how valiant and mighty an arm was his. He accordingly waited cheerfully and happily for the four days to pass, although they seemed like four centuries to him, so impatient was he for the fray.

But let them pass as we do other things, and let us, rather, accompany Sancho, who, half joyful and half sad, was riding along on his gray to rejoin his master, whose company afforded him more pleasure than the governorship of all the islands in this world.

He had not gone far from the island where his government was situated (he was never able to determine whether it was in reality an island, a city, a town, or a village) when, as it happened, he saw coming toward him down the highway half a dozen pilgrims with their staffs, some of those foreigners who go about singing and begging alms.[2] As they approached him they formed in line and, raising their voices in unison, began a song in some language of which Sancho could understand but a single word: "alms." He knew, therefore, what it was they sought, and being naturally extremely charitable, as Cid Hamete tells us, he took out from his saddlebags the half loaf and half cheese with which he had come provided and gave them to the pilgrims, indicating by signs that he had nothing else to offer them. They accepted the gift willingly enough, but kept saying "*Geld! Geld!*"[3]

"I do not understand what you are asking for, good folks," said Sancho.

One of them then took out a purse from his bosom and displayed it, from which Sancho knew that it was money they wanted. Putting a thumb to his throat and extending his hand upward, he gave them to understand that he had not a coin of any kind on him; and then, spurring the gray, he broke through them. As he passed, however, one of them who had been studying him very attentively flung his arms about him and, in excellent Castilian, cried out, "God bless me! What is this I see? Is it possible that I hold in my arms my dear friend and good neighbor Sancho Panza? Yes, there can be no doubt about it, for I'm not asleep nor am I drunk just now."

Sancho was quite taken aback at hearing himself thus called by name and at being embraced by this foreign pilgrim. He stared hard at the fellow for a good long while, without saying a word, but was still unable to recognize him.

Seeing his perplexity, the pilgrim said to him, "How can it be, Sancho Panza, my brother, that you do not recognize your neighbor Ricote, the Moorish shopkeeper of your village?"

Sancho continued to gaze at him harder than ever, and little by little he began to place him. Then, slipping down off the ass, he threw his arms about his townsman's neck.

"Who the devil would ever have known you, Ricote," he said, "in that clown suit you are wearing? Tell me, who has made a Frenchman out of you,[4] and how do you dare come back to Spain, where, if they catch and recognize you, it will go hard with you?"

"Since you did not know who I was, Sancho," replied the pilgrim, "I am safe. No one would recognize me dressed as I am. But let us leave the road and go into that poplar grove over there, where my companions are going to eat and rest. You shall eat with them, for they are very good folk. That will give me a chance to tell you what has happened to me since I left our village in obedience to his Majesty's command that threatened the unfortunate people of my nation with such severe treatment, as you have heard."[5]

Sancho consented, and after Ricote had spoken to the others they went over to the poplar grove, which was at some distance from the highway. There the mendicants cast aside their staffs and threw off their capes or pilgrims' cloaks, being clad now only in their undergarments.[6] They were all fine young fellows, with the exception of Ricote, who was well along in years, and they all carried saddlebags that appeared to be well stocked, at least with those things that are capable of exciting thirst and summoning it from two leagues away. They stretched out on the ground and, making a tablecloth of the grass, set out upon it bread, salt, knives, nuts, bits of cheese, and clean-picked ham-bones which, if they could not be gnawed any longer, could still be sucked. There was also a black substance called caviar, which is made of fish eggs and is a great awakener of thirst.[7] There was no lack of olives, and although they were dried and without seasoning, they were very palatable.

But what made the best showing of all at that feast was half a dozen flasks of wine, each of the pilgrims having produced one from his saddlebags. Even the worthy Ricote, now transformed from a Moor into a German, or Dutchman, brought out one that in size compared favorably with the other five. They all fell to with right hearty appetites, but they ate very slowly, taking up small morsels of food on the end of their knives and savoring every mouthful; and then, at one and the same time, they raised their arms and flasks aloft, with the mouths of the wine bags[8] tight pressed against their own mouths and their eyes fastened upon the heavens as if they were taking aim at the sky. They sat like this for a good while, wagging their heads from side to side as if to indicate the pleasure they found in emptying the contents [9] of the flasks into their stomachs.

Sancho took it all in and was not displeased at what he saw.[10] Indeed, by way of putting into effect the proverb that he knew so well—"When in Rome, do as you see" [11]—he asked Ricote for his flask and took aim along with the others. Four times the skins were hoisted, but the fifth time it was useless, for they were drier than matweed, a circumstance that diminished the mirth which the company thus far had shown. Every now and then someone would take Sancho's right hand and say, "Spaniard and German, all the same, good fellow," [12] and Sancho would reply, "Good fellow, by God," [13] and would burst into a laugh that lasted for an hour, during which time he remembered nothing of what had happened to him in his government; for cares have little jurisdiction while we are eating and drinking.

Finally, when the wine was exhausted, they began to feel drowsy and ended by falling asleep over their table and tablecloth. Ricote and Sancho alone remained awake, for they had eaten more and drunk less, and the Morisco thereupon took his companion to one side, where they seated themselves at the foot of a beech tree, leaving the others buried in sweet slumber. Then it was Ricote began speaking, in purest Castilian, without once falling into his own Moorish tongue.

"Sancho Panza, my friend and neighbor, you know very well how terrified and dismayed all the people of my nation were by his Majesty's edict and proclamation directed against us. To me, at any rate, it seemed as if, even before the time that was granted us for getting out of Spain had expired, I had already suffered the rigor of the law upon my own person and those of my children. And so I decided—and wisely, I think, like one who knows that on a certain date the house in which he lives will be taken from him and who looks for another into which he may move—I decided, as I was about to say, to leave town alone, without my family, and to seek out a place to which I might take them in comfort so that we would not have to depart in last-minute haste like the others.

"For I saw clearly, as did all our elders, that those proclamations were no mere threats as some maintained, but actual laws that were to be put into effect at a specified time. I was compelled to believe this because I knew of the evil and foolish designs of our people,[14] and for this reason it appeared to me to be a divine inspiration that led his Majesty to carry out so bold a resolution. Not that they were all to blame, for some were true Christians, but these latter were so few in number that they were unable to hold out against those that were not. In short, and with good reason, the penalty of banishment was inflicted upon us, a mild and lenient one as some saw it, but for us it was the most terrible one to which we could have been subjected.

"Wherever we may be, it is for Spain that we weep; for, when all is said, we were born here and it is our native land. Nowhere have we met with the reception that we hoped for. In Barbary and other parts of Africa we expected to be received and welcomed with open arms, but that is where we are insulted and treated the worst. We did not know our good fortune until we had lost it; [15] and almost all of us are so anxious to return that most of those, and they are many, who know the language as I do are now coming back here, leaving their wives and young ones behind and without protection, so great is their love for this land.[16] As for me, I can say that I now know and feel what is meant by the saying, 'Sweet is the love of one's country.'

"Well, then, as I have said, I left our town and made my way to France; but although they gave us a very good reception, I wanted to see all there was to be seen and so I went on to Italy and finally reached Germany. There, it seemed to me, we might enjoy a freer life, as the inhabitants are not overly concerned with fine points but each one does very much as he likes, since for the most part there is full liberty of conscience.[17] I took a house in Augsburg, after which I joined these pilgrims, many of whom are in the habit of coming to Spain every year to visit the sanctuaries, which are for them, like the Indies, an unfailing source of profit. They go all over the country, and there is not a town that they do not leave with their stomachs full of food and wine and at least a real in cash, while at the end of their ramblings they have more than a hundred crowns saved. Changing their money into gold, they hide it in the hollow of their staffs or among the patches of their pilgrims' cloaks, or they employ some other device for getting it out of the realm and back to the country where they reside, and this in spite of the guards that are stationed at the posts and passes.

"And now, Sancho, it is my intention to go back and get the treasure that I left buried in the ground. As it is outside the village, I'll be able to do this without danger, and then I will write to my wife and daughter, whom I know to be in Algiers, or will cross over in person from Valencia, and make arrangements to bring them to some French port and from there to Germany, where we will await what God may have in store for us. For I am certain, Sancho, that my daughter, Ricota, and

Francisca Ricota, my wife, are Catholic Christians; and although I am not as strong in the faith as they, I still am more of a Christian than a Morisco and I pray God constantly to open the eyes of my understanding and reveal to me the way in which I may serve Him. What surprises me is that my wife and daughter should have gone to Barbary rather than to France, where they might have lived like Christians."

"You must remember, Ricote," said Sancho, "that it was not for them to decide. It was Juan Tiopieyo, your wife's brother, who took them away, and, being a shrewd Moor,[18] he knew what he was doing. And I can tell you something else: I don't think it is any use for you to go looking for that buried treasure, for we heard that they had taken from your brother-in-law and your wife many pearls and much money in gold that they wanted to carry out of the country." [19]

"That may well be," replied Ricote, "but I am sure, Sancho, that they did not lay hands on my hoard, for, being afraid that something would happen, I told no one where it was. And so, if you want to come with me and help me get it and hide it, I will give you two hundred crowns, for which I know you can find good use, and you know that I know it."

"I would do it," said Sancho, "but I am not at all covetous. To show you that I am not, only this morning I gave up an office in which, before six months had gone by, I might have lined the walls of my house with gold and been eating off silver plates. For this reason, and because, as I see it, I would be betraying my king by showing favor to his enemies, I would not go with you even though you offered me four hundred crowns, cash down."

"And what office was it that you left, Sancho?" asked Ricote.

"I quit being governor of an island," replied Sancho, "and such an island that, I give you my word, you'd have hard work finding its like."

"Where is this island?" Ricote wanted to know.

"Where is it? Why, two leagues from here; it's called the island of Barataria."

"Be off with you, Sancho," said Ricote. "Islands are out there, in the sea; there are none on the mainland."

"What do you mean?" said Sancho. "I am telling you, friend Ricote, that I left there this morning and that yesterday I governed it at my pleasure, like a sagittarius;[20] but, for all of that, I gave it up, for it seemed to me a dangerous trade, that of governor."

"And what did you get out of your government?" Ricote asked.

"I got the knowledge that I am not fit to govern anything, unless it be a herd of cattle. I also learned that the riches to be had from such governments are only to be gained at the loss of rest and sleep and even nourishment; for on islands the governors eat little, especially where they have doctors to look after their health."

"I don't know what you are talking about, Sancho," said Ricote, "but it sounds like nonsense to me. Who would be giving you islands to govern, anyway? Are there no men in the world more capable of governing than you? Stop such prattle, come back to your senses, and make up your mind whether or not you wish to come with me and help me get the buried treasure that I left behind me. As I told you, I will see that you have enough to live on out of it."

"And I have already told *you*, Ricote," said Sancho, "that I will not. Be satisfied with my promise not to betray you. Go your way in Heaven's name and let me go mine; for well-gotten gain may be lost, but ill-gotten gain is bound to be, and its owner with it." [21]

"I don't want to insist, Sancho," said Ricote. "But tell me, were you in our village when my wife, my daughter, and my brother-in-law left?"

"That I was," Sancho assured him, "and I can tell you that your daughter looked so lovely that everybody in the town came out to see her off, and they all said that she was the most beautiful creature in the world. She wept and embraced all her women friends and acquaintances and all the others who were there to bid her farewell, and begged them all to remember her in their prayers to God and to Our Lady, His mother. I was so touched by it that, though I am not much given to tears, I had to shed a few myself. And faith, there were many there who felt like hiding her or going out and snatching her from the arm of the law along the highway, but they were afraid to disobey the king's command. Most concerned of all was Pedro Gregorio, the rich young heir that you know, who, they say, was very fond of your daughter. Since she left he has not been seen in our village, and we all think that he went after her to rescue her, but up to now we have had no word of any kind."

"I suspected all along," said Ricote, "that the young gentleman was in love with her, but I was not disturbed by it. You have doubtless heard, Sancho, that the Morisco women almost never have anything to do in an amorous way with old Christians; and since I believed that my daughter thought more of being a Christian than she did of falling in love, I was not worried by the attentions of this heir."

"God grant it may be so," said Sancho, "for otherwise it would be bad for both of them. And now, friend Ricote, I must leave you, for I wish to reach the place where my master is by nightfall."

"God go with you, brother Sancho. My comrades are stirring, and it is time for us to be on our way."

With this, the two of them embraced, Sancho mounted his gray, Ricote leaned on his staff once more, and thus they parted.

CHAPTER LV. *Of the things that happened to Sancho along the way, with other unsurpassable events.*

AS A RESULT of having spent so much time with Ricote, Sancho was unable to reach the duke's castle that day, although he was within half a league of it when night fell, a night that was dark and overcast. However, as it was summer, he was not greatly concerned and merely drew up at some distance from the road with the intention of waiting until morning; but luck and fate as usual were against him, and so it happened that, just as he was seeking a spot where he would be more comfortable, both he and the gray tumbled into a deep and very dark pit between some old buildings that stood there. Even as he was falling, he prayed to God with all his heart, thinking that surely he would keep on going down and down until he had come to the depths of the abyss; but this was not the case, for at a little more than three fathoms [1] the ass struck bottom and Sancho found himself still seated upon his mount, unharmed in any way.

He felt his body all over and held his breath to make sure that he really was sound of limb with no holes in him anywhere; and then, upon discovering that he was quite all right, with no bones broken and in perfectly good health, he gave no end of thanks to God Our Lord for the mercy that had been shown him, for he had thought that he undoubtedly would be broken into a thousand pieces. He next ran his hands over the walls of the pit to see if it would be possible to get out of it without help from anyone, but all he encountered was a smooth surface without foothold of any kind. He was very much distressed at this, especially when he heard the ass groaning with pain—and no wonder the poor beast did so, nor could he be blamed for it, for the truth is, he was in a very bad way.

"Ah," exclaimed Sancho Panza then, "how many unforeseen things happen at every step to those that live in this wretched world! Who would ever have said that he who yesterday was enthroned as the governor of an island, ordering his servants and vassals about, would today find himself buried in a pit with no one to help him or come to his rescue, no servant or vassal of any sort? My donkey and I are going to have to die here of hunger, unless he dies first of his jolts and bruises and I of sorrow. One thing is certain, I'll not be as lucky as was my master, Señor Don Quixote de la Mancha, when he went down into the cave of that enchanted Montesinos, where he came upon people who entertained him better than if he had been in his own house. Why, it seems as if they had the table already laid for him and the bed made; he saw beautiful and pleasant visions there, but all that I'll see here will be toads and snakes.

"What an unlucky fellow I am! Where have my follies and my fancies brought me? They'll take my bones out of here, whenever it pleases Heaven to have them found, gnawed clean, white, and smooth. And the bones of my good gray along with mine—that way, perhaps, they will be able to make out who we are, at least those who have heard how Sancho Panza and his ass were never parted one from the other. Once again I say: what unlucky wretches we are, seeing that fate would not let us die in our own country, among our own people! There, even if nothing could be done to remedy our misfortune, we'd at least have had someone to grieve for us and close our eyes at the end as we passed away!

"O friend and comrade," he went on, addressing the donkey,[2] "how ill have I repaid your services! Forgive me, and beg fortune as hard as you can to get us out of this miserable plight in which the two of us now find ourselves. I promise you, I'll put a laurel wreath on your head so that you'll look like a poet laureate,[3] and I'll also give you double rations."

Such was the manner in which Sancho Panza voiced his laments, and the ass listened to him but answered not a word,[4] so great was the poor creature's anguish and suffering. Finally the night, filled with moans and wails, came to an end, and by the light of day Sancho perceived that it was absolutely impossible for him to get out of the pit unaided, whereupon he once more began calling out piteously to see if anyone heard him; but it was like crying aloud in the desert, for in all that region there was not a human ear to pay heed, and then it was that he gave himself up for dead. The gray was lying on his back and his master now managed to get him on his feet, although the animal was barely able to stand. Taking out a crust [5] from his saddlebags—for they had shared the misfortune of man and beast—Sancho fed it to his mount, which seemed to appreciate it. As he did so, he remarked as if the gray could understand him, "With bread, all sorrows are good." [6]

Looking about him, he discovered a hole on one side of the pit big enough for a person to squeeze through, and promptly made for it. Creeping along, he found that on the inside the hole was wide and roomy and that it was light enough for him to see, thanks to a ray of sunlight that came in through what might be called the roof, illuminating everything; and he then observed that it expanded at the far end into a spacious cavity. As soon as he saw this, he came back to where the donkey was and, picking up a stone, began knocking the earth away until he had enlarged the opening sufficiently for the beast to be able to pass through without difficulty. Having accomplished this, he took the gray by the halter and led him across the cavern beyond by way of ascertaining if there was any outlet on the other side. He went in darkness a part of the time and at other times without light,[7] but never without fear.

"God Almighty help me!" he said to himself. "This may be hard luck for me, but it would make a good adventure for my master Don Quixote. He would take these depths and dungeons for flowery gardens and Galiana's palace [8] and would expect to come out of this dark narrow place into some meadow all in bloom; but I, poor hopeless wretch, with no one to lend me encouragement, am thinking at every step I take that another hole deeper than the first one is suddenly going to open up under my feet and swallow me. Welcome, evil, if you come alone." [9]

With such thoughts as these in mind he went on until it seemed to him that he had gone a little more than half a league, and then he descried a dim light that came from somewhere and appeared to be daylight, showing that this road which for him was one leading to the other world ended there in an aperture of some kind.

At this point Cid Hamete leaves him and goes back to Don Quixote, who with great elation was waiting for the appointed battle that he was to wage with the one who had robbed Doña Rodríguez' daughter of her honor, a shameful wrong and grievance which he intended to avenge. Having sallied forth one morning to practice his skill at what he had to do in the encounter set for the following day, he was engaged in putting Rocinante through a short gallop or mock charge when the hoofs of his mount came so near the edge of a pit that, had he not reined in sharply, he would never have been able to avoid falling into it. As it was, he stopped just in time and did not fall. Coming up a little nearer to the cavern, but without dismounting, he gazed down into its depths and, as he did so, heard loud cries from somewhere inside it. He listened closely and succeeded in making out what was said.

"Ho, up there! Is there any Christian who hears me, or any charitable knight who will take pity on a sinner buried alive, a poor unfortunate governor without a government?"

It sounded to Don Quixote like Sancho Panza's voice, at which he was greatly astonished. "Who is it down below?" he shouted as loudly as he could. "Who is it that is lamenting in that manner?"

"Who should it be," came the answer, "or who should be lamenting, if not the wretched Sancho Panza, who as a punishment for his sins has the misfortune to be governor of the island of Barataria, and who was formerly squire to the famous knight Don Quixote de la Mancha?"

Upon hearing this Don Quixote was doubly astonished, and his amazement grew as the thought came to him that Sancho Panza must be dead and his soul in torment down there. Carried away by this idea, he called out once more, "I conjure you by all that, as a Catholic Christian, I well may conjure you by, tell me who you are and whether or not you are a soul in torment. Tell me, also, what it is that you would have me do for you; for it is my calling to aid and succor those who are in trouble in this world, and those in the other world as well who are not able to help themselves."

"From what you say," was the reply, "your Grace who is talking to me now must be my master Don Quixote de la Mancha; there is no doubt about it: the very tone of voice tells me it cannot be anybody else."

"I am indeed Don Quixote," said the knight, "he who professes to aid and succor all those in need, both the living and the dead. And so, tell me who you are and do not keep me any longer in suspense. If you are my squire, Sancho Panza, and have died, and if the devils have not carried you off and you by God's mercy are in purgatory, then our holy mother, the Roman Catholic Church, has the means of releasing you from the torments that you are suffering, and I for my part will intercede with her in your behalf in so far as my worldly substance will permit. Therefore declare yourself and tell me who you are."

"By all that's holy!" [10] the voice answered, "and by the birth of anyone your Grace wishes, I swear, Señor Don Quixote de la Mancha, that

I am your squire, Sancho Panza, and that I never have died in all the days of my life. Having left my government owing to circumstances and reasons which it would take too long to explain, I fell last night into this pit where I am now, and the gray with me—he will not let me lie, seeing that, by way of further proof, he is right here beside me."

Nor was this all; it was as if the ass had understood what Sancho said, for he at once began braying so lustily that the whole cavern echoed with the sound.

"A famous witness," observed Don Quixote. "I know that bray as a mother does her child,[11] and I can hear your voice too, my Sancho. Wait for me and I will go to the duke's castle, which is near by, and bring someone to get you out of that pit into which you must have fallen on account of your sins."

"Go, your Grace," said Sancho, "and, for God's sake, come back soon, as I can't stand it here, being buried alive and dying of fear."

Don Quixote thereupon went to the castle to tell the duke and duchess what had happened to his squire. They were not a little surprised, although they could understand Sancho's having fallen, since the cavern had been there from time immemorial. What they could not understand was why he had left his government without notifying them of his coming. Finally, as the saying is,[12] they brought ropes and tackle and by dint of many people and much labor contrived to rescue Sancho Panza and the ass from that darkness and draw them up to the light of day.

Seeing Sancho emerge in such a manner, a student remarked, "That is the way all bad governors ought to leave their governments: like this sinner who comes forth from the depths of the abyss, dead of hunger, pale-faced, and, I'll wager, without a penny to his name."

Sancho overheard him and replied, "It was eight or ten days ago, brother backbiter, that I came to govern the island which they had given me, and not for one hour of that time did I have my fill of bread; the doctors persecuted me and enemies broke my bones and I had no chance to take bribes or collect my dues;[13] and this being so, as indeed it is, I can't see that I deserve to come out in this fashion; but man proposes and God disposes,[14] and different times different manners;[15] let no one say 'I won't drink of this water,'[16] for where you think there is bacon there are no pegs;[17] God knows what I mean and I say no more, though I could if I wanted to."

"Do not be angry at what you hear, Sancho, and do not let it trouble you," said Don Quixote, "for if you do, there will be no end of it. See that your conscience is clear and let them say what they like, since to endeavor to bind the tongues of slanderers is like trying to put doors to the open country. If a governor leaves his office a rich man, they say that he has been a thief; and if he comes out a poor man, they brand him as worthless and a fool."

"Well, this time," replied Sancho, "they'll surely have to set me down as a fool rather than a thief."

Conversing in this manner and surrounded by a crowd of small boys and other people, they reached the castle, where the duke and duchess were waiting for them. Sancho, however, was unwilling to go up and meet the duke until he first had stabled his gray, which, as he remarked, had spent a very bad night. When this had been attended to, he mounted the stairs and knelt before my lord and lady.

"Because," he said, "it was your Highnesses' pleasure and not on account of any merits of my own, I went to govern your island of Barataria. I was naked when I entered upon my government and naked I find myself now, and so I neither lose nor gain. As to whether I governed well or ill, I had witnesses who will say what they will. I answered questions, solved problems, and decided cases at law, and all the while I was dying of hunger to please Doctor Pedro Recio, native of Tirteafuera, doctor to the island and its governor. Enemies fell upon us by night and we were very hard pressed, but the islanders say that it was due to the might of my arm that they came out of it free and victorious, and may God give them health to the extent that they are telling the truth.

"The short of it is that during this time I had a chance to try out the burdens and responsibilities of governing and I find that, by my reckoning, my shoulders cannot bear the weight; it is no load for these ribs of mine, and these are no arrows for my quiver. And so, before the government threw me over, I decided to throw over the government; and yesterday morning I left the island as I found it, with the same streets, houses, and roofs that it had when I came. I asked no one for a loan nor did I try to make any money out of my office; and although I had it in mind to make a few laws, I made none,[18] since I was afraid they would not be kept and then it would be all the same whether I made them or not.

"I left the island, as I have said, with only my gray for company. I fell into a pit but kept on going until, this morning, by the light of the sun, I saw an outlet. It was not so easy to get out of it though, and if Heaven had not sent my master Don Quixote to me, I'd have been there until the end of the world. And so, my lord and lady, the Duke and Duchess, your governor, Sancho Panza, who stands before you here, in the ten days, no more, that he has held the governorship, has come to learn that he would not give anything whatever to rule, not alone an island, but the entire world. Now that I've made this clear, I kiss your Highnesses' feet; and like the small lads who say 'Leap and let me have it,' [19] I give a leap out of my government and pass over to the service of my master Don Quixote; for with him, even though I eat my bread with fear and trembling, at least I get my fill, and in that case it's all the same to me whether it be of carrots or of partridges."

With this, Sancho brought his long speech to a close. Don Quixote had feared that his squire would utter all kinds of nonsense, and when he heard him finish as sensibly as this he gave thanks to Heaven from the bottom of his heart. The duke then embraced Sancho, expressing his regret that the governor had quitted his post so soon and adding that he would provide him with another, there on his estate, that carried with it less responsibility and would prove more profitable. The duchess did the same and gave orders that he be looked after, as he appeared to be suffering from the bruises he had received.

CHAPTER LVI. *Of the tremendous battle such as never before was seen that took place between Don Quixote de la Mancha and the lackey Tosilos in defense of the duenna Doña Rodríguez' daughter.*

THE duke and duchess were not sorry for the joke they had played on Sancho Panza in connection with the government they had given him, especially when, that same day, the major-domo arrived to give them a detailed account of practically everything that Sancho had said and done during the time, ending with a vivid description of the attack upon the island and the governor's fear and departure, all of which provided them with considerable amusement.

After that, as the history goes on to relate, the day of battle came.

Having repeatedly instructed the lackey Tosilos as to how he was to conduct himself so that he would be able to vanquish Don Quixote without killing or wounding him, the duke ordered that the steel tips be removed from the lances; for, as he remarked to his guest, he prided himself upon being a Christian and so could not permit this combat to be waged at such risk and peril to the lives of the participants. The knight, he added, would have to be content with the free field that was offered him upon his host's estate, though even that was against the decree of the holy Council [1] prohibiting such challenges, for which reason it was too dangerous in the present instance to observe to the full all the rigorous provisions governing such encounters.

The knight replied that his Excellency might arrange all matters having to do with this affair in the way that best suited him, and he, Don Quixote, would obey him in everything. The dread day having arrived, then, the duke ordered them to erect a spacious platform facing the courtyard of the castle for the judges of the field and the two duennas, mother and daughter, who were the suppliants in the case; and from all the towns and villages round about a huge throng of people gathered, attracted by the novel character of the combat, for neither the living nor the dead in all that region had ever seen or heard tell of such a one.

The first to enter the field and lists was the master of ceremonies, who surveyed and paced the entire ground very carefully to make sure there was no chance of foul play, no hidden trap that might cause one of the contestants to stumble and fall. Then the duennas came in and took their seats. Wrapped in mantles that covered even their eyes and bosoms, they displayed no little emotion as Don Quixote made his appearance. Shortly afterward, accompanied by many trumpets, the big lackey Tosilos hove in sight at one side of the square. He was mounted upon a powerful steed that shook the whole place and was clad in a suit of stoutly wrought and gleaming armor. His horse looked like one of those that come from Friesland, being broad-backed and of a grayish color, with an arroba [2] of wool hanging from each of his fetlocks.

This brave fighter had been well schooled by his master the duke as to how he was to behave toward Don Quixote de la Mancha, and he had been warned that under no circumstances was he to slay the knight; [3] rather, he was to endeavor to shun the first clash in order to avoid killing him, as he certainly would do if he met him full tilt. He now rode slowly across the square to where the duennas were and remained there for some little while gazing at the one who was asking that he take her as his bride. Meanwhile, the master of ceremonies had called to Don Quixote, who was already present in the lists, and, going over to stand at Tosilos's side, he proceeded to address the duennas, inquiring if they would consent to have Don Quixote de la Mancha represent their cause. They agreed to this, with the understanding that whatever the knight did in their behalf should be looked upon as well done, valid, and binding.

By this time the duke and duchess had taken their places in a gallery overlooking the enclosure, which was filled with a vast multitude waiting to witness this most extraordinary conflict. In accordance with the conditions that had been laid down, if Don Quixote won, his opponent was to have to marry Doña Rodríguez' daughter; and if he was vanquished, the other was to be free of the promise that was claimed of him, without having to give any further satisfaction. The master of ceremonies now apportioned the sun [4] and placed each of them where he was supposed to stand. There was a roll of drums, the air was filled with the sound of trumpets, and the earth trembled underfoot as the crowd looked on anxiously, some hoping for a fortunate outcome while others feared the worst. Commending himself with all his heart to God and to his lady Dulcinea del Toboso, Don Quixote awaited the signal for the charge.

But our lackey had other thoughts in mind; he was thinking only of what I am now about to tell you. It seems that, as he gazed upon his fair enemy, she had impressed him as being the most beautiful woman he had seen in all his life,[5] and the little blind boy who in our street is commonly called Cupid had been unwilling to let slip the opportunity of triumphing over a lackey's heart and had wished to add it to his list of trophies. And so, stealing up very softly, without anyone's seeing him, he discharged an arrow two yards long through the poor fellow's left side, piercing his heart through and through. This he was able to do in perfect safety, for Love is invisible and comes and goes as he likes with no one to call him to account for what he does.

Accordingly, when they came to give the signal for the charge, our lackey was rapt in ecstasy. Thinking of the beauty of her whom he had made the mistress of his liberty, he paid no attention to the sound of the trumpet, but Don Quixote, the moment he heard it, was off on the run, bearing down on his enemy at Rocinante's top speed.

Seeing this, Sancho, good squire that he was, cried out, "May God guide you, O cream and flower of knights-errant! May God give you the victory, since you have the right on your side!"

Although Tosilos saw Don Quixote charging at him, he did not stir a step, but instead called in a loud voice to the master of ceremonies; and when the latter came up to see what was wanted, he said to him, "Sir, is not this battle being fought to decide whether or not I shall marry that young lady?"

"It is," was the answer.

"Well, then," said the lackey, "I would have you know that my conscience hurts me, and I'd be laying a heavy burden on it if I went through with this battle. I therefore yield myself as vanquished and am willing to marry the lady at once."

The marshal of the field was astonished by this speech, and, being one of those who were familiar with the affair as it had been plotted, he did not know what reply to make. Seeing that his adversary was not charging him in turn, Don Quixote had stopped midway in his course. As for the duke, he was unable to make out what was happening until the marshal came to tell him what Tosilos had said, upon hearing which he was amazed and very angry.

While this was going on Tosilos rode over to where Doña Rodríguez sat. "Lady," he called to her, "I am willing to marry your daughter, and I have no desire to obtain by strife and fighting what I can get peacefully, without any danger of death."

"Since that is so," said the valiant Don Quixote when he heard this, "I am free and absolved of my promise. Let them marry, in Heaven's name; and seeing that God has bestowed her, may St. Peter bless the match."

Having come down to the castle courtyard, the duke went up to Tosilos. "Is it true, knight," he asked, "that you yield yourself as vanquished and that, pricked by your uneasy conscience, you wish to marry this maiden?"

"Yes, my lord," replied Tosilos.

"And right he is," put in Sancho Panza, "for what you have to give to the mouse, give to the cat and spare yourself the trouble." [6]

Tosilos, meanwhile, was endeavoring to unlace his helmet and begged them to hurry and help him as it was all he could do to get his breath and he could not stay shut up in that narrow space for so long a time. They removed it for him in great haste, and then his lackey countenance was revealed for all to see.

"It's a trick! A trick!" screamed Doña Rodríguez and her daughter. "They've put Tosilos, lackey to my lord the duke, in the place of the true husband! Justice from God and the King against such cunning as this, not to say villainy!"

"Do not distress yourselves, ladies," said Don Quixote. "This is neither cunning nor villainy, or if it is, it is not the duke who is to blame but those wicked enchanters that persecute me. Enviously fearful that I might win a glorious victory, they have converted your husband's face into that of one who, so you say, is the duke's lackey. Take my advice and, despite the malice of my enemies, go ahead and marry this man, for undoubtedly he is the one you wanted to marry all the time."

As he heard this the duke came near losing his anger and bursting into a fit of laughter. "The things that happen to Señor Don Quixote," he said, "are so extraordinary that I am ready to believe this is not my lackey. But supposing we employ the following stratagem: let us postpone the wedding for, say, a couple of weeks, and in the meantime let us keep this person, concerning whom we are in doubt, in close confinement; it may be that he will then return to his former shape, for the grudge the enchanters hold against Don Quixote cannot last as long as that, especially when they see that these tricks and transformations are doing them so little good."

"Oh, sir," said Sancho, "those scoundrels are used to changing one thing into another where my master is concerned. A knight that he vanquished some time ago, the one called the Knight of the Mirrors, was turned into the bachelor Sansón Carrasco, a native of our village and a great friend of ours; and they changed my lady Dulcinea del Toboso into a peasant lass; and so, I fancy, this lackey is going to have to live and die a lackey all the days of his life."

"Let him be who he may who asks me for my hand," said Rodríguez' daughter, "I thank him for it; for I would rather be a lackey's lawfully wedded wife than the cast-off mistress of a gentleman—although he who deceived me is no gentleman either."

The short of the matter is, as a result of all this talk and all that had happened Tosilos was placed in confinement until they could see what the upshot of his transformation would be. They all acclaimed Don Quixote's victory, although most of them were sadly disappointed at not having seen the combatants pound each other to bits, after they had waited for them so eagerly. In this respect they were like boys who are grieved when the man to be hanged fails to appear, having won a pardon either from the one he has wronged or from the court. The crowd now dispersed, and the ducal pair with Don Quixote returned to the castle, where Tosilos was put under lock and key. As for Doña Rodríguez and her daughter, they were very well pleased, since one way or the other the affair would end in marriage, and that was what Tosilos wanted also.

CHAPTER LVII. *Which treats of how Don Quixote took leave of the duke and of what happened to him in connection with the witty and impudent Altisidora.*

BY NOW Don Quixote had come to feel that it would be well for him to quit a life of idleness such as he was leading in the castle; for he believed he was doing a great wrong in depriving the outside world of his presence, by keeping himself shut up like this and leisurely enjoying all the innumerable comforts and luxuries with which my lord and lady surrounded him as a knight-errant. It seemed to him that he would have to give an accounting to Heaven for this sloth and seclusion; and so it was that one day he begged permission of the ducal pair to take his leave. They granted his request, at the same time showing how very sorry they were to have him go. The duchess then gave Sancho Panza the letters from his wife, at which he burst into tears.

"Who would have thought," he said, "that such great hopes as the news of my government aroused in the bosom of my wife, Teresa Panza, would end with my going back, as I am doing now, to the long-drawn-out adventures of my master Don Quixote de la Mancha? But, for all of that, I am glad to see that my Teresa behaved like herself in sending the acorns to the duchess; for if she had not sent them, I'd have been sorry and she would have been ungrateful. What comforts me is the fact that they can't call that present a bribe, for I already had the governorship when she sent it, and it stands to reason that those who receive a favor should show their gratitude, even if it's only with trifles. The truth is: naked I went into the government and naked I leave it; and that, I may say in all conscience, is no small matter. 'Naked was I born, naked I find myself, and so, I neither win nor lose.'"

Such were Sancho's reflections on the day of his departure. Don Quixote had said farewell to his hosts the night before, and bright and early in the morning he appeared fully armed in the courtyard of the castle. The entire household watched him from the balconies, and even the duke and duchess came out to see him off. Sancho was mounted on his gray, with his saddlebags, his valise, and his store of provisions, and was very happy because the duke's major-domo (the one who had played the part of La Trifaldi) had presented him with a little purse containing two hundred gold crowns. The money was intended for their needs upon the road, but Don Quixote knew nothing of it as yet.

As they all stood looking on in this manner, the witty and impudent Altisidora, from her place among the duchess's other damsels and duennas, suddenly lifted up her voice and began to sing in a mournful tone:

> *Lend ear, wicked knight,*
> *Rein in thy steed;*
> *To punish his flanks*
> *There's surely no need.*
>   *Whom fleest, false one?*
> *I am no dragon bold*
> *But a gentle spring lamb*
> *That is far from the fold.*
>   *Ah, thou hast made mock*
> *Of the fairest of maids*
> *Diana or Venus*
> *E'er glimps'd in their glades.*
>   *O cruel Bireno,*[1] *Aeneas untrue,*
> *May Barabbas go with thee, bring thee heart's rue.*
>
> *In thy pitiless claws,*
> *Ruthless bird of prey,*
> *A lovelorn heart*
> *Thou bearest away.*
>   *Three kerchiefs hast stolen,*
> *Of garters a pair*
> *From legs pure as marble,*
> *So white and so fair.*
>   *Two thousand sad sighs*
> *Thou takest with thee,*
> *If they were but flame,*
> *What Troys there would be!*

O cruel Bireno, Aeneas untrue,
May Barabbas go with thee, bring thee heart's rue.

As for Sancho, thy squire,
May his heart be so fell
Dulcinea will never
Be freed of her spell.
For the fault that is thine
May she bear the pain,
Since the just pay for sinners,[2]
So goes the refrain.
May your greatest adventures
Betray each fond hope;
Forgetting your loved one,
In dreams may you grope.
O cruel Bireno, Aeneas untrue,
May Barabbas go with thee, bring thee heart's rue.

May they take thee for false
From Cadiz to Seville,[3]
From London to England,
And bear thee ill will.
When thou playest at cards,
May thou never hold kings
Nor aces nor sevens,
But lose at all things.
If thy corns thou shouldst trim,
Let it be till they bleed;
If thy molars are pulled,
May the roots all recede.
O cruel Bireno, Aeneas untrue,
May Barabbas go with thee, bring thee heart's rue.

All the while the woebegone Altisidora was singing this song, in the manner that has been described, Don Quixote was gazing at her; and then, without a word in reply, he turned to Sancho.

"By the souls of your ancestors, friend Sancho," he said, "I conjure you to speak the truth. Tell me: do you by any chance have upon your person the three kerchiefs and the garters that this love-sick maid is talking about?"

"The three kerchiefs I have," said Sancho, "but as for the garters, it's over the hills of Ubeda."[4]

The duchess was astonished at Altisidora's brazenness. She had taken her for a bold, sprightly, impudent girl but had never thought that she would carry her impudence to such an extreme as this; and not having been forewarned of the joke, my lady was more amazed than ever. The duke for his part was of a mind to carry on the jest.

"It does not seem fitting to me, Sir Knight," he said, "in view of the hospitality you have been accorded here in my castle, that you should be so bold as to make off with three kerchiefs if nothing more—not to speak of my damsel's garters—an act which indicates an evil disposition on your part and is not in keeping with your reputation. Return the garters, or otherwise I challenge you to mortal combat; and I have no fear, either, that those scoundrelly enchanters will change or transform my features as they did those of Tosilos, my lackey, when he joined battle with you."

"God forbid," replied Don Quixote, "that I should unsheath my sword against your most illustrious person, seeing that I have received so many favors from you. The kerchiefs I will return, for Sancho says that he has them; but it is impossible to return the garters, for the reason that neither I nor he have had them in our possession. If this damsel of yours will look in her hiding places, I am sure she will come upon them. I, my lord the Duke, have never been a thief, nor do I expect to be so long as I live if God does not let me out of His keeping. This maiden speaks as one who is lovelorn, as she herself admits, but, since I am not to blame for that, there is no occasion for me to beg her pardon or your Excellency's. I would merely entreat you to have a better opinion of me and once again grant me permission to continue my journey."

"And God give you a fortunate one, Señor Don Quixote," said the duchess, "so that we may always hear good news of your exploits. Go, then, and God go with you; for the longer you tarry the more you add to the flame in the hearts of these damsels who look upon you. As for this girl of mine, I will so chastise her that she will henceforth offend no more either by look or words."

"O valiant Don Quixote!" exclaimed Altisidora at this point, "there is one word, no more, that I have to say to you and I would have you listen to it: I wish to beg your pardon about the theft of my garters, for, by God and upon my soul, I have them on at this moment; I made the same mistake as the man on the ass who went looking for it."

"What did I tell you?" said Sancho. "I'm a fine one when it comes to concealing stolen property! If I had wanted to do anything like that, I had plenty of chances in my government."

Don Quixote then bowed his head in a farewell to the duke and duchess and all the bystanders, and, turning Rocinante about, followed by Sancho on the ass, he left the castle and took the highroad for Saragossa.

CHAPTER LVIII. *Which tells how adventures came crowding thick and fast on Don Quixote.*

As SOON as Don Quixote found himself in the open country, free to roam at will and without being annoyed by Altisidora's advances, his spirits rose and he felt at peace, ready to take up once more the pursuit of his ideals of chivalry.

"Freedom," he said, turning to Sancho, "is one of the most precious gifts that the heavens have bestowed on men; [1] with it the treasures locked in the earth or hidden in the depths of the sea are not to be compared; for the sake of freedom, as for the sake of honor, one may and should risk one's life, and captivity, on the other hand, is the greatest evil that can befall a human being. [2] You have seen, Sancho, the abundance and luxury in that castle we have just left; yet I assure you that in the midst of those delicious banquets and snow-cooled beverages it seemed to me as though I were in the straits of hunger, since I did not enjoy them with the same freedom as if they had been my own. The obligation to return benefits and favors received is a shackle on the liberty-loving spirit of man. Happy he to whom Heaven gives a slice of bread without his being obliged to thank any other person but only Heaven itself!" [3]

"For all that your Grace says," remarked Sancho, "we ought to be duly grateful for the two hundred gold crowns which the duke's majordomo handed to me in a little purse and which I now carry next my heart as a kind of soothing plaster against a time of need; for we are not always going to find castles where they will entertain us, and some-times we are likely to come upon inns where they will give us a beat-ing."

Talking of this and other subjects, the knight and his squire had gone a little more than a league when they caught sight of a dozen men dressed like workmen and lying upon their cloaks which they had spread out on the green grass of a little meadow. They were engaged in eating, and beside them were a number of white sheets, or such they appeared to be, covering something underneath, objects that were either stand-ing upright or lying flat, with small spaces in between. Coming up to them as they made their meal, Don Quixote greeted them at first very courteously and then inquired what was beneath the cloths.

"Sir," one of the men answered him, "those are images carved in · relief to be used in an altar piece [4] that we are putting up in our village. We keep them covered like that to prevent them from becoming soiled, and we carry them on our shoulders so that they will not be broken." [5]

"If you would be so good," said Don Quixote, "I should like to see them, for images that are transported with such care must surely be fine ones."

"I should think they are!" said another of the men. "You can tell from what they cost; for the truth is, there is not a one of them that is not worth more than fifty ducats; but if you will wait a moment, your Grace, you may see with your own eyes."

Leaving his dinner and rising to his feet, the workman went over and took the cover off the first image, which proved to be one of St. George on horseback, with a dragon coiled at his feet and a lance thrust down its throat, a scene marked by all the ferocity with which it is cus-tomarily depicted. The entire image appeared to be one blaze of gold, as the saying is; and, as he gazed upon it, Don Quixote observed, "This was one of the best knights-errant that the heavenly militia ever had. His name was Don St. George [6] and he was, moreover, a protector of damsels.[7] Let us see this other one."

The man uncovered it, and it was seen to be an image of St. Martin, likewise mounted, and sharing his cloak with the beggar. No sooner had he laid eyes upon it than Don Quixote had a comment to make.

"This knight, also," he said, "was one of the Christian adventurers, and it is my opinion, Sancho, that he was even more liberal than he was valiant,[8] as you may see from the fact that he is here dividing his cloak and giving the beggar half of it; and it undoubtedly must have been winter at the time or otherwise he would have given him all of it, he was so charitable."

"I don't think it was that," said Sancho. "He most likely believed in the proverb that says, 'Brains are required for giving and keeping.' " [9]

Don Quixote laughed at this and then asked them to remove another cloth, beneath which was revealed a likeness of Spain's patron. He too was on horseback and bore a bloodstained sword as he trampled over Moors and human heads.

"Ah!" exclaimed Don Quixote, "this is a real knight and one of Christ's own cohorts. He is Don San Diego Matamoros,[10] the Moor-slayer, one of the most valiant saints and men of arms that this world ever had or Heaven has now."

The next cloth that they lifted covered a figure representing the fall of St. Paul from his horse, along with all the circumstances attendant upon his conversion such as are commonly to be seen upon altar pieces and which were here portrayed so vividly that one would have said that Christ was speaking and Paul answering.

"This man in his day," said Don Quixote, "was the greatest enemy that the Church of Our Lord God had to combat, and he became the greatest champion it will ever have, a knight-errant in life, and in death a steadfast saint, a tireless worker in the Lord's vineyard, teacher of the Gentiles with Heaven for a school [11] and Jesus Christ as instructor and schoolmaster."

There being no more to see, Don Quixote directed them to cover the images once more. "I take it as a good omen, my brothers," he said to the workmen, "to have seen what I have today; for these saints and knights followed the same profession that I do, which is that of arms. The only difference between them and me is that they, being saints, waged a holy warfare, while I fight after the manner of men. They conquered Heaven by force of arms, for Heaven suffereth violence; [12] but, up to now, I do not know what I have won with all the hardships I have endured. However, if my lady Dulcinea were but free of those that she is suffering, it may be that my fortunes would improve, and with a sounder mind [13] I should be able to tread a better path than the one I follow at present."

"May God hear and sin be deaf," said Sancho.[14]

The men were equally astonished by Don Quixote's figure and by his conversation, for they did not understand the half of what he said. Having finished their dinner, they took up the images and, bidding the knight farewell, resumed their journey.

Once again, Sancho was amazed at his master's erudition; it was as if he had never known him before. There surely was not a story in the world, he thought to himself, not a single event that the knight did not have at his fingertips and firmly fixed in his memory. "Truly, sir," he said, "if what happened to us today can be called an adventure, it has been one of the sweetest and pleasantest that we have had in all our wanderings. We have come out of it without any fright or beating, nor have we laid hand to sword or flayed the earth with our bodies or gone hungry. Praise God for having let me see such a one with my own eyes!"

"You are right, Sancho," said Don Quixote, "but you must remember that all times are not alike and do not always take the same course; and what the vulgar commonly call omens (for which there is no rational basis) are to be looked upon by the wise man as being no more than happy accidents. One of these believers in omens will rise in the morning, leave his house, and fall in with a friar of the order of the blessed St. Francis; whereupon, as though he had encountered a griffin, he will turn around and go home. If a Mendoza chances to spill salt on the table, he spills gloom over his heart at the same time,[15] just as if nature were under any obligation to give notice of coming misfortunes through things of such little moment as those mentioned. The man who is at once wise and a Christian ought not to trifle with the will of Heaven. When Scipio came to Africa he stumbled as he leaped ashore, and his soldiers took it for an ill omen, but as he embraced the earth he cried out, 'You will not escape me, Africa, for I hold you tightly in my arms.'[16] And similarly, Sancho, our meeting with these images has been for me simply[17] a very happy occurrence."

"I believe it," said Sancho, "and now I wish your Grace would tell me why it is the Spaniards as they go into battle call upon San Diego Matamoros; crying, 'Santiago, and close, Spain!'[18] Does it mean by any chance that Spain is open and has to be closed, or what kind of talk is this?"[19]

"You are very simple-minded, Sancho," replied Don Quixote. "Look you, God gave Spain that great knight of the Red Cross as her patron and protector, especially in those arduous struggles that the Spaniards had with the Moors; and so it is they call upon him as their defender in all the battles that they join; and very often, in those battles, they have plainly seen him overthrowing, trampling under foot, destroying, and killing the Hagarene[20] cohorts. Many examples of the truth of this will be found recorded in the veracious Spanish histories."

Sancho now changed the subject. "I marvel, sir," he said, "at the impudence of Altisidora, the duchess's damsel. She must have been pierced and sorely wounded by the one they call Cupid, who, they say, is a little blind boy; but though he may be blear-eyed, or, more properly speaking, sightless, if he takes aim at a heart, however small it may be, he is sure to hit it and run it through with his arrows. I have heard it said, on the other hand, that the darts of love are blunted by the modesty and reserve of maidens, but in Altisidora's case it would seem they had been sharpened rather than dulled."

"You must bear in mind, Sancho," said Don Quixote, "that love is no respecter of the conventions nor in its actions does it keep within the bounds of reason, but rather resembles death which without discrimination assails the lofty palaces of kings and the humble shepherd's hut.[21] When love takes complete possession of a heart, the first thing it does is to banish all fear and shame; and thus it was that Altisidora shamelessly declared her passion, awakening thereby no pity in my bosom but only a feeling of embarrassment."

"What cruelty!" exclaimed Sancho. "What unheard-of ingratitude! For myself I can say that at the slightest word of love from her I'd have surrendered and become her slave. Son of a whore! what a heart of marble, what bowels of brass, what a soul of mortar! But I can't imagine what it was that girl saw in your Grace that made her turn slave and offer herself to you. Where was the bold and dashing appearance, the grace of manner, the handsome face—any of these things singly or all of them together—that led her to fall in love with you? To tell the honest truth, I have many times stopped to look your Grace over from the topmost hair of your head down to the soles of your feet and when I do so I see more things to frighten a person than to cause one to love you. I have heard it said that beauty is the first and principal thing where falling in love is concerned, and since your Grace has none at all, I'm sure I don't know why the poor girl did it."

"Do not forget, Sancho," replied Don Quixote, "that there are two kinds of beauty, one being of the soul and the other of the body. That of the soul is revealed through intelligence, modesty, right conduct, generosity, and good breeding, all of which qualities may exist in an ugly man; and when one's gaze is fixed upon beauty of this sort and not upon that of the body, love is usually born suddenly and violently. I, Sancho, can see very well that I am not handsome, but I am also aware that I am not misshapen; and it is enough for a man not to be a monster in order to be well loved, so long as he possesses those other endowments of which I have told you."

Conversing in this manner, they entered a wood alongside the road, when suddenly, without his expecting it, Don Quixote found himself entangled in some nets of green cord that had been strung between the trees; and being unable to imagine what the meaning of it was, he said to Sancho, "It is my opinion that this is going to be one of the rarest adventures that could be conceived. May they slay me if the enchanters who persecute me are not trying to enmesh me, by way of delaying my journey and in revenge for my stern treatment of Altisidora. But let me inform them that even though these nets were made of hardest diamonds in place of green cord, and even though they were stronger than the one in which the jealous god of the forge snared Venus and Mars, I still would break them as if they were fashioned of rushes or cotton thread."

He was about to ride on and burst through them all when without warning there appeared before him from among the trees two most beautiful shepherd lasses—or, at least, they were dressed like shepherdesses, save for the fact that their jackets and peasant skirts [22] were of fine brocade (that is to say, they wore hoop skirts made of tabby and richly embroidered in gold).[23] Their hair, which fell down loose over their shoulders, might well compete with the rays of the sun in brightness and was crowned with garlands of laurel interwoven with red amaranth. They appeared to be between fifteen and eighteen years of age, and the sight of them was such as to fill Sancho with astonishment and Don Quixote with admiration and cause the sun to halt in its course.[24] An uncanny silence held them all, and then, finally, one of the lasses spoke.

"Stop, Sir Knight," she said, "and do not break those nets; for they have been stretched not to do you harm but for our amusement. And since you are bound to ask us why they were put there and who we are, I will answer you in a few words. In a village some two leagues away, where there are many rich gentlefolk and important personages, a number of friends and relatives decided among themselves that they would come here with their sons, wives, daughters, neighbors, acquaintances, and kinsmen to seek diversion in this spot, which is one of the most pleasing to be found in all these parts. It is our intention to set up here a new pastoral Arcadia, with the maidens dressing as shepherdesses and the lads as shepherds. We have been studying two eclogues, one by the famous poet Garcilaso, and the other by the most excellent Camões in his own Portuguese tongue, but we have not as yet acted them.

"We came only yesterday, and we have erected some field tents, as they are called, among the trees on the edge of a brook whose abundant waters fertilize all these meadows. Last night we stretched the nets you see here to snare the foolish little birds that, startled by our clamor, fall into them. If you, sir, would like to be our guest, you will receive a most courteous and hospitable welcome, since for the present all care and melancholy are banished from this place."

"Assuredly, fairest lady," replied Don Quixote, "Actaeon [25] when he surprised Diana at the bath could not have been more amazed and charmed than I at beholding your beauty. I approve the way you have found of amusing yourselves and thank you for your invitation, and if I can serve you in any way, you have but to command with the certainty that you will be obeyed; for my calling is none other than that of showing gratitude and doing good to people of every sort, especially those of high station, as you quite evidently are. If these nets that probably occupy but a small space were spread out over the whole round earth, I still should seek new worlds through which I might pass in order to avoid breaking them. What I say may sound exaggerated, but in order that you may believe it let me tell you that he who gives you this assurance is Don Quixote de la Mancha himself, if by chance that name has reached your ears."

"Ah, my dear," said the other maid, "what great good fortune has befallen us! Do you see this gentleman here before us? I would have you know that he is the bravest, the most lovelorn, and the most courteous of any in this world, if one is to believe the story of his deeds which has been put into print and which I have read. And I will wager that this good man with him is a certain Sancho Panza, his squire, whose drolleries are quite incomparable."

"That is the truth," said Sancho. "I am that droll squire that your Grace is speaking of, and this gentleman is my master, the same Don Quixote de la Mancha that is in the story."

"Oh!" exclaimed the first maiden, "let us beg him to stay, my dear; our fathers and brothers would be delighted to have him, and I too have heard of his valor and his squire's amusing ways. [26] But, above all, they tell me he is the most steadfast and loyal lover that ever was and that his lady is a certain Dulcinea del Toboso to whom all Spain awards the palm of beauty."

"And rightly so," said Don Quixote, "unless it be that your own unrivaled beauty puts hers in doubt. But do not trouble yourselves, ladies, by urging me to stay, for the imperative duties of my profession do not suffer me to rest under any circumstances."

At that moment a brother of one of the maidens came up, dressed like them in gay and costly shepherd attire. They informed him that the gentleman with them was the valiant Don Quixote de la Mancha, and that the other was Sancho, his squire, with whom the young man was already familiar through the history, which he had read. The dashing shepherd then begged the knight to come to their tents, and Don Quixote was compelled to yield.

The beaters now began starting the game, and the nets were soon filled with small birds of various species that, deceived by the color, had fallen into the danger from which they were fleeing. As many as thirty persons gathered there, all of them festively garbed as shepherds and shepherdesses, and within a very short while they all knew who Don Quixote and his squire were, which pleased them greatly, for they too had heard of the knight through the history of his exploits. Making their way to the tents, they found the tables neatly laid with an abundance of choice food, and they honored their guest by according him first place among them as all looked on and marveled at the sight of him.

When the cloth had at last been removed, Don Quixote raised his voice and spoke.

"There are those who will tell you that one of the greatest sins men can commit is pride, but I maintain that ingratitude is worse; and in making this assertion, I am mindful of the common saying to the effect that Hell is full of ingrates. This sin, insofar as possible, I have endeavored to avoid ever since I had the use of my reasoning powers. If I find myself unable to repay the good deeds that have been done me with others in kind, I substitute the desire for the performance; and when this is not enough, I make public the favors I have received, since he who publishes abroad the benefits conferred upon him would surely repay them if it were possible for him to do so. Those that receive are for the most part the inferiors of those that give. Thus God, being the supreme giver, is over all; the gifts of man fall short by an infinite distance of those that He bestows, but gratitude to a certain extent makes up for this shortcoming and deficiency.

"And so, being grateful for the kindness that has been shown me here and being unable to return it in full measure, owing to the limited means at my disposal, I do hereby offer you what lies within my power. I accordingly declare that for two whole days, in the middle of this highway that leads to Saragossa, I will maintain that these ladies disguised as shepherd lasses are the most beautiful and courteous damsels of any in the world, excepting only the peerless Dulcinea del Toboso, sole mistress of my affections, if I may say so without offense to any of the ladies and gentlemen who hear my words."

Sancho had been listening most attentively to everything Don Quixote said, and he now cried out in a loud voice, "Is it possible there are any in the world who would dare to say and swear that this master of mine is a madman? Tell me, you gentlemen shepherds, is there any village curate, however wise and however much of a scholar he may be, who could make the speech you have just heard? Is there any knight-errant, however famous for his bravery, who could make the offer my master has made you?"

Exceedingly angry and red in the face, the knight now turned upon his squire. "Is it possible, Sancho," he said, "that there is anyone in this world who would say that you are not a fool—a fool lined with folly, with I know not what trimmings of cunning and roguery? Who told you to meddle in my affairs and decide whether I am a wise man or a blockhead? Be quiet and do not answer me, but go and saddle Rocinante at once if he is unsaddled, for we are going to put my offer into effect, and, with the right that I have on my side, you may reckon as vanquished all who would contradict me."

He rose from his seat in a rage, his anger plainly visible to the others present, who were amazed by it, being unable to make up their minds as to whether he was mad or sane. They did their best to dissuade him from the proposed challenge, telling him that they were assured of his gratitude and there was no need for him to give fresh proof of his courage as the instances of it contained in the history were quite sufficient. Nevertheless, Don Quixote insisted upon carrying out his intention, and, having mounted Rocinante, grasped his lance, and braced his buckler on his arm, he took his stand in the middle of a highway not far distant from the verdant meadow. Sancho followed on his donkey, with the throng of pastoral revelers hard at his heels, for they were anxious to see what would be the outcome of this vainglorious, unheard-of undertaking.

Having posted himself, then, in the middle of the highway as has been stated, Don Quixote rent the air with such words as these:

"O ye travelers and wayfarers, knights and squires, those on foot and those on horseback, who pass along this road within the next two days, know that Don Quixote de la Mancha, knight-errant, stands here to maintain that the nymphs who inhabit these groves and meadows excel in beauty and in courtesy all others in the world, leaving aside the lady of my heart, Dulcinea del Toboso. And so, let anyone who holds the contrary come on, for I await him on this spot."

Twice he repeated these same words and twice there was no adventurer to hear them. But fate, which was guiding his affairs from better to better, ordained that shortly afterward he should descry down the road a large number of men on horseback, many of them with lances in their hands and all riding hard, in close formation. No sooner did those who were with Don Quixote catch sight of the horsemen than they turned and withdrew some distance from the road; for they knew very well that if they stayed they might incur some danger. Don Quixote alone stood his ground, while Sancho shielded himself behind Rocinante's crupper.

The troop of lancers came on, and one of them who rode ahead of the others cried out to the knight, "Out of the way, devil take you, or these bulls will trample you to pieces!"

"Ha, rabble!" replied Don Quixote, "bulls mean nothing to me, even though they be the fiercest that Jarama breeds upon its banks.[27] Confess at once, ye scoundrels, that it is the truth I have here proclaimed or be prepared to do battle with me!"

The herdsman had no time to reply and the knight did not have time to get out of the way if he had wished to do so, and as a result the wild bulls and the tame leading-oxen[28] and all the many drovers and others who were taking the animals to be penned in a village where the bulls were to be baited[29] the following day—the entire troop, in short, both man and beast, passed over Don Quixote and over Sancho, Rocinante, and the gray as well, knocking them all down and sending them rolling. Sancho was badly mauled, his master was frightened, the ass was battered, and Rocinante was far from sound; but they all finally got to their feet, and, stumbling here and falling there, Don Quixote ran after the herd as fast as he could.

"Stop, scoundrelly rabble!" he shouted. "It is a single knight who awaits you, and he is not one who agrees with those that say 'When the enemy flees, build him a bridge of silver.' "[30]

But the drovers in their haste did not stop for this; indeed, they paid no more attention to his threats than to the clouds of yesteryear. It was weariness that stopped Don Quixote as, filled with rage at being balked of his revenge, he sat down to wait for Sancho, Rocinante, and the ass to reach his side. Then master and man mounted once again, and without turning to bid farewell to the imitation Arcadia they continued on their way with more of shame than pleasure in their mien.

CHAPTER LIX. *Wherein is related an extraordinary experience of Don Quixote's, which may be looked upon as an adventure.*[1]

IT WAS the bright clear water of a spring which they had come upon within the cool shade of a grove that afforded Don Quixote and Sancho their first relief from the dust that covered them and the weariness they felt as a result of the incivility of the bulls; and, having turned both the gray and Rocinante loose, without headstall or bridle, the long-suffering pair, master and man, now sat down beside it. Not, however, before Sancho had hastened over to his saddlebag-pantry and taken out what he was in the habit of calling the "grub," [2] while Don Quixote rinsed his mouth and bathed his face, a proceeding which cooled him off and revived somewhat his sagging spirits. Out of pure disgust he would not eat anything, nor did Sancho out of pure politeness venture to touch any of the victuals before him until his master had acted as taster.[3] But when the latter saw that the knight, lost in thought, had forgotten to lift the food to his mouth, he proceeded to trample under foot any kind of good breeding and, without opening his mouth to say a word,[4] began stowing away in his stomach the bread and cheese that were at hand.

"Eat, friend Sancho," said Don Quixote, "and sustain life, since that is of more importance to you than it is to me. Leave me to die of my thoughts and my misfortunes; for you may know, Sancho, that I was born to live dying and you to die eating. That you may see how true this is, look at me now. Here I am with my name in the history books, a famous man of arms, courteous in my conduct, respected by princes, sought after by damsels, and just when I was expecting palms, triumphs, and crowns, I find myself this morning, as a climax to it all, trodden underfoot, battered, and kicked by a herd of filthy animals. When I think of this, my teeth are blunted, my jaws are numbed, my hands are paralyzed, and I lose all appetite to such an extent that I've a mind to die of hunger, which is the cruelest death there is."

"In that case," observed Sancho, who did not leave off munching all the while, "I take it your Grace does not agree with the proverb that says, 'Let Marta die, but let her die with her belly full.' [5] As for me, I have no intention of killing myself. Rather, I mean to do like the shoemaker, who stretches the leather with his teeth to make it reach as far as he likes. I intend to stretch my life out by eating until I come to the end that Heaven has fixed for it; and let me tell you, sir, there is no greater madness than to despair as your Grace is doing. Take my word for it; after you have had a bite to eat, stretch out for a little nap on this green grass-mattress and you will see how much better you feel when you wake up again."

Finding that Sancho's reasoning was that of a philosopher rather than a fool, Don Quixote decided to take his advice. But first he said to him, "If you will do what I am going to tell you, Sancho, I am certain that I shall feel better and less heavyhearted. What I ask is that while I am sleeping as you have urged me to do, you go off to one side some distance away, lay bare your flesh, and with Rocinante's reins give yourself three or four hundred lashes as a substantial payment on account of the three thousand and some that you have yet to give yourself in order to accomplish Dulcinea's disenchantment. It is no small sorrow to me that the poor lady has to remain bewitched as a result of your carelessness and neglect."

"There is much to be said as to that," replied Sancho. "Let us both sleep for the present, and afterward what is to be is in God's hands. Your Grace should know that this business of a man's flogging himself in cold blood is a hard thing to do, especially when the lashes fall on a body that is as badly nourished and underfed as mine. Let my lady Dulcinea be patient, for when she's least expecting it I'll be whipping myself until I'm as full of holes as a sieve. Until death it's all life; [6] by which I mean to say, there's life in me yet, along with the desire to accomplish what I promised."

Thanking him for this, Don Quixote ate a little and Sancho a good deal, and then they both lay down to sleep, leaving those two constant friends and companions, Rocinante and the gray, to roam at will without restraint of any kind and feed upon the grass in which the meadow abounded. Waking somewhat tardily, they mounted once more and resumed their journey, being in haste to reach an inn which they could see, about a league from where they were, as it appeared. I say inn, for the reason that this was what Don Quixote called it, contrary to his usual custom of calling all inns castles. Drawing up in front of it, they inquired of the landlord if he had a lodging for them and were informed that he did have, one with all the comforts and conveniences that were to be found in Saragossa. When they had dismounted, Sancho carried their store of provisions into a room to which the innkeeper gave him a key; then he took the animals out to the stable, fed them their rations, and returned to see what further orders Don Quixote had for him. The knight was seated upon a stone bench against the wall, and his squire was especially grateful to Heaven that this particular inn had not appeared to him to be a castle.

When the supper hour came they retired to their room, and Sancho then asked the landlord what he had in the way of fare and was told that his mouth should be the measure and he might order anything that pleased him, as this hostelry was provided with birds of the air, fowls of the earth, and fish of the sea.

"We don't need all that," said Sancho. "A couple of roast chickens will be enough for us, for my master has a delicate stomach and eats very little and I'm not too much of a glutton myself."

The innkeeper replied that they had no chickens, the kites having made away with them.

"Well, then, Sir Landlord, have them roast a pullet for us, and be sure it's nice and tender."

"A pullet? My father!" exclaimed their host. "It's the truth I'm telling you that only yesterday I sent more than fifty of them to market in the city; but, outside of pullets, your Grace may have what you wish."

"If that is so, you must have some veal or kid."

"There is none in the house just now, for as it happens we just finished the last of it, but next week we'll have plenty and to spare."

"A lot of good that will do us!" said Sancho. "I'll bet that when we come to the end of all the things you don't have, we'll end up with plenty of bacon and eggs."

"In God's name," said the innkeeper, "my guest is not very sharp-witted! Here I have just told him that I have neither pullets nor hens and he expects me to have eggs. Talk about something else that's good to eat but don't be asking for fancy dishes." [7]

"Body of me!" cried Sancho. "Come to the point, Sir Landlord; tell me what you have and stop all this talk."

"What I really and truly have," replied their host, "is a couple of cow-heels that look like calves' feet, or a couple of calves' feet that look like cow-heels, boiled with chickpeas, onions, and bacon, and right now they're calling 'Eat me! Eat me!'"

"Put them aside for me this minute," said Sancho, "and don't let anybody touch them. I'll pay more than anyone else, for there's nothing that I like better and it makes no difference to me whether they're feet or heels."

"No one will touch them," said the innkeeper, "for I have other guests, persons of quality who bring with them their own cook, butler, and larder."

"They could not be of any better quality than my master," said Sancho, "but the calling he follows does not permit of larders or storerooms; we stretch ourselves out in the middle of a field and fill up on acorns or medlars."

Such was the conversation that Sancho had with the innkeeper, and he did not carry it any further by answering the question which the landlord put to him regarding his master's calling or profession. When the supper hour came Don Quixote withdrew into his room,[8] the landlord brought in the stew-pot just as it was, and the knight straightaway fell to eating. While he was so engaged, he heard voices from the next room, which was separated from his own by a thin partition.

"Upon your life, Señor Don Jerónimo," someone was saying, "while they are bringing our supper, let us read another chapter of the *Second Part of Don Quixote de la Mancha*." [9]

No sooner did he hear his name mentioned than Don Quixote rose to his feet and began listening intently to what they were saying about him.

"Why would your Grace have us read such nonsense as that, Señor Don Juan," came the reply, "seeing that he who has read the First Part of the history of Don Quixote de la Mancha cannot possibly find any pleasure in this second one?"

"For all of that," said Don Juan, "it would be well to read it, since no book is so bad that there is not some good to be found in it. What displeases me most about it is that it depicts Don Quixote as no longer in love with Dulcinea del Toboso." [10]

Hearing this, the knight was filled with anger and resentment; raising his voice, he called out, "Whoever says that Don Quixote has forgotten or ever can forget the peerless Dulcinea del Toboso will have to answer to me, and I will show him with evenly matched weapons how far he is from the truth. Forgetfulness is not a part of his make-up, but constancy is his motto, and his profession is to preserve it with gentle bearing and without doing it any violence whatsoever." [11]

"Who is it that answers us?" came the question from the other room.

"Who should it be," replied Sancho, "if not Don Quixote de la Mancha himself, who will make good all that he has said or may say? For he who is well able to pay doesn't mind giving pledges." [12]

He had no more than said this when two gentlemen, for such they appeared to be, entered the room, one of whom threw his arms about Don Quixote's neck.

"Your appearance," he said, "does not belie your name, nor can your name fail to suggest your appearance. You, sir, are undoubtedly the true Don Quixote de la Mancha, north pole and morning star of knight-errantry despite the one who has sought to usurp your name and obliterate your achievements, as the author of this book which I hand you here has done."

With this, he placed the book which his companion carried in Don Quixote's hands. The knight took it and, without saying a word, began leafing through it, and then after a short while he gave it back, saying, "From the little I have seen of it, I have found three things for which the author deserves to be censured. The first is certain words that I have read in the preface; [13] the second is the fact that the language is that of an Aragonese who frequently omits his articles; [14] and the third (which above all brands him as ignorant) is the mistake he makes, and the falsehood of which he is guilty in the essential part of the story, by stating that the wife of Sancho Panza, my squire, is named Mari Gutiérrez when the name should be Teresa Panza. [15] And it is greatly to be feared that one who errs in so important a matter as this will be wrong in all the other particulars throughout the history."

Sancho now spoke up. "A fine historian he is! He surely must know a lot about our business when he calls my wife, Teresa Panza, Mari Gutiérrez! Take the book again, Señor, and see if I am in it and if they've changed my name too."

"From what I have heard tell, my friend," said Don Jerónimo, "you must be Sancho Panza, Señor Don Quixote's squire."

"That I am," said Sancho, "and I'm proud of it."

"Faith, then," said the gentleman, "this new author does not treat you with that decency that your person displays. He portrays you as a glutton and a simpleton, not at all droll—in short, quite different from the Sancho described in the first part of your master's history." [16]

"May God forgive him," said Sancho. "He'd have done better if he had forgotten all about me and left me in my corner; for let him who is able play the instrument, and St. Peter is well enough off in Rome." [17]

The two gentlemen then invited Don Quixote to come into their room and have supper with them, for they well knew that the inn had nothing suitable for him to eat. The knight, always extremely courteous, yielded to this request, but Sancho remained with the stew-pot and, invested with delegated plenary authority,[18] seated himself at the head of the table, with the landlord sharing the meal, for the latter was no less fond of feet and heels than was the squire.

In the course of the supper Don Juan asked Don Quixote what news he had of the lady Dulcinea del Toboso. Was she married or not, had she given birth or was she with child, or was she still a virgin, preserving her modesty and good name and cherishing amorous thoughts of Señor Don Quixote?

"Dulcinea," replied the knight, "is yet a maid, and my passion for her is more unwavering than ever. Our relations are as unsatisfactory as they were before, and as for her beauty, it has been transformed into that of an unclean peasant lass."

He then went on to tell them, point by point, all about the spell that had been laid upon the lady Dulcinea and what had occurred in the Cave of Montesinos, together with the instructions which the magician Merlin had given for her disenchantment and the lashes that Sancho was to give himself. The two gentlemen were delighted as they listened to Don Quixote's account of these strange events in his history and were at once astonished at the nonsense he talked and the polished manner in which he told the story. At times they would take him for a man of intelligence and at other times for a fool, without being able to make up their minds as to just where they were to place him in the vague realm between sound sense and madness.

Having finished his supper, Sancho left the landlord with his legs wobbling [19] and went to the room where his master was.

"May they slay me, good sirs," he said, "if the author of that book that your Worships have is any friend of mine.[20] He calls me a glutton, if what your Worships say is true, and I only hope he doesn't call me a drunkard as well."

"He does call you something of the sort," said Don Jerónimo, "though I cannot remember just how he puts it. I only know that his language is offensive and, moreover, that he lies, as I can tell by looking at the face of our worthy Sancho, here present."

"Believe me, your Worships," said the squire, "the Sancho and the Don Quixote of that story cannot be the same as those in the history composed by Cid Hamete Benengeli, that is to say, they cannot be ourselves: my master, who is valiant, wise, and in love; and I, who am simple-minded, droll, and neither a glutton nor a drunkard."

"I believe you," said Don Juan; "and if it were possible an order should be issued to the effect that no one is to dare to treat of the affairs of the great Don Quixote unless it be Cid Hamete, the original author— just as Alexander ordered that none but Apelles was to dare paint his portrait."

"Let him who will portray me," said Don Quixote, "but let him not mistreat me; for one very often loses patience when insult is heaped on injury."

"No one," said Don Juan, "can insult Señor Don Quixote without his being able to avenge himself, unless he chooses to ward off the blow with the shield of his patience, which appears to me to be great and strong."

Speaking of these and other things, they spent a good part of the night together, and although Don Juan wanted Don Quixote to read more of the book to see what it contained, he could not persuade him to do so; for the knight stated that he regarded it as read and took it to be altogether silly, adding that if by any chance the author should hear that he had had it in his hands, he did not wish to give him the pleasure of thinking that he, Don Quixote, had perused these pages, for we should keep our thoughts and above all, our eyes away from that which is lewd and obscene. They then asked him what his destination was, and he replied that he was bound for Saragossa, where he proposed to take part in the armored tourney that was customarily held there every year; whereupon Don Juan informed him that this new history told how Don Quixote, whoever he might be, in that same tournament had participated in a tilting at the ring but that the description given had shown a sorry lack of inventiveness, especially with regard to the mottoes of the knights and their liveries, in which regard it was impoverished in the extreme though rich in foolishness.[21]

"For that very reason," said Don Quixote, "I will not set foot in Saragossa but will let the world see how this new historian lies, by showing people that I am not the Don Quixote of whom he is speaking."

"You are quite right in doing so," said Don Jerónimo, "for there are other joustings in Barcelona where Don Quixote can display his valor."

"That is what I have in mind," said the knight; "and now, if your Worships will excuse me, it is time to go to bed, and so I will take my leave, trusting that you will number me among your best friends and faithful servants."

"And me too," said Sancho. "It may be I'll be good for something."

With this, they bade one another farewell and Don Quixote and Sancho retired to their own room, leaving Don Juan and Don Jerónimo marveling still at the strange admixture of good sense and madness they had observed; for the two gentlemen were convinced that these were the true Don Quixote and Sancho, while those the Aragonese author had portrayed were not. The knight was up at an early hour the next morning and took leave of his hosts of the evening before by knocking on the partition. As for Sancho, he paid the landlord handsomely, advising him after this not to praise so highly the accommodations of his hostelry or else to lay in a better stock of provisions.

CHAPTER LX. *Of what happened to Don Quixote on his way to Barcelona.*

THE morning was cool and gave promise of the same kind of day to follow as Don Quixote sallied forth from the inn, having made inquiries as to which was the most direct route to Barcelona without passing through Saragossa; for he was determined to give the lie to that new historian, who, so they told him, had heaped so much abuse upon him.

For the first six days nothing happened to him worthy of being set down in writing; but at the end of that time, having left the highway, he found himself at nightfall in a dense grove of oak or cork trees (on this point Cid Hamete is not as precise as he usually is). Master and man thereupon dismounted and made themselves as comfortable as they could at the foot of the trees, and Sancho, who had had a good noonday meal, lost no time in entering the gates of sleep. Don Quixote, on the other hand, kept awake by his thoughts rather than by hunger, was unable to close his eyes as his mind wandered here and there through a thousand different places. Now it seemed that he was in the Cave of Montesinos and was beholding Dulcinea, transformed into a peasant maid, skipping about and mounting her she-ass; and again the words of Merlin the sage were ringing in his ears, setting forth the conditions to be observed and what was to be done in order to accomplish the lady's disenchantment. He fell into a mood of despair as he thought of the laxness and want of charity displayed by his squire Sancho, who, to his master's knowledge, had given himself but five lashes in all, a very small proportion indeed of the countless number that remained to be administered. This made him feel so sad and vexed that he was led to indulge in the following soliloquy:

"If Alexander the Great cut the Gordian knot, saying, 'To cut comes to the same thing as untying,' and for all of that did not cease to be the universal lord of all Asia, this should apply neither more nor less to the present case, if by way of disenchanting Dulcinea I were to flog Sancho whether he likes it or not. If the remedy lies in his receiving three thousand-odd lashes, what difference does it make to me whether he or someone else inflicts them, seeing that the heart of the matter lies in his receiving them, regardless of where they come from?" [1]

With this idea in mind he went over to his squire, having first taken Rocinante's reins and adjusted them in such a manner that they might be used as a lash. He then began undoing Sancho's points [2] (it is the general belief that there was only the one in front to hold up the breeches), but no sooner had he approached him than Sancho was wide awake.

"What is this? Who is laying hands on me and undressing me?"

"It is I," replied Don Quixote. "I have come to make up for your negligence and relieve my own sufferings. I am going to give you a flogging, Sancho, and so discharge a part of the debt you owe. Dulcinea is pining away, you lead a carefree life, and I die of longing. Untruss yourself, then, of your own free will, for it is my will to give you, here in this out-of-the-way place, not less than a thousand strokes."

"You will do nothing of the sort," said Sancho. "Be quiet, your Grace, or by the living God the deaf shall hear us. The lashes that I owe are to be voluntary, not forced, and just now I don't feel like giving myself any. Your Grace has my word that I will whip and swat myself whenever the notion takes me and that should be enough."

"No, Sancho," said Don Quixote, "I cannot leave it to your courtesy, for you are hardhearted and, for a countryman, have very tender flesh."

He accordingly kept on struggling to undo his squire's trousers; seeing which, Sancho leaped to his feet and charged at him. Grappling with him man to man,[3] he tripped him up and brought him down flat on his back, and then placing his right knee on the knight's chest, he grasped his master's hands and held them in such a way that the poor fellow could neither stir nor breathe.

"How now, traitor?" cried Don Quixote. "So you would rebel against your lord and master, would you, and dare to raise your hand against the one who feeds you?"

"I neither unmake nor make a king," [4] replied Sancho, "but am simply standing up for myself, for I am my own lord. If your Grace will promise me to be quiet and not undertake to flog me for the present, I will let you go free as you like; otherwise not, but

> Here shalt thou die, traitor,
> Doña Sancha's enemy." [5]

Don Quixote gave the promise and swore by the one who was his life and the object of his affections [6] that he would not touch a hair of his squire's garments but would leave the matter of flogging himself entirely to Sancho's own free choice. Sancho then rose and walked away for some little distance. Just as he was about to lean back against another tree, he felt something touching his head, and, raising his hands, he found that it was a pair of feet with shoes and stockings on them. Trembling with fright, he ran over to another tree, and the same thing happened, whereupon he began shouting at the top of his voice, calling upon Don Quixote to come and help him. The knight did so, and when he asked Sancho what had occurred to frighten him, the latter replied that all the trees were full of human feet and legs. His master in turn felt them and at once realized what they were.

"There is no reason to be afraid," he said, "for these feet and legs that you feel but do not see are undoubtedly those of some outlaws and highwaymen who have been strung up here, for it is the custom of the officers of justice to hang them in this manner, twenty or thirty at a time, when they capture them; all of which leads me to believe that we must be near Barcelona." [7]

And he was right. It was daylight now, and, lifting their eyes, they saw that these were indeed the bodies of bandits; but if the sight of the dead was terrifying, they were no less dismayed by the appearance of more than forty living robbers who of a sudden surrounded them, telling them in the Catalan tongue that they should keep quiet and wait until the captain of the band came up. Don Quixote was on foot, his horse unbridled, his lance reposing against a tree; he was, in short, utterly defenseless, and so there was nothing for him to do but fold his arms, bow his head, and conserve his energies for a more favorable time and circumstance. The bandits, meanwhile, went over and searched the donkey, leaving nothing in the saddlebags or the valise, and a lucky thing it was for Sancho that he carried in his girdle the crowns that the duke had given him and those that he had brought from home. As it was, those fine fellows would have stripped him and looked to see what he had hidden between his hide and his flesh if at that moment their captain had not arrived on the scene.

He was a stockily built, swarthy-complexioned man of a little more than average height, apparently about thirty-four years of age and with a stern-looking face. He was mounted on a powerful horse and was clad in a coat of mail, and at his side he carried four pistols of the sort which in that country are known as petronels.[8] Perceiving that his squires (for such is the name given to those that follow this calling) were about to despoil Sancho, he ordered them to desist and was at once obeyed; and thus it was the girdle escaped. He was astonished to observe a lance leaning against a tree and a shield on the ground while the sight of Don Quixote in a suit of armor, standing there in deep dejection, filled him with amazement; it seemed to him that this was the most mournful and melancholy countenance that sorrow's own self could have fashioned.

"Do not be so sad, my good man," he said, going up to him. "You have not fallen into the hands of any cruel Busiris,[9] but into those of Roque Guinart,[10] who is inclined to be merciful rather than stern."

"I am not sad to have fallen into your hands, O valiant Roque," replied Don Quixote, "for your fame on this earth is boundless. What grieves me, rather, is the fact that your soldiers have found me without a bridle on my steed, whereas in accordance with that order of knight-errantry that I profess I am required to be constantly on the alert, serving as my own sentinel at all hours. I would have you know, O great Roque, that had they found me upon my horse, armed with lance and shield, it would not have been so easy for them to subdue me; for I am Don Quixote de la Mancha, with whose exploits the whole world is filled."

Then it was that Roque Guinart came to realize the nature of Don Quixote's infirmity, which had more to do with madness than with boastfulness. Although he had heard the knight's name mentioned a number of times, he had never regarded his deeds as true, since he could not bring himself to believe that such a whim could so take possession of the human heart. For this reason he was very glad indeed to have fallen in with him and to have the opportunity of seeing for himself at close range what he had heard so much about from a distance.

"Valiant knight," he said, "do not be downcast nor look upon this situation in which you find yourself as an unfortunate one; for it may be that through such mischances your crooked fortunes will be straightened out, seeing that Heaven, by strange and unheard-of roundabout ways that men never dreamed of, is accustomed to lift up the fallen and enrich the poor."

Don Quixote was about to thank him when they heard behind them what sounded like a troop of horses. It was, however, but a single horse upon which a young man came riding furiously. He looked to be about twenty, and his attire consisted of a gold-trimmed suit of green damask with breeches and a loose jacket; [11] he wore a cocked hat of the Walloon variety, tight-fitting waxed boots, and gilded spurs, sword, and dagger; in his hands he carried a fowling piece, and at his side was a brace of pistols. Hearing the sound, Roque turned his head to behold the handsome figure, and, riding up to him, the youth addressed him as follows:

"O valiant Roque, I come to seek you out and to find in you if not a cure, at least some relief, for my misfortune. Not to keep you in suspense, for I am aware that you do not recognize me, I will tell you who I am. I am Claudia Jerónima, daughter of Simón Forte, your very good friend and the special enemy of Clauquel Torrellas, who is also your enemy since he is of the rival band. As you know, this Torrellas has a son, Don Vicente Torrellas, or, at any rate, that is what he was called less than a couple of hours ago. But to cut short the story of my misadventure, I will tell you in a few words what he has done to me. He saw me and took a fancy to me, and I listened to and fell in love with him without my father's knowledge; for there is not a woman, however retiring and secluded she may be, who will not find more than enough opportunities for carrying out her reckless desires.

"The short of it is, he promised to be my husband and I gave him my word that I would be his wife, and the matter went no further. Yesterday I learned that, forgetful of what he owed me, he was about to marry another and that the nuptials were to be held this morning, a piece of news that upset me greatly and put an end to my patience. As my father was not in the village at the time, I donned this costume in which you see me and, riding this horse as hard as I could, I caught up with Don Vicente about a league or so from here. Without pausing to indulge in any reproaches or listen to any excuses, I fired this fowling piece at him and these two pistols besides, and to the best of my belief I must have lodged more than two bullets in his body, opening in it doors through which my honor might emerge bathed in his blood. I left him there with his servants, who did not dare undertake to defend him, and came to look for you that you might help me get to France, where I have relatives with whom I can live. And I would also ask you to protect my father lest Don Vicente's kinsmen [12] wreak some monstrous vengeance."

Admiring the beautiful Claudia's dash and spirit and her charming figure, and admiring her as well for what she had done, Roque now spoke to her.

"Come, Señora," he said, "let us go see if your enemy is dead, and afterward we will consider what is best for you."

Don Quixote had been listening attentively to Claudia's words and Roque Guinart's reply. "There is no need," he observed, "for anyone to go to the trouble of defending this lady, as I will take that responsibility upon myself. Give me my horse and my arms and await me here. I will go look for the knight and, living or dead, compel him to keep the promise he made to so beautiful a creature."

"And let no one think that he won't," said Sancho, "for my master is a good hand when it comes to matchmaking. Why, it's not many days ago that he forced another to marry who also wanted to break his word to a certain damsel, and if it had not been for the enchanters who persecuted the fellow and changed his true shape into that of a lackey, the maiden I am telling you about would not be a maid at this minute."

Roque, more concerned with thinking of the beauteous Claudia and her plight than he was with listening to the conversation of master and man, did not hear these remarks. He now ordered his squires to return to Sancho all that they had taken from the gray and to withdraw to that spot where they had spent the night; and, accompanied by the young woman, he then set out at full speed in search of the dead or wounded Don Vicente. When they reached the place where she had come upon her betrothed, they found nothing more than recently spilled blood; but, looking around in all directions, they sighted a number of people on the slope of a hill, which led them to believe, as was the case, that this must be the one they sought and that his servants were carrying him away either to care for his wounds or to bury him. Quickening their pace, Roque and his companion had no difficulty in overtaking the others, who were proceeding very slowly.

They found Don Vicente in the arms of his servants. In a voice that was faint from exhaustion he was calling upon them to let him die, inasmuch as the pain from his wounds would not permit of his going any farther. Flinging themselves from their horses, the pair went over to him. The servants were frightened at Roque's appearance, and Claudia was deeply moved at sight of Don Vicente as, half tenderly half sternly, she knelt beside him and took his hand in hers.

"Had you given me this," she said, "in accordance with our understanding, you would never have found yourself brought to such a pass."

Opening his eyes, the wounded gentleman recognized her. "I perceive plainly enough, O beautiful and deceived lady," he said, "that it is you who have slain me, a punishment that, by reason of the affection I bear you, I did not deserve; for never in thought or deed have I ever wished to offend you, nor would such a thing have been possible."

"Then," said Claudia, "it is not true that you were on your way this morning to wed Leonora, daughter of the rich Balvastro?"

"Most certainly not," replied Don Vicente. "It must have been my evil fortune that brought you such tidings, so that, in your jealous rage, you might be led to take my life; but seeing that I now leave that life in your hands and arms, I look upon my lot as a fortunate one after all.[18] By way of assurance that I speak the truth, press my hand and take me for your husband if you will, since there is no better way in which I may atone for the wrong you fancy I have done you."

Claudia did so, and her own heart was so oppressed that she fell in a faint on Don Vicente's bloodstained bosom even as the death spasm seized him. Roque was perplexed by it all, not knowing what to do. The servants ran for water and with it bathed the faces of the couple, whereupon the young woman recovered from her swoon, but not her bridegroom from his paroxysm, for his life had come to an end. When Claudia saw this and was certain that her beloved husband was no more, she rent the air with her sighs, made the heavens ring with her laments, tore her hair and cast it on the breeze, clawed her face with her hands, and gave all the signs of grief and feeling that could conceivably come from an afflicted bosom.

"O cruel and thoughtless woman," she cried, "how readily did you let yourself be moved to carry out so evil a design! O mad force of jealousy, to what desperate straits do you bring those who accord you a place in their hearts! O my husband, whose misfortune in being mine has taken you from the marriage bed to the grave!"

Claudia's laments were so heart-rending as to bring tears to Roque's eyes, unaccustomed as he was to shedding tears on any occasion whatsoever. The servants wept, Claudia swooned away at every step, and all the region round about appeared to be one vast field of sorrow and misfortune. Roque Guinart ordered the servants to take Don Vicente's body to the village where his father lived, which was not far away, in order that it might be given burial. Claudia informed him that she wished to go to a certain convent where an aunt of hers was the abbess, as she intended to spend the rest of her life there with another and eternal bridegroom, and Roque praised this worthy resolution and offered to escort her to her destination, promising further that he would protect her father against Don Vicente's relatives or anyone else who might seek to attack him.

Claudia, however, would not consent to his accompanying her but thanked him heartily for his kindness and took leave of him in tears. The servants bore the body away and Roque returned to his followers, and thus did the love affair of Claudia Jerónima come to an end. Was such an end to be wondered at, seeing that it was the cruel and invincible power of jealousy that wove the web of her lamentable history?

Roque Guinart found his squires in the place to which he had ordered them to retire, and in the midst of them, mounted on Rocinante, was Don Quixote. The Knight was engaged in making a speech to them in which he sought to persuade them to give up this mode of life which was so dangerous to body and soul; but inasmuch as most of them were Gascons, a rude lot with no respect for law and order,[14] his words had little effect upon them. Roque as he drew up inquired of Sancho if they had returned to him the valuables which they had stripped from the ass, and the squire replied that they had, but that three kerchiefs worth as much as three whole cities, still were missing.

"What are you talking about, man?" said one of the band. "I have them myself, and they are not worth three reales."

"That is true," said Don Quixote, "but my squire values them at the price he has mentioned by reason of the one who gave them to me."

Roque ordered the fellow to give them back at once, after which he lined his men up and had them produce all the clothing, jewels, money, and other objects that they had stolen since the last time they had divided the spoils. Having made a hasty appraisal and reduced to terms of money those items that could not be divided, he split the whole into shares with such equity and exactitude that in not a single instance did he go beyond or fall short of a strict distributive justice. They were all well satisfied with the payment received, indeed they were quite well pleased; and Roque then turned to Don Quixote.

"If I did not observe an absolute impartiality with these fellows," he said, "there would be no living with them."

"From what I have seen here," remarked Sancho, "justice is so good a thing that even robbers find it necessary."

Hearing this, one of the band raised the butt end of an harquebus [15] and would undoubtedly have come down with it on Sancho's head if Roque Guinart had not shouted to him to refrain. Sancho was terrified and made up his mind that from then on he would keep a tightly sewn lip as long as he was in the present company.

At this point one of those squires who had been stationed as sentinels along the highway to see who came and went and report to their chief on what happened, came riding up.

"Sir," he said, "not far from here, along the road to Barcelona, there is a great crowd of people approaching."

"Were you able to make out," Roque asked him, "whether they are the kind that are looking for us or the kind we are looking for?"

"The kind we are looking for," replied the squire.

"Well, then," said Roque, "be on your way, all of you; bring them to me here at once and see that not a one escapes."

The men did as they had been commanded to do, leaving Don Quixote, Sancho, and Roque alone together; and as the three of them waited to see what the squires would bring back, the leader of the band addressed the knight.

"The life we lead," he said, "must appear a strange one to Señor Don Quixote, one filled with strange happenings and adventures and all of them dangerous. I am not at all surprised that it should seem so, for I really must confess that there is no mode of existence that is more restless and laden with anxiety than ours. What led me to adopt such a life was a certain desire for vengeance, which has the power to disturb the quietest of hearts. I am by nature merciful and well meaning, but, as I say, the will to avenge a wrong that was done me so overcomes my virtuous inclinations that I continue in this calling in spite of what my better judgment tells me; and even as one depth calls to another and one sin to another sin, so have the objects of my vengeance come to be linked together in such a manner that I have taken upon myself not merely my own wrongs but those of others as well. But, please God, though I find myself in this bewildering labyrinth, I still have not given up hope of reaching a secure haven in the end."

Don Quixote was amazed to hear Roque express such praiseworthy and well-reasoned sentiments; for among those who follow the highwayman's trade of robbing and killing he had not believed it possible there could be anyone so right-thinking as this.

"Señor Roque," he now replied to him, "the beginning of health lies in a knowledge of one's infirmity, and in the sick man's being willing to take the medicines that the physician prescribes. Your Grace is sick, you know what the disease is from which you are suffering, and Heaven, or, better, God, who is our physician, will provide the remedies to cure you—but not all of a sudden or through any miracle, for they usually do their healing work little by little. Moreover, intelligent sinners are nearer redemption than simple-minded ones, and by what your Grace has said you have shown that you are a man of sense. There is nothing to do, then, but to be of good courage and wait for your sickly conscience to improve. And if your Grace is of a mind to take a short cut and obtain your salvation with ease, then come with me and I will teach you to be a knight-errant. In that life you will meet with so many hardships and misadventures that, if they were to be taken as a penance, they would land you in Heaven in the twinkling of an eye."

Roque laughed at Don Quixote's advice, and then, changing the subject, went on to tell him of the outcome of Claudia Jerónima's affair, which made Sancho feel very sad, for he had been struck by the young woman's beauty, courage, and self-assurance. By this time the squires were back with their prize, consisting of two gentlemen on horseback, two pilgrims on foot, and a coach full of women accompanied by about half a dozen servants, some of whom were mounted while others were not. The squires had them surrounded, and both victors and vanquished preserved a deep silence as they waited for the great Roque Guinart to speak. He now inquired of the gentlemen who they were and whence they came and what money they had on them.

"Sir," one of them answered, "we are two captains of Spanish infantry; our companies are in Naples and we are to embark in four galleys that are said to be in Barcelona with orders for Sicily. We have with us three or four hundred crowns, which is enough to make us feel rich and happy, as it is truly a fortune in view of that poverty to which soldiers are accustomed."

Roque put the same question to the pilgrims as to the captains and was told that they were on their way to take ship for Rome and that they had about sixty reales between them. He also wanted to know who the women in the coach were, whither they were bound, and how much money they had on their persons.

"Those in the coach," one of the men on horseback replied, "are my lady Doña Guiomar de Quiñones, wife of the president of the vicarial court of Naples, her small daughter, a young waiting woman, and a duenna; we six servants are accompanying them, and their money amounts to six hundred pounds."

"That means," said Roque Guinart, "that we have here altogether nine hundred crowns and sixty reales; my soldiers should have about sixty; see how much is coming to each one of them, for I am a poor hand at reckoning."

Upon hearing this, the highwaymen raised a shout: "Long live Roque Guinart, in spite of the thieving rascals [16] that seek his ruin!"

The captains were obviously grieved, the president's lady was downcast, and the pilgrims were by no means happy as they thought of their funds being confiscated. Roque kept them in suspense like this for a short while and then, their distress being visible at the distance of a crossbow shot, he put an end to it by saying to the captains, "Will you be so courteous, your Worships, as kindly to lend me sixty pounds, and will my lady, the president's wife, let me have eighty, to satisfy the members of my band, since the abbot must dine on what he gets by singing? [17] You may then go your way free and unhindered with a safe-conduct which I will give you in order that, should you fall in with other bands of mine that I have scattered around these parts, they may not do you any harm; for it is not my intention to do wrong to soldiers or to any woman, especially persons of quality."

The captains were most eloquent and profuse in thanking Roque for his courtesy and generosity, for such was the way they felt about his leaving them their own money. The lady, Doña Guiomar de Quiñones, wanted to fling herself out of the coach that she might kiss the great man's hands and feet, but he would by no means consent to this; rather, he begged her pardon for the wrong he had done her, explaining that he was forced to comply with the unavoidable exigencies of his unpleasant calling. She thereupon ordered one of her servants to pay over at once the eighty crowns that constituted her share, for the captains had already disbursed their sixty.

The pilgrims were about to give up the pitiably small sum of money that they had on them, but Roque told them to keep quiet, and, turning to his followers he said, "Of these crowns, two go to each one of you, which leaves twenty over; let ten be given to the pilgrims and ten to this worthy squire that he may speak well of the present adventure."

He then had them bring him pen and ink and paper, with which he always went provided, and proceeded to write out a safe-conduct addressed to the leaders of his bands, after which he bade them good-by, leaving the travelers free to go their way as they marveled at his magnanimity, generosity, and unusual conduct, for they regarded him as more like Alexander the Great than a notorious bandit.

"This captain of ours," said one of his men, speaking in a mixture of Gascon and Catalan, "is better suited to be a friar [18] than a highwayman; after this, if he wants to be so liberal, let it be with his own property, not with ours."

The poor wretch did not speak so low but that Roque overheard him, and, drawing his sword, the latter laid the fellow's head open, dividing it almost in two.

"That," he said, "is the way I punish those who are impudent and too free with their tongues."

All his men were stunned by this and did not utter a word, such was the respect they had for him. Then, going off to one side, he wrote a letter to a friend of his in Barcelona, stating that the famous knight, Don Quixote de la Mancha, of whom there was so much talk, was with him at the moment and that he found him to be the most entertaining and sensible man in all the world. He added that, four days from then, which would be on St. John the Baptist's Day,[19] he meant to set him down in the middle of the beach of that city, clad in full armor, mounted on Rocinante his horse, and accompanied by his squire Sancho on an ass, and he wished his correspondent to notify his friends, the Niarros, of this fact so that they might have some diversion with the knight. He would have liked, he said, to deprive his enemies, the Cadells,[20] of this pleasure, but that was impossible since Don Quixote's mad actions and shrewd observations and Sancho Panza's drolleries could not fail to amuse them all. This letter he dispatched by one of his followers, who, exchanging his highwayman's costume for peasant garb, made his way into Barcelona and delivered it to the individual to whom it was addressed.

CHAPTER **LXI**. *Of what happened to Don Quixote upon his entrance into Barcelona, with other matters that contain more truth than wit.*

THREE days and three nights Don Quixote spent with Roque, and if it had been three hundred years the former would still have found plenty to observe and wonder at in the bandit's mode of life. Daybreak would find them in one place, dinnertime in another; they would now flee, not knowing from whom, and now would lie in wait, not knowing what to expect. They slept standing up, interrupting their slumbers to move from one place to another. And all the while they were sending out spies, posting sentinels, and blowing on the matchlocks of their harquebuses, though they had but few of these weapons as all of them [1] carried petronels.

Roque passed the night apart from his followers, keeping them in ignorance of his whereabouts; for the many proclamations which the viceroy of Barcelona had issued against him, putting a price upon his head,[2] made him fearful and uneasy and he did not dare trust anyone, being in dread even of his own men lest they slay him or hand him over to the authorities. It was truly a wretched and a wearying life that he led.

At length, following untraveled roads, short cuts, and secret paths, Roque, Don Quixote, Sancho, and six squires set out for Barcelona, arriving at the beach during the night of St. John's Eve. There the bandit chief embraced his guests and, giving Sancho the ten crowns which he had promised him but which had not as yet been paid, bade them farewell and departed, leaving Don Quixote to sit in the saddle just as he was and wait for the coming of day.

It was not long before the fair Aurora began to show herself on the balconies of the east, bringing joy to the grass and flowers; and if there was nothing about her coming to please the ear, that deficiency was instantly remedied by the sound of many flageolets and drums, and the "Look out, there! Make way! Make way!" of runners who appeared to sally forth from the city. Aurora, meanwhile, was making way for the sun, which was gradually lifting above the horizon's lowest rim a face larger than a shield.

Looking about them in all directions, Don Quixote and Sancho now had their first view of the sea, which impressed them as being very broad and spacious, much larger than the Lakes of Ruidera in La Mancha. They saw the galleys on the beach with their lowered awnings, decked out with streamers and pennants that fluttered in the breeze and swept and kissed the surface of the water, while from aboard the vessels, near and far, bugles, trumpets, and clarions filled the air with a martial melody. The boats now began to move about and engage in a sort of skirmish in the quiet water, and at the same moment a large number of horsemen on handsome mounts with showy liveries came riding from the city and began executing a similar maneuver. The soldiers on the galleys discharged a countless number of rounds of artillery, and their fire was returned by those on the walls and in the forts, the deafening roar of the heavy cannon being answered in turn by the guns amidship. The sea was bright, the earth rejoicing, the air clear save now and then for the smoke from the artillery—in short, everything was such as to infuse all the people gathered there with an unlooked-for sense of pleasure.

As for Sancho, he was unable to make out how those bulky objects moving over the water could have so many feet. But at this point the liveried horsemen with cheers, cries, and Moorish war whoops [3] came galloping up to where Don Quixote waited in astonishment and some alarm.

And then one of them—the one to whom Roque had sent word— raised his voice and cried out to the knight, "Welcome to our city, O mirror, beacon, and north star of all knight-errantry, in the full sense of the word.[4] You are, I repeat, very welcome indeed, O valiant Don Quixote de la Mancha—not the false, not the fictitious, not the apocryphal one that we read of in mendacious histories that have appeared of late, but the true and legitimate one, the real one that Cid Hamete Benengeli, flower of historians, has portrayed for us."

Don Quixote did not utter a word in reply, nor did the horsemen give him a chance to do so. Wheeling their steeds again and again, they and their followers began performing a complicated caracole around him; and he then turned to Sancho and said, "These gentlemen plainly recognized us. I will wager you that they have read our history and that of the Aragonese as well, which was printed not so long ago."

The horseman who had previously addressed the knight now spoke to him once more. "Come with us, Señor Don Quixote," he said, "for we are all at your service, being great friends of Roque Guinart."

"If courtesy begets courtesy," replied Don Quixote, "then that which you display is the daughter or very near relative of the courtesy manifested by the great Roque. Take me wherever you see fit, for I have no other will than yours, especially if you choose to employ it in your service."

The gentleman replied with words equally polite; and then, closing in around him, they all set out for the city to the sound of drums and flageolets. But as they were about to enter the town, the Evil One, who ordains all things evil, and small boys, who are more mischievous than mischief itself, took a hand in the matter. Forcing their way through the crowd, a pair of impudent and prankish urchins lifted up the tails of Rocinante and the gray and inserted a bunch of furze under each of them. When they felt these unaccustomed spurs, the poor animals pressed their tails tightly against their bodies, thereby increasing the pain, and as a result they began leaping and rearing in such a manner that they tossed their riders to the ground. Very much embarrassed by what had happened, Don Quixote ran up to relieve the nag of his plume, and Sancho did the same for his donkey. Those who were serving as the knight's escort would have liked to punish the lads for their impudence, but this was impossible, for the pair were soon lost among the thousands in the crowd.

Master and man then mounted again and, accompanied still by music and cheers, reached the home of their guide, which was very large and imposing, in short, the house of a wealthy gentleman. And here we shall leave them for the present, seeing that Cid Hamete would have it so.

CHAPTER LXII . *Which deals with the adventure of the enchanted head, together with other trifling things that cannot be left untold.*

DON ANTONIO MORENO was the name of Don Quixote's host, a gentleman of wealth and discernment who was fond of amusing himself in an innocent and kindly way. Having taken the knight into his house, he began casting about for some harmless means of bringing out his mad traits; for jests that give pain are no jests at all,[1] and those pastimes that result in hurting another person are not worth while.

The first thing he did, accordingly, was to have Don Quixote remove his armor, which left him clad only in that tight-fitting chamois-skin suit that we have already described and portrayed a number of times; after which, he led him out onto a balcony overlooking one of the principal thoroughfares of the city, in order that the people gathered there, including the small boys, might have a look at him. The crowd stared as if he had been a monkey, while the liveried horsemen once more rode up and down in front of him, as if it was for his special benefit and not to celebrate some festive occasion that they had donned that garb. Sancho, meanwhile, was happy as could be; for it seemed to him that, without his knowing the why or wherefore of it all, he had come upon another Camacho's wedding, another house like that of Don Diego de Miranda's, or another castle like the duke's.

Some of Don Antonio's friends dined with him that day, and they all treated Don Quixote with the utmost respect, showing him the honors due a knight-errant, at which he became so puffed up and self-satisfied that he could not contain himself. As for Sancho's witticisms, they were such that the household servants and all the others present hung upon his every word. When they were seated at the table, their host turned to Sancho.

"We have received word here, my good Sancho," he said, "that you are very fond of *manjar blanco* [2] and forced-meat balls, so fond, indeed, that if there is any left over, you put it away in your bosom for another day." [3]

"No, sir, that is not so," replied Sancho, "for I am more cleanly than greedy, and my master Don Quixote, here present, can very well tell you that the two of us are used to going for a week at a time with nothing to eat but a handful of nuts or acorns. The truth of the matter is that if they happen to give me a heifer, I run with the halter,[4] by which I mean to say, I eat what is set before me and take things as they come; and if anyone says that I eat more than my share or am unclean, you may take my word for it, he's wide of the mark, and I'd put it in a different way if it wasn't for the honorable beards at this table."[5]

"I can assure you," said Don Quixote at this point, "that the sparingness and cleanliness with which Sancho eats might be inscribed and engraved on tablets of bronze, to be preserved as a lasting memorial for future ages. I grant you that when he is hungry he appears to be a bit of a glutton, for then he eats with great haste and chews his food with both cheeks bulging. But he is always scrupulously clean, and during the time that he was governor he became so dainty in his habits that he even used a fork for eating grapes or pomegranate seeds."

"What?" said Don Antonio. "Has Sancho been a governor?"

"Yes," replied Sancho, "governor of an island named Barataria. For ten days I governed it as I saw fit, and during that time I lost my rest and learned to scorn all the governments in the world. I finally ran away from it and fell into a pit, where I gave myself up for dead, but by a miracle I came out alive."

Don Quixote then gave them a detailed account of everything that had happened in connection with Sancho's government, and they all enjoyed it very much. When the cloth had been removed, Don Antonio took his guest by the hand and led him into another room of the house, where the only article of furniture was a table that appeared to be made of jasper, resting upon a pedestal of the same material, while upon it was a head resembling the busts of the Roman emperors and seemingly carved out of bronze. After they had walked around the table many times, Don Antonio spoke.

"Now that I am certain, Señor Don Quixote, that the door is shut and no one can overhear us, I wish," he said, "to tell your Grace of one of the rarest adventures, or, more properly speaking, one of the strangest things, that could be imagined, but upon condition that your Grace keeps it hidden away in the most remote and secret closet of your mind."

"That I swear to do," said Don Quixote, "and by way of further security, I will place a flagstone over it; for I would have your Grace know, Señor Don Antonio"—he had learned his host's name by this time—"that you are talking to one who, though he has ears for hearing, has no tongue for speaking. Hence your Grace may feel safe in transferring to my bosom what you have in yours, knowing full well that I have consigned it to the depths of silence."

"Relying on that promise," said Don Antonio, "I shall astonish your Grace with what you will see and hear, and at the same time relieve myself of the pain I feel at having no one to whom I may confide my secrets, which are not to be entrusted to everybody."

Don Quixote was puzzled as he waited to see what would come of all these precautions. Taking the knight's hand, Don Antonio now passed it over the bronze head and over the entire table, all the way down to the jasper base.

"This head, Señor Don Quixote," he remarked, "was made and fashioned by one of the greatest enchanters and sorcerers in all the world.[6] He was a Pole by birth, a disciple of the famous Escotillo [7] of whom so many marvels are related. He was here in my house, and for the price of a thousand crowns which I gave him he carved the head, which has the property and the virtue of being able to answer all questions that are asked of its ear. By setting up geometrical figures,[8] observing the stars, casting horoscopes, and noting the hour and season, he brought his work to that perfection that we shall see tomorrow; for on Fridays it is mute, and since today is Friday we must wait. In the meantime, your Grace may be deciding what questions you wish to put to it, and I know from experience that it will answer you truly."

Amazed to think that the head should possess such qualities, Don Quixote was inclined to disbelieve his host; but in view of the fact that he would shortly be able to put the matter to a test, he merely thanked Don Antonio for having revealed to him so great a secret. They then left the room, the master of the house locking the door behind him, and went down to the great hall where the other gentlemen were and where Sancho all the while had been telling them of many of the adventures and accidents that had befallen his master.

That afternoon they took Don Quixote out for a ride,[9] not in his armor but dressed for the street, being attired in a greatcoat of tawny-colored cloth which at that season of the year would have made ice itself sweat, while the servants had orders to keep Sancho entertained and not to permit him to leave the house. Don Quixote went mounted, not upon Rocinante, but upon a large even-paced mule with very fine trappings. Having put his greatcoat on him, they sewed a piece of parchment on the back of it with an inscription in large letters: "THIS IS

DON QUIXOTE DE LA MANCHA." From the moment they set out, the placard attracted the attention of all those who had come to behold the spectacle, and the knight for his part was astonished to find so many people gazing at him and calling him by name.

Turning to Don Antonio, who rode alongside him, he said, "Great are the prerogatives of knight-errantry, seeing that it makes the one who follows that calling known and famous in all parts of the earth. If you do not believe me, Señor Don Antonio, your Grace has but to observe the lads of this city, who, though they have never seen me, nevertheless recognize me."

"That is true, Señor Don Quixote," replied Don Antonio; "for just as fire cannot remain hidden or shut away from view, so virtue cannot fail to be recognized for what it is, and that virtue which is attained through the profession of arms shines forth above all others."

It happened, then, that as Don Quixote was riding along in the manner described, to the applause of the multitude, a certain Castilian [10] who had read the placard on the knight's back raised his voice and cried out, "May the devil take you, Don Quixote de la Mancha! What! and aren't you dead from all the clubbings that your ribs have had? You are a madman, but if you kept your madness to yourself it would not be so bad. As it is, you have the faculty of turning into madmen and fools all that have anything to do with you. As proof of this, just look at those gentlemen that are accompanying you. Go back to your home, you crackbrain, attend to your own affairs, see to your wife and children, and leave off these absurdities that eat your brain away and skim off your wits."

"Brother," Don Antonio said to him, "go about your business and do not be giving advice to those that do not ask for it. Señor Don Quixote de la Mancha is quite sane, and we who are with him are not fools. Virtue is to be honored wherever it is met with; so go, and bad luck go with you, and do not be meddling in what does not concern you."

"By God, but your Grace is right," replied the Castilian, "for to give advice to this good man is to kick against the prick; but, for all of that, it is a very great pity to see the good sense they say the fool displays on all other subjects [11] drained off like this through the channel of his knight-errantry. And may the bad luck your Grace wished me really follow me and my descendants if from this day forth, though I live to be older than Methuselah, I give advice to anyone whether he asks for it or not."

With this, the advice-giver went his way, and they resumed their ride; [12] but so great was the eagerness of the small boys and all the rest of the crowd to see what was on the placard that Don Antonio was compelled to take it off under pretense of removing something else. At nightfall they returned home, to find an evening party in progress there; for Don Antonio's wife, a beautiful lady of high station and endowed with wit and gaiety, had invited some of her women friends to come and show honor to her house guest and enjoy his unheard-of variety of madness. A number of them accepted the invitation, a splendid supper was served, and the dancing began about ten o'clock.

Among the ladies were two that, being of a mischievous disposition, were fond of a practical joke, and although they were perfectly respectable they were somewhat free and easy in their ways when it came to playing pranks for the sake of innocent diversion. This pair insisted on Don Quixote's dancing with them so often that they wore him out, not only in body but in spirit as well. He was a sight to see: long, lean, lank, and yellow-looking, clad in his tight-fitting suit, awkward, and, above all, not very light on his feet. The frolicsome ladies made furtive love to him and he, likewise by stealth, rejected their advances; but, finding himself hard pressed by these attentions, he finally raised his voice and cried out, "*Fugite, partes adversae!* [13] Leave me in peace, unwelcome temptations! Away with your passion, ladies; for she who is queen of my heart, the peerless Dulcinea del Toboso, will consent to none other assailing it and laying it low!"

Saying this, he sat down in the middle of the ballroom floor, battered and broken from his exertions as a dancer, and Don Antonio then had them pick him up and carry him off to bed. The first to lay hold to him was Sancho.

"It was an evil hour, my master," he said, "when you tried to dance! Do you think that all brave men and knights-errant can do that? [14] If so, I can tell you that you are mistaken. There are those that would rather slay a giant than cut a caper. Now, if it had been a clog dance [15] I'd have taken your place, for I can tap my heels like a gerfalcon,[16] but when it comes to your fancy steps [17] I'm no good at it."

With these and other remarks Sancho set the company to laughing, and then he went off to put his master to bed, taking care to cover him well that he might sweat out any cold caught by dancing.

The next day Don Antonio decided that it would be well to try out the enchanted head at once, and so, with Don Quixote, Sancho, and a couple of friends, together with the ladies who had worn Don Quixote out with dancing the evening before and who had spent the night there, he shut himself up in the room where the head was. Explaining to them its peculiar properties, which he was to put to the test for the first time that day, he bound them all to secrecy; for, with the exception of Don Antonio's two friends, there was no one who understood the mystery behind the enchantment, and if these two had not been informed of it by the master of the house, they of necessity would have been quite as amazed as the others, so skillfully and artfully was the mechanism contrived.

The first who came up to whisper in the ear of the magic head was Don Antonio himself, who in a low voice, yet not so low but that the rest of them could hear him, said, "Tell me, O head, by the virtue that is in you,[18] what am I thinking of at this moment?"

And without moving its lips the head replied, in a tone so clear and distinct that all were able to make it out, "I am no judge of thoughts."

The entire company was astonished at hearing it speak, in view of the fact that neither around the table nor in all the room was there any human being who could have given the answer.

"How many of us are there here?" was Don Antonio's next question; and the reply, uttered in the same tone of voice, was, "There are you and your wife, two friends of yours, two women friends of hers, a famous knight named Don Quixote de la Mancha, and his squire whose name is Sancho Panza."

This created fresh astonishment, and everyone's hair was standing on end from sheer fright. "I am now convinced," remarked Don Antonio as he turned aside, "that the one who sold you to me did not cheat me, O wise head, talking head, answering and admirable head! Let someone else come up and ask any question that he likes."

Since women ordinarily are extremely curious, the first to do so was one of the friends of Don Antonio's wife. "Tell me, O head," she inquired, "what must I do to be very beautiful?" And the answer was, "Be very modest."

"I ask no more," said the one who had put the question.

She was followed by her companion. "I should like to know, O head, whether my husband loves me or not."

"Observe the way he treats you," came the response, "and judge for yourself."

"There was no need of my asking to learn that," said the married lady as she walked away; "for it goes without saying that the way a person treats you shows the way he feels toward you."[19]

One of Don Antonio's friends was the next questioner. "Who am I?"

"You know who you are."

"That is not what I asked you," said the gentleman. "I wanted you to tell me if you recognized me."

"Yes, I recognize you; you are Don Pedro Noriz."

"That is all I seek to know, as it is enough to assure me, O head, that you know everything."

It was the other friend's turn now. "Tell me, O head, what does my son and heir desire?"

"I have already told you that I am no judge of such things, but, nevertheless, I may inform you that what your son desires is to bury you."

"That is to say," the gentleman replied, " 'What I see with my eyes I point out with my finger.' [20] I have no further questions."

Don Antonio's wife came next. "I do not know, O head, what to ask you. I should merely like to have you tell me if I am to enjoy my good husband for many years to come."

"Yes, you will," was the answer, "for his good health and temperate mode of living promise him a long life-span, which many by their intemperance cut short."

Don Quixote now came forward. "Tell me," he said, "you who do the answering, with regard to my story of what happened to me in the Cave of Montesinos, did it really happen or was it a dream? Will my squire Sancho be sure to receive the lashes that are his due? And will Dulcinea finally be disenchanted?"

"With respect to the cave," the head replied, "there is much to be said on both sides; Sancho's lashes will proceed apace; and the disenchantment of Dulcinea will ultimately be accomplished."

"That is enough," said Don Quixote. "Let me but see Dulcinea freed of the magic spell and it will seem to me that all the good fortune I could wish for has come to me at once."

Sancho was the last, and his question was, "Head, shall I have another government? Shall I ever be through with this poverty-stricken life of a squire? Shall I see my wife and children again?"

"You will govern in your house," the head assured him; "if you return to it, you will see your wife and young ones; and if you leave off serving, you will cease to be a squire."

"That's fine, by God!" exclaimed Sancho. "I could have told myself as much as that. The prophet Perogrullo [21] could not have done better."

"Stupid creature," said Don Quixote, "what answer did you expect? Is it not enough that the replies which this head gives have a bearing on the questions put to it?"

"Yes," said Sancho, "it will do; but I'd have liked it better if it had spoken longer and told me more."

This ended the questions and answers, but it did not end the astonishment they all felt, with the exception of Don Antonio and his friends, who knew the secret of the thing. That secret Cid Hamete Benengeli chose to reveal at once, not wishing to keep the world in suspense or under the impression that there was anything strange and magical about it. He accordingly goes on to state that Don Antonio, in imitation of another head which he had seen in Madrid, the work of an artisan of that city, had had this one made in his own house in order to provide entertainment and astonish the ignorant.

The mechanism was constructed in the following manner. The table was made of wood painted and varnished like jasper, and the pedestal upon which it rested was of the same material, with four projecting eagles' claws to give it greater firmness. The bronze-colored head, which resembled the bust of a Roman emperor, of the kind seen on coins and medals, was entirely hollow, and so was the table on which it stood, into which it fitted so exactly that there was no sign of any juncture. The foot of the table was also hollow, forming a continuation of the throat and chest of the head above, and the whole was connected with another room immediately below. Through the hollow foot, table, throat, and chest there was inserted a tin-plate tube very nicely adjusted and out of sight, while in the lower room was stationed the one who did the answering; he would place his mouth to the tube and voices would then travel up and down it as through an ear trumpet, the words being articulated very clearly and everything being arranged so cleverly that it was impossible to discover the trick.

A nephew of Don Antonio's, an intelligent, sharp-witted student, was the one who gave the responses, and having been previously advised by his uncle as to who were to be present in the room with the head, he had found no difficulty in answering the first question promptly and accurately but had been compelled to resort to guesses in replying to the others. However, being a clever fellow, he acquitted himself in a clever manner. Cid Hamete further tells us that this marvelous contrivance lasted for ten or a dozen days, but as the news spread through the city that Don Antonio had in his house an enchanted head that answered all queries put to it, he, fearing lest word of this should reach the alert ears of those reverend gentlemen, the sentinels of our faith, had explained the matter to the Inquisitors, who had ordered him to smash the mechanism and carry the jest no further, in order that the ignorant rabble might not be scandalized. But in Don Quixote's opinion and that of Sancho, the head remained an enchanted one with the virtues ascribed to it, though the knight was better satisfied than his squire with the answers that it gave.

By way of humoring Don Antonio and keeping Don Quixote entertained, while affording the latter, at the same time, an opportunity to display his absurdities, the gentlemen of the city arranged for a tilting at the ring six days from then, but, owing to circumstances that will be related further on, this event did not take place. In the meantime, Don Quixote wished to go out for a quiet stroll, for he feared that if he went on horseback the small boys would follow him, and so, accompanied only by Sancho and a couple of servants that Don Antonio had furnished him, he set out with this object in view.

As he was going down a certain street he glanced up and saw a sign in large letters over a doorway, reading: "BOOKS PRINTED HERE." This pleased him very much, as he had never seen a printing shop up to that time and had a desire to find out what it was like. Going inside with all his retinue, he saw them drawing proofs here, correcting them there, setting type in one place and making revisions in another—in short, he beheld everything that goes to make up a large establishment of this sort. Going up to one of the cases, he inquired what was being done there, the workmen explained things for him, and, wondering at what he had observed, he passed on. He put the same question to another printer, and the man replied, "Sir, this gentleman here"—and he pointed to an impressive individual with a rather grave look on his face— "has translated a Tuscan book into our Castilian tongue, and I am now engaged in setting the type for it."

"What is the title of the book?" asked Don Quixote.

It was the author [22] who answered. "Sir," he said, "this work in Tuscan is called *Le Bagatelle*." [23]

"And what does *Le Bagatelle* mean in Castilian?"

"*Le Bagatelle*," replied the author, "is equivalent to *los juguetes* [24] in Spanish; and although the title is a humble-sounding one, this book contains much meat and substance."

"I," said Don Quixote, "am somewhat acquainted with Tuscan and pride myself on being able to recite certain stanzas of Ariosto. [25] But tell me, my dear sir, and I ask this not to test your Grace's ability but merely out of curiosity, in the course of your labors have you come upon such a word as *pignatta*?" [26]

"Yes, many times," was the answer.

"And how does your Grace render it into Castilian?"

"How should I render it except by *olla?*" [27]

"Body of me!" exclaimed Don Quixote, "how far advanced your Grace is in the Italian language! I will lay you a good wager that you translate *piace* as *place*, *più* as *más*, *su* as *arriba*, and *giù* as *abajo*." [28]

"I do indeed," said the author, "for those are the proper equivalents."

"And I would venture to take an oath," Don Quixote went on, "that your Grace is not known to the world at large, which always is chary of rewarding men of exceptional ability and works deserving of praise. How many talents have been lost in that way, how many geniuses have been tossed into the corner, how much of real worth has gone unappreciated! But, for all of that, it appears to me that translating from one language into another, unless it be from one of those two queenly tongues, Greek and Latin, is like gazing at a Flemish tapestry with the wrong side out: even though the figures are visible, they are full of threads that obscure the view and are not bright and smooth as when seen from the other side.[29] Moreover, translating from easy languages does not call for either wit or eloquence, any more than does the mere transcription or copying of a document.

"By this," the knight continued, "I do not mean to imply that the task of translating is not a laudable occupation, for a man might employ his time less worthily and with less profit to himself. I make an exception here of those two famous translators: Doctor Cristóbal de Figueroa in his *Pastor Fido* and Don Juan de Jáuregui in his *Aminta*,[30] where happily one may doubt as to which is the translation and which the original. But, your Grace, I should like to know, is this book being printed at your own expense or have you already disposed of the rights to some bookseller?"

"I pay for the printing," said the author, "and I expect to clear at least a thousand ducats on this first edition of two thousand copies, which at two reales apiece ought to sell in no time at all." [31]

"That," said Don Quixote, "is a fine bit of calculation on your Grace's part, but it is plain to be seen that you are not familiar with the ins and outs of the printers and the way in which they all work together.[32] I can promise you that when you find yourself weighted down with two thousand copies, you will be astonished how your body will ache all over, especially if the book happens to be a little out of the ordinary and does not make spicy reading." [33]

"But what would your Grace have me do? Give it to a bookseller who will pay me three maravedis for the rights and think that he is doing me a favor? I do not have books printed to win fame in this world, for I am already well known through my works; it is money that I seek, for without it a fine reputation is not worth a cent." [34]

"Well, good luck and God help you," said Don Quixote; and with this he moved on to another case, where he perceived that they were correcting the proofs of a book entitled *Light of the Soul*.[35]

"These," he said, "are the books that ought to be printed, even though there are many of the sort, for many are the sinners these days,[36] and an infinite number of lights are required for all those that are in darkness."

Going up to another case, he saw that here, too, they were correcting a book, and when he asked the title he was told that it was the *Second Part of the Ingenious Gentleman, Don Quixote de la Mancha*, composed by a certain native of Tordesillas.[37]

"I have heard of this work," he said, "and, in all truth and upon my conscience, I think it ought to be burned to ashes as a piece of impertinence; but Martinmas will come for it as it does for every pig.[38] Fictional tales are better and more enjoyable the nearer they approach the truth or the semblance of the truth, and as for true stories, the best are those that are most true." [39]

Saying this, he stalked out of the printing shop with signs of considerable displeasure.

That same day Don Antonio made arrangements to take him to see the galleys on the beach, and Sancho was delighted at this as he never in his life had beheld such a sight.[40] Their host thereupon notified the commander [41] that he was bringing with him his guest, the famous Don Quixote de la Mancha, of whom that officer and everyone in the city had heard. As for what happened to them aboard the vessels, that will be related in the following chapter.

CHAPTER LXIII . *Of the misfortune that befell Sancho Panza upon his visit to the galleys, and the strange adventure of the beautiful Moorish maiden.*

DON QUIXOTE pondered deeply the reply which the enchanted head had given him. No matter how much he thought about it, he was unable to hit upon the method by which the trick was worked but always came back to the one thing he accepted as being unquestionably true: the promise that Dulcinea would be disenchanted. He turned this over and over in his mind and was very happy in the thought that he would soon be witnessing its fulfillment. As for Sancho, while he hated being a governor, as has been stated, he nonetheless had a desire to give orders once more and be obeyed, such is the misfortune that a position of authority, even if only held in jest, brings with it.

But to come back to our story: That afternoon their host, Don Antonio Moreno, and his two friends with Don Quixote and Sancho repaired to the galleys. The commander had been advised of his good luck in being able to lay eyes upon so famous a pair, and no sooner had they reached the waterfront than all the vessels struck their awnings and the flageolets began to resound. A small boat covered with costly rugs and cushions of crimson velvet was lowered, and the moment Don Quixote set foot in the skiff the commander's galley fired its cannon amidship and all the others did the same. As the knight mounted the starboard ladder, the entire crew saluted him, as is the custom when an important personage comes aboard, crying "*Hu, hu, hu*" three times.

The general—for such we shall call him, seeing that he was a Valencian gentleman of high rank—then gave Don Quixote his hand and embraced him, saying, "This day I shall mark with a white stone [1] as being one of the best I ever expect to enjoy as long as I live, since it has afforded me a sight of Señor Don Quixote de la Mancha—a monument in memory of the occasion [2] when I met the one who, as we can plainly see, contains within himself the sum and substance of all that is worth while in knight-errantry."

Overjoyed at finding himself received in so lordly a manner, Don

Quixote made an equally courteous speech in reply, and they all retired to the poop, which was very well fitted out, and sat down upon the benches there. The boatswain then went to the gangway and with his whistle gave the signal for the crew to strip,[3] which was done in a moment's time. Sancho was astonished to see so many naked men, and he marveled still more as he saw them rig the awning with such speed that it seemed to him as if all the devils in Hell must be working there. This, however, was but gingerbread and cakes [4] compared to what I am about to tell you now.

The squire was seated on the captain's platform next to the foremost rower on the right; and this fellow, having been instructed as to what he was to do, now seized him and, raising him in his arms, started passing him down the line on that side. All the members of the crew were standing ready, and they proceeded to send him flying from one pair of arms to another and from bench to bench so fast that poor Sancho lost the sight of his eyes and undoubtedly must have fancied that it was the demons themselves that were carrying him off; and this did not stop until he had been returned on the left-hand side and set down once more in the poop, bruised and breathless, and sweating all over and unable to imagine what it was that had happened to him.

Upon witnessing this flight without wings on Sancho's part, Don Quixote inquired of the general if it was a customary ceremony in the case of those who came aboard for the first time; for if by any chance it was, he did not intend to follow this calling, as he had no desire to engage in any such exercises; and he further vowed to God that if anyone should lay hands on him for that purpose, he would kick the life out of him. With this, he rose to his feet and grasped his sword.

At that instant they struck the awning and brought down the lateen yard with so tremendous a clatter that Sancho thought the heavens were becoming unhinged and were about to fall upon him, and full of fear he stuck his head between his legs. Don Quixote's own legs, for that matter, were none too steady as he sat huddled and trembling with all the color gone from his face. The crew thereupon hoisted the yard as speedily and noisily as they had lowered it, preserving all the while a dead silence, as though they had neither voice nor breath; following which, the boatswain piped them to weigh anchor, and, leaping upon the middle of the gangway, he began flaying the backs of the rowers as they little by little put out to sea. When Sancho perceived all those ruddy-colored feet in motion—for such he took the oars to be—he started speaking to himself.

"This," he said, "is really magic, and not the kind my master talks about. What have these poor wretches done that they should be whipped like that, and how comes it that this one man who goes along whistling there dares to punish so many of them? I declare, this is Hell or at the very least purgatory."

Don Quixote, meanwhile, had noticed how attentively his squire was taking it all in. "Ah, friend Sancho," he remarked, "how quickly you could finish with the disenchantment of Dulcinea if you would only strip down to the waist and take your place among these gentlemen! For amid the pain and misery of so many you would not feel your own to any great extent; and it might be that the wise Merlin would count each one of these lashes, lustily laid on, as equivalent to ten of those which you must give yourself anyway, sooner or later."

The general was about to ask what was the meaning of this talk of lashes and Dulcinea's disenchantment when a sailor exclaimed, "Monjuich [5] signals that there is a vessel with oars standing offshore to westward."

Hearing this, the general leaped to the gangway and shouted, "Ho, there, my lads, don't let her get away from us! It must be some corsair brigantine from Algiers that the watchtower has signaled."

With this, the three other galleys came up alongside the commander's craft to find out what his orders were. The general commanded two of them to put out to sea while he and the other one would hug the land, and that way the brigantine would not escape them. The crew then began rowing so furiously that the boats appeared to be flying over the water. When the two that had put out from shore had gone a couple of miles or so, they sighted a vessel which they took to be one of fourteen or fifteen banks of oars, as proved to be the case. As soon as it made out the galleys, it took to flight, hoping and expecting to escape by sheer speed; but in this it was mistaken, for the commander's galley was one of the swiftest that sailed the sea and bore down so hard upon the brigantine that those aboard clearly realized there was no chance of their getting away.

The captain, accordingly, was of a mind to stop rowing and surrender, in order not to anger our commander, but fate ordained otherwise; and just as the galley came up near enough for those on the vessel to be able to hear the call to surrender, two drunken *Toraquis*, that is to say Turks, who with a dozen more of their countrymen were on board, discharged their muskets, killing two of our soldiers lined up on the wales. When he saw what had happened, the general swore that he would not leave a man of them alive and immediately attacked with great fury, but the enemy slipped away beneath our oars. The galley darted on past for a considerable distance, and while it was engaged in turning about those aboard the brigantine, seeing their lot was hopeless, hoisted sail and, trusting to the breeze and their oars, once again endeavored to flee. Their exertions, however, did not do them as much good as their rashness did them harm; for our chief galley having overtaken them after a pursuit of a little more than half a mile, we threw our oars over them and captured them all.

The other two galleys now came up and all four with their prize returned to the beach, where a huge crowd was awaiting them to see what they brought with them. The general cast anchor close to shore and, perceiving that the viceroy of the city was there, he ordered the small boat to be lowered to bring him aboard. At the same time he commanded his men to let down the yardarm that he might promptly hang the captain and all the rest of the prisoners, about thirty-six in number, strapping fellows all, and most of them Turkish musketeers. When the general asked who the ship's master was, one of the captives spoke up and answered him in the Castilian tongue, for, as was afterward learned, he was a renegade Spaniard.

"Sir," he said, "this young man that you see here is our captain." And he pointed to one of the most handsome and gallant-looking youths that the human imagination could conceive, a lad who, to all appearances, was under twenty years of age.

"Tell me, foolish dog," the general said to the youth, "what led you to kill two of my soldiers when you saw it was impossible for you to escape? Is this the respect you show to commanders' galleys? Do you not know that valor does not consist in rashness and that faint hopes should make men brave but not foolhardy?"

The captain was about to reply, but the general could not listen to him as the viceroy was already boarding the galley, accompanied by a number of attendants and townspeople.

"So, the hunting was good, Señor General?" said the viceroy.

"How good it was your Excellency will see as soon as I've strung up the game on this yardarm."

"How does it come you are doing that?" the viceroy wished to know.

"Because," said the general, "against all law and reason and military custom they have killed two of my best soldiers, and I have sworn to hang every man of them, especially this youth who is their captain."

As he said this he pointed to the young fellow who stood there, his hands already bound and the rope about his neck, waiting for death.

The viceroy looked the prisoner over and saw how handsome he was, how gallant and modest his bearing, and, the young man's comeliness being his letter of recommendation,[6] he at once felt a desire to spare his life.

"Tell me, Captain," he asked, "are you a Turk by nationality, a Moor, or a renegade?"

To this the youth replied, also in Spanish, "I am neither a Turk, nor a Moor, nor a renegade."

"Then what are you?"

"A Christian woman."

"A woman and a Christian, in such a costume and in such a plight? Why, it is astonishing—scarcely to be believed."

"If you gentlemen," replied the youth, "will suspend my execution while I tell you the story of my life, you will not have to wait too long for your revenge."

Who could have had so hard a heart that it would not have been softened by these words, at least to the extent of listening to what the poor unfortunate lad wished to say? The general told him that he might feel free to speak but that he was not to hope for pardon inasmuch as his guilt was plainly established. Having been granted this permission, the youth began his story.

"I," he said, "am of that race whose misfortunes exceed their prudence, for over it of late has rolled a sea of troubles. I was born of Morisco parents, and in the course of our wanderings I was taken to Barbary by an uncle and aunt[7] of mine. It was of no use my telling them that I was a Christian, which, as a matter of fact, I am—and not one of those pretended or seeming converts but a true believer of the Catholic faith. It did me no good to state this fact to those charged with enforcing our wretched banishment, nor would my kinsfolk believe me; they looked upon it as a lying invention on my part to enable me to remain in the land of my birth, and so it was by force rather than of my own free will that they took me with them.

"I had a Christian mother and a father who was a sensible man and a Christian as well. I imbibed the Catholic faith with my mother's milk. I had a good upbringing, and never in word or deed, to the best of my knowledge, did I give any sign of being a Morisco. And keeping pace with these virtues (for such is the way in which I regard the habits I had formed), my beauty, if I may claim any, grew with the years. Although I lived a very retiring and secluded life, I was not so shut off from the world but that a young gentleman, named Don Gaspar Gregorio,[8] had an opportunity of seeing me. He is the son and heir of one who is the lord of a village next to ours; but it would take too long to tell you how we met and talked and how he fell hopelessly in love with me while I was not wholly indifferent to him—especially since I am fearful every moment that this cruel rope that threatens me will tighten between my tongue and throat.

"And so I will merely say that it was Don Gregorio's desire to accompany me into exile. Knowing our language very well, he mingled with the Moors that came from other villages, and on the way he made friends with my uncle and aunt; for my father, being a prudent and far-sighted man, as soon as he heard of the decree of banishment, had left our village and gone to look for some place in a foreign land that would serve us as a refuge, leaving behind him, concealed and buried in a spot with which I alone am acquainted, many pearls and precious stones, together with a certain sum of money in gold, in the form of cruzados [9] and doubloons. His instructions were that under no circumstances was I to touch this treasure if by any chance they expelled us before he returned. I obeyed his orders, and with my uncle and aunt, as I have said, and other friends and relatives I went to Barbary. It was in Algiers that we settled, but it might as well have been in Hell itself.

"The king of the country heard of my beauty and of the rumor regarding my wealth, and this in a way was fortunate for me. Summoning me before him, he asked what part of Spain I was from and what money and jewels I had brought with me. I told him the name of my village and informed him that the jewels and the money were still buried there, but that I could very easily recover them if I myself were to return for them. Even as I said this I was in dread lest he should be blinded by my beauty rather than by his own covetousness, and while we were conversing in this manner word reached him that I was accompanied by one of the most handsome and gallant youths that could be imagined, whereupon I knew at once that they were speaking of Don Gaspar Gregorio, whose comeliness is beyond all praise. I was greatly disturbed, knowing the danger that Don Gregorio ran; for among those barbarous Turks a handsome boy or youth is more highly esteemed than the most beautiful of women.[10]

"The king ordered them to bring the young man before him that he might have a sight of him, and in the meantime he inquired of me if all

that he had heard was true. As if forewarned by Heaven, I assured him
that it was, but that I wished to inform him that the youth in question
was not a man but a woman like myself, and I begged him to allow me
to go and clothe her in the garments proper to her sex in order that
he might behold her in all her beauty and that she might be less embarrassed at appearing in his presence. He readily consented to my doing so, adding that some other time we would discuss the means by
which I could return to Spain to get the hidden treasure.

"I spoke to Don Gaspar and reminded him of the danger that lay in
his appearing as a man. I then dressed him as a Moorish woman and
that same afternoon conducted him before the king, who was struck
with admiration upon seeing him and announced his intention of keeping the 'girl' as a present for the Grand Seignior.[11] Being afraid of leaving her among the women of his harem as well as distrustful of himself,
he commanded that she be taken to the house where some of the leading
Moorish ladies dwelt, which was done at once. As to the feelings of
both of us (for I cannot deny that I care for him deeply), that is something that may be left to the imagination of any pair of lovers who are
separated.

"The king then arranged that I should return to Spain in this brigantine, accompanied by two Turks, who were the ones that killed your
soldiers. This Spanish renegade"—and she pointed to the one who had
been the first to speak—"also came with me, and I can tell you that I
know well that he is a Christian at heart and that he would much rather
remain in Spain than go back to Barbary. The other members of the
brigantine's crew are Moors and Turks who serve only to man the
oars. As for this greedy and insolent pair, they chose to disregard the
orders they had to set me and this renegade ashore the moment we
reached Spanish soil. We were to be landed in Christian garb, with
which we came provided; but they insisted upon first skirting the coast
to see if they could capture some prize, for they feared that if they
obeyed orders and some accident happened to us we might reveal the
fact that there was a brigantine at sea, in which case, if there chanced
to be any galleys around, they would be taken.

"Last night we sighted this beach and, knowing nothing of these four
vessels, we were discovered, with the result that you have seen. To
make a long story short, Don Gregorio, dressed as a woman, still lives
among women, and his life is clearly in danger, while I stand here with
my hands tied, waiting, or rather, dreading to lose the life of which I
already am weary. That, sirs, is the end of my sad tale, as true as it is un-

fortunate. What I would ask of you is that you let me die like a Christian woman, for, as I have said, I am in no wise guilty of the offense that my people have committed." [12]

As she fell silent her eyes filled with tears, and those of many of the bystanders did so as well. Moved to compassion, the viceroy went up to her and with his own hands undid the rope that bound those of the beautiful Moorish Christian. In the meantime, as she related her story, an aged pilgrim who had come aboard with the viceroy watched her most intently, and she had no sooner finished speaking than he cast himself down at her feet and embraced them.

"O Ana Felix, my unhappy daughter!" he cried in a voice that was broken by innumerable sobs and sighs. "I am your father, Ricote, who has returned to seek you, being unable to live without you, since you are my very soul."

At these words Sancho opened his eyes and looked up, for he had been sitting all the while with his head bowed, brooding over the unpleasant treatment he had experienced; and as he gazed at Ricote he recognized him as the same pilgrim whom he had met the day he left his government, and felt quite sure that this was indeed the old man's daughter.

Freed now of her bonds, the girl embraced her father, mingling her tears with his, as he turned to the general and the viceroy and said, "This, gentlemen, is my daughter, more unfortunate in life than her name would imply. Ana Felix she is called, her surname being Ricote, and she is famed as much for her beauty as for my wealth. I left my native country to go seek in foreign lands someone who would take us in and shelter us, and, having found such a person in Germany, I returned in this pilgrim's guise and in the company of certain other pilgrims of that nation to hunt for my daughter and dig up the treasure hoard which I had left buried here. I found the treasure, which I carry with me, but not my daughter; and now, by this strange turn of events which you have witnessed, I have come upon the most valuable thing I possess, in this my beloved child. If the small amount of blame that attaches to us, and her tears as well as mine, without impairing the integrity of justice, can open the door to mercy, then I beseech you to be merciful to us, since we have never had any thought of offending you, nor do we in any way sympathize with the plottings of our people, who have justly been sent into banishment."

At this point Sancho spoke up. "I know Ricote well," he said, "and I know that what he says about Ana Felix's being his daughter is the truth;

but as to all the other things he has to say about his comings and goings and his good or evil intentions, I do not propose to meddle in that."

All those present were amazed at the strange case. "One by one," said the general, "your tears have prevented me from carrying out my oath. May you live as many years as Heaven has allotted you, beauteous Ana Felix, but these two rash and insolent fellows must pay the penalty for the crime they have committed." And with this he ordered the Turks who had slain his men to be hanged from the yardarm. The viceroy, however, pleaded with him earnestly to spare them, pointing out that their actions savored more of madness than of defiance. The general acceded to his wishes, for deeds of vengeance are seldom executed in cold blood.

They then began laying plans for rescuing Don Gaspar Gregorio from his perilous situation, Ricote offering to put up more than two thousand ducats in the form of pearls and other jewels that were in his possession. Many plans were suggested, but none of them as good as that proposed by the above-mentioned Spanish renegade, who volunteered to go to Algiers in some small craft with about six banks of oars manned by Christian rowers; for he knew where, how, and when he could and should land, and he was also acquainted with the house where Don Gaspar was kept. The general and the viceroy were at first inclined to be doubtful of the renegade and were hesitant about entrusting to his charge the Christians who were to do the rowing, but Ana Felix vouched for him and her father, Ricote, promised that he would come forward with the ransom money in case anything happened to them.

This decision having been reached, the viceroy went ashore and Don Antonio Moreno took the Morisco maid and her father home with him, the viceroy charging him to show them all the hospitality in his power, while for his own part he offered them anything his house contained that might serve for their entertainment, such was the good will and benevolence that Ana Felix's beauty had inspired in his bosom.

CHAPTER LXIV. *Which treats of the adventure that caused Don Quixote the most sorrow of all those that have thus far befallen him.*

DON ANTONIO MORENO'S wife, the history tells us, was very happy to take Ana Felix into her home and she gave the young Moorish woman a most cordial reception, being charmed by her wit and beauty alike, for in both respects the girl was more than ordinarily gifted—indeed, so attractive was she that all the townspeople came to have a look at her, as if they had been summoned by the ringing of a bell.

Don Quixote, meanwhile, remarked to his host that the decision reached with regard to freeing Don Gregorio was not a good one inasmuch as the dangers inherent in the plan outweighed the advantages. It would be better, he said, if he himself were to be set down in Barbary with his arms and steed, as he would surely effect a rescue in spite of all the Moors in the world, just as Don Gaiferos had done in the case of his wife, Melisendra.[1]

"Your Grace," Sancho reminded him, "should remember that it was on the mainland that Don Gaiferos rescued his lady and it was by land that he took her to France; but with us, even supposing that we did rescue Don Gregorio, we'd have no way of getting him back to Spain, since there is an ocean in between."

"There is a remedy for everything except death,"[2] said Don Quixote. "Let them but bring the boat to the strand and we shall be able to embark though all the world try to prevent us."

"It sounds easy to hear your Grace tell it," replied Sancho, "but it's a long way from saying to doing.[3] I'm for leaving it to the renegade; he seems to me to be an honest fellow with plenty of guts."[4]

Don Antonio settled the matter by stating that in case the renegade did not succeed they would resort to the expedient of sending the great Don Quixote. And so, a couple of days later, the rescue party put out in a light craft with six oars on each side, manned by a most valiant crew; and two days after that the galleys set sail for the east, the general having asked the viceroy to be so good as to let him know what happened in connection with Ana Felix and the freeing of Don Gregorio, which that gentleman readily consented to do.

And then, one morning, as Don Quixote went for a ride along the beach, clad in full armor—for, as he was fond of saying, that was his only ornament, his only rest the fight,⁵ and, accordingly, he was never without it for a moment ⁶—he saw approaching him a horseman similarly arrayed from head to foot and with a brightly shining moon blazoned upon his shield.

As soon as he had come within earshot the stranger cried out to Don Quixote in a loud voice, "O illustrious knight, the never to be sufficiently praised Don Quixote de la Mancha, I am the Knight of the White Moon, whose incomparable exploits you will perhaps recall. I come to contend with you and try the might of my arm, with the purpose of having you acknowledge and confess that my lady, whoever she may be, is beyond comparison more beautiful than your own Dulcinea del Toboso. If you will admit the truth of this fully and freely, you will escape death and I shall be spared the trouble of inflicting it upon you. On the other hand, if you choose to fight and I should overcome you, I ask no other satisfaction than that, laying down your arms and seeking no further adventures, you retire to your own village for the space of a year, during which time you are not to lay hand to sword but are to dwell peacefully and tranquilly, enjoying a beneficial rest that shall redound to the betterment of your worldly fortunes and the salvation of your soul. But if you are the victor, then my head shall be at your disposal, my arms and steed shall be the spoils, and the fame of my exploits shall go to increase your own renown. Consider well which is the better course and let me have your answer at once, for today is all the time I have for the dispatching of this business."

Don Quixote was amazed at the knight's arrogance as well as at the nature of the challenge, but it was with a calm and stern demeanor that he replied to him.

"Knight of the White Moon," he said, "of whose exploits up to now I have never heard, I will venture to take an oath that you have not once laid eyes upon the illustrious Dulcinea; for I am quite certain that if you had beheld her you would not be staking your all upon such an issue, since the sight of her would have convinced you that there never has been, and never can be, any beauty to compare with hers. I do not say that you lie, I simply say that you are mistaken; and so I accept your challenge with the conditions you have laid down, and at once, before this day you have fixed upon shall have ended. The only exception I make is with regard to the fame of your deeds being added to my renown, since I do not know what the character of your exploits has been and am quite content with my own, such as they are. Take, then, whichever side of the field you like, and I will take up my position, and may St. Peter bless what God may give." [7]

Now, as it happened, the Knight of the White Moon was seen by some of the townspeople, who informed the viceroy that he was there, talking to Don Quixote de la Mancha. Believing this to be a new adventure arranged by Don Antonio Moreno or some other gentleman of the place, the viceroy at once hastened down to the beach, accompanied by a large retinue, including Don Antonio, and they arrived just as Don Quixote was wheeling Rocinante to measure off the necessary stretch of field. When the viceroy perceived that they were about to engage in combat, he at once interposed and inquired of them what it was that impelled them thus to do battle all of a sudden.

The Knight of the White Moon replied that it was a matter of beauty and precedence and briefly repeated what he had said to Don Quixote, explaining the terms to which both parties had agreed. The viceroy then went up to Don Antonio and asked him if he knew any such knight as this or if it was some joke that they were playing, but the answer that he received left him more puzzled than ever; for Don Antonio did not know who the knight was, nor could he say as to whether this was a real encounter or not. The viceroy, accordingly, was doubtful about letting them proceed, but inasmuch as he could not bring himself to believe that it was anything more than a jest, he withdrew to one side, saying, "Sir Knights, if there is nothing for it but to confess [8] or die, and if Señor Don Quixote's mind is made up and your Grace, the Knight of the White Moon, is even more firmly resolved, then fall to it in the name of God and may He bestow the victory."

The Knight of the White Moon thanked the viceroy most courteously and in well-chosen words for the permission which had been granted them, and Don Quixote did the same, whereupon the latter, commending himself with all his heart to Heaven and to his lady Dulcinea, as was his custom at the beginning of a fray, fell back a little farther down the field as he saw his adversary doing the same. And then, without blare of trumpet or other warlike instrument to give them the signal for the attack, both at the same instant wheeled their steeds about and returned for the charge. Being mounted upon the swifter horse, the Knight of the White Moon met Don Quixote two-thirds of the way and with such tremendous force that, without touching his opponent with his lance (which, it seemed, he deliberately held aloft) he brought both Rocinante and his rider to the ground in an exceedingly perilous fall. At once the victor leaped down and placed his lance at Don Quixote's visor.

"You are vanquished, O knight! Nay, more, you are dead unless you make confession in accordance with the conditions governing our encounter."

Stunned and battered, Don Quixote did not so much as raise his visor but in a faint, wan voice, as if speaking from the grave, he said, "Dulcinea del Toboso is the most beautiful woman in the world and I the most unhappy knight upon the face of this earth. It is not right that my weakness should serve to defraud the truth. Drive home your lance, O knight, and take my life since you already have deprived me of my honor."

"That I most certainly shall not do," said the one of the White Moon. "Let the fame of my lady Dulcinea del Toboso's beauty live on undiminished. As for me, I shall be content if the great Don Quixote will retire to his village for a year or until such a time as I may specify, as was agreed upon between us before joining battle."

The viceroy, Don Antonio, and all the many others who were present heard this, and they also heard Don Quixote's response, which was to the effect that, seeing nothing was asked of him that was prejudicial to Dulcinea, he would fulfill all the other conditions like a true and punctilious knight. The one of the White Moon thereupon turned and with a bow to the viceroy rode back to the city at a mild canter. The viceroy promptly dispatched Don Antonio to follow him and make every effort to find out who he was; and, in the meanwhile, they lifted Don Quixote up and uncovered his face, which held no sign of color and was bathed in perspiration. Rocinante, however, was in so sorry a state that he was unable to stir for the present.

Brokenhearted over the turn that events had taken, Sancho did not know what to say or do. It seemed to him that all this was something that was happening in a dream and that everything was the result of magic. He saw his master surrender, heard him consent not to take up arms again for a year to come as the light of his glorious exploits faded into darkness. At the same time his own hopes, based upon the fresh promises that had been made him, were whirled away like smoke before the wind. He feared that Rocinante was maimed for life, his master's bones permanently dislocated—it would have been a bit of luck if his madness also had been jolted out of him.[9]

Finally, in a hand litter which the viceroy had them bring, they bore the knight back to town. The viceroy himself then returned, for he was very anxious to ascertain who the Knight of the White Moon was who had left Don Quixote in so lamentable a condition.

CHAPTER LXV. *Wherein is revealed who the Knight of the White Moon was, with the freeing of Don Gregorio and other events.*

THE Knight of the White Moon was followed not only by Don Antonio Moreno, but by a throng of small boys as well, who kept after him until the doors of one of the city's hostelries had closed behind him. A squire came out to meet him and remove his armor, for which purpose the victor proceeded to shut himself up in a lower room, in the company of Don Antonio, who had also entered the inn and whose bread would not bake until he had learned the knight's identity. Perceiving that the gentleman had no intention of leaving him, he of the White Moon then spoke.

"Sir," he said, "I am well aware that you have come to find out who I am; and, seeing that there is no denying you the information that you seek, while my servant here is removing my armor I will tell you the exact truth of the matter. I would have you know, sir, that I am the bachelor Sansón Carrasco from the same village as Don Quixote de la Mancha, whose madness and absurdities inspire pity in all of us who know him and in none more than me. And so, being convinced that his salvation lay in his returning home for a period of rest in his own house, I formed a plan for bringing him back.

"It was three months ago [1] that I took to the road as a knight-errant, calling myself the Knight of the Mirrors, with the object of fighting and overcoming him without doing him any harm, intending first to lay down the condition that the vanquished was to yield to the victor's will. What I meant to ask of him—for I looked upon him as conquered from the start—was that he should return to his village and not leave it for a whole year, in the course of which time he might be cured. Fate, however, ordained things otherwise; for he was the one who conquered me and overthrew me from my horse, and thus my plan came to naught. He continued on his wanderings, and I went home, defeated, humiliated, and bruised from my fall, which was quite a dangerous one. But I did not for this reason give up the idea of hunting him up once more and vanquishing him as you have seen me do today.

"Since he is the soul of honor when it comes to observing the ordinances of knight-errantry, there is not the slightest doubt that he will keep the promise he has given me and fulfill his obligations. And that, sir, is all that I need to tell you concerning what has happened. I beg you not to disclose my secret or reveal my identity to Don Quixote, in order that my well-intentioned scheme may be carried out and a man of excellent judgment be brought back to his senses—for a sensible man he would be, once rid of the follies of chivalry."

"My dear sir," exclaimed Don Antonio, "may God forgive you for the wrong you have done the world by seeking to deprive it of its most charming madman! Do you not see that the benefit accomplished by restoring Don Quixote to his senses can never equal the pleasure which others derive from his vagaries? But it is my opinion that all the trouble to which the Señor Bachelor has put himself will not suffice to cure a man who is so hopelessly insane; and if it were not uncharitable, I would say let Don Quixote never be cured, since with his return to health we lose not only his own drolleries but also those of his squire, Sancho Panza, for either of the two is capable of turning melancholy itself into joy and merriment. Nevertheless, I will keep silent and tell him nothing, that I may see whether or not I am right in my suspicion that Señor Carrasco's efforts will prove to have been of no avail."

The bachelor replied that, all in all, things looked very favorable and he hoped for a fortunate outcome. With this, he took his leave of Don Antonio, after offering to render him any service that he could; and, having had his armor tied up and placed upon a mule's back, he rode out of the city that same day on the same horse on which he had gone into battle, returning to his native province without anything happening to him that is worthy of being set down in this veracious chronicle.

Don Antonio informed the viceroy of what Carrasco had told him, and that official was none too well pleased to hear it, since with Don Quixote's retirement all those who had heard of his mad exploits would lose a great deal of enjoyment.

For six days Don Quixote remained in bed, sad and dejected, moody and ill-tempered, as he went over again and again in his mind the unfortunate defeat he had experienced.

Sancho sought to console him, and among other things he said to him, "Raise your head, master, and cheer up a bit if you can. You ought to thank Heaven that, even though you were thrown to earth, you came out of it without a single broken rib. You know that those that give must take,[2] and there is not always bacon where there are stakes.[3] A fig for the doctor; we don't need him to cure this sickness. Let's return home and give up going around looking for adventures in strange lands and places. If you stop to consider, I am the one who stands to lose the most, though your Grace may have more bruises to show. For while I lost all desire to be a governor when I left my government, I still shouldn't mind being a count; but that can never be if your Grace quits the calling of chivalry and gives up the idea of becoming a king. And so it is my hopes go up in smoke."

"Be quiet, Sancho," said his master, "for you know very well that my retirement and seclusion is not to exceed a year, after which time I shall return to my honorable profession, and I cannot fail to win a kingdom, along with some county to bestow on you."

"May God hear you and sin be deaf,"[4] said Sancho. "I have always heard tell that a good hope is better than a bad holding."[5]

At this point Don Antonio entered the room with a great show of satisfaction. "Pay me for good news,[6] Señor Don Quixote," he said. "Don Gregorio and the renegade who went for him are now on the beach! What am I saying? They are already at the viceroy's house and will be here any moment."

Don Quixote was somewhat cheered by this report. "To tell the truth," he said, "I should have been glad, almost, if it had turned out differently, as that would have obliged me to go to Barbary, where by the might of my arm I should have freed not Don Gregorio alone, but all the Christian captives that are there. But what am I thinking of, wretch that I am? Am I not the vanquished one? Am I not the one who was overthrown? Am I not he who cannot take up arms for an entire year? What, then, am I promising, of what do I boast, seeing that I am better fitted to handle the distaff than the sword?"

"Stop talking like that, master," said Sancho. "Let the hen live even though she may have the pip;[7] it's today for thee and tomorrow for me;[8] as to this matter of encounters and blows, you should pay no heed to them, since he who falls today may be on his feet again tomorrow[9] —that is to say, unless he prefers to stay in bed and lose heart instead of plucking up fresh courage for battles to come. So, get up this minute, your Grace, and prepare to receive Don Gregorio; for I think I hear people stirring about, and that means he must already be in the house."

This was the truth. Don Gregorio and the renegade having given the viceroy an account of their crossing, the youth was anxious to see Ana Felix, and so the two men came on to Don Antonio's home. Although he had been clad in a woman's garments when they took him out of Algiers, Gregorio had exchanged them on the boat for those of another captive who had come with them; but whatever the garb he wore, he was plainly a person to be loved, served, and esteemed, for he was extraordinarily handsome and about seventeen or eighteen years of age. Ricote and his daughter went out to meet him, the father with tears and the maiden with becoming modesty. The young couple did not embrace, for where there is much love there should not be too great a freedom of manners. All those present were filled with admiration at Don Gregorio's comeliness and Ana Felix's beauty, but it was silence that spoke for the lovers and their eyes were the tongues that revealed the joy they felt and the purity of their affection.

The renegade then described the means which he had adopted in rescuing Don Gregorio, while the latter told of the perils and straits in which he had found himself during his sojourn among the womenfolk. He did not make a long speech, his words in fact were few, and in this he displayed a wisdom beyond his years. Ricote then paid both the renegade and the rowers very liberally for their services. As for the one who had abjured the Faith, he was soon reunited with the Church through penance and a contrite heart, and from a rotten limb became a sound and clean one. A couple of days later the viceroy and Don Antonio had a discussion as to what should be done to enable Ana Felix and her father to remain in Spain; for it seemed to them there could be no harm in permitting a daughter who was so good a Christian and a father who was seemingly so right-minded to continue residing in the country. Don Antonio even offered to go to the capital and arrange matters, since in any case he had other pressing business that required his presence there, and he dropped a hint to the effect that many difficulties could be overcome by means of favor and bribery.

"No," said Ricote, who was present at this conference, "neither favor nor bribes will be of any avail, for the great Don Bernardino de Velasco, Count of Salazar,[10] whom his Majesty has charged with seeing to our banishment, is not to be moved by entreaties, promises, gifts, or appeals to his sympathy. While it is true that he tempers mercy with justice, nevertheless, perceiving as he does that the entire body of our nation is rotting and corrupt, he would rather make use of the cautery that sears than of the ointment that soothes; and, accordingly, by means of prudence, sagacity, diligence, and the fear that he inspires, he has been able to carry upon his sturdy shoulders the weight of this great undertaking. As a result, all the plottings and schemings, the importunities and wiles, of our people have not succeeded in blinding his Argus-eyes, which are ever on the alert lest some one of us should remain behind in concealment and, like a hidden root, in the course of time come to bear poisonous fruit in a Spain that is now cleansed and freed of that terror that our excessive numbers inspired in it. A heroic resolve, this, on the part of the great Philip III, and what unheard-of wisdom, his entrusting the task to such a one as Don Bernardino de Velasco!"

"At any rate," said Don Antonio, "once I am there I will exert every effort, and let Heaven do as it may see fit. Don Gregorio shall come with me that he may relieve the anxiety his parents must feel on account of his absence, Ana Felix may stay here with my wife or in a convent, and I know that the Señor Viceroy will be pleased to have the worthy Ricote as his guest until we see how I make out with the negotiations."

The viceroy gave his consent to everything, but Don Gregorio, upon hearing what had been suggested, declared that he neither could nor would leave Doña Ana Felix under any circumstances; however, as he had intended in any event to go visit his parents and arrange to return for her, he ended by falling in with the plan that had been agreed upon. And so Ana Felix remained with Don Antonio's wife and Ricote stayed in the viceroy's house.

Two days after Don Antonio's departure Don Quixote and Sancho prepared to leave, the injuries which the knight had sustained in his fall having prevented his taking the road any sooner. There were tears, sighs, sobs, and swoonings as Don Gregorio said good-by to Ana Felix. Ricote offered the former a thousand crowns if he needed them, but all the money the young man would accept was five crowns, which Don Antonio lent him and which he promised to pay back when they reached the capital. The two of them then set out, followed shortly afterward by Don Quixote and Sancho, as we have said. The knight wore no fighting gear now but was dressed for the road, while Sancho went along on foot, the armor being piled upon the ass's back.

CHAPTER LXVI. *Which treats of that which he who reads will see and that which he will hear who listens to a reading of it.*

UPON leaving Barcelona, Don Quixote turned to gaze back at the spot where he had met with his downfall.

"Here," he said, "was Troy; here my ill luck and not my cowardice robbed me of the glory I had won; here it was that fortune practiced upon me her whims and caprices; here my exploits were dimmed; and here, finally, my star set never to rise again."

"Master," said Sancho when he heard this, "brave hearts should be patient in adversity just as they are joyous in prosperity. I am judging by the way I feel about it myself, for when I was a governor I was glad, but now that I am a squire and go on foot I am not sad. For I have heard it said that what they call luck is a drunken wench who does not know her own mind; above all, she is blind and so cannot see what she is doing, nor does she know who it is she is overthrowing or exalting."

"You are quite a philosopher, Sancho," said Don Quixote, "and you speak words of wisdom; I am sure I do not know who has been your teacher. But I can tell you one thing: that there is no such thing as luck in this world, and whatever happens, whether it be good or bad, does not occur by chance but through a special providence of Heaven; hence the saying that each man is the architect of his own fortune.[1] I was the architect of mine, but I did not observe the necessary prudence, and as a result my presumptuousness has brought me to a sorry end. I should have reflected that Rocinante, weak as he is, could not withstand the Knight of the White Moon's powerful steed. In short, I was too daring; I did my best but I was overthrown. However, although I sacrificed my honor, I cannot be accused of failing to keep my word. When I was a knight-errant, valiant and bold, my deeds and the might of my arm supported my reputation, and now that I am an ordinary squire I will back up my word by keeping the promise I have given. Proceed, then, friend Sancho, and let us go to fulfill the year of our novitiate in our native province, for during that period of retirement we shall obtain fresh strength, which will enable us to return to the profession of arms, one that I never can forget."

"Sir," replied Sancho, "it is not so pleasant traveling on foot, and I do not feel equal to any long marches. Suppose that we leave this armor on a tree, in place of some hanged man, and then with me on the gray's back and my feet off the ground, we will go as far at a stretch as your Grace chooses; but there's no use expecting me to do it if I have to walk."

"That is a good idea, Sancho," said Don Quixote. "Let my arms be hung up as a trophy, and round about them on the trees we will carve the inscription that was placed over those that Orlando had borne:

> *These let none move*
> *Who dares not with Orlando his valor prove.*" [2]

"All that," said Sancho, "strikes me as sound sense; and if it wasn't that we'll be needing Rocinante along the road, it might be well to string him up, too."

"But come to think of it," said Don Quixote, "I have no desire to hang either him or the armor, lest it be said, 'For good service an ill reward.'" [3]

"Your Grace is quite right," Sancho agreed, "for, according to the opinion of the wise the fault of the ass is not to be attributed to the pack-saddle. [4] Since it is your Grace that is to blame for what has happened, punish yourself and do not be letting your anger out on that battered and bloody suit of armor, nor on poor, meek Rocinante, nor on my tender feet by trying to make them travel more than is right and proper."

In this and similar conversation they spent the whole of that day and the four succeeding ones without anything happening to interrupt their journey. On the fifth day, as they entered a village, they encountered a great crowd of merrymakers at the door of an inn, for it was a feast day. As Don Quixote approached them a peasant raised his voice and called out, "One of those two gentlemen coming there, who do not know the parties concerned, will tell us what is to be done with regard to our wager."

"That I will gladly do," said Don Quixote, "and in all fairness, if I can understand the matter."

"Well, then, good sir," said the peasant, "it is like this. One of the natives of this village who is so fat that he weighs eleven arrobas [5] has challenged a neighbor of his, who does not weigh more than five, to run a race. The understanding was that they were to run a hundred paces, their weights being equalized, and when the challenger was asked how this was to be done, he replied that the other should put six arrobas of iron on his back, which would even things between the fat man and the lean one."

Before Don Quixote could reply, Sancho spoke up. "No," he said, "that won't do. It is only a few days now since I quit being a governor and a judge, as everybody knows, and so I am used to settling such doubtful points and giving a verdict in all sorts of cases."

"Answer them, then, friend Sancho, by all means," said Don Quixote, "since I am in no mood to give crumbs to a cat,[6] my mind is so excited and upset."

Having thus been granted permission, Sancho addressed himself to the peasants, who were standing around open-mouthed, waiting to hear his opinion.

"Brothers," he began, "what the fat man asks is unreasonable and altogether unjust; for if it is true that the one who is challenged has a right to choose the weapons, it is not proper for him to accept those that will make it impossible for him to come out the winner. Accordingly, it is my opinion that the fat challenger ought to trim, prune, cull, peel off, and tidy up his flesh until he has taken off six arrobas here and there on his body wherever he may think best, and in that manner, being left with five arrobas, he will be on an equal footing with his opponent and the race may be run with the odds even." [7]

"Well, now, I swear," declared one of the peasants who had heard what Sancho said, "this gentleman has spoken like a saint and given judgment like a canon. But you can be sure that the fat one will not be willing to part with a single ounce of flesh, much less six arrobas."

"The best thing would be for them not to run at all," said another. "That way, the lean man will not be battered down under the load, and the fat one will not have to part with his flesh. Let's spend half the wager on wine and take these gentlemen to the tavern where they sell the good stuff,[8] and upon my head be—the cloak when it rains." [9]

"I thank you, gentlemen," replied Don Quixote, "but I cannot pause for a moment; it is sad thoughts and unfortunate circumstances that compel me to appear discourteous and be on my way with all possible speed." Saying which, he gave Rocinante the spur and rode on, leaving the crowd to marvel equally at the knight's strange figure and the wisdom of his servant, for such they took Sancho to be.

"If the man," said one of the peasants, "is as wise as that, what must the master be! I'll lay you a bet that if they're going to Salamanca to study, they will become court judges in no time at all; for it's a joke—all you have to do is to study and study some more, have someone to

back you, and a little luck, and before you know it you find yourself
with a rod of justice in your hand or a miter on your head."

That night master and man spent in the fields, under the open sky,
and the next day, upon continuing their journey, they saw coming
toward them a man on foot with saddlebags about his neck and in his
hand a javelin or pike. In short, he was the very picture of a foot-courier,
and as he approached Don Quixote he quickened his pace and, coming
up to him half on the run, embraced his right thigh, for that was as far
as he could reach.

"O Señor Don Quixote de la Mancha," he exclaimed with a show of
great joy, "how happy at heart my lord the duke will be when he hears
that your Grace is returning to the castle! For he and the duchess are
still there."

"I do not recognize you, my friend," said Don Quixote, "unless you
see fit to tell me who you are."

"I," replied the courier, "am Tosilos, lackey to my lord the duke, the
one who refused to fight with your Grace over the marriage of Doña
Rodríguez' daughter."

"Why, God bless me!" said Don Quixote, "is it possible you are the
one whom my enemies the enchanters transformed into this lackey that
you say you are, in order to cheat me of the honor of winning that
battle?"

"No more of that talk, my good sir," said the courier. "There was no
enchantment about it, nor any change of appearance whatsoever. It
was as Tosilos the lackey that I entered and came out of the lists. I
liked the girl and thought that I could win her without fighting; but
things did not turn out that way, for just as soon as your Grace had
left our castle my lord the duke had them give me a hundred blows
with a club for having disobeyed his orders about the combat. The upshot of it all is: the girl has become a nun, Doña Rodríguez has gone back
to Castile, and I am now on my way to Barcelona with a packet of letters
from my master to the viceroy. If your Grace would like a wee drop,
I have here a gourd full of the best; [10] it's not very cold but it's good
wine, and I also have a few slices of Tronchón cheese, which will serve
as the summoner and awakener of thirst if by any chance it is asleep." [11]

"That suits me," said Sancho. "Let's not stand on ceremony, but let
the good Tosilos pour in spite of all the enchanters in the Indies."

"I must say, Sancho," remarked Don Quixote, "that you are the
biggest glutton on the face of the earth, and the biggest dunce besides
not to be able to see that this courier is enchanted and this Tosilos a false

one. Stay with him and drink your fill, and I will ride on very slowly and wait for you to catch up with me."

With a laugh the lackey unsheathed [12] his gourd and brought out the cheese and a small loaf of bread from the saddlebags, whereupon he and Sancho seated themselves upon the greensward and most peaceably and companionably proceeded to do away with the entire store of provisions, exhibiting so hearty an appetite that they even licked the package of letters because it smelled of cheese.

"Undoubtedly, Sancho my friend," said Tosilos, "this master of yours must be a madman."

"He owes no one anything," [13] replied Sancho, "especially when it comes to the coin of madness. I can see it plainly enough, and I've told him as much, but what good does it do? Above all, now that he's done for; for he has been conquered by the Knight of the White Moon."

Tosilos then begged him to relate what had happened, but Sancho replied that it would be discourteous to keep his master waiting, and there would be time for that another day if they chanced to meet. And shaking out his jacket and brushing the crumbs from his beard, he gave Tosilos an *adiós* and drove the gray forward until he came to where the knight was sitting in the shade of a tree.

CHAPTER LXVII. *How Don Quixote resolved to turn shepherd and lead a rustic life during the year for which he had given his promise, with other events that are truly diverting and that make good reading.*

IF Don Quixote had had a great deal on his mind before his downfall, it was even worse afterward. There he sat in the shade of a tree, as has been said, and thither like flies to honey thoughts came swarming to sting and annoy him. Some of them had to do with Dulcinea's disenchantment, while others were concerned with his forced retirement.

As Sancho reached his master's side, he began praising the generosity of the lackey Tosilos, whereupon Don Quixote said to him, "Is it possible, Sancho, that you still believe him to be a real lackey? You do not seem to remember having seen Dulcinea converted and transformed into a peasant lass and the Knight of the Mirrors into the bachelor Sansón Carrasco, all of which was the work of those enchanters that persecute me. But come now, tell me: did you ask this Tosilos as you call him what, through God's will, has become of Altisidora, whether or not she has wept over my absence or has already consigned to oblivion the love thoughts that tortured her when I was present?"

"The things on my mind," replied Sancho, "had nothing to do with asking foolish questions like that. Body of me! master, is your Grace in any position to be inquiring into the thoughts of others, and especially love thoughts?"

"Look, Sancho," said Don Quixote, "there is a great deal of difference between those actions that are performed out of love and those that are motivated by gratitude. A knight may well withhold his affections, but he cannot be ungrateful. Altisidora, it would seem, cared for me deeply; she gave me those three kerchiefs, as you know; [1] she wept when I departed; she heaped maledictions on my head and, casting modesty aside, bewailed her fate in public; all of which is a sign that she adores me, since lovers when angry usually end by cursing each other. There was no hope I could give her, no treasure I could offer her, for all that I have belongs to Dulcinea, and the treasure of knights-errant is like that of the fairy folk: seeming but unreal. [2] All that I can give her is a place in my memory, without prejudice to that which I reserve for Dulcinea—the Dulcinea to whom you do so grievous a wrong by your remissness in lashing yourself and punishing that flesh of yours (would that I saw it eaten by wolves), which you would keep for the worms rather than devote to the relief of that poor lady."

"Sir," Sancho answered him, "I cannot see what lashing my backside has to do with the disenchanting of the enchanted; it's like saying 'If you have a headache, rub ointment on your knees.' At any rate, I'll venture to swear that in all the histories your Grace has read on the subject of knight-errantry you have never heard of a spell being removed by such means. But however that may be, I'll see to whipping myself whenever I happen to feel like it and when I have an opportunity to do it with some comfort."

"God grant it may be so," said Don Quixote, "and may Heaven give you the grace to remember the obligation you are under to aid my lady, who is at the same time your lady, seeing that you belong to me."

With talk of this sort they jogged along until they came to the place where they had been trampled by the bulls. Don Quixote recognized it at once.

"This," he observed, "is the meadow where we fell in with those gallant and gaily bedecked shepherds and shepherdesses who were endeavoring to imitate and restore the Arcadia of old, a novel idea and an inspired one; and if you approve, Sancho, I would suggest that, at least for the time that I have to live in retirement, we likewise turn shepherds. I will purchase some sheep and all the other things that are necessary to the pastoral life, taking for myself the name of 'the shepherd Quixotiz,' while you will be 'the shepherd Pancino.' Together we will roam the hills, the woods, and the meadows, now singing songs and now composing elegies, drinking the crystal water of the springs or that of the clear running brooks or mighty rivers. The oaks will provide us with an abundance of their delicious fruit,[3] the hardwood trunks of the cork trees will furnish us a seat, the willows will give us shade, the roses will lend their perfume, and the spacious meadows will spread a myriad-colored carpet for our feet; we shall breathe the clean, pure air, and despite the darkness of the night the moon and stars will afford us illumination; song will be our joy, and we shall be happy even in our laments, for Apollo will supply the inspiration for our verses and love will endow us with conceits and we shall be everlastingly famous—not only in this age but for all time to come."

"By God," exclaimed Sancho, "that kind of life squares and corners with me.[4] And what's more, the moment they hear of it the bachelor Sansón Carrasco and Master Nicholas the barber will want to do the same thing and turn shepherds with us. I only hope to God the curate also doesn't take it into his head to enter the fold, seeing that he's so jolly and fond of amusing himself."

"You are quite right," said Don Quixote, "and the bachelor Sansón Carrasco if he joins the flock, as I have no doubt he will, can call himself 'the shepherd Sansonino,' or, it may be, 'the shepherd Carrascón'; barber Nicholas can be 'Niculoso,'[5] just as old Boscán was known as 'Nemoroso.'[6] As for the curate, I do not know what we can call him unless it is something derived from his title, such as 'the shepherd Curiambro.' As for the shepherdesses whose lovers we shall be, we can pick their names as we would pears, and since my lady has one that befits a shepherdess as well as it does a princess, I need not trouble myself with looking for anything better; but you, Sancho, may call yours whatever you choose."

"I will simply call her 'Teresona,' " [7] said Sancho, "seeing that her real name is Teresa and she is big and fat. And, moreover, when I come to sing her praises in my verses, I'll show how chaste my love is, as I don't propose to go looking for fancy bread in other men's houses.[8] It will not be proper for the curate to have a shepherdess, since he must set a good example, but as for the bachelor, his soul is in the palm of his hand."

"God bless me!" cried Don Quixote, "what a life we are going to lead, Sancho my friend! What music we shall hear—the strains of reed flutes,[9] Zamora bagpipes, tabors, timbrels, rebecs! And if amid all these different varieties of music the *albogues* [10] also resound, then practically all the pastoral instruments will be there."

"What are *albogues?*" inquired Sancho. "I never heard tell of them, nor have I ever seen one in all my life."

"*Albogues,*" replied Don Quixote, "are plates resembling brass candlesticks, which, when struck together on the empty or hollow side, make a noise that, if not very agreeable or harmonious, is still not displeasing to the ear and goes well with the rustic character of the bagpipe and tabor. The name is a Moorish one, as are all those in our Castilian tongue that begin with *al,* such as *almohaza, almorzar, alfombra, alguacil, alhucema, almacén, alcancía,*[11] and a few other similar ones. Our language has only three such nouns that end in *i,* and they are *borceguí zaquizamí,* and *maravedí.*[12] As for *alhelí* and *alfaquí,*[13] both the initial *al* and the final *i* show them at once to be Arabic.

"If I speak of this, it is because I was reminded of it by the mention of the word *albogues.* The fact that I myself, as you know, am something of a poet will be of great assistance to us in perfecting ourselves in this way of life,[14] and the bachelor Sansón Carrasco is a very fine one. As for the curate I cannot say, but I will wager you that he must have a bit of the poet in him, and Master Nicholas as well, no doubt, since all barbers, or most of them at any rate, like to strum the guitar and improvise verses. In my songs I shall lament my separation from my loved one, while you may sing your own praises as the constant lover; the shepherd Carrascón will be the rejected swain, and the curate Curiambro may choose whatever theme may suit him best. That way everything will go very well with nothing left to be desired."

"Ah, master," said Sancho, "I am so unlucky I fear the day will never come when I can lead such a life as that. Oh, what neat spoons I'll turn out when I'm a shepherd! [15] What tidbits, creams, garlands, and pastoral odds and ends! [16] If they don't look upon me as a wise man, I'll at least get a reputation for being ingenious! My daughter Sanchica will bring us our dinner to the sheepfold—but wait a minute! She's good-looking and the shepherds are not so simple-minded after all; they have plenty of mischief in them, and I would not have her go for wool and come back shorn.[17] You will find love-making and evil passions in the fields as in the cities, in shepherds' huts as well as in royal palaces. Do away with the cause, you do away with the sin; [18] if the eyes don't see, the heart will not break; [19] and escape from the slaughter is worth more than good men's prayers." [20]

"That will be enough of your proverbs, Sancho," said Don Quixote, "since any one of those you have quoted is sufficient to express your thought. Many times have I advised you not to be so prodigal in your use of them and to observe some degree of moderation, but it appears to be like preaching in the desert: 'My mother whips me and I keep right on.' " [21]

"Your Grace," remarked Sancho, "puts me in mind of the proverb: 'Said the frying pan to the kettle, get away, black-eyes.' [22] You scold me for doing it, and you start stringing them yourself."

"Mark you, Sancho," replied Don Quixote, "when I bring them in they are to the purpose and fit the subject like a ring on the finger; whereas you, in place of introducing them, drag them in by the hair of the head. If I remember rightly, I have told you once before [23] that proverbs are concise maxims drawn from the wisdom and experience of our elders, and the saying that is not appropriate is simply nonsensical. However, no more of this, for darkness is coming on. Let us retire some little distance from the highway to a place where we may spend the night. God knows what tomorrow will bring."

They did so, and had a late supper and a bad one, at which Sancho was greatly put out. He could not help thinking of the hardships of knight-errantry as experienced in the woods and wilds, even though one occasionally met with abundance in homes and castles, as in the houses of Don Diego de Miranda and Don Antonio Moreno and at the wedding of the rich Camacho. But, he reflected, it could not be always day or always night, and so he spent that particular night in sleeping, while his master kept vigil.

CHAPTER LXVIII. *Of the bristly adventure that befell Don Quixote.*

THE night was rather dark. The moon, true enough, was in the sky but not anywhere to be seen; for my lady Diana upon occasion goes for a little stroll in the antipodes, leaving the hills in blackness and the valleys devoid of light. Don Quixote complied with the demands of nature by yielding to his first sleep but not to his second, in which respect he differed from his squire, who never had a second sleep since his first one lasted from night until morning, showing what a good constitution he had and how few cares. Don Quixote's anxieties, on the other hand, kept him awake, to such an extent that he aroused Sancho.

"It amazes me, Sancho," he said, "to see how unconcerned you are. I think you must be made of marble or solid brass without any trace of feeling whatsoever. Here I keep vigil while you sleep, I weep while you sing, I am faint from hunger while you are sluggish and exhausted from pure gluttony. Good servants ought to share the sufferings of their masters and feel for them, if only for the sake of appearances. Behold the calmness of the night and this solitude round about us which invites us to break our sleep by a vigil of some sort. And so, as you live, bestir yourself, go off some little distance from here, and with right good will and courage cheerfully lay on three or four hundred lashes of those that you owe toward Dulcinea's disenchantment.

"I put this in the form of a request, having no desire to come to grips with you as I did the other time, for I know what strength you have in your arms. And then, after you have done this, we will spend the rest of the night singing as I lament my separation and you praise your lover's constancy. In this manner we may at once begin that pastoral life we mean to follow when we reach our own village."

"Master," replied Sancho, "I am no monk to be getting up in the middle of my sleep and disciplining myself, nor do I think I would feel much like singing after the pain I would suffer from the whipping —you can't go from one extreme to another like that. So, let me sleep, your Grace, and do not trouble me about the lashes, or you'll make me swear never to touch a hair of my smock, much less my flesh."

"O hardhearted one!" cried Don Quixote. "O pitiless squire! O what ingratitude for the ill-bestowed bread of mine you have eaten and the favors I have shown and expected to show you! It was through me that you became a governor, and it is owing to me that you may hope soon to become a count or to obtain some title of equal worth; for the fulfillment of that promise will not be long delayed once this year has passed,[1] since I—*post tenebras spero lucem.*" [2]

"I don't know anything about that," said Sancho. "All I know is that while I am asleep I have neither fear nor hope nor troubles nor any concern about glory. Blessings on the one who invented sleep, the cloak that covers all human thoughts, the food that relieves hunger, the water that quenches thirst, the fire that keeps the cold away, the cold that tempers heat—in short, the common currency with which all things are bought, the weight and balance that makes the shepherd equal to the king and that puts the fool on an equal footing with the wise man. There is only one fault to be found with sleep, according to what I've heard, and that is the fact that it resembles death; for between a sleeping man and a dead one there is very little difference." [3]

"Never, Sancho," said Don Quixote, "have I heard you use such polished language as now, which leads me to recognize the truth of the proverb you sometimes quote: 'Not with whom you are bred, but with whom you are fed.' " [4]

"Ha! master," exclaimed Sancho, "upon my word, I'm not the one who's stringing proverbs now; they also drop from your Grace's mouth in pairs and faster than they do from mine. The only thing is that between my sayings and yours there is this difference: yours are always timely and my own are not; but they are all proverbs just the same."

At this point they heard a kind of subdued roar, a harsh and grating sound that spread through all the valleys. Don Quixote at once stood up and laid his hand upon his sword, while Sancho crouched beneath the gray, placing the bundle of armor on one side of him and the packsaddle on the other; for he was quite as alarmed as his master was excited, and was trembling all over. The noise grew in volume as it came near the terrified pair—at least one of them was terrified; as for the other, his valor is well known.

The truth of the matter was, some men were driving to the fair more than six hundred pigs and were continuing their journey even at that hour; and so great was the din the animals created with their grunting and snorting that it deafened the ears of Don Quixote and Sancho, who could not make out what it was. Meanwhile, the grunting herd rushed onward, fanning out far and wide, and without any respect for Don Quixote's person or that of Sancho, either, it passed over both of them, knocking down Sancho's intrenchments, unseating the knight, and sweeping Rocinante off his feet. The trampling, the grunting, and the speed with which the filthy beasts came on threw everybody and everything into confusion and on the ground: the packsaddle, the armor, the ass, Rocinante, Sancho, Don Quixote, and all the rest. Picking himself up as best he could, Sancho asked his master for the sword, saying he wished to slaughter half a dozen of these gentry, these impolite pigs (for by this time he had realized what they were).

"Let them be, my friend," said Don Quixote, "seeing this is but the penalty for my sin; for Heaven justly decrees as punishment for a vanquished knight-errant that he shall be eaten by jackals, stung by wasps, and trampled by swine."

"In that case," said Sancho, "Heaven's way of punishing the squires of vanquished knights must be to have them bitten by flies, eaten up with lice, and attacked by hunger. If we were the sons of those we serve or very near relatives, it would not be so strange if we were to suffer the punishment for their misdeeds even to the fourth generation; but what, after all, have the Panzas to do with the Quixotes? Oh, well, let's settle ourselves again and get what little sleep is left us this night, for God will send the dawn and we will make out somehow."

"Go ahead and sleep, Sancho," said Don Quixote, "since you were born for that purpose. As for me, I was born to keep vigil; and in the time that remains between now and morning I propose to give rein to my longings and find outlet for them in a little madrigal which, without your knowing anything about it, I composed last night."

"If you ask me," replied Sancho, "longings that lead one to make verses can't amount to very much. So, versify all you like, your Grace, and I will get what sleep I can." Saying this, he took what space he required and, huddling down, fell into a dreamless slumber undisturbed by bond or debt or trouble of any kind.

Whereupon, leaning against the trunk of a beech—or it may have been a cork tree, for Cid Hamete Benengeli is not definite on the point —Don Quixote began singing the following air to the accompaniment of his own sighs:

> *Love, when I pause to think*
> *Of the terrible wound that thou hast dealt to me,*
> *To the haven of death I'd flee*
> *And let my troubles in oblivion sink.*

But as the port I near,
Sailing a sea of woe to my anodyne,
Such wondrous joy is mine
That life once more doth live and finds me here.

Life, then, it is that slays
And death restores to me the one I hate—
O strange, unheard-of fate
That juggles life and death and with me plays! [5]

Each of these verses was accompanied by many sighs and not a few
tears, as if the singer's heart were transfixed with grief over his downfall and his separation from Dulcinea.

Day finally came, and as the rays of the sun fell on Sancho's eyes he
awoke, roused and shook himself, and stretched his sluggish limbs. Beholding the damage which the pigs had done to his pantry, he cursed
the drove in no uncertain terms. Then the two of them took to the road
again, and along toward sunset they saw coming toward them about
ten men on horseback and four or five on foot. Don Quixote's heart
gave a leap and Sancho once more was frightened, for the men who
were approaching carried lances and bucklers and appeared to be war-
riors.

"If it were permitted me, Sancho," said Don Quixote, "to make use
of my weapons, if my promise did not keep my arms tied, that crew
coming there would be but cakes and gingerbread for me. [6] But it may
be something other than what we fear."

By this time those on horseback were upon them, and without saying
a word they surrounded Don Quixote, pointing their upraised spears at
his back and bosom and threatening him with death. Putting a finger
to his mouth by way of signifying that silence was called for, one of the
men on foot then seized Rocinante's bridle and led him out of the road,
while his companions drove Sancho and the gray before them, preserving an astonishing silence all the while, as they followed in the
tracks of Don Quixote and his guide. Two or three times the knight
started to inquire where they were taking him and what they wanted of
him, but no sooner had he begun to move his lips than his abductors
threatened to close them with their lance points. The same thing happened with Sancho: the moment he showed signs of talking, one of the
foot attendants would prick him with a goad, and the gray as well, just
as if he too were about to speak.

As night closed in upon them they quickened their pace, and the two prisoners were more afraid than ever, especially when they heard the men saying to them every now and then, "Get on with you, you troglodytes! Be quiet, barbarians! Pay the price, you cannibals! No complaints, you Scythians! Keep your eyes shut, you murderous Polyphemuses, you flesh-eating lions!"

These and other similar epithets tortured the ears of the wretched master and man and caused Sancho to mutter to himself, "So, we are tortolites, are we? So, we are barbers and clouts, bitches that you say 'come, come' to?[7] I don't like those names at all; it's a bad wind for thrashing our corn;[8] misfortune comes upon us all at once like blows on a dog's back,[9] and I only hope this unlucky adventure that threatens us will lead to nothing worse than blows."

As for Don Quixote, he was dumfounded by it all, being at his wits' end to make out what the purpose of this vicious name-calling could be. The only thing of which he was certain was that no good could come of it and there was much to be feared. And then, about an hour past midnight, they arrived at a castle which was quite familiar to him, for it was that of the duke where he had stayed not long before.

"God bless me!" he cried as soon as he recognized the edifice, "and what is the meaning of this? Here is a house in which all is courtesy and graciousness, but for the vanquished good turns into evil and evil into something worse."

Upon entering the principal courtyard of the castle, they found it fitted out in such a manner as to add to their astonishment and increase their fears twofold, as will be seen in the following chapter.

CHAPTER LXIX. *Of the strangest and most extraordinary adventure that has befallen Don Quixote in the entire course of this great history.*

THE horsemen dismounted and together with those on foot at once and in great haste picked up Sancho and Don Quixote bodily and carried them into the courtyard. There nearly a hundred torches, fixed in their sockets, were flaring, while the adjoining galleries were illuminated by more than five hundred lamps, as a result of which, despite the fact that the night was somewhat overcast, the absence of daylight was not noticed. In the middle of the courtyard a funeral mound about two yards high had been reared, completely covered by an enormous black velvet canopy, and on the steps leading up to it more than a hundred white wax tapers in silver candlesticks were shedding their glow. Upon this catafalque lay the lifeless body of a maiden, so lovely as to make even death itself seem beautiful. Her head rested upon a brocade pillow and was crowned with a plaited garland of sweet-smelling flowers of various sorts; her hands were folded over her bosom and between them was a bough of the yellow palm of victory.[1]

At one side of the patio was a stage with two chairs on which were seated two personages who, from the crowns upon their heads and the scepters in their hands, appeared to be kings, whether real ones or not. This stage also was reached by steps, and beside it were two other seats, where those who were carrying the prisoners now deposited Don Quixote and Sancho, preserving a dead silence as they did so and giving the knight and his squire to understand by means of signs that they too were to say nothing. The captives, however, would have been silent even without this admonition, for the astonishment they felt at all the things they beheld was more than sufficient to render them tongue-tied.

Two persons of obvious importance accompanied by a large retinue then mounted the stage, and Don Quixote at once recognized them as his hosts, the duke and duchess. They seated themselves upon two richly adorned chairs alongside the two individuals who looked the part of kings, all of which was cause enough for amazement, not to mention the fact that the knight had discovered the dead woman upon the catafalque to be none other than the beauteous Altisidora. Who would not have been amazed?

As the duke and duchess mounted the stage, Don Quixote and Sancho rose and made a profound obeisance, the ducal pair replying with a slight inclination of their heads. An officer thereupon crossed the courtyard and, going up to Sancho, threw over him a black buckram robe with flames painted on it, and removing the squire's cap he replaced it with a miter of the kind that those under sentence from the Holy Office wear, at the same time whispering in his ear that he was not to open his lips or they would gag him or possibly put him to death. Surveying himself from head to foot, Sancho saw that he was all aflame, but inasmuch as the flames did not burn him he did not give a rap for them. He took off his miter, and when he saw there were devils painted on it he put it back on again.

"So far so good," he muttered. "Those haven't scorched me yet and these haven't carried me off."

Don Quixote also looked him over, and although he was frightened out of his wits he could not help laughing at the figure that Sancho cut. Then, seemingly from beneath the catafalque, there came the low and pleasing sound of flutes, which, unaccompanied by any human voice (for here silence's self kept silent), produced an effect that was at once gentle and amorous; and suddenly, beside the pillow where the head of the "corpse" reclined, there appeared a handsome youth clad like an ancient Roman who, to the sound of a harp which he himself played, began singing in a very sweet, clear voice the two stanzas that follow:

> *While in this court where magic doth hold sway*
> *The fair Altisidora seeks the light*
> *('Twas Don Quixote's cruelty did slay*
> *The hapless maid); while ladies all bedight*
> *In goat-hair garments* [2] *celebrate the day,*
> *With dour duennas dressing for the rite*
> *In robes of baize and wool, my harp I'll play*
> *Better than Thracian bard,* [3] *to hymn her plight.*
>
> > *And not in life alone be this my theme,*
> > *But when my tongue in death is cold and still,*
> > *I mean to raise my voice and thus redeem*
> > *The debt I owe thee, with a right good will.*

Free of its prison cell, on Stygian stream
My constant soul shall try its singing skill
In odes to thee, and in that hour supreme
Roll back oblivion's waters, dark and chill.[4]

"That will do," said one of the "kings" at this point; "proceed no further, divine singer, as it would be an endless task to portray for us now the death and all the graces of the peerless Altisidora. For she is not dead as the ignorant ones think, but lives on by the tongue of fame and through the penance which Sancho Panza here present must endure in order to restore her to the light of this world. And so, O Rhadamanthus, thou who dost sit in judgment with me in Pluto's murky pit,[5] seeing thou dost know all that the inscrutable Fates have decreed in regard to the manner in which this damsel is to be revived, do thou tell us at once in order that the hoped-for boon be no longer deferred."

No sooner had Minos, his fellow judge, said this than Rhadamanthus rose to his feet. "Ho!" he cried, "you officers of this household, great and small, of high and low degree, come one and all and imprint on Sancho's face twenty-four smacks,[6] and give him besides a dozen pinches and half a dozen pinpricks in his back and arms; for upon this ceremony Altisidora's salvation is dependent."

Hearing this, Sancho broke his silence at last. "I swear," he said, "I'd just as soon turn Moor as let this face of mine be slapped or mistreated! Body of me! What has that to do with the resurrection of this damsel? The old woman was fond of blites . . . [7] They enchant Dulcinea and flog me to disenchant her. Altisidora dies of the sickness God sends her, and to bring her back to life they have to give me a couple of dozen smacks, make a sieve of my body with pinpricks, and raise welts on my arms with their pinches. Try those jokes on your brother-in-law;[8] I'm an old dog and it's no use saying *tus, tus* to me." [9]

"Thou shalt die!" shouted Rhadamanthus at the top of his voice. "Relent, thou tiger! Humble thyself, haughty Nimrod! Suffer and be silent, seeing that nothing impossible is asked of thee, and complain not of the hardships involved in this matter. Smacked thou shalt be, pricked full of holes, and pinched until thou dost groan with pain. What, ho, officers! Carry out my behest or ye shall see for what it was ye were born."

At this moment a procession of as many as six duennas was to be seen crossing the courtyard. Four of them wore spectacles and all had their right hands raised with four inches of wrist showing, by way of making them seem longer as is the present fashion.[10] As soon as he caught sight of them Sancho began bellowing like a bull.

"I might allow myself to be manhandled by anybody else," he said, "but to think that I am going to let duennas touch me—nothing of the sort! Cat-claw my face as they did my master's in this very castle, run my body through with burnished dagger points, nip my arms with red-hot pincers—I'll bear it all patiently to please these gentlefolk; but the devil take me if I let duennas lay hands on me!"

It was Don Quixote's turn to break silence now. "Be patient, my son," he said. "Comply with the wishes of these gentlemen, and thank Heaven there is lodged in your person such virtue that through the martyrdom of your flesh you are able to disenchant the enchanted and resurrect the dead."

As the duennas approached him Sancho became more quiet and tractable, and, settling himself comfortably in his chair, he held up his face and beard to the first comer, who gave him a resounding smack, followed by a low bow.

"Less bowing and scraping, Señora Duenna," he said, "and less paint and lotions [11] for, by God, your hands smell of vinegar water." [12]

To make a long story short, all the duennas slapped him and many other members of the household pinched him, but the thing he could not stand was the pinpricks. When it came to that, he rose from his chair with a show of anger and, seizing a lighted torch that stood near by, began laying about him among the duennas and all his other tormentors, crying, "Away with you, ministers of Hell! I am not made of brass so that I do not feel such unusual torture as this!"

Then it was that Altisidora, who must have been tired of lying on her back for so long a time, turned over on her side, beholding which, all the bystanders shouted, with one voice as it were, "Altisidora is alive! Altisidora lives!" And Rhadamanthus commanded Sancho to forego his wrath, seeing that their purpose had now been achieved.

When Don Quixote saw Altisidora stirring, he fell on his knees before Sancho.

"O son of my loins," he said, "for I will not call you squire, now is the time for you to give yourself a few of those lashes that you owe toward Dulcinea's disenchantment. Now, I repeat, is the time, when the virtue that is in you is ripe and may efficaciously accomplish the good that is expected of you."

"That," said Sancho, "to my mind, is trick upon trick and not honey on pancakes. It would be a fine thing to have lashes on top of pinches, slaps, and prickings! You might as well take a big stone, tie it around my neck, and throw me into a well; it doesn't make much difference to me if in order to cure other people's ills I have to be the cow at the wedding.[13] Leave me alone or by God I'll throw everything over, no matter what happens." [14]

Altisidora by now had risen to a sitting posture upon the bier, and at that very instant there was a blare of flutes and flageolets, and all those present cried out, "Long live Altisidora! Long live Altisidora!"

The duke and duchess and the kings Minos and Rhadamanthus then rose, and all of them together, with Don Quixote and Sancho, advanced to receive the maiden and take her down from the catafalque. Acting like one who had just recovered from a swoon, she bowed to the ducal pair and to the kings, and then, with a sidewise glance at Don Quixote, she said, "May God forgive you, heartless knight, for thanks to your cruelty I have been in the other world more than a thousand years as it seems to me. As for you, O most compassionate of all the squires in this world, I thank you for the life I now possess! From this day forth, friend Sancho, you may look upon as yours six chemises of mine which I am presenting to you that you may make yourself as many shirts; and if some of them are a little ragged, at least all of them are clean."

Doffing his miter, Sancho knelt and kissed her hand in return for this favor, and the duke then ordered them to relieve him of that head-piece, and his flame-covered robe as well, and to restore his cap and jacket. Sancho, however, begged to be allowed to keep the accouterments, saying he wished to take them back to his own country as a memento of this most extraordinary event, and the duchess replied that he might do so, adding that he already had reason to know what a great friend of his she was. And, finally, the duke directed that the courtyard be cleared and all should retire to their rooms, with Don Quixote and Sancho being conducted to the ones they had formerly occupied.

CHAPTER LXX. *Which follows the sixty-ninth and treats of matters that cannot be omitted if this history is to be clearly understood.*

SANCHO slept that night on a truckle bed [1] in Don Quixote's chamber. This he would gladly have avoided if he could have, for he knew very well that his master would keep him awake answering questions and he was in no mood for an extended conversation; the pain that he still felt from his recent martyrdom interfered with the free exercise of his tongue, and as a result he would rather have slept alone in a hovel than in this sumptuous room with company of any sort. His apprehensions proved to be justified, for his master began talking the moment they were in bed.

"What do you think, Sancho, of what happened this evening? Great and mighty is the power wielded by one who is scornful in love; for you with your own eyes have seen Altisidora lying there dead, slain not by arrows, or sword, or any warlike weapon, and not by any deadly poison, but solely by thought of the unrelenting disdain that I have always shown her."

"She's welcome to die any time she likes," replied Sancho, "for I didn't make her fall in love and I never in all my life disdained her. As I have said once before, I fail to see what the saving of Altisidora, a maid more whimsical than she is sensible, has to do with the tormenting of Sancho Panza. Now I begin to perceive, clearly and distinctly, that there are such things as enchanters and enchantments in this world, and God deliver me from them since I cannot free myself. But no more of that. I beg your Grace to let me sleep and not ask me any more questions, unless you want me to throw myself out the window."

"Sleep, friend Sancho," said Don Quixote, "providing the pinpricks and pinches you received and the slaps they gave you will let you do so."

"There is no pain," said Sancho, "that can equal those insulting smacks, if for no other reason than that they were given me by those confounded duennas. But again I beg you: let me sleep; for sleep is relief from misery to those who are miserable when they are awake."

"So be it," said Don Quixote, "and God keep you company."

The two of them then dropped off; and Cid Hamete, the author of this great history, takes the opportunity thus afforded him to explain how it was the duke and duchess came to devise the elaborate plot that has been described. It appears that the bachelor Sansón Carrasco had not forgotten how the Knight of the Mirrors had been conquered and overthrown by Don Quixote, an event that had upset all his plans, and he had, accordingly, wished to try his hand again, hoping for better luck the next time. From the page who brought the letter and gift to Teresa Panza, Sancho's wife, he had learned where the knight was and had then once more provided himself with weapons and a horse, taking care to have a white moon painted on his shield. He had transported the armor upon the back of a mule, led by a peasant and not by Tomé Cecial, his former squire, who might be recognized by Sancho or his master.

Upon reaching the duke's castle, he was informed of the road that Don Quixote had taken with the object of participating in the tournament at Saragossa. He also learned of the jokes that had been played upon the knight in connection with Dulcinea's disenchantment, which was to be accomplished at the expense of Sancho's backside. Finally, the duke told him of the trick the squire had played in making his master believe that Dulcinea was under a magic spell and had been transformed into a peasant lass, and how the duchess had ended by convincing Sancho that he was the one that was deceived since Dulcinea really was enchanted. The bachelor marveled at all this and laughed over it no little as he thought of Sancho's shrewdness combined with his simple-mindedness and the extremes to which Don Quixote's madness was capable of carrying him.

The duke requested him, if he found the knight, and whether he succeeded in overcoming him or not, to return and let them know how things turned out. Promising to do so, the bachelor took his departure. Not encountering Don Quixote in Saragossa, he went on, with the result that has already been set forth. Going back to the castle, he gave the duke a full account of the combat, with the conditions that had been laid down, adding that, being a good knight-errant and bent upon keeping his word, the vanquished one was already on his way back to his native village, where he was to remain for a year, in which time it might be that he would be cured of his madness; for this, after all, said the bachelor, was what had led to the assuming of these disguises on his part, since he looked upon it as a pity that so well-intentioned a gentleman should be so insane. With this, he took his leave once more and went on to the village to wait there for Don Quixote, who was coming along the road behind him.

It was then that the duke took occasion to play this joke, so great was the pleasure he derived from everything that had to do with the pair. Sending out a host of retainers on foot and on horseback along all the roads far and near and in every direction from which he thought Don Quixote might be approaching, he gave them orders in case they found the knight to bring him to the castle, either of his own free will or by force. When they came upon him, the servants advised their master of the fact, and, having already decided on all that was to be done, as soon as he received this message the duke ordered that the torches and lamps in the courtyard be lighted and that Altisidora be placed upon the funeral mound with all the pomp and ceremony previously mentioned, all of which was done so skillfully and in so lifelike a manner that it was the next thing to reality itself.

Here, Cid Hamete remarks, it is his personal opinion that the jesters were as crazy as their victims and that the duke and duchess were not two fingers' breadth removed from being fools when they went to so much trouble to make sport of the foolish.

As for these latter, one of them was sleeping soundly and the other was still keeping vigil with his aimless thoughts when daylight came upon them, bringing with it the desire to rise; for whether he was the victor or the vanquished Don Quixote was not slothful and never took a delight in wallowing in the feathers. No sooner was he awake than Altisidora, upon the bidding of her master and mistress, entered the room. To him she was as one returned from the dead, for she wore the same garland as when she lay upon the bier, being clad in a robe of white taffeta with gold flowers; with hair loose-flowing over her shoulders, she leaned upon a cane of very fine black ebony.

Greatly embarrassed by her presence in his chamber, Don Quixote huddled down in the bed, covering himself almost entirely with the sheets and counterpane. Too tongue-tied to speak, he was unable to show her any courtesy whatever. She sat down upon a chair at the head of his bed and, heaving a deep sigh, addressed him in a faint voice but one filled with emotion.

"When women of high station," she said, "and modest, retiring damsels trample on their honor and give free rein to their tongues, breaking through all obstacles to publish abroad the inmost secrets of their hearts, they are indeed in dire straits. I, Señor Don Quixote, am one of these,

hard pressed and overcome by love but, for all of that, so long-suffering and modest that silence broke my heart and I died. Slain by thought of the stern manner in which you have treated me, stonyhearted knight—
Oh, harder far than marble to my plaint! [2]—
I lay dead for two whole days, judging from what I was told by those that looked upon me. And had it not been that love took pity on me, finding a remedy for me in the tortures laid on this worthy squire, I should still be in the other world."

"Love," said Sancho, "might very well have laid them on my donkey instead, and I'd have thanked him for it. But tell me, my lady—and may Heaven provide you with a softer-hearted lover than my master—what did you see in that other world? What is there in Hell, anyway? For, of course, that is where you have to go when you die in despair."

"To tell you the truth," replied Altisidora, "I do not think that I died completely since I did not enter Hell, for once I had done so I should never have been able to leave no matter how much I wished to. The fact is, I only went as far as the gate, where I saw about a dozen devils playing a game of tennis. They were dressed in breeches and doublets and wore Walloon collars trimmed with Flemish bone-lace, with ruffles of the same material that served them as cuffs and with four inches of their arms sticking out in order to make their hands, which carried blazing rackets, appear longer than they were. [3] But what amazed me more than this was the fact that, in place of tennis balls, they made use of what appeared to be books filled with wind and rubbish, which was something strange and marvelous to behold. And I was still further astonished to note that, whereas it is natural for the winners in a game to be glad and the losers sorry, in this case all those that took part were growling, snarling, and cursing all the time."

"That is not to be wondered at," said Sancho, "for, whether they play games or not and whether they win or lose, devils are never satisfied."

"That must be the way it is," agreed Altisidora, "but there is another thing that surprises me, or surprised me then, and that is the fact that no ball was of any use a second time, and it was wonderful to see the constant succession of books, new and old. To one of the brand-new volumes, which was very well bound, they gave such a whack that they knocked the insides out of it and sent the leaves flying in all directions. 'Just see what book that is,' said a devil to his companion, and the other devil replied, 'This is the *Second Part of the History of Don Quixote de la Mancha*, written not by Cid Hamete, the original author, but by an

Aragonese who, according to his own account, is a native of Tordesillas.'

" 'Take it away,' said the other. 'Throw it into the bottomless pit so I shan't have to see it.'

" 'Is it as bad as all that?'

" 'It is so bad,' said the first devil, 'that if I had deliberately set myself to write a worse one, I shouldn't have been able to achieve it.'

"They then went on with their game, batting about other books, but, for my part, on hearing the name of Don Quixote whom I so adore, I made up my mind then and there to remember this vision I had seen."

"It must undoubtedly have been a vision," said Don Quixote, "seeing there is no other in the world who bears that name. The history you speak of has been going from hand to hand for some time but does not stay long anywhere, for everybody gives it a kick and has done with it. I am not disturbed to hear that I am wandering about in fantastic garb in the infernal regions just as I do in the light above, for I am not the one of whom that history treats. If it by chance is a true, faithful, and worthy account, then it will live for ages, but if it is bad, it will not be a far step for it from the cradle to the grave."

Altisidora was about to go on with her reproaches addressed to Don Quixote when he interrupted her. "Lady," he said, "I have told you many times how it grieves me that you should have fastened your affections upon me, since I am not in a position to give you anything but gratitude in return. I was born to belong to Dulcinea del Toboso, and the Fates, if Fates there be, have set me aside for her. Accordingly, to think that the beauty of another can make any impression upon my heart is vain indeed. This frankness on my part should be sufficient to induce you to retire within the bounds of your modesty, as no one is under any obligation to do that which is impossible."

Hearing this, Altisidora became angry and excited. "By the living God, Don Codfish!" she cried. "Soul of a brass mortar, date-stone harder and more obdurate than an ignorant rustic when you ask him to do you a favor and he has made up his mind to the contrary! Just let me throw myself on you and I'll scratch your eyes out! Do you perhaps think, Don Vanquished, Don Cudgeled, that it was for you I died? All that you saw last night was pretense. I am not the woman to let the black of my nail suffer for such a camel as you, not to speak of dying for you!"

"That I can well believe," said Sancho, "for this business of people dying from love is something to laugh at. They may talk about it, but when it comes to doing it—tell that to Judas!" [4]

While they were conversing, the musician, singer, and poet who had rendered the verses given above came in. "Sir Knight," he said with a profound obeisance to Don Quixote, "will your Grace be so good as to count me among your most faithful servants? For I have long been a great admirer of yours and of your famous exploits."

"Will your Grace kindly tell me who you are," said the knight, "that I may show you the courtesy that is your due?"

The youth thereupon informed him that he was the panegyrist of the night before.

"I must say," replied Don Quixote, "that your Grace has an excellent voice, although what you sang did not appear to me to be very much to the purpose; for what have Garcilaso's stanzas to do with this lady's death?" [5]

"Your Grace need not wonder at that," said the musician. "Among the unshorn poets [6] of our day it is customary for each one to write as he pleases and steal from anyone he chooses, whether his borrowings be to the point or not,[7] and there is no absurdity that may not be attributed to poetic license."

Don Quixote was about to make a reply but was interrupted by the entrance of the duke and duchess, who had come to pay him a visit. They had a long and agreeable conversation, in the course of which Sancho made so many droll remarks, and mischievous ones as well, as to leave the lord and lady of the house wondering alike at his sharp-wittedness and his simplicity. Don Quixote begged them to grant him permission to depart that same day, as it was more becoming for van-quished knights like him to dwell in pigsties than in royal palaces. His hosts very amiably acceded to this request, and the duchess then inquired if Altisidora was in his good graces.

"My lady," he replied, "I can assure you that this damsel's affliction is solely due to idleness, the remedy for which is constant and honorable employment. She has just informed me that they wear lace in Hell, and inasmuch as she is skilled at making it, she should keep her hands occu-pied; for when she is busy moving the bobbins back and forth, images of that which she desires will not go flitting across her mind. It is the truth I speak, or such is my opinion and my advice." [8]

"And mine too," put in Sancho, "for in all my life I never knew a lace-maker that died for love. Young ladies who are busy have their minds on their work and not on their lovers. I speak from experience, for when I'm busy with the spade I never think of my old woman—I mean my Teresa Panza—although I love her better than I do my own eyelashes."

"You are quite right, Sancho," said the duchess, "and I will see that my

Altisidora is kept occupied from now on at some kind of needlework, for she is exceedingly clever at it."

"There is no need, my lady," said Altisidora, "of your resorting to that remedy, for the thought of the cruel way in which this scoundrelly vagabond has treated me will efface him from my memory without having recourse to any other means. With your Highnesses' permission, I should like to leave this room in order that my eyes may not have to behold his mournful countenance, his ugly and abominable features."

"That," observed the duke, "reminds me of the saying:

> For he who doth rave, and insults shout,
> Is very near forgiving." [9]

Dabbing at her eyes with a handkerchief as if to wipe the tears away, Altisidora then rose and, with a curtsy to her master and mistress, went out the door.

"Bad luck go with you, poor damsel," said Sancho, "bad luck, I say; for you've fallen in with a soul of matweed and a heart of oak. Now, if it had been me, faith, and another cock would have crowed for you."

This brought an end to the conversation, and Don Quixote proceeded to dress himself, had dinner with his hosts, and took his leave that afternoon.

CHAPTER LXXI. *Of what befell* [1] *Don Quixote and his squire Sancho on the way to their village.*

As THE vanquished and deeply afflicted Don Quixote went his way, he was, on the one hand, overly sad, and, on the other, very happy. His sadness was due to his defeat, while his happiness lay in thinking of the virtue his squire had shown he possessed by resurrecting Altisidora, although it must be admitted he had some difficulty in persuading himself that the lovelorn maiden had really been dead. As for Sancho, he found no cause for rejoicing but was downcast because the damsel had failed to keep her word and give him the chemises.

As he kept going over this in his mind, he turned to his master and said, "Really, sir, I am the most unlucky doctor in all the world. There's many a one that kills the patient he treats, yet insists on being paid even though all he does is write out a prescription for certain medicines which the apothecary—not he—makes up, and in this way he wheedles the sick man out of it.[2] With me, the health of another costs me drops of blood, slaps, pinches, pinpricks, and lashes, and I don't get a penny for it. But I swear, if they bring me any more, they'll have to grease my palm before I cure them; for it is by singing that the abbot gets his dinner,[3] and I can't believe that Heaven has bestowed this power on me in order that I should pass it on to others for nothing."

"You are right, friend Sancho," replied Don Quixote. "It was very wrong of Altisidora not to have given you the chemises she promised you. It is true, the virtue that is in you is *gratis data*, having cost you no effort other than that involved in receiving the torments inflicted on your person; but, nevertheless, I can tell you that, so far as I am concerned, if you want pay for those lashes with which Dulcinea is to be disenchanted, I would gladly compensate you. The only thing is: I am not certain that the cure would be effective if it were paid for, and I would not have the reward interfere with the medicine. But, for all of that, I do not see that there would be any harm in trying; so, think it over, Sancho, and decide upon your price; then administer the flogging and pay yourself off with your own hand, since you are the one who holds my money."

Sancho opened his eyes wide at this offer and pricked up his ears until they stood out a palm's breadth from his head. In his heart he was now quite willing to take a whipping.

"Very well, then, master," he said, "I will hold myself at your Grace's disposition; for I shall be only too glad to gratify your desires so long as I profit by it. If I appear grasping, you must blame it on the love I have for my wife and young ones. Tell me, your Grace, how much is each lash worth to you?"

"Sancho," said Don Quixote, "if I had to pay you in accordance with the great value of the remedy, all the treasure of Venice and the mines of Potosí would not suffice.[4] So, see what you have of mine and put a price on each stroke."

"The strokes," said Sancho, "amount to three thousand three hundred-odd, of which I have already given myself five—that leaves the rest to come. But let the five go for the odd ones; three thousand three hundred at a cuartillo [5] each—and I wouldn't take less if all the world insisted on it—that makes three thousand three hundred cuartillos, or fifteen hundred half-reales, and the three hundred strokes amount to seventy-five reales, which added to the seven hundred and fifty come to eight hundred and twenty-five reales altogether.[6] Deducting these from your Grace's money which I am holding, I'll return home rich and well satisfied even though well flogged; for you don't catch trout [7]—I need say no more."

"O blessed Sancho!" cried Don Quixote, "O kind Sancho! Dulcinea and I will be under obligations to serve you all the days of our life that Heaven may allot us! If she resumes her lost shape—and it is not possible that she should fail to do so—her misfortune will have been her good luck and my downfall a most happy triumph. But tell me, Sancho; when do you propose to begin your discipline? For if you speed it, I will give you an additional hundred reales."

"When?" said Sancho. "Tonight without fail. Let your Grace see to it that we spend the night in the fields, under the open sky, and I will lay my flesh open at the same time."

The night so anxiously awaited by Don Quixote was long in coming; indeed, it seemed to him that the wheels of Apollo's chariot must have broken down and the day was being unduly prolonged, as is always the case with lovers who can never adjust their desires to the course of time.[8] At last they entered a pleasant grove a short distance off the highway, and here, leaving Rocinante's saddle and the ass's packsaddle unused, they stretched themselves out on the green grass and had their supper from Sancho's supply of provisions. Then, having made a powerful and flexible whip out of the donkey's halter, the squire retired for a distance of some twenty paces among a clump of beech trees.

Seeing him set about it so energetically and courageously, his master called after him, "Take care, my friend, that you do not cut yourself to pieces; let there be a space between the lashes, and do not be in such haste that your breath will give out by the time you are half done; by which I mean to say, do not lay on so stoutly that life will fail you before you have attained the desired number. And in order that you may not lose by a card too many or too few,[9] I will stand to one side and keep count on my rosary. May Heaven favor you as your good intentions deserve."

"He who is well able to pay doesn't worry about pledges," [10] was Sancho's answer. "I intend to lay them on in such a way that I will feel them and yet not kill myself; for that, I take it, is where the miracle comes in."

Saying this, he stripped to the waist, snatched up the whip, and began, with Don Quixote counting the strokes. He had given himself six or eight lashes when he began to think that the jest was a somewhat heavy one and the price very cheap. Pausing for a moment, he informed his master that he had made a mistake in his estimate and that each stroke ought to be paid for at the rate of half a real and not a cuartillo.

"Continue, friend Sancho," said Don Quixote, "and don't lose courage, for I am doubling your pay."

"In that case," said the squire, "God be with me and let the lashes rain down."

Rascal that he was, however, he stopped laying them on his shoulders and let them fall on the trees instead, uttering such moans every now and then that it seemed as if each one was tearing his heart out. Don Quixote became alarmed at this, fearing that Sancho by his imprudence would do away with himself before the purpose of the thing had been achieved.

"Upon your life, my friend," he called to him, "let the matter rest there, for this impresses me as being a very harsh remedy and we shall have to be patient: Zamora was not won in an hour.[11] Unless I missed my count, you have already given yourself more than a thousand lashes, and that will do for the present; for, to employ a homespun phrase, the ass will bear the load but not the overload." [12]

"No, no, master," Sancho protested, "I will not have it said of me, 'The money paid, the arm broken.' [13] Stand back a little farther, your Grace, and let me give myself a thousand or so more. A couple of flourishes [14] like this and we'll have done with it, and there'll be cloth to spare."

"Well, then," said Don Quixote, "seeing that you are so well disposed, may Heaven help you. Lay on, for I am going away."

Sancho then returned to his task so intrepidly that before long he had stripped the bark off any number of trees, such was the severity with which he whipped himself. As he dealt a tremendous stroke to one of the beeches he raised his voice and cried, "Here shalt thou die, Samson, and all those that are with you!" [15]

At the sound of this agonized wail and the thud of the cruel lash, Don Quixote came running up and snatched from Sancho's hand the twisted halter that served as a whip. "Fate, my dear Sancho," he said, "will not have you lose your life to please me, for you need it to support your wife and children. Let Dulcinea wait for a better occasion. As for me, content with a hope that is soon to be realized, I will bide my time until you have recovered your strength so that this business may be finished to the satisfaction of all concerned."

"Since your Grace will have it so," said Sancho, "so be it. Throw your cloak [16] over my shoulders if you will, for I am all a-sweat and don't want to catch cold—that is a risk that novices run, you know, when they discipline themselves."

Don Quixote did as requested; stripping to his undergarments, he covered Sancho, who slept until the sun awakened him. They then resumed their journey, which for the time being ended in a village three leagues from there. Dismounting at a hostelry, the knight recognized it for what it was and did not take it to be a castle with a deep moat, turrets, portcullis, and a drawbridge; for ever since he had been overcome in combat he had talked more rationally on all subjects, as will presently be seen.

They were given lodging in a lower room, the walls of which were covered with some old bits of painted serge of the kind found in villages in place of leather hangings. [17] On one of these was depicted, by a very crude hand, the abduction of Helen, when the bold guest bore her off from Menelaus, and on the other was represented the story of Dido and Aeneas, with the queen standing on a high tower and signaling with half a sheet to the fugitive, who was now at sea on a frigate or brigantine. Helen did not appear very reluctant about going, for she was laughing slyly and roguishly, but the beauteous Dido was shedding tears the size of walnuts.

"These two ladies," observed Don Quixote as he surveyed the paintings, "were most fortunate not to have been born in this age, and I, above all men, am unlucky not to have lived in their time. Had I encountered those gentlemen, Troy would not have been burned nor Carthage destroyed, for all I should have had to do would have been to slay Paris, and all the ensuing misfortunes would have been avoided."

"I will wager you," said Sancho, "that before long there will not be an alehouse, inn, tavern, or barbershop where the history of our exploits will not be painted on the walls, [18] but I'd like it done by a better hand than the one that did these."

"Right you are, Sancho," said Don Quixote, "for this painter is like Orbaneja who lived in Ubeda and who, when asked what he was painting, used to reply, 'Whatever it turns out to be'; and if it happened to be a cock, he would write beneath it, 'This is a rooster,' so that it would not be taken for a fox. [19] And it is my opinion, Sancho, that the painter or writer (it is all the same) who brought to light the history of this new Don Quixote that was recently published must be one of this sort: that is to say, he painted or wrote *whatever came out.* Or one might compare him to a poet by the name of Mauleón who was at court some years ago and who was in the habit of answering offhand any and all questions put to him. When someone asked him what *Deum de Deo* meant, he replied, '*Dé donde diere.*' [20]

"But, leaving all this aside, tell me, Sancho, whether or not you mean to have another turn at flogging yourself tonight and whether you prefer that it be indoors or out."

"Upon my word, master," said Sancho, "considering what I mean to do to myself, it makes no difference to me whether it's in a house or in the fields; but, for all of that, I'd prefer that it be among trees, for they seem to keep me company and are a wonderful help in bearing the pain."

"But after all, friend Sancho," said Don Quixote, "you have to recover your strength, and so I think we had best wait until we get back to our village, which will be day after tomorrow at the latest."

Sancho replied that his master should do as he saw fit, but that he himself preferred to get the business over with while his blood was warm and while he had an appetite for it,[21] for there was often danger in delay, pray to God and wield the hammer,[22] one "take" was better than two "I'll give you's," [23] and a bird in the hand was better than a vulture on the wing.[24]

"No more proverbs, Sancho, for God's sake," said Don Quixote. "It would seem that you are back to the *sicut erat* [25] again. Speak plainly, simply, and in a straightforward manner, as I have so often told you, and you will see how much better it will be." [26]

"I don't know what bad luck it is of mine," said Sancho, "but I can't talk without proverbs, and for me they all make sense; [27] but I'll mend my ways if I can."

And with this their conversation ended.

CHAPTER LXXII. *Wherein is related how Don Quixote and Sancho reached their village.*

DON QUIXOTE and Sancho spent the entire day at the village inn, waiting for night to come in order that the one might go out into the fields and finish the task of disciplining himself, while the other witnessed this action, which for him meant the fulfillment of his desires.

Meanwhile, there came riding up to the hostelry a gentleman with three or four servants.

"Here, Señor Don Alvaro Tarfe," said one of the attendants, addressing the person who appeared to be their master, "your Grace may take your siesta, for the lodgings appear to be clean and cool."

"Listen, Sancho," said Don Quixote when he heard this, "it seems to me that when I was leafing through that book containing the second part of my history I came upon the name Don Alvaro Tarfe."

"That may well be," replied Sancho, "but let him dismount and we can ask him about it afterward."

The landlady gave the gentleman a room on the ground floor opposite Don Quixote's and similarly adorned with painted serge. The new arrival then put on a summer coat and, coming out into the portico of the inn, which was wide and airy, he encountered the knight, who was pacing up and down there.[1]

"In which direction is your Grace traveling, gentle sir?" the newcomer inquired.

"I am bound for a near-by village of which I am a native," was the answer. "And your Grace?"

"I, sir," said the gentleman, "am on my way to Granada, which is my own country."

"And a good country it is," said Don Quixote. "But will your Grace please be so good as to inform me of your name, since it is more important than I can tell you that I should know it."

"My name," replied the other guest, "is Don Alvaro Tarfe."

"Well, then," said Don Quixote, "I think your Grace must undoubtedly be the Don Alvaro Tarfe who is spoken of in the *Second Part of the History of Don Quixote de la Mancha* that was recently printed and published by a new author."

"I am the same one," the gentleman assured him, "and the Don Quixote you mention, who is the chief subject of that history, was a very great friend of mine. It was I who took him away from his native heath, or, at least, I induced him to come and attend a tournament that was being held in Saragossa, whither I was bound. The truth of the matter is, I did him many favors and kept him from a flogging at the hands of the executioner as a result of his rash conduct." [2]

"Tell me, Señor Don Alvaro, do I in any way resemble the Don Quixote of whom you are speaking?"

"No, certainly not; in no way whatever."

"And this Don Quixote of yours—did he have with him a squire by the name of Sancho Panza?"

"Yes, he did; and although the fellow had the reputation of being very droll, I never once heard him say anything amusing."

"That I can believe," said Sancho at this point, "for it is not given to everyone to say droll things. The fellow your Grace is talking about, gentle sir, must have been some very great scoundrel, blockhead, and thief all in one; for I am the real Sancho Panza, and my drolleries come faster than rain. If your Grace would put it to the test, you have but to follow me around for at least a year and you will see how they drop from me at every turn—so many of them and of such a sort that, without realizing most of the time what it is I am saying, I bring a laugh to all who hear me. And the real Don Quixote, the famous, the valiant, the wise, the lovelorn, the undoer of wrongs, the guardian of minors and orphans, the protector of widows, the slayer of damsels,[3] he who has for his one and only lady the peerless Dulcinea del Toboso, is this gentleman here present, my master. All other Don Quixotes and all other Sancho Panzas are a mockery and a dream."

"By Heaven if I don't believe you," said Don Alvaro, "for in the course of these few words you have uttered, my friend, you have said more amusing things than are to be found in all the talk I heard from the other Sancho, and I heard a great deal of it. He was more of a glutton than a talker and more stupid than droll. I have no doubt that those enchanters that persecute the good Don Quixote have wished to persecute me through my association with the bad one. But what am I saying? I will venture to take an oath that I left him locked up in a madhouse in Toledo [4] so that they might treat him, and now another Don Quixote appears upon the scene, though quite different from mine."

"I do not know," said our Don Quixote, "whether I am good or not, but I can assure you that I am not 'the bad one'; in proof of which, Señor Don Alvaro Tarfe, I would have your Grace know that I have never been in Saragossa in all the days of my life. When I heard that the imaginary Don Quixote had taken part in the tournament in that city, I resolved not to go there so that I might show all the world it was a lie. I accordingly went straight on to Barcelona, that storehouse of courtesy, haven of wayfarers, fatherland of the brave, avenger of the wronged, home of loyal friendships freely bestowed, and, moreover, in point of beauty and situation, a city without a peer. And while the things that happened to me there were none too pleasant and, indeed, caused me much sorrow, I still have no regrets but am glad that I have seen that town.

"In short, Señor Don Alvaro Tarfe, I am Don Quixote de la Mancha, the one who is known to fame and not the wretch who has sought to usurp my name and do himself honor by thinking my thoughts. And so, I implore your Grace—for I know you must be a gentleman—to make a declaration before the local magistrate [5] to the effect that you have never in all your life laid eyes on me up to now, that I am not the Don Quixote referred to in the Second Part, and that Sancho Panza my squire is not the one that your Grace knew."

"That I will gladly do," said Don Alvaro, "although I must say I am amazed to find that there are two Don Quixotes and two Sanchos so alike in names and so unlike in the way they deport themselves. I will state and affirm, then, that I have not seen what I did see and that what happened to me could not have occurred."

"Your Grace," said Sancho, "is undoubtedly enchanted like my lady Dulcinea del Toboso, and I would to Heaven that your disenchantment depended upon my giving myself another three thousand-odd lashes as I am doing for her sake. I would lay them on without looking for any reward whatever."

"I do not undertsand this matter of lashes," said Don Alvaro; to which Sancho replied that it was a long story but he would be glad to explain if the gentleman by any chance was going their way.

When the dinner hour came Don Quixote and Don Alvaro sat down at table together, and, as chance would have it, the village magistrate accompanied by a notary entered the inn, whereupon the knight laid a petition before him, setting forth that it was necessary for the protection of his, Don Quixote's, rights that the other gentleman there present should make an affidavit. This was to be to the effect that the gentleman in question was not personally acquainted with Don Quixote de la Mancha, also present, and it was to be further stated that this latter person was not the individual referred to in a history entitled *Second Part of Don Quixote de la Mancha*,[6] composed by a certain Avellaneda, native of Tordesillas.

The short of the matter is, the magistrate drew up the document and the affidavit was made with all the legal formalities customary in such cases. Don Quixote and Sancho were very happy over this, just as if it were a matter of great importance to them, and as if their own words and deeds did not reveal clearly enough the difference between the true knight and his squire and the pair of pretenders. There followed then an elaborate exchange of courtesies between Don Alvaro and Don Quixote, with the great Manchegan displaying such good sense and moderation as completely to disabuse the other gentleman of the mistake under which he had been laboring, causing him to feel that he must have been enchanted, now that he had come into contact with a person who was the direct opposite of the one of the same name he had previously known.[7]

As evening came on they all set out from the village, and at a distance of something like half a league their paths separated, Don Quixote taking the road that led to his home and Don Alvaro the other one. In this brief space of time the knight related to his companion how he had been overcome in combat and told him of Dulcinea's enchantment and how it was to be remedied. Don Alvaro was more astonished than ever at all this, and, embracing the two of them, he went his way. Don Quixote and Sancho likewise continued their journey, spending the night in a grove in order to give the squire an opportunity of fulfilling his penance, with the strokes for the most part falling on the bark of the beech trees instead of on his shoulders; for he took care to see to it that the lashes he gave himself were such as would not have disturbed a fly had there been one on him.

Don Quixote, however, was under the same illusion as before and did not miss counting a single stroke, finding that with those of the previous night the total now amounted to three thousand twenty-nine. It seemed as if the sun that morning rose earlier than usual to witness the sacrifice, and with the coming of day they took to the road again, talking all the while of the mistake Don Alvaro had made and congratulating themselves on having secured his affidavit in the presence of a magistrate and in so binding a form.

They traveled all that day and night with nothing occurring worthy of note save for the fact that Sancho completed his task, which made Don Quixote so exceedingly happy that he could scarcely wait for daylight to see if he would meet with his by now disenchanted lady along the highway; and each time that he encountered a woman he would go up to her in the hope of recognizing Dulcinea del Toboso, for he believed that Merlin could not lie and that his promises were infallible. Occupied with such thoughts and anxieties as these, they mounted a slope from the top of which they had a view of their village, at the sight of which Sancho fell on his knees.

"Open your eyes, O beloved homeland," he cried, "and behold your son, Sancho Panza, returning to you. If he does not come back very rich, he comes well flogged. Open your arms and receive also your other son, Don Quixote, who returns vanquished by the arm of another but a victor over himself; and this, so I have been told, is the greatest victory that could be desired. I bring money with me, too; for while they gave me many good lashes, I went mounted like a fine gentleman." [8]

"Leave off that nonsense," said Don Quixote, "and let us go straight on to our village, where we may give our fancies free rein as we plan the pastoral life that we intend to lead."

With this, they descended the other side of the slope and came to the town.

CHAPTER LXXIII. *Of the omens that Don Quixote encountered upon entering his village, with other incidents that embellish and lend credence to this great history.*

As THEY entered the village, Cid Hamete informs us, Don Quixote caught sight of two lads on the communal threshing floor who were engaged in a dispute.

"Don't let it worry you, Periquillo," one of them was saying to the other; "you'll never lay eyes on it again as long as you live."

Hearing this, Don Quixote turned to Sancho. "Did you mark what that boy said, my friend?" he asked. " 'You'll never lay eyes on it [1] again . . .' "

"Well," replied Sancho, "what difference does it make what he said?"

"What difference?" said Don Quixote. "Don't you see that, applied to the one I love, it means I shall never again see Dulcinea."

Sancho was about to answer him when his attention was distracted by a hare that came flying across the fields pursued by a large number of hunters with their greyhounds. The frightened animal took refuge by huddling down beneath the donkey, whereupon Sancho reached out his hand and caught it and presented it to his master.

"*Malum signum, malum signum,*" [2] the knight was muttering to himself. "A hare flees, the hounds pursue it, Dulcinea appears not."

"It is very strange to hear your Grace talk like that," said Sancho. "Let us suppose that this hare *is* Dulcinea del Toboso and the hounds pursuing it are those wicked enchanters that transformed her into a peasant lass; she flees, I catch her and turn her over to your Grace, you hold her in your arms and caress her. Is that a bad sign? What ill omen can you find in it?" [3]

The two lads who had been quarreling now came up to have a look at the hare, and Sancho asked them what their dispute was about. To this the one who had uttered the words "You'll never lay eyes on it again as long as you live," replied that he had taken a cricket cage from the other boy and had no intention of returning it ever. Sancho then brought out from his pocket four cuartos [4] and gave them to the lad in exchange for the cage, which he placed in Don Quixote's hands.

"There, master," he said, "these omens are broken and destroyed, and to my way of thinking, even though I may be a dunce, they have no more to do with what is going to happen to us than the clouds of yesteryear. If I am not mistaken, I have heard our curate say that sensible persons of the Christian faith should pay no heed to such foolish things, and you yourself in the past have given me to understand that all those Christians who are guided by omens are fools.[5] But there is no need to waste a lot of words on the subject; come, let us go on and enter our village."

The hunters at this point came up and asked for the hare, and Don Quixote gave it to them. Continuing on their way, the returning pair encountered the curate and the bachelor Carrasco, who were strolling in a small meadow on the outskirts of the town as they read their breviaries. And here it should be mentioned that Sancho Panza, by way of sumpter cloth,[6] had thrown over his gray and the bundle of armor it bore the flame-covered buckram robe in which they had dressed the squire at the duke's castle, on the night that witnessed Altisidora's resurrection; and he had also fitted the miter over the donkey's head, the result being the weirdest transformation and the most bizarrely appareled ass that ever were seen in this world. The curate and the bachelor recognized the pair at once and came forward to receive them with open arms. Don Quixote dismounted and gave them both a warm embrace; meanwhile, the small boys (boys are like lynxes in that nothing escapes them [7]), having spied the ass's miter, ran up for a closer view.

"Come, lads," they cried, "and see Sancho Panza's ass trigged out finer than Mingo,[8] and Don Quixote's beast is skinnier than ever!"

Finally, surrounded by the urchins and accompanied by the curate and the bachelor, they entered the village and made their way to Don Quixote's house, where they found the housekeeper and the niece standing in the doorway, for the news of their return had preceded them. Teresa Panza, Sancho's wife, had also heard of it, and, half naked and disheveled, dragging her daughter Sanchica by the hand, she hastened to greet her husband and was disappointed when she saw him, for he did not look to her as well fitted out as a governor ought to be.

"How does it come, my husband," she said, "that you return like this, tramping and footsore? You look more like a vagabond than you do like a governor." [9]

"Be quiet, Teresa," Sancho admonished her, "for very often there are stakes where there is no bacon.[10] Come on home with me and you will hear marvels. I am bringing money with me, which is the thing that matters, money earned by my own efforts and without harm to anyone."

"You just bring along the money, my good husband," said Teresa, "and whether you got it here or there, or by whatever means, you will not be introducing any new custom into the world."

Sanchica then embraced her father and asked him if he had brought her anything, for she had been looking forward to his coming as to the showers in May. And so, with his wife holding him by the hand while his daughter kept one arm about his waist and at the same time led the gray, Sancho went home, leaving Don Quixote under his own roof in the company of niece and housekeeper, the curate and the barber.

Without regard to time or season, the knight at once drew his guests to one side and in a few words informed them of how he had been overcome in battle and had given his promise not to leave his village for a year, a promise that he meant to observe most scrupulously, without violating it in the slightest degree, as every knight-errant was obliged to do by the laws of chivalry. He accordingly meant to spend that year as a shepherd, he said, amid the solitude of the fields, where he might give free rein to his amorous fancies as he practiced the virtues of the pastoral life; and he further begged them, if they were not too greatly occupied and more urgent matters did not prevent their doing so, to consent to be his companions. He would purchase a flock sufficiently large to justify their calling themselves shepherds; and, moreover, he would have them know, the most important thing of all had been taken care of, for he had hit upon names that would suit them marvelously well. When the curate asked him what these names were, Don Quixote replied that he himself would be known as "the shepherd Quixotiz," the bachelor as "the shepherd Carrascón," the curate as "the shepherd Curiambro," [11] and Sancho Panza as "the shepherd Pancino."

Both his listeners were dismayed at the new form which his madness had assumed. However, in order that he might not go faring forth from the village on another of his expeditions (for they hoped that in the course of the year he would be cured), they decided to fall in with his new plan and approve it as being a wise one, and they even agreed to be his companions in the calling he proposed to adopt.

"What's more," remarked Sansón Carrasco, "I am a very famous poet, as everyone knows, and at every turn I will be composing pastoral or courtly verses or whatever may come to mind, by way of a diversion for us as we wander in those lonely places; but what is most necessary of all, my dear sirs, is that each one of us should choose the name of the shepherd lass to whom he means to dedicate his songs, so that we may not leave a tree, however hard its bark may be, where their names are not inscribed and engraved as is the custom with lovelorn shepherds."

"That is exactly what we should do," replied Don Quixote, "although, for my part, I am relieved of the necessity of looking for an imaginary shepherdess, seeing that I have the peerless Dulcinea del Toboso, glory of these brookside regions, adornment of these meadows, beauty's mainstay, cream of the Graces—in short, one to whom all praise is well becoming however hyperbolical it may be."

"That is right," said the curate, "but we will seek out some shepherd maids that are easily handled,[12] who if they do not square with us will fit in the corners." [13]

"And," added Sansón Carrasco, "if we run out of names we will give them those that we find printed in books the world over: such as Fílida, Amarilis, Diana, Flérida, Galatea, and Belisarda; [14] for since these are for sale in the market place, we can buy them and make them our own. If my lady, or, rather, my shepherdess, should by chance be called Ana, I will celebrate her charms under the name of Anarda; if she is Francisca, she will become Francenia; if Lucía, Luscinda; for it all amounts to the same thing. And Sancho Panza, if he enters this confraternity, may compose verses to his wife, Teresa Panza, under the name of Teresaina."

Don Quixote had to laugh at this, and the curate then went on to heap extravagant praise upon him for his noble resolution which did him so much credit, and once again he offered to keep the knight company whenever he could spare the time from the duties of his office. With this, they took their leave of him, advising and beseeching him to take care of his health and to eat plentifully of the proper food.

As fate would have it, the niece and the housekeeper had overheard the conversation of the three men, and as soon as the visitors had left they both descended upon Don Quixote.

"What is the meaning of this, my uncle? Here we were thinking your Grace had come home to lead a quiet and respectable life, and do you mean to tell us you are going to get yourself involved in fresh complications—

> Young shepherd, thou who comest here,
> Young shepherd, thou who goest there . . .[15]

For, to tell the truth, the barley is too hard now to make shepherds' pipes of it." [16]

"And how," said the housekeeper, "is your Grace going to stand the midday heat in summer, the winter cold, the howling of the wolves out there in the fields? You certainly cannot endure it. That is an occupation for robust men, cut out and bred for such a calling almost from their swaddling clothes. Setting one evil over against another, it is better to be a knight-errant than a shepherd. Look, sir, take my advice, for I am not stuffed with bread and wine when I give it to you but am fasting and am going on fifty years of age: stay at home, attend to your affairs, go often to confession, be charitable to the poor, and let it be upon my soul if any harm comes to you as a result of it."

"Be quiet, daughters," said Don Quixote. "I know very well what I must do. Take me up to bed, for I do not feel very well; and you may be sure of one thing: whether I am a knight-errant now or a shepherd to be, I never will fail to look after your needs as you will see when the time comes."

And good daughters that they unquestionably were, the housekeeper and the niece helped him up to bed, where they gave him something to eat and made him as comfortable as they could.

CHAPTER LXXIV . *Of how Don Quixote fell sick, of the will that he made, and of the manner of his death.*

INASMUCH as nothing that is human is eternal but is ever declining from its beginning to its close, this being especially true of the lives of men, and since Don Quixote was not endowed by Heaven with the privilege of staying the downward course of things, his own end came when he was least expecting it. Whether it was owing to melancholy occasioned by the defeat he had suffered, or was, simply, the will of Heaven which had so ordained it, he was taken with a fever that kept him in bed for a week, during which time his friends, the curate, the bachelor, and the barber, visited him frequently, while Sancho Panza, his faithful squire, never left his bedside.

Believing that the knight's condition was due to sorrow over his downfall and disappointment at not having been able to accomplish the disenchantment and liberation of Dulcinea, Sancho and the others endeavored to cheer him up in every possible way. The bachelor urged him to take heart and get up from bed that he might begin his pastoral life, adding that he himself had already composed an eclogue that would cast in the shade all that Sannazaro [1] had ever written, and had purchased with his own money from a herdsman of Quintanar two fine dogs to guard the flock, one of them named Barcino and the other Butrón. All this, however, did not serve to relieve Don Quixote's sadness; whereupon his friends called in the doctor, who took his pulse and was not very well satisfied with it. In any case, the physician told them, they should attend to the health of his soul as that of his body was in grave danger.

Don Quixote received this news calmly enough, but not so his housekeeper, niece, and squire, who began weeping bitterly, as if he were already lying dead in front of them. It was the doctor's opinion that melancholy and depression were putting an end to his patient's life. The knight then requested them to leave him alone as he wished to sleep a little, and they complied. He slept for more than six hours at a stretch, as the saying is, and so soundly that the housekeeper and niece thought he would never wake.

At last he did, however, and at once cried out in a loud voice, "Blessed be Almighty God who has given me so many blessings! Truly His mercy is boundless and is not limited or restrained by the sins of men."

The niece listened carefully to what her uncle said, and it seemed to her that he was speaking more rationally than was his wont, at least during his illness.

"Sir," she said to him, "what does your Grace mean? Has something occurred that we know nothing about? What is this talk of mercy and sins?"

"The mercy that I speak of," replied Don Quixote, "is that which God is showing me at this moment—in spite of my sins, as I have said. My mind now is clear, unencumbered by those misty shadows of ignorance that were cast over it by my bitter and continual reading of those hateful books of chivalry. I see through all the nonsense and fraud contained in them, and my only regret is that my disillusionment has come so late, leaving me no time to make any sort of amends by reading those that are the light of the soul. I find myself, niece, at the point of death, and I would die in such a way as not to leave the impression of a life so bad that I shall be remembered as a madman; for even though I have been one, I do not wish to confirm it on my deathbed. And so, my dear, call in my good friends: the curate, the bachelor Sansón Carrasco, and Master Nicholas the barber; for I want to confess my sins and make my last will and testament."

The niece, however, was relieved of this errand, for the three of them came in just then.

"I have good news for you,[2] kind sirs," said Don Quixote the moment he saw them. "I am no longer Don Quixote de la Mancha but Alonso Quijano,[3] whose mode of life won for him the name of 'Good.' I am the enemy of Amadis of Gaul and all his innumerable progeny; for those profane stories dealing with knight-errantry are odious to me, and I realize how foolish I was and the danger I courted in reading them; but I am in my right senses now and I abominate them."

Hearing this, they all three were convinced that some new kind of madness must have laid hold of him.

"Why, Señor Don Quixote!" exclaimed Sansón. "What makes you talk like that, just when we have received news that my lady Dulcinea is disenchanted? And just when we are on the verge of becoming shepherds so that we may spend the rest of our lives in singing like a lot of princes, why does your Grace choose to turn hermit? Say no more, in Heaven's name, but be sensible and forget these idle tales."

"Tales of that kind," said Don Quixote, "have been the truth for me in the past, and to my detriment, but with Heaven's aid I trust to turn them to my profit now that I am dying. For I feel, gentlemen, that death is very near; so, leave all jesting aside and bring me a confessor for my sins and a notary to draw up my will. In such straits as these a man cannot trifle with his soul. Accordingly, while the Señor Curate is hearing my confession, let the notary be summoned."

Amazed at his words, they gazed at one another in some perplexity, yet they could not but believe him. One of the signs that led them to think he was dying was this quick return from madness to sanity and all the additional things he had to say, so well reasoned and well put and so becoming in a Christian that none of them could any longer doubt that he was in full possession of his faculties. Sending the others out of the room, the curate stayed behind to confess him, and before long the bachelor returned with the notary and Sancho Panza, who had been informed of his master's condition, and who, finding the housekeeper and the niece in tears, began weeping with them. When the confession was over, the curate came out.

"It is true enough," he said, "that Alonso Quijano the Good is dying, and it is also true that he is a sane man. It would be well for us to go in now while he makes his will."

At this news the housekeeper, niece, and the good squire Sancho Panza were so overcome with emotion that the tears burst forth from their eyes and their bosoms heaved with sobs; for, as has been stated more than once, whether Don Quixote was plain Alonso Quijano the Good or Don Quixote de la Mancha, he was always of a kindly and pleasant disposition and for this reason was beloved not only by the members of his household but by all who knew him.

The notary had entered along with the others, and as soon as the preamble had been attended to and the dying man had commended his soul to his Maker with all those Christian formalities that are called for in such a case, they came to the matter of bequests, with Don Quixote dictating as follows:

"ITEM. With regard to Sancho Panza, whom, in my madness, I appointed to be my squire, and who has in his possession a certain sum of money belonging to me: inasmuch as there has been a standing account between us, of debits and credits, it is my will that he shall not be asked to give any accounting whatsoever of this sum, but if any be left over after he has had payment for what I owe him, the balance, which will amount to very little, shall be his, and much good may it do him. If when

I was mad I was responsible for his being given the governorship of an island, now that I am of sound mind I would present him with a kingdom if it were in my power, for his simplicity of mind and loyal conduct merit no less."

At this point he turned to Sancho. "Forgive me, my friend," he said, "for having caused you to appear as mad as I by leading you to fall into the same error, that of believing that there are still knights-errant in the world."

"Ah, master," cried Sancho through his tears, "don't die, your Grace, but take my advice and go on living for many years to come; for the greatest madness that a man can be guilty of in this life is to die without good reason, without anyone's killing him, slain only by the hands of melancholy. Look you, don't be lazy but get up from this bed and let us go out into the fields clad as shepherds as we agreed to do. Who knows but behind some bush we may come upon the lady Dulcinea, as disenchanted as you could wish. If it is because of worry over your defeat that you are dying, put the blame on me by saying that the reason for your being overthrown was that I had not properly fastened Rocinante's girth. For the matter of that, your Grace knows from reading your books of chivalry that it is a common thing for certain knights to overthrow others, and he who is vanquished today will be the victor tomorrow."

"That is right," said Sansón, "the worthy Sancho speaks the truth."

"Not so fast, gentlemen," said Don Quixote. "In last year's nests there are no birds this year.⁴ I was mad and now I am sane; I was Don Quixote de la Mancha, and now I am, as I have said, Alonso Quijano the Good. May my repentance and the truth I now speak restore to me the place I once held in your esteem. And now, let the notary proceed:

"ITEM. I bequeath my entire estate, without reservation,⁵ to my niece Antonia Quijana,⁶ here present, after the necessary deductions shall have been made from the most available portion of it to satisfy the bequests that I have stipulated. The first payment shall be to my housekeeper for the wages due her, with twenty ducats over to buy her a dress. And I hereby appoint the Señor Curate and the Señor Bachelor Sansón Carrasco to be my executors.

"ITEM. It is my will that if my niece Antonia Quijana should see fit to marry, it shall be to a man who does not know what books of chivalry are; and if it shall be established that he is acquainted with such books and my niece still insists on marrying him, then she shall lose all that I have bequeathed her and my executors shall apply her portion to works of charity as they may see fit.

"ITEM. I entreat the aforementioned gentlemen, my executors, if by good fortune they should come to know the author who is said to have composed a history now going the rounds under the title of *Second Part of the Exploits of Don Quixote de la Mancha*, to beg his forgiveness in my behalf, as earnestly as they can, since it was I who unthinkingly led him to set down so many and such great absurdities as are to be found in it; for I leave this life with a feeling of remorse at having provided him with the occasion for putting them into writing."

The will ended here, and Don Quixote, stretching himself at length in the bed, fainted away. They all were alarmed at this and hastened to aid him. The same thing happened very frequently in the course of the three days of life that remained to him after he had made his will. The household was in a state of excitement, but with it all the niece continued to eat her meals, the housekeeper had her drink, and Sancho Panza was in good spirits; for this business of inheriting property effaces or mitigates the sorrow which the heir ought to feel and causes him to forget.[7]

Death came at last for Don Quixote, after he had received all the sacraments [8] and once more, with many forceful arguments, had expressed his abomination of books of chivalry. The notary who was present remarked that in none of those books had he read of any knight-errant dying in his own bed so peacefully and in so Christian a manner. And thus, amid the tears and lamentations of those present, he gave up the ghost; that is to say, he died. Perceiving that their friend was no more, the curate asked the notary to be a witness to the fact that Alonso Quijano the Good, commonly known as Don Quixote, was truly dead,[9] this being necessary in order that some author other than Cid Hamete Benengeli might not have the opportunity of falsely resurrecting him and writing endless histories of his exploits.

Such was the end of the Ingenious Gentleman of La Mancha,[10] whose birthplace Cid Hamete was unwilling to designate exactly [11] in order that all the towns and villages of La Mancha might contend among themselves for the right to adopt him and claim him as their own, just as the seven cities of Greece did in the case of Homer. The lamentations of Sancho and those of Don Quixote's niece and his housekeeper, as well as the original epitaphs that were composed for his tomb, will not be recorded here, but mention may be made of the verses by Sansón Carrasco:

> *Here lies a gentleman bold*
> *Who was so very brave*
> *He went to lengths untold,*

> *And on the brink of the grave*
> *Death had on him no hold.*
> *By the world he set small store—*
> *He frightened it to the core—*
> *Yet somehow, by Fate's plan,*
> *Though he'd lived a crazy man,*
> *When he died he was sane once more.*[12]

As for that most wise chronicler, Cid Hamete, he has left us the following address to his pen: [13]

"Here shalt thou remain, hung upon this rack by this brass wire. I know not if thou beest well cut or not, O pen of mine, but here thou shalt live for long ages to come, unless some presumptuous and scoundrelly historians should take thee down to profane thee. But ere they do this thou may'st warn them and say to them as best thou canst:

> *Hands off, o'erweening ones!*
> *Let it by none attempted be;*
> *For this emprise, my lord the King,*
> *Hath been reserved for me.*[14]

"For me alone Don Quixote was born and I for him; it was for him to act, for me to write, and we two are one in spite of that Tordesillesque [15] pretender who had, and may have, the audacity to write with a coarse and ill-trimmed ostrich quill of the deeds of my valiant knight. This is no burden for his shoulders, no subject for his congealed talent; and if perchance thou shouldst come to know him, advise him that he should let Don Quixote's tired and moldering bones rest in their sepulcher and not try to bear him off, contrary to all the laws of death, to Old Castile [16] by raising him from that grave where he really and truly lies stretched out, being quite unable now to sally forth once again on a third expedition. For the two sallies that he did make to the delight and approval of all who heard of them, in foreign countries as well as our own, are sufficient to cast ridicule upon all the ridings forth of knights-errant in times past.

"Doing this, thou shalt fulfill thine obligations as a Christian by giving good counsel to one who wished thee ill, and I shall be the first one to enjoy the fruit of his own writings as fully as he desired, since I have had no other purpose than to arouse the abhorrence of mankind toward those false and nonsensical stories to be met with in the books of chivalry, which, thanks to this tale of the genuine Don Quixote, are already tottering and without a doubt are doomed to fall.[17] *Vale*."

NOTES

Part Two

APPROBATIONS

1. Pausanias alludes to a number of statues of Dionysus that he saw in the course of his travels and also refers to various folk festivals in honor of Bacchus. Schevill states that he has not encountered the work by Bosio mentioned here.

2. In referring to Cicero's *De Legibus*, the writer possibly has in mind Book I, Chapter 8: "*Opus est et cura vacare et negotio.*" The Latin verse quoted is from a well-known work, the *Disticha de Moribus, nomine Catonis inscripta, cum Latina & Hispanica interpretatione* (Schevill cites the edition of London, 1543). The complete distich reads:

> *Interpone tuis interdum gaudia curis,*
> *Ut possis animo quemvis sufferre laborem.*

3. On the Cervantes influence abroad, see *Cervantes, A Tentative Bibliography of His Works,* by Ford and Lansing; *The Influence of Cervantes in France in the Seventeenth Century* by Esther J. Crooks (Baltimore: Johns Hopkins University Press, 1931); and *Cervantes in England* by James Fitzmaurice-Kelly (London, 1905). The reader with German at his command may be referred to *Cervantes und seine Werke nach deutschen Urtheilen* by Edmund Dorer (Leipzig, 1881). Benedetto Croce has dealt with Cervantes in Italy in *Saggi sulla letteratura del Seicento* (Bari, 1911 and 1924), pp. 125 ff.

4. For this incident, see *The Life and Misadventures of Miguel de Cervantes* by Mariano Tomás, pp. 239–40.

5. Schevill believes it possible that Cervantes may have met Márquez Torrez in the palace of the cardinal whom the latter served. Under date of March 26, 1616, the author of *Don Quixote* writes to the Cardinal Archbishop of Toledo, signing himself "your humble servant."

PROLOGUE

1. In the original Spanish editions the Prologue to Part II precedes the Dedication; and inasmuch as the same order is observed in the *Novels* (1613) and the *Comedies and Interludes* (1614), it seems likely that this was also the order followed in the manuscript. (Schevill)

2. The allusion here is to the spurious Second Part of the *Don Quixote*, published in the autumn of 1614 and attributed on the title-page to Alonso Fernández de Avellaneda of Tordesillas. This work was licensed and printed at Tarragona. For a lively account of the Avellaneda episode, the reader may be referred to Tomás's *The Life and Misadventures of Miguel de Cervantes,* pp. 226 ff.

3. A proverb.

4. Reference to the battle of Lepanto (1571) in which Cervantes was wounded.

5. One variety of envy is a mortal sin; the other consists in emulating the good example of another.

6. Cervantes is referring to Lope de Vega, who received holy orders in the spring of 1614, the title of "familiar of the Holy Office," or Inquisition, having probably been bestowed upon him in 1608, or after the First Part of the *Don Quixote* had appeared. The author's argument thus would not hold for Part I. Avellaneda had accused him of attacking Lope from motives of envy.

7. Avellaneda had described the *Exemplary Novels* as "*más satíricas que exemplares, si bien no poco ingeniosas.*"

8. The word in Spanish is "*podenco*" —"a small greyhound." Ormsby renders this by the British term "lurcher." Motteux wrongly has "spaniel."

9. Avellaneda: "Let him complain of my work because of the profits of which I deprive him."

10. No *entremés*, or interlude, bearing this title is known to have been printed, though it may have existed in manuscript form. (Schevill)

11. The *Veintecuatros*, the Twenty-four, was the title given to the municipal authorities, twenty-four in number, of Seville, Granada, and Cordova. (In Lisbon, the *Casa dos Vinte e quatro* was the Court of Aldermen.)

12. A verse satire on the reign of Henry IV.

DEDICATION

1. Don Pedro Fernández Ruiz de Castro y Osorio, seventh Count of Lemos, was known as the patron of Cervantes, Lope de Vega, and other celebrated writers of the period. In 1610 he was appointed Viceroy and Captain-General of Naples and did not return to Spain until July 1616, about three months after Cervantes' death. The interested reader may be referred to an article by Otis H. Green, "The Literary Court of the Conde de Lemos at Naples, 1610–1616," in the *Hispanic Review*, October 1933, pp. 290 ff. Despite the fact that he lived until 1619, the Duke of Béjar to whom Part I is dedicated is not mentioned again by Cervantes. Both patrons, as a matter of fact, disappointed the hopes of the poverty-ridden author of *Don Quixote*.

2. It is possible that the author's whimsy is based upon a historical incident reported to have occurred in the year 1612, when the Chinese monarch is said to have sent a letter to the Spanish crown, employing as messenger a returning barefoot friar. (Fernández Guerra, cited by Schevill.)

CHAPTER I

1. According to Clemencín, this popular phrase is derived from the game of chess.

2. An antique coin worth around ten pesetas; as previously pointed out, the dobla is not to be confused with the gold doblón, or doubloon, worth twenty pesetas.

3. This ballad has not been identified.

4. Ormsby: "*Andar estaciones* prop-erly means to visit certain churches, for the purpose of offering up the prayers required to obtain indulgences."

5. The knights mentioned here are prominent in the Spanish romances of chivalry or in the pages of Ariosto and Boiardo. Turpin's *Cosmography* is a fictitious work. (On Turpin, see Part I, Chapter VI and note 8.) It is Ariosto who traces the descent of the Dukes of Ferrara from Ruggiero.

6. I follow the reading of the first edition, "*no quiero quedar en mi casa.*" Some editions have the reading "*me quiero,*" which has been followed by earlier translators. Ormsby: "And so I will stay where I am." Motteux: "I do design to stay where I am." The "*pues*" which introduces the following clause ("*pues no me saca el capellán*") probably should be "*puesto,*" which would make the meaning clear. (That is, "even though" in place of "since.")

7. The original has "*descubrir*"—"discover." I adopt Schevill's emendation, "*describir.*"

8. In I Samuel 17:4, we read: ". . . Goliath of Gath, whose height was six cubits and a span," that is, six and a half, not seven and a half, cubits, or about nine feet, nine inches.

9. An account of the Sicilian bones is given in Antonio de Torquemada's *Jardín de Flores Raras o Curiosas*. They are also mentioned in Haedo's *Topografía de Argel*.

10. Cervantes is referring to the Spanish version of Pulci's *Morgante Maggiore*, published at Valencia in 1533 under the title of *Libro del Esforzado Gigante Morgante*.

11. Reference to Medoro's devotion to his master, Dardinel. As he knelt beside Dardinel's body, he received a wound of which Angelica cured him.

12. The author here misquotes a couplet from Ariosto: *Orlando Furioso*, XXX, 16.

13. The Andalusian poet is Luis Barahona de Soto, the Castilian is Lope de Vega. The former was the author of a work known as *La Primera Parte de la Angélica*, copies of which will be found in the library of the Hispanic Society of New York and in the British Museum. (See Part I, Chapter VI and note 26.) Copies of Lope's *La Hermosura de An-*

gélica are preserved in the National Library at Madrid and in the British Museum. This work formed the first part of the poet's *Rimas*, printed at Madrid in 1602.

14. The text at this point is very confused and a number of emendations have been suggested. I have followed Pellicer's reading: "*fingidas, o* [*no*] *fingidas*." Schevill suggests that in the manuscript there may possibly have been some other verb in place of the second "*fingidas*."

15. As a matter of fact, the famous poet Góngora did write some satiric verses on this theme, and Quevedo touches on the subject in a heroic poem on Orlando's love and madness.

CHAPTER II

1. The word "*ciudad*" (city) is here employed in the sense of municipal government or council (*ayuntamiento* or *cabildo*). Schevill cites the *Dictionary of the Academy*.

2. "*. . . insulas ni insulos.*" For "island" Don Quixote always says "*insula*," which is the form that occurs in the *Amadis;* but this highbrow term is too much for the housekeeper and the niece, who are used to saying "*isla*."

3. The *hidalgos* (originally, "sons of somebody") were gentlemen by birth, the *caballeros* by station in life.

4. "Don" today is a universal form of address where Spanish is spoken, but in Cervantes' time its use was restricted.

5. Literally, "two yokes" (*yugadas*), the yoke being the amount of land a team of oxen could plow in a day.

6. There was a proverb: "*Hidalgo honrado antes roto que remendado*"—"An honored gentleman goes ragged rather than patched."

7. Proverbial expression.

8. Proverbial expression.

9. In Spanish, "*berenjenas*."

CHAPTER III

1. Only one month is supposed to have elapsed since Don Quixote's return from his wanderings, yet the story of his adventures has already been written and printed and, as we are soon to be told, has been distributed to the extent of some twelve thousand copies. Cervantes, however, is never concerned with discrepancies of this sort, and on the present occasion explains the matter away by having resort to the magician's art.

2. Compare what is said on this subject in Part I, Chapter IX.

3. That is to say, the bachelor was dressed in the garb of the secular clergy. "*Por el hábito de San Pedro*" was a proverbial exclamation. In the Catholic Church the four minor orders of the clergy are *Ostiarius, Lector, Exorcista,* and *Acolytus*.

4. There was no edition of the *Don Quixote* at Antwerp until 1673 and none at Barcelona before 1617. Cervantes may have heard of the edition of Brussels of 1607. (Schevill)

5. Here and in the balance of the chapter Cervantes repeats the various criticisms that were made of Part I.

6. That is, "the day is not yet over," or "life is yet young."

7. The play in the original is on "*grama-*" and "*-tica.*"

8. "*Mezclar berzas con capochos*" was a proverbial expression.

9. Compare Chapter LXXI following (note 19).

10. The Motteux version, as usual, substitutes "orthodox" for "Catholic."

11. The expression as it occurs in other Spanish authors is "*De pajo o de heno mi vientre lleno*"—"With straw or hay I fill my belly."

12. "El Tostado" was Alfonso [Tostado Ribera] de Madrigal, Bishop of Avila, who died in 1450. He is said to have left over sixty thousand written pages, but his works have now been completely forgotten.

13. See the *Epistles* of Pliny the Younger, Book III; he attributes the saying to his uncle, Pliny the Elder. This saying is again cited in Chapter LIX following.

14. "Worthy Homer sometimes nods." See Horace, *Ars Poetica*, 359: "*Indignor quandoque bonus dormitat Homerus.*"

15. "The number of fools is infinite." See the Vulgate, Ecclesiasticus 1:15.

16. See Part I, Chapter XXIII and note 2.

17. "*. . . me pondra en la espina de Santa Lucia*"—an expression meaning to feel the pangs of hunger.

18. Literally, "do penance with him" —"*hazer penitencia con él.*"

CHAPTER IV

1. See Ariosto's *Orlando Furioso,* XXVII, 84, and Boiardo's *Orlando Innamorato,* II, 40.

2. Literally, "raise it a good span higher than what it is."

3. The word employed here is "*ripio,*" a mixture of mortar and gravel for filling the spaces between large stones.

4. It was St. George who aided Pedro I of Aragon to defeat the Moors, at the battle of Alcoraz in 1096. The festival was in celebration of this event.

5. These oaths, "Body of me," "Body of the world," etc., are all milder forms of swearing by the Sacrament (body of Christ). Compare the English expression " 'od's body."

6. The historic battle cry: "*¡Santiago, y cierra España!*"

7. A proverb: "*Quando viene el bien, metelo en casa.*"

8. A proverb.

9. That is, "in the ditch."

10. Cervantes is, of course, being satirical here, but it is likely that he did not have any particular poets in mind.

11. The *décima* was, properly, a ten-line stanza; the *redondilla* was a four-line stanza, the last line rhyming with the first. Poetic acrostics were popular in Cervantes' day.

CHAPTER V

1. A proverb.

2. A proverb.

3. That is, it is better to take someone you know, with all his faults.

4. See Matthew 27:17, 21; Mark 15:11; Luke 23:18.

5. Molière has made use of this scene in Act III of *Le Bourgeois Gentilhomme.* See "Notes on the Spanish Sources of Molière," by Sylvanus Griswold Morley, in *Publications of the Modern Language Association of America,* XIX, 1904, pp. 270–89.

6. An inversion of the proverb "Laws go as kings like." See Part I, Chapter XLV and note 2.

7. This would seem to be the sense of the word "*pazpuerca,*" not "slut." (Schevill)

8. In the original the proverb rhymes:

"*La muger honrada, la pierna quebrada y en casa; y la donzella honesta, el hazer algo es su fiesta.*"

9. The Infanta Uracca was the daughter of Ferdinand I of Castile. Upon being left out of her father's will, she threatened to enter upon a life of ill fame.

10. In Spanish, "*almohadas.*"

11. Literally, "I will dress him up as fine as a palm branch"—"*como un palmito.*"

CHAPTER VI

1. It was necessary to see that neither of the combatants had the sun in his eyes.

2. The *sambenito* was the garment worn by those who, having been tried by the Inquisition, had confessed and repented. It was a yellow linen garment painted over with devils and flames and was worn by the condemned as they went to the stake.

3. The word "*caballero*" has a double meaning: knight and gentleman. In this passage it apparently has the sense of gentleman.

4. The *hidalgos.*

5. These verses are from an elegy by the well-known poet Garcilaso de la Vega, written on the death of the Duke of Alva's brother, Don Bernardino de Toledo. (*Elegía primera,* verses 202–204.)

CHAPTER VII

1. A play on the double meaning of "*ventura*"—"good fortune" and a "venture" or "risk."

2. St. Apollonia, according to tradition, prayed to the Virgin for relief from the toothache and her prayer was granted.

3. "*No hay más que bachillear*"—the noun "*bachiller*" means either a bachelor of arts or a babbler or loquacious person.

4. "*Hablen cartas y callen barbas*"— that is, where there is a written agreement, words are unnecessary. Sancho here indulges, as he not infrequently does, in a string of proverbs.

5. "*Quien destaja no baraja*": prior to Ormsby, English translators had rendered this proverb as "He who cuts does not shuffle." This is due to the fact that both verbs have twofold meanings:

"*destajar*" signifying, at once, "to contract to do a job" and "to cut a deck of cards"; while "*barajar*" means "to shuffle the cards" and, in old Spanish, "to wrangle."

6. Compare our saying "A bird in the hand . . ."

7. In the Spanish this is a rhyming couplet: "*El consejo de la muger es poco,/Y el que no le toma es loco.*"

8. Literally, "you speak pearls today" —"*que hablays oy de perlas.*"

9. "*Tan presto se va el cordero como el carnero*"—that is to say, "goes to the butcher's."

10. These are all popular sayings.

11. More proverbs.

12. This is the reverse of the "bird in hand."

13. Ormsby observes that the truth of this saying "has always been recognized by politicians, diplomatists, and agitators."

14. The original text mentions only the niece as entering at this point—obviously an oversight on the part of author or printer.

15. Popular proverb.

CHAPTER VIII

1. The reference is to Garcilaso's Third Eclogue, verses 53 ff.

2. The Spanish text reads: ". . . deve de andar mi honra a coche acá, cinchado, y, como dicen, al estricote, aquí y allí, barriendo las calles." The phrase "*a coche acá, cinchado*" has been extensively discussed by the commentators. "Literally, 'pig, hog there!' A cry still used by the Manchegan swineherds." (Fitzmaurice-Kelly, note in his edition of Ormsby's translation.) Schevill states that "*coche acá*" is the call used by the swineherd to drive away the hog, while "*cinchado*" seems to apply rather to the ass, but that the meaning is, simply, that Sancho's honor was being mishandled and dragged in the mud ("*maltratada, enlodada*").

3. Schevill suggests that the work alluded to here may have been Vicente Espinel's *Satira contra las Damas de Sevilla.*

4. This is the Pantheon, today known not as All Saints' but as the Tempio di Santa Maria della Rotonda.

5. There is a word play in the Spanish: "*cortesissimo Cortés.*"

6. Don Quixote appears to be speaking of the seven deadly sins.

7. "*Julio*" in Spanish means both "July" and "Julius."

8. According to Ormsby, the allusion is to San Diego de Alcalá, canonized in 1588, and San Salvador de Orta, or San Pedro de Alcántara, canonized in 1562.

9. "*Sucedió cosas que a cosas llegan.*"

CHAPTER IX

1. It is with these words that the old ballad of *Conde Claros* begins: "*Media noche era por filo.*" "*Por filo*" is, literally, "on the line."

2. Not "descended from a hill," as in Motteux, where the word "*monte*" is incorrectly rendered. The allusion is to the grove of oak trees mentioned at the end of the preceding chapter.

3. ". . . *a pierna tendida.*"

4. A proverb.

5. A proverb.

6. Beginning of a popular ballad of the Carolingian cycle which John Gibson Lockhart has translated. The quotation is given here in Lockhart's words. For his version, see the Bohn Popular Library edition of the Motteux *Don Quixote*, Vol. II, pp. 239–42.

7. For an English version of this ballad, "The Moor Calainos," see Lockhart, loc. cit., pp. 543–46.

CHAPTER X

1. These are two well-known proverbs. The first one, in Spanish, commonly reads: "*La verdad adelgaza y no quiebra*"—"The truth runs thin [or fine] but does not break." The Italians say: "*La verità può languire ma non perire*"—"Truth may languish but not perish." The second one occurs in two forms: "*La verdad siempre anda sobre la mentira como el aceite sobre el agua*" —"The truth always rises above a lie as oil above water"; and: "*La verdad como el olio siempre anda en somo*"—"Truth like oil always floats on the top." The Portuguese have the same saying: "*A verdade e o aceite andão de cima*"— "Truth and oil rise to the top." (See Ormsby's list of proverbs.)

The sentences contained in this opening paragraph are transferred by Hartzenbusch to the beginning of Chapter XVII following, as he believes they more properly belong there. Ormsby follows

Hartzenbusch in this. "It would be absurd," he says, "to call Don Quixote's simplicity in the matter of Sancho's mystification about the village girls, mad doings [*locuras*] that go beyond the maddest that can be conceived; while the lion adventure described in Chapter xvii is all through treated as his very maddest freak; one compared with which, as Sancho says, all the rest were 'cakes and fancy bread.'" However, it has seemed best to follow the first edition.

2. Three more proverbs. The one about the bacon and the pegs is misquoted by Sancho; it runs: "Many think there is bacon where there are no pegs"—"*Muchos piensan que hay tocinos donde no hay estacas*"—i.e., no pegs (in the smokehouse) on which to hang the bacon. Compare Part I, Chapter xxv (note 5), and Chapters lv (note 17), lxv (note 3), and lxxiii (note 10) following.

3. These lines are from a popular ballad. "*Con cartas y mensajeros*"—"With letters and messengers."

4. The expression "let the bolt fall" is from a rhyming couplet: "*Allá darás Rayo/En casa de Tamayo*"—"Fall there, O thunderbolt, on Tamayo's house"—the implication being, not on mine.

5. A proverb. The meaning, of course, is to look for the impossible.

6. Salamanca was full of bachelors of arts. The sense of this expression and of "trying to find Marica in Rávena" is to "look for a needle in a haystack."

7. "*No con quien naces,/Sino con quien paces.*" Compare our proverbs: "A man is known by the company he keeps" and "Birds of a feather flock together."

8. Ormsby: "i.e., the lists of bachelors qualified for degrees." Motteux: "As they do professor's chairs, that everybody may know who they belong to."

9. Ormsby: "Ordinary brocade had only a triple border." Motteux: "All cloth of gold above ten rows high." Jarvis: "All cloth of tissue above ten hands deep."

10. In Spanish, Sancho says "*cananeas*" for "*hacaneas*." I have adopted Ormsby's rendering.

11. These speeches of Sancho's may seem decidedly out of character, but this is something of which the author is by no means unaware. Cervantes in Part I was never too greatly concerned with the matter, and in Part II there can be no doubt that he definitely intends to portray a certain growth in character on the part of the squire as well as of the knight. In this connection, see Chapter xii following and note 4. It is conceivable that Sancho, who, however simple-minded he may appear at times, is not dull-witted, may have picked up from his master a good deal of the cant of chivalry and some of Don Quixote's flowery language.

12. This is addressed, not to the ass which the girl rides, but to Sancho. (Shelton and Jarvis take it as applied to the ass.) The expression "*Más jo, que te estrego, burra de mi suegro*" (note the rhyme) is a popular one.

13. An obscure oath.

14. The first edition reads "*Mucho sabeys, mucho podeys y mucho más hazeys*"—"Great is your wisdom, great is your power, and greater yet your deeds." But in place of "*mucho más hazeys*," modern editions read "*mucho mal hazeys*"—"great the harm you do," a reading which has been followed here.

15. ". . . *en agallas alcornoqueñas.*" Ormsby: "into oak galls." Motteux: "into gall nuts." Jarvis: "into cork galls."

16. The *jineta* was a saddle with high pommel and cantle and short stirrups. The expression, to ride "*a la jineta*" has previously occurred.

CHAPTER XI

1. ". . . *con voz no muy desmayada.*" Ormsby wrongly has: "in a weak and faint voice." Motteux is better: "with more spirit than one would have expected."

2. In the original, this is a question: "*quien la vido y la vee aora, ¿qual es el coraçon que no llora?*" Another version is: "*quien me vido y me ve aoras,*" etc. —"who saw me once . . ."

3. In other words, it did not resemble the type of cart or wagon that was common in central and southern Spain.

4. A Toledo dramatist and theatrical manager.

5. The interested reader may be referred to an article by Professor Crawford, "The Devil As a Dramatic Figure

in the Spanish Religious Drama before Lope de Vega," in the *Romanic Review*, September–October 1910, pp. 302 ff., 374 ff. See also Florence Whyte, *The Dance of Death in Spain and Catalonia* (Baltimore: Johns Hopkins University Press, 1931), particularly p. 145. It is thought that this passage may have been inspired by one in the *Amadis of Gaul*, II, xii.

6. ". . . *compañias reales y de titulo*." Motteux mistranslates: "especially if they be of the king's players, or some of the nobles."

7. "*Sopa de arroyo*"—slang for pebbles.

CHAPTER XII

1. Compare our proverb: "A bird in the hand is worth two in the bush." This *refrán* has previously occurred in Part I, Chapter xxxi (note 6); compare Chapters xxxi and lxxi (note 24) following.

2. Literally, "in the comedy and intercourse of this world."

3. It may be of interest to compare Omar Khayyám:

> Impotent pieces of the game he plays
> Upon this checker-board of nights and days.
> Hither and thither moves, and checks and slays,
> And one by one back in the closet lays.

4. See Chapter x preceding, note 11. We have here a clear awareness on Cervantes' part of the growth and deepening of Sancho's character. The squire like his master is a larger person than the one we encounter in Part I.

5. The friendship of Nisus and Euryalus is celebrated in Vergil's *Aeneid*. Pylades, friend and companion of Orestes, is mentioned by Pindar, Sophocles, and other Greek writers.

6. These lines are from a popular ballad included by Pérez de Hita in the *Civil Wars of Granada* (*Guerras Civiles de Granada*).

7. "*De amigo a amigo la chinche. . . .*" The phrase "to have a bug in the eye" —"*tener chinche en el ojo*"—means to keep a watchful eye out; here, the sense is that one friend is wary of the other.

8. These are folklore references on Cervantes' part.

9. We have already had this proverbial expression in Chapters iv (note 7) and xxx of Part I.

10. See Matthew 12:34, and Luke 6:45.

11. I follow the emendation of a number of editors who substitute "*atentos*" for "*atónitos*," which occurs in the first edition. It seems obvious from the context that Don Quixote and Sancho were listening attentively rather than "with astonishment."

12. Ormsby has an interesting note: "The pieces of verse introduced in the Second Part are more or less burlesques, and sometimes, as here and in Chapter xviii, imitations of the affected poetry of the day. The verses in the First Part (except, of course, the commendatory verses, and those at the end of the last chapter) are serious efforts, and evidently regarded by Cervantes with some complacency. The difference is significant."

13. The Tartessians were the inhabitants of the old region known as Tartéside. Tartessus was an ancient maritime town under the Romans.

14. Lockhart draws attention to a similar scene in the *Amadis of Gaul*, II, lxvi.

15. Proverbial expression that has occurred before.

CHAPTER XIII

1. In the title to Chapter xii, Cervantes refers to Don Quixote's new acquaintance as the Knight of the Mirrors, but the significance of this appellation does not become clear until Chapter xiv. Meanwhile, the newcomer is referred to as the Knight of the Wood.

2. Genesis 3:19.

3. A proverb.

4. As has been seen, the fanega is equivalent to about 1.6 bushel.

5. Compare Part I, Chapter xx (note 3), and Chapter xxxvi (note 11) following.

6. A proverb.

7. There is an untranslatable play here on the adjective "*crudo*," which means both "raw" and "cruel."

8. Sancho means to say that his troubles never come singly. A proverbial expression.

9. Here again the author is deepening the motivation of Sancho's character.

10. The sense is "paltry" (Ormsby's translation), not "fresh-water squires,"

as in Motteux. The expression "*de agua y lana*" is the opposite of the one applied to nobles and courtiers: "*de gran estofa*" —"of high quality."

11. That is, large, or close together, or both.

12. Ormsby: "Anyone who has ever watched a Spanish peasant with a *bota* [flask] knows how graphic this is."

13. Ciudad Real was the chief city of La Mancha and center of a winegrowing district, the best-known vintage being Valdepeñas, to which Cervantes in his plays and novels applies the epithet "*El Católico*"—which will explain Sancho's exclamation.

14. This is a popular tale which may have been translated by the Spaniards from some other language. There are traces of it in the southeastern United States. (Schevill) See *Modern Language Notes*, June 1905, p. 183. Cervantes has used the same story in a slightly different form in one of his interludes, *The Election of the Judges of Deganzo* (*Elección de los Alcaldes de Deganzo*).

CHAPTER XIV

1. The "woman" is the enormous statue (of Faith according to some, of Victory according to others) on top of the old Moorish belfry of the Cathedral of Seville.

2. Allusion to certain stone animal figures to be found at Guisando, Avila, and elsewhere. They are said to resemble hippopotamuses rather than bulls. The "Bulls" of Guisando are supposed to mark the site of one of Caesar's victories over the younger Pompey.

3. In the Sierra de Cabra, south of Cordova. It is thought that this may be the shaft of an ancient mine.

4. These lines, incorrectly quoted, are from Alonso de Ercilla's famous poem, the *Araucana* (1569–89), celebrating the struggle of the Spaniards with the indomitable Araucanian Indians of Chile (1, 2).

5. A proverb.

6. Reference to the fine imposed in some confraternities, the wax being for use in churches.

7. According to the commentator Covarrubias, this proverbial expression is derived from rabbit-hunting with the crossbow, the sense being, "let each

hunter look out for his own bolts.'"

8. This proverb occurs several times. See Part II, XLIII (note 17) and LXVII (note 17).

9. The Italians have the proverb: "*Gatto rinchiuso doventa leone.*"

10. "*A esso vos respondemos*" is the form employed by a monarch in response to a petition.

11. The knobs or buttons to keep the spurs from going in too far.

12. A proverb.

13. The text of the first edition is somewhat jumbled here. At least one editor would amend to read: ". . . without any doubt the bachelor Sansón Carrasco . . . is rash and ill advised." I have followed Hartzenbusch and Rodríguez Marín, whose reading is adopted by Schevill.

CHAPTER XV

1. This is a play on the proverb "*Uno piensa el bayo, otro quien le ensilla*"— "The bay is of one mind, he who saddles him of another."

2. Proverbial expression.

CHAPTER XVI

1. Compare Chapter x preceding, where Don Quixote says: "The malign enchanter who doth persecute me hath placed clouds and cataracts upon my eyes. . . ." As Schevill points out, Cervantes evidently forgot here what he had previously written, as the two descriptions of Dulcinea do not correspond.

2. The greatcoat is the *gabán*, worn for hunting and traveling, which had a hood to cover the head. The cap is the *montera* of Central Spain, a headpiece with flaps.

3. See Chapter x preceding and note 16.

4. The first edition has "*caballo*"— "horse" which is obviously out of place in this description of Don Quixote's person. I have accordingly followed the majority of editors, who read "*cuello*"— "neck." Ormsby reads "*cabello*"—"hair" —which also seems inappropriate. Motteux: "the lankness of his horse"; Jarvis: "his lank horse."

5. These lines have previously been quoted, Part I, Chapter XLIX.

6. ". . . *treynta mil vezes de millares.*" Motteux has "thirty thousand

millions more"! Compare Chapter III preceding, where it is stated that "more than twelve thousand copies" were in existence.

7. ". . . *mi atenuada flaqueza.*" Motteux: "my exhausted body."

8. For *"perdigón"*—"partridge"—Clemencín reads *"perdiguero"*—"pointer." But partridges were used as decoys in Andalusia.

9. Ormsby: "first saint in the saddle"; Motteux and Jarvis: "first saint on horseback." It seems desirable to indicate the kind of saddle as the Spanish does. A saint, for that matter, would have been more likely to ride a donkey than a horse.

10. ". . . *los modernos romancistas*"—i.e., moderns who write in Spanish. Motteux, who is even more inaccurate than usual in this chapter, has "modern romancers."

11. Reference to the *justas literarias*, which still lingered on in Cervantes' time.

12. The saying was a popular one in the Renaissance era. Schevill cites Caelius Rhodiganus (1450–1525): *"Vulgo certe iactatur nasci poetam, oratorem fieri"*—"It is commonly said that the poet is born, the orator made."

13. Ovid's beautiful line: *"Est deus in nobis: agitante calescimus illo"*—"There is a god in us, he stirs and we grow warm." (*Fasti*, VI, 5; compare the third book of the *De Arte Amandi*.)

14. Ovid was exiled to Pontus. The original reads: *"islas de Ponto"*—"isles of Pontus"; the correction of "coast" or "shores" for "isles" was made by Clemencín and Hartzenbusch.

15. The laurel tree.

CHAPTER XVII

1. With regard to the beginning of this chapter, see Chapter X preceding and note 1.

2. *"Hombre apercebido, medio combatido"*—literally, "A man who is prepared has his battle half fought." The Italian form of the proverb is nearer to the English: *"Chi è avvisato è armato."*

3. It has been remarked that lions coming from Oran would have been landed at Cartagena, and so would not have been met by Don Quixote and his party on the road to Saragossa.

4. On this knight, see Part I, Chapter XLIX, note 2.

5. The *"perrillo,"* or "little dog," was the trademark of Julian del Rei, famous armorer of Toledo and Saragossa.

6. ". . . *que sepan de tu boca esta hazaña.*" Motteux has: "that they may have an account of this exploit from my own mouth," which is not only a mistranslation but does not make sense.

7. *"Antecogidos del hidalgo."* Motteux: "at the head of them"; Jarvis: "at their head."

8. The knights in the romances of chivalry frequently changed their names. Knight of the Lions was one of the titles of Amadis of Gaul.

9. Variation of the proverb *"Tanto se pierde por carta de más como por carta de menos"*—"As much is lost by a card too many as a card too few." Compare Chapters XXXIII (note 23), XXXVII (note 6), and LXXI (note 9) following.

CHAPTER XVIII

1. These are the opening lines of Garcilaso de la Vega's Tenth Sonnet.

2. *"Borceguíes"*—half-boots or buskins.

3. Shelton's rendering is: "his shoes close on each side"; he reads *"encerrados"*—"closed"—in place of *"enceradaos"*—"waxed"—a reading which Lockhart prefers.

4. The shoulder strap or baldric was easier than a belt around the waist for kidney sufferers.

5. There is a word play here which unfortunately cannot be brought over in translation: *"sus negros requesones que tan blanco pusieron a su amo"*—literally, "his *black* curds which made his master so *white*," the word *"negro"* (black) having here the sense of unlucky, accursed, damnable.

6. Literally, "and take the pulse of what he knows" (i.e., of his wit).

7. Cervantes won a first prize in such a tournament at Saragossa in 1595.

8. The allusion is to a famous and legendary fifteenth-century swimmer of Catania in Sicily, known as Pescecola, who according to the folk tale was finally drowned in the pool of Charybdis when he was tempted by the king to dive twice on the same day on the chance of bringing up a golden cup. He was also known as "Nicolao the Fish."

A work entitled *Account of How Nicolao the Fish Reappeared in the Sea,* etc., was published at Barcelona in 1608.

9. See Horace's *Satires,* 1, iii, 2–3.
Nunquam inducant animum cantare rogati,
Injussi nunquam desistant.
"When asked, they never can bring themselves to sing; unasked, they never can desist."

10. The making of such glosses was a popular diversion with Spanish poets in the sixteenth and seventeenth centuries. Ticknor traces the custom to the poets of Provence, but Lope de Vega asserts that this was a Spanish invention.

11. The poet in question was Liñan de Riaza, who died in 1607. He was the author of a satirical sonnet containing the verse: *"laureado por Chipre y por Gaeta."* (Schevill)

12. This sonnet is seen as a caricature of the Góngora school.

13. Play on *"poetas consumidos"* and *"poeta consumado."* Fitzmaurice-Kelly (notes to the Ormsby translation) observes that "the joke on *'consumidos'* and *'consumado'* is not transferable," and this is doubtless true. The sense of *"consumidos"* is probably "lean" or "emaciated." Ormsby thinks the word may refer to the *"genus irritabile vatum,"* and he renders it as "irritable," although a later edition has "lean poets." Fitzmaurice-Kelly: "It may be that Cervantes uses the . . . word in its secondary sense of 'fretful.' "

14. See Chapter xxii following. The Cave of Montesinos is about six miles from the hamlet of Ruidera, which is some fifteen miles southeast of Argamasilla, amid the lakes where the waters of the Guadiana rise to flow down into the plains of La Mancha.

15. Here, as previously in this chapter, Cervantes in the original changes from the third person to the second (direct address) in the middle of a sentence.

16. See Vergil's *Aeneid,* vi, 853: *"parcere subjectis et debellare superbos."*

17. The word "castle" employed in the title of this chapter appears to hold out a promise, which is not fulfilled, of an adventure similar to those that Don Quixote met with in Part I. What we have, instead, is an episode in keeping with the more serious tone of Part II.

Don Diego de Miranda is essentially the kindly, well-meaning burgher and substantial citizen brought into contact with Don Quixote the dreamer.

CHAPTER XIX

1. *"Un poco de grana blanca."* Motteux mistranslates: "what seemed to be a little white grain"!

2. *"Medias de cordellate"*—grogram stockings.

3. The *zapateadores* do a kind of clog dance (the *zapateado*), in the course of which the dancer strikes the soles of his shoes with the palms of his hands. The *zapateado* (*sapateado*) is also a Portuguese dance and occurs even in the *sertões* or northeastern backlands of Brazil; it is mentioned by Euclides da Cunha.

4. A rhyming proverb: *"Cada oveja con su pareja."* The Portuguese also have it: *"Cada ovelha com sua parelha."*

5. In connection with this defense of the right of parents to arrange marriages for their children, compare Rabelais, Book III, Chapter xlviii (see *The Portable Rabelais,* pp. 507 ff.).

6. Another "rain" of proverbs. The expression, "God will do better than that"—*"Dios lo hará mejor,"* was commonly used in predicting misfortune for oneself or for another. (Rodríguez Marín)

7. Sayago was a district near the Portuguese frontier. The Castilian of Toledo was the standard, as Tuscan was the model for Italians.

8. The old Moorish market place of Toledo.

9. The Cathedral cloisters were a favorite lounging place as a refuge from the heat.

10. Majadahonda is a small village about six miles northwest of Madrid. (Cervantes has "Mahalahonda," probably a printer's error.)

11. Rodríguez Marín remarks that this phrase, *"por mis pecados,"* like *"con perdón"* and *"si no lo han por enojo,"* was greatly abused, being employed in and out of season.

12. Parenthesis supplied.

13. Motteux mistranslates: " 'As for turning my back,' said the artist, 'I won't be obliged to it.' "

14. *"Más espesas que hígado":* the expression is not given in the *Dictionary*

of the Academy. According to Rodríguez Marín, it is a popular one, and
Cejador states: *"Parece hígado, está
como un hígado,* is said of thick choco-
late." Schevill: "May this phrase possibly have its origin in the fact that pigs
and ducks, after they have stuffed themselves with figs, have a liver that is very
much enlarged and thick?" (Translated from the Spanish note.) Ormsby:
"thicker than hops or hail." Motteux:
"laid on like any lion."

15. The element of humorous exaggeration is not frequent in Cervantes as
it is in a Renaissance writer like Rabelais, for example, but it sometimes
does occur, as here. The same may be
said of the pretense of exactness, likewise introduced occasionally with humorous intent.

16. *"Diestros"*—fencing experts.

17. To "fall off one's donkey"—*"caer
de su burro,"* is to admit that one has
been in the wrong.

18. That is, of course, all except Don
Quixote and Sancho. Cervantes is never
meticulous about such details.

19. The place in question is referred
to sometimes as a "village"—*"aldea"* or
"lugar"—sometimes as a "town"—
"pueblo."

20. The one who had not gone after
the sword.

CHAPTER XX

1. Rodríguez Marín raises the question as to whether the entire episode of
Camacho's wedding may not be a
reminiscence of an event that actually
occurred at which Cervantes had been
present or of which he had heard an account. The records show that there was
a Don Pedro Camacho de Villavicencio
who was known as "El Rico," or "the
Rich," and who on August 15, 1507,
drew up a will that was remarkable for
the amount of property of which it disposed. (See Rodríguez Marín's edition
of *Don Quixote,* Vol. VI, p. 10.)

2. The first edition has *"duerme,"* an
imperative form, followed by most
translators, but I have adopted Schevill's
reading of *"duermes"* (indicative) as
more in consonance with the text.

3. The Spanish word is *"juncos,"*
which ordinarily means "rushes," but
which is here equivalent to *"junquillos."*
(See Rodríguez Marín.)

4. A coin worth four copper maravedis, corresponding roughly to the
British farthing.

5. This expression has occurred twice
before: Chapter III preceding and Part I,
Chapter XXX.

6. Hero of one of the Carolingian
ballads.

7. There was a popular saying: "Singing and dancing do not make up a trous-
seau"—*"Cantar y bailar no componen
ajuar."*

8. The wine here is measured by
weight, the arroba amounting to 25.4
pounds. In liquid measure, the quantity
represented is between six and seven
gallons.

9. The Spanish word is *"Interés,"*
which Ormsby renders as "Interest,"
Motteux as "Wealth." "Worldly
Wealth" seems a little nearer to the
meaning.

10. This was the usual apparel of savages on the stage in Cervantes' time.

11. In a cockfight the winner was
called *"El Rey,"* or "the Cock."

12. *"A la barba de las habilidades de
Basilio!"* There has been considerable
discussion as to the meaning of the
phrase *"a la barba,"* but it would seem
to apply to one who was "stuck" with
paying for others. According to Rodríguez Marín, the expression is equivalent
to *"Pierda y pague Basilio . . ."*
Ormsby: "A fig for the accomplishments of Basilio!" Motteux: ". . . a fig
for his abilities, say I." The French
translator, Cardaillac, has: ". . . *nargue
des talents de Basile!"* Tieck: *"Schade
was um Basilios Geschicklichkeiten!"*
(See Schevill.)

13. A proverb.

14. A proverb.

15. Literally, "people would rather
take the pulse of having than of knowing." There is a Spanish popular song:

> *Más vale saber que haber
> Dice la común sentencia;
> Que el sabio puede ser rico,
> Y el rico no compra ciencia.*

"Knowing is worth more than having,
the common saying goes; for the wise
man may be rich but the rich man cannot purchase wisdom." (Rodríguez
Marín) Here, as frequently, Sancho reverses the proverb.

16. The allusion, of course, is to

Horace's famous and beautiful lines (*Odes*, I, IV, 13–14).

> *Pallida mors aequo pulsat pede*
> *pauperum tabernas*
> *regumque turres.*

Cervantes has quoted these lines in the Prologue to Part I.

17. I have followed the majority of editors since 1738, who supply a verb here—*"tuvieras."*

CHAPTER XXI

1. The *"patena"* is a large medal, somewhat like a locket, that is worn by country women.

2. Ormsby: "The richest ordinary velvet being three-pile." With regard to the "palm-green" cloth that Quiteria wears, here as in the preceding chapter ("dresses of palm-leaf green"), in my rendering of *"palmilla"* I have followed Dr. Francisco del Rosal whose unpublished *Vocabulario* is cited by Rodríguez Marín and who states that the term was originally applied to cloth *"de color verde claro, que es el de la hoja de la palma."* Covarrubias asserts that the *palmilla* was a pigeon-blue cloth manufactured especially at Cuenca (*palmilla* being equivalent to *palomilla*, from *paloma*, a pigeon or dove), and he notes that there were also green varieties (*palmillas verdes*) of this same cloth and that it is possible that a palm was originally woven into the border of it.

3. *". . . que puede passar por los bancos de Flandes."* This expression has occasioned a great deal of discussion. It has commonly been taken as referring to the shoals off the Flemish coast, a peril that was dreaded by Spanish sailors. Others have seen an allusion to the monetary banks of exchange of the Low Countries (Lope de Vega employs it in this sense). Still others believe the reference is to the *bancos* upon which beds, tables, etc., in the home were placed. See the extended notes by Rodríguez Marín and Schevill. The latter seems to sum the matter up when he states: ". . . it appears that Sancho meant to say of Quiteria that, by reason of her youth and beauty, her wealth, and other endowments (of an up-and-coming lass) the young lady was in a position to brave the perils of matrimony and the hazardous life of a married woman." (Translated from the Spanish note.)

4. But Don Quixote has never seen Dulcinea.

5. *"Tenia . . . el alma en los dientes"* —literally, "had his soul in his teeth."

6. A play on the expression "soul in his teeth" (see preceding note). Literally, "had his soul on his tongue rather than in his teeth."

7. Similar episodes occur in other works of the time.

8. Matthew 19:6; Mark 10:9.

9. Motteux slurs this passage: " . . . Basil, whose virtues, in spite of his poverty, had secured him many friends . . ."

10. This may sound like a modernism, but it is absolutely literal: *"hombre de valor y de pelo en pecho."*

CHAPTER XXII

1. Proverbs 12:4: "A virtuous woman is a crown to her husband: but she that maketh him ashamed is a rottenness in his bones." Compare Proverbs 31:10: "Who can find a virtuous woman? for her price is far above rubies."

2. This statement may be noted in view of Don Quixote's devotion to Dulcinea. Rodríguez Marín is inclined to think it the incoherence of a madman, but it is just as likely that it is to be explained by Cervantes' usual carelessness in such matters.

3. *"A qué quieres, boca."*

4. The obviously missing adverb has been supplied.

5. A proverb.

6. For the Giralda of Seville, see Chapter XIV preceding and note 1. The Angel of the Magdalena was a weather-vane on the Church of the Magdalena at Salamanca. The Vecinguerra Conduit was the sewer draining the Potro quarter of Cordova (the quarter of the Horse Fountain; see Part I, Chapter III and note 1). On the Bulls of Guisando, see Chapter XIV preceding and note 2. With the exception of Sierra Morena, the other names are those of fountains in Madrid.

7. Virgilius Polydorus (Virgilio Polidoro) was an Italian historian, born at Urbino around 1470. He spent more than fifty years of his life in England, where he rose to a high position in the ecclesiastical hierarchy. His most im-

portant work is one on English history, *Anglicae Historiae Libri XXVI*, published at Basel in 1534 (a copy exists in the British Museum). Among his other works was one entitled *De Inventoribus Rerum* (*On the Inventors of Things*). He died at Urbino in 1550.

8. Reference to syphilis and unctions of mercury.

9. In the sense of acrobat.

10. An old ballad line. Compare Cervantes' poetic address to his pen at the end of the *Don Quixote;* see also the end of Chapter XXIX (note 9), Chapter XXXIX (note 2), and the beginning of Chapter XLI following.

11. A proverb.

12. Cervantes' word here is *"sima,"* a deep cavern, an abyss, or a chasm. The possibility that this may have been an ancient mine shaft has already been noted.

13. What Sancho means is the Virgin of the Rock of France (Peña de Francia). The allusion is to a site between Salamanca and Ciudad Rodrigo where an image of the Virgin was discovered in the fifteenth century; a Dominican monastery was later erected on the spot.

14. The Trinity of Gaeta refers to a chapel dedicated to the Holy Trinity on the promontory of Gaeta, to the north of Naples.

15. Ormsby's rendering of *"valentón del mundo"* seems the best to be had.

16. Compare Psalms 102:11, 103:15, 109:23, 144:4; and Ecclesiastes 6:12. As Calderón was to put it: *"La vida es sueño y sueño de sueño"*—"Life is a dream and a dream of a dream."

17. These are characters from the literature of chivalry. Montesinos is the protagonist of the "Ballads of Montesinos." Durandarte was his cousin and the brother of Count Dirlos (see Chapter XX preceding and note 6). Belerma was Durandarte's lady, and Guadiana was his squire, transformed by Merlin into the river of that name. The "daughters of Ruidera" are the Lakes of Ruidera (see Chapter XVIII preceding and note 14).

CHAPTER XXIII

1. Scholars have not been able to identify this personage.

2. Merlin was Welsh, though the Bretons tried to claim him. Malory in his *Morte d'Arthur* calls him "a devil's son." Compare the verses in Chapter XXXV following.

3. Covarrubias (*Tesoro de la Lengua Castellana*, under the word *"Corazón"*) makes this observation: "Timorous animals have a proportionately larger heart than others, animals such as the hare, the deer, the mouse, and similar ones mentioned by Aristotle, *lib.* 3, *De Partibus Animalium;* and so, when we say by way of praise that a man or animal has a great heart [great courage], we do not mean that his heart is great in size but in ardor . . ." (Cited by Schevill.)

4. According to Clemencín, Cervantes, copying from memory, has here mingled and altered two old ballads, one of which begins:

O Belerma! O Belerma!
Por mi mal fuiste engendrada.

"O Belerma! O Belerma! for my woe thou wert begotten." For the legend of the heart, compare the French *Roman du Châtelain de Couci* and see the account given by Gaston Paris, *Histoire Littéraire de la France* (Paris, 1890), Vol. 28, pp. 252 ff. A reminiscence of Orlando's sword, Durandal, or Durendal, has been seen in the name Durandarte. Durandarte is also said to have been the name of the sword carried by Bramante, who was slain by Charlemagne at Toledo.

5. According to this passage, the number of the lakes was ten. In Chapter XVIII preceding, Cervantes speaks of "the seven lakes that are commonly known as the Lakes of Ruidera." Clemencín says there are fifteen; other authorities say eleven.

6. The two lakes ("nieces") are in the upper portion of the valley in question where the province of Murcia and the former province of New Castile met. They were within the domain of the Order of St. John.

7. The Guadiana flows underground for a part of its course. See Part I, Chapter XVIII and note 11.

8. A proverb.

9. A proverbial saying among card players.

10. A proverb.

11. For a slightly different version of

this proverb, see Chapter x preceding and note 7.

12. In the original there is a play here on *"vino"*—"wine"—and *"vino"*—"he came." Allusion to a ballad some lines of which have been given in Part I, Chapter XIII. For Quintañona, see Chapter XIII and note 1.

13. Reference to the Fuggers of Bavaria. Founded by Johannes Fugger in the fourteenth century, the family in the course of three hundred years came to own some sixty estates. In the Renaissance era the Fuggers of Augsburg were celebrated bankers and financiers. The reader may be referred to R. Ehrenberg's *Capital and Finance in the Age of the Renaissance: A Study of the Fuggers* (London, 1928). Motteux: "if I had all the treasures which Croesus possessed."

14. See Part I, Chapter v and note 1.

15. The "seven parts of the world" was a familiar concept of the age. The Infante Pedro was the second son of John I of Portugal and brother of Prince Henry the Navigator. He traveled widely in Europe and the East between 1416 and 1428. An account of his voyages was published at Lisbon in 1554 and was popular in Spain.

CHAPTER XXIV

1. See Catherine Perry Hargrave, *A History of Playing Cards and a Bibliography of Cards* (Boston: Houghton Mifflin, 1930).

2. A tribute in passing to Cervantes' patron, the Count of Lemos.

3. The text of the first edition is confused here, although what the author wrote, or meant to write, is clear enough (Schevill thinks something may have been dropped from the manuscript by the printer). After stating that "they all three made straight for the hostelry, where they arrived a little before nightfall," the text continues: "The cousin proposed to Don Quixote that they go up to it [*que llegassen a ella*] and have a drink, and no sooner did Sancho Panza hear this than he turned his gray's head toward the hermitage [*a la hermita*]." Editors have made the obvious transposition of the pronoun *"ella"* and *"la hermita,"* and Rodríguez Marín helpfully suggests that the clause "where they arrived a little before nightfall" should be regarded as parenthetical. In

addition, for purposes of translation, I have supplied "on the way" and have rendered *"dixo"* as a pluperfect—"had proposed."

4. *"Una sotahermitaño"* (in modern Spanish one would say *sotaermitaña*). Rodríguez Marín: "In this sub-hermit one may behold the brazen countenance of the anchorite's Magdalen."

5. "Little of the best"—*"de lo caro"*; literally, of the dearest. "Cheap water" —*"agua barata."* There were two classes of taverns in Cervantes' time: those that sold *de lo barato* and the ones that dispensed *de lo caro.* The former sold only *vino ordinario;* the latter, few in number (there are said to have been not more than eight at the beginning of the seventeenth century), could serve both varieties. (Rodríguez Marín)

6. A fashion said to have been introduced by the Duke of Lerma, who suffered from bunions. (Ormsby)

7. The *seguidilla* was a seven-line stanza with a special rhythm.

8. The word means "niggardliness." In the original: *"espilorceria."*

9. See Don Quixote's speech on this subject, Part I, Chapter XXXVIII.

10. It is not known where Cervantes got this, but it was not from Terence.

11. The original has *"sobrino"*— "nephew," an obvious slip on Cervantes' part.

CHAPTER XXV

1. Proverbial expression denoting impatience. Motteux: "Don Quixote was on thorns to know . . ."

2. *"Regidor"*—an officer in charge of finances.

3. *"Dadme albricias."* The word *"albricias"* is still in use in this sense.

4. *". . . los dexos, muchos y apresurados."* Ormsby: "your finishing notes come thick and fast."

5. *"En bueno mano está,"* an expression used when urged to have a drink. Literally, "It [the glass] is in a good hand."

6. A proverb.

7. The reader interested in the subject may be referred to *A Book of Marionettes,* by Helen H. Joseph (New York: Viking Press, 1929). For the puppet theater in Cervantes' time, the student should consult Armando Cotarelo

y Vallador, *El teatro de Cervantes* (Madrid, 1915), pp. 574 ff.

8. Cervantes means the Monte Aragon region, in the eastern part of La Mancha, near the Cuenca Mountains, later part of the province of Cuenca.

9. Gayfer, King of Bordeaux, was one of Charlemagne's chieftains. Melisendra (properly, Melisenda) was Charlemagne's daughter who was held captive by the Moors. The story is told in the Spanish *cancioneros*, or ballad collections, from which Cervantes takes it.

10. "Gallant man" (*"hombre galante"*) is the Italian *"galantuomo."* "Good companion" is *"buon compagno,"* which Cervantes carries over as *"bon compaño."* The latter expression is used again in Chapter LIV following. Such foreign phrases are not as out of place as they might seem in the mouth of a provincial innkeeper, since he well may have picked them up as a soldier in the Italian wars.

11. In the original Don Quixote says this in transliterated Italian: *"qué pexe pillamo (che pesce pigliamo)."*

12. *"¡Voto a rus!"* The meaning of this obviously mild oath or exclamation remains a mystery to the commentators.

13. *"Señor Monissimo."*

14. Giantess in the *Amadis of Gaul.*

15. The original reads *"porque lo devo"*—literally, "because I owe it" [to him], and Rodríguez Marín suggests this may have a meaning which becomes clear when the identity of the puppet master is later disclosed; see Chapter XXVII following.

16. There is a word play here which is impossible to carry over. Sancho mistakes Don Quixote's *"pacto"* for *"patio"* and *"espreso"* for *"espeso,"* which means sometimes "thick" and sometimes "dirty" or "slovenly."

17. Reference to judicial, or divinatory, astrology. The "figures" are horoscopes.

18. John 10:38: ". . . though ye believe not me, believe the works."

CHAPTER XXVI

1. This verse is from Gregorio Hernández de Velasco's Spanish translation of Vergil's *Aeneid*, published in 1555. See the *Aeneid*, II, 1: *"Conticuere omnes, intentique ora tenebant."* On the use

made by Cervantes of the *Aeneid*, see Schevill's "Studies in Cervantes, III, Vergil's Aeneid," in the *Transactions of the Connecticut Academy*, 1908.

2. In the year 1905 a puppet show based upon the story of Melisendra was staged at the Ateneo in Madrid, in connection with the three-hundredth anniversary of the publication of *Don Quixote*. (Rodríguez Marín)

3. These verses are not from one of the old ballads but are the opening lines of a set of octaves of later date, discovered by Pellicer in the National Library at Madrid. As for the game mentioned here, the expression in the original is *"jugando a las tablas"*—"playing at tables," corresponding to the French *"aux tables,"* found in Rabelais and other writers. The table games included chess, draughts (checkers), backgammon, and dice. See L. Sainéan: *La Langue de Rabelais* (Paris, 1922), Vol. I, p. 287. It would appear that the game that Gayfer is playing is tricktrack (*tric-trac*), or backgammon. Motteux: "draughts"; Ormsby: "playing at the tables."

4. Line from a ballad attributed to Miguel Sanchez, printed in the third part of Durán's collection, the *Romancero General.*

5. In the *Chanson de Roland*, Roland's (Orlando's) sword is named Durandal.

6. This is Marsiles of the *Chanson de Roland*, a historical personage. Sansueña is a city mentioned in the romances of chivalry and identified by Cervantes as the modern Saragossa. Later in the chapter he refers to "King Marsilio of Saragossa."

7. These verses are found in a *jácara*, or humorous ballad, of Quevedo. (Clemencín)

8. From a ballad in the Durán collection. (Schevill)

9. Góngora has a humorous ballad the theme of which is: how Melisendra must have suffered on this ride.

10. Is this, possibly, a criticism of the dramatists of the day?

11. This is literal. Motteux: "Christian lovers," which is not a bad rendering. Ormsby: "faithful lovers."

12. These lines are from one of the Rodrigo ballads.

13. A proverb.

14. *"Pillar la mona"*—"catch the she-ape"—is slang for getting drunk.

CHAPTER XXVII

1. See Part I, Chapter XXII ff.
2. See Part I, Chapter XXIII and note 2, and Part II, Chapter III.
3. See Chapter IV preceding and note 1. For the siege of Albraca, see Part I, Chapter X.
4. See Part I, Chapter XXX and note 6.
5. Cervantes seems to have been under the mistaken impression that the Mancha de Aragon region (see Chapter XXV preceding and note 8) was a part of the kingdom of Aragon. (Ormsby)
6. *". . . como un pequeño sardesco."* A *sardesco* is a pony or small ass; colloquially, the word means "rude" or "stubborn." Motteux: "a very Sardinian for stubbornness."
7. The terms *"regidor"* (see Chapter XXV preceding and note 2) and *"alcalde"* cannot be rendered with complete accuracy. The *regidores* were aldermen or councilmen; the *alcalde* was the mayor or a judge or justice of the peace.
8. Don Diego Ordoñez de Lara was a Castilian knight in the service of King Sancho II. Vellido (Bellido) Dolfos was an enemy spy who by a ruse slew the monarch beneath the walls of Zamora. This treacherous act was avenged by Don Diego, a near kinsman of the victim. The story is told in the *Chronicle of the Cid* and in one of the old ballads. See the Ballads of the Cid in Menéndez y Pelayo's *Antologia;* also, Durán's *Romancero General,* No. 791, and the *Cancionero de Romances* (Antwerp, 1550).
9. The original has *"panes"*—"loaves," but Ormsby adopts the reading "fishes." Lockhart, in his note on this passage in the Motteux version, renders a few lines from the *Chronicle of the Cid,* which include the imprecation "May all your harvests rot."
10. *"Pueblo de la Reloxa (Reloja)."* There has been much argument among commentators as to the identification of this "Clocktown." Rodríguez Marín, who has an extended note and an appendix on the subject, is of the opinion that there were two Clocktowns, one of which he identifies as the hamlet of Espartinas near Seville, adding that "To this day, in Espartinas, it is dangerous to ask *'¿Que hora es?'*—'What time is it?'"
11. The *Cazoleros,* or "Scullions," were the inhabitants of Valladolid and derived their name from a townsman, Cazalla, who was burned as a Lutheran in 1559. The "Eggplant-growers" (*Berenjeros,* from *berenjenas,* eggplants) were the Toledans. The "Whalers" (*Balenatos*) were the residents of Madrid, so called because they were supposed to have mistaken a packsaddle floating down the flooded Manzanares for a whale. The identity of the "Soapmen" (*Jaboneros*) is uncertain.
12. Compare our Declaration of Independence: ". . . our Lives, our Fortunes, and our Sacred Honor."
13. Compare the three just conditions under which war may be waged as set forth by St. Thomas Aquinas, *Summa Theologica,* II, ii, Quaest. 40 (1), De Bello. These conditions are: the authorization of the ruler; a just cause; a right intention.
14. Matthew 5:44: "Love your enemies . . . do good to them that hate you . . ." Compare Luke 6:27 and 35.
15. Matthew 11:30.
16. *"No se me dava dos ardites."*

CHAPTER XXVIII

1. This proverb has occurred in Part I, Chapter XXV.
2. There is a confused text here in the first edition. The original reads ". . . que yo pondré silencio en mis rebuznos; pero no en dexar de dezir," which is in contradiction to the obvious sense of the passage. I have followed Schevill in dropping the *"en"* and supplying *"puedo"*: ". . . pero no puedo dexar de dezir."
3. Both the Spaniards and the Portuguese have this proverb.
4. *"En vuestra mano esta escudillar."* Allusion to pouring broth from the *olla,* or stew-pot. (Rodríguez Marín)
5. Cervantes forgets that Sancho did not accompany Don Quixote on the first sally.
6. In Chapter II preceding the name of the bachelor's father is given as Bartolomé. Some commentators see in this an instance of Sancho's poor memory (his memory, as a matter of fact, was very good); others ascribe the discrepancy to Cervantes' carelessness; others

still see in Tomé a shortened form (based upon sound) of Bartolomé.

7. This proverb is also found in Part I, Chapter LII.

8. In the Spanish, a rhyming proverb: *"Quien yerra y se enmienda/A Dios se encomienda."*

CHAPTER XXIX

1. Commentators have objected that Don Quixote and Sancho, traveling as they did, could not possibly have covered the distance between the Cave of Montesinos and the banks of the Ebro (something over two hundred miles) in less than ten or fifteen days, in place of the five days which the author allows them for the journey. But Rodríguez Marín observes that, with the exigencies of earning a livelihood, which prevented him even from correcting his manuscript, Cervantes had no time to spend upon geographical minutiae.

2. A proverb.

3. These malapropisms of Sancho are, it goes without saying, the despair of any translator. In such cases it is almost always impossible to render the passage literally. Here, the word play is on *"longinquos"* (*"caminos"*) and Sancho's *"logicuos."*

4. The Riphaean Mountains, a range in northernmost Scythia, are frequently mentioned by classic authors.

5. Play on *"linea"*—"line," and *"leña"* —"wood."

6. The original reads ". . . *según el cómputo de Ptolomeo, que fué el mayor cosmógrafo . . ."* Out of this Sancho makes: ". . . *puto y gafo* [literally, "leprous whoreson"], *con la añadidura de meon o meo, o no sé como."*

7. Ormsby: "In the *Theatrum orbis terrarum* of Abraham Ortelius (Antwerp, 1600), this phenomenon is said to be observable immediately after passing the Azores."

8. Don Quixote asks: *"¿. . . has topado algo?"* and Sancho replies: *"Y aun algos."* This answer has since become proverbial and the expression has even found its way into the *Dictionary of the Academy.* (Rodríguez Marín)

9. See Chapter XXII preceding, note 10.

10. ". . . *dos barcadas como estas."*

CHAPTER XXX

1. This is literal: *"con un sillón de plata."* Ormsby: "a silver-mounted sidesaddle." Jarvis: "A sidesaddle of cloth of silver."

2. Literally, "kiss the hands of her great beauty."

3. See Chapter XIV preceding and note 5.

4. Rhyming proverb: *"En casa llena/ Presto se guisa la cena."* Portuguese: *"Na casa cheia, asinha se faz a cea."*

5. *"A vuestra encumbrada altanería y fermosura." "Altanería"* means both "haughtiness" and "hawking." Motteux: "your hawking beauty."

6. On this speech of Sancho's see Chapter X preceding, note 11.

7. The commentator Pellicer has identified Don Quixote's hosts as the Duke and Duchess of Villahermosa, who had a country place in this region. In the year 1905, in connection with the celebration of the three-hundredth anniversary of the publication of Part I of the *Don Quixote,* the Duchess of Villahermosa observed the occasion by staging an elaborate fiesta, having medals struck and paying the printing costs of a handsome Cervantes album, *Album Cervantino Aragonés* (Madrid, 1905). See Rodríguez Marín's note.

8. A proverb.

9. The text is obscure at this point. I have followed Schevill.

10. *"Escudero andado."*

CHAPTER XXXI

1. There is a rhyme in the original:
Quando de Bretaña vino,
que damas curauan del,
y dueñas del su rozino.
Compare the lines in Part I, Chapters II and XIII.

2. The Spanish word is *"juglar,"* corresponding to the French *"jongleur,"*— "a mountebank." According to the *Dictionary of the Academy,* a *juglar* in the sixteenth century was one who "for money and before the people sang, danced, or performed tricks and clownish acts."

3. The "fig" was originally a gesture of contempt made by closing the fist and inserting the thumb between the index and middle fingers. (Covarrubias)

4. Somewhat freely: ". . . *no per-*

derá vuessa merced la quinola de sus años por punto menos."

5. The Spanish *montera.*

6. Pellicer states that Cervantes here gives an accurate picture of the luxury maintained by Spanish grandees of the period.

7. It is believed that the author had in mind a particular cleric. Some say it was the Duke of Béjar's chaplain, who did his best to persuade that nobleman to refuse Cervantes' dedication of Part I. (See Rodríguez Marín and Ormsby.)

8. *"A buen salvo está el que repica":* the sense of this proverb is that while the bell-ringer may sound the alarm, he himself is safe in the belfry.

9. In connection with an exchange of compliments, it was a popular form of courtesy to repeat the previous speaker's words, applying them to him. (Rodríguez Marín) This particular form of word play was not uncommon in the Renaissance; compare Rabelais, Book III, Chapter IX (*The Portable Rabelais,* pp. 424–27). See also the colloquy of Erasmus entitled "Echo."

10. Tembleque is a town in La Mancha. "Hurry back from Tembleque, brother" has come to be a proverbial expression addressed to a long-winded storyteller.

11. This story may have been based upon a real-life incident. (Rodríguez Marín)

12. *"Nora tal* [en hora tal]." Euphemism for *"noramala* [en hora mala]"— "in an evil hour."

CHAPTER XXXII

1. *"Togados"*—literally, toga-wearers. Rodríguez Marín sees here the classic antithesis between *togae* and *arma*— compare Cicero: *"Cedant arma togae"* (*De Officiis,* I, xxii). Cervantes, through the mouth of Don Quixote, is fond of dwelling on the theme of arms versus letters.

2. *"Auiendose criado algunos en la estrecheza de algun pupilage."* Previous English-language translators have taken *"estrecheza"* in the sense of "narrow-mindedness" instead of its other meaning, "poverty." Ormsby: "having been brought up in all the straitness of some seminary." Motteux and Jarvis overlook the reflexive *"auiendose criado"* and as

a result get the meaning wrong. Motteux: "having trained up a few pupils straightly"; Jarvis: "a poor pedagogue, who never saw more of the world," etc. Rodríguez Marín points out that the allusion is to the hunger endured by poor students in the schools.

3. Another echo of Garcilaso, passage quoted in Chapter VI preceding.

4. *"El ancho campo de la ambición."* Ormsby suggests emending *"ancho campo"* to read *"ancho camino"*— "broad road." "It would be absurd," he says, "to talk of the broad field of flattery or hypocrisy, and a narrow path is naturally the opposite of a broad road, not of a broad field." However, to this translator, "broad field" seems quite in keeping with the concept of ambition, and in the process of translation the difficulty may be solved by supplying "road" and "way" in the phrase and clause that follow, as has been done here.

5. Calderón (in his *Cervantes Vindicado*) is inclined to believe that Sancho threw in the verb *"perseverar"* simply for its sonorous, high-sounding effect. Hartzenbusch and Benjumea substitute *"persuadir"*—"persuade." See Rodríguez Marín's note.

6. The Portuguese also have this proverb.

7. See Chapter X preceding and note 7.

8. See "Urganda the Unknown," prefatory verses to Part I.

9. Personage in the *Orlando Innamorato* of Boiardo.

10. So-called "Neapolitan soap" (*jabón napolitano*) was manufactured in the households of princes and the nobility. There are in existence a number of curious sixteenth-century recipes for making it. Among the elements that went into its composition were wheat bran, milk of poppies, goat's milk, marrow of deer, bitter almonds, and sugar. (Rodríguez Marín)

11. The proverb ran: *"Bueno es vivir para ver,"* our "Live and learn."

12. A proverb.

13. Parrhasius, Timanthes, and Apelles were famous Greek painters of the fourth and fifth centuries B.C.; Lysippus was a fourth-century Greek sculptor.

14. Don Quixote uses the form *"demostina"* instead of the more usual *"de-*

mosteniana"—"Demosthenian." (Clemencín)

15. On the Sayago region, see Chapter xix preceding and note 7.

16. Oriana was the lady of Amadis of Gaul. Alastrajarea, in the chivalric romances, was the wife of the prince Don Falanges of Astra. On Queen Madásima, see Part I, Chapters xxiv and xxv.

17. This proverb has occurred in Part I, Chapters iv (note 3) and xlvii (note 11).

18. Compare Chapter vi preceding.

19. Reference to nautical terminology.

20. See Part I, Chapter xxxi.

21. For the slaying of Orlando (Roland) by Bernardo del Carpio, see Part I, the beginning of Chapter xxvi. On the Twelve Peers, see Part I, Chapter xlix.

22. Part I, Chapters xlv ff.

23. According to Clemencín, who based his information on old records, there were no noble houses in El Toboso, nor even small gentry, the population being made up of Moorish peasants. There has been some discussion, which has arrived nowhere, as to whether or not there was a real-life prototype of Dulcinea.

24. See Part I, Chapter xli and note 9.

25. A proverbial expression, according to the *Dictionary of the Academy*.

26. Allusion to the agility of these birds, according to Rodríguez Marín. The phrase puzzled Ormsby.

27. Rhyming proverb: *"Ni hagas cohecho,/Ni pierdas derecho."*

28. *"Con lexia mas clara"*—literally, "with clearer lye" (Ormsby). Motteux: "cleaner suds"; Jarvis's "clearer suds" is better.

29. A cosmetic water that, according to an old recipe preserved in the National Library of Madrid, consisted of a distillation of red and white roses, trefoil, red poppies, lavender root, honeysuckle, orange blossoms, white lilies, thyme, carnations, and orange rind. Directions as to the method of manufacturing it are also given. (See Rodríguez Marín.) It is of interest to compare the *eau d'ange* which Rabelais mentions in connection with the Abbey of Thélème (see Book I, end of Chapter xl or *The Portable Rabelais*, p. 210). According to M. Paul Dorveaux, *eau d'ange* was *"eau*

distillé de myrte" (see the Lefranc critical edition, *Œuvres de Rabelais* [Paris, 1913], Tome Second, p. 421, note 38).

30. In place of *"ceremonias,"* I adopt the reading *"cirimonias,"* to accord with the duchess's subsequent speech. It is not unlikely that this was what Cervantes wrote.

31. Don Quixote's overrefined language here is explained by Clemencín as being a parody on that of a bully of Seville.

32. The *penante*, or slender, narrow-mouthed jar, held but a small quantity of wine.

33. Commentators seem to have overlooked the fact that when Don Quixote and Sancho first caught sight of the ducal pair, it was "as they emerged from a wood at sunset" (see the beginning of Chapter xxx preceding); yet at the end of the present chapter, Don Quixote goes off to take a siesta. Apparently under the impression that the time is night, Ormsby has: "it's about as likely . . . as that it's now midnight," by way of an attempt at clarifying the sense (the original reads *"como aora es noche"*). Motteux has a gross mistranslation: "which I will put up with as it is now night."

34. *"Que me trasquilen a cruzes."* I follow Rodríguez Marín, who interprets this expression as meaning, "to cut the hair crudely and unevenly." He cites Correas: *Vocabulario de Refranes.* This is said to have been the manner in which the hair of fools was trimmed.

35. See note 30 preceding.

CHAPTER XXXIII

1. Reference to the famous ivory seat which the Cid won by the capture of Valencia. "When the Cid returned to Castile, the king, Don Alfonso, invited him to take a seat beside him, and when the Cid out of modesty refused, his Majesty ordered him to sit upon the ivory chair." (Clemencín, quoting the old chronicle.)

2. See Part I, Chapter xxvi.

3. A proverbial expression used in connection with a speaker who wanders far afield. (Covarrubias) Ubeda was a small town in the upper Guadalquivir valley. The region is not particularly hilly, and the origin of the expression is obscure.

4. "*Es agradecido.*" Clemencín suggests that this be emended to "*soy agradecido*"—"I am grateful," but there appears to be no good reason for the change. Ormsby (edition of 1885) has: "I'm grateful," but the edition of his translation by Fitzmaurice-Kelly reads: "he is free-handed" (*agradecido* sometimes has this meaning in old Spanish). Motteux: "he is grateful." Jarvis: "he returns my love."

5. Jarvis: "nothing in the world can part us but the sexton's spade and shovel."

6. This proverb occurs again in Chapter LIII (note 11) following.

7. "*Limiste de Segovia.*" Segovia was noted for its manufacture of fine cloth. Rabelais (Book IV, Chapter VI) has the form "*limestre*," and Ménage (*Dictionnaire Etymologique*) states: "The serge of *Limestre* is said to derive its name from the one who first manufactured it, but there is no proof of this. It is a serge that is made today at Rouen, and at Darnetal near Rouen, and was formerly made in Spain, also, being of fine Spanish wool." (See Sainéan, *La Langue de Rabelais*, Vol. II, pp. 226–27.)

8. This paragraph consists of a string of proverbs.

9. We have this proverb in English.

10. See Part I, Chapter XXVII and note 1.

11. See Chapter VI preceding.

12. The duenna is quoting another version of a ballad, "*Despues que el rey don Rodrigo,*" that appears in the *cancioneros* (*Cancionero de Romances* of Antwerp and Durán's *Romancero General*, No. 606).

13. Commentators have seen a confused text here, finding it difficult to make sense out of the conclusion of this sentence, but the idea seems to be that Sancho will be constantly improving his lot. Both Motteux and Jarvis mistranslate; Motteux: "you will not give it up for one of triple brocade"; Jarvis: "for which he would refuse one of brocade three stories high."

14. Rhyming proverb: "*A quien cuece y amasa,/No le hurtes hogaza.*" This is something like our "Don't kill the goose that lays the golden egg."

15. Propitiatory sounds addressed to a dog ("nice doggy"). The Spanish proverb runs: "*A perro viejo no hay*

'*tus, tus*'"—"There's no use in saying '*tus, tus*' to an old dog."

16. These are all proverbs.

17. The duchess is imitating Sancho's way of talking.

18. A proverb.

19. Reference to the *Disticha*, a well-known school text, of Dionysius Cato.

20. Miguel Verino was the author of a collection of moral couplets, the *De Puerorum Moribus Disticha*, which was in wide use in European schools and, according to Lockhart, writing in the nineteenth century, was "still used as a textbook in some of the English schools." Dying young, Verino was the subject of a Latin epitaph by Politian which began: "*Michael Verinus florentibus occidit annis.*" Commentators point out that there is nothing surprising in the duchess's being able to quote Latin, as this was by no means an uncommon accomplishment with Spanish ladies of high rank in Cervantes' time. The Duchess of Villahermosa, who may have been the prototype of Cervantes' character, was a woman of broad culture.

21. Ormsby: "The commonplace explanation is that we should not trust to appearances." The Portuguese have this proverb and its converse: "*Debaixo de bom saio está o homem máo*"—"Under a good cloak is a bad man."

22. Sancho means to say that he never gets drunk. Motteux: "though I wear breeches, I don't ill use them."

23. Compare Chapter XVII (note 9) preceding and Chapter XXXVII following.

24. "*En las cortesias jumentiles y assininas.*"

CHAPTER XXXIV

1. It was Sancho, not Don Quixote, who related the Montesinos episode.

2. Favila succeeded his father Pelayo on the throne. As Ormsby points out, however, he was hardly a "Gothic king," as that line properly ends with Rodrigo. According to an old Spanish chronicle, he was slain by a boar (not bears) that he sought to subdue by bodily strength alone, unaided by his huntsmen, in the animal's lair.

3. This comparison of war and the chase is common with Renaissance writers, particularly the Spaniards.

4. The expression "*y vereeis como os*

vale vn pan por ciento" has puzzled commentators and translators. Rodríguez Marín states that the sense is "to obtain great profit from an exercise or pursuit." Ormsby gives it this meaning: "and you will find the good of it." Motteux takes it in a different sense: "you shall see how plain fare agrees with you."

5. Compare the proverb quoted in Chapter v (note 8) preceding: "The respectable woman has a broken leg and stays at home." Sancho here turns it to his own use. It occurs again in Chapter XLIX (note 17) following.

6. *Standard Dictionary:* "A game of cards, antedating and essentially like poker." Ormsby: "The game (*triunfo envidado*) seems to have been more like 'all fours.'" For some inexplicable reason Motteux has: "a game of trumps at Christmas."

7. *"Del dicho al hecho,/Hay gran trecho."*

8. Cervantes seems especially fond of this saying. It has occurred in Chapters XIV (note 5) and XXX (note 3) preceding, and recurs in Chapters LIX (note 12) and LXXI (note 10) following.

9. Proverb with assonant rhyme: *"Mas vale á quien Dios ayuda/Que quien mucho madruga."*

10. Jarvis: "the belly carries the legs, and not the legs the belly."

11. The *Comendador Griego* was Hernán Núñez de Guzmán, a learned Hellenist who held the chair of Greek at the University of Salamanca and who was a commander of the Order of Santiago, whence his title—not "Greek commentator," as Motteux and others have it. He left a manuscript collection of proverbs which was published after his death, the *Refranes ó Proverbios en Romance*, etc. (Salamanca, 1555).

12. The Moslem cry *"Le ilah ile alah"* —"There is no divinity but God" ("there is no god but Allah").

13. At the beginning of the chapter we are told that Sancho himself had come to believe this.

14. Ormsby: "In the carts described, wheels and axle are all in one piece. They are in use to this day in the Asturias, and their creaking may be heard on a still evening miles away. The country folk there maintain it has the effect Cervantes mentions."

15. See the prefatory verses to Part I.

CHAPTER XXXV

1. The phrase *"vn disciplinante de luz"* cannot be rendered accurately in English except by a tedious circumlocution. The literal sense is "penitents of light." There were two classes of penitents in the confraternities: the *disciplinantes de luz* and the *disciplinantes de sangre*, or "blood penitents." The former marched in processions, carrying lighted tapers; the latter were flagellants. (Rodríguez Marín)

2. *"Ni pesada ni por pesar."*

3. Sancho says *"abernuncio"* in place of *"abrenuncio,"* an expression meaning "far be it from me" or "fie on that!" The Latin form of the word is *"abrenuntio,"* from *"abrenuntiare"*—"to renounce," as, for example, to renounce the devil and all his works, in baptism (it is used in this sense by the fifth-century Christian writer Salvianus). Both Motteux and Jarvis have the rather meaningless rendering: "I pronounce it."

4. *"Alma de cántaro"*—idiomatic for "fool."

5. Inmate of a school for orphan lads.

6. *"A Dios rogando/Y con el mazo dando."* In the sense of "work and pray." In his list of proverbs in the *Don Quixote*, Ormsby cites a number of sayings corresponding to this one to be found in other European languages. Italian: *"Invoca i santi e da di piglio all' aratro"*—"Invoke the saints and lay a hand to the plough." French: *"Dieu donne fil à toile ourdie"*—"God provides thread for the web with a warp." There is also the Latin: *"Dii facientes adjuvant"*—"The gods help the doers" ("God helps him who helps himself").

7. Compare Chapter VII (note 6) preceding and LXXI (note 23) following.

8. In the sense of something fitting, a suitable accompaniment.

9. *"Que no son todos los tiempos unos"*—literally, "that all times are not the same."

10. *"Como de boluereme cazique."* Jarvis: "as much to the thing as to turn Turk." Motteux: "I have no more stomach for it than to be among the men-eaters." Ormsby: "as little fancy for it as for turning cacique." "Cacique" is, literally, a West Indian chief.

11. See Chapter x (note 2) preceding. The Portuguese also have the proverb.

12. See Chapter II (note 7) preceding.

13. *"Si algunos . . . fueren de mosqueo."* *"Mosqueo"* is the act of driving flies away.

CHAPTER XXXVI

1. *"La letra con sangre entra"*—proverbial with schoolmasters of the time.

2. This theological heresy was suppressed by the Inquisition in the majority of the editions of *Don Quixote* printed in Spain following the edition of Valencia in 1616.

3. This expression, which has come to be a proverb, apparently derives from someone who had been whipped through the streets mounted on an ass.

4. This is literal. Ormsby: "take care that nobody speaks evil of thee behind thy back."

5. *"Pon lo tuyo en consejo, y unos diran. . . ."* Rodríguez Marín: *"Lo tuyo, lo mio,* and *lo suyo* are vulgar euphemisms for the pudenda, abundant examples of which are to be found in our sixteenth-century writers." Previous translators appear to have been unaware of this or else have glossed it over.

6. See Chapter XXXI (note 8) preceding and Chapter XLIII (note 10) following.

7. See Part I, Chapter XX (note 9).

8. *". . . tengo de comer las manos tras él"*—literally, *". . . after it."* The expression is one denoting great eagerness.

9. *"Su calongía"*—literally, "canonry." (Modern Spanish: *"calonjía."*)

10. The word in Spanish is *"orégano"* —"wild marjoram," an allusion to the proverb that has already occurred in Part I, Chapter XXI (note 2): *"Plegue á Dios que orégano sea,/Y no se nos vuelva alcaravea—*"Please God that it be marjoram and not turn out to be caraway." The connection is somewhat obscure; some would here read *"orógano,"* or *"oroganoso,"* from *"oro"*—"gold," and *"gana"*—"desire." At any rate, for purposes of translation, "gold-seeker" would seem to be near enough. Motteux also employs it.

11. Compare Chapter XIII (note 5) preceding and Part I, Chapter XX (note 3).

12. The name Trifaldín was formed by Cervantes after the Truffaldin of Boiardo's *Orlando Innamorato* and Ariosto's *Orlando Furioso.* *"Truffar"* in Italian, Spanish *"trufar,"* means "to cheat" or "hoax." (Rodríguez Marín)

13. Commentators are not agreed as to what country is meant. Possibly a mythical one.

14. Imitation of the Latin *Dixi* with which academic orations were terminated.

CHAPTER XXXVII

1. Play on the name Trifaldi and *"tres faldas"*—"three skirts."

2. See Chapter V preceding (note 6) and Part I, Chapter XLV (note 2).

3. A proverb.

4. A number of editors, including Fitzmaurice-Kelly and Hartzenbusch, have emended *"barbero"* to *"boticario"* —"apothecary," as more in consonance with the text; but "barber" may be due to ideational attraction, suggested by clipping and scissors.

5. A proverb.

6. Compare Chapters XVII (note 9) and XXXIII (note 23) preceding, where the proverb was quoted differently: "It is better to lose by a card too many than a card too few."

7. "A word to the wise," etc. There are a number of forms of the proverb in Latin and other languages: *"Dictum* (or *verbum) sapienti"*; *"Intelligenti pauca"*; in French: *"A bon entendeur salut"*; Portuguese: *"A bom entendedor, poucas palavras."*

CHAPTER XXXVIII

1. Variety of cloth worn by some religious orders and by women of the people in some provinces. (*Dictionary of the Academy,* cited by Rodríguez Marín.)

2. *"De delgado canequí"*—a cotton or calico cloth of East Indian origin. (*Dictionary of the Academy,* cited by Rodríguez Marín.)

3. Martos is a town in Andalusia, southwest of Jaen. It was noted for the size of the chickpeas produced in that region. (Rodríguez Marín)

4. *"Lobos,"* hence, Lobuna.

5. From *"zorro, zorra"*—"fox."

6. The meaning of this verbal slip becomes apparent later, when the identity of the "countess" is revealed. In Spanish the play is on the masculine and feminine forms, "*criado*" and "*criada*," and is not so obvious as in English.

7. "*Antes que salga a la placa de vuestros oydos, por no dezir orejas*"—literally, "before it emerges into the public place of your hearing, not to say ears."

8. Play on the Latin superlative ending, "-*issimus*." Fitzmaurice-Kelly, in his notes on Ormsby sees a satire on the "*culto*" literary style of the period.

9. The old commentators see this as originally the expression of a eunuch, who was "not so much interested in the ornamentation of his body as in that of his soul." Correas, in his dictionary of proverbs, *Vocabulario de Refranes*, goes so far as to identify "a certain gentleman, a young student, native of Avila, named Ortiz." (See Rodríguez Marín's note.)

10. See Chapter XXXVI preceding, note 13.

11. This imaginary island has been referred to in Part I, Chapter XVIII (Don Quixote's adventure with the sheep).

12. Southern point of the East Indian peninsula.

13. Lockhart (notes to Motteux) thinks it strange that Cervantes should employ as the name of his countess a term signifying a figure of speech; but the appellations of heroes and heroines in the romances of chivalry are fanciful in the extreme.

14. In connection with these accomplishments, see Chapter VI preceding.

15. This *redondilla* is translated from the Italian of Serafino Aquilano (Serafino of Aquila), whose poems were printed at Venice in 1502; there is a copy in the Bibliothèque Nationale in Paris. (Schevill) The original is itself an imitation of the Spanish verse form.

16. See *The Republic*, Books III and X.

17. Allusion to the ballad of that title.

18. It may be assumed that Cervantes is here criticizing, or satirizing, the affected character of much of the poetry of his age—which, it is to be remembered, was the age of Góngora and his followers. The "conceit" was the thing with poets of the time. Indeed, the literary manner known as "*conceptismo*" would appear to be rather deeply embedded in the Spanish temperament.

19. The author of the original form of this stanza (it is quoted a little differently here) was the Comendador Escrivá; it appeared in the *Cancionero General* of Hernando del Castillo in 1511. Edgar Allan Poe cites the stanza in his burlesque piece, "How to Write an Article for Blackwoods."

20. On this measure, see Chapter XXIV preceding, note 7.

21. Name applied to remote and uninhabited islands. Torquemada employs it in this sense in his *Jardín de Flores Curiosas.* (Rodríguez Marín) See Schevill's *Ovid and the Renaissance in Spain*, p. 176.

22. The Tibar is a river in Arabia; the phrase "*oro de tibar*" signifies superrefined gold. Panchaia, a part of Arabia Felix, is mentioned by Vergil, *Georgics*, II, 139: "*Totaque thuriferis Panchaia pinguis arenis.*" On the balsam, see Pliny's *Natural History*.

CHAPTER XXXIX

1. "Who, speaking of such things, could restrain his tears?" Vergil's *Aeneid*, II, 6–8. The passage reads, in full:

> *Quis talia fando*
> *Myrmidonum, Dolopumve, aut*
> *duri miles Ulixi*
> *Temperet a lacrimis?*

2. The idea of a particular adventure being reserved for a particular knight is frequently stressed. See Chapter XXII preceding, note 10.

3. "Civil" is probably to be taken here in the sense of "miserable." (Rodríguez Marín)

CHAPTER XL

1. "*Responde a las tacitas.*" A word is lacking in the original. I follow Clemencín in reading "*preguntas*"—"questions."

2. "*Apostaré yo que no tienen hazienda para pagar a quien las rape.*"

3. Ladies in Cervantes' time actually removed hair in this fashion. Rodríguez Marín quotes a recipe for "removing hair from the forehead and face or any other part," found in the manuscript section of the National Library at Madrid.

4. This also is true to life. (Rodríguez Marín)

5. There is an untranslatable word play here: *"oliscan a terceras, auiendo dexado de ser primas."* If one were to take *"terceras"* and *"primas"* in their literal signification, the rendering would be: "have a third-rate smell, having ceased to be first-rate." But *"prima"* also means "cousin," and *"terceira"* is a term for "procuress," while the verb *"oliscar,"* according to the *Dictionary of the Academy,* has the sense of "smell bad." Motteux: "their odor is somewhat third-rate." Ormsby's rendering does not seem to say anything: "most of them have a flavor of agents that have ceased to be principals."

6. *"Las caualgaduras que son de retorno."* According to Covarrubias, *"mulas de retorno"* are "mules that come back without a load." But the phrase appears to be equivalent to *"mulas de alquiler"*—"beasts for hire." (Schevill)

7. For the story of Pierres and Magalona, see Part I, Chapter XLIX, note 6.

8. "Clavileño," from *"clavo"*—"nail" or "spike" (*"clavija"* — "peg"), and *"leño"*—"log."

9. Compare the *"mediocritas aurea,"* or "golden mean," of Horace (*Odes,* II, x, 5–6). The concept is a common one with the Latin writers.

10. This proverb has occurred in Part I, Chapter XXII (note 4).

11. According to Correas (*Vocabulario de Refranes,* cited by Rodríguez Marín), the sense of this proverbial expression is "great loss," "damage," or "sorrow."

12. *"Si pensassen por ello ser reynas."* Motteux mistranslates: "though they were to be queens thereby." In connection with the use of the pronoun *vos,* see Part I, Chapter LI.

CHAPTER XLI

1. Compare the "savages" or "wild men" at Camacho's wedding; see Chapter XX preceding, note 10.

2. Motteux is in error here: "that he will not use anything but his sword," etc.

3. It has been previously stated that the peg was in the forehead. Ormsby notes that in the case of the magic horse in the *Arabian Nights* the guiding peg

was located in the neck; he also alludes to Chaucer's "Stede of bras"—"Ye moten trill a pin stont in his ere."

4. *"Ni . . . insula, ni insulos."* *"Insulos"* is here used jocosely for *"insulanos"*—"islanders." (Rodríguez Marín)

5. The first of these two proverbs has occurred in Part I, Chapters XXIX and XLVI; it recurs in Chapter LXXI following. The second has been quoted in Chapter IV (note 7) preceding, and appears again in Chapters L (note 16) and LXII (note 4) following.

6. This proverb recurs in Chapters LIII (note 8) and LIX (note 17) following. The Portuguese also have it.

7. See Chapter XXII preceding, note 14.

8. This is a proverb with us.

9. The word play here is untranslatable. Don Quixote says: *"eres hombre veridico,"* and Sancho, mistaking *"veridico"* for *"verdico (verdecico)"*—"greenish," replies: *"No soy verde, sino moreno"*—"I am not green but brownskinned." For once, at least, I have adopted a rendering from Motteux as the best available one: "I believe thou art trusty"—"I am not rusty but sunburnt." Ormsby: "Thou art veracious" —"I'm not voracious."

10. Don Quixote has his mythology somewhat confused. The Palladium was an image or statue of Pallas that, according to legend, fell from Heaven at Troy and during the Trojan war was borne off by Ulysses and Diomedes because the fate of the city depended on its possession.

11. *"Sendos paternostres y sendas auemarias."* Motteux: "with two Paternosters and two Ave-Marias."

12. Clemencín notes that Pierres, Magalona's husband, was king of Naples, not of France. Hartzenbusch makes the emendation: "queen of Naples."

13. Some editors (Benjumea and Fitzmaurice-Kelly) here read *"legión"* in place of *"región."* Rodríguez Marín thinks it may have been a slip of the tongue on Sancho's part.

14. Peralvillo was a place near Ciudad Real where the Holy Brotherhood executed its prisoners.

15. The licentiate Torralba was tried by the Inquisition in 1528 on charges of dealing in magic. His trial became famous in story and song.

16. Elsewhere (in his *Persiles y Sigismunda*) Cervantes states that the Torre di Nona is a prison, not a street. (Schevill)

17. Charles, Constable of Bourbon under Francis I, who went over to the side of the Emperor Charles V and aided in the defeat of the French monarch at Pavia in 1525. He died two years later, in the first assault on Rome by the imperial army. See the account in Benvenuto Cellini's *Autobiography*. For an account of Bourbon's treason, the reader may be referred to *Marguerite of Navarre*, by Samuel Putnam (New York: Coward-McCann, 1935).

18. "*Para cogerla, por mas que se remonte.*" Motteux is wrong: "to seize it more strongly from a height."

19. The great Portuguese navigator known to us as Magellan.

20. "*Por contento y satisfecho a toda su voluntad.*" The expression is one used by notaries, something like "for value received." Cervantes employs it in a legal document in connection with the sale of two of his comedies, under date of March 5, 1585. (Rodríguez Marín)

21. Reference is to the Pleiades.

22. The original contains a redundancy that does not go well in English: "*son como vnos alhelies y como vnas flores*—"are like so many gillyflowers and so many flowers." Rodríguez Marín points out that this double form of comparison is characteristic of the popular speech.

CHAPTER XLII

1. "*Tengo de prouar a que sabe el ser governador.*" Motteux misses the sense: "I wish to prove that I know how to be a governor."

2. Compare Sancho's letter to his wife in Chapter XXXVI preceding (see note 8 to that chapter).

3. The Christus was the cross preceding the alphabet in school primers, and "not to know the Christus" was an expression signifying complete ignorance.

4. Allusion to the school text, known as the *Disticha de Moribus*, etc., of Dionysius Cato (see Chapter XXXIII preceding and note 19).

5. Cervantes' phrase here, "*mar proceloso,*" has the flavor of classical Latinity. Compare St. Augustine (*De*

Civitate Dei, v, 22): "*procellossimum pelagus.*"

6. It was the custom of fathers to begin their exhortations to their sons (either by word of mouth or in writing) with this biblical maxim. (Rodríguez Marín) Compare Psalms 111:10, and Proverbs 1:7 and 9:10.

7. Allusion to the well-known fable of Aesop and Phaedrus.

8. The reference here is to the peacock's lordly tail; when it looks down at its feet, the bird is supposed to be ashamed. The image is a popular one with the Spanish mystics. (Rodríguez Marín)

9. This passage has proved confusing to editors and commentators. I have followed the reading suggested by Schevill.

10. Cervantes here alters an old saying that went: "*La sangre se hereda, y el vicio se pega*"—"Blood is inherited and vice sticks." Compare the remarks of Dorotea, in Part I, Chapter XXXVI: "true nobility consists in virtue."

11. Begging friars would refuse alms but suggest that they might be thrown into their hoods: "*No quiero, no quiero; pero echádmelo en la capilla, ó en el sombrero*"—"I do not want any, I do not want any; but throw it into my hood or into my hat." The text literally reads: "... or as the 'I don't want any' of your hood." Ormsby: "... or for the hood of thy 'won't have it.'" Motteux: "... as ... a cape to cover bribery."

CHAPTER XLIII

1. This was a comparison applied to black, unclean nails rather than to long ones. That such nails were common in Cervantes' time is indicated by the frequency with which writers employ the phrase "*negro de uña*"—"black of a nail," a phrase that occurs later in this chapter. (Rodríguez Marín)

2. See Suetonius's *Life of Julius Caesar*, Chapter 45.

3. The smell of garlic was regarded as the mark of the countryman. (Rodríguez Marín)

4. This is the second time that this significant statement has occurred. In Chapter XXVI preceding, it is put into the mouth of Master Pedro of the puppets.

5. The proverb runs: *"Come poco y cena mas poco."* Another version is: *"Come poco y cena mas,/Duerme en alto y vivirás"*—"Eat little [for the midday meal], have a little more for supper, sleep at the top of the house, and you will live [long]."

6. In his *Tesoro de la lengua castellana,* published four years before the second part of *Don Quixote* appeared, Covarrubias lists the words *"regoldar"*—"to belch," and *"regveldo (regüeldo)"*—"belching," but says nothing against their use though he condemns the practice for which they stand as "a discourtesy and boorishness, especially when done in front of persons to whom respect is to be shown." (Rodríguez Marín)

7. Cervantes clearly believed that the people were the makers of language. Compare Horace, *Ars Poetica,* 71–72: ". . . *si volet usus,/quem penes arbitrium est et ius et norma loquendi.*"

8. See Chapter xxx preceding (note 4).

9. See Chapter vii preceding (note 5).

10. See Chapter xxxi (note 8) and Chapter xxxvi (note 6) preceding.

11. A proverb; compare Chapter lviii (note 9) following.

12. Proverb: *"Castígame mi madre, y yo trómpogelas."*

13. See Chapter xxxiii preceding and note 3.

14. Don Quixote has uttered this proverb before, in conversing with the Princess Micomicona, Part I, Chapter xlvi.

15. This proverb is repeated in Chapter lxiv (note 2) following. The Italians also have it.

16. The proverb reads in full: "He whose father is a judge goes to court with assurance." The *Dictionary of the Academy* lists the phrase *"tener el padre alcalde"*—"have a judge for a father."

17. The proverb "Many go for wool and come back shorn" has been quoted in Chapter xiv (note 8) preceding, and in Part I, Chapter vii (note 4); it is repeated in Chapter lxvii (note 17) following.

18. *"A quien Dios quiere bien, la casa le sabe."* There is some doubt as to the meaning here, whether it is "his house knows it" or "the house is sweet to him"; and Hartzenbusch in place of

"casa" would read *"caza"*—"the chase," with the sense: "his hunting is successful." However, if one is to follow Covarrubias, the reading given above would seem to be the preferred one. (See Rodríguez Marín.)

19. One thinks of some of the "success" maxims of the American "self-made man."

20. Compare Chapter xx (note 13) preceding.

21. *"Del hombre arraigado,/No te verás vengado."*

22. This saying originally read *"al buen callar llaman santo"*—"To keep silent well is called holy." *"Santo,"* with the old spelling *"sancto,"* was transformed into *"Sancho"*; and Sancho Panza proceeds to apply it to himself. (See Rodríguez Marín.)

23. Rhyming proverb: *"Entre dos muelas cordales,/Nunca pongas tus pulgares."* Ormsby cites the Italian: *"Tra l'incudine e il martello,/Man non metta chi ha cervello"*—"Between the hammer and the anvil he does not put his hand who has a head."

24. Compare Part I, Chapter xx (note 13).

25. See Matthew 7:3–4 and Luke 6: 41–42.

26. In place of *"la muerta"*—"the dead woman," an older reading of the proverb has *"la Muerte"*—"Death." (Ormsby)

27. Rodríguez Marín notes a jocular variation: "The wise man knows more in his house than the fool in the house of another."

CHAPTER XLIV

1. Ormsby: "The original, bringing a charge of misinterpretation against its translator, is a confusion of ideas that it would not be easy to match."

2. In the text: *"la del Capitán cautiuo"*—"The Story of the Captive Captain"; but in Part I (see the title of Chapter xl) the tale is referred to as "The Captive's Story"—*"La Historia del Cautiuo."*

3. Cervantes is here alluding to those who had criticized him for the introduction of these stories in Part I, and in a manner is justifying their presence there. That he took these tales seriously is indicated by the remark concerning their craftsmanship in the next sentence.

In the introduction to his translation of *Don Quixote*, Ormsby observes: "He [Cervantes] had these stories ready written, and it seemed a good way of disposing of them; it is by no means unlikely that he mistrusted his own powers of extracting from Don Quixote and Sancho material enough to fill a book; but, above all, it is likely that he felt doubtful of his venture. It was an experiment in literature . . . he could not tell how it would be received; and it was well, therefore, to provide his readers with something of the sort they were used to, as a kind of insurance against total failure. The event did not justify his diffidence. The public . . . skimmed the tales hastily and impatiently, eager to return to the adventures of Don Quixote and Sancho; and the public has ever since done much the same."

4. In connection with these counsels that Don Quixote gives to Sancho, it has been pointed out that Cervantes is indebted to the *Galateo Español* of Gracián Dantisco, published at Barcelona in 1593. A copy of this work is preserved in the British Museum.

5. Professor Schevill thinks that the author may be indebted in this island episode to a passage in the second part of the *Amadis of Gaul*.

6. The phrase *"en justo y creyente"* —literally, "as a righteous man and a believer," has the idiomatic sense of "immediately," "at once." In English, in order to bring out the full flavor and meaning of the expression, it is necessary to give it a double translation.

7. The cap is the *montera*. "Watered camlet" (*chamelote de aguas*), according to Covarrubias, is camlet whose sheen is reminiscent of sea waves.

8. The *jineta*. The Spanish gentry had adopted this saddle from the Moors.

9. Or brand-new—*"flamantes."*

10. Two fanegas. The sense here is, of course, figurative.

11. The Spanish word *"soledad"* here has the sense of the Portuguese *"saudades,"* an expression that is untranslatable in its fullness of meaning, signifying as it does a vague nostalgic longing, half pleasant, half sad. In other words, it was more than mere aloneness that Don Quixote felt. (See Rodríguez Marín's note.)

12. Motteux expands as usual: "if they come into my chamber, they must fly in at the window."

13. I follow Schevill's reading in this passage.

14. The allusion is to the poet, Juan de Mena, known as "the Spanish Ennius." He was born at Cordova in 1512. In his poem "El Laberinto," the following *copla* (No. 227) occurs:

> O vida segura, la mansa pobreza,
> dadiva santa desagradecida!

"O the blessed life, meek poverty, holy gift unappreciated." Ormsby: "I suspect there is a touch of malice in the words 'the great Cordovan poet.' To hear any other poet but Góngora so described would have made a Góngorist foam at the mouth."

15. See I Corinthians 7:30-31, and II Corinthians 7:10.

16. Cervantes here employs a word, *"pantalia,"* the sense of which is unknown. I follow Schevill in taking it as referring to patches, since we are told in the next paragraph that "the patch on his shoe can be seen a league away."

17. There are numerous allusions to this custom in Spanish writers of the period. The toothpick was a mark of gentility. (See Rodríguez Marín.)

18. "Than a stain [*mancilla*] in the heart."

19. This is a burlesque ballad with assonant rhymes in the second and fourth verses. I have not attempted to imitate the assonance as Ormsby has.

20. Imitation of a passage in Vergil's *Aeneid*, iv, 366–67.

21. Inasmuch as these rivers meet, the effect is intended to be farcical. (Clemencín)

22. These gifts heighten the farcical tone of the piece: silver slippers, damask breeches, etc.

23. Reference to one of the crown jewels known as "La Sola," or the unmatchable one. Pellicer: "It was fished up in the Southern Sea, in 1515, and when the palace at Madrid burned, it was lost along with other most precious gems, in the year 1734."

24. This expression was too much for the editors Hartzenbusch and Benjumea, who emended *"los cabellos, como lirios"* to read *"los cabellos, como el oro"*—"golden locks."

25. *"Madama"* is a Gallicism, employed jocosely.

26. See the adventure in the inn, Part I, Chapter xxvi.

27. The expression *"cozido ó asado"* signifies "in whatever way it may be (*de cualquier manera que sea*)." (Rodríguez Marín)

CHAPTER XLV

1. *"Meneo dulce de las cantimploras."* Covarrubias defines the *"cantimplora"* as "a copper jug with a very long neck for cooling water or wine, by placing or burying the jug in the snow or moving it about in a vat containing snow." And Pellicer comments: "by the heat of the sun (which the author is here apostrophizing) thirst is excited in summer, which makes it necessary to shake the coolers." The effect is intended to be farcical.

2. Of Thymbra, or Thymbre, a city in Troas that contained a temple of Apollo; hence, Thymbraeus, "The Thymbraean," came to be one of the god's epithets.

3. Ormsby: "Hartzenbusch thinks that this outburst is a caricature of a passage in some poem of the day, and that such imitations are not uncommon in *Don Quixote*. If so, we cannot wonder at it that Cervantes was not beloved by the high-flying poets of the period."

4. See Aristotle's *Physics*, ii, 2.

5. Pellicer identifies Sancho's "island" as Alcalá del Ebro, on the peninsula formed by the bend of the Ebro River. Ormsby observes: "The critics have been much exercised by the identification of Baratria, which has always been with the cervantistas a favorite hunting ground for political allusions."

6. In modern Spanish, *"barato"* is an adjective meaning "cheap," but in old Spanish it is also a noun signifying "a jest." Like Ormsby, I adopt this latter reading. Motteux: "because the government cost him so cheap."

7. Compare Teresa Panza's remarks in Chapter v preceding.

8. The abuse of the title of "Don" by those without the worldly means to live up to it was frequently commented upon in Cervantes' day.

9. It was originally the custom to beg the pardon of those present when some unclean or vile subject was mentioned.

Later, such expressions of apology came to be interjected without rhyme or reason.

10. Rodríguez Marín believes that Cervantes is alluding sarcastically to the quality of clothing (and food as well) furnished to prisoners.

11. The case of the drover's purse comes later in the chapter. The author, apparently, had originally put it first and then changed the order but neglected to elide this reference. (Rodríguez Marín) Ormsby in his translation changes the order of the incidents.

12. *"Por hazerle plazer y buena obra"* —a notary's phrase.

13. This was the procedure known in civil law as *"juramento decisorio,"* when one party agreed to abide by what the other swore. (Rodríguez Marín)

14. The rod of justice held by Sancho. It was lowered in order that the witness might place his hand upon the cross of the rod and take his oath upon it.

15. Commentators are agreed that this episode is taken from the Life of St. Nicholas of Bari as inserted in the *Golden Legend* of Jacobo de Voragine, thirteenth-century Archbishop of Genoa.

16. See note 9 above.

17. Literally, "other cats in my beard."

18. This anecdote appeared in printed form as early as 1550, in the devotional work of Francisco de Osuna, *Norte de los Estados*, published at Burgos in that year. There are other traces of the story that go back as far as 1531. (See the note by Rodríguez Marín.)

CHAPTER XLVI

1. This paragraph is omitted by Ormsby in his translation on the ground that the lines "are repeated with some trifling changes in Chapter L, which is obviously their proper place, while they come in very awkwardly here."

2. *"Vihuela"* — not "lute" as in Motteux.

3. Another burlesque ballad with assonant rhymes. See Chapter xliv preceding, note 19.

4. The original has *región*, clearly a printer's error.

5. *"Azeyte de Aparicio"*—an ointment said to have been named after its in-

ventor, while others see "*Aparicio*" as a corruption of "*hyperico*." Hypericum, in any event, was one of the ingredients. Ormsby: "oil of John's wort."

CHAPTER XLVII

1. "*Como juego de maessecoral*"—literally, "like a trick of Master Coral." According to Covarrubias, the expression derives from the fact that charlatans and jugglers, stripping off their cloaks and jackets, were in the habit of performing in doublets of the hue of red coral.

2. Cervantes is here caricaturing a custom that actually existed in Spain: that of having physicians present at the tables of princes to advise what foods should be eaten and to see that royal appetites were restrained. This is attested by a document brought to light by the Society of Spanish Bibliophiles. (See Rodríguez Marín's note.)

3. Clemencín states that "physicians formerly applied this term to a certain subtle and balsamic humor which, so they believed, conferred vigor and elasticity upon the fibers that make up the bodily texture." Covarrubias cites Albertus Magnus: "*humidum est vitae qualitas et potentia.*"

4. Doctor Recio is not quoting Hippocrates. There was a prevalent saying to the effect: "*Omnis saturatio* [or: *indigestio*] *mala, panis autem pessima*"— "All surfeit [indigestion] is bad, but that of bread is the worst of all." The doctor substitutes "partridges" for "bread." (Schevill)

5. "*Manjar peliagudo*"—"*peliagudo*" also means "difficult" or "dangerous."

6. The olla-podrida is a highly seasoned dish of meat and vegetables cooked in a bulging, wide-mouthed pot or jar known as an *olla*. The term has been carried over into English.

7. "*Cañutillos de suplicaciones.*" This is the thin, rolled wafer known in modern Spanish as "*barquillo.*"

8. This is a village in La Mancha (not an imaginary one as some have supposed) that has disappeared from the modern maps. The doctor locates it with a fair degree of accuracy. The name literally means "Be off with you." The physician's name, "Agüero," means "omen," which accounts for Sancho's

play upon it: "Mal-Agüero" — "bad omen."

9. The University of Osuna has been referred to in Chapter 1 preceding. Founded in 1549, it existed until 1820. In its prime it was an important cultural center. (Schevill)

10. Literally, "I will place them upon my head"; compare Part I, Chapter VI and note 10.

11. See note 8 above.

12. The Biscayans were prominent in the royal service under Charles V and Philip II. They were noted for their ability and loyalty and many of them held secretarial posts. (See Rodríguez Marín's note.)

13. Literally, "newborn."

14. "*De muerte adminicula y pessima, como es la de la hambre.*" "*Adminicula*" is a word of Latin derivation that seems out of place in Sancho's mouth and that makes not too much sense here. Most translators, in various languages, e.g., Ormsby in English, have rendered it as "slow death." Tieck: "*ein schlimmster und schmählichster Tod.*" Motteux: "evil death."

15. Compare Chapter XXXIII preceding, and Part I, Chapter VI.

16. Compare Chapter XXXIV preceding: "it's the tripes that carry the feet, not the feet the tripes."

17. "*Alma de cántaro.*"

18. Compare the French peasant's expression "*bon comme le pain.*" For the European peasant in general, bread, which is the staple article of his daily diet, has a significance that is almost sacramental.

19. "*Perlesía*" is "paralysis" or "palsy." "*Perlerines*" connotes "*perlas*"—"pearls."

20. Rodríguez Marín cites the popular sayings: "*Quien feo ama, hermoso le parece*"—"An ugly person whom one loves appears beautiful"; and "*El escarabajo llama á sus hijos granos de oro*"— "The black beetle calls its young ones grains of gold."

21. This passage is somewhat obscure. Like Ormsby, I have followed the reading of Professor Juan Calderón (*Cervantes Vindicado*).

CHAPTER XLVIII

1. It was customary to attribute physical defects to "the hand of God." (Rodríguez Marín)

2. "*Cebolluda labradora.*" The adjective "*cebolluda*" means "bulbous," or having the characteristics of an onion ("cebolla"). Ormsby: "a clumsy country wench." Motteux: "a rank country wench."

3. A reminiscence of Garcilaso's Third Eclogue; see Chapter VIII preceding and note 1.

4. "*Antes os la dará roma que aguileña.*" Motteux has the sense: "he will rather tempt a man with an ugly object than with a beautiful one." According to Rodríguez Marín, this is the tag of a popular tale of Andalusia.

5. "*La que ofrecen essas reuerendissimas tocas.*" Motteux makes a bad blunder: "that which the most respectful pledges offer."

6. The distinction was a necessary one in Cervantes' time, the western part of the principality being known as Asturias de Oviedo, while the far eastern portion was called Asturias de Santillana.

7. "*Era montañés*"—that is, from the mountainous region north of Castile and León, known as the "Montaña."

8. The hand-borne litter or sedan chair.

9. Pellicer locates this gate, famous in its day, as having been at the point where the Calle de los Milaneses and the Calle de Santiago began. According to Rodríguez Marín, it was burned in 1582 and shortly afterward was completely torn down, but the name, as in the case of the well-known Puerta del Sol, remained attached to the spot.

10. That is, to the barber-surgeon.

11. Rodríguez Marín believes this episode is taken from the *Floresta Española* of Melchor de Santa Cruz.

12. "*Dança como el pensamiento, bayla como vna perdida.*" In order to render this passage clearly, it is necessary to expand somewhat upon the Spanish text. As Lockhart points out in his notes to Motteux, there is a distinction (which previous translators have ignored) between the *danza,* or courtly dance, and the *baile,* or dance of the people. Ormsby: "dances quick as thought, foots it like a gypsy." Motteux: "dances like a thought, trips like a mad one."

13. Literally, a "tradesman's ear"— "*orejas de mercader.*"

14. This comparison has occurred in Part I, Chapter XII. Ormsby, doubtless inadvertently, omits the clause.

15. This is the old medicine speaking, with its conception of bodily "humors," its practice of blood-letting, etc. Webster defines an issue as "a discharge, or flux, of blood"; and, "an artificial ulcer made, as by incision, to secure discharge of pus." The Spanish term is "*fuente*"—literally, "spring" or "fountain."

CHAPTER XLIX

1. In Cervantes' time there were a number of popular treatises in Spanish on Hippocrates and his aphorisms. (Schevill)

2. "Olla-podrida" literally means a "rotten pot." See Chapter XLVII preceding, note 6.

3. A proverb.

4. See Chapter XXXII (note 27) preceding and Chapter LI (note 10) following.

5. See Chapter XIV preceding, note 7.

6. The general sense of this expression is: there is disorder, or a disturbance, somewhere. (Schevill. See also the note by Rodríguez Marín.)

7. Compare Chapter XLIII preceding.

8. "*Tener respeto a la religion y a la honra de los religiosos.*" Ormsby: "to respect religion and honor its ministers," rather than Motteux's evasive rendering: ". . . and honor religious men." Rodríguez Marín observes that "we have here an excellent program of government, set forth in only four lines of type." Whether or not one agrees with this, there can be little doubt that Sancho is voicing Cervantes' own view of government and society.

9. This is a slip; Sancho had already supped.

10. The Spanish word "*barato*" used here refers to a gift made to onlookers or servants out of the common fund (our modern "kitty" in a poker game) or out of the winner's gains. (Rodríguez Marín)

11. Nothing is known of this particular sharper. (Schevill) For Cacus, see Prologue to Part I, note 8.

12. "*Auia de saber con quantas entraua la romana.*"

13. "*Barato*" again.

14. "*Algún oficial*"—"oficial" here has

the sense of *"artesano"*—"artisan" (Rodríguez Marín); not "under officers," as Motteux has it.

15. The garment here referred to is the *saltaembarca*, which appears to have been a sort of seaman's jacket open at the sides; compare the Italian *saltambarco*, a peasant's jacket. (See Rodríguez Marín's note.)

16. That is, with reeds employed as lances or javelins in a mock tournament.

17. Compare Chapter v (note 8) and Chapter xxxiv (note 5) preceding.

18. Rhyming proverb: *"La mujer y la gallina/Por andar se pierden aina."*

19. A proverb.

CHAPTER L

1. "Teresa Sancha" in the original.

2. The literal reading is "making public the Aranjuez of her issues [fountains]." The fountains of Aranjuez were famous ones. On issues, see Chapter xlviii preceding, note 15.

3. On the text at this point, see Chapter xlvi preceding, note 1.

4. Ormsby: "Argamasilla is the only village in La Mancha where such a sight could be seen; an arm of the Guadiana flows past it."

5. Tag of one of the old Cid ballads, *"A Calatrava la Vieja."* There are references in other ballads to this mode of punishment inflicted upon light women, and a number of later Spanish writers refer to it. (See Rodríguez Marín's note.)

6. For this expression, compare Chapters xxxii and xxxiv preceding.

7. A proverb.

8. Literally, "you have but to open your mouth, and your mouth will be the measure."

9. A similar expression has occurred in Chapter xlii preceding.

10. The Spanish dry measure, the "celemín," is roughly equivalent to a peck.

11. Aubrey Bell, in his *Cervantes* (pp. 12–13), cites this passage as an instance of what he elsewhere (p. 42) calls "the independent and happy poverty of the peasant."

12. *"Como vn pino de oro."* A "pino de oro" was a small ornament or trinket stuck in the hair. (Rodríguez Marín)

13. The Spanish word here is *"papahigo."* According to Covarrubias, the *papahigo* was a half-mask covering the face and used by travelers as a protection against the air and the cold. Duffield has: "travel with his face in a mask." Jarvis: "travel with a cape to his cap." Motteux is wrong: "go with an umbrella over his head"; and Ormsby is ambiguous: "take the road with a sunshade."

14. Literally, "a bad year and a bad month."

15. Rhyming proverb: *"Andeme yo caliente,/Y ríase la gente."*

16. This proverb has occurred before; see Chapters iv (note 7) and xli (note 5) preceding, and Chapter lxii (note 4) following.

17. Sound made in coaxing a dog; see Chapter xxxiii preceding, note 15.

18. Rhyming proverb: *"Vióse el perro/En bragas de cerro,/Y no conoció su compañero"*—"The dog saw himself in hempen breeches and did not know his companion." A variation is: "The countryman [*el villano*] saw himself . . . and was proud as proud could be [*y fiero que fiero*]." Compare the Italian: *"Villano nobilitato non conosce suo parentato"*—"A rustic made a noble does not know his [own] relatives."

19. "Augustine doubts [it]." An expression employed by casuists and students discussing dogmatic questions. (Rodríguez Marín)

20. On this proverb, see Chapter x preceding, note 1.

21. Master Pedro has quoted this biblical injunction, Chapter xxv preceding (see note 18).

22. *"Cual el tiempo, tal el tiento"*—"As the time [occasion], so the behavior." Compare the proverb quoted in Chapter iv (note 8) preceding: "Manners change when honors come."

23. Literally, "do penance with me." Compare Chapter iii (note 18) preceding.

CHAPTER LI

1. Literally, "a question"; *"vna pregunta"* here has the sense of a difficult problem. These subtleties enjoyed a great vogue in the schools of the day. (Schevill)

2. This paradox is a very old one, going back to the ancient Greek logicians. (Compare the story of the King of the Crocodiles, the Epimenides Paradox,

etc.) See the discussion by Bertrand Russell and Alfred North Whitehead, *Principia Mathematica*, Vol. I, p. 61. The Theory of Logical Types invented by Russell represents the first means of circumventing all the known paradoxes within a completely formalized logical system. Other methods have been proposed, and a good deal of investigation of this subject has been made by modern mathematical logicians. (For this note I am indebted to my son, Hilary Whitehall Putnam.)

3. Clemencín and Hartzenbusch recall that Sancho on two previous occasions (Chapters XXXVI and XLIII preceding) has stated that he did know how to sign his name. Hartzenbusch, always free with his emendations, accordingly would read: "*Si supiera mejor firmar*" —"If I knew how to sign my name better."

4. Motteux has the literal rendering: "I will snuff them away to air"—"*yo las despauilaré en el aire.*"

5. Compare Psalms 113:7: "He raiseth up the poor out of the dust, and lifteth the needy out of the dunghill."

6. There were a number of forms of this proverb: "Trim a bough and it will look like a young man," etc. (Rodríguez Marín)

7. See the well-known fable by Phaedrus.

8. Schevill notes that the germ of this thought is to be found in Plato himself (*Phaedo*, XL): "If you would follow my advice, think not of Socrates but of the truth." The saying is commonly attributed to Aristotle, being a free rendering of a passage in his *Nicomachean Ethics*. Compare the Spanish proverb: "*Amigo Pedro, amigo Juan, pero más amiga la verdad*"—"Pedro is a friend, Juan is a friend, but a greater friend is the truth."

9. The name, as has been seen, means "be off with you" or "take yourself off."

10. A variation on the proverb "Take no bribe and surrender no right." See Chapters XXXII (note 27) and XLIX (note 4) preceding.

11. As previously noted, the fanega (hanega) was roughly equivalent to 1.6 bushels.

12. Speaking of the dire poverty which the author of *Don Quixote* endured, Aubrey F. G. Bell (*Cervantes*, p. 43) observes: "He had suffered . . .

from the insults of market-women, whose fierce loquacity covered a falseness in their weights."

13. "*De haldas o de mangas*"—literally, "by skirts or sleeves"; the expression commonly means, in colloquial usage, "in one way or another," "by hook or crook," etc. Pellicer notes that the words have the secondary meaning of "fees and gifts." That is, the fees and gifts that Sancho would receive as governor.

14. Here we have something very like modern price-control and wage-fixing. Apparently there was a "servant problem" then, as now.

15. "*Coplas.*"

16. Lockhart (notes to Motteux) calls attention to an address to the throne by Herrera, physician to Philip III, on the state of mendicity in Madrid, with particular reference to the abuses perpetrated by the blind or false-blind.

CHAPTER LII

1. This proverb has occurred in Part I, Chapter XXII.

2. Allusion to amulets and other charms worn in the lists to bring victory. (Rodríguez Marín)

3. "*Su mal andante hija.*" Ormsby: "her unlucky daughter"; Motteux: "her forsaken daughter."

4. The expression in the original is "*bien desseada*"—"much longed for," a popular formula at the beginning of a letter, which the acolyte who serves as copyist employs even though Teresa previously had not known that the duchess existed. (Rodríguez Marín)

5. "*De meter este buen dia en mi casa*"—literally, "to take this fine day into my house." Allusion to the proverb: "When good luck comes along, open the door and let it in [take it into your house]." See Chapter IV preceding, and note 7.

6. This would mean that the loaf cost about five cents, and meat about ten cents the pound.

7. "*Y a Roma por todo*"—proverbial expression.

8. "*Vuestra pomposidad*"—used with farcical effect.

9. Professor Schevill notes that this son does not appear as a character in the story, though he is mentioned a number of times; he thinks it strange that Teresa

does not refer to the lad in her letter to his father.

10. Cervantes himself had had more than one unfortunate experience as a tax collector and was even imprisoned as a result of his muddled accounts.

11. A linen lace made with bobbins.

12. A little over three cents.

13. "A small municipality in the province of Teruel, diocese of Saragossa, now forgotten in the guidebooks and travel narratives." (Schevill, translated from the Spanish note.)

CHAPTER LIII

1. Compare the famous line of Shakespeare: "And thus the whirligig of time brings in his revenges." (*Twelfth Night*, Act V, Scene 1.)

2. The text here may not appear to make sense, but it is what Cervantes wrote: "*la primauera sigue al verano, el verano al estío, el estío al otoño, y el otoño al invierno, y el invierno a la primauera.*"

"*Verano*" and "*estío*" both mean "summer"; I have rendered the latter as "harvest season"—Ormsby has "fall." Needless to say, this passage has occasioned a lively controversy among editors and commentators. Some translators have followed the original while others have adopted the emendation of the Academy: "spring is followed by summer"—"*a la primavera sigue el verano,*" etc. Jarvis: "spring is succeeded by summer." Motteux: "spring precedes summer." Like Ormsby and Duffield, I have left the passage as it stands. Professor Schevill believes Cervantes wrote it in this manner for one of several possible reasons. I agree with Duffield that the author's intention was probably humorous, a desire to poke fun at the "Mohammedan philosopher," Cid Hamete.

3. Some editors, among them Hartzenbusch and Rodríguez Marín, emend the text to read "swifter than the wind." Schevill retains the reading found in the first edition.

4. Literally, "about reinforcements" —"*de socorros.*"

5. The term "*lanterna*" is here employed humorously for "*faro*"— "beacon." (Rodríguez Marín) The "north pole" is an allusion to the mariner's compass.

6. Scaling ladders.

7. "*Me hago agua*"—"I am turning to water."

8. This proverb has occurred in Chapter XLI (note 6) preceding, and occurs again in Chapter LIX (note 17) following.

9. The "*gazpacho*" is a kind of cold broth made with bread, olive oil, water, vinegar, garlic, onions, etc.

10. Compare Chapter VIII preceding, and Part I, Chapter XXV. The proverb occurs again in Chapters LV and LVII following.

11. Allusion to the proverb: "To her harm the ant grew wings." Compare Chapter XXXIII (note 6) preceding.

12. See Chapter XIX preceding and note 4.

13. The Portuguese also have this proverb. Motteux is wrong: "Let no one stretch his legs the more, however wide the sheet may be."

14. It was seven days, not ten, according to the statement made earlier in the chapter.

CHAPTER LIV

1. Play on the expression "*mentir por la barba*" (or, "*por mitad de la barba*") —"to lie in [by] one's beard."

2. There are many allusions to this custom by Spanish writers.

3. In the original, "*Guelte, Guelte.*"

4. The term "*franchones,*" "*franchotes,*" or "*franchutes*" was derogatorily applied to those foreigners who roamed over Spain as beggars, peddlers, knife-grinders, castrators of animals, etc. These words are not in the dictionary but are used by many good writers. "*Franchute*" (which might be rendered as "Frenchy") is still in common use. (See the note by Rodríguez Marín.)

5. Reference to the royal decrees which commanded the Moors in Spain, under penalty of death, to be ready to sail for Africa on three days' notice. The edict affecting the kingdoms of Granada, Murcia, and Andalusia and the city of Hornachos was issued on December 9, 1609; the one for Castile, Estremadura, and La Mancha was proclaimed on July 10, 1610; and others followed down through the year 1613. (Rodríguez Marín)

A standard account is given by Florencio Janer, in his *Condición Social de los Moriscos de España* (Madrid, 1857), pp. 72 ff. Cervantes further touches on the subject in his *novela,* the *Colloquy of the Dogs.* He himself appears, in general, to have been against the Moors, though this passage might be taken as indicating a certain sympathy with their sufferings. In the *novela* referred to, he is much more bitter. See the angry notes on the subject by Ormsby and by John Gibson Lockhart (notes to Motteux).

6. In modern Spanish the phrase *"en pelota"* commonly means "stark naked" (equivalent to *"en cueros"*), but here the meaning is "in nether garments"— *"ropas menores,"* or "in trousers and doublet"—*"en calzas y en jubón."* (Rodríguez Marín)

7. The stress on excitants to thirst reminds one of Rabelais.

8. *"Botas"*—small leather wine bags.

9. In the original: "the entrails."

10. Variation on a line from an old and well-known ballad, "Mira Nero de Tarpeya" (Durán's *Romancero General,* No. 571): *"Y él de nada se dolía."*

11. *"Cuando a Roma fueres,/Haz como vieres."* Compare our version: "When in Rome, do as the Romans do."

12. *"Espanol y tudesqui tuto vno: bon compaño"*—"a mixture of bad Italian and Spanish." On the expression *"bon compaño,"* see Chapter xxv preceding and note 10.

13. *"Bon compaño, jura Di."*

14. The excuse for the royal decrees banishing the Moriscos was the alleged discovery of a conspiracy between the Moors of the peninsula and the Barbary corsairs to restore the Moorish monarchy in Spain.

15. A proverb: "The good is not known until it is lost."

16. This is historically accurate. Many of the Moors did come back, and it was necessary to repeat the expulsion order.

17. A contrast to the Germany we have come to know in modern times!

18. *"Fino moro."* Ormsby: "a true Moor." Motteux: "a rank Moor."

19. The Moors at first were permitted to take a certain amount of property with them.

20. As Schevill observes, this expression sounds out of place in Sancho's mouth, but he may have got it from Don Quixote, who in turn found it in the books of chivalry. In gypsy jargon a sagittarius was one who was whipped through the streets.

21. A variation of this proverb is: "The devil takes the well-gotten gain, and takes the ill-gotten and its owner too."

CHAPTER LV

1. *"A poco mas de tres estados."* Covarrubias defines the estado as "a certain measure, of the height of a man. . . . The depth of wells or other deep places is measured by estados." As a measure of length, the estado is 1.85 yards. "Fathom" is the nearest equivalent in English.

2. Phrase supplied by the translator.

3. This is yet another of those expressions that sound a little out of place in Sancho's mouth, but he undoubtedly got it from Don Quixote.

4. For this bit of humor, compare Part I, Chapter xxx. Cervantes is here imitating Boiardo in the *Orlando Innamorato.*

5. But Sancho was supposed to have given his bread and cheese to the pilgrims. "If Cervantes, as some critics maintain, had written the *Quixote* slowly and carefully, would he not have discovered in it such contradictions as this?" (Rodríguez Marín)

6. Compare Chapter xiii (note 3) preceding: "for troubles are less where there is bread."

7. This, of course, is humorous, but Clemencín suspects it is an error.

8. Covarrubias: "A very ancient edifice on the banks of the River Tagus, near Toledo. . . . Galiana was a Moorish princess. . . . Hence, a proverbial expression, applied to those who are not content with the quarters assigned them: *to want Galiana's palace."*

9. Another reading of this proverb is: "Welcome, but not so if you come alone." (In the original, a matter of punctuation.)

10. *"¡Voto a tal!"*

11. Literally, "as if I had given birth to it."

12. Allusion to an old Ballad, "Doña Urraca, aquesa infanta" (Durán's *Romancero General,* No. 807).

13. See Chapter xxxii preceding, note 27.

14. A proverb with the Spaniards as with us.

15. Teresa has quoted this proverb, Chapter L (note 22) preceding.

16. The Portuguese add: "nor eat of this bread."

17. See Part I, Chapter XXV (note 5). This proverb also occurs in Part II, Chapter X (note 2) and again in Chapters LXV (note 3) and LXXIII (note 10).

18. What of Sancho's "Constitutions" (see Chapter LI preceding)?

19. Reference to a children's game. There is some uncertainty as to how it was played. Rodríguez Marín believes it is the modern game of "four corners" (cuatro esquinas, or cuatro cantillos).

CHAPTER LVI

1. Allusion to the Council of Trent (ended 1563), statute of the twenty-fifth session, canon 19, directed against knightly dueling of this sort.

2. The arroba, as has been seen, was 25.6 pounds.

3. This repetition of what has been said earlier in the chapter (such repetitions, as the reader will have noted, are by no means infrequent in Cervantes) might possibly be taken by the captious as further evidence of careless or hasty writing.

4. See Chapter VI preceding, note 1.

5. The question arises: how could the lackey have seen the young woman's face when she was so heavily veiled?

6. A proverb.

CHAPTER LVII

1. For the story of Bireno and his mistress, Olimpia, whom he deserted on a desert island, see Cantos IX and X of the Orlando Furioso (compare the legend of Theseus and Ariadne). It also forms the subject of a popular ballad given in Durán's Romancero General.

2. A proverb. Literally, "the just often pay for sinners in my country."

3. Literally, "from Seville to Marchena, from Granada to Loja, from London to England." Marchena is in the province of Seville and Loja in the province of Granada. I have here taken a hint from Ormsby, who has "from Seville to Cadiz."

4. On this expression, see Chapter XXXIII preceding, note 3.

CHAPTER LVIII

1. Compare the verse quoted in the Prologue to Part I: "Non bene pro toto libertas venditur auro." As Rodríguez Marín notes, this was a favorite theme with Spanish poets of the Golden Age.

2. Having himself been a prisoner of the Moors in Algiers and in jail on a number of occasions, Cervantes could speak from experience.

3. Clemencín: "A beautiful thought eloquently expressed, and how appropriate to Cervantes' own unfortunate, poverty-stricken situation!"

4. A "retablo" is the carved work at the back of an altar.

5. This was the customary way of transporting images from one parish to another. (Rodríguez Marín)

6. This application of "Don" to the name of a saint was not original with Cervantes. Rodríguez Marín calls attention to a twelfth-century poem in which the expression "Don Iesuchristo" (Don Jesus Christ) occurs.

7. St. George, according to legend, slew the dragon to save the king's daughter.

8. "Fué mas liberal que valiente"— literally, "more liberal than valiant." I have followed Rodríguez Marín in taking this phrase as equivalent to "aún más liberal"—"even more liberal." Ormsby: "generous rather than valiant." Jarvis and Motteux: "more liberal than valiant."

9. Compare Chapter XLIII (note 11) preceding.

10. San Diego, or Santiago, is St. James (San Jaime, San Jacobo), the patron saint of Spain.

11. See II Corinthians 12:2–4.

12. Quotation from Matthew 11:12.

13. "Adobandoseme el juyzio." Is this a flash of insight with regard to the state of his mental faculties such as Don Quixote appears to have on several occasions?

14. A popular expression by way of wishing one success in an undertaking. (Rodríguez Marín)

15. This superstition is said to have been prevalent in the Mendoza family. Quevedo refers to it in his Book of All Things (Libro de Todas las Cosas): "If you spill the salt and . . . are (a Mendoza), rise from the table without eating . . . and that way the omen with respect to the salt will be fulfilled; for a misfortune always follows, and it is a misfortune not to eat." Such supersti-

tions, according to Covarrubias, ran in families.

16. This incident, apocryphal or not, is related in Suetonius's *Life of Julius Caesar*, which had appeared in Spanish translation in 1596. See also Livy, I, 56, and Herodotus, VI.

17. Word supplied by the translator to make the sense clearer.

18. "*¡Santiago, y cierra Espana!*" See Chapter IV (note 6) preceding. The sense is "close in upon them" or "attack."

19. The commentators note that Don Quixote does not really answer Sancho's question; and, indeed, it is rather strange that Sancho should ask it, seeing that he himself, in a preceding chapter (IV), has quoted this battle cry as if he understood it very well.

20. Allusion to the tradition that the Moors (Arabs) are descended from Hagar (see the Old Testament).

21. The author appears to be particularly fond of this passage from Horace (*Odes*, I, iv, 13–14), as he makes use of it a number of times, beginning with the Prologue to Part I.

22. "*Sayas.*"

23. According to Rodríguez Marín, the author means to say that the jackets were of brocade and the skirts (*sayas*) of gold-embroidered tabby. This "*tabí de oro*" was a more expensive material than plain tabby; at Seville, in 1627, a little later than when Cervantes wrote, a yard was worth forty-three reales.

24. Ormsby observes: "Hartzenbusch protests that Cervantes can never have written this; but his pen does undoubtedly sometimes indulge in a flourish of the kind." The fact is, the image of the sun halting in its course is taken from a popular love song. (Rodríguez Marín)

25. The first edition has *Anteón* (Antaeus). Authors of the time commonly confused the two names.

26. "*He oido yo dezir de su valor y de sus gracias lo mismo que tu me has dicho.*" Most translators have taken the "*gracias*" as referring to Don Quixote; but a couple of paragraphs above the author has employed the same word with reference to Sancho ("drolleries"). It would seem to be a case of lack of clarity in the writing. Ormsby makes the distinction that I do: "the valor of the one and the drolleries of the other."

27. The Jarama River and the Tagus meet at Aranjuez.

28. These tame oxen (*cabestros*) were employed in driving the bulls from pasture.

29. That is, in a bull fight. Literally, "were to be run."

30. A proverb.

CHAPTER LIX

1. The title is somewhat freely rendered.

2. "*Condumio.*" According to Covarrubias, an old word used by the peasantry to denote food (meat) prepared to be eaten with bread. Ormsby: "the prog"; Jarvis and Motteux: "his sauce."

3. "*A que su señor hiziesse la salua.*" Allusion to the custom formerly observed in the houses of the nobility and other important personages, of having the butler ("*maestresala*"—"*pregustator*") taste the food before his master and the rest of the company did. Here it is Don Quixote who is supposed to be acting as Sancho's "taster."

4. That is, he opened it only to eat, not to talk.

5. Rhyming proverb: "*Muera Marta, y muera harta.*"

6. A proverb: "*Hasta la muerte todo es vida.*"

7. The original has "*y dexesse de pedir gallinas*"—"and don't be asking for hens." Rodríguez Marín is convinced this is an erratum; I follow his emendation: "*gullurías.*"

8. Don Quixote and Sancho were supposed to have gone to their room before the conversation with the innkeeper occurred.

9. Allusion to the spurious continuation of Part I by Fernández de Avellaneda. Rodríguez Marín: "Cervantes was thinking of writing this chapter when there came to hand the *Second Volume of the Ingenious Gentleman, Don Quixote de la Mancha,* supposedly written by Alonso Fernández de Avellaneda and published at Tarragona, in 1614." See the Prologue to Part II.

10. Ormsby: "Avellaneda in chap. II of his continuation makes Aldonza Lorenzo write to Don Quixote threatening him with a beating for calling her Princess and Dulcinea, and Don Quixote, stung by her ingratitude, resolves to look out for another mistress."

11. "*Guardarla con suavidad y sin ha-zerse fuerça alguna.*" Ormsby finds it "difficult to make sense" of this passage. He accordingly adopts Hartzenbusch's suggested emendation: "*su vida*" for "*suavidad*" and "*tuerto*" for "*fuerça.*" Ormsby renders: "his profession to maintain the same with his life and never wrong it." Schevill and Rodríguez Marín make no comment, and indeed it seems that such a translation as I have given would solve the problem.

12. Compare Chapters XIV (note 5), XXX (note 3), and XXXIV (note 8) preceding, and Chapter LXXI (note 10) following.

13. See the Prologue to Part II. The author of the spurious *Don Quixote*, it will be remembered, had taunted Cervantes with being an old man, with one hand missing, etc.

14. Schevill is puzzled by this statement. "To what is Cervantes referring?" he asks. "How are we to judge the style of an author from a text that is poorly printed and, certainly, marred by the usual proportion of printer's errors?" (From the Spanish note.)

15. It was Cervantes himself who, in Part I, Chapter VII, called Sancho's wife Mari Gutiérrez; a few lines above, in the same chapter, he had referred to her as Juana Gutiérrez, and in Part I, Chapter LII, she is Juana Panza.

16. In this chapter the author clearly reveals his own conception of Sancho's character, and we can see the respect that he had for the squire and the peasant type in general. This is a point that Aubrey F. G. Bell stresses throughout in his *Cervantes.* Sancho is neither a glutton nor a drunkard nor a vulgar buffoon; he is "*gracioso*"—"droll," which is something quite different. This is one of the chief sins of Motteux and certain other English language translators who would make him out to be a cockney clown.

17. For the second of these two proverbs, see Chapters XLI (note 6) and LIII (note 8) preceding.

18. "*Con mero mixto imperio.*" A juridical formula, according to Covarrubias.

19. "*Hecho equis*"—that is, with his legs forming the letter X.

20. "*El autor . . . [no] quiere que no comamos buenas migas juntos.*" A free translation.

21. Ormsby: "In chapter XI Avellaneda gives an account of Don Quixote's tilting at the ring in the Coso at Saragossa, and so prolix and encumbered with details that his admirer, M. Germond de Lavigne, was forced to leave it out." The reference is to De Lavigne's French translation (Paris, 1853).

CHAPTER LX

1. Don Quixote forgets that the lashes must be voluntarily inflicted, a fact of which Sancho later reminds him.

2. A point was a tie or string with an aglet, used in the sixteenth and seventeenth centuries to join parts of the costume, such as doublet and hose.

3. "*Se abraçó con el a braço partido.*" There has been some discussion as to the meaning of the expression "*a braço [brazo] partido,*" but, according to the *Dictionary of the Academy,* it has reference to a struggle "with the arms alone, without the use of weapons."

4. Reminiscence of an old historical ballad, "Los fieros cuerpos revueltos" (Durán, *Romancero General,* No. 978). The allusion is to the assassination of Peter the Cruel by his brother, Henry of Trastamara, aided by the latter's page, Bertrand du Guesclin (Beltrán Duguesclin), who as he tripped the monarch up exclaimed, "*Ni quito ni pongo rey; pero ayudo a mi senor*"—"I neither overthrow nor set up a king, but am aiding my lord."

5. Verses from another ballad, "A cazar va Don Rodrigo" (Durán, op. cit., No. 691).

6. "*Por vida de sus pensamientos.*" Ormsby and Motteux render this literally: "by the life of his thoughts." Jarvis: "by the life of his best thoughts."

7. Clemencín remarks that this is a commentary on the state of law and order in the province of Catalonia in that period.

8. The "petronel" was a fifteenth-century portable firearm resembling a large-caliber carbine.

9. The first edition has "Osiris," which, Hartzenbusch notes, is an error or slip of the pen on the author's part; but, as Rodríguez Marín remarks, the slip may be Roque Guinart's and not Cervantes'. Ormsby: "The Busiris who

with Memphian chivalry and perfidious hate pursued the sojourners of Goshen." ⸨See Milton's *Paradise Lost*, I, 307.)

10. Roque Guinart (properly, Roca Guinarda) was a Catalan bandit who achieved considerable notoriety about the time Cervantes wrote. By 1610 he ñad united under his command some two hundred followers. The portrait of him given here appears to be a fairly faithful one. "Despite his evil way of life, he won the warm sympathy of all Spain." (Rodríguez Marín) For an authoritative work on the subject, the special student may be referred to *Perot Roca Guinarda, Historia d'aquest bandoler*, by Lluis Maria Soler y Terol (Manresa, 1909).

11. The "*saltaembarca*"; see Chapter XLIX preceding and note 15.

12. The first edition has "*los muchos de don Vicente.*" I follow the reading of a number of editors: "*deudos*"—"kinsmen," which agrees with the reference later in the chapter to Don Vicente's "*parientes*"—"relatives."

13. The original reads "*para que, zelosa, me quitasses la vida, la qual pues la dexo en tus manos y en tus braços, tengo mi suerte por venturosa.*" Clemencín and other editors have found difficulty in making sense of the passage, due, as Rodríguez Marín observes, to an error in punctuation. Ormsby omits the clause, "*la qual,*" etc. Motteux has the correct translation.

14. "*Gente rústica y desbaratada.*"

15. The "harquebus" was a firearm having a matchlock operated by a trigger and supported for firing by a hook.

16. "*Lladres*"—Catalan for "thieves."

17. Proverb: "*El abad de lo que canta yanta.*" Portuguese: "*Abbade donde canta, dahi janta*"—"Where the abbot sings, there he dines." Compare our "sing for your supper."

18. "*Frade.*"

19. Hartzenbusch points out that this ought to be the day of the beheading of John the Baptist, or August 29, since, according to the dates of the letters written at the duke's place, the feast of the saint's nativity, June 24, was already past.

20. The Niarros and the Cadells were two rival bands; Roque belonged to the former.

CHAPTER LXI

1. The first edition has "*todos*"—"all." Hartzenbusch and some other editors read "*casi todos*"—"nearly all," a reading which Rodríguez Marín feels it is necessary to adopt. Schevill retains "*todos.*"

2. According to the work on Roca Guinarda by Soler y Terol (see note 10 to the preceding chapter), one of these proclamations offered a reward of a thousand pounds in the coin of Barcelona, to be paid out of the royal treasury, along with other inducements, for the capture of the bandit dead or alive.

3. "*Lililies*"—on this war cry, see Chapter XXXIV preceding, note 12.

4. "*Donde mas largamente se contiene*"—a legal phrase used in certain oaths.

CHAPTER LXII

1. A proverb.

2. Rodríguez Marín: "An appetizing dish consisting of breast of fowl, especially of hen, with rice flour, milk, and sugar, the recipe for which the reader will find in the *Libro del arte de cozina* of Diego Granado, Madrid, 1599. . . . The name was applied to this dish as far back as 1420."

3. Allusion to a passage in Chapter XII of the spurious *Don Quixote*.

4. This proverb has occurred in Chapters IV (note 7), XLI (note 5), and L (note 16) preceding.

5. A clear expression of Cervantes' attitude toward Sancho and his resentment of the manner in which Avellaneda treats the squire.

6. "There are many stories in European folklore having to do with talking heads; the eminent Roger Bacon, in the thirteenth century, who was looked upon as a necromancer, fashioned a similar one." (Schevill, from the Spanish note.) "The first *brazen head* on record is that famous one possessed by Albertus Magnus, which was broken into a thousand shivers by his disciple Thomas Aquinas, whose self-possession entirely deserted him on hearing the sayings of the head. The great Albert exclaimed on beholding the accident, '*Periit opus triginta annorum.*' Beckman, in his *History of Inventions*, says that this is all that has been recorded con-

cerning the first and most famous of all the brazen heads. Friar Bacon, in our own country, and the Marquess de Villena, in Spain, passed for having in their possession similar marvels of unholy mechanism. But I believe the *Invisible Girl*, that some years ago made the tour of all the capitals of Europe, has at last revealed all the mystery of all the brazen heads that ever existed; and Cervantes, in the text, seems to have anticipated all the capabilities of such a device." (Lockhart, notes to Motteux.)

See the play by Robert Greene: *The Honorable History of Friar Bacon and Friar Bungay* (1592). The special student will find a number of research references in Schevill.

7. "Michael Scott; it is not known where he was born nor where he died (around 1232); he studied at Paris and Oxford, learned Arabic in Toledo, and translated various texts and commentaries on Aristotle from the Arabic into the Latin; among his own books are: *De sole et luna; De chiromantia;* and *De physiognomia et de hominis procreatione;* in Dante's *Inferno*, xx, 115–17, he appears among the magicians." (Schevill, from the Spanish note.)

The lines from Dante to which Schevill refers are the following:

Quell'altro che ne' fianchi è così poco
Michele Scotto fu, che veramente,
Delle magiche frode, seppe il gioco.

The other, who looks about the flanks so slim,
Was Michael Scott; and verily he knew
The circle of magic and its frauds to limn.

(Lawrence Binyon translation.)
See J. W. Brown, *Life and Legend of Michael Scott* (Edinburgh, 1897); and C. H. Haskins, *Studies in the History of Medical Science* (Cambridge: Harvard University Press, 1924). Other commentators, however, including Bowle and Pellicer, have denied that the Escotillo mentioned by Cervantes is the thirteenth-century Michael Scott. Ormsby adopts this latter view, to the effect that the individual in question is one Michele Escoto, or Escotillo, a native of Parma, who as an astrologer and magician enjoyed a great reputation in the Low Countries in the time of Alexander Farnese. Rodríguez Marín dismisses the subject with: "The annotators of *Don Quixote* cite various astrologers and sorcerers named *Escoto*. I shall not pause here to conjecture as to which of them Cervantes must be referring." (Clasicos Castellanos edition of the *Don Quixote,* edited by Rodríguez Marín, Vol. VIII, p. 139.)

8. "*Guardó rumbos*": "*rumbos*" here has the sense of "*rombos*," or geometrical figures, as the latter term is employed by Merlin in his poetic speech in Chapter xxxv preceding. (Rodríguez Marín) Ormsby, accordingly, is in error: "observed the points of the compass."

9. "*Sacaron a passear.*" Ormsby: "took Don Quixote out for a stroll." But one does not speak of a stroll on horseback. A little further on Ormsby renders "*passeo*" more properly as "excursion."

10. Clemencín raises the question as to why these words are put into the mouth of a Castilian, and believes that the answer is "because Don Quixote's experiences must have been better known in Castile than in other regions"; but Rodríguez Marín thinks the author means to emphasize that "it was not a Catalan but a Castilian who spoke thus to Don Quixote, a son of the people."

11. The original has "on all subjects" —"*en todas las cosas.*"

12. Ormsby again has "stroll."

13. "Flee, ye adversaries!" A formula of the Church in exorcising evil spirits.

14. In the original: "Do you think that all brave men are *danzadores* and that all knights-errant are *bailarines?*" The distinction here, which cannot be brought out in English without a cumbersome circumlocution, is one that has been previously noted between the *danza,* or formal, stately dance of the nobility, and the *baile,* or dance of the people.

15. Reference to the *zapateado;* see Chapter xix preceding and note 3. Jarvis and Motteux: "shoe-jig"; Ormsby: "shoe-fling."

16. For this expression, see Chapter xxxii preceding and note 26. The sense is "agile as a gerfalcon."

17. "*En lo del dançar no doy puntada*": reference to the *danza* again.

18. This was an expression employed in folk tales.

19. Rodríguez Marín cites the proverb: "*El amor y la fe en las obras se ve*"—"Love and faith are shown by their works."

20. Proverbial expression.

21. Perogrullo was a legendary character who prophesied the obvious. Samples of his oracular(?) utterances are to be found in the collection known as *Cantos populares españoles:* "If you would have the ladies come after you, when you go walking place yourself in front of them." Another specimen: "It will be a sign, if you talk, that you have a tongue; and if you have molars, it will show you are not without them; and it is certain that if you go to the mirror you will see your face," etc. (Cited by Rodríguez Marín.)

22. Properly, the translator.

23. In the text: "*Le Bagatele.*" It is not known whether any Italian work with this title ever existed or not. Professor Schevill states that he has gone through any number of Italian and Spanish works without coming upon any trace of *Le Bagatelle.* In Cervantes' time there were numerous volumes of this sort variously labeled as collections of pleasantries, novels, tales, fables, entertaining deeds and sayings, jests, apothegms, miscellanies, etc. Schevill further draws attention to the fact that this is an imaginary printing shop and that the Barcelona editions of the spurious *Don Quixote* and of the work entitled *Light of the Soul,* referred to later on, are nonexistent ones.

24. That is, "trifles."

25. The text reads: "*me precio de cantar*"—"I pride myself on being able to sing," etc. That Cervantes owed a considerable debt to the *Orlando Furioso* as to other works that belong to the literature of chivalry, no reader of the *Don Quixote* can fail to observe; and according to Aubrey F. G. Bell (*Cervantes,* p. 19), during his five years' residence in Italy he had "learned sufficient Italian to read the poems of Ariosto and Tasso in the original." His recollections of the language, however, to employ Professor Schevill's word, are marked by a certain "nebulousness" ("*nebulosidad*") and would appear to be auditory rather than visual, as is indicated by his habit of transliterating and Hispanicizing Italian vocables: thus, "*compagno*" becomes "*compaño*," "*pignatta*" becomes "*piñata*," "*piace*" is rendered as "*piache,*" etc.

26. *Piñata* in the text. An earthenware cooking-pot.

27. Stew-pot.

28. "*Piace (place)*" is "pleases"; "*più (más)*" is "more"; "*su (arriba)*" is "up"; and "*giù (abajo)*" is "down."

29. This comparison had been made use of by Diego de Mendoza, author of *Lazarillo de Tormes,* and by Luis Zapata in the preface to his translation of Horace's *Ars Poetica,* published in 1591. Compare Cervantes' observations on the translation of poetry, in Part I, Chapter VI. Alexander Pope in one of his letters approves the idea.

30. The *Pastor Fido* is the work of Battista Guarini (Venice, 1590); the Spanish translation by Cristóbal Suárez de Figueroa was first published at Naples in 1602, and in a differing form was printed again at Valencia in 1609. Jáuregui's version of Torquato Tasso's *Aminta* was published at Rome in 1607; a second edition appeared at Seville in 1618.

31. Clemencín remarks that this is bad arithmetic. A thousand ducats is a sum equivalent to eleven thousand reales; at six reales the copy the returns on an edition of two thousand would amount to twelve thousand reales; but this leaves only a thousand reales—a very small sum—for the cost of paper, printing, and all other expenses.

32. Lockhart observes: "It is amusing to see, in many passages of his works, how completely Cervantes understood the tricks of the booksellers of his time." As Clemencín notes, these remarks would be out of place in the mouth of a gentleman of Argamasilla; it is obviously Cervantes himself who is speaking. The author also touches on the subject in his novels, *The Licentiate Vidriera* and *Persiles and Sigismunda.*

33. "*Si el libro es un poco abieso.*" One thinks here of the American Thoreau carrying home the unsold copies of his first book, *A Week on the Concord and Merrimack Rivers,* and remarking that he now had a library of nine hundred books, some seven hundred of which he himself had written!

34. *"No vale vn quatrín."*

35. Work by the Dominican friar, Felipe de Meneses, first published at Seville in 1555; there were a number of later editions, but none is known to have been printed at Barcelona. The title read: *Light of the Christian Soul against Blindness and Ignorance,* etc.

36. *"Son muchos los pecadores que se vsan."* Motteux mistranslates: "for sinners that use them are many."

37. *"Un tal vezino de Tordesillas"*—literally, "a certain neighbor." The title-page of Avellaneda's work identified him as *"natural de la villa de Tordesillas"*—"a native. . . ."* The correct title of Avellaneda's work is *The Ingenious Gentleman, Don Quixote de la Mancha, Which contains his third sally and is the fifth part of his adventures* (Tarragona, 1614). See the English translations by Captain John Stevens (London, 1705) and William Yardley (London, 1784).

"It was hardly judicious in Cervantes," says Ormsby, "to credit his enemy with a second edition, but he seems to lose his head whenever he thinks of Avellaneda and his insults; and from this on he apparently thinks of little else. From Chapter LIX to the end, indeed, there is a decided falling off. The story is at once hurried and spun out, and in the episodes of Claudia and Ana Felix he drops into the tawdry style of the novels in the First Part. It is only when he touches earth in Sancho Panza that he recovers anything like his old vigor."

38. It was the custom to kill pigs on St. Martin's Day. The proverb ran: *"A cada puerco le llega su San Martín"*—"To every pig comes its Martinmas."

39. A statement of the basic spirit of realism that animates Cervantes' art.

40. Sancho had viewed the galleys when he and his master were first set down on the beach.

41. The *"cuatralbo"* was an officer in command of four galleys.

CHAPTER LXIII

1. Compare Chapter x preceding, where, when Sancho returns from his supposed interview with Dulcinea, Don Quixote says to him, "What is it, Sancho, my friend? Am I to be able to mark this day with a white stone or a black one?"

2. *"Tiempo y señal que nos muestra que en el se encierra,"* etc. Hartzenbusch emends to read: *"tipo y señal";* which Ormsby, who adopts his reading, renders as "pattern and image." I have followed Rodríguez Marín, who sees *"tiempo"* as referring to the day or occasion and *"señal"* to the white stone.

3. *"Que la chusma hiziesse fueraopa."* According to the *Dictionary of the Academy, "Ropa afuera!"*—"Clothes off!"—was an expression employed to advise the rowers to make ready. According to Covarrubias, it was used when they had to row lustily (*"con hígado"*).

4. Compare Sancho's use of this expression in Part I, Chapter XVII; it has occurred a number of times.

5. The citadel of Barcelona.

6. Rodríguez Marín points out that this concept is not Cervantes' own but Aristotle's.

7. *"Por dos tios mios."* Previous translators have rendered as "two uncles of mine"; but Rodríguez Marín, whom I have followed, states that this must refer to Juan Tiopieyo and his wife; for, as Clemencín notes, Ricote, in the story that he tells in Chapter LIV preceding, mentions only one uncle.

8. In Chapter LIV preceding, this young man is referred to as Don Pedro Gregorio; and in this present chapter, it will be noted, he is variously called Don Gaspar Gregorio, Don Gregorio, and Don Gaspar. Rodríguez Marín thinks this may possibly be a double name, like Juan José, Pedro Antonio, etc., and considers this "a fresh indication of the carelessness with which Cervantes wrote."

9. The cruzado was an old Castilian coin of gold, silver, or copper, so called because it had a cross on the obverse side. There was also a Portuguese cruzado.

10. Clemencín observes that such a remark is scarcely becoming in the mouth of a damsel of twenty. Rodríguez Marín: "And the same may be said of the words a few lines below: 'I spoke to Don Gaspar and reminded him of the danger that lay in his appearing as a man.'"

11. That is, the Sultan.

12. For the nature of this "offense," see Chapter LIV preceding, note 14.

CHAPTER LXIV

1. See Chapter XXV preceding (note 9).

2. Compare Chapter XLIII preceding (note 15).

3. See Chapter XXXIV preceding (note 7).

4. This is literal: "*de muy buenas entrañas.*"

5. Compare Part I, Chapter II (note 6).

6. Motteux is inaccurate: "without them [arms] he never felt that he was himself at all."

7. "*A quien Dios se la diere, San Pedro se la benediga*": from the marriage ceremony.

8. That is, confess that the other is in the right.

9. In the original there is an untranslatable pun on the double sense of "*deslocado*"—"dislocated" and "cured of madness" (from "*loco*"—"mad").

CHAPTER LXV

1. Certain commentators have expended a great deal of time and energy in an attempt to establish a chronology for *Don Quixote;* but as Don Antonio Eximeno observes in his *Apologia de Miguel de Cervantes,* etc. (Madrid, 1806), cited by Menéndez y Pelayo and Rodríguez Marín: "Cervantes' geography and that of every author of works of the imagination is largely fanciful, and the time element of the fable is as imaginary as the fable itself."

2. "*Donde las dan las toman*"—literally, "where they give them, they take them." A proverb. Ormsby renders literally; Motteux: "they that give must take."

3. A variation on the proverb that has occurred a number of times: "Many think to find bacon where there are no pegs."

4. Compare Chapter LVIII preceding.

5. See Chapter VII preceding.

6. "*Albricias.*"

7. See Chapter V preceding.

8. Rhyming proverb: "*Hoy por ti y mañana por mí.*"

9. A proverb.

10. Philip III's officer charged with the expulsion of the Moriscos of La Mancha.

CHAPTER LXVI

1. This saying will be found in Sallust's *Oration on Caesar,* 1, 1: "*Sed res docuit id verum esse quod in carminibus Appius ait, fabrum esse suae quemque fortunae.*"

2. From the *Orlando Furioso,* IV, 57. See Part I, Chapter XIII and note 3.

3. A proverb.

4. The Portuguese have the same proverb in a slightly different form: "*Com raiva do asno tornase á albarda*" —"With rage one turns from the ass to the packsaddle."

5. The arroba being twenty-five pounds, the fat man's weight was two hundred and seventy-five.

6. An expression used in connection with persons of small consequence. (Correas: *Vocabulario de Refranes.*)

7. This anecdote is not original with Cervantes; it will be found in the *Floresta Española* of Melchor de Santa Cruz, who, according to Bowle, took it from the Italian writer Alciato's *De singulari certamine liber* (Venice, 1544), a Spanish translation of which was published at Antwerp in 1558(?).

8. "*A la taberna de lo caro*": on this expression and the different classes of wines and taverns in the Spain of that era, see Chapter XXIV preceding and note 5.

9. This starts off as a juridical phrase, employed by someone who is going bond for another, and ends jocosely with a popular proverb.

10. "*De lo caro.*"

11. On the cheese of Tronchón, see Chapter LII preceding and note 13. These "awakeners of thirst" once more remind one of Rabelais.

12. That is, removed the cover from it ("*dessembaynó su calabaça*").

13. There is a pun in the original that is hopelessly untranslatable, based upon the double meaning of the verb "*deber*": "ought" or "must," and "to owe." Tosilos says: ". . . *deue de ser vn loco*"; and Sancho replies: "*¿Como deue? . . . no deue nada á nadie.*" By attempting to render it, other translators have succeeded only in writing bad English.

CHAPTER LXVII

1. It was Sancho who had filched the kerchiefs without his master's knowledge. See Chapter LVII preceding.

2. There was a popular saying to the effect that "fairy treasure ["*los tesoros de los duendes*"] is converted into a coal," and Covarrubias states that the expression refers to "all possessions that are consumed and done away with in an unaccountable manner." Ormsby notes that "the Spanish *duendes* are . . . more akin to brownies than fairies."

3. That is, acorns. Clemencín observes that "acorns do not merit such an epithet."—"Apparently," says Rodríguez Marín, "he [Clemencín] has never tasted those acorns, for there are such, that are better than the best almonds."

4. Like a cornerstone in a building. The expression is a common one in Cervantes. Rodríguez Marín thinks it was a popular saying current at the time.

5. The first edition has "*Miculoso*," which most editors have changed to "*Niculoso*."

6. The allusion is to Garcilaso de la Vega's First Eclogue. Boscán is seen as Garcilaso himself. There is a play on the Spanish "*bosque*" and the Latin "*nemus*"—a grove.

7. "Big Teresa," *-ona* being an augmentative suffix.

8. "*Buscar pan de trastrigo*"—literally, to look for better bread than that made of wheat; this was a proverbial expression signifying a quest for something out of the ordinary.

9. The "*churumbela*" was a wind instrument made of a reed and resembling a flageolet.

10. There is a difference of opinion among commentators as to what kind of instrument, properly speaking, is signified by *albogues*. According to the description given here, *albogues* were a kind of cymbals, but others say the term refers to a wind instrument. (See the note in Cejador.)

11. The reader unacquainted with Spanish may possibly be interested in the meaning of these words: *almohaza* —a currycomb; *almorzar*—to breakfast or lunch; *alfombra*—a carpet; *alguacil* —a constable; *alhucema*—lavender; *almacén*—shop; *alcancía*—bank or money-box. Schevill notes that not all these words are of Arabic origin, *almorzar*, for example, being from the Latin *admorsus* (*admordere*), that is to say, a "bite." He gives a number of philo-logical references for those interested in the subject. As Clemencín remarks, the Arabic employs *al* as an article, "which we affix to certain Latin vocables, and this is the reason why we do not recognize them as our own."

12. *Borceguí*—a buskin or half-boot, *zaquizamí*—a garret; *maravedí*—the coin.

13. *Alhelí* — gillyflower; *alfaquí* — teacher of the Koran.

14. The text in the original is somewhat obscurely (or carelessly) worded, and this has led to a number of proposed emendations, but the sense of the passage is clear enough.

15. "*Qué polidas cuchares tengo de hazer.*" Jarvis has a suggestive rendering, though outside the text: "Oh, what neat wooden spoons shall I make when I am a shepherd!" Motteux: "Oh, how I shall make the spoons shine when I see me a shepherd!"

16. Jarvis: "What curds and cream! what garlands! what pretty knick-nacks!"

17. Variation on the proverb: "Many go for wool," etc. See Part I, Chapter VII, and Part II, Chapters XIV (note 8) and XLIII (note 17).

18. A proverb.

19. Ormsby cites the Plattdeutsch: "*Wat de oogen nich seht dat kränkt de hart ook nich.*"

20. Compare Part I, Chapter XXI (note 11).

21. Compare Chapter XLIII (note 12) preceding.

22. "*Quítate allá, ojinegra.*" The original form of the saying was "*Tirte allá, culnegra*"—"Be off with you, blackbottom." It is in this form that the proverb is preserved among Jews of Spanish origin. (Rodríguez Marín)

23. See Part I, Chapters XXI and XXXIX.

CHAPTER LXVIII

1. Ormsby, probably by oversight, omits this clause.

2. This is from the Vulgate, Job 17:12: "After darkness I hope for light." The words appear on the title page of Parts I and II of the original edition of the *Don Quixote* and certain other works put out by the same publisher, Juan de la Cuesta.

3. One cannot but recall here Shakespeare's famous lines (*Macbeth*, Act II, Scene 2):

Sleep that knits up the ravell'd
sleave of care,
The death of each day's life, sore
labour's bath,
Balm of hurt minds, great nature's
second course,
Chief nourisher in life's feast.

And a little later in the same play (Act II, Scene 3): "Shake off this downy sleep, death's counterfeit . . ." Compare Keats's "Endymion":

O magic sleep! O comfortable
bird,
That broodest o'er the troubled
sea of the mind
Till it is hush'd and smooth! O
unconfined
Restraint! imprisoned liberty!
great key
To golden palaces.

It may also be of interest to cite J. G. Saxe's humorous lines from "Early Rising":

"God bless the man who first invented sleep!"
So Sancho Panza said and so
say I;
And bless him, also, that he
didn't keep
His great discovery to himself,
nor try
To make it,—as the lucky fellow
might—
A close monopoly by patent-
right.

4. For this proverb, see Chapter x preceding, note 7, and Chapter XXXII (note 7).

5. Miguel de Unamuno, in his *Life of Don Quixote and Sancho* (see the translation by Homer P. Earle, New York, 1927), a running commentary on Cervantes' masterpiece, becomes even more dithyrambic than usual in discussing these lines, finding that they hold the most deeply hidden and intimate essence of the Quixotic spirit; but, as it happens, Don Francisco Rodríguez Marín has shown the verses in question to be taken from a Spanish translation of Pietro Bembo's *Gli Asolani*, an edition of which was published at Venice as early as 1515, the Spanish version appearing at Salamanca in 1551. (See the extended note in Rodríguez Marín.)

6. Compare Chapters II (note 8), XVII, and LXIII (note 4) preceding.

7. Motteux is at his typical worst here: "Trollopites, barbers, and Andrew Hodge-podge, and bitchlings." Ormsby slurs the passage: "We, tortolites, barbers, animals! I don't like those names at all. . . ."

8. A proverb.

9. Proverbial expression.

CHAPTER LXIX

1. According to the *Dictionary of the Academy*, to bury a woman with a palm ("*enterrar con palma*") was "to bury her in a state of virginity." Rodríguez Marín: "The old custom of placing a palm in the hands of dead virgins has come down to our day." He quotes a stanza from the *Cantos Populares Españoles*, containing the line: "*Muero moza y llevo palma*"—"I die a maid and carry off the palm." Ormsby: "The dried palm branch preserved from Easter Sunday that may be seen in almost every Spanish house."

2. "*Picote.*" Covarrubias: "A coarse goatskin cloth, so rough that it pricks you when you touch it, whence the name *picote*." (From "*picar*"—"to prick.") Not "sables" as in Ormsby. With regard to the "robes of baize and wool"—"*de vayeta y de anascote*," which the duennas wear, "*anascote*" is a woolen stuff that resembles serge. Ormsby has: "in baize and bombazine."

3. The allusion, of course, is to Orpheus.

4. The second of these stanzas is from Garcilaso de la Vega's Third Eclogue. Schevill observes that Garcilaso was a poet whom Cervantes imitated. The rhyme scheme in the original is ababacbcc.

5. Minos, Aeacus, and Rhadamanthus were the mythical judges of the infernal regions. The phrase "Pluto's murky pit" —"*las cabernas lóbregas de Dite*," will be found in Merlin's speech, Chapter XXXV preceding.

6. "*Veynte y quatro mamonas.*" "*Mamona*," properly speaking, is the gesture that consists in laying five fingers on someone's beard as a sign of contempt (Covarrubias); but here the word obviously implies more than that, and "smack" would seem to be the appropriate rendering.

7. Beginning of the proverb: "The old woman liked the blites and left

neither green nor dry." Motteux: "The old woman tickled herself with trifles." (!)

8. A proverb.

9. For this expression, see Chapter XXXIII preceding, note 15.

10. In the words of the poet Virués, "long, smooth, white, delicate hands (*blancas, largas, suaves, delicadas*)" were the fashion then as small ones were in a later era. (See the note in Rodríguez Marín.)

11. "*Menos mudas.*"

12. Vinegar water (*vinagrillo*) was a cosmetic lotion composed of vinegar, eggs, sweet limes, and honey. (Rodríguez Marín)

13. Proverbial expression signifying one who serves as the butt for the jests of others or upon whom they impose.

14. "*Que la arroje y lo eche todo á treze, aunque no se venda.*" Motteux: "Let me be, or by Heaven I will fling out, and do it all in a lump, though it be lost labour."

CHAPTER LXX

1. "*Vna carriola*"—a bed on wheels that may be pushed under another bed.

2. From Garcilaso's First Eclogue, verse 57.

3. On long hands, see the preceding chapter.

4. "*Crealo Iudas*"—literally, "let Judas believe it." Some commentators have seen here a reminiscence of Horace, *Satires*, I, v, 100–101: ". . . *credat Iudaeus Apella, non ego*"—"let the Jew Apella believe it, not I"; but Schevill thinks that such an allusion is out of the question considering that Sancho is the speaker.

5. The stanza quoted in the preceding chapter.

6. "*Los intonsos poetas*": the sense of *intonso* is "ignorant," "unpolished." Ormsby: "callow poets."

7. This habit of borrowing from another poet's work was a common one and was not looked upon as being in the least disreputable. In one of Lope de Vega's sonnets the following lines occur:

> De Garcilaso es este verso, Juana.
> Todos hurtan: paciencia!

"This verse, Juana, is from Garcilaso. Everybody filches: think nothing of it!"

8. Compare the advice which the

knight gives Altisidora in the ballad that he sings in Chapter XLVI preceding.

9. These verses are from a ballad in Durán's *Romancero General*, No. 107. They had become a proverb.

CHAPTER LXXI

1. This is literal: "*De lo que á Don Quixote sucedió.*" Ormsby: "of What Passed between Don Quixote and His Squire," etc., which perhaps more nearly reflects the contents of the chapter.

2. "*Y cátalo cantusado*": there has been much discussion as to the meaning of the verb "*cantusar*," which still, apparently, remains obscure. I have followed the majority of commentators, who take it as synonymous with "*engatusar*," signifying "to get something out of someone by wheedling" (*Dictionary of the Academy*). Clemencín takes "*cantusado*" as equivalent to "*despachado*" or "*concluído*," an interpretation adopted by Ormsby: "and, there, his labour is over." Motteux, on the other hand, has: "which they do not make up but the apothecary, and which they have got to know by cheating."

3. See Chapter LX preceding and note 17.

4. Both "the treasure of Venice" and "the mines of Potosí" were proverbial expressions denoting fabulous wealth. Potosí (now in western Bolivia) is noted for its silver mines.

5. One-quarter of a real.

6. Schevill estimates that Sancho's fee would amount to 61.1 gold crowns. Rodríguez Marín: "Sancho surely was quick at turning cuartillos into reales! And with the same speed Cervantes must have cast up his own accounts hundreds of times during the years when he was engaged in cash transactions with purveyors, finance officers, constables, muleteers, millers, etc."

7. The proverb in full reads: "Trout are not caught with dry breeches"— "*No se toman truchas/A bragas enjutas.*"

8. "*Los enamorados, que jamás ajustan la cuenta de sus desseos*": it is possible the reading here should be: "who are always unreasonable" (Rodríguez Marín suggests this). I have finally decided, however, to follow Hartzenbusch's emendation: "*que jamás ajustan con el*"

tiempo la cuenta de sus desseos." Ormsby does the same: "lovers, who never make the reckoning of their desires agree with time." Motteux: "as is always the case with lovers who never make allowance for the reckoning of their desires."

9. Allusion to the proverb quoted several times before (see Chapters XVII [note 9], XXXIII [note 23], and XXXVII [note 6], preceding): "As much is lost by a card too many as a card too few."

10. Compare Chapters XIV (note 5), XXX (note 3), XXXIV (note 8), and LIX (note 12), preceding.

11. Rhyming proverb: "*No se ganó Zamora,/En una hora.*" This all but impregnable fortress held out for a very long time, and in the course of the siege King Sancho II lost his life. The Portuguese have the same saying. Compare our "Rome was not built in a day."

12. A proverb.

13. Rhyming proverb: "*A dineros pagados,/Brazos quebrados,*" the sense being: no more work to be had out of a person after he has been paid for it.

14. "*Dos levadas*": "*levada*" is a fencing term, meaning a salute or flourish with the foil.

15. Rodríguez Marín states that in his native Andalusia he has heard the saying: "Here shall die Samson with all the Philistines!"

16. The *ferreruelo* was a short cloak without a cape.

17. Rodríguez Marín: "Leather hangings (*guadamecies* or *guadameciles*) were employed as a wall covering in summer, especially in Andalusia, but during the winter their place was taken by tapestries. . . . Tapestries, however, were an expensive luxury for the poor, who in place of them and at all seasons made use of silk serges [or twill], a kind of coarse frieze adorned with painted or embroidered figures or landscapes."

18. Sancho's prophecy has been more than fulfilled. Today the image of the Ingenious Gentleman and his squire is to be found everywhere in Spain.

19. Cervantes forgets that he has already narrated this anecdote in Chapter III preceding.

20. Literally, "I gave whence I shall give."

21. "*Quando estaua picado el molino*": I have adopted the meaning given by Correas (*Vocabulario de Refranes*).

22. See Chapter XXXV preceding and note 6.

23. Compare Chapters VII (note 6) and XXXV (note 7) preceding.

24. Compare Part I, Chapter XXXI (note 6), and Part II, Chapters XII (note 1) and XXXI.

25. "As it was" (in the beginning).

26. "*Y veras como te vale vn pan por ciento*": for this expression, see Chapter XXXIV preceding, note 4.

27. Play on the double meaning of "*razón*": "a word," and "reason" or "sense."

CHAPTER LXXII

1. This is reminiscent of a scene in the first chapter of the spurious *Don Quixote*. It was Bowle who first noted a number of such references throughout the present chapter.

2. See Avellaneda, Chapter IX.

3. That is, by spurning them in love, as in the case of Altisidora.

4. The institution known as the Casa del Nuncio, an asylum for the insane founded in 1483 by Francisco Ortiz, Canon of Toledo and Apostolic Nuncio.

5. The alcalde.

6. As previously pointed out (Chapter LXII preceding, note 37), this is not the correct title of Avellaneda's work.

7. Here, as not infrequently throughout this work, a free translation, paraphrastic and sometimes slightly expanded, is rendered necessary by the impossible name-repetitions of the original.

8. See the beginning of Sancho's letter to his wife, Chapter XXXVI preceding and note 3.

CHAPTER LXXIII

1. "*No la has de ver,*" etc.: it will be noted that the pronoun "*la*" is feminine, referring to the cricket cage ("*jaula de grillos*") mentioned a little later.

2. A Latin phrase used by medical writers. Bowle cites Avicena: "*Si non videt infirmus et non audit est* SIGNUM MALUM."

3. "Meeting with a hare, even when it was not being chased by hounds, was looked upon, and still is today, as a bad omen." Meeting with a wolf, on the other hand, was a good omen. (Rodríguez Marín)

4. A small coin worth four maravedis.

5. See Don Quixote's remarks on superstitions and omens in Chapter LVIII preceding.

6. The *"repostero"* was properly a covering ornamented with a coat of arms.

7. Rodríguez Marín thinks this may be reminiscent of the proverb *"Los criados son enemigos no excusados* [or, *enemigos pagados*]"—"Servants are inescapable [or paid] enemies."

8. *"Más galán que Mingo"* was a popular saying that derived originally from the opening lines of a fifteenth-century satire, the *Mingo Revulgo*. Rodríguez Marín points out that there is a humorous play here on the double sense of the preposition *de* in certain phrases ["ass of a Sancho Panza"—"beast of a Don Quixote"].

9. Word play on *"governador"*—"governor," and *"desgovernado,"* which means either deprived of government or a lawless individual.

10. Once again an allusion to the proverb "Many think to find bacon where there are no stakes"; compare Part I, Chapter xxv (note 5), and Part II, Chapters x (note 2), LV (note 17), and LXV (note 3).

11. The first edition here has "Curambro." Compare Chapter LXVII preceding.

12. *"Pastoras mañeruelas"*: according to Covarrubias, *"mañeruelos"* was a term applied to ponies that readily allowed themselves to be handled and subdued. "The comparison of shepherd maids to horses and ponies goes well with the curate's jovial humor." (Schevill, from the Spanish note.)

13. *"Si no nos quadraren, nos esquinen."*

14. These are names from the literature of pastoral romance; compare Part I, Chapter xxv.

15. Lines from an old Christmas carol which will be found in the ballad collection of Francisco de Ocaña.

16. A proverb.

CHAPTER LXXIV

1. Jacapo Sannazaro, Neapolitan poet (1458–1530), was the author of the *Arcadia* (see the edition published at Torino in 1888).

2. Literally, "pay me for good news" —*"dadme albricias,"* an expression that has occurred a number of times before.

3. With regard to Don Quixote's real name, see Part I, Chapter I. There the name is given as Quijana (Quixana).

4. Rhyming proverb: *"En los nidos de antaño/No hay pajaros hogaño."*

5. *"A puerta cerrada"*—literally, "my entire estate from the doors inward," a popular expression still employed in Andalusia and elsewhere. (Rodríguez Marín)

6. It was a custom among the people, in the case of women, to give a feminine termination to a name with a masculine ending. (Rodríguez Marín)

7. Ormsby: "This piece of commonplace cynicism, so uncalled for and so inconsistent with what has gone before, is, I imagine, regretted by most of Cervantes' readers. The conclusion of the *Don Quixote*, it must be confessed, is not worthy of the book or of its author. After the quiet pathos and dignity of Don Quixote's death, the shrill note of the scolding once more administered to the wretched Avellaneda falls like a discord on the reader's ear, and Samson [Sansón] Carrasco's doggerel does not tend to allay the irritation." The thought expressed here is to be found in a number of Spanish proverbs and verses: "The weeping of the heir is dissimulated laughter"—*"El llanto del heredero es risa disimulada"*; "Dead man to the grave, the living to the loaf"—*"El muerto al hoyo, y el vivo al bollo."* (See Rodríguez Marín's note.)

8. Reference to the rites of penance, communion, and extreme unction.

9. Previous translators have taken the phrase *"muerto naturalmente"* as signifying a death by natural causes in opposition to a violent one; but, as Rodríguez Marín points out, the proper sense is "actually or wholly dead," as is shown by the fact that the expression was used even of condemned persons who had been put to death by the executioner.

10. Rodríguez Marín: "Don Quixote's death is as touching and saddening as that of a person who has really existed and for whom we have felt a profound affection. 'What a worthy madman,' the reader exclaims to himself, 'in this rascally world of ours where there are so many wicked ones of sound mind!'"

11. See Part I, Chapter I and note I. For a work in English on the geography

of the region, see August F. Jaccaci, *On the Trail of Don Quixote, Being a Record of Rambles in the Ancient Province of La Mancha* (London, 1897). The reader of Spanish may be referred to the lecture by Antonio Blazquez, *La Mancha en Tiempo de Cervantes* (Madrid, 1905).

12. Clemencín and others have objected to the introduction of these lines here. They are a doggerel imitation of the epitaphs composed by village poets.

13. Sannazaro concludes his *Arcadia* with an apostrophe to his flute.

14. The last two verses are from a ballad on the death of Alonso de Aguilar (*Guerras Civiles de Granada*, 1, xvii).

The ballad in question has been translated by Lockhart.

15. Of Tordesillas.

16. At the close of the spurious *Don Quixote*, Avellaneda tells how the knight, after being released from the madhouse of Toledo, "purchased for himself another and better steed and made a tour of Old Castile, where stupendous and never-before-heard-of adventures befell him," etc.

17. This proved to be true. No new romance of chivalry appeared after *Don Quixote* and only a few of the old ones were reprinted. The last work in this category was the *Policisne de Boecia*, published at Valladolid in 1602.

BIBLIOGRAPHY

I

List of the Principal English-Language Translations of "Don Quixote"

The History of the Valorovs and Wittie Knight-Errant Don Qvixote of the Mancha. Translated out of the Spanish. London: Printed by William Stansby for Ed Blovnt and W. Barret, 1612. Pp. xii + 594. (Part I of the version by Thomas Shelton.)

The History of Don Quichote. London: Edward Blount, 1620. Vol. I: pp. xii + 572; Vol. II: pp. viii: + 504. (Parts I and II of the Shelton.)

There have been numerous reprints of this version, the latest being that of the Ashendene Press in 1927–28 (London, 2 vols.). In 1923 there appeared to be something like a Shelton revival, three editions appearing in that year: those by the Navarre Society and Macmillan & Company in London, and the one by the George H. Doran Company in New York (2 vols., 3 vols., and 1 vol., respectively). The Navarre Society edition has a preface by F. J. Harvey Darton; and the American printing, reproducing the Constable & Company London edition of the preceding year, contains a distinguished introduction by J. B. Trend and the illustrations of Jean de Bosschère. This translation, with an introduction by the noted American scholar J. D. M. Ford, was included in the Harvard Classics (New York: P. F. Collier & Son, 1909), Vol. 14. A four-volume edition, with introductions by James Fitzmaurice-Kelly, was published in the Tudor Translations (London: David Nutt, 1896), Vols. 13–16. Another four-volume edition, published at London by Gibbings & Company and at Philadelphia by the J. B. Lippincott Company in 1895 and 1901, has a preface by Justin Huntley McCarthy. A number of the eighteenth-century editions (London, 1725, 1731, 1733, and 1740) have engravings by Charles-Antoine Coypel. The four-volume edition published at London by T. Fisher Unwin in 1906 and at New York by Charles Scribner's Sons, 1906–1907, has the illustrations of Daniel Vierge and an introduction by Royal Cortissoz. It was the edition of 1725 (London: R. Knaplock) that was revised by Captain John Stevens.

The history of the most renowned Don Quixote of La Mancha and his trusty squire Sancho Panza. Now made into English according to the humour of our modern language. London: T. Hodgkin, 1687. Pp. 616.

Version by John Phillips. One printing only.

The history of the renown'd Don Quixote de la Mancha. Translated from the original Spanish by several hands, and publish'd by Peter Motteux. London: Sam Buckley, 1700. 4 vols.

The four-volume edition published at London in 1725 was the first to be revised by J. Ozell. This revision has been used as the basis for a number of modern editions (London: John Lane, 1930; London: Nonesuch Press, 1930; New York: The Modern Library, 1930). John Gibson Lockhart's notes and "Life of Cervantes" first appeared in the Edinburgh edition of 1822. They have been reprinted five or six times and may be found along with Lockhart's ballad renderings in Bohn's Popular Library (London: G. Bell and Sons, 1913, 2 vols.). A special edition of Part I of the Motteux-Ozell version with Salvador Dali's illustrations was published in New York by The Illustrated Modern Library in 1946.

The Life and Exploits of the Ingenious Gentleman Don Quixote de la Mancha. Translated from the original Spanish of Miguel de Cervantes Saavedra by Charles Jarvis. London: J. and R. Tonson and R. Dodsley, 1742. 2 vols.

As stated in the Introduction, this translation has been about the most popular of all—in England if not in America—having run through close to a hundred printings. The latest would seem to be that of Frederick Warne & Company in 1933 (London, 1 vol.). The edition put out by Dodd, Mead & Company in 1925 (New York, 1 vol.) contains the W. Heath Robinson illustrations, which first appeared in the one-volume London Bliss & Sands edition of 1897; and in 1928 the same firm brought out the Jarvis text with illustrations by Arthur Boyd Houghton. The Jarvis was edited, with notes and introduction, by James Fitzmaurice-Kelly (London and New York: H. Frowde, 1907 and 1912). It was published as Vols. 25–26 in Morley's Universal Library (London: George Routledge & Sons, 1885), with an introduction by Henry Morley. It has been something of a favorite with artists, among its illustrators being Gustave Doré, Tony Johannot, George Cruikshank, Arthur Boyd Houghton, and W. Heath Robinson.

The History of the Renowned Don Quixote de la Mancha. Translated from the original Spanish of Miguel de Cervantes Saavedra. London: J. Cooke, 1744. 2 vols.

Abridgment by Charles Henry Wilmot. There was one reprinting, in 1774(?). Ormsby mistakes this second printing for the first.

The History and Adventures of the Renowned Don Quixote. Translated from the Spanish of Miguel de Cervantes Saavedra, by Tobias George Smollett. To which is added some account of the author's life. Illustrated by 28 copper plates designed by Hayman. London: A. Millar, T. Osborne, J. Rivington, 1755. 2 vols.

Although Ormsby characterizes this version as "a mere bookseller's speculation," it has had some thirty-odd printings, though few in the last hundred years. Its popularity was due in good part, no doubt, to the reputation as a humorist possessed by the author of *Humphrey Clinker* and *Roderick Random*.

The History of the Renowned Don Quixote de la Mancha. Translated into English by George Kelly. To which are added notes on the more difficult passages. London: E. Carpenter and A. Bridgman, 1769. 4 vols.

One printing only.

Don Quixote de la Mancha. Translated from the Spanish of Miguel de Cervantes Saavedra by Mary Smirke. Engravings by Robert Smirke. London: T. Cadell and W. Davies, 1818. 4 vols.

There were two London reprintings, in 1847 and 1853. The fourth printing (New York: D. Appleton & Company, 1855) is described as "A Revised translation based on those of Motteux, Jarvis and Smollett."

The History of Don Quixote. Translated and edited by J. W. Clarke, and with a biographical notice of Cervantes by T. Teignmouth Shore. Illustrated by Gustave Doré. London: Cassell, Petter & Galpin, 1864–67. 1 vol.

There were five reprints, 1870–1906.

The Ingenious Knight Don Quixote de la Mancha. A new translation by Alexander James Duffield, with notes of John Bowle, Juan Antonio Pellicer, Diego Clemencín, and others. London: C. K. Paul & Company, 1881. 3 vols.

Compare the one-volume edition of the *Don Quixote* put out by Charles Scribner's Sons (New York, 1902; reprinted in 1909) and "Edited from the translations of Duffield and Shelton, by Mary E. Burt and Lucy L. Cable."

The Ingenious Gentleman Don Quixote of La Mancha, by Miguel de Cervantes Saavedra. Translated into English, with introduction and notes, by John Ormsby. London: Smith, Elder & Company, 1885. 4 vols.

This edition has enjoyed a deserved popularity in America. Of the sixteen reprints, 1885–1936, thirteen were by publishing houses in New York or Boston. and one of the others, the Macmillan edition of 1899, was published in London and New York. There was a Glasgow printing, edited by Fitzmaurice-Kelly, in 1901; and the Ormsby translation illustrated by Enric C. Ricart was brought out in Barcelona, in two volumes, in 1933. The latest printing is the one-volume edition by Grosset (New York, 1936). The work was published by the Limited Editions Club in two volumes in 1933; by the Thomas Y. Crowell Company in 1932 in two volumes; by Alfred A. Knopf in 1926 in two volumes; and by Dodd, Mead & Company in 1916 in four volumes. The Knopf edition has an introduction by George Edward Woodberry. The Ormsby version was a favored one for school use at the turn of the century, and there are a number of editions designed for younger readers. The Dodd, Mead & Company edition first published in 1893 has Cruikshank illustrations.

The Ingenious Gentleman Don Quixote of La Mancha. A new edition, done into English with notes, original and selected, and a new life of the author, by Henry Edward Watts. London: B. Quaritch, 1888. 5 vols.

This version was reprinted at London, in four volumes, in 1895 and was published in New York, in two volumes, in 1898, by D. Appleton & Company, with a critical and biographical introduction by Joseph O'Connor. A four-volume edition with etchings by Adolphe Lalauze was brought out at Philadelphia by G. Barrie some time in the early 1900's (date uncertain).

The Imaginative Gentleman Don Quixote de la Mancha. Translated into English by Robinson Smith. London: George Routledge & Sons; New York: E. P. Dutton; 1908(?). 1 vol.

There was a second London printing in 1910, and a third, "with a new life of Cervantes, notes and appendices," in 1914. The fourth London printing, 1914, was termed a "second edition"; and in 1932 the Hispanic Society of America brought out what is described as a "new edition," bearing the title *The Visionary Gentleman Don Quixote de la Mancha.* This last-mentioned edition is in two volumes. It has been out of print for some time.

II

Principal Spanish Editions Made Use of in the Preparation of this Translation

Don Quixote de la Mancha. Madrid: V. Suárez, Gráficas Reunidas, 1928–41. 4 vols.

This is the edition of the *Don Quixote* by Professor Rudolph Schevill in the *Obras Completas de Miguel de Cervantes Saavedra* edited by Schevill and Professor Adolfo Bonilla y San Martín of the University of Madrid. (See the Introduction and note 38.)

El ingenioso hidalgo Don Quijote de la Mancha. Nueva edición crítica con el comento refundido y mejorado y más de setecientas notas dispuestas por F. Rodríguez Marín. Madrid: Tipografía de la Revista de Archivos, 1927–28. 7 vols.

This critical edition with its vast number of notes runs to a total of more than 3500 pages.

El ingenioso hidalgo Don Quijote de la Mancha. Edición y notas de F. Rodríguez Marín. Madrid: La Lectura, 1911–13. 8 vols.

This is Rodríguez Marín's first and more popular edition, in the Clásicos Castellanos series, where it constitutes Vols. IV, VI, VIII, X, XIII, XVI, XIX, and XXII.

El ingenioso hidalgo Don Quixote de la Mancha, compuesto por Miguel de Cervantes. Edición crítica con variantes, notas y el diccionario de todas las palabras

usadas en la inmortal novela, por Don Clemente Cortejón. Continuada por Juan Givanel i Mas, y Juan Suñé Benajes. Madrid: V. Suárez, 1905-13. 6 vols.
On Cortejón, see the Introduction.

III

Early Spanish Editions of "Don Quixote" Referred to in the Notes

(For other earlier Spanish editions see Section V, following.)

El Ingenioso Hidalgo Don Quixote de la Mancha. Compuesto por Miguel de Cervantes Saavedra, Dirigido al Duque de Beiar, Marques de Gibraleón, Conde de Benalcaçar, y Benares, Visconde de la Puebla de Alcozer, Señor de las villas de Capilla, Curiel, y Burgillos. Año 1605, con privilegio, en Madrid, por Juan de la Cuesta. Vendese en casa de Francisco de Robles, librero del Rey, nro Señor.

This is the first edition of Part I. A second edition with the same title (save for a couple of printer's errors and the addition of the words *"de Castilla, Aragon y Portual"* after the *Privilegio*) appeared in the same year. There are substantial variations in the body of the text to differentiate it from the other printing and establish it as the second one; but it has been mistaken for the first by such scholars as Ticknor, Bowle, and others. A third La Cuesta edition was brought out in 1608. Inasmuch as it is by Cervantes' own publisher, it is referred to in the notes to this translation as the "third edition," although the two editions of Lisbon and that of Valencia (see the Introduction and note 12) and the edition of Brussels (see the item following) had appeared in the meanwhile. In the erroneous belief that the author was responsible for the textual changes to be found in this edition, scholars for long regarded it as the definitive one.

El Ingenioso Hidalgo Don Quixote de la Mancha, etc. En Bruselas por Roger Velpius. Año 1607. (Part I.)

This is what is known as the "edition of Brussels" and is so referred to in the notes to the present translation. It was reprinted in 1611 and 1617. Attempts are made at a correction of Cervantes' text, particularly with reference to the theft of the ass.

Segunda Parte del Ingenioso Cavallero Don Quijote de la Mancha por Miguel de Cervantes Saavedra, autor de su primera parte. Dirigida a D. Pedro Fernández de Castro Conde de Lemos. . . . Año 1615. Con Privilegio en Madrid, por Juan de la Cuesta.

This is the first edition of part II. It is a quarto volume of 584 pages. Note the change in the title from *Hidalgo* to *Caballero*, probably due to inadvertency.

Segunda Parte del Ingenioso Cavallero Don Quijote de la Mancha, etc. En Bruselas por Humberto Antonio, impresor jurado. Año 1616. (The Brussels edition of Part II.)

NOTE. The complete Don Quixote in Spanish did not appear until 1637, more than twenty years after its author's death, in the form of two wretchedly printed quarto volumes from the press of Francisco Martínez at Madrid. A Brussels edition of 1662 and one at Antwerp, 1697, are much better from the typographical point of view.

IV

Continental Translations of "Don Quixote" Cited in the Notes to this Version

FRENCH

L'ingenievx Don Qvixote de la Manche. Composé par Michel de Cervantès, tradvit fidellement d'espagnole en françois, et dedié au Roy par César Ovdin. Paris: Iean Fouet, 1614. 1 vol.

Le valevrevx Don Qvixote de la Manche; ov, L'histoire de ses grands exploicts d'armes, fideles amours, et aduentures estranges. Traduit fidèlement de l'espagnole de Michel de Cervantès & dedié au Roy par César Ovdin. Paris: Iean Fouet, 1616. 1 vol. (Part I.)

Scholars have come to realize (Rodríguez Marín among them) that César Oudin, a Frenchman who was a teacher of Spanish, had a good knowledge of the Spanish of Cervantes' time. In 1618 François de Rosset published his translation of Part II, and from 1633 on the combined Oudin-Rosset rendering of the complete work became the standard one; it was brought out again as late as 1936, under the editorship of Jean Cassou (Paris: Nouvelle Revue Française); there were also editions by Flammarion in 1912 and 1926. Other French versions include a popular but unsatisfactory abridgment by Florian; one by H. Bouchon Dubournial, which Brunet condemned, and one by De l'Aulnaye, which he praised; one by the Abbé Lejeune; the well-known one by Louis Viardot (1836); and others. Ormsby in his bibliography gives the printing of 1616 as the first one.

ITALIAN

L'ingegnoso cittadino Don Chisciotte della Mancia. Tradotto di spagnuolo in italiano, da Lorenzo Franciosini Fiorentino. Venetia: Andrea Baba, 1625.

Franciosini, like Oudin, had the advantage of being a contemporary of the author. His version was reprinted at Venice and elsewhere a number of times, down to the early part of the nineteenth century. In 1832–33 it was published in an eight-volume edition at Milan, revised by L. Toccagni. There has been no subsequent printing. For some reason or other there have not been a great many translations of the *Don Quixote* in Italian.

GERMAN

Don Kichote de la Mantzscha. Juncker Harnisch auss Fleckenland, auss hispanischer Spraach in Hochteutsche versetzt, durch Pahsch Basteln von der Sohle. Cöthen, 1621.

This is only a partial translation—twenty-two chapters. It was reprinted at Frankfurt in 1648. The latest of the three editions is the one of Frankfurt, 1928, with a study by Hermann Tiemann. The first complete German version, by an anonymous hand, appeared at Basel and Frankfurt in 1682.

Leben und Thaten des scharfsinnigen Edlen Don Quixote von der Manche von Miguel de Cervantes Saavedra. Übersetzt von Ludwig Tieck. Berlin: Johann Friedrich Unger, 1799–1801. 4 vols.

From the literary point of view this is by far the most interesting of the German versions, and it is also the most popular. The appearance of Tieck's *Don Quixote* had a considerable influence upon the Romantic movement, and in particular upon Heinrich Heine. Ormsby admits that the translation is a spirited one but adds that "the spirit is not quite the spirit of Cervantes." He also finds that Tieck is inclined to take too many liberties with the text, and, indeed, it is true that this rendering has a certain lusty and expansive quality that is often to be found in the works of the Romantics; but for all of that it remains an admirable piece of German prose. Ormsby further criticizes the use of *scharfsinnig* in the title, remarking that *sinnreich*, which had been employed by Dietrich Wilhelm Soltau in his version (Königsberg, 1800–1801) is nearer to the Spanish *ingenioso*.

NOTE. The latest German translation is the four-volume one by Ludwig Braunfels (Stuttgart, 1884), which Ormsby praises rather highly. It was reprinted at Strassburg in 1905 and at Berlin in 1923; see also the two-volume version based upon Braunfels and Florian and edited by Hermann Tiemann (Hamburg-Leipzig, 1925?).

V

A List of the Principal Commentators and Lexicographers Cited in the Notes to this Translation

(For convenient reference, this list has been arranged alphabetically.)

Academy Edition. *El ingenioso Hidalgo Don Quixote de la Mancha, etc.* Madrid: Joaquín de Ibarra, 1780.

This is the edition by the Spanish Royal Academy, in four large quarto volumes with plates. A laudable attempt is made at a definitive text, but too much reliance is placed on the third edition of 1608. Two years later (1782) the Academy brought out a less pretentious edition in four small octavo volumes. A third edition (6 vols., 16mo) appeared in 1787; there was a fourth edition (4 vols., 8vo) in 1819, reprinted in 1832; and in 1836 Little and Brown of Boston published the Academy text with emendations by Francis Sales (1 vol. 8vo, with plates.)

Bowle, Rev. John. *Historia del famoso cavallero, etc.* London and Salisbury: E. Easton, 1781.

Originally published in six quarto volumes, this edition is famous for its notes.

Calderon, Juan. *Cervantes vindicado en ciento y quince pasajes del texto del ingenioso hidalgo Don Quixote de la Mancha que no han entendido o que han entendido mal, algunos de sus comentadores y críticos.* Prólogo y notas de Luis Usoz del Rio. Madrid: J. Martín Alegría, 1854. Pp. xxiii + 256.

Cejador y Frauca, Julio. *La lengua de Cervantes. Gramática y diccionario de la lengua castellana en "El ingenioso hidalgo Don Quixote de la Mancha."* Prólogo de Rufino José Cuervo. Madrid: Tipografía de Jaime Ratés, 1905–1906. 2 vols.

On this work see the Introduction.

Clemencín, Diego. *El ingenioso hidalgo Don Quixote de la Mancha . . . comentado por D. Clemencín.* Madrid: D. E. Aguado, 1833–39.

A new and critical edition of this valuable work was brought out by Rodríguez Marín at Barcelona in 1915.

Correas, Gonzalo. *Vocabulario de refranes y frases proverbiales y otras formulas comunes de lengua castellana, en que van todos los impresos antes y otra gran copia que juntó el Maestro Gonzalo Correas.* Madrid: Tipografía de la Revista de Archivos, Bibliotecas y Museos, 1924. 3 vols.

Another modern edition of this work is that published at Madrid, by Tipografía de Jaime Ratés in 1906.

Cortejón y Lucas, Clemente. See Section II preceding.

Covarrubias, Horacio Sebastián de. *Tesoro de la lengua castellana, o española, según la impresión de 1611, con las adiciones de Benito Remigio Noydens publica-*

das en la de 1674; edición preparada por Martín de Riguer. . . . Barcelona: S. A. Horta, 1943.

First published during Cervantes' lifetime, in 1611, Covarrubias's *Tesoro* has much light to throw on the language of *Don Quixote.*

Dictionary of the Academy. Diccionario de la lengua española, compuesto por la Real Academia Española. Madrid: Talleres Espasa-Calpe, S.A., 1939. 1 vol.

This is the sixteenth edition; the first appeared in 1726 with the title *Diccionario de la lengua castellana.*

Fitzmaurice-Kelly, James. *The Complete Works of Miguel de Cervantes Saavedra.* Glasgow: Gowans & Gray, 1901–1903. 7 vols. Vols. III–VI, the *Don Quixote,* translated by John Ormsby.

See Fitzmaurice-Kelly's notes on the Ormsby version.

Hartzenbusch, Juan Eugenio. *El ingenioso hidalgo Don Quixote de la Mancha.* Edición corregida con especial estudio de la primera. Argamasilla de Alba: Riva-deneyra, 1863. 4 vols.

Jarvis, Charles. See Section I preceding.

Lockhart, John Gibson. *The History of the Ingenious Gentleman Don Quixote of La Mancha.* Translated from the Spanish by Motteux. A new edition with copious notes, and an essay on the life and writings of Cervantes, by John Gibson Lockhart. Edinburgh: A. Constable & Company; London: Hurst, Robinson & Company, 1822. 5 vols.

See the note on the Motteux version in Section I preceding and also the Introduction. A reprint of this item was brought out by J. M. Dent & Sons, London and Toronto, and E. P. Dutton & Company, New York, in 1906. Lockhart's notes and his essay on Cervantes will be found in the Everyman's Library edition (London: J. M. Dent & Sons, 1910), and in Bohn's Popular Library (London: G. Bell & Sons, 1913).

Ormsby, John. See Section I preceding and the Introduction.

Pellicer, Juan Antonio. *El ingenioso hidalgo Don Quixote de la Mancha, etc.* Corregida de nuevo, con nuevas notas, con nuevas viñetas, con nuevo análisis y con la vida del autor por J. A. Pellicer. Madrid: G. de Sancha, 1783–1802. 10 vols.

The latest edition of this work is that published at Madrid, 1905, 1 vol., pp. cxxvii + 896.

Rodríguez Marín, Francisco. See Section II preceding and the Introduction.

Schevill, Rudolph. See Section II preceding and the Introduction.

Shelton, Thomas. See Section I preceding and the Introduction.